W9-BVR-391

THE MARK TWAIN PAPERS

AUTOBIOGRAPHY OF MARK TWAIN

VOLUME 2

The Mark Twain Project is an editorial and publishing program of The Bancroft Library, working since 1967 to create a comprehensive critical edition of everything Mark Twain wrote.

This volume is the second one in that edition to be published simultaneously in print and as an electronic text at http://www.marktwainproject.org. The textual commentaries for all Mark Twain texts in this volume are published *only* there.

THE MARK TWAIN PAPERS

AUTOBIOGRAPHY OF MARK TWAIN

VOLUME 2

BENJAMIN GRIFFIN AND
HARRIET ELINOR SMITH, EDITORS

Associate Editors
Victor Fischer
Michael B. Frank
Sharon K. Goetz
Leslie Diane Myrick

A publication of the Mark Twain Project of The Bancroft Library

UNIVERSITY OF CALIFORNIA PRESS
BERKELEY LOS ANGELES LONDON

Frontispiece: Photograph by Underwood and Underwood, 1907, Tuxedo Park, New York.

University of California Press, one of the most distinguished university presses in the United States, enriches lives around the world by advancing scholarship in the humanities, social sciences, and natural sciences. Its activities are supported by the UC Press Foundation and by philanthropic contributions from individuals and institutions. For more information, visit http://www.ucpress.edu.

University of California Press
Berkeley and Los Angeles, California

University of California Press, Ltd.
London, England

All texts by Mark Twain in *Autobiography of Mark Twain, Volume 2* have been published previously, by permission of the Mark Twain Foundation, in the Mark Twain Project's *Microfilm Edition of Mark Twain's Literary Manuscripts Available in the Mark Twain Papers, The Bancroft Library, University of California, Berkeley* (Berkeley: The Bancroft Library, 2001), and some texts have been published previously in one or more of the following: Albert Bigelow Paine, editor, *Mark Twain's Autobiography* (New York: Harper and Brothers, 1924); Bernard DeVoto, editor, *Mark Twain in Eruption* (New York: Harper and Brothers, 1940); Charles Neider, editor, *The Autobiography of Mark Twain, Including Chapters Now Published for the First Time* (New York: Harper and Brothers, 1959). Unless otherwise noted, all illustrations are reproduced from original documents in the Mark Twain Papers of The Bancroft Library, University of California, Berkeley.

Twain, Mark, 1835–1910
[Autobiography]
Autobiography of Mark Twain, Volume 2 / editors: Benjamin Griffin , Harriet Elinor Smith ;
associate editors: Victor Fischer, Michael B. Frank, Sharon K. Goetz, Leslie Diane Myrick
p. cm. — (The Mark Twain Papers)
"A publication of the Mark Twain Project of The Bancroft Library."
Includes bibliographical references and index.
ISBN 978-0-520-27278-1 (cloth : alk. paper)
1. Twain, Mark, 1835–1910. 2. Authors, American—19th century—Biography. I. Griffin, Benjamin, 1968– II. Smith, Harriet Elinor. III. Fischer, Victor, 1942– IV. Frank, Michael B. V. Goetz, Sharon K. VI. Myrick, Leslie Diane. VII. Bancroft Library. VIII. Title.
PS1331.A2 2010
818'.4'0924dc22 2009047700
Manufactured in the United States of America

19 18 17 16 15 14 13 12 11 10
10 9 8 7 6 5 4 3 2 1

The paper used in this publication meets the minimum requirements of ANSI/NISO Z39.48-1992 (R 1997) (*Permanence of Paper*).

Editorial work for this volume has been supported by a generous gift to the Mark Twain Project of The Bancroft Library from the

KORET FOUNDATION

and by matching and outright grants from the

NATIONAL ENDOWMENT
FOR THE HUMANITIES,
an independent federal agency.

Without that support, this volume could not have been produced.

The Mark Twain Project at the University of California, Berkeley, gratefully acknowledges generous support from the following, for editorial work on the *Autobiography of Mark Twain* and for the acquisition of important new documents:

The University of California, Berkeley, Class of 1958
Members of the Mark Twain Luncheon Club
The Barkley Fund
Phyllis R. Bogue
The Mark Twain Foundation
Robert and Beverly Middlekauff
Peter K. Oppenheim

The Beatrice Fox Auerbach Foundation Fund at the Hartford Foundation for Public Giving
The House of Bernstein, Inc.
Helen Kennedy Cahill
Kimo Campbell
Lawrence E. Crooks
Mrs. Henry Daggett
Les and Mary De Wall
The Renee B. Fisher Foundation
Ann and David Flinn
Peter B. and Robin Frazier
Virginia Robinson Furth
Stephen B. Herrick
The Hofmann Foundation
Don and Bitsy Kosovac
Watson M. and Sita Laetsch
Edward H. Peterson
Roger and Jeane Samuelsen

The Benjamin and Susan Shapell Foundation
Janet and Alan Stanford
Montague M. Upshaw
Jeanne and Leonard Ware
Sheila M. Wishek
Patricia Wright, in memory of Timothy J. Fitzgerald
Peter and Midge Zischke

and

The thousands of individual donors over the past fifty years
who have helped sustain the ongoing work
of the Mark Twain Project.

The publication of this volume has been made possible by a gift to the University of California Press Foundation by

WILSON GARDNER COMBS

FRANK MARION GIFFORD COMBS

in honor of

WILSON GIFFORD COMBS

BA 1935, MA 1950, University of California, Berkeley

MARYANNA GARDNER COMBS

MSW 1951, University of California, Berkeley

The University of California Press
gratefully acknowledges the support of

The Mark Twain Foundation

The Sydney Stern Memorial Trust

John G. Davies

and the Humanities Endowment Fund
of the UC Press Foundation

CONTENTS

List of Dictations *xiv*
Acknowledgments *xvii*

AUTOBIOGRAPHY OF MARK TWAIN *1*

Explanatory Notes *457*

Appendixes
Samuel L. Clemens: A Brief Chronology *649*
Family Biographies *652*
Previous Publication *656*

Note on the Text *661*
Word Division in This Volume *663*
References *665*
Index *697*

Photographs follow page 300

LIST OF DICTATIONS

1906 Autobiographical Dictations, April–December

2 April *3*
3 April *6*
4 April *11*
5 April *18*
6 April *23*
9 April *27*
10 April *33*
11 April *37*
21 May *46*
23 May *49*
24 May *52*
26 May *57*
28 May *60*
29 May *64*
31 May *68*
1 June *71*
2 June *74*
4 June *80*
6 June *97*
7 June *100*
11 June *108*
12 June *111*
13 June *114*
14 June *118*
18 June *121*
19 June *128*
20 June *130*
22 June *132*
23 June *136*
25 June *140*
17 July *143*
30 July *148*
31 July *151*
6 August *158*
7 August *160*
8 August *162*
10 August *167*
11 August *171*
13 August *176*
15 August *177*
27 August *179*
28 August *182*
29 August *188*
30 August *195*
31 August *199*
3 September *214*
4 September *219*
5 September *222*
7 September *225*
10 September *229*
2 October *235*
3 October *240*
4 October *243*
5 October *245*
8 October *247*
9 October *250*
10 October *251*
11 October *255*
12 October *256*
15 October *257*
16 October *260*
30 October *262*
7 November *266*
8 November *269*
19 November *273*
20 November *277*
21 November *281*
22 November *283*
23 November *286*
24 November *288*
30 November *292*
1 December *297*
2 December *301*
3 December *304*
5 December *306*
6 December *309*
13 December *312*
17 December *315*
18 December *317*
19 December *320*
20 December *324*
21 December *326*
26 December *334*
27 December *342*
28 December *346*
29 December *356*

1907 **Autobiographical Dictations, January–February**

6 January *359*	28 January *387*	12 February *433*
9 January *361*	29 January *400*	19 February *434*
15 January *370*	30 January *409*	25 February *436*
17 January *374*	1 February *413*	26 February *442*
22 January *376*	4 February *415*	27 February *445*
23 January *380*	11 February *430*	28 February *454*

ACKNOWLEDGMENTS

Editorial work on the *Autobiography of Mark Twain* began some eight years ago and is expected to continue for another two. But acquiring the collective skills, expertise, and materials that allow us to do the work has taken much longer: more than four decades of editorial labor on every aspect of Mark Twain's writings, made possible by the continuous support, since 1967, of the National Endowment for the Humanities, an independent federal agency. We thank the Endowment for that long-standing, patient, and generous support, of which its two most recent outright and matching grants are but a small part. With equal fervor, we thank the Koret Foundation for its recent generous grant in support of editorial and production work on the *Autobiography,* all of which has gone (or will go) to satisfy the matching component of the Endowment's recent grants.

For their continuing support of work on the *Autobiography* and for help in acquiring important original documents for the Mark Twain Papers, we thank those institutions and individuals listed on pages ix–x. The Mark Twain Project has been sustained over the years in so many ways by so many people that we are obliged to thank them as one large group, much as we would prefer to name every individual and institution who has contributed. Much of the Endowment's recent support of the Mark Twain Project has been in the form of funds matching the generous gifts of individuals and foundations. For donations ranging from five dollars to five million dollars, we thank all our loyal and generous supporters. Without their donations, the Project would long ago have ceased to exist, and would certainly not be producing the *Autobiography* edition today.

That said, we must nevertheless single out for special thanks a heroic undertaking to create an endowment supporting the present and future work of the Mark Twain Project by the alumni of the University of California, Berkeley, Class of 1958, led by Roger and Jeane Samuelsen, Edward H. Peterson, and Don and Bitsy Kosovac. In 2008, as a fiftieth reunion gift to the University, the Class endowed the Mark Twain Project with a dedicated fund of $1 million. We renew our thanks to each and every member of the Class for their unprecedented generosity. And we also acknowledge here the creation of two smaller endowment funds in support of the Project by the estates of Phyllis R. Bogue and Peter K. Oppenheim. These efforts to create long-term private support for the Project have fundamentally altered the way we pay for this work.

Central to all our recent fundraising efforts has been the Mark Twain Luncheon Club, organized twelve years ago by Watson M. (Mac) Laetsch, Robert Middlekauff, and the late Ira Michael Heyman, three of the wisest administrators ever to help manage the Berkeley campus. The leadership of the Club has been unflagging and indispensable; we thank them for it and for a thousand other forms of help. The Club now has a newsletter, produced for us by Ron Kolb and Pamela Patterson, who have our continuing thanks. We also thank the Club's nearly one hundred members for their loyal financial and moral support of the Project, and on their behalf we extend thanks to the dozens of visiting speakers who have addressed the Luncheon Club members over the years. Thanks also to David Duer, the director of development in the Berkeley University Library, for his always wise and judicious counsel, and for his heroic labors in raising financial support for the Project. Last but not least, we thank the Berkeley campus for granting the Project relief from indirect costs on its grants from the Endowment. We are grateful for this and all other forms of support from our home institution.

We thank the staff of the University Library and The Bancroft Library at Berkeley, especially Thomas C. Leonard, University Librarian; Elaine Tennant, the James D. Hart Director of The Bancroft Library; and Peter E. Hanff, its Deputy Director, all of whom serve on the Board of Directors of the Mark Twain Project. To them and to the other members of the Board—Frederick Crews, Mary C. Francis, Michael Millgate, Alison Mudditt, George A. Starr, and G. Thomas Tanselle—we are indebted for every kind of moral and intellectual support.

Scholars and archivists at other institutions have been vital to editorial work on this volume. Barbara Schmidt, an independent scholar whose invaluable website devoted to Mark Twain research (www.twainquotes.com) consistently delivers the goods, has freely and generously shared information and documents with us. Kevin Mac Donnell, an expert dealer and collector of Mark Twain documents, has been generous as ever. We would also like to thank the following scholars, librarians, and archivists who assisted us with research, documents, and permissions: Jim Boulden; Tara Brady; Lee Brumbaugh, of the Nevada Historical Society; Donald Hoffmann; Sally Hobby Owen; Lance Heidig, of Cornell University Library; Patti Philippon, of the Mark Twain House and Museum, Hartford; Steve Courtney, also of that House; Dean M. Rogers, of Vassar College Libraries; Nancy Sherbert, Kansas Historical Society, Topeka; Henry Sweets, of the Mark Twain Boyhood Home and Museum, Hannibal; Eva Tucholka, of Culver Pictures; and Mark Woodhouse, of the Center for Mark Twain Studies at Elmira College.

The enthusiasm of our sponsoring editor at UC Press, Mary C. Francis, is an inspiration to us. We are grateful for the tireless help of Kathleen MacDougall, our highly skilled copy editor and project manager, who contributed much to the accuracy of the editorial matter and was a guiding hand at every stage of the production process. Sandy Drooker has designed the book with her usual skill and sensitivity, effectively supporting the editors' request for a slightly larger type size than was used in *Volume 1;* Sam Rosenthal has expertly supervised the printing and binding process. Alex Dahne, publicity director at UC Press, has been our friendly, acute guide in the world of public relations.

The Mark Twain Project's editions are always the product of a complex and sustained collaboration among the editors. We thank (and ought to have thanked sooner) Richard E. Bucci, former member of the staff, for his skillful assistance in helping us decide how to edit texts that were dictated rather than inscribed, which comprise almost all of the *Autobiography*. Associate editors Victor Fischer and Michael B. Frank have contributed to every aspect of the editorial work, drawing on their more than forty years of experience at the Project. They carried out original research for and drafted much of the annotation, and assisted with the painstaking preparation and checking required to produce accurate texts, apparatus, and index. The expertise and energy of associate editors Sharon K. Goetz and Leslie Diane Myrick have been essential in many ways. They have created technological supports that lighten the editors' labors, and that make possible the simultaneous digital publication of this and our other editions online at www.marktwainproject.org. None of us would be able to carry on without the quiet contributions of the Project's administrative assistant, Neda Salem. On our behalf she has handily navigated the thickets of bureaucracy, organized daily office matters, and patiently and skillfully answered the hundreds of requests for information and copies of documents which the Project receives from Mark Twain enthusiasts around the world.

B. G. H. E. S.

AUTOBIOGRAPHY OF MARK TWAIN

An exciting
1849-51. [illegible] event in [illegible] vil-
nibal),
was the ar[illegible] the mesmerize
the year [illegible] 185[illegible] that I
not sure, [illegible] the month
s May; th[illegible] detail has surviv
ear of fifty [illegible] pair of
onnected little incid[illegible] th
th have served to keep the
mory of it green for me all th
incidents of no consequenc
worth embalming, yet my
mory has preserved them care
y & flung away things of real
e to give them space & make
comfortable. The truth is, a
an's memory has no more

Monday, April 2, 1906

Government of new Territory of Nevada—Governor Nye and the practical jokers—Mr. Clemens begins journalistic life on Virginia City *Enterprise*—Reports legislative sessions—He and Orion prosper—Orion builds twelve-thousand-dollar house—Governor Nye turns Territory of Nevada into a State.

PROMOTION FOR BARNES, WHOM TILLMAN BERATED

Had Woman Ejected from White House; to be Postmaster.

MERRITT GETS NEW PLACE

Present Postmaster at Washington to be Made Collector at Niagara—Platt Not Consulted.

Special to The New York Times.

WASHINGTON, March 31.—President Roosevelt surprised the capital this afternoon by announcing that he would appoint Benjamin F. Barnes as Postmaster of Washington, to succeed John A. Merritt of New York. Mr. Merritt, who for several years has been Postmaster here, has been chosen for Collector of the Port of Niagara, succeeding the late Major James Low.

Mr. Barnes is at present assistant secretary to the President. Only a short time ago he figured extensively in the newspapers for having ordered the forcible ejection from the White House of Mrs. Minor Morris, a Washington woman who had called to see the President. What attracted attention to the case was not the ejection itself, but the violence with which it was performed.

Mrs. Morris, who had been talking to Barnes in an ordinary conversational tone, and with no indications of excitement, so far as the spectators observed, was seized by two policemen and dragged by the arms out of the building and across the asphalt walk in front of the White House, a distance corresponding to that of two ordinary city blocks. During a part of the journey a negro carried her by the feet. Her dress was torn and trampled.

She was locked up on a charge of disorderly conduct, and when it was learned that she would be released on that charge a policeman, a relative of Barnes's, was sent to the House of Detention to prefer a charge of insanity against her so that she would have to be held. She was held accordingly until two physicians had examined her and pronounced her sane. He was denounced by Mrs. Morris, by various newspapers, and by Mr. Tillman in the Senate.

The appointment of Barnes to be Postmaster so soon after this incident has created endless talk here. It is taken to be the President's way of expressing confidence in Barnes and repaying him for the pain he suffered as a result of the newspaper criticisms of his course.

Orion Clemens again. To continue.

The Government of the new Territory of Nevada was an interesting menagerie.

1861

Governor Nye was an old and seasoned politician from New York—politician, not statesman. He had white hair; he was in fine physical condition; he had a winningly friendly face and deep lustrous brown eyes that could talk as a native language the tongue of every feeling, every passion, every emotion. His eyes could out-talk his tongue, and this is saying a good deal, for he was a very remarkable talker, both in private and on the stump. He was a shrewd man; he generally saw through surfaces and perceived what was going on inside without being suspected of having an eye on the matter.

When grown-up persons indulge in practical jokes, the fact gauges them. They have lived narrow, obscure, and ignorant lives, and at full manhood they still retain and cherish a job lot of left-over standards and ideals that would have been discarded with their boyhood if they had then moved out into the world and a broader life. There were many practical jokers in the new Territory. I do not take pleasure in exposing this fact, for I liked those people; but what I am saying is true. I wish I could say a kindlier thing about them instead—that they were burglars, or hat-rack thieves, or something like that, that wouldn't be utterly uncomplimentary. I would prefer it, but I can't say those things, they would not be true. These people were practical jokers, and I will not try to disguise it. In other respects they were plenty good enough people; honest people; reputable and likable. They played practical jokes upon each other with success, and got the admiration and applause and also the envy of the rest of the community. Naturally they were eager to try their arts on big game, and that was what the Governor was. But they were not able to score. They made several efforts, but the Governor defeated these efforts without any trouble and went on smiling his pleasant smile as if nothing had happened. Finally the joker-chiefs of Carson City and Virginia City conspired together to see if their combined talent couldn't win a victory, for the jokers were getting into a very uncomfortable place. The people were laughing at them, instead of at their proposed victim. They banded themselves together to the number of ten and invited the Governor to what was a most extraordinary attention in those days—pickled oyster-stew and champagne—luxuries very seldom seen in that region, and existing rather as fabrics of the imagination than as facts.

The Governor took me with him. He said disparagingly,

"It's a poor invention. It doesn't deceive. Their idea is to get me drunk and leave me under the table, and from their standpoint this will be very funny. But they don't know me. I am familiar with champagne and have no prejudices against it."

The fate of the joke was not decided until two o'clock in the morning. At that hour the Governor was serene, genial, comfortable, contented, happy, and sober, although he was so full that he couldn't laugh without shedding champagne tears. Also, at that hour the last joker joined his comrades under the table, drunk to the last perfection. The Governor remarked,

"This is a dry place, Sam, let's go and get something to drink and go to bed."

The Governor's official menagerie had been drawn from the humblest ranks of his constituents at home—harmless good fellows who had helped in his campaigns, and now they had their reward in petty salaries payable in greenbacks that were worth next to nothing. Those boys had a hard time to make both ends meet. Orion's salary was eighteen hundred dollars a year, and he couldn't even support his dictionary on it. But the Irishwoman who had come out on the Governor's staff charged the menagerie only ten dollars a week apiece for board and lodging. Orion and I were of her boarders and lodgers; and so, on these cheap terms the silver I had brought from home held out very well.

At first I roamed about the country seeking silver, but at the end of '62 or the beginning of '63 when I came up from Aurora to begin a journalistic life on the Virginia City *Enterprise,* I was presently sent down to Carson City to report the legislative session. *1862 or '63* Orion was soon very popular with the members of the legislature, because they found that whereas they couldn't usually trust each other, nor anybody else, they could trust him. He easily held the belt for honesty in that country, but it didn't do him any good in a pecuniary way, because he had no talent for either persuading or scaring legislators. But I was differently situated. I was there every day in the legislature to distribute compliment and censure with evenly balanced justice and spread the same over half a page of the *Enterprise* every morning, consequently I was an influence. I got the legislature to pass a wise and very necessary law requiring every corporation doing business in the Territory to record its charter in full, without skipping a word, in a record to be kept by the Secretary of the Territory—my brother. All the charters were framed in exactly the same words. For this record-service he was authorized to charge forty cents a folio of a hundred words for making the record; also five dollars for furnishing a certificate of each record, and so on. Everybody had a toll-road franchise but no toll-road. But the franchise had to be recorded and paid for. Everybody was a mining corporation, and had to have himself recorded and pay for it. Very well, we prospered. The record-service paid an average of a thousand dollars a month, in gold.

Governor Nye was often absent from the Territory. He liked to run down to San Francisco every little while and enjoy a rest from Territorial civilization. Nobody complained, for he was prodigiously popular. He had been a stage-driver in his early days in New York or New England, and had acquired the habit of remembering names and faces, and of making himself agreeable to his passengers. As a politician this had been valuable to him, and he kept his arts in good condition by practice. By the time he had been Governor a year, he had shaken hands with every human being in the Territory of Nevada, and after that he always knew these people instantly at sight and could call them by name. The whole population, of twenty thousand persons, were his personal friends, and he could do anything he chose to do and count upon their being contented with it. Whenever he was absent from the Territory—which was generally—Orion served his office in his place, as Acting Governor, a title which was soon and easily shortened to "Governor." Mrs. Governor Clemens enjoyed being a Governor's wife. No one on this planet ever enjoyed a distinction more than she enjoyed that one. Her delight in being the head of society was so frank that it disarmed criticism, and even envy. Being the Governor's wife and head of society, she looked for a proper kind of house to live in—a house commensurate with these dignities—and she easily persuaded Orion to build that house. Orion could be persuaded to do anything. He recklessly built and furnished a house at a cost of twelve thousand dollars, and there was no other house in that sage-brush capital that could approach this property for style and cost.

When Governor Nye's four-year term was drawing to a close, the mystery of why he had ever consented to leave the great State of New York and help inhabit that jack-rabbit desert was solved: he had gone out there in order to become a United States Senator. All that was now necessary was to turn the Territory into a State. He did it without any difficulty. That patch of sand and that sparse population were not well fitted for the heavy burden of a state government, but no matter, the people were willing to have the change, and so the Governor's game was made.

Orion's game was made too, apparently, for he was as popular because of his honesty as the Governor was for more substantial reasons; but at the critical moment the inborn capriciousness of his character rose up without warning, and disaster followed.

Tuesday, April 3, 1906

The Barnes incident again—Barnes appointed to postmastership of Washington—Mr. Clemens prepares speech on King Leopold of Belgium, but suppresses it after learning that our Government will do nothing in the matter—Intends to speak at Majestic Theatre on "The American Gentleman" but is defeated by length of first part of program—Theodore Roosevelt *the* American gentleman—Mark Twain letter sells for forty-three dollars at Nast sale—Report cabled that Mr. Clemens was dying, in London—Reporters interview him for American papers.

BARNES'S APPOINTMENT
ANGERS WASHINGTON

"White House Strong-Arm Methods," Says a Local Newspaper.

SENATE MAY HOLD IT UP

New Postmaster Characterized as a Carpetbagger—Citizens Say Selection Is an Insult.

Special to The New York Times.

WASHINGTON, April 2.—The President's selection of Benjamin F. Barnes, his assistant secretary, to be Postmaster of Washington has raised a storm. It is being criticised as a "carpetbag" appointment, Barnes being a New Jersey man. Members of the House and Senate criticise it, and it is reported that an effort will be made to defeat the confirmation.

The feeling on the subject is shown to-night in the appearance of The Evening Star, the Administration's strongest supporter in the city press. The Barnes matter breaks out all over the paper. First, there is a cartoon representing the President handing the District of Columbia an April fool cigar, which explodes, the face of Barnes appearing in the smoke, while the President shouts "April Fool!" Next there are three columns of interviews with prominent citizens of the District and members of Congress, all condemning the appointment.

The leading editorial article is devoted to the subject, and says that the President has rewarded "his tactless and too strenuous bouncer" by giving him the Washington Post Office at double his present salary. The Star says:

"There remain, logically, to be rewarded at the expense of the District, the policemen who shared with Mr. Barnes the honors in the Morris drag-out. What shall their harvest be—a local Judgeship, Commissionership, or Superintendency of Police?"

The Star prints a string of clippings from other papers ridiculing the appointment. Then, all over the editorial page are scattered detached paragraphs like these:

> The application of White House strong-arm methods to the local Postal Service may relieve the patrons of the office of the necessity of licking their own stamps.
>
> Much as Oyster Bay approves of the President it would rise in indignation if he used his influence to supplant its local men in local offices.
>
> The April Fool wag becomes less violent as the years go by. His style of humor is but seldom exploited to any shocking extent. The recent appointment of a Postmaster for Washington offers a contrary argument, but it is only one of those exceptions which prove the rule.
>
> When in future your letters seem to have been hit by a cyclone, passed through a train wreck, and run through a sausage machine you will know that they have come out of the Washington Post Office. But don't go to the Post Office to complain unless in need of exercise. Ladies should observe extreme caution in this matter.
>
> Some of the President's local proteges are as enthusiastic for Mr. Barnes as they were for the whipping post not long ago.
>
> There is a strong feeling that in the matter of appointments Niagara Falls has very much the better of the transaction.

The last reference is to the transfer of Postmaster Merritt to Niagara Falls to make room for Mr. Barnes. Finally The Star prints letters from citizens to the editor protesting against the appointment.

Among the interviews with prominent citizens is one with R. Ross Perry, a leading lawyer, who says: "Apparently the President thinks this district should be governed as the Romans governed a conquered province." D. William Oyster calls it "an insult to our community." Mason W. Richardson says: "We seem to have no rights that are worthy of respect." John Ridout says, "in view of the temperament of Mr. Barnes, as disclosed in the Morris incident, the prospect for satisfactory interviews between him and citizens acting in the exercise of their right to criticise the administration of his office is not encouraging."

So far as I can remember, I have kept track of the Barnes incident by occasionally inserting an informing clipping from the newspapers. If anything is lacking from this procession of signal-posts it is the President's letter of some weeks ago. Maybe I inserted it. Possibly I didn't. But it is no matter. Either way will do. It was splendidly brutal,

1906

frankly heartless. It contained not a word of pity for the abused lady; and an equally striking feature of it was that it contained not a word of pity for the President himself. Surely everybody else pitied him, and was ashamed of him. It contained not a word of rebuke, nor even of criticism of Barnes's conduct, and its approval of it was so pronounced that the spirit of it amounted to praise.

And now the President has appointed this obscene slave to the postmastership of Washington. The daring of it—the stupid blindness of it—is amazing. It would be unbelievable if it emanated from any human being in the United States except our incredible President.

When Choate and I agreed to speak at Carnegie Hall on the 22d of January, along with Booker Washington, in the interest of his Tuskegee Institute, I at first took that thief and assassin, Leopold II King of the Belgians, as my text, and carefully prepared a speech—wrote it out in full, in fact, several weeks beforehand. But when the appointed date was drawing near I began to grow suspicious of our Government's attitude toward Leopold and his fiendishnesses. Twice I went to Washington and conferred with the State Department. Then I began to suspect that the Congo Reform Association's conviction that our Government's pledged honor was at stake in the Congo matter was an exaggeration; that the Association was attaching meanings to certain public documents connected with the Congo which the strict sense of the documents did not confirm. A final visit to the State Department settled the matter. The Department had kept its promise, previously made to the President and to me, that it would examine into the matter exhaustively and see how our Government stood. It was found that of the fourteen Christian Governments pledged to watch over Leopold and keep him within treaty limits, our Government was not one. Our Government was only sentimentally concerned, not officially, not practically, not by any form of pledge or promise. Our Government could interfere in the form of prayer or protest, but so could a Sunday-school. I knew that the Administration was going to be properly and diplomatically polite, and keep out of the muddle; therefore I privately withdrew from the business of agitating the Congo matter in the United States, and wrote the Boston branch that I thought it would be a pity to wring the hearts of this nation further with the atrocities Leopold was committing upon those helpless black natives of the Congo, since this would be to harrow up the feelings of the nation to no purpose—since the nation itself could do nothing save through its Government, and the Government would of course do nothing.

So I suppressed that speech and delivered one in its stead on another subject. But before selecting that subject I examined another one and prepared a speech upon it. If that speech had had a title I suppose it would have been "What is an American Gentleman?" Or maybe it would have been "America, the Land of the Free and the Home of the Brave and of the Ill-mannered"—or possibly it might have been "The Unpolite Nation." I did not throw the speech away, but saved it, hoping for the right occasion.

The right occasion arrived, a few weeks ago, when I was to speak in the Majestic Theatre on Sunday afternoon to a couple of thousand male Young Christians who might take an interest in hearing the views of an expert upon the qualities required to constitute an American gentleman. But I was defeated again. The program was of the customary sort, where many persons are giving their time and labor to a great cause without salary and each must be allowed to step out and dangle himself before the audience by way of remuneration. A man who couldn't speak, spoke. And a woman who couldn't sing, sang. Another man who couldn't speak, spoke. A mixed string-and-piano-band made some noises, and when the house rejoiced that the affliction was over, the band took it for an encore and did the noises over again. Then a man who couldn't read, read a chapter from the Bible—and so this chaos went on and on. And every now and then God in His inscrutable wisdom would turn that singer loose again. I thought my turn would never come. At last when it did arrive I saw that I must cut myself down by half; that instead of allowing myself an hour, I must put up with 50 per cent of that. The result was that I talked upon a text—a good text, too—dropped by one of those speakers who couldn't speak, and who didn't know he had dropped it, and never missed it. And so once more my exposition of what the American gentleman should be got suppressed.

Now then all this has been fortunate. Still, all good things come to him who waits. I have waited, because I couldn't help it, but my reward has come just the same. I don't have to say, now, what the American gentleman should be—the whole ground can be covered with half a sentence, and an hour's laborious talk saved by just stating what the American gentleman is. He is Theodore Roosevelt, President of the United States.

I am not jesting, but am in deep earnest, when I give it as my opinion that our President is *the* representative American gentleman—of to-day. I think he is as distinctly and definitely the representative American gentleman of to-day as was Washington the representative American gentleman of his day. Roosevelt is the whole argument for and against, in his own person. He represents what the American gentleman ought not to be, and does it as clearly, intelligibly, and exhaustively as he represents what the American gentleman *is*. We are by long odds the most ill-mannered nation, civilized or savage, that exists on the planet to-day, and our President stands for us like a colossal monument visible from all the ends of the earth. He is fearfully hard and coarse where another gentleman would exhibit kindliness and delicacy. Lately, when that slimy creature of his, that misplaced doctor, that dishonored Governor of Cuba, that sleight of hand Major General, Leonard Wood, penned up six hundred helpless savages in a hole and butchered every one of them, allowing not even a woman or a child to escape, President Roosevelt—representative American gentleman, First American gentleman—put the heart and soul of our whole nation of gentlemen into the scream of delight which he cabled to Wood congratulating him on this "brilliant feat of arms," and praising him for thus "upholding the honor of the American flag."

Roosevelt is far and away the worst President we have ever had, and also the most admired and the most satisfactory. The nation's admiration of him and pride in him and worship of him is far wider, far warmer, and far more general than it has ever before lavished upon a President, even including McKinley, Jackson, and Grant.

Is the Morris-Barnes incident closed? Possibly yes; possibly no. We will keep an eye on it and see. For the moment, there seems to be something like a revolt there in Washington among half a dozen decent people and one newspaper, but we must not build too much upon this. It is but a limited revolt, and can be vituperated into silence by that vast patriot band of cordial serfs, the American newspaper editors.

This is from this morning's paper:

MARK TWAIN LETTER SOLD.

Written to Thomas Nast, It Proposed a Joint Tour.

A Mark Twain autograph letter brought $43 yesterday at the auction by the Merwin-Clayton Company of the library and correspondence of the late Thomas Nast, cartoonist. The letter is nine pages note-paper, is dated Hartford, Nov. 12, 1877, and is addressed to Nast. It reads in part as follows:

Hartford, Nov. 12.

My Dear Nast: I did not think I should ever stand on a platform again until the time was come for me to say "I die innocent." But the same old offers keep arriving that have arriven every year, and been every year declined—$500 for Louisville, $500 for St. Louis, $1,000 gold for two nights in Toronto, half gross proceeds for New York, Boston, Brooklyn, &c. I have declined them all just as usual, though sorely tempted as usual.

Now, I do not decline because I mind talking to an audience, but because (1) traveling alone is so heart-breakingly dreary, and (2) shouldering the whole show is such cheer-killing responsibility.

Therefore I now propose to you what you proposed to me in November, 1867—ten years ago, (when I was unknown,) viz.: That you should stand on the platform and make pictures, and I stand by you and blackguard the audience. I should enormously enjoy meandering around (to big towns—don't want to go to little ones) with you for company.

The letter includes a schedule of cities and the number of appearances planned for each.

This is as it should be. This is worthy of all praise. I say it myself lest other competent persons should forget to do it. It appears that four of my ancient letters were sold at auction, three of them at twenty-seven dollars, twenty-eight dollars, and twenty-nine dollars respectively, and the one above mentioned at forty-three dollars. There is one very gratifying circumstance about this, to wit: that my literature has more than held its own as regards money value through this stretch of thirty-six years. I judge that the forty-three-dollar letter must have gone at about ten cents a word, whereas if I had written it to-day its market rate would be thirty cents—so I have increased in value two or three hundred per cent. I note another gratifying circumstance—that a letter of General Grant's sold at something short of eighteen dollars. I can't rise to General Grant's lofty place in the estimation of this nation, but it is a deep happiness to me to know that when it comes to epistolary literature he can't sit in the front seat along with me.

This reminds me—nine years ago, when we were living in Tedworth Square, London, a report was cabled to the American journals that I was dying. I was not the one. It was another Clemens, a cousin of mine,—Dr. J. Ross Clemens, now of St. Louis—who was due to die but presently escaped, by some chicanery or other characteristic of the tribe of Clemens. The London representatives of the American papers began to flock in, with American cables in their hands, to inquire into my condition. There was nothing the matter with me, and each in his turn was astonished, and disappointed, to find me reading and smoking in my study and worth next to nothing as a text for transatlantic news. One of these men was a gentle and kindly and grave and sympathetic Irishman, who hid his sorrow the best he could, and tried to look glad, and told me that his paper, the *Evening Sun,* had cabled him that it was reported in New York that I was dead. What should he cable in reply? I said—

"Say the report is greatly exaggerated."

He never smiled, but went solemnly away and sent the cable in those words. The remark hit the world pleasantly, and to this day it keeps turning up, now and then, in the newspapers when people have occasion to discount exaggerations.

The next man was also an Irishman. He had his New York cablegram in his hand—from the New York *World*—and he was so evidently trying to get around that cable with invented softnesses and palliations that my curiosity was aroused and I wanted to see what it did really say. So when occasion offered I slipped it out of his hand. It said,

"If Mark Twain dying send five hundred words. If dead send a thousand."

Now that old letter of mine sold yesterday for forty-three dollars. When I am dead it will be worth eighty-six.

Wednesday, April 4, 1906

The Morris case again—Scope of this autobiography, a mirror—More about Nast sale; laurels for Mr. Clemens—Clippings in regard to Women's University Club reception; Mr. Clemens comments on them—Vassar benefit at Hudson Theatre; Mr. Clemens meets many old friends.

MRS. MORRIS CASE IN SENATE.

Nomination of Barnes Opens Way for an Inquiry.

Special to The New York Times.

WASHINGTON, April 3.—Criticism of the appointment of Mr. Roosevelt's Assistant Secretary, B. F. Barnes, to be Postmaster of Washington continues. It now seems likely that the appointment may have a hard time in passing the Senate. Barnes's action in having Mrs. Minor Morris put out of the White House is the chief ground of opposition. The Senate Committee on Post Offices and Post Roads has determined to investigate Barnes's action in the Morris case, and eye witnesses of the affair have been summoned to appear before the committee to-morrow and tell what they saw. This is the same investigation which Mr. Tillman requested and which the Senate refused to grant. It now comes as the result of the President's action in appointing Barnes Postmaster. The witnesses who are to appear before the committee were not asked to testify in the investigation which the President made when he decided that Barnes's course was justified.

There was much speculation to-day as to who Mr. Barnes's successor as Assistant Secretary would be. The Evening Star to-night devotes a column and a half to suggestions on the subject, saying that the leading candidates are John L. McGrew, a clerk in the White House offices; Warren Young, Chief Executive Clerk; M. C. Latta, the President's personal stenographer; James J. Corbett of New York, Robert Fitzsimmons, Augustus Ruhlin, and James J. Jeffries.

The article is illustrated with two pictures of Corbett and Fitzsimmons.

That is neat, and causes me much gentle delight. The point of that whole matter lies in the last four names that are mentioned in it. These four men are prize-fighters—the most celebrated ones now living.

Is the incident now closed? Again we cannot tell. The smell of it may linger in American history a thousand years yet.

This autobiography of mine differs from other autobiographies—differs from *all* other autobiographies, except Benvenuto's, perhaps. The conventional biography of all the ages is an open window. The autobiographer sits there and examines and discusses the people that go by—not all of them, but the notorious ones, the famous ones; those that wear fine uniforms, and crowns when it is not raining; and very great poets and great statesmen—illustrious people with whom he has had the high privilege of coming in contact. He likes to toss a wave of recognition to these with his hand as they go by, and he likes to notice that the others are seeing him do this, and admiring. He likes to let on that in discussing these occasional people that wear the good clothes he is only interested in interesting his reader, and is in a measure unconscious of himself.

But this autobiography of mine is not that kind of an autobiography. This autobiography of mine is a mirror, and I am looking at myself in it all the time. Incidentally I notice the people that pass along at my back—I get glimpses of them in the mirror—and whenever they say or do anything that can help advertise me and flatter me and raise me in my own estimation, I set these things down in my autobiography. I rejoice when a king or duke comes my way and makes himself useful to this autobiography, but they are rare customers, with wide intervals between. I can use them with good effect as lighthouses and monuments along my way, but for real business I depend upon the common herd.

Here is some more about the Nast sale:

30 CENTS FOR McCURDY POEM.

Other Literary Curiosities from the Nast Collection at Auction.

The sale of autograph letters, wash drawings, pencil and pen and ink sketches, the property of the late Thomas Nast, the cartoonist, was continued yesterday by the Merwin-Clayton Company.

Five letters from Theodore Roosevelt as Police Commissioner, Colonel of the Rough Riders, Governor, and President, to Mr. Nast, thanking him for sketches and expressing warm friendship for the cartoonist, brought prices ranging from $1.50 to $2.25.

Richard A. McCurdy's autograph letter and original autograph poem addressed to Nast, with a typewritten copy of the poem, brought 30 cents the lot.

The following letter written by Gen. Philip H. Sheridan to Nast was bid in at $12.25 by J. H. Manning, a son of the late Daniel Manning:

May 12, 1875.

Dear Nast:

It is true. I will be married on the 30th of June coming unless there is a slip between the cup and the lip, which is scarcely possible. I will not have any wedding for many reasons, among them the recent death of my father.

I am very happy, but wish the d—d thing was over. Yours truly,

SHERIDAN.

P.S. and M.I.—I send the inclosed for your oldest. Please send me yours to be kept for mine. P. H. S.

A letter written by Lincoln, and which was laid over a piece of white silk bearing a faded red stain, sold for $38. The attached certificate stated that the silk was from the dress of Laura Keene, worn on the night of Lincoln's assassination, and that the stain was made by his blood.

Gen. W. T. Sherman's letter to Nast, dated March 9, 1879, indorsing a testimonial of the cartoonist's services to the army and navy, sold for $6.

A scrapbook containing sketches of Lincoln, Sumner, Greeley, Walt Whitman, and many water color sketches, brought $75.

A sketch of William M. Tweed and his companion, Hunt, under arrest, brought $21. Two companion Christmas sketches by Nast, representing a child telephoning to Santa Claus, brought $43 each. A sketch of Gen. Grant was bid in for $36. A sketch of the "G.O.P." elephant brought $28. A sketch representing the Saviour, full face, with nimbus, brought $65.

An autograph photograph of Theodore Roosevelt, dated 1884, was bid in at $5.

It is a great satisfaction to me to notice that I am still ahead—ahead of Roosevelt, ahead of Sherman, ahead of Sheridan, even ahead of Lincoln. These are fine laurels, but they will not last. A time is coming when some of them will wither. A day will come when a mere scratch of Mr. Lincoln's pen will outsell a whole basketful of my letters. A time will come when a scratch of the pens of those immortal soldiers, Sherman and Sheridan, will outsell a thousand scratches of mine, and so I shall enjoy my supremacy now, while I may. I shall read that clipping over forty or fifty times, now, while it is new and true, and let the desolating future take care of itself.

I omit this morning's stirring news from Russia to make room for this half-column clipping, because the clipping is about me.

MARK TWAIN TALKS TO COLLEGE WOMEN

Says He'll Only Speak to Alumnae After This.

TELLS THAT TWICHELL STORY

Five Hundred Women Shook Hands with Him and Showered Him with Pretty Speeches.

The Women's University Club and Mark Twain entertained each other yesterday. The club gave a reception, with the author as the guest of honor, and the entire club and a good many of its relatives and friends turned out to meet him. There were 500 of them at least, and each one had something to say to Mr. Clemens when she shook hands with him.

Some one who was looking on said that a good many "repeated" and went up twice to shake hands.

Mr. Clemens in the course of a long life has had other experiences in which college girls have had a part, and he was somewhat reminiscent. The girls he talked to yesterday were some of them grandchildren of other girls he had met in other days.

"I don't have to say anything, do I?" said one girl, who had not been able to think up an interesting remark, as she shook hands with the guest of honor.

"No, indeed," said Mr. Clemens, "I'm shy that way myself."

"I have been waiting since I was three years old for this," said another girl. "It was as long ago as that that my father pointed out the pictures in 'Innocents Abroad' to me."

"I bring a message from two little girls," said an older woman. "They want you to write another story as nice as 'The Prince and the Pauper,' and send them the first copy," and Mark Twain gayly promised that he would.

Mr. Clemens had promised to speak at the club, but, having a cold, asked to be excused. He was persuaded, however, to "tell a yarn."

They brought in a little platform that had been in readiness for the address, but he was not satisfied with it.

"I don't think that is high enough," he said, "because I can't tell what people are thinking unless I see their faces." Then at his request they brought a chair, which was placed on the platform, and he stood on it. The veteran author never spoke to a more appreciative audience.

"I am not here, young ladies, to make a speech," he said, "but what may look like one in the distance. I don't dare to make a speech, for I haven't made any preparations, and if I tried it on an empty stomach—I mean an empty mind—I don't know what iniquity I might commit.

"On the 19th of this month, at Carnegie Hall, I am going to take formal leave of the platform for ever and ever, as far as appearing for pay is concerned and before people who have to pay to get in, but I have not given up for other occasions.

"I shall now proceed to infest the platform all the time under conditions that I like—when I am not paid to appear and when no one has to pay to get in, and I shall only talk to audiences of college girls. I have labored for the public good for many years, and now I am going to talk for my own contentment."

Then Mr. Clemens told his "yarn."

It was a yarn about a walking tour with the Rev. Joseph Twichell that the public has found entertaining. The college women appeared to be entertained by it.

MARK TWAIN ADORED BY THE COLLEGE GIRLS AT WOMEN'S UNIVERSITY CLUB.

MARK TWAIN WAS WREATHED IN GIRLS.

Five Hundred at Women's University Club Hung About Their Universal Sweetheart.

COULDN'T SEE THEM ALL, SO HE MOUNTED A CHAIR.

Fed Him on Ices to Keep Up His Drooping Energies Between "Repeating" Delegations.

Mark Twain has the college-girl habit!

He is not discriminating about the college. He loves them all! He admitted it yesterday at the Women's University Club to about five hundred of them. If he melted into momentary tenderness over Barnard he excused it by saying that, if not his greatest, it was his latest love.

From 4 to 6 Mr. Clemens was wreathed about with girls, and as happy as a king. He looked into their faces with quizzical eyes, laid a detaining hand on a shoulder now and again, while he invented a story to draw a smile from a pair of pretty lips. And when he could not see enough of them he mounted a chair to have his horizon bounded by girls—girls in Easter bonnets and charming frocks; girls all blushes and delight in the presence of their universal sweetheart.

His Heart Is True.

"On the 19th of this month," said Mark, "I am going to take my formal leave of the platform forevermore at Carnegie Hall. That is as far as appearing for pay is concerned. But I have not really left the platform at all. I shall proceed to get on it as often as I desire when the conditions are what I like. I mean when nobody who pays can get there, and nobody is in the house except young ladies from the colleges."

Shouts interrupted him.

"I have labored for the public good," continued Mr. Clemens, shaking his leonine mane prodigiously, "for thirty-five or forty years. I propose to work for my personal contentment the rest of the time." His smile included them all. Mr. Clemens had not intended to address his girls collectively. As he explained, he "never liked to make a speech without preparation, because it was impossible to tell what kind of iniquity he might wander into on an empty stomach—that is, mind." But the pressure was too much for him. He had come to be the guest of honor and have the privilege of talking to all the college women individually.

There he stood at the head of the long drawing-room of the club-house on Madison Square North, with Miss Maida Castelhun, the President, a vision in black jetted lace over blue silk, to support him on the right—and the support was quite literal at times. Miss Cutting, of Vassar, in white, was at his left to make the introductions, while Miss Hervy, of the Entertainment Committee, fed Mr.

Clemens's drooping energies with occasional tid-bits from the refreshment room, and kept a vigilant eye out for "repeaters" among those who greeted him.

Fed Him Charlottes.

It was a beautiful sight to see Miss Hervy's tall figure, the tail of her light gray gown thrown over her arm, bearing down through the throng like a ship under full sail with a charlotte russe held aloft in a white gloved hand.

"Mr. Clemens must have this before he says another word," she would exclaim and the line halted while the humorist meekly devoured her offering. He shamelessly encouraged the repeaters.

"I met a lady I had seen the other day at Vassar," he said, as he held a Vassar hand, "and found I had to construct things all over again, for she is now a grandmother. Perhaps I am seeing some of her grand-daughters now. It is terrible mixing, you know."

Some of them declared they had waited for this moment all their lives. One whispered as she passed:

"I don't have to say anything, do I?"

"No," replied Mr. Clemens, "I'm shy about that sort of thing, myself."

"Won't you tell the Blue Jay story?"

"I've been brought up on 'Tom Sawyer.'"

"Won't you do us another 'Prince and the Pauper'" were some of the speeches hailed upon him.

One Touch of Nature.

But the best was the little freshman who rushed up with dancing eyes, gave his hand an energetic squeeze and asked:

"Say, have you had an ice in there?—they're perfectly fine."

When Mark Twain promised to "yarn" for them, a small platform was brought in.

"But I want a chair," he said. "I can't see what you are doing out there."

A dozen hands were extended to help him up and he told the story of Twichell and himself, when for three hours and a half he hunted for a lost sock in the desert of a German bedroom "like a modern Sahara."

Then he sat down on his chair and the girls grouped themselves at his feet.

It is evident that this reporter was there. He didn't see everything, and he didn't hear everything, but he saw and heard the most of the show, and he saw and heard with considerable accuracy, too. He is right when he says I have the college-girl habit. I was never without it. Susy's Biography shows, incidentally, that I had it twenty years ago and more. I had it earlier than that, as Smith College can testify. That Vassar episode was damaged by that old goat who was President there at the time, but nothing can ever damage the lovely vision of the Vassar girls of that mixed delightful and devilish day. It was a lovely vision, and it does not fade out of my memory.

Day before yesterday all Vassar, ancient and modern, packed itself into the Hudson Theatre, and I was there. The occasion was a benefit arranged by Vassar and its friends to raise money to aid poor students of that College in getting through the college course. I was not aware that I was to be a feature of the show, and was distressed and most uncomfortably inflamed with blushes when I found it out. Really the distress and the blushes were manufactured, for at bottom I was glad. When the ladies started to lead me through the house to the stage, when the performance was over, I was so coy that everybody admired, and was moved by it. I do things like that with an art that deceives even the hardened and experienced cynic. It has taken me a long time and has cost me much practice to perfect myself in that art, but it was worth the trouble. It makes me the most winning old thing that ever went among confiding girls. I held a reception on that stage for an hour or two, and all Vassar, ancient and modern, shook hands with me. Some of the moderns were too beautiful for words, and I was very friendly with those. I was so hoping somebody would want to kiss me for my mother, but I didn't dare to suggest it myself. Presently, however, when it happened, I did what I could to make it contagious, and succeeded. This required art, but I had it in stock. I *seemed* to take the old and the new as they came, without discrimination, but I averaged the percentage to my advantage, and without anybody's suspecting, I think.

Among that host I met again as many as half a dozen pretty old girls whom I had met in their bloom at Vassar that time that Susy and I visited the College so long ago. Yesterday, at the University Club, almost all the five hundred were of the young and lovely, untouched by care, unfaded by age. There were girls there from Smith, Wellesley, Radcliffe, Vassar and Barnard, together with a sprinkling of college girls from the South, from the Middle West and the Pacific coast.

I delivered a moral sermon to the Barnard girls at Columbia University a few weeks ago, and now it was like being among old friends. There were dozens of Barnard girls there, scores of them, and I had already shaken hands with them at Barnard. As I have said, the reporter heard many things there yesterday, but there were several which he didn't hear. One sweet creature wanted to whisper in my ear, and I was nothing loth. She raised her dainty form on tiptoe, lifting herself with a grip of her velvet hands on my shoulders and put her lips to my ear and said "How do you like being the belle of New York?" It was so true, and so gratifying, that it crimsoned me with blushes, and I could make no reply. The reporter lost that.

Two girls, one from Maine, the other from Ohio, were grandchildren of fellow-passengers who sailed with me in the *Quaker City* in the "Innocents Abroad" excursion thirty-nine years ago. We had a pleasant chat of course. Then a middle-aged lady shook hands and said,

"In something approaching the same way, Mr. Clemens, I also am an old friend of yours, for one of my oldest and most intimate friends was also a fellow-passenger of yours in the *Quaker City*—Mrs. Faulkner."

By anticipation, my face was beginning to light up. That name blew it out as if it had been a candle. It was a pity that that lady hadn't penetration enough to realize that this was a good time to drop the matter, or change the subject. But no, she had no more presence of mind than I should have had in her place. There was a pair of us there. She was out of presence of mind, and I couldn't help her because I was out of it too. She didn't know what to say, so she said the wrong thing. She said,

"Why, don't you remember Mrs. Faulkner?"

I didn't know what to say, and so I said the wrong thing. I exposed the fact that I didn't remember that name. She tottered where she stood. I tottered where I stood. Neither of us could say anything more, and the fact that there was a pack and jam of eager young watchers and listeners all about us didn't in the least modify the difficulty for us. She melted into the crowd and disappeared, leaving me pretty uncomfortable—and, if signs go for anything, she was uncomfortable herself. People are always turning up who have known me in the distant past, and sometimes it is so but usually it isn't. This is the first time, however, that I have ever heard of a *Quaker City* passenger who had never seen that ship. There was no Mrs. Faulkner among the *Quaker City*'s people.

Thursday, April 5, 1906

Miss Mary Lawton the rising sun, Ellen Terry the setting sun—Ellen Terry's farewell banquet, on fiftieth anniversary—Mr. Clemens's cablegram—Mr. Clemens has fine new idea for a play; Mr. Hammond Trumbull squelches it—Orion Clemens is defeated as Secretary of State—At Mr. Camp's suggestion Mr. Clemens speculates unfortunately—Mr. Camp offers to buy Tennessee Land for two hundred thousand dollars. Orion refuses—Mr. Clemens just discovers that he still owns a thousand acres of the Tennessee Land—Orion comes East, gets position on Hartford *Evening Post*—After various business ventures he returns to Keokuk and tries raising chickens.

Am I standing upon the world's back and looking east toward the rising sun and west toward the setting sun? That is a handsome figure! I wonder if it has been used before. It probably has. Most things that are said have been said before. In fact all things that are said have been said before. Moreover they have been said many millions of times. This is a sad thing for the human race that sits up nine nights in the week to admire its own originality. The race has always been able to think well of itself, and it doesn't like people who throw bricks at its naïve self-appreciation. It is sensitive upon this point. The other day I furnished a sentiment in response to a man's request—to wit:

"The noblest work of God?" Man.

"Who found it out?" Man.

I thought it was very good, and smart, but the other person didn't.

But I must get back to the back of the world and look east and west again at those suns. One of them is Miss Mary Lawton, an American young lady who has been training herself for the stage; and at last we hope and believe we see an opening for her. We strongly believe that hers will be a great name some day. Fay Davis, a famous and popular actress who is playing the chief rôle in a serious and impressive drama called—never mind the name, I have forgotten it—wishes to retire from the piece as soon as a competent successor can be found; and at Daniel Frohman's suggestion I cabled London two or three days ago and asked Charles Frohman if he would let Miss Lawton try that part. That is the sun which is apparently about to rise; the sun which is about to set is Ellen Terry, who has been a queen of the English stage for fifty years, and will retire from it on the 28th of this month, which will be the fiftieth anniversary. She will retire in due form at a great banquet in London, and cablegrams meet for the occasion will flow in upon the banqueteers from old friends of hers in America and other formerly distant regions of the earth—there are no distant regions now. The American cablegrams are being collected by a committee in New York, and by request I have furnished mine. To do these things by cable, at twenty-five cents a word, is the modern way and the only way. They could go by post at no expense, but it wouldn't be good form. [Privately I will remark that they *do* go by mail—dated to suit the requirements.]

> Age has not withered, nor custom staled, the admiration and affection I have felt for you so many many years. I lay them at your honored feet with the strength and freshness of their youth upon them undiminished.

She is a lovely character, as was also Sir Henry Irving, who lately departed this life. I first knew them thirty-four years ago in London, and thenceforth held them in high esteem and affection.

When I ushered in that large figure, a while ago, about the world's back and the rising and sinking suns, and exposed a timid doubt as to the freshness of that great figure, that timidity was the result of an experience of mine a quarter of a century ago. One day a splendid inspiration burst in my head and scattered my brains all over the farm—we were spending the summer at Quarry Farm that summer. That explosion fertilized the farm so that it yielded double crops for seven years. That wonderful inspiration of mine was what seemed to me to be the most novel and striking basic idea for a play that had ever been imagined. I was going to write that play at once, and astonish the world with it; and I did, indeed, begin upon the work immediately. Then it occurred to me that as I was not well acquainted with the history of the drama it might be well for me to make sure that this idea of mine was really new before I went further. So I wrote Hammond Trumbull, of Hartford, and asked him if the idea had ever been used on the stage. Hammond Trumbull was the learned man of America at that time, and had been so regarded by both hemispheres for a good many years. I knew that he would know all about it. I waited a week and then his answer came. It covered several great pages of foolscap written in Trumbull's small and beautiful hand, and the pages consisted merely of a list of titles of plays in which that new idea of mine had been used, in about sixty-seven countries. I do not remember how many thousand plays were mentioned in the list. I only remember that he hadn't written down all the titles, but had only furnished enough for a sample. And I also remember that the earliest play in the invoice was a Chinese one and was upwards of twenty-five hundred years old.

That figure of mine—standing on the back of the world and watching the rising and the declining suns—is really stately, is really fine, but I am losing confidence in it. Hammond Trumbull is dead. But if he were with us now he could probably furnish me with a few reams of samples.

Orion Clemens—Resumed.

1864–65

There were several candidates for all the offices in the gift of the new State of Nevada save two—United States Senator, and Secretary of State. Nye was certain to get a Senatorship, and Orion was so sure to get the Secretaryship that no one but him was named for that office. But he was hit with one of his spasms of virtue on the very day that the Republican party was to make its nominations in the Convention, and refused to go near the Convention. He was urged, but all persuasions failed. He said his presence there would be an unfair and improper influence, and that if he was to be nominated the compliment must come to him as a free and unspotted gift. This attitude would have settled his case for him without further effort, but he had another attack of virtue on the same day, that made it absolutely sure. It had been his habit for a great many years to change his religion with his shirt, and his ideas about temperance at the same time. He would be a teetotaler for a while and the champion of the cause; then he would change to the other side for a time. On nomination day he suddenly changed from a friendly attitude toward whisky—which was the popular attitude—to uncompromising teetotalism, and went absolutely dry. His friends besought and implored, but all in vain. He could not be persuaded to cross the threshold of a saloon. The paper next morning contained the list of chosen nominees. His name was not in it. He had not received a vote.

His rich income ceased when the State government came into power. He was without an occupation. Something had to be done. He put up his sign as attorney at law, but he got no clients. It was strange. It was difficult to account for. I cannot account for it—but if I were going to guess at a solution I should guess that by the make of him he would examine both sides of a case so diligently and so conscientiously that when he got through with his argument neither he nor a jury would know which side he was on. I think that his client would find out his make in laying his case before him, and would take warning and withdraw it in time to save himself from probable disaster.

I had taken up my residence in San Francisco about a year before the time I have just been speaking of. One day I got a tip from Mr. Camp, a bold man who was always making big fortunes in ingenious speculations and losing them again in the course of six months by other speculative ingenuities. Camp told me to buy some shares in the "Hale and Norcross." I bought fifty shares at three hundred dollars a share. I bought on a margin, and put up 20 per cent. It exhausted my funds. I wrote Orion and offered him half, and asked him to send his share of the money. I waited and waited. He wrote and said he was going to attend to it. The stock went along up pretty briskly. It went higher and higher. It reached a thousand dollars a share. It climbed to two thousand, then to three thousand; then to twice that figure. The money did not come, but I was not disturbed. By and by that stock took a turn and began to gallop down. Then I wrote urgently. Orion answered that he had sent the money long ago—said he had sent it to the Occidental Hotel. I inquired for it. They said it was not there. To cut a long story short, that stock went on down until it fell below the price I had paid for it. Then it began to eat up the margin, and when at last I got out I was very badly crippled.

When it was too late, I found out what had become of Orion's money. Any other human being would have sent a check, but he sent gold. The hotel clerk put it in the safe and went on vacation, and there it had reposed all this time enjoying its fatal work, no doubt. Another man might have thought to tell me that the money was not in a letter, but was in an express package, but it never occurred to Orion to do that.

Later, Mr. Camp gave me another chance. He agreed to buy our Tennessee land for two hundred thousand dollars, pay a part of the amount in cash and give long notes for the rest. His scheme was to import foreigners from grape-growing and wine-making districts in Europe, settle them on the land, and turn it into a wine-growing country. He knew what Mr. Longworth thought of those Tennessee grapes, and was satisfied. I sent the contracts and things to Orion for his signature, he being one of the three heirs. But they arrived at a bad time—in a doubly bad time, in fact. The temperance virtue was temporarily upon him in strong force, and he wrote and said that he would not be a party to debauching the country with wine. Also he said how could he know whether Mr. Camp was going to deal fairly and honestly with those poor people from Europe or not?—and so, without waiting to find out, he quashed the whole trade, and there it fell, never to be brought to life again. The land, from being suddenly worth two hundred thousand dollars, became as suddenly worth what it was before—nothing, and taxes to pay. I had paid the taxes and the other expenses for some years, but I dropped the Tennessee Land there, and have never taken any interest in it since, pecuniarily or otherwise, until yesterday.

I had supposed, until yesterday, that Orion had frittered away the last acre, and indeed that was his own impression. But a gentleman arrived yesterday from Tennessee and brought a map showing that by a correction of the ancient surveys we still own a thousand acres, in a coal district, out of the hundred thousand acres which my father left us when he died in 1847. The gentleman brought a proposition; also he brought a reputable and well-to-do citizen of New York. The proposition was that the Tennesseean gentleman should sell that land; that the New York gentleman should pay all the expenses and fight all the lawsuits, in case any should turn up, and that of such profit as might eventuate the Tennesseean gentleman should take a third, the New Yorker a third, and Sam Moffett and his sister (Mrs. Charles L. Webster), and I—who are the surviving heirs—the remaining third.

This time I hope we shall get rid of the Tennessee Land for good and all and never hear of it again.

1867

I came East in January 1867. Orion remained in Carson City perhaps a year longer. Then he sold his twelve-thousand-dollar house and its furniture for thirty-five hundred in greenbacks at about 60 per cent discount. He and his wife took first-class passage in the steamer for New York. In New York they stopped at an expensive hotel; explored the city in an expensive way; then fled to Keokuk, and arrived there about as nearly penniless as they were when they had migrated thence in July '61. About 1871 or '72 they came to New York. They were obliged to go somewhere. Orion had been trying to make a living in the law ever since he had arrived from the Pacific coast, but he had secured only two cases. Those he was to try free of charge—but the possible result will never be known, because the parties settled the cases out of court without his help.

1871

I had bought my mother a house in Keokuk. I was giving her a stated sum monthly, and Orion another stated sum. They all lived together in the house. Orion could have had all the work he wanted, at good wages, in the composing-room of the *Gate City,* (a daily paper) but his wife had been a Governor's wife and she was not able to permit that degradation. It was better, in her eyes, that they live upon charity.

But, as I say, they came East and Orion got a job as proof-reader on the New York *Evening Post* at ten dollars a week. They took a single small room, and in it they cooked, and lived on that money. By and by Orion came to Hartford and wanted me to get him a place as reporter on a Hartford paper. Here was a chance to try my scheme again, and I did it. I made him go to the Hartford *Evening Post,* without any letter of introduction, and propose to scrub and sweep and do all sorts of things for nothing, on the plea that he didn't need money but only needed work, and that that was what he was pining for. Within six weeks he was on the editorial staff of that paper at twenty dollars a week, and he was worth the money. He was presently called for by some other paper at better wages, but I made him go to the *Post* people and tell them about it. They stood the raise and kept him. It was the pleasantest berth he had ever had in his life. It was an easy berth. He was in every way comfortable. But ill luck came. It was bound to come.

A new Republican daily was to be started in Rutland, Vermont, by a stock company of well-to-do politicians, and they offered him the chief editorship at three thousand a year. He was eager to accept. His wife was equally eager—no, twice as eager, three times as eager. My beseechings and reasonings went for nothing. I said,

"You are as weak as water. Those people will find it out right away. They will easily see that you have no back-bone; that they can deal with you as they would deal with a slave. You may last six months, but not longer. Then they will not dismiss you as they would dismiss a gentleman: they will fling you out as they would fling out an intruding tramp."

It happened just so. Then he and his wife migrated to that persecuted and unoffending Keokuk once more. Orion wrote from there that he was not resuming the law; that he thought that what his health needed was the open air, in some sort of outdoor occupation; that his old father-in-law had a strip of ground on the river border a mile above Keokuk with some sort of a house on it, and his idea was to buy that place and start a chicken farm and provide Keokuk with chickens and eggs, and perhaps butter—but I don't know whether you can raise butter on a chicken farm or not. He said the place could be had for three thousand dollars cash, and I sent the money. He began to raise chickens, and he made a detailed monthly report to me, whereby it appeared that he was able to work off his chickens on the Keokuk people at a dollar and a quarter a pair. But it also appeared that it cost a dollar and sixty cents to raise the pair. This did not seem to discourage Orion, and so I let it go. Meantime he was borrowing a hundred dollars per month of me regularly, month by month. Now to show Orion's stern and rigid business ways—and he really prided himself on his large business capacities—the moment he received the advance of a hundred dollars at the beginning of each month, he always sent me his note for the amount, and with it he sent, *out of that money, three months' interest* on the hundred dollars at 6 per cent per annum, these notes being always for three months. I did not keep them of course. They were of no value to anybody.

As I say, he always sent a detailed statement of the month's profit and loss on the chickens—at least the month's loss on the chickens—and this detailed statement included the various items of expense—corn for the chickens, a bonnet for the wife, boots for himself, and so on; even carfares, and the weekly contribution of ten cents to help out the missionaries who were trying to damn the Chinese after a plan not satisfactory to those people. But at last when among those details I found twenty-five dollars for pew-rent I struck. I told him to change his religion and sell the pew.

Friday, April 6, 1906

Mr. Clemens's present house unsatisfactory because of no sunshine—Mr. Clemens meets Etta in Washington Square—Recalls ball-room in Virginia City forty-four years ago—Orion resumed; he invents wood-sawing machine; invents steam canal-boat; his funny experience in bath-tub—Bill Nye's story—Orion's autobiography—His death.

This house is No. 21 Fifth Avenue, and stands on the corner of 9th street within a couple of hundred yards of Washington Square. It was built fifty or sixty years ago by Renwick, the architect of the Roman Catholic Cathedral. It is large, and every story has good and spacious rooms. Something more than a year ago, Clara and Katy, (the housekeeper,) examined it and greatly liked it. They did not superficially examine it, but examined it in detail, and the more they searched it the better they liked it. It was then my turn to act, and instead of taking it for a year, with an option or two, I took it for three years and signed the contract. We put the furniture in, then moved in ourselves, and made a discovery straightway. There was not a window in the whole house, either on the Fifth Avenue front or on the long 9th street side, that had ever known what a ray of sunshine was like. It was a bad business, and too late to correct it. The entire house is in shadow at all seasons of the year except dead summertime. The sun gets in then, but as there wouldn't ever be anybody in the house at that time of the year, it is no advantage.

Nobody thrives in this house. Nobody profits by our sojourn in it except the doctors. They seem to be here all the time. We must move out and find a house with some sunshine in it.

Yesterday I went down to Washington Square, turned out to the left to look at a house that stands on the corner of the Square and University Place. Presently I stepped over to the corner of the Square to take a general look at the frontage of the house. While crossing the street I met a woman, and was conscious that she recognized me, and it seemed to me that there was something in her face that was familiar to me. I had the instinct that she would turn and follow me and speak to me, and the instinct was right. She was a fat little woman, with a gentle and kindly but aged and homely face, and she had white hair, and was neatly but poorly dressed. She said,

"Aren't you Mr. Clemens?"

"Yes," I said, "I am."

She said, "Where is your brother Orion?"

"Dead," I said.

"Where is his wife?"

"Dead," I said; and added, "I seem to know you, but I cannot place you."

She said "Do you remember Etta Booth?"

I had known only one Etta Booth in my lifetime, and that one rose before me in an instant, and vividly. It was almost as if she stood alongside of this fat little antiquated dame in the bloom and diffidence and sweetness of her thirteen years, her hair in plaited braids down her back and her fire-red frock stopping short at her knees. Indeed I remembered Etta very well. And immediately another vision rose before me, with that child in the centre of it and accenting its sober tint like a torch with her red frock. But it was not a quiet vision; not a reposeful one. The scene was a great ball-room in some ramshackle building in Gold Hill or Virginia City, Nevada. There were two or three hundred stalwart men present and dancing with cordial energy. And in the midst of the turmoil Etta's crimson frock was swirling and flashing; and she was the only dancer of her sex on the floor. Her mother, large, fleshy, pleasant and smiling, sat on a bench against the wall in lonely and honored state and watched the festivities in placid contentment. She and Etta were the only persons of their sex in the ball-room. Half of the men represented ladies, and they had a handkerchief tied around the left arm so that they could be told from the men. I did not dance with Etta, for I was a lady myself. I wore a revolver in my belt, and so did all the other ladies—likewise the gentlemen. It was a dismal old barn of a place, and was lighted from end to end by tallow-candle chandeliers made of barrel-hoops suspended from the ceiling, and the grease dripped all over us. That was in the beginning of the winter of 1862. It has taken forty-four years for Etta to cross my orbit again.

1862

I asked after her father.

"Dead," she said.

I asked after her mother.

"Dead," she said.

Another question brought out the fact that she had long been married, but had no children. We shook hands and parted. She walked three or four steps, then turned and came back, and her eyes filled, and she said,

"I am a stranger here, and far from my friends—in fact I have hardly any friends left. Nearly all of them are dead. I must tell my news to you. I *must* tell it to somebody. I can't bear it by myself, while it is so new. The doctor has just told me that my husband can live only a very little while, and I was not dreaming it was so bad as this."

Orion Resumed.

I think the poultry experiment lasted about a year, possibly two years. It had then cost me six thousand dollars. It is my impression that Orion was not able to give the farm away, and that his father-in-law took it back as a kindly act of self-sacrifice.

Orion returned to the law business, and I suppose he remained in that harness off and on for the succeeding quarter of a century, but so far as my knowledge goes he was only a lawyer in name, and had no clients.

1890

My mother died, in her eighty-eighth year, in the summer of 1890. She had saved some money, and she left it to me, because it had come from me. I gave it to Orion and he said, with thanks, that I had supported him long enough and now he was going to relieve me of that burden, and would also hope to pay back some of that expense, and maybe the whole of it. Accordingly, he proceeded to use up that money in building a considerable addition to the house, with the idea of taking boarders and getting rich. We need not dwell upon this venture. It was another of his failures. His wife tried hard to make the scheme succeed, and if anybody could have made it succeed she would have done it. She was a good woman, and was greatly liked. Her vanity was pretty large and inconvenient, but she had a practical side too, and she would have made that boarding-house lucrative if circumstances had not been against her.

Orion had other projects for recouping me, but as they always required capital I stayed out of them, and they did not materialize. Once he wanted to start a newspaper. It was a ghastly idea, and I squelched it with a promptness that was almost rude. Then he invented a wood-sawing machine and patched it together himself, and he really sawed wood with it. It was ingenious; it was capable; and it would have made a comfortable little fortune for him; but just at the wrong time Providence interfered again. Orion applied for a patent and found that the same machine had already been patented and had gone into business and was thriving.

Presently the State of New York offered a fifty-thousand-dollar prize for a practical method of navigating the Erie Canal with steam canal-boats. Orion worked at that thing two or three years, invented and completed a method, and was once more ready to reach out and seize upon imminent wealth when somebody pointed out a defect: his steam canal-boat could not be used in the wintertime; and in the summertime the commotion its wheels would make in the water would wash away the State of New York on both sides.

Innumerable were Orion's projects for acquiring the means to pay off his debt to me. These projects extended straight through the succeeding thirty years, but in every case they failed. During all those thirty years his well-established honesty kept him in offices of trust where other people's money had to be taken care of, but where no salary was paid. He was treasurer of all the benevolent institutions; he took care of the money and other property of widows and orphans; he never lost a cent for anybody, and never made one for himself. Every time he changed his religion the church of his new faith was glad to get him; made him treasurer at once, and at once he stopped the graft and the leaks in that church. He exhibited a facility in changing his political complexion that was a marvel to the whole community. Once the following curious thing happened, and he wrote me all about it himself.

One morning he was a Republican, and upon invitation he agreed to make a campaign speech at the Republican mass meeting that night. He prepared the speech. After luncheon he became a Democrat and agreed to write a score of exciting mottoes to be painted upon the transparencies which the Democrats would carry in their torchlight procession that night. He wrote these shouting Democratic mottoes during the afternoon, and they occupied so much of his time that it was night before he had a chance to change his politics again; so he actually made a rousing Republican campaign speech in the open air while his Democratic transparencies passed by in front of him, to the joy of every witness present.

He was a most strange creature—but in spite of his eccentricities he was beloved, all his life, in whatsoever community he lived. And he was also held in high esteem, for at bottom he was a sterling man.

Whenever he had a chance to get into a ridiculous position he was generally competent for that occasion. When he and his wife were living in Hartford, at the time when he was on the staff of the *Evening Post,* they were boarders and lodgers in a house that was pretty well stocked with nice men and women of moderate means. There was a bath-room that was common to the tribe, and one Sunday afternoon when the rest of the house was steeped in restful repose, Orion thought he would take a bath, and he carried that idea to a more or less successful issue. But he didn't lock the door. It was his custom, in summer weather, to fill the long bath-tub nearly full of cold water and then get in it on his knees with his nose on the bottom and maintain this pleasant attitude a couple of minutes at a time. A chambermaid came in there, and then she rushed out and went shrieking through the house,

"Mr. Clemens is drowned!"

Everybody came flying out of the doors, and Mrs. Clemens rushed by, crying out in agony,

"How do you know it is Mr. Clemens?"

And the chambermaid said, "I don't."

It reminds me of Bill Nye, poor fellow,—that real humorist, that gentle good soul. Well, he is dead. Peace to his ashes. He was the baldest human being I ever saw. His whole skull was brilliantly shining. It was like a dome with the sun flashing upon it. He had hardly even a fringe of hair. Once somebody admitted astonishment at his extraordinary baldness.

"Oh" he said "it is nothing. You ought to see my brother. One day he fell overboard from a ferry-boat and when he came up a woman's voice broke high over the tumult of frightened and anxious exclamations and said, 'You shameless thing! And ladies present! Go down and come up the other way.'"

About twenty-five years ago—along there somewhere—I suggested to Orion that he write an autobiography. I asked him to try to tell the straight truth in it; to refrain from exhibiting himself in creditable attitudes exclusively, and to honorably set down all the incidents of his life which he had found interesting to him, including those which were burned into his memory because he was ashamed of them. I said that this had never been done, and that if he could do it his autobiography would be a most valuable piece of literature. I said I was offering him a job which I could not duplicate in my own case, but I would cherish the hope that he might succeed with it. I recognize now that I was trying to saddle upon him an impossibility. I have been dictating this autobiography of mine daily for three months; I have thought of fifteen hundred or two thousand incidents in my life which I am ashamed of, but I have not gotten one of them to consent to go on paper yet. I think that that stock will still be complete and unimpaired when I finish these memoirs, if I ever finish them. I believe that if I should put in all or any of those incidents I should be sure to strike them out when I came to revise this book.

Orion wrote his autobiography and sent it to me. But great was my disappointment; and my vexation, too. In it he was constantly making a hero of himself, exactly as I should have done and am doing now, and he was constantly forgetting to put in the episodes which placed him in an unheroic light. I knew several incidents of his life which were distinctly and painfully unheroic, but when I came across them in his autobiography they had changed color. They had turned themselves inside out, and were things to be intemperately proud of. In my dissatisfaction I destroyed a considerable part of that autobiography. But in what remains Miss Lyon has discovered passages which she finds interesting, and I shall quote from them here and there and now and then, as I go along.

1898

While we were living in Vienna in 1898 a cablegram came from Keokuk announcing Orion's death. He was seventy-two years old. He had gone down to the kitchen in the early hours of a bitter December morning; he had built the fire, and had then sat down at a table to write something, and there he died, with the pencil in his hand and resting against the paper in the middle of an unfinished word—an indication that his release from the captivity of a long and troubled and pathetic and unprofitable life was mercifully swift and painless.

Monday, April 9, 1906

Letter from French girl enclosing cable about "Huck Finn"—The Juggernaut Club—Letter from Librarian of Brooklyn Public Library in regard to "Huckleberry Finn" and "Tom Sawyer"—Mr. Clemens's reply—The deluge of reporters trying to discover contents of that letter.

This morning's mail brings me from France a letter from a French friend of mine, enclosing this New York cablegram.

MARK TWAIN INTERDIT

NEW-YORK, 27 mars. *(Par dépêche de notre correspondant particulier.)*—Les directeurs de la bibliothèque de Brooklyn ont mis les deux derniers livres de Mark Twain à l'index pour les enfants au-dessous de quinze ans, les considérant comme malsains.

Le célèbre humoriste a écrit à des fonctionnaires une lettre pleine d'esprit et de sarcasme. Ces messieurs se refusent à la publier, sous le prétexte qu'ils n'ont pas l'autorisation de l'auteur de le faire.

The letter is from a French girl who lives at St. Dié, in Joan of Arc's region. I have never seen this French girl, but she wrote me about five years ago and since then we have exchanged friendly letters three or four times a year. She signs herself Hélène Picard, French Member. "French Member" will be better understood after I shall have explained it. The reference is to the Juggernaut Club. I invented the Juggernaut Club. I am the only male member of it. No other person of my sex is eligible to membership. My humble title is Chief Servant of the Juggernaut Club—but it is a good deal of a deception. I am the real boss. I am the power behind the throne, on the throne, and in front of it, and no combination of votes is worth anything against mine. The ballot is secret, anyway. Nobody knows who votes for who, except myself. It is great fun. I have the constitution and by-laws somewhere, but I cannot put my hand on that document just now. There are several members, and I make these several members *think* there are a couple of dozen in the club. One of the strictest of the rules is that there shall be but one member in a country, never two. That member represents that country until she dies. She cannot resign, and she cannot be turned out. This French girl highly values her great and exclusive position as representative of France, and usually she does not sign herself Member for France, but simply signs no name at all, but just signs "France." Among the membership is a reigning queen, a queen who is in very good standing, too, or she couldn't stay in this club. I am the only person connected with the club who knows the name or residence of any other member of the club. My wife knew the names and countries of the membership, but that was because she and I were really one person and there were no secrets. Sometimes I was that person, sometimes she was that person. Sometimes it took both of us together to constitute that person. When I was going to appoint the American member I consulted her, and although she was not a member and had not the slightest authority in the club, she arbitrarily vetoed that girl and appointed another one in her stead. This was mutiny. This was insubordination. This was usurpation, but it had to stand, and it did.

The reason I named the club after Juggernaut, was, because I held that god in most sincere admiration and reverence, and I wanted to do him honor. He has always been misrepresented in Christian countries. When I was a Sunday-school boy we were taught to abhor him as being a sort of malignant and bloody monster, whereas if there is a better god anywhere than Juggernaut I have not heard of him. All the movements of his spirit are kind, gentle, merciful, beautiful, lovable. His temple is visited by pilgrims of all ranks, from one end of India to the other, and when they step their feet over the threshold of his temple, all caste, all nobility, all royalty, all inequalities, all rank, station, wealth, cease to exist for the time being—utterly cease, and have no existence. The street-sweeper and the sovereign prince, the outcast, the mendicant, and the millionaire all stand upon the one level, and may touch each other and may eat from the same dish and drink from the same cup without defilement. For the time being, those pilgrims constitute a perfect democracy, the only perfect democracy that has ever existed in the earth or ever *will* exist in it. It would improve the other gods to go to school to Juggernaut. I have never seen any subordinate member of the club except the American one.

"France" writes good English. She closes her letter with this paragraph:

> Something in a newspaper that I read this morning has surprised me very much. I have cut it out because, often, these informations are forged and, if this is the case, the slip of paper will be my excuse. Please, allow me to smile, my dear unseen Friend! I cannot imagine for a minute that you have been very sorry about it.—In France, such a measure would have for immediate result to make every one in the country buy these books, and I—for one,—am going to get them as soon as I go through Paris, perfectly sure that I'll find them as wholesome as all you have written. I know your pen well. I know it has never been dipped in anything but clean, clear ink.

I must go back now to that French cablegram. Its information is not exactly correct, but it is near enough. "Huck Finn" and "Tom Sawyer" are not recent books. "Tom" is more than thirty years old. The other book has been in existence twenty-one years. When "Huck" appeared, twenty-one years ago, the public library of Concord, Massachusetts, flung him out indignantly, partly because he was a liar and partly because after deep meditation and careful deliberation he made up his mind on a difficult point, and said that if he'd got to betray Jim or go to hell, he would go to hell—which was profanity, and those Concord purists couldn't stand it.

After this disaster, "Huck" was left in peace for sixteen or seventeen years. Then the public library of Denver flung him out. He had no similar trouble until four or five months ago—that is to say, last November. At that time I received the following letter.

> SHEEPSHEAD BAY BRANCH
> BROOKLYN PUBLIC LIBRARY
> 1657 SHORE ROAD
>
> BROOKLYN-NEW YORK, Nov. 19th, '05.
>
> Dear Sir,
>
> I happened to be present the other day at a meeting of the children's librarians of the Brooklyn Public Library. In the course of the meeting it was stated that copies of "Tom Sawyer" and "Huckleberry Finn" were to be found in some of the children's rooms of the system. The Sup't of the Children's Dep't—a conscientious and enthusiastic young woman—was greatly shocked to hear this, and at once ordered that they be transferred to the adults' department. Upon this I

shamefacedly confessed to having read Huckleberry Finn aloud to my defenceless blind people, without regard to their age, color, or previous condition of servitude. I also reminded them of Brander Matthews's opinion of the book, and stated the fact that I knew it almost by heart, having got more pleasure from it than from any book I have ever read, and reading is the greatest pleasure I have in life. My warm defence elicited some further discussion and criticism, from which I gathered that the prevailing opinion of Huck was that he was a deceitful boy who said "sweat" when he should have said "perspiration." The upshot of the matter was that there is to be further consideration of these books at a meeting early in January which I am especially invited to attend. Seeing you the other night at the performance of "Peter Pan" the thought came to me that you (who know Huck as well as I—you *can't* know him better or love him more—) might be willing to give me a word or two to say in witness of his good character tho he "warn't no more quality than a mud cat."

I would ask as a favor that you regard this communication as confidential, whether you find time to reply to it or not; for I am loath for obvious reasons to bring the institution from which I draw my salary into ridicule, contempt or reproach.

Yours very respectfully,
Asa Don Dickinson.
(In charge Department for the Blind
and Sheepshead Bay Branch, Brooklyn Public Library.)

That was a very private letter. I didn't know the author of it, but I thought I perceived that he was a safe man, and that I could venture to write a pretty private letter in return and trust that he would not allow its dreadful contents to leak out and get into the newspapers. I wrote him on the 21st.

21 Fifth Ave.
Nov. 21, 1905.

Dear Sir:

I am greatly troubled by what you say. I wrote Tom Sawyer and Huck Finn for adults exclusively, and it always distresses me when I find that boys and girls have been allowed access to them. The mind that becomes soiled in youth can never again be washed clean; I know this by my own experience, and to this day I cherish an unappeasable bitterness against the unfaithful guardians of my young life, who not only permitted but compelled me to read an unexpurgated Bible through before I was 15 years old. None can do that and ever draw a clean sweet breath again this side of the grave. Ask that young lady—she will tell you so.

Most honestly do I wish I could say a softening word or two in defence of Huck's character, since you wish it, but really in my opinion it is no better than those of Solomon, David, Satan, and the rest of the sacred brotherhood.

If there is an Unexpurgated in the Children's Department, won't you please help that young woman remove Huck and Tom from that questionable companionship?

Sincerely yours—
(Signed) S. L. Clemens.

I shall not show your letter to any one—it is safe with me.

A couple of days later I received this handsome rejoinder in return.

Sheepshead Bay Branch
BROOKLYN PUBLIC LIBRARY
1657 Shore Road

Brooklyn-New York, Nov. 23rd, '05.

Dear Sir,

Your letter rec'd. I am surprised to hear that you think Huck and Tom would have an unwholesome effect on boys and girls. But relieved to hear that you would not place them in the same category with many of the scriptural reprobates. I know of one boy who made the acquaintance of Huck in 1884, at the age of eight, and who has known him intimately ever since, and I can assure you he is not an atom the worse for the 20 years' companionship. On the contrary he will always feel grateful to Huck's father—I don't mean Pap—for the many hours spent with him and Jim, when sickness and sorrow were forgotten.

Huckleberry Finn was the first book I selected to read to my blind (for selfish reasons I am afraid), and the amount of innocent enjoyment it gave them, has never been equalled by anything I have since read.

Thanking you for the almost unhoped for courtesy of your reply, I am

Yours very respectfully,
Asa Don Dickinson.

Four months drifted tranquilly by. Then there was music! There came a freshet of newspaper reporters and they besieged poor Miss Lyon all day. Of course I was in bed. I am always in bed. She barred the stairs against them. They were bound to see me, if only for a moment, but none of them got by her guard. They said a report had sprung up that I had written a letter some months before to the Brooklyn Public Library; that according to that report the letter was pungent and valuable, and they wanted a copy of it. They said the head officials of the Brooklyn Library declared that they had never seen the letter and that they had never heard of it until the reporters came and asked for it. I judged by this that my man—who was not in the head library, but in a branch of it—was keeping his secret all right, and I believed he could be trusted to continue to keep that secret, for his own sake as well as mine. That letter would be a bombshell for me if it got out—but it would hoist him, too. So I felt pretty confident that for his own sake, if for no other, he would protect me.

Miss Lyon had a hard day of it, but I had a most enjoyable one. She never allowed any reporter to get an idea of the nature of the letter; she smoothed all those young fellows down, in her tactful and fascinating and diplomatic way, and sent them away mightily pleased with her, but empty. Each time that she repulsed an enemy she came up stairs, told me all about it and what the enemy had said, and how ingeniously he had pleaded, and we had very good times together. Once she had three of these persuasive envoys on her hands at once—but no matter. She beat the whole battery and they got nothing.

They renewed the assault next day, but I told her to never mind—human nature would win the victory for us. There would be an earthquake somewhere, or a municipal upheaval *here,* or a threat of war in Europe—something would be sure to happen in the way of a big excitement that would call the boys away from No. 21 Fifth Avenue for twenty-four hours, and that would answer every purpose; they wouldn't think of that letter again, and we should have peace.

I knew the reporters would get on the right track very soon, so I wrote Mr. Dickinson and warned him to keep his mouth hermetically sealed. I told him to be wise and wary. His answer bears date March 28th.

Bay Ridge Branch
BROOKLYN PUBLIC LIBRARY
73d Street and Second Avenue
Telephone No. 338 Bay Ridge

Brooklyn-New York, Mar. 28, '06.

Dear Mr. Clemens,

Your letter of the 26th inst. rec'd this moment. As I have now been transferred to the above address, it has been a long time reaching me.

I have tried to be wary and wise and am very grateful to you for your reticence. The poor old B.P.L. has achieved some very undesirable notoriety. I thought my head was coming off when I heard from my chief on the telephone night before last. But yesterday he began to be amused, I think, at the tea pot tempest.

Last night I reached home at 11.30 and found a Herald man sitting on the steps, leaning his head against the door post. He had been there since 7.30 and said he would cheerfully sit there till morning if I would give him the least hint of the letter's contents. But I was wise and wary.

At the January meeting it was decided not to place Huck and Tom in the *Children's* rooms along with "Little Nellie's Silver Mine" and "Dotty Dimple at Home." But the books have not been "restricted" in any sense whatever. They are placed on open shelves among the adult fiction, and any child is free to read adult fiction if he chooses.

I am looking forward with great eagerness to seeing and hearing you tomorrow night at the Waldorf. As I have a wild scheme for a national library for the blind, they have been generous enough to place a couple of boxes at my disposal. The "young lady" whom you mentioned in your letter—the Sup't of the Children's Dep't—and several other B.P.L.'s, I hope will be present.

I am very sorry to have caused you so much annoyance through reporters, but be sure that I have said nothing nor will say anything to them about the contents of that letter. And please don't you tell on me!

Yours very respectfully,
Asa Don Dickinson.

I saw him at the Waldorf the next night, where Choate and I made our public appeal in behalf of the blind, and found him to be a very pleasant and safe and satisfactory man.

Now that I have heard from France, I think the incident is closed—for it had its brief run in England, two or three weeks ago, and in Germany also. When people let "Huck Finn" alone he goes peacefully along, damaging a few children here and there and yonder, but there will be plenty of children in heaven without those, so it is no great matter. It is only when well-meaning people expose him that he gets his real chance to do harm. Temporarily, then, he spreads havoc all around in the nurseries and no doubt does prodigious harm while he has his chance. By and by, let us hope, people that really have the best interests of the rising generation at heart will become wise and not stir Huck up.

Tuesday, April 10, 1906

Child's letter about "Huckleberry Finn" being flung out of Concord Library—Ambassador White's autobiography—Mr. Clemens's version of the Fiske-Cornell episode—Another example of his great scheme for finding employment for the unemployed—This client wins the Fiske lawsuit.

When "Huck Finn" was flung out of the Concord Public Library twenty-one years ago, a number of letters of sympathy and indignation reached me—mainly from children, I am obliged to admit—and I kept some of them so that I might re-read them now and then and apply them as a salve to my soreness. I have overhauled those ancient letters this morning and among them I find one from a little girl who resents that library's treatment of Huck and then goes innocently along and gives me something more of a dig than even the library had done. She says,

> I am eleven years old, and I live on a farm near Rockville, Maryland. Once this winter we had a boy to work for us named John. We lent him "Huck Finn" to read, and one night he let his clothes out of the window and left in the night. The last we heard from him he was out in Ohio; and father says if we had lent him "Tom Sawyer" to read he would not have stopped on this side of the ocean.

Bless her gentle heart, she was trying to cheer me up; and her effort is entitled to the praise which the country journalist conferred upon the Essex band after he had praised the whole Fourth of July celebration in detail, and had exhausted his stock of compliments. But he was obliged to lay something in the nature of a complimentary egg, and with a final heroic effort he brought forth this:

"The Essex band done the best they could."

I have been reading another chapter or two in Ambassador White's autobiography, and I find the book charming, particularly where he talks about me. I find any book charming that talks about me. I am expecting this one of mine to do something in that line, and it is my purpose that it shall not lose sight of that subject long at a time. Mr. White was the first President of Cornell University, and he gives the University's side of the Willard Fiske trouble. I stopped at that point. I didn't read his version, for I want to give another version first, and as this version may conflict with his, I wish to set it down now before its complexion shall have a chance to undergo a change by coming in contact with his version.

This brings me back to another example of my great scheme for finding work for the unemployed. The famous Fiske-Cornell episode of a quarter of a century ago grew up in this way. About fifty years ago, when Willard Fiske was a poor and untaught and friendless boy of thirteen, he and Bayard Taylor took steerage passage in a sailing ship and crossed the ocean. They found their way to Iceland, and Willard Fiske remained there a year or two. He acquired the Norse languages and perfected himself in them. He also became an expert scholar in the literature of those languages. By and by he returned to America, and while still a very young man and hardly of age, he got a place as instructor in that kind of learning in the infant Cornell University. This seat of learning was at Ithaca, New York, and Mr. McGraw was a citizen of that little town. He had made a fortune in the electric telegraph, and it was his purpose to leave a large part of it to the University. He had a lovely young daughter, and she and young Fiske fell in love with each other. They were aware of this; the girl's parents were aware of it; the University was aware of it; Ithaca was aware of it. All these parties expected Fiske to propose, but he didn't do it. There was no way to account for it, and so all the parties, including the girl, went on from month to month and year to year in a condition of suppressed surprise, waiting for the mystery to solve itself. Which it still didn't do. At last Mr. McGraw died, and the fact developed that he had left no will. Therefore the daughter was sole heir. However she knew what her father's intention had been, so she turned over to the University a good part of the fortune and thus made the intention good.

The years drifted along and the relations between Fiske and Miss McGraw remained the same. But there was no proposal. Fiske had a quite definite reason for not proposing. It was that he was very poor and the girl very rich, and he was not willing to seem to marry her for her money. This was good morals, good principle, good sentiment—but it was not business. Things remained just in this way for years and years, and the devotion of the couple to each other went along unimpaired by time. At last, when they were well stricken in years, and when Miss McGraw had developed pulmonary consumption, she invited Fiske and Charles Dudley Warner and his wife to make a trip up the Nile with her in the old-fashioned dahabieh, a trip which occupied a matter of three months. Miss McGraw had already been on the other side of the ocean several months, and she had been buying all sorts of beautiful things; pictures, sculpture, costly rugs, and so on, wherewith to adorn a little palace which she was building in Ithaca.

At last there on board the dahabieh a sorrowful time came—for Miss McGraw's malady was making great progress and it was manifest that she could not live long. Then she came out frankly and said she wanted to marry Fiske so that she could leave her fortune to him. Fiske wanted to marry her, but his ideas remained unimpaired in his heart and head and he was not willing to accept the fortune. The Warners wrought with him. They used their best persuasions. He was as anxious for the marriage as was Miss McGraw, but he wouldn't accept the fortune. At last he was persuaded to a modification of the terms. He was willing to accept the little palace and its furnishings and three hundred thousand dollars; he would accept nothing more. The marriage took place. Mrs. Fiske made a will, and in the will she left the palace and its furnishings and three hundred thousand dollars to her husband, Willard Fiske. She left the residue of the fortune to Cornell University.

By and by Fiske arrived at an understanding of the fact that he had not acted wisely. The income of three hundred thousand dollars was wholly inadequate. He could not live in the Ithaca house on any such income as that. He did not try to live in it. There it stood, with all those beautiful things in it which Miss McGraw had gathered in her travels in Europe, and Fiske lived elsewhere—lived most comfortably elsewhere—lived where three hundred thousand dollars was really a fortune, and he was entirely satisfied. He lived in Italy. He was as dear and sweet a soul as I have ever known. His was a character which won friends for him, and whoso became his friend remained so, ever afterward.

Now followed this curious circumstance. Cornell had received by Mrs. Fiske's will a noble addition to its endowment—two million dollars, if I remember rightly. No doubt Cornell University was satisfied. But the University's lawyers, picking and searching around through Mrs. Fiske's will, found a defect in it which neither Mrs. Fiske nor Charley Warner, who drew the will, suspected was there. It was something about "residue." It was the opinion of those lawyers that the University might claim the little palace and its rich equipment, and make the claim good in a court of law.

The claim was put forward. Fiske and Warner were outraged by this insolence, this greed. Both knew that it was the desire of the dying wife that her husband should live in that house and have the sacred companionship of those things which had been selected by her own hands for its adornment. Both knew that but for Fiske's stubborn resistance he would have had not only the house but a great sum of money besides, and now that the University proposed to take the house away from Fiske—well, it was time for the worm to turn. The worm turned. Fiske was the worm. Fiske resisted the University's claim and the University brought suit.

Now then, I must go back to a point antedating the bringing of this suit three or four years. One day in Hartford a young fellow called and wanted to see me. I think he said he was from Canada. He said he had a strong desire, an irresistible desire, to become a lawyer, and he thought that if he could get some work to do that would support him, he could meantime use his off hours, if he had any, in studying Blackstone. He thought he could be a journalist. He thought he could at least become a good reporter, and his idea was to get me to use my influence with the Hartford newspaper people to the end that he might get the sort of chance he was after.

I said "Certainly, I will get you a berth in any newspaper in the town. Choose your own paper."

He was very grateful. These clients of mine always are, until they learn the conditions. I furnished him the conditions in the same old way. He considered a moment and then said,

"How simple that is; how sure it is; how certain it is; how actually infallible it is, human nature being constructed as it is—how is it that that has not been thought of before?" Then he added, as he went out of the door, "I choose the *Courant,* and I will have the job before night."

About three months afterward he came out to report progress. He had moved along so briskly, from sweeper-out, up through the several grades, that he was now on the editorial staff; and was very happy, particularly as staff work allowed him a good deal of off time for the study of the law, and the law was where his high ambition lay.

I come back now to that Fiske lawsuit. We had gone to Elmira one summer to spend the summer, as usual, at Quarry Farm, and we were visiting Mrs. Clemens's family down in the town for a while. A young man called and said he would like to see me. I went to the library and saw him there. It was the young man of whom I have been talking, but as I had not seen him for three or four years I did not at first recall him. He said that while he was on the *Courant* he saved all the money he could, and studied the law diligently in his off hours—that now, recently, he had given up journalism and was going to make a break into the law; that he had canvassed the field and had decided that he would become office assistant to David B. Hill of Elmira, New York—that is to say, he had decided to do this, evidently without requiring Mr. Hill to state whether he wanted it so or not. Hill was a very distinguished lawyer and a big politician, a man of vast importance and influence—and he is still that to-day, in his old age. The application was made and Hill said promptly that he didn't need anybody's assistance. But young Bacon said he didn't want any pay, he only wanted a chance to work; he could support himself. He would do anything that could be of any assistance to Mr. Hill, even to sweeping out the office; that he wanted to work, and he wanted to be near a man like Hill because he was determined to become a lawyer. Well, as he was not expensive, and showed a determination that pleased Hill, Hill gave him office room. Very well, the usual thing happened, the thing that always happens. Little by little Bacon got to beguiling out of Hill things to do, and presently Hill was furnishing him the things to do without any beguilement.

"Now then," Bacon said, "Mr. Clemens, I've got a chance—I've got a chance."

Professor Willard Fiske brought his case to Mr. Hill. Mr. Hill examined it carefully and declined to take it. He said Fiske had no case, and therefore he did not wish to take it merely to lose it. Fiske insisted, and presently Hill said, "Well, here's this young fellow here in my office. If he wants to take your case, all right; I will advise him and help him to the best of my ability without charge;" and he asked if Fiske was willing to put the case into Bacon's hands. Fiske did it.

Then young Bacon had this happy idea. There being nothing for Fiske in the apparent conditions, he went to the University charter to see what he might find there. He found a very pleasant thing there; to use a phrase of the day, he struck oil in that charter. He brought the charter to Mr. Hill and showed him this large fact: that Cornell University was not privileged to accept or to acquire any property if, at the time, it already possessed property worth three millions of dollars. Cornell University possessed property worth more than that at the time that Mrs. Fiske made her will, and it still possessed that amount.

Hill said "Well, Bacon, the case is yours—that is to say, well, Bacon, the case is Fiske's. It is the University, now, that has no show."

Bacon won the case. It was his first case. He charged Fiske a hundred thousand dollars for his services. Fiske handed him the check, and his thanks therewith.

I didn't see Bacon again for some years—I don't know how many—and then he told me that that first lawsuit of his was also his last one; that that first fee of his was the only one he had ever received; that he had hardly pocketed that check until he ran across a most charming young widow possessed of a great fortune and he took them both in.

I think I will say nothing more about my great scheme for providing jobs for the unemployed. I think I have proven that it is a good and effective scheme.

Wednesday, April 11, 1906

Mr. Frank Fuller and his enthusiastic launching of Mr. Clemens's first New York lecture—Results not in fortune but in fame—Leads to a lecture tour under direction of Redpath—Clipping in regard to Frank Fuller, and Mr. Clemens's comments—Olive Logan clipping and Mr. Clemens's comments—Mr. Clemens's feeling toward suicides.

I am not glancing through my books to find out what I have said in them. I refrain from glancing through those books for two reasons; first—and this reason always comes first in every matter connected with my life—laziness. I am too lazy to examine the books. The other reason is—well, let it go. I had another reason, but it has slipped out of my mind while I was arranging the first one. I think it likely that in the book called "Roughing It" I have mentioned Frank Fuller. But I don't know, and it isn't any matter.

When Orion and I crossed the continent in the overland stage-coach, in the summer of 1861, we stopped two or three days in Great Salt Lake City. I do not remember who the Governor of Utah Territory was at that time, but I remember that he was absent—which is a common habit of Territorial Governors, who are nothing but politicians who go out to the outskirts of countries and suffer the privations there in order to build up States and come back as United States Senators. But the man who was acting in the Governor's place was the Secretary of the Territory, Frank Fuller—called Governor, of course, just as Orion was in the great days when he got that accident-title through Governor Nye's absences. Titles of honor and dignity once acquired in a democracy, even by accident and properly usable for only forty-eight hours, are as permanent here as eternity is in heaven. You can never take away those titles. Once a justice of the peace for a week, always "judge" afterward. Once a major of militia for a campaign on the Fourth of July, always a major. To be called colonel, purely by mistake and without intention, confers that dignity on a man for the rest of his life. We adore titles and heredities in our hearts, and ridicule them with our mouths. This is our democratic privilege.

1861

Well, Fuller was Acting Governor, and he gave us a very good time during those two or three days that we rested in Great Salt Lake City. He was an alert and energetic man; a pushing man; a man who was able to take an interest in anything that was going—and not only that, but take five times as much interest in it as it was worth, and ten times as much as anybody else could take in it—a very live man.

I was on the Pacific coast thereafter five or six years, and returned to the States by the way of the Isthmus in January '67. In the previous year I had spent several months in the Sandwich Islands for the Sacramento *Union,* and had returned to San Francisco empty as to cash but full of information—information proper for delivery from the lecture platform. My letters from the Islands had given me a large notoriety—local notoriety. It did not extend eastward more than a hundred miles or so, but it was a good notoriety to lecture on, and I made use of it on the platform in San Francisco and amassed twelve or fifteen hundred dollars in the few nights that I labored for the instruction and amusement of my public. Fifteen hundred dollars was about half—the doorkeeper got the rest. He was an old circus man and knew how to keep door.

1867

When I arrived in New York I found Fuller there in some kind of business. He was very hearty, very glad to see me, and wanted to show me his wife. I had not heard of a wife before; had not been aware that he had one. Well he showed me his wife, a sweet and gentle woman with most hospitable and kindly and winning ways. Then he astonished me by showing me his daughters. Upon my word, they were large and matronly of aspect, and married—he didn't say how long. Oh, Fuller was full of surprises. If he had shown me some little children, that would have been well enough, and reasonable. But he was too young-looking a man to have grown children. Well, I couldn't fathom the mystery and I let it go. Apparently it was a case where a man was well along in life but had a handsome gift of not showing his age on the outside.

Governor Fuller—it is what all his New York friends called him now, of course—was in the full storm of one of his enthusiasms. He had one enthusiasm per day, and it was always a storm. He said I must take the biggest hall in New York and deliver that lecture of mine on the Sandwich Islands—said that people would be wild to hear me. There was something catching about that man's prodigious energy. For a moment he almost convinced me that New York was wild to hear me. I knew better. I was well aware that New York had never heard of me, was not expecting to hear of me, and didn't want to hear of me—yet that man almost persuaded me. I protested, as soon as the fire which he had kindled in me had cooled a little, and went on protesting. It did no good. Fuller was sure that I should make fame and fortune right away without any trouble. He said leave it to him—just leave everything to him—go to the hotel and sit down and be comfortable—he would lay fame and fortune at my feet in ten days.

I was helpless. I was persuadable, but I didn't lose *all* of my mind, and I begged him to take a very small hall, and reduce the rates to side-show prices. No, he would not hear of that—said he would have the biggest hall in New York City. He would have the basement hall in Cooper Institute, which seated three thousand people and there was room for half as many more to stand up; and he said he would fill that place so full, at a dollar a head, that those people would smother and he could charge two dollars apiece to let them out. Oh, he was all on fire with his project. He went ahead with it. He said it shouldn't cost me anything. I said there would be no profit. He said,

"Leave that alone. If there is no profit that is my affair. If there is profit it is yours. If it is loss, I stand the loss myself, and you will never hear of it."

He hired Cooper Institute, and he began to advertise this lecture in the usual way—a small paragraph in the advertising columns of the newspapers. When this had continued about three days I had not yet heard anybody or any newspaper say anything about that lecture, and I got nervous.

"Oh," he said, "it's working around underneath. You don't see it on the surface." He said "Let it alone, now, let it work."

Very well, I allowed it to work—until about the sixth or seventh day. The lecture would be due in three or four days more—still I was not able to get down underneath, where it was working, and so I was filled with doubt and distress. I went to Fuller and said he must advertise more energetically.

He said he would. So he got a barrel of little things printed that you hang on a string—fifty in a bunch. They were for the omnibuses. You could see them swinging and dangling around in every omnibus. My anxiety forced me to haunt those omnibuses. I did nothing for one or two days but sit in 'buses and travel from one end of New York to the other and watch those things dangle, and wait to catch somebody pulling one loose to read it. It never happened—at least it happened only once. A man reached up and pulled one of those things loose, said to his friend,

"Lecture on the Sandwich Islands by Mark Twain. Who can that be, I wonder"—and he threw it away and changed the subject.

I couldn't travel in the omnibuses any more. I was sick. I went to Fuller and said,

"Fuller, there is not going to be anybody in Cooper Institute that night, but you and me. It will be a dead loss, for we shall both have free tickets. Something must be done. I am on the verge of suicide. I would commit suicide if I had the pluck, and the outfit." I said, "You must paper the house, Fuller. You must issue thousands of complimentary tickets. You *must* do this. I shall die if I have to go before an empty house that is not acquainted with me and that has never heard of me, and that has never traveled in the 'bus and seen those things dangle."

"Well," he said, with his customary enthusiasm, "I'll attend to it. It shall be done. I will paper that house, and when you step on the platform you shall find yourself in the presence of the choicest audience, the most intelligent audience, that ever a man stood before in this world."

And he was as good as his word. He sent whole basketsful of complimentary tickets to every public-school teacher within a radius of thirty miles of New York—he deluged those people with complimentary tickets—and on the appointed night they all came. There wasn't room in Cooper Institute for a third of them. The lecture was to begin at half past seven. I was so anxious that I had to go to that place at seven. I couldn't keep away. I wanted to see that vast vacant Mammoth Cave and die. But when I got near the building I found that all the streets for a quarter of a mile around were blocked with people, and traffic was stopped. I couldn't believe that those people were trying to get into Cooper Institute, and yet that was just what was happening. I found my way around to the back of the building and got in there by the stage door. And sure enough, the seats, the aisles, the great stage itself, were packed with bright-looking human beings raked in from the centres of intelligence—the schools. I had a deal of difficulty to shoulder my way through the mass of people on the stage, and when I had managed it and stood before the audience, that stage was full. There wasn't room enough left for a child.

I was happy, and I was excited beyond expression. I poured the Sandwich Islands out onto those people with a free hand, and they laughed and shouted to my entire content. For an hour and fifteen minutes I was in paradise. From every pore I exuded a divine delight—and when we came to count up we had thirty-five dollars in the house.

Fuller was just as jubilant over it as if it had furnished the fame and the fortune of his prophecy. He was perfectly delighted, perfectly enchanted. He couldn't keep his mouth shut for several days.

"Oh," he said, "the fortune didn't come in—that didn't come in—that's all right. That's coming in later. The fame is already here, Mark. Why, in a week you'll be the best known man in the United States. This is no failure. This is a prodigious success."

That episode must have cost him four or five hundred dollars, but he never said a word about that. He was as happy, as satisfied, as proud, as delighted, as if he had laid the fabled golden egg and hatched it.

He was right about the fame. I certainly did get a working quantity of fame out of that lecture. The New York newspapers praised it. The country newspapers copied those praises. The lyceums of the country—it was right in the heyday of the old lyceum lecture system—began to call for me. I put myself in Redpath's hands, and I caught the tail-end of the lecture season. I went West and lectured every night, for six or eight weeks, at a hundred dollars a night—and I now considered that the whole of the prophecy was fulfilled. I had acquired fame, and also fortune. I don't believe these details are right, but I don't care a rap. They will do just as well as the facts. What I mean to say is, that I don't know whether I made that lecturing excursion in that year or whether it was the following year. But the main thing is that I made it, and that the opportunity to make it was created by that wild Frank Fuller and his insane and immortal project.

All this was thirty-eight or thirty-nine years ago. Two or three times since then, at intervals of years, I have run across Frank Fuller for a moment—only a moment, and no more. But he was always young. Never a gray hair; never a suggestion of age about him; always enthusiastic; always happy, and glad to be alive. Last fall his wife's brother was murdered in a horrible way. Apparently a robber had concealed himself in Mr. Thompson's room, and in the night had beaten him to death with a club. A couple of months ago I ran across Fuller on the street, and he was looking so very, very old, so withered, so mouldy, that I could hardly recognize him. He said his wife was dying of the shock caused by the murder of her brother; that nervous prostration was carrying her off, and she could not live more than a few days—so I went with him to see her.

She was sitting upright on a sofa, and was supported all about with pillows. Now and then she leaned her head for a little while on a support. Breathing was difficult for her. It touched me, for I had seen that picture so many, many times. During two or three months Mrs. Clemens sat up like that, night and day, struggling for breath. When she was made drowsy by opiates and exhaustion she rested her head a little while on a support, just as Mrs. Fuller was doing, and got naps of two minutes' or three minutes' duration.

I did not see Mrs. Fuller alive again. She passed to her rest about three days later.

The thing which has brought Frank Fuller into my mind is this half-column of matter which I have scissored from this morning's paper. I never get a chance to hunt among my old note-books for texts for this autobiography, for the reason that every day the newspaper furnishes me a couple of dozen, and I never can catch up at this rate.

STRANGE SEQUEL TO BLACKMAILING CASE.

Louis R. Fuller Learns for First Time that He Is Not Rich Dr. Fuller's Son.

When Louis R. Fuller, Yale graduate and society favorite in New York and Boston, appeared in the Centre Street Police Court yesterday as complainant against Homer Hawkins, No. 101 West Eighty-eighth street, whom he accused of attempted blackmail and assault, he learned for the first time that he is only the adopted son of Dr. Frank Fuller, millionaire president of the Health Food Company, No. 61 Fifth avenue.

Hawkins had sent a letter to Louis R. Fuller, demanding $500 under penalty of disclosing confidential information to a Mr. Rowbotham, whose daughter is engaged to marry Fuller. His arrest followed. When Hawkins was arraigned yesterday, Magistrate Whitman held him in $2,500 bail on the blackmail charge and in an additional $500 bail on a charge of carrying concealed weapons. Mrs. Ellen Faxon, mother of Homer Hawkins, was in court to aid her son. It was the first time she had seen Louis R. Fuller, her brother by adoption. She begged him not to press the charge.

"Don't you know that he is of Dr. Fuller's own flesh and blood?" she exclaimed, "and that you are his uncle only by adoption?"

Louis R. Fuller did not know at first what to say. It was the first intimation he had ever had that he was not Dr. Fuller's own son. Then looking the woman straight in the eye he said:

"Your son had no business to do what he did; I am going to press the charge."

Mrs. Faxon's Story.

When Mrs. Faxon was seen by a World reporter at her home, after a futile effort to get bail for her son, she said:

"While I do not approve of my boy's action, when the true facts come out very few persons will blame him for what he did. My father and my mother separated in 1868. Two years later my mother died. I married, and with my husband and an only sister went to California to live. There Homer was born. His father died shortly after his birth. A few years later I married my present husband, Frank Faxon, who is now in Southern California.

"Twenty years ago I learned that my father had married Miss Anna Thompson, of Portsmouth, N.H. She was a sister of the late Jacob H. Thompson, who was found murdered in his room in the St. James Hotel. One child was born to them. This child died and a year later a boy, now known as Louis R. Fuller, was adopted. Who he was or where he came from I do not know.

"As my boy neared manhood he began to ask about his grandparents. I told him the true story. Three years ago Homer came to New York and visited his grandfather. He then learned that his uncle by adoption was being educated at Yale. From that day to this he has been a changed boy. His grandfather sent him back to California to keep him from meeting Louis.

Meets Father After Thirty Years.

"When I found myself almost penniless two years ago I went to my father's summer home at Madison, N.J., and met him for the first time in thirty years. My stepmother told me that New York was not big enough for us both. Since then I have been earning a living as a seamstress.

"It made Homer's heart bleed to think that another was usurping the comfort and love that belonged to us."

Dr. Fuller and his adopted son occupy fine apartments at the Allston, No. 17 East Thirty-eighth street. They were not at home last night. Mrs. Fuller died of nervous prostration last February, never having recovered from the shock following her brother's death.

New York *World.*

That clipping is full of mystery for me. The lady says "My father and my mother separated in 1868." It was in the previous year that Fuller showed me his wife—the one that died the other day—and also astonished me with those portly and matronly daughters of his. I seem to gather, now, that there had been an earlier Mrs. Fuller, and that the unexplained daughters were of that vintage. Fuller didn't tell me he had ever had another wife. I think this lady must be wrong in her dates. I think the separation must have occurred before 1867, and not in 1868. The lady says "separated." She doesn't say divorced. Well, let it go. I can't straighten it out. According to my reading of this account Louis Fuller is not entirely accounted for. But let that go. It is no matter. If he was adopted by Fuller, or by anybody else, it must have been in his infancy—because if the adopter had waited, he would have considered the developed Louis not much of an asset and would have left him for some other speculator. But never mind. Let the whole thing go. It is beginning to tangle my head. The most that I get out of the whole matter is that the Fuller life, like all other lives that climb up into old age or thereabouts, is a tragedy. It is a pity to grow old, because you know that the tragedy is always hanging over you, and if you don't get out of life by some fortunate accident it will fall on you pretty surely. I wonder how old Fuller is. More than eighty, I imagine—yet he never looked old until lately.

I will disengage my mind from this dismal subject and see if I can't find a cheerfuler one among this morning's clippings.

No, it is a failure. There is nothing very cheerful about the one I hold in my hand.

It is headed "Olive Logan has Husband Arrested." I doubt if I have thought of Olive Logan or encountered her name for a good thirty years and more. She belongs 'way back yonder in that brief period among the lyceum days, when a new kind of female lecturer invaded the platform. The previous kind had been the Anna Dickinson kind, women who had something to say; and could say it well; women who were full of talent; women who talked straight out of their hearts and could powerfully move an audience with their eloquence. Then came the Olive Logan kind: women who hadn't anything to say, and couldn't have said it if they had had anything to say; women who invaded the platform to show their clothes. They were living fashion-plates. All over the country the women filled the lecture halls to look at those clothes, and they brought their husbands along. The men didn't want to go, but they had to.

A woman had to have a name before Redpath would launch her upon the lecture platform. Olive Logan set herself the task of manufacturing a reputation. For a season or two she wrote inane, affected, and valueless stuff for obscure periodicals. As a method of creating fame that proved to be a dead failure. Then she began the most curious—the most curious—well, I can't think of the word I want—let it go. What she began was this. She married a penny-a-liner (whose name I have forgotten) and he handed around little two-line items amongst the newspapers and got them inserted—like this:

"Olive Logan has taken the Hunter mansion at Cohasset for the summer."

Now why should that interest anybody? But it did. There wasn't any truth in it, but the reader couldn't know that. He had never heard of Olive Logan, but surely Olive Logan wouldn't be mentioned in that matter-of-course way unless she was a celebrity, and therefore the reader found himself in the unsatisfactory position of being ignorant of a thing he ought to know. Dear me, Olive Logan couldn't take the Hunter mansion, or any other mansion. She couldn't take a shack, and pay the rent.

Then there would be another item presently:

"Olive Logan is at least independent. She has boldly deserted the world-famous Parisian male milliner, Worth, and has ordered her gowns for next season from his new but prosperous rival, Savarin."

That item would flit from paper to paper throughout the United States. Persons reading it would take it for granted that Olive Logan was a celebrated and important person, although he had not been quite aware of it before, so far as he could remember. But that item would impress him, if he was a woman, and do it every time. A person who could boldly desert Worth must be something not far short of a duchess.

These items followed each other in procession straight along, week by week, through the year. There was never a word of explanation of who Olive Logan might be or of what she had done to earn fame. The items were never of the slightest consequence to any one, since they merely referred to Olive Logan's clothes and the summer residences she was supposed to take, with now and then an opinion on some subject which she was not acquainted with. These opinions were flung out in the same matter-of-course way that distinguished the items about the clothes:

"Olive Logan has expressed the opinion that transcendentalism, even as a Bostonian interest, is passing away."

Now this curious thing actually happened—and I am alive to swear to it—that at the end of this kind of persistent itemizing of this unknown adventuress, Redpath was able to put her on the platform at a hundred dollars a night and send her all over this country. She wasn't worth ten cents a week, but she soared from town to town throughout the United States for three or four or five years, at the regular lecture rate of a hundred dollars a night. She was actually famous. There is no doubt about it. Her name was familiar to everybody. Every man was familiar with Olive Logan's name; every woman was familiar with it—and there wasn't a human being in the entire United States who could answer if you asked him "What is her fame based on? What is it that she has done?" You would paralyse a person by asking him that question. He would think for an instant that he could easily tell what her fame rested upon, but just a single second of reflection was sure to convince him that whereas he never had thought of it before, the fact was that he hadn't any idea in the world who Olive Logan was or what she had done. She had built up a great, a commercially valuable name, on absolute emptiness; built it up upon mere remarks about her clothes and where she was going to spend the summer, and her opinions about things that nobody had asked her to express herself about. It was the emptiest reputation that was ever invented in this world. Of course she couldn't go to the same town the third time. The first time her house would be filled. The audience would go away aware that they had got nothing whatever for their money. The second time the house would be filled with the rest of the people who hadn't seen her, but that exhausted that town. There were no more idiots left. The Lyceum Committee of the town would know that as an attraction Olive Logan had ceased to exist. She was not sent for again. And, as I have said, I haven't heard of Olive Logan for a whole lifetime. And now she turns up in this morning's paper under that heading, "Olive Logan has Husband Arrested."

OLIVE LOGAN HAS HUSBAND ARRESTED.

Famous Lecturer, Authoress and Actress Declares that He Drinks and Neglects Her.

Olive Logan, lecturer, authoress, actress, stage beauty of thirty years ago, appeared as a suppliant in the Harlem police court yesterday afternoon. She is sixty-seven years old, white-haired, tottering and very deaf. Magistrate Cornell did not catch her name, but her charming voice and exquisite use of the English language caught his attention. He sent a policeman with her into an adjoining corridor to shout into her ear-trumpet and get her story.

"I want a warrant," said the aged woman, "for my husband, James O'Neill Logan. We live at No. 2568 Seventh avenue. He is always drinking."

The magistrate issued a summons, and when the man was brought to court in the afternoon his condition was so bad that he was ordered into custody until to-day.

"We are terribly in debt," said Mrs. Logan to the reporters. "My husband is employed at Ellis Island, but the saloons get his money, and he often comes home without a cent. We are in danger of being dispossessed. We have no money to buy food. I am so weak with the infirmities of age that I can no longer write. It is only as a last resort that I have appealed to the court."

Magistrate Cornell will make an order in the case to-day.

Olive Logan was born in Elmira, N.Y., on April 22, 1839. She gained fame as a writer and lecturer, and in 1872 she was married to William Wirt Sikes, appointed by President Grant Consul to Cardiff, Wales. He died in London in 1883. Mrs. Sikes always clung to her first name. She was a protege of the late Augustin Daly, who trained her for the stage. She wrote "Surf; or, Life at Long Branch," dramatized Wilkie Collins's "Armadale" and made a metrical translation of Francois Coppee's "Le Passant."

Mrs. Logan said James O'Neill was her office boy in London twenty-five years ago. When he grew up he became her secretary.

"He came to America with me," she said, "and we decided to be married, although I was twenty-two years older than he. The first ten years of our married life were a dream of happiness. He is a fine fellow, and I love him still. His drinking has ruined us."

Why, dear me, she was born in Elmira, New York, it appears—the town where my wife was born and where we spent our summers for sixteen years. The town where was also born the first distinctly and rollickingly humorous book that was ever written by an American woman, "The Widow Bedott." That book was written by a girl eighteen years old. It is now forgotten, but it swept this continent with a hurricane of laughter when it first came out.

And here I find the name of that husband of hers, that penny-a-liner without salary or local habitation or name, who did the itemizing and created Olive Logan's fame. I remember his name perfectly now, William Wirt Sikes. And of course he would be appointed a Consul to some part of this planet, because he was not needed in this country. We have certainly furnished this world with whole regiments, battalions, and divisions of ignorant, characterless, and chuckle-headed Consuls who have exhibited the United States to a wondering foreign public, and who ought not to have had any salary. Nor fees. They ought to have charged admission—a shilling, say, to foreigners desiring to examine our political product. Olive Logan's present husband, it appears, is named James O'Neill, and was her office boy in London a quarter of a century ago. She was twenty-two years older than he was. The first ten years of their married life was "a dream of happiness." He has taken to hard drinking.

Well, you see it is another tragedy. You've only got to live long enough and your tragedy will arrive. I didn't think, thirty-five years ago, that the day could ever come when my heart would soften toward Olive Logan, and that I would put my hands before my eyes if she were drowning, so as not to see it; but now I do pity her—I do pity her. Her tragedy has come, and I have to be sorry for her, and I am sorry. If she were drowning I would not look—but I would not pull her out. I would not be a party to that last and meanest unkindness, treachery to a would-be suicide. My sympathies have been with the suicides for many, many years. I am always glad when the suicide succeeds in his undertaking. I always feel a genuine pain in my heart, a genuine grief, a genuine pity, when some scoundrel stays the suicide's hand and compels him to continue his life.

In this morning's paper, a woman living in California—her husband living in Washington, an employee of the Government—takes the life of her son, fourteen years old, with gas; tries to die with him; is found on her knees at his bedside, unconscious, nearly gone. The people who thus find her, instead of going out and shutting the door, as I would have done, drag her out of the place and into the fresh air and summon a doctor, and that doctor commits the crime of bringing her back to life, with all that that means for her. Her husband lost to her through the fascinations of some department clerk in Washington; her boy gone out of this world, and happy; nothing left in this world of a penny's value for her—the tragedy of her life brought upon her when she has not yet reached the tragedy age. And look at that doctor's comment! He says he "entertains hopes of her recovery." He ought to be shot. I entertain hopes that to-morrow morning's paper will bring news that she is on her way to the cemetery, where she can have peace.

Dublin, New Hampshire, Monday, May 21, 1906

Early experiences as an author—Publishing of "The Jumping Frog" in volume of sketches—Meeting Carleton in Lucerne—His apology for having refused to publish Mr. Clemens's book of sketches—Difficulties attending the bringing out of "The Innocents Abroad."

We are to abide here in the green solitude of the woods and hills for the next five months.

1867

My experiences as an author began early in 1867. I came to New York from San Francisco in the first month of that year and presently Charles H. Webb, whom I had known in San Francisco as a reporter on the *Bulletin,* and afterward editor of *The Californian,* suggested that I publish a volume of sketches. I had but a slender reputation to publish it on, but I was charmed and excited by the suggestion and quite willing to venture it if some industrious person would save me the trouble of gathering the sketches together. I was loth to do it myself, for from the beginning of my sojourn in this world there was a persistent vacancy in me where the industry ought to be. (Ought to was is better, perhaps, though the most of the authorities differ as to this.)

Webb said I had some reputation in the Atlantic States, but I knew quite well that it must be of a very attenuated sort. What there was of it rested upon the story of "The Jumping Frog." When Artemus Ward passed through California on a lecturing tour, in

1865–66

1865 or '66, I told him the "Jumping Frog" story, in San Francisco, and he asked me to write it out and send it to his publisher, Carleton, in New York, to be used in padding out a small book which Artemus had prepared for the press and which needed some more stuffing to make it big enough for the price which was to be charged for it.

It reached Carleton in time, but he didn't think much of it, and was not willing to go to the type-setting expense of adding it to the book. He did not put it in the waste-basket, but made Henry Clapp a present of it, and Clapp used it to help out the funeral of his dying literary journal, *The Saturday Press.* "The Jumping Frog" appeared in the last number of that paper, was the most joyous feature of the obsequies, and was at once copied in the newspapers of America and England. It certainly had a wide celebrity, and it still had it at the time that I am speaking of—but I was aware that it was only the frog that was celebrated. It wasn't I. I was still an obscurity.

Webb undertook to collate the sketches. He performed this office, then handed the result to me, and I went to Carleton's establishment with it. I approached a clerk and he bent eagerly over the counter to inquire into my needs; but when he found that I had come to sell a book and not to buy one, his temperature fell sixty degrees and the old-gold intrenchments in the roof of my mouth contracted three-quarters of an inch and my teeth fell out. I meekly asked the privilege of a word with Mr. Carleton, and was coldly informed that he was in his private office. Discouragements and difficulties followed, but after a while I got by the frontier and entered the holy of holies. Ah, now I remember how I managed it! Webb had made an appointment for me with Carleton; otherwise I never should have gotten over that frontier. Carleton rose and said brusquely and aggressively,

"Well, what can I do for you?"

I reminded him that I was there by appointment to offer him my book for publication. He began to swell, and went on swelling and swelling and swelling until he had reached the dimensions of a god of about the second or third degree. Then the fountains of his great deep were broken up, and for two or three minutes I couldn't see him for the rain. It was words, only words, but they fell so densely that they darkened the atmosphere. Finally he made an imposing sweep with his right hand which comprehended the whole room and said,

"Books—look at those shelves! Every one of them is loaded with books that are waiting for publication. Do I want any more? Excuse me, I don't. Good morning."

Twenty-one years elapsed before I saw Carleton again. I was then sojourning with my family at the Schweitzerhof, in Lucerne. He called on me, shook hands cordially, and said at once, without any preliminaries,

"I am substantially an obscure person, but I have at least one distinction to my credit of such colossal dimensions that it entitles me to immortality—to wit: I refused a book of yours, and for this I stand without competitor as the prize ass of the nineteenth century."

It was a most handsome apology, and I told him so, and said it was a long delayed revenge but was sweeter to me than any other that could be devised; that during the lapsed twenty-one years I had in fancy taken his life several times every year, and always in new and increasingly cruel and inhuman ways, but that now I was pacified, appeased, happy, even jubilant; and that thenceforth I should hold him my true and valued friend and never kill him again.

I reported my adventure to Webb, and he bravely said that not all the Carletons in the universe should defeat that book; he would publish it himself on a 10 per cent royalty.

And so he did. He brought it out in blue and gold, and made a very pretty little book of it. I think he named it "The Celebrated Jumping Frog of Calaveras County, and Other Sketches," price $1.25. He made the plates and printed and bound the book through a job printing-house, and published it through the American News Company.

In June I sailed in the *Quaker City* Excursion. I returned in November, and in Washington found a letter from Elisha Bliss of the American Publishing Company of Hartford, offering me 5 per cent royalty on a book which should recount the adventures of the excursion. In lieu of the royalty, I was offered the alternative of ten thousand dollars cash upon delivery of the manuscript. I consulted A. D. Richardson and he said "take the royalty." I followed his advice and closed with Bliss. By my contract I was to deliver the manuscript in July of 1868. I wrote the book in San Francisco and delivered the manuscript within contract time. Bliss provided a multitude of illustrations for the book, and then stopped work on it. The contract date for the issue went by, and there was no explanation of this. Time drifted along and still there was no explanation. I was lecturing all over the country; and about thirty times a day, on an average, I was trying to answer this conundrum:

1868

"When is your book coming out?"

I got tired of inventing new answers to that question, and by and by I got horribly tired of the question itself. Whoever asked it became my enemy at once, and I was usually almost eager to make that appear.

As soon as I was free of the lecture field I hastened to Hartford to make inquiries. Bliss said that the fault was not his; that he wanted to publish the book but the directors of his Company were staid old fossils and were afraid of it. They had examined the book, and the majority of them were of the opinion that there were places in it of a humorous character. Bliss said the house had never published a book that had a suspicion like that attaching to it, and that the directors were afraid that a departure of this kind could seriously injure the house's reputation; that he was tied hand and foot, and was not permitted to carry out his contract. One of the directors, a Mr. Drake—at least he was the remains of what had once been a Mr. Drake—invited me to take a ride with him in his buggy, and I went along. He was a pathetic old relic, and his ways and his talk were also pathetic. He had a delicate purpose in view and it took him some time to hearten himself sufficiently to carry it out, but at last he accomplished it. He explained the house's difficulty and distress, as Bliss had already explained it. Then he frankly threw himself and the house upon my mercy and begged me to take away "The Innocents Abroad" and release the concern from the contract. I said I wouldn't—and so ended the interview and the buggy excursion. Then I warned Bliss that he must get to work or I should make trouble. He acted upon the warning, and set up the book and I read the proofs. Then there was another long wait and no explanation. At last toward the end of July (1869 I think), I lost patience and telegraphed Bliss that if the book was not on sale in twenty-four hours I should bring suit for damages.

1869

That ended the trouble. Half a dozen copies were bound and placed on sale within the required time. Then the canvassing began, and went briskly forward. In nine months the book took the publishing house out of debt, advanced its stock from twenty-five to two hundred, and left seventy thousand dollars' profit to the good. It was Bliss that told me this—but if it was true, it was the first time that he had told the truth in sixty-five years. He was born in 1804.

Wednesday, May 23, 1906

Webb states that "Jumping Frog" has been favorably received but that he has made nothing on it because of dishonesty of American News Company—Mr. Clemens makes contract with American Publishing Company for "The Innocents Abroad" and suppresses the publication of "Jumping Frog" by Webb—Afterwards discovers from the American News Company that Webb had swindled him—Terms of contract with Bliss for "Roughing It" and "A Tramp Abroad."

But I must go back to Webb. When I got back from the *Quaker City* Excursion, in November 1867, Webb told me that the "Jumping Frog" book had been favorably received by the press and that he believed it had sold fairly well, but that he had found it impossible to get a statement of account from the American News Company. He said the book had been something of a disaster to him, since he had manufactured it with his own private funds and was now not able to get any of the money back because of the dishonest and dodging ways of the News Company.

1867

I was very sincerely sorry for Webb; sorry that he had lost money by befriending me; also, in some degree sorry that he was not able to pay me my royalties.

I made my contract for "The Innocents Abroad" with the American Publishing Company. Then, after two or three months had gone by, it occurred to me that perhaps I was violating that contract, there being a clause in it forbidding me to publish books with any other firm during a term of a year or so. Of course that clause could not cover a book which had been published before the contract was made; anybody else would have known that. But I didn't know it, for I was not in the habit of knowing anything that was valuable; and I was also not in the habit of asking other people for information. It was my ignorant opinion that I was violating the Bliss contract, and that I was in honor bound to suppress the "Jumping Frog" book and take it permanently out of print. So I went to Webb with the matter. He was willing to accommodate me upon these terms: that I should surrender to him such royalties as might be due me; that I should also surrender to him, free of royalty, all bound and unbound copies which might be in the News Company's hands; also that I should hand him eight hundred dollars cash; also that he should superintend the breaking up of the plates of the book, and for that service should receive such bounty as the type founders should pay for the broken plates as old type-metal. Type-metal was worth nine cents a pound, and the weight of the plates was about forty pounds. One may perceive by these details that Webb had some talent as a trader.

After this Webb passed out of the field of my vision for a long time. But meantime chance threw me in the way of the manager of the American News Company, and I asked him about Webb's difficulties with the concern and how they had come about. He said he didn't know of any difficulties. I then explained to him that Webb had never been able to collect anything from the Company. In turn, he explained to me that my explanation was not sound. He said the Company had always furnished statements to Webb, at the usual intervals, and had accompanied them with the Company's check to date. By his invitation, I went with him to his office, and by his books and accounts he proved to me that what he had said was true. Webb had collected his dues and mine, regularly, from the beginning, and had pocketed the money. At the time that Webb and I had settled, he was owing me six hundred dollars on royalties. The bound and unbound "Jumping Frogs" which he had inherited from me at that time had since been sold, and the result had gone into his pocket—part of it being six hundred more that should have come to me on royalties.

To sum up, I was now an author; I was an author with some little trifle of reputation; I was an author who had published a book; I was an author who had not become rich through that publication; I was an author whose first book had cost him twelve hundred dollars in unreceived royalties, eight hundred dollars in blood money, and three dollars and sixty cents smouched from old type-metal. I was resolved, from that moment, that I would not publish with Webb any more—unless I could borrow money enough to support the luxury.

By and by, when I became notorious through the publication of "The Innocents Abroad," Webb was able to satisfy the public—first, that he had discovered me; later, that he had created me. It was quite generally conceded that I was a valuable asset to the American nation and to the great ranks of literature; also that for the acquisition of this asset a deep debt of gratitude was due from the nation and the ranks—to Webb.

By and by Webb and his high service were forgotten. Then Bliss, and the American Publishing Company, came forward and established the fact that they had discovered me; later, that they had created me; therefore that some more gratitude was due. In the course of time there were still other claimants for these great services. They sprang up in California, Nevada, and around generally, and I came at last to believe that I had been more multitudinously discovered and created than any other animal that had ever issued from the Deity's hands.

Webb believed that he was a literary person. He might have gotten this superstition accepted by the world if he had not extinguished it by publishing his things. They gave him away. His prose was enchantingly puerile; his poetry was not any better; yet he kept on grinding out his commonplaces at intervals until he died, two years ago, of over-cerebration. He was a poor sort of a creature, and by nature and training a fraud. As a liar he was well enough, and had some success but no distinction, because he was a contemporary of Elisha Bliss and when it came to lying Bliss could overshadow and blot out a whole continent of Webbs, like a total eclipse.

1872 About 1872 I wrote another book, "Roughing It." I had published "The Innocents" on a 5 per cent royalty, which would amount to about twenty-two cents per volume. Proposals were coming in now from several other good houses. One offered 15 per cent royalty; another offered to give me *all* of the profits and be content with the advertisement which the book would furnish the house. I sent for Bliss, and he came to Elmira. If I had known as much about book publishing then as I know now, I would have required of Bliss 75 or 80 per cent of the profits above cost of manufacture, and this would have been fair and just. But I knew nothing about the business and had been too indolent to try to learn anything about it. I told Bliss I did not wish to leave his corporation, and that I did not want extravagant terms. I said I thought I ought to have half the profit above cost of manufacture, and he said with enthusiasm that that was exactly right, exactly right. He went to his hotel and drew the contract and brought it to the house in the afternoon. I found a difficulty in it. It did not name "half profits," but named a 7½ per cent royalty instead. I asked him to explain that. I said that that was not the understanding. He said "No, it wasn't," but that he had put in a royalty to simplify the matter—that 7½ per cent royalty represented fully half the profit and a little more, up to a sale of a hundred thousand copies; that after that, the Publishing Company's half would be a shade superior to mine.

I was a little doubtful, a little suspicious, and asked him if he could swear to that. He promptly put up his hand and made oath to it, exactly repeating the words which he had just used.

It took me nine or ten years to find out that that was a false oath, and that 7½ per cent did not represent one-fourth of the profits. But in the meantime I had published several books with Bliss on 7½ and 10 per cent royalties, and of course had been handsomely swindled on all of them.

In 1879 I came home from Europe with a book ready for the press—"A Tramp Abroad." I sent for Bliss and he came out to the house to discuss the book. I said that I was not satisfied about those royalties, and that I did not believe in their "half profit" pretenses; that this time he must put the "half profit" in the contract and make no mention of royalties—otherwise I would take the book elsewhere. He said he was perfectly willing to put it in, for it was right and just, and that if his directors opposed it and found fault with it he would withdraw from the concern and publish the book himself—fine talk, but I knew that he was master in that concern and that it would have to accept any contract that had been signed by him. This contract lay there on the billiard table with his signature attached to it. He had ridden his directors rough-shod ever since the days of "The Innocents Abroad," and more than once he had told me that he had made his directors do things which they hadn't wanted to do, with the threat that if they did not comply he would leave the Company's service and take me along with him.

1879

I don't know how a grown person could ever be so simple and innocent as I was in those days. It ought to have occurred to me that a man who could talk like that must either be a fool or convinced that I was one. However, I was the one. And so, even very simple and rudimentary wisdoms were not likely to find their way into my head.

I reminded him that his Company would not be likely to make any trouble about a contract which had been signed by him. Then, with one of his toothless smiles, he pointed out a detail which I had overlooked, to wit: the contract was with Elisha Bliss, as a private individual, and the American Publishing Company was not mentioned in it.

He told me afterward that he took the contract to the directors and said that he would turn it over to the Company for one-fourth of the profits of the book together with an increase of salary for himself and for Frank, his son, and that if these terms were not satisfactory he would leave the Company and publish the book himself—whereupon the directors granted his demands and took the contract. The fact that Bliss told me these things with his own mouth is unassailable evidence that they were not true. Six weeks before the book issued from the press Bliss told the truth once, to see how it would taste, but it overstrained him and he died.

When the book had been out three months there was an annual meeting of the stockholders of the Company and I was present, as a half-partner in the book. The meeting was held in the house of a neighbor of mine, Newton Case, a director in the Company from the beginning. A statement of the Company's business was read, and to me it was a revelation. Sixty-four thousand copies of the book had been sold, and my half of the profit was thirty-two thousand dollars. In 1872 Bliss had made out to me that 7½ per cent royalty—some trifle over twenty cents a copy—represented one-half of the profits, whereas at that earlier day it hardly represented a sixth of the profits. Times were not so good now, yet it took all of fifty cents a copy to represent half.

1872

Well, Bliss was dead and I couldn't settle with him for his ten years of swindlings. He has been dead a quarter of a century now. My bitterness against him has faded away and disappeared. I feel only compassion for him, and if I could send him a fan I would.

When the balance sheets exposed to me the rascalities which I had been suffering at the hands of the American Publishing Company I stood up and delivered a lecture to Newton Case and the rest of the conspirators——

Thursday, May 24, 1906

Mr. Clemens tries to buy his contracts from the American Publishing Company and finally takes his next book, "Old Times on the Mississippi," to James R. Osgood, who published it by subscription and made a failure of it—Osgood next published "The Prince and Pauper"—Mr. Clemens buys numerous patents, losing on all of them; also stock in Hartford Accident Insurance Company—Description of Senator Jones—Mr. Clemens refuses to buy telephone stock.

—meaning the rest of the directors.

My opportunity was now come to right myself and level up matters with the Publishing Company, but I didn't see it, of course. I was seldom able to see an opportunity until it had ceased to be one. I knew all about that house now, and I ought to have remained with it. I ought to have put a tax upon its profits for my personal benefit, the tax to continue until the difference between royalties and half profits should in time return from the Company's pocket to mine, and the Company's robbery of me be thus wiped off the slate. But of course I couldn't think of anything so sane as that, and I didn't. I only thought of ways and means to remove my respectability from that tainted atmosphere. I wanted to get my books out of the Company's hands and carry them elsewhere. After a time I went to Newton Case—in his house as before—and proposed that the Company cancel the contracts and restore my books to me free and unencumbered, the Company retaining as a consideration the money it had swindled me out of on "Roughing It," "The Gilded Age," "Sketches Old and New," and "Tom Sawyer."

Mr. Case demurred at my language, but I told him I was not able to modify it; that I was perfectly satisfied that he and the rest of the Bible Class were aware of the fraud practised on me in 1872 by Bliss—aware of it when it happened, and consenting to it by silence. He objected to my calling the Board of Directors a Bible Class. And I said then it ought to stop opening its meetings with prayer—particularly when it was getting ready to swindle an author. I was expecting that Mr. Case would deny the charge of guilty knowledge and resent it, but he didn't do it. That convinced me that my charge was well founded; therefore I repeated it, and proceeded to say unkind things about his theological seminary. I said,

1872

"You have put seventy-five thousand dollars into that factory and are getting a great deal of praise for it, whereas *my* share in that benefaction goes unmentioned—yet I *have* a share in it, for of every dollar that you put into it, a portion was stolen out of my pocket."

He returned no thanks for these compliments. He was a dull man and unappreciative.

Finally I tried to buy my contracts, but he said it would be impossible for the Board to entertain a proposition to sell, for the reason that nine-tenths of the Company's livelihood was drawn from my books and therefore its business would be worth nothing if they were taken away. At a later time Judge What's-his-name, a director, told me I was right; that the Board did know all about the swindle which Bliss had practised upon me at the time that the fraud was committed.

As I have remarked, I ought to have remained with the Company and leveled up the account. But I didn't. I removed my purity from that mephitic atmosphere and carried my next book to James R. Osgood of Boston, formerly of the firm of Fields, Osgood and Company. That book was "Old Times on the Mississippi." Osgood was to manufacture the book at my expense; publish it by subscription, and charge me a royalty for his services. Osgood was one of the dearest and sweetest and loveliest human beings to be found on the planet anywhere, but he knew nothing about subscription publishing, and he made a mighty botch of it. He was a sociable creature, and we played much billiards, and daily and nightly had a good time. And in the meantime his clerks ran our business for us and I think that neither of us inquired into their methods or knew what they were doing. That book was a long time getting built; and when at last the final draft was made upon my purse I realized that I had paid out fifty-six thousand dollars upon that structure. Bliss could have built a library for that money. It took a year to get the fifty-six thousand back into my pocket, and not very many dollars followed it. So this first effort of mine to transact that kind of business on my own hook was a failure.

Osgood tried again. He published "The Prince and Pauper." He made a beautiful book of it, but all the profit I got out of it was seventeen thousand dollars.

Next, Osgood thought he could make a success with a book in the *trade.* He had been trained to trade-publishing. He was a little sore over his subscription attempts, and wanted to try. I gave him "The White Elephant," which was a collection of rubbishy sketches, mainly. I offered to bet he couldn't sell ten thousand copies in six months, and he took me up—stakes five dollars. He won the money, but it was something of a squeeze. However, I think I am wrong in putting that book last. I think that that was Osgood's first effort, not his third. I should have continued with Osgood after his failure with "The Prince and the Pauper," because I liked him so well, but he failed, and I had to go elsewhere.

Meantime I had been having an adventure on the outside. An old and particular friend of mine unloaded a patent on me, price fifteen thousand dollars. It was worthless, and he had been losing money on it a year or two, but I did not know those particulars, because he neglected to mention them. He said that if I would buy the patent he would do the manufacturing and selling for me. So I took him up. Then began a cash outgo of five hundred dollars a month. That raven flew out of the ark regularly every thirty days, but it never got back with anything, and the dove didn't report for duty. After a time, and half a time, and another time, I relieved my friend and put the patent into the hands of Charles L. Webster, who had married a niece of mine and seemed a capable and energetic young fellow. At a salary of fifteen hundred a year he continued to send the raven out monthly, with the same old result to a penny.

At last, when I had lost forty-two thousand dollars on that patent I gave it away to a man whom I had long detested and whose family I desired to ruin. Then I looked around for other adventures. That same friend was ready with another patent. I spent ten thousand dollars on it in eight months. Then I tried to give that patent to the man whose family I was after. He was very grateful, but he was also experienced by this time, and was getting suspicious of benefactors. He wouldn't take it, and I had to let it lapse.

Meantime, another old friend arrived with a wonderful invention. It was an engine, or a furnace, or something of the kind, which would get out 99 per cent of all the steam that was in a pound of coal. I went to Mr. Richards of the Colt Arms Factory and told him about it. He was a specialist and knew all about coal and steam. He seemed to be doubtful about this machine, and I asked him why. He said because the amount of steam concealed in a pound of coal was known to a fraction, and that my inventor was mistaken about his 99 per cent. He showed me a printed book of solid pages of figures; figures that made me drunk and dizzy. He showed me that my man's machine couldn't come within 90 per cent of doing what it proposed to do. I went away a little discouraged. But I thought that maybe the book was mistaken, and so I hired the inventor to build the machine on a salary of thirty-five dollars a week, I to pay all expenses. It took him a good many weeks to build it. He visited me every few days to report progress, and I early noticed by his breath and gait that he was spending thirty-six dollars a week on whisky, and I couldn't ever find out where he got the other dollar.

Finally, when I had spent five thousand on this enterprise, the machine was finished, but it wouldn't go. It did save 1 per cent of the steam that was in a pound of coal, but that was nothing. You could do it with a tea-kettle. I offered the machine to the man whose family I was pursuing, but without success. So I threw the thing away and looked around for something fresh. But I had become an enthusiast on steam, and I took some stock in a Hartford company which proposed to make and sell and revolutionize everything with a new kind of steam pulley. The steam pulley pulled thirty-two thousand dollars out of my pocket in sixteen months, then went to pieces and I was alone in the world again, without an occupation.

But I found one. I invented a scrap-book—and if I do say it myself, it was the only rational scrap-book the world has ever seen. I patented it and put it in the hands of that old particular friend of mine who had originally interested me in patents, and he made a good deal of money out of it. But by and by, just when I was about to begin to receive a share of the money myself, his firm failed. I didn't know his firm was going to fail—he didn't say anything about it. One day he asked me to lend the firm five thousand dollars and said he was willing to pay 7 per cent. As security he offered the firm's note. I asked for an endorser. He was much surprised, and said that if endorsers were handy and easy to get at, he wouldn't have to come to me for the money, he could get it anywhere. That seemed reasonable, and so I gave him the five thousand dollars. They failed inside of three days—and at the end of two or three years I got back two thousand dollars of the money.

That five thousand dollars had a history. Early in 1872 Joe Goodman wrote me from California that his friend Senator John P. Jones was going to start a rival, in Hartford, to the Travelers Accident Insurance Company, and that Jones wanted Joe to take twelve thousand of the stock and had said he would see that he did not lose the money. Joe now proposed to transfer this opportunity to me, and said that if I would make the venture he was sure Jones would protect me from loss. So I took the stock and became a director. Jones's brother-in-law, Lester, had been for a long time actuary in the Travelers Company. He was now transferred to our Company and we began business. There were five directors. Three of us attended every Board meeting for a year and a half. At the end of eighteen months the Company went to pieces and I was out of pocket twenty-three thousand dollars. Jones was in New York tarrying for a while at a hotel which he had bought, (the St. James), and I sent Lester down there to see if he could get the twenty-three thousand dollars. But he came back and reported that Jones had been putting money into so many things that he was a good deal straitened and would be glad if I would wait a while. I did not suspect that Lester was drawing upon his fancy, but it was so. He hadn't said anything to Jones about it. But his tale seemed reasonable, because I knew that Jones had built a line of artificial-ice factories clear across the Southern

States—nothing like it this side of the great Wall of China. I knew that the factories had cost him a million dollars or so, and that the people down there hadn't been trained to admire ice and didn't want any and wouldn't buy any—that therefore the Chinese Wall was an entire loss and failure. I also knew that Jones's St. James Hotel had ceased to be a profitable house because Jones, who was a big-hearted man with ninety-nine parts of him pure generosity—and that is the case to this day—had filled his hotel from roof to cellar with poor relations gathered from the four corners of the earth—plumbers, bricklayers, unsuccessful clergymen, and, in fact, all the different kinds of people that knew nothing about the hotel business. I was also aware that there was no room in the hotel for the public, because all its rooms were occupied by a multitude of other poor relations gathered from the four corners of the earth, at Jones's invitation, and waiting for Jones to find lucrative occupations for them. I was also aware that Jones had bought a piece of the State of California with some spacious city sites on it; with room for railroads, and with a very fine and spacious and valuable harbor on its city front, and that Jones was in debt for these properties. Therefore I was content to wait a while. Among other things, I also knew this: that whereas Jones had promised to save Joe Goodman from loss, he was under no such promise to me.

As the months drifted by, Lester now and then volunteered to go and see Jones on his own hook. His visits produced nothing. The fact is, Lester was afraid of Jones and felt a delicacy about troubling him with my matter while he had so many burdens on his shoulders. He preferred to pretend to me that he had seen Jones and had mentioned my matter to him, whereas in truth he had never mentioned it to him at all. At the end of two or three years Mr. Slee of our Elmira coal firm proposed to speak to Jones about it and I consented. Slee visited Jones and began in his tactful and diplomatic way to lead up to my matter, but before he had got well started Jones glanced up and said,

"Do you mean to say that that money has never been paid to Clemens?"

He drew his check for twenty-three thousand at once; said it ought to have been paid long ago, and that it would have been paid the moment it was due if he had known the circumstances. There are not many John P. Joneses in the world.

1877

This was in the spring of 1877. With that check in my pocket I was prepared to seek sudden fortune again. The reader, deceived by what I have been saying about my adventures, will jump to the conclusion that I sought an opportunity at once. I did nothing of the kind. I was the burnt child. I wanted nothing further to do with speculations. General Hawley sent for me to come to the *Courant* office. I went there with my check in my pocket. There was a young fellow there who said that he had been a reporter on a Providence newspaper, but that he was in another business now: that he was with Graham Bell, and was agent for a new invention called the telephone. He believed there was great fortune in store for it and wanted me to take some stock. I declined. I said I didn't want anything more to do with wildcat speculation. Then he offered the stock to me at twenty-five. I said I didn't want it at any price. He became eager—insisted that I at least take a trifle of it—five hundred dollars' worth. He said he would sell me as much as I wanted for five hundred dollars—offered to let me gather it up in my hands and measure it in a plug hat—said I could have a whole hatful for five hundred dollars. But I was the burnt child, and I resisted all these temptations—resisted them easily—went off with my check intact, and next day lent five thousand of it, on an unendorsed note, to my friend who was going to go bankrupt three days later, as I have already stated.

About the end of the year (or possibly in the beginning of 1878) I put up a telephone wire from my house down to the *Courant* office, the only telephone wire in town, and the *first* one that was ever used in a private house in the world, for practical purposes.

1878

That young man couldn't sell *me* any stock, but he sold a few hatfuls of it to an old dry-goods clerk in Hartford for five thousand dollars. That five thousand was that clerk's whole fortune. He had been half a lifetime saving it. It is strange how foolish people can be, and what ruinous risks they can take when they want to get rich in a hurry. I was sorry for that man when I heard about it. I thought I might have saved him if I had had an opportunity to tell him about my experiences.

We sailed for Europe on the 10th of April, 1878. We were gone fourteen months, and when we got back one of the first things we saw was that clerk driving around in a sumptuous barouche with liveried servants all over it in piles—and his telephone stock was emptying greenbacks into his premises at such a rate that he had to handle them with a shovel. It is strange the way the ignorant and inexperienced so often and so undeservedly succeed when the informed and the deserving fail.

To return to my adventures in the publishing business.

Saturday, May 26, 1906

Mr. Clemens becomes his own publisher and makes Webster general agent in firm of Webster and Company, Publishers—Webster publishes "Huckleberry Finn" successfully—Whitford of firm of Alexander and Green draws the contract—Lecture tour with George Cable—Farewell address on 19th of April.

As I have already remarked, I had imported my nephew-in-law, Webster, from the village of Dunkirk, New York, to conduct that original first patent-right business for me, at a salary of fifteen hundred dollars. That enterprise had lost forty-two thousand dollars for me, so I thought this a favorable time to close it up. I proposed to be my own publisher now, and let young Webster do the work. He thought he ought to have twenty-five hundred dollars a year while he was learning the trade. I took a day or two to consider the matter and study it out searchingly. So far as I could see, this was a new idea. I remembered that printers' apprentices got *no* salary. Upon inquiry I found that this was the case with stone masons, brick masons, tinners, and the rest. I found that not even lawyers or apprenticed doctors got any salary for learning the trade. I remembered that on the river an apprentice pilot not only got nothing in the way of salary but he also had to pay some pilot a sum in cash which he didn't have—a large sum. It was what I had done myself. I had paid Bixby a hundred dollars, and it was borrowed money. I was told by a person who said he was studying for the ministry that even Noah got no salary for the first six months—partly on account of the weather and partly because he was learning navigation.

The upshot of these thinkings and searchings of mine was that I believed I had secured something entirely new to history in Webster. And also I believed that a young backwoodsman who was starting life in New York without any equipment of any kind, without proved value of any kind, without prospective value of any kind, yet able without blinking an eye to propose to learn a trade at another man's expense and charge for this benefaction an annual sum greater than any President of the United States had ever been able to save out of his pay for running the most difficult country on the planet, after Ireland, must surely be worth securing—and instantly—lest he get away. I believed that if some of his gigantic interest in No. 1 could be diverted to the protection of No. 2, the result would be fortune enough for me.

I erected Webster into a firm—a firm entitled Webster and Company, Publishers—and installed him in a couple of offices at a modest rental, on the second floor of a building somewhere below Union Square, I don't remember where. For assistants he had a girl, and perhaps a masculine clerk of about eight-hundred-dollar size. For a while Webster had another helper. This was a man who had long been in the subscription-book business, knew all about it, and was able to teach it to Webster—which he did—I paying the cost of tuition. I am talking about the early part of 1884 now. I handed Webster a competent capital and along with it I handed him the manuscript of "Huckleberry Finn." Webster's function was general agent. It was his business to appoint sub-agents throughout the country. At that time there were sixteen of these sub-agencies. They had canvassers under them who did the canvassing. In New York City Webster was his own sub-agent.

1884

Before ever any of these minor details that I am talking about had entered into being, the careful Webster had suggested that a contract be drawn and signed and sealed before we made any real move. That seemed sane, though I should not have thought of it myself—I mean it *was* sane *because* I had not thought of it myself. So Webster got his friend Whitford to draw the contract. I was coming to admire Webster very much, and at this point in the proceedings I had one of those gushing generosities surge up in my system; and before I had thought, I had tried to confer upon Webster a tenth interest in the business in addition to his salary, free of charge. Webster declined promptly—with thanks, of course, the usual kind. That raised him another step in my admiration. I knew perfectly well that I was offering him a partnership interest which would pay him two or three times his salary within the next nine months, but he didn't know that. He was coldly and wisely discounting all my prophecies about "Huckleberry Finn's" high commercial value. And here was this new evidence that in Webster I had found a jewel, a man who would not get excited; a man who would not lose his head; a cautious man; a man who would not take a risk of any kind in fields unknown to him. Except at somebody else's expense, I mean.

The contract was drawn, as I say, by Whitford. Dunkirk, New York, produced Whitford as well as Webster, and has not yet gotten over the strain. Whitford was privileged to sign himself "of the firm of Alexander and Green." Alexander and Green had a great and lucrative business and not enough conscience to damage it—a fact which came out rather prominently last year when the earthquake came which shook the entrails out of the three great Life Insurance Companies. Alexander and Green had their offices in the Mutual Building. They kept a job lot of twenty-five lawyers on salary, and Whitford was one of these. He was good-natured, obliging, and immensely ignorant, and was endowed with a stupidity which by the least little stretch would go around the globe four times and tie.

That first contract was all right. There was nothing the matter with it. It placed all obligations, all expenses, all liability, all responsibilities upon *me,* where they belonged.

It was a happy combination, Webster and Whitford. The amount that the two together didn't know about anything was to me a much more awful and paralysing spectacle than it would be to see the Milky Way get wrecked and drift off in rags and patches through the sky. When it came to courage, moral or physical, they hadn't any. Webster was afraid to venture anything in the way of business without first getting a lawyer's assurance that there was nothing jailable about it. Whitford was consulted so nearly constantly that he was about as much a member of the staff as was the girl and the subscription expert. But as neither Webster nor Whitford had had any personal experience of money, Whitford was not an expensive incumbent, though he probably thought he was.

At the break of the autumn I went off with George W. Cable on a four months' reading-campaign in the East and West—the last platform work which I was ever to do in this life in my own country. I resolved at the time that I would never rob the public from the platform again unless driven to it by pecuniary compulsions. After eleven years the pecuniary compulsions came, and I lectured all around the globe.

Ten years have since lapsed, during which time I have only lectured for public charities and without pay. On the 19th of last month I took a public and formal leave of the platform—a thing which I had not done before—in a lecture on Robert Fulton for the benefit of the Robert Fulton Memorial Fund.

I seem to be getting pretty far away from Webster and Whitford, but it's no matter. It is one of those cases where distance lends enchantment to the view. Webster was successful with "Huckleberry Finn," and a year later handed me the firm's check for fifty-four thousand five hundred dollars, which included the fifteen thousand dollars capital which I had originally handed to him.

Once more I experienced a new birth. I have been born more times than anybody except Krishna, I suppose.

Monday, May 28, 1906

Mr. Clemens calls on General Grant just as he is about to sign contract with the Century Company for publication of his Memoirs on 10 per cent royalty—Mr. Clemens dissuades him, and finally decides to publish them himself—Terms upon which they were published.

Webster conceived the idea that he had discovered me to the world, but he was reasonably modest about it. He did much less cackling over his egg than Webb and Bliss had done.

It had never been my intention to publish anybody's books but my own. An accident diverted me from this wise purpose. That was General Grant's memorable book. One night in the first week of November 1884 I had been lecturing in Chickering Hall and was walking homeward. It was a rainy night, and but few people were about. In the midst of a black gulf between lamps, two dim figures stepped out of a doorway and moved along in front of me. I heard one of them say,

1884

"Do you know General Grant has actually determined to write his Memoirs and publish them? He has said so, to-day, in so many words."

That was all I heard—just those words—and I thought it great good luck that I was permitted to overhear them.

In the morning I went out and called on General Grant. I found him in his library with Colonel Fred Grant, his son. The General said, in substance, this:

"Sit down and keep quiet until I sign a contract"—and added that it was for a book which he was going to write.

Fred Grant was apparently conducting a final reading and examination of the contract, to himself. He found it satisfactory, and said so, and his father stepped to the table and took up the pen. It might have been better for me, possibly, if I had let him alone, but I didn't. I said,

"Don't sign it. Let Colonel Fred read it to me first."

Colonel Fred read it, and I said I was glad I had come in time to interfere. The Century Company was the party of the second part. It proposed to pay the General 10 per cent royalty. Of course this was nonsense—but the proposal had its source in ignorance, not dishonesty. The great Century Company knew all about magazine publishing; no one could teach them anything about that industry; but, at that time, they had had no experience of subscription publishing, and they probably had nothing in their minds except trade-publishing. They could not even have had any valuable experience in trade-publishing, or they would not have asked General Grant to furnish a book on the royalty commonly granted to authors of no name or repute.

I explained that these terms would never do; that they were all wrong, unfair, unjust. I said,

"Strike out the 10 per cent and put 20 per cent in its place. Better still, put 75 per cent of the net returns in its place."

The General demurred, and quite decidedly. He said they would never pay those terms.

I said that that was a matter of no consequence, since there was not a reputable publisher in America who would not be very glad to pay them.

The General still shook his head. He was still desirous of signing the contract as it stood.

I pointed out that the contract as it stood had an offensive detail in it which I had never heard of in the 10 per cent contract of even the most obscure author—that this contract not only proposed a 10 per cent royalty for such a colossus as General Grant, but it also had in it a requirement that out of that 10 per cent must come some trivial tax for the book's share of clerk hire, house rent, sweeping out the offices, or some such nonsense as that. I said he ought to have three-fourths of the profits and let the publisher pay running expenses out of his remaining fourth.

The idea distressed General Grant. He thought it placed him in the attitude of a robber—robber of a publisher. I said that if he regarded that as a crime it was because his education had been neglected. I said it was not a crime, and was always rewarded in heaven with two halos. Would be, if it ever happened.

The General was immovable, and challenged me to name the publisher that would be willing to have this noble deed perpetrated upon him. I named the American Publishing Company of Hartford. He asked if I could prove my position. I said I could furnish the proof, by telegraph, in six hours—three hours for my dispatch to go to Hartford, three hours for Bliss's jubilant acceptance to return by the same electric gravel-train—that if he needed this answer quicker I would walk up to Hartford and fetch it.

The General still stood out. But Fred Grant was beginning to be persuaded. He proposed that the Century contract be laid on the table for twenty-four hours, and that meantime the situation be examined and discussed. He said that this thing was not a matter of sentiment; it was a matter of pure business, and should be examined from that point of view alone. His remark about sentiment had a bearing. The reason was this. The broking firm of Grant and Ward—consisting of General Grant, Mr. Ward (called for a time the "Little Napoleon of Finance") and Ward's confederate, Fish—had swindled General Grant out of every penny he had in the world. And at a time when he did not know where to turn for bread, Roswell Smith, head of the Century Company, offered him five hundred dollars per article for four magazine articles about certain great battles of the Civil War. The offer came to the despairing old hero like the fabled straw to the drowning man. He accepted it with gratitude, and wrote the articles and delivered them. They were easily worth ten thousand dollars apiece, but he didn't know it. Five hundred dollars apiece seemed to him fabulous pay for a trifle of pleasant and unlaborious scribbling.

He was now most loth to desert these benefactors of his. To his military mind and training it seemed disloyalty. If I remember rightly his first article lifted the Century's subscription list from a hundred thousand copies to two hundred and twenty thousand. This made the Century's advertisement pages, for that month, worth more than double the money they had ever commanded in any previous month. At a guess, I should say that this increase of patronage was worth, that month, eight thousand dollars. This is a safe estimate, a conservative estimate.

The doubled subscription list established in that month was destined to continue for years. It was destined to increase the magazine's advertisement income about eight or ten thousand dollars a month during six years. I have said that each of General Grant's articles was worth ten thousand dollars instead of five hundred. I could say that each of the four articles was worth twenty-five thousand dollars and still be within bounds.

I began to tout for the American Publishing Company. I argued that that Company had been first in the field as applicants for a volume of Grant Memoirs, and that perhaps they ought to have a chance at a bid before the Century Company. This seemed to be news to General Grant. But I reminded him that once during the apparently wonderfully prosperous days of the firm of Grant and Ward I called upon him in his private office one day, helped him to consume his luncheon, and begged him to write his Memoirs and give them to the American Publishing Company. He had declined at the time, and most decidedly, saying he was not in need of money, and that he was not a literary person and could not write the Memoirs.

I think we left the contract matter to stew for that time, and took it up again the next morning. I did a good deal of thinking during the interval. I knew quite well that the American Publishing Company would be glad to get General Grant's Memoirs on a basis of three-quarters profit for him, to one-quarter for themselves. Indeed I knew quite well that there was not a publisher in the country—I mean a publisher experienced in the subscription publishing business—who would not be glad to get the book on those terms. I was fully expecting to presently hand that book to Frank Bliss and the American Publishing Company and enrich that den of reptiles—but the sober second thought came then. I reflected that that Company had been robbing me for years and building theological factories out of the proceeds, and that now was my chance to feed fat the ancient grudge I bore them.

At the second conference with the General and Fred, the General exhibited some of the modesty which was so large a feature of his nature. General Sherman had published his Memoirs in two large volumes, with Scribners, and that publication had been a notable event. General Grant said:

"Sherman told me that his profits on that book were twenty-five thousand dollars. Do you believe I could get as much out of my book?"

I said I not only believed but I *knew* that he would achieve a vastly greater profit than that—that Sherman's book was published in the trade; that it was a suitable book for subscription distribution, and ought to have been published in that way; that not many books were suitable to that method of publishing, but that the Memoirs of such illustrious persons as Sherman and Grant were peculiarly adapted to that method; that a book which contained the right material for that method would harvest from eight to ten times as much profit by subscription as it could be made to produce by trade sale.

The General had his doubts that he could gather twenty-five thousand dollars' profit from his Memoirs. I inquired why. He said he had already applied the test, and had secured the evidence and the verdict. I wondered where he could have gotten such evidence and such a verdict, and he explained. He said he had offered to sell his Memoirs out and out to Roswell Smith for twenty-five thousand dollars, and that the proposition had so frightened Smith that he hardly had breath enough left in his clothes to decline with.

Then I had an idea. It suddenly occurred to me that I was a publisher myself. I had not thought of it before. I said,

"Sell *me* the Memoirs, General. I am a publisher. I will pay double price. I have a check-book in my pocket; take my check for fifty thousand dollars now, and let's draw the contract."

General Grant was as prompt in declining this as Roswell Smith had been in declining the other offer. He said he wouldn't hear of such a thing. He said we were friends, and if I should fail to get the money back out of his book— He stopped there, and said there was no occasion to go into particulars, he simply would not consent to help a friend run any such risk.

Then I said,

"Give me the book on the terms which I have already suggested that you make with the Century people—20 per cent royalty, or, in lieu of that, 75 per cent of the profits on the publication to go to you, I to pay all running expenses such as salaries, etc., out of my fourth."

He laughed at that, and asked me what my profit out of that remnant would be.

I said, a hundred thousand dollars in six months.

He was dealing with a literary person. He was aware, by authority of all the traditions, that literary persons are flighty, romantic, unpractical, and, in business matters, do not know enough to come in when it rains, or at any other time. He did not say that he attached no value to these flights of my imagination, for he was too kindly to say hurtful things, but he might better have said it, because he looked it with ten-fold emphasis, and the look covered the whole ground. To make conversation, I suppose, he asked me what I based this dream upon—if it had a basis.

I said,

"I base it upon the difference between your literary commercial value and mine. My first two books sold a hundred and fifty thousand copies each—three dollars and a half per volume in cloth, costlier volumes at a higher price according to binding—average price of the hundred and fifty thousand, four dollars apiece. I know that your commercial value is easily four times as great as mine; therefore I know it to be a perfectly safe guess that your book will sell six hundred thousand single volumes, and that the clear profit to you will be half a million dollars, and the clear profit to me a hundred thousand."

We had a long discussion over the matter. Finally General Grant telegraphed for his particular friend, George W. Childs of the Philadelphia *Ledger,* to come up to New

York and furnish an opinion. Childs came. I convinced him that Webster's publishing machinery was ample and in good order. Then Childs delivered the verdict, "Give the book to Clemens." Colonel Fred Grant endorsed and repeated the verdict, "Give the book to Clemens." So the contract was drawn and signed, and Webster took hold of his new job at once.

By my existing contract with Webster he merely had a salary of twenty-five hundred dollars a year. He had declined to accept, gratis, of an interest in the business, for he was a cautious person and averse from running risks. I now offered him, gratis, a tenth share in the business—the contract as to other details to remain as before. Then, as a counter proposition, he modestly offered this: that his salary be increased to thirty-five hundred dollars a year; that he have 10 per cent of the profits accruing from the Grant book, and that I furnish all the capital required at 7 per cent.

I said I should be satisfied with this arrangement.

Then he called in his pal, Whitford, who drew the contract. I couldn't understand the contract—I never could understand any contract—and I asked my brother-in-law, General Langdon, a trained business man, to understand it for me. He read it and said it was all right. So we signed it and sealed it. I was to find out later that the contract gave Webster 10 per cent of the profits on the Grant book *and* 10 per cent interest in the profits of the whole business—but not any interest in such losses as might occur.

The news went forth that General Grant was going to write his Memoirs, and that the firm of Charles L. Webster and Company would publish them. The announcement produced a vast sensation throughout the country. The nation was glad, and this feeling poured itself heartily out in all the newspapers. On the one day, young Webster was as unknown as the unborn babe. The next day he was a notoriety. His name was in every paper in the United States. He was young, he was human, he naturally mistook this transient notoriety for fame; and by consequence he had to get his hat enlarged. His juvenile joy in his new grandeur was a pretty and pleasant spectacle to see. The first thing he did was to move out of his modest quarters and secure quarters better suited to his new importance as the most distinguished publisher in the country.

Tuesday, May 29, 1906

Webster's fine new quarters—Mr. Clemens calls on General Grant when he hears that his sore throat has been pronounced cancer—General Grant tells him of the ways in which Ward deceived him.

His new quarters were on the second or third floor of a tall building which fronted on Union Square, a commercially aristocratic locality. His previous quarters had consisted of two good-sized rooms. His new ones occupied the whole floor. What Webster really needed was a cubby-hole up a back street somewhere, with room to swing a cat in—a long cat—this cubby-hole for office work. He needed no storage rooms, no cellars. The printers and binders of the great Memoir took care of the sheets and the bound volumes for us, and charged storage and insurance. Conspicuous quarters were not needed for that mighty book. You couldn't have hidden General Grant's publisher where the agent and the canvasser could not find him. The cubby-hole would have been sufficient for all our needs. Almost all the business would be transacted by correspondence. That correspondence would be with the sixteen general agents, none of it with their ten thousand canvassers.

However, it was a very nice spread that we made, as far as spaciousness and perspective went. These were impressive—that is, as impressive as nakedness long drawn out and plenty of it could be. It seemed to me that the look of the place was going to deceive country people and drive them away, and I suggested that we put up a protecting sign just inside the door: "Come in. It is not a rope walk."

It was a mistake to deal in sarcasms with Webster. They cut deep into his vanity. He hadn't a single intellectual weapon in his armory, and could not fight back. It was unchivalrous in me to attack with mental weapons this mentally weaponless man, and I tried to refrain from it, but couldn't. I ought to have been large enough to endure his vanities, but I wasn't. I am not always large enough to endure my own. He had one defect which particularly exasperated me, because I didn't have it myself. When a matter was mentioned of which he was ignorant, he not only would not protect himself by remarking that he was not acquainted with the matter, but he had not even discretion enough to keep his tongue still. He would say something intended to deceive the hearers into the notion that he knew something about that subject himself—a most unlikely condition, since his ignorance covered the whole earth like a blanket, and there was hardly a hole in it anywhere. Once in a drawing-room company some talk sprang up about George Evans and her literature. I saw Webster getting ready to contribute. There was no way to hit him with a brick or a Bible, or something, and reduce him to unconsciousness and save him, because it would have attracted attention—and therefore I waited for his mountain to bring forth its mouse, which it did as soon as there was a vacancy between speeches. He filled that vacancy with this remark, uttered with tranquil complacency:

"I've never read any of his books, on account of prejudice."

Before we had become fairly settled in the new quarters, Webster had suggested that we abolish the existing contract and make a new one. Very well, it was done. I probably never read it nor asked anybody else to read it. I probably merely signed it and saved myself further bother in that way. Under the preceding contracts Webster had been my paid servant; under the new one I was his slave, his absolute slave, and without salary. I owned nine-tenths of the business; I furnished all the capital; I shouldered all the losses; I was responsible for everything—but Webster was sole master. This new condition and my sarcasms changed the atmosphere. I could no longer give orders, as before. I could not even make a suggestion with any considerable likelihood of its acceptance.

General Grant was a sick man, but he wrought upon his Memoirs like a well one, and made steady and sure progress.

Webster throned himself in the rope walk and issued a summons to the sixteen general agents to come from the sixteen quarters of the United States and sign contracts.

They came. They assembled. Webster delivered the law to them as from Mount Sinai. They kept their temper wonderfully, marvelously. They furnished the bonds required. They signed the contracts, and departed. Ordinarily they would have resented the young man's arrogances, but this was not an ordinary case. The contracts were worth to each general agent a good many thousands of dollars. They knew this, and the knowledge helped them to keep down their animosities.

Whitford was on hand. He was always at Webster's elbow. Webster was afraid to do anything without legal advice. He could have all the legal advice he wanted, because he had now hired Whitford by the year. He was paying him ten thousand dollars a year out of my pocket. And indeed Whitford was worth part of it—the two-hundredth part of it. It was the first time he had ever earned anything worth speaking of, and he was content. The phrase "worth speaking of" is surplusage. Whitford had never earned anything. Whitford was never destined to earn anything. He did not earn the ten thousand dollars nor any part of it. In two instances his services proved a pecuniary damage to the firm. His other services were inconsequential and unnecessary. The bookkeeper could have performed them.

1884–85

During the winter of 1884 and '85 General Grant fell on the ice and hurt himself, and rheumatism followed. Cable and I were out on the platform in the West during the winter. By and by our program brought us to New York for a day or two, and I saw in the paper that a sore throat from which General Grant had been suffering for a time had turned out to be cancer—malignant and incurable. I went to the house and found him muffled in a thick dressing-gown and sitting in an arm-chair. He looked miserably sick. One of his specialists was present, Shrady or Douglas; Douglas, I think—Douglas, I am sure. The newspapers had laid the cancer to excessive smoking. I said:

"General, this is a warning to the rest of us."

He shook his head, and Douglas said,

"No, it isn't a warning to anybody. This is not a result of smoking. Smoking has never hurt General Grant, and it will never hurt you. No one knows how long this cancer poison has been lurking in General Grant's system—many and many a year, perhaps. All it needed at any time was a sufficient opportunity to develop itself, and the development would ensue. Without such sufficient opportunity he could live to a hundred, and die unaware that there was such a thing as cancer poison in him."

The thing that furnished the opportunity was the shame and humiliation and mental misery inflicted upon General Grant by the robberies committed upon confiding clients by Fish and Ward of the firm of Grant and Ward. It was the unimpeachable credit and respectability of his name and character that enabled them to swindle the public. They could not have done it on their own reputations. It was General Grant's mental miseries that gave the cancer poison its opportunity. It was not tobacco.

At that time, and for some time afterward, General Grant was able to use his voice, and he now began to tell me some of Ward's performances. It was plain that he thought he ought to be ashamed of having been gulled and deceived by such a man as Ward, and wanted to find a justification or palliation for the confidence which he had misplaced in

Ward. It was most pathetic to hear this old lion, who had been brought so low by a hyena, trying to explain why it was natural that he should trust a hyena, he being innocently ignorant of the ways of that kind of an animal. He said, in substance:

"You would have done as I did, Clemens. He would have deceived you as easily as he deceived me. He would have deceived anybody who was ignorant of the intricacies of finance and commercial ways and methods. Indeed he would have deceived men that *were* acquainted with those intricacies and those methods, and he did it. The proof is in the testimony given before the courts. It is in the testimony of at least one such man which was never given in court at all. That man was so ashamed of having been duped by such a poor creature as Ward that he suffered a loss of three hundred thousand dollars, out of which sum Ward had swindled him—suffered the loss and kept still, and avoided the witness box. Now then, when such a man as that could be deceived by Ward, is it to be wondered at that he was able to deceive me? Now consider Ward's ways, and see how ingeniously deceptive they were. Let me go into particulars for a moment. He used to sit there in his private office and accept investments from people, waste that money, throw it away, lose it—and when a statement was due the investor, furnish it promptly, and along with it a handsome profit on the investment, the investment and the profit and everything connected with it being drawn from some other investor who had just been in and left his money to be speculated with. I will give you an instance. When our firm was at the very top wave of prodigal prosperity, as I supposed, and as everybody supposed (whereas it was not making a cent, but was losing money) one of the very sharpest and most successful brokers in this town bustled into our office one day and said,

"'Ward, I am just taking the steamer for Europe and back to get a breath of fresh air. Here's ten thousand dollars. Do you think you can do anything with it in so short a time?'

"Ward said nonchalantly, 'Oh, perhaps. If you want to leave it I'll see what we can do.'

"The man left his check and bustled out again. Ward used that check to pay some customer a dividend on an investment that hadn't earned a penny. Thirty days later that broker bustled in again and said,

"'Well, anything happened?'

"Ward said, as nonchalantly as ever,

"'Well, not much, but something'—carelessly drew a check and handed it to the man.

"The man said, 'Good gracious! A hundred per cent profit in thirty days!' He handed the check back to Ward and said 'That's a good enough hen for me. Set her again.'"

General Grant said that Ward's depredations upon him and upon the Grant relationship were exhaustively complete. He said,

"I had laid up four hundred thousand dollars. Ward got it all. He questioned me about the outlying kin, and wherever he found a member of it that had saved up something in a stocking he sent for it and got it. In one case, a poor old female relative of mine had scrimped and saved until she had something like a thousand dollars laid up for the rainy day of old age. Ward took it without a pang."

Presently came the memorable 4th of March, 1885—forever memorable to me for a picture which it brought. *1885*

Thursday, May 31, 1906

The lovely morning and the majestic Mount Monadnock—Mr. Clemens speaks freely in this autobiography because he speaks from the grave—Does not believe in immortality—Webster a Jew—Bill taken up in Congress on last day of Arthur's term by which Grant was again made a General—Grant's indifference to eulogies.

This is a magnificent morning. This shady front porch is the right vantage-ground to dictate from. There isn't a softer, peacefuller prospect than this anywhere in the earth. There isn't a bluer sky, even over Sweden. There isn't a more bewitching arrangement of white cloudlets to be found in any sky this side of Australia. Monadnock is so close by, in the divine atmosphere of this morning, that I almost think I could stretch out and rest my elbow in the crotch of its twin peaks as in a crutch. Monadnock is always impressive, always majestic, always beautiful, with a beauty whose phases are as manifold as those that are working their enchantments upon that valley yonder, which stretches away and away, on a morning like this, until its hundred shades of green melt into blue, and the blue becomes a dream and melts and mingles with the base of heaven under the remote horizon.

This is not a time nor a place to damn Webster, yet it must be done. It is a duty. Let us proceed. It is not my purpose, in this history, to be more malicious toward any person than I am. I am not alive. I am dead. I wish to keep that fact plainly before the reader. If I were alive I should be writing an autobiography on the usual plan. I should be feeling just as malicious toward Webster as I am feeling this moment—dead as I am—but instead of expressing it freely and honestly, I should be trying to conceal it; trying to swindle the reader, and not succeeding. He would read the malice between the lines, and would not admire me. Nothing worse will happen if I let my malice have frank and free expression. The very reason that I speak from the grave is that I want the satisfaction of sometimes saying everything that is in me instead of bottling the pleasantest of it up for home consumption. I can speak more frankly from the grave than most historians would be able to do, for the reason that whereas they would not be able to *feel* dead, howsoever hard they might try, I myself am able to do that. They would be making believe to be dead. With me, it is not make-believe. They would all the time be feeling, in a tolerably definite way, that that thing in the grave which represents them is a conscious entity; conscious of what it was saying about people; an entity capable of feeling shame; an entity capable of shrinking from full and frank expression, for they believe in immortality. They believe that death is only a sleep, followed by an immediate waking, and that their spirits are conscious of what is going on here below and take a deep and continuous interest in the joys and sorrows of the survivors whom they love and don't.

But I have long ago lost my belief in immortality—also my interest in it. I can say, now, what I could not say while alive—things which it would shock people to hear; things which I could not say when alive because I should be aware of that shock and would certainly spare myself the personal pain of inflicting it. When we believe in immortality we have a reason for it. Not a reason founded upon information, or even plausibilities, for we haven't any. Our reason for choosing to believe in this dream is that we desire immortality, for some reason or other, I don't know what. But I have no such desire. I have sampled this life, and it is sufficient. Another one would be another experiment. It would proceed from the same source as this one. I should have no large expectations concerning it, and if I may be excused from assisting in the experiment I shall be properly grateful. Annihilation has no terrors for me, because I have already tried it before I was born—a hundred million years—and I have suffered more in an hour, in this life, than I remember to have suffered in the whole hundred million years put together. There was a peace, a serenity, an absence of all sense of responsibility, an absence of worry, an absence of care, grief, perplexity; and the presence of a deep content and unbroken satisfaction in that hundred million years of holiday which I look back upon with a tender longing and with a grateful desire to resume, when the opportunity comes.

It is understandable that when I speak from the grave it is not a spirit that is speaking; it is a nothing; it is an emptiness; it is a vacancy; it is a something that has neither feeling nor consciousness. It does not know what it is saying. It is not aware that it is saying anything at all, therefore it can speak frankly and freely, since it cannot know that it is inflicting pain, discomfort, or offence of any kind.

Some people had a prejudice against Webster which I did not share. They disapproved of him because he was a Jew. At least they said he was a Jew, and they professed to know that he was a Jew. I have no prejudices against Jews. I have nothing that resembles a prejudice against Jews. To me, Jews are just merely human beings, and to my mind the difference between one human being and another is not a matter of the slightest consequence. As between a crocodile and an alligator there is no real choice, to my mind, therefore why should there be a choice between Jew and Christian—or between anybody and anybody else? To be a human being of any kind is a hard enough lot, and unpleasant and disreputable in the best of circumstances. Therefore why should a man think more of himself, being a Christian, than he thinks of his neighbor who has escaped that privilege?

One of these prejudiced people said to me that he could not abide Webster because he was a Jew. It seemed to me an unkind feeling, and I explained to him that I was destitute of it, and tried to reason him into coming up and standing with me on my higher and nobler plane. I said I would always try to be just to any human being, in any circumstances, and be as prompt and interested in getting him out of the way as if I had a personal interest in accomplishing it. However, I am wandering from Webster and the Grant Memoirs, which is my subject for the present.

I am talking freely about Webster because I am expecting my future editors to have judgment enough and charity enough to suppress all such chapters in the early editions of this book, and keep them suppressed, edition after edition, until all whom they could pain shall be at rest in their graves. But after that, let them be published. It is my desire, and at that distant date they can do no harm.

I go back, now, to the concluding sentence of yesterday's dictation.

In the history of the United States there had been one officer bearing that supreme and stately and simple one-word title, "General." Possibly there had been two. As to that I do not remember. In the long stretch of years lying between the American Revolution and our Civil War, that title had had no existence. It was an office which was special in its nature. It did not belong among our military ranks. It was only conferrable by Act of Congress and upon a person specially named in the Act. No one could inherit it. No one could succeed to it by promotion. It had been conferred upon General Grant, but he had surrendered it to become President. He was now in the grip of death, with the compassionate and lamenting eyes of all the nation upon him—a nation eager to testify its gratitude to him by granting any wish that he might express. It was known to his friends that it was the dearest ambition of his heart to die a General. On the last day of Mr. Arthur's term and of the Congress then sitting, a bill to confer the title was taken up, at the last moment. There was no time to lose. Messengers were sent flying to the White House. Mr. Arthur came in all haste to the Capitol. There was great anxiety and excitement. And, after all, these strenuous efforts were instituted too late! In the midst of the taking of the vote upon the bill the life of the Congress expired. No, would have expired—but some thoughtful person turned the clock back half an hour, and the bill went through! Mr. Arthur signed it at once, and the day was saved.

The news was dispatched to General Grant by telegram, and I was present, with several others, when it was put into his hands. Every face there betrayed strong excitement and emotion—except one, General Grant's. He read the telegram, but not a shade or suggestion of a change exhibited itself in his iron countenance. The volume of his emotion was greater than all the other emotions there present combined, but he was able to suppress all expression of it and make no sign.

1879

I had seen an exhibition of General Grant's ability to conceal his emotions once before, on a less memorable occasion. This was in Chicago, in 1879, when he arrived there from his triumphal progress around the globe, and was fêted during three days by Chicago and by the first army he commanded—the Army of the Tennessee. I sat near him on the stage of a theatre which was packed to the ceiling with surviving heroes of that army, and their wives. When General Grant, attended by other illustrious Generals of the war, came forward and took his seat, the house rose, and a deafening storm of welcome burst forth which continued during two or three minutes. There wasn't a soldier on that stage who wasn't visibly affected, except the man who was being welcomed, Grant. No change of expression crossed his face.

Then the eulogies began. Sherman was present, Sheridan was present, Schofield, Logan, and half a dozen other bearers of famous military names were there. The orators always began by emptying Niagaras of glory upon Grant. They always came and stood near him, and over him, and emptied the Niagara down on him at short range, but it had no more effect upon him than if he had been a bronze image. In turn, each orator passed from Grant to Sherman, then to Sheridan, and to the rest, and emptied barrels of inflamed praise upon each. And in every case it was as if the orator was emptying fire upon the man, the victim so writhed and fidgeted and squirmed and suffered. With a spy-glass you could have picked out the man that was being martyrized, at a distance of three miles. Not one of them was able to sit still under the fiery deluge of praise except that one man, Grant. He got his Niagara every quarter of an hour for two hours and a half, and yet when the ordeal was over he was still sitting in precisely the same attitude which he had assumed when he first took that chair. He had never moved a hand or foot, head, or anything. It would have been a sufficiently amazing thing to see a man sit without change of position during such a stretch of time without anything whatever on his mind, nothing to move him, nothing to excite him; but to see this one sit like that for two hours and a half under such awful persecution, was an achievement which I should not have believed, if I had not seen it with my own eyes.

Friday, June 1, 1906

General Grant wishes Mr. Clemens's opinion of the literary quality of his Memoirs—Mr. Clemens places them side by side with Caesar's "Commentaries"—Depew's best speech—Buckner's visit to General Grant—General Grant's death—Success of the Memoirs, and Webster's enlarged head—Webster suspects his bookkeeper, Scott.

Whenever galley-proofs or revises went to General Grant, a set came also to me. General Grant was aware of this. Sometimes I referred to the proofs casually, but entered into no particulars concerning them. By and by I learned, through a member of the household, that he was disturbed and disappointed because I had never expressed an opinion as to the literary quality of the Memoirs. It was also suggested that a word of encouragement from me would be a help to him. I was as much surprised as Columbus's cook could have been to learn that Columbus wanted his opinion as to how Columbus was doing his navigating. It could not have occurred to me that General Grant could have any use for anybody's assistance or encouragement in any work which he might undertake to do. He was the most modest of men, and this was another instance of it. He was venturing upon a new trade, an uncharted sea, and stood in need of the encouraging word, just like any creature of common clay. It was a great compliment that he should care for my opinion, and should desire it, and I took the earliest opportunity to diplomatically turn the conversation in that direction and furnish it without seeming to lug it in by the ears.

By chance, I had been comparing the Memoirs with Caesar's "Commentaries" and was qualified to deliver judgment. I was able to say, in all sincerity, that the same high merits distinguished both books—clarity of statement, directness, simplicity, unpretentiousness, manifest truthfulness, fairness and justice toward friend and foe alike, soldierly candor and frankness, and soldierly avoidance of flowery speech. I placed the two books side by side upon the same high level, and I still think that they belonged there. I learned afterward that General Grant was pleased with this verdict. It shows that he was just a man, just a human being, just an author. An author values a compliment even when it comes from a source of doubtful competency.

This reminds me of the most telling speech I ever listened to—the best speech ever made by the capable Depew, and the shortest. Although General Grant was a vivacious and interesting talker when none were present but familiar friends, it was his habit to keep his jaws locked when strangers were about. It was difficult to get him to venture even half a dozen words on a public occasion. He would keep his seat, when called upon to speak, and would leave the toast-master to make his excuses for him. That fine speech of Depew's was made at a banquet in honor of General Grant. Depew always came late to banquets, in those early days, and this time he arrived just as the chairman was finishing an impassioned eulogy of the guest of the occasion. Depew came striding up the centre of the house, and just as he reached the middle the chairman sat down, in the midst of the usual cyclone of cries for "Grant, Grant, General Grant!"

General Grant said "There's Depew. Let him respond for me."

Depew stopped where he was, and without pause or hesitation said, with fine impressiveness, in substance, this:

"Respond for *him?* It is not necessary. No felicity of words can so eloquently speak as can the silence and the visible person of a man whose name will still be familiar upon the lips of men when twenty centuries shall have come and gone."

That was the substance of what he said, not the words. The language was finished, perfect, moving, flawless. Depew was the prince of after-dinner orators during thirty years. He made some hundreds of happy and distinguished speeches, but I think his briefest one was his best. He is dying now, and under a cloud—a pity, too, that such should be his fate after so long a career of great and uninterrupted popularity.

General Grant wrought heroically with his pen while his disease made its steady inroads upon his life, and at last his work stood completed. He was moved to Mount McGregor, and there his strength passed gradually away. Toward the last, he was not able to speak, but used a pencil and small slips of paper when he needed to say anything.

I went there to see him once, toward the end, and he asked me with his pencil, and evidently with anxious solicitude, if there was a prospect that his book would make something for his family.

I said that the canvass for it was progressing vigorously, that the subscriptions and the money were coming in fast, that the campaign was not more than half completed yet—but that if it should stop where it was there would be two hundred thousand dollars coming to his family. He expressed his gratification, with his pencil.

When I was entering the house, the Confederate General, Buckner, was leaving it.

1840

Buckner and Grant had been fellow cadets at West Point, about 1840. I think they had served together in the Mexican war, a little later. After that war Grant (then a Captain in the regular army) was ordered to a military post in Oregon. By and by he resigned and came East and found himself in New York penniless. On the street he met Buckner, and borrowed fifty dollars of him. In February 1862 Buckner was in command of the Confederate garrison of Fort Donelson. General Grant captured the fortress, by assault, and took fifteen thousand prisoners. After that, the two soldiers did not meet again until that day at Mount McGregor, twenty-three years later.

1862

Several visitors were present, and there was a good deal of chaffing and joking, some of it at Buckner's expense. Finally General Buckner said,

"I have my full share of admiration and esteem for Grant. It dates back to our cadet days. He has as many merits and virtues as any man I am acquainted with, but he has one deadly defect. He is an incurable borrower, and when he wants to borrow he knows of only one limit—he wants what you've got. When I was poor he borrowed fifty dollars of me; when I was rich he borrowed fifteen thousand men."

General Grant died at Mount McGregor on the 23d of July.

In September or October the Memoirs went to press. Several sets of plates were made; the printing was distributed among several great printing establishments; a great number of steam presses were kept running night and day on the book; several large binderies were kept at work binding it. The book was in sets of two volumes—large octavo. Its price was nine dollars in cloth. For costlier bindings the price was proportionately higher. Two thousand sets in tree-calf were issued at twenty-five dollars per set.

The book was issued on the 10th of December, and I turned out to be a competent prophet. In the beginning I had told General Grant that his book would sell six hundred thousand single volumes, and that is what happened. It sold three hundred thousand sets. The first check that went to Mrs. Grant was for two hundred thousand dollars; the next one, a few months later, was for a hundred and fifty thousand. I do not remember about the subsequent checks, but I think that in the aggregate the book paid Mrs. Grant something like half a million dollars.

Webster was in his glory. In his obscure days his hat was No. 6¼; in these latter days he was not able to get his head into a barrel. He loved to descant upon the wonders of the book. He liked to go into the statistics. He liked to tell that it took thirteen miles of gold leaf to print the gilt titles on the book backs; he liked to tell how many thousand tons the three hundred thousand sets weighed. Of course that same old natural thing happened: Webster thought it was *he* that sold the book. He thought that General Grant's great name helped, but he regarded himself as the main reason of the book's prodigious success. This shows that Webster was merely human, and merely a publisher. All publishers are Columbuses. The successful author is their America. The reflection that they—like Columbus—didn't discover what they expected to discover, and didn't discover what they started out to discover, doesn't trouble them. All they remember is that they discovered America; they forget that they started out to discover some patch or corner of India.

A Mr. Scott was Webster's bookkeeper. Back in the summer, when the subscription money had begun to pour in in a great and steady stream of bank-bills, sent by express, Webster told me he was suspicious of Scott and was going to lay a trap for him. He was going to pass some marked bank notes through his hands and see if they would stick.

Saturday, June 2, 1906

Examination of the books and punishment of Scott, who had stolen twenty-six thousand dollars—Webster refuses books which Mr. Clemens wishes published and accepts worthless ones—Finally he takes drugs, and Mr. Clemens buys him out—He is succeeded by Hall—Webster accepted Stedman's "Library of American Literature" which caused the firm to fail—Mr. Clemens starts on his lecturing tour around the world and in thirteen months pays off all his indebtedness—J. W. Paige, and the type-setting machine.

I suspected that that bookkeeper, Scott, was going to have an uncomfortable time. Whenever Webster got a fellow human being by the scruff of the neck, so to speak—a human being who was helpless, a human being who could be strangled without in any way endangering the strangler—the strangulation was exceedingly likely to ensue.

Charles L. Webster was one of the most assful persons I have ever met—perhaps the most assful. The times when he had an opportunity to be an ass and failed to take advantage of it were so few that, in a monarchy, they would have entitled him to a decoration. The thing which he had proposed concerning Scott—the laying of the time-worn trap in the form of marked money—was a good common-sense idea, and as it offered Webster a chance to play detective, and snoop and spy around and catch somebody committing sin, I expected him to set that project in operation at once. He was very fond of detective work. There wasn't a detective in America—at least a distinguished one—that knew less about it than Webster did. He was about on a level with Sherlock Holmes.

Webster did not set the trap—why he didn't is beyond my guess. His suspicions had not been removed. They continued alive. As the months went by, rumors floated over from Jersey to the effect that Scott was become a very fast and very popular young man in his town; that he was starting social clubs of various kinds and making himself useful to them as manager or director or president, and so on; that he was the life and soul of these clubs; that he was a valuable supporter of the livery stables; that the life he was leading was an expensive one—for him, or for somebody—but a profitable one for his community.

Three or four months after Webster had proposed to set that trap the time came for an examination of the books by expert accountants, in the interest of Mrs. Grant. Webster ordered the examination. The experts came, and Scott lavished his assistance upon them. He got out the books and spread them open. He would fetch a sweep down a column in the journal, point to the total at the bottom, skip to the ledger, show that the total in the ledger tallied with the total in the journal. The whole examination was over in a little while. The experts went away satisfied. Webster was satisfied—and as for Scott, he was probably something more than satisfied.

But Fred Grant was not satisfied. He had heard those rumors. By the authority in him vested as representative of three-fourths of the partnership in the book, he ordered another examination, without giving any notice of it. He selected the expert accountants himself, and they stepped into Scott's domain armed and equipped for business, and unexpected. They called for the books. Scott bustled around, got them out, as before, began as before to sweep his finger down a journal column and then show the accountant that the journal and the ledger tallied. But he got in only one sample of his help. The expert coldly explained to him that *he* knew how to examine books and didn't need the assistance of a bookkeeper who was personally interested in the examination.

Webster was looking on. He said that the color went out of poor Scott's face, and he looked very sick. He excused himself from further attendance—said he would go home and lie down. The expert found that Scott had stolen twenty-six thousand dollars. Webster and the other tadpole, Whitford, were now in a high state of excitement and effectiveness. Whitford set himself the task of fetching Scott before the grand jury, with the idea of hanging him, which couldn't be done for that kind of an offence, but Whitford didn't know it. Webster set himself the task of finding out what sort of a record lay back of Scott—a thing which he might better have done before he hired him. But, as I have said, Webster was one of the most assful persons I have ever known. He got at Scott's record without any difficulty. It was easy to trace him from employment to employment. In fact you could trace him from one employment to the next by the stolen money which he had dripped along the road. Poor Scott was sent to the penitentiary for five years—or nine—I don't remember which. It was another instance of sending up the wrong man. It ought to have been Webster.

Webster had been hating me pretty venomously on account of the sarcasms which I had tried to entertain him with at the time that he hired his fine new quarters in Union Square. His detestation of me had solidified and become permanent and insoluble when the latest contract had made him master and me his slave. I was not able to understand why he had not hunted Scott down when he first suspected him, for that was his nature. In trying to solve the riddle I arrived at the charitable conclusion that Webster was willing to have the concern robbed because it cost me nine dollars where it cost him one. I have always been charitable in my judgments of people, and that was my guess as an explanation of Webster's long continued indifference in the Scott matter. There seemed evidence that that might be the explanation, when the matter used to cross my mind in later times. For instance, whereas the book had been distributed among the group of regular general agents, here and there, in great centres of population throughout the country, we had reserved the New York general agency for ourselves. It was a matter quite easily handled, and was worth to us a profit of thirty thousand dollars. By and by Webster, as autocrat, and without consulting me, generously gave the whole profit of this general agency to the Grants, not even requiring them to pay part of the salaries and other general agency expenses. I think he was willing to stand his three-thousand-dollar part of the sacrifice so long as I had to stand twenty-seven thousand—besides he might find some way to recoup, whereas I couldn't.

Three-fourths of the twenty-six thousand dollars stolen by Scott had to be made good to the Grants, since the money was taken after it was already in our possession. This expense had been put upon us by Webster's stupidity and mismanagement, but that did not discourage him from appealing to me beseechingly and tearfully to pay to him his share of that loss out of my pocket. He had originally been intended for a mendicant, and he knew the trade by instinct. He could beg like a professional. I am the most assful person I have ever been acquainted with, and I granted his prayer, although I was not able to see how his tenth of the deficit of eighteen or nineteen thousand dollars could amount to four thousand. But apparently it did. He was a master hand at figures when he was figuring for C. L. Webster.

In the early days, when the general agents were being chosen, he conferred one of the best western general agencies upon an ex-preacher, a professional revivalist whom God had deposited in Iowa for improprieties of one kind and another which had been committed by that State. All the other candidates for agencies warned Webster to keep out of that man's hands, assuring him that no sagacities of Whitford, or anybody else, would be able to defeat that revivalist's inborn proclivity to steal. Their persuasions went for nothing. Webster gave him the agency. We furnished him the books. He did a thriving trade. He collected a gross sum of thirty-six thousand dollars, and Webster never got a cent of it.

It is no great marvel to me that Mrs. Grant got a matter of half a million dollars out of that book. The miracle is that it didn't run her into debt. It was fortunate for her that we had only one Webster. It was an unnatural oversight in me that I didn't hunt for another one.

Let me try to bring this painful business to a close. One of the things which poisoned Webster's days and nights was the aggravating circumstance that whereas he, Charles L. Webster, was the great publisher—the greatest of publishers—and my name did not appear anywhere as a member of the firm, the public persisted in regarding me as the substance of that firm and Webster the shadow. Everybody who had a book to publish offered it to me, not to Webster. I accepted several excellent books, but Webster declined them every time, and he was master. But if anybody offered *him* a book, he was so charmed with the compliment that he took the book without examining it. He was not able to get hold of one that could make its living.

Joe Jefferson wrote me and said he had written his autobiography and he would like me to be the publisher. Of course I wanted the book. I sent his letter to Webster and asked him to arrange the matter. Webster did not decline the book. He simply ignored it, and brushed the matter out of his mind. He accepted and published two or three war books that furnished no profit. He accepted still another one: distributed the agency contracts for it, named its price (three dollars and a half in cloth) and also agreed to have the book ready by a certain date, two or three months ahead. One day I went down to New York and visited the office and asked for a sight of that book. I asked Webster how many thousand words it contained. He said he didn't know. I asked him to count the words, by rough estimate. He did it. I said,

"It doesn't contain words enough for the price and dimensions, by four-fifths. You will have to pad it with a brick. We must start a brickyard, and right away, because it is much cheaper to make bricks than it is to buy them in the market."

It set him in a fury. Any little thing like that would have that effect. He was one of the most sensitive creatures I ever saw, for the quality of the material that he was made of.

He had several books on hand—worthless books which he had accepted because they had been offered to him instead of to me—and I found that he had never counted the words in any of them. He had taken them without examination. Webster was a good general agent, but he knew nothing about publishing, and he was incapable of learning anything about it. By and by I found that he had agreed to resurrect Henry Ward Beecher's "Life of Christ." I suggested that he ought to have tried for Lazarus, because that had been tried once and we knew it could be done. He was exasperated again. He certainly was the most sensitive creature that ever was, for his make. He had also advanced to Mr. Beecher, who was not in prosperous circumstances at the time, five thousand dollars on the future royalties. Mr. Beecher was to revamp the book—or rather I think he was to finish the book. I think he had just issued the first of the two volumes of which it was to consist when that ruinous scandal broke out and suffocated the enterprise. I think the second volume had not been written, and that Mr. Beecher was now undertaking to write it. If he failed to accomplish this within a given time he was to return the money. He did not succeed, and the money was eventually returned.

Webster kept back a book of mine, "A Yankee at the Court of King Arthur," as long as he could, and finally published it so surreptitiously that it took two or three years to find out that there was any such book. He suppressed a compilation made by Howells and me, "The Library of Humor," so long, and finally issued it so clandestinely, that I doubt if anybody in America ever did find out that there was such a book.

William M. Laffan told me that Mr. Walters, of Baltimore, was going to have a sumptuous book made which should illustrate in detail his princely art collection; that he was going to bring the best artists from Paris to make the illustrations; that he was going to make the book himself and see to it that it was made exactly to his taste; that he was going to spend a quarter of a million dollars on it; that he wanted it issued at a great price—a price consonant with its sumptuous character, and that he wanted no penny of the proceeds. The publisher would have nothing to do but distribute the book and take the whole of the profit. Laffan said,

"There, Mark, you can make a fortune out of that without any trouble at all, and without risk or expense."

I said I would send Webster down to Baltimore at once. I tried to do it, but I never succeeded. Webster never touched the matter in any way whatever. If it had been a second-hand dog that Mr. Walters wanted published, he would have only needed to apply to Webster. Webster would have broken his neck getting down to Baltimore to annex that dog. But Mr. Walters had applied to the wrong man. Webster's pride was hurt, and he would not look at Mr. Walters's book. Webster had immense pride, but he was short of other talents.

Webster was the victim of a cruel neuralgia in the head. He eased his pain with the new German drug, phenacetine. The physicians limited his use of it, but he found a way to get it in quantity: under our free institutions anybody can poison himself that wants to and will pay the price. He took this drug with increasing frequency and in increasing quantity. It stupefied him and he went about as one in a dream. He ceased from coming to the office except at intervals, and when he came he was pretty sure to exercise his authority in ways perilous for the business. In his condition, he was not responsible for his acts.

Something had to be done. Whitford explained that there was no way to get rid of this dangerous element except by buying Webster out. But what was there to buy? Webster had always promptly collected any money that was due him. He had squandered, long ago, my share of the book's profit—a hundred thousand dollars. The business was gasping, dying. The whole of it was not worth a dollar and a half. Then what would be a fair price for me to pay for a tenth interest in it? After much consultation and much correspondence, it transpired that Webster would be willing to put up with twelve thousand dollars and step out. I furnished the check.

Webster's understudy and business manager had now been for some time a young fellow named Frederick J. Hall, another Dunkirk importation. We got all our talent from that stud-farm at Dunkirk. Poor Hall meant well, but he was wholly incompetent for the place. He carried it along for a time with the heroic hopefulness of youth, but there was an obstruction which was bound to defeat him sooner or later. It was this:

Stedman, the poet, had made a compilation, several years earlier, called "The Library of American Literature"—nine or ten octavo volumes. A publisher in Cincinnati had tried to make it succeed. It swallowed up that publisher, family and all. If Stedman had offered me the book I should have said "Sold by subscription and on the instalment plan, there is nothing in this book for us at a royalty above 4 per cent, but, in fact, it would swamp us at any kind of royalty, because such a book would require a cash capital of several hundred thousand dollars, and we haven't a hundred thousand."

But Stedman didn't bring the book to me. He took it to Webster. Webster was delighted and flattered. He accepted the book on an 8 per cent royalty, and thereby secured the lingering suicide of Charles L. Webster and Company. We struggled along two or three years under that deadly load. After Webster's time, poor little Hall struggled along with it and got to borrowing money of a bank in which Whitford was a director—borrowing on notes endorsed by me and renewed from time to time. These notes used to come to me in Italy for renewals. I endorsed them without examining them, and sent them back. At last I found that additions had been made to the borrowings, without my knowledge or consent. I began to feel troubled. I wrote Mr. Hall about it and said I would like to have an exhaustive report of the condition of the business. The next mail brought that exhaustive report, whereby it appeared that the concern's assets exceeded its liabilities by ninety-two thousand dollars. Then I felt better. But there was no occasion to feel better, for the report ought to have read the other way. Poor Hall soon wrote to say that we needed more money and must have it right away, or the concern would fail.

I sailed for New York. I emptied into the till twenty-four thousand dollars which I had earned with the pen. I looked around to see where we could borrow money. There wasn't any place. This was in the midst of the fearful panic of '93. I went up to Hartford to borrow—couldn't borrow a penny. I offered to mortgage our house and grounds and furniture for any small loan. The property had cost a hundred and sixty-seven thousand dollars, and seemed good for a small loan. Henry Robinson said,

"Clemens, I give you my word, you can't borrow three thousand dollars on that property."

Very well, I knew that if that was so, I couldn't borrow it on a basketful of government bonds. Webster and Company failed. The firm owed me about sixty thousand dollars, borrowed money. It owed Mrs. Clemens sixty-five thousand dollars, borrowed money. Also it owed ninety-six creditors an average of a thousand dollars or so apiece. The panic had stopped Mrs. Clemens's income. It had stopped my income from my books. We had but nine thousand dollars in the bank. We hadn't a penny wherewith to pay the Webster creditors. Henry Robinson said,

"Hand over everything belonging to Webster and Company to the creditors, and ask them to accept that in liquidation of the debts. They'll do it. You'll see that they'll do it. They are aware that you are not individually responsible for those debts, that the responsibility rests upon the firm as a firm."

I didn't think much of that way out of the difficulty, and when I made my report to Mrs. Clemens she wouldn't hear of it at all. She said,

"This is my house. The creditors shall have it. Your books are your property—turn them over to the creditors. Reduce the indebtedness in every way you can think of—then get to work and earn the rest of the indebtedness, if your life is spared. And don't be afraid. We shall pay a hundred cents on the dollar, yet."

It was sound prophecy. Mr. Rogers stepped in, about this time, and preached to the creditors. He said they could not have Mrs. Clemens's house—that she must be a preferred creditor, and would give up the Webster notes for sixty-five thousand dollars, money borrowed of her. He said they could not have my books; that they were not an asset of Webster and Company; that the creditors could have everything that belonged to Webster and Company; that I would wipe from the slate the sixty thousand dollars I had lent to the Company, and that I would now make it my task to earn the rest of the Webster indebtedness, if I could, and pay a hundred cents on the dollar—but that this must not be regarded as a promise.

In a conversation with Mr. Rogers and a couple of lawyers, in those days, one of the men said,

"Not 5 per cent of the men who become ruined at fifty-eight ever recover." Another said, with enthusiasm, "Five per cent! None of them ever recover." It made me feel very sick.

1894 That was in '94, I believe—though it may have been in the beginning of '95. However, Mrs. Clemens and Clara and I started, on the 15th of July, 1895, on our lecturing raid around the world. *1895* We lectured and robbed and raided for thirteen months. I wrote a book and published it. I sent the book-money and lecture-money to Mr. Rogers as fast as we captured it. He banked it and saved it up for the creditors. We implored him to pay off the smaller creditors straightway, for they needed the money, but he wouldn't do it.

He said that when I had milked the world dry he would take the result and distribute it, pro rata, among the Webster people.

1898 At the end of '98 or the beginning of '99 Mr. Rogers cabled me, at Vienna,

"The creditors have all been paid a hundred cents on the dollar. There is eighteen thousand five hundred dollars left. What shall I do with it?"

I answered, "Put it in Federal Steel"—which he did, all except a thousand dollars, and took it out again in two months with a profit of 125 per cent.

There—thanks be! A hundred times I have tried to tell this intolerable story with a pen, but I never could do it. It always made me sick before I got half way to the middle of it. But this time I have held my grip and walked the floor and emptied it all out of my system, and I hope to never hear of it again.

It would not be right for me to pretend that the speculations which I was talking *1886* about the other day ended my speculative career. During 1886, and the four succeeding years, while Webster was sitting on my financial nest and hatching ruin for me, I was assisting in the work at my end of the line, Hartford. I entered into an arrangement with a descendant of Judas Iscariot by the name of J. W. Paige, a natural liar and thief, to build a type-setting machine, I to furnish the money. Let us not dwell upon this. The machine was a failure. It was a beautiful machine—the most wonderful creation that has ever issued from a human being's brain. It stands in Cornell University, a monument of human ingenuity and stupidity—the ingenuity was Paige's, the stupidity was mine. I spent a hundred and seventy thousand dollars on it. More than two-thirds of it came out of Mrs. Clemens's pocket. We pulled through——

Monday, June 4, 1906

Two years ago to-morrow occurred the death of Mrs. Clemens—Mrs. Clemens's illness, and the journey around the world—The house in West 10th street and the overtaxing of Mrs. Clemens's strength—Three months in the Adirondacks—House at York Harbor—Journey there in Mr. Rogers's yacht—Mrs. Clemens's fear of heart trouble—Howells's visit, and the curious story which he related.

To-morrow will be the 5th of June, a day which marks the disaster of my life—the death of my wife. It occurred two years ago, in Florence, Italy, whither we had taken her in the hope of restoring her broken health.

The dictating of this autobiography, which was begun in Florence in the beginning *1904* of 1904, was soon suspended because of the anxieties of the time, and I was never moved *1906* to resume the work until January 1906, for I did not see how I was ever going to bring myself to speak in detail of the mournful episodes and experiences of that desolate interval and of the twenty-two months of wearing distress which preceded it. I wish to bridge over that hiatus, now, with an outline sketch. I can venture nothing more as yet.

Mrs. Clemens had never been strong, and a thirteen months' journey around the world seemed a doubtful experiment for such a physique as hers, but it turned out to be a safe one. When we took the train westward-bound at Elmira on the 15th of July, 1895, *1895* we moved through blistering summer-heats, and, by and by, through summer-heats with the heat of burning forests added. This for twenty-three days—I lecturing every night. Notwithstanding these trying conditions, Mrs. Clemens reached Vancouver in as good health as she was when she began the journey. From that day her health seemed improved, although the summer continued thereafter for five months without a break. It was summer at the Sandwich Islands. We reached Sydney, Australia, thirty-four degrees south of the equator, in October, just when the Australian summer was getting well under way. It was summer during our whole stay in Australia, New Zealand, and Tasmania. It was still summer when we sailed from Melbourne on the 1st of January '96. It was blistering summer in Ceylon, of course, as it always is. It was supposed by the English residents of Bombay to be winter there, when we reached that city in January, but we couldn't recognize that our climate had ever changed since our departure from Elmira in mid-July. It was still summer to us all over India until the 17th of March, when an English physician in Jeypore told us to fly for Calcutta and get out of India immediately, because the warm weather could come at any time, now, and it would be perilous for us. So we sweltered along through the "cold weather," as they called it there, clear from Rawal Pindi to Calcutta, and took ship for South Africa—and still Mrs. Clemens's health had steadily improved. She and Clara went with me all over my lecture course in South Africa, except to Pretoria, and she never had a day's illness.

We finally finished our lecture-raid on the 14th of July '96, sailed for England the *1896* next day, and landed at Southampton on the 31st. A fortnight later Mrs. Clemens and Clara sailed for home to nurse Susy through a reported illness, and found her in her coffin in her grandmother's house.

The diminished family presently joined me in England. We lived in London, in Switzerland, in Vienna, in Sweden, and again in London, until October 1900. And when *1900* at that time we took ship, homeward bound, Mrs. Clemens's health and strength were in better condition than they had ever been before since she was sixteen years old and met with the accident which I have before mentioned in a previous chapter.

We took No. 14 West 10th street, just out of Fifth Avenue, for a year, and there the overtaxing of Mrs. Clemens's strength began. The house was large; housekeeping was a heavy labor—as indeed it always is in New York—but she would not have a housekeeper. She had resisted, and successfully resisted, all my persuasions in that direction from the day that we were married. Social life was another heavy tax upon her strength. In the drive and rush and hurly-burly of the mid-winter New York season, my correspondence grew beyond my secretary's strength and mine, and I found that Mrs. Clemens was trying to ease our burden for us. One day I wrote thirty-two brief letters with my own hand, and then found, to my dismay, that Mrs. Clemens had written the same number. She had added this labor to her other labors, and they were already too heavy for her.

By the following June this kind of life, after her nine and a half years of tranquil and effortless life in Europe, began to exhibit effects. Three months' repose and seclusion in the Adirondacks did her manifest good. Then we took a house in Riverdale-on-the-Hudson. It was a large house, and again the housekeeping burden was heavy. Early in 1902 she was threatened with a nervous break down, but soon the danger seemed past.

At the end of June we secured a furnished house in the outskirts of York Harbor for the summer. Mr. Rogers brought his *Kanawha,* the fastest steam yacht in American waters, cast anchor and sent the launch ashore at our river front, and Mrs. Clemens and Jean and I went down to embark. I found, then, that Mrs. Clemens was not taking a servant along. This was because she was so afraid of being an inconvenience and an incumbrance to Mr. Rogers. It was too bad. She could have had the whole ship and welcome. Jean's health was bad, and she would need much attention. This service would fall upon Mrs. Clemens. My services would be of a stupid and ignorant sort, and worthless. It was too late. She had arranged to ship the entire household and all the baggage by rail to York Harbor.

It was lovely weather, and we sped over the sparkling seas like a bird, chasing all craft in sight, and sending them all astern, one by one. But these delights were not for Mrs. Clemens. She had to stay below and take care of Jean. As night fell we took refuge from heavy weather in the harbor of New London. Mrs. Clemens did not get much rest or sleep, because of Jean. The next morning we sailed to Fairhaven. That was Mrs. Clemens's opportunity to lie at rest on board the yacht, two or three hours, while the rest of us went ashore and visited Mr. Rogers's family at his country place. But she elected to go ashore. She fatigued herself in many ways. She continued to add to these fatigues by nursing Jean during the rest of the voyage to York Harbor.

Once again, here was opportunity to rest, but she would not rest. She could not rest. She never was intended to rest. She had the spirit of a steam engine in a frame of flesh. It was always racking that frame with its tireless energy; it was always exacting of it labors that were beyond its strength. Her heart soon began to alarm her. Twelve years before, two Hartford physicians of high repute had ordered her to the baths of Aix-les-Bains, and had told her that with care she would live two years. Two physicians of Aix-les-Bains said that with care she would live longer than that. Physicians of repute in Rome, Florence, and Berlin had given her the usual two years—and at Nauheim (Germany) the physician lowest in the published and authorized list of physicians chartered by that Bath, examined Mrs. Clemens and told me that there was nothing very serious the matter with her; that she would probably live a good many years yet. I was affronted. I was indignant that this ignorant apprentice should be allowed to play with people's lives, and I paid his bill and discharged him on the spot, without a recommendation. Yet he was the only physician of the dozen whose prediction was worth anything. When we took up our residence in York Harbor Mrs. Clemens had outlived all the other predictions by eleven years.

But, as I have said, she became alarmed about her heart, in York Harbor, early in

July. Her alarm increased rapidly. Within a fortnight she began to dread driving out. Anything approaching swift motion terrified her. She was afraid of descending grades, even such slight ones as to be indeterminable and imperceptible in the summer twilights. She would implore the coachman not only to walk his horses down those low and imperceptible hills, but she watched him with fear and distress, and if the horses stepped out of a walk for only a moment she would seize me on one side and the carriage on the other, in an ecstasy of fright. This was the condition of things all through July.

Now comes a curious thing. Howells was living at Kittery Point, three-quarters of an hour away by trolley, and one day in July or early in August he made his second visit to us. It was afternoon, and Mrs. Clemens's resting time. She was up stairs in her room. Howells and I sat on the veranda overlooking the river and chatting, and presently he drifted into the history of a pathetic episode in the life of a friend of his, one or two of whose most moving features were soon to find strange duplication in Mrs. Clemens's case.

While he sat there that afternoon telling the curious story, neither of us suspected that it was prophetic, yet it was.

I at once wrote it out in the form of a tale—using fictitious names, of course—and sent it to *Harper's Monthly.* I here append it.

Was it Heaven? Or Hell?

I

"You told a *lie?*"

"You confess it—you actually confess it—you told a lie!"

II

The family consisted of four persons: Margaret Lester, widow, aged thirty-six; Helen Lester, her daughter, aged sixteen; Mrs. Lester's maiden aunts, Hannah and Hester Gray, twins, aged sixty-seven. Waking and sleeping, the three women spent their days and nights in adoring the young girl; in watching the movements of her sweet spirit in the mirror of her face; in refreshing their souls with the vision of her bloom and beauty; in listening to the music of her voice; in gratefully recognizing how rich and fair for them was the world with this presence in it; in shuddering to think how desolate it would be with this light gone out of it.

By nature—and inside—the aged aunts were utterly dear and lovable and good, but in the matter of morals and conduct their training had been so uncompromisingly strict that it had made them exteriorly austere, not to say stern. Their influence was effective in the house; so effective that the mother and the daughter conformed to its moral and religious requirements cheerfully, contentedly, happily, unquestioningly. To do this was become second nature to them. And so in this peaceful heaven there were no clashings, no irritations, no fault-findings, no heart-burnings.

In it a lie had no place. In it a lie was unthinkable. In it speech was restricted to absolute truth, iron-bound truth, implacable and uncompromising truth, let the resulting consequences be what they might. At last, one day, under stress of circumstances, the darling of the house sullied her lips with a lie—and confessed it, with tears and self-upbraidings. There are not any words that can paint the consternation of the aunts. It was as if the sky had crumpled up and collapsed and the earth had tumbled to ruin with a crash. They sat side by side, white and stern, gazing speechless upon the culprit, who was on her knees before them with her face buried first in one lap and then the other, moaning and sobbing, and appealing for sympathy and forgiveness and getting no response, humbly kissing the hand of the one, then of the other, only to see it withdrawn as suffering defilement by those soiled lips.

Twice, at intervals, Aunt Hester said, in frozen amazement,

"You told a *lie?*"

Twice, at intervals, Aunt Hannah followed with the muttered and amazed ejaculation,

"You confess it—you actually confess it—you told a lie!"

It was all they could say. The situation was new, unheard-of, incredible; they could not understand it, they did not know how to take hold of it, it approximately paralysed speech.

At length it was decided that the erring child must be taken to her mother, who was ill, and who ought to know what had happened. Helen begged, besought, implored that she might be spared this further disgrace, and that her mother might be spared the grief and pain of it; but this could not be: duty required this sacrifice, duty takes precedence of all things, nothing can absolve one from a duty, with a duty no compromise is possible.

Helen still begged, and said the sin was her own, her mother had had no hand in it,—why must she be made to suffer for it?

But the aunts were obdurate in their righteousness, and said the law that visited the sins of the parent upon the child was by all right and reason reversible; and therefore it was but just that the innocent mother of a sinning child should suffer her rightful share of the grief and pain and shame which were the allotted wages of the sin.

The three moved toward the sick-room.

At this time the doctor was approaching the house. He was still a good distance away, however. He was a good doctor and a good man, and he had a good heart, but one had to know him a year to get over hating him, two years to learn to endure him, three to learn to like him, and four or five to learn to love him. It was a slow and trying education, but it paid. He was of great stature; he had a leonine head, a leonine face, a rough voice, and an eye which was sometimes a pirate's and sometimes a woman's, according to the mood. He knew nothing about etiquette, and cared nothing about it; in speech, manner, carriage, and conduct he was the reverse of conventional. He was frank, to the limit; he had opinions on all subjects; they were always on tap and ready for delivery, and he cared not a farthing whether his listener liked them or didn't. Whom he loved he loved, and manifested it; whom he didn't love he hated, and published it from the house-tops. In his young days he had been a sailor, and the salt airs of all the seas blew from him yet. He was a sturdy and loyal Christian, and believed he was the best one in the land, and the only one whose Christianity was perfectly sound, healthy, full-charged with common sense, and had no decayed places in it. People who had an axe to grind, or people who for any reason wanted to get on the soft side of him, called him The Christian,—a phrase whose delicate flattery was music to his ears, and whose capital T was such an enchanting and vivid object to him that he could *see* it when it fell out of a person's mouth even in the dark. Many who were fond of him stood on their consciences with both feet and brazenly called him by that large title habitually, because it was a pleasure to them to do anything that would please him; and with eager and cordial malice his extensive and diligently cultivated crop of enemies gilded it, beflowered it, expanded it to "The *Only* Christian." Of these two titles, the latter had the wider currency; the enemy, being greatly in the majority, attended to that. Whatever the doctor believed, he believed with all his heart, and would fight for it whenever he got the chance; and if the intervals between chances grew to be irksomely wide, he would invent ways of shortening them himself. He was severely conscientious, according to his rather independent lights, and whatever he took to be a duty he performed, no matter whether the judgment of the professional moralists agreed with his own or not. At sea, in his young days, he had used profanity freely, but as soon as he was converted he made a rule, which he rigidly stuck to ever afterwards, never to use it except on the rarest occasions, and then only when duty commanded. He had been a hard drinker at sea, but after his conversion he became a firm and outspoken teetotaler, in order to be an example to the young, and from that time forth he seldom drank; never, indeed, except when it seemed to him to be a duty,—a condition which sometimes occurred a couple of times a year, but never as many as five times.

Necessarily such a man is impressionable, impulsive, emotional. This one was, and had no gift at hiding his feelings; or if he had it he took no trouble to exercise it. He carried his soul's prevailing weather in his face, and when he entered a room the parasols or the umbrellas went up—figuratively speaking—according to the indications. When the soft light was in his eye it meant approval, and delivered a benediction; when he came with a frown he lowered the temperature ten degrees. He was a well-beloved man in the house of his friends, but sometimes a dreaded one.

He had a deep affection for the Lester household, and its several members returned this feeling with interest. They mourned over his kind of Christianity, and he frankly scoffed at theirs; but both parties went on loving each other just the same.

He was approaching the house—out of the distance; the aunts and the culprit were moving toward the sick-chamber.

III

The three last named stood by the bed; the aunts austere, the transgressor softly sobbing. The mother turned her head on the pillow; her tired eyes flamed up instantly with sympathy and passionate mother-love when they fell upon her child, and she opened the refuge and shelter of her arms.

"Wait!" said Aunt Hannah, and put out her hand and stayed the girl from leaping into them.

"Helen," said the other aunt, impressively, "tell your mother all. Purge your soul; leave nothing unconfessed."

Standing stricken and forlorn before her judges, the young girl mourned her sorrowful tale through to the end, then in a passion of appeal cried out:

"Oh, mother, can't you forgive me? won't you forgive me?—I am so desolate!"

"Forgive you, my darling? Oh, come to my arms!—there, lay your head upon my breast, and be at peace. If you had told a thousand lies—"

There was a sound—a warning—the clearing of a throat. The aunts glanced up, and withered in their clothes—there stood the doctor, his face a thundercloud. Mother and child knew nothing of his presence; they lay locked together, heart to heart, steeped in immeasurable content, dead to all things else. The physician stood many moments glaring and glooming upon the scene before him; studying it, analyzing it, searching out its genesis; then he put up his hand and beckoned to the aunts. They came trembling to him and stood humbly before him and waited. He bent down and whispered:

"Didn't I tell you this patient must be protected from all excitement? What the hell have you been doing? Clear out of the place!"

They obeyed. Half an hour later he appeared in the parlor, serene, cheery, clothed in sunshine, conducting Helen, with his arm about her waist, petting her, and saying gentle and playful things to her; and she also was her sunny and happy self again.

"Now, then," he said, "good-bye, dear. Go to your room, and keep away from your mother, and behave yourself. But wait—put out your tongue. There, that will do—you're as sound as a nut!" He patted her cheek and added, "Run along now; I want to talk to these aunts."

She went from the presence. His face clouded over again at once; and as he sat down he said:

"You two have been doing a lot of damage—and maybe some good. Some good, yes—such as it is. That woman's disease is typhoid! You've brought it to a show-up, I think, with your insanities, and that's a service—such as it is. I hadn't been able to determine what it was before."

With one impulse the old ladies sprang to their feet, quaking with terror.

"Sit down! What are you proposing to do?"

"Do? We must fly to her. We—"

"You'll do nothing of the kind; you've done enough harm for one day. Do you want to squander all your capital of crimes and follies on a single deal? Sit down, I tell you. I have arranged for her to sleep; she needs it; if you disturb her without my orders, I'll brain you—if you've got the materials for it."

They sat down, distressed and indignant, but obedient, under compulsion. He proceeded:

"Now, then, I want this case explained. *They* wanted to explain it to me—as if there hadn't been emotion and excitement enough already. You knew my orders; how did you dare to go in there and get up that riot?"

Hester looked appealingly at Hannah; Hannah returned a beseeching look at Hester—neither wanted to dance to this unsympathetic orchestra. The doctor came to their help. He said,

"Begin, Hester."

Fingering at the fringes of her shawl, and with lowered eyes, Hester said, timidly:

"We should not have disobeyed for any ordinary cause, but this was vital. This was a duty. With a duty one has no choice; one must put all lighter considerations aside and perform it. We were obliged to arraign her before her mother. She had told a lie."

The doctor glowered upon the woman a moment, and seemed to be trying to work up in his mind an understanding of a wholly incomprehensible proposition; then he stormed out:

"She told a lie! *Did* she? God bless my soul! I tell a million a day! And so does every doctor. And so does everybody—including you—for that matter. And *that* was the important thing that authorized you to venture to disobey my orders and imperil that woman's life! Look here, Hester Gray, this is pure lunacy; that girl *couldn't* tell a lie that was intended to injure a person. The thing is impossible—absolutely impossible. You know it yourselves—both of you; you know it perfectly well."

Hannah came to her sister's rescue:

"Hester didn't mean that it was that kind of a lie, and it wasn't. But it was a lie."

"Well, upon my word, I never heard such nonsense! Haven't you got sense enough to discriminate between lies? Don't you know the difference between a lie that helps and a lie that hurts?"

"*All* lies are sinful," said Hannah, setting her lips together like a vise; "all lies are forbidden."

The Only Christian fidgeted impatiently in his chair. He wanted to attack this proposition, but he did not quite know how or where to begin. Finally he made a venture:

"Hester, wouldn't you tell a lie to shield a person from an undeserved injury or shame?"

"No."

"Not even a friend?"

"No."

"Not even your dearest friend?"

"No. I would not."

The doctor struggled in silence a while with this situation; then he asked,

"Not even to save him from bitter pain and misery and grief?"

"No. Not even to save his life."

Another pause. Then,

"Nor his soul."

There was a hush—a silence which endured a measurable interval—then Hester answered, in a low voice, but with decision,

"Nor his soul."

No one spoke for a while; then the doctor said,

"Is it with you the same, Hannah?"

"Yes," she answered.

"I ask you both—why?"

"Because to tell such a lie, or any lie, is a sin, and could cost us the loss of our own souls—*would,* indeed, if we died without time to repent."

"Strange . . . strange . . . it is past belief." Then he asked, roughly, "Is such a soul as that *worth* saving?" He rose up, mumbling and grumbling, and started for the door, stumping vigorously along. At the threshold he turned and rasped out an admonition: "Reform! Drop this mean and sordid and selfish devotion to the saving of your shabby little souls, and hunt up something to do that's got some dignity to it! *Risk* your souls! risk them in good causes; then if you lose them, why should you care? Reform!"

The good old gentlewomen sat paralysed, pulverized, outraged, insulted, and brooded in bitterness and indignation over these blasphemies. They were hurt to the heart, poor old ladies, and said they could never forgive these injuries.

"Reform!"

They kept repeating that word resentfully. "Reform—and learn to tell lies!"

Time slipped along, and in due course a change came over their spirits. They had completed the human being's first duty—which is to think about himself until he has exhausted the subject, then he is in a condition to take up minor interests and think of other people. This changes the complexion of his spirits—generally wholesomely. The minds of the two old ladies reverted to their beloved niece and the fearful disease which had smitten her; instantly they forgot the hurts their self-love had received, and a passionate desire rose in their hearts to go to the help of the sufferer and comfort her with their love, and minister to her, and labor for her the best they could with their weak hands, and joyfully and affectionately wear out their poor old bodies in her dear service if only they might have the privilege.

"And we shall have it!" said Hester, with the tears running down her face. "There are no nurses comparable to us, for there are no others that will stand their watch by that bed till they drop and die, and God knows we would do that."

"Amen," said Hannah, smiling approval and endorsement through the mist of moisture that blurred her glasses. "The doctor knows us, and knows we will not disobey again; and he will call no others. He will not dare!"

"Dare?" said Hester, with temper, and dashing the water from her eyes; "he will dare anything—that Christian devil! But it will do no good for him to try it this time—but, laws! Hannah, after all's said and done, he is gifted and wise and good, and he would not think of such a thing. . . . It is surely time for one of us to go to that room. What is keeping him? Why doesn't he come and say so?"

They caught the sound of his approaching step. He entered, sat down, and began to talk.

"Margaret is a sick woman," he said. "She is still sleeping, but she will wake presently; then one of you must go to her. She will be worse before she is better. Pretty soon a night-and-day watch must be set. How much of it can you two undertake?"

"All of it!" burst from both ladies at once.

The doctor's eyes flashed, and he said, with energy:

"You *do* ring true, you brave old relics! And you *shall* do all of the nursing you can, for there's none to match you in that divine office in this town; but you can't do all of it, and it would be a crime to let you." It was grand praise, golden praise, coming from such a source, and it took nearly all the resentment out of the aged twins' hearts. "Your Tilly and my old Nancy shall do the rest—good nurses both, white souls with black skins, watchful, loving, tender,—just perfect nurses!—and competent liars from the cradle. . . . Look you! keep a little watch on Helen; she is sick, and is going to be sicker."

The ladies looked a little surprised, and not credulous; and Hester said:

"How is that? It isn't an hour since you said she was as sound as a nut."

The doctor answered, tranquilly,

"It was a lie."

The ladies turned upon him indignantly, and Hannah said,

"How can you make an odious confession like that, in so indifferent a tone, when you know how we feel about all forms of—"

"Hush! You are as ignorant as cats, both of you, and you don't know what you are talking about. You are like all the rest of the moral moles: you lie from morning till night, but because you don't do it with your mouths, but only with your lying eyes, your lying inflections, your deceptively misplaced emphasis, and your misleading gestures, you turn up your complacent noses and parade before God and the world as saintly and unsmirched Truth-Speakers, in whose cold-storage souls a lie would freeze to death if it got there! Why will you humbug yourselves with that foolish notion that no lie is a lie except a spoken one? What is the difference between lying with your eyes and lying with your mouth? There is none; and if you would reflect a moment you would see that it is so. There isn't a human being that doesn't tell a gross of lies every day of his life; and you—why, between you, you tell thirty thousand; yet you flare up here in a lurid hypocritical horror because I tell that child a benevolent and sinless lie to protect her from her imagination, which would get to work and warm up her blood to a fever in an hour, if I were disloyal enough to my duty to let it. Which I should probably do if I were interested in saving my soul by such disreputable means.

"Come, let us reason together. Let us examine details. When you two were in the sick-room raising that riot, what would you have done if you had known I was coming?"

"Well, what?"

"You would have slipped out and carried Helen with you—wouldn't you?"

The ladies were silent.

"What would be your object and intention?"

"Well, what?"

"To keep me from finding out your guilt; to beguile me to infer that Margaret's excitement proceeded from some cause not known to you. In a word, to tell me a lie—a silent lie. Moreover, a possibly harmful one."

The twins colored, but did not speak.

"You not only tell myriads of silent lies, but you tell lies with your mouths—you two."

"*That* is not so!"

"It is so. But only harmless ones. You never dream of uttering a harmful one. Do you know that that is a concession—and a confession?"

"How do you mean?"

"It is an unconscious concession that harmless lies are not criminal; it is a confession that you constantly *make* that discrimination. For instance, you declined old Mrs. Foster's invitation last week to meet those odious Higbies at supper—in a polite note in which you expressed regret and said you were very sorry you could not go. It was a lie. It was as unmitigated a lie as was ever uttered. Deny it, Hester—with another lie."

Hester replied with a toss of her head.

"That will not do. Answer. Was it a lie, or wasn't it?"

The color stole into the cheeks of both women, and with a struggle and an effort they got out their confession:

"It was a lie."

"Good—the reform is beginning; there is hope for you yet; you will not tell a lie to save your dearest friend's soul, but you will spew out one without a scruple to save yourself the discomfort of telling an unpleasant truth."

He rose. Hester, speaking for both, said, coldly:

"We have lied; we perceive it; it will occur no more. To lie is a sin. We shall never tell another one of any kind whatsoever, even lies of courtesy or benevolence, to save any one a pang or a sorrow decreed for him by God."

"Ah, how soon you will fall! In fact, you have fallen already; for what you have just uttered is a lie. Good-bye. Reform! One of you go to the sick-room now."

IV

Twelve days later.

Mother and child were lingering in the grip of the hideous disease. Of hope for either there was little. The aged sisters looked white and worn, but they would not give up their posts. Their hearts were breaking, poor old things, but their grit was steadfast and indestructible. All the twelve days the mother had pined for the child, and the child for the mother, but both knew that the prayer of these longings could not be granted. When the mother was told—on the first day—that her disease was typhoid, she was frightened, and asked if there was danger that Helen could have contracted it the day before, when she was in the sick-chamber on that confession visit. Hester told her the doctor had poo-poo'd the idea. It troubled Hester to say it, although it was true, for she had not believed the doctor; but when she saw the mother's joy in the news, the pain in her conscience lost something of its force—a result which made her ashamed of the constructive deception which she had practised, though not ashamed enough to make her distinctly and definitely wish she had refrained from it. From that moment the sick woman understood that her daughter must remain away, and she said she would reconcile herself to the separation the best she could, for she would rather suffer death than have her child's health imperiled. That afternoon Helen had to take to her bed, ill. She grew worse during the night. In the morning her mother asked after her:

"Is she well?"

Hester turned cold; she opened her lips, but the words refused to come. The mother lay languidly looking, musing, waiting; suddenly she turned white and gasped out,

"Oh, my God! what is it? is she sick?"

Then the poor aunt's tortured heart rose in rebellion, and words came:

"No—be comforted; she is well."

The sick woman put all her happy heart in her gratitude:

"Thank God for those dear words! Kiss me. How I worship you for saying them."

Hester told this incident to Hannah, who received it with a rebuking look, and said, coldly,

"Sister, it was a lie."

Hester's lips trembled piteously; she choked down a sob, and said,

"Oh, Hannah, it was a sin, but I could not help it. I could not endure the fright and the misery that were in her face."

"No matter. It was a lie. God will hold you to account for it."

"Oh, I know it, I know it," cried Hester, wringing her hands, "but even if it were now, I could not help it. I know I should do it again."

"Then take my place with Helen in the morning. I will make the report myself."

Hester clung to her sister, begging and imploring.

"Don't, Hannah, oh, don't—you will kill her."

"I will at least speak the truth."

In the morning she had a cruel report to bear to the mother, and she braced herself for the trial. When she returned from her mission, Hester was waiting, pale and trembling, in the hall. She whispered,

"Oh, how did she take it—that poor, desolate mother?"

Hannah's eyes were swimming in tears. She said,

"God forgive me, I told her the child was well!"

Hester gathered her to her heart, with a grateful "God bless you, Hannah!" and poured out her thankfulness in an inundation of worshiping praises.

After that, the two knew the limit of their strength, and accepted their fate. They surrendered humbly, and abandoned themselves to the hard requirements of the situation. Daily they told the morning lie, and confessed their sin in prayer; not asking forgiveness, as not being worthy of it, but only wishing to make record that they realized their wickedness and were not desiring to hide it or excuse it.

Daily, as the fair young idol of the house sank lower and lower, the sorrowful old aunts painted her glowing bloom and her fresh young beauty to the wan mother, and winced under the stabs her ecstasies of joy and gratitude gave them.

In the first days, while the child had strength to hold a pencil, she wrote fond little love-notes to her mother, in which she concealed her illness; and these the mother read and re-read through happy eyes wet with thankful tears, and kissed them over and over again, and treasured them as precious things under her pillow.

Then came a day when the strength was gone from the hand, and the mind wandered, and the tongue babbled pathetic incoherences. This was a sore dilemma for the poor aunts. There were no love-notes for the mother. They did not know what to do. Hester began a carefully studied and plausible explanation, but lost the track of it and grew confused; suspicion began to show in the mother's face, then alarm. Hester saw it, recognized the imminence of the danger, and descended to the emergency, pulling herself resolutely together and plucking victory from the open jaws of defeat. In a placid and convincing voice she said:

"I thought it might distress you to know it, but Helen spent the night at the Sloanes'. There was a little party there, and although she did not want to go, and you so sick, we persuaded her, she being young and needing the innocent pastimes of youth, and we believing you would approve. Be sure she will write the moment she comes."

"How good you are, and how dear and thoughtful for us both! Approve? Why, I thank you with all my heart. My poor little exile! Tell her I want her to have every pleasure she can—I would not rob her of one. Only let her keep her health, that is all I ask. Don't let that suffer; I could not bear it. How thankful I am that she escaped this infection—and what a narrow risk she ran, Aunt Hester! Think of that lovely face all dulled and burnt with fever. I can't bear the thought of it. Keep her health. Keep her bloom! I can see her now, the dainty creature—with the big blue earnest eyes; and sweet, oh, so sweet and gentle and winning! Is she as beautiful as ever, dear Aunt Hester?"

"Oh, more beautiful and bright and charming than ever she was before, if such a thing can be"—and Hester turned away and fumbled with the medicine bottles, to hide her shame and grief.

V

After a little, both aunts were laboring upon a difficult and baffling work in Helen's chamber. Patiently and earnestly, with their stiff old fingers, they were trying to forge the required note. They made failure after failure, but they improved little by little all the time. The pity of it all, the pathetic humor of it, there was none to see; they themselves were unconscious of it. Often their tears fell upon the notes and spoiled them; sometimes a single misformed word made a note risky which could have been ventured but for that; but at last Hannah produced one whose script was a good enough imitation of Helen's to pass any but a suspicious eye, and bountifully enriched it with the petting phrases and loving nicknames that had been familiar on the child's lips from her nursery days. She carried it to the mother, who took it with avidity, and kissed it, and fondled it, reading its precious words over and over again, and dwelling with deep contentment upon its closing paragraph:

"Mousie darling, if I could only see you, and kiss your eyes, and feel your arms about me! I am so glad my practising does not disturb you. Get well soon. Everybody is good to me, but I am so lonesome without you, dear mamma."

"The poor child, I know just how she feels. She cannot be quite happy without me; and I—oh, I live in the light of her eyes! Tell her she must practise all she pleases; and, Aunt Hannah—tell her I can't hear the piano this far, nor her dear voice when she sings: God knows I wish I could. No one knows how sweet that voice is to me; and to think—some day it will be silent! What are you crying for?"

"Only because—because—it was just a memory. When I came away she was singing 'Loch Lomond.' The pathos of it! It always moves me so when she sings that."

"And me, too. How heart-breakingly beautiful it is when some youthful sorrow is brooding in her breast and she sings it for the mystic healing it brings. . . . . Aunt Hannah?"

"Dear Margaret?"

"I am very ill. Sometimes it comes over me that I shall never hear that dear voice again."

"Oh, don't—don't, Margaret! I can't bear it!"

Margaret was moved and distressed, and said, gently:

"There—there—let me put my arms around you. Don't cry. There—put your cheek to mine. Be comforted. I wish to live. I will live if I can. Ah, what could she do without me! . . . Does she often speak of me?—but I know she does."

"Oh, all the time—all the time!"

"My sweet child! She wrote the note the moment she came home?"

"Yes—the first moment. She would not wait to take off her things."

"I knew it. It is her dear, impulsive, affectionate way. I knew it without asking, but I wanted to hear you say it. The petted wife knows she is loved, but she makes her husband tell her so, every day, just for the joy of hearing it. . . . She used the pen this time. That is better; the pencil marks could rub out, and I should grieve for that. Did you suggest that she use the pen?"

"Y-no—she—it was her own idea."

The mother looked her pleasure, and said:

"I was hoping you would say that. There was never such a dear and thoughtful child! . . . Aunt Hannah?"

"Dear Margaret?"

"Go and tell her I think of her all the time, and worship her. Why—you are crying again. Don't be so worried about me, dear; I think there is nothing to fear, yet."

The grieving messenger carried her message, and piously delivered it to unheeding ears. The girl babbled on unaware; looking up at her with wondering and startled eyes flaming with fever, eyes in which was no light of recognition—

"Are you—no, you are not my mother. I want her—oh, I want her! She was here a minute ago—I did not see her go. Will she come? will she come quickly? will she come now? . . . There are so many houses . . . and they oppress me so . . . and everything whirls and turns and whirls . . . oh, my head, my head!"—and so she wandered on and on, in her pain, flitting from one torturing fancy to another, and tossing her arms about in a weary and ceaseless persecution of unrest.

Poor old Hannah wetted the parched lips and softly stroked the hot brow, murmuring endearing and pitying words, and thanking the Father of all that the mother was happy and did not know.

VI

Daily the child sank lower and steadily lower toward the grave, and daily the sorrowing old watchers carried gilded tidings of her radiant health and loveliness to the happy mother, whose pilgrimage was also now nearing its end. And daily they forged loving and cheery notes in the child's hand, and stood by with remorseful consciences and bleeding hearts, and wept to see the grateful mother devour them and adore them and treasure them away as things beyond price, because of their sweet source, and sacred because her child's hand had touched them.

At last came that kindly friend who brings healing and peace to all. The lights were burning low. In the solemn hush which precedes the dawn vague figures flitted soundless along the dim hall and gathered silent and awed in Helen's chamber, and grouped themselves about her bed, for a warning had gone forth, and they knew. The dying girl lay with closed lids, and unconscious, the drapery upon her breast faintly rising and falling as her wasting life ebbed away. At intervals a sigh or a muffled sob broke upon the stillness. The same haunting thought was in all minds there: the pity of this death, the going out into the great darkness, and the mother not here to help and hearten and bless.

Helen stirred; her hands began to grope wistfully about as if they sought something—she had been blind some hours. The end was come; all knew it. With a great sob Hester gathered her to her breast, crying, "Oh, my child, my darling!" A rapturous light broke in the dying girl's face, for it was mercifully vouchsafed her to mistake those sheltering arms for another's; and she went to her rest murmuring, "Oh, mamma, I am so happy—I so longed for you—now I can die."

Two hours later Hester made her report. The mother asked,

"How is it with the child?"

"She is well."

VII

A sheaf of white crêpe and black was hung upon the door of the house, and there it swayed and rustled in the wind and whispered its tidings. At noon the preparation of the dead was finished, and in the coffin lay the fair young form, beautiful, and in the sweet face a great peace. Two mourners sat by it, grieving and worshiping—Hannah and the black woman Tilly. Hester came, and she was trembling, for a great trouble was upon her spirit. She said,

"She asks for a note."

Hannah's face blanched. She had not thought of this; it had seemed that that pathetic service was ended. But she realized now that that could not be. For a little while the two women stood looking into each other's face, with vacant eyes; then Hannah said,

"There is no way out of it—she must have it; she will suspect, else."

"And she would find out."

"Yes. It would break her heart." She looked at the dead face, and her eyes filled. "I will write it," she said.

Hester carried it. The closing line said:

"Darling Mousie, dear sweet mother, we shall soon be together again. Is not that good news? And it is true; they all say it is true."

The mother mourned, saying:

"Poor child, how will she bear it when she knows? I shall never see her again in life. It is hard, so hard. She does not suspect? You guard her from that?"

"She thinks you will soon be well."

"How good you are, and careful, dear Aunt Hester! None goes near her who could carry the infection?"

"It would be a crime."

"But you *see* her?"

"With a distance between—yes."

"That is so good. Others one could not trust; but you two guardian angels—steel is not so true as you. Others would be unfaithful; and many would deceive, and lie."

Hester's eyes fell, and her poor old lips trembled.

"Let me kiss you for her, Aunt Hester; and when I am gone, and the danger is past, place the kiss upon her dear lips some day, and say her mother sent it, and all her mother's broken heart is in it."

Within the hour Hester, raining tears upon the dead face, performed her pathetic mission.

VIII

Another day dawned, and grew, and spread its sunshine in the earth. Aunt Hannah brought comforting news to the failing mother, and a happy note, which said again, "We have but a little time to wait, darling mother, then we shall be together."

The deep note of a bell came moaning down the wind.

"Aunt Hannah, it is tolling. Some poor soul is at rest. As I shall be soon. You will not let her forget me?"

"Oh, God knows she never will!"

"Do not you hear strange noises, Aunt Hannah? It sounds like the shuffling of many feet."

"We hoped you would not hear it, dear. It is a little company gathering, for—for

Helen's sake, poor little prisoner. There will be music—and she loves it so. We thought you would not mind."

"Mind? Oh, no, no—oh, give her everything her dear heart can desire. How good you two are to her, and how good to me. God bless you both, always!"

After a listening pause:

"How lovely! It is her organ. Is she playing it herself, do you think?" Faint and rich and inspiring the chords floated to her ears on the still air. "Yes, it is her touch, dear heart; I recognize it. They are singing. Why—it is a hymn! and the sacredest of all, the most touching, the most consoling. . . . It seems to open the gates of paradise to me. . . . If I could die now. . . ."

Faint and far the words rose out of the stillness—

Nearer, my God, to Thee,
Nearer to Thee,
E'en though it be a cross
That raiseth me.

With the closing of the hymn another soul passed to its rest, and they that had been one in life were not sundered in death. The sisters, mourning and rejoicing, said,

"How blessed it was that she never knew."

IX

At midnight they sat together, grieving, and the angel of the Lord appeared in the midst transfigured with a radiance not of earth; and speaking, said:

"For liars a place is appointed. There they burn in the fires of hell from everlasting unto everlasting. Repent!"

The bereaved fell upon their knees before him and clasped their hands and bowed their gray heads, adoring. But their tongues clung to the roof of their mouths, and they were dumb.

"Speak! that I may bear the message to the chancery of heaven and bring again the decree from which there is no appeal."

Then they bowed their heads yet lower, and one said:

"Our sin is great, and we suffer shame; but only perfect and final repentance can make us whole; and we are poor creatures who have learned our human weakness, and we know that if we were in those hard straits again our hearts would fail again, and we should sin as before. The strong could prevail, and so be saved, but we are lost."

They lifted their heads in supplication. The angel was gone. While they marveled and wept he came again; and bending low, he whispered the decree.

X

Was it heaven? Or hell?

Wednesday, June 6, 1906

The celebrations at York Harbor—Mrs. Clemens's failing health—She entertains, for the last time, the beautiful "American foreigner" introduced by Carmen Sylva—The return to Riverdale in invalid's car—The season of unveracity.

In York Harbor.

York Harbor consists of a widely scattered cluster of independent little villages called York, York Harbor, York Village, York Centre, West York, East York, South York—I think those are the names, but I am not certain, and it is not important. The whole of them together are bunched under one simple, rational name, York. About the 6th of August a celebration broke out among these hives—a celebration in commemoration of the two hundred and fiftieth anniversary of the institution of municipal self-constituted government on the continent of America. For two or three days there were quaint back-settlement processions, mass meetings, orations, and so on, by day, and fireworks by night.

Mrs. Clemens was always young, and these things had a strong interest for her. She even took more interest in my speeches than I took in them myself. During three days she went about behind horses in the daytime, and by boat at night, seeing and hearing and enjoying all that was going on. She was over-exerting herself, overtaxing her strength, and she began to show it. With difficulty I persuaded her to forego the grand performances of the closing night, and we observed their firework effects from the piazza, across the intervening distance of two or three miles. But my interference had come too late. The overtaxing of her strength had already been over-sufficient.

The next afternoon was the last she ever spent in this life as a person personally and intimately connected with this world's affairs. It was the last time she was to receive and entertain a visitor. This visit promised to be commonplace, and instantly and easily forgetable, but by grace of my native talent for making innocent and discomforting blunders, it wasn't. The visitor was a lady. She had forwarded to us a letter of introduction and now she was come, upon our invitation, to spend the afternoon and dine with us. She was a beautiful creature. She said she was thirty years old and had been married fifteen years. Her manner, and her English, would have convicted her of being of foreign origin, and if any evidence were needed to clinch the conviction and justify the verdict, it was present in her alien and unpronounceable name, which no inexperienced Christian might try to pronounce and live. Yet she was not a foreigner at all. She was American born, of native American parents. Her tongue had never known any language but the American language until she married that unpronounceable foreigner, at fifteen, in Paris. Her English was quaint and pretty, graceful, and understandable, but it was not English.

The letter of introduction which she had forwarded to me was one of those formidable great missives which are the specialty of royalty, and it was from the Queen of Rumania. It said that the bearer and her husband, who was a Rumanian nobleman, had resided at the Rumanian court for fifteen years, where the husband had held an important post under the Government. The letter spoke affectionately of the wife. It also said that she was a highly accomplished musician and competent to teach, and that she was returning to her own country in the hope of being able to earn a living there by teaching. Her Majesty thought that perhaps I could be useful in finding classes for this exiled friend of hers. Carmen Sylva's letter was in English, a language of which she is a master, and the letter explained why these people, so comfortably nested in her court and in her affections for fifteen years, were suddenly become exiles, wanderers in the earth, friendless, forlorn, and driven to earn their bread by the sweat of their accomplishments. But just as we were going to find out *what* it was that had caused this disaster—if it was a disaster—just as my wife and I had reached the summit of eagerness to get at the kernel of that interesting secret, the Queen delivered that kernel in *French.* It was a single phrase—two or three words—but they made a combination which we had never encountered before and which we were not able to cipher out the meaning of. The Queen said in substance—I have forgotten the exact words—that the husband had been obliged to resign his post, or posts, and retire from the court on account of—then followed that fiendish French sentence. For a moment I was so exasperated that I wished I never had learned the French language—plainly a language likely to fail a person at the crucial moment.

At mid-afternoon Mrs. Clemens, the beautiful American foreigner, and I, sat grouped together and chatting on the piazza. I had in my hand the current *North American Review,* fresh, enticing, inviting, with the fragrance of the printer's ink still breathing from its pages and making me long to open it and see what was in it. That court-bred creature had her eyes about her. She was accustomed to reading people's concealed feelings and desires by help of treacherous exterior indications such as attitude, fidgets, and so on. She saw what was the matter with me, and she most winningly and beseechingly asked me to open the magazine and read aloud. I was most cordially grateful. I opened the magazine, and the first thing that attracted me was an article by an Austrian prince on Dueling in Court and Military circles on the Continent of Europe. It profoundly interested me, and I read along with vigor and emphasis. The Prince was hostile to the dueling system. He told of the measures which were being taken by generals and great nobles in Austria—particularly in Austria, I think—to abolish the system. In the course of his uncompromising indictment of the system he remarked upon the fact that no important official on the continent of Europe could decline a challenge, from any motive whatever, and not by that act cover himself and his family with shame and disgrace and be thenceforth spurned and ignored by the society in which they moved, and even by their friends.

I happened to lift my eyes—that poor woman's face was as white as marble! The French phrase stood translated! I did not read any more, and we hurriedly changed to some other topic.

As I have said, this was the last incident in Mrs. Clemens's social life—a life in which she had been active and which she had enjoyed with all her heart from the days of her young girlhood. It was the last incident—it closed that volume. It prefaced the next and final volume of her existence in this earth.

At seven the next morning (August the 11th) I was wakened by a cry. I saw Mrs. Clemens standing on the opposite side of the room, leaning against the wall for support, and panting. She said "I am dying."

I helped her back to the bed and sent for Dr. Leonard, a New York physician. He said it was a nervous break down, and that nothing but absolute rest, seclusion, and careful nursing, could help her. That was the beginning. During the twenty-two succeeding months she had for society, physicians and trained nurses only, broadly speaking.

The next sixty days were anxious ones for us. When we entered the month of October, it was a question if we could get her back to Riverdale. We could not venture transportation by Mr. Rogers's yacht. She would not be able to endure the sea effect. At last we resolved to try the rather poor contrivance called an invalid's car. I call it a poor contrivance because while it is spacious, and has plenty of room in it for all the friends and nurses and physicians you need, it has one very great defect—the invalid's bed is stationary and immovable, and responds to every jump and jerk and whirl of the train, whereas if it were suspended from the roof by elastic ropes, hammock fashion, the invalid would never feel a jolt or a quiver. We secured a special train to take this car to Boston and around Boston. Then we hitched it to a regular express train which delivered us in the Grand Central Station in New York on time. A locomotive stood ready and waiting, and in fifteen minutes it delivered us at our home, Riverdale.

The Siege and Season of Unveracity.

The burly English butler carried Mrs. Clemens up stairs to her bed and left her there with the trained nurse. When he closed that bedroom door he shut the truth out from that bed-chamber forever more. The physician, Dr. Moffat, came once or twice a day and remained a few minutes. If any doctor-lies were needed he faithfully furnished them. When the trained nurse was on duty she furnished such lies as were needful. Clara stood a daily watch of three or four hours, and hers was a hard office indeed. Daily she sealed up in her heart a dozen dangerous truths, and thus saved her mother's life and hope and happiness with holy lies. She had never told her mother a lie in her life before, and I may almost say that she never told her a truth afterward. It was fortunate for us all that Clara's reputation for truthfulness was so well established in her mother's mind. It was our daily protection from disaster. The mother never doubted Clara's word. Clara could tell her large improbabilities without exciting any suspicion, whereas if I had tried to market even a small and simple one the case would have been different. I was never able to get a reputation like Clara's. It would have been useful to me now, but it was too late to begin the labor of securing it, and I furnished no information in the bed-chamber. But my protection lay in the fact that I was allowed in the bed-chamber only once a day, then for only two minutes. The nurse stood at the door with her watch in her hand and turned me out when the time was up.

My room was next to Mrs. Clemens's, with a large bath-room between. I could not talk with her, but I could correspond by writing. Every night I slipped a letter under the bath-room door that opened near her bed—a letter which contained no information about current events, and could do no harm. She responded, with pencil, once or twice a day—at first at some length, but as the months dragged along and her strength grew feebler, she put her daily message of love in trembling characters upon little scraps of paper, and this she continued until the day she died.

I have mentioned that Clara's post was difficult, and indeed it was.

Thursday, June 7, 1906

The difficulties of Clara's position during her mother's and Jean's illness—The Susy Crane letter—Mr. Clemens's version of Mr. Howells's story—Taking Mrs. Clemens to Florence, and her death, there.

Several times, in letters written to friends, in those days, I furnished illustrations of the difficulties of Clara's position. One of these letters was written to Susy Crane at the end of 1902, two months and a half after we had come back from York Harbor.

Some days before Christmas, Jean came in from a long romp in the snow, in the way of coasting, skeeing, and so on, with the young Dodges, and she sat down, perspiring, with her furs on, and was presently struck with a violent chill. She fell into the doctor's hands at once, and by Christmas Eve was become very ill. The disease was double pneumonia. From that time onward, to and beyond the date of this letter, her case was alarming. During all this time her mother never suspected that anything was wrong. She questioned Clara every day concerning Jean's health, spirits, clothes, employments and amusements, and how she was enjoying herself; and Clara furnished the information right along, in minute detail—every word of it false, of course. Every day she had to tell how Jean dressed; and in time she got so tired of using Jean's existing clothes over and over again, and trying to get new effects out of them, that finally, as a relief to her hard-worked invention she got to adding imaginary clothes to Jean's wardrobe, and would probably have doubled it and trebled it if a warning note in her mother's comments had not admonished her that she was spending more money on these spectral gowns and things than the family income justified.

Of course Jean had to have a professional nurse, and a woman named Tobin was engaged for that office. Jean's room was at the other end of the house from her mother's quarters; and so, doctors and nurses could come and go without their presence being detected by Mrs. Clemens. During the middle, or the end, of January, Jean had become able to be about, and the doctor ordered a change of scene for her. He said she must be taken South, to Old Point Comfort, and this was done. Katy and Miss Tobin accompanied her, and she remained at Old Point Comfort several weeks. The orders were to stay six weeks, but neither Jean nor Katy could endure that trained nurse, and they returned to Riverdale before the term was up.

During the whole of Jean's absence Mrs. Clemens was happy in the thought that she was on the premises; that she was in blooming health; that she was having as joyous a time as any young girl in the region. Clara kept her mother posted, every day, concerning Jean's movements. On one day she would report Jean as being busy with her wood-carving; the next day she would have Jean hard at work at her language-studies; the day after, she would report Jean as being busy typewriting literature for me. In the course of time she got as tired of these worn stage-properties as she had of Jean's clothes, before.

I will here insert the Susy Crane letter.

Clara's Day.

In bed, 9 p.m.
Riverdale, Dec. 29/02.

Susy dear, two hours ago, Clara was recounting her day to me. Of course I can't get any of it right, there's so much detail; but with your York Harbor experience of the hardships attendant upon sick-room lying, you will get an idea, at any rate, of what a time that poor child has every day, picking her way through traps and pitfalls, and just barely escaping destruction two or three times in every hour.

[To-day. Jean's other lung attacked; a crisis expected to-night—Dr. Janeway to be summoned in the morning. Our doctor is to stay all night.]

Of course Clara does not go to her Monday lesson in New York to-day, on Jean's account—but FORGETS that fact, and enters her mother's room (where she has no business to be,) toward train-time, *dressed in a wrapper.*

Livy. Why Clara, aren't you going to your lesson?

Clara. (Almost caught). Yes.

Livy. In that costume?

Cl. Oh, no.

L. Well, you can't make your train, it's impossible.

Cl. I know, but I'm going to take the other one.

L. Indeed *that* won't do—you'll be ever so *much* too late for your lesson.

Cl. No, the lesson-time has been put an hour later. [*Lie.*]

L. (Satisfied. Then suddenly). But Clara, that train and the late lesson together will make you late to Mrs. Hapgood's luncheon.

Cl. No, the train leaves fifteen minutes earlier than it used to. [*Lie.*]

L. (Satisfied). Tell Mrs. Hapgood etc. etc. etc. *(which Clara promises to do).* Clara dear, after the luncheon—I hate to put this on you—but *could* you do two or three little shopping-errands for me?—it is a pity to send Miss Lyon all the way to New York for so little.

Cl. Oh, it won't trouble me a bit—I can do it. *(Takes a list of the things she is to buy—a list which she will presently hand to Miss Lyon and send her to New York to make the purchases).*

L. (Reflectively). What is that name? Tobin—Toby—no, it's Tobin—Miss Tobin.

Cl. (Turning cold to the marrow, but exhibiting nothing—Miss Tobin is Jean's trained nurse). What about Tobin—or Miss Tobin? Who is it?

L. A nurse—trained nurse. They say she is very good, and not talkative. Have you seen her?

Cl. (Desperately—not knowing anything to say in this mysterious emergency). Seen her? A Miss Tobin? No. Who is it?

L. (To Clara's vast relief). Oh, *I* don't know. The doctor spoke of her—and praised her. I suppose it was a hint that we need another. But I didn't respond, and he dropped the matter. Miss Sherry is enough; we don't need another. If he approaches you about it, discourage him. I think it is time you were dressing, dear—remember and tell Mrs. Hapgood what I told you.

[*Exit Clara—still alive—finds Miss Sherry waiting in the hall. They rehearse some lies together for mutual protection. Clara goes and hovers around in Jean's part of the house and pays her frequent visits of a couple of minutes but does not allow her to talk. At 3 or 4 p.m. takes the things Miss Lyon has brought from New York; studies over her part a little, then goes to her mother's room.*]

Livy. It's very good of you, dear. Of course if I had known it was going to be so snowy and drizzly and sloppy I wouldn't have asked you to buy them. Did you get wet?

Cl. Oh, nothing to hurt.

L. You took a cab, both ways?

Cl. Not from the station to the lesson—the weather was good enough till that was over.

L. Well, now, tell me everything Mrs. Hapgood said.

[*Clara tells her a long story, avoiding novelties and surprises and anything likely to inspire questions difficult to answer; and of course detailing the menu, for if it had been the feeding of the five thousand, Livy would have insisted on knowing what kind of bread it was and how the fishes were served. By and by, while talking of something else—*]

Livy. CLAMS!—in the end of December. Are you sure it was clams?

Cl. I didn't say cl— I meant blue-points.

L. (Tranquillized). It seemed odd. What is Jean doing?

Cl. She said she was going to do a little typewriting. [*Lie, of course; Jean being hardly alive.*]

L. Has she been out to-day?

Cl. Only a moment, right after luncheon. She was determined to go out again, but—

L. How did you know she was out?

Cl. (Saving herself in time). Katy told me. She was determined to go out again in the rain and snow, but I persuaded her to stay in.

L. (With moving and grateful admiration). Clara you *are* wonderful! the wise watch you keep over Jean, and the *influence* you have over her; it's so lovely of you, and I tied here and can't take care of her myself. *(And she goes on with these undeserved praises till Clara is expiring with shame).* How did John Howells seem yesterday?

Cl. Oh, he was very well. Of course it seemed pretty desolate in that big dining room with only two at table.

L. Why only *two?*

Cl. (Stupidly). Well—er—papa doesn't count.

L. But doesn't Jean count?

Cl. (Almost caught again). Why, yes, she *counts* of course,—makes up the number—but she doesn't say anything—never talks.

L. Did she walk with you?

Cl. A little way. Then we met the Dodges and she went off coasting with them.

L. (Wonderingly). Sunday?

Cl. (Up a stump for a moment). Well, they don't *every* Sunday. They didn't last Sunday.

[*Livy was apparently satisfied. Jean said, some weeks ago, that Clara is the only person who can tell her mother an* improbable *lie and get it believed; and that it is because Clara has never before told her any lies.*]

L. When did Mark Hambourg come?

Cl. Just as John was leaving.

L. I kept waiting to hear the piano. Wasn't it dull for him with no music? Why didn't you take him to the piano?

Cl. I did offer, but he had a headache. [*Lie.*]

[*The piano is too close to Jean—it would have disturbed her.*]

This is a pretty rude sketch, Aunt Sue, and all the *fine* things are left out—I mean the exceedingly close places which Clara is constantly getting into and then slipping out *just* alive by a happy miracle of impromptu subterfuge and fraud. The whole thing would be funny, if it were not so heart-breakingly pathetic and tragic.

I have the strongest desire to call you to us, but the doctor wouldn't let you see Livy; and if he did—but he wouldn't.

Dec. 30. 6 a.m.—(which is about dawn). I have been up to Jean's room, and find all quiet there—Jean sleeping. Miss Tobin whispered, "She has had a *splendid* night." The doctor (and Clara) had put in an appearance a couple of times in the night and gone back to bed, finding things going well.

SLC

When one considers that Clara had been practising these ingenuities for two months and a half, and that she was to continue to practise them daily for a year and a half longer, one gets something of a realizing sense of the difficulties and perils of the office she was filling. I will furnish here another sample.

Letter to Reverend Joseph H. Twichell.

Riverdale-on-the-Hudson
The Last day of a—in some respects—
Tough Year, being A.D. 1902.

Dear Joe—

It is 10 a.m., and the post has just brought your good greeting of yesterday. Yesterday at mid-afternoon there was a memorable episode: I was in Livy's presence two minutes and odd, (the trained nurse holding the watch in her hand) for the first time in three and a half months.

Livy was radiant! (And I didn't spoil it by saying, "Jean is lying low with pneumonia these seven days.")

[A good deal of the rest of the week, Joe, can be found in my Christmas story (*Harper's*) entitled "Was it Heaven? Or Hell?" which is largely a true story and was written in York Harbor in August or September.]

In that story mother and daughter are ill, and the lying is attended to by a pair of aged aunts—assisted by the doctor, of course, though I suppress his share to make the story short. In this Riverdale home the liars are the doctor, Clara, and Miss Sherry (Livy's trained nurse). Those are the regulars. I am to see Livy again to-day for two or three minutes, and it is possible that she may say "Who was it you were talking with at breakfast?—I made out a man's voice." (And confuse me.) (The man was the doctor; he spends his nights here with Jean, and is not due to visit Livy until noon—he lives two or three miles away.) She sent Miss Sherry down to ask that question, during breakfast. We three consulted, and sent back word it was a stranger. It will be like Livy to ask me what stranger it was. Therefore I am to go prepared with a stranger calculated to fill the bill.

Yesterday morning the doctor left here at nine and made his rounds in Yonkers, then came back and paid Livy his usual noon visit; but this morning he had a patient or so within half a mile of here, and to save travel he thought it would be a good idea to go straight up to Livy from the breakfast table; so he sent up to say he had called in passing, and couldn't he come up and see Livy *now?* Of course she said yes, and he went up. He ought to have kept still; but some devil of injudacity moved him to say—

"Mr. Clemens says you are looking distinctly better than when he last saw you, in York."

Livy was back at him instantly:

"Why—have you seen him? How did you come to see him since yesterday afternoon?"

Luckily the doctor did not exhibit the joggle she had given him, but said composedly—

"I ran across him in the hall a minute ago when I came in."

So then he had to get Miss Sherry outside and arrange with her to tell me that that was how he came to know my opinion of the patient's looks. To make doubly sure he hunted me up and told me himself; then called Clara and instructed *her;* for although her watch is not in the forenoon, she takes Miss Sherry's place a little while every morning while Miss Sherry goes down and plans Livy's food for the day with the cook.

I am to see Livy a moment every afternoon until she has another bad night; and I stand in dread, for with all my practice I realize that in a sudden emergency I am but a poor clumsy liar, whereas a fine alert and capable emergency-liar is the only sort that is worth anything in a sick-chamber.

Now, Joe, just see what reputation can do. All Clara's life she has told Livy the truth and now the reward comes: Clara lies to her three and a half hours every day, and Livy takes it all at par, whereas even when I tell her a truth it isn't worth much without corroboration.

Clara's talents are worked plenty hard enough without this new call upon them—Jean. Of course we do not want Jean to know her own danger, and that the doctor is spending his nights thirty feet from her. Yesterday at sunrise Clara carried an order from him to Jean's nurse; and being worn and not at her brightest self, she delivered it in Jean's hearing. At once Jean spoke up:

"What is the doctor doing here—is mamma worse?"

It brought Clara to herself, and she said—

"No. He telephoned this order late last night, and said let it go into effect at six or seven this morning."

This morning Clara forgot herself again. She was in a long hall that leads past Jean's room, and called out to Katy about something, "Take it to the doctor's room!"

Then she flew to explain to Jean with an explanatory lie, and was happy to find that Jean was asleep and hadn't heard.

I wish Clara were not so hard driven—so that she could take a pen and put upon paper all the details of one of her afternoons in her mother's room. Day before yesterday (Monday), for instance. We were all desperately frightened and anxious about Jean (both lungs affected, temperature 104$\frac{2}{5}$, with high pulse and blazing fever), the whole household moving aimlessly about with absent and vacant faces—and Clara sitting miserable at heart but outwardly smiling, and telling her happy mother what good times Jean was having, coasting and carrying on out in the snow with the Dodges these splendid winter days! * * * *

Joe, Livy is the happiest person you ever saw. And she has had it all to herself for a whole week. What a week! So full of comedy and pathos and tragedy!

Jean had a good night last night, and she is doing as well as in the circumstances can be expected.

Joe, don't let those people invite me—I couldn't go. I have canceled all engagements, and shan't accept another for a year.

There'll be a full report of that dinner*—issued by Colonel Harvey as a remembrancer—and of course he will send it to all the guests. If he should overlook you—which he won't—let me know.

Soon my brief visit is due. I've just been up, listening at Livy's door. For the first time in months I heard her break into one of her girlish old-time laughs. With a word I could freeze the blood in her veins!

P.S. 1902.

Dec. 31, 4 p.m. A great disappointment. I was sitting outside Livy's door, waiting. Clara came out a minute ago and said Livy is not so well, and the nurse can't let me see her to-day. And Clara whispered other things. In the effort to find a new diversion for Jean, she pretended she had sent her down to a matinée in New York this afternoon. Livy was pleased, but at once wanted the name of the play. Clara was aground. She was afraid to name one—in fact couldn't for the moment think of any name. Hesitances won't do; so she said Jean hadn't mentioned the name of it, but was only full of seeing Fay Davis again.

That was satisfactory, and the incident was closed. Then—

"Your father is willing to go with you and Jean to-morrow night?" (To Carnegie Hall.)

"Oh, yes. He is reformed since you are sick; never grumbles about anything he thinks you would like him to do. He's all alacrity to do the most disagreeable things. You wouldn't recognize him, now. He's spoiling himself—getting so vain of himself he—"

And so on and so on—fighting for time—time to think up material. She had sent back the tickets a week ago, with a note explaining why we couldn't come; the thing had passed out of her mind, and to have it sprung upon her out of the hoary past in this sudden way was a perilous matter and called for wariness. (It is my

* My sixty-seventh birthday. M.T.

little juvenile piece "The Death-Wafer," which Livy loves; and longs to hear about it from an eye-witness.)

"Who else is going?"

"Mary Foote and—and Miss Lyon and—and Elizabeth Dodge—and—I think that is all."

"Why—has Jean invited Elizabeth and not her *sister?*"

(Clara had forgotten there was a sister, and was obliged to explain that she didn't really remember, but believed Jean *had* mentioned the sister.)

"Well, to make sure, speak to her about it. But is that all she has invited? It is a great big box, and the management have been very kind. It mustn't have a thin look."

And so Livy began to worry.

"Oh, don't you bother, Mousie. You can depend on Jean to have it full. She mentioned names, but I had the cook on my hands and wasn't paying attention."

And at this point, sure enough, I fell heir to *my* share; for Clara said—

"Day after to-morrow she'll want to know *all* about it. *I* can't furnish details, they've gone out of my head. You must post me thoroughly, to-morrow."

She had to get back to Livy's room, then—and perhaps explain what kept her so long.

This is a perplexing place. Livy knows the story, and I don't. I wrote it three years ago, or more. I think I will suggest some such procedure as this—to Clara:

"*Generalize*—keep *generalizing*—about the scenery, and the costumes, and how bluff and fine the old Lord Protector was, and how pretty and innocently audacious the child was, and how pathetically bowed and broken the poor parents were, and all that, and how *perfectly* natural and accurate the Tower of London looked—work the Tower hard, Livy knows the Tower well—work it for all it's worth—keep whirling it in—every time you get stuck, say 'Oh, but the Tower! ah, the Tower!' And keep your ears open—your *mother* will furnish the details, without knowing it. She'll mention the child's climbing up into Cromwell's lap uninvited—and you must break into the middle of her sentence and say 'Oh, you should have *seen* it!' and she'll say, 'When the child put the red wafer into her own father's hand—' you will break in and say, 'Oh, Mousie, it was too pitiful for anything—you could hear the whole house sob;' and she'll say, 'Was the child equal to her part when she flew to Cromwell and dragged him out and stamped her foot and—' you must break in and say 'It was great! and when he said *"Obey! she spoke by my voice; the prisoner is pardoned—set him free!"* you ought to have *been* there! it was just grand!'"*

Mark.

1903.

Jan. 1/03. The doctor did not stay last night. Just as I was beginning to dress for dinner Livy's nurse came for me, and I saw the patient four minutes. She was in great spirits—like twenty-five years ago.

She has sent me a New-Year greeting this morning, and has had a good night.

Jean has had a good night, and does not look to me so blasted and blighted as on the previous days. She sleeps all the time. Temperature down to within a shade of normal, this morning. Everything looking well here (unberufen!)

Mark.

*June, 1906. Clara followed the instructions, and succeeded.

Jan. 28.

Livy had a slight backset yesterday, so the doctor has just told me he is going to shut off my daily visit for a few days. It will distress her, and may have an ill effect at first; but later, results will show the wisdom of it no doubt.

Katy's absence at Old Point Comfort with Jean makes a new difficulty: Livy charges Clara with orders for Katy every day. For months Katy has prepared special dishes for Livy, and now Livy wants her stirred up—she is growing careless in her cooking the past few days and isn't up to standard! By gracious *we* can't counterfeit Katy's cookery!

Yours ever,
Mark.

Jean is enjoying herself very well at Old Point Comfort. Clara has asked Judy to come up, and we are hoping she will say yes.

The story ("Was it Heaven—or Hell?") appeared in the Christmas *Harper* when Jean's life was hanging by a thread (as we all knew), but while she was taking joyous and active part in the Christmas fêtes and festivities of the neighborhood (as her mother supposed). The mother inquired into all the festivities with that lively interest which was so characteristic of her. She wanted all the details. She wanted all the names. If it was a young people's party, or fête, or dance, she wanted to know. If it was at William E. Dodge's house, or if it was at Cleveland Dodge's, or if it was at George W. Perkins's house, she had to have the house, the nature of the entertainment, the names of the participants, and all about it. Clara furnished these particulars; and while her mother's face beamed with pleasure in the thought of the brave time Jean was having, Clara sat there with her still heart listening—if a heart can listen. She knew that Jean might be dying at that moment.

Italy.

Toward the end of October we carried Mrs. Clemens aboard ship, her excellent nurse, Miss Sherry, accompanying us. We reached Florence on the 9th of November. We conveyed our patient to that odious Villa di Quarto. I have already told a sufficiency of the history of our eight months' occupancy of that infamous place. I will not inflict upon myself the useless pain of filling out the remaining months of it.

Mrs. Clemens was doomed from the beginning, but she never suspected it—*we* never suspected it. She had been ill many times in her life, but her miraculous recuperative powers always brought her out of these perils safely. We were full of fears and anxieties and solicitudes all the time, but I do not think we ever really lost hope. At least, not until the last two or three weeks. It was not like *her* to lose hope. We never expected her to lose it—and so at last when she looked me pathetically in the eyes and said "You believe I shall get well?" it was a form which she had never used before, and it was a betrayal. Her hope was perishing, and I recognized it.

During five months I had been trying to find another and satisfactory villa, in the belief that if we could get Mrs. Clemens away from the Villa di Quarto and its fiendish associations, the happier conditions would improve both the health of her spirit and that of her body. I found many villas that had every desired feature save one or two, but the lacking one or two were always essentials—features necessary to the well-being of the invalid. But at last, on Saturday the 4th of June, I heard of a villa which promised to meet all the requirements. Sunday afternoon Jean and I drove to it, examined it, and came home satisfied—more than satisfied, delighted. The purchase price was thirty thousand dollars cash, and we could have possession at once.

We got back home at five in the afternoon, and I waited until seven with my news. I was allowed to have fifteen minutes in the sick-room two or three times a day—the last of these occasions being seven in the evening—and I was also privileged to step in for a single moment at nine in the evening and say good night. At seven that evening I was at the bedside. I described the villa, exhibited its plans, and said we would buy it to-morrow if she were willing, and move her to it as soon as she could bear the journey. She was pleased. She was satisfied. And her face—snow white, marble white, these latter weeks—was radiant. I overstayed my time fifteen minutes—a strenuously forbidden trespass. As I was passing out at the door which was furthest from her bed, it was borne in upon her that, by rights, I had forfeited my privilege of coming at nine to say good night. I think so, because she kissed her hand at me and said "You'll come again?" I said "Yes."

I came again at nine. As I entered I saw Katy and the trained nurse, one on each side of Mrs. Clemens, who was sitting up in bed—she had not lain down for two months—and they were apparently supporting her. But she was dead. She must have died as I entered the door. She had been blessedly unaware that her end was near. She had been gaily chatting with Katy and the nurse a moment before I entered the room.

We brought her home. And in the library of her father's house, and upon the same spot where she had stood, a young girl bride, thirty-five years before, her coffin now rested. Mr. Twichell, who had assisted at her marriage, was there to say the farewell words.

Monday, June 11, 1906

The beautiful morning—Noble situation of the house—Its one defect, loneliness—The visit of the deer—Sympathy with Adam and Eve in Garden of Eden—Irruption of Vesuvius—Earthquake in San Francisco.

After a week of silence and inanition I hardly know where to take up this thread again. This veranda is not the best workshop in the world, particularly in such superb weather as this. The skies are enchantingly blue. The world is a dazzle of sunshine. Monadnock is closer to us than usual by several hundred yards. The vast extent of spreading valley is intensely green—the lakes as intensely blue. And there is a new horizon—a remoter one than we have known before, for beyond the mighty half-circle of hazy mountains that form the usual frame of the picture, rise certain shadowy great domes that are unfamiliar to our eyes. Certainly this house is nobly situated. It stands solitary, reserved, and well satisfied with itself, in the midst of its hundred or so of acres of grass and grove, and from this high throne looks out upon that spacious paradise of which I have been talking.

But there is a defect—only one, but it is a defect which almost entitles it to be spelled with a capital D. This is the defect of loneliness. We have not a single neighbor, who is a neighbor. Nobody lives within two miles of us except Franklin MacVeagh, and he is the furthest off of any, because he is in Europe. My social life has to be limited to the friends who come to me. I can't very well go to them, because I don't like driving, and I am much too indolent to walk. The rest of the household walk and drive, daily, and thereby they survive. But I am not surviving. I am in a trance. When I have dictated a couple of hours in the forenoon I don't know what to do with myself until ten o'clock next day. Sometimes the household are so melancholy that it ceases to be pathetic and becomes funny. Some member of it has given the house a Masonic name, The Lodge of Sorrow.

I feel for Adam and Eve now, for I know how it was with them. I am existing, broken hearted, in a Garden of Eden, and in a household consisting of six or eight persons—yet I feel as Alexander Selkirk felt, who had to cheer himself with sorrowful poetry because there was no other way to put in the time, and he said:

> Oh Solitude, where are the charms that sages have seen in thy face?
> Better live in the midst of alarms than dwell in this horrible place.

Adam would have said it. Adam would have written it and left it on record—if he could have spelled the words. The Garden of Eden I now know was an unendurable solitude. I know that the advent of the serpent was a welcome change—anything for society. I would have welcomed him. I would have done anything I could think of to make him comfortable and get him to stay. He could have had all the apples, if I had to go without, myself.

I never rose to the full appreciation of the utter solitude of this place until a symbol of it—a compact and visible allegory of it—furnished me the lacking lift three days ago. I was standing alone on this veranda, in the late afternoon, mourning over the stillness, the far-spreading, beautiful desolation, and the absence of visible life, when a couple of shapely and graceful deer came sauntering across the grounds and stopped, and at their leisure impudently looked me over, as if they had an idea of buying me as bric-à-brac. Then they seemed to conclude that they could do better for less money, elsewhere, and they sauntered indolently away, and disappeared among the trees. It sizes up this solitude. It is so complete, so perfect, that even the wild animals are satisfied with it. Those dainty creatures were not in the least degree afraid of me.

There have been some large vacancies in this work of mine. Early in April came the great irruption of Vesuvius and electrified the world. After the lapse of perhaps a week, we began to get the elaborate particulars, along with photographs that made them understandable. My first thought was, "Here is a chance to show that old news is quite as interesting as fresh news, provided it shall come in the form of a narrative furnished by an eye-witness." I thought I would get the account by the Younger Pliny of the overwhelming of Herculaneum and Pompeii in A.D. 79 and put it in this book, where it would be, and remain, interesting, as long as the book might last. But straightway the thing happened which I might have known would happen—the newspapers came out with the Younger Pliny's narrative. It not only happened now, but it will happen again and again every time there is a great irruption of Vesuvius, so long as newspapers and magazines continue to exist, until Vesuvius shall go permanently dry—even though it be a hundred thousand years.

So there was no occasion to put the Younger Pliny into this book. He will always be heard from when the occasion comes, without need of help from me. I was dictating about other matters at the time, and trying hard to catch up to the current date. Therefore I allowed that irruption to wait until I could get a proper chance at it. But meantime I went on collecting and preserving, day after day, the daily accounts of the progress of the irruption, and, therewith, the pictures forwarded by eye-witnesses.

But before in my dictating I was able to catch up and begin on the irruption, came the mighty news of the obliteration of San Francisco by earthquake and fire, and Vesuvius vanished instantly and completely from my interest and from the interest of the world. San Francisco filled the whole world, from horizon to horizon, and there was no more Vesuvius. Never in all history, I suppose, was a world-interest so suddenly and so completely extinguished.

The first hint of the disaster which had befallen San Francisco reached me in such an extravagant form that I took it for an impudent invention, and it did not hold my attention ten minutes. It came to me by telephonic message from a friend down in the city. He simply said: "San Francisco was destroyed by an earthquake at five o'clock this morning. Two thousand lives lost." But by nightfall "extra" after "extra" began to appear and the news to take on the semblance of reality. Certain definite details were furnished. The next morning's papers contained news of a convincing character—although there was not much of it, for the reason that the earthquake and the fire together had almost totally abolished railway and telegraphic communication with San Francisco from the outside.

I began to accumulate pictures and narratives again. I threw away all my Vesuvian accumulations to make room for the San Franciscan collections. But in a few days these had become a mountain, and the thing was hopeless. I destroyed my San Franciscan accumulations and stopped harvesting that kind of material. It occurred to me that there were certain good reasons why I could properly and wisely excuse myself from becoming a historian of that disaster. It happened to occur to me that inasmuch as this was the only instance in history of the destruction of a very great city by fire and earthquake, it would stand alone among disasters; conspicuous, awful, sublime, forever visible to men, forever unforgetable—and would so remain even if the aid of the book and the newspaper were denied it. However, this aid would not be wanting. No, it will have that help for all time to come. A thousand years from now there will still be whole libraries about the destruction of San Francisco. There will still be acres of pictures—photographic and authentic—illustrating the disaster. I recognize that I can quite safely leave San Francisco out of this book, and that is what I shall do.

Tuesday, June 12, 1906

The San Francisco earthquake—Madame Sembrich's experience—The strange absence of fear shown by all who were shaken up by the earthquake—Mr. Clemens speaks of the great San Franciscan earthquake which occurred when he was living there—He learns through Mr. Richard Williams of the safety of Steve and Jim Gillis.

During fifty-six years, the whole great globe has been continuously contributing to the population of San Francisco, therefore its destruction was a matter of personal concern to families scattered everywhere upon the globe's surface. Its population, of four hundred thousand, represented all the races of men, pretty nearly. There is not another city of just its size in the world whose destruction could send dread and terror to anything like so many and so widely scattered hearthstones. New York seemed now to be suddenly swarming with ex-Californians, and with relatives and intimate friends of existing Californians. Everybody I met seemed to have personal grounds for his interest in the disaster. Some had a pecuniary interest in it. One friend of mine who had been living long in New York on a liberal income furnished by San Franciscan property, had lost the most of his possessions and been obliged to remove from expensive quarters to cheap ones in a humble flat. A week before the calamity a young couple, of independent means, dined at my table, and they were full of pleasant anticipations of an excursion around the world which they were preparing to make. Their fortune was in San Francisco. Ten days after the calamity they were aware that they were paupers; they were now seeking employment, for wages. They quickly found it—the wife in New York, the husband in Montana.

It is thirty-eight years since I last saw San Francisco and was engaged in advancing its prosperity, at thirty or forty dollars a week on the *Morning Call,* as chief and only reporter. In my day I knew everybody in San Francisco—including the most of the dogs and cats—because of my newspaper connection; but now I could not seem to call to mind any of my friends of that early day who would be likely to have been spared thirty-eight years to enjoy the earthquake. After much thinking and recalling, I did dig up out of my memory three or four old friends whom I had reason to believe were still alive; also I established a personal connection in another way. About a week before the disaster the husband of Madame Sembrich visited me at 21 Fifth Avenue—the rented house which we call our home—and brought Madame Sembrich's autograph album, which I was under contract to her to sign. As he was going away he said:

"It will interest you to know that my wife, with the rest of the Grand Opera Company, is arriving in San Francisco to-day."

As it turned out, she was not only arriving, but had arrived. And not only had she arrived, but at the time of our conversation the earthquake had shaken her out of the eighth story of her hotel, in night costume, and now she was camping in a public park. The earthquake shook her out of her bed and upset all the furniture in her room. She fled down the rocking stairs nearly to the street, then climbed up to her quarters again to get her jewels, made the descent a second time, this time to the street level, where she found the hotel entrance clogged with fallen building material. Then, being unhappy in her scant apparel, she made the ascent once more to get something, I don't know what—a hair-pin, I suppose. What I am arriving at is this: that with the globe apparently going to pieces, everything jostling and cracking and crumbling and making a muffled and thunderous clamor of unaccustomed noises, that charming and dainty and delicate and refined little creature was not frightened.

According to innumerable personal accounts of reputable witnesses, the passion of fear was strangely absent at the time of that cataclysm—yet we have the impression that the fright communicated by an earthquake is the most terrible of all frights, and spares nobody. I do not know how to account for this radical change. I was in what was called the "Great Earthquake" in San Francisco a long time ago, and I remember that everybody who came under my notice during the sharp half-minute joggle that it lasted was frightened—except myself. I was not frightened because I didn't know it was an earthquake. It shook me up violently, and I fell against a house on the street corner; but I supposed, for the moment, that it was a riot inside the house. That interested me instantly and intensely, because I was a newspaper reporter, and was thankful. A moment or two later I recognized that it was an earthquake, and was arranging to get frightened, when I realized that the time for it had gone by, and that it was not now worth while. That earthquake produced two deaths—a lady died from sheer fright, and a young man was so demented with fright that he jumped out of a window and was killed.

My attention is called to this matter of the absence of fright as exhibited in this recent earthquake, by a published letter of Professor William James, the philosopher, who was visiting at Stanford University, and who noted the wide prevalence of that astonishing absence of panicky fear. To him it was an extraordinary thing, and unaccountable. It is not discoverable in the history of any preceding earthquake, in America or elsewhere. Professor James was shaken out of his quarters, but had no feeling of fright or fear. He was merely strongly and absorbingly interested in the event as being a remarkable one, a memorable one, and one worth going far to experience. He speaks of an undergraduate who was sleeping in the fourth story of a massive stone dormitory of the University, and who was plunged from his bed down through the four floors and into the basement, where he lay imprisoned in wreckage, but not frightened,—and not hurt, so far as he knew—only surprised, with a surprise tinged with regret, for it was hardly five o'clock in the morning and he hadn't finished his sleep. He worked his way up through the crazy ruins, reached what was left of his room in the fourth story, accumulated remnants of his clothes from here, there, and yonder, covered his nakedness with them, and went off to see what had been happening to other people. He was still unaware that he was hurt, yet before noon he was in the hospital, and it took him a week or two there to get mended up so that he could get out and on his feet again.

As I say, I dug out of my memory several friends of the days of thirty-eight years ago, to get anxious about. One was Joe Goodman. He is safe—nothing happened to him. Another was "little Ward," who was a compositor on the *Morning Call* in my time—and he used to go with little Steve Gillis and me to the beer saloons in Montgomery street when work was over, at two o'clock in the morning, and where I used to sit around till dawn and have a restful, pleasant time, while little Ward and Steve—weighing ninety-five pounds each—good-naturedly picked quarrels with any strangers over their size who seemed to need entertainment, and they always thrashed those strangers with their fists. I never knew them to suffer a defeat. They never assisted each other. If one had offered to assist the other against some overgrown person, it would have been an affront, and a battle would have followed between that pair of little friends—a battle which would have continued for years and could never have been decided, because those boys were absolutely equally matched in scientific fisticuffs. We three were about of an age—I twenty-nine, and they twenty-seven.

Thinking over these hallowed memories I presently remembered that little Ward sent a bullet through his head several years ago, when he had reached the age of sixty-five. My solicitude was now diminished to little Steve Gillis and his brother Jim. As I have before remarked, I had been a boarder in their parents' house for a year or two, in those days, and was very intimate with the young sons and daughters of the family. I was presently to learn that the Gillis boys were safe. One day a card was brought up to my room, the address upon which was "Richard Williams, San Francisco." I had the proprietor of it brought up to my den at once, for I wanted to make inquiries. He was tall, broad shouldered, muscular; with a strong jaw and a determined face, gentlemanly in his dress and manners, and apparently about forty years old. He wore no beard, and his face was a fearful spectacle to look upon. It was a riot and confusion of broad and slick scars, which overlapped each other like the scales of a fish—the sort of scars that fire makes. I said to myself, "He doesn't need to put San Francisco on his card. Anybody will know that he is back, recently, from there, or from Perdition; for he never could have got that work of art from any but one or the other of those places; they don't turn out that complete and perfect kind, elsewhere—in this world or anywhere else." It was a brutal rudeness to stare at him, but I couldn't help it. There was a fascination—a grisly fascination—about his aspect which made it impossible for me to keep my eyes off his face; and I think that wherever he goes he must find that the rest of the world are like me—they can't resist.

He said, "Mr. Clemens, you don't know me. You've never seen me. But I am the eldest son of the eldest of the Gillis sisters."

"Oh impossible," I said, "why they were nothing but young girls."

"Yes," he said, "so they were, but they didn't stay so."

"Well," I said, "I see how it is. Those young girls have remained young girls in my memory all this time, but they could have grown up in the meantime; it has happened before. Well, it does seem very strange that you, a great stalwart man, should actually be the offspring of one of those young creatures. How old are you?"

He said he was thirty-seven, but was often taken to be older.

He told me that his uncles, little Steve Gillis and Jim, were both in the hospital at the time of the earthquake and the fire, and that although the hospitals had turned out to be particularly fatal places at the time of the catastrophe because the inmates were not able to aid in their own rescue, Jim and Steve had escaped. That was natural. They are the bravest of the brave. You might break their legs and their backs, too, and they would fight their way out of a danger that would be fatal to ordinary men with all their bones about them in good repair.

I am going to confess that I don't know to this day how he got those scars. I had a delicacy about asking him how he got them. I knew there were only just the two places, hell or San Francisco, and so— Moreover, I knew that if he had any sensitiveness about it he would throw me out of the window. He looked like just that determined kind of a man. I wish I knew whether he was in that San Francisco fire and got burned up and escaped—but I never shall know.

Wednesday, June 13, 1906

The days of reporting on the *Morning Call*—The advent of Smiggy McGlural and the *resignation* of Mr. Clemens—Destruction of *Morning Call* building in recent earthquake—Good times with Bret Harte in *Morning Call* office.

How wonderful are the ways of Providence! But I will take that up later.

In those days—about forty years ago—I was a reporter on the *Morning Call* of San Francisco. I was more than that—I was *the* reporter. There was no other. There was enough work for one, and a little over, but not enough for two—according to Mr. Barnes's idea, and he was the proprietor, and therefore better situated to know about it than other people. By nine in the morning I had to be at the police court for an hour and make a brief history of the squabbles of the night before. They were usually between Irishmen and Irishmen, and Chinamen and Chinamen, with now and then a squabble between the two races, for a change. Each day's evidence was substantially a duplicate of the evidence of the day before, therefore the daily performance was killingly monotonous and wearisome. So far as I could see, there was only one man connected with it who found anything like a compensating interest in it, and that was the court interpreter. He was an Englishman who was glibly familiar with fifty-six Chinese dialects. He had to change from one to another of them every ten minutes, and this exercise was so energizing that it kept him always awake—which was not the case with the reporters. Next, we visited the higher courts, and made notes of the decisions which had been rendered the day before. All the courts came under the head of "regulars." They were sources of reportorial information which never failed. During the rest of the day we raked the town from end to end, gathering such material as we might, wherewith to fill our required column—and if there were no fires to report, we started some. At night we visited the six theatres, one after the other: seven nights in the week, three hundred and sixty-five nights in the year. We remained in each of those places five minutes, got the merest passing glimpse of play and opera, and with that for a text we "wrote up" those plays and operas, as the phrase goes, torturing our souls every night, from the beginning of the year to the end of it, in the effort to find something to say about those performances which we had not said a couple of hundred times before. There has never been a time, from that day to this (forty years), that I have been able to look at even the outside of a theatre without a spasm of the dry gripes, as "Uncle Remus" calls it—and as for the inside, I know next to nothing about that, for in all this time I have seldom had a sight of it, nor ever had a desire in that regard which couldn't have been overcome by argument.

After having been hard at work from nine or ten in the morning until eleven at night scraping material together, I took the pen and spread this muck out in words and phrases, and made it cover as much acreage as I could. It was fearful drudgery—soulless drudgery—and almost destitute of interest. It was an awful slavery for a lazy man, and I was born lazy. I am no lazier now than I was forty years ago, but that is because I reached the limit forty years ago. You can't go beyond possibility.

Finally there was an event. One Sunday afternoon I saw some hoodlums chasing and stoning a Chinaman who was heavily laden with the weekly wash of his Christian customers, and I noticed that a policeman was observing this performance with an amused interest—nothing more. He did not interfere. I wrote up the incident with considerable warmth and holy indignation. Usually I didn't want to read, in the morning, what I had written the night before; it had come from a torpid heart. But this item had come from a live one. There was fire in it, and I believed it was literature—and so I sought for it in the paper next morning with eagerness. It wasn't there. It wasn't there the next morning, nor the next. I went up to the composing-room and found it tucked away among condemned matter on the standing galley. I asked about it. The foreman said Mr. Barnes had found it in a galley-proof and ordered its extinction. And Mr. Barnes furnished his reasons—either to me or to the foreman, I don't remember which; but they were commercially sound. He said that the *Call* was like the New York *Sun* of that day: it was the washerwoman's paper—that is, it was the paper of the poor; it was the only cheap paper. It gathered its livelihood from the poor, and must respect their prejudices, or perish. The Irish were the poor. They were the stay and support of the *Morning Call;* without them the *Morning Call* could not survive a month—and they hated the Chinamen. Such an assault as I had attempted could rouse the whole Irish hive, and seriously damage the paper. The *Call* could not afford to publish articles criticising the hoodlums for stoning Chinamen.

I was lofty in those days. I have survived it. I was unwise, then. I am up-to-date now. Day before yesterday's New York *Sun* has a paragraph or two from its London correspondent which enables me to locate myself. The correspondent mentions a few of our

American events of the past twelvemonth, such as the limitless rottenness of our great insurance companies, where theft has been carried on by our most distinguished commercial men as a profession; the exposures of conscienceless graft—colossal graft—in great municipalities like Philadelphia, St. Louis, and other large cities; the recent exposure of million-fold graft in the great Pennsylvania Railway system—with minor uncoverings of commercial swindles from one end of the United States to the other; and finally to-day's lurid exposure, by Upton Sinclair, of the most titanic and death-dealing swindle of them all, the Beef Trust, an exposure which has moved the President to demand of a reluctant Congress a law which shall protect America and Europe from falling, in a mass, into the hands of the doctor and the undertaker. According to that correspondent, Europe is beginning to wonder if there is really an honest male human creature left in the United States. A year ago, I was satisfied that there was no such person existing upon American soil—except myself. That exception has since been rubbed out, and now it is my belief that there isn't a single male human being in America who is honest. I held the belt all along, until last January. Then I went down, with Rockefeller and Carnegie and a group of Goulds and Vanderbilts and other professional grafters, and swore off my taxes like the most conscienceless of the lot. I was a great loss to America, because I was irreplaceable. It is my belief that it will take fifty years to produce my successor. I believe the entire population of the United States—exclusive of the women—to be rotten, as far as the dollar is concerned. Understand, I am saying these things as a dead person. I should consider it indiscreet in any live one to make these remarks publicly.

But, as I was saying, I was loftier forty years ago than I am now, and I felt a deep shame in being situated as I was—slave of such a journal as the *Morning Call.* If I had been still loftier I would have thrown up my berth and gone out and starved, like any other hero. But I had never had any experience. I had *dreamed* heroism, like everybody, but I had had no practice, and I didn't know how to begin. I couldn't bear to begin with starving. I had already come near to that once or twice in my life, and got no real enjoyment out of remembering about it. I knew I couldn't get another berth if I resigned. I knew it perfectly well. Therefore I swallowed my humiliation and stayed where I was. But whereas there had been little enough interest attaching to my industries, before, there was none at all now. I continued my work, but I took not the least interest in it, and naturally there were results. I got to neglecting it. As I have said, there was too much of it for one man. The way I was conducting it now, there was apparently work enough in it for two or three. Even Barnes noticed that, and told me to get an assistant, on half wages. There was a great hulking creature down in the counting-room—good-natured, obliging, unintellectual—and he was getting little or nothing a week and boarding himself. A graceless boy of the counting-room force who had no reverence for anybody or anything, was always making fun of this beachcomber, and he had a name for him which somehow seemed intensely apt and descriptive—I don't know why. He called him Smiggy McGlural. I offered the berth of assistant to Smiggy, and he accepted it with alacrity and gratitude. He went at his work with ten times the energy that was left in me. He was not intellectual, but mentality was not required or needed in a *Morning Call* reporter, and so he conducted his office to perfection. I gradually got to leaving more and more of the work to McGlural. I grew lazier and lazier, and within thirty days he was doing almost the whole of it. It was also plain that he could accomplish the whole of it, and more, all by himself, and therefore had no real need of me.

It was at this crucial moment that that event happened which I mentioned a while ago. Mr. Barnes discharged me. It was the only time in my life that I have ever been discharged, and it hurts yet—although I am in my grave. He did not discharge me rudely. It was not in his nature to do that. He was a large, handsome man, with a kindly face and courteous ways, and was faultless in his dress. He could not have said a rude, ungentle thing to anybody. He took me privately aside and advised me to resign. It was like a father advising a son for his good, and I obeyed.

I was on the world, now, with nowhere to go. By my Presbyterian training, I knew that the *Morning Call* had brought disaster upon itself. I knew the ways of Providence, and I knew that this offence would have to be answered for. I could not foresee when the penalty would fall nor what shape it would take, but I was as certain that it would come, sooner or later, as I was of my own existence. I could not tell whether it would fall upon Barnes or upon his newspaper. But Barnes was the guilty one, and I knew, by my training, that the punishment always falls upon the innocent one, consequently I felt sure that it was the newspaper that at some future day would suffer for Barnes's crime.

Sure enough! Among the very first pictures that arrived, in the fourth week of April—there stood the *Morning Call* building towering out of the wrecked city, like a Washington Monument; and the body of it was all gone, and nothing was left but the iron bones! It was then that I said "How wonderful are the ways of Providence!" I had known it would happen. I had known it for forty years. I had never lost my confidence in Providence during all that time. It was put off longer than I was expecting, but it was now comprehensive and satisfactory enough to make up for that. Some people would think it curious that Providence should destroy an entire city of four hundred thousand inhabitants to settle an account of forty years' standing, between a mere discharged reporter and a newspaper, but to me there was nothing strange about that, because I was educated, I was trained, I was a Presbyterian, and I knew how these things are done. I knew that in Biblical times, if a man committed a sin, the extermination of the whole surrounding nation—cattle and all—was likely to happen. I knew that Providence was not particular about the rest, so that He got somebody connected with the one He was after. I remembered that in the Magnalia a man who went home swearing, from prayer-meeting one night, got his reminder within the next nine months. He had a wife and seven children, and all at once they were attacked by a terrible disease, and one by one they died in agony, till at the end of a week there was nothing left but the man himself. I knew that the idea was to punish the man, and I knew that if he had any intelligence he recognized that that intention had been carried out, although mainly at the expense of other people.

In those ancient times the counting-room of the *Morning Call* was on the ground floor; the office of the Superintendent of the United States Mint was on the next floor above, with Bret Harte as private secretary of the Superintendent. The quarters of the editorial staff and the reporter were on the third floor, and the composing-room on the fourth and final floor. I spent a good deal of time with Bret Harte in his office after Smiggy McGlural came, but not before that. Harte was doing a good deal of writing for *The Californian*—contributing "Condensed Novels" and sketches to it, and also acting as editor, I think. I was a contributor. So was Charles H. Webb; also Prentice Mulford; also a young lawyer named Hastings, who gave promise of distinguishing himself in literature some day. Charles Warren Stoddard was a contributor. Ambrose Bierce, who is still writing acceptably for the magazines to-day, was then employed on some paper in San Francisco—*The Golden Era,* perhaps. We had very good times together—very social and pleasant times. But that was after Smiggy McGlural came to my assistance; there was no leisure before that. Smiggy was a great advantage to me—during thirty days. Then he turned into a disaster.

It was Mr. Swain, Superintendent of the Mint, who discovered Bret Harte. Harte had arrived in California in the '50s, twenty-three or twenty-four years old, and had wandered up into the surface diggings of the camp at Yreka, a place which had acquired its curious name—when in its first days it much needed a name—through an accident. There was a bakeshop with a canvas sign which had not yet been put up but had been painted and stretched to dry in such a way that the word bakery showed through and was reversed. A stranger read it wrong end first, Yreka, and supposed that that was the name of the camp. The campers were satisfied with it and adopted it.

Harte taught school in that camp several months. He also edited the weekly rag which was doing duty as a newspaper. He spent a little time also in the pocket-mining camp of Jackass Gulch (where I tarried, some years later, during three months). It was at Yreka and Jackass Gulch that Harte learned to accurately observe and put with photographic exactness on paper the woodland scenery of California and the general country aspects—the stage-coach, its driver and its passengers, and the clothing and general style of the surface-miner, the gambler, and their women; and it was also in these places that he learned, without the trouble of observing, all that he didn't know about mining, and how to make it read as if an expert were behind the pen. It was in those places that he also learned how to fascinate Europe and America with the quaint dialect of the miner—a dialect which no man in heaven or earth had ever used until Harte invented it. With Harte it died, but it was no loss. By and by he came to San Francisco. He was a compositor, by trade, and got work in the *Golden Era* office at ten dollars a week.

Thursday, June 14, 1906

Entirely about Bret Harte—his appearance, dress, writings, etc.

Harte was paid for setting type only, but he lightened his labors and entertained himself by contributing literature to the paper, uninvited. The editor and proprietor, Joe Lawrence, never saw Harte's manuscripts, because there weren't any. Harte spun his literature out of his head while at work at the case, and set it up as he spun. *The Golden Era* was ostensibly and ostentatiously a literary paper, but its literature was pretty feeble and sloppy, and only exhibited the literary forms, without really being literature. Mr. Swain, the Superintendent of the Mint, noticed a new note in that *Golden Era* orchestra—a new and fresh and spirited note that rose above that orchestra's mumbling confusion and was recognizable as music. He asked Joe Lawrence who the performer was, and Lawrence told him. It seemed to Mr. Swain a shame that Harte should be wasting himself in such a place and on such a pittance, so he took him away, made him his private secretary, on a good salary, with little or nothing to do, and told him to follow his own bent and develop his talent. Harte was willing, and the development began.

Bret Harte was one of the pleasantest men I have ever known. He was also one of the unpleasantest men I have ever known. He was showy, meretricious, insincere; and he constantly advertised these qualities in his dress. He was distinctly pretty, in spite of the fact that his face was badly pitted with smallpox. In the days when he could afford it—and in the days when he couldn't—his clothes always exceeded the fashion by a shade or two. He was always conspicuously a little more intensely fashionable than the fashionablest of the rest of the community. He had good taste in clothes. With all his conspicuousness there was never anything really loud nor offensive about them. They always had a single smart little accent, effectively located, and that accent would have distinguished Harte from any other of the ultra-fashionables. Oftenest it was his necktie. Always it was of a single color, and intense. Most frequently, perhaps, it was crimson—a flash of flame under his chin; or it was indigo blue, and as hot and vivid as if one of those splendid and luminous Brazilian butterflies had lighted there. Harte's dainty self-complacencies extended to his carriage, and gait. His carriage was graceful and easy, his gait was of the mincing sort, but was the right gait for him, for an unaffected one would not have harmonized with the rest of the man and the clothes.

He hadn't a sincere fibre in him. I think he was incapable of emotion, for I think he had nothing to feel with. I think his heart was merely a pump, and had no other function. I am almost moved to say I *know* it had no other function. I knew him intimately in the days when he was private secretary on the second floor and I a fading and perishing reporter on the third, with Smiggy McGlural looming doomfully in the near distance. I knew him intimately when he came East five years later, in 1870, to take the editorship of the proposed *Lakeside Magazine,* in Chicago, and crossed the continent through such a prodigious blaze of national interest and excitement that one might have supposed he was the Viceroy of India on a progress, or Halley's comet come again after seventy-five years of lamented absence.

I knew him pretty intimately thenceforth until he crossed the ocean to be Consul, first at Crefeld, in Germany, and afterwards in Glasgow. He never returned to America. When he died, in London, he had been absent from America and from his wife and daughters twenty-six years.

This is the very Bret Harte whose pathetics, imitated from Dickens, used to be a godsend to the farmers of two hemispheres on account of the freshets of tears they compelled. He said to me once, with a cynical chuckle, that he thought he had mastered the art of pumping up the tear of sensibility. The idea conveyed was that the tear of sensibility was oil, and that by luck he had struck it.

Harte told me once, when he was spending a business-fortnight in my house in Hartford, that his fame was an accident—an accident that he much regretted for a while. He said he had written "The Heathen Chinee" for amusement; then had thrown it into the waste-basket; that presently there was a call for copy to finish out the *Overland Monthly* and let it get to press. He had nothing else, so he fished the "Chinee" out of the basket and sent that. As we all remember, it created an explosion of delight whose reverberations reached the last confines of Christendom, and Harte's name, from being obscure to invisibility in the one week, was as notorious and as visible, in the next, as if it had been painted on the sky in letters of astronomical magnitude. He regarded this fame as a disaster, because he was already at work on such things as "The Luck of Roaring Camp," a loftier grade of literature, a grade which he had been hoping to presently occupy with distinction in the sight of the world. "The Heathen Chinee" did obstruct that dream, but not for long. It was presently replaced by the finer glory of "The Luck of Roaring Camp," "Tennessee's Partner," and those other felicitous imitations of Dickens. In the San Franciscan days Bret Harte was by no means ashamed when he was praised as being a successful imitator of Dickens; he was proud of it. I heard him say, myself, that he thought he was the best imitator of Dickens in America, a remark which indicates a fact, to wit: that there were a great many people in America, at that time, who were ambitiously and undisguisedly imitating Dickens. His long novel, "Gabriel Conroy," is as much like Dickens as if Dickens had written it himself.

It is a pity that we cannot escape from life when we are young. When Bret Harte started East in his new-born glory, thirty-six years ago, with the eyes of the world upon him, he had lived all of his life that was worth the living. He had lived all of his life that was to be respectworthy. He had lived all of his life that was to be worthy of his *own* respect. He was entering upon a miserable career of poverty, debt, humiliation, shame, disgrace, bitterness, and a world-wide fame which must have often been odious to him, since it made his poverty and the shabbiness of his character conspicuous beyond the power of any art to mercifully hide them. There was a happy Bret Harte, a contented Bret Harte, an ambitious Bret Harte, a hopeful Bret Harte, a bright, cheerful, easy-laughing Bret Harte, a Bret Harte to whom it was a bubbling and effervescent joy to be alive. That Bret Harte died in San Francisco. It was the corpse of that Bret Harte that swept in splendor across the continent; that refused to go to the Chicago banquet given in its honor because there had been a breach of etiquette—a carriage had not been sent for it; that resumed its eastward journey leaving behind the grand scheme of the *Lakeside Monthly* in sorrowful collapse; that undertook to give all the product of its brain for one year to the *Atlantic Monthly* for ten thousand dollars—a stupendous sum in those days—furnished nothing worth speaking of for the great pay, but collected and spent the money before the year was out, and then began a dismal and harassing death-in-life of borrowing from men and living on women which was to cease only at the grave.

Monday, June 18, 1906

The five letters written by three women, twenty-seven years ago, and Mr. Clemens's comments upon them—Bret Harte again.

Let me consider that I have now been dead five hundred years. It is my desire, and indeed my command, that what I am going to say now shall not be permitted to see the light until the edition of A.D. 2400. At that distant date the things which I am about to say will be commonplaces of the time, and barren of offence, whereas if uttered in our day they could inflict pain upon my friends, my acquaintances, and thousands of strangers whom I have no desire to hurt, and could get me ostracized, besides, and cut off from all human fellowship—and the ostracism is the main thing. I am human, and nothing could persuade me to do any bad deed—or any good one—that would bring that punishment upon me.

What I am going to say is not new, except to utterance. I think every person in Christendom of average intelligence has thought the things which I am going to say, many and many a time. He is thoroughly familiar with them, in his secret heart, and would gladly and promptly utter them and publish them if he had been dead five hundred years; but all these thousands and thousands of human beings of above average intelligence are like myself, they have not the courage to come out and tell their deep secret to their neighbor, (who possesses the same secret down in the depths of his heart, also, though he never lets on). It is against nature for a person to have the courage to get himself spurned and avoided; and these millions, along with me, are keeping the great secret, each one thinking he is the only one that has it, and hoping that the others will not find it out and crucify him.

My spirit is a little stirred, but I am trying to keep it from appearing at its full temperature in my words. During five years I have had in my possession a sack of old letters to which I attached no value. They were letters from strangers to each other, in the main, Smiths and Joneses and the like, wholly unknown to the world and to me, persons of not the slightest interest to anybody. I was never expecting to become industrious enough to overhaul that sack and examine its contents, but now that I am doing this autobiography the joys and the sorrows of everybody, high and low, rich and poor, famous and obscure, are dear to me. I can take their heart affairs into my heart as I never could before. In becoming my own biographer I realize that I have become the biographer of Tom, Dick, and Harry, the voiceless. I recognize that Tom and I are intimates; that be he young or be he old, he has never felt anything that I have not felt; he has never had an emotion that I am a stranger to.

Before I got up this morning I brought that ancient bag to the bed, and the first envelope I pulled out was a find. It contained five letters written by three obscure women twenty-seven years ago. They embody a pitiful romance. One of the women is evidently old, and has a good use of language but no education. No. 2 is evidently elderly, and apparently has some education. No. 3 is evidently young, and has had but little schooling, but has a native gift of expression which is very striking. I think it very remarkable and very interesting to see how well you know these three women after you have carefully studied their letters a while. I think that the three characters stand out as strongly and distinctly as they would in the book of a trained novelist after he had devoted seventeen pages to painting their portraits for us. The three are strangers to me. I had never heard of them until this morning. The poor little romance is twenty-seven years old, yet the artless art of the ignorant authors of it has made it stir me as if the incidents had happened yesterday; and not to strangers, but to personal friends of mine.

1879
Three Rivers Oct 5
Mich

Mrs Williams
Dear Lady

Permit a stranger to address a few lines of inquiry to you in regard to Mrs Hunt who stoped with you last winter. She was in poor health and was confined at your home—— She is a widdow and has a little boy with her named Earnest She bcame intimate with a *Married man* here and got in trouble by him, then suddenly left saying she was going to Kansas City where she has relatives but instead she went to Detroit and said she was boarding with Mrs Williams. Now what I wish to know is this what story did she tell you in regard to herslf and circumstances &c did she have a *living child* and what did she do with it was it male of female?

I will assure you by answering my questions and writing whatever you wish will be kept strictly confidental if you wish it. I think from the tenor of her letters she must have been verry ungrateful for your kindness when she was friendless. I will quote a passage from one of her letters "Mrs Williams pretends to be a christian woman but the love for *gain* is stronger than her religeon and when I could not pay her $50 extra she forgot herself as a lady or a christian and said hard things."

I am a relative of hers but do not wish to screne her in doing wrong, but would like to know how much truth or how many untruths she has told while with you. She pretends she has nothing *living,* but I have reason to think othewise. By giving this your earliest attention you will confer a great favor on an unknown friend

Yours Respecfly
Mrs Wm Griffiths
Three Rivers
Mich

From the Same to the Same.

excuse pencil)
Oct 13th 1879
Three Rivers
Mich

Mrs Williams
Detroit—
Dear Madam

Yours of the 9th was duly recd and many thanks for your kindness and prompt answer— You have failed to answer the most important part of my letter concerning the child— I will ask again will you please answer them—

When she left you house did she take the child with her, what did she inted to do with it, was it *Male or female* what was the name of the man she told you who was the father of it? Those are plain questions and I trust you as a Lady of honer and integrity and will do as you would wish to be done by— Be assured that no trouble will ever come to you in consequence of it— I have good reasons for wishing to know these things as I know all the rest from her own pen. She givs me the name of a man but I have reason to doubt her word. She has told different stories and I dont consider her *word good for anything* I do not blame you for doing as you did by her but I think your confidence was misplaced and she illtreated you for your kindness to her——

I will give you *just one* illustration— You say she did *not board* with you—you allso say she went away in *your debt*

I have in my possesion a bill of her own making while at your house saying like this.

Indebtedness *paid* from 24 of Dec to 6th of March—— Commencing (10 weeks board $8. per week $80) &c and other things carried out in the same way untill it figures up to nearly $200—two hundred dollars and to *my* certain knowledge she had over two hundred from here while at your house, and was abuntently able to have paid all that you required of her——you say *she* said the last she heard from this *man* he was in Canada the one that she tells me I dont think he was ever in Canada in his life I am anxious to hear the name she told you to see how they will corispond— If you will be kind enough to answer ths early, you may heare from me again—

Resectfly your Friend
Mrs Wm Griffiths

From the Girl to Mrs. Williams.

Kansas City*

My Dear Mrs Williams

I have been so Ill both in mind and body that I found it impossible to write you before. I arrived in Chicago at 6 am the next morning and as soon as I could went to bed and was not able to leave there untill the last of the next week. I was fearful that I was being taxed beyond my strength to endure and such is the case I am so nervous that I cannot control my hand in writing. My kind friends in C— have done nobly such kindness I did not look for, little Bessie is well cared for which of course help's me although, I cannot help longing to have her myself. I have never heard a word from Mr H since I left your home and cannot learn where he is the most I have learned has been that he was in Canida I presume like the *coward* and *villain* that he has proved himself to be he will stay away, if possible I expect to go to Colorado. I am so miserable that I do not have very much ambition. I feel the necessity of trying to battle with this great trouble, and do something and with God's help I hope I shall succeed, no one but him know's what I have suffered and do now.

Ernest is well is very much pleased with the West, he has gone to sabbath School. The weather is and has been rather cool for the time of year. I may stay here untill July I cannot decide yet what I had better do. I hope your health has improved

with kind regards
Mrs S M Hunt
East 17th st
Kansas City
Mo

* Probably March or April. (M.T.)

From Mrs. Williams to the Girl.

Detroit. October 16. 1879

Mrs Sylvia Hunt—

I received your letter from Kansas City some months ago. Since then have received some letters from Three Rivers Michigan—which have somewhat surprised me.

It seems you reported there that you *boarded* with us at $8.00 per week—that as you left I demanded $50.00 and that I professed to be a Christian but my love for money was stronger than my religion Etc. Etc. It would take too long to quote at length.

Mrs Hunt you know the circumstances under which I took you—on your part—and you know very well you paid but a nominal sum for your accommodations while you were well—but nothing like what you aught to have paid concidering the deception you practiced to get to stay until after your confinement.

Concerning the *hard things* I said to you—you know all I said and *I* know all I said.

I promised to keep your secret—and up to this date nothing has gone from me—rather us—for Mr W. knew all. We seldom speak of you in any way—but since you have chosen to misrepresent so many things (and you have done it because this person writing could not know any other way than through you,] again I say since you have chosen to mis represent things as you have and had the money to the amount of over two hundred dollars sent you while at our house and since you have chosen to act as you have—I must say I feel under no obligations to keep from answering certain questions that have been asked me.

We thought it but proper to give you this notice before I write again (I have answered one letter to Three Rivers, but answered no questions in that—now another is before me.

Respectfully, &c.
Mrs M. E. Williams

From the Girl to Mrs. Williams.

Oct 18th
Kansas City

Mrs Williams

I am so grateful to you for writing to me and giving me an opportunity to defend myself from Parties who seem determined to injure all they can. When I came here I was Heart broken so my Sister said she would never thought I was the same person and I told her all I do not think I could of lived but for her kindness and support, sometime ago I rec'd a letter, stating that letter's from those I was with at D *explaining every thing,* demanding also money for indebtedness &c, which I had left unpaid was rec'd and that there was no use to think I was safe as they knew everything. I was *dumb* with surprize I felt your demand upon me for $50.00 keenly but at the same time I thought you had the impresion that I could get all the money I wanted and as I did not get away when I expected to you might as well have pay for it, and I did not lay up a hard thought. I have many hours sat and thought of my home at that time and thankful to think I was not thrown among those who I could not trust when I rec'd the letter I replyed by writing to my Sister telling her of the Ill treatment rec'd from Mr H &c when it came to my sickness I said like this that it was to sad for me to say anything about I would and must draw a vail over that forever. I felt deeply hurt to think you had as I supposed written to them and although your name was never mentioned in a letter I ever wrote to anyone (Ernest at one time in writing to his Cousin said Mr Williams where we lived had the nicest Black cow he ever saw) and I did not think anything of it as I had not one thought of trying to deceive anyone in regard to my name, place or anything accept Mr H I was told before I left C— to go to D to never let him know the names of anyone but to do the best could, and make him pay at the rate of $8 00 or $9 00 pr wk for board and send all the bill's I could so as to get all the money I could from him it is utterly false that I had $200 while at your house I had of my own money $65.00 which I got and Mr H did not send me but $25.00 that I had to use while there. If I had not had that of my own I would of been obliged to of applyed for aid he does not know to day how I ever lived or paid as I found he did not get the 3 last letter's I wrote with bill statements containing board bill at $8.00 pr wk and other bill's as large as could be made, in one of those letter's I said like this which I wrote with a demand for money. I shall not be able to leave here under the circumstances which I expected, meaning I was to late, and urged the necessity of imediate releif for Mrs W. I never expected to remain at your house and had my mind not been so troubled I should of seen I had made a wrong estimate of time I am sorry I did not show you the letter I wrote to Dr F telling him to have everything ready for my comfort through sickness, and at the same time telling him of your great kindness to me and also his reply trying to cheer me and saying God he knew was with me as so many kind friend's were with me then my letter telling him of my mistake and sickness. I am sure you would not doubt me then in regard to my staying, those 3 letter's fell into the hand's of *Mr H's wife* in place of his and I found she took them to my sister as there was no name to them to see if it was my writing. She then thought she would find out what they meant, and had my Sister write, as also did she, professing to know all and making me think you had written to her and told all, in replying to my Sister, I said I had felt I was with Christan people but you had made me feel and doubt that there was any at all I felt you had told them and tried to get money that I said I thought your asking me for the $50.00 and them the other that your love for money was the greatest. I never mentioned your name then I said Parties my Sister here has seen all the letter's I have re'cd and all I write and I can prove all I say to you if you wish when I paid you the $10.00 I knew not what I would do as when I arrived in C— I had only money enough to pay my fare here and 95 cts over and walked to the depot to save that, where I boarded they trusted me and the first work I was able to do I sent the money to pay it and Dr F knew all, and but for their aid, I could not of left there under the painful circumstances I had to, as I had no money, and I have never rec'd one ct since nor had a letter from Mr H since before I was sick all I have now I have to work for what is to come in future may if ever I get it be to late to ever help me any my Sister at home then coppied the 3 letter's and sent them to my Sister here we then knew we had judged you wrong and I am glad it is so and at the same time sorry I said what I did, although I felt I had good reason then to say it Mrs H did not think it would show the deception she wrote me and found she was obliged to let me alone I have no mean's to defend myself with and it will be best to say nothing. What they have said in regard to my *Character* is False and utterly without any foundation—made up lies which I do not feel they would care to be made to prove as Mrs W there can no one *prove* one thing whereever I have been all these yrs I can prove every hr of time how and who with it was spent but Mr H made an attempt to prove that I was not all right I wish the letter I wrote him about that had fell into his wife's hand's she would never made an attempt to do what she seem's anxious she say's to my Sister she hated her husbanded she knew he was mean enough to do anything, at the same time she want's to know all and in order to do so has taken what I wrote to my Sister in reply to what I thought you had written) and then the 3 letter's from them put the indebtedness for board which I sent as I told you to him in order to get money and wrote to you or got someone to so as to make you feel I had done you an injustice and to get you to tell her all your name they got from E's letter no other way, had I mean's I would, go home and settle with them I would and could put Mr H in a place where he would be obliged to work as I have proof's that would do it my Sister here know's of thing's that happened when I was a child that my Father had forbidden her to go with him she is older than me but she never told me although say's many times has thought what if he should take advantage of my being alone and injure me, as she knew he alway's professed to be such a friend to me. I wish I knew how I could make him pay me $200 or 3—or—5—my Sister think's it best for me to keep still and in writing say nothing about it she will go home this winter I think, and I have friend's there that will not beleive me to be bad as they know me and been with me my life has alway's been a quiet one and have alway's worked hard there is in every place as you know gossipper's and a class of people who feast upon all that tend's to be low and tell lies and is such a habit with them they think and really beleive what they say. I care not for them, although it is not pleasant as I wrote my Sister I was glad I never for one moment felt unhappy for anything I had done wrong in my conscience was clear my unhapiness was caused from the wrong other's had done to me. Mrs W I thank you kindly for writing to me and ask your pardon for doubting you and am willing to trust you now whatevr they write to deceive

Yours respectfully
Mrs S M Hunt, Kansas City
Mo

I did not understand about the hard word's I do not remember that we had any and I cannot recall anything of the kind it is not strange I my poor head is so presed I feel wild sometimes and I have such a battle with myself as the cry for revenge keep's a battle in my mind

I have an uncompromising detestation of that old cat who writes the first letter. I feel disrespectfully toward that machine-made Christian who writes the second one. I think that *in her heart* she turned the friendless refugee and the baby into the street in the raw March weather; and so I hold her guilty to the hilt for that uncommitted inhuman act, and I am sure she would have *committed* it if she could have done it without falling under the artificial censure of the community. I call it artificial because I think that perhaps the majority of the community would have secretly approved the act while publicly denouncing it. I think this because it is human nature—wrought upon by established conventions—to privately exult over certain kinds of baseness and ungenerosity while publicly censuring them to keep on the good side of Mrs. Grundy.

All my sympathies and my compassion are for the betrayed and abused ignorant and trusting young widow, who was as yet too young to know the human race, and I hope that she and her children are long ago dead—a wish and a prayer which I reserve for the good and the deserving alone. I believe every word she says. I think No. 1 is a scheming old malignant. I have already said what I think of No. 2. I discover neither lies nor furtivenesses in the young woman's letter, but only straight and open sincerities—except in one or two particulars which I am unwilling to regard as serious possible departures from cast-iron fact. When she says she has always led a quiet life and has worked hard, I believe it. When she says her conscience absolves her, I believe that too. I think she means that she was tempted beyond her strength by a man whom she had known familiarly in her early girlhood, and that by some inborn instinct she realized that *she did not create her own nature,* that *she did not create its limitations,* and that when those limitations were overpassed she was *not strictly responsible for the consequences.* There are human laws against her conduct, but her conduct transgresses no law of Nature, and the *laws of Nature take precedence of all human laws.* The purpose of *all* human laws is one—*to defeat the laws of Nature.* This is the case among all the nations, both civilized and savage. It is a grotesquerie, but when the human race is not grotesque it is because it is asleep and losing its opportunity.

That young woman's letter exhibits the fact that she has had very little schooling. It is unlikely that she has had much practice with the pen, yet how moving and convincing are her simple phrases, her unstudied eloquence! Her letter is *literature*—good literature—and the most practised pen cannot surpass it, out of the best-trained head. She speaks from the heart; and the heart has no use for the artifices of training or education or dramatic invention when it has a tale to tell.

I am forgetting Bret Harte—but let him go until another time. This new interest has superseded him, and by the law of this biography the newest and warmest interest always has the floor, and takes precedence of all other matters. I shall finish with Bret Harte by and by, for I am prejudiced against him and feel that I can talk about him impartially. In some of his characteristics he reminds me of God. I do not mean of any and every god among the two or three millions of gods that our race has been manufacturing since it nearly ceased to be monkeys—I mean our own God. I do not mean that Mighty One, that Incomparable One that created the universe and flung abroad upon its horizonless ocean of space its uncountable hosts of giant suns—fleets of the desert ether, whose signal lights are so remote that we only catch their latest flash when it has been a myriad of years on its way—I mean the little God whom we manufactured out of waste human material; whose portrait we accurately painted in a Bible and charged its authorship upon Him; the God who created a universe of such nursery dimensions that there would not be room in it for the orbit of Mars (as it is now known to the infant class in our schools) and put our little globe in the centre of it under the impression that it was the only really important thing in it.

Tuesday, June 19, 1906

About the character of God, as represented in the New and the Old Testaments.

Our Bible reveals to us the character of our God with minute and remorseless exactness. The portrait is substantially that of a man—if one can imagine a man charged and overcharged with evil impulses far beyond the human limit; a personage whom no one, perhaps, would desire to associate with, now that Nero and Caligula are dead. In the Old Testament His acts expose His vindictive, unjust, ungenerous, pitiless and vengeful nature constantly. He is always punishing—punishing trifling misdeeds with thousand-fold severity; punishing innocent children for the misdeeds of their parents; punishing unoffending populations for the misdeeds of their rulers; even descending to wreak bloody vengeance upon harmless calves and lambs and sheep and bullocks, as punishment for inconsequential trespasses committed by their proprietors. It is perhaps the most damnatory biography that exists in print anywhere. It makes Nero an angel of light and leading, by contrast.

It begins with an inexcusable treachery, and that is the keynote of the entire biography. That beginning must have been invented in a pirate's nursery, it is so malign and so childish. To Adam is forbidden the fruit of a certain tree—and he is gravely informed that if he disobeys he shall die. How could that be expected to impress Adam? Adam was merely a man in stature; in knowledge and experience he was in no way the superior of a baby of two years of age; he could have no idea of what the word death meant. He had never seen a dead thing; he had never heard of a dead thing before. The word meant nothing to him. If the Adam child had been warned that if he ate of the apples he would be transformed into a meridian of longitude, that threat would have been the equivalent of the other, since neither of them could mean anything to him.

The watery intellect that invented the memorable threat could be depended on to supplement it with other banalities and low grade notions of justice and fairness, and that is what happened. It was decreed that all of Adam's descendants, to the latest day, should be punished for the baby's trespass against a law of his nursery fulminated against him before he was out of his diapers. For thousands and thousands of years, his posterity, individual by individual, has been unceasingly hunted and harried with afflictions in punishment of the juvenile misdemeanor which is grandiloquently called Adam's Sin. And during all that vast lapse of time, there has been no lack of rabbins and popes and bishops and priests and parsons and lay slaves eager to applaud this infamy, maintain the unassailable justice and righteousness of it, and praise its Author in terms of flattery so gross and extravagant that none but a God could listen to it and not hide His face in disgust and embarrassment. Hardened to flattery as our Oriental potentates are, through long experience, not even they would be able to endure the rank quality of it which our God endures with complacency and satisfaction from our pulpits every Sunday.

We brazenly call our God the source of mercy, while we are aware, all the time, that there is not an authentic instance in history of His ever having exercised that virtue. We call Him the source of morals, while we know by His history and by His daily conduct, as perceived with our own senses, that He is totally destitute of anything resembling morals. We call Him Father, and not in derision, although we would detest and denounce any earthly father who should inflict upon his child a thousandth part of the pains and miseries and cruelties which our God deals out to His children every day, and has dealt out to them daily during all the centuries since the crime of creating Adam was committed.

We deal in a curious and laughable confusion of notions concerning God. We divide Him in two, bring half of Him down to an obscure and infinitesimal corner of the world to confer salvation upon a little colony of Jews—and only Jews, no one else—and leave the other half of Him throned in heaven and looking down and eagerly and anxiously watching for results. We reverently study the history of the earthly half, and deduce from it the conviction that the earthly half has reformed, is equipped with morals and virtues, and in no way resembles the abandoned, malignant half that abides upon the throne. We conceive that the earthly half is just, merciful, charitable, benevolent, forgiving, and full of sympathy for the sufferings of mankind and anxious to remove them. Apparently we deduce this character not by examining facts, but by diligently declining to search them, measure them, and weigh them. The earthly half requires us to be merciful, and sets us an example by inventing a lake of fire and brimstone in which all of us who fail to recognize and worship Him as God are to be burned through all eternity. And not only *we,* who are offered these terms, are to be thus burned if we neglect them, but also the earlier billions of human beings are to suffer this awful fate, although they all lived and died without ever having heard of Him or the terms at all. This exhibition of mercifulness may be called gorgeous. We have nothing approaching it among human savages, nor among the wild beasts of the jungle. We are required to forgive our brother seventy times seven times, and be satisfied and content if on our death-bed, after a pious life, our soul escape from our body before the hurrying priest can get to us and furnish it a pass with his mumblings and candles and incantations. This example of the forgiving spirit may also be pronounced gorgeous.

We are told that the two halves of our God are only seemingly disconnected by their separation; that in very fact the two halves remain one, and equally powerful, notwithstanding the separation. This being the case, the earthly half—who mourns over the sufferings of mankind and would like to remove them, and is quite competent to remove them at any moment He may choose—satisfies Himself with restoring sight to a blind person, here and there, instead of restoring it to all the blind; cures a cripple, here and there, instead of curing all the cripples; furnishes to five thousand famishing persons a meal, and lets the rest of the millions that are hungry remain hungry—and all the time He admonishes inefficient man to cure these ills which God Himself inflicted upon him, and which He could extinguish with a word if He chose to do it, and thus do a plain duty which He had neglected from the beginning and always will neglect while time shall last. He raised several dead persons to life. He manifestly regarded this as a kindness. If it was a kindness it was not just to confine it to a half a dozen persons. He should have raised the rest of the dead. I would not do it myself, for I think the dead are the only human beings who are really well off—but I merely mention it, in passing, as one of those curious incongruities with which our Bible history is heavily overcharged.

Whereas the God of the Old Testament is a fearful and repulsive character, He is at least consistent. He is frank and outspoken. He makes no pretense to the possession of a moral or a virtue of any kind—except with His mouth. No such thing is anywhere discoverable in His conduct. I think He comes infinitely nearer to being respectworthy than does His reformed self, as guilelessly exposed in the New Testament. Nothing in all history—nor even His massed history combined—remotely approaches in atrocity the invention of hell.

His heavenly self, His Old Testament self, is sweetness and gentleness and respectability, compared with His reformed earthly self. In heaven He claims not a single merit, and hasn't one—outside of those claimed by His mouth—whereas in the earth He claims every merit in the entire catalogue of merits, yet practised them only now and then, penuriously, and finished by conferring hell upon us, which abolished all His fictitious merits in a body.

Wednesday, June 20, 1906

The defects about Bibles—Remarks about the Immaculate Conception.

There are one or two curious defects about Bibles. An almost pathetic poverty of invention characterizes them all. That is one striking defect. Another is that each pretends to originality, without possessing any. Each borrows from the others, and gives no credit, which is a distinctly immoral act. Each, in turn, confiscates decayed old stage-properties from the others, and with naïve confidence puts them forth as fresh new inspirations from on high. We borrow the Golden Rule from Confucius, after it has seen service for centuries, and copyright it without a blush. When we want a Deluge we go away back to hoary Babylon and borrow it, and are as proud of it and as satisfied with it as if it had been worth the trouble. We still revere it and admire it, to-day, and claim that it came to us direct from the mouth of the Deity; whereas we know that Noah's flood never happened, and couldn't have happened. The flood is a favorite with Bible-makers. If there is a Bible—or even a tribe of savages—that lacks a General Deluge it is only because the religious scheme that lacks it hadn't any handy source to borrow it from.

Another prime favorite with the authors of sacred literature and founders of religions is the Immaculate Conception. It had been worn threadbare before we adopted it as a fresh new idea—and we admire it as much now as did the original conceiver of it when his mind was delivered of it a million years ago. The Hindoos prized it ages ago when they acquired Krishna by the Immaculate process. The Buddhists were happy when they acquired Gautama by the same process twenty-five hundred years ago. The Greeks of the same period had great joy in it when their Supreme Being and his cabinet used to come down and people Greece with mongrels half human and half divine. The Romans borrowed the idea from Greece, and found great happiness in Jupiter's Immaculate Conception products. We got it direct from Heaven, by way of Rome. We are still charmed with it. And only a fortnight ago, when an Episcopal clergyman in Rochester was summoned before the governing body of his Church to answer the charge of intimating that he did not believe that the Savior was miraculously conceived, the Rev. Dr. Briggs, who is perhaps the most daringly broad-minded religious person now occupying an American pulpit, took up the cudgels in favor of the Immaculate Conception, in an article in the *North American Review,* and from the tone of that article it seemed apparent that he believed he had settled that vexed question, once and for all. His idea was that there could be no doubt about it, for the reason that the Virgin Mary knew it was authentic because the Angel of the Annunciation told her so. Also, it must have been so, for the additional reason that Jude—a later son of Mary, the Virgin, and born in wedlock—was still living and associating with the adherents of the early Church many years after the event, and that he said quite decidedly that it was a case of Immaculate Conception; therefore it must be true, for Jude was right there in the family and in a position to know.

If there is anything more amusing than the Immaculate Conception doctrine, it is the quaint reasonings whereby ostensibly intelligent human beings persuade themselves that the impossible fact is proven.

If Dr. Briggs were asked to believe in the Immaculate Conception process as exercised in the cases of Krishna, Osiris, Buddha, and the rest of the tribe, he would decline, with thanks, and probably be offended. If pushed, he would probably say that it would be childish to believe in those cases, for the reason that they were supported by none but human testimony, and that it would be impossible to prove such a thing by human testimony, because if the entire human race were present at a case of Immaculate Conception they wouldn't be able to tell when it happened, nor whether it happened at all—and yet this bright man with the temporarily muddy mind is quite able to believe an impossibility whose authenticity rests entirely upon human testimony—the testimony of but one human being, the Virgin herself, a witness not disinterested, but powerfully interested; a witness incapable of knowing the fact as a fact, but getting all that she supposed she knew about it at second-hand,—at second-hand from an entire stranger, an alleged angel, who could have been an angel, perhaps, but also could have been a tax collector. It is not likely that she had ever seen an angel before, or knew their trade-marks. He was a stranger. He brought no credentials. His evidence was worth nothing at all to anybody else in the community. It is worth nothing, to-day, to any but minds which are like Dr. Briggs's—which have lost their clarity through mulling over absurdities in the pious wish to dig something sane and rational out of them. The Immaculate Conception rests wholly upon the testimony of a single witness—a witness whose testimony is without value—a witness whose very existence has nothing to rest upon but the assertion of the young peasant wife whose husband needed to be pacified. Mary's testimony satisfied him, but that is because he lived in Nazareth, instead of New

York. There isn't any carpenter in New York that would take that testimony at par. If the Immaculate Conception could be repeated in New York to-day, there isn't a man, woman, or child, of those four millions, who would believe in it—except perhaps some addled Christian Scientist. A person who can believe in Mother Eddy wouldn't strain at an Immaculate Conception, or six of them in a bunch. The Immaculate Conception could not be repeated successfully in New York in our day. It would produce laughter, not reverence and adoration.

To a person who doesn't believe in it, it seems a most puerile invention. It could occur to nobody but a god that it was a large and ingenious arrangement, and had dignity in it. It could occur to nobody but a god that a divine Son procured through promiscuous relations with a peasant family in a village could improve the purity of the product, yet that is the very idea. The product acquires purity—purity absolute—purity from all stain or blemish,—through a gross violation of both human law and divine, as set forth in the constitution and by-laws of the Bible. Thus the Christian religion, which requires everybody to be moral and to obey the laws, has its very beginning in immorality and in disobedience to law. You couldn't purify a tomcat by the Immaculate Conception process.

Apparently, as a pious stage-property, it is still useful, still workable, although it is so bent with age and so nearly exhausted by overwork. It is another case of begats. What's-his-name begat Krishna, Krishna begat Buddha, Buddha begat Osiris, Osiris begat the Babylonian deities, they begat God, He begat Jesus, Jesus begat Mrs. Eddy. If she is going to continue the line and do her proper share of the begatting, she must get at it, for she is already an antiquity.

There is one notable thing about our Christianity: bad, bloody, merciless, money-grabbing and predatory as it is—in our country, particularly, and in all other Christian countries in a somewhat modified degree—it is still a hundred times better than the Christianity of the Bible, with its prodigious crime—the invention of hell. Measured by our Christianity of to-day, bad as it is, hypocritical as it is, empty and hollow as it is, neither the Deity nor His Son is a Christian, nor qualified for that moderately high place. Ours is a terrible religion. The fleets of the world could swim in spacious comfort in the innocent blood it has spilt.

Friday, June 22, 1906

The brutal Russian massacres of the Jews—Compares ancient and modern massacres—Tendency of present generation to turn its attention to war—Evil influence of the Bible upon children—Present God and religion will not last.

For two years, now, Christianity has been repeating, in Russia, the sort of industries in the way of massacre and mutilation with which it has been successfully persuading Christendom in every century for nineteen hundred years, that it is the only right and true religion—the one and only religion of peace and love. For two years, now, the ultra-Christian Government of Russia has been officially ordering and conducting massacres of its Jewish subjects. These massacres have been so frequent that we have become almost indifferent to them. The accounts of them hardly affect us more than do accounts of corners in a railroad stock in which we have no money invested. We have become so used to their described horrors that we hardly shudder now when we read of them.

Here are some of the particulars of one of the latest efforts of these humble twentieth century disciples to persuade the unbeliever to come into the fold of the meek and gentle Savior.

> Horrible details have been sent out by the correspondent of the Bourse Gazette, who arrived in Bialystok in company with Deputy Schepkin on Saturday, and who managed to send his story by a messenger Sunday afternoon. The correspondent, who accompanied Schepkin directly to the hospital escorted by a Corporal's guard, says he was utterly unnerved by the sights he witnessed there.
>
> "Merely saying that the bodies were mutilated," the correspondent writes, "fails to describe the awful facts. The faces of the dead have lost all human resemblance. The body of Teacher Apstein lay on the grass with the hands tied. In the face and eyes had been hammered three-inch nails. Rioters entered his home, killing him thus, and then murdered the rest of his family of seven. When the body arrived at the hospital it was also marked with bayonet thrusts.
>
> "Beside the body of Apstein lay that of a child of 10 years, whose leg had been chopped off with an axe. Here also were the dead from the Schlachter home, where, according to witnesses, soldiers came and plundered the house and killed the wife, son, and a neighbor's daughter and seriously wounded Schlachter and his two daughters.
>
> "I am told that soldiers entered the apartments of the Lapidus brothers, which were crowded with people who had fled from the streets for safety, and ordered the Christians to separate themselves from the Jews. A Christian student named Dikar protested and was killed on the spot. Then all of the Jews were shot.
>
> "From the wounded in the hospital the correspondent heard many pitiable stories, all of the same general tenor. Here is the account of a badly wounded merchant named Nevyazhiky:
>
> "'I live in the suburbs. Learning of the pogrom, I tried to reach the town through the fields, but was intercepted by roughs. My brother was killed, my arm and leg were broken, my skull was fractured, and I was stabbed twice in the side. I fainted from loss of blood, and revived to find a soldier standing over me, who asked: "What, are you still alive! Shall I bayonet you?" I begged him to spare my life. The roughs again came, but spared me, saying: "He will die; let him suffer longer."'"
>
> The correspondent, who adopts the bitterest tone toward the Government, holds that the pogrom undoubtedly was provoked, and attributes the responsibility to Police Lieutenant Sheremetieff. He declares that not only the soldiers, but their officers, participated, and that he himself was a witness as late as Saturday to the shooting down of a Jewish girl from the window of a hotel by Lieut. Miller of the Vladimir Regiment. The Governor of the Province of Grodno, who happened to be passing at the moment, ordered an investigation.

The pulpit and the optimist are always talking about the human race's steady march toward ultimate perfection. As usual, they leave out the statistics. It is the pulpit's way—the optimist's way.

Is there any discoverable advance toward moderation between the massacre of the Albigenses and these massacres of Russian Jews? There is one difference. In elaborate cruelty and brutality the modern massacre exceeds the ancient one. Is any advance discoverable between Bartholomew's Day and these Jewish massacres? Yes. The same difference again appears: the modern Russian Christian and his Czar have advanced to an extravagance of bloody and bestial atrocity undreamed of by their crude brethren of three hundred and thirty-five years ago.

The Gospel of Peace is always making a good deal of noise with its mouth; always rejoicing in the progress it is making toward final perfection, and always diligently neglecting to furnish the statistics. George III reigned sixty years, the longest reign in English history, up to his time. When his revered successor, Victoria, turned the sixty-year corner—thus scoring a new long-reign record—the event was celebrated with great pomp and circumstance and public rejoicing in England and her colonies. Among the statistics fetched out for general admiration were these: that for each year of the sixty of her reign, Victoria's Christian soldiers had fought in a separate and distinct war. Meantime, the possessions of England had swollen to such a degree, by depredations committed upon helpless and godless pagans, that there were not figures enough in Great Britain to set down the stolen acreage and they had to import a lot from other countries.

There are no peaceful nations now, except those unhappy ones whose borders have not been invaded by the Gospel of Peace. All Christendom is a soldier-camp. During all the past generation, the Christian poor have been taxed almost to starvation-point to support the giant armaments which the Christian Governments have built up, each to protect itself from the rest of the brotherhood and, incidentally, to snatch any patch of real estate left exposed by its savage owner. King Leopold II of Belgium—probably the most intensely Christian monarch, except Alexander VI, that has escaped hell thus far—has stolen an entire kingdom in Africa, and in fourteen years of Christian endeavor there has reduced the population of thirty millions to fifteen, by murder, mutilation, overwork, robbery, rapine—confiscating the helpless native's very labor, and giving him nothing in return but salvation and a home in heaven, furnished at the last moment by the Christian priest.

Within this last generation each Christian power has turned the bulk of its attention to finding out newer and still newer, and more and more effective ways of killing Christians—and, incidentally, a pagan now and then—and the surest way to get rich quickly, in Christ's earthly kingdom, is to invent a gun that can kill more Christians at one shot than any other existing gun.

Also, during the same generation, each Christian Government has played with its neighbors a continuous poker game, in the naval line. In this game France puts up a battleship; England sees that battleship, and goes it one battleship better; Russia comes in and raises it a battleship or two—*did,* before the untaught stranger entered the game and reduced her stately pile of chips to a damaged ferry-boat and a cruiser that can't cruise. We are in it, ourselves, now. This game goes on, and on, and on. There is never a new shuffle; never a new deal. No player ever calls another's hand. It is merely an unending game of put up, and put up, and put up; and by the law of probabilities, a day is coming when no Christians will be left on the land, except the women. The men will be all at sea, manning the fleets.

This singular game, which is so costly and so ruinous, and so silly, is called statesmanship—which is different from assmanship on account of the spelling. Anybody but a statesman could invent some way to reduce these vast armaments to rational and sensible and safe police proportions, with the result that thenceforth all Christians could sleep in their beds unafraid, and even the Savior could come down and walk on the seas, foreigner as He is, without dread of being chased by Christian battleships.

Has the Bible done something still worse than drench the planet with innocent blood? To my mind it has—but this is only an opinion, and it may be a mistaken one. There has never been a Protestant boy nor a Protestant girl whose mind the Bible has not soiled. No Protestant child ever comes clean from association with the Bible. This association cannot be prevented. Sometimes the parents try to prevent it, by not allowing the children to have access to the Bible's awful obscenities, but this only whets the child's desire to taste that forbidden fruit, and it does taste it—seeks it out secretly and devours it with a strong and grateful appetite. The Bible does its baleful work in the propagation of vice among children, and vicious and unclean ideas, daily and constantly, in every Protestant family in Christendom. It does more of this deadly work than all the other unclean books in Christendom put together; and not only more, but a thousand-fold more. It is easy to protect the young from those other books, and they are protected from them. But they have no protection against the deadly Bible.

Is it doubted that the young people hunt out the forbidden passages privately, and study them with pleasure? If my reader were here present—let him be of either sex or any age, between ten and ninety—I would make him answer this question himself—and he could answer it in only one way. He would be obliged to say that by his own knowledge and experience of the days of his early youth, he knows positively that the Bible defiles all Protestant children, without a single exception.

Do I think the Christian religion is here to stay? Why should I think so? There had been a thousand religions before it was born. They are all dead. There had been millions of gods before ours was invented. Swarms of them are dead and forgotten long ago. Ours is by long odds the worst God that the ingenuity of man has begotten from his insane imagination—and shall He and His Christianity be immortal, against the great array of probabilities furnished by the theological history of the past? No. I think that Christianity, and its God, must follow the rule. They must pass on, in their turn, and make room for another God and a stupider religion. Or perhaps a better than this? No. That is not likely. History shows that in the matter of religions, we progress backward, and not the other way. No matter, there will be a new God and a new religion. They will be introduced to popularity and acceptance with the only arguments that have ever persuaded any people in this earth to adopt Christianity, or any other religion that they were not born to: the Bible, the sword, the torch, and the axe—the only missionaries that have ever scored a single victory since gods and religions began in the world. After the new God and the new religion have become established in the usual proportions—one-fifth of the world's population ostensible adherents, the four-fifths pagan missionary field, with the missionary scratching its continental back complacently and inefficiently—will the new converts believe in them? Certainly they will. They have always believed in the million gods and religions that have been stuffed down their midriffs. There isn't anything so grotesque or so incredible that the average human being can't believe it. At this very day there are thousands upon thousands of Americans of average intelligence who fully believe in "Science and Health," although they can't understand a line of it, and who also worship the sordid and ignorant old purloiner of that gospel—Mrs. Mary Baker G. Eddy, whom they do absolutely believe to be a member, by adoption, of the Holy Family, and on the way to push the Savior to third place and assume occupancy of His present place, and continue that occupancy during the rest of eternity.

Saturday, June 23, 1906

Concerning the character of the real God.

Let us now consider the real God, the genuine God, the great God, the sublime and supreme God, the authentic Creator of the *real* universe, whose remotenesses are visited by comets only—comets unto which incredibly distant Neptune is merely an outpost, a Sandy Hook to homeward bound spectres of the deeps of space that have not glimpsed it before for generations—a universe not made with hands and suited to an astronomical nursery, but spread abroad through the illimitable reaches of space by the fiat of the real God just mentioned; that God of unthinkable grandeur and majesty, by comparison with whom all the other gods whose myriads infest the feeble imaginations of men are as a swarm of gnats scattered and lost in the infinitudes of the empty sky.

When we think of such a God as this, we cannot associate with Him anything trivial, anything lacking dignity, anything lacking grandeur. We cannot conceive of His passing by Sirius to choose our potato for a footstool. We cannot conceive of His interesting Himself in the affairs of the microscopic human race and enjoying its Sunday flatteries, and experiencing pangs of jealousy when the flatteries grow lax or fail, any more than we can conceive of the Emperor of China being interested in a bottle of microbes and pathetically anxious to stand well with them and harvest their impertinent compliments. If we could conceive of the Emperor of China taking an intemperate interest in his bottle of microbes, we should have to draw the line there; we could not, by any stretch of imagination, conceive of his selecting from these innumerable millions a quarter of a thimbleful of Jew microbes—the least attractive of the whole swarm—and making pets of them and nominating them as his chosen germs, and carrying his infatuation for them so far as to resolve to keep and coddle them alone, and damn all the rest.

When we examine the myriad wonders and glories and charms and perfections of this infinite universe (as we know the universe now), and perceive that there is not a detail of it—from the blade of grass to the giant trees of California, nor from the obscure mountain rivulet to the measureless ocean; nor from the ebb and flow of the tides to the stately motions of the planets—that is not the slave of a system of exact and inflexible law, we seem to know—not suppose nor conjecture, but *know*—that the God that brought this stupendous fabric into being with a flash of thought and framed its laws with another flash of thought, is endowed with limitless power. We seem to know that whatever thing He wishes to do, He can do that thing without anybody's assistance. We also seem to know that when He flashed the universe into being He foresaw everything that would happen in it from that moment until the end of time.

Do we also know that He is a moral being, according to our standard of morals? No. If we know anything at all about it, we know that He is destitute of morals—at least of the human pattern. Do we know that He is just, charitable, kindly, gentle, merciful, compassionate? No. There is no evidence that he is any of these things,—whereas each and every day, as it passes, furnishes us a thousand volumes of evidence, and indeed proof, that he possesses none of these qualities.

When we pray, when we beg, when we implore, does He listen? Does He answer? There is not a single authentic instance of it in human history. Does He silently refuse to listen—refuse to answer? There is nothing resembling proof that He has ever done anything else. From the beginning of time, priests, who have imagined themselves to be His appointed and salaried servants, have gathered together their full numerical strength and simultaneously prayed for rain, and never once got it, when it was not due according to the eternal laws of Nature. Whenever they got it, if they had had a competent Weather Bureau they could have saved themselves the trouble of praying for that rain, because the Bureau could have told them it was coming, anyhow, within twenty-four hours, whether they prayed or saved their sacred wind.

From the beginning of time, whenever a king has lain dangerously ill, the priesthood and some part of the nation have prayed in unison that the king be spared to his grieving and anxious people (in case they were grieving and anxious, which was not usually the rule) and in no instance was their prayer ever answered. When Mr. Garfield lay near to death, the physicians and surgeons knew that nothing could save him, yet at an appointed signal all the pulpits in the United States broke forth with one simultaneous and supplicating appeal for the President's restoration to health. They did this with the same old innocent confidence with which the primeval savage had prayed to his imaginary devils to spare his perishing chief—for that day will never come when facts and experience can teach a pulpit anything useful. Of course the President died, just the same.

Great Britain has a population of forty-one millions. She has eighty thousand pulpits. The Boer population was a hundred and fifty thousand, with a battery of two hundred and ten pulpits. In the beginning of the Boer war, at a signal from the Primate of all England, the eighty thousand English pulpits thundered forth a titanic simultaneous supplication to their God to give the embattled English in South Africa the victory. The little Boer battery of two hundred and ten guns replied with a simultaneous supplication to the same God to give the Boers the victory. If the eighty thousand English clergy had left their prayers unshed and gone to the field, they would have got it—whereas the victory went the other way, and the English forces suffered defeat after defeat at the hands of the Boers. The English pulpit kept discreetly quiet about the result of its effort, but the indiscreet Boer pulpit proclaimed with a loud and exultant voice that it was *its* prayers that had conferred the victory upon the Boers.

The British Government had more confidence in soldiers than in prayer—therefore instead of doubling and trebling the numerical strength of the clergy, it doubled and trebled the strength of its forces in the field. Then the thing happened that always happens—the English whipped the fight, a rather plain indication that the Lord had not listened to either side, and was as indifferent as to who should win as He had always been, from the day that He was evolved, down to the present time—there being no instance on record where He has shown any interest at all in any human squabble, nor whether the good cause won out or lost.

Has this experience taught the pulpit anything? It has not. When the Boer prayers achieved victory—as the Boers believed—the Boers were confirmed once more in their trust in the power of prayer. When a crushing finality of defeat overwhelmed them, later, in the face of their confident supplications, their attitude was not altered, nor their confidence in the righteousness and intelligence of God impaired.

Often we see a mother who has been despoiled, little by little, of everything she held dear in life but a sole remaining dying child; we have seen her, I say, kneeling by its bed and pouring out from a breaking heart beseechings to God for mercy that would get glad and instant answer from any man who had the power to save that child,—yet no such prayer has ever moved a God to pity. Has that mother been convinced? Sometimes—but only for a little while. She was merely a human being, and like the rest—ready to pray again in the next emergency; ready to believe again that she would be heard.

We know that the real God, the Supreme God, the actual Maker of the universe, made everything that is in it. We know that He made all the creatures, from the microbe and the brontosaur down to man and the monkey, and that he knew what would happen to each and every one of them, from the beginning of time to the end of it. In the case of each creature, big or little, He made it an unchanging law that that creature should suffer wanton and unnecessary pains and miseries every day of its life—that by that law these pains and miseries could not be avoided by any diplomacy exercisable by the creature; that its way, from birth to death, should be beset by traps, pitfalls, and gins, ingeniously planned and ingeniously concealed; and that by another law every transgression of a law of Nature, either ignorantly or wittingly committed, should in every instance be visited by a punishment ten-thousandfold out of proportion to the transgression. We stand astonished at the all-comprehensive malice which could patiently descend to the contriving of elaborate tortures for the meanest and pitifulest of the countless kinds of creatures that were to inhabit the earth. The spider was so contrived that she would not eat grass, but must catch flies, and such things, and inflict a slow and horrible death upon them, unaware that her turn would come next. The wasp was so contrived that he also would decline grass and stab the spider, not conferring upon her a swift and merciful death, but merely half paralysing her, then ramming her down into the wasp den, there to live and suffer for days, while the wasp babies should chew her legs off at their leisure. In turn, there was a murderer provided for the wasp, and another murderer for the wasp's murderer, and so on throughout the whole scheme of living creatures in the earth. There isn't one of them that was not designed and appointed to inflict misery and murder on some fellow creature and suffer the same, in turn, from some other murderous fellow creature. In flying into the web the fly is merely guilty of an indiscretion—not a breach of any law—yet the fly's punishment is ten-thousandfold out of proportion to that little indiscretion.

The ten-thousandfold law of punishment is rigorously enforced against every creature, man included. The debt, whether made innocently or guiltily, is promptly collected by Nature—and in this world, without waiting for the ten-billionfold additional penalty appointed—in the case of man—for collection in the next.

This system of atrocious punishments for somethings and nothings begins upon the helpless baby on its first day in the world, and never ceases until its last one. Is there a father who would persecute his baby with unearned colics and the unearned miseries of teething, and follow these with mumps, measles, scarlet fever, and the hundred other persecutions appointed for the unoffending creature? And then follow these, from youth to the grave, with a multitude of ten-thousandfold punishments for laws broken either by intention or indiscretion? With a fine sarcasm, we ennoble God with the title of Father—yet we know quite well that we should hang His style of father wherever we might catch him.

The pulpit's explanation of, and apology for, these crimes, is pathetically destitute of ingenuity. It says they are committed for the benefit of the sufferer. They are to discipline him, purify him, elevate him, train him for the society of the Deity and the angels—send him up sanctified with cancers, tumors, smallpox, and the rest of the educational plant; whereas the pulpit knows that it is stultifying itself, if it knows anything at all. It knows that if this kind of discipline is wise and salutary, we are insane not to adopt it ourselves and apply it to our children.

Does the pulpit really believe that we can improve a purifying and elevating breed of culture invented by the Almighty? It seems to me that if the pulpit honestly believed what it is preaching, in this regard, it would recommend every father to imitate the Almighty's methods.

When the pulpit has succeeded in persuading its congregation that this system has been really wisely and mercifully contrived by the Almighty to discipline and purify and elevate His children whom He so loves, the pulpit judiciously closes its mouth. It doesn't venture further, and explain why these same crimes and cruelties are inflicted upon the higher animals—the alligators, the tigers, and the rest. It even proclaims that the beasts perish—meaning that their sorrowful life begins and ends here; that they go no further; that there is no heaven for them; that neither God nor the angels, nor the redeemed, desire their society on the other side. It puts the pulpit in a comical situation, because in spite of all its ingenuities of explanation and apology it convicts its God of being a wanton and pitiless tyrant in the case of the unoffending beasts. At any rate, and beyond cavil or argument, by its silence it condemns Him irrevocably as a malignant master, after having persuaded the congregation that He is constructed entirely out of compassion, righteousness, and all-pervading love. The pulpit doesn't know how to reconcile these grotesque contradictions, and it doesn't try.

In His destitution of one and all of the qualities which could grace a God and invite respect for Him, and reverence, and worship, the real God, the genuine God, the Maker of the mighty universe, is just like all the other gods in the list. He proves, every day, that He takes no interest in man, nor in the other animals, further than to torture them, slay them, and get out of this pastime such entertainment as it may afford—and do what He can not to get weary of the eternal and changeless monotony of it.

Monday, June 25, 1906

Only hearsay evidence that there is to be a heaven hereafter—Christ does not prove that He is God—Takes up the human race—Man a machine, and not responsible for his actions.

It is to these celestial bandits that the naïve and confiding and illogical human rabbit looks for a heaven of eternal bliss, which is to be his reward for patiently enduring the want and sufferings inflicted upon him here below—unearned sufferings covering terms of two or three years, in some cases; five or ten years in others; thirty, forty, or fifty in others; sixty, seventy, eighty, in others. As usual, where the Deity is Judge, the rewards are vastly out of proportion to the sufferings—and there is no system about the matter anyhow. You do not get any more heaven for suffering eighty years than you get if you die of the measles, at three.

There is no evidence that there is to be a heaven hereafter. If we should find, somewhere, an ancient book in which a dozen unknown men professed to tell all about a blooming and beautiful tropical paradise secreted in an inaccessible valley in the centre of the eternal icebergs which constitute the Antarctic continent—not claiming that they had seen it themselves, but had acquired an intimate knowledge of it through a revelation from God—no Geographical Society in the earth would take any stock in that book; yet that book would be quite as authentic, quite as trustworthy, quite as valuable, evidence as is the Bible. The Bible is just like it. Its heaven exists solely upon hearsay evidence—evidence furnished by unknown persons; persons who did not prove that they had ever been there.

If Christ had really been God, He could have proved it, since nothing is impossible with God. He could have proved it to every individual of His own time and of our time, and of all future time. When God wants to prove that the sun and the moon may be depended upon to do their appointed work every day and every night, He has no difficulty about it. When He wants to prove that man may depend upon finding the constellations in their places every night—although they vanish and seem lost to us every day—He has no difficulty about it. When He wants to prove that the seasons may be depended upon to come and go according to a fixed law, year after year, He has no difficulty about it. Apparently He has desired to prove to us beyond cavil or doubt many millions of things, and He has had no difficulty about proving them all. It is only when He apparently wants to prove a future life to us that His invention fails, and He comes up against a problem which is beyond the reach of His alleged omnipotence. With a message to deliver to men which is of infinitely more importance than all those other messages put together, which He has delivered without difficulty, He can think of no better medium than the poorest of all contrivances—a book. A book written in two languages—to convey a message to a thousand nations—which, in the course of the dragging centuries and eons, must change and change and become finally wholly unintelligible. And even if they remained fixed, like a dead language, it would never be possible to translate the message with perfect clearness into any one of the thousand tongues, at any time.

According to the hearsay evidence, the character of every conspicuous god is made up of love, justice, compassion, forgiveness, sorrow for all suffering and desire to extinguish it. Opposed to this beautiful character—built wholly upon valueless hearsay evidence—is the absolutely authentic evidence furnished us every day in the year, and verifiable by our eyes and our other senses, that the real character of these gods is destitute of love, mercy, compassion, justice, and other gentle and excellent qualities, and is made up of all imaginable cruelties, persecutions, and injustices. The hearsay character rests upon evidence only—exceedingly doubtful evidence. The real character rests upon proof—proof unassailable.

Is it logical to expect of gods whose unceasing and unchanging pastime is the malignant persecution of innocent men and animals, that they are going to provide an eternity of bliss, presently, for these very same creatures? If King Leopold II, the Butcher, should proclaim that out of each hundred innocent and unoffending Congo negroes he is going to save one from humiliation, starvation, and assassination, and fetch that one home to Belgium to live with him in his palace and feed at his table, how many people would believe it? Everybody would say "A person's character is a permanent thing. This act would not be in accordance with that butcher's character. Leopold's character is established beyond possibility of change, and it could never occur to him to do this kindly thing."

Leopold's character *is* established. The character of the conspicuous gods is also established. It is distinctly illogical to suppose that either Leopold of Belgium or the heavenly Leopolds are ever going to think of inviting any fraction of their victims to the royal table and the comforts and conveniences of the regal palace.

According to hearsay evidence, the conspicuous gods make a pet of one victim in a hundred—select him arbitrarily, without regard to whether he's any better than the other ninety-nine or not—but damn the ninety-nine through all eternity, without examining into their case. But for one slight defect this would be logical, and would properly reflect the known character of the gods—that defect is the gratuitous and unplausible suggestion that one in a hundred is permitted to pull through. It is not likely that there will be a heaven hereafter. It is exceedingly likely that there will be a hell—and it is nearly dead certain that nobody is going to escape it.

As to the human race. There are many pretty and winning things about the human race. It is perhaps the poorest of all the inventions of all the gods, but it has never suspected it once. There is nothing prettier than its naïve and complacent appreciation of itself. It comes out frankly and proclaims, without bashfulness, or any sign of a blush, that it is the noblest work of God. It has had a billion opportunities to know better, but all signs fail with this ass. I could say harsh things about it, but I cannot bring myself to do it—it is like hitting a child.

Man is not to blame for what he is. He didn't make himself. He has no control over himself. All the control is vested in his temperament—which he did not create—and in the circumstances which hedge him round, from the cradle to the grave, and which he did not devise and cannot change by any act of his will, for the reason that he has no will. He is as purely a piece of automatic mechanism as is a watch, and can no more dictate or influence his actions than can the watch. He is a subject for pity, not blame—and not contempt. He is flung head over heels into this world without ever a chance to decline, and straightway he conceives and accepts the notion that he is in some mysterious way under obligations to the unknown Power that inflicted this outrage upon him—and thenceforth he considers himself responsible to that Power for every act of his life, and punishable for such of his acts as do not meet with the approval of that Power—yet that same man would argue quite differently if a human tyrant should capture him and put chains upon him and make him a slave. He would say that the tyrant had no right to do that; that the tyrant had no right to put commands upon him of any kind, and require obedience; that the tyrant had no right to compel him to commit murder and then put the responsibility for the murder upon him. Man constantly makes a most strange distinction between man and his Maker, in the matter of morals. He requires of his fellow man obedience to a very creditable code of morals, but he observes without shame or disapproval his God's utter destitution of morals.

God ingeniously contrived man in such a way that he could not escape obedience to the laws of his passions, his appetites, and his various unpleasant and undesirable qualities. God has so contrived him that all his goings out and comings in are beset by traps which he cannot possibly avoid, and which compel him to commit what are called sins—and then God punishes him for doing these very things which from the beginning of time He had always intended that he should do. Man is a machine, and God made it—without invitation from any one. Whoever makes a machine, here below, is responsible for that machine's performance. No one would think of such a thing as trying to put the responsibility upon the machine itself. We all know perfectly well—though we all conceal it, just as I am doing, until I shall be dead, and out of reach of public opinion—we all know, I say, that God, and God alone, is responsible for every act and word of a human being's life between cradle and grave. We know it perfectly well. In our secret hearts we haven't the slightest doubt of it. In our secret hearts we have no hesitation in proclaiming as an unthinking fool anybody who thinks he believes that he is by any possibility capable of committing a sin against God—or who thinks he thinks he is under obligations to God and owes Him thanks, reverence, and worship.

New York, July 17, 1906

Five or six weeks ago, when I was dictating those chapters of this autobiography which detail my disastrous adventures with Charles H. Webb, my first publisher; the American Publishing Company, my second publisher; and Charles L. Webster, my third publisher, I was by no means suspecting that I was on the eve of a disastrous adventure with still another publisher, the great corporation of Harper and Brothers. Perhaps disastrous is not just the term for this last adventure; possibly ridiculous is the better word. There was a sort of dignity about my adventure with Elisha Bliss, junior, of the American Publishing Company, in 1872, but that quality is quite lacking in this present one with Harper and Brothers. Bliss, in beguiling me into the belief that in changing the agreed wording of the contract for "Roughing It" from "half profit over and above cost of manufacture" to a specified royalty, was setting a trap for me, whereby he expected to rob me of about thirty thousand dollars, a trick which succeeded, as I have already explained. There was a sort of dignity about that, for the reason that thirty thousand dollars was a great sum of money to that poor little publishing company, and worth the sinful trouble which Bliss took to acquire it. In the present instance, the trap which Mr. Duneka set for me could result in a pecuniary advantage to Harper and Brothers of only ten or twelve thousand dollars, I imagine, and therefore, as I have suggested, the trick lacked dignity.

My experiences with Webb, and Bliss, and Webster stand as abiding proof that when it comes to examining a contract and understanding it, I am an incapable. I have shown that I misread and misunderstood those contracts in every instance. My present experience is excellent evidence that I have no more ability in understanding a contract to-day than I had then. I wonder who is really the man hurt in a swindle—eventually: the perpetrator of it or the confiding ass who suffers from it? Bliss captured my thirty thousand dollars, but I made it cost him a quarter of a million thirteen years afterward. However, never mind this conundrum, I must get to the beginning of my subject.

The beginning was three years ago. I was anxious to get my books concentrated in one publisher's hands. The Harpers had half of them, and the American Publishing Company had the other half. Collier wanted to publish a cheap edition of them by subscription, and he offered to guarantee a sale of forty thousand sets a year. A concentration of the books in one publisher's hands I presently found to be impossible, but Duneka said that he would be quite willing to give Bliss the subscription rights in the Harper books if Bliss would give him in return the trade rights in the Bliss books. Duneka said that he had made this very offer to Bliss two years before. I said I didn't see any reason why Bliss should not accept these terms. I placed the matter before Bliss, and at first he was willing, but when I went back to Duneka with that word, Duneka was no longer willing himself; he had heard of the Collier offer, and had changed his mind. That was my first experience of Mr. Duneka's facility in going back on his word.

At the end of 1902 I wrote some Christian Science articles, and published three of them in the *North American Review.* The rest of the articles were not to be published serially, but were to be joined to the first three and issued in book form; and that announcement was made. Duneka had the remaining matter set up and forwarded to me in the form of galley-proofs. I read and revised these and put the book in shape for the composing-room. I took it to Mr. Duneka; he did not break out into any enthusiasms about it, in fact he looked embarrassed. I inquired as to what might be the matter, and he developed the fact that he was afraid of the Christian Scientists. He said they were growing very strong, and would it be to my interest to publish such a book and antagonize this growing power? also, would it be to the interest of Harper and Brothers to antagonize that power? I said that if he was afraid, I didn't wish to push a dangerous book upon him, and I would publish it elsewhere; but he said "No; by no means no, if the book must be published, we wish to publish it ourselves." But I said I didn't want a publisher who was afraid, and I would rather take it elsewhere. Also, I said that my interest in a book lay in the writing of it, so it was not a matter of great consequence to me whether it was published or not. Let it be suppressed. But how was it to be suppressed? The announcement had gone forth that it was to be published in book form at once. How was the suppression to be managed? Mr. Duneka said that that would be very easy, not a line need go into print about it; that he would privately inform the trade that it was found that the book could not be issued in time for the spring trade, therefore its publication had been postponed until the fall. He said that by that time the trade would have forgotten that there was any such book, and we should not hear anything more about it. It was then agreed that Mr. Duneka should quiet the book down and prepare it for its grave without letting anything get into print about it. This was a distinct understanding, a plain and straightforward agreement, yet my back was hardly turned before a notice to this effect appeared in the *Publishers' Weekly* of April 11th, 1903:

> Neither Harper and Brothers nor the *North American Review* will publish Mark Twain's Christian Science book. All orders have been canceled.

Only one interpretation can be put upon this language: that Harper and Brothers had refused my book, and were offensively proud of having done it. This was my second experience with Mr. Duneka as a promise-keeper.

He probably supposed that I would never see that notice, and in fact it was not likely that I would see it; but a Pittsburgh bookseller sent it to me, and inquired why I had lost my grip and was afraid to issue the book. That was three years ago. Inquiries followed, by letter, from persons in this country and in England, and I explained to them that the publication of the book was not my affair, that it was in the hands of Harper and Brothers, and they could best explain why it was not issued. Then other letters began to come from these inquirers, which said that upon application to Harper and Brothers for an explanation of why the book was not issued, the reply was that I had desired them to suppress the book.

I attributed all these slynesses to Mr. Duneka, who is the manager at Harpers, and could tell the inquirers the truth if he wanted to, and could prevent the dissemination of spurious information if he so desired. The inquiries continued to come, and at last I suggested that perhaps it would be best to issue the book. Then Mr. Duneka had a happy idea, and said he would make that book volume XXIV of my Collected Works, and sell it only to persons ordering a whole set, and in that way no mention of the book would get into print, and no harm would be done. Mr. Duneka has reiterated his promise to get out of the scrape in that way several times. Up to date he has not kept his word, and I have never suspected him of intending to keep it. As late as three months ago, one of these inquiry-letters came to me from England. I referred the writer to Harper and Brothers. They answered him, and promptly put the blame on me, as usual.

Some time ago I wrote an unfriendly article about the Butcher, King Leopold of Belgium, and offered it to Mr. Duneka. He accepted it, and thought he ought to publish it as soon as possible, because he had employed Mr. Nevinson to make a tour through Portuguese Africa and expose the cruelties which the Portuguese were perpetrating upon the helpless blacks there, and my article would have an opportunity to precede Mr. Nevinson's exposures and break the road in front of him. But the article did not appear. It continued to fail to appear, and kept on failing to appear. Finally, Mr. Nevinson's first article appeared, and the position was changed—he was breaking ground for me. I thought I knew what the trouble was. Mr. Duneka is a Roman Catholic, and anything like a criticism of that Church, or of an individual connected with it, gives Mr. Duneka the dry gripes. Finally, I asked him when that article was going to appear. He explained that Mr. Nevinson's articles were ended now, and it would be very bad policy to follow them with my article, because I would overshadow him and blot him out. This was very complimentary, but I was not fishing for compliments, and it was not altogether satisfactory. When Mr. Duneka needs a pretext for not doing a thing he is handy in finding one. When time and circumstances take the tuck out of that pretext, he is handy in finding a fresh one to take its place. I have noticed these ingenuities more than once, and have admired them. It was plain that Mr. Duneka was afraid of that article. He is interesting. He grows more and more interesting every day. He has inspirations which could enter no human head but his own. A short story called "A Horse's Tale," which will begin in the August number of *Harper's Magazine,* has for its principal stage the bull ring in Spain. In the proof sheets Mr. Duneka suggested that we change Spain to Mexico, and have the performance there. The fact that the performance could not perform in Mexico with any considerable effect did not trouble Mr. Duneka. What he was shuddering about was that in the story the Spanish priests hurried through their sacred functions on Sundays in order to get to the bull ring in time to see the butcheries. The fact that this was merely a fact and not an invention could not reconcile Mr. Duneka to its publication. I judge that that was the trouble with him; he did not explain what the trouble was. There could be nothing else in the story that could explain his attitude. I have half a dozen novels half finished, and now and then as the years go by I add a chapter or two to one or another of them as the notion strikes me, and if I live forty years I shall finish several of the six. Last summer, Mr. Duneka wanted to look at one of these stories, a story whose scene is laid in the Middle Ages, and in it he found a drunken and profane Catholic priest—a spectacle which was as common in Europe four hundred years ago as Dunekas are in hell to-day. Of course it made him shudder, and he wanted that priest reformed or left out. Mr. Duneka seems to do four-fifths of the editing of everything that comes to Harper and Brothers for publication, and he certainly has a good literary instinct and judgment as long as his religion does not get into his way.

My experience has taught me that Mr. Duneka's statements are not valuable, that his promises are not to be relied upon, and that he is very timid, even pathetically timid; but that he would set a trap for me, and try to cheat me out of a small sum of money is a new departure in his character. I never suspected him of any disposition to pick my pocket, until now.

My contract with the Harpers of three years ago puts all my books permanently in their possession; not only my old books, but also any new books which I may write. The old books are listed in that contract, and among them appears "Mark Twain's Library of Humor." The Harpers pay me one and the same royalty upon all those old books (20 per cent). Now if Harper and Brothers choose to renew the dress of any one of these old books and put it on the market, they do not have to ask me for permission; they can do it without saying anything to me. They would only need to pay me the 20 per cent royalty. They could issue the old "Library of Humor" without saying anything to me about it, though they would know when they did it that I would be very much obliged to them if they did nothing of the kind. I made up that book a good many years ago, at a time when I thought that such a book would be valuable and popular. I took the utmost pains with its preparation. I also paid out money in order that the work might be well done—five thousand dollars. I got two experts to help me, Mr. Howells and Charles Hopkins Clark, now editor of the Hartford *Courant.* I bought all the humorous books I could find. Mr. Clark read them carefully through, marking each article with a capital "A," or "B," or "C," according to whether it was his first, second, or third choice. Then Mr. Howells went over the indicated articles, and marked his first and second choice. Then I went over them myself and made the final choice. A great deal of honest work was expended upon the book. It has lain out of print now for as many as seven years, and I have had no desire to see it dug up and sent adrift again. Mr. Duneka said that he had heard that a "pirate" out West was going to republish the book, on the plea that its abandonment for so many years had nullified the copyright. Therefore, he thought we ought to beat that game by *"ostensibly"* republishing the book ourselves, in the interest of my reputation, and beat that "pirate." He told me that we should only need to set up that old book again (the plates were long ago destroyed), and issue it in some exceedingly cheap form, and make a merely *"ostensible"* publication of it (not a real publication), put a few copies on sale, and this game would beat the "pirate." I said "Go ahead and do it," for I was not aware that I was now dealing with a "pirate" close at home. I thought he proposed to make it a fifty-cent book in paper covers. I cannot swear that he said that, but I can swear that that was the impression which he gave me, and I know that he *intended* to give me that impression. Then he said that as there was "no money in the book for either of us" (those are his words), he would not be able to pay me much of a royalty. I said I was indifferent as to that—make the royalty what he pleased. He suggested 3 per cent. I wrote him and consented to that. By and by he sent me a paper to sign, and of course I signed it; also, of course, I did just as I did with those ancient publishers: read it without studying it; that would inevitably happen, particularly with Mr. Duneka, whose honesty I had not doubted. I made several contracts with Bliss after the fatal one, but I was always suspecting him then, and I examined those contracts very carefully; but I don't examine contracts carefully when I think I am dealing with a man who is clean and honest. I shall be ready for Mr. Duneka next time. This paper which I signed had one detail in it which I did not notice, and to which I would have attached no importance if I had noticed it. That detail privileges Mr. Duneka to add some new matter to that old book and "bring it up to date." If I had been suspecting Mr. Duneka, that might have made me stop and think, and also wonder why you *want* new matter in a book which is not really being published, but only *"ostensibly"* published? why you *want* to bring a book "up to date" when there is "no money in it for either of us"? but, as I say, I never noticed that phrase, and if I had noticed it, I should have thought it was only one of Mr. Duneka's heaven-sent inspirations and had nothing in it.

About the end of last April, Mr. Duneka began to vomit "Libraries of Humor" upon the public, and by and by I noticed two things: that these libraries were *not* my old book, and that the price was *not* cheap. Before I could rise to the size of the game Mr. Duneka was playing, he had spewed out three of these volumes and was ready to spew another. I have never examined one of these books further than to read through the Table of Authors who had furnished the material. I saw that they were modern authors. It may turn out that Mr. Duneka has put in one, or two, or three articles from the old book, but if this is true, it is neither according to the original agreement between him and me, nor in accordance with the paper which I signed. He has advertised the book largely, enthusiastically, shoutingly. He has called it "Mark Twain's Library of Humor," which it is *not.* He has advertised me as being the *"editor"* of it, whereas I had nothing to do with its construction, nor have I ever edited a line of it.

When an author is wholly unknown, his royalty is, as a rule, 10 per cent; when he is better known it reaches 15 per cent; and when he is widely known it is 20 per cent. If Mr. Duneka had published the old book as it stood, without speaking to me, our contract would oblige him to pay me 20 per cent; but he shrewdly beguiled me into the notion that the book was not being really *published,* that there was "no money in it for his house or for me," and that therefore, in the circumstances, 3 per cent would be enough to pay me. I didn't care whether he paid me *any* per cent or not, I was not interested in the matter; but if he had come to me and said that he proposed to get up a "Library of Humor" himself, a new one, full of fresh matter, and that he would like to get me to put my name to it as the constructor and editor of it; and that he was going to advertise it largely, charge six dollars for it, (which is *double* the price of *my* old "Library"), and sell as many sets as he could, would he venture to ask me to accept 3 per cent royalty as pay for my share of this contemptible crime, this bare-faced proposal to swindle the public with a book which was not mine in any sense? It is unbelievable. If I try to imagine Macmillan, or Scribner, or Doubleday, or any other respectable publisher, proposing to me to let him put my name on a book which I did not make, and accept of 3 per cent royalty, or 10 per cent, or 20 per cent, or 100 per cent, I find myself unable to conceive of such a romance. None of these publishers would think of asking me to assume the fatherhood of a book which I was neither to prepare nor to edit, and accept eighteen cents as my reward out of a selling price of six dollars.

I have directed Mr. Duneka, through my legal counsel, to suppress that fraudulent book at once, and stop robbing the public under my name, and he has promised to do so. The situation is unthinkably grotesque. The book has been out such a little while that the profit on it cannot have amounted to more than ten or twelve thousand dollars. Mr. Duneka would know that I would repudiate the book as soon as I recognized its character. He could hope to get nothing out of it but that ten or twelve thousand dollars, and he would then have to shelve it; and so, as I say, it is unthinkable that the manager of a millionaire concern like the Harper Corporation would be willing to destroy the pleasant relations existing between the Corporation and me for so small a sum as ten or twelve thousand dollars. It would seem that none but a fool would think of such an idea as that, and yet I may be mistaken—possibly it is wisdom. In these days of big graft, and little graft, and universal graft, it is difficult to say what is wisdom and what isn't. It is a marvelous spectacle, an incredible spectacle, this millionaire corporation filching pennies from its own child! It seems to me that this is reducing graft to its cheapest and meanest terms.

Monday, July 30, 1906

Mr. Clemens returns to Dublin after a four or five weeks' vacation spent partly in New York attending to business matters connected with "Library of Humor," and partly at Fairhaven with Mr. Rogers—The Laura Wright episode; first meeting on Mississippi steamboat, and letter just received.

I am back again in this country house in the New Hampshire hills after an absence of four or five weeks—since about the 25th of June. The chapter which precedes the present one, and which is dated New York July 17th, explains the cause of this absence. I dictated that chapter in New York, at the time, in order that I might get the details crystallized into language while they were fresh in my mind.

The sudden spewing of that "Library of Humor" upon an unoffending public, under my name and ostensibly by my authority, was one of the most unexpected things that has ever happened to me. For cool impudence and cold rascality, I doubt if the match of it can be found anywhere in the history of book publishing. I went down to New York full of a warm desire to make trouble, but of course I consulted H. H. Rogers before committing any overt acts, for many years of edifying experience have taught me that whenever in a matter of business I proceed without first taking Mr. Rogers's judgment upon the matter, I do the wrong thing. In the present case, he advised that I make no public trouble; no public exposure of Mr. Duneka. He said that an exposure of Duneka would be an exposure of the House of Harper and Brothers, whereas the House of Harper and Brothers was not present to defend itself, since Colonel Harvey, the head of it, was in Europe. Edward Lauterbach, my legal counsel, being of the like opinion, no noise was made.

Mr. Lauterbach telephoned Duneka to come and talk about the matter. Duneka was deposited in one of Mr. Lauterbach's offices, and Lauterbach wanted me to go in there and talk with him. I said he had already advised me not to make any trouble—still I was willing to take the new advice, but thought it would be best if I should first rehearse before Lauterbach and the Harper lawyer, Larkin, who was present, the remarks I should make to Mr. Duneka. I rehearsed—and they both said "Try it in a church first"—and they agreed that I could do more good staying out of that conference than by trying to assist it.

I had several points to make, but was quite willing to confine myself to the principal one and leave the others alone until the head of the Corporation should get back from England, which would be in the course of a week or two. That principal point was the instant suppression of that bastard book and the destruction of the plates and all copies of the book that were in the Harpers' hands. That was all that I required of Mr. Duneka, and he was effusively glad to comply, and was full of apologies and regrets for what he had done.

While waiting for Harvey's return from England, I lived on board Mr. Rogers's yacht, nights, lying at anchor far down the Bay, where it was cool, returning to the city at breakfast-time, mornings, and living at home, at 21 Fifth Avenue, during the days, whence I transacted such other business as came my way, by telephone. Fridays, at 9 a.m., we sailed for Fairhaven, Massachusetts, Mr. Rogers's country home, a trip of about eight hours, by that smart boat. We spent the Saturday, and half of each Sunday, there, then sailed for New York again at lunch-time, Sundays. It was the pleasantest vacation I have ever had in my life, and I was not gratified when my business finally released me and permitted me to get back to the hills and go to work.

One day in Fairhaven, while playing billiards with a member of the family, a chance remark called to my mind an early sweetheart of mine, and I fell to talking about her. I hadn't seen her for forty-eight years; but no matter, I found that I remembered her quite vividly, and that she possessed a lively interest for me notwithstanding that prodigious interval of time that had spread its vacancy between her and me. She wasn't yet fifteen when I knew her. It was in the summertime, and she had gone down the Mississippi from St. Louis to New Orleans as guest of a relative of hers who was a pilot on the *John J. Roe,* a steamboat whose officers I knew very well, as I had served a term as steersman in that boat's pilot-house. She was a freighter. She was not licensed to carry passengers, but she always had a dozen on board, and they were privileged to be there because they were not registered; they paid no fare; they were guests of the Captain, and nobody was responsible for them if anything of a fatal nature happened to them. It was a delightful old tug, and she had a very spacious boiler-deck—just the place for moonlight dancing and daylight frolics, and such things were always happening. She was a charmingly leisurely boat, and the slowest one on the planet. Up-stream she couldn't even beat an island; down-stream she was never able to overtake the current. But she was a love of a steamboat. Mark Leavenworth, her captain, was a giant, and hospitable and good-natured, which is the way of giants. Zeb, his brother, was another giant possessed of the same qualities, and of a laugh which could be heard from Vicksburg to Nebraska. He was one of the pilots, and Beck Jolly was another. Jolly was very handsome, very graceful, very intelligent, companionable—a fine character—and he had the manners of a duke. If that is too strong I will say a viscount. Beck Jolly was a beautiful creature to look at. But it's different now. I saw him four years ago, and he had white hair, and not much of it; two sets of cheeks; a cataract of chins; and by and large he looked like a gasometer. The clerks, the mates, the chief steward, and all officials, big and little, of the *John J. Roe,* were simple-hearted folk and overflowing with good-fellowship and the milk of human kindness. They had all been reared on farms in the interior of Indiana, and they had brought the simple farm ways and farm spirit to that steamboat and had domesticated it there. When she was on a voyage there was nothing in her to suggest a steamboat. One didn't seem to be on board a steamboat at all. He was floating around on a farm. Nothing in this world pleasanter than this can be imagined.

At the time I speak of I had fallen out of the heaven of the *John J. Roe* and was steering for Brown, on the swift passenger packet, the *Pennsylvania,* a boat which presently blew up and killed my brother Henry. On a memorable trip, the *Pennsylvania* arrived at New Orleans, and when she was berthed I discovered that her stern lapped the fo'castle of the *John J. Roe.* I went aft, climbed over the rail of the ladies' cabin, and from that point jumped aboard the *Roe,* landing on that spacious boiler-deck of hers. It was like arriving at home at the farm-house after a long absence. It was the same delight to me to meet and shake hands with the Leavenworths and the rest of that dear family of steamboating backwoodsmen and hay-seeds as if they had all been blood kin to me. As usual, there were a dozen passengers, male and female, young and old; and as usual they were of the hearty and likable sort affected by the *John J. Roe* farmers. Now, out of their midst, floating upon my enchanted vision, came that slip of a girl of whom I have spoken—that instantly elected sweetheart out of the remotenesses of interior Missouri—a frank and simple and winsome child who had never been away from home in her life before, and had brought with her to these distant regions the freshness and the fragrance of her own prairies.

I can state the rest, I think, in a very few words. I was not four inches from that girl's elbow during our waking hours for the next three days. Then there came a sudden interruption. Zeb Leavenworth came flying aft shouting "The *Pennsylvania* is backing out." I fled at my best speed, and as I broke out upon that great boiler-deck the *Pennsylvania* was gliding sternward past it. I made a flying leap and just did manage to make the connection, and nothing to spare. My toes found room on the guard; my finger-ends hooked themselves upon the guard-rail, and a quartermaster made a snatch for me and hauled me aboard.

That comely child, that charming child, was Laura M. Wright, and I could see her with perfect distinctness in the unfaded bloom of her youth, with her plaited tails dangling from her young head and her white summer frock puffing about in the wind of that ancient Mississippi time—I could see all this with perfect distinctness when I was telling about it over the billiard table in Fairhaven last Saturday. And I finished with the remark "I never saw her afterward. It is now forty-eight years, one month and twenty-seven days, since that parting, and no word has ever passed between us since."

I reached home from Fairhaven last Wednesday and found a letter from Laura Wright. It shook me to the foundations. The plaited tails fell away; the peachy young face vanished; the fluffy short frock along with it; and in the place of that care-free little girl of forty-eight years ago, I imagined the world-worn and trouble-worn widow of sixty-two. Laura's letter was an appeal to me for pecuniary help for herself and for her disabled son, who, as she incidentally mentioned, is thirty-seven years old. She is a school-teacher. She is in need of a thousand dollars, and I sent it.

It is an awful world—it is a fiendish world. When I knew that child her father was an honored Judge of a high court in the middle of Missouri, and was a rich man, as riches were estimated in that day and region. What had that girl done, what crime had she committed, that she must be punished with poverty and drudgery in her old age? However, let me get right away from this subject before I get warmed up and say indiscreet things—BeJesus!

Tuesday, July 31, 1906

Colonel Harvey arrives to-night—Letter from Clara Clemens—Mr. Clemens receives copy of Mr. Duneka's "Library of Humor"—Seventy-eight other humorists contained therein—Letter from Mr. Orr referring to "1601"—Three letters from John Hay referring to same—Mr. Clemens's reply—Mr. Clemens tells why he wrote "1601" and what it is, and of the private printing of several copies.

Colonel Harvey will arrive here to-night, to remain a day or two, and we shall have no trouble in straightening out the tangle which has been made in our affairs.

Since I got back here I have received a letter from my daughter Clara, who is spending her summer at Norfolk, Connecticut, and I shall at once dispatch a copy of it to Howells, for it contains a miracle which he and I were talking privately about last year—a compliment from child to father. We were remarking upon the fact that illustrious authors can by their talents compel compliments from everybody but their own children. We are so close to them that our magnitude does not impress them. It is a commonplace to them, and does not thrill, does not stun, does not overawe. Naturally, we particularly want the compliments which we can't get. When at last it comes spontaneously from the child—a thing which almost never happens—we are not merely gratified beyond all reason, but are struck dumb with pleasant astonishment. I shall insert Clara's compliment here, where it can't get lost.

> Uncle Joe* came to see me to-day and I really can't imagine what prompted him to do such a generous thing, but I appreciated it though I found no way to prove or even express it.
>
> He reminded me more than ever of you in his vivid, dramatic, moving, masterly way of painting an impressionist picture whenever he spoke—you two are alike also in tones of voice and anticipatory gesture. I had a rich enjoyment in his visit and felt very much like the kings that command private amusements that they share with no one.
>
> Uncle Joe sent you his love and spoke warmly of your Howells article which I have just this minute read with utmost delight. It has led me to read "Venetian Days"—or rather to the intention of reading it—as soon as I can procure it, and has given me many minutes of laughter over the delicious criticism of stage-directions. Of course your thoughts are funny in themselves, but not commandingly funny till you have dressed them up in that never-failing style of yours. The extract from "Venetian Days" is so beautiful that when one has finished it one seems to have been lying on a floating support of snowflakes, and one dreads to leave it, in the same way that one hates to be pulled from a moment of reverie at sea, when, half hypnotized, one's vague thoughts seem to move deliciously with the waves.

The western pirate of whom Duneka had heard rumor has really published his book, and my copyright lawyer has sent me a copy of it—a great fat, coarse, offensive volume, not with my name on it as perpetrator, but with its back inflamed with a big picture of me in lurid colors; placed there, of course, to indicate that I am the author of the crime. This book is a very interesting curiosity, in one way. It reveals the surprising fact that within the compass of these forty years wherein I have been playing professional humorist before the public, I have had for company seventy-eight other American humorists. Each and every one of the seventy-eight rose in my time, became conspicuous and popular, and, by and by, vanished. A number of these names were as familiar in their day as are the names of George Ade and Dooley to-day—yet they have all so completely passed from sight now that there is probably not a youth of fifteen years of age in the country whose eye would light with recognition at the mention of any one of the seventy-eight names.

This book is a cemetery; and as I glance through it I am reminded of my visit to the cemetery in Hannibal, Missouri, four years ago, where almost every tombstone recorded

* Reverend Joseph H. Twichell—"uncle" by courtesy.

a forgotten name that had been familiar and pleasant to my ear when I was a boy there fifty years before.

In this mortuary volume I find Nasby, Artemus Ward, Yawcob Strauss, Derby, Burdette, Eli Perkins, the "Danbury News Man," Orpheus C. Kerr, Smith O'Brien, Josh Billings, and a score of others, maybe twoscore, whose writings and sayings were once in everybody's mouth but are now heard of no more, and are no longer mentioned. Seventy-eight seems an incredible crop of well-known humorists for one forty-year period to have produced, and yet this book has not harvested the entire crop—far from it. It has no mention of Ike Partington, once so welcome and so well known; it has no mention of Doesticks, nor of the Pfaff crowd—nor of Artemus Ward's numerous and perishable imitators; nor of three very popular Southern humorists whose names I am not able to recall; nor of a dozen other sparkling transients whose light shone for a time but has now, years ago, gone out.

Why have they perished? Because they were merely humorists. Humorists of the "mere" sort cannot survive. Humor is only a fragrance, a decoration. Often it is merely an odd trick of speech and spelling, as in the case of Ward and Billings and Nasby and the "Disbanded Volunteer," and presently the fashion passes, and the fame along with it. There are those who say a novel should be a work of art solely, and you must not preach in it, you must not teach in it. That may be true as regards novels, but it is not true as regards humor. Humor must not *professedly* teach, it must not professedly preach; but it must do both if it would live forever. By forever, I mean thirty years. With all its preaching it is not likely to outlive so long a term as that. The very things it preaches about, and which are novelties when it preaches about them, can cease to be novelties and become commonplaces in thirty years. Then that sermon can thenceforth interest no one.

I have always preached. That is the reason that I have lasted thirty years. If the humor came of its own accord and uninvited, I have allowed it a place in my sermon, but I was not writing the sermon for the sake of the humor. I should have written the sermon just the same, whether any humor applied for admission or not. I am saying these vain things in this frank way because I am a dead person speaking from the grave. Even I would be too modest to say them in life. I think we never become really and genuinely our entire and honest selves until we are dead—and not then until we have been dead years and years. People ought to start dead, and then they would be honest so much earlier.

Among the letters awaiting me when I got back from New York was this one:

Cleveland June 28 1906

My dear Sir

Having seen some letters of the late John Hay, copies of which I enclose, I am somewhat anxious to know the title of the piece mentioned, or whether it is printed in your published writings.

Did you know Alexander Gunn, to whom Hay's letters were addressed?

An answer at your convenience will greatly oblige.

Very truly yours
Chas. Orr

The letters referred to by Mr. Orr are the following:

June 21 1880

Dear Gunn

Are you in Cleveland for all this week? If you will say yes by return mail I have a masterpiece to submit to your consideration which is only in my hands for a few days.

Yours, very much worritted by the depravity of Christendom,

Hay

Letter No. 2 discloses Hay's own high opinion of the effort and his deep concern for its safety.

June 24 1880

My dear Gunn

Here it is. It was written by Mark Twain in a serious effort to bring back our literature and philosophy to the sober and chaste Elizabethan standard. But the taste of the present day is too corrupt for anything so classic. He has not yet been able even to find a publisher. The Globe has not yet recovered from Downey's inroad, and they won't touch it.

I send it to you as one of the few lingering relics of that race of appreciative critics who know a good thing when they see it.

Read it with reverence and gratitude and send it back to me; for Mark is impatient to see once more his wandering offspring.

Yours
HAY

No. 3 makes it quite clear that Gunn had confirmed the judgment of Hay.

Washington DC July 7 1880

My dear Gunn

I have your letter, and the proposition which you make to pull a few proofs of the masterpiece is highly attractive, and of course highly immoral. I cannot properly consent to it, and I am afraid the great man would think I was taking an unfair advantage of his confidence. Please send back the document as soon as you can, and if, in spite of my prohibition, you take these proofs, save me one.

Very truly yours
John Hay

I replied to Mr. Orr as follows:

Dublin, New Hampshire.
July 30, 1906.

Dear Mr. Orr:

I cannot thank you enough for sending me copies of John Hay's notes to Mr. Gunn. In the matter of humor, what an unsurpassable touch John Hay had! I may have known Alexander Gunn in those ancient days, but the name does not sound familiar to me.

The title of the piece is "1601." The piece is a supposititious conversation which takes place in Queen Elizabeth's closet in that year, between the Queen and Shakspeare, Ben Jonson, Francis Bacon, Beaumont, Sir Walter Raleigh, the Duchess of Bilgewater, and one or two others; and is not—as John Hay mistakenly supposes—"a serious effort to bring back our literature and philosophy to the sober and chaste Elizabethan standard;" no, the object was only a serious attempt to reveal to Rev. Joe Twichell the picturesqueness of parlor conversation in Elizabeth's time; therefore if there is a decent or delicate word findable in it, it is because I overlooked it. I hasten to assure you that it is *not* printed in my published writings.

"1601" was so be-praised by the archeological scholars of a quarter of a century ago, that I was rather inordinately vain of it. At that time it had been privately printed in several countries, among them Japan. A sumptuous edition on large paper, rough-edged, was made by Lieut. C. E. S. Wood at West Point—an edition of 50 copies—and distributed among popes and kings and such people. In England copies of that issue were worth 20 guineas when I was there six years ago, and none to be had. I thank you again, and am,

Yours very truly,
S. L. Clemens.

Dear me, but John Hay's letters do carry me back over a long stretch of time! Joe Twichell's head was black then; mine was brown. To-day both are as white and sparkly as a London footman's.

"1601" was a letter which I wrote to Twichell, about 1876, from my study at Quarry Farm one summer day when I ought to have been better employed. I remember the incident very well. I had been diligently reading up for a story which I was minded to write—"The Prince and the Pauper." I was reading ancient English books with the purpose of saturating myself with archaic English to a degree which would enable me to do plausible imitations of it in a fairly easy and unlabored way. In one of these old books I came across a brief conversation which powerfully impressed me, as I had never been impressed before, with the frank indelicacies of speech permissible among ladies and gentlemen in that ancient time. I was thus powerfully impressed because this conversation seemed *real,* whereas that kind of talk had not seemed real to me before. It had merely seemed Rabelaisian—exaggerated, artificial, made up by the author for his passing needs. It had not seemed to me that the blushful passages in Shakspeare were of a sort which Shakspeare had actually heard people use, but were inventions of his own—liberties which he had taken with the facts, under the protection of a poet's license.

But here at last was one of those dreadful conversations which commended itself to me as being absolutely real, and as being the kind of talk which ladies and gentlemen did actually indulge in in those pleasant and lamented ancient days now gone from us forever. I was immediately full of a desire to practise my archaics, and contrive one of those stirring conversations out of my own head. I thought I would practise on Twichell. I have always practised doubtful things on Twichell from the beginning, thirty-nine years ago.

So I contrived that meeting of the illustrious personages in Queen Elizabeth's private parlor, and started a most picturesque and lurid and scandalous conversation between them. The Queen's cup-bearer, a dried-up old nobleman, was present to take down the talk—not that he wanted to do it, but because it was the Queen's desire and he had to. He loathed all those people because they were of offensively low birth, and because they hadn't a thing to recommend them except their incomparable brains. He dutifully set down everything they said, and commented upon their words and their manners with bitter scorn and indignation. I put into the Queen's mouth, and into the mouths of those other people, grossnesses not to be found outside of Rabelais, perhaps. I made their stateliest remarks reek with them, and all this was charming to me—delightful, delicious—but their charm was as nothing to that which was afforded me by that outraged old cup-bearer's comments upon them.

It is years since I have seen a copy of "1601." I wonder if it would be as funny to me now as it was in those comparatively youthful days when I wrote it. It made a fat letter. I bundled it up and mailed it to Twichell in Hartford. And in the fall, when we returned to our home in Hartford and Twichell and I resumed the Saturday ten-mile walk to Talcott Tower and back, every Saturday, as had been our custom for years, we used to carry that letter along. There was a grove of hickory trees by the roadside, six miles out, and close by it was the only place in that whole region where the fringed gentian grew. On our return from the Tower we used to gather the gentians, then lie down on the grass upon the golden carpet of fallen hickory leaves and get out that letter and read it by the help of these poetical surroundings. We used to laugh ourselves lame and sore over the cup-bearer's troubles. I wonder if we could laugh over them now? We were so young then!—and maybe there was not so much to laugh at in the letter as we thought there was.

However, in the winter Dean Sage came to Twichell's on a visit, and Twichell, who was never able to keep a secret when he knew it ought to be revealed, showed him the letter. Sage carried it off. He was greatly tickled with it himself, and he wanted to know how it might affect other people. He was under the seal of confidence, and could not show the letter to any one—still he wanted to try it on a dog, as the stage phrase is, and he dropped it in the aisle of the smoking-car accidentally, and sat down near-by to wait for results. The letter traveled from group to group around the car, and when he finally went and claimed it, he was convinced that it possessed literary merit. So he got a dozen copies privately printed in Brooklyn. He sent one to David Gray, in Buffalo; one to a friend in Japan; one to Lord Houghton, in England; and one to a Jewish rabbi in Albany, a very learned man and an able critic and lover of old-time literatures.

"1601" was privately printed in Japan and in England, and by and by we began to hear from it. The learned rabbi said it was a masterpiece in its verities and in its imitation of the obsolete English of Elizabeth's day. And the praises delivered to me by the poet, David Gray, were very precious. He said "Put your name to it. Don't be ashamed of it. It is a great and fine piece of literature and deserves to live, and will live. Your 'Innocents

Abroad' will presently be forgotten, but this will survive. Don't be ashamed; don't be afraid. Leave the command in your will that your heirs shall put on your tombstone these words, and these alone: *'He wrote the immortal "1601".'*"

When we sailed for Europe in 1891 I left those sumptuous West Point copies hidden away in a drawer of my study, where I thought they would be safe. We were gone nearly ten years, and whenever anybody wanted a copy I promised it—the promise to be made good when we should return to America. In Berlin I promised one to Rudolph Lindau, of the Foreign Office. He still lives, but I have not been able to make that promise good. I promised one to Mommsen, and one to William Walter Phelps, who was our Minister at the Berlin court. These are dead, but maybe they don't miss "1601" where they are. When I went lecturing around the globe I promised "1601" pretty liberally—these promises all to be made good when I should return home.

In 1890 I had published in *Harper's Monthly* a sketch called "Luck," the particulars of which had been furnished to Twichell by a visiting English army chaplain. The next year, in Rome, an English gentleman introduced himself to me on the street and said "Do you know who the chief figure in that 'Luck' sketch is?" "No," I said, "I don't." "Well," he said, "it is Lord Wolseley—and don't you go to England if you value your scalp." In Venice another English gentleman said the same to me. These gentlemen said "Of course Wolseley is not to blame for the stupendous luck that has chased him up ever since he came shining out of Sandhurst in that most unexpected and victorious way, but he will recognize himself in that sketch, and so will everybody else, and if you venture into England he will destroy you."

In 1900, in London, I went to the Fourth of July banquet, arriving after eleven o'clock at night, at a time when the place was emptying itself. Choate was presiding. An English admiral was speaking, and some two or three hundred men were still present. I was to speak, and I moved along down behind the chairs which had been occupied by guests, toward Choate. These chairs were now empty. When I had reached within three chairs of Choate, a handsome man put out his hand and said "Stop. Sit down here. I want to get acquainted with you. I am Lord Wolseley." I was falling, but he caught me, and I explained that I was often taken that way. We sat and chatted together and had a very good time—and he asked me for a copy of "1601," and I was very glad to get off so easy. I said he should have it as soon as I reached home.

We reached home the next year, and not a sign of those precious masterpieces could be found on the premises anywhere. And so all those promises remain unfulfilled to this day. Two or three days ago I found out that they have reappeared, and are safe in our house in New York. But I shall not make any of those promises good until I shall have had an opportunity to examine that masterpiece and see whether it really is a masterpiece or not. I have my doubts—though I had none a quarter of a century ago. In that day I believed "1601" was inspired.

Monday, August 6, 1906

Goes back to the failure of Charles L. Webster and Company—First meeting with H. H. Rogers—His sympathy, and assistance—Mr. Clemens in three years pays off a hundred cents on the dollar.

Let us go back three months, now, and take up—no, let him wait. I could not do him justice this morning, for I feel at peace with all the human race. It is best to wait for a more favorable time. We must not be inadequate with that man—we must boil him in oil. I know I get these soft spells too often, but I was born so—I cannot change my disposition. By my count, estimating from the time when I began these dictations two years ago, in Italy, I have been in the right mood for competently and exhaustively feeding fat my ancient grudges in the cases of only thirteen deserving persons—one woman and twelve men. It makes good reading. Whenever I go back and re-read those little biographies and characterizations it cheers me up, and I feel that I have not lived in vain. The work was well done. The art of it is masterly. I admire it more and more every time I examine it. I do believe I have flayed and mangled and mutilated those people beyond the dreams of avarice.

Those chapters will not see print for fifty or seventy-five years to come—but that is no matter, my enjoyment was in the writing of them, not in the unhappiness they could afford to those people or their children. I should like to read them privately to those people, and I shall hope for that opportunity; but their families have done me no harm, and my heirs and assigns must not publish any of those chapters while any of the wives and children are still living. They have my permission to publish them after that. I don't mind grandchildren and great-grandchildren, and they themselves won't mind. I did not write those malignant chapters in malice entirely—a part of my motive was to do those people good. It seemed to me that if I could read the chapters to them privately it would go far to acclimate them for the Hereafter.

No, I could not do that man justice this morning. Let him go. I seem to be out of vitriol; I suppose I have sprung a leak somewhere. I seem to be full of peace, affection, and the joy of life. Let us go back to history, and resume where we left off, six or seven weeks ago, with the failure of Charles L. Webster and Company.

My wife and I realized that we were really ruined this time, and quite completely. In my account, in a previous chapter, of the many fortunes which I had for years been wasting in foolish speculations, I have not intimated that the losses ever seriously embarrassed us, and indeed they did not. But the case was different now. In six or seven years Charles L. Webster and Company and James W. Paige the composing-machine adventurer, had between them swallowed up a quarter of a million dollars, half of it mine, half of it my wife's. The great panic of '93–'94 was on. Our incomes, like most other people's, were crippled. Moreover, we were under the heavy burden of debt left behind by the dead Webster firm. It was in these black days that I stumbled accidentally upon H. H. Rogers one evening in the lobby of the Murray Hill Hotel, whither Dr. Clarence C. Rice and I had gone on some errand or other, I do not now remember what. However, Henry Rogers interested himself in my troubles at once, and set himself the task of piloting me out of them. It was not a holiday job, for even a Standard Oil veteran; but his was a cool and capable head, and he was not disturbed by the complications and perplexities that were driving me toward insanity. It cost him several weeks of diligent hard work, and one trip to Chicago, to pull me out of the Paige entanglement and set that matter permanently straight. It cost him five years of intricate and bothersome work to pull me out of the Webster complications and abolish them out of my life for good and all.

Personally I never had anything to do with straightening out those involved and vexatious Webster complexities. I sat around idle; sometimes here, sometimes with the family in Europe, and latterly decorating the globe's circumference with a garland of lectures, delivered in the interest of the Webster creditors. He did the whole of it himself. We were not legally liable for much of that great Webster indebtedness, but Mrs. Clemens and I considered ourselves morally liable for the whole of it, and we believed that if I could have four years' time I could earn enough to pay it all off at a hundred cents on the dollar. I was only fifty-eight; I was in good repair; and we elected to pay a hundred cents. Now I wish to make particular note of this fact: of all our business friends, there was only *one* who approved the hundred cents proposition, encouraged us in it, and said "Hold your grip and go ahead." That was Henry Rogers. We held our grip and went ahead. In something short of three years we earned the money—forwarding it to Mr. Rogers as fast as we acquired it—and then we were out of debt. We had paid a hundred cents on the dollar, and owed no one a penny.

In the beginning Mrs. Clemens wanted to turn over her house to the creditors—land, furniture and all—a property which had cost more than a hundred and fifty thousand dollars, and which she had paid for out of her own pocket. She was determined to do this, but Mr. Rogers would not permit it—and of course I wouldn't. It cost her a pang to relinquish that idea, but she was not able to help herself.

I have said in a previous chapter that at the meeting of Webster creditors Mr. Rogers insisted on making Mrs. Clemens a preferred creditor, and in giving her my copyrights in satisfaction of an indebtedness of sixty-five thousand dollars which she had lent to Webster and Company upon the firm's notes, from time to time. He secured his point, and the copyrights went to Mrs. Clemens. That was the far-sightedest thing Mr. Rogers has ever done for me. All values were flat at that time; no kind of property was salable; you couldn't even give it away to a really bright and intelligent person. My books were no exception to the rule. They seemed permanently dead. I was not able to regard them as property. But Mr. Rogers stood to it that when the panic should be over they would revive, and would presently furnish a steady income and be as valuable as before. It turned out that he was right.

It is odd that he, a man of affairs, a purely business man, a man whose intellectual activities had been concerned all his life solely with finance and vast material commercial operations, should have been able to forecast with such certainty and such confidence the future of such a thing as a pile of paralysed old books. It is odd, and yet it is hardly surprising, for he carries a most remarkable head upon his shoulders, and it has long ago ceased to surprise me when it does surprising things. I think he was the only person alive who considered those old books a valuable asset, but the result has verified his judgment. Within two or three years after the prediction the books had revived and had begun to furnish my family an ample support; time has not diminished the figure, but enlarged it. My wife and I could have been persuaded to let the copyrights go; but nothing would have come of it, for Mr. Rogers would not have allowed the books to get away from us, and he is a very willful man. *He* is the reason that my literature affords a generous support for my children, and will continue to afford it after I am gone until the Government needs their bread and butter and takes it from them under the only dishonorable copyright law that exists upon the planet outside of England.

Tuesday, August 7, 1906

Mr. Clemens expresses his gratitude to Mr. Rogers—Describes the man as one of the three handsomest men in America.

Who saves my soul does me a service; who saves my family's bread and butter does me a service that is worth thirty of it. For I am well acquainted with my soul, and know its value to a farthing. To Reverend Joseph H. Twichell I owe thanks for the impending halo, to Mr. Rogers I owe gratitude. A person's soul is not an asset of serious importance, now that hell has become so doubtful. In this world we can get along without it, and many, many of us do. Its condition and prospects interest us in a colorless and perfunctory way, Sundays, but do not go to the heart and set a grip upon it. It is the peril of the wife and children's bread and butter that does that. When the bread and butter of one's dearest in all the world is in danger, that person realizes that he stands in the presence of a tremendous *reality,* and that by comparison with this sharp and searching exigency, the saving of his soul is a light matter and can be put off to another time. I will take up these theological aspects in a future chapter and thresh them out—but for the present I will return to business.

There are many and various kinds of sacrifice which a person can make for his friend, but I think the highest and greatest of them is his sacrifice of time and labor in the cause. Mr. Rogers gave a part of his time, daily, during several weeks, to the straightening out of my Paige entanglements; he gave many weeks of his time to the arranging of an agreement between the American Publishing Company and the Harpers whereby I got the use of my Harper books in a completed set to be issued by the former Company; he had the Webster matter on his hands for five years; three years ago he labored at another contract between the two publishing firms and myself during a good many weeks, and at last got it accomplished and signed—a contract which released me from slavery to two masters and left me in the happier condition of servant to only one—the Harper Corporation. Any one who has served two masters in this world will understand the almost inestimable value of this modification.

Mr. Rogers's time is worth several thousand dollars an hour, and I have had almost daily use of it for thirteen years; he has not charged me anything for it, therefore I stand morally indebted to him in the sum of several millions of dollars. He could have sold it to great corporations for that—but I am aware that he is always squandering his time and talent and labor in a spendthrift fashion upon his friends, and so I argue that he gets more pleasure and more satisfaction out of working for his friends for nothing than he would get out of working for those other people at Standard Oil wages.

Mr. Rogers is a very handsome man, symmetrically formed, compactly constructed; he is warm-hearted, affectionate, and as sensitive as a woman. He has a wellspring of humor in him that never runs dry, and an infallible perception of humor in others. He is sixty-seven years old by the almanac, but otherwise only twenty-five, and is as lively and companionable as any other youth of his age. When he is conducting a stern business matter with his peers, his eye knows how to take care of its affairs, but when none but friends are around it is as frank and as candid as an eagle's; and out of it looks—if my affection is not deceiving me—the spirit of that which resides within: high-mindedness, honor, honesty.

His pictures do not do him justice. It is the common fault of pictures. Thirteen years ago, when I first knew him, he and two others were the especially handsome men of America. Those others were Choate and Twichell. I was not in the competition at that time. I think that those three are still the handsomest men in America, though this cannot be determined by their pictures, because of the inadequacy of pictures in general. Half an hour ago a darling little creature, in summer frock and with her hair hanging in plaited tails down her back, arrived here, and I put my arm around her shoulders and snuggled her head against my breast and inquired, and acquired, her name. Presently she said,

"I have never seen you before, but I knew you by your pictures."

Then she nestled her head back, tilted up her face, and looked sweetly up and added,

"But they are not half so beautiful as you are."

I was aware of it before, but to please her I pretended that it was a discovery, and that this was the first time any one had exhibited so delicate and so just a penetration.

Those three men are extravagantly and satisfyingly handsome, but I doubt if Henry Rogers is second in the competition. It is an old saying that whatever is unpleasant in a person's character and disposition will come out at sea, and that if he has any disagreeable infirmities of temper he will not be able to conceal them on shipboard. I have made a great many voyages with Mr. Rogers and his friends in his yacht, and his character and disposition always stood the test. He was always genial, always courteous, always diligently thoughtful of others. On land it is the same. Consider that most temper-trying game—billiards. When Mr. Rogers painstakingly tries for an easy shot and misses it a couple of yards and I burst into an unfeeling laugh, he does not resent it, he only leans on his cue and looks wounded, and says "I should be sorry to have a disposition like yours."

One would think I am painting an angel; but it is only a future one. If there is a better man among us, a cleaner man, a kindlier man, a man with fewer faults, I have not met him.

In mid-July, 1895, Mrs. Clemens and Clara and I started on our lecturing and book-making money-grubbing raid around the globe, and every day we melted a layer off the Webster debt. At the end of two and a half years we had earned the necessary money, then Mr. Rogers paid off all of the ninety-six creditors at one sitting. We still had ten thousand dollars in bank in London, and eighteen thousand five hundred dollars left over in his hands in New York. We were living in Vienna. I sent over and asked him to bet on Federal Steel with the eighteen thousand five hundred dollars. He bought the stock, and after two or three months he sold it for considerably more than twice the figure he had paid for it. The wolf has not molested our door since. Whenever I have trusted Mr. Rogers to invest my savings for me I have prospered; but nearly every time that I have stealthily and clandestinely crept into the market and invested them on my own judgment I have got struck by lightning.

Now let us go back to the beginning and see if we can adequately do up that man—No. 14 in the blatherskite gallery. No, gentle stenographer, put up your pencil—this is not the time. I don't seem to be loaded—and when I take hold of him I want to warm him up so competently that when he lands at his final home Satan will be obliged to say "You can come in if you like, but after what you have been through with my nephew we've nothing fresh to offer you here."

The man has done me no harm, but I have never liked his complexion.

Wednesday, August 8, 1906

The effrontery of amateur literary efforts—The playing of charades to-night—From Susy's Biography: the presentation of "The Prince and Pauper" at Mr. Warner's house.

There is one great trouble about dictating an autobiography, and that is the multiplicity of texts that offer themselves when you sit down and let your mouth fall open and are ready to begin. Sometimes the texts come flooding from twenty directions at once, and for a time you are overwhelmed with this Niagara and submerged and suffocated under it. You can use only one text at a time, and you don't know which one to choose out of the twenty—still you must choose; there is no help for it, and you choose with the understanding that the nineteen left over are probably left over for good, and lost, since they may never suggest themselves again. But this time a text is forced upon me. This is mainly because it is the latest one that has suggested itself in the last quarter of an hour, and therefore the warmest one, because it has not had a chance to cool off yet. It is a couple of amateur literary offerings. From old experience I know that amateur productions, offered ostensibly for one's honest cold judgment, to be followed by an uncompromisingly sincere verdict, are not really offered in that spirit at all. The thing really wanted and expected is compliment and encouragement. Also, my experience has taught me that in almost all amateur cases compliment and encouragement are impossible—if they are to be backed by sincerity.

I have this moment finished reading this morning's pair of offerings, and am a little troubled. If they had come from strangers I should not have given myself the pain of reading them, but should have returned them unread, according to my custom, upon the plea that I lack an editor's training and therefore am not qualified to sit in judgment upon any one's literature but my own. But this morning's harvest came from friends, and that alters the case. I have read them, and the result is as usual: they are not literature. They do contain meat, but the meat is only half cooked. The meat is certainly there, and if it could pass through the hands of an expert cook the result would be a very satisfactory dish indeed. One of this morning's samples does really come near to being literature, but the amateur hand is exposed with a fatal frequency, and the exposure spoils it. The author's idea is, in case I shall render a favorable verdict, to offer the manuscript to a magazine.

There is something about this naïve intrepidity that compels admiration. It is a lofty and reckless daring which I suppose is exhibited in no field but one—the field of literature. We see something approaching it in war, but approaching it only distantly. The untrained common soldier has often offered himself as one of a forlorn hope and stood cheerfully ready to encounter all its perils—but we draw the line there. Not even the most confident untrained soldier offers himself as a candidate for a brigadier-generalship, yet this is what the amateur author does. With his untrained pen he puts together his crudities and offers them to all the magazines, one after the other—that is to say, he proposes them for posts restricted to literary generals who have earned their rank and place by years and even decades of hard and honest training in the lower grades of the service.

I am sure that this affront is offered to no trade but ours. A person untrained to shoemaking does not offer his services as a shoemaker to the foreman of a shop—not even the crudest literary aspirant would be so unintelligent as to do that. He would see the humor of it; he would see the impertinence of it; he would recognize as the most commonplace of facts that an apprenticeship is necessary in order to qualify a person to be tinner, bricklayer, stone mason, printer, horse-doctor, butcher, brakeman, car conductor, midwife—and any and every other occupation whereby a human being acquires bread and fame. But when it comes to doing literature, his wisdoms vanish all of a sudden and he thinks he finds himself now in the presence of a profession which requires no apprenticeship, no experience, no training—nothing whatever but conscious talent and a lion's courage.

We do not realize how strange and curious a thing this is until we look around for an object lesson whereby to realize it to us. We must imagine a kindred case—the aspirant to operatic distinction and cash, for instance. The aspirant applies to the management for a billet as second tenor. The management accepts him, arranges the terms, and puts him on the pay-roll. Understand, this is an imaginary case; I am not pretending that it has happened. Let us proceed.

After the first act the manager calls the second tenor to account, and wants to know. He says:

"Have you ever studied music?"

"A little—yes, by myself, at odd times, for amusement."

"You have never gone into regular and laborious training, then, for the opera, under the masters of the art?"

"No."

"Then what made you think you could do second-tenor stunts in 'Lohengrin'?"

"I thought I could. I wanted to try. I seemed to have a voice."

"Yes, you have a voice, and with five years of diligent training under competent masters you could be successful, perhaps, but I assure you you are not ready for second tenor yet. You have a voice; you have presence; you have a noble and childlike confidence; you have a courage that is stupendous, and even superhuman. These are all essentials, and they are in your favor, but there are other essentials in this great trade, which you still lack. If you can't afford the time and labor necessary to acquire them, leave opera alone and try something which does not require training and experience. Go away, now, and try for a job in surgery."

Surgery. What does that remind me of? All our thoughts come from the outside. They come always by suggestion. We never originate one ourselves. It ought not to take me five minutes to trace out the origin of this one—surgery. . . . I see now where it originated, I see it without spending even so much as two minutes upon it. It comes from the charades. There is to be a surgeon in the charades to-night. I am to be that surgeon; I had forgotten it. But it will be an easy part, although I don't know anything about surgery; as easy as authorship to an amateur. We have taken with energy to charading, of late. About once a week we get together the youths and maidens of the region, to the number of fifteen or twenty, and after supper we play impromptu charades until bedtime. We are busy choosing the words for to-night, and the household are busy contriving the costumes. A quite variegated talent is required in these performances. You have to act several parts in the course of an evening. The charaders are divided into two squads; the leaders are chosen beforehand; then, when we are ready to begin, the leaders choose a subordinate, turn about, until the panel is exhausted. Meantime, the leaders have selected the words that are to be played. While one squad is playing, the other squad acts as audience. I am to lead one side this evening, and have chosen four words, to wit: cocktail, champagne, catastrophe—and another, I can't recall it now, but I've got it on a piece of paper up stairs. If my side plays two charades and the other side two, that is all that we shall have time for; but we generally select more words than we are going to need, in order that we may have a choice. On our side, to-night, we shall get no further than those two drinks—cocktail and champagne—because it will take all the time at our side's disposal, these being long-winded charades, the kind that string out pretty liberally in performance. There is going to be opportunity for a wide spread of histrionic talent. I am to be a rooster, a surgeon, a teacher of reading, spelling, arithmetic, geography, singing, and the art of story-telling (with an illustration). I am to be several other things, also. I am to be a teething child, nine months old, in long clothes; also an Indian chief; also an emperor in a party of emperors; also some other things too tedious to describe. Necessarily there is going to be a good deal of noise and fun—there always is.

It brings back the lost and lamented days of a quarter of a century ago—days which I have already described in earlier chapters of this autobiography—when the children were little creatures and we and the children of the neighbors used so often to play impromptu charades. Naturally this reminds me of Susy's Biography, and that it is months since we have taken a text from it, because such a multitude of things have forced themselves into these talks through the compulsion of passing and flying interests, and have crowded the Biography out of our minds. But we will look at it now and draw a remark or two from it.

From Susy's Biography.

> Papa went to Europe to lecture and after staying in Scotland and England and making a flying tripp through Ireland he returned home with mamma.
>
> Last winter papa was away for many months reading with Mr. G. W. Cable, and while he was gone we composed a plan of surprising him when he came home by acting scenes from "The Prince and Pauper."* It took us a great while to commit all that was necesary but at last we were almost ready and we expected him to come home the next day on which evening we had planned to surprise him. But we received a telegram from him stating that he would reach Hartford "to-day at two o'clock." We were all dismayed for we were by no means prepared to receive him and the library was strune with costumes which were to be tried on for the last time and we had planned a dress rehearsal over at Mr. Warners for that afternoon.
>
> But mamma gathered the things up as quickly as possible and hustled them into the mahogany-room. Soon we heard the carriage roll over the pavement in front of the house and we all rushed to the doore. After we had partially gotten over our surprise and delight at seeing papa we all went into the library. We all sat with papa a little while and then mamma dissapeared into the mahogany-room. Clara and I sat with papa a while so as to prevent his being surprised of our seemingly uncalled for disertion of him. But soon we too had to withdraw to the mahogany-room so as to help mamma sew on bucles onto slippers and pack costumes into a clothes-basket. Papa was left all alone; exept that one of us every once in a while would slipp in and stay with him a little while. Any one but papa would have wondered at mamma's unwonted absence but papa is so absence minded, he very seldom notices things as accurately as other people do; although I do not believe in this instance he could have been wholly without suspicion.† At last he went up to the billiard-room and Jean went with him. Mamma as a special favor let Jean into this secret on condition that she would not breathe a whisper to any one on the subject, especially to papa, and Jean had promised but when alone up in papa's room, it was very hard for her not to tell papa the whole thing. As it was she was undecided whether to tell him or not. She did go so far as to begin with "It's a secret, papa," and then dropping varius other hints about the secret and she went so far that papa said afterwards that if he had been any one else he should have guessed it in a minute.

* Dramatized from the book by her mother. S.L.C.

† But I was. S.L.C.

At ½ past three o'clock we all started for Mr. Warners house, there to have our rehearsal. Jean and the nurse went with us, so papa was left absolutely alone.

The next day the first information that papa got was that he was invited for the evening and he did not know that anything unusual was going to happen until he sat before the curtain.

We got through the scenes quite successfully and had some delightful dancing afterwards. After we had danced for about ½ an hour mamma seemed in quite a hurry to get home, so we put on our things and started for home. When we entered the library a lady was sitting in one of the arm-chairs. I did not recognize her and wondered why mamma did not introduce me to her, but on drawing nearer to her chair I saw it was Aunt Clara Spaulding!

Mamma told Aunt Clara that we would have the "Prince and Pauper" again in a few weeks so she could see it. So it was decided that we should have it again in a few weeks.

At length the time was sett and we were nearly prepared, when Frank Warner who took the "Miles Hendon" part got a severe cold and could not play it, so papa said that he would take the part. Papa had only three days to learn the part in, but still we were all sure that he could do it. The scene that he acted in was the scene between Miles Hendon and the Prince, "The Prithee pour the water!" scene. I was the Prince and papa and I rehearsed together two or three times a day for the three days before the appointed evening. Papa acted his part beautifully and he added to the scene, making it a good deal longer. He was inexpressibly funny, with his great slouch hat and gait! Oh such a gait! Papa made the Miles Hendon scene a splendid success and every one was delighted with the scene, and papa too. We had great great funn with our "Prince and Pauper" and I think we none of us shall forget how imensely funny papa was in it. He certainly could have been an actor as well as an author.*

I have already described that monumental night in an earlier chapter of this autobiography. In the quoted passages you have an exhibition of that thing which I was talking about a while ago—untrained, inexperienced amateur authorship. It has merits, and very noticeable ones. This time the result is literature. The writer is a child, and we do not want a child to write as a grown person writes. The proprieties, the accuracies, and the reserves which we require of the grown person we will not endure in the child. Susy is all alive with her subject. Her heart is in it, and her interest is so intense that she makes us see the episodes as she saw them, and also makes us see her very self in the flesh, her glad self, her eager self, her excited self, with the flush in her cheeks and the glow in her eyes. If it were a grown person writing, we would not have it; it would not be literature. But as it stands, it is literature, and no grown person, trained or untrained, can successfully imitate it: the innocent simplicities and childish eagernesses and exaltations which give it its charm and make literature of it, would elude him.

If we only had Susy here to-night!

*Susy's opinion stands now justified, and mightily reinforced, after sixteen or seventeen years, for at dinner the other night, after I had told about—I forget what—Sir Henry Irving let fall the same remark. *Riverdale, November 1901.* S.L.C.

Friday, August 10, 1906

Clipping from *Westminster Gazette,* criticising statement in "Diary of Eve" and calling it irreverent—Mr. Clemens replies to this—Mr. Higbie's manuscript—Mr. Clemens's reply to him—Extract from Mr. Higbie's essay.

This morning's mail brings me this clipping from the *Westminster Gazette,* which is one of the brightest and ablest of the London journals.

MARK TWAIN TRIPPING.

> Even a professional humorist may be called upon to suffer a laugh at his own expense. "Mark Twain," in his somewhat irreverent "Diary of Eve" (Harper's), is guilty of an amusing error. Alluding to the naming by Adam of the brute creation, the "mother of all living" is made to suggest that but for her tactful prompting and assistance the feat would never have been accomplished. As a matter of fact, the naming of the "fowl of the air" and the "beast of the field" was performed prior to the forming of woman, which was indeed, as the famous humorist would have known had he taken the trouble to read carefully the second chapter of Genesis, a consequence of the former transaction, for we are told (Gen. ii., 20): "And Adam gave names to all cattle, and to the fowl of the air, and to every beast of the field; but for Adam there was not found an help meet for him." It is always well to be sure of one's ground—even before attempting a joke.

This depresses me. It always saddens the professional lightning-bug when he flares up under the mole's nose and finds that the mole doesn't know that anything has happened. The *Westminster*'s man is unaware of the privileges of our profession. He thinks we must stick to the facts, when we use them, and not profane them; whereas by the privileges of our order we are independent of facts; we care nothing for them, in a really religious way. If in their integrity they will not work into our scheme with the kind of effect which we wish to produce, we re-arrange them to meet the requirements of the occasion. When we are hot with the fires of production we would even distort the facts of the multiplication-table, let alone the facts of Genesis. We have no inflamed respect for facts. We could keep our head and be calm in their presence even if one in thirty-five of them was true. Even if I had known the unimportant fact that it was not Eve who named the animals, I should have coldly ignored it, in the interest of art. I should have altered the fact to suit my fiction. If I had felt it best to turn the whole fable of creation inside out, I would have done it without compunction. The *Gazette* says: "It is always well to be sure of one's ground—even before attempting a joke." We look at it the other way. One of our principal by-laws says "Do not try to be sure of your audience before attempting a joke; it will always contain at least one person whose quartz its diamond drill cannot penetrate."

As to my irreverence, I am sure I was never irreverent in my life; I am also sure that no irreverent person has ever existed in the earth. It is not the privilege of governments, or laws, or churches, or even editors, to tell us what we must revere. In this matter we may choose for ourselves, and we always do. We do not revere Mahomet; we do not revere the gods of India; we do not hold in awe the mosques, the temples, and the other things that are sacred in the eyes of those peoples. And we are not found fault with for assuming this attitude. All our fellow-citizens forgive us for it and concede that we are merely exercising an indisputable right. Then those fellow-citizens face the other way, and naïvely require us to revere *their* sacred things and personages. They even pass laws exacting this reverence of us—laws which punish us if we decline to obey them. These fine intelligences talk about freedom of conscience, and then tell our consciences how to act, under pain of penalties! In permitting us to withhold reverence from the sacred things and personages of India and Turkey, and from the sacred personages and things of Rome and Greece, these citizens grant us the right to withhold our reverence from any other sacred things and personages, here or elsewhere.

Properly, no such thing as irreverence is possible. No man can be irreverent toward the things which *he* holds sacred in his heart—the thing is impossible; but he is free to say disagreeable things about any other person's gods and Bibles—even those of the Indians, the Turks, the Romans and the Greeks. No one denies him this right. Certainly, then, the word *irreverence* is a word which has no meaning, and no rightful place in the dictionary, since it describes something which has never existed and is never going to exist. I revere a number of things, and I never speak of them disrespectfully, nor even think of them disrespectfully. If I should do either of these things my act could be described as *irreverence;* but as it is not possible for me to do them the word is impotent and meaningless in my case, as it is in all other cases. I repeat, there are things which are sacred to me and which I hold in reverence—but I do not count Adam and Eve in this list, nor their fabulous history.

At last we have heard from Higbie, and there is no denying that I am depressed. Higbie is the silver miner who was my cabin-mate in Aurora, Esmeralda, during two or three months, forty-five years ago. We talked about him in a chapter away back yonder in the winter, or the spring. He was proposing to write for the New York *Herald,* upon guarded invitation, some account of his life and mine out on the frontier in the long ago, and he proposed to pass his manuscript through my hands to see if I might like what he was going to say about me.

It was then that a warm old-comrade impulse surged up in me and disordered my judgment. I encouraged him. It was wrong to do this—wrong and foolish. I ought to have reserved my reply until my judgment could have a chance to cool down and get straightened out—and of course I didn't do that. I jumped at once to a conclusion, and, by all the laws of human experience, it was necessarily an erroneous one. I remembered Higbie perfectly well—a most kindly, engaging, frank, unpretentious, unlettered, and utterly honest, truthful, and honorable giant; practical, unimaginative, destitute of humor, well endowed with good plain common sense, and as simple-hearted as a child. Under the warrant of these facts, I jumped to a conclusion—the apparently entirely trustworthy conclusion that the real Higbie,—the genuine Higbie, the engaging Higbie, the unhumorous Higbie, the unimaginative Higbie—would appear in his manuscript and win the heart of every reader. It ought to have occurred to me that no human being who attempts literature for the first time can be his natural self—but it didn't. I imagined Higbie telling about those old days in the simple and unaffected language of a Robinson Crusoe, and charging his words with the honesty, the truthfulness and the sincerity that were born in him. Such a narrative could not fail to be inviting and acceptable; I knew this perfectly well. Now then, how could an artificial Higbie ever occur to me? I could not imagine such a thing. I could as easily have imagined the silver and gold amalgam in a retort turning to slag and rubbish—and yet that is what happened to Higbie when he took the unaccustomed pen in his hand. The natural Higbie, the real Higbie, the delightful Higbie, the honest Higbie, the truthful Higbie, the sincere Higbie, the childlike Higbie, went up in the vapor of the quicksilver and left nothing behind but slag—just slag, only slag, and not worth thirty cents a ton in any market of the precious metals.

In Higbie's essay there are seventeen thousand five hundred words; thirteen thousand of the words are such extravagant distortions of the actual facts that hardly an unimpeachable grain of truth is discoverable in them. This Higbie of seventy-five immature years is not the splendid and stalwart Higbie I cabined with forty-four years ago. His paper is headed "A Little Experience in Nevada and Surrounding Country in the Early Sixties, Leading up to My Acquaintance with Samuel L. Clemens, 'Mark Twain.'" His Introduction, of four thousand words, leads gradually up to me, and is an unadorned statement of his goings and comings, and sounds true—doubtless is true. Then he encounters me, and the newly-born literary artist sets his fancy afire and the conflagration begins. Evidently he sat down with my book "Roughing It" before him and reproduced every detail of my Esmeralda chapters from it, translating each and every detail into his own language. Manifestly, when those texts gave out he filled in with his fancies, and whenever he fetched me on the stage he evidently felt the necessity of bursting into frenzies of humor, and he did it. It is sad, it is pathetic; Higbie was always gravity, seriousness, practicality itself. I can almost imagine a humorous camel, but a humorous Higbie is beyond my strength.

If only Higbie were a stranger! Then I could write him an uncharitable letter and return his manuscript to him—but we can't treat friends in that way. We have to write them gently; we have to write them candidly, too. Therefore we do it, but we do not enjoy it. It *hurts,* and we are glad when the uncomfortable task is achieved. I have written Higbie the following letter, which will not see print until years after both of us are dead.

Dublin, New Hampshire.

Dear Higbie:

I have read it, and the fact is, I am greatly disappointed. It is mainly second-hand news, worked over. In "Roughing It" I have already told about the Wide-West blind lead; and about your locating it; and about our dreams of what we would do when we got the money; and about your going cementing and my going off to nurse Nye; and about the relocating of the blind lead; and about my joining the staff of the "Enterprise;" and about Lake Mono; and about the robbery on the divide—and so forth and so on. To make the retelling of these things valuable there is only one way, not two: *they must be better told than I told them.* You have not done that, and any editor would say so at once; and he would add that he *could not use matter, anyway, that had already been used.* I exhausted that ore-pile, and left nothing behind but waste rock.

You have invented some new things—such as the flap-jacks and the ball—but any editor would strike them out, because such things are without value except when funny, and you have not made them funny. And how could you? You are a straight, honest, practical, sincere man, and no schooling, no training, no diligence would ever qualify you to write humorously—it is out of your line; and even if it were not, you could not pick up that exacting art in a day.

You have made me pretty ridiculous, but I shan't mind that if the editors will buy your MS. But I clearly perceive that it would damage its chances for me to offer it to them, for the reason that they would certainly ask me for a paragraph in praise of it and I could not furnish it. In print I have never praised anything which I could not praise with heartiness and sincerity. For in my way I am as honest as you are, Cal.

But there is one thing I can do, and this I will gladly do if you say the word: I can send it to the Herald, through my literary agent, and he can say you passed it through my hands to see if there was anything in it that would wound me, and that I found it innocent of reproach in that respect. Shall I do that? Let me hear from you, old friend.

Sincerely yours,
S. L. Clemens.

In justice to Higbie—for it may be that his humor will appeal to others, although it has gone over my head—I here append his flap-jack episode—an episode which resembles his extravagant ball, in this: that neither of them happened. Both are exudations of his unschooled fancy.

At that time I was very fond of hot-cakes—slap-jacks the miners called them—and when alone would have them every morning as they could be made very quick with good flour, yeast powder, and water. The first slap-jacks made after Sam's arrival, there was nothing said and I supposed he liked them as well as myself, so we had hot-cakes several mornings in succession. I thought I discovered a frown of disapproval at those cakes, but he said nothing. When I happened to be at home at mid-day we would have slap-jacks for both breakfast and dinner, and when I was sure he didn't like them we had them three times a day regular with no dishes on the side. I was wondering what would happen next and ran away with the foolish idea that I had him in a tight place and would compel him to go to work and cook something for himself that he liked rather than feed on flap-jacks three times a day forever.

At that time I was not aware of the resources of the man or his disinclination for any kind of physical exertion and supposed that any kind of a mortal under the circumstances would pitch in and cook some kind of a dish that would suit his taste. Not he. So with desperation in every fiber I would renew the attack and make it my particular business to be home at every meal and stack up in front of him a pile of flap-jacks as high as his head and in diameter the size of a large frying-pan. I went on the principle of quantity versus quality. I couldn't help but admire his patience and perseverance, but saw that the barometer was low and a storm brewing, and proceeded to batten down hatches, take in sail, and make everything snug before the gale struck: and as an extra safeguard pilled more cakes on the table as ballast.

With a fearful scowl and a glance of contempt and defiance at that pile of cakes, he leaned back from the table and opened up that innocent mound of flap-jacks.

"Hot-cakes," he says, "hot-cakes three times a day the year round. Why man they would ruin the digestive organs of the most able-bodied ostrich that ever roamed the wilds of Africa." Then he went into a learned dissertation on the injurious effects of yeast powders in combination with flour and water straight; that it would ruin the constitution of any man alive to keep that kind of a diet up for any length of time; and with other very decisive opinions on the subject. All this time I had been stowing away hot-cakes for dear life with the inward conviction that he was coming to time. In fact had eaten more than I should otherwise have done in order to give him time to finish his eloquent discussion. As a final appeal he says, "For Heavens sake man, lets have a change. Hot cakes, hot-cakes! Straight three times a day with nothing on the side. Why I never heard of such a thing."

By this time I was nearly exploding with hot-cakes and laughter, but I said, "All right, Sam. I am so fond of hot-cakes myself that I think nothing about the wants of others and if there is anything you would particularly like our credit is good up at the store. Get anything you like and fix it up to suit yourself and it will suit me."

"Thats the talk," he says, "we'll have a change to-morrow. Good lord man. its a wonder we are alive to-day stuffing ourselves with nothing but hot-cakes," and in a mollified tone "I will admit you make fine large cakes and use great skill in tossing them into the air and catching them upside down in that frying-pan, but as a regular diet three times a day the year round, I will admit my constitution will not stand the strain."

Saturday, August 11, 1906

Man incapable of originating a thought; simply receives suggestions from the outside—Note to Andrew Carnegie, asking for hymn-book—The pension for John T. Lewis—Mr. Rogers's doubt as to the existence of John T. Lewis—Two letters from Lewis—Kipling comes to America—Visits Mr. Clemens in Elmira.

From the beginning of time, philosophers of all breeds and shades have been beguiled by the persuasions of man's bulkiest attribute, vanity, into believing that a human being can originate a thought in his own head. I suppose I am the only person who knows he can't. In my own person I have studied him most carefully these many years—indeed for a quarter of a century—and I now know beyond doubt or question that his mind is quite incapable of inventing a thought, and is strictly limited to receiving suggestions from the outside and manufacturing second-hand thoughts out of them. The expert in hypnotism takes pride in the notion that in powerfully moving his subject by suggestion, he has discovered a new thing, whereas no human being has ever been moved to any act or idea by any force *except* suggestion. The reason that I can come to this dictation-industry every morning unprepared with a text, is that I know quite well that somebody's passing remark, or a paragraph in the newspaper, or a letter in the mail, will suggest something which will remind me of something in my life's experiences and will surely furnish me, by this process, one or more texts.

The first thing I notice in this morning's paper is a note which I wrote to Andrew Carnegie some years ago, and which, for a certain reason, flashes John T. Lewis into my mind, although Lewis is not mentioned in the note.

> My dear Mr. Carnegie,—I see by the papers that you are very prosperous. I want to get a hymn-book. It costs six shillings. I will bless you, God will bless you, and it will do a great deal of good.
>
> Yours truly,
> Mark
>
> P.S.—Don't send me the hymn-book; send me the six shillings.

The note suggests that fine old colored friend, John T. Lewis, because of the suspicious form of it. Many a stranger would think that the hymn-book was only a blind; that at bottom I didn't really want the hymn-book, but only wanted to get my hands on the money. Such a suspicion would do me wrong. I only wanted the hymn-book. I was most anxious to get it, but I wanted to select it myself. If I had succeeded in getting the money I would have bought a hymn-book with it and not any other thing. Although I have no evidence but my own as to this, I believe it to be trustworthy and sufficient. I am speaking from my grave, and it is not likely that I would break through the sod with an untruth in my mouth.

It is a strange thing, when you come to examine it—Andrew Carnegie has built a Peace Palace on the other side, for the housing of that great and beneficent modern institution, the Hague Tribunal, at a cost of ten million dollars; he has built, and endowed with ten millions, that other most noble and inestimably valuable benefaction, the Carnegie Institute; he has established a permanent fund of fifteen million dollars for the dignified and respectable maintenance of veterans of both sexes who have devoted their long lives to the higher grades of teaching, and in their old age find themselves poor, forlorn, and without support—a benefaction of so fine and gracious a sort that it brings the moisture to one's eyes to think of it; he has distributed eighty million dollars' worth of free libraries around about the planet for the intellectual elevation of men of all grades and creeds and colors—and yet when he could save a tottering soul from destruction with six shillings' worth of hymn-book, he turns coldly away and leaves that soul to perish. Truly there are a good many different kinds of people in the world, and Andrew Carnegie is one of them. If not several.

The unworded doubt which his silence cast upon the purity of my intentions was duplicated, in another way, by another man, Henry Rogers. In a previous chapter I have told how John T. Lewis saved the lives of a rich man's wife and daughter, thirty years ago, when not another man in the State could have done it, and was rewarded with thanks—repeated thanks, lots of thanks, plenty of thanks. About five years ago the rheumatism took hold of him and he was not able to get a livelihood out of his farm. It took all the money he could make to pay the interest on the money he borrowed in that ancient day—a loan which I mentioned when I was speaking of it before. Something had to be done for his relief, therefore Susy Crane and Jean and I contributed a monthly sum, in the form of a pension, so that he might live the rest of his days without work. I offered Henry Rogers a chance to enlarge that pension, and he was quite willing, and said he would send his check to John T. Lewis on the first of every month.

I said no, I was not very busy, make the check to my order.

He said "Not on your life"—or words to that effect.

He did not stop with that injurious remark, but suggested that it was more than likely that there wasn't any such colored man as John T. Lewis. I offered to bring witnesses, but he said he believed he could do better by getting some one else to select the witnesses. I think he is the stubbornest man, about some things, I have ever known—the stubbornest and the most suspicious. He was determined to draw the checks to John T. Lewis's order, and it was only by tiring him out that at last I got him to draw them to mine. But he always disbelieved in John T. Lewis. I got myself spaciously photographed alongside of John T. Lewis, standing in front of the farm-house, at Susy Crane's farm. It did not convince him; he merely looked sad, and framed it and hung it up in his private office at 26 Broadway, and labeled it "The Imaginary John T. Lewis"—and there it hangs yet; hangs there looking so honest that it would convince any but an implacably prejudiced mind.

I pledge my honor I always sent the money to Lewis. Moreover, I sent it through Susy Crane, who delivered it to him, month by month, in person; and to this she will testify, knowing me well enough to know that if she declines I will make trouble. The pension set Lewis up quite to his content; made a tranquilly care-free and happy man of him, and thenceforth he claimed that he was the only absolutely independent man in the county.

As you perceive, it is the Carnegie spirit over again—with this difference: John T. Lewis did get Henry Rogers's money, but I never got the hymn-book.

While I was taking a long and comfortable and unearned holiday at Fairhaven, a few weeks ago, the following letter arrived at Dublin from Quarry Farm. It brought the news of Lewis's death, and added certain particulars. I call attention, with a just pride, to the title which it confers upon me. All who know me—except perhaps Henry Rogers and Andrew Carnegie—will grant that I deserve it. It is a matter of pride to me to reflect that I acquired it without the help of a hymn-book. I do not know that I am surprised to find by the letter that Lewis was a Dunker Baptist. He was born one, in Maryland, but when I first knew him, something more than a generation ago, he had sampled every religion in the market, in turn, had found none of them equal to the task of saving a soul like his, and had at last joined the Free-Thinkers and found rest for his spirit. I think it quite likely that in the long lapse of years between that time and this he went back over his course, taking a bite out of each old friendly religion as he went, and finally fetched up in Dunkerdom, whence in his childhood he had started out on his long and adventurous salvation-excursion.

Quarry Farm.
Elmira, N.Y.
July 23, 1906.

Dear and Holy Samuel,

Several weeks ago I received a call from Lewis which should have fallen to your lot instead of mine; for, all the half hour, as I stood under the vines on the front porch visiting with Lewis, you were in my mind. He was half reclining in a low open wagon, into which he could climb, and out of which he could easily roll.

Lewis began by saying, "You have been very kind to me, and I thought it was not quite fair for me to slip away without telling you I was failing. And I wanted to talk with you about getting one of my own people to preach the funeral sermon. The nearest Dunker Baptist minister is in Brooklyn, a white man, and I want if possible to get him to come up here for a few days to learn about my character, so that he can speak intelligently at the funeral. Would you be willing to give a little something toward it, and maybe some other friends would."

While a worldly ambition of this nature did not strongly appeal to me, it was the request of a dying friend and I said yes, I would help bear the expense.

Lewis then said it would be a great comfort to talk with one of his own faith, which was easy to understand. He then said, "Would you be willing to give him a meal if he comes?" "Certainly," I promised, and after a little talk about when I should pay the rent of his farm, he went on to get his mail, his precious checks, and see his Doctor.

The Doctor forbade his going to town, but after a few days of rest Lewis was again on the road, impressing all who saw him with his feebleness. Perhaps ten days ago he gave up the trips when I made all the calls, as he went steadily down. He was always cheerful, and seemed not to suffer much pain, told stories, and was able to eat almost everything.

Three days ago a new difficulty appeared, on account of which his Doctor said he must go to the Hospital for care, such as it was quite impossible to give in his home.

He died on the way there.

With love,
Susan L. Crane.

After a few days the following interesting letter arrived:

Friday, July 27.

Dear Holy Samuel,

Now that two days are passed, it seems hardly worth while to tell you of the funeral of Lewis, save that I promised.

At the hour named a goodly company of colored and white friends gathered at the parlors of the undertaker, where all the arrangements were made in good order.

There was a long silent wait, after which Mr. Harrington, the undertaker, said that Mr. Hough, of Brooklyn who was expected, failed to come—and Mrs. Harrington would read a paper prepared by Mr. Lewis which would explain why they did not secure the services of some one else.

There were facts concerning Lewis's birth, his life in various places, his joining the Dunker church, followed by the statement that *unless some brother of his own denomination could preach his funeral sermon he wished his body to be buried without ceremony, as he did not recognize as Christians any who did not follow the explicit teaching of the Lord.*

This was a surprise, there was a chill, a silence, and for an instant I felt excluded from all possibility of future rescue.

A Psalm and the Lord's Prayer closed the simple, suitable service.

Think of it! A will strong enough to exclude all but the Dunkers! still, Lewis prayed for you and Mr. Rogers, and you may be Dunkers yet.

He was deeply and sincerely grateful to you, and had this not been as true as it was, yours was a good, a beautiful thought, faithfully put into action, year after year when you were unable to see the comfort, the blessing you were conferring. This has been my privilege, and I am thankful the struggles are ended for the lonely man.

The old hill folks are nearly all gone.

Most lovingly yours,
Susan L. Crane.

I am glad he prayed for Henry Rogers; and it would have been well enough if he had given Carnegie a lift, too.

Lewis's last estate reminds me of David Gray's, and is an impressive revelation of the strength and persistency of impressions made upon the human mind in the early years, when its feelings and emotions are fresh, young, and strong, and before it is capable of reasoning. At five years of age David Gray was a strenuous Presbyterian; at thirty-five he had long been a pronounced agnostic—not to put it stronger. He died as strenuous a Presbyterian as he had been when he was five years old and an expert theologian.

This morning's cables contain a verse or two from Kipling, voicing his protest against a liberalizing new policy of the British Government which he fears will deliver the balance of power in South Africa into the hands of the conquered Boers. Kipling's name, and Kipling's words always stir me now—stir me more than do any other living man's. But I remember a time, seventeen or eighteen years back, when the name did not suggest anything to me, and only the words moved me. At that time Kipling's name was beginning to be known here and there, in spots, in India, but had not traveled outside of that empire. He came over and traveled about America, maintaining himself by correspondence with Indian journals. He wrote dashing, free-handed, brilliant letters, but no one outside of India knew about it.

On his way through the State of New York, he stopped off at Elmira and made a tedious and blistering journey up to Quarry Farm in quest of me. He ought to have telephoned the farm first; then he would have learned that I was at the Langdon homestead, hardly a quarter of a mile from his hotel. But he was only a lad of twenty-four, and properly impulsive—and he set out, without inquiring, on that dusty and roasting journey up the hill. He found Susy Crane and my little Susy there, and they came as near making him comfortable as the weather and the circumstances would permit——

Monday, August 13, 1906

Kipling's visit to Mr. Clemens's in Elmira, continued—Some of his books mentioned.

The group sat on the veranda, and while Kipling rested and refreshed himself he refreshed the others with his talk—talk of a quality which was well above what they were accustomed to; talk which might be likened to footprints, so strong and definite was the impression which it left behind. They often spoke wonderingly of Kipling's talk, afterward, and they recognized that they had been in contact with an extraordinary man; but it is more than likely that they were the only persons who had perceived that he was extraordinary. It is not likely that they perceived his full magnitude; it is most likely that they were Eric Ericsons who had discovered a continent but did not suspect the horizonless extent of it. His was an unknown name, and was to remain unknown for a year yet; but Susy kept his card and treasured it as an interesting possession. Its address was Allahabad. No doubt India had been to her an imaginary land, up to this time; a fairyland, a dreamland, a land made out of poetry and moonlight for the Arabian Nights to do their gorgeous miracles in; and doubtless Kipling's flesh and blood and modern clothes realized it to her for the first time, and solidified it. I think so because she more than once remarked upon its incredible remoteness from the world that we were living in, and computed that remoteness and pronounced the result with a sort of awe—fourteen thousand miles, or sixteen thousand, whichever it was. Kipling had written upon the card a compliment to me. This gave the card an additional value in Susy's eyes, since as a distinction it was the next thing to being recognized by a denizen of the moon.

Kipling came down, that afternoon, and spent a couple of hours with me, and at the end of that time I had surprised him as much as he had surprised me—and the honors were easy. I believed that he knew more than any person I had met before, and I knew that he knew I knew less than any person he had met before—though he did not say it; and I was not expecting that he would. When he was gone, Mrs. Langdon wanted to know about my visitor. I said,

"He is a stranger to me, but he is a most remarkable man—and I am the other one. Between us, we cover all knowledge; he knows all that can be known, and I know the rest."

He was a stranger to me, and to all the world, and remained so for twelve months; then he became suddenly known, and universally known. From that day to this he has held this unique distinction: that of being the only living person, not head of a nation, whose voice is heard around the world the moment it drops a remark; the only such voice in existence that does not go by slow ship and rail but always travels first-class—by cable.

About a year after Kipling's visit in Elmira, George Warner came into our library one morning, in Hartford, with a small book in his hand, and asked me if I had ever heard of Rudyard Kipling. I said,

"No."

He said I would hear of him very soon, and that the noise he was going to make would be loud and continuous. The little book was the "Plain Tales," and he left it for me to read, saying it was charged with a new and inspiriting fragrance and would blow a refreshing breath around the world that would revive the nations. A day or two later he brought a copy of the London *World* which had a sketch of Kipling in it, and a mention of the fact that he had traveled in the United States. According to this sketch, he had passed through Elmira. This remark, added to the additional fact that he hailed from India, attracted my attention—also Susy's. She went to her room and brought his card from its place in the frame of her mirror, and the Quarry Farm visitor stood identified.

I am not acquainted with my own books, but I know Kipling's—at any rate I know them better than I know anybody else's books. They never grow pale to me; they keep their color; they are always fresh. Certain of the ballads have a peculiar and satisfying charm for me. To my mind, the incomparable Jungle Books must remain unfellowed permanently. I think it was worth the journey to India to qualify myself to read "Kim" understandingly and to realize how great a book it is. The deep and subtle and fascinating charm of India pervades no other book as it pervades "Kim;" "Kim" is pervaded by it as by an atmosphere. I read the book every year, and in this way I go back to India without fatigue—the only foreign land I ever day-dream about or deeply long to see again.

Wednesday, August 15, 1906

First school days—Praying for gingerbread.

My school days began when I was four years and a half old. This was at Hannibal, Missouri, a place which at that time was either a large village or a small town, I hardly know which. There were no public schools in Missouri in those early days, but there were two private schools in Hannibal—terms twenty-five cents per week per pupil, and collect it if you can. Mrs. Horr taught the children, in a small log house at the southern end of Main street; Mr. Sam Cross taught the young people of larger growth in a frame schoolhouse on the hill. I was sent to Mrs. Horr's school, and I remember my first day in that little log house with perfect clearness, after these sixty-five years and upwards; at least I remember an episode of that first day. I broke one of the rules, and was warned not to do it again, and was told that the penalty for a second breach was a whipping. I presently broke the rule again, and Mrs. Horr told me to go out and find a switch and fetch it. I was glad she appointed me, for I believed I could select a switch suitable to the occasion with more judiciousness than anybody else. In the mud I found a cooper's shaving of the old-time pattern—oak, two inches broad, a quarter of an inch thick, and rising in a shallow curve at one end. There were nice new firm-bodied shavings of the same breed close by, but I took this one, although it was rotten. I carried it to Mrs. Horr, presented it, and stood before her in an attitude of meekness and resignation which seemed to me calculated to win favor and sympathy;

but it did not happen. She divided a long look of strong disapprobation equally between me and the rotten shaving; then she called me by my entire name, Samuel Langhorne Clemens—probably the first time I had ever heard it all strung together in one procession—and said she was ashamed of me. I was to learn, later, that when a teacher calls a boy by his entire name it means trouble. She said she would try and appoint a boy with a better judgment than mine in the matter of switches, and it saddens me yet to remember how many faces lighted up with the hope of getting that appointment. Jim Dunlap got it, and when he returned with the switch of his choice I recognized that he was an expert. For sixty-five years I have wanted to expose him to infamy, and I do it now with a large and healing satisfaction.

Mrs. Horr was a New England lady of middle age, with New England ways and principles, and she always opened school with prayer and a chapter from the New Testament; also she explained the chapter with a brief talk. In one of these talks she dwelt upon the text "Ask and ye shall receive," and said that whosoever prayed for a thing with earnestness and strong desire need not doubt that his prayer would be answered. I was so forcibly struck by this information, and so gratified by the opportunities which it offered, that this was probably the first time I had heard of it. I thought I would give it a trial. I believed in Mrs. Horr thoroughly, and I had no doubts as to the result. I prayed for gingerbread. Margaret Kooneman, who was the baker's daughter, brought a slab of gingerbread to school every morning; she had always kept it out of sight before, but when I finished my prayer and glanced up, there it was in easy reach, and she was looking the other way. In all my life I believe I never enjoyed an answer to prayer more than I enjoyed that one; and I was a convert, too. I had no end of wants and they had always remained unsatisfied, up to that time, but I meant to supply them, and extend them, now that I had found out how to do it.

But this dream was like almost all the other dreams we indulge in in life—there was nothing in it. I did as much praying, during the next two or three days, as any one in that town, I suppose, and I was very sincere and earnest about it too, but nothing came of it. I found that not even the most powerful prayer was competent to lift that gingerbread again, and I came to the conclusion that if a person remains faithful to his gingerbread and keeps his eye on it, he need not trouble himself about your prayers.

Something about my conduct and bearing troubled my mother, and she took me aside and questioned me concerning it with much solicitude. I was reluctant to reveal to her the change that had come over me, for it would grieve me to distress her kind heart, but at last I confessed, with many tears, that I had ceased to be a Christian. She was heartbroken, and asked me why.

I said it was because I had found out that I was a Christian for revenue only, and I could not bear the thought of that, it was so ignoble.

She pressed me to her breast and comforted me. I gathered, from what she said, that if I would continue in that condition I would never be lonesome.

Monday, August 27, 1906

Two instances of remarkable memory for names and faces—General Grant's and King Edward's.

Several weeks ago, in Chapter XLI, I spoke of how rare a thing a good memory for names and faces is. I wish to recall now, under that head, an incident or two.

About the middle of the last quarter of the last century I received a distressed letter from my London publisher, in which he said that the Internal Revenue Office had sent him a bill of ten pounds, a tax due upon my English copyrights. Mr. Chatto was a good deal troubled about this, and asked me what course he should pursue. He said that in all his experience the like of this case had not occurred before; that this was the first he had heard that a foreign copyright was taxable. I asked him to refrain from arguing the matter, pay the bill, charge it to me, then ask the Internal Revenue Office to tell us all about it. Chatto had said that there was no mention of a copyright tax in the English statutes, so I was full of an infantile curiosity to know under what title or designation my literature—and mine alone—had been found worthy of this high distinction.

Several weeks went by; then I received from that Internal Revenue Office a sheet of brown wrapping-paper the size of a quilt, and on it was pasted, or printed, some hundreds of numbered paragraphs in small type, each paragraph specifying by name a taxable article, and also specifying the tax that had been inflicted upon it. It took me a long time to read all the paragraphs, and when I got through it seemed to me that not one purchasable or sellable article in use in our modern civilization had escaped the sharp eye of the law-maker. Every individual thing, great and small, from the brass pin to the ocean liner, had been searched out and required to contribute to the revenues of the State. No, there was one thing that had been overlooked, and apparently only one—copyright had not been mentioned.

I wrote the Internal Revenue and asked under what head my copyrights had been taxed, and he replied that they had been taxed by authority of Paragraph D, Section 14. I examined Paragraph D, Section 14, with an eager curiosity, and was grieved to find that the British Government had coldly singled me out from all the multitude of foreign authors and had levied upon my literature under the head of *"Classified Products of Gas Factories."* I do not remember that those were the exact words, but I have correctly delivered the sense of them. I was regarded by those unfeeling people in the Revenue Office as a literary gas factory.

To amuse myself, I wrote a letter to Queen Victoria about this matter. It was a rambling, good-natured, leather-headed letter, such as a copiously ignorant person, reared in the backwoods of a democracy and innocent of the restrictions of high etiquette, might write, in a purely friendly way, to a crowned head. In it I stated the details of my grievance and suggested that my humiliating misfortune could not have happened if her Majesty had been at home and attending to her manifold duties in her proverbially faithful way; and I think I implored her to take hold of my case personally, and require the Revenue

Office to remove the attainder—if it was an attainder—and restore to me my abolished dignity. With the innocence of a person acquainted only with the unartful diplomacy of the farm and the corner grocery, I tried to get on the good side of her Majesty with a few compliments. I said I had called upon her at Buckingham Palace once, and had been greatly disappointed in not finding her in, but would call again some day and hope for better fortune. I said I had never had the honor of personal acquaintanceship with any member of the Royal Family except the Lord Mayor, but that I had once had the pleasure of meeting the Prince of Wales. It was one day when I was coming down the Strand on top of a 'bus and he was coming up the Strand at the head of a temperance procession, and he would probably remember me because I had on my new frieze overcoat with brass buttons—and so on, a lot of other nonsense of this calibre. About this time the Harpers applied to me for some nonsense, and I sent this screed and they published it in the Drawer, under the head of "An Open Letter to the Queen."

However, I am getting too far along. There is another matter which perhaps I should have mentioned first. In the beginning of General Grant's first term as President, I came East from the Pacific Coast to bring the manuscript of "The Innocents Abroad," and in the course of business I went down to Washington. Near the White House, one morning, I encountered Senator Stewart of Nevada. He asked me if I would like to see the President. Naturally I said I would. General Grant was the tallest figure in Christendom, at that time, and I had never seen him. I supposed that Stewart merely meant to intrude me into the White House and furnish me a distant look at the President. That he would actually introduce me was a thing which could not occur to me, for I was a totally unknown and inconsequential wanderer from the distant Pacific; the President had never heard of me, and couldn't by any possibility feel any interest in me. Stewart went blundering into the President's private office, by authority of a rude privilege sacred to Senators. There was no one there but the President. He was bent over his desk and was busily writing. He had on a long and much wrinkled and crumpled linen duster, whose tails he had liberally used as a pen-wiper—so liberally, indeed, that the multitude of black streaks suggested the flight of Saxon arrows at the battle of Senlac. With native American independence of the proprieties, Stewart marched me forward, stood over the President, and said—

"Mr. President, allow me to introduce to you Mr. Clemens."

The President slowly raised his head, turned his face, and looked sternly up at me for as much as an hour and a half, without winking. I do not mean that it was really that long; I only mean that it seemed that long. When I had endured it as long as I could, and when it seemed to me that somebody must rupture that devastating silence or I should die, I said hesitatingly,

"Mr. President, I am embarrassed—are you?"

Then the faintest twinkle flickered in his eye for just a single moment—and I and it vanished so nearly together that nobody could have told which of us got off the premises first.

Years afterward I had a telegraphic call to go out to Chicago and attend a great Grant banquet and respond to the toast of "The Babies." General Grant was arriving from the Pacific, after his memorable circumnavigation of the globe, and he was to be entertained in proper state and splendor, during three days, by the Army of the Tennessee, which was the first army he had ever commanded. In an earlier chapter I have already told how Chicago was packed and jammed with people during those three days. I arrived in the evening. There was to be a grand procession the next morning. At ten o'clock on the said morning I crowded my way through the packed halls and corridors of the hotel, and presently arrived at a place on the second floor where a spacious platform had been built out and decorated with flags. It seemed to me that that would be a good vantage-ground from which to view the procession. It was empty; it looked inviting, and I walked out on it. As far away as I could see, in every direction, the sidewalks, the windows and the roofs were black and parti-colored with masses of human beings of the two sexes. That platform had been built for General Grant; those people knew it, and when I stepped out there they took me for him, and in my life I have never had so enthusiastic a welcome as that one, nor one which made me prouder, or gave me more delight. The music of a distant band came floating down on the air and I looked up the street and saw the procession coming. Lieutenant General Phil Sheridan, in full uniform, was riding at the head of it, and a vast wave of welcome and applause moved with him and marked his progress, step by step, as he came. When he had arrived within fifty or a hundred yards of my platform the Mayor of Chicago, linked arm in arm with General Grant, marched out upon the platform, followed by many generals in uniform, and by the Reception Committee, gay and fine in the fluttering badges of their office. The Mayor saw me there, and it turned out that his notions of etiquette were no better than those betrayed by Senator Stewart on the only other time that I had seen the hero of our great war, for instead of taking me to General Grant, he brought General Grant to me, and said:

"General, allow me to introduce to you Mr. Clemens."

General Grant fixed that same stern look upon my face which had congealed the blood in it in a bygone day; he allowed it to do its crumbling and disintegrating work upon me for an hour and a half—then he said,

"Mr. Clemens, I am not embarrassed—are you?"

However, I have wandered far from my other incident; I must get back to it. In 1891 or '92 we were spending the summer at Nauheim, in Germany, and one day Twichell and I mounted the tally-ho coach and went over to Homburg to watch the crowd of invalids take the waters at the springs. There I ran across the British Ambassador to the Court of Berlin, whom I knew very well, and he asked me if I would like to meet the Prince of Wales. There could be but one answer. He said the Prince was around somewhere, and he would go and find him. He ought to have taken me with him, but not even ambassadors know as much about etiquette as I do. He disappeared among the shrubbery, and presently appeared again escorting the present King of England. He introduced me to him and I said the proper thing, for I have been carefully trained, and I always know what the proper thing to say is. I said,

"I am very glad to know your Royal Highness."

He said,

"Mr. Clemens, I am very glad to meet you—again."

The word gave me a little start. It saddened me, too, for it seemed plain that he was mistaking me for some other random commoner. I said,

"Why, have you met me before, sir?"

He smiled a very pleasant smile and said,

"Why yes, don't you remember the time when you were coming down the Strand on top of the 'bus and I was coming up the Strand at the head of a temperance procession, and you had on your new frieze overcoat with the brass buttons?"

As I have already said, the ability to remember names and faces is a most rare one—and I think that the two illustrations of it which I have placed before the reader are especially and particularly extraordinary. And I think that the case of the King is still more extraordinary than that of General Grant, for the King remembered my face although he had never really seen it before at all.

When the people drink the Homburg waters the regulations framed by the doctors require them to walk a mile in order to enlarge the effects. The Prince started on his mile and invited me to accompany him. I have had much social commerce with royalties in my time, and I have always found them quite human and pleasant and unpretentious. The Prince of Wales was rather especially so. His talk was easy, and happy, and flowing, and it was traversed by a spontaneous and delicate vein of humor that gave it a charm not to be overlooked or underestimated by the professional humorist. He was perfectly natural and human; and if he was at any time embarrassed by my presence I was not able to discover it. I could easily have been embarrassed by his, but, by grace of his courtesy, I was not.

I wonder if he has ever read W. W. Jacobs's "Dialstone Lane." I hope so. It is a book which all monarchs gifted with an appreciation of light and delicate and bubbling and inexhaustible humor ought to read, and thereby relieve for a time the weight of the burdens they bear. I think it is the one purely humorous story in our language that hasn't a defect.

Tuesday, August 28, 1906

Higbie's reply to Mr. Clemens's criticism of his article— The holiday at Bar Harbor, where an incident brings to Mr. Clemens's memory his scheme for teaching impromptu oratory, which he tried long ago at the Fellow-Craftsmen's Club—The same scheme is tried on board Mr. Rogers's yacht at Bar Harbor.

Higbie's reply has come, and I recognize with satisfaction that I was not mistaken about him. He hid himself, temporarily, behind his sad attempt at literature, and was odiously artificial. But the real Higbie, the genuine Higbie, the manly Higbie, the common-sense Higbie, was there all the time; and in his letter just received he has come out from behind that mask and is his own self again, and lovable and welcome. I was uncompromisingly frank with him—I had to be, and he was worthy of that honorable treatment. He has taken his medicine like a man, and I believed he would.

This letter of his is in strong and agreeable contrast with his deadly literature. His literature is not literature, but his letter is. His literature came from a vacuum; his letter comes from his heart. Speech that comes from the heart is sure to be literature; there is no power in artless spelling and uncouth phrasing that can take that great quality out of it. It is a refreshment, in a world of insincerities and shallow vanities, to come across a man who can ask for a criticism and mean it when he asks it. I shall leave his spelling untinkered, for, being honest spelling, it has a dignity of its own. This cannot hurt him, for it will not see print while he is alive. Higbie and his letters and his literature will have interest for readers in the far future, when they shall have gathered about them the mellowing haze of a long perspective. Let them lie here and wait. Their day will come.

> Greenville, Plumas Co., California.
> Aug. 18, 1906.
>
> S. L. Clemens.
> Dublin, N.H.
>
> Yours of no date rec. Am not much disapointed that you condemn the article. I had sense enough to see for myself, that it was a crude affair, and sent it to you for aprovel, or condemnation, and am glad you condemn it, for the reason that you saw something that would mak you rediculous, and all the money in North America wouldnt tempt me to have it published for that reason alone. I saw so much trash in Publications lately that I ran away with the foolish Idea that mine might pass muster, that was a poor excuse for not having a higher Ideal of good Literature wasent it? What part did you consider made you rediculous? I certainly had no intention to do so, but I sent it you for that verry purpose, and dont you think for a moment, that I take offence at your critisism. I asked for it, and got it straight from the shoulder, and thank you for it. I may be foolish enough to re-write it some time, and perhaps get it in better shape, in mean time let it rest.
>
> With great respt
> C. H. Higbie.

I have been away on a holiday for ten days, at sea in Mr. Rogers's yacht with some other young people, and when we were lying at anchor at Bar Harbor an incident occurred that fetched up out of the sub-cellars of my memory a matter which had lain buried there and forgotten for a quarter of a century.

In that old day somebody started a club called the Fellow-Craftsmen's Club, and I attended its first banquet, upon invitation. I think it was its last banquet, too, as I have never heard of it since. It probably died that night—and it may be that I helped to kill it. There were sixty-five men present, and Gilder was in the chair. Gilder was pretty young at that time, and pretty timid, and correspondingly diffident—not ungraceful qualities, and they still adorn him in a modified degree. Major J. B. Pond was alive in those days, and very much alive. He had been a lecture agent for some years, and was always diligently fussing around in the interest of his vocation and inflicting new talent upon the public. In the matter of pushing and advertising and over-praising his clients he was conscienceless. During the banquet I asked him to go and say to Gilder, in his private ear, that he had brought with him a young Southerner, unknown, but full of talent, who had invented a scheme for teaching impromptu oratory, and it would be a great benevolence to a struggling young fellow if Gilder would allow him to get up there and explain his invention and persuade the Fellow-Craft Club to take him under its wing and find him some classes to teach.

It was a gross and degraded proposition, in every way indelicate and offensive, and naturally it shocked Gilder, who tried to beg off; but Pond stuck to him and I can see the pair yet—the vast Pond bending over the lean and gentle Gilder, buzzing industriously at his ear—and Gilder making pathetic gestures revealing what he was suffering. Gilder said,

"Pond, I can't think of such a thing. Can't you see, yourself, that it is unthinkable? It is an atrocity. These people wouldn't stand it for a moment. You are always trying to crowd your goods in everywhere that there is a chance to advertise them, but this is no place for it. It would be indecent. If I should try to intrude this obscure adventurer upon these men they would rightly regard it as an impertinence, and they would resent it. Now go away, and drop the matter."

But Pond didn't go away. He still buzzed and buzzed, and begged and implored, and at last Gilder surrendered. When speech-making time came he got up and haltingly and hesitatingly informed the banqueteers that there was present among them an unknown young man from the South who would like the privilege of placing before them an invention of his for qualifying novices to get up, upon call, and make speeches upon any subject without previous preparation, and without diffidence or embarrassment. This young man——

Mr. Pond sang out,

"Langhorne—Mr. Samuel Langhorne."

These are my first two names, but nobody happened to notice that. Gilder proceeded,

"With your permission, gentlemen, I will ask Mr. Langhorne—"

He got no further. He was interrupted by a rising wave of dissent which went on rising until it broke into a storm. Gilder stood there defeated, and uncertain as to what he might better do—but I got up at that point, and, being recognized, was most heartily received, because the club thought they were now rid of Mr. Langhorne, and consequently they were properly grateful. I said something like this:

"I am Langhorne—that is my middle name. I am the inventor of the scheme which has been mentioned, and I think it a good one and likely to be of great benefit to the world; still this hope may be disappointed, and therefore I can't afford to use my real name, lest in trying to acquire a new and possibly valuable reputation I destroy the valuable one which I already possess, and yet fail to replace it with a new one. I propose to take classes and teach, under this apparently fictitious name. I wish to describe my scheme to you and prove its value by illustration. The scheme is founded upon a certain fact—a fact which long experience has convinced me *is* a fact, and not a fiction of my imagination. That fact is this: those speakers who are called upon at a banquet after the regular toasts have been responded to, are generally merely called upon by name and requested to get up and talk—that is all. No text is furnished them and they are in a difficult situation, apparently—but only apparently. The situation is not difficult at all, in fact, for they are usually men who know that they may be possibly called upon, therefore they go to the banquet prepared—after a certain fashion. The speeches which these volunteers make are all of a pattern. They consist of three first-rate anecdotes—first-water jewels, so to speak, set in the midst of a lot of rambling and incoherent talk, where they flash and sparkle and delight the house. The speech is made solely for the sake of the anecdotes whereas they shamelessly pretend that the anecdotes are introduced upon sudden inspiration, to illustrate the reasonings advanced in the speech. There *are* no reasonings in the speech. The speech wanders along in a random and purposeless way for a while; then, all of a sudden, the speaker breaks out as with an unforeseen and happy inspiration and says 'How felicitously what I have just been saying is illustrated in the case of the man who'—then he explodes his first anecdote. It's a good one—so good that a storm of delighted laughter sweeps the house and so disturbs its mental balance for the moment that it fails to notice that the anecdote didn't illustrate what the man had been saying—didn't illustrate anything at all, indeed, but was dragged in by the scruff of the neck and had no relation to the subject which the speaker was pretending to talk about. He doesn't allow the laughter to entirely subside before he is off and hammering away at his speech again. He doesn't wait, because that would be dangerous. It would give the house time to reflect; then it would see that the anecdote did not illustrate anything. He goes flitting airily along in his speech in the same random way as before, and presently has another of those inspirations and breaks out again with his 'How felicitously what I have just been saying is illustrated in the case of the man who'—then he lets fly his second anecdote, and again the house goes down with a crash. Before it can recover its senses he is away again, and cantering gaily toward the home stretch, filling the air with a stream of empty words that have no connection with anything; and finally he has his third inspiration, introduced with the same set form, 'How felicitously what I have just been saying is illustrated in the case of the man who'—then he lets fly his last and best anecdote and sits down under tempests and earthquakes of laughter, and everybody in his neighborhood seizes his hand and shakes it cordially and tells him it was a splendid speech—splendid.

"That is my scheme. I hope to get classes. I shall charge a high rate, because the pupil will need but one lesson. By grace of a single lesson I will make it possible for the novice who has never faced an audience in his life to rise to his feet, upon call, without trepidation or embarrassment and make an impromptu speech upon any subject that can be mentioned, without preparation of any kind, and also without even any knowledge of the subject which may be chosen for him. He shall always be ready, for he shall always have his three anecdotes in his pocket, written on a card, and thus equipped he shall never fail. I beg you to give me a text and let me prove what I have been saying—any text, any subject will do—all subjects are alike under my system. Give me a text."

There was a good deal of buzzing among the membership—then somebody spoke up and said,

"There is a nigger in this woodpile somewhere. There is collusion. This is a put-up hand. He's got a confederate here who will furnish him a text that has already been agreed upon. We want to beat that game."

Somebody else spoke up and said,

"There is only one way to beat it. Let every man present choose a text and write it on a piece of paper, not allowing any one else to see it—then pass a hat and collect the texts. The hat shall be held so high, when it reaches Gilder, that he can't look into it and make a selection; he must reach up and take out the first slip of paper his fingers touch—and that shall be this fraud's text, and will beat his game."

So the hat was passed, and everybody dropped a text into it. When it got to Gilder he reached up, took out a slip of paper and read from it "Portrait Painting."

The house was delighted, and shouted with a happy unanimity,

"Now then go ahead and let us see where you will come out with your scheme." I said,

"It is a good enough text. I want no better. I've already told you that all texts are alike, under this noble system. All that I need to do now is to talk a straight and uninterrupted stream of irrelevancies which shall ostensibly deal learnedly and instructively with the subject of portrait painting. The stream must not break anywhere; I must never hesitate for a word, because under this scheme the orator that hesitates is lost; it can give the house a chance to collect its reasoning faculties, and that is a thing which must not happen."

I began with the earliest known example of the art of portrait painting—that picture in outline of the extinct mammoth which primeval man carved upon the bone of a deer's horn, and which is treasured in a French museum. After elaborating that a little I passed to the distemper portraits, six thousand years old, furnished us by an Egyptian cemetery; then to the figures carved at a later date upon the monoliths and tombs of Egypt; then said, with enthusiasm "How felicitously what I have just been saying is illustrated in the case of the man who reached his home at two o'clock in the morning and his wife said plaintively 'Oh John, when you've had whisky enough why don't you ask for sarsaparilla?'—and he said 'Why, Maria, when I have had whisky enough I can't *say* sarsaparilla.'"

I did not wait for the full results, but plunged into my speech again and brought it along down, step by step, enlarging upon the results of the several stages, and when I got to Daguerre's monumental invention I discoursed upon it with a violence of enthusiasm that was startling to hear—notwithstanding it was about destitute of sense and coherence—then had one of those sudden inspirations, and exclaimed with feeling,

"How felicitously what I have just been saying is illustrated in the case of the man who arrived at his house at that usual unfortunate hour in the super-early morning, and stood there and watched his portico rising and sinking and swaying and reeling, and at last, when it swung around into his neighborhood he made a plunge and scrambled up the steps and got safely onto the portico, stood there watching his dim house rise and fall and swing and sway, until the front door came his way and he made a plunge and got in, and scrambled up the long flight of stairs, but at the topmost step instead of planting his foot upon it he only caught it with his toe, and down he tumbled, and rolled and thundered all the way down the stairs, fetched up in a sitting posture on the bottom step with his arm braced around the friendly newel-post and said 'God pity the poor sailors out at sea on such a night as this.'"

Then I went warbling along on my portrait painting and presently introduced my third and finest anecdote, using the same set form of introduction as before, and sat down triumphant, my great system proved and established.

But sorrow followed, and disaster. The first man called upon to speak was the brand-new district attorney, a man glib enough before judges and juries, but it was mainly a literary crowd that he was confronting now, and he showed timidity. He talked along hesitatingly, uncomfortably, unhappily; and presently it was plain that he was trying to lead up to an anecdote and didn't know how to manage it. Then the house broke out, from one end to the other, with encouragements. They said,

"Fetch it out! fetch it out! How felicitously what you have just been saying is illustrated in the case of the man who— Let her fly!"

He tried to work up to his anecdote, but the encouragements always broke out in time to scare him and shut him off, so he never got to his anecdote at all. He surrendered, and sat down.

The same thing happened to the next man, the new postmaster of Brooklyn. He struggled manfully along and approached his anecdote from four or five different directions, but always the house helped him along so enthusiastically that they frightened him off and he never reached his goal. He sat down defeated. Five other men were called upon, in turn, and each in turn declined to take a chance in that insurrection. Finally General Horace Porter was called up, and he got away with the honors of the evening. Let the house encourage and storm as they would, he stood to his guns, serene and unafraid. He told seven anecdotes, and introduced every one of them with the proper formula—"How felicitously," etc.

At Bar Harbor we invited half a dozen charming young ladies and as many charming young gentlemen to come aboard and take luncheon with us. On the evening preceding the luncheon our young people discussed the matter, on the quarter-deck aft, and devised ways and means to make the luncheon go off in a lively way. My ancient oratorical scheme came into my head and we concluded to try it. Next day, at the end of the luncheon, I got up and asked for a text, and those young rascals invited me to talk upon "Marriage Engagements." I recognized the villainy of it, for there were two engaged couples present, but I had to stick to my contract, and I did it.

It was plenty good enough fun—at least it was good enough fun for the others, though the couples and I could have enjoyed another text more. However, I took it out of one of the criminals—a lovely young creature who sat at my right, and with whom I was upon terms which permitted a considerable degree of latitude. I said that I hoped to have the young gentlemen in my oratorical class, and that I also had a scheme of instruction in a beautiful and neglected art which I hoped would appeal to the young ladies and persuade them to make up a class for me and cultivate their powers in that gracious art. I said that my scheme was to teach what I called the Classified Blush—the Graduated Blush. I said that there was hardly a young lady in the land who knew how to blush in anything like an expert way—they blushed carelessly, ignorantly, thoughtlessly; they over-blushed, they under-blushed; they seldom exhibited a blush which was exactly proportioned to the dimensions of the compliment which called it forth. I was sure that after a young lady had taken a dozen lessons from me she could blush accurately every time; that she would cease from furnishing a mild and almost colorless No. 1 blush when the compliment was of so handsome a nature that it properly called for a No. 6, or possibly a rich and radiant and crimson No. 14. I said,

"Now here at my side sits a young lady to whom I have given nineteen lessons, and I will prove to you that she is an expert. When I call for a No. 1 she'll not make the mistake of furnishing a No. 4, which would be overdoing it. When I call for No. 10, No. 14, and so on, you will see the exactly proper and requisite sunset-flush rise in these beautiful cheeks—there, just that casual little remark, you see, brings a No. 2. Now if you will look into her lovely blue eyes, if you will examine her charming features, her satin skin, her tawny hair, the fine intelligence which beams in her face—there now, look at that! Here where I touch her cheek with my finger an inch in front of her dainty ear, is the meridian which marks the degrees reaching from 1 to 5. See the color steal toward 5. Now it crosses it. Keep your eye on it. I move my finger forward toward her delicate nostril—see the rich blood follow it! When I tell you that hers is the loveliest form, the loveliest spirit that perhaps exists in the world to-day, that she is a darling of the darlings——but I need go no further. The blush has reached her nostril and her collar, and is a No. 16—the most engaging blush, the most charming blush, the most beautiful blush that can adorn the face of any earthly angel, save and except No. 31, which is the last and final possibility, and is called the 'San Francisco, or the Combined Earthquake and Conflagration.' I will now produce that blush."

But I didn't. It isn't right, and it isn't fair to carry vengeance too far. It seemed to me that that little witch and I were about even, and so I elected to be just and stand pat.

Wednesday, August 29, 1906

Letter from lady in regard to story, "A Horse's Tale," and Mr. Clemens's reply—Project for composite story—Two letters from lady who tried to aid San Francisco sufferers by contributing her brother's wife's "oll woole" suit—Reminiscences of Captain Ned Wakeman, and extract from his letter to Mr. Twichell.

In this morning's mail comes a letter from a stranger, which carries me back to what I was saying a couple of days ago when we were discussing Higbie's letter. Higbie's letter came from his heart, and I suggested that when the heart has something to say the product is literature, no matter whether the phrasing loyally follows accepted literary forms or splendidly ignores them, as the freshet ignores the dam. This lady's letter is from the heart, and it is in good English—educated English—but her heart would have delivered its message with as sure and moving a touch if she had never had a day's schooling in her life. We have seen this exemplified in Chapter XXXI, where we quoted an ignorant and eloquent letter written by a wronged and grieving western girl twenty-seven years ago.

I wish to insert here several letters of this kind, and in this way lead up to an occurrence of a week or two ago. We will begin with this morning's letter.

Sound Beach, Conn.
August 25, 1906.

Dear "Mark Twain"—

Please dont write any more such heart-breaking stories. I have just been reading Soldier Boy's story in Harpers. I dont think I would have read it had I known what was to come to Soldier Boy.

You used to write so differently. The note of pathos, of tragedy, of helpless pain creeps in now, more and more insistent. I fancy life must have taken on its more somber colours for you, and what you feel is reflected in what you write

You belong to all of us—we of America—and we all love you and are proud of you, but you make our hearts ache sometimes.

When your story of the poor dog was published in Harpers I read it and I cant tell you what I felt. I have never re-read it and I try not to remember it, but I cant help it. And now this story of Soldier Boy. It sinks into my heart. I feel like stretching out my hand to you and saying "I, too, feel these things, the dumb helpless pain of all the poor animals, and my soul protests against it, mightily but impotently, like yours."

I hope there is a heaven for animals somewhere, where they wont have to be with men, and you hope so too, dont you?

Dont think I am hysterical, notoriety seeking, or a crank. I am neither, only just poor and common-place—and—no longer young, but I *feel* all these things.

I beg to subscribe myself,

Most respectfully yours,
(Mrs) Lillian R. Beardsley.

To
Mr. Samuel L. Clemens.
By, Harper and Bros.
New York City.

I have explained my case to the lady as follows:

Dublin, New Hampshire.
Aug. 28.

Dear Madam:

I know it is a pity to wring the poor human heart, and it grieves me to do it; but it is the only way to move some people to reflect.

The "Horse's Tale" has a righteous purpose. It was not written for publication here, but in Spain. I was asked to write it to assist a band of generous ladies and gentlemen of Spain who have set themselves the gracious task of persuading the children of that country to renounce and forsake the cruel bull-fight. This in the hope that these children will carry on the work when they grow up. It is a great and fine cause, and if this story, distributed abroad in Spain in translation can in any degree aid it, I shall not be sorry that I complied with the request with which I was honored.

Sincerely yours,
S. L. Clemens.

Let us go on with our argument.

Several weeks ago the editor of *Harper's Bazar* projected a scheme for a composite story. A family was to tell the story. The father was to begin it, and, in turn, each member of the family was to furnish a chapter of it. There was to be a boy in the family, and I was invited to write his chapter. I was afraid of the scheme because I could not tell, beforehand, whether the boy would take an interest in it or not. Experience has taught me, long ago, that if *I* tell a boy's story—or anybody else's—it is never worth printing; it comes from the head, not the heart, and always goes into the waste-basket. To be successful, and worth printing, the imagined boy would have to tell his story *himself,* and let me act merely as his amanuensis. I did not tell the "Horse's Tale," the horse told it himself, through me. If he hadn't done that it wouldn't have been told at all. When a tale tells itself there is no trouble about it; there are no hesitancies, no delays, no cogitations, no attempts at invention; there is nothing to do but hold the pen and let the story talk through it and say, after its own fashion, what it desires to say.

Mr. Howells began the composite tale. He held the pen, and through it the father delivered his chapter—therefore it was well done. A lady followed Howells, and furnished the old-maid sister's chapter. This lady is of high literary distinction; she is nobly gifted; she has the ear of the nation, and her novels and stories are among the best that the country has produced; but *she* did not tell those tales, she merely held the pen and they told themselves—of this I am convinced. I am also convinced of another thing—that she did not act as amanuensis for the old-maid sister, but wrote the old-maid sister's chapter out of her own head, without any help from the old maid. The result is a failure. It is a piece of pure literary manufacture, and has the shop-marks all over it.

Thus far, the boy has not applied to me. I am ready to hold the pen for him in case he shall desire it, but he must tell his story himself. If I should try to tell it for him it would be poorly done, and would damage my reputation. I cannot afford to damage my reputation for the sake of a boy I am not acquainted with, and who is so dim and shadowy in my mind as this one is.

I now arrive at a couple of letters which were handed to me by a neighbor yesterday—a man of good character and established veracity—and he gives me his word of honor that they are genuine; otherwise I should say they are too good to be true. They flow delightfully along without a break anywhere, from beginning to end, the genial and happy stream suffering not even the momentary interruption of a comma, from the first word to the last. The spelling is so free, so independent, so majestically lawless, that Susy's is a slave to rule by comparison with it. The source of these letters is this:

When the appeal for clothing for the sufferers by the San Francisco fire and earthquake went abroad over the land the kind-hearted writer of these letters took a suit of clothes belonging to her brother's wife and carried them to the Armory in her town and generously devoted them to the cause, delivering them to Miss Blank Blank, chairman of the committee in charge of the matter, and receiving in return Miss Blank's cordial thanks. This is letter No. 1:

> Miss Blank dear freind i took some Close into the armerry and give them to you to Send too the suffrers out to California and i Hate to truble you but i got to have one of them Back it was a black oll woole Shevyott With a jacket to Mach trimed Kind of Fancy no 38 Burst measure and passy menterry acrost the front And the color i woodent Trubble you but it blonged to my brothers wife and she is Mad about It I thoght she was willin but she want she says she want done with it and she was goin to Wear it a Spell longer she ant so free harted as what i am and she Has got more to do with Than i have having a Husband to Work and slave For her i gess you remember Me I am shot And stout and light complected i torked with you quite a spell about the suffrars and said it Was offul about that erth quake i shoodent wondar if they had another one rite off seeine general Condision of the country is Kind of Explossive i hate to take that Black dress away from the suffrars but i will hunt round And see if i can get another One if i can i will call to the armerry for it if you will jest lay it asside so no more at present from your True freind.
> i liked your
> appearance very Much.

She wrote that divine letter on the 1st of May. On the following day she got a note from Miss Blank grieving over the fact that the brother's wife's all-wool suit of clothes had unfortunately passed out of her hands before the letter requiring its return had reached her. She was sincerely sorry that this calamity had been added to the San Franciscan disaster, and was also sorry that there seemed no way to repair the damage. On the 3d, she received the following reply in rebuttal. Both of this good soul's letters are winning and eloquent—splendidly and stirringly eloquent—in spite of their departure from the customary shop-worn literary forms, and in spite of their paralysing originality, and I think it is because they came not out of that good woman's head—in any large degree—but right out of her heart.

> Providence R. I.
> May the 3th 1906
>
> Miss Blank dear frei-
> nd i got your Letter all Right now dont you worry eny More about the Black Sute when I told Mame what you said she felt reel Bad about your fretin over it and she says good lord, she must think im meaner than dirt i give Her one of them feathar boars such as is all the Go and she was tickled to death over it and it kind of made it up to her about loosing the Sute she is reel amable By nature but she has ben orful

> tried this spring what with one thing and Another and she ant herself Jim says to me one day go slow for a spell with Mame she is orful tried what with the young ones and the spring cleening and a fire broke out in our bacement that thretend to lose our little all the same weak As the california erthguake every one Has there trubles an take it right strate throgh our crosses ant eny hevyer thane we can Bare theys a hire power that waches Over us and protects us from injerry i hope you have had good luck about your good work no more at present from yure true freind.

I am glad I have lived to read those letters. They are a benefaction. They have brightened my life and made me glad to continue it for the present—indefinitely, in fact, if I may have the privilege of hearing further from the writer of them from time to time. There is a charm about their limpid and flowing simplicity and their abounding and spirit-stirring eagerness which is graciously and benignantly satisfying to me. To my mind they are altogether delicious, and I think it would be hard to match them in the literature of any age or of any country.

Still pursuing our subject, I will now insert an extract from a letter written by Captain Ned Wakeman to the Reverend Joseph H. Twichell twenty or twenty-five years ago. I first knew Captain Wakeman thirty-nine years ago. I made two voyages with him, and we became fast friends. He was a great burly, handsome, weatherbeaten, symmetrically built and powerful creature, with coal black hair and whiskers, and the kind of eye which men obey without talking back. He was full of human nature, and the best kind of human nature. He was as hearty and sympathetic and loyal and loving a soul as I have found anywhere, and when his temper was up he performed all the functions of an earthquake, without the noise. He was all sailor, from head to heel; and this was proper enough, for he was born at sea, and, in the course of his sixty-five years, he had visited the edges of all the continents and archipelagoes, but had never been on land except incidentally and spasmodically, as you may say. He had never had a day's schooling in his life, but had picked up worlds and worlds of knowledge at second-hand, and none of it correct. He was a liberal talker, and inexhaustibly interesting. In the matter of a wide and catholic profanity he had not his peer on the planet while he lived. It was a deep pleasure to me to hear him do his stunts in this line. He knew the Bible by heart, and was profoundly and sincerely religious. He was always studying the Bible when it was his watch below, and always finding new things, fresh things, and unexpected delights and surprises in it—and he loved to talk about his discoveries and expound them to the ignorant. He believed that he was the only man on the globe that really knew the secret of the Biblical miracles. He had what he believed was a sane and rational explanation of every one of them, and he loved to teach his learning to the less fortunate.

I have said a good deal about him in my books. In one of them I have told how he brought the murderer of his colored mate to trial in the Chincha Islands before the assembled captains of the ships in port, and how when sentence had been passed he drew the line there. He had intended to capture and execute the murderer all by himself, but had been persuaded by the captains to let them try him with the due formalities, and under the forms of law. He had yielded that much, though most reluctantly, but when the captains proposed to do the executing also, that was too much for Wakeman, and he struck. He hanged the man himself. He put the noose around the murderer's neck, threw the bight of the line over the limb of a tree, and made his last moments a misery to him by reading him nearly into premature death with random and irrelevant chapters from the Bible.

He was a most winning and delightful creature. When he was fifty-three years old he started from a New England port, master of a great clipper ship bound around the Horn for San Francisco, and he was not aware that he had a passenger, but he was mistaken as to that. He had never had a love passage, but he was to have one now. When he was out from port a few weeks he was prowling about some remote corner of his ship, by way of inspection, when he came across a beautiful girl, twenty-four or twenty-five years old, prettily clothed and lying asleep with one plump arm under her neck. He stopped in his tracks and stood and gazed, enchanted. Then he said,

"It's an angel—that's what it is. It's an angel. When it opens its eyes, if they are blue I'll marry it."

The eyes turned out to be blue, and the pair were married when they reached San Francisco. The girl was to have taught school there. She had her appointment in her pocket—but the Captain saw to it that that arrangement did not materialize. He built a little house in Oakland—ostensibly a house, but really it was a ship, and had all a ship's appointments, binnacle, scuppers, and everything else—and there he and his little wife lived an ideal life during the intervals that intervened between his voyages. They were a devoted pair, and worshiped each other. By and by there were two little girls, and then the nautical paradise was complete.

When the Captain told me about that first encounter with his passenger he got out the pictures of his family, and he had previously described them, in the extravagant way which was natural to him, as being beautiful beyond the power of words to describe; but this time he had not overstated the case. The trio really were beautiful beyond the power of words to describe, and also sweet and winning beyond expression.

Captain Ned Wakeman was honored and beloved by San Franciscans as not many men have been honored and loved. He met with reverses, and when he died he left his family in straitened circumstances. I was living in Hartford at the time, and some one in San Francisco wrote me and said that as I was known to be an old and warm friend of the Captain it was desired that I should write a paragraph for publication in the *Alta California,* proposing a subscription of several thousand dollars for the benefit of his family. I did it, of course. I do not now remember what the proposed sum was, but Ralston, the banker, took the matter up and raised it in an hour. It was good evidence of the respect and affection in which the veteran was held.

Captain Wakeman had a fine large imagination, and he once told me of a visit which he had made to heaven. I kept it in my mind, and a month or two later I put it on paper—this was in the first quarter of 1868, I think. It made a small book of about forty thousand words, and I called it "Captain Stormfield's Visit to Heaven." Five or six years afterward I showed the manuscript to Howells and he said, "Publish it."

But I didn't. I had turned it into a burlesque of "The Gates Ajar," a book which had imagined a mean little ten-cent heaven about the size of Rhode Island—a heaven large enough to accommodate about a tenth of 1 per cent of the Christian billions who had died in the past nineteen centuries. I raised the limit; I built a properly and rationally stupendous heaven, and augmented its Christian population to 10 per cent of the contents of the modern cemeteries; also, as a volunteer kindness I let in a tenth of 1 per cent of the pagans who had died during the preceding eons—a liberty which was not justifiable, because those people had no business there; but as I had merely done it in pity, and out of kindness, I allowed them to stay. Toward the end of the book my heaven grew to such inconceivable dimensions on my hands that I ceased to apply poor little million-mile measurements to its mighty territories, and measured them by light-years only! and not only that, but a million of them linked together in a stretch.*

In the thirty-eight years which have since elapsed I have taken out that rusty old manuscript several times and examined it with the idea of printing it, but I always concluded to let it rest. However, I mean to put it into this Autobiography now.† It is not likely to see the light for fifty years, yet, and at that time I shall have been so long under the sod that I shan't care about the results.

I used to talk to Twichell about Wakeman, there in Hartford, thirty years ago and more, and by and by a curious thing happened. Twichell went off on a vacation, and as usual he followed his vacation-custom—that is to say, he traveled under an alias, so that he could associate with all kinds of disreputable characters and have a good time, and nobody be embarrassed by his presence, since they wouldn't know that he was a clergyman. He took a Pacific mail ship and started South for the Isthmus. Passenger traffic in that line had ceased almost entirely. Twichell found but one other passenger on board. He noticed that that other passenger was not a saint, so he went to foregathering with him at once, of course. After that passenger had delivered himself of about six majestically and picturesquely profane remarks Twichell (alias Peters) said,

"Could it be, by chance, that you are Captain Ned Wakeman of San Francisco?"

His guess was right, and the two men were inseparable during the rest of the voyage. One day Wakeman asked Peters-Twichell if he had ever read the Bible. Twichell said a number of things in reply—things of a rambling and non-committal character, but, taken in the sum, they left the impression that Twichell—well, never mind the impression; suffice it that Wakeman set himself the task of persuading Twichell to read that book. He also set himself the task of teaching Twichell how to understand the miracles. He expounded to him, among other miracles, the adventure of Isaac with the prophets of Baal. Twichell could have told him that it wasn't Isaac, but that wasn't Twichell's game,

* "*Light-year.*" This is without doubt the most stupendous and impressive phrase that exists in any language. It is restricted to astronomy. It describes the distance which light, moving at the rate of 186,000 miles per second, travels in our year of fifty-two weeks.

† *Three hours later.* I have just burned the closing two-thirds of it. M.T.

and he didn't make the correction. It was a delicious story, and it is delightful to hear Twichell tell it. I have printed it in full in one of my books—I don't remember which one.

Perhaps these prefatory words will answer well enough as an introduction to that extract from Wakeman's letter to Twichell which I mentioned a while ago. I shall not meddle with Captain Wakeman's spelling and construction, but put in the extract exactly as it came from his pen.

> Christmas day. Cal.
> Brooklyn, East Oakland
>
> Rev. Joseph. H. Twichell. Sir—last Eve right in the Midst of Enjoying all the pleasure there is or can be, round the Christmas tree that unlike any other Tree I Ever see, Bears Fruit in Every Clime which is the finest and the greatest variety and of Most Excellent flavour that I ever knew, it is a Golden fruit of a Devoted Mothers Love and Effection towards five of the Most Beautiful Children you ever see, and in effect far excells any other Tree there is in the world, as I was enjoying, hugely the happy emotions of the Bigger Children as they with difficulty restrained their Joyish feelings, as they Plucked the fruit that God had sent them and turning towards their mother with all the tenderest words of Love and Effection and with Eyes that was beaming of what my Poor Pensel cannot Portray, whilst the little ones ran Perfectly frantic with Joy Btueen the Tree and ma-ma Lap, and I was enjoying in a cosy Parlor of our little Hut, that which filled me with feelings of not only Present but Past, it was in watching that heavenly Smile which now and again Broke out in a hearty Girlish Laugh on the most Beatic Countinance of a Mother 40 years old that I Ever see, just at this time your letter was put into my hands, the Perusal of which I can assure you added much to my unbounded pleasure to hear from you so soon and from my old friend Don Carlos Flucha which Brought Back Volumes of Pleasant Remissises, all Bound in Gilt, any one of which were in the hand of our Mutual friend Mark Twain would make a Small Book Bound in Calf.

Thursday, August 30, 1906

Mr. Clemens's method of writing stories—Tells how some of his stories were commenced, how they were sometimes left for several years unfinished—Some of them have never been finished—Trouble with telephones—Miss Lyon's long-distance message to Clara Clemens—Mr. Scovel gives a clause of telephone law.

I was never willing to destroy "Captain Stormfield's Visit to Heaven." Now and then, in the past thirty years, I have overhauled my literary stock and transferred some of it to the fire, but "Stormfield's Visit" always escaped. Secretly and privately I liked it, I couldn't help it. But never mind about that, I wish to speak of something else now.

There has never been a time in the past thirty-five years when my literary shipyard hadn't two or more half-finished ships on the ways, neglected and baking in the sun;

generally there have been three or four; at present there are five. This has an unbusiness-like look, but it was not purposeless, it was intentional. As long as a book would write itself I was a faithful and interested amanuensis, and my industry did not flag; but the minute that the book tried to shift to *my* head the labor of contriving its situations, inventing its adventures and conducting its conversations, I put it away and dropped it out of my mind. Then I examined my unfinished properties to see if among them there might not be one whose interest in itself had revived, through a couple of years' restful idleness, and was ready to take me on again as amanuensis.

It was by accident that I found out that a book is pretty sure to get tired, along about the middle, and refuse to go on with its work until its powers and its interest should have been refreshed by a rest and its depleted stock of raw materials reinforced by lapse of time. It was when I had reached the middle of "Tom Sawyer" that I made this invaluable find. At page 400 of my manuscript the story made a sudden and determined halt and refused to proceed another step. Day after day it still refused. I was disappointed, distressed, and immeasurably astonished, for I knew quite well that the tale was not finished, and I could not understand why I was not able to go on with it. The reason was very simple—my tank had run dry; it was empty; the stock of materials in it was exhausted; the story could not go on without materials; it could not be wrought out of nothing. When the manuscript had lain in a pigeon-hole two years I took it out, one day, and read the last chapter that I had written. It was then that I made the great discovery that when the tank runs dry you've only to leave it alone and it will fill up again, in time, while you are asleep—also while you are at work at other things, and are quite unaware that this unconscious and profitable cerebration is going on. There was plenty of material now, and the book went on and finished itself without any trouble.

Ever since then, when I have been writing a book I have pigeon-holed it without misgivings when its tank ran dry, well knowing that it would fill up again without any of my help within the next two or three years, and that then the work of completing it would be simple and easy. "The Prince and the Pauper" struck work in the middle, because the tank was dry, and I did not touch it again for two years. A dry interval of two years occurred in "The Connecticut Yankee at the Court of King Arthur." A like interval has occurred in the middle of other books of mine. Two similar intervals have occurred in a story of mine called "Which Was It?" In fact, the second interval has gone considerably over time, for it is now four years since that second one intruded itself. I am sure that the tank is full again now, and that I could take up that book and write the other half of it without a break or any lapse of interest—but I shan't do it. The pen is irksome to me. I was born lazy, and dictating has spoiled me. I am quite sure I shall never touch a pen again; therefore that book will remain unfinished—a pity, too, for the idea of it is (actually) new and would spring a handsome surprise upon the reader, at the end.

There is another unfinished book, which I should probably entitle "The Refuge of the Derelicts." It is half finished, and will remain so. There is still another one, entitled "The Adventures of a Microbe During Three Thousand Years—by a Microbe." It is half finished and will remain so. There is yet another—"The Mysterious Stranger." It is more than half finished. I would dearly like to finish it, and it causes me a real pang to reflect that it is not to be. These several tanks are full now, and those books would go gaily along and complete themselves if I would hold the pen, but I am tired of the pen.

There was another of these half-finished stories. I carried it as far as thirty-eight thousand words four years ago, then destroyed it for fear I might some day finish it. Huck Finn was the teller of the story, and of course Tom Sawyer and Jim were the heroes of it. But I believed that that trio had done work enough in this world and were entitled to a permanent rest.

In Rouen, in '93, I destroyed fifteen thousand dollars' worth of manuscript, and in Paris, in the beginning of '94, I destroyed ten thousand dollars' worth—I mean, estimated as magazine stuff. I was afraid to keep those piles of manuscript on hand, lest I be tempted to sell them, for I was fairly well persuaded that they were not up to standard. Ordinarily there would have been no temptation present, and I would not think of publishing doubtful stuff—but I was heavily in debt then, and the temptation to mend my condition was so strong that I burnt the manuscripts to get rid of it. My wife not only made no objection, but encouraged me to do it, for she cared more for my reputation than for any other concern of ours. About that time she helped me put another temptation behind me. This was an offer of sixteen thousand dollars a year, for five years, to let my name be used as editor of a humorous periodical. I praise her for furnishing her help in resisting that temptation, for it is her due. There was no temptation about it, in fact, but she would have offered her help, just the same, if there had been one. I can conceive of many wild and extravagant things when my imagination is in good repair, but I can conceive of nothing quite so wild and extravagant as the idea of my accepting the editorship of a humorous periodical. I should regard that as the saddest (for me) of all occupations. If I should undertake it I should have to add to it the occupation of undertaker, to relieve it in some degree of its cheerlessness. I could edit a serious periodical with relish and a strong interest, but I have never cared enough about humor to qualify me to edit it or sit in judgment upon it.

There are some books that refuse to be written. They stand their ground, year after year, and will not be persuaded. It isn't because the book is not there and worth being written—it is only because the right form for the story does not present itself. There is only one right form for a story, and if you fail to find that form the story will not tell itself. You may try a dozen wrong forms, but in each case you will not get very far before you discover that you have not found the right one—then that story will always stop and decline to go any further. In the story of "Joan of Arc" I made six wrong starts, and each time that I offered the result to Mrs. Clemens she responded with the same deadly criticism—silence. She didn't say a word, but her silence spoke with the voice of thunder. When at last I found the right form I recognized at once that it was the right one, and I knew what she would say. She said it, without doubt or hesitation.

In the course of twelve years I made six attempts to tell a simple little story which I knew would tell itself in four hours if I could ever find the right starting-point. I scored six failures; then one day in London I offered the text of the story to Robert McClure, and proposed that he publish that text in the magazine and offer a prize to the person who should tell it best. I became greatly interested and went on talking upon the text for half an hour; then he said,

"You have told the story yourself. You have nothing to do but put it on paper just as you have told it."

I recognized that this was true. At the end of four hours it was finished, and quite to my satisfaction. So it took twelve years and four hours to produce that little bit of a story, which I have called "The Death-Wafer."

To start right is certainly an essential. I have proved this too many times to doubt it. Twenty-five or thirty years ago I began a story which was to turn upon the marvels of mental telegraphy. A man was to invent a scheme whereby he could synchronize two minds, thousands of miles apart, and enable them to freely converse together through the air without the aid of a wire. Four times I started it in the wrong way, and it wouldn't go. Three times I discovered my mistake after writing about a hundred pages. I discovered it the fourth time when I had written four hundred pages—then I gave it up and put the whole thing in the fire.

I have mentioned an unfinished book which might be entitled "The Refuge of the Derelicts." In the manuscript the story has no title, but begins with *a pretty brusque remark* by an ancient admiral, who is Captain Ned Wakeman under a borrowed name. This reminds me of something.

Four or five months ago, in the New York home, I learned by accident that we had been having a good deal of trouble with our telephones. The family get more or less peace and comfort out of concealing vexations from me on account of the infirmities of my temper, and it would be only by accident that I could find out that the telephones were making trouble. Upon inquiry I discovered that my tribe had been following the world's usual custom—they had applied for relief to the Telephone Company's subordinates. This is always a mistake. The only right way is to apply to the President of a corporation; your complaint receives immediate and courteous attention then. I called up the headquarters and asked the President to send some one to my house to listen to a complaint. One of the chief superintendents came—Mr. Scovel. The complaint occupied but a minute of our time. Then he sat by the bed and we smoked and chatted half an hour very pleasantly. I remarked that often and often I would dearly like to use the telephone myself, but didn't dare to do it because when the connection was imperfect I was sure to lose my temper and swear—and while I would like to do that, and would get a good deal of satisfaction out of it, I couldn't venture it because I was aware that by telephone law the Company can remove your telephone if you indulge yourself in that way.

Mr. Scovel gladdened me by informing me that I could allow myself that indulgence without fear of injurious results, for there wouldn't be any, there being a clause in the law which allowed me that valuable privilege. Then he quoted that clause and made me happy.

Two or three months ago I wanted that nameless manuscript heretofore mentioned, and I asked my secretary to call up my New York home on the long-distance and tell my daughter Clara to find that manuscript and send it to me. The line was not in good order, and Miss Lyon found great difficulty in making Clara understand what was wanted. After a deal of shouting back and forth Clara gathered that it was a manuscript that was wanted, and that she would find it among the manuscriptural riffraff in my study somewhere. Then she wanted to know by what sign she would recognize it. She asked for the title of it.

Miss Lyon—using a volume of voice which should have carried to New York without the telephone's help, said—

"It has no title. It begins with a remark."

It took some time to make Clara understand that. Then she said,

"What is the remark?"

Miss Lyon shouted—

"Tell him to go to hell."

Clara. "Tell him to go—where?"

Miss Lyon. "To hell."

Clara. "I can't get it. Spell it."

Miss Lyon. "H-E-L-L."

Clara. "Oh, *hell.*"

I was troubled, not by the ear-splitting shouting, which I didn't mind, but by the character of the words that were going over that wire and being listened to in every office on it, and for a moment I was scared and said,

"Now they'll take our telephone out, on account of this kind of talk."

But the next moment I was comfortable again, because I remembered that blessed clause in the telephone law which Mr. Scovel had quoted to me, and which said:

"In employing our telephones no subscriber shall be debarred from using his native language."

Friday, August 31, 1906

Mr. Clemens appoints two pupils and tries his scheme for Spontaneous Oratory at the Dublin club house—Tells of his second lecture and the repetition of the Horace Greeley story—Tells the same thing later at Chickering Hall—The series of seven photographs of Mr. Clemens—Letter from his long-vanished sweetheart, Laura Wright—Reminiscences of her; of Youngblood, the pilot; and of Davis, the mate—Letter offering tour in vaudeville.

Around about here, in the New Hampshire woods and hills, are scattered a couple of dozen summer resorters, who own their houses and who come here every summer, some of them from as far away as Chicago and St. Louis. They have a modest and pretty club house for dances and other diversions, and two or three times a month they meet there and are entertained with music, lectures, and so on, furnished by the home talent. The home talent consists of distinguished artists, college professors, historians, and so on—and I am a part of it myself. My turn having arrived now, I mean to exploit my system of "Spontaneous Oratory" to-morrow afternoon, and see how it will go. Yesterday I appointed a couple of pupils—Messrs. Brush and Smith—explained the game to them, and required them to be on hand to-morrow with three good anecdotes apiece. I shall ask the audience for a subject, and we three will debate it in accordance with the principles of my system. I believe the performance will be elevating and instructive. I know it will if my pupils bring good anecdotes, and if they shall always remember to introduce each anecdote *with one and the same set formula monotonously—without changing a word.* I will furnish the formula; repetition of it will do the rest.

For repetition is a mighty power in the domain of humor. If frequently used, nearly any *precisely worded and unchanging formula* will eventually compel laughter if it be gravely and earnestly repeated, at intervals, five or six times. I undertook to prove the truth of this, forty years ago, in San Francisco, on the occasion of my second attempt at lecturing. My first lecture had succeeded to my satisfaction. Then I prepared another one, but was afraid of it because the first fifteen minutes of it was not humorous. I felt the necessity of preceding it with something which would break up the house with a laugh and get me on pleasant and friendly terms with it at the start, instead of allowing it leisure to congeal into a critical mood, since that could be disastrous. With this idea in mind, I prepared a scheme of so daring a nature that I wonder now that I ever had the courage to carry it through. San Francisco had been persecuted for five or six years with a silly and pointless and unkillable anecdote which everybody had long ago grown weary of—weary unto death. It was as much as a man's life was worth to tell that mouldy anecdote to a citizen. I resolved to begin my lecture with it, and keep on repeating it until the mere repetition should conquer the house and make it laugh. That anecdote is in one of my books.

There were fifteen hundred people present, and as I had been a reporter on one of the papers for a good while I knew several hundred of them. They loved me, they couldn't help it; they admired me; and I knew it would grieve them, disappoint them, and make them sick at heart to hear me fetch out that odious anecdote with the air of a person who thought it new and good. I began with a description of my first day in the overland coach; then I said,

"At a little 'dobie station out on the plains, next day, a man got in and after chatting along pleasantly for a while he said 'I can tell you a most laughable thing indeed, if you would like to listen to it. Horace Greeley went over this road once. When he was leaving Carson City he told the driver, Hank Monk, that he had an engagement to lecture at Placerville and was very anxious to go through quick. Hank Monk cracked his whip and started off at an awful pace. The coach bounced up and down in such a terrific way that it jolted the buttons all off of Horace's coat and finally shot his head clean through the roof of the stage, and then he yelled at Hank Monk and begged him to go easier—said he warn't in as much of a hurry as he was a while ago. But Hank Monk said "Keep your seat, Horace, I'll get you there on time!"—and you bet he did, too, what was left of him!'"

I told it in a level voice, in a colorless and monotonous way, without emphasizing any word in it, and succeeded in making it dreary and stupid to the limit. Then I paused and looked very much pleased with myself, and as if I expected a burst of laughter. Of course there was no laughter, nor anything resembling it. There was a dead silence. As far as the eye could reach that sea of faces was a sorrow to look upon; some bore an insulted look; some exhibited resentment, my friends and acquaintances looked ashamed, and the house, as a body, looked as if it had taken an emetic.

I tried to look embarrassed, and did it very well. For a while I said nothing, but stood fumbling with my hands in a sort of mute appeal to the audience for compassion. Many did pity me—I could see it. But I could also see that the rest were thirsting for blood. I presently began again, and stammered awkwardly along with some more details of the overland trip. Then I began to work up toward my anecdote again with the air of a person who thinks he did not tell it well the first time, and who feels that the house will like it the next time, if told with a better art. The house perceived that I was working up toward the anecdote again, and its indignation was very apparent. Then I said,

"Just after we left Julesburg, on the Platte, I was sitting with the driver and he said 'I can tell you a most laughable thing indeed if you would like to listen to it. Horace Greeley went over this road once. When he was leaving Carson City he told the driver, Hank Monk, that he had an engagement to lecture at Placerville and was very anxious to go through quick. Hank Monk cracked his whip and started off at an awful pace. The coach bounced up and down in such a terrific way that it jolted the buttons all off of Horace's coat and finally shot his head clean through the roof of the stage, and then he yelled at Hank Monk and begged him to go easier—said he warn't in as much of a hurry as he was a while ago. But Hank Monk said "Keep your seat, Horace, I'll get you there on time!"—and you bet he did, too, what was left of him!'"

I stopped again, and looked gratified and expectant, but there wasn't a sound. The house was as still as the tomb. I looked embarrassed again. I fumbled again. I tried to seem ready to cry, and once more, after a considerable silence, I took up the overland trip again, and once more I stumbled and hesitated along—then presently began again to work up toward the anecdote. The house exhibited distinct impatience, but I worked along up, trying all the while to look like a person who was sure that there was some mysterious reason why these people didn't see how funny the anecdote was, and that they must see it if I could ever manage to tell it right, therefore I must make another effort. I said,

"A day or two after that we picked up a Denver man at the cross-roads and he chatted along very pleasantly for a while. Then he said 'I can tell you a most laughable thing indeed, if you would like to listen to it. Horace Greeley went over this road once. When he was leaving Carson City he told the driver, Hank Monk, that he had an engagement to lecture at Placerville and was very anxious to go through quick. Hank Monk cracked his whip and started off at an awful pace. The coach bounced up and down in such a terrific way that it jolted the buttons all off of Horace's coat and finally shot his head clean through the roof of the stage, and then he yelled at Hank Monk and begged him to go easier—said he warn't in as much of a hurry as he was a while ago. But Hank Monk said "Keep your seat, Horace, I'll get you there on time!"—and you bet he did, too, what was left of him!'"

All of a sudden the front ranks recognized the sell, and broke into a laugh. It spread back, and back, and back, to the furthest verge of the place; then swept forward again, and then back again, and at the end of a minute the laughter was as universal and as thunderously noisy as a tempest.

It was a heavenly sound to me, for I was nearly exhausted with weakness and apprehension, and was becoming almost convinced that I should have to stand there and keep on telling that anecdote all night, before I could make those people understand that I was working a delicate piece of satire. I am sure I should have stood my ground and gone on favoring them with that tale until I broke them down, for I had the unconquerable conviction that the monotonous repetition of it would infallibly fetch them some time or other.

A good many years afterward there was to be an Authors' Reading at Chickering Hall, in New York, and I thought I would try that anecdote again, and see if the repetition would be effective with an audience wholly unacquainted with it, and who would be obliged to find the fun solely in the repetition, if they found it at all, since there would be not a shred of anything in the tale itself that could stir anybody's sense of humor but an idiot's. I sat by James Russell Lowell on the platform, and he asked me what I was going to read. I said I was going to tell a brief and wholly pointless anecdote in a dreary and monotonous voice, and that therein would consist my whole performance. He said,

"That is a strange idea. What do you expect to accomplish by it?"

I said,

"Only a laugh. I want the audience to laugh."

He said "Of course you do—that is your trade. They will require it of you. But do you think they are going to laugh at a silly and pointless anecdote drearily and monotonously told?"

"Yes," I said, "they'll laugh."

Lowell said "I think you are dangerous company. I am going to move to the other end of this platform and get out of the way of the bricks."

When my turn came I got up and exactly repeated—and most gravely and drearily—that San Francisco performance of so many years before. It was as deadly an ordeal as ever I have been through in the course of my checkered life. I never got a response of any kind until I had told that juiceless anecdote in the same unvarying words *five times;*

then the house saw the point and annihilated the heart-breaking silence with a most welcome crash. It revived me, and I needed it, for if I had had to tell it four more times I should have died—but I would have done it, if I had had to get somebody to hold me up. The house kept up that crash for a minute or two, and it was a soothing and blessed thing to hear.

Mr. Lowell shook me cordially by the hand, and said,

"Mark, it was a triumph of art! It was a triumph of grit, too. I would rather lead a forlorn hope and take my chances of a soldier's bloody death than try to duplicate that performance."

He said that during the first four repetitions, with that mute and solemn and wondering house before him, he thought he was going to perish with anxiety for me. He said he had never been so sorry for a human being before, and that he was cold, all down his spine, until the fifth repetition broke up the house and brought the blessed relief.

The following post-card has been issued this morning to our summer resorters, and I think that if we fail in other ways, in our debate, the day will be saved anyhow by six or eight repetitions of that formula "How felicitously what I have just been saying is illustrated in the case of the man who—"

> At the Club, on Saturday, September the 1st, Mr. Mark Twain will reveal and explain the true secret of after-dinner speaking, and in a single lesson will teach novices, by a method of his own, how to speak successfully and acceptably upon any topic whatsoever, without embarrassment, without previous preparation, and even without knowledge of the subject.
>
> After his explanation there will be a debate between himself and his pupils, Messrs. George Brush and Joseph Smith, in illustration of his method.
>
> The exhibition will begin at 4 p.m.

The pictures which Mr. Paine made on the portico here several weeks ago, have been developed, and are good. For the sake of the moral lesson which they teach, I wish to insert a set of them here for future generations to study, with the result, I hope, that they will reform, if they need it—and I expect they will. I am sending half a dozen of these sets to friends of mine who need reforming, and I have introduced the pictures to them with this formula:

> This series of photographs registers with scientific precision, stage by stage, the progress of a moral purpose through the mind of the human race's Oldest Friend.

No. 1

Shall I learn to be good?

. . . . .
. . . . .

I will sit here and think it over.

Truly Yours
Mark Twain

Sept. '06.

No. 2
There do seem
to be so many
diffi....

3
3
And yet if I should
really try . . . .

No. 4.
. . . . and just put my whole heart in it . . . . . .

No. 5
.... But then I couldn't
break the Sab.....

No. 6.
.... and there's so
many other privileges,
that.... perhaps.....

7
Oh, never mind,
I reckon I'm good enough
just as I am.

At last we have heard again from my long-vanished little fourteen-year-old sweetheart of nearly fifty years ago. It had begun to look very much as if we had lost her again. She was drifting about among old friends in Missouri, and we couldn't get upon her track. We supposed that she had returned to her home in California, where she teaches school, and we sent the check there. It traveled around during two months and finally found her, three or four days ago, in Columbia, Missouri. She has written a charming letter, and it is full of character. Because of the character exhibited, I find in her, once more at sixty-three, the little girl of fourteen of so long ago.

When she went back up the river, on board the *John J. Roe,* in that ancient day which I have already spoken of in a previous chapter, the boat struck a snag in the night and was apparently booked to find the bottom of the Mississippi in a few minutes. She was rushed to the shore, and there was great excitement and much noise. Everybody was commanded to vacate the vessel instantly. This was done,—at least for the moment no one seemed to be missing. Then Youngblood, one of the pilots, discovered that his little niece was not among the rescued. He and old Davis, the mate, rushed aboard the sinking boat and hammered on Laura's door, which they found locked, and shouted to her to come out—that there was not a moment to lose.

She replied quite calmly that there was something the matter with her hoop-skirt, and she couldn't come yet. They said,

"Never mind the hoop-skirt. Come without it. There is no time to waste upon trifles."

But she answered, just as calmly, that she wasn't going to come until the skirt was repaired and she was in it. She kept her word, and came ashore, at her leisure, completely dressed.

I was thinking of this when I was reading her letter this morning, and the thought carried me so far back into the hoary past that for the moment I was living it over again, and was again a heedless and giddy lad, with all the vast intervening stretch of years abolished—and along with it my present condition, and my white head. And so, when I presently came upon the following passage in her letter it hit me with an astonishing surprise, and seemed to be referring to somebody else:

> But I must not weary you nor take up your valuable time with my chatter. I really forget that I am writing to one of the world's most famous and sought-after men, which shows you that I am still roaming in the Forest of Arden.

And so I am a hero to Laura Wright! It is wholly unthinkable. One can be a hero to other folk, and in a sort of vague way understand it, or at least believe it, but that a person can really be a hero to a near and familiar friend, is a thing which no hero has ever yet been able to realize, I am sure.

She has been visiting the Youngbloods. It revives in me some ancient and tragic memories. Youngblood was as fine a man as I have known. In that day he was young, and had a young wife and two small children—a most happy and contented family. He was a good pilot, and he fully appreciated the responsibilities of that great position. Once when a passenger boat upon which he was standing a pilot's watch was burned on the Mississippi, he landed the boat and stood to his post at the wheel until everybody was ashore and the entire after part of the boat, including the after part of the pilot-house, was a mass of flame; then he climbed out over the breast-board and escaped with his life, though badly scorched and blistered by the fire. A year or two later, in New Orleans, he went out one night to do an errand for the family and was never heard of again. It was supposed that he was murdered, and that was doubtless the case, but the matter remains a mystery yet.

That old mate, Davis, was a very interesting man. He was past sixty, and his bush of hair and whiskers would have been white if he had allowed them to have their own way, but he didn't. He dyed them, and as he only dyed them four times a year he was generally a curious spectacle. When the process was successful, his hair and whiskers were sometimes a bright and attractive green; at other times they were a deep and agreeable purple; at still other times they would grow out and expose half an inch of white hair. Then the effect was striking, particularly as regards his whiskers, because in certain lights the belt of white hair next to his face would become nearly invisible; then his bush of whiskers did not seem to be connected with his face at all, but quite separated from it and independent of it. Being a chief mate, he was a prodigious and competent swearer, a thing which the office requires. But he had an auxiliary vocabulary which no other mate on the river possessed, and it made him able to persuade indolent roustabouts more effectively than did the swearing of any other mate in the business, because while it was not profane, it was of so mysterious and formidable and terrifying a nature that it sounded five or six times as profane as any language to be found on the fo'castle anywhere in the river service. Davis had no education beyond reading and something which so nearly resembled writing that it was reasonably well calculated to deceive. He read, and he read a great deal, and diligently, but his whole library consisted of a single book. It was Lyell's "Geology," and he had stuck to it until all its grim and rugged scientific terminology was familiar in his mouth, though he hadn't the least idea of what the words meant, and didn't care what they meant. All he wanted out of those great words was the energy they stirred up in his roustabouts. In times of extreme emergency he would let fly a volcanic irruption of the old regular orthodox profanity mixed up and seasoned all through with imposing geological terms, then formally charge his roustabouts with being Old Silurian Invertebrates out of the Incandescent Anisodactylous Post-Pliocene Period, and damn the whole gang in a body to perdition.

People are always wounding my dignity. Every now and then some ignorant person afflicts me in that way. I was once a lecturer, but I have reformed long ago. I have discarded all such degradations and have tried to make the world understand that I am now a stately person who has retired from all small things and sits upon a summit apart—a great and shining literary light who deals substantially with nothing on a lower plane than the sun and the constellations. And so when a letter such as came in this morning's mail reaches me, it drags me down from my summit and humiliates me.

Read this irreverent letter and reflect upon it. Think of a person proposing a tour in vaudeville to a man of my proportions! He wants to arrange a tour, he says, in which he could give me three consecutive weeks and one week of rest. He has no shame. He says he could give me as many weeks as I might desire, and that he would simply want a "sixteen to twenty minute monologue or lecture as you might choose to call it, and twice a day."

Why doesn't he propose a clog-dance and done with it? He thinks I would enjoy such an engagement—thinks it will be a new field for me and show me a new set of faces; also he thinks the best part of the whole thing would be the "renumeration." It is a good enough word, but it could not be more offensive to me if he had spelled it right. He thinks he can secure me a very "tidy sum" per week.

But read the letter. I am wounded to the heart, and I cannot go on with it. If this man shall chance to hear of our Spontaneous Oratory experiment, he will probably affront me again.

The Boyle Agency
INTERNATIONAL
VAUDEVILLE AND DRAMATIC
31 WEST 31ST STREET

NEW YORK August 24, 1906

Samuel L. Clemmens, Esq., (Mark Twain)
21 Fifth Avenue, New York
My Dear Mr. Clemens:—

I should like to suggest to you a tour in vaudeville. I shall be able to arrange a tour in which we could give you say three consecutive weeks and one week of rest. I could give you as many weeks as you might desire beginning September 24 or the first week of October. I make this explanation, as I feared you could consider vaudeville too strenuous. We would simply want a sixteen to twenty minute monologue or lecture as you might choose to call it, and twice a day. Some of the weeks would include Sunday and some of them would mean only six days. I am very sure that you would enjoy such an engagement. It will be a new field for you, and would show you a new set of faces. The best part of the whole thing would be the renumeration. I am very sure that I can secure for you a very tidy sum per week. I name, of course, Hammerstein's and the Percy G. Williams' houses in this city and Brooklyn, and the highest class vaudeville houses in other cities East of Chicago. Kindly give this matter your earnest thought and let me know what you think you would like for this kind of an engagement per week.

Trusting that you are enjoying the best of health and that I may have a favorable reply from you, I am

Very truly yours,
B. Butler Boyle

Monday, September 3, 1906

The debate at the Dublin club house—Spontaneous Oratory good scheme for ocean liner entertainments—Susy's Biography—The sum in arithmetic—Sour Mash, and the other cats—A tribute to General Grant.

We carried out our project at the club on Saturday afternoon, and were very well satisfied with it. We had a narrow platform against one end of the hall, and on it three chairs in a row for the accommodation of myself and my pupils. I explained my system to the house—a system whereby I could teach the novice, with a single lesson, how to make impromptu speeches of a satisfactory and successful character upon any and all occasions without timidity, without embarrassment, and even without doubt or solicitude as to the result. I said that my two pupils—the artists George Brush and Joseph Smith—could not really be said to have received a lesson, as yet, but that the explanation which I had just been making would qualify them to get up and address this house, when called upon, and do it to the house's contentment—because each of them had two or three anecdotes in his vest pocket, and inasmuch as the anecdotes are the essential feature of my system of Spontaneous Oratory, the resulting speeches would necessarily be successful. I said that my system had never been subjected to the severe test of a debate before, but that it would nevertheless be found able to competently meet this emergency.

I said that we were now ready to begin as soon as the audience would favor us with a subject for discussion. After a brief conference with others, Professor Henderson offered us this question for debate:

> If it were decreed that one of the sexes must be exterminated, which one could best be spared?

I said it was an admirable selection and offered a difficult question for settlement, but that its difficulties had no terrors for us; we should settle it, and settle it permanently, within an hour and a quarter.

I elected to open the debate myself, and maintain that the planet could better get along without the men than without the women. I appointed Mr. Brush to attack this position and devote his best reasoning powers to a defence of the male sex's superior claims to preservation. I appointed Mr. Smith to follow, on either side of the question or on both sides of it, according to his desire and the movements of his spirit.

We carried the debate through with a good quality of seriousness; also with animation; with deep feeling at times, together with occasional outbreaks of vindictiveness and vituperation. Each man's speech ended with an excellent anecdote which professed to illustrate what the speaker had just been saying, but didn't illustrate it of course—didn't illustrate what he had been saying nor what anybody else had been saying this year.

Brush assumed the character and manner of an old German professor, and searched the deeps of the subject, assisting himself with irruptions of scientific terms clothed in the dead languages; and his grave mingling of earnestness and absurdity was a fine exhibition of art, and very effective.

Mr. Smith assumed the precise and ornate style of the experienced disputant of the old-time village debating society, and exhibited with good art the confidence and complacency that are born of an established reputation.

We got through in a short hour and a quarter, and then I was convinced that we had made a valuable discovery. I was sure that whereas country clubs usually find it difficult to provide fortnightly entertainments of a really entertaining sort with the home talent at their disposal, they need now only do debates, on our plan, to insure an excellent nonsense-entertainment every time.

I am moved to offer our scheme to the attention of the sea-going public. It ought to be adopted in the liners, and given the place which has been occupied for generations, on the night before reaching port, by those dreary exhibitions of ship-going talent—the trial by jury, which is always a witless and extravagant exhibition; and the "concert," which consists of speeches made up of compliments to the ship and its officers, amateur music which does not enthuse, and over-impassioned recitations of "Curfew Shall Not Ring To-night," with other worn and ancient distresses. I believe there is nothing in all the range of steamship entertainments that is so empty, noisy, pointless and frantic, as the trial by jury. I have read one, lately, which some maniac took down in shorthand and published. Without doubt it was sufficiently stupid when it happened; it was sure to be still stupider when exposed to cold print. A better day is coming, I hope, when at last the recitations and the trial by jury will be abolished from the sea and the Spontaneous Debate elected to fill their place. To make those other things endurable, talent and experience in the performers is necessary; to make a Spontaneous Debate delightful, neither talent nor experience is necessary—nothing is necessary but a stream of earnest and incoherent words interrupted at intervals by an illustrative good anecdote which does not illustrate anything. Words are plenty; so are good anecdotes. These being present in any gathering of human beings, the Spontaneous Debate cannot fail.

From Susy's Biography.

1884

The other day we were all sitting, when papa told Clara and I that he would give us an arithmetic example; he began "If A byes a horse for $100—" "$200" Jean interrupted; the expression of mingled surprise and submission on papa face, as he turned to Jean and said "Who is doing this example, Jean?" was inexpressibly funny. Jean laughed and papa continued "If A byes a horse for $100—" "$200" Jean promptly interrupted; papa looked perplexed and mamma went into convulsions of laughter. It was plain to us all that papa would have to change his summ to $200. So he accordingly began "If A byes a horse for $200 and B byes a mule for $140 and they join in co-partnership and trade their creatures for a piece of land at $480 how long will it take a lame man to borrow a silk umbrella?"

Susy does not furnish the answer—and now, after the lapse of twenty years, I find that I am not able to furnish it myself. It is one of those losses which we may mourn but cannot repair.

> Papa's great care now is Sour Mash (the cat) and he will come way down from his study on the hill to see how she is getting along.

It was quite natural for me to do it, for I had a great admiration for Sour Mash, and a great affection for her, too. She was one of the institutions of Quarry Farm for a good many years. She had an abundance of that noble quality which all cats possess, and which neither man nor any other animal possesses in any considerable degree—independence. Also she was affectionate, she was loyal, she was plucky, she was enterprising, she was just to her friends and unjust to her enemies—and she was righteously entitled to the high compliment which so often fell from the lips of John T. Lewis—reluctantly, and as by compulsion, but all the more precious for that:

"Other Christians is always worrying about other people's opinions, but Sour Mash don't give a damn."

Indeed she was just that independent of criticism, and I think it was her supreme grace. In her industries she was remarkable. She was always busy. If she wasn't exterminating grasshoppers she was exterminating snakes—for no snake had any terrors for her. When she wasn't catching mice she was catching birds. She was untiring in her energies. Every waking moment was precious to her; in it she would find something useful to do—and if she ran out of material and couldn't find anything else to do she would have kittens. She always kept us supplied, and her families were of a choice quality. She herself was a three-colored tortoise-shell, but she had no prejudices of breed, creed, or caste. She furnished us all kinds, all colors, with that impartiality which was so fine a part of her make. She allowed no dogs on the premises except those that belonged there. Visitors who brought their dogs along always had an opportunity to regret it. She hadn't two plans for receiving a dog guest, but only one. She didn't wait for the formality of an introduction to any dog, but promptly jumped on his back and rode him all over the farm. By my help she would send out cards, next day, and invite that dog to a garden party, but she never got an acceptance. The dog that had enjoyed her hospitalities once was willing to stand pat.

> A few months after the last "Prince and Pauper" we started for the farm. The farm is Aunt Susy's home and where we stay in the summer. It is situated on the top of a high hill overlooking the vally of Elmira. In the winter papa sent way to Kansas for a little donkey for us to have at the farm, and when we got to the farm we were delighted to find the donky in good trimm and ready to have us ride her. But she has proved to be very balky and to have to make her go by walking in front of her with a handful of crackers.

The creature was no bigger than a calf, yet when she chose to balk she could not be budged from her position by any arts that the children were master of. I said it was because they were not decided enough with her; that they lacked confidence in their power to move her and she was aware of it and took advantage of the situation. I said that all she needed on her back was a person equipped with confidence and decision of character—then she would know her place. I jumped on the creature's back, by way of an object lesson, but went over her head in the same instant and landed on my own back. The children were astonished, but I said it was nothing, I could do it every time.

In those days I was more musical than I am now in my old age, and could out-bray any donkey in the region, and give him points. The children admired this performance beyond measure, and they often had me at it and raising the echoes of the hills and the valleys. They were always eager to have me show off my talent before company, but I was diffident and got out of it upon one pretense or another. They wanted me to set my bray to poetry, and I did it; did it most grandly, too, in their opinion, for they were charitable critics. It was wonderfully good poetry, just as poetry, but was prodigiously improved by the bray. The donkey's name was Cadichon. I cannot call to mind who furnished that name, but it was the children that furnished the pronunciation. They called it Kiditchin, with the emphasis on the middle syllable.

From Susy's Biography.

Papa wrote a little poem about her which I have and will put in here, it is partly German and partly English.

Kiditchin.

O du lieb' Kiditchin,
Du bist ganz bewitchin,
Waw-----he!

In summer days Kiditchin
Thou'rt dear from nose to britchin
Waw-----he!

No dought thoult get a switchin
When for mischief thou'rt itchin'
Waw-----he!

But when youre good Kiditchin
You shall feast in James's kitchen
Waw-----he!

O now lift up thy song—
Thy noble note prolong,—
Thou living Chinese gong!

Waw--he! waw--he-waw!
Sweetest donkey man ever saw.

There are eleven cats at the farm here now, and papa's favorite a Tortoise Shell he has named "Sour Mash" and a little spotted one "Famine." It is very pretty to see what papa calls the cat prosession it was formed in this way. Old Minnie-cat headed, (the mother of all the cats) next to her came aunt Susie, then Clara on the donkey, accompanied by a pile of cats, then papa and Jean hand in hand and a pile of cats brought up the rear, Mamma and I made up the audience.

Our varius occupations are as follows. Papa rises about ½ past 7 in the morning, breakfasts at eight, writes plays tennis with Clara and me and tries to make the donkey go in the morning, does varius things in P.M., and in the evening plays tennis with Clara and me and amuses Jean and the donkey.

Mamma rises about ¼ to eight, breakfasts at eight, teaches Jean German reading from 9–10, reads German with me from 10–11— Then she reads studdies or visits with aunt Susie for a while, and then she reads to Clara and I till lunch time things connected with English history for we hope to go to England next summer, while we sew. Then we have lunch. She studdies for about half an hour or visits with aunt Susie, then reads to us an hour or more, then studdies writes reads and rests till supper time. After supper she sits out on the porch and works till eight o'clock, from eight o'clock till bedtime she plays whist with papa and after she has retired she reads and studdies German for a while.

Clara and I do most every thing from practicing to donkey riding and playing tag, while Jean's time is spent in asking mamma what she can have to eat.

It is Jean's birth day to day. She is 5 yrs. old. Papa is away to-day and he telegraphed Jean that he wished her 65 happy returns. Papa has just written something about General Grant. I will put it in here.*

General Grant.

Any one who has had the privilege of knowing General Grant personaly will recognize how justly General Beale recently outlined his great, simple, beautiful nature. Thirteen hundred years ago, as the legends of King Arthur's Round table have it, Sir Launcelot, the flower of Cristian chivalry, the knight without a peer, lay dead in the castle of Joyous Gard. With a loving and longing heart his brother the knight Sir Ector de Maris had been seeking him patiently for seven lagging years, and now he arrived at this place at nightfall and heard the chanting of monks over the dead. In the quaint and charming English of nearly four hundred years ago the story says,—

"And when Sir Ector heard such noise and light in the quire of Joyous Gard he alight, and put his horse from him, and came into the quire and there he saw men sing and weep. And all they knew Sir Ector but he knew not them. Then went Sir Bors unto Sir Ector and told him how there lay his brother Sir Launcelot dead: and then Sir Ector threw his shield, sword, and helm from him; and when he beheld Sir Launcelot's visage, he fell down in a swoon: and when he awaked it were hard for any tongue to tell the doleful complaints that he made for his brother."

Then follows his tribute—a passage whose noble and simple eloquence had not its equal in English literature until the Gettysburg Speech took its lofty place beside it. The words drew a portrait 13 centuries ago; they draw its twin to-day without the alteration of a syllable:

"Ah Launcelot, thou were head of all Christian knights! And now I dare say, thou Sir Launcelot, there thou liest, that thou were never matched of earthly knight's hands; and thou were the courtliest knight that ever bare shield; and thou were the truest friend to thy friend that ever bestrode horse; and thou were the truest lover, of a sinful man, that ever loved woman; and thou were the kindest man

* Written by request—for Susy's Biography. S.L.C.

> that ever strake with sword; and thou were the goodliest person that ever came among press of knights; and thou were the meekest man and the gentlest that ever ate in hall among ladies; and thou were the sternest knight to thy mortal foe that ever put spear in rest."

Tuesday, September 4, 1906

The supremacy of the house-fly.

There is one thing which fills me with wonder and reverence every time I think of it—and that is the confident and splendid fight for supremacy which the house-fly makes against the human being. Man, by his inventive ingenuity, has in the course of the ages, by help of diligence and determination, found ways to acquire and establish his mastery over every living creature under the vault of heaven—except the house-fly. With the house-fly he has always failed. The house-fly is as independent of him to-day as he was when Adam made his first grab for one and didn't get him. The house-fly defies all man's inventions for his subjugation or destruction. No creature was ever yet devised that could meet man on his own level and laugh at him and defy him, except the house-fly. In ancient times man's dominion over animated nature was not complete; but, detail by detail, as the ages have drifted by, his inventive genius has brought first one and then another of the unconquerables under his dominion: first the elephant and the tiger, and then the lion, the hippopotamus, the bear, the crocodile, the whale, and so on. One by one man's superiors in fight have succumbed and hauled down the flag. Man is confessed master of them all, now. There isn't one of them—there isn't a single species—that can survive if man sets himself the task of exterminating it—the house-fly always excepted. Nature cannot construct a monster on so colossal a scale that man can't find a way to exterminate it as soon as he is tired of its society. Nature cannot contrive a creature of the microscopicalest infinitesimality and hide it where man cannot find it—find it and kill it. Nature has tried reducing microbes to the last expression of littleness, in the hope of protecting and preserving by this trick a hundred deadly diseases which she holds in warmer affection than she holds any benefit which she has ever conferred upon man, but man has circumvented her and made her waste her time and her effort. She has gone on pathetically and hopefully reducing her microbes until at last she has got them down so fine that she can conceal a hundred million of them in a single drop of a man's blood—but it is all in vain. When man is tired of his microbes he knows how to find them and exterminate them. It is most strange, but there stands the simple truth: of all the myriad of creatures that inhabit the earth, including the Christian dissenter, not one is beyond the reach of the annihilatory ingenuity of scientific man—except the house-fly.

It is a most disastrous condition. If all the troublesome and noxious creatures in the earth could be multiplied a hundred-fold, and the house-fly exterminated as compensation, man should be glad and grateful to sign the contract. We should be infinitely better off than we are now. One house-fly, all by itself, can cause us more distress and misery and exasperation than can any dozen of the other vexations which Nature has invented for the poisoning of our peace and the destruction of our comfort. All human ingenuities have been exhausted in the holy war against the fly, and yet the fly remains to-day just what he was in Adam's time—independent, insolent, intrusive, and indestructible. Flypaper has accomplished nothing. The percentage of flies that get hitched to it is but one in the hundred, and the other ninety-nine assemble as at a circus and enjoy the performance. Slapping flies with a wet towel results in nothing valuable beyond the exercise. There are not two marksmen in fifty that can hit a fly with a wet towel at even a short range, and this method brings far more humiliation than satisfaction, because there is an expression about the missed fly which is so eloquent with derision that no operator with sensitive feelings can continue his labors after his self-respect is gone—a result which almost always follows his third or fourth miss. Anger and eagerness disorder his aim. Under these influences he delivers a slat which would get a dog every time, yet misses the fly mysteriously and unaccountably—does not land on the fly's territory at all. Then the fly smiles that cold and offensive smile which is sacred to the fly, and the man is conquered, and gives up the contest. Poisonous powders have been invented for the destruction of noxious insects; they kill the others, but the fly prefers them to sugar. No method of actually exterminating the fly and getting your house thoroughly rid of him has ever been discovered. When our modern fashion of screening all the doors and windows was introduced, it was supposed that we were now done with the fly, and that we had defeated him at last, along with the mosquito. It was not so. Those other creatures have to stay outside nowadays, but the fly remains a member of the family just as before.

A week or two ago we hunted down every fly in my bedroom and took his life; then we closed the doors and kept them closed night and day. I believed I was now rid of the pest for good and all, and I was jubilant. It was premature. When I woke the next morning there was a congregation of flies all about me waiting for breakfast—flies that had been visiting the hog-pen, and the hospital, and all places where disease, decay, corruption and death are to be found, and had come with their beaks and their legs fuzzy with microbes gathered from wounds and running sores and ulcers, and were ready and eagerly waiting to wipe off these accumulations upon the butter, and thus accomplish the degraded duty wherewith Nature—man's persistent and implacable enemy—had commissioned them.

It was matter for astonishment. The screens were perfect; the doors had been kept closed; how did the creatures get into the room? Upon consultation it was determined that they must have come down the chimney, since there was certainly no other entrance to the place available. I was jubilant once more, for now I believed that we could infallibly beat the fly. Militarily speaking, we had him in the last ditch. That was our thought. At once we had a fine wire screen constructed and fitted closely and exactly into the front of the fireplace, whereby that entrance was effectually closed. During the day we destroyed all the flies in the room. At night we laid the wood fire and placed the screen. Next morning I had no company for breakfast and was able to eat it in peace at last. The fire had been lighted and was flaming hospitably and companionably up. Then presently I saw that our guess as to how the flies got in had been correct, for they had now begun to come down the chimney, in spite of the fire and smoke, and assemble on the inside of the screen. It was almost unbelievable that they had ventured to descend through all that fire and smoke, but that is what they had done. I suppose there is nothing that a fly is afraid of. His daring makes all other courage seem cheap and poor. Now that I know that he will go through fire to attain his ends it is my conviction that there are no perils for him in this earth that he does not despise.

But for my deep prejudices, I should have admired those daring creatures. I should have felt obliged to admire them. And indeed I would have admired them anyway if they could have departed a little from the inborn insolence and immodesty of their nature and behaved themselves in a humble and winning Christian way for once. But they were flies, and they couldn't do that. Their backs were scorching with the heat—I knew it, I could see it—yet with an ill-timed and offensive ostentation they pretended to like it. It is a vain, mean-spirited and unpleasant creature. You cannot situate a fly in any circumstances howsoever shameful and grotesque that he will not try to show off.

We assailed the screen with brooms and wet towels and things and tried to dislodge those flies and drive them into the fire, but it only amused them. A fly can get amusement out of anything you can start. They took it for a game, and they played it with untiring assiduity and enjoyment. As always, they came out ahead. As always, man gave it up and the fly prevailed. It was cold, and by and by we were obliged to take away the screen so that we could mend the fire. Then they all plunged into the room with a hurrah and said they were glad to see us, and explained that they would have come earlier but that they had been delayed by unforeseen circumstances.

However, we have hopes. By noon the fire had been out a couple of hours, the screen had been replaced, and there were no flies on the inside of it. This meant a good deal—it seemed to mean a good deal, at any rate—and so we have a new scheme now. When we start a fire mornings, hereafter, we shan't mend it again that day. I will freeze, rather. As many flies may come down and gather on the screen and show off as may desire to do it, but there they will remain. We shan't admit them to the room again, and when the fire goes down they will retire up the chimney and distribute elsewhere the wanton and malicious persecutions for which they were created.

The flea never associates with me—has never shown even a passing desire for my company, and so I have none but the friendliest feeling toward him. The mosquito troubles me but little, and I feel nothing but a mild dislike for him. Of all the animals that inhabit the earth, the air, and the waters, I hate only one—and that is the house-fly. But I do hate him. I hate him with a hatred that is not measurable with words. I always spare the snake and the spider, and the others, and would not intentionally give them pain, but I would go out of my way, and put aside my dearest occupation, to kill a fly, even if I knew it was the very last one. I can even bear to see a fly suffer, for an entire minute—even two minutes, if it is one that I have spent an hour hunting around the place with a wet towel—but that is the limit. I would like to see him suffer a year, and would do it, and gladly, if I could restrict the suffering to himself; but after it reaches a certain point, and the bulk of it begins to fall to my share, I have to call a halt and put him out of his misery, for I am like the rest of my race—I am merciful to a fellow-creature upon one condition only: that its pain shall not confer pain upon *me.*

I have watched the human race with close attention for five and twenty years now, and I know beyond shadow of doubt that we can stand the pain of another creature straight along, without discomfort, until its pain gives *us* pain. Then we become immediately and creditably merciful. I suppose it is a pity that we have no higher motive for sparing pain to a fellow creature, still it is the cold truth—we have no higher one. We have no vestige of pity, not a single shred of it, for any creature's misery until it reaches the point where the contemplation of it inflicts misery upon ourselves. This remark describes every human being that has ever lived.

After improving my marksmanship with considerable practice with a towel, this morning, I slapped a couple of flies into the wash-bowl. With deep satisfaction I watched them spin around and around in the water. Twice they made land and started to climb up the bowl, but I shoved them back with fresh satisfaction and plunged them under with my finger, with more satisfaction. I went on gloating over their efforts to get out of their trouble. Twice more they made land, and in both instances I restored them to their activities in the water. But at last their struggles relaxed and the forlorn things began to exhibit pitiful signs of exhaustion and despair. This pathetic spectacle gave *me* pain, and I recognized that I had reached my limit. I cared not a rap for their sufferings so long as they furnished enjoyment for me, but when they began to inflict pain upon me, that was another matter. The conditions had become personal. I was human, and by the law of my make it was not possible for me to allow myself to suffer when I could prevent it. I had to put the flies out of their troubles, I couldn't help it. I turned a soap-dish over them, and when I looked under it half an hour later I perceived that the spiritual part of them had ascended to the happy hunting grounds of their fathers.

Wednesday, September 5, 1906

Items from the Children's Record, showing their different characteristics.

It is years since I have examined the Children's Record. I have turned over a few of its pages this morning. This book is a record in which Mrs. Clemens and I registered some of the sayings and doings of the children, in the long ago, when they were little chaps. Of course we wrote these things down at the time because they were of momentary interest—things of the passing hour, and of no permanent value—but at this distant day I find that they still possess an interest for me and also a value, because it turns out that they were registrations of character. The qualities then revealed by fitful glimpses, in childish acts and speeches, remained as a permanency in the children's characters in the drift of the years, and were always afterward clearly and definitely recognizable.

There is a masterful streak in Jean that now and then moves her to set my authority aside for a moment and end a losing argument in that prompt and effective fashion. And here in this old book I find evidence that she was just like that before she was quite four years old.

From the Children's Record.

Quarry Farm,
July 7, 1884.

Yesterday evening our cows (after being inspected and worshiped by Jean from the shed roof for an hour,) wandered off down into the pasture, and left her bereft. I thought I was going to get back home, now, but that was an error. Jean knew of some more cows, in a field somewhere, and took my hand and led me thitherward. When we turned the corner and took the right-hand road, I saw that we should presently be out of range of call and sight; so I began to argue against continuing the expedition, and Jean began to argue in favor of it—she using English for light skirmishing, and German for "business." I kept up my end with vigor, and demolished her arguments in detail, one after the other, till I judged I had her about cornered. She hesitated a moment, then answered up sharply:

"Wir werden nichts mehr darüber sprechen!" (We won't talk any more about it!)

It nearly took my breath away; though I thought I might possibly have misunderstood. I said:

"Why, you little rascal! Was hast du gesagt?"

But she said the same words over again, and in the same decided way. I suppose I ought to have been outraged; but I wasn't, I was charmed. And I suppose I ought to have spanked her; but I didn't, I fraternized with the enemy, and we went on and spent half an hour with the cows.

That incident is followed in the Record by the following paragraph, which is another instance of a juvenile characteristic maintaining itself into mature age. Susy was persistently and conscientiously truthful throughout her life, with the exception of one interruption covering several months, and perhaps a year. This was while she was still a little child. Suddenly—not gradually—she began to lie; not furtively, but frankly, openly, and on a scale quite disproportioned to her size. Her mother was so stunned, so nearly paralysed for a day or two, that she did not know what to do with the emergency. Reasonings, persuasions, beseechings, all went for nothing; they produced no effect; the lying went tranquilly on. Other remedies were tried, but they failed. There is a tradition that success was finally accomplished by whipping. I think the Record says so, but if it does it is because the Record is incomplete. Whipping was indeed tried, and was faithfully kept up during two or three weeks, but the results were merely temporary; the reforms achieved were discouragingly brief.

Fortunately for Susy, an incident presently occurred which put a complete stop to all the mother's efforts in the direction of reform. This incident was the chance discovery in Darwin of a passage which said that when a child exhibits a sudden and unaccountable disposition to forsake the truth and restrict itself to lying, the explanation must be sought away back in the past; that an ancestor of the child had had the same disease, at the same tender age; that it was irremovable by persuasion or punishment, and that it had ceased as suddenly and as mysteriously as it had come, when it had run its appointed course. I think Mr. Darwin said that nothing was necessary but to leave the matter alone and let the malady have its way and perish by the statute of limitations.

We had confidence in Darwin, and after that day Susy was relieved of our reformatory persecutions. She went on lying without let or hindrance during several months, or a year; then the lying suddenly ceased, and she became as conscientiously and exactingly truthful as she had been before the attack, and she remained so to the end of her life.

The paragraph in the Record to which I have been leading up is in my handwriting, and is of a date so long posterior to the time of the lying-malady that she had evidently forgotten that truth-speaking had ever had any difficulties for her.

> Mama was speaking of a servant who had been pretty unveracious, but was now "trying to tell the truth." Susy was a good deal surprised, and said she shouldn't think anybody would have to *try* to tell the truth.

In the Record the children's acts and speeches quite definitely define their characters. Susy's indicated the presence of mentality—thought—and they were generally marked by gravity. She was timid, on her physical side, but had an abundance of moral courage. Clara was sturdy, independent, orderly, practical, persistent, plucky—just a little animal, and very satisfactory. Charles Dudley Warner said Susy was made of mind, and Clara of matter.

When Motley, the kitten, died, some one said that the thoughts of the two children need not be inquired into, they could be divined: that Susy was wondering if this was the *end* of Motley, and had his life been worth while; whereas Clara was merely interested in seeing to it that there should be a creditable funeral.

In those days Susy was a dreamer, a thinker, a poet and philosopher, and Clara——well, Clara wasn't. In after years a passion for music developed the latent spirituality and intellectuality in Clara, and her practicality took second and, in fact, even third place, with the result that nowadays she loses purses and fans, and neglects things, and forgets orders, with a poet's facility. Jean was from the beginning orderly, steady, diligent, persistent; and remains so. She picked up languages easily, and kept them.

After ten years of unremitting labor under the best masters, domestic and foreign, Clara will make her public début as a singer on the concert stage seventeen days hence.

> *Susy aged eleven, Jean three.* Susy said the other day when she saw Jean bringing a cat to me of her own motion, "Jean has found out already that mamma loves morals and papa loves cats."

It is another of Susy's remorselessly sound verdicts.

As a child, Jean neglected my books. When she was nine years old Will Gillette invited her and the rest of us to a dinner at the Murray Hill Hotel in New York, in order that we might get acquainted with Mrs. Leslie and her daughters. Elsie Leslie was nine years old, and was a great celebrity on the stage. Jean was astonished and awed to see that little slip of a thing sit up at table and take part in the conversation of the grown people, capably and with ease and tranquillity. Poor Jean was obliged to keep still, for the subjects discussed never happened to hit her level; but at last the talk fell within her limit and she had her chance to contribute to it. "Tom Sawyer" was mentioned. Jean spoke gratefully up and said,

"I know who wrote that book—Harriet Beecher Stowe!"

> One evening Susy had prayed, Clara was curled up for sleep; she was reminded that it was her turn to pray now. She said "Oh one's enough," and dropped off to slumber.
>
> *Clara five years old.* We were in Germany. The nurse, Rosa, was not allowed to speak to the children otherwise than in German. Clara grew very tired of it; by and by the little creature's patience was exhausted, and she said "Aunt Clara, I *wish* God had made Rosa in English."
>
> *November 30, 1878. Clara four years old, Susy six.* This morning when Clara discovered that this is my birthday, she was greatly troubled because she had provided no gift for me, and repeated her sorrow several times. Finally she went musing to the nursery and presently returned with her newest and dearest treasure, a large toy horse, and said "You shall have this horse for your birthday, papa."
>
> I accepted it with many thanks. After an hour she was racing up and down the room with the horse, when Susy said,
>
> "Why Clara, you gave that horse to papa, and now you've tooken it again."
>
> *Clara.* "I never give it to him for *always;* I give it to him for his *birthday.*"
>
> In Geneva, in September, I lay abed late one morning, and as Clara was passing through the room I took her on my bed a moment. Then the child went to Clara Spaulding and said,
>
> "Aunt Clara, papa is a good deal of trouble to me."
>
> "Is he? Why?"
>
> "Well, he wants me to get in bed with him, and I can't do that with jelmuls (gentlemen)—I don't like jelmuls anyway."
>
> "What, you don't like gentlemen! Don't you like Uncle Theodore Crane?"
>
> "Oh yes, but he's not a jelmul, he's a friend."

Friday, September 7, 1906

The statement made at the banquet of the Ends of the Earth Club, "We are of the Anglo-Saxon race," etc.—Our public and private mottoes and morals—Mr. Clemens's tribute to British Premier Campbell-Bannerman on his seventieth birthday—Meeting Labouchere—Anecdote of the lost deed which was to have been presented to Prince of Wales.

For good or for evil, we continue to educate Europe. We have held the post of instructor for more than a century and a quarter now. We were not elected to it, we merely took it. We are of the Anglo-Saxon race. At the banquet, last winter, of that organization which calls itself the Ends of the Earth Club, the chairman, a retired regular army officer of high grade, proclaimed in a loud voice, and with fervency,

"We are of the Anglo-Saxon race, and when the Anglo-Saxon wants a thing *he just takes it.*"

That utterance was applauded to the echo. There were perhaps seventy-five civilians present and twenty-five military and naval men. It took those people nearly two minutes to work off their stormy admiration of that great sentiment; and meanwhile the inspired prophet who had discharged it—from his liver, or his intestines, or his esophagus, or wherever he had bred it—stood there glowing and beaming and smiling, and issuing rays of happiness from every pore—rays that were so intense that they were visible, and made him look like the old-time picture in the almanac of the man who stands discharging signs of the zodiac in every direction, and so absorbed in happiness, so steeped in happiness, that he smiles and smiles, and has plainly forgotten that he is painfully and dangerously ruptured and exposed amidships, and needs sewing up right away.

The soldier man's great utterance, interpreted by the expression which he put into it, meant, in plain English—

"The English and the Americans are thieves, highwaymen, pirates, and we are proud to be of the combination."

Out of all the English and Americans present, there was not one with the grace to get up and say he was ashamed of being an Anglo-Saxon, and also ashamed of being a member of the human race, since the race must abide under the presence upon it of the Anglo-Saxon taint. I could not perform this office. I could not afford to lose my temper and make a self-righteous exhibition of myself and my superior morals that I might teach this infant class in decency the rudiments of that cult, for they would not be able to grasp it; they would not be able to understand it.

It was an amazing thing to see—that boyishly frank and honest and delighted outburst of enthusiasm over the soldier prophet's mephitic remark. It looked suspiciously like a revelation—a secret feeling of the national heart surprised into expression and exposure by untoward accident; for it was a representative assemblage. All the chief mechanisms that constitute the machine which drives and vitalizes the national civilization were present—lawyers, bankers, merchants, manufacturers, journalists, politicians, soldiers, sailors—they were all there. Apparently it was the United States in banquet assembled, and qualified to speak with authority for the nation and reveal its private morals to the public view.

The initial welcome of that strange sentiment was not an unwary betrayal, to be repented of upon reflection; and this was shown by the fact that whenever, during the rest of the evening, a speaker found that he was becoming uninteresting and wearisome, he only needed to inject that great Anglo-Saxon moral into the midst of his platitudes to start up that glad storm again. After all, it was only the human race on exhibition. It has always been a peculiarity of the human race that it keeps two sets of morals in stock—the private and real, and the public and artificial.

Our public motto is "In God We Trust," and when we see those gracious words on the trade-dollar (worth sixty cents) they always seem to tremble and whimper with pious emotion. That is our public motto. It transpires that our private one is "When the Anglo-Saxon wants a thing *he just takes it.*" Our public morals are touchingly set forth in that stately and yet gentle and kindly motto which indicates that we are a nation of gracious and affectionate multitudinous brothers compacted into one—"*e pluribus unum.*" Our private morals find the light in the sacred phrase "Come, *step* lively!"

We imported our imperialism from monarchical Europe; also our curious notions of patriotism—that is, if we have any principle of patriotism which any person can definitely and intelligibly define. It is but fair then, no doubt, that we should instruct Europe, in return for these and the other kinds of instruction which we have received from that source.

Something more than a century ago we gave Europe the first notions of liberty it had ever had, and thereby largely and happily helped to bring on the French Revolution and claim a share in its beneficent results. We have taught Europe many lessons since. But for us, Europe might never have known the interviewer; but for us certain of the European states might never have experienced the blessing of extravagant imposts; but for us the European Food Trust might never have acquired the art of poisoning the world for cash; but for us her Insurance Trusts might never have found out the best way to work the widow and orphan for profit; but for us the long delayed resumption of Yellow Journalism in Europe might have been postponed for generations to come. Steadily, continuously, persistently, we are Americanizing Europe, and all in good time we shall get the job perfected. At last, after long waiting, London journalism has adopted our fashion of gathering sentiments from everywhere whenever anything happens that a sentiment can be coined out of. Yesterday arrived this cablegram:

> British Premier Campbell-Bannerman celebrates seventieth birthday tomorrow. London *Tribune* requests tribute.

I furnished it, to wit:

> To His Excellency, the British Premier—
>
> Congratulations, not condolences. Before seventy we are merely respected, at best, and we have to behave all the time, or we lose that asset; but after seventy we are respected, esteemed, admired, revered, and don't have to behave unless we want to. When I first knew you, honored sir, one of us was hardly even respected.
>
> Mark Twain.

A great and brave statesman, and a charming man. I met him first at Marienbad, in Austria, half a generation ago. In the years that have since elapsed I have met him frequently in London, at private dinners in his own house and elsewhere, and at banquets. In Vienna, in '98, we lived in the same hotel for a time, and the intercourse was daily and familiar. I hope that this explanation will in a measure justify the form of the tribute which I have just quoted. Now that I come to think of it, I am not quite sure that anything could really justify me in addressing the acting king of the British Empire in such an irreverent way, but I didn't think of that when I was putting the words together. I had before me only the companionable comrade of the earlier days, when he was only an important member of Parliament and I was not respected, because I was a bankrupt.

In Marienbad he introduced me to Labouchere, and for a number of days I helped that picturesque personality walk off his mineral water up and down the promenade. His vocabulary, and his energetic use of it, were an unqualified and constant delight to me. Two or three years later, at Homburg, I came across his wife, in the throng of medicinal-water drinkers, and eagerly asked where I might find her husband. She said he was not there, he was in London. I expressed my honest grief, and said I would rather hear him swear than hear an archbishop pray. She had been a great actress in her time, and she knew how to say with effect the thing she had to say, when her heart was in it. Her face lighted with pleasure at the honest admiration which I had expressed for her husband's power, and she said:

"Oh you never saw him at his best. Mr. Clemens, you ought to see him at home mornings, during the session, standing before the table ready for breakfast, with his back to the fire and his hands parting his coat-tails for the comfort of the warmth—you should hear him break out and curse the Opposition, name by name, and wind up with his comprehensive and unvarying and eloquent formula, 'the *sons* of bitches!'"

I last met Sir Henry at a small dinner party, six years ago, at the house of the Nestor of Parliament of that day. Among the guests were Sir William Vernon Harcourt, leader of the Opposition. I had not seen him for twenty-seven years, but of course I recognized him. The caricatures would make that sure. I asked him if he remembered me, and he said,

"Certainly, it is only twenty-seven years since I saw you last."

At that time I was beginning to realize that I was old, and I said I hoped that he was either older than I or that he would at least strain a point and say he was, because it had been so long since I had come across any one whose years exceeded mine that I was getting depressed, and needed comfort. He said,

"Well, examine your English history and decide. When I was nine years old I was crossing London Bridge when I heard the tolling bells announce the death of William IV."

I said, "I am grateful. You have renewed my youth, and if there is anything you desire, even to the half of my kingdom, name it. I have been the oldest man in the earth for months; I am glad to take second place for a while."

After dinner one of the men present said he could tell the company a curious thing if they would keep it to themselves, and let it be confidential—at least as far as regarded names and dates. He said he was acting as an official, at a function some years before, where the Prince of Wales—the present King—was to receive in state the deed of a vast property which had been conferred upon the nation by a wealthy citizen. It was the narrator's duty to formally hand the deed to the Prince in an envelope.

When everything was about ready for the presentation his clerk came to him, pale and agitated, and informed him in a whisper that the deed had disappeared! It was not in the safe; they had ransacked the place and could find no trace of it. It was a ghastly situation; something must be done, and done promptly. The narrator whispered to the clerk:

"Rush!—fold up a *Daily News,* shove it into an official envelope, and fetch it here."

This was done. The official committee of noblemen and gentlemen, bareheaded, and with the narrator at its head, solemnly approached the Prince where he stood supported by his imposing retinue, and with awe inspiring formalities the *Daily News* was placed in his hands, whereupon he pronounced, in carefully prepared and impressive words, the nation's profound gratitude to the wealthy citizen for this precious and memorable gift. It was not even a new paper, it was two days old.

The narrator closed with the statement that even unto that day the lost deed had never been found.

Monday, September 10, 1906

Plan of this autobiography—Satire on Captain Sellers—Mr. Clemens published no literature until forty years ago—Two letters from Mr. Alden and one from Mr. Rees in regard to "Snodgrass" papers—Mr. Clemens's comments on same.

I have not yet finished about the British Premier and his seventieth birthday, but I will let that go over until another day and talk about a matter of immediate interest—an interest born of Saturday's mail.

As I have several times remarked before, in the course of these dictations, it is the foundation principle of this autobiography that it shall drop a subject, whether it be finished or not, the moment a subject of warmer interest shall intrude itself. I think I have also said that the foundation plan or principle of this autobiography is that no subject shall ever be continued after one of a sharper and fresher interest for me has come clamoring into my mind. In fact, this autobiography is substantially a conversation, albeit I do all the conversing myself. In a conversation of two hours' duration, subject after subject is touched upon and discussed for a few minutes, but is never completed; it is always dropped in the middle to make way, in turn, for a subject of newer interest which has been suggested by a remark dropped by the talker who for the moment has the floor. The other autobiographies patiently and dutifully follow a planned and undivergent course through gardens and deserts and interesting cities and dreary solitudes, and when at last they reach their appointed goal they are pretty tired—and they have been frequently tired during the journey, too. But this is not that kind of autobiography. This one is only a pleasure excursion, and it sidetracks itself anywhere that there is a circus, or a fresh excitement of any kind, and seldom waits until the show is over, but packs up and goes on again as soon as a fresher one is advertised.

In a chapter which I dictated five months ago, I made a little outline-sketch, in which I strung together certain facts of my life and named the dates of their occurrence. I stated that in 1849, in Hannibal, Missouri, when I was a child of fourteen, my brother went away on a journey, and I edited one issue of his weekly newspaper for him without invitation, and when he got back it took him several weeks to quiet down and pacify the people whom my writings had excited. That was fifty-seven years ago. I did not meddle with a pen again, so far as I can remember, until ten years later—1859. I was a cub pilot on the Mississippi River then, and one day I wrote a rude and crude satire which was leveled at Captain Isaiah Sellers, the oldest steamboat pilot on the Mississippi River, and the most respected, esteemed, and revered. For many years he had occasionally written brief paragraphs concerning the river and the changes which it had undergone under his observation during fifty years, and had signed these paragraphs "Mark Twain" and published them in the St. Louis and New Orleans journals. In my satire I made rude game of his reminiscences. It was a shabby poor performance, but I didn't know it, and the pilots didn't know it. The pilots thought it was brilliant. They were jealous of Sellers, because when the gray-heads among them pleased their vanity by detailing in the hearing of the younger craftsmen marvels which they had seen in the long ago on the river, Sellers was always likely to step in at the psychological moment and snuff them out with wonders of his own which made their small marvels look pale and sick. However, I have told all about this in "Old Times on the Mississippi."

1849

1859

The pilots handed my extravagant satire to a river reporter, and it was published in the New Orleans *True Delta.* That poor old Captain Sellers was deeply wounded. He had never been held up to ridicule before; he was sensitive, and he never got over the hurt which I had wantonly and stupidly inflicted upon his dignity. I was proud of my performance for a while, and considered it quite wonderful, but I have changed my opinion of it long ago. Sellers never published another paragraph nor ever used his nom de guerre again.

1859–62

Between 1859 and the summer of 1862 I left the pen strictly alone. I then became a newspaper reporter in Nevada, but I wrote no literature. I confined myself to writing up the inconsequential happenings of Virginia City for the *Territorial Enterprise.* I wrote no literature until 1866, when a little sketch of mine called "The Jumping Frog" was published in a perishing literary journal in New York and killed it on the spot.

1866

Now then, if I know my own history, I never wrote and never published a line of literature until forty years ago. If I know my own history, I never had any leaning toward literature, nor any desire to meddle with it, nor had ever flourished a literary pen save by accident—and then only twice—up to forty years ago.

Now then I have arrived at that subject whose fresh new interest has sidetracked my reminiscences of the British Premier and postponed their completion—for the present—while I consider this new and delicious matter furnished by Saturday's mail. First in order come the following letters, two by Mr. Alden, editor of *Harper's Monthly,* and one by a Mr. Thomas Rees:

Editorial Rooms, Harper's Magazine
Harper & Brothers
Franklin Square, New York

September 6, 1906.

Dear Mark:

I received a few weeks ago from Mr. Thomas Rees some manuscripts offered for sale to us, purporting to be copies of "Snodgrass" papers contributed by you some fifty years ago to a newspaper published by his father. I returned them with a letter of which I send you a copy—also a copy of a letter I have just received from him. I think you should have cognizance of this correspondence.

The offer of the manuscripts was accompanied by an affidavit sworn to by Mr. Rees, Sr., attesting to your authorship.

Yours faithfully,
H. M. Alden

COPY of Mr. Alden's letter to Mr. Thomas Rees.

August 27, 1906.

Dear Mr. Rees:

We cannot publish the "Snodgrass" letters you send us, as they have no interest to our readers as the productions of "Snodgrass," and we could not put them forth as the productions of "Mark Twain" because that would be untrue. Even the suggestion that "Snodgrass" died and was buried and arose again as "Mark Twain" would be a distinct injury to Mr. Clemens, after he had so utterly and deliberately discarded the earlier pen-name. It certainly would be a manifest impropriety. In any case I venture to suggest that Mr. Clemens should be consulted before any attempt is made to publish these things.

Very truly yours,
(Signed) H. M. Alden.

Mr. Thomas Rees,
Illinois State Register,
Springfield, Illinois.

COPY of Mr. Thomas Rees's letter, manager of the *Illinois State Register.*

Springfield, Ill., Sept. 4, 1906.

H. M. Alden,
C/o Harper Bros., Pubs.,
New York City.

Dear Sir:

I acknowledge hereby the receipt of the manuscripts of the Clemens "Snodgrass" articles. Please accept my thanks for their prompt return. I notice you advise at the close of your letter reading, "In any case I venture to suggest that Mr. Clemens should be consulted before any attempt is made to publish these things." While as a matter of courtesy, in case I should conclude to publish the same, I might communicate with Mr. Clemens, I do not know that he has any rights in the premises, nor that there is anything in the ethics of the situation that call for a compliance with your advice.

Mr. Clemens wrote these articles under contract with my father and my elder brother more than half a century ago. He was paid for the same and thereby parted entirely with any right that he might have had in them at that time. They were published in a daily newspaper without being copyrighted, and thereby became public property. The only rights that I have in the premises that are not possessed by the general public, is the fact that I know where to find the text and have an affidavit of their genuineness. If I should lay the matter of the publication of these articles before Mr. Clemens and he should request or forbid that I should publish the same, it would in no way protect him against the other eighty million people in the United States that might be disposed to take up the work. And no history of Mr. Clemens's life will be complete without at least reference to these particular articles and his former pen name.

However, I am under lasting obligations for your kind advice.

Yours respectfully,
(Signed) Thomas Rees.

To me this is a most interesting thing, because it is such a naïve exposure of certain traits in human nature—traits which are in everybody, no doubt, but which only about one man in fifty millions is willing to lay bare to the public view. The rest of the fifty millions are restrained by pride from making the exposure. Did I write the rubbish with which Mr. Rees charges me? I suppose not. I have no reason to suppose that I wrote it, but I can't say, and I don't say, that I didn't write it. I can only say that since by Mr. Rees's count I was only eighteen or nineteen years old at the time, it must have been a colossal event in my life, and one likely to be remembered by me for a century. I am astonished that it has left no impression, nor any sign of an impression, upon my memory. If a Far-Western lad of eighteen or nineteen had, all by himself and in his own name, *entered into a solemn contract*—a contract to do or suffer anything, little or big—he would have put aside all other concerns, temporal and eternal, and made a house-to-house visitation throughout the village and told everybody, even to the cats and dogs, about it, and it would have made him celebrated. Celebrity is what a boy or a youth longs for more than for any other thing. He would be a clown in a circus; he would be a pirate, he would sell himself to Satan, in order to attract attention and be talked about and envied. True, it is the same with every grown-up person; I am not meaning to confine this trait to the boys. But there is a distinction between the boy and the grown person—the boys are all Reeses. That is to say, they lack caution; they lack wisdom; they are innocent; they are frank; and when they have an opportunity to expose traits which they ought to hide they don't know enough to resist.

Up to the time that I was eighteen or nineteen years old, no Far-Western boy of that age had ever achieved the glory of *making a contract* about something or other and signing it. If I did it I was the only one. I hope I did it, because I would like to know, even at seventy-one, that I was not commonplace even when I was a child—that I was not only not commonplace, but was the only lad in the Far West that wasn't. I cannot understand why it is that if I did it, it has left no impression upon my memory. Every boy and girl in the town would have pointed me out, daily, and said with envy and admiration and malice:

"There he goes! That's the boy that *made a contract*."

I would have hunted up stragglers, and couples, and groups and gangs of boys and girls, every day, in order to pass them by with studied modesty and unconsciousness, and hear them say:

"He's the one! He *made the contract!*"

Those happy experiences would have made a record upon my memory, I suppose. Indeed I almost know that they would have done it.

At a very much earlier age than that, I was made the recipient of a considerably smaller distinction by Mrs. Horr, my school-teacher, and I have never forgotten it for a moment since, nor ceased to be vain of it. I was only five years old, and had been under her ministrations only six months when she, inspired by something which she honestly took to be prophecy, exclaimed in the hearing of several persons that I would one day be "*President of the United States, and would stand in the presence of kings unabashed.*" I carried that around personally, from house to house, and was surprised and hurt to find how few people there were, in that day, who had a proper reverence for prophecy, and confidence in it. But no matter—the circumstance bedded itself in my memory for good and all. Therefore I cannot see how that much larger thing, that actual thing, that visible and palpable thing—a *contract,* an imposing and majestic *contract*—could have entered into my life at the maturer age of eighteen or nineteen and then flitted away forever and left no sign that it had ever been there.

When I examine the next detail I am surprised again. According to the affidavit of what is left, at this distant day, of the elder Mr. Rees, the contract required him to *pay* me for my infant literature; also that I *received the payment.* These things are unthinkable. In that day there was no man in the United States, sane or insane, who could have dreamed of such a thing as wanting an unknown lad who had never written a line of literature in his life to furnish him some literature; and not only furnish him some literature but ask him to take *pay* for it! It is true that in that ancient day everybody wrote ostensible literature. There were no exceptions then, there are none now. Everybody wrote for the local paper, and was glad to get in gratis—publication was sufficient pay. There were a few persons in America—fifteen perhaps, maybe twenty-five—who were so widely known as writers that they could demand remuneration of the periodicals for their output and get it, but there were no Clemenses in that clan; there were no juveniles in it; no unknown lads lost in the remotenesses of the wild and woolly West who could ask for pay for their untrained scribblings and get it.

1853

In 1853, which is "more than fifty years ago," my brother was hit a staggering blow by a new idea—an idea that had never been thought of in the West by any person before—the idea of hiring a literary celebrity to write an original story for his Hannibal newspaper *for pay!* He wrote East and felt of the literary market, but he met with only sorrows and discouragements. He was obliged to keep within the limit of his purse, and that limit was narrowly circumscribed. What he wanted was an original story which could be continued through three issues of his weekly paper and cover a few columns of solid bourgeois each time. He offered a sum to all the American literary celebrities of that day, in turn, but, in turn, Emerson, Lowell, Holmes, and all the others declined.

At last a celebrity of about the third degree took him up—with a condition. This was a Philadelphian, Homer C. Wilbur, a regular and acceptable contributor to *Sartain's Magazine* and the other first-class periodicals. He said he could not write an original story for the sum offered—*which was five dollars*—but would translate one from the French for that sum. My brother took him up, and sent the money—I don't remember now where he got it. The story came. We made an immense noise over it. We bragged in double-great-primer capitals, readable at thirty yards without glasses, that we had bought it and *paid* for it—proudly naming the sum—and we ran it through four numbers of the paper, increasing the subscription list by thirty-eight copies, payable in turnips and cord-wood; and it took all of three months for the excitement to quiet down.

Important as this memorable enterprise was, *no contract* passed between the parties. The whole thing was done by letters—just mere ordinary letters—fourteen or fifteen I suppose; and each person paid the other person's postage. It was a fashion of the day. Postage was ten cents, and we didn't prepay because the letter might never arrive and the money would be wasted. Nothing passed but just letters—mere ordinary letters. My brother trusted the great author, the great author trusted my brother. Signed and sealed *contracts* for periodical literature have never been known in this country, nor heard of in any other, except in the one single instance which we have under consideration this morning. The elder Rees, professional affidaviter, had the monopoly of that novelty. He wouldn't trust even an obscure child of nineteen in so stately a matter as a bucketful of literary slops, without a contract that would hold that lad and be good for fifty years.

According to the professional affidaviter, I was *paid* for those writings. If it was money, I wonder what the sum was. I know perfectly well, by the Wilbur case, and by the difference between Wilbur's fame and my obscurity, it couldn't have been over thirty cents for the bucketful, and I know also that it must have included the bucket. But if the pay was delivered in the universal currency of the Far West, it couldn't have been cord-wood, because cord-wood was never hauled in smaller lots than half-cords, and a half-cord would have been worth a dollar and a quarter, and would have covered more literature than even a reckless and improvident Rees would have been willing to enter into a solemn contract for. If it was eggs, I got six dozen; if it was watermelons I got three; if it was bar-soap I got five bars; if it was tallow-candles I got thirty; if it was soda-water I got six glasses; if it was ice-cream I got three saucers—and the colic. I have no recollection of ever getting those riches. If I got any of them I know I got them in instalments, and wide apart; for in that day any so noble an irruption of wealth as three plates of cream, all paid down in one single instalment, would have been an event so electrifying and so exalting that it would stay caked in my memory three centuries.

The common human trait which the Reeses have laid bare for inspection—and which the rest of the nations of the earth carefully conceal for shame, and pretend that they do not possess it—is the trait which urges a man to sacrifice all his pride, all his delicacy, all his decency, when his eye falls upon an unprotected dollar—a spectacle which sometimes takes the manhood out of him and leaves behind it nothing but the animal. Affidavits are nothing to this kind of a person; they come cheap; he would make a hundred a day for thirty cents apiece. This kind of person is gratefully ready to dig up a crime or a foolishness that has been condoned and forgotten by the merciful for fifty years, if he can get a dollar and a half out of it. It is fatal for his kind to have the luck to trace home to an esteemed and respected white-headed woman a forgotten disgrace whereby she tarnished her good name in her girlhood, for he will remorselessly expose it if there is half a handful of soiled dollars in it for him. It is out of the breed of Reeses that the world gets its Burkes and Hares. But the Burkes and Hares are to be pitied, not reviled. They only obey the law of their nature. They did not make their nature; they are not responsible; and no humane person will permit himself to say harsh things about them. It would be impossible for me to say abusive things about these modern Burkes and Hares of the Middle West. They must have bread to eat, and their ways of acquiring it are limited. As is natural, they acquire it in those ways which give them the most pleasure, the most satisfaction, the most contentment. They dig up dead reputations and sell the rotten product for food, and eat the food. Their ancestors, Burke and Hare, dug up the dead in the cemeteries and sold the corpses for bread and ate the bread; which is another way of saying they fed upon the dead. The Reeses are only Burkes and Hares deprived of their natural trade by the obstructive modern legal conditions under which they exist.

I may have written those papers, but it is not at all likely that I did. In any case, I have no recollection of it, and must let it stand at that. But one thing I will quite confidently maintain, in spite of all the affidavits of all the Burkes and Hares, and that is that when the affidaviter says that there was a *contract,* and that I was *paid* for the work, those two statements are plain straightforward falsehoods; and what is more, and worse, they are poorly devised, unplausible, and inartistic. As works of art, even a Rees ought to be ashamed of them, I think.

Tuesday, October 2, 1906

Another stolen holiday, including banquet-speech in New York and visit to Norfolk, Connecticut—In a letter received this morning friend calls Mr. Clemens "the blessedest 'accident' I have yet met with in my life"—Mr. Clemens reviews the series of "accidents" during his life which have led up to meeting this friend.

I have been to New York and to Fairhaven again on another stolen holiday—sixteen or seventeen days, this time. My summer seems to have been passed mainly in stolen holidays; pretext-holidays. With the exception of a banquet-speech in New York on the 19th of September, and a visit to Norfolk, Connecticut, to witness my daughter Clara's début as a singer, I believe these many weeks of holidays were secured to me by pretext alone. The pretexts were pretty thin, as a rule—however, I have no regrets. In all my seventy years I have not often had a holiday when I really wanted one.

The morning mail brings me a letter from a young woman in New York, in which I find the remark, "You are the blessedest 'accident' I have yet met with in my life." This brings back to my mind a conversation which I had with her a week ago, and I wish to recall some of the details of it, because they illustrate a philosophy of mine—or a superstition of mine, if you prefer that word. I had been able to do for her what she regarded as a great service, and, frankly speaking, I realized that it was, although it was a service which had cost me so little in the way of effort that the time and labor involved did not entitle it to a compliment. She said:

"You have accomplished this for me, and I am not acquainted with another person who could have done it. It was a happy accident that I accidentally met you last April—no, not an accident, there being no such things as accidents—it was ordered."

"Ordered by whom? Or by what?"

"By the Power that watches over us and commands all events."

"Issuing the orders from day to day?"

"Perhaps so. Yes, I suppose that is the way."

Anno Mundi 1

I said "I believe that only one command has ever been issued, and that that command was issued in the beginning of time—in the first second of time; that that command resulted in an act; in Adam's first act—if there was an Adam—and that from that act sprang another act as a natural and unavoidable consequence—let us say it was Eve's act—and that from *that* act proceeded *another* act of one of these two persons as an unavoidable consequence; and that now the chain of natural and unavoidable happenings being started, there has never been a break in it from that day to this; and so, in my belief, Adam's first act was the origin and cause of the service which I have been enabled to do for you, and I am quite sure that if Adam's first act, howsoever trifling it may have been, had taken a different form, no matter how trifling a form, the entire chain of human events for all these thousands of years would have been changed; in which case it is most unlikely that you and I would ever have met. Indeed it is most unlikely that *both* of us would have been born in the same land. The very slightest change in Adam's first act could have resulted in your being an Eskimo and I a Hottentot; and could also have resulted in your being born five centuries ago and in my birth being postponed until century after next.

"I am not jesting. I have studied these things a long time and I positively believe that the first circumstance that ever happened in this world was the parent of every circumstance that has happened in this world since; that God ordered that first circumstance and has never ordered another one from that day to this. Plainly, then, I am not able to conceive of such a thing as the thing which we call an *accident*—that is to say, an event without a cause. Each event has its own place in the eternal chain of circumstances, and whether it be big or little it will infallibly cause the *next* event, whether the next event be the breaking of a child's toy or the destruction of a throne. According to this superstition of mine, the breaking of the toy is fully as important an event as the destruction of the throne, since without the breaking of the toy the destruction of the throne would not have happened.

"But I like that word accident, although it is, in my belief, absolutely destitute of meaning. I like it because it is short and handy, and because it answers so well and so conveniently, and so briefly, in designating happenings which we should otherwise have to describe as odd, curious, interesting, and so on, and then add some elaboration to help out our meaning. And so for convenience sake, let us say it was an accident that you and I met last April, and that out of that accident grew, in a quite natural way, the linked series of accidents which led up to and made possible the service which I have had the good fortune to render you. Accident is a word which I constantly make use of when I am talking to myself about the chain of incidents which has constituted my life.

"I will undertake to go back, now, and give name and date to some of these accidents. *1841* When I was six years old, and my brother Henry four, he had the erysipelas, and when he was getting well of it Nature provided him with a new skin. I liked the old one and I wished I could have it. I was prodigiously interested in the peeling process. The skin of one of his heels came off, and was tough and stiff and resembled a cup, and it hung by only a shred of skin. I wanted it to play with, but, young as I was, I had a good deal of judgment and I knew that I couldn't get it by asking for it—therefore I must think up some more judicious way. When at last I was alone with him for a moment, there was my chance. The time was brief; there was no scissors handy, and I pulled that heel-cup loose by force. Henry was hurt by this operation and he cried—cried much louder than was necessary, as it seemed to me, considering how small was his loss and how great my gain; but I was mainly troubled because it attracted attention, and brought rebuke for me and punishment.

"If I had the kind of memory I would like to have, I could recall what the punishment produced in the way of a *next* link in my chain, and could then go on, link by link, all down my seventy years, and prove to my perfect satisfaction that nothing has ever happened to me in all that time which could have happened to me if I had let that heel-cup alone. I haven't any idea what the links were that led down to the heel-cup event and produced it, neither can I supply from my memory the long series of events stretching down through the next six years and caused by it—but in my twelfth year *1847* another incident happened. My father died, and I was taken from school and put in a printing-office. I was likely to remain there forever. I had to have an accident in order to get out of it. My elder brother came up from St. Louis and furnished it by providing me *1850* an equally unpromising place in a printing-office of his own.

"Nothing but another accident could get me free and give me another start. Circumstances enabled me to furnish it myself. I ran away from home and was gone a year. *1853* A series of accidents—that is to say, circumstances—shipped me to St. Louis, then to New York, then to Philadelphia, then to Muscatine, Iowa, then to Keokuk; and by this time I was twenty-one years old. I was likely to remain in Keokuk forever, but another *1856* accident, decreed by Adam's first act and thereby made unavoidable, came to my rescue. I had been longing to explore the Amazon River and open its head-waters to a great trade in coca, but I hadn't any money to get to the Amazon with. But for the accident thrown in my way, at this time, by Adam's first act, I should never have even got started toward the Amazon. That accident was a fifty-dollar bill. I found it in the street on a winter's morning. I advertised it in order to find the owner, and then I immediately left for Cincinnati for fear I might succeed if I waited. At Cincinnati I took passage in the *Paul Jones* for New Orleans, on my way to the Amazon. When I had been in New Orleans a couple of days my money was all gone and I had found out that there was no ship leaving for the Amazon that year, nor any likelihood that a ship would be leaving for the Amazon during the next century.

1857

"It was imperatively necessary that another accident should come to my help. Exactly at the moment foreordained by Adam's first act it arrived. On the way down the river I had gotten acquainted with one of the pilots of the *Paul Jones,* and I went to him now and begged him to make a pilot of me. It was by accident that I had made his acquaintance. Ordinarily he would not have wanted my society in the pilot-house, and would have enabled me to find it out; but on the day that I entered it one of *his* accidents happened to be due. He was suffering from a malady, or a pain of some kind, and was hardly able to stand at the wheel, so he was grateful for my advent. He gave the wheel to me and sat on the high bench and superintended my efforts while I learned how to steer. Thenceforth to New Orleans I steered for him every day all through his watch. If he hadn't had that pain I should not have made his acquaintance, and my entire career, down to this day, would have been changed, and by a new train of accidents I should have drifted into the ministry or the penitentiary, or the grave, or somewhere, and should not have been heard of again.

"When the war broke out, three or four years later, I had been a pilot a couple of years or more, and was receiving so sumptuous a wage that I regarded myself as a rich man. I was without occupation now; the river was closed to navigation; it was time for another accident to happen or I should be drifting toward the ministry and the penitentiary again. Of course the accident happened. My elder brother was appointed Secretary of the new Territory of Nevada, and as I had to pay his passage across the continent I went along with him to see if I could find something to do out there on the frontier. By and by I went out to the Humboldt mines. The expedition was a failure. In the middle of '61 I went down to the Esmeralda mines and scored another failure. By and by I found myself shoveling sand in a quartz mill at ten dollars a week and board. I lasted two weeks and was obliged to quit, the labor was so intolerably heavy and my muscles so incompetent.

1861

"Once more there was no outlook, and I stood upon the very verge of the ministry or the penitentiary—nothing could save me but a new accident. Of course it happened. In those days everybody that had a mining claim wrote descriptions of it and prophecies concerning its future richness, and published them in the Virginia City *Enterprise,* and I had been doing the like with my worthless mining claims. Now then, just as a new accident was imperatively necessary to save me from the ministry and the penitentiary, it happened. Chief Justice Turner came down there and delivered an oration. I was not present, but I knew his subject and I knew what he would say about it, and how he would say it, and that into it he would inject all his pet quotations. I knew that he would scatter through it the remark about somebody's lips having been sweetened by 'the honey of the bees of Hymettus,' and the remark that 'Whom the gods would destroy they first make mad,' and the one which says 'Against the stupid, even the gods strive in vain.' He had a dozen other pet prettinesses and I knew them all, for I had heard him orate a good many times. He had an exceedingly flowery style, and I knew how to imitate it. He could charm an audience an hour on a stretch without ever getting rid of an idea. Every now and then he would wind up an empty sentence with a flourish and say, *'Again,'* and then go on with another emptiness which he pretended was a confirmation of the preceding one. At the end he would say, *'To sum up'*—and then go on and smoothly and eloquently sum up everything he hadn't said, and his audience would go away enchanted.

"I didn't hear his speech, as I have already said, but I made a report of it, anyway, and got in all the pet phrases; and although the burlesque was rather extravagant, it was easily recognizable by the whole Territory as being a smart imitation. It was published in the *Enterprise,* and just in the nick of time to save me. That paper's city editor was going East for three months and by return mail I was offered his place for that interval.

1862

"That accident had in it prodigious consequences for me, although I did not suspect it at the time, of course. Like all our other accidents, it happened on the minute, on the second, on the fraction of a second. No accident ever comes late; it always arrives precisely on time. When that one happened I had never been so near the ministry in my life.

"I took that berth, and during my occupancy of it I had to go to Carson City, the capital, and report the proceedings of the legislature. Every Sunday I wrote a letter to the paper, in which I made a resumé of the week's legislative work, and in order that it might be readable I put no end of seasoning into it. I signed these letters 'Mark Twain.'

1864

"Signing them in that way was another accident which had been decreed by Adam's first act. It was the cause of my presently drifting out of journalism and into literature. I could go on, now, and trace everything that has ever happened to me since, in all these forty years, straight back to that accident. Out of it grew, two years later, the accident which gave me a correspondence-job to live on when I was discharged from the San Francisco *Morning Call;* out of that correspondence grew the accident of my being sent to the Sandwich Islands for the Sacramento *Union;* out of that accident grew a notoriety which enabled me to mount the lecture platform when I was once more penniless and pointed for the ministry; out of the lecture accident resulted my opportunity to join the *Quaker City* Excursion; out of that excursion grew the accident of an invitation to write 'The Innocents Abroad' and become profitably notorious all over America; out of that same accident grew the accident of my stepping into Charley Langdon's stateroom one day when the ship lay at anchor in the Bay of Smyrna and finding on his table a likeness of his sister, whom I was to seek out within the year and marry two years later; out of this happy accident resulted a thousand other happy accidents, link after link, year after year, until the chain reached down to you and your affairs, a week ago, and enabled me to do you a service which you believe could not have been done for you by any other person with whom you are acquainted. To my mind, it is absolutely certain that if ever a link, a single link, a link of the most apparently trifling sort, in the chain that stretches back from me to Adam, had ever been broken, there is no likelihood, nor even a remote possibility, that you and I would ever have looked into each other's faces in this life."

1866

1867

1906

Wednesday, October 3, 1906

Clara Clemens's début in Norfolk, Connecticut—The episode of her crib catching fire when she was seven years old—The two other fires on the two following days—Rosa's promptness in rescuing the children—Rosa's marriage, and her experience with the scarecrow and the crows.

Yesterday I mentioned that on the 22d of September I went up to Norfolk, Connecticut, from New York, and witnessed my daughter Clara's début as a singer. She had sung in public once before, but that was in Italy in a class of a dozen other girls—a music teacher's exhibition—and of course the house was full of approving and uncritical papas and mammas and brothers and sisters and aunts and cousins and uncles, and it was not a real début, and had few of the terrors of a real début. It was two years and a half ago. In Norfolk Clara was two-thirds of the entire show. The other third consisted, according to custom, of interlardings of instrumental music. She showed good nerve. She was frozen stiff with stage-fright, but it was not detectable.

She always had plenty of nerve. I think I have several times touched upon this fact in earlier chapters. Once when she was seven years old she came near being burnt up one morning, but she was more interested in the tumult and excitement than she was in the danger. As far as the peril was concerned, she was as indifferent as if she had a paid-up fire policy on her life. She had the diphtheria, and had been removed to our room so that her mother might have her under her eye all the time. She was in her crib, and over the crib had been built a tent of blankets; on the floor was an alcohol lamp, which supplied heat to a vessel filled with lactic acid and lime; from this vessel a spout discharged the medicated steam into the tent. It was early morning. The season was winter, and the weather was very cold. Mrs. Clemens left the room for a moment, and then one of those accidents happened which had been decreed by Adam's first act—or, at any rate, was an unavoidable result of that act. The lamp set the blanket-tent and the bedding on fire. Rosa, the German nurse, entered at that moment. The flames were streaming up round about the child, but that did not make Rosa lose her head—nothing ever did, during the twelve years that she was in our service. She went at the work of rescue with that fine intelligence which begins at the right end instead of the wrong end. She first snatched Clara from the crib and put her on the bed; then she flung up a window; next she gathered the burning tent in her hands and carried it there and flung it out; next she carried the burning mattress and bedding to the window and threw them out; finally she enveloped the child in wraps. She did all these things in their proper order, giving each service its right and proper place in the list. Rosa was a swift person, and she accomplished these several things in about the space of time it would have taken me to think out one of them and start out to hunt up somebody to do it. Clara was not badly scorched, and she enjoyed all the details of the stirring incident. (This was Rosa's testimony.) She also enjoyed the tumult and the excited ejaculations which followed when her mother and I and the entire household, big and little, swarmed into the room a few moments later. We got the impression that she would like to have it all done over again.

While I am back in that distant time I will go on and tell about what happened the next morning, and the morning after. On the first of these two mornings Jean, a baby of one year's experience of life, was asleep in her crib in the nursery, under a tall canopy of flimsy white muslin, or some such material. The crib was in front of a brisk wood fire, and the whole fireplace-front was covered by a spark-arrester in the form of a screen of fine copper wires—wires that were so close together that you could hardly insert a knife-blade between them—nevertheless a spark was discharged through this obstruction, and it lit on the slope of that canopy and set it afire. It was about breakfast-time, and no one was in the room. The Polish wet-nurse ought to have been there, but she wasn't; she wasn't, because Adam's first act had created a chain of events which made it impossible for her to be there at that time. But she presently entered and saw the canopy blazing up. She was not a Rosa, and she lost her head at once, what there was of it, and went screaming out of the place. The screams brought Rosa, and she flew into the room and snatched Jean out and put her on the bed; next she ran and threw up a window; then she carried the burning mattress and bed-clothes to the window and threw them out, along with what was left of the canopy; next she threw water on the crib and on the wood-work at the base of the wall—for both were on fire—and finally she clothed Jean in wraps, and was then all through and ready for the household to swarm in and make a tumult, as usual.

With the practice which Rosa had now accumulated, she could have saved a child from a burning crib every morning for the rest of her life, and never put any detail of the incident in the wrong place in the list. Jean had suffered two or three burns, but they were of small consequence.

The next morning, just before breakfast-time, Susy, aged nine, was practising at the piano in the schoolroom, which adjoined the nursery. At one end of the room a fire of large logs was burning. Susy was at the other end of the room with her back toward the fire. A log burned in two and the ends fell and scattered coals around about the heavy wood-work which supported the mantelpiece, and set it on fire. Just at the right moment the barber entered that room. This had been made necessary and unavoidable by Adam's first act, and could never have happened if Adam had done something other than the thing which he did do. No one was likely to enter that room at that hour. The barber had never entered it before; he had always shaved me in a bedroom on the ground floor, but this time, in obedience to Adam's arrangement, that room was in possession of a guest, and George, the colored butler, had sent the barber up to the schoolroom with instructions to abide there in peace until I should come. He made no outcry when he saw the flames climbing to the mantelpiece, but brought water from the nursery bath-room and extinguished them. If Adam had delayed him even three or four minutes, the house could not have been saved.

Our family has never had many adventures, and so we have always set a high value on the three which I have described; and the value of them to us has been greatly enhanced by the fact that they were not scattered over a period of months or years, but all happened in a bunch in three consecutive days.

Rosa was a remarkable girl. She was very lively, and active, and spirited, with a strong sense of humor, and she had a rollicking laugh that came easily and was as catching as the smallpox. You would not expect such a character to be cool and prompt and effective in an emergency, but she was. I have not met her match for coolness and clear-headedness and wisdom in times of excitement and peril. Once when Clara was four years old we were living for a time on the third floor of a hotel in Baden-Baden, and one morning a middle-aged German chambermaid appeared in our room, white-faced and trembling, and tried to tell us something, but was so frightened that she couldn't speak. While we waited—which was the natural thing for ordinary people to do—Rosa didn't, but slipped out, without a word, and found Clara entertaining herself in a most questionable way. She had crowded her small body through the pillars of the marble balustrade, and had then faced about and clasped her hands around a pillar, with her back overhanging the marble pavement of the lobby, three stories below. Rosa approached her nonchalantly, and said,

"Wait here, Clärchen, I am going to bring you something pretty—no, maybe I better take you with me. It is at the other end of the hall."

Then she lifted the child over the balusters, brought her and delivered her into the arms of her mother, and then sat down and cried.

She saved Clara again the next summer, in America. It was at the seaside, and a number of children attended by their nurses were playing in the water. I was sitting on a little precipice twenty-five feet high overlooking the scene. Rosa and Susy were sitting on the sand at some little distance from Clara. A girl seven or eight years old began to splash water in Clara's face; this bewildered the child and partially strangled her, and in struggling to get away from the persecution she fell on her face, and so remained, helplessly struggling. Of course this meant death, unless a rescue was prompt. The nursery maids stood appalled, and through fright they were not able to move a limb. There was no way for me to get down that precipice without breaking my neck. But after a moment Rosa saw what had happened, and she came flying and rushed in and dragged the child ashore. Clara has had other alarming adventures by water, and if I had been the right kind of a father I would have taken out both fire and marine insurance on her long ago.

When Rosa had been with us twelve years she married a young farmer whose place was near Susy Crane's "Quarry Farm." The couple put in a corn crop, and when it was sprouting the crows came and began to dig up the result. There was no scarecrow, but Rosa had a superannuated old gingham umbrella, and she spread it and stuck it up amidst the corn-sprouts for a scarecrow. Then she sat down on the porch very much pleased with her cunning idea. But there was a surprise awaiting her. It began to rain, and the crows pulled up the corn-sprouts and took them under the umbrella to eat them! Rosa's sense of humor enabled her to enjoy that episode to the full.

Thursday, October 4, 1906

Miss Clara Clemens's début as a concert singer, at Norfolk, Connecticut, September 22d—Mr. Clemens's talk—Difference between speeches and talks.

It was my purpose, yesterday morning, to talk about Clara's début, and about that only, but of course I soon wandered from the track—however, it is no matter; as I have said before, there is no law back of this autobiography which requires me to ever talk about a thing which I was intending to talk about, if in the meantime I chance to get interested in something else. I will return to that début now.

When the fact transpired that Clara was to sing in Norfolk on the 22d, the Associated Press and the newspapers took it up, and although some of them printed Clara's portrait, and in that way made her prominent above me, all of them touched her *name* rather lightly in the display-heads but put "Mark Twain's daughter" in very large letters. This was vinegar for Clara, but saccharin for me, for I had been pretending for two years that for her there could be no glory comparable to the glory of being my daughter, and that therefore she ought to suppress herself and sail altogether under my name. Naturally, she wouldn't listen to this most reasonable suggestion, but perversely wanted to succeed upon her own merit or not at all. In Florence, two years ago, she thought she had suppressed me in the bills, but at the last moment the management treacherously intruded me, and she sang (mainly) as Mark Twain's daughter. Our skirmishings have continued ever since, and they have had a real joy for me and a vexation for her which was not wholly fictitious.

When she was leaving for Norfolk on the 21st I begged her to let me go up there, the next day, and lead her out on the platform, but she wouldn't allow it. She evidently believed I was in earnest. She said I would get all the welcome and she none. But when our old Katy came back from depositing her on board her train, she said that Clara's courage had weakened, and she had concluded that she would prefer to face her first audience under her father's protection. This would be unwise, and of course must not happen, but I thought I would keep up the game, anyway. When she arrived in Norfolk, Mrs. R.W. Gilder, who was mothering her, promptly decided that it wouldn't do for me to lead her out. Her manager also said it mustn't even be thought of. Other friends said the same. Very well, who was to convey this decision to me? Neither Clara nor the others were willing to bell this cat.

When I arrived in Norfolk at noon on the 22d, Clara timidly suggested that if I led her out I would have to answer the call for a speech, and she thought it ought to be very brief. I pretended to be greatly gratified with even this small chance to show off, and eagerly said I would confine myself to saying merely these words:

"I should be most glad to respond, but Mr. Luckstone, who was to accompany me on the trombone, has unfortunately caught cold and is not able to keep his engagement."

Clara was much relieved, and said that if I would restrict myself to that she would be content. But when she reported this to the manager there was more trouble. He said:

"It will not do. They will not let him stop with that, and if he gets to talking he will be so charmed with himself that he may never get through at all; and meantime you will be standing there gradually wilting away to nothing. This is our show, not his, and if we don't keep him off the platform, somehow or other, he will take it away from us."

Clara asked him to convey this decision to me, but he said he was too young to approach my white head with such a mission. Mr. Luckstone declined on the same terms, and so did the others. But Rodman Gilder, aged twenty-three, spoke up and said he would tell me. They all admired his pluck, and were properly thankful. They left for the hall at seven in the evening in a quite happy and grateful frame of mind, and when Rodman and I followed them, an hour and a half later, he said:

"Mr. Clemens, they don't want you to lead Miss Clara out."

I said, "Why I never intended to"—and we dropped the subject there and took up another one.

When we arrived, Rodman reported, but those people were so set in their belief that I was going to raid their show that they didn't credit Rodman's statement, but placed guards over the greenroom and the stage entrances to bar me out.

They gave us seats in the third row, and I awaited Clara's appearance without much apprehension, for I judged that in case her vocalization should not be up to standard, her youth and her beauty would carry her to success anyway, for she *is* beautiful, I concede it myself, who shouldn't. She was heartily received, and when she had reached the middle of her first number Mr. Luckstone, at the piano, turned his head over his shoulder and beamed upon her, and Miss Gordon, who sat breathless and trembling with anxiety at my right, whispered,

"That means approbation!—she's perfectly safe now."

And it was true. She gathered strength and confidence from that time forth, and carried the house with her to the end. From the beginning of the evening to the finish she was frozen with stage-fright, but she had concealed it so well that, with all my stage experience, I had not suspected it, and I am sure that no one in the house had detected it. That was good grit, and characteristic of her native pluck.

At the finish she was recalled a couple of times; then Miss Gordon and I made a plunge for the stage—both of us to congratulate her, and I to show off and get my share of the glory. When we reached the stage she was coming on in answer to a third call, and I kissed her, with calculated effusion and ostentation, but the audience thought it was only a stage kiss, a pretended kiss, and they shouted:

"*Do* it—*do* it!"

I led her off the stage to the greenroom, and then, in answer to a call for myself, she led *me* on, thus reversing my original program.

I didn't make a speech, but only talked. I talked fifteen or twenty minutes; and that is the disaster that could have happened if my vicious original program had been carried out—a procedure which I had never at any time proposed to myself, of course.

In our trip around the world Clara had heard me make a great many speeches, and so when she said of this one "it is the happiest talk you have ever made," I said she was a competent judge and I could endorse her verdict. My talk was reported in the newspapers, and by consequence I now have an opportunity to say something which I have long wanted to say. It is this:

It is proper enough to publish *speeches*—real speeches, artistic speeches—for by reason of their nicely calculated form and graceful phrasing they read well in print and convey the speaker's whole meaning; but a *talk* is a very different thing, and ought never to be printed. It never reads well; print kills it. An easy-going talk is as effective with an audience as the best of speeches, but its effectiveness proceeds from an art which is all its own, and is quite different from the speaker's art. A fine speech may be badly delivered, yet read perfectly in print, for the delivery is not there to mar it; but it is the *delivery* that makes a talk effective, not the phrasing. The speaker says *all* the words of his speech, and they are all necessary; nothing is left unsaid to be supplied by the hearer's intelligence; but in a talk many a word is left out and many a sentence left unfinished; because, when the house breaks into applause or laughter in the middle of a talker's sentence, he recognizes that it has caught his idea, and so he doesn't finish the sentence; the stenographer doesn't finish it for him, and it goes into print in that broken and incomprehensible form. The talker leaves out many a word and supplies its place with something much better—a look, an emphasis, an inflection, a pause, a fictitious hesitation for a word, the ghost of a gesture—in a word, the best and most effective parts of a talk are *acted,* not spoken. The acting cannot be conveyed in print, therefore the juice of the talk has disappeared and nothing but the dry husk remains.

Clara thought that that was a very felicitous talk of mine, and I was willing to admit it. But in print it was altogether the flattest piece of rubbish I have seen in a year. It was an extinguished lightning-bug.

Friday, October 5, 1906

Authorship of the two letters concerning San Francisco sufferers traced to Miss Grace Donworth—Letter from Miss Anne Stockbridge.

Several weeks ago I injected into one of these chapters a couple of odd and comical letters concerning a contribution of clothing for the sufferers by the San Francisco catastrophe. The spelling was painstakingly bad, therefore suspiciously bad; but the neighbor who gave me the copies was able to vouch for their genuineness. He is a man whose word is above reproach, and so I was obliged to believe the letters genuine and I did believe it. *I* was satisfied, but my mind, fussing at the matter independently while I was busy with other things, wasn't. It disturbed me with one protest after another, until I asked my neighbor to take measures to reinforce his verification of the genuineness of the letters. He did so. He interviewed the gentleman who had furnished the copies, and he said he knew them to be genuine for his sister had given them to him with the positive assertion that they were of that character. I used one of them in a speech before the Associated Press, the other night, in New York, and in the speech I, in my turn, vouched for the genuineness of the document. The speech was published, and one of the results of the publication is the following letter, which arrived a day or two ago.

Stockbridge Hall
Yarmouth, Me.
Sept. 27. 1906.

My dear Mr. Clemens,

I am the "dear friend" in the letter handed to you lately by Mr. S. B. Pearmain, who tells me that the names of the sender and receiver were cut out by him. If they had not been cut out the letter would have been written by "Jennie Allen" to "Miss Anny Stokbridge."

When I let Mr. Pearmain have my letters, through my brother, Mr. Stockbridge of the University Club, Boston, to show you, neither my brother nor I expected they would be published in any paper. My brother tells me that he told Mr. Pearmain that if they were to be shown to any considerable number of people it would be better to have the names suppressed. I find, however, in the issue of the New York Times for September twentieth the first letter complete with the exception of the names. I thought it was a most fitting and appropriate subject for your discussion at the Associated Press Co. dinner, but how do you think "Jennie" would like it, if she chanced to see the paper?

After the receipt of letter number two, a friend wrote asking "Jennie" to go to Maine for the summer. I am going to have a fotograf copy of that one which I should like to send to you. It is in some respects funnier than the others, and only a fotograf copy can do justice to the cacography and the ornamentation.

I then thought I would call on "Jennie." I had become quite interested in her, but on consulting my street directory, I was dismayed to find there was no such street in Providence.

My next shock came when I had returned to me, from the Dead Letter office, a letter addressed to "Jennie" with the remark "No such person to be found." This happened, you understand, after I had allowed my brother to lend the letters to Mr. Pearmain. I was now thoroughly aroused, and went over my list of friends to see if any one of them could have been bright enough to write these letters which had been accepted as genuine by scores of people to whom I had read them.

At last I hit upon a lady from Machias, Maine, Miss Grace Donworth, who had been at the "Armerry" with me while we were collecting the clothing for the Californians. She heard me read the first letter and also heard me say I had written to "Jennie."

Also as good fortune would have it some one did call for me at the Armory who was a stranger to every one. I was not there at the time, so you see I was deceived myself.

At first Miss Donworth was non-committal but at last acknowledged the authorship and has since sent me some notes, continuing Jennie's story, which are irresistibly funny, and which bring in other characters such as one runs across in Maine. . . . .

Very truly yours,
Anne W. Stockbridge.
257 Benefit St.
Providence, R.I.

It shows that the human race doesn't change, but remains as easily deceived and as eager to be deceived as it always was. If I remember rightly, Chatterton deceived Horace Walpole with his Rowley inventions, and he would as certainly have deceived you and me with them. The Ireland forgeries were accepted by astute Shaksperean scholars in a past generation, and their like would win the suffrage of Shaksperean scholars to-day. In very truth, "Jennie's" over-elaborated, inartistic, and unscientific forgeries ought not to have deceived anybody, for now that we know them to be fakes we promptly perceive that there is little or no plausibility about them; yet they deceived the scores of persons to whom they were shown. The Book of Mormon, engraved upon metal plates, was dug up out of the ground in some out-of-the-way corner of Canada by Joseph Smith, a man of no repute and of no authority, and upon this extravagantly doubtful document the Mormon Church was built, and upon it stands to-day and flourishes. "Science and Health" was sent down from heaven to Mother Eddy, after having been sent up there by Brother Quimby, and upon "Science and Health" stands the great and growing and prosperous Christian Science Church to-day. Evidently one of the least difficult things in the world, to-day, is to humbug the human race.

"Jennie's" letters are an innocent fraud, and a quite justifiable one, since they make pleasant reading and can harm no one. They are to be multiplied and a book is to be made of them. It may be that the book will prosper better as a genuine work than as a fake, and so I will keep the secret by not publishing this chapter at the present time.

Monday, October 8, 1906

Item from Susy's Biography about Sour Mash—Mr. Clemens describes the three kittens which he rented for the summer and will return to their home when he goes back to the city—Their characteristics likened to the characteristics of human beings—The ugliness of masculine attire.

From Susy's Biography.

Papa says that if the collera comes here he will take Sour Mash to the mountains. *1885*

This remark about the cat is followed by various entries, covering a month, in which Jean, General Grant, the sculptor Gerhardt, Mrs. Candace Wheeler, Miss Dora Wheeler, Mr. Frank Stockton, Mrs. Mary Mapes Dodge, and the widow of General Custer appear and drift in procession across the page, then vanish forever from the Biography; then Susy drops this remark in the wake of the vanished procession:

Sour Mash is a constant source of anxiety, care, and pleasure to papa.

I did, in truth, think a great deal of that old tortoise-shell harlot; but I haven't a doubt that in order to impress Susy I was pretending agonies of solicitude which I didn't honestly feel. Sour Mash never gave me any real anxiety; she was always able to take care of herself, and she was ostentatiously vain of the fact; vain of it to a degree which often made me ashamed of her, much as I esteemed her.

Many persons would like to have the society of cats during the summer vacation in the country, but they deny themselves this pleasure because they think they must either take the cats along when they return to the city, where they would be a trouble and an incumbrance, or leave them in the country, houseless and homeless. These people have no ingenuity, no invention, no wisdom; or it would occur to them to do as I do: *rent* cats by the month for the summer, and return them to their good homes at the end of it. Early last May I rented a kitten of a farmer's wife, by the month; then I got a discount by taking three. They have been good company for about five months now, and are still kittens—at least they have not grown much, and to all intents and purposes are still kittens, and as full of romping energy and enthusiasm as they were in the beginning. This is remarkable. I am an expert in cats, but I have not seen a kitten keep its kittenhood nearly so long before.

These are beautiful creatures—these triplets. Two of them wear the blackest and shiniest and thickest of sealskin vestments all over their bodies except the lower half of their faces and the terminations of their paws. The black masks reach down below the eyes, therefore when the eyes are closed they are not visible; the rest of the face, and the gloves and stockings, are snow white. These markings are just the same on both cats—so exactly the same that when you call one the other is likely to answer, because they cannot tell each other apart. Since the cats are precisely alike, and can't be told apart by any of us, they do not need two names, so they have but one between them. We call both of them Sackcloth, and we call the gray one Ashes. I believe I have never seen such intelligent cats as these before. They are full of the nicest discriminations. When I read German aloud they weep; you can see the tears run down. It shows what pathos there is in the German tongue. I had not noticed, before, that all German is pathetic, no matter what the subject is nor how it is treated. It was these humble observers that brought the knowledge to me. I have tried all kinds of German on these cats; romance, poetry, philosophy, theology, market reports; and the result has always been the same—the cats sob, and let the tears run down, which shows that all German is pathetic. French is not a familiar tongue to me, and the pronunciation is difficult, and comes out of me incumbered with a Missouri accent; but the cats like it, and when I make impassioned speeches in that language they sit in a row and put up their paws, palm to palm, and frantically give thanks. Hardly any cats are affected by music, but these are; when I sing they go reverently away, showing how deeply they feel it. Sour Mash never cared for these things. She had many noble and engaging qualities, but at bottom she was not refined, and cared little or nothing for theology and the arts.

It is a pity to say it, but these cats are not above the grade of human beings, for I know by certain signs that they are not sincere in their exhibitions of emotion, but exhibit them merely to show off and attract attention—conduct which is distinctly human, yet with a difference: they do not know enough to conceal their desire to show off, but the grown human being does. What is ambition? It is only the desire to be conspicuous. The desire for fame is only the desire to be continuously conspicuous and attract attention and be talked about.

These cats are like human beings in another way: when Ashes began to work his fictitious emotions, and show off, the other members of the firm followed suit, in order to be in the fashion. That is the way with human beings; they are afraid to be outside; whatever the fashion happens to be, they conform to it, whether it be a pleasant fashion or the reverse, they lacking the courage to ignore it and go their own way. All human beings would like to dress in loose and comfortable and highly colored and showy garments, and they had their desire until a century ago, when a king, or some other influential ass, introduced sombre hues and discomfort and ugly designs into masculine clothing. The meek public surrendered to the outrage, and by consequence we are in that odious captivity to-day, and are likely to remain in it for a long time to come.

Fortunately the women were not included in the disaster, and so their graces and their beauty still have the enhancing help of delicate fabrics and varied and beautiful colors. Their clothing makes a great opera-audience an enchanting spectacle, a delight to the eye and the spirit, a Garden of Eden for charm and color. The men, clothed in dismal black, are scattered here and there and everywhere over the Garden like so many charred stumps, and they damage the effect but cannot annihilate it.

In summer we poor creatures have a respite, and may clothe ourselves in white garments; loose, soft, and in some degree shapely; but in the winter—the sombre winter, the depressing winter, the cheerless winter, when white clothes and bright colors are especially needed to brighten our spirits and lift them up—we all conform to the prevailing insanity and go about in dreary black, each man doing it because the others do it, and not because he wants to. They are really no sincerer than Sackcloth and Ashes. At bottom the Sackcloths do not care to exhibit their emotions when I am performing before them, they only do it because Ashes started it.

I would like to dress in a loose and flowing costume made all of silks and velvets, resplendent with all the stunning dyes of the rainbow, and so would every sane man I have ever known; but none of us dares to venture it. There is such a thing as carrying conspicuousness to the point of discomfort; and if I should appear on Fifth Avenue on a Sunday morning, at church time, clothed as I would like to be clothed, the churches would be vacant and I should have all the congregations tagging after me, to look, and secretly envy, and publicly scoff. It is the way human beings are made; they are always keeping their real feelings shut up inside, and publicly exploiting their fictitious ones.

Next after fine colors, I like plain white. One of my sorrows, when the summer ends, is that I must put off my cheery and comfortable white clothes and enter for the winter into the depressing captivity of the shapeless and degrading black ones. It is mid-October now, and the weather is growing cold up here in the New Hampshire hills, but it will not succeed in freezing me out of these white garments, for here the neighbors are few, and it is only of crowds that I am afraid. I made a brave experiment, the other night, to see how it would feel to shock a crowd with these unseasonable clothes, and also to see how long it might take the crowd to reconcile itself to them and stop looking astonished and outraged. On a stormy evening I made a talk before a full house, in the village, clothed like a ghost, and looking as conspicuous, all solitary and alone on that platform, as any ghost could have looked; and I found, to my gratification, that it took the house less than ten minutes to forget about the ghost and give its attention to the tidings I had brought.

I am nearly seventy-one, and I recognize that my age has given me a good many privileges; valuable privileges; privileges which are not granted to younger persons. Little by little I hope to get together courage enough to wear white clothes all through the winter, in New York. It will be a great satisfaction to me to show off in this way; and perhaps the largest of all the satisfactions will be the knowledge that every scoffer, of my sex, will secretly envy me and wish he dared to follow my lead.

That mention that I have acquired new and great privileges by grace of my age, is not an uncalculated remark. When I passed the seventieth milestone, ten months ago, I instantly realized that I had entered a new country and a new atmosphere. To all the public I was become recognizably old, undeniably old; and from that moment everybody assumed a new attitude toward me—the reverent attitude granted by custom to age—and straightway the stream of generous new privileges began to flow in upon me and refresh my life. Since then I have lived an ideal existence; and I now believe what Choate said last March, and which at the time I didn't credit: that the best of life begins at seventy; for then your work is done; you know that you have done your best, let the quality of the work be what it may; that you have earned your holiday—a holiday of peace and contentment—and that thenceforth, to the setting of your sun, nothing will break it, nothing interrupt it.

Tuesday, October 9, 1906

Item from Susy's Biography about visit to Onteora—Description of the primitive inhabitants.

From Susy's Biography.

> Mamma and papa have returned from Onteora and they have had a delightful visit. Mr. Frank Stockton was down in Virginia and could not reach Onteora in time, so they did not see him, and Mrs. Mary Mapes Dodge was ill and couldn't go to Onteora, but Mrs. General Custer was there and mamma said that she was a very attractive, sweet appearing woman.

Onteora was situated high up in the Catskill Mountains, in the centre of a far-reaching solitude. I do not mean that the region was wholly uninhabited; there were farm-houses here and there, at generous distances apart. Their occupants were descendants of ancestors who had built the houses in Rip Van Winkle's time, or earlier; and those ancestors were not more primitive than were this posterity of theirs. The city people were as foreign and unfamiliar and strange to them as monkeys would have been, and they would have respected the monkeys as much as they respected these elegant summer resorters. The resorters were a puzzle to them, their ways were so strange and their interests so trivial. They drove the resorters over the mountain roads and listened in shamed surprise at their bursts of enthusiasm over the scenery. The farmers had had that scenery on exhibition from their mountain roosts all their lives, and had never noticed anything remarkable about it. By way of an incident: a pair of these primitives were overheard chatting about the resorters, one day, and in the course of their talk this remark was dropped,

"I was a-drivin' a passel of 'em round about yisterday evenin', quiet ones, you know, still and solemn, and all to wunst they busted out to make your hair lift, and I judged hell was to pay. Now what do you reckon it was? It wa'n't anything but jest one of them common damned yaller sunsets."

In those days——

Wednesday, October 10, 1906

The visit to Onteora—Dinner at Mrs. Dodge's—Mr. Clemens's method of quieting the racket at table—Some of the practical jokes which Dean Sage played on Mr. Twichell.

I couldn't finish, yesterday. It was one of those exasperating times when the brain is clogged and muddy and the words refuse to come: a body may know quite well what he wants to say; the idea in his mind may have shape and form, but by no ingenuity can the right words be found for the phrasing. Sometimes dogged persistency and determined effort will eventually improve the conditions and turn on the words and make them flow, but this does not often happen. The thing that does happen is that you may lose your temper, break some furniture, and quit for the day. That is what happened yesterday. When the words will not come there is always a good reason for it, and always the same reason—broken sleep the night before.

Susy has named a number of the friends who were assembled at Onteora at the time of our visit, but there were others—among them Laurence Hutton, Charles Dudley Warner, and Carroll Beckwith, and their wives. It was a bright and jolly company. *1890* Some of those choice spirits are still with us; the others have passed from this life: Mrs. Clemens, Susy, Mr. Warner, Mary Mapes Dodge, Laurence Hutton, Dean Sage—peace to their ashes! Susy is in error in thinking Mrs. Dodge was not there at that time; we were her guests.

We arrived at nightfall, dreary from a tiresome journey; but the dreariness did not last. Mrs. Dodge had provided a home-made banquet, and the happy company sat down to it, twenty strong, or more. Then the thing happened which always happens at large dinners, and is always exasperating: everybody talked to his elbow-mates and all talked at once, and gradually raised their voices higher, and higher, and higher, in the desperate effort to be heard. It was like a riot, an insurrection; it was an intolerable volume of noise. Presently I said to the lady next me—

"I will subdue this riot, I will silence this racket. There is only one way to do it, but I know the art. You must tilt your head toward mine and seem to be deeply interested in what I am saying; I will talk in a low voice; then, just because our neighbors won't be able to hear me, they will *want* to hear me. If I mumble long enough—say two minutes—you will see that the dialogues will one after another come to a standstill, and there will be silence, not a sound anywhere but my mumbling."

Then in a very low voice I began:

"When I went out to Chicago, eleven years ago, to witness the Grant festivities, there was a great banquet on the first night, with six hundred ex-soldiers present. The gentleman who sat next me was Mr. Medill, proprietor of the Chicago *Tribune.* He was very hard of hearing, and he had a habit common to deaf people of shouting his remarks instead of delivering them in an ordinary voice. He would handle his knife and fork in reflective silence for five or six minutes at a time and then suddenly fetch out a shout that would make you jump out of the United States."

By this time the insurrection at Mrs. Dodge's table—at least that part of it in my immediate neighborhood—had died down, and the silence was spreading, couple by couple, down the long table. I went on in a lower and still lower mumble, and most impressively—

"During one of Mr. Medill's mute intervals, a man opposite us approached the end of a story which he had been telling his elbow-neighbor. He was speaking in a low voice—there was much noise—I was deeply interested, and straining my ears to catch his words—stretching my neck, holding my breath, to hear, unconscious of everything but the fascinating tale. I heard him say, 'At this point he seized her by her long hair—she shrieking and begging—bent her neck across his knee, and with one awful sweep of the razor——'

"'HOW DO YOU LIKE CHICA-A-AGO!!!'"

That was Medill's interruption, hearable at thirty miles. By the time I had reached that place in my mumblings Mrs. Dodge's dining room was so silent, so breathlessly still, that if you had dropped a thought anywhere in it you could have heard it smack the floor.* When I delivered that yell the entire dinner company jumped as one person, and punched their heads through the ceiling, damaging it, for it was only lath and plaster, and it all came down on us, and much of it went into the victuals and made them gritty, but no one was hurt. Then I explained why it was that I had played that game, and begged them to take the moral of it home to their hearts and be rational and merciful thenceforth, and cease from screaming in mass, and agree to let one person talk at a time and the rest listen in grateful and unvexed peace. They granted my prayer, and we had a happy time all the rest of the evening; I do not think I have ever had a better time in

*This was tried. I well remember it. M.T., *Oct., '06.*

my life. This was largely because the new terms enabled me to keep the floor—now that I had it—and do all the talking myself. I do like to hear myself talk. Susy has exposed this in her Biography of me.

Dean Sage was a delightful man, yet in one way a terror to his friends, for he loved them so well that he could not refrain from playing practical jokes on them. We have to be pretty deeply in love with a person before we can do him the honor of joking familiarly with him. Dean Sage was the best citizen I have known in America. It takes courage to be a good citizen, and he had plenty of it. He allowed no individual and no corporation to infringe his smallest right and escape unpunished. He was very rich, and very generous, and benevolent, and he gave away his money with a prodigal hand; but if an individual or a corporation infringed a right of his, to the value of ten cents, he would spend thousands of dollars' worth of time and labor and money and persistence on the matter, and would not lower his flag until he had won his battle or lost it.

He and Reverend Joe Twichell had been classmates in college, and to the day of Sage's death they were as fond of each other as a pair of sweethearts. It follows, without saying, that whenever Sage found an opportunity to play a joke upon Twichell, Twichell was sure to suffer. In '73, when Reverend Henry Ward Beecher was being tried in Brooklyn, the luster of his name and the national interest in the scandal involved in the trial brought Congregational clergymen to Brooklyn from all over America, and kept the Brooklyn streets populous with clerical coats and clerical white cravats as long as the trial lasted. Twichell went there to help watch the trial, and of course was a guest in the Sage mansion. Twichell and Sage would walk down the street daily with arms locked—Twichell of course wearing the costume that advertised his sacred office to all spectators—and whenever they got within earshot of a group of clergymen Sage would burst out with an impassioned irruption of profanity, slap Twichell on the back, and say approvingly,

1873

"Your very remark, Dominie, and you never said a truer thing in your life!"

Along about 1873 Sage fell a victim to an attack of dysentery which reduced him to a skeleton, and defied all the efforts of the physicians to cure it. He went to the Adirondacks and took Twichell with him. Sage had always been an active man, and he couldn't idle any day wholly away in inanition, but walked every day to the limit of his strength. One day, toward nightfall, the pair came upon a humble log cabin which bore these words painted upon a shingle: "Entertainment for Man and Beast." They were obliged to stop there for the night, Sage's strength being exhausted. They entered the cabin, and found its owner and sole occupant there, a rugged and sturdy and simple-hearted man of middle age. He cooked supper and placed it before the travelers—salt junk, boiled beans, corn bread and black coffee. Sage's stomach could abide nothing but the most delicate food, therefore this banquet revolted him, and he sat at the table unemployed, while Twichell fed ravenously, limitlessly, gratefully; for he had been chaplain in a fighting regiment all through the war, and had kept in perfection the grand and uncritical appetite and splendid physical vigor which those four years of tough fare and activity had furnished him. Sage went supperless to bed, and tossed and writhed all night upon a shuck mattress that was full of attentive and interested corn-cobs. In the morning Joe was ravenous again, and devoured the odious breakfast as contentedly and as delightedly as he had devoured its twin the night before. Sage sat upon the porch, empty, and contemplated the performance and meditated revenge. Presently he beckoned to the landlord and took him aside and had a confidential talk with him. He said,

"I am the paymaster. What is the bill?"

"Two suppers, fifty cents; two beds, thirty cents; two breakfasts, fifty cents—total a dollar and thirty cents."

Sage said, "Go back and make out the bill, and fetch it to me here on the porch. Make it thirteen dollars."

"Thirteen dollars! Why it's impossible! I am no robber. I am charging you what I charge everybody. It's a dollar and thirty cents, and that's all it is."

"My man, I've got something to say about this as well as you. It's thirteen dollars. You'll make out your bill for that, and you'll *take* it, too, or you'll not get a cent."

The man was troubled, and said, "I don't understand this. I can't make it out."

"Well, I understand it. I know what I am about. It's thirteen dollars, and I want the bill made out for that. There's no other terms. Get it ready and bring it out here. I will examine it and be outraged. You understand? I will dispute the bill. You must stand to it; you must refuse to take less. I will begin to lose my temper; you must begin to lose yours. I will call you hard names; you must answer with harder ones. I will raise my voice; you must raise yours. You must go into a rage—foam at the mouth, if you can; insert some soap, to help it along. Now go along and follow your instructions."

The man played his assigned part, and played it well. He brought the bill and stood waiting for results. Sage's face began to cloud up, his eyes to snap, and his nostrils to inflate like a horse's; then he broke out with—

"*Thirteen dollars!* You mean to say that you charge thirteen dollars for these damned inhuman hospitalities of yours? Are you a professional buccaneer? Is it your custom to——"

The man burst in with spirit: "Now I don't want any more out of you—that's a plenty. The bill is thirteen dollars, and you'll *pay* it—that's all. A couple of characterless adventurers, bilking their way through this country and attempting to dictate terms to a gentleman! a gentleman who received you supposing you were gentlemen yourselves, whereas in my opinion hell's full of——"

Sage broke in—

"Not another word of that!—I won't have it. I regard you as the lowest down thief that ever——"

"Don't you use that word again! By —— I'll take you by the neck and——"

Twichell came rushing out, and just as the two were about to grapple he pushed himself between them and began to implore—

"Oh Dean, don't, *don't!*—now Mr. Smith, control yourself! Oh, think of your family, Dean!—think what a scandal——"

But they burst out with maledictions, imprecations, and all the hard names they could dig out of the rich accumulations of their educated memories, and in the midst of it the man shouted,

"When *gentlemen* come to this house, I treat them *as* gentlemen. When people come to this house with the ordinary Christian appetites of gentlemen, I charge them a dollar and thirty cents for what I furnished you; but when a man brings a hellfired Famine here that gorges a barrel of pork and four barrels of beans at two sittings—"

Sage broke in, in a voice that was eloquent with remorse and self-reproach,

"I never thought of that, and I ask your pardon; I am ashamed of myself and of my friend. Here's your thirteen dollars, and my apologies along with it."

Thursday, October 11, 1906

From Susy's Biography.

> Mamma has given me a very pleasant little newspaper scrap about papa, to copy. I will put it in here.

I also will insert it, because it is a part of Susy's little book, and because it contains compliments for me from James Redpath. Compliments from Redpath were worth having.

> I saw a rather disparaging paragraph the other day that recalled an incident of the Grant obsequies. I was at the Fifth Avenue Hotel at night, when the large halls were crowded with a mob of American celebrities. As we were looking toward the great staircase I saw James Redpath throw a kiss to a man going up, who turned with a friendly smile and tossed back a similar salutation. "Who is that?" I asked. "That," said Mr. Redpath, "is the man who made death easy for Gen. Grant." "Who—Shrady or Douglas?"* "No" said our friend "it is Mr. Clemens—Mark Twain. If it had not been for him Grant's death-bed would have been haunted by the fear of poverty for his wife and children. I wish" he added "I could tell all I know about Mark's noble and knightly generosity. But I learned it only under the seal of confidence. Mark deliberately allows men who would have driven a hard bargain with Grant to malign him when he could crush them by a simple statement. But I tell you the time will come when, if the newspaper reports of this day are read people will ask why Mark Twain was not given the chief place in the procession. He did more than any living man to make Grant die without dread or regret. Mark is a better man than he is an author and there is no doubt, I guess, that he is great with his pen." I recall this remark as I saw Mark sneeringly referred to the other day.

The chief ingredients of Redpath's make-up were honesty, sincerity, kindliness, and pluck. He wasn't afraid. He was one of Ossawatomie Brown's right-hand men in

* Physicians. S.L.C.

the "bleeding Kansas" days; he was all through that struggle. He carried his life in his hands, and from one day to another it wasn't worth the price of a night's lodging. He had a small body of daring men under him, and they were constantly being hunted by the "jayhawkers," who were pro-slavery Missourians, guerrillas, modern free lances——

Friday, October 12, 1906

Redpath and the jayhawker chief at the press dinner in Boston.

I broke off there yesterday, in the middle of a sentence, because I saw that my word-stream was dammed up again, and I couldn't make it flow.

I can't think of the name of that dare-devil guerrilla who led the jayhawkers and chased Redpath up and down the country, and, in turn, was chased by Redpath. By grace of the chances of war, the two men never met in the field, though they several times came within an ace of it.

Ten or twelve years later, Redpath was earning his living in Boston as chief of the lecture business in the United States. Fifteen or sixteen years after his Kansas adventures I became a public lecturer, and he was my agent. Along there somewhere was a press dinner, one November night, at the Tremont Hotel in Boston, and I attended it. I sat near the head of the table, with Redpath between me and the chairman; a stranger sat on my other side. I tried several times to talk with the stranger, but he seemed to be out of words and I presently ceased from troubling him. He was manifestly a very shy man, and, moreover, he might have been losing sleep the night before.

The first man called up was Redpath. At the mention of the name the stranger started, and showed interest. He fixed a fascinated eye on Redpath, and lost not a word of his speech. Redpath told some stirring incidents of his career in Kansas, and said, among other things:

"Three times I came near capturing the gallant jayhawker chief, and once he actually captured *me,* but didn't know me and let me go, because he said he was hot on Redpath's trail and couldn't afford to waste time and rope on inconsequential small-fry."

My stranger was called up next, and when Redpath heard his name he, in turn, showed a startled interest. The stranger said, bending a caressing glance upon Redpath and speaking gently—I may even say sweetly—

"You realize that I was that jayhawker chief. I am glad to know you now and take you to my heart and call you friend"—then he added, in a voice that was pathetic with regret, "but if I had only known you then, what tumultuous happiness I should have had in your society!—while it lasted."

I lost my sleep again last night; it is plain that the mill will not grind, to-day; I give it up and shall not try to dictate again until next Monday.

Monday, October 15, 1906

Item from Susy's Biography about Sour Mash and the flies—Mrs. Clemens's experiment for destroying the flies in the Hartford house—Soap-bubble item from Susy's Biography; Mr. Clemens's comments—Mr. Clemens's experience in learning to ride high bicycle—Letters regarding his fiftieth birthday.

From Susy's Biography.

September 9th, 1885

Mamma is teaching Jean a little natural history and is making a little collection of insects for her. But mamma does not allow Jean to kill any insects she only collects those insects that are found dead. Mamma has told us all, perticularly Jean, to bring her all the little dead insects that she finds. The other day as we were all sitting at supper Jean broke into the room and ran triumfantly up to Mamma and presented her with a plate full of dead flies. Mamma thanked Jean very enthusiastically although she with difficulty concealed her amusement. Just then Sour Mash entered the room and Jean believing her hungry asked Mamma for permission to give her the flies. Mamma laughingly consented and the flies almost immediately dissapeared.

Sour Mash's presence indicates that this adventure occurred at Quarry Farm. Susy's Biography interests itself pretty exclusively with historical facts; where they happen is not a matter of much concern to her. When other historians refer to the Bunker Hill Monument they know it is not necessary to mention that that monument is in Boston. Susy recognizes that when she mentions Sour Mash it is not necessary to localize her. To Susy, Sour Mash is the Bunker Hill Monument of Quarry Farm.

Ordinary cats have some partiality for living flies, but none for dead ones; but Susy does not trouble herself to apologize for Sour Mash's eccentricities of taste. This Biography was for *us,* and Susy knew that nothing that Sour Mash might do could startle us or need explanation, we being aware that she was not an ordinary cat, but moving upon a plane far above the prejudices and superstitions which are law to common catdom.

Once in Hartford the flies were so numerous for a time, and so troublesome, that Mrs. Clemens conceived the idea of paying George* a bounty on all the flies he might kill. The children saw an opportunity here for the acquisition of sudden wealth. They supposed that their mother merely wanted to accumulate dead flies, for some aesthetic or scientific reason or other, and they judged that the more flies she could get, the happier she would be; so they went into business with George on a commission. Straightway the dead flies began to arrive in such quantities that Mrs. Clemens was pleased beyond words with the success of her idea. Next, she was astonished that one house could furnish so many. She was paying an extravagantly high bounty, and it presently began to look as if by this addition to our expenses we were now probably living beyond our income. After a few days there was peace and comfort; not a fly was discoverable in the house; there wasn't a

* The colored butler.

straggler left. Still, to Mrs. Clemens's surprise, the dead flies continued to arrive by the plateful, and the bounty-expense was as crushing as ever. Then she made inquiry, and found that our innocent little rascals had established a Fly Trust, and had hired all the children in the neighborhood to collect flies on a cheap and unburdensome commission.

Mrs. Clemens's experience in this matter was a new one for her, but the governments of the world had tried it, and wept over it, and discarded it, every half-century since man was created. Any government could have told her that the best way to increase wolves in America, rabbits in Australia, and snakes in India, is to pay a bounty on their scalps. Then every patriot goes to raising them.

From Susy's Biography.

September 10th, 1885

> The other evening Clara and I brought down our new soap bubble water and we all blew soap bubles. Papa blew his soap bubles and filled them with tobacco smoke and as the light shone on them they took very beautiful opaline colors. Papa would hold them and then let us catch them in our hand and they felt delightful to the touch the mixture of the smoke and water had a singularly pleasant effect.

It is human life. We are blown upon the world, we float buoyantly upon the summer air a little while, complacently showing off our grace of form and our dainty iridescent colors; then we vanish with a little puff, leaving nothing behind but a memory—and sometimes not even that. I suppose that at those solemn times when we wake in the deeps of the night and reflect, there is not one of us who is not willing to confess that he is really only a soap-bubble, and as little worth the making.

I remember those days of twenty-one years ago, and a certain pathos clings about them. Susy, with her manifold young charms and her iridescent mind, was as lovely a bubble as any we made that day—and as transitory. She passed, as they passed, in her youth and beauty, and nothing of her is left but a heart-break and a memory. That long-vanished day came vividly back to me a few weeks ago when, for the first time in twenty-one years, I found myself again amusing a child with smoke-charged soap-bubbles.

1885

Susy's next date is November 29th, 1885, the eve of my fiftieth birthday. It seems a good while ago. I must have been rather young for my age then, for I was trying to tame an old-fashioned bicycle nine feet high. It is to me almost unbelievable, at my present stage of life, that there have really been people willing to trust themselves upon a dizzy and unstable altitude like that, and that I was one of them. Twichell and I took lessons every day. He succeeded, and became a master of the art of riding that wild vehicle, but I had no gift in that direction and was never able to stay on mine long enough to get any satisfactory view of the planet. Every time I tried to steal a look at a pretty girl, or any other kind of scenery, that single moment of inattention gave the bicycle the chance it had been waiting for, and I went over the front of it and struck the ground on my head or my back before I had time to realize that something was happening. I didn't always go over the front way; I had other ways, and practised them all; but no matter which way was chosen for me there was always one monotonous result—the bicycle skinned my leg and leapt up into the air and came down on top of me. Sometimes its wires were so sprung by this violent performance that it had the collapsed look of an umbrella that had had a misunderstanding with a cyclone. After each day's practice I arrived at home with my skin hanging in ribbons, from my knees down. I plastered the ribbons on where they belonged, and bound them there with handkerchiefs steeped in Pond's Extract, and was ready for more adventures next day. It was always a surprise to me that I had so much skin, and that it held out so well. There was always plenty, and I soon came to understand that the supply was going to remain sufficient for all my needs. It turned out that I had nine skins, in layers, one on top of the other like the leaves of a book, and some of the doctors said it was quite remarkable.

I was full of enthusiasm over this insane amusement. My teacher was a young German from the bicycle factory, a gentle, kindly, patient creature, with a pathetically grave face. He never smiled; never made a remark; he always gathered me tenderly up when I plunged off, and helped me on again without a word. When he had been teaching me twice a day for three weeks I introduced a new gymnastic—one that he had never seen before—and so at last a compliment was wrung from him, a thing which I had been risking my life for days to achieve. He gathered me up and said mournfully:

"Mr. Clemens, you can fall off a bicycle in more different ways than any person I ever saw before."

From Susy's Biography.

November 29th, 1885

Papa will be fifty years old tomorrow, and among his numerous presents The Critick sent him a delightful notice of his semi centenial; containing a poem to him by Dr. Holmes a paragraph from Mr. F. R. Stockton, one from Mr. C. D. Warner, and one from Mr. J. C. Harris (Uncle Remus).

Papa was very much pleased and so were we all. I will put the poem and paragraphs in here.

The Critic.

Mark Twain's Semi-Centennial.

Mark Twain will be half-a-hundred years old on Monday. Within the past half-century he has done more than any other man to lengthen the lives of his contemporaries by making them merrier, and it looks as if he were going to do even more good in this way within the next fifty years than in those just ended. We print below a few letters of condolence from writers whose pens, like his, have increased 'the stock of harmless pleasures,' and whom we have reminded of the approach of Mr. Clemens's first semi-centennial.

My dear Mr. Clemens:

In your first half-century you have made the world laugh more than any other man. May you repeat the whole performance and 'mark twain!' Yours very truly,

Frank R. Stockton.

Charlottesville, Va.

My dear Neighbor:

You may think it an easy thing to be fifty years old, but you will find it not so easy to stay there, and your next fifty years will slip away much faster than those just accomplished. After all, half a century is not much, and I wouldn't throw it up to you now, only for the chance of saying that few living men have crowded so much into that space as you, and few have done so much for the entertainment and good-fellowship of the world. And I am glad to see that you wear your years as lightly as your more abundant honors. Having successfully turned this corner, I hope that we shall continue to be near neighbors and grow young together. Ever your friend,

Chas. Dudley Warner.

Tuesday, October 16, 1906

Reminiscences of Charles Dudley Warner and Uncle Remus—Anecdote of Jim Wolf and the wasps.

Warner is gone. Stockton is gone. I attended both funerals. Warner was a near neighbor, from the autumn of '71 until his death, nineteen years afterward. It is not the privilege of the most of us to have many intimate friends—a dozen is our aggregate—but I think he could count his by the score. It is seldom that a man is so beloved by both sexes and all ages as Warner was. There was a charm about his spirit, and his ways, and his words, that won all that came within the sphere of its influence. Our children adopted him while they were little creatures, and thenceforth, to the end, he was "Cousin Charley" to them. He was "Uncle Charley" to the children of more than one other friend. Mrs. Clemens was very fond of him, and he always called her by her first name—shortened. Warner died, as she died, and as I would die—without premonition, without a moment's warning.

Uncle Remus still lives, and must be over a thousand years old. Indeed I know that this must be so, because I have seen a new photograph of him in the public prints within the last month or so, and in that picture his aspects are distinctly and strikingly geological, and one can see that he is thinking about the mastodons and the plesiosaurians that he used to play with when he was young.

It is just a quarter of a century since I have seen Uncle Remus. He visited us in our home in Hartford and was reverently devoured by the big eyes of Susy and Clara,—for I made a deep and awful impression upon the little creatures, who knew his book by heart through my nightly declamation of its tales to them—by revealing to them privately that he was the real Uncle Remus whitewashed so that he could come into people's houses the front way.

He was the bashfulest grown person I have ever met. When there were people about he stayed silent, and seemed to suffer until they were gone. But he was lovely, nevertheless; for the sweetness and benignity of the immortal Remus looked out from his eyes, and the graces and sincerities of his character shone in his face.

It may be that Jim Wolf was as bashful as Harris. It hardly seems possible, yet as I look back fifty-six years and consider Jim Wolf, I am almost persuaded that he was. He was our long slim apprentice in my brother's printing-office in Hannibal. However, in an earlier chapter I have already introduced him. He was the lad whom I assisted with uninvited advice and sympathy the night he had the memorable adventure with the cats. He was seventeen, and yet he was as much as four times as bashful as I was, though I was only fourteen. He boarded and slept in the house, but he was always tongue-tied in the presence of my sister, and when even my gentle mother spoke to him he could not answer save in frightened monosyllables. He would not enter a room where a girl was; nothing could persuade him to do such a thing. Once when he was in our small parlor alone, two majestic old maids entered and seated themselves in such a way that Jim could not escape without passing by them. He would as soon have thought of passing by one of Harris's plesiosaurians ninety feet long. I came in presently, was charmed with the situation, and sat down in a corner to watch Jim suffer, and enjoy it. My mother followed, a minute later, and sat down with the visitors and began to talk. Jim sat upright in his chair, and during a quarter of an hour he did not change his position by a shade—neither General Grant nor a bronze image could have maintained that immovable pose more successfully. I mean as to body and limbs; with the face there was a difference. By fleeting revealments of the face I saw that something was happening—something out of the common. There would be a sudden twitch of the muscles of the face, an instant distortion, which in the next instant had passed and left no trace. These twitches gradually grew in frequency, but no muscle outside of the face lost any of its rigidity, or betrayed any interest in what was happening to Jim. I mean if something *was* happening to him, and I knew perfectly well that that was the case. At last a pair of tears began to swim slowly down his cheeks amongst the twitchings, but Jim sat still and let them run; then I saw his right hand steal along his thigh until half way to his knee, then take a vigorous grip upon the cloth.

That was a *wasp* that he was grabbing! A colony of them were climbing up his legs and prospecting around, and every time he winced they stabbed him to the hilt—so for a quarter of an hour one group of excursionists after another climbed up Jim's legs and resented even the slightest wince or squirm that he indulged himself with, in his misery. When the entertainment had become nearly unbearable, he conceived the idea of gripping them between his fingers and putting them out of commission. He succeeded with many of them, but at great cost, for, as he couldn't see the wasp, he was as likely to take hold of the wrong end of him as he was the right; then the dying wasp gave him a punch to remember the incident by.

If those ladies had stayed all day, and if all the wasps in Missouri had come and climbed up Jim's legs, nobody there would ever have known it but Jim and the wasps and me. There he would have sat until the ladies left.

When they finally went away we went up stairs and he took his clothes off, and his legs were a picture to look at. They looked as if they were mailed all over with shirt-buttons, each with a single red hole in the centre. The pain was intolerable—no, would have been intolerable, but the pain of the presence of those ladies had been so much harder to bear that the pain of the wasps' stings was quite pleasant and enjoyable by comparison.

Jim never could enjoy wasps. I remember once——

Tuesday, October 30, 1906

Mr. Clemens plays practical joke on Jim Wolf—Wasps in his bed—From Susy's Biography—Tributes to Mr. Clemens on his fiftieth birthday from Oliver Wendell Holmes and Uncle Remus—Depression which the fiftieth year brought to James Russell Lowell and Major General Franklin—Mr. Clemens not affected by it.

I remember a circumstance in support of this conviction of mine; it preceded the episode which I have just recorded. In those extremely youthful days I was not aware that practical joking was a thing which, aside from being as a rule witless, is a base pastime and disreputable. In those early days I gave the matter no thought, but indulged freely in practical joking without stopping to consider its moral aspects. During three-fourths of my life I have held the practical joker in limitless contempt and detestation; I have despised him as I have despised no other criminal, and when I am delivering my opinion about him the reflection that I have been a practical joker myself seems to increase my bitterness rather than to modify it.

One afternoon, ages ago when I was fourteen or fifteen years old, I found the upper part of the window in Jim Wolf's bedroom thickly cushioned with wasps. Jim always slept on the side of his bed that was against the window. I had what seemed to me a happy inspiration: I turned back the bed-clothes and brushed the wasps down and collected a few hundred of them on the sheet on that side of the bed, then turned the covers over them and made prisoners of them. I made a deep crease down the centre of the bed to protect the front side from invasion by them, and then at night I offered to sleep with Jim. He was willing.

I made it a point to be in bed first, to see if my side of it was still a safe place to rest in. It was. None of the wasps had passed the frontier. As soon as Jim was ready for bed I blew out the candle and let him climb in in the dark. He was talking, as usual, but I couldn't answer, because by anticipation I was suffocating with laughter, and although I gagged myself with a hatful of the sheet I was on the point of exploding all the time. Jim stretched himself out comfortably, still pleasantly chatting; then his talk began to break, and become disjointed; separations intervened between his words, and each separation was emphasized by a more or less sudden and violent twitch of his body, and I knew that the immigrants were getting in their work. I knew I ought to evince some sympathy, and ask what was the matter, but I couldn't do it safely, because I should laugh if I tried. Presently he stopped talking altogether—that is, on the subject which he had been pursuing, and said,

"There is something in this bed."

I knew it, but held my peace. He said,

"There's thousands of them."

Then he said he was going to find out what it was. He reached down and began to explore. The wasps resented this intrusion and began to stab him all over and everywhere. Then he said he had captured one of them and asked me to strike a light. I did it, and when he climbed out of bed his shirt was black with half-crushed wasps dangling by one hind leg, and in his two hands he held a dozen prisoners that were stinging and stabbing him with energy, but his grit was good and he held them fast. By the light of the candle he identified them, and said,

"Wasps!"

It was his last remark for the night. He added nothing to it. In silence he uncovered his side of the bed and, dozen by dozen, he removed the wasps to the floor and beat them to a pulp with the bootjack, with earnest and vindictive satisfaction, while I shook the bed with mute laughter—laughter which was not all a pleasure to me, for I had the sense that his silence was ominous. The work of extermination being finally completed, he blew out the light and returned to the bed and seemed to compose himself to sleep—in fact he did lie stiller than anybody else could have done in the circumstances.

I remained awake as long as I could, and did what I could to keep my laughter from shaking the bed and provoking suspicion, but even my fears could not keep me awake forever, and I finally fell asleep and presently woke again—under persuasion of circumstances. Jim was kneeling on my breast and pounding me in the face with both fists. It hurt—but he was knocking all the restraints of my laughter loose; I could not contain it any longer, and I laughed until all my body was exhausted, and my face, as I believed, battered to a pulp.

Jim never afterward referred to that episode, and I had better judgment than to do it myself, for he was a third longer than I was, although not any wider.

I played many practical jokes upon him, but they were all cruel and all barren of wit. Any brainless swindler could have invented them. When a person of mature age perpetrates a practical joke it is fair evidence, I think, that he is weak in the head and hasn't enough heart to signify.

I have wandered far from my semi-centennial. Susy inserts a poem by Oliver Wendell Holmes and a greeting from Uncle Remus (Joel Chandler Harris).

From Susy's Biography.

To Mark Twain
(*ON HIS FIFTIETH BIRTHDAY*).

AH Clemens, when I saw thee last,—
We both of us were younger,—
How fondly mumbling o'er the past
Is Memory's toothless hunger!

So fifty years have fled, they say,
Since first you took to drinking,—
I mean in Nature's milky way,—
Of course no ill I'm thinking.

But while on life's uneven road
  Your track you've been pursuing,
What fountains from your wit have flowed—
  What drinks you have been brewing!

I know whence all your magic came,—
  Your secret I've discovered,—
The source that fed your inward flame—
  The dreams that round you hovered:

Before you learned to bite or munch
  Still kicking in your cradle,
The Muses mixed a bowl of punch
  And Hebe seized the ladle.

Dear babe, whose fiftieth year to-day
  Your ripe half-century rounded,
Your books the precious draught betray
  The laughing Nine compounded.

So mixed the sweet, the sharp, the strong,
  Each finds its faults amended,
The virtues that to each belong
  In happier union blended.

And what the flavor can surpass
  Of sugar, spirit, lemons?
So while one health fills every glass
  Mark Twain for Baby Clemens!

Nov. 23d, 1885. Oliver Wendell Holmes.

To the Editors of The Critic:

There must be some joke about this matter, or else fifty years are not as burdensome as they were in the days when men were narrow-minded and lacked humor—that is to say, when there was no Mark Twain to add salt to youth and to season old age. In those days a man at fifty was conceded to be old. If he had as many enemies as he had grandchildren it was thought that he had lived a successful life. Now Mark Twain has no grandchildren, and his enemies are only among those who do not know how to enjoy the humor that is inseparable from genuine human nature.

I saw Mr. Twain not so very long ago piloting a steamboat up and down the Mississippi River in front of New Orleans, and his hand was strong and his eye keen. Somewhat later I heard him discussing a tough German sentence with little Jean—a discussion in which the toddling child probably had the best of it,—but his mind was clear, and he was bubbling over with good humor. I have seen him elsewhere and under other circumstances, but the fact that he was bordering on fifty years never occurred to me.

And yet I am glad that he is fifty years old. He has earned the right to grow old and mellow. He has put his youth in his books, and there it is perennial. His last book is better than his first, and there his youth is renewed and revived. I know that some of the professional critics will not agree with me, but there is not in our fictive literature a more wholesome book than 'Huckleberry Finn.' It is history, it is romance, it is life. Here we behold human character stripped of all tiresome details; we see people growing and living; we laugh at their humor, share their griefs; and, in the midst of it all, behold we are taught the lesson of honesty, justice and mercy.

But this is somewhat apart from my purpose; it was my desire simply to join THE CRITIC in honoring the fiftieth anniversary of an author who has had the genius to be original, and the courage to give a distinctively American flavor to everything he has ever written.

JOEL CHANDLER HARRIS.

Twenty-one years have gone by since then, but they have had absolutely no effect upon my spiritual constitution; they have left not a single trace upon it; on the contrary, I seem to feel several years younger than I felt then. When a man reaches fifty, age seems to suddenly descend upon him like a black cloud. He feels immeasurably old—very much older than he is ever to feel again, I am sure. I doubt if any person ever crosses his fiftieth parallel without experiencing what I have just described. Once when I was visiting Howells in Cambridge, a long time ago, he glanced through the window and said,

"Be careful now; don't mention age; keep clear away from subjects that can suggest it. Here comes James Russell Lowell. He has just arrived at his half-century and thinks he is a thousand years old. He is under a depression which he cannot shake off. He is miserable with the realization that he is at last old—old beyond escape, old beyond cure; but he keeps his black secret shut up within, and perhaps is not aware that it is exposing itself on the outside, in his carriage and expression, as effectively as he could expose it by speech. Just at present his age is the only thing he thinks about and the only thing he won't talk about."

It was true. Mr. Lowell talked to us about many things during the next hour, but age was not one of them.

Several years later another instance came under my notice. Major General Franklin, who had been one of McClellan's favorite generals in the Civil War, arrived at his fiftieth year, and his life-long cheerfulness suddenly deserted him as completely as if it had been a garment which he had discarded. He sat an evening through at the Monday Evening Club and when it came his turn to speak he excused himself, and during the evening no utterance escaped him but now and then a profound sigh. But within a couple of months he had resumed his youth again and had forgotten that he was old. There was evidence of this at the club. He illustrated his part of the discussion with war reminiscences of a cheerful sort, just as had been his common habit before the fifty-year bolt struck him down. One of his illustrations was the following incident. I have forgotten what he employed it to illustrate, but I remember the incident very well. He was telling about the rout at the first Bull Run, and was describing the wild flight of the soldiery and how they flung knapsacks, muskets, and everything away as they fled, and how they sought protection from the bullets wherever they could find it. He found one of his soldiers lying at full length in a gully, and said to him,

"Come out of that, you rabbit! Come out of it and try to be a man!"

But the soldier said tranquilly "Yes, you want the place yourself, you son of a bitch!"

Lowell regained his cheerfulness and went to his death a cheerful soul at seventy-two. Franklin reached a greater age, I think, but the depressions which his fiftieth year brought him passed quickly and did not return.

I do not perceive that my fifty-seven added years have brought serious depressions to me, if any at all, but if they have, they have failed to last. I am aware that I am very old now, but I am also aware that I have never been so young as I am now, in spirit, since I was fourteen and entertained Jim Wolf with the wasps. I am only able to perceive that I am old by a mental process; I am altogether unable to feel old in spirit. It is a pity, too, for my lapses from gravity must surely often be a reproach to me. When I am in the company of very young people I always feel that I am one of them, and they probably privately resent it.

Wednesday, November 7, 1906

Simplified Spelling.

The first time I was in Egypt a Simplified Spelling epidemic had broken out, and the atmosphere was electrical with feeling engendered by the subject. This was four or five thousand years ago—I do not remember just how many thousand it was, for my memory for minor details has suffered some decay in the lapse of years. I am speaking of a former state of existence of mine, perhaps my earliest reincarnation; indeed I think it was the earliest. I had been an angel previously, and I am expecting to be one again—but at the time I speak of I was different.

The Simplifiers had risen in revolt against the hieroglyphics. An uncle of Cadmus who was out of a job had come to Egypt and was trying to introduce the Phenician alphabet and get it adopted in place of the hieroglyphics. He was challenged to show cause, and he did it to the best of his ability. The exhibition and discussion took place in the Temple of Astarte, and I was present. So also was the Simplified Committee, with Croesus as foreman of the Revolt—not a large man physically, but a simplified speller of acknowledged ability. The Simplifiers were few; the Opposition were multitudinous. The Khedive was the main backer of the Revolt, and this magnified its strength and saved it from being insignificant. Among the Simplifiers were many men of learning and distinction, mainly literary men and members of college faculties; but all ranks and conditions of men and all grades of intellect, erudition, and ignorance, were represented in the Opposition.

As a rule, the speeches on both sides were temperate and courteous, but now and then a speaker weakened his argument with personalities, the Revolters referring to the

Opposition as fossils, and the Opposition referring to the Revolters as "those cads," a smart epithet coined out of the name of Uncle Cadmus.

Uncle Cadmus began with an object lesson, with chalk, on a couple of blackboards. On one of them he drew in outline a slender Egyptian in a short skirt, with slim legs and an eagle's head in place of a proper head, and he was carrying a couple of dinner pails, one in each hand. In front of this figure he drew a toothed line like an excerpt from a saw; in front of this he drew three skeleton birds of doubtful ornithological origin; in front of these he drew a partly constructed house, with lean Egyptians fetching materials in wheelbarrows to finish it with; next he put in some more unclassified birds; then a large king, with carpenter's shavings for whiskers and hair; next he put in another king jabbing a mongrel lion with a javelin; he followed this with a picture of a tower, with armed Egyptians projecting out of the top of it and as crowded for room as the cork in a bottle; he drew the opposing army below, fierce of aspect but much out of drawing, as regards perspective: they were shooting arrows at the men in the tower, which was poor military judgment, because they could have reached up and pulled them out by the scruff of the neck. He followed these pictures with line after line of birds and beasts and scraps of saw-teeth and bunches of men in the customary short frock, some of them doing things, the others waiting for the umpire to call game; and finally his great blackboard was full from top to bottom. Everybody recognized the invocation set forth by the symbols: it was the Lord's Prayer.

It had taken him forty-five minutes to set it down. Then he stepped to the other blackboard and dashed off "Our Father which art in heaven," and the rest of it, in graceful Italian script, spelling the words the best he knew how in those days, and finished it up in four minutes and a half.

It was rather impressive.

He made no comment at the time, but went to a fresh blackboard and wrote upon it in hieroglyphics:

"At this time the King possessed of cavalry 214,580 men and 222,631 horses for their use; of infantry 16,341 squadrons together with an emergency-reserve of all arms, consisting of 84,946 men, 321 elephants, 37,264 transportation carts, and 28,954 camels and dromedaries."

It filled the board, and cost him twenty-six minutes of time and labor. Then he repeated it on another blackboard in Italian script and Arabic numerals, and did it in two minutes and a quarter. Then he said,

"My argument is before you. One of the objections to the hieroglyphics is that it takes the brightest pupil nine years to get the forms and their meanings by heart; it takes the average pupil sixteen years; it takes the rest of the nation all their days to accomplish it—it is a life sentence. This cost of time is much too expensive. It could be employed more usefully in other industries, and with better results.

"If you will renounce the hieroglyphics and adopt written words instead, an advantage will be gained. By you? No, not by you. You have spent your lives in mastering the hieroglyphics, and to you they are simple, and the effect pleasant to the eye, and even beautiful. You are well along in life; it would not be worth your while to acquire the new learning; the aspect of it would be unpleasant to you; you will naturally cling with affection to the pictured records which have become beautiful to you through habit and use, and which are associated in your mind with the moving legends and tales of our venerable past and the great deeds of our fathers, which they have placed before you indestructibly engraved upon stone. But I appeal to you in behalf of the generations which are to follow you, century after century, age after age, cycle after cycle. I pray you consider them and be generous. Lift this heavy burden from their backs. Do not send them toiling and moiling down to the twentieth century still bearing it, still oppressed by it. Let your sons and daughters adopt the words and the alphabet, and go free. To the youngest of them the hieroglyphics have no hallowed associations; the words and the alphabet will not offend their eyes; custom will quickly reconcile them to it, and then they will prefer it—if for no other reason, for the simple reason that they will have had no experience of any method of communication considered by others comelier or better. I pray you let the hieroglyphics go, and thus save millions of years of useless time and labor to a hundred and fifty generations of posterity that are to follow you.

"Do I claim that the substitute which I am proposing is without defect? No. It has a serious defect. My fellow Revolters are struggling for one thing, and for one thing only—the shortening and simplifying of the spelling. That is to say, they have not gone to the *root* of the matter—and in my opinion the reform which they are urging is hardly worth while. The trouble is not with the spelling; it goes deeper than that; it is with the *alphabet.* There is but one way to scientifically and adequately reform the orthography, and that is by reforming the alphabet; then the orthography will reform itself. What is needed is that each letter of the alphabet shall have a perfectly definite sound, and that this sound shall never be changed or modified without the addition of an accent, or other visible sign, to indicate precisely and exactly the nature of the modification. The Germans have this kind of an alphabet. Every letter of it has a perfectly definite sound, and when that sound is modified an *umlaut* or other sign is added to indicate the precise shade of the modification. The several values of the German letters can be learned by the ordinary child in a few days, and after that, for ninety years, that child can always correctly spell any German word it hears, without ever having been taught to do it by another person, or being obliged to apply to a spelling book for help.

"But the English alphabet is a pure insanity. It can hardly spell any word in the language with any large degree of certainty. When you see the word *chaldron* in an English book, no foreigner can guess how to pronounce it; neither can any native. The reader knows that it is pronounced *chaldron*—or *kaldron,* or *kawldron*—but neither he nor his grandmother can tell which is the right way without looking in the dictionary; and when he looks in the dictionary the chances are a hundred to one that the dictionary itself doesn't know which is the right way, but will furnish him all three and let him take his choice. When you find the word *bow* in an English book, standing by itself and without any informing text built around it, there is no American nor Englishman alive, nor any dictionary, that can tell you how to pronounce that word. It may mean a gesture of salutation, and rhyme with cow; and it may also mean an obsolete military weapon, and rhyme with blow. But let us not enlarge upon this. The sillinesses of the English alphabet are quite beyond enumeration. That alphabet consists of nothing whatever except sillinesses. I venture to repeat that whereas the English orthography needs reforming and simplifying, the English alphabet needs it two or three million times more."

Uncle Cadmus sat down, and the Opposition rose and combated his reasonings in the usual way. Those people said that they had always been used to the hieroglyphics; that the hieroglyphics had dear and sacred associations for them; that they loved to sit on a barrel under an umbrella in the brilliant sun of Egypt and spell out the owls and eagles and alligators and saw-teeth, and take an hour and a half to the Lord's Prayer, and weep with romantic emotion at the thought that they had, at most, but eight or ten years between themselves and the grave for the enjoyment of this ecstasy; and that then possibly these Revolters would shove the ancient signs and symbols from the main track and equip the people with a lightning-express reformed alphabet that would leave the hieroglyphic wheelbarrow a hundred thousand miles behind and have not a damned association which could compel a tear, even if tears and diamonds stood at the same price in the market.

Thursday, November 8, 1906

From Susy's Biography: Mr. Clemens thinks he will write no more books—Mr. Clemens's inability to remember faces of friends—The exquisite faces and landscapes which his mind draws and paints when he is half asleep—He has not yet written himself out; prefers dictating—Mrs. Riggs recalls the episode of F. Hopkinson Smith selling the original manuscripts at auction—The artists' dinner for Hopkinson Smith.

From Susy's Biography.

Feb. 12, '86.

Mamma and I have both been very much troubled of late because papa since he has been publishing Gen. Grant's book has seemed to forget his own books and work entirely, and the other evening as papa and I were promonading up and down the library he told me that he didn't expect to write but one more book, and then he was ready to give up work altogether, die, or do anything, he said that he had written more than he had ever expected to, and the only book that he had been pertickularly anxious to write was one locked up in the safe down stairs, not yet published.*

But this intended future of course will never do, and although papa usually

* It isn't yet. Title of it, "Captain Stormfield's Visit to Heaven." S.L.C.

> holds to his own opinions and intents with outsiders, when mamma realy desires anything and says that it must be, papa allways gives up his plans (at least so far) and does as she says is right (and she is usually right, if she dissagrees with him at all). It was because he knew his great tendency to being convinced by her, that he published without her knowledge that article in the "Christian Union" concerning the government of children. So judging by the proofs of past years, I think that we will be able to persuade papa to go back to work as before, and not leave off writing with the end of his next story. Mamma says that she sometimes feels, and I do too, that she would rather have papa depend on his writing for a living than to have him think of giving it up.

I have a defect of a sort which I think is not common; certainly I hope it isn't: it is rare that I can call before my mind's eye the form and face of either friend or enemy. If I should make a list, now, of persons whom I know in America and abroad—say to the number of even an entire thousand—it is quite unlikely that I could reproduce five of them in my mind's eye. Of my dearest and most intimate friends, I could name eight whom I have seen and talked with four days ago, but when I try to call them before me they are formless shadows. Jean has been absent, this past eight or ten days, at a Sanatorium in the country, and I wish I could reproduce her in the mirror of my mind, but I can't do it. There was a dinner party here last night, all old friends of ours. I recall how Mrs. Kate Douglas Wiggin Riggs looked; also how Dorothea Gilder looked; but I can get only blurred and scarcely recognizable glimpses of Norman Hapgood and Mrs. Hapgood, Mr. Riggs, and Clara Clemens.

It may be that this defect is not constitutional, but a result of life-long absence of mind and indolent and inadequate observation. Once or twice in my life it has been an embarrassment to me. Twenty years ago, in the days of Susy's Biography, there was a dispute one morning at the breakfast table about the color of a neighbor's eyes. I was asked for a verdict, but had to confess that if that valued neighbor and old friend had eyes I was not sure that I had ever seen them. It was then mockingly suggested that perhaps I didn't even know the color of the eyes of my own family, and I was required to shut my own at once and testify. I was able to name the color of Mrs. Clemens's eyes, but was not able to even suggest a color for Jean's, or Clara's, or Susy's.

This defect seems to be out of place with me. It would seem to indicate that I have no sense of form and proportion or I would have memory of them, since each faculty has a memory of its own. I think I ought to be able to recall forms and faces, because, although I can neither draw nor paint, my mind often draws and paints the most exquisite and the most faultless faces—faces of strangers always—when I am almost asleep but yet dimly conscious of my surroundings. These faces are very small. In size and quality they are like the old-fashioned ivory miniatures; like, but not just like, for they are much more dainty and charming and beautiful than any ivory miniatures that I have ever seen; by contrast with them the ivory miniature is coarse and unspiritual.

I may not have a monopoly in this kind of art, but I have an idea that more people lack it than possess it. My half-asleep mind has drawn and painted for me thousands upon thousands of these lovely faces, but I think I can say with certainty that not once has the face of a friend or an acquaintance appeared among them. It is a pity, for if my dead could come back in that gracious form, that weird art would have a priceless value for me.

There is another form of picture-making which my mind, when I am but half conscious, shares with the rest of the world, I suppose; that is the production of faces of about half normal size in black and white, never in color; faces that laugh, faces that grin, faces that swiftly undergo all sorts of pleasant and unpleasant contortions; faces that continuously dissolve away and vanish, but instantly reappear with new features and with new "stunts" to exhibit, to use the slang phrase. With me, these faces, like the miniature faces, are always new to me; they never favor me with a countenance which I have ever seen before.

The landscapes which rise upon my drowsing mind properly belong with the miniatures, for they are projected on a very small scale. They seem close by, but they look as they would look to a Gulliver in Lilliput. There will be a lake; there will be a rim of delicate mountains steeped in soft sunlight; there will be little bays with miniature white sand beaches; there will be capes and headlands projecting into the dimpling blue water; and the whole landscape—lake, mountains and all—will be so little that it will look as if it might be framed and hung upon the wall.

All this talk is suggested by Susy's remark: "The other evening as papa and I were promonading up and down the library"—— Thank God I can see *that* picture! and it is not dim, but stands out clear in the unfaded light of twenty-one years ago. In those days Susy and I used to "promonade" daily up and down the library, with our arms about each other's waists, and deal in intimate communion concerning affairs of State, or the deep questions of human life, or our small personal affairs.

It was quite natural that I should think I had written myself out when I was only fifty years old, for everybody who has ever written has been smitten with that superstition at about that age. Not even yet have I really written myself out. I have merely stopped writing because dictating is pleasanter work, and because dictating has given me a strong aversion to the pen, and because two hours of talking per day is enough, and because— But I am only damaging my mind with this digging around in it for pretexts where no pretext is needed, and where the simple truth is for this one time better than any invention, in this small emergency. I shall never finish my five or six unfinished books, for the reason that by forty years of slavery to the pen I have earned my freedom. I detest the pen, and I wouldn't use it again to sign the death-warrant of my dearest enemy.

Fifteen years ago.... However I am reminded of something that occurred here at dinner last night; in fact I am reminded of several things that occurred here at dinner last night. Mrs. Riggs seemed to me to be almost as young and beautiful as she was a quarter of a century ago, and certainly she was as bright and charming as ever she was in her life. I couldn't look at her without thinking of F. Hopkinson Smith, successful novelist, acceptable public reader, acceptable after-dinner talker, acceptable water-color artist, acceptable architect, and of high repute as a builder of lighthouses and great iron bridges. I couldn't possibly ever look at Mrs. Riggs and not instantly think of F. Hopkinson

Smith. About a dozen years ago there was a great gathering one night at Sherry's, in aid of one of those charities where a crowd gets together at an expensive place like that and spends four thousand dollars for things to eat and collects thirty-seven dollars and a half for the charity—usually by an auction sale of things which nobody values and nobody wants. The auction this time was of original manuscripts, presumably in autograph form. F. Hopkinson Smith was the auctioneer. In those days his reputation as a writer was just barely budding; he was hardly known, but he probably didn't know it. He certainly is a man of many talents, and good ones, too, but several of them are not as good as he thinks they are. He began the auction with a literary production of his own, a short story. It was a typewritten manuscript; it was merely autographed at the end. He made proclamation, and, to encourage the house, he started the bidding himself—at fifty dollars for the property. He auctioned away very energetically, and with good staying power, and finally succeeded in selling the asset at an advance upon his own bid. Then he put up an original manuscript of Mrs. Riggs's, all in her own handwriting; but as he didn't start the bidding this time there was an embarrassed pause, he barking away vigorously all through it but not raising a bid, for the people had been discouraged by the pace he had set. By and by somebody had the courage to start a bid—two dollars and a half—and Smith worked and sweated over it most manfully, because he had by this time realized what a mistake he had made in the beginning and what a particularly unpleasant mistake it was for all concerned—and everybody in the house was concerned.

Well, never mind what the final result was—it is gone from my memory, and was never important anyway. At the end of the evening Mrs. Riggs and Mrs. Mary Mapes Dodge met in the dressing-room, and Mrs. Dodge said with immense enthusiasm,

"Kate Douglas Wiggin, there aren't any words that can express the admiration I feel for you. It was wonderful that you could hold your temper, in the circumstances; it was marvelous that you didn't break out and tell that man what you thought of him."

Mrs. Riggs said,

"Oh yes, yes, I wanted to, but you know I am a lady, and I have to be so damned particular!"

And I can't ever think of Smith without thinking of a luncheon party of artists which gathered itself together in Chase's spacious and sumptuous studio years and years ago when Hopkinson Smith's large fame as an artist had just begun to flicker and spit and make itself vaguely visible in the twilight of public observation. He was at the luncheon, and, being new, the artists were very kind to him, very complimentary, and did everything they could to make him feel at home. It may be that in trying so hard to be sufficiently kind they overdid it. At any rate, when the speeches had been going on for a good while, an artist who had been unconsciously and unintentionally qualifying himself to take a chance in the debate, rose up and stood with roving and genial eye, and supporting his general unsteadiness by leaning his forefinger on the table; he licked his lips several times, and then said,

"I've (hic) been hearing a tiresome complimentary lot about this Mr. Hop-skip-and-jumpkinson Smith; and if *he* ain't too tired I (hic) want to see him get up and *do* it!"

Monday, November 19, 1906

Susy's spelling—More remarks about Simplified Spelling.

From Susy's Biography.

> Ever since papa and mamma were married, papa has written his books and then taken them to mamma in manuscript and she has expergated them. Papa read "Huckleberry Finn" to us in manuscript just before it came out, and then he would leave parts of it with mamma to expergate, while he went off up to the study to work, and sometimes Clara and I would be sitting with mamma while she was looking the manuscript over, and I remember so well, with what pangs of regret we used to see her turn down the leaves of the pages, which meant that some delightfully dreadful part must be scratched out. And I remember one part pertickularly which was perfectly fascinating it was dreadful, that Clara and I used to delight in, and oh with what dispair we saw mamma turn down the leaf on which it was written, we thought the book would be almost ruined without it. But we gradually came to feel as mamma did.

It would be a pity to replace the vivacity and quaintness and felicity of Susy's innocent free spelling with the dull and petrified uniformities of the spelling book. Nearly all the grimness is taken out of the "expergating" of my books by the subtle mollification accidentally infused into the word by Susy's modification of the spelling of it.

I remember the special case mentioned by Susy, and can see the group yet—two-thirds of it pleading for the life of the culprit sentence that was so fascinatingly dreadful and the other third of it patiently explaining why the court could not grant the prayer of the pleaders; but I do not remember what the condemned phrase was. It had much company, and they all went to the gallows; but it is possible that that specially dreadful one which gave those little people so much delight was cunningly devised and put into the book for just that function, and not with any hope or expectation that it would get by the expergator alive. It is possible, for I had that custom.

Susy's quaint and effective spelling falls quite opportunely into to-day's atmosphere, which is heavy with the rumblings and grumblings and mutterings of the Simplified Spelling Reform. Andrew Carnegie started this storm, a couple of years ago, by moving a simplifying of English orthography, and establishing a fund for the prosecution and maintenance of the crusade. He began gently. He addressed a circular to some hundreds of his friends, asking them to simplify the spelling of a dozen of our badly spelt words—I think they were only words which end with the superfluous *ugh.* He asked that these friends use the suggested spellings in their private correspondence.

By this, one perceives that the beginning was sufficiently quiet and unaggressive; but of course the newspapers got hold of it; and they got as much fun out of it as they could have gotten out of a funeral, or any of the other things which to the average newspaper mind are particularly ludicrous.

Next stage: a small committee was appointed, with Brander Matthews for managing director and spokesman. It issued a list of three hundred words, of average silliness as to spelling, and proposed new and sane spellings for these words. The President of the United States, unsolicited, adopted these simplified three hundred officially, and ordered that they be used in the official documents of the Government. It was now remarked, by all the educated and the thoughtful except the clergy, that Sheol was to pay. This was most justly and comprehensively descriptive. The indignant British lion rose, with a roar that was heard across the Atlantic, and stood there on his little isle, gazing, red-eyed, out over the glooming seas, snow-flecked with driving spindrift, and lashing his tail—a most scary spectacle to see.

The lion was outraged because we, a nation of children, without any grown-up people among us, and with no property in the language, but using it merely by courtesy of its owner the English nation, were trying to defile the sacredness of it by removing from it peculiarities which had been its ornament and which had made it holy and beautiful for ages.

In truth there is a certain sardonic propriety in preserving our orthography, since ours is a mongrel language which started with a child's vocabulary of three hundred words, and now consists of two hundred and twenty-five thousand; the whole lot, with the exception of the original and legitimate three hundred, borrowed, stolen, smouched from every unwatched language under the sun, the spelling of each individual word of the lot locating the source of the theft and preserving the memory of the revered crime.

Why is it that I have intruded into this turmoil and manifested a desire to get our orthography purged of its asininities? Indeed I do not know why I should manifest any interest in the matter, for at bottom I disrespect our orthography most heartily, and as heartily disrespect everything that has been said by anybody in defence of it. Nothing professing to be a defence of our ludicrous spellings has had any basis, so far as my observation goes, except sentimentality. In these "arguments" the term venerable is used instead of mouldy, and hallowed instead of devilish; whereas there is nothing properly venerable or antique about a language which is not yet four hundred years old, and about a jumble of insane spellings which were grotesque in the beginning, and which grow more and more grotesque with the flight of the years.

However, I like to have a hand in whatever is going on, and so I took a hand in the Spelling Reform and made a speech upon the subject before the Associated Press delegates, last September, in these words:

> I am here to make an appeal to the nations in behalf of the Simplified Spelling. I have come here because they cannot all be reached except thru you. There are only two forces that can carry light to all the corners of the globe—only two—the sun in the heavens and the Associated Press down here. I may seem to be flattering the sun, but I do not mean it so; I am meaning only to be just and fair all around. You speak with a million voices; no one can reach so many races, so many hearts and intellects, as you—except Rudyard Kipling, and he cannot do it without your help. If the Associated Press will adopt and use our simplified forms, and thus spread them to the ends of the earth, covering the whole spacious planet with them as with a garden of flowers, our difficulties are at an end.

Every day of the 365 the only pages of the world's countless newspapers that are read by all the human beings and angels and devils that can read, are those pages that are built out of Associated Press dispatches. And so I beg you, I beseech you—oh, I implore you to spell them in our simplified forms. Do this daily, constantly, persistently, for three months—only three months—it is all I ask. The infallible result?—victory, victory all down the line. For by that time all eyes here and above and below will have become adjusted to the change and in love with it, and the present clumsy and ragged forms will be grotesque to the eye and revolting to the soul. And we shall be rid of phthisis and phthisic and pneumonia and pneumatics, and diphtheria and pterodactyl, and all those other insane words which no man addicted to the simple Christian life can try to spell and not lose some of the bloom of his piety in the demoralizing attempt. Do not doubt it.

Do I seem to be seeking the good of the world? That is the idea. It is my public attitude; privately I am merely seeking my own profit. We all do it, but it is sound and it is virtuous, for no public interest is anything other or nobler than a massed accumulation of private interests. In 1883, when the Simplified Spelling movement first tried to make a noise, I was indifferent to it; more—I even irreverently scoffed at it. What I needed was an object lesson, you see. It is the only way to teach some people. Very well, I got it. At that time I was scrambling along, earning the family's bread on magazine work at seven cents a word, compound words at single rates, just as it is in the dark present. I was the property of a magazine, a seven-cent slave under a boiler-iron contract. One day there came a note from the editor requiring me to write ten pages on this revolting text: "Considerations concerning the alleged subterranean holophotal extemporaneousness of the conchyliaceous superimbrication of the ornithorhyncus, as foreshadowed by the unintelligibility of its plesiosaurian anisodactylous aspects."

Ten pages of that. Each and every word a seventeen-jointed vestibuled railroad train. Seven cents a word. I saw starvation staring the family in the face. I went to the editor, and I took a stenographer along so as to have the interview down in black and white, for no magazine editor can ever remember any part of a business-talk except the part that's got graft in it for him and the magazine. I said, "Read that text, Jackson, and let it go on the record; read it out loud." He read it: "Considerations concerning the alleged subterranean holophotal extemporaneousness of the conchyliaceous superimbrication of the ornithorhyncus as foreshadowed by the unintelligibility of its plesiosaurian anisodactylous aspects."

I said, "You want ten pages of those rumbling, great long summer thunder-peals and you expect to get them at seven cents a peal?"

He said, "A word's a word, and seven cents is the contract; what are you going to do about it?"

I said, "Jackson, this is cold-blooded oppression. What's an average English word?"

He said, "Six letters."

I said, "Nothing of the kind; that's French, and includes the spaces between the words; an average English word is four letters and a half. By hard honest labor I've dug all the large words out of my vocabulary and shaved it down till the average is three letters and a half. I can put 1,200 words on your page, and there's not another man alive that can come within two hundred of it. My page is worth $84 to me. It takes exactly as long to fill your magazine page with long words as it does with short ones—four hours. Now then, look at the criminal injustice of this requirement of yours. I am careful, I am economical of my time and labor. For the family's sake I've got to be. So I never write 'metropolis' for seven cents, because I can get the same money for 'city.' I never write 'policeman,' because I can get the same price for 'cop.' And so on and so on. I never write 'valetudinarian' at all, for not even hunger and wretchedness can humble me to the point where I will do a word like that for seven cents; I wouldn't do it for fifteen. Examine your shameful text, please; count the words."

He counted, and said it was twenty-four. I asked him to count the letters. He made it 203.

I said, "Now, I hope you see the whole size of your contemplated crime. With my vocabulary I would make sixty words out of those 203 letters, and get $4.20 for it; whereas for your inhuman twenty-four I would get only $1.68. Ten pages of these sky-scrapers of yours would pay me only about $300; in my simplified vocabulary the same space and the same labor would pay me $840. I do not wish to work upon this scandalous job by the piece, I want to be hired by the year." He coldly refused. I said:

"Then for the sake of the family, if you have no feeling for me, you ought at least to allow me overtime on that word 'extemporaneousness.'" Again he coldly refused. I seldom say a harsh word to any one, but I was not master of myself then, and I spoke right out and called him an anisodactylous plesiosaurian conchyliaceous ornithorhyncus, and rotten to the heart with holophotal subterranean extemporaneousness. God forgive me for that wanton crime; he lived only two hours!

From that day to this I have been a devoted and hard-working member of that heaven-born institution, the International Association for the Prevention of Cruelty to Authors, and now I am laboring with the Simplified Committee, and with my heart in the work.

Now then, let us look at this mighty question reasonably, rationally, sanely—yes, and calmly, not excitedly. What is the real function, the essential function, the supreme function, of language? Isn't it merely to convey ideas and emotions? Certainly. Then if we can do it with words of fonetic brevity and compactness, why keep the present cumbersome forms? But can we? Yes. I hold in my hand the proof of it. Here is a letter written by a woman, right out of her heart of hearts. I think she never saw a spelling book in her life. The spelling is her own. There isn't a waste letter in it anywhere: it reduces the fonetics to the last gasp—it squeezes the surplusage out of every word—there's no spelling that can begin with it on this planet outside of the White House. And as for the punctuation, there isn't any. It is all one sentence, eagerly and breathlessly uttered, without break or pause in it anywhere. The letter is absolutely genuine—I have the proofs of that in my possession. I can't stop to spell the words for you, but you can take the letter presently and comfort your eyes with it:—

"Miss —— dear freind i took some Close into the armerry and give them to you to Send too the suffrers out to California and i Hate to truble you but i got to have one of them Back it was a black oll woole Shevyott With a jacket to Mach trimed Kind of Fancy no 38 Burst measure and passy menterry acrost the front And the color i woodent Trubble you but it belonged to my brothers wife and she is Mad about It. I thoght she was willin but she want she says she want done with it and she was going to Wear it a Spell longer she ant so free harted as what i am and she Has got more to do with Than i have having a Husband to Work and slave For her i gess you remember Me I am shot and stout and light complected i torked with you quite a spell about the suffrars and said it was orful about that erth quake I shoodent wondar if they had another one rite off seeine general Condision of the country is Kind of Explossive i hate to take that Black dress away from the suffrars but i will hunt round And see if i can get another One if i can i will call to the armerry for it if you will jest lay it asside so no more at present from your True freind. i liked your appearance very Much."

Now you see what Simplified Spelling can do. It can convey any fact you need to convey; and it can pour out emotions like a spellbinder. I beg you, I beseech you, to adopt our spelling, and print all your dispatches in it.

Now, I wish to say just one entirely serious word:

I have reached a time of life, seventy years and a half, where none of the concerns of this world have much interest for me personally. I think I can speak dispassionately upon this matter, because, in the little while that I have got to remain here I can get along very well with these old-fashioned forms, and I don't propose to make any trouble about it at all.

There are eighty-two millions of us people that use this orthography, and it ought to be simplified in our behalf, but it is kept in its present condition to satisfy a million people who like to have their literature in the old form. That looks to me to be rather selfish, and we keep the forms as they are while we have got a hundred thousand people coming in here from foreign countries every month and they have got to struggle with this orthography of ours, and it keeps them back and damages their citizenship for years until they learn to spell the language, if they ever do learn. There is really no argument against reform except merely sentimental argument.

People say it is the spelling of Chaucer and Spenser and Shakspeare and a lot of other people who did not know how to spell anyway, and it has been transmitted to us and we preserved it and wish to continue to preserve it because of its ancient and hallowed associations. If that argument is good, then it would be a good argument not to banish the flies and the cockroaches from hospitals because they have been there so long that the patients have got used to them and they feel a tenderness for them on account of the associations.

Tuesday, November 20, 1906

Georgia Cayvan dead—Some details of her career—The pension scheme for raising money for charity—Instance where it worked: Helen Keller—Mr. Ellsworth's attempt to raise money, by written applications, for Major Pond's little boy, which did not work.

Georgia Cayvan is dead. I find this in the morning paper. She was close upon fifty years old. It is another tragedy. Apparently, broadly speaking, life is just that, simply that—a tragedy; with a dash of comedy distributed through it, here and there, to heighten the pain and magnify it, by contrast. I knew Georgia Cayvan thirty years ago.

She was so young, then, and so innocent and ignorant, that life was a joy to her. She did not need to say so in words; it beamed from her eyes and expressed itself—almost shouted itself—in her attitudes, her carriage, the tones of her voice, and in all her movements. It was refreshment to a jaded spirit to look at her. She was a handsome creature; I remember her very well indeed. She was just starting in life; just making tentative beginnings toward earning her bread. She had taken lessons in the Delsarte elocutionary methods, and was seeking pupils, with the idea of teaching that art. She came to our house in Hartford every day, during a month or two, and her class came there to learn. Presently she tried her hand as a public reader. Once, when she was to read to the young ladies in Miss Porter's celebrated school in Farmington, eight miles back in the country, I went out there and heard her. She was not yet familiar enough with the arbitrary Delsarte gestures to make them seem easy and natural, and so they were rather machine-like, and marred her performance; but her voice and her personality saved the day and won the praises of the house.

The stage was her dream and her ambition. She presently got engagements in New York, and soon began to rise in popular favor. Her advancement was rapid; she quickly acquired a wide reputation and became a welcome figure upon every stage between New York and San Francisco. She commanded high pay; she was a pet of prosperity; her high place seemed permanently established; consequently she was envied, which was natural. Years went by; her health failed; she was obliged to retire from the stage; her name no longer appeared in print, and she was presently forgotten. By and by she was able to appear again, for a little while, but the days of her good fortune were over; she showed age and care; her form had lost its grace, and to her houses she was a stranger; they were cold, and their coldness quenched her fires. She could not play against this frost, which was more than a frost, and deadlier, since the feeling evinced was that of compassion—the most fatal of all the attitudes an audience can assume.

She again retired from the stage, discouraged and with broken health, and again her name passed out of print. Presently it was discovered that her mind was affected, and that she was wholly without means. But she had been generous, in her prosperous days, toward actors smitten with misfortune, and now her generosity bore fruit. The profession flocked to her relief, and quickly raised a fund sufficient to keep her in comfort during the rest of her days. She has remained in a private asylum for the insane ever since, and now good fortune is hers once more after these eleven dragging years of melancholy darkness, for she is dead. It is a pathetic history.

Actors can always raise a fund for their unfortunates, they being able by their genius and accomplishments to furnish an equivalent for every dollar the friend and the stranger may contribute, but what other profession can do it? Raising a fund for a benevolent object is one of the most difficult enterprises that this life furnishes. As much as thirty years ago, I had already acquired experience enough in the solemn joys of raising charity funds to enable me to retire from that business permanently. Mrs. Clemens and I undertook, at various times, to raise several funds of the kind, of several thousand dollars each, but we had no success, and had to contribute the whole of the funds ourselves, to "save our face." This was expensive. That was one difficulty; another difficulty was that the fund-raising idea is a stupid one by the very nature of it. So we retired from that business and invented a better system—a more rational system—and reduced it to a code, and put it in writing, for future guidance. This was a pension system.

The idea was this: a rich man who could afford a subscription of a thousand dollars quite easily, wouldn't contribute it; he wouldn't spare it out of his business; neither was he willing to cut down his children's estate to that degree. But we argued that perhaps he would contribute the *interest* on a thousand dollars annually, for a time, and that if he paid the fifty dollars in instalments, quarterly, he wouldn't miss, nor mind, the small periodical outgo of twelve dollars and a half. We also argued that the man to whom a hundred dollars in a lump was a matter of consequence, would not contribute so considerable a sum to a fund, but could be persuaded to contribute the interest upon such a sum once a year toward a pension account.

The pension scheme succeeded to our entire satisfaction. When we asked a person to contribute the interest on a certain sum we asked him to contribute it annually for as many years as he would, but with the distinct understanding that he could withdraw his name, without prejudice, whenever he chose to do it, and without apology or explanation; but give us timely notice, so that we could supply his place with another benefactor, and thus keep the pension aggregate unimpaired.

As the years went by we now and then recommended the pension system to persons who called to get subscriptions for a fund, and we were gratified to see that whenever they tried our system it succeeded. I call to mind a couple of instances of comparatively recent years.

One was the case of Helen Keller. I will come to it presently. I first met Helen Keller, that wonderful creature, when she was fourteen years old. It was at Laurence Hutton's house, one rainy Sunday afternoon. She had then been under the loving care and competent instruction of Miss Sullivan for seven years. When Miss Sullivan undertook the case, Helen was seven years old, and had been stone blind, deaf, and dumb, for five years and a half. To educate such a child was certainly a formidable undertaking, and nearly equivalent to trying to educate a graven image; but Miss Sullivan was a pastmaster of Dr. Howe's methods, and by heroic pluck and perseverance she gradually introduced the blessed light into that darkened mind. In seven years she made a scholar out of that child. To-day Helen Keller is one of the best educated women in the world. She is a college graduate, and is a competent scholar in Greek, Latin, German, French, and mathematics; she is familiar with the literature of those languages, and not many persons can write so ably, so gracefully, and so eloquently as she—witness the letter which she wrote me last March, and which I copied into this autobiography at the time.

Three or four years after the visit to Laurence Hutton's house—a visit which I have described at considerable length in an earlier chapter of this autobiography—I was sojourning in London with my family. I received a letter from Hutton, stating that disaster had befallen Helen; that the wealthy gentleman who had been her and her teacher's support for a number of years, and who had intended to make provision for them in his will, had suddenly died intestate, leaving Helen and Miss Sullivan destitute. Hutton was proposing to raise a fund of fifty thousand dollars, the income of which was to go to the support of the two women, and he asked me if I could raise a part of this fund in London. I wrote him that it would take him a good while to raise the fifty thousand dollars, and that meantime the beneficiaries would need money. Then I detailed to him the pension scheme, and suggested that he conduct both schemes at the same time, and told him I thought the pension scheme would succeed at once, and that the fund scheme would drag.

After a week or two he wrote that the fund scheme was dragging, but that he had acquired in a single afternoon a pension list of twenty-five hundred dollars a year, the interest on fifty thousand dollars, and that a fund would not be needed. One man on that list pledged twelve hundred dollars a year, the interest on twenty-five thousand dollars, and in the ten years which have since elapsed his contribution has aggregated twelve thousand dollars. He still pays it. He does not feel, or mind, this gradual outgo; but if he had been asked to contribute five thousand dollars in a lump to a fund, he would have declined.

When J. B. Pond, the lecture agent, died, three or four years ago, he left no estate. Ellsworth, of the Century Company, undertook to raise a fund of twelve or fifteen thousand dollars, the interest on it to be devoted to the school and college expenses of Pond's little boy. Ellsworth wrote and asked me to subscribe, and said he was going to apply to the hundred, or hundred and fifty, or two hundred, professionals, of one kind and another, for whose exhibitions Pond had acted as agent during twenty years. He was going to apply to these people by letter. I wrote him that he would not be able to raise any such fund—certainly not by letter. I proposed my pension scheme, and pledged myself for fifty dollars a year for five years, and begged him to try the system, but not by letter. It must be done in person, and face to face with the victim. But he preferred his own plan, and proceeded to raise his twelve- or fifteen-thousand-dollar fund by letter. From Sir Henry M. Stanley he received a gift of one hundred dollars, and a like contribution from two or three others of Pond's most shining stars; but he got no more than a hundred dollars from any client except me, and I would not have contributed my two hundred and fifty dollars in a lump sum.

Stanley's lecture tour in the United States, after he returned from finding and rescuing Emin Pacha, was Pond's one really brilliant triumph of his twenty years' service as a lecture agent. For once, Pond was brave. He offered Stanley a hundred and ten thousand dollars for a hundred and ten nights, all expenses paid, and he came out of the campaign a clear hundred and ten thousand to the good himself.

I knew Stanley well for thirty-seven years—from the day that he stenographically reported a lecture of mine in St. Louis, for a local newspaper, until his death in 1904—and I know that if Ellsworth had sent a persuasive representative to talk with him on a pension basis, he would have pledged a hundred dollars a year indefinitely, and without hesitation.

When Ellsworth got through with his effort to raise a fund of twelve or fifteen thousand dollars, he had secured sixteen hundred, and was a sad, sad man. It is possible that he sometimes admiringly reflects, now, that I am a wise person. As for me, I wish there were some more of us in the world, for I find it lonesome.

Wednesday, November 21, 1906

Father Hawley, and the meeting at which he presided in Hartford, thirty years ago—showing the ill effects of having too many orators when trying to raise money by public speaking.

Before I close this talk about methods of raising money for charities, I wish to speak of one very common method which I have not yet mentioned. It is exploited with considerable frequency in every community in the Christian world. A public meeting is called, and orators appointed to move the audience to tears and charity. The scheme is good, and when it is well managed the results are about all that could be desired. But oftener than otherwise, I think, mismanagement is the rule. Commonly, instead of enlisting one strong speaker whose whole heart is in his work, and then promptly shutting off his oratory the moment that he has worked up the house to the highest attainable point of enthusiasm for the cause, three or four—or half a dozen—minor speakers are added to the list, and they weary the house; they exasperate it; and the results for the charity are deplorable.

I am now once more reasoning from experience, not hearsay—an experience which makes me unhappy now, and has made me unhappy every time it has risen upon my memory in the long stretch of thirty years since it burnt for itself a habitation there. It is an incident of the Hartford days. A Mr. Hawley was the city missionary—a man with a big generous heart, a charitable heart; a man whose pity went spontaneously out to all that suffer, and who labored in behalf of the poor, the forsaken, the forlorn, and the helpless, with an eager and tireless zeal not matchable among men, I think, except where the object is the acquiring of somebody else's money upon gratifyingly hard and sordid terms. He was not a clergyman, nor an officer in any church; he was merely a plain, ordinary Christian; but he was so beloved—not to say worshiped—by all ranks and conditions of his fellow-citizens that he was called "Father" by common consent. It was a title of affection, and also of esteem and admiration; and his character and conduct conferred a new grace and dignity upon that appellation.

Father Hawley collected money, clothing, fuel, food, and other necessaries of life for the people, and personally attended to the distribution of these things among the Hartford poor—not among the professional paupers; he left those to the city government, and to the regular charity organizations, and confined his efforts to the seeking out in garrets and cellars of worthy and honest poor families and individuals who had fallen into poverty through stress of circumstances but endured their miseries in silence and concealment, and would not beg. All the year long, day and night, Father Hawley prosecuted his still-hunt after the sick and hungry of this class, and once annually he summoned the city and gave an account of his stewardship.

That was always a great night in Hartford, a memorable night. There was no house that could hold the people, but as many got in as could find sitting room or standing-space, for when Hawley set out to tell of the pitiful things he had seen in the cellars and the garrets there was no eloquence like to his; not even the coldest heart in the house could listen unmoved.

I was present at one of these annual assemblages, and although it was a matter of thirty years ago, I find no difficulty in remembering it. The house was packed to suffocation. When Hawley came forward upon the platform, the house rose, with one impulse, and greeted him with a storm of welcome which continued during a minute or more. Then he began his report—not with a flourish, not with wordy embroideries and decorations, but quietly, without gestures, and in the simplest words. He stood there like another Wendell Phillips—indeed, he reminded me of Wendell Phillips; and it is not too high praise to say, that in his way, and on his own specialty, he was that master's peer. Wendell Phillips used to stand motionless, and seemingly emotionless, and deliver gentle and simple sentences that blighted and blasted, and which drove his hearers to almost uncontrollable fury. And in the same way, Father Hawley, standing solitary, and still, and gestureless, told in the simplest language tales of sorrow, and suffering, and grief, and unearned misery, which wrung the hearts of his house and made their tears flow like rain.

At the end of twenty minutes, that packed audience was beside itself; it was beside itself in the sense that it was lifted above itself, exalted to lofty and generous and hitherto unknown altitudes of feeling; and every individual there was eager and anxious and aching to put his hand in his pocket and contribute every penny he had to the cause for which Father Hawley was pleading. I was like the rest. I had four hundred dollars in my pocket, in bills. I wanted somebody to come and get it; and I wished I had any rag of paper that I could write a check upon. That man had so stirred my compassion for his poor that my emotions had overmastered me, and I was in a sense insane. If they had passed the plate at that supreme moment, that vast audience would have gone forth from that place beggars, paupers, proper subjects for Father Hawley's own benevolent ministrations.

But no—always when there is a chance for an ass to work his gift, that ass is always there. He was there on that night to help mismanage the enterprise and defeat it. Father Hawley may have talked a half hour, in making his report, but I think it was not so much. When he sat down the house was wild to impoverish itself for the cause. But four speakers followed him, and then the fatigue began; also the cooling process—that is, the pocket-books began to cool, but not the hides of their owners—far from it! By this time every man was sweltering; and it will never be known how hot the place really was, because there was only one thermometer, and it vomited its quicksilver out at the top and left no record of what it had scored.

The first speaker abolished my desire to get a piece of paper and do a check; the second one reduced my proposed four-hundred-dollar contribution to two hundred; the third and fourth reduced it to nothing; and at last, when the plate did get to me I put in a button and took out ten cents.

This experience, taken along with others of a similar sort, has convinced me that when a public call for a benevolence is resorted to, the very first thing to be considered and cared for is the management of it. A *professional* manager ought to be engaged, and paid for his services. Under amateur management, mismanagement is almost always the rule, I believe; with the result, as I think, that the right moment for passing the plate is missed, and, by consequence, dimes collected where dollars could have been secured if the orators had been gagged at the time that they ought to have received that attention. The management ought always to provide gags, and they ought always to be applied when the proper time arrives.

Thursday, November 22, 1906

The international copyright bills before Congress in '86—Mr. Clemens supported the Chace Bill—The young physician (now very old) who by drawing quaint pictures and writing original poems persuaded his little patients to take his odious mixtures, and who afterwards had these published in book form and is still living on income from his book, as he is a citizen of an honest country, Germany. Mr. Clemens will be seventy-one next week. His copyrights will soon begin to expire, therefore he must continue writing.

From Susy's Biography.

Feb. 12, '86.

Papa has long wanted us to have an international copywright in this country, so two or three weeks ago, he went to Washington to see what he could do to influence the government in favor of one. Here is a newspaper's description of the hearing of the Senate that he attended. Jan. 30, '86.

The Outlook for International Copyright.

WASHINGTON, January 30.—It is the impression of those who have followed the hearing in international copyright that the Senate Committee on Patents will report favorably the bill with the "printers' amendment," which is advocated by General Hawley, by Senator Chace, by Mr. Clemens, and other publishers who are also authors, and is accepted by the representative of the Typographical Union, which, as the agent of that Union somewhat grandiloquently told the Committee, through its affiliation with the Knights of Labor, speaks for from 4,000,000 to 5,000,000 people. Although it was clearly demonstrated to the Committee by Mr. Lowell and others that the American author is the only laborer who is obliged to

> compete with those who are not paid anything, the influence of the book manufacturers, and of labor unions, and of the various protected interests, is so strong in Congress that those who boast that they are "practical legislators" will not support a bill solely on the ground that, as Mr. Lowell put it, "it is a measure of morality and justice." It is not, however, measures of morality and justice that can control the most votes. Mr. Clemens, in his humorous way, during the hearing said a very practical thing, in accordance with which the Committee is very likely to act. He said that while the American author has a great interest in American books, there are a great many others who are interested in book-making in its various forms, and the "other fellows" are the larger part.

There were two international copyright bills before Congress at the time: (1) the Chace Bill, which recognized the claims of American printers and binders, and other trades which had acquired vested rights in the business of book-making, and (2) the Hawley Bill, which ignored these claims. It did not seem to me that Congress could properly abolish those rights; therefore in speaking before the Senate Committee I supported *1891* the Chace Bill. It was finally passed, and in the summer of 1891 it went into effect. It was a lame, poor bill, as regards the rights and interests of foreign authors, but this can be said with truth, and emphatically, of any copyright law, either foreign or domestic, that has ever come into being since the invention of printing—except in Germany, France, Italy, Sweden, Norway, Russia, and some other countries, civilized, half civilized, and savage. Of unmentioned governments there remain two, Great Britain and the United States. Neither of these has ever passed a copyright bill which was not conspicuously distinguished for ignorance, robbery, and silliness. As I have said, the Chace Bill was a lame poor affair, yet it was a great improvement upon any that had ever passed through the criminal Congressional mill before. It had its share of silliness and villainy, but it could not be British nor American without these characteristics.

Somewhere about 1888 or '89, if my memory is correct, I went, one day, and paid *1888 or '89* my respects to the venerable author of "Struwwelpeter." He was very old, not far short of eighty, I think. When he was a young physician and just getting into practice, his methods were the methods of that ancient time—that is to say, if a patient had any blood in him he pumped it out, and then filled up his body, a dipperful at a time, with bitter and nauseating and odious mixtures compounded of ordure, and dead men's fat, and the dried livers of toads, and ipecac, and calomel, and raisins, and spices, and lemon juice, and sugar, and spiders, and sewage, and asafetida, and molasses, and some of the blood that had been pumped out of the sufferer the day before. In some cases the patient survived; but in cases where the patient was a little child, the physician and the mother met with difficulty, and obstruction, and resistance, and sobs, and tears, and pleadings, when the dipperful of filth was offered and the pair of touched and sympathetic executioners implored the child to swallow it.

By and by the young physician discovered a new and powerful persuader, by accident. He did not know how to draw, and that was the valuable part of his discovery, for he drew a child that was so unlike any child that God had been able to design up to that time, that when the little patient by whose bed he was watching got a glimpse of it, that child was excited and delighted to the verge of convalescence. The young physician did not know how to write poetry, and that was another inestimably valuable addition to his discovery, for when he appended to the picture some lines of poetry, they were so far beyond human help, in their abandoned unliterariness, that when they were read to the patient they completed the cure. To make it still completer, the young physician offered to make another picture, and purge himself of another poem, if the child would agree to swallow the offered dipperful of slush without murmuring. The child was glad to sign the contract.

From that day forth, the young physician moved upon all suffering nurseries equipped with pencil and paper and water-colors, and he had no more trouble with the children. He could draw a picture and do a poem in five minutes, and he was always able to trade these fascinatingly dreadful manufactures to his little patients on the terms just indicated. He kept his drawings and poems, in order that he might administer them, from time to time, to children that had not yet seen them but needed their persuasions, and by and by his accumulation of these things sufficed to fill a small table-drawer. Crude as the pictures were, and unconventional and fearfully original as the poetry was, they were smart and witty and humorous, and to children they were limitlessly captivating. Somebody suggested to the young doctor that he publish these works in a little book. He did it. The little book was a primer, and was sold at a price which brought it within reach of even the leanest purse—four or five cents, I should say, I do not remember exactly. The sale was prodigious, and it has never ceased from being that in any year from that time till to-day.

In the course of time it came to pass that the doctor stood in need of the income produced by that accidentally begotten primer, and when I saw him, in his old age, that income was his sole support. But it was sufficient. At that time his book was more than fifty years old—I should say fifty-five—but he was a citizen of an honest country, and his Government sat tranquilly by and saw him buy his bread with his own money without making any attempt to rob him of it, for by the German law the copyright term was fifty years, and as many more years added to that as the author might live; whereas if he had been of the English or American breed of Christians, and product of the English and American breed of civilization, I should not have seen him, for he would have been already a dozen years in the poor house, and meantime his and other publishers would have been stealing his children's share of the profits of his book, with his Government standing by and approving.

I am nearly seventy-one. I shall be seventy-one a week from now. I have supported myself by my own labor during every year for fifty-nine years. If I were living under an honorable government I could retire from work, now, and take a holiday for the two or three years that possibly remain of my life; but I am not privileged to do that, because five years from now my copyrights will begin to expire, under the forty-two-year limit, and the publishers and their confederate, the Government, will begin to steal from my children the bread which I have earned for them; therefore instead of taking a vacation,

I must dictate these memoirs and build them as a protecting fortress around and about my twenty-five books, and by this means confer upon those books the equivalent of another twenty-eight years' copyright.

I should like to stop dictating and blaspheme a while, now, but I must not do it—I have reformed, until day after to-morrow.

Friday, November 23, 1906

Mr. Clemens tells of his idea in regard to international copyright, which he disclosed to Dr. Oliver Wendell Holmes thirty-five years ago.

I was supposing that I had said, yesterday, all that I wanted to say about copyright, but I was probably mistaken. This morning's mail brings a printed circular from Thorvald Solberg, Register of Copyrights, Washington, conveying notice of the fact that the Senate and House Committees on Patents will resume hearings upon the pending Copyright Bill on December 7th and 8th, and that the two Committees will sit conjointly in the Senate Reading Room at the Library of Congress. Mr. Solberg requests that those persons desiring to be heard will as soon as possible notify his office, stating the amount of time they will require and the particular provisions of the bill upon which they will desire to speak.

This softly, sweetly, gently, wafts me back, as upon perfumed zephyrs, to the dim and dreamy and devilish past. Reminiscences connected with copyright-anguishes crop up all around me, and I am surprised to find that I have foolishly wasted in this drunken and nefarious traffic so many hours that might have been usefully employed. Thirty-five years ago, an idea, in the line of international copyright, was born to me in Hartford, and I took the first train and carried it, proud and rejoicing, to Boston, and exposed it to Dr. Oliver Wendell Holmes for his homage and admiration. This idea was very simple in construction—even a Congressman could have understood it. It was based upon principle, and it ignored policy, as being unworthy to travel in its high company. It proposed that our copyright law should be so amended as to extend each and every one of its protections and benevolences to all foreign authors upon the same terms as those enjoyed by the American author; that this apparent grace should be extended not as a grace but as the foreign author's *right,* thus putting the foreign author's clothes and his book upon the same basis—as being his property, and not righteously and fairly filchable from him by any government, Christian or pagan. And finally, this recognition of the foreign author's right to his property was to be a *gratis* act; nothing was to be required of any foreign government in return; the act was to be a simple act of justice, and unsullied and undegraded by any trading and trafficking in, and selling of, said justice.

Dr. Holmes laughed at this project most cruelly and cordially. He said it was Utopian; that governments didn't deal in gratis contributions of pecuniarily valuable graces; that governments did not trade in dreams and romance; that they did not give something for nothing; that it had been their settled policy, from the beginnings of civilization—and earlier, for that matter—to always require something for something in a trade with a foreign government, and also always to try to get two somethings for one something, and accomplish it if humanly possible. He said that if our Government should do this juvenile thing, all the other Christian governments would laugh at it, and would gladly accept our sentimental charity and chuckle over it, and never dream of furnishing anything in return.

I was sorry to learn that apparently it is only Christian *peoples* that stand for Christian morals and teach them from the pulpit, and in the schools, and that Christian *governments,* placed in power by these same moral people, have no public morals, but deride them, and do it frankly, openly, aboveboard, and even boastfully. I was only half as old, then, as I am now, and I did not know, then, as I know now, that our American governments, municipal, state, and federal, are very poor in *public* morals, while the men that constitute these governments are in most cases properly equipped with private morals and live up to them in private life.

I contended that my plan was a good one, even as a measure of policy; that while it might be very true that the English *Government* might laugh in its sleeve at our romantic exhibition of justice and cleanliness, the English *people's* attitude would be very different; that they would be ashamed to receive a common justice at our hands without a return, and would demand that for shame's sake, and for decency's sake, we be met half way, and British honor and fairness be saved from reproach. I used that argument, but, at the same time, I really cared not a farthing about a foreign return of our fair-dealing. In my capacity as just a human being, I was not able to conceive of myself entering into an agreement with another human being to leave his property unstolen provided he would respect mine in the same way; and governments being nothing more than assemblages of human beings representative of the people, and ostensibly selected for character and intelligence, I was not able to understand how they could propagate thieving, encourage it, applaud it, and stubbornly refuse to respect property rights, and still keep their own self-respect.

I ventured another argument. I said we had been living on stolen English literature ever since the discovery of America by Columbus; that we were still living upon it and in that way teaching our people to envy and worship kings, emperors, dukes, high birth, hereditary privilege, and many other offensively undemocratic things; that we were still stealing this unwholesome literature, and thereby rooting and establishing monarchical and aristocratic ideals in the hearts of our nation; and yet, most incongruously, parents, schools, colleges, universities, and Fourth of July stump orators were all engaged in deriding and abusing these very ideals and trying to train the nation in a wholesome disrespect for them. I said that just at the present time England ought to be very glad, and indeed eager, to accept my proposition, because we were stealing fifty books from her where she stole one from us; but that a time could come, and probably would come, when this condition of things would be reversed; when her population would no longer be only a third short of our own, but would have well nigh disappeared under our swarming accumulations of the human animal, and we should be furnishing fifty books to *her* one, and anxiously and prayerfully wishing an international copyright law could be arranged on a moral basis, leaving policy out.

However, I did not convince Dr. Holmes. He made game of all my notions, and I went back home very much wilted, and dropped the international copyright scheme out of my mind. I had not mentioned it to any one except Dr. Holmes, and I was glad of that, and made up my mind that I would not furnish anybody else an opportunity to laugh at me. But as it turned out, I had not been so very unstatesmanlike after all. Fourteen years later the Hawley International Copyright Bill, which I have already spoken of, came before Congress, and it was just my scheme over again. But it stood no chance; we were a Christian nation with private and effective Christian morals; our Government was a Christian government with Christian public morals, and a moral Hawley Bill stood no more chance there than it would have stood in that place whither so many Congresses have gone, and will go.

Saturday, November 24, 1906

More about international copyright—Congresses and Parliaments made up of men who know nothing about the matter—Mr. Clemens disputes with Lord Thwing his statement that there is no property in ideas.

I believe that our Heavenly Father invented man because he was disappointed in the monkey. I believe that whenever a human being, of even the highest intelligence and culture, delivers an opinion upon a matter apart from his particular and especial line of interest, training, and experience, it will always be an opinion of so foolish and so valueless a sort that it can be depended upon to suggest to our Heavenly Father that the human being is another disappointment, and that he is no considerable improvement upon the monkey. Congresses and Parliaments are not made up of authors and publishers, but of lawyers, agriculturalists, merchants, manufacturers, bankers, and so on. When bills are proposed affecting these great industries, they get prompt and intelligent attention, because there are so many members of the law-making bodies who are personally and profoundly interested in these things and ready to rise up and fight for or against them with their best strength and energy. These bills are discussed and explained by men who know all about the interests involved in them; men recognized as being competent to explain and discuss and furnish authoritative information to the ignorant. As a result, perhaps no important English or American statutes are uncompromisingly and hopelessly idiotic except the copyright statutes of these two countries. The Congresses and the Parliaments are always, and must always remain, in the condition of the British Parliaments of seventy-five and eighty years ago, when they were called upon to legislate upon a matter which was absolutely new to the whole body of them and concerning which they were as strictly and comprehensively ignorant as the unborn child is of theology. There were no railroad men in those Parliaments; the members had to inform themselves through the statements made to them by Stephenson, and they considered him a visionary, a half-lunatic, possibly even ass and poet. Through lack of previous knowledge and experience of railway matters, they were unable to understand Stephenson. His explanations, so simple to himself, were but a fog to those well-meaning legislators; so far as they were concerned, he was talking riddles, and riddles which seemed to be meaningless; riddles which seemed also to be dreams and insanities. Still, being gentlemen, and kindly and humane, they listened to Stephenson patiently, benevolently, charitably, until at last, in a burst of irritation, he lost his prudence and proclaimed that he would yet prove to the world that he could drive a steam locomotive over iron rails at the impossible speed of twelve miles an hour! That finished him. After that, the law-makers imposed upon themselves no further polite reserves, but called him, frankly, a dreamer, a crank, a lunatic.

Copyright has always had to face what Stephenson faced—bodies of law-makers absolutely ignorant of the matter they were called upon to legislate about; also absolutely unteachable, in the circumstances, and bound to remain so—themselves and their successors—until a day when they shall be stockholders in publishing houses and personally interested in finding out something about authorship and the book trade—a day which is not at all likely to arrive during the term of the present geological epoch.

Authors sometimes understand their side of the question, but this is rare; none of them understands the publisher's side of it. A man must be both author and publisher, and experienced in the scorching griefs and trials of both industries, before he is competent to go before a Copyright Committee of Parliament or Congress and afford it information of any considerable value. A thousand, possibly ten thousand, valuable speeches have been made in Congresses and Parliaments upon great corporation interests, for the men who made them had been competently equipped by personal suffering and experience to treat those great matters intelligently; but, so far as I know, no publisher of great authority has ever sat in a law-making body and made a speech in his trade's interest that was worth remembering, or that has been remembered. So far as I know, only one author has ever made a memorable speech before a law-making body in the interest of his trade—that was Macaulay. I think his speech is called great to this day, by both authors and publishers; whereas the speech is so exhaustively ignorant of its subject, and so trivial and jejune in its reasonings, that to the person who has been both author and publisher it ranks as another and formidable evidence, and possibly even proof, that in discarding the monkey and substituting man, our Father in Heaven did the monkey an undeserved injustice.

Consider a simple example: if you could prove that only twenty idiots are born in a century, and that each of them, by special genius, was able to make an article of commerce which no one else could make; and which was able to furnish the idiot, and his descendants after him, an income sufficient for the modest and economical support of half a dozen persons, there is no Congress and no Parliament in all Christendom that would dream of descending to the shabbiness of limiting that trifling income to a term of years, in order that it might be enjoyed thereafter by persons who had no sort of claim upon it. I know that this would happen, because all Congresses and Parliaments have a kindly feeling for idiots, and a compassion for them, on account of personal experience and heredity. Neither England nor America has been able to produce, in a century, any more than twenty authors whose books have been able to outlive the copyright limit of forty-two years, yet the Congresses and the Parliaments stick to the forty-two-year limit greedily, intensely, pathetically, and do seem to believe, by some kind of insane reasoning, that somebody is in some way benefited by this trivial robbery inflicted upon the families of twenty authors in the course of a hundred years. The most uncompromising and unlimited stupidity can invent nothing stupider than this; not even the monkey can get down to its level.

In a century we have produced two hundred and twenty thousand books; not a bathtub-full of them are still alive and marketable. The case would have been the same if the copyright limit had been a thousand years. It would be entirely safe to make it a thousand years, and it would also be properly respectable and courteous to do it.

When I was in London seven years ago, I was haled before the Copyright Committee of the House of Lords, who were considering a bill to add eight entire years to the copyright limit, and make it fifty. One of the ablest men in the House of Lords did the most of the question-asking—Lord Thwing—but he seemed to me to be a most striking example of how unintelligent a human being can be when he sets out to discuss a matter about which he has had no personal training, and no personal experience. There was a long talk—but I wish to confine myself to a single detail of it. Lord Thwing asked me what I thought would be a fair and just copyright limit. I said a million years—that is to say, copyright in perpetuity. The answer seemed to outrage him; it quite plainly irritated him. He asked me if I was not aware of the fact that it had long ago been decided that there could be no property in ideas, and that as a book consisted merely of ideas, it was not entitled to rank as property or enjoy the protections extended to property. I said I was aware that somebody, at some time or other, had given birth to that astonishing superstition, and that an ostensibly intelligent human race had accepted it with enthusiasm, without taking the trouble to examine it and find out that it was an empty inspiration and not entitled to respect. I added that in spite of its being regarded as a fact, and as also well charged with wisdom, it had not been respected by any Parliament or Congress since Queen Anne's time; that in her day, by the changing of perpetual copyright to a limited copyright of fourteen years, its claim as property was *recognized;* that the retaining of a limit of any kind—of even fourteen years, for instance—was a recognition of the fact that the ideas of which a book consisted were property.

Lord Thwing was not affected by these reasonings—certainly he was not convinced. He said that the fact remained that a book, being merely a collocation of ideas, was not in any sense property, and that no book was entitled to perpetual existence as property, or would ever receive that grace at the hands of a legislature entrusted with the interests and well-being of the nation.

I said I should be obliged to take issue with that statement, for the reason that perpetual copyright was already existent in England, and had been granted by a Parliament or Parliaments entrusted with the duty of protecting the interests and well-being of the nation. He asked for the evidence of this, and I said that the New and Old Testaments had been granted perpetual copyright in England, and that several other religious books had also been granted perpetual copyright in England, and that these perpetual copyrights were not enjoyed by the hungry widows and children of poor authors, but were the property of the press of Oxford University, an institution quite well able to live without this charitable favoritism. I was vain of this unanswerable hit, but I concealed it.

With the gentleness and modesty which were born in me, I then went on and pleaded against the assumption that a book is not properly property because it is founded upon ideas, and is built of ideas from its cellar to its roof. I said it would not be possible for anybody to mention to me a piece of property of any kind which was not based in the same way, and built from cellar to roof out of just that same material—ideas.

Lord Thwing suggested real estate. I said there was not a foot of real estate on the globe whose value, if it had any, was not the result of ideas, and of nothing except ideas. I could have given him a million instances. I could have said that if a man should take an ignorant and useless dog and train him to be a good setter, or a good shepherd dog, the dog would now be a more or less valuable property, and would be salable at a more or less profitable figure, and that this acquired value would be merely the result of an idea practically and intelligently applied—the idea of making valuable a dog that had previously possessed no value. I could have said that the smoothing-iron, the wash-tub, the shingle or the slate for a roof, the invention of clothing, and all the improvements that the ages have added, were all the results of men's thinkings and men's application of ideas; that but for these ideas, these properties would not have existed; that in all cases they owe their existence to ideas, and that in this way they become property, and valuable. I could have said that but for those inspirations called ideas, there would be no railways, no telegraphs, no printing-press, no phonographs, no telephones—no anything in the whole earth that is called property and has a value. I did say that that holy thing—real estate—that sacred thing which enjoys perpetual copyright everywhere, is like all other properties—its value is born of an idea, and every time that that value is increased it is because of the application of further ideas to it, and for no other reason. I said that if by chance there were a company of twenty white men camping in the middle of Africa, it could easily happen that while all of the twenty realized that there was not an acre of ground in the whole vast landscape in view at the time that possessed even the value of a discarded oyster can, it could also happen that there could be one man in that company equipped with ideas—a far-seeing man who could perceive that at some distant day a railway would pass through this region and that this camping-ground would infallibly become the site of a prosperous city, of flourishing industries. It could easily happen that that man would be bright enough to gather together the black chiefs of the tribes of that region and buy that whole district for a dozen rifles and a barrel of whisky, and go home and lay the deeds away for the eventual vast profit of his children. It could easily come true that in time that city would be built and that land made valuable beyond imagination, and the man's children rich beyond their wildest dreams, and that this shining result would proceed from that man's *idea,* and from no other source; that if there were any real justice in the world, the ideas in a book would rank breast to breast with the ideas which created value for real estate and all other properties in the earth, and then it would be recognized that an author's children are as fairly entitled to the results of his ideas as are the children of any brewer in England, or of any owner of houses and lands and perpetual-copyright Bibles.

Monday, November 30, 1906

From Susy's Biography, item about the ducks—Mr. Clemens tells of his young ducks that had their feet chewed by snapping turtles—Billy Rice's version of "There is a happy land," and Mr. Clemens's recollections of the first negro-minstrel shows.

From Susy's Biography.

> Jean and Papa were walking out past the barn the other day when Jean saw some little newly born baby ducks, she exclaimed as she perceived them "I dont see why God gives us so much ducks when Patrick kills them so."

Susy is mistaken as to the origin of the ducks. They were not a gift, I bought them. I am not finding fault with her, for that would be most unfair. She is remarkably accurate in her statements as a historian, as a rule, and it would not be just to make much of this small slip of hers; besides I think it was a quite natural slip, for by heredity and habit ours was a religious household, and it was a common thing with us whenever anybody did a handsome thing, to give the credit of it to Providence, without examining into the matter. This may be called automatic religion—in fact that is what it is; it is so used to its work that it can do it without your help or even your privity; out of all the facts and statistics that may be placed before it, it will always get the one result, since it has never been taught to seek any other. It is thus the unreflecting cause of much injustice. As we have seen, it betrayed Susy into an injustice toward me. It had to be automatic, for she would have been far from doing me an injustice when in her right mind. It was a dear little biographer, and she meant me no harm, and I am not censuring her now, but am only desirous of correcting in advance an erroneous impression which her words would be sure to convey to a reader's mind. No elaboration of this matter is necessary; it is sufficient to say *I* provided the ducks.

It was in Hartford. The greensward sloped down hill from the house to the sluggish little river that flowed through the grounds, and Patrick, who was fertile in good ideas, had early conceived the idea of having home-made ducks for our table. Every morning he drove them from the stable down to the river, and the children were always there to see and admire the waddling white procession; they were there again at sunset to see Patrick conduct the procession back to its lodgings in the stable. But this was not always a gay and happy holiday-show, with joy in it for the witnesses; no, too frequently there was a tragedy connected with it, and then there were tears and pain for the children. There was a stranded log or two in the river, and on these certain families of snapping turtles used to congregate and drowse in the sun and give thanks, in their dumb way, to Providence for benevolences extended to them. It was but another instance of misplaced credit; it was the young ducks that those pious reptiles were so thankful for—whereas they were *my* ducks. I bought the ducks.

When a crop of young ducks, not yet quite old enough for the table but approaching that age, began to join the procession, and paddle around in the sluggish water, and give thanks—not to me—for that privilege, the snapping turtles would suspend their songs of praise and slide off the logs and paddle along under the water and chew the feet of the young ducks. Presently Patrick would notice that two or three of those little creatures were not moving about, but were apparently at anchor, and were not looking as thankful as they had been looking a short time before. He early found out what that sign meant—a submerged snapping turtle was taking his breakfast, and silently singing his gratitude. Every day or two Patrick would rescue and fetch up a little duck with incomplete legs to stand upon—nothing left of their extremities but gnawed and bleeding stumps. Then the children said pitying things and wept—and at dinner we finished the tragedy which the turtles had begun. Thus, as will be seen, it was really the turtles that gave us "so much ducks." At my expense.

From Susy's Biography.

Papa has written a new version of "There is a happy land" it is—

"There is a boarding house
Far, far away,
Where they have ham and eggs,
Three times a day,
Oh dont those boarders yell
When they hear the dinner-bell,
They give that land-lord rats
Three times a day."

Again Susy has made a small error. It was not I that wrote the song. I heard Billy Rice sing it in the negro-minstrel show, and I brought it home and sang it—with great spirit—for the elevation of the household. The children admired it to the limit, and made me sing it with burdensome frequency. To their minds it was superior to the "Battle Hymn of the Republic."

How many years ago that was! Where now is Billy Rice? He was a joy to me, and so were the other stars of the nigger show—Billy Birch, David Wambold, Backus, and a delightful dozen of their brethren, who made life a pleasure to me forty years ago, and later. Birch, Wambold, and Backus are gone years ago; and with them departed to return no more forever, I suppose, the real nigger show—the genuine nigger show, the extravagant nigger show—the show which to me had no peer and whose peer has not yet arrived, in my experience. We have the grand opera; and I have witnessed, and greatly enjoyed, the first act of everything which Wagner created, but the effect on me has always been so powerful that one act was quite sufficient; whenever I have witnessed two acts I have gone away physically exhausted; and whenever I have ventured an entire opera the result has been the next thing to suicide. But if I could have the nigger show back again, in its pristine purity and perfection, I should have but little further use for opera. It seems to me that to the elevated mind and the sensitive spirit, the hand-organ and the nigger show are a standard and a summit to whose rarified altitude the other forms of musical art may not hope to reach.

I remember the first negro-minstrel show I ever saw. It must have been in the early '40s. It was a new institution. In our village of Hannibal, on the banks of the Mississippi, we had not heard of it before, and it burst upon us as a glad and stunning surprise.

The show remained a week, and gave a performance every night. Church members did not attend these performances, but all the worldlings flocked to them, and were enchanted. Church members did not attend shows out there in those days.

The minstrels appeared with coal-black hands and faces, and their clothing was a loud and extravagant burlesque of the clothing worn by the plantation slave of the time; not that the rags of the poor slave were burlesqued, for that would not have been possible; burlesque could have added nothing in the way of extravagance to the sorrowful accumulation of rags and patches which constituted his costume; it was the form and color of his dress that was burlesqued. Standing collars were in fashion in that day, and the minstrel appeared in a collar which engulfed and hid the half of his head and projected so far forward that he could hardly see sideways over its points. His coat was sometimes made of curtain calico, with a swallow-tail that hung nearly to his heels and had buttons as big as a blacking-box. His shoes were rusty, and clumsy, and cumbersome, and five or six sizes too large for him. There were many variations upon this costume, and they were all extravagant, and were by many believed to be funny.

The minstrel used a very broad negro dialect; he used it competently, and with easy facility, and *it* was funny—delightfully and satisfyingly funny. However, there was one member of the minstrel troupe of those early days who was not extravagantly dressed, and did not use the negro dialect. He was clothed in the faultless evening costume of the white society-gentleman, and used a stilted, courtly, artificial, and painfully grammatical form of speech, which the innocent villagers took for the real thing as exhibited in high and citified society, and they vastly admired it and envied the man who could frame it on the spot, without reflection, and deliver it in this easy and fluent and artistic fashion. "Bones" sat at one end of the row of minstrels, the banjo sat at the other end, and the dainty gentleman just described sat in the middle. This middle-man was the spokesman of the show. The neatness and elegance of his dress, the studied courtliness of his manners and speech, and the shapeliness of his undoctored features, made him a contrast to the rest of the troupe, and particularly to "Bones" and "Banjo." "Bones" and "Banjo" were the prime jokers, and whatever funniness was to be gotten out of paint and exaggerated clothing, they utilized to the limit. Their lips were thickened and lengthened with bright red paint to such a degree that their mouths resembled slices cut in a ripe watermelon.

The original ground plan of the minstrel show was maintained without change for a good many years. There was no curtain to the stage in the beginning; while the audience waited they had nothing to look at except the row of empty chairs back of the footlights; presently the minstrels filed in and were received with a whole-hearted welcome; they took their seats, each with his musical instrument in his hand; then the aristocrat in the middle began with a remark like this:

"I hope, gentlemen, I have the pleasure of seeing you in your accustomed excellent health, and that everything has proceeded prosperously with you since last we had the good fortune to meet."

"Bones" would reply for himself, and go on and tell about something in the nature of peculiarly good fortune that had lately fallen to his share; but in the midst of it he would be interrupted by "Banjo," who would throw doubt upon his statement of the matter; then a delightful jangle of assertion and contradiction would break out between the two; the quarrel would gather emphasis, the voices would grow louder and louder, and more and more energetic and vindictive, and the two would rise and approach each other, shaking fists and instruments, and threatening bloodshed, the courtly middle-man, meantime, imploring them to preserve the peace and observe the proprieties—but all in vain, of course. Sometimes the quarrel would last five minutes, the two contestants shouting deadly threats in each other's faces, with their noses not six inches apart—the house shrieking with laughter, all the while, at this happy and accurate imitation of the usual and familiar negro quarrel—then finally the pair of malignants would gradually back away from each other, each making impressive threats as to what was going to happen the "next time" each should have the misfortune to cross the other's path; then they would sink into their chairs and growl back and forth at each other across the front of the line until the house had had time to recover from its convulsions and hysterics, and quiet down.

The aristocrat in the middle of the row would now make a remark which was surreptitiously intended to remind one of the end men of an experience of his of a humorous nature, and fetch it out of him—which it always did. It was usually an experience of a stale and mouldy sort, and as old as America. One of these things, which always delighted the audience of those days until the minstrels wore it threadbare, was "Bones's" account of the perils which he had once endured during a storm at sea. The storm lasted so long that in the course of time all the provisions were consumed. Then the middle-man would inquire anxiously how the people managed to survive. "Bones" would reply,

"We lived on eggs."

"You lived on eggs! Where did you get eggs?"

"Every day, when the storm was so bad, the captain laid *to*."

During the first five years, that joke convulsed the house; but after that, the population of the United States had heard it so many times that they respected it no longer, and always received it in a deep and reproachful and indignant silence—along with others of its calibre which had achieved disfavor by long service.

The minstrel troupes had good voices, and both their solos and their choruses were a delight to me as long as the negro show continued in existence. In the beginning, the songs were rudely comic—such as "Buffalo Gals," "Camptown Races," "Old Dan Tucker," and so on; but a little later, sentimental songs were introduced—such as "The Blue Juniata," "Sweet Ellen Bayne," "Nelly Bly," "A Life on the Ocean Wave," "The Larboard Watch," etc.

The minstrel show was born in the early '40s, and it had a prosperous career for about thirty-five years; then it degenerated into a variety show, and was nearly all variety show with a negro act or two thrown in incidentally. The real negro show has been stone dead for thirty years. To my mind, it was a thoroughly delightful thing, and a most competent laughter-compeller, and I am sorry it is gone.

As I have said, it was the worldlings that attended that first minstrel show in Hannibal. Ten or twelve years later the minstrel show was as common in America as the Fourth of July, but my mother had never seen one. She was about sixty years old by this time, and she came down to St. Louis with a dear and lovely lady of her own age, an old citizen of Hannibal—Aunt Betsey Smith. She wasn't anybody's aunt, in particular; she was aunt to the whole town of Hannibal; this was because of her sweet and generous and benevolent nature, and the winning simplicity of her character. Like my mother, Aunt Betsey Smith had never seen a negro show. She and my mother were very much alive; their age counted for nothing; they were fond of excitement, fond of novelties, fond of anything going that was of a sort proper for members of the church to indulge in. They were always up early to see the circus procession enter the town, and to grieve because their principles did not allow them to follow it into the tent; they were always ready for Fourth of July processions, Sunday-school processions, lectures, conventions, camp-meetings, wakes, revivals in the church—in fact, for any and every kind of dissipation that could not be proven to have anything irreligious about it—and they never missed a funeral. In St. Louis, they were eager for novelties, and they applied to me for help. They wanted something exciting and proper. I told them I knew of nothing in their line except a Convention which was to meet in the great hall of the Mercantile Library and listen to an exhibition and illustration of native African music by fourteen missionaries who had just returned from that dark continent. I said that if they actually and earnestly desired something instructive and elevating, I would recommend the Convention, but that if at bottom they really wanted something frivolous, I would look further. But no, they were charmed with the idea of the Convention, and were eager to go. I was not telling them the strict truth, and I knew it at the time, but it was no great matter; it is not worth while to strain one's self to tell the truth to people who habitually discount everything you tell them, whether it is true or isn't.

The alleged missionaries were the Christy minstrel troupe—in that day one of the most celebrated of such troupes, and also one of the best. We went early, and got seats in the front bench. By and by, when all the seats on that spacious floor were occupied, there were sixteen hundred persons present. When the grotesque negroes came filing out on the stage in their extravagant costumes, the old ladies were almost speechless with astonishment. I explained to them that the missionaries always dressed like that in Africa.

But Aunt Betsey said, reproachfully, "But they're niggers!"

I said "That is no matter; they are Americans in a sense, for they are employed by the American Missionary Society."

Then both the ladies began to question the propriety of their countenancing the industries of a company of negroes, no matter what their trade might be—but I said that they could see, by looking around, that the best people in St. Louis were present, and that certainly they would not be present if the show were not of a proper sort.

They were comforted, and also quite shamelessly glad to be there. They were happy, now, and enchanted with the novelty of the situation; all that they had needed was a pretext of some kind or other to quiet their consciences, and their consciences were quiet now—quiet enough to be dead. They gazed on that long curved line of artistic mountebanks with devouring eyes. The middle-man began. Presently he led up to that old joke which I was telling about a while ago. Everybody in the house except my novices had heard it a hundred times; a frozen and solemn and indignant silence settled down upon the sixteen hundred, and poor "Bones" sat there in that depressing atmosphere and went through with his joke. It was brand-new to my venerable novices, and when he got to the end, and said, "We lived on eggs," and followed it by explaining that every day during the storm the captain "laid *to,*" they threw their heads back and went off into heart-whole cackles and convulsions of laughter that so astonished and delighted that great audience that it rose in a solid body to look, and see who it might be that had not heard that joke before. The laughter of my novices went on and on till their hilarity became contagious, and the whole sixteen hundred joined in and shook the place with the thunders of their joy. Aunt Betsey and my mother achieved a brilliant success for the Christy minstrels that night, for all the jokes were as new to them as they were old to the rest of the house. They received them with screams of laughter, and passed the hilarity on, and the audience left the place sore and weary with laughter and full of gratitude to the innocent pair that had furnished to their jaded souls that rare and precious pleasure.

December 1, 1906

Mr. Clemens's early experiments with mesmerism.

An exciting event in our village (Hannibal), was the arrival of the mesmerizer. I think the year was 1850. As to that I am not sure, but I know the month—it was May; that detail has survived the wear of fifty-five years. A pair of connected little incidents of that month have served to keep the memory of it green for me all this time; incidents of no consequence, and not worth embalming, yet my memory has preserved them carefully

1849–51

and flung away things of real value to give them space and make them comfortable. The truth is, a person's memory has no more sense than his conscience, and no appreciation whatever of values and proportions. However, never mind those trifling incidents; my subject is the mesmerizer, now.

He advertised his show, and promised marvels. Admission as usual: twenty-five cents, children and negroes half price. The village had heard of mesmerism, in a general way, but had not encountered it yet. Not many people attended, the first night, but next day they had so many wonders to tell that everybody's curiosity was fired, and after that for a fortnight the magician had prosperous times. I was fourteen or fifteen years old—the age at which a boy is willing to endure all things, suffer all things, short of death by fire, if thereby he may be conspicuous and show off before the public; and so, when I saw the "subjects" perform their foolish antics on the platform and make the people laugh and shout and admire, I had a burning desire to be a subject myself. Every night, for three nights, I sat in the row of candidates on the platform, and held the magic metal disk in the palm of my hand, and gazed at it and tried to get sleepy, but it was a failure; I remained wide awake, and had to retire defeated, like the majority. Also, I had to sit there and be gnawed with envy of Hicks, our journeyman; I had to sit there and see him scamper and jump when Simmons the enchanter exclaimed "See the snake! see the snake!" and hear him say, "My, how beautiful!" in response to the suggestion that he was observing a splendid sunset; and so on—the whole insane business. I couldn't laugh, I couldn't applaud; it filled me with bitterness to have others do it, and to have people make a hero of Hicks, and crowd around him when the show was over, and ask him for more and more particulars of the wonders he had seen in his visions, and manifest in many ways that they were proud to be acquainted with him. Hicks—the idea! I couldn't stand it; I was getting boiled to death in my own bile.

On the fourth night temptation came, and I was not strong enough to resist. When I had gazed at the disk a while I pretended to be sleepy, and began to nod. Straightway came the professor and made passes over my head and down my body and legs and arms, finishing each pass with a snap of his fingers in the air, to discharge the surplus electricity; then he began to "draw" me with the disk, holding it in his fingers and telling me I could not take my eyes off it, try as I might; so I rose slowly, bent and gazing, and followed that disk all over the place, just as I had seen the others do. Then I was put through the other paces. Upon suggestion I fled from snakes; passed buckets at a fire; became excited over hot steamboat-races; made love to imaginary girls and kissed them; fished from the platform and landed mud-cats that outweighed me—and so on, all the customary marvels. But not in the customary way. I was cautious at first, and watchful, being afraid the professor would discover that I was an impostor and drive me from the platform in disgrace; but as soon as I realized that I was not in danger, I set myself the task of terminating Hicks's usefulness as a subject, and of usurping his place.

It was a sufficiently easy task. Hicks was born honest; I, without that incumbrance—so some people said. Hicks saw what he saw, and reported accordingly; I saw more than was visible, and added to it such details as could help. Hicks had no imagination, I had a double supply. He was born calm, I was born excited. No vision could start a rapture in him, and he was constipated as to language, anyway; but if I saw a vision I emptied the dictionary onto it and lost the remnant of my mind into the bargain.

At the end of my first half hour Hicks was a thing of the past, a fallen hero, a broken idol, and I knew it and was glad, and said in my heart, Success to crime! Hicks could never have been mesmerized to the point where he could kiss an imaginary girl in public, or a real one either, but I was competent. Whatever Hicks had failed in, I made it a point to succeed in, let the cost be what it might, physically or morally. He had shown several bad defects, and I had made a note of them. For instance, if the magician asked "What do you see?" and left him to invent a vision for himself, Hicks was dumb and blind, he couldn't see a thing nor say a word, whereas the magician soon found that when it came to seeing visions of a stunning and marketable sort I could get along better without his help than with it. Then there was another thing: Hicks wasn't worth a tallow dip on mute mental suggestion. Whenever Simmons stood behind him and gazed at the back of his skull and tried to drive a mental suggestion into it, Hicks sat with vacant face, and never suspected. If he had been noticing, he could have seen by the rapt faces of the audience that something was going on behind his back that required a response. Inasmuch as I was an impostor I dreaded to have this test put upon me, for I knew the professor would be "willing" me to do something, and as I couldn't know what it was, I should be exposed and denounced. However, when my time came, I took my chance. I perceived by the tense and expectant faces of the people that Simmons was behind me willing me with all his might. I tried my best to imagine what he wanted, but nothing suggested itself. I felt ashamed and miserable, then. I believed that the hour of my disgrace was come, and that in another moment I should go out of that place disgraced. I ought to be ashamed to confess it, but my next thought was, not how I could win the compassion of kindly hearts by going out humbly and in sorrow for my misdoings, but how I could go out most sensationally and spectacularly.

There was a rusty and empty old revolver lying on the table, among the "properties" employed in the performances. On May-day, two or three weeks before, there had been a celebration by the schools, and I had had a quarrel with a big boy who was the school-bully, and I had not come out of it with credit. That boy was now seated in the middle of the house, half way down the main aisle. I crept stealthily and impressively toward the table, with a dark and murderous scowl on my face, copied from a pirate romance, seized the revolver suddenly, flourished it, shouted the bully's name, jumped off the platform, and made a rush for him and chased him out of the house before the paralysed people could interfere to save him. There was a storm of applause, and the magician, addressing the house, said, most impressively—

"That you may know how really remarkable this is, and how wonderfully developed a subject we have in this boy, I assure you that without a single spoken word to guide him he has carried out what I mentally commanded him to do, to the minutest detail. I could have stopped him at a moment in his vengeful career by mere exertion of my will, therefore the poor fellow who has escaped was at no time in danger."

So I was not in disgrace. I returned to the platform a hero, and happier than I have ever been in this world since. As regards mental suggestion, my fears of it were gone. I judged that in case I failed to guess what the professor might be willing me to do, I could count on putting up something that would answer just as well. I was right, and exhibitions of unspoken suggestion became a favorite with the public. Whenever I perceived that I was being willed to do something I got up and did something—anything that occurred to me—and the magician, not being a fool, always ratified it. When people asked me, "How *can* you tell what he is willing you to do?" I said, "It's just as easy," and they always said admiringly, "Well, it beats *me* how you can do it."

Hicks was weak in another detail. When the professor made passes over him and said "his whole body is without sensation now—come forward and test him, ladies and gentlemen" the ladies and gentlemen always complied eagerly, and stuck pins into Hicks, and if they went deep Hicks was sure to wince, then that poor professor would have to explain that Hicks "wasn't sufficiently under the influence." But I didn't wince; I only suffered, and shed tears on the inside. The miseries that a conceited boy will endure to keep up his "reputation!" And so will a conceited man; I know it in my own person, and have seen it in a hundred thousand others. That professor ought to have protected me, and I often hoped he would, when the tests were unusually severe, but he didn't. It may be that he was deceived as well as the others, though I did not believe it nor think it possible. Those were dear good people, but they must have carried simplicity and credulity to the limit. They would stick a pin in my arm and bear on it until they drove it a third of its length in, and then be lost in wonder that by a mere exercise of will-power the professor could turn my arm to iron and make it insensible to pain. Whereas it was not insensible at all; I was suffering agonies of pain.

After that fourth night, that proud night, that triumphant night, I was the only subject. Simmons invited no more candidates to the platform. I performed alone, every night, the rest of the fortnight. In the beginning of the second week I conquered the last doubters. Up to that time a dozen wise old heads, the intellectual aristocracy of the town, had held out, as implacable unbelievers. I was as hurt by this as if I were engaged in some honest occupation. There is nothing surprising about this. Human beings feel dishonor the most, sometimes, when they most deserve it. That handful of over-wise old gentlemen kept on shaking their heads all the first week, and saying they had seen no marvels there that could not have been produced by collusion; and they were pretty vain of their unbelief, too, and liked to show it and air it, and be superior to the ignorant and the gullible. Particularly old Dr. Peake, who was the ringleader of the irreconcileables, and very formidable; for he was an F.F.V., he was learned, white-haired and venerable, nobly and richly clad in the fashions of an earlier and a courtlier day, he was large and stately, and he not only seemed wise, but was what he seemed, in that regard. He had great influence, and his opinion upon any matter was worth much more than that of any other person in the community. When I conquered him, at last, I knew I was undisputed master of the field; and now, after more than fifty years, I acknowledge, with a few dry old tears, that I rejoiced without shame.

The Clemenses' house on Farmington Avenue, Hartford, winter 1880.

Clara as Lady Jane Grey and Margaret (Daisy) Warner as the pauper in the prince's clothing for the *Prince and the Pauper* play, Hartford, March 1886. Photograph by Horace L. Bundy.

Onteora, New York, 1890: Carroll Beckwith, W. F. Clarke, Dora Wheeler, R. Heber Newton, Laurence Hutton, Mary Mapes Dodge, Candace Wheeler, Brander Matthews, Lillie Hamilton French, Eleanor V. Hutton, S. L. Clemens, and Mary Knight Wood. The Mark Twain House and Museum, Hartford.

Susy and Samuel Clemens in costume after enacting the story of Hero and Leander, on the porch at Onteora, 1890.

Clemens and Laurence Hutton on the Huttons' porch, Onteora, New York, 1890.

Carroll Beckwith and his portrait of Clemens, Onteora, New York, 1890.

Olivia, Samuel, and Clara Clemens, James B. Pond, and Mrs. Pond on the North American lecture tour, July–August 1895. Courtesy of Kevin Mac Donnell.

Susan Crane, Mrs. James B. Pond, James B. Pond, Jr., Susy Clemens, and the dogs, Osman and Bruce, at Quarry Farm, Elmira, New York, 15 September 1895. Photograph by James B. Pond. Mark Twain Archive, The Center for Mark Twain Studies, Elmira College.

Clemens on the back lawn at Dollis Hill House, 1900.

Samuel and Olivia Clemens, Dollis Hill House, 1900: "Mamma and Papa under the oaks and beeches where we always sat and had our tea." Photograph and description by Jean Clemens.

"The Lair" at Lower Saranac Lake, New York, 1901, "with a glimpse of the lake and the bathing-tent." Photograph and description by Jean Clemens.

An unidentified servant, Olivia, Clara, and Jean Clemens on the porch at "The Lair," Lower Saranac Lake, 1901. Photograph by Frederick W. Rice.

Henry Huttleston Rogers.

H. H. Rogers's mansion in Fairhaven, Massachusetts.

Samuel and Olivia Clemens on the porch at Quarry Farm, 1903. The Mark Twain House and Museum, Hartford.

Clemens with John T. Lewis in Elmira, 1 July 1903. Photograph by Thomas E. Marr.

Clemens in the billiard room at 21 Fifth Avenue, New York, 1905 or 1906. Photograph by Underwood and Underwood.

Katy Leary in Jean's study, 21 Fifth Avenue, New York, January 1905. Photograph by Jean Clemens.

Josephine Hobby, Clemens's stenographer and typist for the Autobiographical Dictations, in her automobile driving costume, Greenwich, Connecticut, ca. 1906. Courtesy of Sally Hobby Owen.

Alden birthday dinner, 10 November 1906: Richard Watson Gilder, editor of the *Century Magazine;* Woodrow Wilson, president of Princeton University; William Dean Howells, author and former editor of the *Atlantic Monthly;* Henry Mills Alden, editor of *Harper's Monthly;* George Harvey, owner and editor of the *North American Review* and *Harper's Weekly;* Thomas Bailey Aldrich, author and former editor of the *Atlantic Monthly;* the Rt. Rev. Ethelbert Talbot, bishop of the Episcopal Diocese of Central Pennsylvania; and Edmund Clarence Stedman, poet and critic (*Harper's Weekly* 50 [15 Dec 1906]: 1815).

Elisha Bliss, Jr., of the American Publishing Company, ca. 1879. Photograph by H. J. Rodgers. The Mark Twain House and Museum, Hartford.

Frank Bliss of the American Publishing Company, 1890s. Photograph by DeLamater and Son. The Mark Twain House and Museum, Hartford.

Charles L. Webster, 1884 (*MTBus,* facing 154).

Frederick A. Duneka, general manager of Harper and Brothers, at the Alden dinner, 10 November 1906 (*Harper's Weekly* 50 [15 Dec 1906]: 1819).

Clemens and Joseph H. Twichell on the RMS *Bermudian,* January 1907. Photograph by Isabel Lyon.

Clemens and Twichell in Bermuda, January 1907. Photograph by Isabel Lyon.

Laura Wright at the age of sixteen, May 1861.

James Redpath in Kansas Territory in the 1850s as a correspondent for the New York *Tribune*. Kansas State Historical Society.

Captain Edgar (Ned) Wakeman and his wife, Mary Lincoln Wakeman. The Bancroft Library, University of California, Berkeley.

Bret Harte in the late 1870s or early 1880s. Photograph by Napoleon Sarony.

Joel Chandler Harris, New York, 1906. Photograph by Underwood and Underwood.

Mollie and Orion Clemens, Keokuk, Iowa, 1897. Photograph by Wales Studio. Nevada Historical Society, Reno.

Four generations, 18 June 1882: Jane Lampton Clemens, Annie Moffett Webster, Jean Webster, and Pamela A. (Clemens) Moffett. Special Collections, Vassar College Library.

Clara Clemens, New York, ca. 1894. Photograph by Joseph Gaylord Gessford. The Mark Twain House and Museum, Hartford.

Jean Clemens and "The Professor," Kaltenleutgeben, Austria, 1898. Photograph by Fritz Knozer. The Mark Twain House and Museum, Hartford.

Susy Clemens, Florence, 1892. Photograph by Mademoiselles Angiolini.

December 2, 1906

Mr. Clemens's experiments in mesmerism, continued.

In 1847 we were living in a large white house on the corner of Hill and Main streets—a house that still stands, but isn't large now, although it hasn't lost a plank; I saw it a year ago and noticed that shrinkage. My father died in it in March of the year mentioned, but our family did not move out of it until some months afterward. Ours was not the only family in the house, there was another—Dr. Grant's. One day Dr. Grant and Dr. Reyburn argued a matter on the street with sword-canes, and Grant was brought home multifariously punctured. Old Dr. Peake calked the leaks, and came every day for a while, to look after him. The Grants were Virginians, like Peake, and one day when Grant was getting well enough to be on his feet and sit around in the parlor and talk, the conversation fell upon Virginia and old times. I was present, but the group were probably quite unconscious of me, I being only a lad and a negligeable quantity. Two of the group—Dr. Peake and Mrs. Crawford, Mrs. Grant's mother—had been of the audience when the Richmond theatre burned down thirty-six years before, and they talked over the frightful details of that memorable tragedy. These were eye-witnesses, and with their eyes I saw it all with an intolerable vividness: I saw the black smoke rolling and tumbling toward the sky, I saw the flames burst through it and turn it red, I heard the shrieks of the despairing, I glimpsed their faces at the windows, caught fitfully through the veiling smoke, I saw them jump to their death, or to mutilation worse than death. The picture is before me yet, and can never fade.

1847

In due course they talked of the colonial mansion of the Peakes, with its stately columns and its spacious grounds, and by odds and ends I picked up a clearly defined idea of the place. I was strongly interested, for I had not before heard of such palatial things from the lips of people who had seen them with their own eyes. One detail, casually dropped, hit my imagination hard. In the wall, by the great front door, there was a round hole as big as a saucer—a British cannon ball had made it, in the War of the Revolution. It was breath-taking; it made history real; history had never been real to me before.

Very well, three or four years later, as already mentioned, I was king-bee and sole "subject" in the mesmeric show; it was the beginning of the second week; the performance was half over; just then the majestic Dr. Peake, with his ruffled bosom and wristbands and his gold-headed cane, entered, and a deferential citizen vacated his seat beside the Grants and made the great chief take it. This happened while I was trying to invent something fresh in the way of a vision, in response to the professor's remark—

"Concentrate your powers. Look—look attentively. There—don't you see something? Concentrate—concentrate! Now then—describe it."

Without suspecting it, Dr. Peake, by entering the place, had reminded me of the talk of three years before. He had also furnished me capital and was become my confederate, an accomplice in my frauds. I began on a vision, a vague and dim one (that was part of the game at the beginning of a vision, it isn't best to see it too clearly at first, it might look as if you had come loaded with it.) The vision developed, by degrees, and gathered swing, momentum, energy! It was the Richmond fire. Dr. Peake was cold, at first, and his fine face had a trace of polite scorn in it; but when he began to recognize that fire, that expression changed, and his eyes began to light up. As soon as I saw that, I threw the valves wide open and turned on all the steam, and gave those people a supper of fire and horrors that was calculated to last them one while! They couldn't gasp, when I got through—they were petrified. Dr. Peake had risen, and was standing,—and breathing hard. He said, in a great voice—

"My doubts are ended. No collusion could produce that miracle. It was totally impossible for him to know those details, yet he has described them with the clarity of an eye-witness—and with what unassailable truthfulness God knows I know!"

I saved the colonial mansion for the last night, and solidified and perpetuated Dr. Peake's conversion with the cannon ball hole. He explained to the house that I could never have heard of that small detail, which differentiated this mansion from all other Virginian mansions and perfectly identified it, therefore the fact stood proven that I had *seen* it in my vision. Lawks!

It is curious. When the magician's engagement closed there was but one person in the village who did not believe in mesmerism, and I was the one. All the others were converted, but I was to remain an implacable and unpersuadable disbeliever in mesmerism and hypnotism for close upon fifty years. This was because I never would examine them, in after life. I couldn't. The subject revolted me. Perhaps because it brought back to me a passage in my life which for pride's sake I wished to forget; though I thought—or persuaded myself I thought—I should never come across a "proof" which wasn't thin and cheap, and probably had a fraud like me behind it.

The truth is, I did not have to wait long to get tired of my triumphs. Not thirty days, I think. The glory which is built upon a lie soon becomes a most unpleasant incumbrance. No doubt for a while I enjoyed having my exploits told and retold and told again in my presence and wondered over and exclaimed about, but I quite distinctly remember that there presently came a time when the subject was wearisome and odious to me and I could not endure the disgusting discomfort of it. I am well aware that the world-glorified doer of a deed of great and real splendor has just my experience; I know that he deliciously enjoys hearing about it for three or four weeks, and that pretty soon after that he begins to dread the mention of it, and by and by wishes he had been with the damned before he ever thought of doing that deed; I remember how General Sherman used to rage and swear over "When we were marching through Georgia," which was played at him and sung at him everywhere he went; still, I think I suffered a shade more than the legitimate hero does, he being privileged to soften his misery with the reflection that his glory was at any rate golden and reproachless in its origin, whereas I had no such privilege, there being no possible way to make mine respectable.

How easy it is to make people believe a lie, and how hard it is to undo that work again! Thirty-five years after those evil exploits of mine I visited my old mother, whom I had not seen for ten years; and being moved by what seemed to me a rather noble and perhaps heroic impulse, I thought I would humble myself and confess my ancient fault. It cost me a great effort to make up my mind; I dreaded the sorrow that would rise in her face, and the shame that would look out of her eyes; but after long and troubled reflection, the sacrifice seemed due and right, and I gathered my resolution together and made the confession.

To my astonishment there were no sentimentalities, no dramatics, no George Washington effects; she was not moved in the least degree; she simply did not believe me, and said so! I was not merely disappointed, I was nettled, to have my costly truthfulness flung out of the market in this placid and confident way when I was expecting to get a profit out of it. I asserted, and re-asserted, with rising heat, my statement that every single thing I had done on those long-vanished nights was a lie and a swindle; and when she shook her head tranquilly and said she knew better, I put up my hand and *swore* to it—adding a triumphant "*Now* what do you say!"

It did not affect her at all; it did not budge her the fraction of an inch from her position. If this was hard for me to endure, it did not begin with the blister she put upon the raw when she began to put my sworn oath out of court with *arguments* to prove that I was under a delusion and did not know what I was talking about. Arguments! Arguments to show that a person on a man's outside can know better what is on his inside than he does himself! I had cherished some contempt for arguments before, I have not enlarged my respect for them since. She refused to believe that I had invented my visions myself; she said it was folly: that I was only a child at the time and could not have done it. She cited the Richmond fire and the colonial mansion and said they were quite beyond my capacities. Then I saw my chance! I said she was right—I didn't invent those, I got them from Dr. Peake. Even this great shot did no damage. She said Dr. Peake's evidence was better than mine, and he had said in plain words that it was impossible for me to have heard about those things. Dear, dear, what a grotesque and unthinkable situation: a confessed swindler convicted of honesty and condemned to acquittal by circumstantial evidence furnished by the swindled!

I realized, with shame and with impotent vexation, that I was defeated all along the line. I had but one card left, but it was a formidable one. I played it—and stood from under. It seemed ignoble to demolish her fortress, after she had defended it so valiantly; but the defeated know not mercy. I played that master card. It was the pin-sticking. I said solemnly—

"I give you my honor, a pin was never stuck into me without causing me cruel pain."

She only said—

"It is thirty-five years. I believe you do think that, *now,* but I was there, and I know better. You never winced."

She was so calm! and I was so far from it, so nearly frantic.

"Oh, my goodness!" I said, "let me *show* you that I am speaking the truth. Here is my arm; drive a pin into it—drive it to the head—I shall not wince."

She only shook her gray head and said with simplicity and conviction—

"You are a man, now, and could dissemble the hurt; but you were only a child then, and could not have done it."

And so the lie which I played upon her in my youth remained with her as an unchallengeable truth to the day of her death. Carlyle said "a lie cannot live." It shows that he did not know how to tell them. If I had taken out a life policy on this one the premiums would have bankrupted me ages ago.

December 3, 1906

Mesmerism continued—The Baron F. incident.

One evening we dined with the C.'s, (in Vienna, in 1897), and after dinner a number of friends of the family dropped in to smoke and chat; among them G., who had dined with the X.'s. He brought with him an incident. It was to this effect. When dinner was announced a guest was still lacking—the Baron F., a cousin of Herr X. Ten minutes later he had not yet arrived; then he was given up, and the company went to the table. Between soup and fish the Baron arrived and was ushered in—a large and strongly built man about fifty years old, with iron gray hair and a harsh and hard face. With a perfunctory word of excuse for his tardiness he took his seat and began to unfold his napkin; in the midst of this function he stopped, and began to stare across the table at a Mr. B., a visiting Englishman of grave mien and middle age. As he stared his countenance darkened, and assumed an expression of hatred of the most bitter and uncompromising kind; the napkin fell from his hands, and he got up abruptly and stalked out of the room. X., astonished, left his bewildered guests and followed, to see what the matter was. He found the Baron gloving himself for departure. He was not exactly frothing at the mouth, but was near to doing it. In answer to X.'s anxious inquiries, he said—

1897

"No, give yourself no concern, it isn't anything that's happened here—it dates back, away back. I can't be mistaken, that's an Englishman and his name is B. Isn't it so?"

"Yes."

"Well, I've seen him only once before, and it's twenty-seven years ago, but I know him, I would recognize him in Siberia, in Sahara, in hell! How fortunate that I couldn't reach him—I don't wish to be a murderer!"

"Why, what was the trouble? What did he do?"

"Do? Oh, oh, oh, it's too horrible to think of! Out of my way—don't detain me; do you want me to kill him?"

That was the incident, and that was all that G. knew. Enough to heat our curiosity to the sizzling point, and raise a world of excited wondering and guessing; and valuable to that degree in a smoking-klatch, but we had to wait several days before we got the tale's sequel. Which was this.

In 1870 B. was living in London. He was a young fellow with an alert and inquiring mind and a sharp appetite for novelties. He had taken up mesmerism—as it was then called—and was doing with it many of the strange things afterward done by Charcot under its other name of hypnotism. One evening B. was exhibiting some of these marvels in the house of an eminent man of science, and had brought with him for the purpose subjects whom he had experimented upon before. A gentleman present begged him to come to his house in Sydenham, and give a similar exhibition before friends of his. B. said—

"I will, on this condition: that you provide a dozen persons, for experiment, whom you know, but who shall be strangers to me; this in order that collusion cannot be charged. I may not be able to affect any of them, but out of the dozen I can expect to affect one or two at least."

The condition was accepted, and the day appointed. But the day before the date chosen, the gentleman sent a note saying he had failed to get anybody to consent, and begging B. to bring subjects himself.

B. took with him a young man who was an easy subject, and whom he had often mesmerized before. The two went upon a platform which had been arranged at the end of a drawing-room, and faced a company of forty men—some young, some middle-aged; some fashionable and frivolous, some of a graver stamp; some sarcastic of aspect, the others blandly unfriendly. B. noted this unpleasant atmosphere and was sorry he had not exacted the original terms. He tried to recover that lost ground by inviting the gentlemen present to provide him with subjects from their number, and said he would regard it as a great favor if his request could be complied with. He waited, but got only silence—there was no other response.

He then mesmerized his young man, and made him mistake salt for sugar, sugar for salt, chalk for alum, alum for chalk, water for brandy, brandy for milk, and so on; made him see ships sailing on the sea, houses on fire, battles, horse-races, and all such things—and all through these performances the audience smiled contempt, and a group of young fashionables, one of whom was standing, and leaning indolently against the wall, uttered low-voiced ejaculations: "Humbug!" "charlatan!" etc. It was intended that B. should hear, and he heard. He expected his host to interfere and protect him from these insults, and glanced a hint or two at him; but evidently the host was afraid. B. recognized that if he was to have any protection he must furnish it himself. He tried to locate one of those affronts and make sure of the mouth it came from, but he was never quick enough. The dandy who leaned against the wall seemed to be the ringleader, but B. was not sure of it. He went on with his demonstrations, growing angrier and angrier all the while, and the offensive comments continued. He now said—

"I will now make this subject's body as rigid as iron; and will ask any that doubt, to come on the platform and examine him and test him."

He stretched the young man in the air, with his head upon one table and his heels upon another, and no support between, and invited the doubters to come and apply their tests. No one moved. There was an ejaculation: "Just a tuppenny juggler and his hired pal!"

This time B. spotted the utterer; it was the young fashionable who was leaning against the wall. He limbered up his subject with a few passes, then turned to the audience and said—

"I was invited to come here, I did not invite myself. I was invited as a gentleman, to meet gentlemen; you best know why the host's part of the contract has not been fulfilled. You lack the courage to come on this platform and submit to tests in your own persons, yet you have the courage—being many—to insult me, who am but one, and—as you think—not able to resent it. You do not believe in mesmerism; you do not believe in the genuineness of my demonstrations; you shall have a test that will convince you. I require the person leaning against the wall to come here."

He bent his gaze upon the person, who gazed back—gazed and still gazed, B. beckoning—beckoning, drawing him, the audience watching.

"Now then—come!"

The new subject moved slowly forward, with his eyes fixed upon B.'s, and arrived upon the platform.

"Stop!" The man stopped. "Get up and stand in this chair." The man obeyed. "What do you see?—the ocean?" The man nodded his head dreamily. "Is it at your feet? do you see the waves washing in?" More nods. "Do you not notice how hot it is? Why do you wear such heavy clothes in such weather? Throw them off and take a plunge—it will do you good." The man took off his coat. "Now your vest—throw it down. Now your trowsers—throw them down. Now your shirt. Now the underclothes. There—plunge! Stop!" B. turned to the house and continued:

"Here stands one unbeliever—a Mayfair man—a society man—a swell—a smirking lady-killer—a perfumed drawing-room dandy, contemptuous of other people's feelings and sensitive about his own, proud of his prettiness, vain of his charms—here they all are before you, stark naked! As he is, so shall you be; so help me God I will now strip every coward of you to the skin!"

But he didn't. There was a wild rush and scramble, and the place was vacant in a minute. The naked man was Baron F.

Wednesday, December 5, 1906

"A Yankee at the Court of King Arthur" written to contrast English life of the Middle Ages with modern civilization—Arraignment of King Leopold II—His character contrasted with character of lawyer who cared for John Marshall Monument Fund.

From Susy's Biography.

Feb. 22 '86.

Yesterday evening papa read to us the beginning of his new book, in manuscript, and we enjoyed it very much, it was founded on a New Englanders visit to England in the time of King Arthur and his round table.

That book was an attempt to imagine, and, after a fashion, set forth, the hard conditions of life for the laboring and defenceless poor in bygone times in England, and, incidentally, contrast these conditions with those under which the civil and ecclesiastical pets of privilege and high fortune lived in those times. I think I was purposing to contrast that English life—not just the English life of Arthur's day, but the English life of the whole of the Middle Ages—with the life of modern Christendom and modern civilization—to the advantage of the latter, of course. That advantage is still claimable, and does creditably and handsomely exist everywhere in Christendom—if we leave out Russia and the royal palace of Belgium. The royal palace of Belgium is still what it has been for fourteen years—the den of a wild beast—King Leopold II—who for money's sake mutilates, murders, and starves, half a million of friendless and helpless poor natives in the Congo State every year, and does it by the silent consent of all the Christian powers except England; none of them lifting a hand or a voice to stop these atrocities, although thirteen of them are by solemn treaty pledged to the protecting and uplifting of those wretched natives. In fourteen years, Leopold has deliberately destroyed more lives than have suffered death on all the battle-fields of this planet for the past thousand years. In this vast statement I am well within the mark—several millions of lives within the mark. It is curious that the most advanced and most enlightened century of all the centuries the sun has looked upon, should have the ghastly distinction of having produced this mouldy and piety-mouthing hypocrite; this bloody monster whose mate is not findable in human history anywhere, and whose personality will surely shame hell itself when he arrives there—which will be soon, let us hope and trust.

The conditions under which the poor lived in the Middle Ages were hard enough, but those conditions were heaven itself as compared with those which have obtained in the Congo State for these past fourteen years. I have mentioned Russia. Cruel and pitiful as was life throughout Christendom in the Middle Ages, it was not so cruel, not so pitiful, as is life in Russia to-day. In Russia, for three centuries, the vast population has been ground under the heels, and for the sole and sordid advantage of, a procession of crowned assassins and robbers who have all deserved the gallows. Russia's hundred and thirty millions of miserable subjects are much worse off, to-day, than were the poor of the Middle Ages whom we so pity. We are accustomed, now, to speak of Russia as mediaeval, and as standing still in the Middle Ages, but that is flattery. Russia is 'way back of the Middle Ages; the Middle Ages are a long way in front of her, and she is not likely to catch up with them so long as the Czardom continues to exist.

To-day's news from that horrible country moves me to blush for having said hard and harsh things about the life of the poor in the Middle Ages, in the book called "A Connecticut Yankee at the Court of King Arthur."

SELLING WIVES FOR BREAD.

Horrors of Famine in Russian Provinces Along the Volga.

Special Cable Despatch to THE SUN.

ST. PETERSBURG, Dec. 4.—The newspapers are publishing terrible accounts of the famine in the Volga governments, in seven of which millions of people are said to be dying of starvation. The Tartars are said to be suffering equally with the Russians.

In the village of Tetyusehi eight Tartar maidens have been sold to dealers in white slaves from the Caucasus at prices that ranged from $34 to $92. Russian peasants near Astrakhan are taking their wives to that city and compelling them to enter the brothels, the husbands receiving about $14 in each case.

I must stop, now, and consult a note-book or two, and find something complimentary to the human race to take this unpleasant taste out of my mouth. John Cadwalader, a distinguished lawyer of Philadelphia, furnished me such a note, four or five years ago. I don't know where to look for it, but I can furnish its chief details from memory.

Seventy-one years ago, in my birth year, 1835, the illustrious John Marshall, Chief-Justice of the United States Supreme Court, died in Philadelphia. A meeting of the bar was called, and a committee was appointed to solicit subscriptions for a monument to commemorate the event. The honor of subscribing was to be restricted to the legal profession; all the lawyers in America were to be asked to subscribe, and all subscriptions were to be limited to one dollar. A young lawyer of the time—whose name I cannot now recall—was appointed to receive the subscriptions and receipt for them. The dollars began presently to flow in from all about the Union. Then the thing happened which always happens: a prodigious new event of some kind or other suddenly absorbed the interest and attention of the whole nation and drove the matter of the monument out of everybody's mind. When this happened, the dollars stopped coming, and the stoppage came so early that only a trifling sum had by that time been accumulated—somewhere in the neighborhood of three thousand dollars.

1835

Fifty years afterward, the young subscription-gatherer already mentioned died in the harness, a plodding, honest, aged, and undistinguished lawyer. In his will he had named John Cadwalader as one of the executors. Cadwalader found the dead man's papers in perfect order, and so clearly and painstakingly classified, indexed, and labeled, that they afforded an accurate and exhaustive view of the old man's affairs. Among these papers was one which noted the investment of the Monument Fund, dating from the time that the fund had been received, fifty years before. The investment had been made in interest-bearing, gilt-edged securities; presently these had been sold and the result reinvested in the same safe kind of securities. This selling and reinvesting had gone on from year to year for fifty years; in all cases the securities were named, and the interest, and the old bank where the accumulation was deposited was also named. The footing-up showed that there now stood to the credit of the Chief-Justice Marshall Monument Fund in that bank money and securities exceeding the sum of fifty thousand dollars. Cadwalader was so astonished that he rather doubted the evidence of his eyes, and was afraid that he had been beguiling himself with a fairy-tale. He went to the bank and asked if the Monument Fund really had a credit there of above fifty thousand dollars, and was told that the sum was there, and subject at any time to the draft of the Monument Fund.

Cadwalader hastened from the place, for his presence was due at the annual meeting of the Philadelphia bar. He arrived there excited, and full of his great news. He immediately rose to furnish it, but at the same moment Philadelphia's most revered, beloved, and illustrious old lawyer, Daniel O'Dogherty, rose to speak. Cadwalader really had the floor, but bowed, gave precedence to O'Dogherty, and sat down. Then a curious and striking thing happened.

O'Dogherty reminded the bar of a great event which had occurred in Philadelphia half a century before—the death of John Marshall, Chief-Justice of the Supreme Court of the United States. He said it was a reproach to the bar of Philadelphia that this event had not long ago been signalized in some way. Then he moved that now, and on the spot, the bar sponge out that reproach; that before any other business was entered upon, or even mentioned, measures be taken to raise fifty thousand dollars for a monument to John Marshall. He supported his motion in a moving and eloquent speech which roused great enthusiasm, and when he sat down there were cries of "Motion! motion!" from all over the house. The chairman proceeded to put the motion; it was seconded; then Cadwalader got up as if to speak to it, and began by saying,

"To take measures, sir, to raise this fifty thousand dollars is happily not necessary—it is already raised!"

Then he went on and told the charmed and astonished house the story which I have just narrated. It takes the bitter taste out of my mouth to recall that beautiful incident.

The resulting Marshall monument is in the Capitol grounds at Washington.

Thursday, December 6, 1906

Clara's pious remark when her wounded hand was being treated—Jean's remark when Mr. Clemens received dinner invitation from Emperor Wilhelm II—The Emperor's dinner—The official of the Foreign Office, and how he got a desired vacation, and retained it.

From Susy's Biography.

Feb. 27, Sunday.

Clara's reputation as a baby was always a fine one, mine exactly the contrary. One often related story conscerning her braveness as a baby and her own opinion of this quality of hers is this. Clara and I often got slivers in our hands and when mama took them out with a much dreaded needle, Clara was always very brave, and I very cowardly. One day Clara got one of these slivers in her hand, a very bad one, and while mama was taking it out, Clara stood perfectly still without even wincing; I saw how brave she was and turning to mamma said "Mamma isn't she a brave little thing! presently mamma had to give the little hand quite a dig with the needle and noticing how perfectly quiet Clara was about it she exclaimed, Why Clara! you *are* a brave little thing! Clara responded "No bodys braver but God!"—

Clara's pious remark is the main detail, and Susy has accurately remembered its phrasing. The three-year-older's wound was of a formidable sort, and not one which the mother's surgery would have been equal to. The flesh of the finger had been burst by a cruel accident. It was the doctor that sewed it up, and to all appearances it was he, and the other independent witnesses, that did the main part of the suffering; each stitch that he took made Clara wince slightly, but it shriveled the others.

I take pride in Clara's remark, because it shows that although she was only three years old, her fireside teachings were already making her a thinker—a thinker and also an observer of proportions. I am not claiming any credit for this. I furnished to the children worldly knowledge and wisdom, but was not competent to go higher, and so I left their spiritual education in the hands of the mother. A result of this modesty of mine was made manifest to me in a very striking way, some years afterward, when Jean was nine years old. We had recently arrived in Berlin, at the time, and had begun housekeeping in a furnished apartment. One morning at breakfast a vast card arrived—an invitation. To be precise, it was a command from the Emperor of Germany to come to dinner. During several months I had encountered socially, on the Continent, men bearing lofty titles; and all this while Jean was becoming more and more impressed, and awed, and subdued, by these imposing events, for she had not been abroad before, and they were new to her—wonders out of dreamland turned into realities. The imperial card was passed from hand to hand, around the table, and examined with interest; when it reached Jean she exhibited excitement and emotion, but for a time was quite speechless; then she said,

"Why papa, if it keeps going on like this, pretty soon there won't be anybody left for you to get acquainted with but God."

It was not complimentary to think I was not acquainted in that quarter, but she was young, and the young jump to conclusions without reflection.

Necessarily, I did myself the honor to obey the command of the Emperor Wilhelm II. Prince Heinrich, and six or eight other guests were present. The Emperor did most of the talking, and he talked well, and in faultless English. In both of these conspicuousnesses I was gratified to recognize a resemblance to myself—a very exact resemblance; no, almost exact, but not quite that—a modified exactness, with the advantage in favor of the Emperor. My English, like his, is nearly faultless; like him I talk well; and when I have guests at dinner I prefer to do all the talking myself. It is the best way, and the pleasantest. Also the most profitable for the others.

I was greatly pleased to perceive that his Majesty was familiar with my books, and that his attitude toward them was not uncomplimentary. In the course of his talk he said that my best and most valuable book was "Old Times on the Mississippi." I will refer to that remark again, presently.

An official who was well up in the Foreign Office at that time, and had served under Bismarck for fourteen years, was still occupying his old place, under Chancellor Caprivi. Smith, I will call him of whom I am speaking, though that is not his name. He was a special friend of mine, and I greatly enjoyed his society, although in order to have it it was necessary for me to seek it as late as midnight, and not earlier. This was because government officials of his rank had to work all day, after nine in the morning, and then attend official banquets in the evening; wherefore they were usually unable to get life-restoring fresh air and exercise for their jaded minds and bodies earlier than midnight; then they turned out, in groups of two or three, and gratefully and violently tramped the deserted streets until two in the morning. Smith had been in the government service, at home and abroad, for more than thirty years, and he was now sixty years old, or close upon it. He could not remember a year in which he had had a vacation of more than a fortnight's length; he was weary all through to the bones and the marrow, now, and was yearning for a holiday of a whole three months—yearning so longingly and so poignantly that he had at last made up his mind to make a desperate cast for it and stand the consequences, whatever they might be. It was against all rules to *ask* for a vacation—quite against all etiquette; the shock of it would paralyse the Chancellery; stern etiquette and usage required another form: the applicant was not privileged to ask for a vacation: he must send in his *resignation.* The chancellor would know that the applicant was not really trying to resign, and didn't want to resign, but was merely trying in this left-handed way to get a vacation.

The night before the Emperor's dinner I helped Smith take his exercise, after midnight, and he was full of his project. He had sent in his resignation that day, and was trembling for the result; and naturally, because it might possibly be that the chancellor would be happy to fill his place with somebody else, in which case he could accept the resignation without comment and without offence. Smith was in a very anxious frame of mind; not that he feared that Caprivi was dissatisfied with him, for he had no such fear; it was the Emperor that he was afraid of; he did not know how he stood with the Emperor. He said that while apparently it was Caprivi who would decide his case, it was in reality the Emperor who would perform that service; that the Emperor kept personal watch upon everything, and that no official sparrow could fall to the ground without his privity and consent; that the resignation would be laid before his Majesty, who would accept it or decline to accept it, according to his pleasure, and that then his pleasure in the matter would be communicated by Caprivi. Smith said he would know his fate the next evening, after the imperial dinner; that when I should escort and protect his Majesty into the large salon contiguous to the dining room, I would find there about thirty men—cabinet ministers, admirals, generals, and other great officials of the Empire—and that these men would be standing talking together in little separate groups of two or three persons; that the Emperor would move from group to group and say a word to each, sometimes two words, sometimes ten words; and that the length of his speech, whether brief or not so brief, would indicate the exact standing in the Emperor's regard, of the man accosted; and that by observing this thermometer an expert could tell, to half a degree, the state of the imperial thermometer in each case; that in Berlin, as in the imperial days of Rome, the Emperor was the sun, and that his smile or his frown meant good fortune or disaster to the man upon whom it should fall. Smith suggested that I watch the thermometer while the Emperor went his rounds of the groups, and said that if his Majesty talked four minutes with any person there present, it meant high favor, and that the sun was in the zenith, and cloudless, for that man.

I mentally recorded that four-minute altitude, and resolved to see if any man there on that night stood in sufficient favor to achieve it.

Very well. After the dinner I watched the Emperor while he passed from group to group, and privately I timed him with a watch. Two or three times he came near to reaching the four-minute altitude, but always he fell short a little. The last man he came to was Smith. He put his hand on Smith's shoulder and began to talk to him; and when he finished, the thermometer had scored seven minutes! The company then moved toward the smoking-room, where cigars, beer, and anecdotes would be in brisk service until midnight, and as Smith passed me he whispered,

"That settles it. The chancellor will ask me how much of a vacation I want, and I shan't be afraid to raise the limit. I shall call for six months."

Smith's dream had been to spend his three months' vacation—in case he got a vacation instead of the other thing—in one of the great capitals of the Continent—a capital whose name I shall suppress, at present. The next day the chancellor asked him how much of a vacation he wanted, and where he desired to spend it. Smith told him. His prayer was granted, and rather more than granted. The chancellor augmented his salary and attached him to the German Embassy of that selected capital, giving him a place of high dignity bearing an imposing title, and with nothing to do except attend banquets of an extraordinary character at the Embassy, once or twice a year. The term of his vacation was not specified; he was to continue it until ordered to come back to his work in the Foreign Office. This was in 1891. Eight years later Smith was passing through Vienna, and he called upon me. There had been no interruption of his vacation, as yet, and there was no likelihood that an interruption of it would occur while he should still be among the living. We all dream nice dreams, but we don't all get them fulfilled in this pleasant way.

1891

1899

December 13, 1906

As regards the coming American monarchy. It was before Mr. Root had been heard from that the chairman of the banquet said:

"In this time of unrest it is of great satisfaction that such a man as you, Mr. Root, is chief adviser of the President."

Mr. Root then got up and in the most quiet and orderly manner touched off the successor to the San Francisco earthquake. As a result, the several State governments were well shaken up and considerably weakened. Mr. Root was prophesying. He was prophesying, and it seems to me that no shrewder and surer forecasting has been done in this country for a good many years.

He did not say, in so many words, that we are proceeding, in a steady march, toward eventual and unavoidable replacement of the republic by monarchy; but I suppose he was aware that that is the case. He notes the several steps, the customary steps, which in all the ages have led to the consolidation of loose and scattered governmental forces into formidable centralizations of authority; but he stops there, and doesn't add up the sum. He is not unaware that heretofore the sum has been ultimate monarchy, and that the same figures can fairly be depended upon to furnish the same sum whenever and wherever they can be produced, so long as human nature shall remain as it is; but it was not needful that he do the adding, since any one can do it; neither would it have been gracious in him to do it.

In observing the changed conditions which in the course of time have made certain and sure the eventual seizure by the Washington Government of a number of State duties and prerogatives which have been betrayed and neglected by the several States, he does not attribute those changes and the vast results which are to flow from them to any thought-out policy of any party or of any body of dreamers or schemers, but properly and rightly attributes them to that stupendous power—*Circumstance*—which moves by laws of its own, regardless of parties and policies, and whose decrees are final, and must be obeyed by all—and will be. The railway is a Circumstance, the steamship is a Circumstance, the telegraph is a Circumstance. They were mere happenings; and to the whole world, the wise and the foolish alike, they were entirely trivial, wholly inconsequential; indeed silly, comical, grotesque. No man, and no party, and no thought-out policy said, "Behold, we will build railways and steamships and telegraphs, and presently you will see the condition and way of life of every man and woman and child in the nation totally changed; unimaginable changes of law and custom will follow, in spite of anything that anybody can do to prevent it."

The changed conditions have come, and Circumstance knows what is following, and will follow. So does Mr. Root. His language is not unclear, it is crystal:

"Our whole life has swung away from the old State centres and is crystallizing about national centres."

". . . . the old barriers which kept the States as separate communities are completely lost from sight."

". . . . that [State] power of regulation and control is gradually passing into the hands of the national government."

"Sometimes by an assertion of the inter-State commerce power, sometimes by an assertion of the taxing power, the national government is taking up the performance of duties which under the changed conditions the separate States are no longer capable of adequately performing."

"We are urging forward in a development of business and social life which tends more and more to the obliteration of State lines and the decrease of State power as compared with national power."

"It is useless for the advocates of State rights to inveigh against . . . the extension of national authority in the fields of necessary control where the States themselves fail in the performance of their duty."

He is not announcing a policy; he is not forecasting what a party of planners will bring about; he is merely telling what the people will require and compel. And he could have added—which would be perfectly true—that the people will not be moved to it by speculation and cogitation and planning, but by *Circumstance*—that power which arbitrarily compels all their actions, and over which they have not the slightest control.

"The end is not yet."

It is a true word. We are on the march, but at present we are only just getting started.

If the States continue to fail to do their duty as required by the people—

". . . . *constructions of the Constitution will be found* to vest the power where it will be exercised—in the national government."

I do not know whether that has a sinister meaning or not, and so I will not enlarge upon it lest I should chance to be in the wrong. It sounds like ship-money come again, but it may not be so intended.

Human nature being what it is, I suppose we must expect to drift into monarchy by and by. It is a saddening thought, but we cannot change our nature: we are all alike, we human beings; and in our blood and bone, and ineradicable, we carry the seeds out of which monarchies and aristocracies are grown: worship of gauds, titles, distinctions, power. We have to worship these things and their possessors, we are all born so, and we cannot help it. We have to be despised by somebody whom we regard as above us, or we are not happy; we have to have somebody to worship and envy, or we cannot be content. In America we manifest this in all the ancient and customary ways. In public we scoff at titles and hereditary privilege, but privately we hanker after them, and when we get a chance we buy them for cash and a daughter. Sometimes we get a good man and worth the price, but we are ready to take him anyway, whether he be ripe or rotten, whether he be clean and decent, or merely a basket of noble and sacred and long-descended offal. And when we get him the whole nation publicly chaffs and scoffs—and privately envies; and also is proud of the honor which has been conferred upon us. We run over our list of titled purchases every now and then, in the newspapers, and discuss them and caress them, and are thankful and happy.

Like all the other nations, we worship money and the possessors of it—they being our aristocracy, and we have to have one. We like to read about rich people in the papers; the papers know it, and they do their best to keep this appetite liberally fed. They even leave out a foot-ball bull-fight now and then to get room for all the particulars of how—according to the display-heading—"Rich Woman Fell Down Cellar—Not Hurt." The falling down the cellar is of no interest to us when the woman is not rich, but no rich woman can fall down cellar and we not yearn to know all about it and wish it was us.

In a monarchy the people willingly and rejoicingly revere and take pride in their nobilities, and are not humiliated by the reflection that this humble and hearty homage gets no return but contempt. Contempt does not shame them, they are used to it, and they recognize that it is their proper due. We are all made like that. In Europe we easily and quickly learn to take that attitude toward the sovereigns and the aristocracies; moreover, it has been observed that when we get the attitude we go on and exaggerate it, presently becoming more servile than the natives, and vainer of it. The next step is to rail and scoff at republics and democracies. All of which is natural, for we have not ceased to be human beings by becoming Americans, and the human race was always intended to be governed by kingship, not by popular vote.

I suppose we must expect that unavoidable and irresistible Circumstances will gradually take away the powers of the States and concentrate them in the central government, and that the republic will then repeat the history of all time and become a monarchy; but I believe that if we obstruct these encroachments and steadily resist them the monarchy can be postponed for a good while yet.

Monday, December 17, 1906

The coincidence of the Kaiser's and the portier's appreciation of "Old Times on the Mississippi," expressed almost in the same moment—The coincidence of Mr. Clemens's reflecting on the definition of the word civilization, and then picking up the morning paper and finding his very ideas set forth by a writer who attributed the marrow of his remarks to Mr. Clemens.

As I have already remarked, "Old Times on the Mississippi" got the Kaiser's best praise. It was after midnight when I reached home; I was usually out until toward midnight, and the pleasure of being out late was poisoned, every night, by the dread of what I must meet at my front door—an indignant face, a resentful face, the face of the portier. The portier was a tow-headed young German, twenty-two or -three years old, and it had been for some time apparent to me that he did not enjoy being hammered out of his sleep, nights, to let me in. He never had a kind word for me, nor a pleasant look. I couldn't understand it, since it was his business to be on watch and let the occupants of the several flats in at any and all hours of the night. I could not see why he so distinctly failed to get reconciled to it.

The fact is, I was ignorantly violating, every night, a custom in which he was commercially interested. I did not suspect this. No one had told me of the custom, and if I had been left to guess it, it would have taken me a very long time to make a success of it. It was a custom which was so well established and so universally recognized, that it had all the force and dignity of law. By authority of this custom, whosoever entered a Berlin house after ten at night must pay a trifling toll to the portier for breaking his sleep to let him in. This tax was either two and a half cents or five cents, I don't remember which; but I had never paid it, and didn't know I owed it, and as I had been residing in Berlin several weeks, I was so far in arrears that my presence in the German capital was getting to be a serious disaster to that young fellow.

I arrived from the imperial dinner sorrowful and anxious, made my presence known, and prepared myself to wait in patience the tedious minute or two which the portier usually allowed himself to keep me tarrying—as a punishment. But this time there was no stage wait; the door was instantly unlocked, unbolted, unchained, and flung wide; and in it appeared the strange and welcome apparition of the portier's round face all sunshine and smiles and welcome, in place of the black frowns and hostility that I was expecting. Plainly he had not come out of his bed: he had been waiting for me, watching for me. He began to pour out upon me in the most enthusiastic and energetic way a generous stream of German welcome and homage, meanwhile dragging me excitedly to his small bedroom beside the front door; there he made me bend down over a row of German translations of my books and said,

"There—you wrote them! I have found it out! By God, I did not know it before, and I ask a million pardons! That one there, the 'Old Times on the Mississippi,' is the best book you ever wrote."

The usual number of those curious accidents which we call coincidences have fallen to my share in this life, but for picturesqueness this one puts all the others in the shade: that a crowned head and a portier, the very top of an empire and the very bottom of it, should pass the very same criticism and deliver the very same verdict upon a book of mine—and almost in the same hour and the same breath—is a coincidence which out-coincidences any coincidence which I could have imagined with such powers of imagination as I have been favored with; and I have not been accustomed to regard them as being small or of an inferior quality. It is always a satisfaction to me to remember that whereas I do not know, for sure, what any other nation thinks of any one of my twenty-three volumes, I do at least know for a certainty what one nation of fifty millions thinks of one of them, at any rate; for if the mutual verdict of the top of an empire and the bottom of it does not establish, for good and all, the judgment of the entire nation concerning that book, then the axiom that we can get a sure estimate of a thing by arriving at a general average of all the opinions involved, is a fallacy.

Speaking of coincidences, one has come my way this morning. While my breakfast was cooling off at my bedside, I was puzzling once more over how one might define the word civilization in a single phrase, unencumbered by confusing elaborations. Necessarily, one could not hope to describe the edifice itself in a phrase, nor in a hundred phrases; but one might hope to squeeze into a phrase the foundation of the edifice, the basis upon which all the elaborations are built toward the sky. By and by I concluded to word the phrase like this: "civilization is a condition wherein every man is of necessity both a master and a slave."

It means forced labor, compulsory labor—every man working for somebody else while imagining that he is working for himself, and at the same time living upon the work of other men who think they are working for themselves and not for him. I do not know of any one, from the emperor down to the rag-picker, who under the hard conditions of civilization is not both master and slave, and who is not obliged to do work which he does not want to do, but does the work because he is a slave, and his master requires it of him and is able to compel him to do it. I seem to have been an exception, for forty years. I seem to work only when I please, and to do no work that I don't want to do. But a moment's reflection shows me that this applies only to my trade. But even this detail will not bear examination. Several times a year I do literary work which I do not want to do, but feel that I cannot escape it; also many times a year I attend banquets and make speeches, whereas I would never attend a banquet nor make a speech if in my condition of slavery I could avoid it, and have my own way. Many things go to the building of that irksome and unsatisfactory condition which we call civilization, but I am satisfied that the whole edifice rests upon the basis of enforced slavery. I find only one man who does only the work which he likes to do—and therefore works not at all, for work which one enjoys is not work, but play: that man is the uncivilized man, the savage. In a fine and large degree he is no man's slave; he is only a master, a slave owner, and his slave is his wife. She does all the work; she gathers the wood and builds the fire and cooks the food; she jerks the beef; she tans the skins and makes the clothes; she puts up the tents and takes them down; she packs the ponies and moves the camp, and on the move she walks and her husband rides. He seldom does any work, but hunts and fishes and goes to war, and to him it is all play and pleasure. I have an impression amounting almost to conviction that the conditions of his life are worth more than six of our civilizations.

When I had finished these philosophizings and was ready to begin upon my cold breakfast, I took up the *Sun* and found an editorial in it which could have been written with my belated thinkings for a text. It was quite a striking coincidence, and it seemed to me that the writer was an unusually wise person and profound and sane thinker. Then I read the rest of his article and found that he was crediting the meat and marrow of his conclusions to me. At first I was not able to recall the connection; then I perceived that he had in his mind the whitewashing of the fence in "Tom Sawyer." I was afraid he was going to overlook something; I was afraid he was going to imagine that I had originated the idea, and that would have been a mistake, for I have never originated an idea, and I have never heard of anybody who had originated one. But he did not make the mistake. He suggested that without any doubt these notions had been held and discussed by other wise persons thousands of years ago.

Tuesday, December 18, 1906

Mr. Clemens and Mr. Paine go to Washington, in company with the members of the League Committee, to plead for the extension of the Copyright Bill.

I went to Washington, a fortnight ago, at the suggestion of the Committee of the Copyright League, to help nurse the amended bill through its initial examination by the Patent Committees of the House and the Senate. Mr. Paine made the trip with me. We had the League Committee for company on board the train—a committee composed of two publishers, a poet, and Robert Underwood Johnson. The publishers were William Appleton and George Haven Putnam, fine men, both, and choice examples of their calling. The poet was Mr. Bowker. No, I am in error; it was two publishers and two poets, for Underwood Johnson is himself a poet, though that is not his regular line; neither is it Bowker's; both of these singers earn their bread by surer handicrafts. They live upon salaries—Johnson as one of the editors of the *Century Magazine,* Bowker as something connected with a railroad. Both of these poets have published modest volumes of verse, and possess copies; both are hard workers for an enlarged literary copyright, and have given their steady and earnest labors to this cause in the Copyright League for years without salary, and without having any pecuniary interest in the proposed lengthened term of literary copyright.

I believe that if we could go back over the past two centuries since England waylaid the author, in Queen Anne's time, and robbed him of his poor little rights, we should find that from that day to this the long struggle to regain those rights for the author has been conducted, almost exclusively, not by the authors who would be benefited by the restoration, but by minor poets whose poems were perishable and evanescent; poets who had little or no use for a copyright of any kind, let alone an extended one. These benefactors, so far as my knowledge and experience go, never get any real help from the small handful of authors who could be pecuniarily benefited by a liberal life-term for books.

When I went to Washington sixteen years ago, to help just such a committee as this one in the nursing of an international copyright bill through the House of Representatives, James Russell Lowell, I think, was the only author who appeared there whose books promised to outlive the forty-two-year limit—except myself. At the hearing before the Patent Committee of the Senate, Mr. Lowell appeared just once, for fifteen minutes. He made a strong and striking speech, then disappeared, and was seen no more. Howells didn't come; Edward Everett Hale didn't come; Thomas Bailey Aldrich didn't come; as I have already said, none of the ten or twenty authors personally and really interested in getting justice for American and foreign authors came forward to assist, except Lowell and myself. Underwood Johnson was of the League Committee in that old day. The international bill was passed, and became law. This victory was attributed to Johnson, and the grateful French Government decorated him with the Legion of Honor for it, and he still wears in his buttonhole that red thread which distinguishes the member of the Legion of Honor from that remnant of the human race who have failed to get it. It makes me jealous; it makes me spiteful toward Underwood Johnson; it embitters me against the French; for Underwood Johnson didn't win that victory, I did it myself. When a legislative body is not acquainted with the interests and rights and wrongs of authorship, these things must be explained to the members before they can be expected to understand the situation; explaining by documents is not worth while; no member can find time to read them; explaining by speeches before a hard-worked committee is not worth while, for the committee cannot in turn convey the acquired information to the rest of the House otherwise than by speeches, and speeches are not effective when they concern a matter in which the House feels no interest.

Copyright is a thing which all legislative bodies are ignorant of and unfamiliar with, and there is only one way to get a copyright measure through Congress—that is by canvassing the Congress individual by individual, and enlightening each in his turn. I did that sixteen years ago. I did not go to the homes, hotels, and boarding-houses of the members, for that would have taken three months. Sunset Cox smuggled me in on the floor of the House, where of course I had no right to be and would have been turned out if the sergeant-at-arms had chosen to see me; but neither the sergeant nor the Speaker paid any attention to me, and so I got into no trouble. Sunset Cox supplied me with Democrats, two and three and four at a time; Mr. John D. Long supplied me with Republicans, and in three or four hours I had had personal contact and conversation with almost every member of the House. As argument I used only two or three essential points. It was not difficult to make them clear and comprehensible, and I made them so. The commonest remark that fell upon my ear, all through those hours, was—

"I have had no time to examine this matter, Mr. Clemens, and I did not understand it before, but I will vote for the bill now."

The bill went through, and a grateful France decorated Underwood Johnson, the poet. However I suppose I ought to be fair, and for this once I will be. It was because of the existence and industries of Underwood Johnson that an international copyright bill was devised and brought before Congress. But for Underwood Johnson, there would have been no bill; but for the bill I should not have been there—and so, a fair and righteous distribution of the honors requires that Underwood Johnson get half the credit and I the other half. If he will give me half of his red thread I will withdraw from him all bitterness, all animosity, all spitefulness, all envy.

This new bill proposes to change the present legal life of a book (which is forty-two years) to the author's life and fifty years after. Underwood is working as hard for it as ever. He and Bowker appeared before the double committee on the first day's hearing and made speeches; Howells was there also, not to speak, but in order that the ten or twenty American authors actually interested in extension of copyright might have a representation in the flesh. I did not attend that first sitting, but I attended next day's sitting, at five in the afternoon, and spoke. The place was crowded, and the two committees had been patiently listening to reasonings and wranglings all day long, and they had listened to the like the whole of the previous day. When Congressmen perform their whole duty in this devoted way the spectacle furnishes the outsider a new light on the legislator's life, and with it a very sincere admiration for men who can labor like that in causes which cannot interest them, and must, of necessity, bore them.

I did not go to Washington to make a speech. The speech was merely an incident, an accident, and not a part of the committee's previously arranged program. My business in Washington, and my desire, was to put in force a private project of my own—a repetition of my industries of sixteen years before: I wanted to talk to the members of the House, man to man. Mr. Speaker Cannon would not overstrain his powers by smuggling me into the House, but he said he would make a fair compromise in the interests of my mission; he would give me his private room in the Capitol, and also his colored messenger to run errands for me. This was very convenient. It was really better than exploiting my canvass on the floor of the House. The colored servant was Neal. I had known him sixteen years before, when I was lobbying for the international bill. Neal has served a procession of Speakers of the House which stretches back without a break for forty years. He knows every member as well as he knows the members of his own family. Before I had talked with any more than twenty members I perceived that they felt no hostility toward the extension of literary copyright—that is to say, book copyright—but were not at all pleased with the bill's attempt to intrude mechanical musical devices, and other things whose interests belong in the Patent Office and had no proper connection with copyright. As soon as I felt convinced that this was really and truly the attitude of the House toward the bill I ceased from urging the whole bill and thenceforth urged only the literary end of it. I talked with a hundred and eighty members of Congress that day, and satisfied myself that if the musical feature of the bill could be eliminated the bill would pass. Afterward I talked with the chairmen of the Senate and House Committees that had the bill in charge, and found that they were tired of the music, and were already considering a project to report the bill with the musical foolishness left out. I ceased from my labors then, leaving two hundred and six members uncanvassed, the temper of the hundred and eighty already canvassed convincing me that the temper of the House was friendly enough toward literary copyright and could be depended upon to remain so without any further persuasions of mine.

December 19, 1906

Mr. Clemens gives his reasons for insisting upon an extension of the Copyright Bill—arranged in the form of an interview with a member of Congress.

.... That was an odd mission of mine to Washington. I arrive at this deduction by a critical examination of the matters involved in it. Instead of compacting them into a solid block, and thus confusing and dimming them, I will try to make them clear by separating them through the handy process of question and answer. I will imagine myself as undergoing examination by a member of Congress who desires to qualify himself to vote upon the Copyright Bill by inquiring into the particulars of the interests involved.

Question. Mr. Clemens, you are here to represent—whom?

Answer. The authors.

Q. All authors?

A. No. There are perhaps ten thousand American authors, but I have appointed myself to represent only twenty-five of them.

Q. Why only twenty-five out of the ten thousand?

A. Because all but the twenty-five are amply protected by the copyright law now in existence.

Q. How do you mean?

A. The new bill proposes to extend the copyright-life of a book *beyond the existing limit,* which is forty-two years. It is possible that the books of twenty-five living authors may still be selling profitably when they reach the age of forty-two years; the books of the other ten thousand, amounting to an annual output of five or six thousand volumes, will all be dead and forgotten long before the forty-two-year limit is reached; therefore of our ten thousand authors only twenty-five are pecuniarily interested in an extension of the existing copyright limit.

Q. Mr. Clemens, are there other persons interested in the making of books, and pecuniarily affected by copyright laws?

A. Yes. To begin with, the publishers.

Q. How many publishers are there?

A. About three hundred. They publish an annual output of five or six thousand new books, and presumably the result is an average profit of a thousand dollars upon each—say an aggregate of five or six million dollars; presumably also, they get as much more *out of books whose copyrights are dead, and on which they pay no royalties to authors or their families,* but filch the author's share and add it to their own.

Q. It is not the authors, then, that get the bulk of the money resulting from authorship?

A. No. Far from it! The ten thousand cannot be expected to produce, each, more than half a book a year. Authorship is not their trade. If one of these makes a thousand dollars out of his book—and sometimes he does—it takes him two years to do it; while he is making five hundred dollars out of his book his publisher may publish forty other books, and make forty thousand dollars.

Q. By this it would appear that authorship is mainly important to the publisher, not to the author?

A. It is true. Pecuniarily, no one concerned is perhaps so little interested in authorship as are our ten thousand authors. Fortunately for them, they do not get their living by authorship; they get it in other and securer ways; with them authorship is a side issue, a pastime.

Q. Very well then, as I understand it authorship is worth several millions a year to publishers, and worth next to nothing to the main body of authors. Is that it?

A. Yes, that is what I am meaning.

Q. Then it seems plain that authorship is one of the most trifling of all imaginable trades. I cannot call to mind another trade that matches it for pecuniary humbleness. Do you know of one?

A. No—none except whitewashing fences; and even that would be a better trade, if you could exercise it in the winter as well as in the summer.

Q. There are still others who are pecuniarily interested in the making of books? Name them.

A. At a guess, two thousand book-compositors, earning a wage of two million and a half dollars a year—

Q. Go on.

A. Some hundreds of printing-press men and boys—

Q. Proceed.

A. Some hundreds or thousands of binders, paper-makers and printing-ink manufacturers.

Q. Go on.

A. Some scores of illustrators, photographers, and engravers.

Q. Go on.

A. Some hundreds of box-makers, packers, porters, and employees of the railways and express companies.

Q. You have footed up a formidable army: Mr. Clemens, is there anybody in the country who is *not* pecuniarily interested in the making of books?

A. Yes sir—the authors. The ten thousand.

Q. Let us now get back to the beginning and add up results. Some thousands of persons and their families are greatly and importantly interested in the making of books; you have granted that these thousands are all well protected by the existing copyright law—protected beyond possibility of hurt; you have conceded that all of the ten thousand authors except the specialized twenty-five, are amply protected by the law as it stands, since their books will never live out the forty-two-year limit, and could therefore not be advantaged by extending it. Now then, I wish to ask you a serious question. You have proven that in representing the twenty-five you represent *the smallest interest, the poorest little interest, the most microscopic interest, that has ever intruded itself upon the attention of a legislative body in this age or any other.* This interest has been intruding and complaining, persistently, for two centuries, in England and America, and in that period has wasted the valuable time of Parliaments and Congresses—time so valuable, so precious, that if you should reduce that valuable time to dollars and cents the aggregate would amount to millions and millions of dollars, and would build fifty battleships and equip for war a hundred thousand soldiers. Mr. Clemens, how do you excuse the continued and persistent agitation of this matter?

A. I excuse it for reasons which seem to me to justify it. In the first place, upon the grounds of our moral law. Our moral laws endow us with certain rights; one of these is the right to hold and enjoy, unchallenged and unmolested, property created by our honest industries; and this endowment is not discriminated, but comes to us all alike, all in equal measure. It does not give this property-right to publisher, butcher, land-owner, corporation, shoemaker, tailor, and deny it to the author; *it includes the author.* It is every man's right—his *right,* and not a benevolence conferred upon him by legislatures. The moral law existed before copyright, and in authority *supersedes any usurping statute that can be inflicted by the legislature.* Legislatures can by force of arbitrary power rob an author by statute, but no casuistry can keep that robbery from being a crime. It is lawful crime, legalized crime, but *it remains crime just the same.* The clause in the Constitution of the United States which denies perpetual property in an author's book is a *crime,* and an *excuser and defender and propagator of crime*—and the fact that it is part of the Constitution in no wise relieves it from that stain, and from merited contempt. The publisher who withholds royalty from a book that has passed the forty-two-year limit under the plea that the Constitution and Congress have granted him permission to commit this degraded crime is not any less a thief than he would be if the property which he is stealing was protected property. In one of our cities there is a firm of publishers that make and sell copyright-expired books only. There are several partners in the firm, and one of them told a friend of mine that his share of the profits of this nefarious trade amounts to forty thousand dollars a year. That person ranks as a most respectable man, but to my mind he belongs in jail, with the other thieves. The late Baron Tauchnitz was the only publisher I have ever known who was above seizing and using property which did not belong to him, the only publisher I have known in whose reach the author's widow and orphan could safely leave unwatched their poor little literary belongings. Yet the name he commonly went by, in an ignorant world, was "that *pirate!*" I personally know that he would not put upon his book-list a book which he had not bought and paid for, whether its copyright was alive or was dead. He knew that no Constitution and no statute can take away perpetual property-right in an author's book, but can only act as a *thief's confederate* and by brute force protect the thief while he steals it. I know of no American publisher who is not a pirate; I will gamble that if there is a publisher anywhere who is not a pirate it is Tauchnitz's son.

With your permission I will venture yet another reason for not being ashamed to come here in the interest of that grotesquely small band—the twenty-five authors who could be benefited by the requested extension of the copyright limit to the life of the author and fifty years after. It is this: almost the most prodigious asset of a country, and *perhaps its most precious possession,* is its native literary product—when that product is fine and noble and enduring. Whence comes this enduring literature? It comes from the *twenty-five,* and from no other source! In the course of a century—and not in any briefer time—the contemporaneous twenty-five may produce from their number one or two, or three, authors whose books can outlast a hundred years. It will take the recurrent successors of the twenty-five several centuries to build a hundred imperishable books; those books become the recognized classics of that country, and are pointed to by the nation with exultant and eloquent pride. *Am I claiming too much when I claim that such a literature is a country's most valuable and most precious possession?* I think not. Nations pride themselves upon the splendors of their deeds of arms, statesmanship, conquest; and when they can point back, century after century, and age after age, to the far-stretching perspective of a great history, their pride is beyond expression in words; *but it all exists by grace of one thing—one thing alone—the country's literature.* It is a country's literature that preserves the country's achievements, which would otherwise perish from the memories of men. When we call to mind that stately line—

"The glory that was Greece, and the grandeur that was Rome"—

we should remember with respect and with reverence that if the great literatures of Greece and Rome had by some catastrophe been blotted out, *the inspiring histories of those countries would be vacant to the world to-day;* the lessons which they left behind, and which have been the guide and teacher of the world for centuries upon centuries would have been as utterly lost to us as if they had never had an existence. It is because of the great literatures of the ancient world, and because of those literatures alone, that the poet can sing of the glory that was Greece and the grandeur that was Rome, and thrill us with the sublimity of his words. It is not *foreign* literatures that sing a country's glories and give them immortality—*only the country's own literature will perform that priceless service.* It were worth a Congress's while to spend upon a copyright law time worth the cost of even a hundred battleships if the result of it might some day be the breeding and nourishing of a Shakspeare. Italy has many battleships; she has many possessions which she is proud of, but far and away above them all she holds in pride one incomparable possession, one name—DANTE!

I represent only twenty-five persons, it is true; only twenty-five out of eighty-five millions; considered commercially I represent the meanest interest that could ever intrude itself upon the time and attention of Congresses and Parliaments, in this age or in any future one, but I am not ashamed of my mission.

Thursday, December 20, 1906

Captain Osborn tells to Bret Harte, in a Californian restaurant, his adventure of falling overboard and his rescue— A tramp overhears him, claims to be his rescuer, is liberally rewarded, and afterwards discovered to be an impostor.

Six months ago, when I was recalling early days in San Francisco, I broke off at a place where I was about to tell about Captain Osborn's odd adventure at the "What Cheer," or perhaps it was at another cheap feeding-place—the "Miners' Restaurant." It was a place where one could get good food on the cheapest possible terms, and its popularity was great among the multitudes whose purses were light. It was a good place to go to to observe mixed humanity. Captain Osborn and Bret Harte went there one day and took a meal, and in the course of it Osborn fished up an interesting reminiscence of a dozen years before and told about it. It was to this effect:

He was a midshipman in the navy when the Californian gold craze burst upon the world and set it wild with excitement. His ship made the long journey around the Horn and was approaching her goal, the Golden Gate, when an accident happened.

"It happened to me," said Osborn. "I fell overboard. There was a heavy sea running, but no one was much alarmed about me, because we had on board a newly patented life-saving device which was believed to be competent to rescue anything that could fall overboard, from a midshipman to an anchor. Ours was the only ship that had this device; we were very proud of it, and had been anxious to give its powers a practical test. This thing was lashed to the garboard-strake of the main-to'gallant mizzen-yard amidships,* and there was nothing to do but cut the lashings and heave it over; it would do the rest. The cry of 'Man overboard!' brought the whole ship's company on deck. Instantly the lashings were cut and the machine flung joyously over. Damnation, it went to the bottom like an anvil! By the time that the ship was brought to and a boat manned, I was become but a bobbing speck on the waves half a mile astern, and losing my strength very fast; but by good luck there was a common seaman on board who had practical ideas in his head and hadn't waited to see what the patent machine was going to do, but had run aft and sprung over after me the moment the alarm was cried through the ship. I had a good deal of a start

* Can this be correct? I think there must be some mistake. M.T.

of him, and the seas made his progress slow and difficult, but he stuck to his work and fought his way to me, and just in the nick of time he put his saving arms about me when I was about to go down. He held me up until the boat reached us and rescued us. By that time I was unconscious, and I was still unconscious when we arrived at the ship. A dangerous fever followed, and I was delirious for three days; then I came to myself and at once inquired for my benefactor, of course. He was gone. We were lying at anchor in the Bay and every man had deserted to the gold-mines except the commissioned officers. I found out nothing about my benefactor but his name—Burton Sanders—a name which I have held in grateful memory ever since. Every time I have been on the Coast, these twelve or thirteen years, I have tried to get track of him, but have never succeeded. I wish I could find him and make him understand that his brave act has never been forgotten by me. Harte, I would rather see him and take him by the hand than any other man on the planet."

At this stage or a little later there was an interruption. A waiter near-by said to another waiter, pointing,

"Take a look at that tramp that's coming in. Ain't that the one that bilked the house, last week, out of ten cents?"

"I believe it is. Let him alone—don't pay any attention to him; wait till we can get a good look at him."

The tramp approached timidly and hesitatingly, with the air of one unsure and apprehensive. The waiters watched him furtively. When he was passing behind Harte's chair one of them said,

"He's the one!"—and they pounced upon him and proposed to turn him over to the police as a bilk. He begged piteously. He confessed his guilt, but said he had been driven to his crime by necessity—that when he had eaten the plate of beans and slipped out without paying for it, it was because he was starving, and hadn't the ten cents to pay for it with. But the waiters would listen to no explanations, no palliations; he must be placed in custody. He brushed his hand across his eyes and said meekly that he would submit, being friendless. Each waiter took him by an arm and faced him about to conduct him away. Then his melancholy eyes fell upon Captain Osborn, and a light of glad and eager recognition flashed from them. He said,

"Weren't you a midshipman once, sir, in the old *Lancaster?*"

"Yes," said Osborn. "Why?"

"Didn't you fall overboard?"

"Yes, I did. How do you come to know about it?"

"Wasn't there a new patent machine aboard, and didn't they throw it over to save you?"

"Why yes," said Osborn, laughing gently, "but it didn't do it."

"No sir, it was a sailor that done it."

"It certainly was. Look here, my man, you are getting distinctly interesting. Were you of our crew?"

"Yes sir, I was."

"I reckon you may be right. You do certainly know a good deal about that incident. What is your name?"

"Burton Sanders."

The Captain sprang up, excited, and said,

"Give me your hand! Give me both your hands! I'd rather shake them than inherit a fortune!"—and then he cried to the waiters, "Let him go!—take your hands off! He is my guest, and can have anything and everything this house is able to furnish. I am responsible."

There was a love-feast, then. Captain Osborn ordered it regardless of expense, and he and Harte sat there and listened while the man told stirring adventures of his life and fed himself up to the eyebrows. Then Osborn wanted to be benefactor in his turn, and pay back some of his debt. The man said it could all be paid with ten dollars—that it had been so long since he had owned that amount of money that it would seem a fortune to him, and he should be grateful beyond words if the Captain could spare him that amount. The Captain spared him ten broad twenty-dollar gold pieces, and made him take them in spite of his modest protestations; and gave him his address and said he must never fail to give him notice when he needed grateful service.

Several months later Harte stumbled upon the man in the street. He was most comfortably drunk, and pleasant and chatty. Harte remarked upon the splendidly and movingly dramatic incident of the restaurant, and said, "How curious and fortunate and happy and interesting it was that you two should come together, after that long separation, and at exactly the right moment to save you from disaster and turn your defeat by the waiters into a victory. A preacher could make a great sermon out of that, for it does look as if the hand of Providence was in it."

The hero's face assumed a sweetly genial expression, and he said,

"Well now, it wasn't Providence this time. I was running the arrangements myself."

"How do you mean?"

"Oh, I hadn't ever seen the gentleman before. I was at the next table, with my back to you the whole time he was telling about it. I saw my chance, and slipped out and fetched the two waiters with me and offered to give them a commission out of what I could get out of the Captain if they would do a quarrel act with me and give me an opening. So then, after a minute or two I straggled back, and you know the rest of it as well as I do."

Friday, December 21, 1906

Mainly from Susy's Biography—About the "Christian Union" article; the mother's methods of punishment, etc., with a few comments by Mr. Clemens.

I wish to insert here some pages of Susy's Biography of me in which the biographer does not scatter, according to her custom, but sticks pretty steadily to a single subject until she has fought it to a finish.

From Susy's Biography.

Feb. 27, '86.

Last summer while we were in Elmira an article came out in the "Christian Union" by name "What ought he to have done" treating of the government of children, or rather giving an account of a fathers battle with his little baby boy, by the mother of the child and put in the form of a question as to whether the father disciplined the child corectly or not; different people wrote their opinions of the fathers behavior, and told what they thought he should have done. Mamma had long known how to disciplin children, for in fact the bringing up of children had been one of her specialties for many years. She had a great many theories, but one of them was, that if a child was big enough to be nauty, it was big enough to be whipped and here we all agreed with her. I remember one morning when Dr. ——— came up to the farm he had a long discussion with mamma, upon the following topic. Mamma gave *this* as illustrative of one important rule for punishing a child. She said we will suppose the boy has thrown a handkerchief onto the floor, I tell him to pick it up, he refuses. I tell him again, he refuses. Then I say you must either pick up the handkerchief or have a whipping. My theory is never to make a child have a whipping and pick up the handkerchief too. I say "If you do not pick it up, I must punish you," if he doesn't he gets the whipping, but *I* pick up the handkerchief, if he does he gets no punishment. I tell him to do a thing if he disobeys me he is punished for so doing, but not forced to obey me afterwards."

When Clara and I had been very nauty or were being very nauty, the nurse would go and call Mamma and she would appear suddenly and look at us (she had a way of looking at us when she was displeased as if she could see right through us) till we were ready to sink through the floor from embarasment, and total absence of knowing what to say. This look was usually followed with "Clara" or "Susy what do you mean by this? do you want to come to the bath-room with me?" Then followed the climax for Clara and I both new only too well what going to the bath-room meant.

But mamma's first and foremost object was to make the child understand that he is being punished for *his* sake, and because the mother so loves him that she cannot allow him to do wrong; also that it is as hard for her to punish him as for him to be punished and even harder. Mamma never allowed herself to punish us when she was angry with us she never struck us because she was enoyed at us and felt like striking us if we had been nauty and had enoyed her, so that she thought she felt or would show the least bit of temper toward us while punnishing us, she always postponed the punishment until *she* was no more chafed by our behavior. She never humored herself by striking or punishing us because or while she was the least bit enoyed with us.

Our very worst nautinesses were punished by being taken to the bath-room and being whipped by the paper cutter. But after the whipping was over, mamma did not allow us to leave her until we were perfectly happy, and perfectly understood why we had been whipped. I never remember having felt the least bit bitterly toward mamma for punishing me. I always felt I had deserved my punishment, and was much happier for having received it. For after mamma had punished us and shown her displeasure, she showed no signs of further displeasure, but acted as if we had not displeased her in any way.

Ordinary punishments answered very well for Susy. She was a thinker, and would reason out the purpose of them, apply the lesson, and achieve the reform required. But it was much less easy to devise punishments that would reform Clara. This was because she was a philosopher who was always turning her attention to finding something good and satisfactory and entertaining in everything that came her way; consequently it was sometimes pretty discouraging to the troubled mother to find that after all her pains and thought in inventing what she meant to be a severe and reform-compelling punishment, the child had entirely missed the severities, through her native disposition to get interest and pleasure out of them as novelties. The mother, in her anxiety to find a penalty that would take sharp hold and do its work effectively, at last resorted, with a sore heart, and with a reproachful conscience, to that punishment which the incorrigible criminal in the penitentiary dreads above all the other punitive miseries which the warden inflicts upon him for his good—solitary confinement in the dark chamber. The grieved and worried mother shut Clara up in a very small clothes-closet and went away and left her there—for fifteen minutes—it was all that the mother-heart could endure. Then she came softly back and listened—listened for the sobs, but there weren't any; there were muffled and inarticulate sounds, but they could not be construed into sobs. The mother waited half an hour longer; by that time she was suffering so intensely with sorrow and compassion for the little prisoner that she was not able to wait any longer for the distressed sounds which she had counted upon to inform her when there had been punishment enough and the reform accomplished. She opened the closet to set the prisoner free and take her back into her loving favor and forgiveness, but the result was not the one expected. The captive had manufactured a fairy cavern out of the closet, and friendly fairies out of the clothes hanging from the hooks, and was having a most sinful and unrepentant good time, and requested permission to spend the rest of the day there!

From Susy's Biography.

But Mamma's oppinions and ideas upon the subject of bringing up children has always been more or less of a joke in our family, perticularly since Papa's article in the "Christian Union," and I am sure Clara and I have related the history of our old family paper-cutter, our punishments and privations with rather more pride and triumph than any other sentiment, because of Mamma's way of rearing us.

When the article "What ought he to have done?" came out Mamma read it, and was very much interested in it. And when papa heard that she had read it he went to work and secretly wrote his opinion of what the father ought to have done. He told Aunt Susy, Clara and I, about it but mamma was not to see it or hear any thing about it till it came out. He gave it to Aunt Susy to read, and after Clara and I had gone up to get ready for bed he brought it up for us to read. He told what he thought the father ought to have done by telling what mamma would have done. The article was a beautiful tribute to mamma and every word in it true. But still in writing about mamma he partly forgot that the article was going to be published, I think, and expressed himself more fully than he would do the second time he wrote it; I think the article has done and will do a great deal of good, and I think it would have been perfect for the family and friend's enjoyment, but a little bit too private to have been published as it was. And Papa felt so too, because the very next day or a few days after, he went down to New York to see if he couldn't get it back before it was published but it was too late, and he had to return without it. When the Christian Union reached the farm and papa's article in it all ready and waiting to be read to mamma papa hadn't the courage to show it to her (for he knew she wouldn't like it at all) at first, and he didn't but he might have let it go and never let her see it, but finally he gave his consent to her seeing it, and told Clara and I we could take it to her, which we did, with tardiness, and we all stood around mamma while she read it, all wondering what she would say and think about it.

She was too much surprised, (and pleased privately, too) to say much at first, but as we all expected publicly, (or rather when she remembered that this article was to be read by every one that took the Christian Union) she was rather shocked and a little displeased.

Clara and I had great fun the night papa gave it to us to read and then hide, so mamma couldn't see it, for just as we were in the midst of reading it mamma appeared papa following anxiously and asked why we were not in bed? then a scuffle ensued for we told her it was a secret and tried to hide it; but she chased us wherever we went, till she thought it was time for us to go to bed, then she surendered and left us to tuck it under Clara's matress.

A little while after the article was published letters began to come in to papa crittisizing it, there were some very pleasant ones but a few very disagreable. One of these, the very worst, mamma got hold of and read, to papa's great regret, it was full of the most disagreble things, and so very enoying to papa that he for a time felt he must do something to show the author of it his great displeasure at being so insulted. But he finally decided not to, because he felt the man had some cause for feeling enoyed at, for papa had spoken of him, (he was the baby's father) rather slightingly in his Christian Union Article.

After all this, papa and mamma both wished I think they might never hear or be spoken to on the subject of the Christian Union article, and whenever any has spoken to me and told me "How much they did enjoy my father's article in the Christian Union" I almost laughed in their faces when I remembered what a great variety of oppinions had been expressed upon the subject of the Christian Union article of papa's.

The article was written in July or August and just the other day papa received quite a bright letter from a gentleman who has read the C.U. article and gave his opinion of it in these words.

It is missing. She probably put the letter between the leaves of the Biography and it got lost out. She threw away the hostile letters, but tried to keep the pleasantest one for her book; surely there has been no kindlier biographer than this one. Yet to a quite creditable degree she is loyal to the responsibilities of her position as historian—not eulogist—and honorably gives me a quiet prod now and then. But how many, many, many she has withheld that I deserved! I could prize them now; there would be no acid in her words, and it is loss to me that she did not set them all down. Oh, Susy, you sweet little biographer, you break my old heart with your gentle charities!

I think a great deal of her work. Her canvases are on their easels, and her brush flies about in a care-free and random way, delivering a dash here, a dash there and another yonder, and one might suppose that there would be no definite result; on the contrary I think that an intelligent reader of her little book must find that by the time he has finished it he has somehow accumulated a pretty clear and nicely shaded idea of the several members of this family—including Susy herself—and that the random dashes on the canvases have developed into portraits. I feel that my own portrait, with some of the defects fined down and others left out, is here; and I am sure that any who knew the mother will recognize her without difficulty, and will say that the lines are drawn with a just judgment and a sure hand. Little creature though Susy was, the penetration which was born in her finds its way to the surface more than once in these pages.

Before Susy began the Biography she let fall a remark now and then concerning my character which showed that she had it under observation. In the Record which we kept of the children's sayings there is an instance of this. She was twelve years old at the time. We had established a rule that each member of the family must bring a fact to breakfast—a fact drawn from a book or from any other source; any fact would answer. Susy's first contribution was in substance as follows. Two great exiles and former opponents in war met in Ephesus—Scipio and Hannibal. Scipio asked Hannibal to name the greatest general the world had produced.

"Alexander"—and he explained why.

"And the next greatest?"

"Pyrrhus"—and he explained why.

"But where do you place yourself, then?"

"If I had conquered you I would place myself before the others."

Susy's grave comment was—

"That *attracted* me, it was just like papa—he is so frank about his books."

So frank in admiring them, she meant.

March 14th, '86.

Mr. Laurence Barrette and Mr. and Mrs. Hutton were here a little while ago, and we had a very interesting visit from them. Papa said Mr. Barette never had acted so well before when he had seen him, as he did the first night he was staying with us. And Mrs. ——— said she never had seen an actor on the stage, whom she more wanted to speak with.

Papa has been very much interested of late, in the "Mind Cure" theory. And in fact so have we all. A young lady in town has worked wonders, by using the "Mind Cure" upon people; she is constantly busy now curing peoples deseases in this way—and curing her own even, which to me seems the most remarkable of all.

A little while past, papa was delighted with the knowledge of what he thought the best way of curing a cold, which was by starving it. This starving did work beautifully, and freed him from a great many severe colds. Now he says it wasn't the starving that helped his colds, but the trust in the starving, the mind cure connected with the starving.

I shouldn't wonder if we finally became firm believers in Mind Cure. The next time papa has a cold, I haven't a doubt, he will send for Miss Holden the young lady who is doctoring in the "Mind Cure" theory, to cure him of it.

Mamma was over at Mrs. George Warners to lunch the other day, and Miss Holden was there too. Mamma asked if anything as natural as near-sightedness could be cured she said oh yes just as well as other deseases.

When mamma came home, she took me into her room, and told me that perhaps my near-sightedness could be cured by the "Mind Cure" and that she was going to have me try the treatment any way, there could be no harm in it, and there might be great good. If her plan succeeds there certainly will be a great deal in "Mind Cure" to my oppinion, for I am *very* near sighted and so is mamma, and I never expected there could be any more cure for it than for blindness, but now I dont know but what theres a cure for *that.*

It was a disappointment; her nearsightedness remained with her always. She was born with it, no doubt; yet, strangely enough she must have been four years old, and possibly five, before we knew of its existence. It is not easy to understand how that could have happened. I discovered the defect by accident. I was half way up the hall stairs one day at home, and was leading her by the hand, when I glanced back through the open door of the dining room and saw what I thought she would recognize as a pretty picture. It was "Stray Kit," the slender, the graceful, the sociable, the beautiful, the incomparable, the cat of cats, the tortoise-shell, curled up as round as a wheel and sound asleep on the fire-red cover of the dining table, with a brilliant stream of sunlight falling across her. I exclaimed about it, but Susy said she could see nothing there, neither cat nor table-cloth. The distance was so slight—not more than twenty feet, perhaps—that if it had been any other child I should not have credited the statement.

March 14th, '86.

Clara sprained her ankle, a little while ago, by running into a tree, when coasting, and while she was unable to walk with it she played solotaire with cards a great deal. While Clara was sick and papa saw her play solotaire so much, he got very much interested in the game, and finally began to play it himself a little, then Jean took it up, and at last *mamma,* even played it ocasionally; Jean's and papa's love for it rapidly increased, and now Jean brings the cards every night to the table and papa and mamma help her play, and before dinner is at an end, papa has gotten a separate pack of cards, and is playing alone, with great interest. Mamma and Clara next are made subject to the contagious solatair, and there are four solotarireans at the table; while you hear nothing but "Fill up the place" etc. It is dreadful! after supper Clara goes into the library, and gets a little red mahogany table, and placing it under the gas fixture seats herself and begins to play again, then papa follows with another table of the same discription, and they play solatair till bed-time.

We have just had our Prince and Pauper pictures taken; two groups and some little single ones. The groups (the Interview and Lady Jane Grey scene) were pretty good, the lady Jane scene was perfect, just as pretty as it could be, the Interview was not so good; and two of the little single pictures were very good indeed, but one was very bad. Yet on the whole we think they were a success.

Papa has done a great deal in his life I think, that is good, and very remarkable, but I think if he had had the advantages with which he could have developed the gifts which he has made no use of in writing his books, or in any other way for other peoples pleasure and benefit outside of his own family and intimate friends, he could have done *more* than he has and a great deal more even. He is known to the public as a humorist, but he has much more in him that is earnest than that is humorous. He has a keen sense of the ludicrous, notices funny stories and incidents knows how to tell them, to improve upon them, and does not forget them. He has been through a great many of the funny adventures related in "Tom Sayer" and in "Huckleberry Finn," *himself* and he lived among just such boys, and in just such villages all the days of his early life. His "Prince and Pauper is his most orriginal, and best production; it shows the most of any of his books what kind of pictures are in his mind, usually. Not that the pictures of England in the 16th Century and the adventures of a little prince and pauper are the kind of things he mainly thinks about; but that *that* book, and those pictures represent the train of thought and imagination he would be likely to be thinking of to-day, to-morrow, or next day, more nearly than those given in "Tom Sawyer or "Huckleberry Finn."*

Papa can make exceedingly bright jokes, and he enjoys funny things, and when he is with people he jokes and laughs a great deal, but still he is more interested in earnest books and earnest subjects to talk upon, than in humorous ones.†

When we are all alone at home, nine times out of ten, he talks about some very earnest subject, (with an ocasional joke thrown in) and he a good deal more often talks upon such subjects than upon the other kind.

He is as much of a Pholosopher as anything I think. I think he could have done a great deal in this direction if he had studied while young, for he seems to enjoy reasoning out things, no matter what; in a great many such directions he has greater ability than in the gifts which have made him famous.

Thus at fourteen she had made up her mind about me, and in no timorous or uncertain terms had set down her reasons for her opinion. Fifteen years were to pass before any other critic—except Mr. Howells, I think—was to re-utter that daring opinion and print it. Right or wrong it was a brave position for that little analyzer to take. She never withdrew it afterward, nor modified it. She has spoken of herself as lacking physical courage, and has evinced her admiration of Clara's; but she had moral courage, which is the rarest of human qualities, and she kept it functionable by exercising it. I think that in questions of morals and politics she was usually on my side; but when she was not she had her reasons and maintained her ground. Two years after she passed out of my life I wrote a philosophy. Of the three persons who have seen the manuscript only one understood it, and all three condemned it. If she could have read it, she also would have condemned it, possibly,—probably, in fact—but she would have understood it. It would have had no difficulties for her on that score; also she would have found a tireless pleasure in analyzing and discussing its problems.

* It is so yet. M.T.

† She has said it well and correctly. Humor is a subject which has never had much interest for me. This is why I have never examined it, nor written about it nor used it as a topic for a speech. A hundred times it has been offered me as a topic in these past forty years, but in no case has it attracted me. M.T.

March 23, '86.

The other day was my birthday, and I had a little birthday party in the evening and papa acted some very funny charades with Mr. Gherhardt, Mr. Jesse Grant (who had come up from New York and was spending the evening with us) and Mr. Frank Warner. One of them was "on his knees" honys-sneeze. There were a good many other funny ones, all of which I dont remember. Mr. Grant was very pleasant, and began playing the charades in the most delightful way.

Susy's spelling has defeated me, this time. I cannot make out what "honys sneeze" stands for. Impromptu charades were almost a nightly pastime of ours, from the children's earliest days—they played in them with me when they were only five or six years old. As they increased in years and practice their love for the sport almost amounted to a passion, and they acted their parts with a steadily increasing ability. At first they required much drilling; but later they were generally ready as soon as the parts were assigned, and they acted them according to their own devices. Their stage-facility and absence of constraint and self-consciousness in the "Prince and Pauper" was a result of their charading practice.

At ten and twelve Susy wrote plays, and she and Daisy Warner and Clara played them in the library or up stairs in the schoolroom, with only themselves and the servants for audience. They were of a tragic and tremendous sort, and were performed with great energy and earnestness. They were dramatized (freely) from English history, and in them Mary Queen of Scots and Elizabeth had few holidays. The clothes were borrowed from the mother's wardrobe and the gowns were longer than necessary, but that was not regarded as a defect. In one of these plays Jean (three years old, perhaps) was Sir Francis Bacon. She was not dressed for the part, and did not have to say anything, but sat silent and decorous at a tiny table and was kept busy signing death-warrants. It was a really important office, for few entered those plays and got out of them alive.

March 26. Mamma and Papa have been in New York for two or three days, and Miss Corey has been staying with us. They are coming home to-day at two o'clock.

Papa has just begun to play chess, and he is very fond of it, so he has engaged to play with Mrs. Charles Warner every morning from 10 to 12, he came down to supper last night, full of this pleasant prospect, but evidently with something on his mind. Finally he said to mamma in an appologetical tone, Susy Warner and I have a plan.

"Well" mamma said "what now, I wonder?"

Papa said that Susy Warner and he were going to name the chess men after some of the old bible heroes, and then play chess on Sunday.

April 18, '86.

Mamma and papa Clara and Daisy have gone to New York to see the "Mikado." They are coming home to-night at half past seven.

Last winter when Mr. Cable was lecturing with papa, he wrote this letter to him just before he came to visit us.

Everett House
New York Jan. 21/84.

Dear Uncle,

That's one nice thing about me, I never bother any one, to offer me a good thing twice. You dont ask me to stay over Sunday, but then you dont ask me to leave Saturday night, and knowing the nobility of your nature as I do—thank you, I'll stay till Monday morning.*

Your's and the dear familie's
George W. Cable.

It seems a prodigious while ago! Two or three nights ago I dined at Andrew Carnegie's with a score of other men, and at my side was Cable—actually an old man, really an old man, that once so young chap! Sixty-two years old, frost on his head, seven grandchildren in stock, and a brand-new wife to re-begin life with!

Wednesday, December 26, 1906

Mr. Clemens's experiments in phrenology with Fowler; also in palmistry—General verdict, he had no sense of humor—His speech before the copyright committees of Congress.

I lately received a letter from England from a gentleman whose belief in phrenology is strong, and who wonders why phrenology has apparently never interested me enough to move me to write about it. I have explained, as follows:

21 Fifth Avenue.
Dec. 18, 1906.

Dear Sir:

I never did profoundly study phrenology; therefore I am neither qualified to express an opinion about it nor entitled to do so. In London, 33 or 34 years ago, I made a small test of phrenology for my better information. I went to Fowler under an assumed name, and he examined my elevations and depressions and gave me a chart which I carried home to the Langham Hotel and studied with great interest and amusement—the same interest and amusement which I should have found in the chart of an impostor who had been passing himself off for me, and who did not resemble me in a single sharply defined detail. I waited 3 months and went to Mr. Fowler again, heralding my arrival with a card bearing both my name and my nom de guerre. Again I carried away an elaborate chart. It contained several sharply defined details of my character, but it bore no recognizable resemblance to the earlier chart. These experiences gave me a prejudice against phrenology which has lasted until now. I am aware that the prejudice should have been against Fowler, instead of against the art; but I am human and that is not the way that prejudices act.

* Cable never traveled Sundays.—M.T., Dec. 22, 1906.

In America, forty or fifty years ago, Fowler and Wells stood at the head of the phrenological industry, and the firm's name was familiar in all ears. Their publications had a wide currency, and were read and studied and discussed by truth-seekers and by converts all over the land. One of the most frequent arrivals in our village of Hannibal was the peripatetic phrenologist, and he was popular, and always welcome. He gathered the people together and gave them a gratis lecture on the marvels of phrenology, then felt their bumps and made an estimate of the result, at twenty-five cents per head. I think the people were almost always satisfied with these translations of their characters—if one may properly use that word in this connection; and indeed the word is right enough, for the estimates really were translations, since they conveyed seeming facts out of apparent simplicities into unsimple technical forms of expression, although as a rule their meanings got left behind on the journey. Phrenology found many a bump on a man's head, and it labeled each bump with a formidable and outlandish name of its own. The phrenologist took delight in mouthing these great names; they gurgled from his lips in an easy and unembarrassed stream, and this exhibition of cultivated facility compelled the envy and admiration of everybody. By and by the people became familiar with these strange names and addicted to the use of them, and they batted them back and forth in conversation with deep satisfaction—a satisfaction which could hardly have been more contenting if they had known for certain what the words meant.

It is not at all likely, I think, that the traveling expert ever got any villager's character quite right, but it is a safe guess that he was always wise enough to furnish his clients character-charts that would compare favorably with George Washington's. It was a long time ago, and yet I think I still remember that no phrenologist ever came across a skull in our town that fell much short of the Washington standard. This general and close approach to perfection ought to have roused suspicion, perhaps, but I do not remember that it did. It is my impression that the people admired phrenology and believed in it, and that the voice of the doubter was not heard in the land.

I was reared in this atmosphere of faith and belief and trust, and I think its influence was still upon me, so many years afterward, when I encountered Fowler's advertisements in London. I was glad to see his name, and glad of an opportunity to personally test his art. The fact that I went to him under a fictitious name is an indication that not the whole bulk of the faith of my boyhood was still with me; it looks like circumstantial evidence that in some way my faith had suffered impairment in the course of the years. I found Fowler on duty, in the midst of the impressive symbols of his trade. On brackets, on tables, on shelves, all about the room, stood marble-white busts, hairless, every inch of the skull occupied by a shallow bump, and every bump labeled with its imposing name, in black letters.

Fowler received me with indifference, fingered my head in an uninterested way, and named and estimated my qualities in a bored and monotonous voice. He said I possessed amazing courage, an abnormal spirit of daring, a pluck, a stern will, a fearlessness that were without limit. I was astonished at this, and gratified, too; I had not suspected it before; but then he foraged over on the other side of my skull and found a hump there which he called "caution." This hump was so tall, so mountainous, that it reduced my courage-bump to a mere hillock by comparison, although the courage-bump had been so prominent, up to that time—according to his description of it—that it ought to have been a capable thing to hang my hat on; but it amounted to nothing, now, in the presence of that Matterhorn which he called my Caution. He explained that if that Matterhorn had been left out of my scheme of character, I would have been one of the bravest men that ever lived—possibly the bravest—but that my cautiousness was so prodigiously superior to it that it abolished my courage and made me almost spectacularly timid. He continued his discoveries, with the result that I came out safe and sound, at the end, with a hundred great and shining qualities; but which lost their value and amounted to nothing because each of the hundred was coupled up with an opposing defect which took the effectiveness all out of it. However, he found a *cavity,* in one place; a cavity where a bump would have been in anybody else's skull. That cavity, he said, was all alone, all by itself, occupying a solitude, and had no opposing bump, however slight in elevation, to modify and ameliorate its perfect completeness and isolation. He startled me by saying that that cavity represented the total absence of the sense of humor! He now became almost interested. Some of his indifference disappeared. He almost grew eloquent over this America which he had discovered. He said he often found bumps of humor which were so small that they were hardly noticeable, but that in his long experience this was the first time he had ever come across a *cavity* where that bump ought to be.

I was hurt, humiliated, resentful, but I kept these feelings to myself; at bottom I believed his diagnosis was wrong, but I was not certain. In order to make sure, I thought I would wait until he should have forgotten my face, and the peculiarities of my skull, and then come back and try again, and see if he had really known what he had been talking about, or had only been guessing. After three months I went to him again, but under my own names this time. Once more he made a striking discovery—the cavity was gone, and in its place was a Mount Everest—figuratively speaking—thirty-one thousand feet high, the loftiest bump of humor he had ever encountered in his life-long experience! I went from his presence prejudiced against phrenology, but it may be, as I have said to the English gentleman, that I ought to have conferred the prejudice upon Fowler, and not upon the art which he was exploiting.*

Eleven years ago, on board a ship bound for Europe, William T. Stead made a photograph of my right hand, and afterwards, in London, sent replicas of it to twelve palmists, concealing from them my name, and asking them to make and send to him estimates of the character of the owner of the hand. The estimates were furnished, and Stead published six or seven of them in his magazine. By those estimates I found that my make-up was about like anybody else's; I did not seem to differ much from other people; certainly in no prominent and striking way—except in a single detail. In none of the estimates was the word humor mentioned—if my memory is not mistreating

* *Feb. 10,* 1907. The English gentleman was not really a gentleman: he sold my private letter to a newspaper.

me—except in one; in that one the palmist said that the possessor of that hand was totally destitute of the sense of humor.

Two years ago, Colonel Harvey took prints of my two hands and sent them to six professional palmists of distinguished reputation here in New York City; and he, also, withheld my name, and asked for estimates. History repeated itself. The word humor occurred only once in the six estimates, and then it was accompanied by the definite remark that the possessor of the hands was destitute of the sense of humor. Now then, I have Fowler's estimate; I have the estimates of Stead's six or seven palmists; I have the estimates of Harvey's half-dozen: the evidence that I do not possess the sense of humor is overwhelming, satisfying, convincing, incontrovertible—and at last I believe it myself.

The speech which I made before the copyright committees of Congress a week or two ago has arrived from Washington, in a Congressional document, and I will put it in here. It is pretty crazily reported, but no matter; it contains the points, and that is the essential thing.

Statement of Mr. Samuel L. Clemens.

Mr. Clemens. I have read the bill. At least I have read such portions of it as I could understand; and indeed I think no one but a practised legislator can read this bill and thoroughly understand it, and I am not a practised legislator.

Necessarily I am interested particularly and especially in the part of the bill which concerns my trade. I like the bill, and I like that proposed extension from the present limit of copyright-life of forty-two years to the author's life and fifty years after. I think that will satisfy any reasonable author, because it will take care of his children. Let the grandchildren take care of themselves. "Sufficient unto the day." That would satisfy me very well. That would take care of my daughters, and after that I am not particular. I shall then long have been out of this struggle and independent of it. Like *all* the trades and occupations of the United States, ours is represented and protected in that bill. I like it. I want them to be represented and protected and encouraged. They are all worthy, all important, and if we can take them under our wing by copyright, I would like to see it done. I should like to have you encourage oyster culture in it, and anything else that comes into your minds. I have no illiberal feeling toward the bill. I think it is just, I think it is righteous, and I hope it will pass without reduction or amendment of any kind.

I am aware that copyright must have a term, must have a limit, because that is required by the Constitution of the United States, which sets aside the earlier constitution, which we call the Decalogue. The Decalogue says that you shall not take away from any man his property. I do not like to use the harsher Scriptural phrase, "Thou shalt not steal." But the laws of England and America do take away property from the owner. They select out the people who create the literature of the land. They always talk handsomely about the literature of the land; they always say what a monumental thing a great literature is. In the midst of their enthusiasm they turn around and do what they can to crush it, discourage it, and put it out of existence. I know that we must have that limit. But forty-two years is too much of a limit. I do not know why there should be a limit at all. I am quite unable to guess why there should be a limit to the possession of the product of a man's labor. There is no limit to real estate. As Dr. Hale has just suggested, you might just as well, after you had discovered a coal mine and worked it forty-two years, have the Government step in and take it away—under what pretext?

The excuse for a limited copyright in the United States is that an author who has produced a book and has had the benefit of it for that term has had the profit of it long enough, and therefore the Government takes the property, which does not belong to it, and generously gives it to the eighty-eight millions. That is the idea. If it did that, that would be one thing. But it does not do anything of the kind. It merely takes the author's property, merely takes from his children the bread and profit of that book, and gives the publisher *double* profit. The publisher and some of his confederates who are in the conspiracy rear families in affluence, and they continue the enjoyment of these ill-gotten gains generation after generation. They live forever, the publishers do.

As I say, this limit is quite satisfactory to me—for the author's life, and fifty years after. In a few weeks, or months, or years I shall be out of it. I hope to get a monument. I hope I shall not be entirely forgotten. I shall subscribe to the monument myself. But I shall not be caring what happens if there is fifty years' added life of my copyright. My copyrights produce to me annually a good deal more money than I have any use for. But those children of mine have use for it. I can take care of myself as long as I live. I know half a dozen trades, and I can invent half a dozen more. I can get along. But I like the fifty years' extension, because that benefits my two daughters, who are not as competent to earn a living as I am, because I have carefully raised them as young ladies who don't know anything and can't do anything. So I hope Congress will extend to them that charity which they have failed to get from me.

Why, if a man who is mad—not mad, but merely strenuous—about race suicide should come to me and try to get me to use my large political and ecclesiastical influence for the passage of a bill by this Congress limiting families to twenty-two children by one mother, I should try to calm him down. I should reason with him. I should say to him, "That is the very parallel to the copyright limitation by statute. Leave it alone. Leave it alone and it will take care of itself." There are only one or two couples at one time in the United States that can reach that limit. Now, if they reach that limit let them go on. Make the limit a thousand years. Let them have all the liberty they want. You are not going to hurt anybody in that way.

The very same with copyright. One author per lustrum produces a book which can outlive the forty-two-year limit and that is all. This nation cannot produce three authors per lustrum who can create a book that will outlast forty-two years. The thing is demonstrably impossible. It cannot be done. To limit copyright is to take the bread out of the mouths of the children of that one author per lustrum, century in and century out. That is all you get of limiting copyright.

I made an estimate once when I was to be called before the Copyright Committee of the House of Lords, as to the output of books, and by my estimate we had issued and published in this country since the Declaration of Independence two hundred and twenty thousand books. What was the use of protecting those books by copyright? They are all gone. They had all perished before they were ten years old. There is only about one book in a thousand that can outlive forty-two years of copyright. Therefore why put a limit at all? You might just as well limit a family to twenty-two. It will take care of itself. If you try to recall to your minds the number of men in the nineteenth century who wrote books in America which books lived forty-two years you will begin with Fenimore Cooper, follow that with Washington Irving, Harriet Beecher Stowe, and Edgar A. Poe, and you will not go far until you begin to find that the list is sharply limited. You come to Whittier and Holmes and Emerson, and you find Howells and Thomas Bailey Aldrich, and then the list gets pretty thin and you question if you can find twenty persons in the United States in a whole century who have produced books that could outlive or did outlive the forty-two-year limit. You can take all the authors in the United States whose books have outlived the forty-two-year limit and you can seat them on one of those benches there. Allow three children to each of them, and you certainly can put the result down at a hundred persons and seat them in three more benches. That is the insignificant number whose bread and butter are to be taken away. For what purpose? For what profit to anybody?

Nobody can tell what that profit is. It is only those books that will outlast the forty-two-year limit that have any value after ten or fifteen years. The rest are all dead. Then you turn those few books into the hands of the pirate—into the hands of the legitimate publisher—and they go on and get the profit that properly should have gone to wife and children. I do not think that is quite right. I told you what the idea was in this country for a limited copyright.

The English idea of copyright, as I found, was different, when I was before the committee of the House of Lords. The spokesman was a very able man, Lord Thwing, a man of great reputation, but he didn't know anything about copyright and publishing. Naturally he didn't, because he hadn't been brought up to this trade. It is only people who have had intimate personal experience with the triumphs and griefs of an occupation who know how to treat it and get what is justly due.

Now that gentleman had no purpose or desire in the world to rob anybody of anything, but this was the proposition—fifty years' extension—and he asked me what I thought the limit of copyright ought to be.

"Well," I said, "perpetuity." I thought it ought to last forever.

Well he didn't like that idea much. I could see some resentment in his manner, and he went on to say that the idea of a perpetual copyright was illogical, and so forth, and so on. And here was his reason: *that it has long ago been decided that ideas are not property,* that there can be no such thing as *property in ideas.*

I said there was property in ideas before Queen Anne's time; it was recognized that books had perpetual copyright up to her day. Dr. Hale has explained, a moment ago, why they reduced it to fourteen years in Queen Anne's time. That is a very charitable explanation of that event. I never heard it before. I thought a lot of publishers had got together and got it reduced. But I accept Dr. Hale's more charitable view, for he is older than I am, but not much older, and knows more than I do, but not much more.

That there could be no such thing as property in an intangible idea, was his position. He said, "What is a book? A book is just built from base to roof of ideas, and there can be no property in them."

I said I wished he could mention any kind of property existing on this planet, that had a pecuniary value, which value was not derived from an idea or ideas—*solely.*

"Well," he said, "landed estate—real estate."

"Why," I said, "take an assumed case, of a dozen Englishmen traveling through South Africa—they camp out; eleven of them see nothing at all; they are mentally blind. But there is one in the party who knows what that near-by harbor means, what this lay of the land means; to him it means that some day—you cannot tell when—a railway will come through here, and there on that harbor a great city will spring up. *That is his idea.* And he has *another* idea, and so, perhaps, he trades his last bottle of Scotch whisky and a horse blanket to the principal chief of that region for a piece of land the size of Pennsylvania. There is the value of an idea *applied to real estate.* That day will come, as it was to come when the Cape-to-Cairo Railway should pierce Africa and cities should be built; there was some smart person who bought the land from the chief and received his everlasting gratitude, just as was the case with William Penn, who bought for forty dollars' worth of stuff the giant area of Pennsylvania. He did a righteous thing. We have to be enthusiastic over it, because that was a thing that had never happened before probably. There again was the *application of an idea to real estate.* Every *improvement* that is put upon real estate is the result of an *idea* in somebody's head. A sky-scraper is another idea. The railway was another idea. The telephone and all those things are merely *symbols* which *represent ideas.* The wash-tub was the result of an idea. The thing hadn't existed before. There is no penny's-worth of property on this earth that does not derive its pecuniary value from *ideas* and association of ideas applied and applied and applied again and again and again, as in the case of the steam engine. You have several hundred people contributing their ideas to the improvement and the final perfection of that great thing, whatever it is—telephone, telegraph, and all."

A book *does* consist solely of ideas, from the base to the summit, *like any other property,* and should not be put under the ban of any restriction, but should be the property of the author and his heirs forever and ever, just as a butcher shop is, or—*anything,* I don't care what it is. It all has the same basis. The law should recognize the right of perpetuity in this and every other kind of property. Yet for this property I do not ask that at all. Fifty years from now I shall not be here. I am sorry, but I shall not be here. Still, I should like to see the limit extended.

Of course we have to move by slow stages. When an event happens in this world, like that of 1714, under Queen Anne, it is a disaster, yet all the world imagines there was an element of justice in it. They do not know why they imagine it, but it is because somebody else has said so. The slow process of recovery has continued until our day, and will keep constantly progressing. First, fourteen years was added, and then a renewal for fourteen years; then you encountered Lord Macaulay, who made a speech on copyright when it was about to achieve a life of sixty years, which kept it at forty-two—a speech that was read and praised all over the world by everybody who did not know that Lord Macaulay did not know what he was talking about. So he inflicted this disaster upon his successors in the authorship of books. The recovery of our lost ground has to undergo regular and slow development—evolution.

Here is this bill, one instance of it. Make the limit the author's life and fifty years after, and, fifty years from now, Congress will see that that has not convulsed the world; has not destroyed any San Francisco. No earthquakes concealed in it anywhere. It has harmed nobody. It has merely fed some starving author's children. Mrs. Stowe's two daughters were close neighbors of mine, and—well, they had their living very much limited.

That is about all I was to say, I believe. I have some notes—I don't know in which pocket I put them—and probably I can't read them when I find them.

There was another thing that came up in that committee meeting. Lord Thwing asked me on what ground I could bring forth such a monstrosity as that—the idea of a perpetual copyright on literature.

He said, "England does not do that." That was good argument. If England doesn't do a thing, that is all right. Why should anybody else? England doesn't do it. England stands for limited copyright, and will stand for limited copyright, and not give unlimited copyright to anybody's books.

I said, "You are excepting one book."

He said, "No; there is no book in England that has perpetual copyright."

I said, "Yes; there is one book in England that has perpetual copyright, and that is the Bible."

He said, "There is no such copyright on the Bible in England."

But I had the documents with me, and I was able to convince him that not only does England confer perpetual copyright upon the Old and New Testaments, but also on the Revised Scriptures, and also on four or five other theological books, and confers those perpetual copyrights and the profits that may accrue not upon some poor author and his children, but upon the well-to-do Oxford University Press, which can take care of itself without perpetual copyright. There was that one instance of injustice, the discrimination between the author of the present day and the author of thousands of years ago, whose copyright had really expired by the statute of limitations.

I say again, as I said in the beginning, I have no enmities, no animosities toward this bill. This bill is plenty righteous enough for me. I like to see all these industries and arts propagated and encouraged by this bill. This bill will do that, and I do hope that it will pass and have no deleterious effect. I do seem to have an extraordinary interest in a whole lot of arts and things. The bill is full of those that I have nothing to do with. But that is in line with my generous, liberal nature. I can't help it. I feel toward those same people the same wide charity felt by the man who arrived at home at two o'clock in the morning from the club. He was feeling perfect satisfaction with life—was happy, was comfortable. There was his house weaving and weaving and weaving around. So he watched his chance, and by and by when the steps got in his neighborhood he made a jump and climbed up on the portico. The house went on weaving. He watched his door, and when it came around his way he plunged through it. He got to the stairs, went up on all fours. The house was so unsteady he could hardly reach the top step; his toe hitched on that step, and of course he crumpled all down and rolled all the way down the stairs and fetched up at the bottom with his arm around the newel-post; and he said, "God pity the poor sailors out at sea on a night like this!"

Thursday, December 27, 1906

Mind Cure comments—The sketch entitled "Luck," and the meeting with Lord Wolseley, the hero of the sketch.

From Susy's Biography.

> April 19.
>
> Yes the Mind Cure *does* seem to be working wonderfully, papa who has been using glasses now, for more than a year, has laid them off entirely. And my near-sightedness is realy getting better. It seems marvelous! When Jean has stomack ache Clara and I have tried to divert her, by telling her to lie on her side and try Mind Cure. The novelty of it, has made her willing to try it, and then Clara and I would exclaim about how wonderful it was it was getting better! And she would think it realy was finally, and stop crying, to our delight.
>
> The other day mamma went into the library and found her lying on the sofa with her back toward the door. She said "Why Jean what's the matter? dont you feel well? Jean said that she had a little stomack ache, and so thought she would lie down. Mamma said "Why dont you try mind cure?" "I am" Jean answered.

It is true that the Mind Cure worked wonders. For a million years the mind has been, in a large degree, master of the body, and has been able to heal many of the body's ailments. When the physician undertakes to cure you he requires you to continue the medicines until the cure has been effected; he would not promise a cure hampered by the understanding that you were to take the medicines when you pleased, and discontinue them at your convenience. In like manner, I suppose that the mind cannot do its healing effectively except it be kept steadily at its work, and its professional requirements be faithfully observed. Take a case of insomnia, for instance. The mind can cure that, and with certainty, under certain conditions—let us say under a single condition: that the patient shall keep watch and not allow his thoughts to interest themselves for a single instant in any distressing or harassing subject. This is all that is necessary to defeat insomnia, and the method is easy and simple—I mean as a rule. There are sorrows and troubles which the beginner's mind is not able to contend with successfully when those powerful aids—training and experience—are lacking; but to the trained mind, the long-experienced mind, the case is different; it seldom encounters a trouble which it cannot drive out of its client's thoughts and furnish him healing sleep and peace in its place. I am not speaking from hearsay, but from personal experience; and not from a brief experience, but from the continuous practice and experience of many years.

To divert the mind from a physical pain, or from a mental one, by the introduction of a new interest, *must* bring relief, because the mind cannot give full and effective attention to two subjects at the same time. The mind cannot get full satisfaction out of the most entertaining pain if you break in upon its vicious pleasures with a sudden and startling interruption. When you burn yourself, the mind centres all its attention upon the pain, to the exclusion of all other interests, and by this cunning method intensifies it and exaggerates it; but if the stove-pipe comes clattering down with a crash, the mind is diverted to that cataclysm for the moment, and the pain ceases. If the event were not a falling stove-pipe, but a rocking, and cracking, and crumbling sky-scraper in a San Francisco earthquake, and the sufferer were on the twentieth floor and it took him half an hour to pick his way down to the ground, through a rain of dropping plaster and brickbats, he would never feel a twinge of pain from his burn during the whole transit.

The mind cannot heal broken bones; and doubtless there are many other physical ills which it cannot heal, but it can greatly help to modify the severities of all of them, without exception, and there are mental and nervous ailments which it can wholly heal, without the help of physician or surgeon. Apparently there are many breeds of mental healing, to judge by the names applied to it—such as the Faith Cure, the Prayer Cure, Mental Healing, Christian Science, and so on—but I suspect, and indeed I also believe, that these are all one and the same thing, and do not need any but one name—Mind Cure. I think it is not a modern discovery. I think it has done its beneficent work in all the ages for a million years, among both the savage and the civilized. I think that all men, for a million years, have used it every day, unconsciously; that we all still use it daily, unconsciously; and that the physician is always making use of it when he says the hopeful and cheering word to his patient.

My family soon got interested in other matters, and we presently ceased to keep our minds at their beneficent work upon our ailments, and therefore never found out just how much or how little our minds could be depended upon to benefit us. We certainly did persuade ourselves that our eyes were helped, and for a time I got along quite well enough without my glasses, but by and by I resumed them, and have not since discarded them. If Susy and her mother got rid, or partially rid, of their nearsightedness, it was only for a time; they became interested in other matters and the defect returned, and remained with them to the last. I feel quite certain that Christian Science heals many physical and mental ills; but I also feel just as certain that it could call itself by any other name and do the same work without any diminution of its effectiveness.

From Susy's Biography.

> The other night papa read us a little article, which he had just written entitled "Luck," it was very good we thought.

That sketch is in some book of mine, and I wish I had it by me, so that I could refresh my memory as to its details; but the book is up stairs, therefore we will let it go. The details are very curious and interesting. I wish it understood that I am now speaking from my grave, and that it is my desire, and also my command, that my heirs and assigns shall keep out of print what I am now about to say until I shall have been fertilizing the earth for twenty-five or thirty years. The genesis of the sketch is as follows:

About twenty-one years ago, Rev. Mr. Twichell came over to our house one evening, full of a tale which he wanted to tell. It was the tale that is set forth in that sketch, and I jotted it down at once, so that I might be sure to get the details right. An English clergyman, on his travels, had been putting in the day with Twichell; both of them had been chaplains in fighting regiments, and they had been having a pleasant time exchanging war reminiscences. In the course of the talk the Englishman told the tale that is narrated in the sketch. He would not name the hero of the sketch, and he defeated all of Joe's theologically sly and ingenious efforts to get at that forbidden name. The Englishman was himself the chaplain of the sketch, and he said that, incredible, unbelievable, unthinkable, as the details of it were, they were nevertheless true.

I wrote the sketch and read it to the family. It naturally had a vivid interest for them, because they were privately aware that it was history; whereas to the outside reader it would pass for merely a more or less ingenious collocation of not very plausible inventions. It made enough of an impression upon Susy to move her to mention it in the Biography.

I doubted the story—I couldn't help it; but Twichell did not doubt it. He said that the English chaplain was manifestly a sincere and truthful man, and that he was also as manifestly troubled about his confederate share in the lucky hero's astonishing adventures. I put the manuscript in my pigeon-holes, and there it lay for six years, along with half a dozen other sketches and short stories; then, when we were about to start in the summer of 1891 for a long sojourn in Europe, I took those old sketches out and sold them to the magazines. The "Luck" sketch appeared in *Harper's* about the end of that year. A year and a half or two years afterward, I was going along the street one day in Rome, when an English gentleman stopped me, named me, asked if he was right in his guess, and when I said he was, we dropped into conversation and took a long walk together. By and by, when we had become pretty well acquainted, and the ice was all melted, he said,

"Mr. Clemens, shall you go to England?"

I said "It is likely, but I don't know. My wife arranges the itinerary and saves me all that kind of trouble. I think it quite likely that we shall go."

He said "Shall you take your tomahawk with you?"

"Why yes, if it shall seem best."

"Well it will. Be advised. Take it with you."

"Why?"

"Because of that sketch of yours entitled 'Luck.' That sketch is current in England, and you will surely need your tomahawk."

"What makes you think so?"

"I think so because the hero of the sketch will naturally want your scalp, and will probably apply for it. Be advised. Take your tomahawk along."

"Why, even with it I shan't stand any chance, because I shan't know him when he applies, and he will have my scalp before I know what his errand is."

"Come, do you mean to say that you don't know who the hero of that sketch is?"

There was surprise and incredulity in his tone. I said,

"Indeed I haven't any idea who the hero of the sketch is."

"Very well; *he* knows who the hero of it is, and so does everybody in England, from the throne down. The tale is true. You have set down the facts veraciously; they were all known before you printed them; they were talked about privately long ago, but you are the first to make a public matter of them; also, you have added a detail to that history—you have added the chaplain. Nobody was able to guess, before, how that hero ever happened to get his start on his extraordinary career. The start had to be a miracle, apparently, but nobody could guess what the miracle was. The chaplain was the only man in the world, except the hero, who knew that deep and all-resolving secret. You have let it out, and now the career that followed is explained, justified, made plausible—let us say made possible. It was possible before, because it had happened, but it was not realizably possible until you revealed the crucial secret. Now then, you are speaking seriously when you tell me you don't know who the hero of that sketch is?"

"Yes, I am speaking seriously. I haven't any idea who it is. Who is it?"

"The high chief and topmost summit of the armies of England—Field-Marshall Lord Wolseley!"

It nearly took my breath away. Several times, during the next two or three years, I had similar conversations with Englishmen on the Continent. They always said "It is Wolseley. Everybody knew those curious facts before you printed them."

Nine years after I printed that sketch we were sojourning in London, and I went down into the city late on a Fourth of July night to attend a Fourth of July dinner, of Americans and Englishmen, and make a speech. It was so late when I arrived that half the guests had already departed, and only about two hundred remained. Choate was presiding, and was making a speech introductory of a British admiral. All of the row of chairs to his left, which had been occupied by distinguished guests, were vacant save one. I was passing along behind that row, intending to choose one of those seats, when I was accosted by that isolated celebrity, who put out his hand and said, smiling pleasantly and cordially,

"Oh sit down here by me, Mr. Clemens. I've been wanting to know you a long time. I am Lord Wolseley."

It caught me unprepared, and scared me so that I went white—so white that the rays from my face made the electric lights look yellow; but I sat down, and presently grew composed, and we had a most pleasant and friendly good time together; and if he had ever heard of that sketch of mine he did not manifest it in any way, and at twelve, midnight, I took my scalp home intact.

Friday, December 28, 1906

From Susy's Biography: some of the stories Mr. Clemens used to tell; tribute to Mr. Clemens from Andrew Lang; Mr. Clemens's speech for Booth dinner; the game of pegs for remembering dates; Mr. Clemens is found laughing over his own book—He comments upon this; also upon the mystery of style—Impossible for an author to conceal his own peculiar style—The coincidence of Dr. Holmes reading of death of relative, remarking that his name was incorrect because Dr. Holmes's father, who baptized him, had lost the slip of paper on which name was written, and the finding of the slip by Dr. Holmes immediately afterwards—The coincidence of the Bessie Stone letter and the coming upon "Mary" in "Huck Finn" immediately after.

From Susy's Biography.

The stories of prevailing interest which Papa tells us is "Jim and the strainin rag" and "Whoop says I." "Jim and the strainin rag" is simply a discription of a little scene way out west; but he tells it in such a funny way, that it is captivating.

"Jim and the strainin Rag"

"Aunt Sal!—Aunt Sal! Jim's gone got the new strainin rag roun his sore schin. a.s. you Jim, take that ar strainin rag off you sore schin, an renc it out, I allers did dispise nastiness."

"Whoop Says She."

Good morning Mrs. O'Callahan. What is it yer got in yer basket? Fish says she. They stinc says I. You lie, says she. Ter Hell says I. *Whoop!* says she—(and then the ingagement was on.)

Susy meant well, but in this monologue (which is from one of Charles Reade's books, I think), she has made some important omissions—among them the point of the thing. But it's no matter. The late Mr. Bunce used to recite it in the billiard room occasionally, to relieve his feelings when the game was going against him. There was a good deal of it, and he placed the scene of it in a magistrate's court, where the speaker was explaining to the judge how a row originated, and how no one was in fault but the badly battered Bridget O'Callahan, who was of a quarrelsome disposition and ever ready to take umbrage at the least little thing. Mr. Bunce threw prodigious energy and fire into the recitation, and his acting appealed to Susy's histrionic predilections. Mr. Bunce's "whoo-oop!" was the gem of the performance, and no one could do it as he did it.

The "Strainin' Rag" was a reminiscence of my boyhood-life among the slaves, and it is probable that one of its attractions for the children was, that the reciting of it was not permissible on the premises. The forbidden has always had value, for both the young and the old. Susy's way of spelling shin seems to me to lift that lowly word above the commonplace.

> We all played a game of croquet yesterday evening, and aunt Clara and I beat papa and Clara, to our perfect satisfaction.
>
> By Andrew Lang.
>
> Mark Twain has reached his fiftieth birthday, and has been warmly congratulated on his "Jubilee" by most of the wits of his native land. As the Ettrick Shepherd said to Wordsworth, when first they met "I'm glad you'r so young a man" so one might observe to Mark, and wish he were still younger. But his genious is still young, and perhaps never showed so well, with such strength and variety, such varacity and humor, as in his latest book "Huckleberry Finn." Persons of extreemly fine culture may have no taste for Mark, when he gets among pictures and holy places, Mark is all himself, and the most powerful and diverting writer I think of his American contemporaries. Here followeth, rather late, but heartily well meant, a tribute to Mark on his Jubilee:
>
> For Mark Twain
>
> To brave Mark Twain, across the sea,
> The years have brought his jubilee.
> One hears it, half in pain,
> That fifty years have passed and gone,
> Since danced the merry star that shone
> Above the babe Mark Twain.
>
> How many, and many a weary day,
> When sad enough were we, Mark's way,
> (Unlike the Laureates Marks)
> Has made us laugh until we cried
> And, sinking back exhausted, sighed
> Like Gargery Wot larks!
>
> We turn his pages and we see
> The Mississippi flowing free;
> We turn again and grin
> Oer all Tom Sayer did and planned
> With him of the ensanguined hand,
> With Huckleberry Finn!
>
> Spirit of Mirth, whose chime of bells,
> Shakes on his cap, and sweetly swells
> Across the Atlantic main,
> Grant that Mark's laughter never die,
> That men through many a century
> May chucle oer Mark Twain!

Susy was properly and justly proud of Andrew Lang's affectionate hand-shake from over the ocean, and her manuscript shows that she copied his words with grateful and painstaking care, yet in spite of her loyal intentions she has raised his spelling to the sunny altitudes of her own, those fair heights where the free airs blow. But no harm is done; if she had asked of him the privilege she would have had it. Even to that quaint ennobling of the word chuckle, in the last line.

For Booth Dinner.

(This speech was given to Susy, and never used or printed, for the Long Clam had bedridden me. M.T.)

Although I am debarred from making a speech, by circumstances which I will presently explain, I yet claim the privilege of adding my voice to yours in deep and sincere welcome and homage to Edwin Booth; of adding my admiration of his long and illustrious career and blemishless character; and thereto my gratification in the consciousness that his great sun is not yet westering, but stands in full glory in the zenith.

I wish to ask your attention to a statement, in writing. It is not safe or wise to trust a serious matter to off-hand speech—especially when you are trying to explain a thing. Now, to make a clean breast, and expose the whole trouble right at the start, I have been entertaining a stranger; I have been at it two days and two nights, and am worn, and jaded, and in fact defeated. He may be known to some of you. He is classified in natural history as the Long Clam, and in my opinion is the most disastrous fish that swims the sea. If you don't know him personally, let him alone; take him at hearsay, and meddle no further. He is a bivalve. When in his ulster, he is shaped like a weaver's shuttle, but there the resemblance ends: the weaver's shuttle travels, but the Long Clam abides; and you can digest a weaver's shuttle, if you wait, and pray. It is your idea, of course, to entertain yourself with the Long Clam, so you lay him on a bed of coals; he opens his mouth like a carpet-sack and smiles; this looks like mutual regard, and you think you are friends, but it is not so; that smile means, "It is your innings now—I'll see you later." You swallow the Long Clam—and history begins. It begins, but it begins so remotely, so clandestinely that you don't know it. You have several hours which you can't tell from repose. Then you go to bed. You close your eyes and think you are gliding off to sleep. It is at this point that the Long Clam rises up and goes to the bat. The window rattles; the Long Clam calls your attention to it. You whirl out of bed and wedge the sash—the wrong sash. You get nearly to sleep; the sash rattles again. The Long Clam reminds you. You whirl out and pound in some more wedges. You plunge into bed with emphasis; a sort of bogus unconsciousness begins to dull your brain; then some water begins to drip somewhere. Every drop that falls, hurts. You think you will try Mind Cure on that drip and so neutralize its effects. This causes the Long Clam to smile. You chafe and fret for fifteen minutes, then you earthquake yourself out of bed and explore for that drip with a breaking heart, and language to match. But you never find it. When you go to bed this time, you understand that your faculties are all up for the night, there is business on hand, and you have got to superintend. The procession begins to move. All the crimes you have ever committed, and which you supposed you had forgotten, file past—and every one of them carries a banner. The Long Clam is on hand to comment. All the dead and buried indignities you have ever suffered, follow; they bite like fangs, they burn like fire. The Long Clam is getting in his work, now. He has dug your conscience out and occupied the old stand; and you will find that for real business, one Long Clam is worth thirty consciences. The rest of that night is slow torture at the stake. There are lurid instants at intervals, occupied by dreams; dreams that stay only half a second, but they seem to expose the whole universe, and disembowel it before your eyes; other dreams that sweep away the solar system and leave the shoreless void occupied from one end to the other by just you and the Long Clam. Now you know what it is to sit up with a Long Clam. Now you know what it is to try to entertain a Long Clam. Now you know what it is to keep a Long Clam amused; to try to keep a Long Clam from feeling lonesome; to try to make a Long Clam satisfied and happy. As for me, I would rather go on an orgy with anybody in the world than a Long Clam; I would rather never have any fun at all than try to get it out of a Long Clam. A Long Clam doesn't know when to stop. After you've had all the fun you want the Long Clam is just getting fairly started. In my opinion there is too much company about a Long Clam. A Long Clam is more sociable than necessary. I've got this one along yet. It's two days, now, and this is the third night, as far as I've got. In all that time I haven't had a wink of sleep that didn't have an earthquake in it, or a cyclone, or an instantaneous photograph of Sheol. And so all that is left of me is a dissolving rag or two of former humanity and a fading memory of happier days; the rest is Long Clam. That is the explanation. That is why I don't make a speech. I am perfectly willing to make speeches for myself, but I am not going to make speeches for any Long Clam that ever fluttered. Not after the way I've been treated. Not that I don't respect the Long Clam, for I do. I consider the Long Clam by long odds the capablest creature that swims the salt sea; I consider the Long Clam the Depew of the watery world, just as I consider Depew the Long Clam of the great world of intellect and oratory. If any of you find life uneventful, lacking variety, not picturesque enough for you, go into partnership with a Long Clam.

Biography Continued.

Mr. W. D. Howells, and his daughter Pilla have been here, to visit us, and we have enjoyed them very much. They arived Saturday at half past two and staid till Sunday night. Sunday night at supper papa and Mr. Howells began to talk about the Jews. Mr. Howells said that in "Silas Lapham" he wrote a sentence about a Jew, that was perfectly true, and he meant no harm to the Jews in saying it, it was true, and he saw no reason why it should not be recognized as fact. But after the story came out in the Century, two or three Jews wrote him, saying in a very plaintive and meek way, that they wished he wouldn't say that about them, he said that after he received these letters his consious pricked him very much for having said what he did.

At last one of these Jews wrote him asking him to take that sentence out of the story when it came out in book form; Mr. Howells said he thought the Jews were a persecuted race, and a race already down. So he decided to take out the sentence, when the story appeared in book form.

Papa said that a Mr. Wood an equantance of his, new a rich Jew who read papa's books a great deal. One day this Jew said that papa was the only great humorist who had ever written without poking some fun against a Jew and that as the Jews were such a good subject for fun and funny ridicule, he had often wondered why in all his stories, not one said or had anything in it against the Jews. And he asked Mr. Wood the next time he saw papa to ask him how this happened.

Mr. Wood soon did see papa, and spoke to him upon this subject. Papa at first did not know himself why it was that he had never spoken unkindly of the Jews in any of his books, but after thinking awhile he decided that the Jews had always seemed to him a race much to be respected; also they had suffered much, and had been greatly persecuted; so to ridicul or make fun of them, seemed to be like attacking a man that was already down, and of course that fact took away whatever there was funny in the ridicule of a Jew.

He said it seemed to him, the Jews ought to be respected very much, for two things perticularly, one was that they never begged, that one never saw a Jew begging, another was that they always took care of their poor, that although one never heard of a Jewish orphans home, there must be such things, for the poor Jews seemed always well taken care of.

He said that once the ladies of a orphans home wrote him asking if he would come to Chicago* and lecture for the benefit of the orphans. So papa went, and read for their benefit. He said that they were the most forlorn looking little wretches ever seen. The ladies said they had done everything possible, but could not raise enough money, and they said that what they realy most needed was a bath tub. So they said that as their last resource they decided to write to him asking him to lecture for them, to see if in that way they could not raise a little money.

And they said what was most humiliating about their lack of means was that right next door, there was a Jewish Orphans home which had everything that was needed to make it comfortable. They said that this home was also a work of charity, but that they never knew of its begging for anything of any one outside a Jew. They said no one (hardly) knew that it was Jewish home, exept they who lived right next door to it, and that very few knew there was such a building in the city.

Stonington.—
May 3, 1886.

Mr. Samuel L. Clemens.

My dear Sir,

When I remember how my dear father Dr. Todd of Pittsfield, Mass. was almost driven to dispair by the silly

Susy probably lost the rest of the letter. The rest of her page is blank.

The following letter—evidently from Virginia—has no date and no signature.

* Cleveland, not Chicago. S.L.C.

Soon after the war, a dear friend in Baltimore sent me a copy of Mark Twain's "Inocents Abroad," it was the first copy, that reached the valley, possibly the first in Virginia.

All of our household read it, I lent it to our friends, and at length nearly every body in the village had read it.

The book was so much enjoyed by people who were sick or sad, that it came to be considered a remedy for all cases where it could be taken, and we sent it about to people who as the prayer book says were troubled in mind, body or "estate," a discription which seemed to most Virginians in those sad and weary days. After I came to Lynchburgh the book, was sent out on its travells again, and was litterally worn out in the service. It was long past being sewed or glued, when it started on its last journey; but many of the fragments were still readable, and I tied them together again, and sent it to a nice young colored girl, to give to her sick Mother to read.

I have long hoped some good Yankee, would be inspired to send me a new copy. Several of Mark Twain's books I should like much to have for my library. And I think they would do a great deal of good. At one time a lady lived near me, whose daily life was so exeptionally severe and wearing, that only a woman remarkably strong in mind and body, could have stood the strain. I once lent her a copy of "Roughing It," which had been loaned to me, with permission to use it a while in my library. For a long time I could not enduce my careburdened friend to return the book, though I begged earnestly for it. She said that volume was her chief resource, and comfort, when worn out with her arduous duties, and she could not do without it. A Minister to whom I chanced to repeat this remark, meaning to show the value of the book, said grimly "she had better read her bible!" I could not agree with him, as I knew my friend did not neglect her religious duties, and made the bible her rule of conduct, and thought she did well, to turn to Mark Twain for diversion.

May 6, '86.

Papa has contrived a new way for us to remember dates. We are to bring to breakfast every morning a date, without fail, and now they are to be dates from English historie. At the farm two summers ago he drove pegs into the ground all around the place representing each king's reign following each other according. Then we used to play games running between these different pegs till finally we knew when each king or queen reigned and in refference to the kings preceeding them.

Among the principal merits of the games which we played by help of the pegs were these—that they had to be played in the open air, and that they compelled brisk exercise. The pegs were driven in the sod along the curves of the road that wound through the grounds and up the hill toward my study. They were white, and were two and a half feet high. Each peg represented an English monarch and the date of his accession. The space between pegs was measured off with a tape-line, and each foot of it covered a year of a reign. William the Conqueror's peg stood in front of the house; twenty-one feet away stood the peg of William Rufus; thirteen feet from that one stood the first Henry's peg; thirty-five feet beyond it stood Stephen's peg—and so on. One could stand near the Conqueror and have all English history skeletonized and land-marked and mile-posted under his eye. To the left, around a curve, the reigns were visible down to Runnymede; then, at the beginning of a straight piece of road stood the peg of Henry III, followed by an impressive stretch of vacancy, with the peg of the first Edward at the end of it. Then the road turned to the right and came up to the end of the reign of the fifth Henry; then it turned to the left and made a long flight up the hill, and ended—without a peg—near the first corner of my study. Victoria's reign was not finished, yet; many years were to elapse before the peg of her successor would be required.

The vacancies between the pegs furnished an object-lesson; their position in the procession another. To read that James I reigned from 1603 until 1625, and William II from 1087 till 1100, and George III from 1760 till 1820 gives no definite impression of the length of the periods mentioned, but the long and short spaces between the pegs of these kings conveyed a quite definite one through the eye to the mind. The eye has a good memory. Many years have gone by, and the pegs have disappeared, but I still see them, and each in its place; and no king's name falls upon my ear without my seeing his pegs at once and noticing just how many feet of space he takes up along the road.

> The other day, mamma went into the library and found papa sitting there reading a book, and roaring with laughter over it. She asked him what he was reading, he answered that he hadn't stopped to look at the title of the book, and went on reading; she glanced over his shoulder at the cover, and found it was one of his own books.

That is another of Susy's unveilings of me. Still, she did not garble history but stated a fact.

I do not remember what book of mine I was reading that day, but I remember the circumstance very well, although it was so many years ago. It was a quiet and peaceful Sunday afternoon, and Mrs. Clemens sat by the wood fire in the library, deeply interested in a book. I sat in the bay window on the opposite side of the room, and I took a book at random from the shelves there and began to read it, with the scandalous result recorded by Susy. I suppose I ought to have been ashamed when I found that the book which had been so delighting me was my own, and it is just possible that I tried to soften my case by *saying* I was ashamed; but at bottom I wasn't, I was gratified. I judged that in feeling and manifesting high and cordial approval and admiration of the book, I had paid it a higher compliment than could have been paid it by any other critic. It was an old book; I do not know which one, but I know that it was one of the first two written by me; therefore it was twelve or fifteen years old. Necessarily, I had changed a good deal in that stretch of time; necessarily my manner of phrasing had considerably changed, and so it was rather a marvelous thing that I should still be able to like the book, or, indeed, any considerable part of it. Of course there was many and many a passage in it that would have affronted and offended me, but by luck I didn't happen upon those, and I am sure I paid myself a very high compliment when I found any at all that did not arouse my hostility.

I soon forget my books after I have finished writing them. As a rule, years elapse before I glance at them again; then they are quite new to me. I can read them as a stranger would, and when I come upon a good thing in them I am as quick and competent to recognize it as any other stranger would be.

Style is a mysterious thing. It seems to be a part of the man, and a thing which he cannot get wholly away from by any art. It seems to leak from his pen in spite of him. Unquestionably, by watchfulness he can disguise his style, apparently—successfully and effectively, throughout a book—but only apparently; the success will not be complete; it will not be perfect; somewhere in the book his watchfulness will relax, and his pen will deliver itself of a phrase that will betray him to any one who is well acquainted with his style. I know this by experience. Ten or twelve years ago, when I sold to the Harpers the serial rights in the book called "Personal Recollections of Joan of Arc," I did not want the authorship to be known, because I did not wish to swindle the public. At that time, my nom de guerre placed upon a book meant to everybody that the book was of a humorous nature; to put it upon a serious book, like the "Joan," would beguile many persons into buying it who would not have been willing to spend their money upon serious books from my pen. The story reached to the third month in the magazine with the anonymity still safe, but the next instalment contained indiscretions of phrasing which were promptly recognized as coming from my shop. Many letters came to the Harpers charging me with the authorship of the book, and after that they put my name to it, with my consent. As a protection to the public, I was going to publish "The Prince and the Pauper" anonymously, but the children, and their mother, persuaded me out of it. Perhaps it was just as well, for there are things in it which would have been recognized by many persons as bearing my trade-mark. Style is apparently, then, as natural and as unconscious, and as difficult to successfully get rid of for any considerable time, as a person's gait and carriage. Two years ago, I wrote in a carefully disguised fashion an article whose authorship I wished should not be discovered. I submitted it to Clara, and in the middle of it she found a phrase which she said anybody would know me by. She was right, and it had to come out—a pity, too, for the careless and unpremeditated phrasings which are so sure to be stamped with the trade-mark of character are usually the ones which are best worth preserving.

A quarter of a century ago, when Thomas Bailey Aldrich succeeded Mr. Howells as editor of the *Atlantic Monthly,* he found in the safe an unsigned contribution by me which had been lying there a couple of years; but he recognized it as mine by the handwriting. He published it, unsigned, and sent me a check. I read two-thirds of the article and regretfully made preparation to return the check with the information that I was not the author of it; then I proceeded to finish the reading, for I found it interesting. Almost immediately my eye fell upon a sentence which brought out of me the remark "There isn't any one alive that would have said it in just that way but myself. I did write the article, and I'll cash the check."

These reminiscences bring to my mind some others which in a way are akin to them. Many years ago, when Jean was perhaps eight years old, Mrs. Clemens and I made a flying visit to Quarry Farm, three or four hundred miles away, leaving the rest of the family and the servants at home. Katy reported conditions to us by telegraph, every day, using a formula which she never changed, and which she had reported by telegraph scores of times when she had been left in charge of the children:

"Children all well and happy. KATY."

Long ago as that was, we had a telephone in our house. Katy telephoned her daily message to the telegraph office, but after a while the operators saved her breath for her. They came to know her voice, and when she would call the office the operator would speak up and say, with the rising inflection proper to an interrogation,

"Children all well and happy, Katy?"

"Yes."

That ended it, and the transmitter went to the hook.

There is something strange and wonderful about a woman's intuitions. The telegram continued to arrive in exactly the same words, daily, for a week; then Mrs. Clemens became uneasy, and she said,

"You must take the next train for Hartford; something is wrong there."

I am merely a man, and of course I wanted a reason for her opinion. She said she hadn't any, except that the telegrams had latterly not affected her as they had been accustomed to do. I remarked that there had been no change in the wording, but she said—— No matter, the fact remained that they were now filling her with vague apprehensions that all was not right, and I must go, and go at once.

I did it. When I arrived at home, twenty-four hours later, it was afternoon. In the hall I found the evening paper, and I stood there a moment to read a short paragraph which had attracted my attention. It announced the death, in Boston, of a relative of Dr. Oliver Wendell Holmes, a man whose name escapes me—but it went on to say that Dr. Holmes had learned of the death from the *Evening Transcript,* and that thereupon he said to a friend,

"This relative had just turned his fiftieth year; here is his name, a name part of which was not really his, but he had to carry it fifty years because he was baptized under it. My father baptized him, and when he was ready to confer the name he found that he had mislaid the slip of paper upon which it was written, so he had to trust to memory, with the result that he got the middle name wrong; it should have been Wendell."

Then Dr. Holmes went to his brother's house to confer about the funeral. This was the house which their father had lived in fifty years before. Dr. Holmes had been in the library a thousand times since, but this time when he entered it he walked to one of the shelves, took out a book at random, blew the dust from it, and gave it a shake, and out dropped the slip of paper that his father had mislaid when he misnamed that child fifty years before. It was remarked that Dr. Holmes was not surprised that he had been moved to take out that particular book and not another, because many times, before, he had been moved to obey seeming commands delivered to him by inanimate objects.

That interested me, for many a time inanimate objects had required service of me and gotten it—at least the requirement had quite plainly seemed to come from those unsentient objects, and from no other accountable source.

While I stood in the hall with the newspaper in my hand, the postman arrived, and when I went up to call on Jean I carried the letters with me. I found Jean sitting up in her crib, in the middle of the nursery, and Katy at her side, reading aloud to her. Mrs. Clemens's instinct had been correct; Jean had been dangerously ill, and the physician had persuaded Katy to continue the usual telegram, he believing that the child would recover, and that it would be wise, and well for Mrs. Clemens's health's sake, to keep the bad news from her. Jean was safe now, and getting along very well. After my conversation with Katy she quitted the room and left me in charge. The book that she had been reading was lying open, face down, on Jean's feet. I took it up and began to read where I judged Katy had left off; then I began to laugh. I read on, and continued to break into explosions of admiring and grateful laughter, until I was interrupted by an ejaculation from Jean. She had an outraged look in her face, and she said in a tone of sharp reproach,

"Papa!"

"Why Jean," I said, "what are your objections? I think it's the brightest book I ever saw. Why it's just charming."

Jean did not melt. She said austerely, indignantly, uncompromisingly,

"Papa, you ought to be ashamed to talk like that about your own book."

But I was innocent. The book was "Huckleberry Finn," but I had not recognized it. I had been paying myself another fine and great and unbought compliment. I read fifteen or twenty minutes, then gave Jean a rest, and took up the letters. They were from strangers, as usual, but the superscription upon one of them had a vaguely and far distant familiar look to it. I opened it and turned to the signature. It was "Bessie Stone."

It carried me back eighteen years in a flash. Away back there in the first months of our marriage, a couple of little Massachusetts schoolgirls wrote a joint letter to me which was full of innocent sweet pieties, and of gentle solicitude for me; and the burden of its message was an appeal to me to amend my ways, now, and lead a better life. I was amused at having the character of my life thus candidly exposed to me by these dear little schoolgirls of fourteen and fifteen years, but I was touched by it, too, for its intent was kindly; its solicitude was sincere and honest, and I did not fail to return the best answer I could, and put into it my quite genuine thanks. I was cautious, though; I was careful; I did not commit myself; I did not promise to lead a better life, for I could not have promised it honestly. I didn't want to lead a better life, and I knew I wasn't going to try; but I couldn't wound and distress and disappoint those sweet little creatures, so I vaguely intimated that I was busy now, that I had a good deal on my hands, and that I should be obliged to postpone this reform for a time, but that I was not going to forget it; no, I should keep it in mind, and——so on, and so on. I wrote the best letter I could, without pledging myself to an upright way of life, which I knew very well I couldn't stand.

The little schoolgirls wrote again; I answered; they wrote again; I answered; they wrote a third time; I answered. The intervals between letters were growing a little wider, and a little wider, all the time. They kept pleading with me to pray—that was one of the main things; they dwelt upon that patiently and persistently, and I did the best I could, in the circumstances, without definitely compromising myself. So at last the correspondence came to an end, I still postponing, and the children finally disheartened, I suppose.

Now then, after a lapse of eighteen years since the day of that correspondence, I opened this letter—still in that original round schoolgirl hand, with not a noticeable change in it in any particular—and in it I found a jubilant note of gladness. Bessie Stone said something like this—I don't remember her words:

"Our pleadings with you about prayer, so long ago, have borne fruit at last. I know it must be on account of those pleadings that Mary came to be a child of prayer, and the thought made me oh, so happy, oh, so grateful!"

I couldn't make anything out of that. I was acquainted with a good many Marys, but I couldn't call to mind one that was specially distinguished in the way indicated, and so I was not able to guess who this Mary could be that Bessie Stone was talking about, or in what way her and her friend's spiritual wrestlings with me had brought this unknown Mary to this pass.

Jean required me to read again, so I put Bessie out of my mind and picked up "Huckleberry Finn" again, and before I had read ten sentences I came upon that very Mary, and her prayer.

This incident would have startled me at any time, but the force of the surprise was doubled and quadrupled through following so swiftly upon the Dr. Holmes incident of a similar character. I have not seen "Huckleberry Finn" since, so far as I remember, and so I do not know whereabouts in the book Mary's prayer is mentioned, and, in fact, I don't remember Mary at all.

Saturday, December 29, 1906

The end of Susy's Biography: the trip to Keokuk—Mr. Clemens speaks of the journey—Mentions hearing the leadsmen's calls on the Mississippi steamboat—He sees his mother, then, for the last time in life—Gives the details of the romance of her life.

From Susy's Biography.

June 26, '86.

We are all of us on our way to Keokuk to see Grandma Clemens, who is very feeble and wants to see us, and pertickularly Jean who is her name sake. We are going by way of the lakes, as papa thought that would be the most comfortable way.

We went by way of the lakes, and it was a very pleasant and satisfactory excursion. We spent a day or two in Duluth, and a day or two in St. Paul and Minneapolis; then we boarded a Mississippi steamboat and went down the river to Keokuk. In my book called "Old Times on the Mississippi" I have explained that "mark twain" is the leadsman's cry for two fathoms—twelve feet—and have also explained how I came to adopt that phrase as a nom de guerre. If the children had ever been acquainted with these not very important facts, they had forgotten them by the time that they arrived on board that

Mississippi steamboat. A little after nightfall we entered a shoal crossing. I was standing alone on the hurricane-deck, astern, and I heard the big bell forward boom out the call for the leads. A moment later the night wind was bringing to me out of the distance, and faintly and musically, the leadsmen's long-drawn chant—sounds which had once been so familiar to me, and which had in them now the charm and witchery and pathos which belong with memories of a life that has been lived, and will come back no more:

"By the d-e-e-p four!"

"Quarter less four!"

"H-a-l-f three!"

"M-a-r-k three!"

"H-a-l-f twain!"

"Quarter-r-r twain!"

"Mark under water twain!"

"M-a-r-k twain!"

"M-a-r-k t-w-a-i-n!"

"M-a-r-k t-w-a-i-n!"

And so it went on, and on, the quaint and welcome old music beating softly upon my ear, and working its enchantments upon my spirit. Then suddenly Clara's little figure burst upon me out of the darkness, and she assailed me in a voice that was intense with rebuke and reproach,

"Papa!"

"Well, dear?"

"I have hunted all over the whole boat for you. Don't you know they are calling you?"

We remained in Keokuk a week, and this was the last time that I saw my aged mother in life. Her memory was decaying; indeed, for matters of the moment it was about gone; but her memories of the distant past remained, and she was living mainly in that far away bygone time; and so the secret of her life—the great secret, the romance of her life—was presently revealed by her lips, unconsciously and unknowingly. Orion's wife had been the recipient of this confidence, and she had kept it strictly to herself, but she felt it right and fair that I should share it with her, and so she told me about it; no, I am wrong in my dates; she did not tell me about it at that time, but at a later time, when I went West to attend my mother's funeral.

It can do no harm to set it down here, for it will not see print until years after all of us who have a personal interest in it shall have passed from this life. All through my boyhood I had noticed that the attitude of my father and mother toward each other was that of courteous, considerate, and always respectful, and even deferential, friends; that they were always kind toward each other, thoughtful of each other, but that there was nothing warmer; there were no outward and visible demonstrations of affection. This did not surprise me, for my father was exceedingly dignified in his carriage and speech, and in a manner he was austere. He was pleasant with his friends, but never familiar; and so, as I say, the absence of exterior demonstration of affection for my mother had no surprise for me. By nature she was warm-hearted, but it seemed to me quite natural that her warm-heartedness should be held in reserve in an atmosphere like my father's.

As I have said, my mother's memory for immediate events failed in the closing years of her life. When she was eighty-five or eighty-six years old a Medical Convention took place in a river town some distance north of Keokuk—Burlington, Iowa. Doctors came to the Convention from many parts of the United States, among them a physician verging toward ninety years of age—Dr. Gwynn, I have forgotten his first name. It was in midsummer. My mother, for her safety's sake, was kept under watch in those days, but one day when the watch was for the moment relaxed she disappeared. She was gone two days, and during this time no trace of her could be found; then she reappeared looking tired and worn, and sad. What had been happening was this: she had found Dr. Gwynn's name in the list of delegates to the Burlington Convention; she had slipped away and wandered to the river and taken passage for Burlington in the steamboat. The Convention's labors were nearly finished. She went to the principal hotel and asked eagerly for Dr. Gwynn. She was informed that he had taken his departure for Kentucky the day before. She made no comment except with her face and eyes, which revealed that she had suffered a deep disappointment. She returned to Keokuk, and then her injured mind betrayed her, and in the privacy of the home she told Orion's wife a secret which she had carried in her heart for more than sixty years. It was this:

When she was a girl of twenty, in Lexington, Kentucky, she became engaged to a fine young fellow who was making his sure and steady way toward prosperity and acceptance as a physician. They were passionately fond of each other. Young John M. Clemens had been a suitor for her hand, but had been rejected. There was to be a ball in a town five or ten miles away. In that day that young girl had a passion for dancing, and, indeed, for everything else that had charm and pleasure and vigorous life in it. She wanted Gwynn to take her to the ball; he was not able to do it; he said his duties required him to remain at his post, and he must not desert it. The young girl was grievously disappointed, and she upbraided him for his lack of devotion. He defended himself, and the incident ended in a lovers' quarrel. He had hardly turned his back when my appointed father appeared on the scene. He once more begged her to marry him, and in her anger she said she would, but it must be instantly, lest her mind undergo a change, since she was not marrying him for love, but to spite Gwynn.

For more than sixty years she had grieved in secret for the crime committed against herself and another in a moment of unreflecting passion. It is as pathetic a romance as any that has crossed the field of my personal experience in my long lifetime.

From Susy's Biography.

July 4,
We have arived in Keokuk after a very pleasant

So ends the loving task of that innocent sweet spirit—like her own life, unfinished, broken off in the midst. Interruptions came, her days became increasingly busy with studies and work, and she never resumed the Biography, though from time to time she gathered materials for it. When I look at the arrested sentence that ends the little book, it seems as if the hand that traced it cannot be far—is gone for a moment only, and will come again and finish it. But that is a dream; a creature of the heart, not of the mind—a feeling, a longing, not a mental product: the same that lured Aaron Burr, old, gray, forlorn, forsaken, to the pier, day after day, week after week, there to stand in the gloom and the chill of the dawn gazing seaward through veiling mists and sleet and snow for the ship which he knew was gone down—the ship that bore all his treasure, his daughter.

Hamilton, Bermuda, January 6, 1907

The power of association to bring back a lost word or name, as shown on the Bermuda trip when Mr. Clemens and Mr. Twichell recall Miss Kirkham's name—Mr. Clemens's dream, born of the association of Mr. Twichell's remarks about aerial navigation and the reading of the statistics of the railway accidents compiled by the United States Government.

"That reminds me." In conversation we are always using that phrase, and seldom or never noticing how large a significance it bears. It stands for a curious and interesting fact, to wit: that sleeping or waking, dreaming or talking, the thoughts which swarm through our heads are almost constantly, almost continuously, accompanied by a like swarm of reminders of incidents and episodes of our past. A man can never know what a large traffic this commerce of association carries on in his mind until he sets out to write his autobiography; he then finds that a thought is seldom born to him that does not immediately remind him of some event, large or small, in his past experience. Quite naturally these present remarks remind me of various things, among others this: that sometimes a thought, by the power of association, will bring back to your mind a lost word or a lost name which you have not been able to recover by any other process known to your mental equipment. Yesterday we had an instance of this.

Reverend Joseph H. Twichell is with me on this flying trip to Bermuda. He was with me on my last visit to Bermuda, and to-day we were trying to remember when it was; we thought it was somewhere in the neighborhood of thirty years ago, but that was as near as we could get at the date. Twichell said that the landlady in whose boarding-house we sojourned in that ancient time could doubtless furnish us the date, and we must look her up. We wanted to see her, anyway, because she and her blooming daughter of eighteen were the only persons whose acquaintance we had made at that time, for we were traveling under fictitious names, and people who wear aliases are not given to seeking society and bringing themselves under suspicion. But at this point in our talk we encountered an obstruction: we could not recall the landlady's name. We hunted all around through our minds for that name, using all the customary methods of research, but without success; the name was gone from us, apparently permanently. We finally gave the matter up, and fell to talking about something else. The talk wandered from one subject to another, and finally arrived at Twichell's school days in Hartford—the Hartford of something more than half a century ago—and he mentioned several of his schoolmasters, dwelling with special interest upon the peculiarities of an aged one named Olney. He remarked that Olney, humble village schoolmaster as he was, was yet a man of superior parts, and had published text-books which had enjoyed a wide currency in America in their day. I said I remembered those books, and had studied "Olney's Geography" in school when I was a boy. Then Twichell said,

"That reminds me—our landlady's name was a name that was associated with school-books of some kind or other fifty or sixty years ago. I wonder what it was. I believe it began with K."

Association did the rest, and did it instantly. I said,

"Kirkham's Grammar!"

That settled it. Kirkham was the name; and we went out to seek for the owner of it. There was no trouble about that, for Bermuda is not large, and is like the earlier Garden of Eden, in that everybody in it knows everybody else, just as it was in the serpent's headquarters in Adam's time. We easily found Miss Kirkham—she that had been the blooming girl of a generation before—and she was still keeping boarders; but her mother had passed from this life. She settled the date for us, and did it with certainty, by help of a couple of uncommon circumstances, events of that ancient time. She said we had sailed from Bermuda on the 24th of May 1877, which was the day on which her only nephew was born—and he is now thirty years of age. The other unusual circumstance—she called it an unusual circumstance, and I didn't say anything—was that on that day the Rev. Mr. Twichell (bearing the assumed name of Peters) had made a statement to her which she regarded as a fiction. I remembered the circumstance very well. We had bidden the young girl good-bye and had gone fifty yards, perhaps, when Twichell said he had forgotten something (I doubted it,) and must go back. When he rejoined me he was silent, and this alarmed me, because I had not seen an example of it before. He seemed quite uncomfortable, and I asked him what the trouble was. He said he had been inspired to give the girl a pleasant surprise, and so had gone back and said to her—

"That young fellow's name is not Wilkinson—that's Mark Twain."

She did not lose her mind; she did not exhibit any excitement at all, but said quite simply, quite tranquilly,

"Tell it to the marines, Mr. Peters—if that should happen to be *your* name."

It was very pleasant to meet her again. We were white-headed, but she was not; in the sweet and unvexed spiritual atmosphere of the Bermudas one does not achieve gray hairs at forty-eight.

I had a dream last night, and of course it was born of association, like nearly everything else that drifts into a person's head, asleep or awake. On board ship, on the passage down, Twichell was talking about the swiftly developing possibilities of aerial navigation, and he quoted those striking verses of Tennyson's which forecast a future when air-borne vessels of war shall meet and fight above the clouds and redden the earth below with a rain of blood. This picture of carnage and blood and death reminded me of something which I had read a fortnight ago—statistics of railway accidents compiled by the United States Government, wherein the appalling fact was set forth that on our 200,000 miles of railway we annually kill 10,000 persons outright and injure 80,000. The war-ships in the air suggested the railway horrors, and three nights afterward the railway horrors suggested my dream. The work of association was going on in my head, unconsciously, all that time. It was an admirable dream, what there was of it.

In it I saw a funeral procession; I saw it from a mountain peak; I saw it crawling along and curving here and there, serpent-like, through a level vast plain. I seemed to see a hundred miles of the procession, but neither the beginning of it nor the end of it was within the limits of my vision. The procession was in ten divisions, each division marked by a sombre flag, and the whole represented ten years of our railway activities in the accident line; each division was composed of 80,000 cripples, and was bearing its own year's 10,000 mutilated corpses to the grave: in the aggregate 800,000 cripples and 100,000 dead, drenched in blood!

On board ship. January 9, 1907

Mr. Clemens's four maxims apropos of an incident which has just occurred—Description of Bermuda.

There has been an incident—an incident of a common sort—an incident of an exceedingly common sort—an incident of a sort which always troubles me, grieves me, and makes me weary of life and long to lie down in the peaceful grave and be at rest. Such incidents usually move me to try to find relief in the building of a maxim. It is a good way, because if you have luck you can get the venom out of yourself and into the maxim; then comfort and a healed spirit follow. Maxims are not easy to make; they do not come in right shape at the first call; they are creatures of evolution, of development; you have to try several plans before you get one that suits you, or even comes fairly near to suiting you. I have made four attempts at this maxim, to wit:

1. If it is *so* funny you can't tell it without laughing, don't tell it: spare your listener.

2. If you can laugh at it yourself while you are telling it, you may know by that sign that it is not funny—to others.

3. When you laugh at your own funny things you are asking alms for their poverty.

4. When the hen has laid a joke she does the laughing herself. There be human beings that are as vulgar.

The relief is not perfect, but it will have to do. I do not feel as axiomatic as usual to-day.

That is a pleasant country—Bermuda—and close by and easy to get to. There is a fine modern steamer admirably officered; there is a table which even the hypercritical could hardly find fault with—not even the hypercritical could find fault with the service. On board there is constant communication with the several populations of the planet—if you want it—through the wireless telegraph, and the trip to Bermuda is made in two days. Many people flit to that garden in winter and spring, and heal their worn minds and bodies in its peaceful serenities and its incomparable climate, and it is strange that the people of our Northern coasts go there in mere battalions, instead of in armies. The place is beautiful to the eye; it is clothed in flowers; the roads and the boating are all that can be desired; the hotels are good; the waters and the land are brilliant with spirit-reviving sunshine; the people, whether white, black, or brown, are courteous and kindly beyond the utmost stretch of a New York imagination. If poverty and wretchedness exist, there is no visible evidence of it. There is no rush, no hurry, no money-getting frenzy, no fretting, no complaining, no fussing and quarreling; no telegrams, no daily newspapers, no railroads, no tramways, no subways, no trolleys, no L's, no Tammany, no Republican party, no Democratic party, no graft, no office-seeking, no elections, no legislatures for sale; hardly a dog, seldom a cat, only one steam-whistle; not a saloon, nobody drunk; no W.C.T.U.; and there is a church and a school on every corner. The spirit of the place is serenity, repose, contentment, tranquillity—a marked contrast to the spirit of America, which is embodied in the urgent and mannerless phrase "Come step lively," a phrase which ought to be stamped on our coinage in place of "In God We Trust." The former expression is full of character, whereas the latter has nothing to recommend it but its bland and self-complacent hypocrisy.

I think it must be the fret and fever of our American life that is responsible for our atrocious manners. No other civilized nation is so uncourteous, so hard, so ungentle, so ill-bred, as ours. We wear several impressive titles—conferred by ourselves, of course—whereby we publish to the world that we are the only free and independent nation; that our land is the special and particular land of the free and home of the brave, and so forth, and so on; but we cannot seem to get anybody outside of our frontiers to recognize these titles, except in a doubting and half-hearted way; whereas what we want, and urgently need, is a title which shall be accepted and ratified with enthusiasm by the rest of the Christian world—a title not claimable by any other nation, a title able to hold its own unchallenged in all weathers. I believe I could think up the right title if I had time. Naturally it would be a title claiming for us the distinction of being *the* Unpolite Nation, but in fairness I should be obliged to make one reserve, one exception—the cabmen of Boston. Boston is the most courteous of American cities, perhaps, and I think it quite likely, at least possible, that of all Boston guilds the guild of cabmen stands about at the head in this regard. Anyway, with thirty-seven years' experience to draw upon, I have never yet encountered an uncourteous Boston cabman. Of such is the kingdom of heaven, as I look at it. I am not claiming to be courteous myself, for in truth I am not. I am an American. I am as national as the eagle itself.

What Bermuda can do for a person in three short days, in the way of soothing his spirit and setting him up physically, and in giving his life a new value by temporarily banishing the weariness and the sordidness out of it, is wonderful—if that is not too strong a word, and I think it isn't. Bronchitis disappears there in twenty-four hours; and it is the same with sore throats, and kindred ailments, and they do not return until the patient gets back home; yet Bermuda is neglected; not many Americans visit it. I suppose it is too near-by. It costs too little trouble and exertion to get to it. It ought to be as far away as Italy; then we would seek it, no doubt, and be properly thankful for its existence. However, there is this much to be said for Americans: that when they go to Bermuda once, they are quite sure to go again; and some among the especially wise acquire the habit of it. I know one American who has spent nine seasons there. Consider this—if you are tired, and depressed, and half sick: you can reach that refuge inside of two days, and a week or two there will bring back your youth and the lost sunshine of your life, and stop your doctor's bills for a year.

Dublin, New Hampshire, Summer-end, 1905.

As concerns interpreting the Deity. This line of hieroglyphs was for fourteen years the despair of all the scholars who labored over the mysteries of the Rosetta stone:

After five years of study Champollion translated it thus:

> *Therefore let the worship of Epiphanes be maintained in all the temples; this upon pain of death.*

That was the twenty-fourth translation that had been furnished by scholars. For a time it stood. But only for a time. Then doubts began to assail it and undermine it, and the scholars resumed their labors. Three years of patient work produced eleven new translations; among them, this, by Grünfeldt, was received with considerable favor:

> *The horse of Epiphanes shall be maintained at the public expense; this upon pain of death.*

But the following rendering, by Gospodin, was received by the learned world with yet greater favor:

> *The priest shall explain the wisdom of Epiphanes to all the people, and these shall listen with reverence, upon pain of death.*

Seven years followed, in which twenty-one fresh and widely varying renderings were scored—none of them quite convincing. But now, at last, came Rawlinson, the youngest of all the scholars, with a translation which was immediately and universally recognized as being the correct version, and his name became famous in a day. So famous, indeed, that even the children were familiar with it; and such a noise did the achievement itself make that not even the noise of the monumental political event of that same year—the Flight from Elba—was able to smother it to silence. Rawlinson's version reads as follows:

> *Therefore, walk not away from the wisdom of Epiphanes, but turn and follow it; so shall it conduct thee to the temple's peace, and soften for thee the sorrows of life and the pains of death.*

Here is another difficult text:

It is demotic—a style of Egyptian writing and a phase of the language which had perished from the knowledge of all men twenty-five hundred years before the Christian era. But the scholars of our day have penetrated its secret. The above text baffled them, however, for twenty-two years, and in that time they framed forty-six versions of it before they hit upon the right one—which is this:

> *It is forbidden the unconsecrated to utter foolish and irreverent speeches concerning sacred things: this privilege, by decree of the Holy Synod, being restricted to the clergy.*

Our red Indians have left many records, in the form of pictures, upon our crags and boulders. It has taken our most gifted and painstaking students two centuries to get at the meanings hidden in these pictures; yet there are still two little lines of hieroglyphs among the figures grouped upon the Dighton Rocks which they have not succeeded in interpreting to their satisfaction. These:

The suggested solutions of this riddle are practically innumerable; they would fill a book.

Thus we have infinite trouble in solving man-made mysteries; it is only when we set out to discover the secrets of God that our difficulties disappear. It was always so. In antique Roman times it was the custom of the Deity to try to conceal His intentions in the entrails of birds, and this was patiently and hopefully continued century after century, although the attempted concealment never succeeded, in a single recorded instance. The augurs could read entrails as easily as a modern child can read coarse print. Roman history is full of the marvels of interpretation which these extraordinary men performed. These strange and wonderful achievements move our awe and compel our admiration. Those men could pierce to the marrow of a mystery instantly. If the Rosetta-stone idea had been introduced it would have defeated them, but entrails had no embarrassments for them. But entrails have gone out, now—entrails and dreams. It was at last found out that as hiding-places for the divine intentions they were inadequate.

> A part of the wall of Velletri having in former times been struck with thunder, the response of the soothsayers was, that a native of that town would some time or other arrive at supreme power. *Bohn's Suetonius,* p. 138.

"Some time or other." It looks indefinite, but no matter, it happened, all the same; one needed only to wait, and be patient, and keep watch, then he would find out that the thunder-stroke had Caesar Augustus in mind, and had come to give notice.

There were other advance-advertisements. One of them appeared just before Caesar Augustus was born, and was most poetic and touching and romantic in its feelings and aspects. It was a dream. It was dreamed by Caesar Augustus's mother, and interpreted at the usual rates:

> Atia, before her delivery, dreamed that her bowels stretched to the stars, and expanded through the whole circuit of heaven and earth. *Suetonius,* p. 139.

That was in the augur's line, and furnished him no difficulties, but it would have taken Rawlinson and Champollion fourteen years to make sure of what it meant, because they would have been surprised and dizzy. It would have been too late to be valuable, then, and the bill for service would have been barred by the statute of limitations.

In those old Roman days a gentleman's education was not complete until he had taken a theological course at the seminary and learned how to translate entrails. Caesar Augustus's education received this final polish. All through his life, whenever he had poultry on the menu he saved the interiors and kept himself informed of the Deity's plans by exercising upon those interiors the arts of augury.

> In his first consulship, while he was observing the auguries, twelve vultures presented themselves, as they had done to Romulus. And when he offered sacrifice, the livers of all the victims were folded inward in the lower part; a circumstance which was regarded by those present who had skill in things of that nature, as an indubitable prognostic of great and wonderful fortune. *Suetonius,* p. 141.

"Indubitable" is a strong word, but no doubt it was justified, if the livers were really turned that way. In those days chicken livers were strangely and delicately sensitive to coming events, no matter how far off they might be; and they could never keep still, but would curl and squirm like that, particularly when vultures came, and showed interest in that approaching great event and in breakfast.

II.

We may now skip eleven hundred and thirty or forty years, which brings us down to enlightened Christian times and the troubled days of King Stephen of England. The augur has had his day and has been long ago forgotten; the Christian priest has fallen heir to his trade.

King Henry is dead; Stephen, that bold and outrageous person, comes flying over from Normandy to steal the throne from Henry's daughter. He accomplished his crime, and Henry of Huntingdon, a priest of high degree, mourns over it in his Chronicle. The Archbishop of Canterbury consecrated Stephen: "wherefore the Lord visited the Archbishop with the same judgment which he had inflicted upon him who struck Jeremiah the great priest: he died within a year."

Stephen's was the greater offence, but Stephen could wait; not so the Archbishop, apparently.

> The kingdom was a prey to intestine wars; slaughter, fire and rapine spread ruin throughout the land; cries of distress, horror and woe rose in every quarter.

That was the result of *Stephen's* crime. These unspeakable conditions continued during nineteen years. Then Stephen died as comfortably as any man ever did, and was honorably buried. It makes one pity the poor Archbishop, and wish that he, too, could have been let off as leniently. How did Henry of Huntingdon know that the Archbishop was sent to his grave by judgment of God for consecrating Stephen? He does not explain. Neither does he explain why Stephen was awarded a pleasanter death than he was entitled to, while the aged King Henry, his predecessor, who had ruled England thirty-five years to H. H.'s and the people's strongly-worded satisfaction, was condemned to close his life in circumstances most distinctly unpleasant, inconvenient, and disagreeable:

> Meantime, the remains of King Henry lay still unburied in Normandy. His corpse was carried to Rouen, where his bowels, with his brain and eyes, were deposited. The body being slashed by knives, and copiously sprinkled with salt, was sewn up in ox hides to prevent the ill effluvia, which so tainted the air as to be pestilential to the bystanders. Even the man who was hired by a large reward to sever the head with an axe and extract the brain, which was very offensive, died in consequence, although he wore a thick linen veil; so that *he was the last of that great multitude King Henry slew.** The corpse being then carried to Caen, was deposited in the church where his father was interred; but notwithstanding the quantity of salt which had been used, and the folds of skin in which it was wrapped, so much foul matter continually exuded that it was caught in vessels placed under the bier, in emptying which the attendants were affected with horror and faintings. *Bohn's Henry of Huntingdon,* p. 262.

This is probably the most uninspiring funeral that is set down in history. There is not a detail about it that is attractive. It is difficult to believe that we are reading about a king, there is something so humble, so unpretending, so unregal, about the whole spectacle, something so simply human and unconventional. We hear nothing of tears, of regret, of a sense of loss, of a reluctance to say farewell, we have only a picture of cold and perfunctory persons who are there by invitation, not by intrusion, and who have no wish to remain longer than courtesy requires. It is one of the saddest funerals there is any account of. There does not appear to have been any music; yet music would have tempered it, music would have made it beautiful, if they could have thought of anything

* The reader will please skip what now follows. M.T.

appropriate to play. But I suppose there was no old music that would quite do, none that would be harmonious, and no time to think out any new music and compose it. It would be difficult, of course, and could take a good while, no doubt, on account of the conditions. It seems to have been just the funeral for *Stephen,* and even at this far distant day it is matter of just regret that by an indiscretion the wrong man got it.

Whenever God punishes a man, Henry of Huntingdon knows why it was done, and tells us; and his pen is eloquent with admiration; but when a man has earned punishment and escapes, he does not explain. He is evidently puzzled, but he does not say anything. I think it is often apparent that he is pained by these discrepancies, but loyally tries his best not to show it. When he cannot praise, he delivers himself of a silence so marked that a suspicious person could mistake it for suppressed criticism. However, he has plenty of opportunities to feel contented with the way things go—his book is full of them.

> King David of Scotland . . . . . under color of religion caused his followers to deal most barbarously with the English. They ripped open pregnant women, tossed children on the points of spears, butchered priests at the altars, and, cutting off the heads from the images on crucifixes, placed them on the bodies of the slain, while in exchange they fixed on the crucifixes the heads of their victims. Wherever the Scots came, there was the same scene of horror and cruelty: women shrieking, old men lamenting, amid the groans of the dying and the despair of the living.

But the English got the victory.

> Then the chief of the men of Lothian fell, pierced by an arrow, and all his followers were put to flight. For the Almighty was offended at them, and their strength was rent like a cobweb.

Offended at them for what? For committing those fearful butcheries? No, for that was the common custom on both sides, and not open to criticism. Then was it for doing the butcheries "under cover of religion?" No, that was not it; religious feeling was often expressed in that fervent way all through those old centuries. The truth is, He was not offended at "them" at all; He was only offended at their King, who had been false to an oath. Then why did not He put the punishment upon the King instead of upon "them?" It is a difficult question. One can see by the Chronicle that the "judgments" fell rather customarily upon the wrong person, but Henry of Huntingdon does not explain why. Here is one that went true; the chronicler's satisfaction in it is not hidden:

> In the month of August Providence displayed its justice in a remarkable manner; for two of the nobles who had converted monasteries into fortifications, expelling the monks, their sin being the same, met with a similar punishment. Robert Marmion was one, Godfrey de Mandeville the other. Robert Marmion issuing forth against the enemy was slain under the walls of the monastery, being the only one who fell, though he was surrounded by his troops. Dying excommunicated, he became subject to death everlasting. In like manner earl Godfrey was singled out among his followers, and shot with an arrow by a common foot-soldier. He made

> light of the wound, but he died of it in a few days, under excommunication. See here the like just judgment of God, memorable through all ages!

This exultation jars upon me; not because of the death of the men, for they deserved that, but because it is death eternal, in white-hot fire and flame. It makes my flesh crawl. I have not known more than three men, or perhaps four, in my whole lifetime, whom I would rejoice to see writhing in those fires for even a year, let alone forever. I believe I would relent before the year was up, and get them out if I could. I could sit and watch a dog that I didn't like, several years, but not forever. I often put a dog on the fire and hold him down with the tongs, and enjoy his yelps and moans and strugglings and supplications, but with a man it would be different, I think. I think that in the long run, if his wife and babies, who had not harmed me, should come crying and pleading, I couldn't stand it; I know I should forgive him and let him go, even if he had violated a monastery. Henry of Huntingdon has been watching Godfrey and Marmion fry, nearly seven hundred and fifty years, now, but I couldn't do it, I know I couldn't. I am soft and gentle in my nature, and I should have forgiven them seventy and seven times, long ago. And I think God has; but this is only surmise, and not authoritative, like Henry of Huntingdon's interpretations. I could learn to interpret, but I have never tried, I get so little time.

All through his book Henry exhibits his familiarity with the intentions of God, and with the reasons for the intentions. Sometimes—very often, in fact—the act follows the intention after such a wide interval of time, that one wonders how Henry could fit one act out of a hundred to one intention out of a hundred and get the thing right, every time, when there was such abundant choice among acts and intentions. Sometimes a man offends the Deity with a crime, and is punished for it thirty years later; meantime he has committed a million other crimes: no matter, Henry can pick out the one that brought the worms. Worms were generally used in those days for the slaying of particularly wicked people. This has gone out, now, but in old times it was a favorite. It always indicated a case of "wrath." For instance, ...

> the just God avenging Robert Fitzhildebrand's perfidy, a worm grew in his vitals, which, gradually gnawing its way through his intestines, fattened on the abandoned man till, tortured with excruciating sufferings and venting himself in bitter moans, he was by a fitting punishment brought to his end; (p. 400).

It was probably an alligator, but we cannot tell; we only know it was a particular breed, and only used to convey wrath. Some authorities think it was an ichthiosaurus, but there is much doubt. Anyway, it has gone out, now, thanks be.

However, one thing we do know; and that is, that that worm had been due years and years. Robert F. had violated a monastery once; he had committed unprintable crimes since, and they had been permitted—under disapproval—but the ravishment of the monastery had not been forgotten nor forgiven, and the worm came at last.

Why were these reforms put off in this strange way? What was to be gained by it? Did Henry of Huntingdon really know his facts, or was he only guessing? Sometimes I am half persuaded that he is only a guesser, and not a good one. The divine wisdom must surely be of a better quality than he makes it out to be.

Five hundred years before Henry's time some forecasts of the Lord's purposes were furnished by a pope, who perceived, by certain perfectly trustworthy signs furnished by the Deity for the information of His familiars, that the end of the world was

> . . . . about to come. But as this end of the world draws near, many things are at hand which have not before happened, as changes in the air, terrible signs in the heavens, tempests out of the common order of the seasons, wars, famines, pestilences, earthquakes in various places; all which will not happen in our days, but after our days all will come to pass.

Still, the end was so near that these signs were "sent before in order that we may be careful for our souls and be found prepared to meet the impending judgment."

That was thirteen hundred years ago. This is really no improvement upon the work of the Roman augurs. Has the trade of interpreting the Lord's matters gone out, discouraged by the time-worn fact that nobody succeeds at it? No, it still flourishes; there was never a century nor a country that was short of experts who knew the Deity's mind and were willing to reveal it. Whenever there has been an opportunity to attribute to Him reasonings and conduct which would make a half-witted human being ridiculous, there has always been an expert ready and glad to take advantage of it. Quotation from newspaper several months old:

> **GOD BEHIND THIS WAR.**
>
> **It Is His Way of Destroying Tyranny, Dr. Hillis Says.**
>
> Preaching yesterday morning in Plymouth Church, Brooklyn, on "Christ at Once the Ideal Radical and the Ideal Conservative," the Rev. Dr. Newell Dwight Hillis referred to Russia as an example of the false conservative in politics, and declared that God, who as a radical only destroyed for the sake of safety, was destroying the idea of tyranny through war.
>
> "Look to the Far East," said Dr. Hillis. "God's ploughshare of war is running through the nations and the old and false idea of tyranny is being turned up and under. Yet, when the thunderstorm has passed, does any man doubt that the air will be sweeter and purer? You say all the East is filled with destruction. It is because God's army is on the march. You do not hear the trumpet call, but God is the guide. Peace is to be the future of the people, oppression is to be destroyed, and government is to be for and by all the people."

So God's plowshare has got started at last. But is there any occasion to fly into ecstasies of admiration over it? The villainies, the slaughters and the tyrannies which have so suddenly dawned upon the Deity and excited His Brooklyn interpreter to such an indecorous degree have been known to the very cats for three hundred years. If these villainies are wrong, they were wrong three centuries ago; if they are worth the Deity's attention now, they were worth it three centuries ago; if they are legitimate matter to rouse the divine wrath now, they were not otherwise three centuries ago; if it is fine and great to stamp out these tyrannies now, it would have been infinitely finer and greater to do it three centuries ago; if it is matter for high Brooklyn commendation that the deep miseries of the hungry and oppressed Russian millions have awakened pity at last, it should be matter for high Brooklyn regret that it was not awakened at the start, instead of away down at this late day, after more than four hundred billion of those poor creatures have been oppressed into their graves.

Brooklyn praise is half slander. No, it is more than that, it is whole slander. To charge upon a man—and not a smart man at that—such a devastating record of immortal stupidities as this, would subject the utterer of the charge to a criminal libel suit, and quite properly, but any one can slander the Deity who has been lawfully consecrated to that work. But not you, and not me. We should be accused of irreverence.

> God's army is on the march. You do not hear the trumpet-call, but God is the guide. . . . oppression is to be destroyed.

All this noise about an army and a plow,—belated—all this inflamed jubilation over a mixed military and agricultural expedition which is only just now getting started when it is already three centuries overdue. It would not do for a person to praise me for being three centuries late at a fire with my hook and ladder company; I should not like it.

In view of the fact that it takes the Rawlinsons, the Champollions and the Indian experts years and years to dig the meaning out of the modestest little batch of hieroglyphs; and that in interpreting the intentions of God the Roman augurs never scored a single demonstrable success; and that from their day to ours all attempts by men to lay bare to us the mind of the Deity have as signally failed, it seems to me that now is a good time for the interpreting-trade to take a rest. If it goes on trying (in its way) to magnify the wisdom of God, there will come a time by and by when there will not be any left to magnify.

Mark Twain.

Tuesday, January 15, 1907

The process which may turn our republic into a monarchy—We have the two Roman conditions: stupendous wealth, and the corn and oil pensions—that is to say, vote bribes—The amazing additions to the pension list commented upon; also, letter from "A Union Veteran."

The human race was always interesting, and we know, by its past, that it will always continue so. Monotonously. It is always the same; it never changes. Its circumstances change from time to time, for better or worse, but the race's *character* is permanent, and never changes. In the course of the ages it has built up several great and worshipful civilizations, and has seen unlooked-for circumstances slyly emerge, bearing deadly gifts which looked like benefits, and were welcomed—whereupon the decay and destruction of each of these stately civilizations has followed. It is not worth while to try to keep history from repeating itself, for man's character will always make the preventing of the repetitions impossible. Whenever man makes a large stride in material prosperity and progress, he is sure to think that *he* has progressed, whereas he has not advanced an inch; nothing has progressed but his circumstances. *He* stands where he stood before. He knows more than his forebears knew, but his intellect is no better than theirs, and never will be. He is richer than his forebears, but his character is no improvement upon theirs. Riches and education are not a permanent possession; they will pass away, as in the case of Rome, and Greece, and Egypt, and Babylon; and a moral and mental midnight will follow—with a dull long sleep and a slow re-awakening. From time to time he makes what looks like a change in his character, but it is not a real change; and it is only transitory, anyway. He cannot even invent a religion and keep it intact; circumstances are stronger than he and all his works; circumstances and conditions are always changing, and they always compel him to modify his religions to harmonize with the new situation.

For twenty-five or thirty years I have squandered a deal of my time—too much of it perhaps—in trying to guess what is going to be the process which will turn our republic into a monarchy, and how far off that event might be. Every man is a master and also a servant, a vassal. There is always some one who looks up to him and admires and envies him; there is always some one to whom he looks up and admires and envies. This is his nature; this is his character; and it is unchangeable, indestructible; therefore republics and democracies are not for such as he; they cannot satisfy the requirements of his nature. The inspirations of his character will always breed circumstances and conditions which must in time furnish him a king and an aristocracy to look up to and worship. In a democracy he will try, and honestly, to keep the crown away, but Circumstance is a powerful master, and will eventually defeat him.

Republics have lived long, but monarchy lives forever. By our teaching, we learn that vast material prosperity always brings in its train conditions which debase the morals and enervate the manhood of a nation—then the country's liberties come into the market and are bought, sold, squandered, thrown away, and a popular idol is carried to the throne upon the shields or shoulders of the worshiping people, and planted there in permanency. We are always being taught—no, formerly we were always being taught—to look at Rome, and beware. The teacher pointed to Rome's stern virtue, incorruptibility, love of liberty, and all-sacrificing patriotism—this when she was young and poor; then he pointed to her later days, when her sun-bursts of material prosperity and spreading dominion came, and were exultingly welcomed by the people, they not suspecting that these were not fortunate glories, happy benefits, but were a disease, and freighted with death. The teacher reminded us that Rome's liberties were not auctioned off in a day, but were bought slowly, gradually, furtively, little by little; first with a little corn and oil for the exceedingly poor and wretched; later with corn and oil for voters who were not quite so poor; later still with corn and oil for pretty much every man that had a vote to sell—exactly our own history over again. At first we granted deserved pensions, righteously, and with a clean and honorable motive, to the disabled soldiers of the Civil War. The *clean* motive began and ended there. We have made many and amazing additions to the pension list, but with a motive which dishonors the uniform and the Congresses which have voted the additions—the sole purpose back of the additions being the purchase of votes. It is corn and oil over again, and promises to do its full share in the eventual subversion of the republic and the substitution of monarchy in its place. The monarchy would come, anyhow, without this, but this has a peculiar interest for us, in that it prodigiously hastens the day. We have the two Roman conditions: stupendous wealth, with its inevitable corruptions and moral blight, and the corn and oil pensions—that is to say, vote-bribes, which have taken away the pride of thousands of tempted men and turned them into willing alms-receivers and unashamed.

It is curious—curious that physical courage should be so common in the world, and moral courage so rare. A year or two ago a veteran of the Civil War asked me if I did not sometimes have a longing to attend the annual great Convention of the Grand Army of the Republic and make a speech. I was obliged to confess that I wouldn't have the necessary moral courage for the venture, for I would want to reproach the old soldiers for not rising up in indignant protest against our Government's vote-purchasing additions to the pension list, which is making of the remnant of their brave lives one long blush. I might try to say the words, but would lack the grit and would fail. It would be one tottering moral coward trying to rebuke a housefull of like breed—men merely as timid as himself, but not any more so.

Well, there it is—I am a moral coward, like the rest; and yet it is amazing to me that out of the hundreds and thousands of physically dauntless men who faced death without a quiver of the nerves on a hundred bloody fields, not one solitary individual of them all has had courage enough to rise up and bravely curse the Congresses which have degraded him to the level of the bounty-jumper and the bastards of the same. Everybody laughs at the grotesque additions to the pension fund; everybody laughs at the grotesquest of them all, the most shameless of them all, the most transparent of them all, the only frankly lawless one of them all—the immortal Executive Order 78. Everybody laughs—privately; everybody scoffs—privately; everybody is indignant—privately; everybody is ashamed to look a real soldier in the face; but none of them exposes his feelings publicly. This is perfectly natural, and wholly inevitable, for it is the nature of man to hate to say the disagreeable thing. It is his character; it has always been so; his character cannot change; while he continues to exist it will never change by a shade.

I have been moved to these uncomfortable reflections by a communication in this morning's *Sun* signed "A Union Veteran." It begins with this remark:

> I see that the Senate has passed the service pension bill with no opposing votes. And I suppose that's all right.

Passed it unanimously—and doubtless with enthusiasm. Evidently some one has invented a new excuse to bilk the Treasury, and at the same time further degrade the honorable calling of the real soldier. This veteran thinks it's all right. It is a pity that he could say that, for the rest of his letter shows that he once had worthier notions, and that the pension plague has undermined them and brought them low. He says:

> Personally I don't believe in service pensions. I think that if a man incurred any disability in the service he ought to get whatever pension is due him to the last cent. He is entitled to that by the contract; but a service pension strikes me differently.

No one will doubt the soundness and sanity and fairness of his view. He continues:

> When Uncle Sam settled with me at the end of my term of service I felt that that closed our accounts definitely and finally. I had agreed on my part to serve for so much a month and a bounty of $100 when I was mustered out; and I got it all, and I considered that that was the end of it.

And indeed it was the end of it, so far as cleanliness goes. After that, the vote-buying began. It continues to-day; it will continue to continue until the remains of every cat, with her descendants, that has been owned by a sutler or a soldier, from Bunker till the monarchy comes in, shall have been added to the pension list. Then there will be more pensioners than population, and we shall be ready for the monarchy as a relief, a refuge, a savior from our vote-buying, mendicant-creating politicians. He continues:

> A few years after the war Congress gave to all veteran soldiers an additional bounty of $100. Why it did this, I don't know; politics, maybe; but it passed out $100 apiece all 'round—

Then he adds: "and I took mine, though I didn't feel I was entitled to it." It was there that the undermining of his manhood began; it was a thing calculated to undermine any one's manhood to whose not too plenty bread and butter a hundred dollars was an important matter. You would have taken it. I would have taken it. We should have felt ashamed; but we could have taken it next time, and afterward, with less and less sense of shame, and by and by we would begin to ask for it; then beg for it; then demand it, and insist upon it. By that time we should have irrevocably lost an inestimably valuable jewel from our character, and the Government would be to blame for it, not us.

Hear him again—see his moral disintegration going on; notice his character decay and crumble under the temptations devised for it by a treacherous Government:

> But now comes the service pension. As I feel about it now I shall not take it. But you can't tell. I took that $100 additional bounty, and I may take the service pension, but I don't think so.

He doesn't think so, and it is to his credit, after the assaults which have been made in these twenty or thirty years upon his self-respect by a conscienceless Government—but when the new bribe comes, in the form of visible cash, he will fall again, just as you and I would; and again the Government will be to blame for it. Hear him once more:

> My service in the army never did me any harm. On the contrary it helped me in many ways and I am prouder of it than of anything else I ever did or ever could do. . . . . I have served in the army in my country's defence in time of war, and I feel that by that service I have been raised to the highest rank of citizenship; and with that honor I am satisfied.

Isn't it a pity to degrade and demoralize a man with a character like that! What punishment can expiate such a crime committed by the Government and condoned—by silence—by the nation? Perhaps there will be no adequate punishment except the monarchy which it is inviting, and for which it is preparing the way in the sure and effective Roman fashion.

I would never venture to talk like this if I were alive. It is only by keeping steadily in my mind that my Autobiography is not to be published until I am dead, that I am enabled to force myself to say the things I think, instead of merely saying the things which I wish the reader to *think* I think—which is the live man's way, and is a part of every man's character, and cannot be changed while he is alive.

The veteran whom I have been quoting makes a suggestion. It is that the pensions be now extended to the Confederate soldiers. The Government will be grateful for that idea: it will now proceed to dicker for the South's vote—and its manhood.

January 17, 1907

About Helen Keller, who dined with Mr. Clemens yesterday evening—Her wonderful intellect, etc.—Some lines written about her by Susan Coolidge.

Helen Keller dined with us yesterday evening. She was accompanied by Mr. and Mrs. Macy. Mrs. Macy became her first teacher in the neighborhood of twenty years ago, and has been at her side ever since. Helen Keller is the eighth wonder of the world; Mrs. Macy is the ninth. Mrs. Macy's achievement seems to me to easily throw all previous miracles into the shade and take the importance out of them. Helen was a lump of clay, another Adam—deaf, dumb, blind, inert, dull, groping, almost unsentient: Miss Sullivan blew the breath of intelligence into her and woke the clay to life. But there the parallel ends. From that point onward there is no twinship between Adam and Helen; in fact the twinship does not reach quite that far, for neither light nor intelligence was blown into Adam's clay, but only the breath of physical life. Adam began his career without an intellect, and there is no evidence that he ever acquired one. Helen is quite a different kind of Adam. She was born with a fine mind and a bright wit, and by help of Miss Sullivan's amazing gifts as a teacher this mental endowment has been developed until the result is what we see to-day: a stone deaf, dumb, and blind girl who is equipped with a wide and various and complete university education—a wonderful creature who sees without eyes, hears without ears, and speaks with dumb lips. She stands alone in history. It has taken all the ages to produce a Helen Keller—and a Miss Sullivan. The names belong together; without Miss Sullivan there had been no Helen Keller.

At dinner the stream of conversation flowed gaily along without let or hindrance, the deaf, dumb, and blind girl taking her full share in it, and contributing her full share of jest and repartee and laughter. Every remark made was reported to Helen by Mrs. Macy with the fingers of one hand, and so rapidly that by the time the utterer of it had reached his last word, Mrs. Macy had delivered that word into Helen's hand, so there was no waiting, there were no intervals. This is a wonderful thing, for the reason that Mrs. Macy does not use shorthand forms, but spells each word out. Her fingers have to move as swiftly as do the fingers of a pianist. The eye of the witness is not quick enough to follow their movements.

Helen's talk sparkles. She is unusually quick and bright. The person who fires off smart felicities seldom has the luck to hit her in a dumb place; she is almost certain to send back as good as she gets, and almost as certainly with an improvement added.

I had not met her for a long time. In the meantime, she has become a woman. By this I mean that whereas formerly she lived in a world which was unreal—a sort of half world, a moon with only its bright and beautiful side presented to her, and its dark and repulsive side concealed from her—I think she now lives in the world that the rest of us know. I think that this is not wholly a guess. I seemed to notice evidences all along that it is a fact. I think she is not now the Helen Keller whom Susan Coolidge knew, and about whom she wrote, with such subtle pathos and charm:

> Behind her triple prison-bars shut in
> She sits, the whitest soul on earth to-day.
> No shadowing stain, no whispered hint of sin,
> Into that sanctuary finds the way.

That was all true in those earlier days. When I first knew Helen she was fourteen years old, and up to that time all soiling and sorrowful and unpleasant things had been carefully kept from her. The word death was not in her vocabulary, nor the word grave. She was indeed "the whitest soul on earth"—the poet's words had said the truth. "To her mind—

> The world is not the sordid world we know;
> It is a happy and benignant spot
> Where kindness reigns, and jealousy is not."

I am sure she has lost that gracious world, and now inhabits the one we all know—and deplore. The poet's description of Helen's face is vivid, and as exactly true as it is vivid:

Like a strange alabaster mask her face,
  Rayless and sightless, set in patience dumb,
  Until like quick electric currents come
The signals of life into her lonely place;
Then, like a lamp just lit, an inward gleam
  Flashes within the mask's opacity,
  The features glow and dimple suddenly,
And fun and tenderness and sparkle seem
  To irradiate the lines once dull and blind,
While the white slender fingers reach and cling
With quick imploring gestures, questioning
  The mysteries and the meanings.

Seen once, the moving and eloquent play of emotion in her face is forever unforgettable. I have not seen the like of it in any other face, and shall not, I know. One would suppose that delicate sound vibrations could not reach her save through some very favorable medium—like wood, for instance—but it is not so. Once yesterday evening, while she was sitting musing in a heavily tufted chair, my secretary began to play on the orchestrelle. Helen's face flushed and brightened on the instant, and the waves of delighted emotion began to sweep across it. Her hands were resting upon the thick and cushion-like upholstery of her chair, but they sprang into action at once, like a conductor's, and began to beat the time and follow the rhythm.

Tuesday, January 22, 1907

Authorship of the lines beginning "Love Came at Dawn"—Also authorship of lines inscribed on Susy's gravestone—Mr. Clemens will try his billiard scheme for winning bets from Mr. Dooley when he comes to play billiards on Friday—Tells how he tried it on Mr. George Robinson, long ago.

In an earlier chapter I inserted some verses beginning "Love Came at Dawn" which had been found among Susy's papers after her death. I was not able to say that they were hers, but I judged that they might be, for the reason that she had not enclosed them in quotation marks according to her habit when storing up treasures gathered from other people. Stedman was not able to determine the authorship for me, as the verses were new to him, but the authorship has now been traced. The verses were written by William Wilfred Campbell, a Canadian poet, and they form a part of the contents of his book called "Beyond the Hills of Dream."

The authorship of the beautiful lines which my wife and I inscribed upon Susy's gravestone was untraceable for a time. We had found them in a book in India, but had lost the book, and with it the author's name. But in time an application to the editor of

Notes and Queries furnished me the author's name,* and it has been added to the verses upon the gravestone.

Last night, at a dinner party where I was present, Mr. Peter Dunne Dooley handed to the host several dollars, in satisfaction of a lost bet. I seemed to see an opportunity to better my condition, and I invited Dooley, apparently disinterestedly, to come to my house Friday and play billiards. He accepted, and I judge that there is going to be a deficit in the Dooley treasury as a result. In great qualities of the heart and brain, Dooley is gifted beyond all propriety. He is brilliant; he is an expert with his pen, and he easily stands at the head of all the satirists of this generation—but he is going to walk in darkness Friday afternoon. It will be a fraternal kindness to teach him that with all his light and culture, he does not know all the valuable things; and it will also be a fraternal kindness to him to complete his education for him—and I shall do this on Friday, and send him home in that perfected condition.

I possess a billiard secret which can be valuable to the Dooley sept after I shall have conferred it upon Dooley—for a consideration. It is a discovery which I made by accident, thirty-eight years ago, in my father-in-law's house in Elmira. There was a scarred and battered and ancient billiard table in the garret, and along with it a peck of checked and chipped balls, and a rackful of crooked and headless cues. I played solitaire up there every day with that difficult outfit. The table was not level, but slanted sharply to the southeast; there wasn't a ball that was round, or would complete the journey you started it on, but would always get tired and stop half way and settle, with a jolty wobble, to a standstill on its chipped side. I tried making counts with four balls, but found it difficult and discouraging, so I added a fifth ball, then a sixth, then a seventh, and kept on adding until at last I had twelve balls on the table and a thirteenth to play with. My game was caroms—caroms solely—caroms plain, or caroms with cushion to help—anything that could furnish a count. In the course of time I found to my astonishment that I was never able to run fifteen, under any circumstances. By huddling the balls advantageously in the beginning, I could now and then coax fourteen out of them, but I couldn't reach fifteen by either luck or skill. Sometimes the balls would get scattered into difficult positions and defeat me in that way; sometimes if I managed to keep them together I would freeze; and always when I froze, and had to play away from the contact, there was sure to be nothing to play at but a wide and uninhabited vacancy.

One day Mr. Dillon called on my brother-in-law, on a matter of business, and I was asked if I could entertain him a while, until my brother-in-law should finish an engagement with another gentleman. I said I could, and took him up to the billiard table. I had played with him many times at the club, and knew that he could play billiards tolerably well—only tolerably well—but not any better than I could. He and I were just a match. He didn't know our table; he didn't know those balls; he didn't know those warped and

* Robert Richardson, deceased, of Australia.

headless cues; he didn't know the southeastern slant of the table, and how to allow for it. I judged it would be safe and profitable to offer him a bet on my scheme. I emptied the avalanche of thirteen balls on the table and said,

"Take a ball and begin, Mr. Dillon. How many can you run with an outlay like that?"

He said, with the half-affronted air of a mathematician who has been asked how much of the multiplication table he can recite without a break,

"I suppose a million—eight hundred thousand, anyway."

I said "You shall have the privilege of placing the balls to suit yourself, and I want to bet you a dollar that you can't run fifteen."

I will not dwell upon the sequel. At the end of an hour his face was red, and wet with perspiration; his outer garments lay scattered here and there over the place; he was the angriest man in the State, and there wasn't a rag or remnant of an injurious adjective left in him anywhere—and I had all his small change.

When the summer was over we went home to Hartford, and one day Mr. George Robinson arrived from Boston with two or three hours to spare between then and the return train, and as he was a young gentleman to whom we were in debt for much social pleasure, it was my duty, and a welcome duty, to make his two or three hours interesting for him. So I took him up stairs and set up my billiard scheme for his comfort. Mine was a good table, in perfect repair; the cues were in perfect condition; the balls were ivory, and flawless—but I knew that Mr. Robinson was my prey, just the same, for by exhaustive tests with this outfit I had found that my limit was thirty-one. I had proved to my satisfaction that whereas I could not fairly expect to get more than six or eight or a dozen caroms out of a run, I could now and then reach twenty and twenty-five, and after a long procession of failures finally achieve a run of thirty-one; but in no case had I ever got beyond thirty-one. Robinson's game, as I knew, was a little better than mine, so I resolved to require him to make thirty-two. I believed it would entertain him. He was one of these brisk and hearty and cheery and self-satisfied young fellows who are brimful of confidence, and who plunge with grateful eagerness into any enterprise that offers a showy test of their abilities. I emptied the balls on the table and said,

"Take a cue and a ball, George, and begin. How many caroms do you think you can make out of that layout?"

He laughed the laugh of the gay and the care-free, as became his youth and inexperience, and said,

"I can punch caroms out of that bunch a week without a break."

I said "Place the balls to suit yourself, and begin."

Confidence is a necessary thing in billiards, but over-confidence is bad. George went at his task with much too much lightsomeness of spirit and disrespect for the situation. On his first shot he scored three caroms; on his second shot he scored four caroms; and on his third shot he missed as simple a carom as could be devised. He was very much astonished, and said he would not have supposed that careful play could be needed with an acre of bunched balls in front of a person.

He began again, and played more carefully, but still with too much lightsomeness; he couldn't seem to learn to take the situation seriously. He made about a dozen caroms, and broke down. He was irritated with himself now, and he thought he caught me laughing. He didn't. I do not laugh publicly at my client when this game is going on; I only do it inside—or save it for after the exhibition is over. But he thought he had caught me laughing, and it increased his irritation. Of course I knew he thought I was laughing privately—for I was experienced; they all think that, and it has a good effect; it sharpens their annoyance and debilitates their play.

He made another trial and failed. Once more he was astonished; once more he was humiliated—and as for his anger, it rose to summer-heat. He arranged the balls again, grouping them carefully, and said he would win this time, or die. When a client reaches this condition it is a good time to damage his nerve further, and this can always be done by saying some little mocking thing or other that has the outside appearance of a friendly remark—so I employed this art. I suggested that a bet might tauten his nerves, and that I would offer one, but that as I did not want it to be an expense to him, but only a help, I would make it small—a cigar, if he were willing—a cigar that he would fail again; not an expensive one, but a cheap native one, of the Crown Jewel breed, such as is manufactured in Hartford for the clergy. It set him afire all over! I could see the blue flame issue from his eyes. He said,

"Make it a hundred!—and no Connecticut cabbage-leaf product, but Havanas, twenty-five dollars the box!"

I took him up, but said I was sorry to see him do this, because it did not seem to me right or fair for me to rob him under our own roof, when he had been so kind to us. He said, with energy and acrimony,

"You take care of your own pocket, if you'll be so good, and leave me to take care of mine."

And he plunged at the congress of balls with a vindictiveness which was infinitely contenting to me. He scored a failure—and began to undress. I knew it would come to that, for he was in the condition now that Mr. Dooley will be in at about that stage of the contest on Friday afternoon. A clothes-rack will be provided for Mr. Dooley to hang his things on, as fast as he shall from time to time shed them. George raised his voice four degrees and flung out the challenge—

"Double or quits!"

"Done," I responded, in the gentle and compassionate voice of one who is apparently getting sorrier and sorrier.

There was an hour and a half of straight disaster after that, and if it was a sin to enjoy it, it is no matter—I did enjoy it. It is half a lifetime ago, but I enjoy it yet, every time I think of it. George made failure after failure. His fury increased with each failure as he scored it. With each defeat he flung off one or another rag of his raiment, and every time he started on a fresh inning he made it "double or quits" once more. Twice he reached thirty and broke down; once he reached thirty-one and broke down. These "nears" made him frantic, and I believe I was never so happy in my life, except the time, a few years later, when the Reverend J. H. Twichell and I walked to Boston and he had the celebrated conversation with the hostler at the Inn at Ashford, Connecticut.

At last, when we were notified that Patrick was at the door to drive him to his train, George owed me five thousand cigars at twenty-five cents apiece, and I was so sorry I could have hugged him. But he shouted,

"Give me ten minutes more!" and added stormily, "it's double or quits again, and I'll win out free of debt or owe you ten thousand cigars, and you'll pay the funeral expenses."

He began on his final effort, and I believe that in all my experience among both amateurs and experts I have never seen a cue so carefully handled in my lifetime as George handled his upon this intensely interesting occasion. He got safely up to twenty-five, and then ceased to breathe. So did I. He labored along, and added a point, another point, still another point, and finally reached thirty-one. He stopped there, and we took a breath. By this time the balls were scattered all down the cushions, about a foot or two apart, and there wasn't a shot in sight anywhere that any man might hope to make. In a burst of anger and confessed defeat, he sent his ball flying around the table at random, and it crotched a ball that was packed against the cushion and sprang across to a ball against the bank on the opposite side, and counted!

His luck had set him free, and he didn't owe me anything. He had used up all his spare time, but we carried his clothes to the carriage and he dressed on his way to the station, greatly wondered at and admired by the ladies, as he drove along—but he got his train.

I am very fond of Mr. Dooley, and shall await his coming with affectionate and pecuniary interest.

P.S. Saturday. He has been here. Let us not talk about it.

Wednesday, January 23, 1907

Mr. Clemens's strange luck in playing his first games of bowling, fifteen-ball pool, and "Quaker."

The proverb says that Providence protects children and idiots. This is really true. I know it because I have tested it in my own person. It did not protect George through the most of his campaign, but it saved him in his last inning, and the veracity of the proverb stood confirmed.

I have several times been saved by this mysterious interposition, when I was manifestly in extreme peril. It has been common, all my life, for smart people to perceive in me an easy prey for selfish designs, and I have walked without suspicion into the trap set for me, yet have often come out unscathed, against all the likelihoods. More than forty years ago, in San Francisco, the office staff adjourned, upon conclusion of its work at two o'clock in the morning, to a great bowling establishment where there were twelve alleys. I was invited, rather perfunctorily, and as a matter of etiquette—by which I mean that

1865

I was invited politely, but not urgently. But when I diffidently declined, with thanks, and explained that I knew nothing about the game, those lively young fellows became at once eager and anxious and urgent to have my society. This flattered me, for I perceived no trap, and I innocently and gratefully accepted their invitation. I was given an alley all to myself. The boys explained the game to me, and they also explained to me that there would be an hour's play, and that the player who scored the fewest ten-strikes in the hour would have to provide oysters and beer for the combination. This disturbed me very seriously, since it promised me bankruptcy, and I was sorry that this detail had been overlooked in the beginning. But my pride would not allow me to back out now, so I stayed in, and did what I could to look satisfied and glad I had come. It is not likely that I looked as contented as I wanted to, but the others looked glad enough to make up for it, for they were quite unable to hide their evil joy. They showed me how to stand, and how to stoop, and how to aim the ball, and how to let fly; and then the game began. The results were astonishing. In my ignorance I delivered the balls in apparently every way except the right one; but no matter—during half an hour I never started a ball down the alley that didn't score a ten-strike, every time, at the other end. The others lost their grip early, and their joy along with it. Now and then one of them got a ten-strike, but the occurrence was so rare that it made no show alongside of my giant score. The boys surrendered at the end of the half hour, and put on their coats and gathered around me and in courteous, but sufficiently definite, language expressed their opinion of an experience-worn and seasoned expert who would stoop to lying and deception in order to rob kind and well-meaning friends who had put their trust in him under the delusion that he was an honest and honorable person. I was not able to convince them that I had not lied, for now my character was gone, and they refused to attach any value to anything I said. The proprietor of the place stood by for a while saying nothing, then he came to my defence. He said,

"It looks like a mystery, gentlemen, but it isn't a mystery after it's explained. That is a *grooved* alley; you've only to start a ball down it any way you please and the groove will do the rest; it will slam the ball against the northeast curve of the head pin every time, and nothing can save the ten from going down."

It was true. The boys made the experiment, and they found that there was no art that could send a ball down that alley and fail to score a ten-strike with it. When I had told those boys that I knew nothing about that game I was speaking only the truth, but it was ever thus, all through my life: whenever I have diverged from custom and principle and uttered a truth, the rule has been that the hearer hadn't strength of mind enough to believe it.

A quarter of a century ago I arrived in London to lecture a few weeks under the management of George Dolby, who had conducted the Dickens readings in America five or six years before. He took me to the Albemarle and fed me, and in the course of the dinner he enlarged a good deal, and with great satisfaction, upon his reputation as a player of fifteen-ball pool, and when he learned by my testimony that I had never seen the game played, and knew nothing of the art of pocketing balls, he enlarged more and

1873

more, and still more, and kept on enlarging, until I recognized that I was either in the presence of the very father of fifteen-ball pool or in the presence of his most immediate descendant. At the end of the dinner Dolby was eager to introduce me to the game and show me what he could do. We adjourned to the billiard room and he framed the balls in a flat pyramid and told me to fire at the apex ball and then go on and do what I could toward pocketing the fifteen, after which he would take the cue and show me what a pastmaster of the game could do with those balls. I did as required. I began with the diffidence proper to my ignorant estate, and when I had finished my inning all the balls were in the pockets and Dolby was burying me under a volcanic irruption of acid sarcasms.

So I was a liar, in Dolby's belief. He thought he had been sold, and at a cheap rate; but he divided his sarcasms quite fairly and quite equally between the two of us. He was full of ironical admiration of his childishness and innocence in letting a wandering and characterless and scandalous American load him up with deceptions of so transparent a character that they ought not to have deceived the housecat. On the other hand, he was remorselessly severe upon me for beguiling him, by studied and discreditable artifice, into bragging and boasting about his poor game in the presence of a professional expert disguised in lies and frauds, who could empty more balls in billiard pockets in an hour than he could empty into a basket in a day.

In the matter of fifteen-ball pool I never got Dolby's confidence wholly back, though I got it in other ways, and kept it until his death. I have played that game a number of times since, but that first time was the only time in my life that I have ever pocketed all the fifteen in a single inning.

My unsuspicious nature has made it necessary for Providence to save me from traps a number of times. Thirty years ago, a couple of Elmira bankers invited me to play the game of "Quaker" with them. I had never heard of the game before, and said that if it required intellect, I should not be able to entertain them. But they said it was merely a game of chance, and required no mentality—so I agreed to make a trial of it. They appointed four in the afternoon for the sacrifice. As the place, they chose a ground-floor room with a large window in it. Then they went treacherously around and advertised the "sell" which they were going to play upon me.

1876

I arrived on time, and we began the game—with a large and eager free-list to superintend it. These superintendents were outside, with their noses pressed against the window-pane. The bankers described the game to me. So far as I recollect, the pattern of it was this: they had a pile of Mexican dollars on the table; twelve of them were of even date, fifty of them were of odd dates. The bankers were to separate a coin from the pile and hide it under a hand, and I must guess "odd" or "even." If I guessed correctly, the coin would be mine; if incorrectly, I lost a dollar. The first guess I made was "even," and was right. I guessed again, "even," and took the money. They fed me another one and I guessed "even" again, and took the money. I guessed "even" the fourth time, and took the money. It seemed to me that "even" was a good guess, and I might as well stay by it, which I did. I guessed "even" twelve times, and took the twelve dollars. I was doing as they secretly desired. Their experience of human nature had convinced them that any human being as innocent as my face proclaimed me to be, would repeat his first guess if it won, and would go on repeating it if it should continue to win. It was their belief that an innocent would be almost sure at the beginning to guess "even," and not "odd," and that if an innocent should guess "even" twelve times in succession and win every time, he would go on guessing "even" to the end—so it was their purpose to let me win those twelve even dates and then advance the odd dates, one by one, until I should lose fifty dollars, and furnish those superintendents something to laugh about for a week to come.

But it did not come out in that way; for by the time I had won the twelfth dollar and last even date, I withdrew from the game because it was so one-sided that it was monotonous, and did not entertain me. There was a burst of laughter from the superintendents at the window when I came out of the place, but I did not know what they were laughing at nor whom they were laughing at, and it was a matter of no interest to me anyway. Through that incident I acquired an enviable reputation for smartness and penetration, but it was not my due, for I had not penetrated anything that the cow could not have penetrated.

Mr. Clemens shows that poor billiard tables and bowling alleys furnish better amusement, and require more skill than good ones—examples: billiard table at Jackass Gulch and bowling alley at Bateman's Point.

The last quarter of a century of my life has been pretty constantly and faithfully devoted to the study of the human race—that is to say, the study of myself, for, in my individual person, I am the entire human race compacted together. I have found that there is no ingredient of the race which I do not possess in either a small way or a large way. When it is small, as compared with the same ingredient in somebody else, there is still enough of it for all the purposes of examination. In my contacts with the species I find no one who possesses a quality which I do not possess. The shades of difference between other people and me serve to make variety and prevent monotony, but that is all; broadly speaking, we are all alike; and so by studying myself carefully and comparing myself with other people, and noting the divergences, I have been enabled to acquire a knowledge of the human race which I perceive is more accurate and more comprehensive than that which has been acquired and revealed by any other member of our species. As a result, my private and concealed opinion of myself is not of a complimentary sort. It follows that my estimate of the human race is the duplicate of my estimate of myself.

I am not proposing to discuss all of the peculiarities of the human race, at this time; I only wish to touch lightly upon one or two of them. To begin with, I wonder why a man should prefer a good billiard table to a poor one; and why he should prefer straight cues to crooked ones; and why he should prefer round balls to chipped ones; and why he should prefer a level table to one that slants; and why he should prefer responsive cushions to the dull and unresponsive kind. I wonder at these things, because when we examine the matter we find that the essentials involved in billiards are as competently and exhaustively furnished by a bad billiard outfit as they are by the best one. One of the essentials is amusement. Very well, if there is any more amusement to be gotten out of the one outfit than out of the other, the facts are in favor of the bad outfit. The bad outfit will always furnish 30 per cent more fun for the players and for the spectators than will the good outfit. Another essential of the game is that the outfit shall give the players full opportunity to exercise their best skill, and display it in a way to compel the admiration of the spectators. Very well, the bad outfit is nothing behind the good one in this regard. It is a difficult matter to correctly estimate the eccentricities of chipped balls and a slanting table, and make the right allowance for them and secure a count; the finest kind of skill is required to accomplish the satisfactory result. Another essential of the game is that it shall add to the interest of the game by furnishing opportunities to bet. Very well, in this regard no good outfit can claim any advantage over a bad one. I know, by experience, that a bad outfit is as valuable as the best one; that an outfit that couldn't be sold at auction for seven dollars is just as valuable for all the essentials of the game as an outfit that is worth a thousand.

I acquired some of this learning in Jackass Gulch, California, more than forty years ago. Jackass Gulch had once been a rich and thriving surface-mining camp. By and by its gold deposits were exhausted; then the people began to go away, and the town began to decay, and rapidly; in my time it had disappeared. Where the bank, and the city hall, and the church, and the gambling dens, and the newspaper office, and the streets of brick blocks had been, was nothing now but a wide and beautiful expanse of green grass, a peaceful and charming solitude. Half a dozen scattered dwellings were still inhabited, and there was still one saloon of a ruined and rickety character struggling for life, but doomed. In its bar was a billiard outfit that was the counterpart of the one in my father-in-law's garret. The balls were chipped, the cloth was darned and patched, the table's surface was undulating, and the cues were headless and had the curve of a parenthesis—but the forlorn remnant of marooned miners played games there, and those games were more entertaining to look at than a circus and a grand opera combined. Nothing but a quite extraordinary skill could score a carom on that table—a skill that required the nicest estimate of force, distance, and how much to allow for the various slants of the table and the other formidable peculiarities and idiosyncrasies furnished by the contradictions of the outfit. Last winter, here in New York, I saw Hoppe and Schaefer and Sutton and the three or four other billiard champions of world-wide fame contend against each other, and certainly the art and science displayed were a wonder to see; yet I saw nothing there in the way of science and art that was more wonderful than shots which I had seen Texas Tom make on the wavy surface of that poor old wreck in the perishing saloon at Jackass Gulch forty years before. Once I saw Texas Tom make a string of seven points on a single inning!—all calculated shots, and not a fluke or a scratch among them. I often saw him make runs of four, but when he made his great string of seven, the boys went wild with enthusiasm and admiration. The joy and the noise exceeded that which the great gathering at Madison Square produced when

Sutton scored five hundred points at the eighteen-inch game, on a world-famous night last winter. With practice, that champion could score nineteen or twenty on the Jackass Gulch table; but to start with, Texas Tom would show him miracles that would astonish him; also it might have another handsome result: it might persuade the great experts to discard their own trifling game and bring the Jackass Gulch outfit here and exhibit their skill in a game worth a hundred of the discarded one, for profound and breathless interest, and for displays of almost superhuman skill.

In my experience, games played with a fiendish outfit furnish ecstasies of delight which games played with the other kind cannot match. Twenty-seven years ago my budding little family spent the summer at Bateman's Point, near Newport, Rhode Island. It was a humble and comfortable boarding place, well stocked with sweet mothers and little children, but the male sex was scarce; however, there was another young fellow besides myself, and he and I had good times—Higgins was his name, but that was not his fault. He was a very pleasant and companionable person. On the premises there was what had once been a bowling alley. It was a single alley, and it was estimated that it had been out of repair for sixty years—but not the balls, the balls were in good condition; there were forty-one of them, and they ranged in size from a grapefruit up to a lignum-vitae sphere that you could hardly lift. Higgins and I played on that alley day after day. At first, one of us located himself at the bottom end to set up the pins in case anything should happen to them, but nothing happened. The surface of that alley consisted of a rolling stretch of elevations and depressions, and neither of us could, by any art known to us, persuade a ball to stay on the alley until it should accomplish something. Little balls and big, the same thing always happened—the ball left the alley before it was half way home and went thundering down alongside of it the rest of the way and made the gamekeeper climb out and take care of himself. No matter, we persevered, and were rewarded. We examined the alley, noted and located a lot of its peculiarities, and little by little we learned how to deliver a ball in such a way that it would travel home and knock down a pin or two. By and by we succeeded in improving our game to a point where we were able to get all of the pins with thirty-five balls—so we made it a thirty-five-ball game. If the player did not succeed with thirty-five, he had lost the game. I suppose that all the balls, taken together, weighed five hundred pounds, or maybe a ton—or along there somewhere—but anyway it was hot weather, and by the time that a player had sent thirty-five of them home he was in a drench of perspiration, and physically exhausted.

Next, we started cocked hat—that is to say, a triangle of three pins, the other seven being discarded. In this game we used the three smallest balls and kept on delivering them until we got the three pins down. After a day or two of practice we were able to get the chief pin with an output of four balls, but it cost us a great many deliveries to get the other two; but by and by we succeeded in perfecting our art—at least we perfected it to our limit. We reached a scientific excellence where we could get the three pins down with twelve deliveries of the three small balls, making thirty-six shots to conquer the cocked hat.

Having reached our limit for daylight work, we set up a couple of candles and played at night. As the alley was fifty or sixty feet long, we couldn't see the pins, but the candles indicated their locality. We continued this game until we were able to knock down the invisible pins with thirty-six shots. Having now reached the limit of the candle game, we changed and played it left-handed. We continued the left-handed game until we conquered its limit, which was fifty-four shots. Sometimes we sent down a succession of fifteen balls without getting anything at all. We easily got out of that old alley five times the fun that anybody could have gotten out of the best alley in New York.

One blazing hot day, a modest and courteous officer of the regular army appeared in our den and introduced himself. He was about thirty-five years old, well built and militarily erect and straight, and he was hermetically sealed up in the uniform of that ignorant old day—a uniform made of heavy material, and much properer for January than July. When he saw the venerable alley, and glanced from that to the long procession of shining balls in the trough, his eye lit with desire, and we judged that he was our meat. We politely invited him to take a hand, and he could not conceal his gratitude; though his breeding, and the etiquette of his profession, made him try. We explained the game to him, and said that there were forty-one balls, and that the player was privileged to extend his inning and keep on playing until he had used them all up—repeatedly—and that for every ten-strike he got a prize. We didn't name the prize—it wasn't necessary, as no prize would ever be needed or called for. He started a sarcastic smile, but quenched it, according to the etiquette of his profession. He merely remarked that he would like to select a couple of medium balls and one small one, adding that he didn't think he would need the rest.

Then he began, and he was an astonished man. He couldn't get a ball to stay on the alley. When he had fired about fifteen balls and hadn't yet reached the cluster of pins, his annoyance began to show out through his clothes. He wouldn't let it show in his face; but after another fifteen balls he was not able to control his face; he didn't utter a word, but he exuded mute blasphemy from every pore. He asked permission to take off his coat, which was granted; then he turned himself loose, with bitter determination, and although he was only an infantry officer he could have been mistaken for a battery, he got up such a volleying thunder with those balls. Presently he removed his cravat; after a little he took off his vest; and still he went bravely on. Higgins was suffocating. My condition was the same, but it would not be courteous to laugh; it would be better to burst, and we came near it. That officer was good pluck. He stood to his work without uttering a word, and kept the balls going until he had expended the outfit four times, making four times forty-one shots; then he had to give it up, and he did; for he was no longer able to stand without wobbling. He put on his clothes, bade us a courteous good-bye, invited us to call at the Fort, and started away. Then he came back, and said,

"What is the prize for the ten-strike?"

We had to confess that we had not selected it yet.

He said, gravely, that he thought there was no occasion for hurry about it.

I believe Bateman's alley was a better one than any other in America, in the matter of the essentials of the game. It compelled skill; it provided opportunity for bets; and if you could get a stranger to do the bowling for you, there was more and wholesomer and delightfuler entertainment to be gotten out of his industries than out of the finest game by the best expert, and played upon the best alley elsewhere in existence.

Monday, January 28, 1907

Senator Clark of Montana, and the dinner given in his honor at the Union League Club because of his having lent to the club a million dollars' worth of European pictures.

In the middle of the afternoon, day before yesterday, a particular friend of mine, whom I will call Jones for this day and train only, telephoned, and said he would like to call for me at half past seven and take me to a dinner at the Union League Club. He said he would send me home as early as I pleased, he being aware that I am declining all invitations this year, and for the rest of my life, that make it necessary for me to go out at night—at least to places where speeches are made and the sessions last until past ten o'clock. But Jones is a very particular friend of mine, and therefore it cost me no discomfort to transgress my rule and accept his invitation; no, I am in error—it did cost me a pang, a decided pang, for although he said that the dinner was a private one, with only ten persons invited, he mentioned Senator Clark of Montana as one of the ten. I am a person of elevated tone, and of morals that can bear scrutiny, and am much above associating with animals of Mr. Clark's breed. I am sorry to be vain—at least I am sorry to expose the fact that I am vain—but I do confess it and expose it; I cannot help being vain of myself for giving such a large proof of my friendship for Jones as is involved in my accepting an invitation to break bread with such a person as Clark of Montana. It is not because he is a United States Senator—it is at least not wholly because he occupies that doubtful position—for there are many Senators whom I hold in a certain respect, and would not think of declining to meet them socially, if I believed it was the will of God. We have lately sent a United States Senator to the penitentiary, but I am quite well aware that of those who have escaped this promotion there are several who are in some regards guiltless of crime—not guiltless of all crimes, for that cannot be said of any United States Senator, I think, but guiltless of some kinds of crime. They all rob the Treasury by voting for iniquitous pension bills in order to keep on good terms with the Grand Army of the Republic, and with the Grand Army of the Republic, junior, and with the Grand Army of the Republic, junior, junior, and with other great-grandchildren of the war—and these bills distinctly represent crime, and violated senatorial oaths. However, while I am willing to waive moral rank and associate with the moderately criminal among the Senators—even including Platt and Chauncey Depew—I have to draw the line at Clark of Montana. He has bought legislatures and judges as other men buy food and raiment. By his example, he has so excused and so sweetened corruption that, in Montana, it no longer has an offensive smell. His history is known to everybody; he is as rotten a human being as can be found anywhere under the flag; he is a shame to the American nation, and no one has helped to send him to the Senate who did not know that his proper place was the penitentiary, with a chain and ball on his legs. To my mind, he is the most disgusting reptile that the republic has produced since Tweed's time.

I went to the dinner, which was served in a small private room of the club, with the usual piano and fiddlers present to make conversation difficult, and comfort impossible. I found that the Montana criminal was not merely a guest, but that the dinner was given in his honor. While the feeding was going on two of my elbow-neighbors supplied me with information concerning the reasons for this tribute of respect to Mr. Clark. Mr. Clark had lately lent to the Union League Club, which is the most powerful political club in America, and perhaps the richest, a million dollars' worth of European pictures for exhibition. It was quite plain that my informant regarded this as an act of almost superhuman generosity. One of my informants said, under his breath, and with awe and admiration, that if you should put together all of Mr. Clark's several generosities to the club, including this gaudy one, the cost to Mr. Clark, first and last, would doubtless amount to a hundred thousand dollars. I saw that I was expected to exclaim, applaud, and adore, but I was not tempted to do it, because I had been informed, five minutes earlier, that Clark's income, as stated under the worshiping informant's breath, was thirty million dollars a year. Human beings have no sense of proportion. A benefaction of a hundred thousand dollars subtracted from an income of thirty million dollars, is not a matter to go into hysterics of admiration and adulation about. If I should contribute ten thousand dollars to a cause, it would be one-ninth of my past year's income, and I could feel it; as matter for admiration, and wonder, and astonishment, and gratitude, it would far and away outrank a contribution of twenty-five million dollars from the Montana jailbird, who would still have a hundred thousand dollars a week left over from his year's income to subsist upon. It reminded me of the only instance of benevolence exploded upon the world by the late Jay Gould, that I had ever heard of. When that first and most infamous corrupter of American commercial morals was wallowing in uncountable stolen millions, he contributed five thousand dollars for the relief of the stricken population of Memphis, Tennessee, at a time when an epidemic of yellow fever was raging in that city. Mr. Gould's contribution cost him no sacrifice; it was only the income of the hour which he daily spent in prayer—for he was a most godly man—yet the storm of worshiping gratitude which welcomed it all over the United States, in the newspaper, the pulpit, and in the private circle, might have persuaded a stranger that for a millionaire American to give five thousand dollars to the dead and dying poor—when he could have bought a circuit judge with it—was the noblest thing in American history, and the holiest.

In time, the President of the Art Committee of the club rose and began with that aged and long-ago discredited remark that there were not to be any speeches on this occasion, but only friendly and chatty conversation; then he went on, in the ancient and long-ago discredited fashion, and made a speech himself—a speech which was well calculated to make any sober hearer ashamed of the human race. If a stranger had come in at that time he might have supposed that this was a divine service, and that the Divinity was present. He would have gathered that Mr. Clark was about the noblest human being the great republic had yet produced, and the most magnanimous, the most self-sacrificing, the most limitlessly and squanderingly prodigal benefactor of good causes living in any land to-day. And it never occurred to this worshipper of money, and money's possessor, that in effect Mr. Clark had merely dropped a dime into the League's hat. Mr. Clark couldn't miss his benefaction any more than he could miss ten cents.

When this wearisome orator had finished his devotions, the President of the Union League got up and continued the service in the same vein, vomiting adulations upon that jailbird which, estimated by any right standard of values, were the coarsest sarcasms, although the speaker was not aware of that. Both of these orators had been applauded all along, but the present one ultimately came out with a remark which I judged would fetch a cold silence, a very chilly chill; he revealed the fact that the expenses of the club's loan exhibition of the Senator's pictures had exceeded the income from the tickets of admission; then he paused—as speakers always do when they are going to spring a grand effect—and said that at that crucial time Senator Clark stepped forward, of his own motion, and put his hand in his pocket and handed out fifteen hundred dollars wherewith to pay half of the insurance on the pictures, and thus the club's pocket was saved whole. I wish I may never die, if the worshippers present at this religious service did not break out in grateful applause at that astonishing statement; and I wish I may never permanently die, if the jailbird didn't smile all over his face and look as radiantly happy as he will look some day when Satan gives him a Sunday vacation in the cold-storage vault.

Finally, while I was still alive, the President of the club finished his dreary and fatiguing marketing of juvenile commonplaces, and introduced Clark, and sat down. Clark rose to the tune of the "Star-Spangled Banner"—no, it was "God Save the King," frantically sawed and thumped by the fiddlers and the piano; and this was followed by "For he's a jolly good fellow," sung by the whole strength of the happy worshippers. A miracle followed. I have always maintained that no man could make a speech with nothing but a compliment for a text, but I know now that a reptile can. Senator Clark twaddled, and twaddled, and twaddled along for a full half hour with no text but those praises which had been lavished upon his trifling generosities; and he not only accepted at par all these silly praises, but added to them a pile—praising his own so-called generosities and magnanimities with such intensity and color that he took the pigment all out of those other men's compliments and made them look pallid and shadowy. With forty years' experience of human assfulness and vanity at banquets, I have never seen anything of the sort that could remotely approach the assfulness and complacency of this coarse and vulgar and incomparably ignorant peasant's glorification of himself.

I shall always be grateful to Jones for giving me the opportunity to be present at these sacred orgies. I had believed that in my time I had seen at banquets all the different kinds of speech-making animals there are, and also all the different kinds of people that go to make our population, but it was a mistake. This was the first time I had ever seen men get down in the gutter and frankly worship dollars, and their possessors. Of course I was familiar with such things, through our newspapers, but I had never before heard men worship the dollar with their mouths, or seen them on their knees in the act.

Palm Readings.

The editor of *Harper's Monthly* has submitted prints of my hands to several New York palmists of the first repute, (hiding my name from them, of course), with a view to testing their art. Ostensibly that is the idea. This is the second time an editor has tried this plan of getting at supposed concealed places in my character. Mr. Stead tried it nine years ago. He sent prints of my hands—without revealing my name—to seven English palmists, and published the results. The "readings" were smoothly worded, but cautious, very cautious and wary. Wary, and cleverly indefinite. It could not be denied that they fitted me; but they would have fitted the rest of the human race just as well. The sentences had a deceptively smart look of saying something, but upon examination that apparent something faded out and vanished, like breath from a razor. In the whole accumulation there was only one dead-certain and absolutely definite assertion—to wit: "The possessor of these hands is destitute of the sense of humor."

1905

I believed this to be an error. I believed that this chiropodist had something the matter with him. Certainly it was curious, most curious. By reputation—and notoriously—I possessed that missing quality; and not only possessed it, but in extravagant, exaggerated, and even monstrous bulk; yet my hand, while naïvely giving away all my minor and hardly-discernible characteristics, had been able to entirely hide my sole prominent hump from the watchful expert. It was as if a blind naturalist should feel and name all the little animals in the menagerie and then overlook the elephant. None of the seven palmists found the elephant—full grown. Several of them found him, but only dog-size.

An examination of the following estimates of me will show that the New York palmists have overlooked the elephant, too. This persuades me that the human hand is not to be trusted, except in minor matters. I think Shakspeare's hand would have glibly and frankly given away all of Shakspeare's inconspicuous and inconsequential qualities, but kept his main secret loyally unrevealed. I wonder why a hand acts like that? There doesn't seem to be any sense in it; nor any fairness. To return to the experience of nine years ago.

"Destitute of the sense of humor." I could not seem to get over the pain of that unkind verdict. And besides, it was as good as repeated, and rubbed in, by the ominous and offensive silence of the six other verdicts: they gave me a fair and reasonable share of all the other qualities, but never mentioned humor at all. A friend came in—he was a stern and hard person, and as cold as a frog—and he asked me what I was crying about, and I told him about those lies and slanders, and he said I ought to be ashamed of myself to be such a baby at sixty; and then he went on and pointed out to me a thing which I had not thought of before—to wit, the vast force, the cumulative force, the convincing force of a *unanimous* verdict, when arrived at by seven dispassionate and unbribed experts, each working independently of the others, in the fear of God, none of them aware of my name, and all of them with reputations to sustain and families to support. He said that to any intelligent person such a verdict must be final and conclusive; he said that this verdict could not be a lie, but *could* be an "exposure"—and *was.* He said he had always believed I was not a humorist, and that I would some day be found out, and now it had happened. He said that by low artifices I had been deceiving and robbing the people for a quarter of a century; then, after an uncomfortable pause, he asked me if I could hold up my hand and look him in the eye and say this was not so. I tried to do it; but because I couldn't, on account of rheumatism and strabismus, he said I stood self-convicted. What he chose to call my "confession" awakened his pity, and he urged me to reform and begin a better life, but I tried to appease him with argument. I said it might be that the palmists had been misled by my hand; that if they had known whose hand it was they might have noticed things in it which they had overlooked this time; and I even offered to go in person before another jury of palmists and make a new and fairer trial, and see how it would come out. But he said it was a foolish idea, and brushed it away. Still, I think there was reason in it. It is so with the phrenologist: he can tell better when he knows you. I am sure of this; for in London, once, I went to Fowler as "John B. Smith" and he found no humor in me—said there was an excavation where the humor-bump should have been—yet when I went to him three months later as "Mark Twain" he said frankly and with enthusiasm that there was a pyramid in that place. Now, since knowing me helped a phrenologist, why might it not help a palmist?

Reading by Niblo.

1. According to the science of Palmistry, this is a Philosophic type of hand.

2. The subject is beyond doubt a great Student, a Thinker and Reformer, broad minded, with a liberal religious sentiment without reference to creed or form.

3. He is progressive and far-seeing, courageous in an emergency, but frequently timid where there is no need of action or quick thought. With him an emergency is an inspiration.

4. His sense of justice is very keen; harshness to others amounting to personal injury to himself. He is sensitive, impressionable and reticent, hence is not easily understood by his associates.

5. Disposition ordinarily is excellent. He is submissive rather than aggressive, yet radical and determined at heart. His manner is gentle, only becoming brusque or nonchalant when stirred to self defence.

6. Independence is the special prerogative of this hand. True the shattered line of Fate marks many hours of darkness and discouragement, but his pride and determination invariably lead him forth into the light, and the harassed spirit rises higher and stronger because of Fate's very resistance. This gift of buoyancy is not only an endowment of the spirit, but an inheritance of the flesh as well.

7. He is proud, honest and sincere, of a generous nature, with more respect to actions than to the results, ambitious of doing and achieving, and possessing great determination in the line of his efforts. His own success is not sufficient but all for whom he cares must push on with him.

8. Self reliance, internal courage, with an intuitive knack of sounding public sentiment render him capable of becoming a successful leader in the financial

and political world, a supporter of any and all innovations that tend toward advancement.

9. An absolute reverence for confidence reposed, is one of the strongest characteristics of this man.

10. Loss of faith would not entail pessimism, however, for he is not one who requires a fixed creed to buoy him up. His superabundant buoyancy of spirit, often compels success where a less confident heart would fail. "The World turns aside to let him pass who knows whither he is going"—and this man knows. His early life is not marked fortunate; menaced by reverses until near his 16th year. After that period excellent things were in store for him.

11. His line of intuition is distinctly marked, showing keen judgment, an excellent judge of character, especially regarding matters of honor or dishonor.

12. The strong line of benevolence is indicative of a charitable nature, giving only for the sake of giving. His hand is expressive of considerable wealth, due in a great measure to his own efforts in life.

13. Fortunately he is not constitutionally frail. Excellently endowed with physical force, he will reach beyond the proverbial limit of life without serious interruption. This strong hold on life he inherits. His death will not take place in the land of his birth.

14. Judging from the condition of the heart line, together with the splendidly developed mount of Venus, his loves are strong and his emotions intense. There will be two great affections satisfied in his life.

15. His mental tastes are extremely refined, fond of gratifying the senses to this extent—appreciates beauty, harmony, color, form, etc.

16. He will meet with his greatest success in middle life, the early years serve merely to "Sow the Seed," enrich the mind and sound the resources of this naturally vacillating individual.

Respectfully,
Niblo.

I am required to edit Mr. Niblo's Report.

1. Philosophic mind. True.

2.*a.* Student of morals, and of man's nature—in that sense, yes, I am a student, for that study is interesting and enticing, and requires no painful research, no systematic labor, no midnight-oil effects. But I have never been a student of anything which required of me wearying and distasteful labor. It is for this reason that the relations between me and the multiplication table are strained.

b. The rest of the paragraph is true, in detail and in mass. In the line of high philosophics I was always *a* thinker, but was never regarded by the world as *the* thinker until the course of nature retired Mr. Spencer from the competition.

3.*a.* "Progressive and far-seeing." I acknowledge it.

b. "Courageous in an emergency." That is too general. There are many kinds of emergencies: we are all good in one or two kinds; some are good in several kinds; but the person who is prompt and plucky in all emergencies is—well, non-existent. He has never lived. If a man were drowning, I would promptly jump in after him; but if he were falling from a tenth-story window I shouldn't know enough to stand from under. You perceive?

I am a good and confident swimmer, and have had several emergency-experiences in the water which were of an educating kind, but I have never had a person try to fall on me out of a sky-scraper. Do you get the idea? The philosophy of it is this: emergency-courage is rather a product of experience than a birthright. No person, when new and fresh, has emergency-courage enough to set a grip on his purse the first time he is offered a chance to cheaply buy a patent that is going to revolutionize steam—no, it is the subsequent occasions that find him ready with his gun. I repeat—the palmist has been too general. He should have named the *kind* of emergencies which find my courage ready and unappalled. I am not saying he could not have done this; and there is one thing which in fairness I *must* concede: that where brevity is required of the palmist, he is obliged to generalize, he cannot particularize.

4. Again. Generalized, this is true of no one; particularized, it is true of everybody. Harshness to Mr. Henry A. Butters of Long Valley would not grieve my spirit, the spectacle of the King of the Belgians dangling from the gibbet where he belongs would make me grateful. I (along with the whole race) am sensitive (to ridicule and insult); impressionable (where the sex is concerned); reticent (where inconvenient truths are required of me).

5. Again. Generalized thus, this fits the great majority of the human race—including me. It fits the worm, too—to a dot. Read it carefully over, and you will see.

6. I hope that the first sentence is true. Independence of mind is so rare in the world that it may almost be said to be non-existent. I have never known a man who possessed it in any considerable degree. Many thoughtless and shallow people despise the cat—but the cat has it; the cat is the only creature that greatly and grandly possesses it. The last sentence of the paragraph—like the first one—is sharply definite, and is as true as it is definite. I am sure that my buoyancy of spirit is above the average, but is it soberly believable that that fact is set down in the lines of my hand, as by print? My sister, who died at a great age, had the same spirit all her life: would Mr. Niblo have discovered it in her hand? My mother, who died at a great age (eighty-eight), possessed it; it never failed her between the cradle and the grave. Was it written down in her hand? My brother, who died at a great age, possessed not a vestige of it. He moved through a cloud of gloom and depression all his days. Could Mr. Niblo have read that pathetic secret in his hand? I wish I had prints of the family's hands; I would submit them to judgment with a warm curiosity.

7. We are *all* proud, in one way or another; we are all honest in some ways and dishonest in others; we are all sincere at times and insincere at other times; we are all ambitious, along one or two narrow lines, but indifferent along all the others. We must throw No. 7 into the generalization-basket.

8. My fondness for experiments and innovations is really above the average, I believe. My mother was like that; my sister, who was an interested and zealous invalid during sixty-five years, tried all the new diseases as fast as they came out, and always enjoyed the newest one more than any that went before; my brother had accumulated forty-two brands of Christianity before he was called away. Yes, I think the closing clause of No.

8 is correct. But the rest of the paragraph contains errors, particularly the part about political and financial leadership. No kind of leadership could ever be in my line. It would curtail my freedom; also it would make me work when I did not want to work. My nature would fret and complain and rebel, and I should fail.

10. Last sentence. No one ever said a truer thing. Up to the age of seven I was at the point of death nearly all the time, yet could never make it. It made the family tired. Particularly my father, who was of a fine and sensitive nature, and it was difficult for him to bear up under disappointments. In the next eight years—I am speaking the truth, I give you my word of honor—I was within one gasp of drowning *nine* different times, and in addition was thrice brought to the verge of death by doctors and disease; yet it was all of no use, nothing could avail, it was just one reverse after another, and here I am to this day. With every hope long ago blighted. Are these the reverses that stand written in my hand? I know of no others, of that early time.

13. First sentence. Seems so, from the revelations which I have just made. But how does he find it out from the flat print of my hand? It is very curious. I have seldom been sick since I was fifteen; I am sixty-nine now. Third sentence: the inheritance is from my mother's side. She was a Lampton. No Lampton ever died prematurely, except by courtesy of the sheriff.

Reading by Mr. Fletcher.

1. This is a hand of strong and marked personality; one in which many phases of decided ability are depicted, in fact it would be possible to read it from at least three points of view, and find a complete history in each.

2. The left hand shows many possibilities of a widely varying character, and not all in harmony with each other by any means. The right hand, however, shows that these have been used by mental determination to build up a personality that is full of force and ability, and one that relies absolutely upon itself. In no sense a dependent hand. In no sense a negative hand. Impressionable without question, but these impressions are recognized then selected, and then *directed.* They rarely, if ever, are the controlling factor. The *Ego* rules, and directs the abilities, instead of being *swayed* by the emotions, strong as these are on occasions. It is distinguished by great originality of thought; demonstrates marked powers of concentration, and never gives up what is undertaken no matter how great the opposition. There is, however, considerable irritability evidenced over delay, or the power of others to grasp situations readily, since this mind takes in at a glance the beginning and the end. Details are dealt with as a whole, rather than being patiently considered. There is no doubt about the conclusions being usually correct. The remarkable record for the past 15 years undoubtedly demonstrates that the palms show many plans that are from time to time suggested, but the fingers could never find the time or opportunities to execute one half of them. No one ever opened door for this hand and said "Come in, this is the way, and here is a garden already for you."

2. It has found its own door, made its own way, and planted every tree and shrub there is in the garden, and there are a great many. To be sure, at times the sun has shone benignly and the growth has been accordingly rapid, and this will continue to the end.

3. This is a nervous, energetic, determined hand, with, at times, a charm of personality, or magnetism about it that could compass almost any result. This will continue to the end. It might suffer itself to a great degree, in a quiet way; it would never *intentionally* cause suffering to others. It is too considerate and humanitarian for that. It will never be satisfied with itself, no matter how great the meed of praise from others may be. The unattained will ever loom up before it, even while others are speaking words of highest commendation.

4. Its interests will always be of a large and comprehensive character. The tendency is ever to attempt too much for one thought to lead up to another, whereby still greater possibilities will be revealed. It's a hand while kindly and generous to a fault with others is never overkind or considerate of itself. The life line is long and well defined, showing inherited longevity from one side of the family. Illnesses are few, but with extraordinary power of reaction. The nervous energy is at times tremendous, and rises on occasions to heights that carry all before it.

5. The head line shows great pride and ambition, and a marked power of concentration of the energies to a given point. There is little pleasure in the victories of yesterday. It's always the work of the tomorrow that engages this mind. The intellectual qualities are of a high order, the result of years of careful and severe training, yet it is quite possible for this mind to move in a groove, and not be always *characterized by the spirit of strict justice.*

6. Again this same line gives strong artistic and refined tendencies, and a tendency also to temporary depression which, however, *deters* the hand not a jot from the work undertaken.

7. Opposition, and some times, marked personal antagonism are also much evidenced, but instead of changing the purpose they have for the most part strengthened and intensified it. This hand brooks little interference from anyone, yet respects authority in the true sense of the word.

8. The heart line shows strong affections and warm sympathies for the few and great fidelity to all obligations. It is ever willing to do more than requested. It holds friendship as one of the most sacred things in the world, although betrayed more than once by friends. The domestic side is not discussed in this reading. This hand ought to be at touch with many people either in public life, or in very close connection with it. It certainly has the power of swaying opinions. The hand is eminently successful, and yet the full measure of its just recognition is before rather than behind it. Its work lives long after its activities.

9. There is the strong will that goes with this type of hand which in many instances borders upon obstinacy, and simply will *not* be moved from a purpose. This is especially true when any principle is at stake. It is absolutely protected from danger although not infrequently at touch with it.

10. A hand that has made, and is destined to continue to make a strong impression upon the public mind and yet remain indifferent to it.

Paragraph 2. "Relies absolutely upon itself; in no sense a dependent hand, in no sense a negative hand." Certainly that is definite enough. And notches the edge of the bull's-eye, too, let us hope; I am not here to discourage compliments. "Distinguished by great originality of thought." I could not deny the accuracy of that and be honest. "Never gives up what is undertaken, no matter how great the opposition." That is definite; there is no uncertain ring about it. But it is not true. Indeed, it is very far from being true. I call to mind not an episode in my life indicating in me—on even a single occasion—the presence of an unconquerable persistency. *"The remarkable record of the past fifteen years"*—very good, that far; stupendously good; to me those years were quite over-remarkable: in worry, in apprehension, in grief, in misfortune piled upon misfortune, disaster upon disaster, the fifteen outdid all the fifty-four that preceded them put together. If the palmist had only stopped at that point! He would have scored handsomely—albeit indefinitely; but when he goes on to explain *why* the fifteen were remarkable, it is a most sad drop from the impressive to the commonplace, and the result of that indiscreet drop is that the remarkableness of the fifteen entirely disappears. "Many plans suggested—no time or opportunity to execute the half of them;" dear me, it happens to *everybody,* there is nothing remarkable about it.

4. "Long life-line; inherited longevity from one side of the family; illnesses are few." All definite and correct. He and Mr. Niblo are in agreement upon these points.

8. First sentence. I hope it is true; also, I believe it is.

9. "Will not be moved from a purpose when a principle is at stake." Perhaps it comes near to being true; still, I think it is a little too sweeping, and a trifle too strong.

10. "Indifferent?" No, that would be against nature. The man who has made either a good impression or a bad one upon the public mind may be outwardly tranquil about it, but never inwardly indifferent.

Reading by Mr. Perin.

1. This is the hand of a good man.

2. In these very few words I could characterize the tendencies and ambitions of this hand.

3. By careful examination of the lines and marks I find this person to be between the age of fifty-five and sixty.

4. The Line of Health shows a fair development of physical strength and his body should never be unduly taxed.

5. The Line of the Head in the left hand shows a powerful brain, he is a natural genius and an intellectual giant.

6. This man should have become a Judge.

7. He is made of the finest clay, is high minded, has a will of steel hardly ever asking or taking advice.

8. His judgment can be fully relied upon.

9. The Line of the Heart as well as the Circle of Mercury in the right hand shows him to be extremely tender hearted, at the same time strong in his convictions.

10. The second phalange of the third finger combined with the Mount of Saturn shows considerable energy, he is self-possessed and his presence of mind is remarkable.

11. The Line of Respiration on the base of the Mount of Jupiter shows that his lungs demand a liberal supply of oxygen.

12. The Line of Blood Circulation shows him to have regular heart beats, and a strong and steady pulsation of blood.

13. The Mount of Luna shows him to be exquisitely moulded, honorable and faithful.

14. The Circle of Venus shows his love of mankind.

15. The Line of Intuition in the left hand between the third and little finger shows him to be a great judge of human nature.

16. There is a very distinctive mark near the Mount of Venus which proves him to be very accurate, he remembers dates perfectly, can judge fairly well of time, while the Mount of Venus proves his love for home.

17. His Line of Constructiveness shows him to be fond of contriving new ways of doing things.

18. He is prolific in ideas, he is very skilled to construct sentences in speech or writing.

19. His Literary Line shows profound ability.

20. The shape of the third finger shows him to be a forceful and magnetic speaker.

21. The Line of Sublimity proves his fondness of the sublime in nature, yet he is not moved to enthusiasm by grandeur.

22. The Line of Muscular temperament shows his moral faculties well balanced, and he shall never need help to keep him in the path of rectitude.

23. The first phalange of the little finger and the Mount of Mercury proves this man to be a philosopher.

24. The thumb of the left hand proves love for children and pets, and the Line of Approbativeness shows ambition and that he desires to write his name on the scroll of fame, but that he is not blinded by the glare of popularity.

25. He is decided and determined, persevering and very firm of purpose.

26. He is industrious and progressive, and any obstacle only stimulates him to greater action.

27. The Line of Secretiveness shows him to be very reserved, and the Line of Conscientiousness which is exceedingly well marked in the centre of the left hand shows that he would never swerve from his conception of right, and that he has the habit to sit in judgment upon his own acts and deeds of others, showing little mercy to the wrong doer.

28. He is a law unto himself.

29. The Line of Benevolence proves this man to be generous to a fault, and that he has a heart too big for his purse.

30. Nothing gives him greater pleasure than bestowing.

31. He is very sympathetic.

32. The Line of Mirthfulness shows him to be fond of joking, and that he enjoys jokes, and laughs at good ones.

33. The Line of Causality shows reasoning, thinking, and that he possesses a very comprehensive mind.

34. The Line of Comparison shows that he can trace the relation between the known and unknown with unerring exactness.

35. In conclusion I desire to speak of his Line of Faith which proves that he will become at least ninety-five years old.

36. The lower part of the Line of Faith with the triangle below the Mount of Mercury shows that his past life has been very honorable, that he is a self made man, and that he has been a public servant serving his fellow men with the most beautiful tendencies and convictions.

37. But, the very best part of his life is yet to come.

38. He will be called upon and it will be expected of him to perform such deeds that will bring him honor, and his countrymen satisfaction and gratification.

39. I have absolutely no idea to whom this hand belongs, if the imprint was properly taken I am absolutely convinced that it is the hand of an ideal man.

(Signed) DR. CARL L. PERIN, PH.D.

1. "Good man," large man, little man. Phrases of this kind have no meaning. They furnish no definite measure of the thing mentioned. There was never an average man whom these phrases would not fit. Every average man is good—by comparison with one or another of his neighbors; and large or little, by comparison with undergrowns and overgrowns.

2. This abolishes No. 1. It exposes the fact that I am not good, but am merely equipped with certain "tendencies and ambitions" in that direction—size of the tendencies and ambitions not specified.

3. That is the age of my spirit, not of my body.

4. A little vague. Does it mean that when a person possesses average physical strength his body should never be unduly taxed? If that is it, then it ought to have specified the circumstances under which it *should* be unduly and recklessly taxed. In case the emergency should arise.

5. Definite—also accurate.

6. Definite. But on the whole doubtful, I think.

7. That about the clay is all right.

8. Fatally indefinite. Judgment of what—not stated. Apples? literature? weather? whisky? theology? hotels? emperors? oysters? horses? As regards emperors and weather my judgment is better than any other person's, but as regards all other things I know it to be bad.

9. The first clause of the sentence is true, but what has the rest of the sentence to do with it? I am tender-hearted *notwithstanding* I have strong convictions—convictions of what? and why couldn't I be tender-hearted without having any convictions at all, or any teeth, or real estate? "Convictions" is manifestly the wrong word. It may easily be that I am tender-hearted notwithstanding I am bald-headed, for of course that could mean something, but I don't think "convictions" means anything, in that place.

10. I have already remarked upon the emptiness of phrases like "presence of mind" when used in a general and unparticularized way.

11. Exactly and remarkably true—of everybody's lungs.

12. Does it mean that I have a strong pulse? In that case it is an error. I have a sort of a kind of a pulse, it is true, but not every doctor can find it and swear to it. The Marienbad specialist felt around over my breast and back and abdomen and said with quite unnecessary frankness that he could not *prove* that I hadn't a heart, but that if I had one it would be an advantage to trade it for a potato.

13. "Exquisitely moulded." It is hereditary in the family. Exquisitely moulded and attractive, people often say. Some have thought me the most attractive thing in the

universe except that mysterious and wonderful force which draws all matter toward its throne in the sun, the Attraction of Gravitation; others go even further, and think I am that sublime force itself. These commonly speak of me as the Centre of Gravity. Over great stretches of the earth's surface I am known by no name but that—the Centre of Gravity. It pleases me and makes me happy, but I often feel that it may not be true. God knows. It is not for me to say.

15. If this is not a heedless use of words—if human *nature* is really meant and not *character*—this is the best guess yet. The *nature* of man is the one sole thing that I do know, down to the bottom. I know the secretest secrets of man's heart, I know all its impulses, its deep workings, its shallow workings, its honesties, its sincerities, its conscious shams, its unconscious shams, its innocent self-delusions, its boundless and bottomless vanities. That is to say, I know my own heart perfectly. I have studied it through years and years of eager and consuming interest, and I know it to be the average heart. In other words, I know the *machine* that is shut up inside of a man, and what it *can* do; but I can't tell by the look of the man's outside what it *will* do. Some can tell, by a look at the outside, which parts of the hidden machine—the good ones or the evil ones—get the most work to do; these are the observers who are able to read *character,* these are the people who are able to judge *men.* I am not of those. I am a pretty poor judge of men by their outsides; I can seldom tell a Butters from an honest man by looking at him. A Countess Massiglia cannot deceive me, it is true, but that is nothing; that species cannot even deceive a detective.

16. "Remembers dates perfectly." Now that is distinctly curious. I do remember dates pretty well—rather unusually well, perhaps—but there is nothing else that I can keep in my memory. Am I to believe that my hand knows that odd fact and is able to communicate it to a palmist?

18. I will think this over and see if it is true, before committing myself.

19 and 20. It would be useless for me to deny these; few would believe me.

21. If the first half of the remark is true, it goes without saying that the other half isn't.

23. Philosopher again. This is cumulative evidence, and has high value. It is easy to see that there is something in palmistry. I wrote a philosophy six years ago, after studying my subject fifteen years. All this time I have kept that manuscript hidden away in a secret place, lest its character become known and I get exterminated. And now my hand has betrayed my secret. It is a strange kind of treachery, and not pleasant.

25 and 26. I have examined this vague generalization in my comments upon Mr. Niblo's "reading."

27. I am not conspicuously reserved; and not secretive at all, except when I have been doing things which are better left unpublished. We are all like that.

28. We will allow that slander to pass.

29 and 30. Pretty wide of the mark. Even if it were true, how would my right hand know what my left hand doeth? It is my right hand that is under examination, and is quite too "fresh." It knows nothing about the matter.

32. "Fond of joking. Laughs at good ones." Is *that* all? It describes the entire human

race. So, that elephant has shrunken to next-to-nothing-and-none-to-carry again. The preceding experts overlooked him altogether. I think it is not kind.

33. This takes away some of the pain, but not all of it.

34. But this removes the last pang. If I can do that, I am satisfied. To be called a philosopher has pleased me; to be recognized as a theologian fills my cup.

35. They all agree upon long life for me. I do not much mind the ninety-five, but I do not like the "at least." Ninety-five is plenty; if I may, I will stand pat at that.

NOTE. To none of the experts has my hand revealed the fact that I have a passion for music—a passion restricted to a *single kind* of music: the sombre, the solemn, the melancholy. Indeed, music is not even mentioned. It seems very curious, very strange, that my hand should be so reserved about my couple of dearly-prized and stately possessions, Music and Humor.

Has there been a mistake? Is it not possible that the experts got my hand-prints mixed with other people's hand-prints, and have examined some of those for mine and have not examined mine at all? I think it possible; indeed I know it is, for it is a thing which has happened in at least one case, to my knowledge. It occurred in Italy, and is celebrated. Americans who were sojourning in Italy in those days, will remember the stir it made, the joy, the laughter, the rain of delighted tears! The expert mixed his hand-prints, and by accident attached his reading of Queen Marguerite's to the Countess Raybaudi-Massiglia's prints—with electrifying results! It painted the Queen's character as it was, and is: lofty, just, merciful, honest, honorable, gracious, generous, gentle, stainless—and then innocently labeled it with the notorious American's name!

Tuesday, January 29, 1907

Comments on the hand "readings" which precede this instalment—Mr. Clemens's recent visit to the German clairvoyant, who tells him some correct details of his life—All the experts agree that he is to live to very old age—Appointment with Wilkerson, who says same thing about long life—Remarks about the New Orleans fortune-teller, and letter mentioned which Mr. Clemens wrote to Orion at the time in regard to the visit.

Those hand "readings" were made two years ago, at the suggestion of Colonel Harvey, who wanted them for *Harper's Weekly*. I was to comment upon the "readings;" then Harvey was to comment upon my comments, with the best severity he could command. I liked the scheme. I pressed my hands upon an inked roller in the printing-office; then pressed them upon sheets of white paper; the reproductions were sharp and clear. These were sent to the experts, (with no name attached,) and when the "readings" founded upon them reached Harvey I wrote out my comments upon them, but Harvey went on neglecting his end of the agreement until the manuscript was mislaid and the matter forgotten. But last week a circumstance recalled it to my mind, and we made a search and found my copy of it among my accumulation of unused manuscripts. That circumstance was this: I was invited to come to the house of an acquaintance up town and witness the performance of a clairvoyant who was said to possess extraordinary powers. I gladly went. I found twenty ladies there, but none of the other sex except the host and the clairvoyant. The clairvoyant was a portly middle-aged gentleman with a smooth round face and honest eyes, good eyes, candid eyes. His manner was Germanically simple, unaffected, and engaging. He was on his feet, talking. His English was good, with just enough of his own nationality about it to give it a pleasant alien flavor. There was one vacant place; it was in the middle of a short sofa, between two ladies whom I did not know, but who whispered their names to me and made me properly and comfortably welcome. Ladies generally do this, for I have a winning way with me which I learned in a hand-book of etiquette. The clairvoyant had distributed a number of slips of paper among the ladies, and had asked them to write questions upon the slips and crumple them up in their hands and wait until he called for them. He presently began the call. He said to a lady,

"Please hold up your fist, with your paper gripped in it, and I will tell you what you have written."

The lady held up her fist, and the clairvoyant said,

"I cannot make out this writing very well; there is a word in it which I do not know. If I see it right, it is c-r-o-i-s-e-t." (The ladies all laughed.) The clairvoyant continued: "You laugh at my spelling, but that is as I see it, although I may be wrong. The question says, 'Shall I receive it in time from Croiset?' "

A quiet, happy, and unanimous laugh followed this, and the clairvoyant said:

"Now I understand; Croiset is the name of a person, and that person is making a gown for the lady and she wishes to know if she is going to receive it in time—the time stipulated. I am glad to be able to inform her that she will receive it in time."

The lady was asked if the reading was correct, and she said it was. After this, several fists were held up; the clairvoyant read their contents; the accuracy of his readings was verified by inspection. Three of these papers were passed to me, and I saw that the clairvoyant had read them correctly. No doubt all the others present were familiar with this kind of miracle, but as I had never encountered it before, it filled me with wonder and admiration. By and by the clairvoyant said,

"But this is monotonous. I would like to do something better—something better entitled to your attention. I would like to tell a little part of somebody's biography. Would that gentleman permit it, in his case?"—indicating me. "I do not know his name; I have never seen him before; I have never heard of him; he is a total stranger to me, but if he will go into a private room with me I will tell him some of his history."

It didn't ring true. It probably didn't ring true to anybody present there. I knew it could easily be true, nevertheless, and that it was not fair to give hospitality to my suspicions; still he had seemed to me to protest too much. I said I should be glad to go to the private room with him, so we went. He tore some slips from a small pad, and said,

"Write on one of them the maiden name of your mother. Write upon each of the others a question—any question you please." He pulled aside the cloth and exposed the naked surface of the polished mahogany table. He said "You must have nothing underneath the paper but a hard surface like that. If you wrote upon a soft surface the pencil would leave an indentation which a person with an abnormally delicate touch could read with his fingers."

Then he stepped to the other side of the room and said to a housemaid who was at some kind of work there, "Sprechen Sie Deutsch?" The girl said she couldn't speak it much, but she could understand it. Then the conversation went on, in German, and I presently said,

"I have finished."

He said "Crumple the slips of paper up, put one of them in your vest pocket, hide one in your spectacle-case, shove another inside of your glove, and hold the other two in your fists."

I did as he directed. Then he came and sat at the table and rapidly wrote some sentences on a pad, then turned the pad upside-down, and said:

"Your mother's maiden name was Jane Lampton. Is that so?"

"Yes."

"She had nine children?"

"Yes, I think she had. I know she had eight, and I think there were nine."

"In what part of this procession was your place?"

"I was No. 5, if there were eight children; I was No. 6, if there were nine."

"Were you twelve years old when you began to earn your living?"

"Yes."

"Were you thirty-four when you married?"

"Yes."

"You became the father of four children?"

"Yes."

Then he said, "The paper in your vest pocket gives your mother's maiden name, Jane Lampton; the one in your spectacle-case asks how many children she had; the one in your glove—"

And so on. I took the crumpled papers from their concealment and found that he had located them correctly, and had delivered their contents with accuracy. He then turned his pad right-side up and handed it to me. What he had written upon it was this:

> Your mother, Jane Lampton, had nine children and you were her sixth child. At the age of twelve years you began to earn your own way of living and when thirty-four years old you married and became the father of four children, and you have surprised many people who have known you from childhood, by your success.

I was full of astonishment—an astonishment which lasted me the rest of the afternoon; but at dinner, in the evening, when I was telling about this adventure, a new suspicion rose in my mind, for I remembered that only a week or two ago I had published a chapter of this Autobiography in which I had stated my mother's maiden name, and the names of her children, up to eight, and that either in that chapter or in one which preceded it, I had told how old I was when I began to earn my own living, and all about my marriage and my children. And so my doubts crowded in upon me and spoiled the pleasure which the clairvoyant's surprising performance had furnished me.

Still there was one remark of his whose interest for me survived. He said it over twice, and assured me that it would come exactly true. This is it:

"You will live to be ninety-eight years, ten months, and two days old, and will not have a serious illness in all that time, and you will die in a foreign land."

This had an interest for me—a distinctly depressing interest—for I do not wish to live forever, either here or elsewhere. It had another interest for me, too, for I remembered that those experts whose "readings" of my hands, two years ago, I have already mentioned, had been in irritating and offensive agreement upon that very thing—my liability to overstay my time here—much as they differed about me in other regards. One of them had said I was to outlive the Scriptural time-limit, and it has since come true. Another, whom I will call Wilkerson, which is not his name, said I had a long life-line; and the third expert—whom I take to be a man without a conscience—said I would live to be ninety-five.

This vicious unanimity moved me to examine into the matter further, so I made an appointment with Wilkerson and went to his place, under my own proper name, and he examined my hands for me. He said he had seen me more than once on the platform, years ago, and had often wanted to read my hands. During the next hour he told me all about my character, and I found that it still remained about as he had discovered it to be two years ago. Of course he couldn't refrain from malignities about my old-age possibilities; toward the end, I was going to ask him about them, but he forestalled me, and said,

"You will live to be close upon a century old, and you will not die in your own country."

In the course of our talk, coincidences were mentioned. He said,

"When your secretary telephoned me about this appointment, yesterday evening, I had just read in the evening paper of the death of Mrs. Hooker; it brought you to my mind, for of course you would know Mrs. Hooker, you and she being residents of Hartford for so many years." I said,

"Now we have come upon another coincidence. Fifteen minutes before my secretary telephoned you, she had answered a long-distance telephone call from Dr. Hooker in Hartford, asking me to act as a pall-bearer at his mother's funeral. And there is still another one. Mr. Paine has been at his country home for a week, and on Thursday my secretary was writing him, and asked me if I had any word to send. At five o'clock on the previous afternoon I had fallen up the front steps of this house and peeled off from my starboard shin a ribbon of skin three inches long. This disaster being still in my mind, where it had persistently and urgently been for twenty-four hours, I said,

"'Tell him I am sorry he fell and skinned his shin at five o'clock yesterday afternoon.'

"When his answering letter came, next day, it said,

"'I *did* fall and skin my shin at five o'clock yesterday afternoon, but how did Mr. Clemens find it out?'"

These shin-skinnings had actually occurred at the same hour, on the same day, and if it were not so serious a matter, it would be funny.

Two years ago, when my secretary was examining my brother Orion's autobiography, she found in it a copy of a letter which I had written from a steamboat on the Mississippi River to my brother Orion in February 1861 when I was twenty-five years old—as I cipher it. I was born almost at the extreme end of 1835, and I hope to never be born again, it is so much trouble to me to cipher from my birth-date and find out how old I am; oftener than any other way, I am a year out in the calculation one way or the other. Evidently my letter had impressed Orion very much, and he had copied it faithfully, word for word, and put it into his autobiography. It was an account of a visit which I had paid to a fortune-teller in New Orleans, by request of an old Hannibal friend of ours, Mrs. Holliday, who was always consulting fortune-tellers and believing everything they said. The day after my visit to Mr. Wilkerson we hunted up that old letter, to find out what my character had been forty-six years ago, and how long that New Orleans experimenter had condemned me to hold down this planet. I will append that letter here, and it will be seen that that woman, in that early day, had postponed my funeral until the completion of my eighty-sixth year,—so there is one thing that all the experts agree upon in my case: I am not to die young. Very well, let it go. I do not care anything more about it.

The New Orleans lady did certainly paint my brother's character with astonishing accuracy. She could not have done her work any better if she had had access to the chapter which I dictated about Orion's character a few months ago, and which was lately published in the *North American Review*. According to my letter, this lady began to read me at once, and very volubly—as if she had a great deal to say and not time enough at her disposal to say it in; according to my letter she was impatient of my interruptions. These things would indicate that she didn't ask me any questions, but read me off-hand out of her own head. I am obliged to accept my own testimony, because I am not able at this distant day to refute it. I know that fortune-tellers who followed after her, in later years, did not read me off-hand, but befooled me into talking, and that afterward, when I came to think their performances over, I was vexed with myself by discovering that they hadn't furnished me any information at first hand, but had slyly pumped it out of me, in my innocence and credulity, and then had handed it back to me as being original discoveries of their own, and had astonished me with the wonderful results of their penetration. If my own testimony in the New Orleans lady's case is true and trustworthy, she was surely a marvelous creature. She did not deal much in prophecy, and what she did furnish in that line was poor—so poor that I could have beaten it myself; but she was undeniably and quite strikingly accurate when she was dealing with my history and with my brother's character. Her references to my sweetheart, and her description of the sweetheart, and of how our estrangement was brought about, is so exactly in accordance with the facts, that I feel sure she pumped these things out of me without my being aware of it; anybody can be tempted to talk about his sweetheart, the only thing that is difficult is to get him to stop some time or other. The sweetheart was Laura Wright—the same who wrote me a letter last summer, from California, and from whom I had not heard for forty-seven years. I injected her, and that incident, into this Autobiography at that time.

I now offer for examination the letter which I wrote my brother Orion forty-six years ago.

> I have just received the following letter from Sam:
>
> Steamer "Alonzo Child."
> Cairo, Ill., Feb. 6th, 1861
>
> My Dear Brother:
>
> After promising Mrs. Holliday a dozen times (without anything further than a *very* remote intention of fulfilling the same)—to visit the fortune teller, Madame Caprell—I have at last done so. We lay in New Orleans a week, and towards the last, novelties began to grow alarmingly scarce; I did not know what to do next. Will Bowen had given the matter up, and gone to bed for the balance of the trip; the Captain was on the Sugar Levee, and the clerks were out on business. I was revolving in my mind another foray among the shipping in search of beautiful figure-heads or paragons of nautical architecture, when I happened to think of Mrs. Holliday; and as the Devil never comes unattended, I naturally thought of Madame Caprell immediately after, and then I started toward the St. Charles Hotel for the express purpose of picking up one of the enchantress's bills, with a view to ascertaining her whereabouts. The bill said 37 Conti, above Tchoupitoulas—terms, $2 for gentlemen in my situation, i.e., unaccompanied by a lady.
>
> Arrived at the place, the bell was answered by a middle-aged lady (who certainly pitied me—I saw it in her eye), who kindly informed me that I was at the wrong door—turn to the left. Which I did. And stood in the Awful Presence. She's a very pleasant little lady—rather pretty—about 28—say 5 feet 2¼—would weigh 116—has black eyes and hair—is polite and intelligent—uses good language, and talks much faster than *I* do.
>
> She invited me into the little back parlor, closed the door; and we were—alone. We sat down facing each other. Then she asked my age. And then she put her hand before her eyes a moment, and commenced talking as if she had a good deal to say and not much time to say it in. Something after this style:
>
> Yours is a watery planet; you gain your livelihood on the water; but you should have been a lawyer—there is where your talents lie; you might have distinguished yourself as an orator; or as an editor; you have written a great deal; you write well—but you are rather out of practice; no matter—you will be *in* practice some day; you have a superb constitution; and as excellent health as any man in the world; you have great powers of endurance; in your profession, your strength holds out against the longest sieges without flagging; still, the upper part of your lungs—the top of them, is slightly affected—and you must take more care of yourself; you do not drink, but you use *entirely* too much tobacco; and you must stop it; mind, not moderate, but *stop* the use of it, totally; then I can almost promise you 86, when you will surely die; otherwise, look out for 28, 31, 34, 47 and 65; be careful—for you are not

of a long-lived race, that is, on your *father's* side; you are the only healthy member of your family, and the only one in it who has anything like the certainty of attaining to a great age—so, stop using tobacco, and be careful of yourself; in nearly all respects, you are the best sheep in your flock; your brother has an excellent mind, but it is not as well balanced as yours; I should call yours the best mind, altogether; there is more unswerving strength of will, and set purpose, and determination and energy in you, than in all the balance of your family put together; in some respects you take after your father, but you are much *more* like your mother, who belongs to the long-lived, energetic side of the house.

S.L.C. But madam, you are too fast—you have given me too much of these qualities.

Madame. No, I have not. Don't interrupt me. I am telling the truth. And I'll prove it. Thus: you never brought all your energies to bear upon an object, but what you accomplished it—for instance, you are self-made, self-educated.

S.L.C. Which proves nothing.

Madame. Don't interrupt. When you sought your present occupation, you found a thousand obstacles in your way—obstacles which would have deterred nineteen out of any twenty men—obstacles unknown,—not even suspected by any save you and me, since you keep such matters to yourself,—but you fought your way through them, during a weary, weary length of time, and never flinched or quailed, nor ever once wished to give over the battle—and hid the long struggle under a mask of cheerfulness, which saved your friends anxiety on your account. To do all this requires the qualities which I have named.

S.L.C. You flatter well, madam.

Madame. Don't interrupt! Up to within a short time, you had always lived from hand to mouth—now you are in easy circumstances—for which you need give credit to no one but yourself. The turning point in your life occurred in 1847–8.

S.L.C. Which was?—

Madame.—a death, perhaps; and this threw you upon the world and made you what you are; it was always intended that you should make yourself; therefore, it was well that this calamity occurred as early as it did. You will never die of water, although your career upon it in the future seems well sprinkled with misfortune; but I *entreat* you to remember this: no matter *what* your circumstances are, in September of the year in which you are 28, *don't* go *near* the water—I will *not* tell you why, but by all that is true and good, I charge you, while that month lasts, keep away from the water—

(Which she repeated several times, with much show of earnestness—"make a note on't," and let's see how much the woman knows.)

[The italics are Sam's, as he made them 20 years ago. O.C.]

Madame. Your life will be menaced in the years I have before mentioned—will be in *imminent* peril when you are 31: if you escape, then when you are 34—neither 47 nor 65 looks so badly; you will continue upon the water for some time yet; you will not retire finally until ten years from now; *two* years from now, or a little more, *a child will be born to you!*

S.L.C. Permit me to hope, madam, in view of this prospective good luck, that I may also have the good-fortune to be *married* before that time.

Madame. Well, you are a free-spoken young man. You will be married within two years. *Of course* you will.

(Make another note, Orion—I think I've caught her up a played-out chute on a falling river this time—but who knows?)

Madame. And *mind*—your whole future welfare depends upon your getting married as soon as you can; don't smile—don't *laugh*—for it is just as true as truth itself; if you fail to marry within two years from now, you will regret that you paid so little attention to what I am saying; don't be foolish, but go and marry—your future depends upon it; you can get the girl you have in your eye, if you are a better man than her mother—*she* (the girl) is; the old gentleman is not in the way, but the mother is decidedly *cranky,* and much in the way; *she* caused the trouble and produced the coolness which has existed between yourself and the young lady for so many months past—and you ought to break through this ice; *you* won't commence, and the girl won't—you are both entirely too proud—a well-matched pair, truly; the young lady is—

S.L.C. But I didn't ask after the young lady, madam, and I don't want to hear about her.

Madame. There, just as I said—*she* would have spoken to me just as you have done. For shame! I must go on. She is 17—not remarkably pretty, but very intelligent—is educated, and accomplished—and has property—5 feet 3 inches—is slender—dark brown hair and eyes—you don't want to see her? Oh, no—but you will, nevertheless, before this year is out—here in New Orleans (mark that), too—and then—look out! The fact of her being so far away now—which is the case, is it not?—doesn't affect the matter. You will marry *twice*—your first wife will live—(I have forgotten the number of years. S.L.C.)— Your second choice will be a widow—your family, finally, all told, will number *ten* children—

S.L.C. Slow!—madam, slow!—and stand by to ship up!—for I know you are out of the channel.

Madame. Some of them will live and some will not—

S.L.C. There's consolation in the latter, at least.

Madame. Yes, ten is the number.

S.L.C. You must think I am fond of children.

Madame. And you *are,* although you pretend the contrary—which is an ugly habit; quit it; I grant you that you do not like to *handle* them, though. What is your brother's age? 33,—and a lawyer?—and in pursuit of an office? Well, he stands a better chance than the other two, and, he *may* get it—he must do his best—and not trust too much to others, either—which is the very reason why he is so far behind, now; he never *does* do anything if he can get anybody else to do it for him; which is bad; he never goes steadily on till he attains an object, but nearly always drops it when the battle is half won; he is too visionary—is always flying off on a new hobby; this will never do—tell him I said so. He is a good lawyer—a *very* good lawyer—and a fine speaker—is very popular, and much respected, and makes many friends; but although he retains their friendship, he loses their confidence, by displaying his instability of character; he wants to speculate in lands, and *will,* some day, with very good success; the land he has now will be very valuable after a while—

S.L.C. Say 250 years hence, or thereabouts, madam—

Madame.—No—less time—but never mind the land, that is a secondary consideration—let him drop that for the present, and devote himself to his business and politics, with all his might, for he must hold offices under Government, and 6 or 8 years from this time, he will run for Congress. You will marry, and will finally live in the South—do not live in the North-West; you will not succeed well; you will live in the South, and after a while you will possess a good deal of property—retire at the end of ten years—after which your pursuits will be literary—try the law—you will certainly succeed. I am done, now. If you have any questions to ask, ask them freely, and if it be in my power I will answer without reserve—without reserve.

I asked a few questions of minor importance—paid her $2 and left—under the decided impression that going to the fortune-teller's was just as good as going to the opera, and cost scarcely a trifle more—*ergo,* I will disguise myself and go again, one of these days, when other amusements fail.

Now isn't she the devil? That is to say, isn't she a right smart little woman? I have given you almost her very language to me, and nothing have I extenuated, nor set down aught in malice. Whenever she said anything pointed about you, she would ask me to tell you of it, so that you might profit by it—and confound me if I don't think she read you a good deal better than she did me. That Congress business amused me a little, for she wasn't far wide of the mark you set yourself, as to time. And father's death in '47–8, and the turning-point in my life, were very good. I wonder if there is a past and future chronological table of events in a man's life written in his forehead for the special convenience of these clairvoyants? She said father's side of the house was not long-lived, but that *he* doctored himself to death. I do not know about that, though. She said that up to 7 years, I had no health, and then mentioned several dates after that when my health had been very bad. But that about that girl's mother being "cranky," and playing the devil with me, *was* about the neatest thing she performed—for although I have never spoken of the matter, I happen to know that she spoke truth. The young lady has been beaten by the old one, though—through the romantic agency of intercepted letters, and the girl still thinks *I* was in fault—and always will, I reckon, for I don't see how she'll ever find out the contrary. And the woman had the impudence to say that although I was eternally falling in love, still, when I went to bed at night, I somehow always happened to think of Miss Laura before I thought of my last new flame—and it always would be the case [which will be very comfortable, won't it, when both she and I (like one of Dickens' characters) are Another's?] But hang the woman, she *did* tell the truth, and I won't deny it. But she said *I* would speak to Miss Laura first—but I'll stake my last button on it she missed it there.

So much for Madame Caprell. Although of course, I have no faith in her pretended powers, I listened to her for half an hour with the greatest interest, and I am willing to acknowledge that she said some very startling things, and made some wonderful guesses. Upon leaving she said I must take care of myself; that it had cost me several years to build up my constitution to its present state of perfection, and now I must watch it. And she would give me this motto: "L'ouvrage de l'année est détruit dans un jour,"—which means, if you don't know it, "The work of a year is destroyed in a day."

We shall not go to St. Louis. We turn back from here, to-morrow or next day. When you want money, let mother know, and she will send it. She and Pamela are always fussing about small change, so I sent them a hundred and twenty *quarters* yesterday—fiddler's change enough to last till I get back, I reckon.

Sam.

Comments—by Orion.

1. The italics are as Sam made them 20 years ago.

2. Sam smoked too much for many years, and still smokes.

3. My mother's mother died when my mother was 13 years of age. Her father died at the age of 63. Her grandfather on her father's side lived beyond 60, and his widow beyond 80. On my father's side his father was killed accidentally when my father was 7 years old. My father's mother lived beyond 60. My father died at 48. My mother is now (1880) 78. My father may have hastened the ending of his life by the use of too much medicine. He doctored himself from my earliest remembrance. During the latter part of his life he bought Cook's pills by the box and took one or more daily. In taking a pill he held it between his right thumb and forefinger, turned his head back, cast the pill to the root of his tongue, and from a glass of water in his left hand, took a sup and washed down the bitter dose.

4. Sam was delicate when a child.

5. My father died March 24, 1847, Sam being then 11 years of age. My mother soon took him from school, and set him to learning the printing business.

6. I have carefully compared this copy with the original, to be certain that it is word for word the same.

Wednesday, January 30, 1907

Decaying political and commercial morals of the United States—The press no longer the palladium of our liberties—Mr. Guggenheim chosen Senator for Colorado by a bought legislature—The little unfinished tale of the Rev. Mr. X. who discovered a first-edition Shakspeare—Mr. Clemens finishes the tale—And shows the difference between this man and the late Hammond Trumbull.

The political and commercial morals of the United States are not merely food for laughter, they are an entire banquet. The human being is a curious and interesting invention. It takes a Cromwell and some thousands of preaching and praying soldiers and parsons ten years to raise the standards of English official and commercial morals to a respectworthy altitude, but it takes only one Charles II a couple of years to pull them down into the mud again. Our standards were fairly high a generation ago, and they had been brought to that grade by some generations of wholesome labor on the part of the nation's multitudinous teachers; but Jay Gould, all by himself, was able to undermine the structure in half a dozen years; and in thirty years his little band of successors—the Senator Clarks, and their kind—have been able to sodden it with decay from roof to cellar, and render it shaky beyond repair, apparently.

Before Jay Gould's time there was a fine phrase, a quite elegant phrase, that was on everybody's lips, and everybody enjoyed repeating it, day and night, and everywhere, and of enjoying the thrill of it: "The press is the palladium of our liberties." It was a serious saying, and it was a true saying, but it is long ago dead, and has been tucked safely away in the limbo of oblivion. No one would venture to utter it now except as a sarcasm.

Mr. Guggenheim has lately been chosen United States Senator by a bought legislature in Colorado—which is almost the customary way, now, of electing United States Senators. Mr. Guggenheim has purchased his legislature and paid for it. By his public utterances, it is plain that the general political rottenness has entered into him and saturated him, and he is not aware that he has been guilty of even an indelicacy, let alone a gross crime. In many instances the palladium of our liberties has nothing but compliment for him, and justification. The Denver *Post,* which is recognized as the principal and most trustworthy reflector of the public opinion of his State, says:

> It is true that Mr. Guggenheim spent a large sum of money, but he only followed the precedents set in many other States. There is nothing essentially wrong in what he has done. Mr. Guggenheim will make the best Senator Colorado has ever had. His election will result in bringing to Colorado what the State needs, capitalists and population of the desirable quality. Mr. Guggenheim will get for Colorado many improvements which Tom Patterson failed to obtain from Washington. He is just the man for the place. There is no use trying to reform the world. They have been trying that for two thousand years and haven't succeeded. Mr. Guggenheim is the choice of the people and they ought to have him, even if he spent a million dollars. The issue of the election was Tom Patterson and Simon Guggenheim, and the people chose Guggenheim. The Denver *Post* bows to the will of the people.

Mr. Guggenheim, in buying what an obsolete phrase called senatorial "honors," did not buy the entire legislature, but practised the customary economy and bought only enough of it to elect him. This has been resented by some of the unbought; they offered a motion to inquire into the methods by which his election was achieved, but the bought majority not only voted the motion down but actually *sponged it from the records.* It looks like sensitiveness, but it probably isn't; it is human nature, that even the most conscienceless thieves do not like to be pilloried in the Rogues' Gallery.

A Little Tale.

It was told me the other night by one of the guests present at the service of praise given by the Union League Club in adulation of Senator Clark, the fragrant. He said:

The Reverend Elliot B.X., of the City of XX, is an eager and passionate collector of rare books; by grace of his wife's wealth, he is able to exploit his passion freely. Several years ago he was traveling through a sparsely settled farming country, and he stopped at a farm-house to rest, or feed, or something. It was a poor little humble place, but the farmer and his wife and their two little children seemed contented and happy. Presently the clergyman's attention was attracted by a large book which in their play the little children were using as a stool. It seemed to be a family Bible. Mr. X. was troubled to see the Scriptures used in such a way; also, the ancient aspect of the book inflamed his book-collecting lust, and he took up the volume and examined it. An earthquake of sudden joy shook him from dome to cellar—the book was a Shakspeare, first-edition, and in good repair!

As soon as he was able to compose himself, he asked the farmer where he got the book. The farmer said it had been in the possession of his people in New England no one knew how many years or generations, and that when he removed to the West to find a new home he brought the book along merely because it was a book; one doesn't throw books away.

Mr. X. asked him if he would sell it. The farmer said "Yes," that he would like to trade it for a book or two of some other character—books of a fresher interest than this one.

Mr. X. said he would take it home, then, and——

Somebody broke into the conversation at this point and it was not resumed. I went home thinking about the unfinished tale, and in bed I continued to think about it. It was an interesting situation, and I was sorry the interruption had occurred; then, as I was not sleepy, I thought I would finish the tale myself. I knew it would be easy to do, because such tales always move along a certain well defined course and they all fetch up at one and the same goal at the end.

I must go back for a moment, for I have forgotten a detail. The book had furnished the clergyman not merely one joyful earthquake, but two, for in it he found what was manifestly Shakspeare's autograph—a prodigious find, there being only two others known to be in existence on the planet! Along with Shakspeare's name was another name—Ward. Without doubt this name would be a help in tracing the book's pedigree and in establishing its authenticity.

As I have said, it would be easy to furnish the tale, so I began to think it out. I thought it out to my satisfaction—as follows:

My Version.

Upon his arrival at home, the clergyman examined the latest quotations of the rare-book market and found that perfect copies of first-edition Shakspeares had advanced 5 per cent since the autumn quotations of the previous year, therefore the farmer's copy was worth $7,300; also, he found that the standing offer of $55,000 for an authentic autograph of Shakspeare had been advanced to $60,000. He returned humble and fervent thanks for the happy fortune which had thrown these treasures in his way, and he resolved to add them to his collection, and thus make that collection illustrious and establish its renown forever; so he sent his check for $67,300 to the farmer, whose astonishment and gratitude were beyond his ability to express in words.

I was very well satisfied with my version, and not unproud of it; wherefore I was eager to get hold of the rest of the other version and see if I had fallen into any discrepancies. I hunted up the narrator, and he furnished me what I wanted, as follows:

Conclusion of the First Version.

The gigantic find proved to be genuine, and worth many thousands of dollars in the market; indeed the value of the autograph was quite beyond estimate in dollars, there being American multimillionaires who would be glad to pay three-fourths of a year's income for it. The generous clergyman did not forget the poor farmer, but sent him an encyclopedia and eight hundred dollars.

Caesar's ghost! I was disappointed, and said so. A discussion followed, in which several of us took part, I maintaining that the clergyman had not been generous to the farmer, but had taken advantage of his ignorance to rob him; the others insisted that the clergyman's knowledge was a valuable acquisition which had been earned by study and diligence, and that he was entitled to all the profit he could get out of it—that there was no call for him to give away that valuable knowledge to a person who had been interesting himself in potatoes, and corn, and hogs, when he might have been devoting his leisure hours to acquiring the same knowledge which had turned out to be so valuable to the clergyman. I was not persuaded, but still insisted that the transaction was not fair to the farmer, and that he ought to have had half of the value of his book and the autograph anyway. I believed I would have allowed him half, and I said so. I could not be sure of this, but I at least believed it. Privately I *knew* that in my first burst of emotion, if I had been in the clergyman's place, I would have given the farmer the entire value; that when the burst of emotion had had time to modify, I would have reduced the farmer's share by 10 per cent; that when the second burst had had time to cool off a little the farmer's share would suffer another shrinkage; and if there should be still further extensions of time for cooling off, I thought it more than likely that I should end by sending the farmer the Cyclopedia and stopping there; for this would be the way of the human race, and I am the human race compacted and crammed into a single suit of clothes, but quite able to represent its entire massed multitude in all its moods and inspirations.

But there are exceptions; I am aware of that; I do not represent those exceptions, but only the massed generality of the race. The late Hammond Trumbull of Hartford was an exception. He was a very great scholar and a very fine human being. If he had used his vast knowledge commercially, he could have made himself rich out of it, but he didn't; he never made a penny out of it at the expense of some other person's ignorance; he was always ready to help the poor possessor of any rare and precious thing, out of his store of knowledge, and he did it gladly, and without charge. I remember an instance: twenty years after the war a lady wrote him from the South that among the flotsam and jetsam left unappropriated by the Union soldiers when they destroyed her father's house in the war time was a copy of the Eliot Indian Bible; that she had been told it was worth a hundred dollars; that she had also been told that Mr. Trumbull would know the book's value, and would be able to advise her in the matter; that she was poor, and the hundred dollars would be an important sum for her.

Trumbull replied that if the volume was perfect the British Museum would take it at its standing price, which was a thousand dollars. He asked the lady to send the book to him, which she did. It turned out to be a perfect copy, and he sent her the money, without rebate.

I recall an instance of the other sort: a poverty-stricken sister, or other female relative of Audubon, possessed a copy, in perfect condition, of Audubon's great book, and she wished to sell it, for she was very poor. Among collectors it had an established price, which was a thousand dollars, but she did not know that. She offered it to a professor in a university, who *did* know it, and he gave her a hundred dollars for it; and not only did he play this swindle upon her, but had no more wit and no more heart than to boast about it afterwards.

Friday, February 1, 1907

Cowboy's fine letter to Helen Keller—
Mr. Clemens comments upon such literature.

Last summer I dictated some remarks upon a subject which I find myself unable to describe in a single phrase. I was talking about a letter twenty-seven years old, which had fallen into my hands by accident—a letter written by a western girl who was in deep trouble—a moving letter, a pathetic letter, couched in wrecked and ruined grammar and spelling, but eloquent with the eloquence which comes from the heart, and is always imperial, whether it be clothed in rags or in cloth of gold; also I quoted and discussed a letter a quarter of a century old, written by Captain Ned Wakeman, spelt, punctuated, and constructed as only that extraordinary mariner could spell, punctuate, and construct—a letter out of his heart, and as rich in the eloquence of sincerity and feeling as was the western girl's. I also remarked upon a passage in Susy's Biography of me—a passage from her heart, and sweetly eloquent—and spelt as only Susy could spell.

In this talk I was trying to show that when the heart speaks it has no use for the conventions; it can rise above them, and the result is *literature,* and not to be called by any less dignified name. I think I was also proposing to show that sometimes the productions of the unschooled mind get even an added grace and power out of fresh and free and lawless grammar and orthography. If that was my position, I consider it strongly reinforced by a letter which has come to my hands this morning; it was written to Helen Keller something more than three years ago, at the time that she published her history of her life, and it came from a cowboy in the Far West, whose spelling, grammar, and construction do most engagingly set at easy and unembarrassed defiance all the laws that govern those artificialities; but the result is unqualifiedly satisfactory, just the same, and miles and miles above the reach of criticism; it comes out of a sound good heart, and out of a most wise and level head, and is *literature*—and not commonplace literature, but literature of a high class; the architect of it is a thinker, an observer, a philosopher, and has also a touch of poetry in him: he perceives why Helen is happy, and the reason for it; he has not failed to perceive that Miss Sullivan (Mrs. Macy,) is a wonderful woman, and, in her way, as wonderful as Helen herself. There is an irresistible charm about his simple and natural fashion of employing the technicalities of his trade in his reflections upon Helen and her teacher—those reflections wherein he shrewdly notes a mental kinship between Helen and the blind steer, and wherein he approves of Miss Sullivan's theory as being right and judicious in the education of a colt—Helen being the colt; likewise a "bronco." His interest and his sympathy proceed from his heart—that good heart which moved him to teach the little "Gurman" boy and girl "United States." It will be noticed that some of his words and names get a deliciousness from his fresh and unconventional spellings of them which they never possessed before—for instance, his new rendering of Booker Washington's patronymic. It is fine to see his great and just admiration of Miss Sullivan and her marvelous work; after he has signed his letter he still has to come back to it in a postscript. And it is pleasant to see that he is his natural and incomparable self to the last, and doesn't have to go away from home to find a telling figure whereby to express his thought. It is long since I have seen so delightful a letter as his; it is literature, high literature, and not to be successfully imitated by any art taught in the schools or known to the trained journeyman of the trade; it ranks away up side by side with Susy's Biography and Captain Ned Wakeman's letter. Read it.

16 Miles By. Elko, Nev. Nov. 29 1903.
Miss Helen Keller
Dear Friend
I sent to Dubleday and Page, New York, for your book, and have just finished reading it. As I am batching and the Evenings drag I thought I rite you and tell you how very interesting your book is. I enjoyed reding it. And Miss Sulivan Letters are just fine. You seemd to be as Happy as all the rest of the Girls, you ought to be becose you cant see the Cloudy days. Reding your Book puts me in mind of a large Drove of Cattle I hurded one Sumer, there was a Blind 2 year Old Steer in the bunch and he seemed to do as well as the rest. he would go through the gates and timber and over Ruff places and would get lost from the rest. Iff the Wind was in the South he would feed on the North Side. and Vice Versey. he was always out to one side and near the middle of the bunch. Iff he wanted to Get on the other side he would drop behind never go in Front. I used to watch him and wonder how he always new when I was close. But what we lack somebody else makes up, for instant a Eastern Man comes West and they call him a Tender Foot. And when a Western Man goes East they call him a Yap. I see in the Kansas City Star that the President of Harvard Coladge says when a Western Man goes East he ought to take a good Wash. He for gets that the Watter here is used up for Eregation.

Some day in the future I expect you will rite another Book on your Life, Unless you get a Man. iff you do it will take your hole Life to Train him. Don't you think it would be very interesting to your Readers to have a sketch on Miss Sullivan Life or rather on her Gurlhud days in your book you speak of her being nearly Blind. Id like to Reed of her parrents, I think she has don more for Education and the People than Miss Francis Wilard. She is a grand Woman and you ought to Sing her prases all of your Life.

I think your little Black plamate Marthy Washington iff she had such a Woman as Miss Sulivan for a Teacher and Gardian her chance would of bin good to have

bin a second Bucker Washington. I see in the paper that when that Duke told King Edward he was ingadged to Miss May Golet the King sed he was glad of it. He sed Ingland neded her money.
Our country needs more Wimmen like your Teacher. She give up her prospects it seems of a home and famly to be a Teacher, and as a Teacher for the Blind she is surly next the top of the Lader. And she has kept you Climing Climing. Her theory of teaching Children is all rite I think I was Teaching a little Gurman Boy and Girl United States in S. Dakota and after reding Miss Sulivan letter I can see now that they lurned Inglish faster runing around the place with me than in School I broke Horses all my life and I think Miss Sulivan theory is all rite in a Colt let them lurn by Experence.

I think when she went to Alabama and took charge of that little Bronco it proved it

B. B. Page

P.S.

When Lue Dilen beet the World record at Memphis, Tenn, They didn forget to Name her *Driver.*

Monday, February 4, 1907

Reminiscences of Bret Harte, brought to mind by recent happenings: his unsuccessful attempt to correct proof of an obituary; the meeting with the rough miner on the steamboat, who congratulates him upon having written "The Luck of Roaring Camp"—Bret Harte a bad man, and an incorrigible borrower.

In these days things are happening which bring Bret Harte to my mind again; they rake up memories of him which carry me back thirty and forty years. He had a curious adventure once, when he was a young chap new to the Pacific coast and floating around seeking bread and butter. He told me some of his experiences of that early day. For a while he taught a school in the lively gold-mining camp of Yreka, and at the same time he added a trifle to his income by editing the little weekly local journal for the pair of journeymen typesetters who owned it. His duties as editor required him to read proof. Once a galley-slip was laid before him which consisted of one of those old-time obituaries which were so dismally popular all over the United States when we were still a soft-hearted and sentimental people. There was half a column of the obituary, and it was built upon the regulation plan; that is to say, it was made up of superlatives—superlatives wherewith the writer tried to praise Mrs. Thompson, the deceased, to the summit of her merit, the result being a flowery, overheated, and most extravagant eulogy, and closing with that remark which was never missing from the regulation obituary: "Our loss is her eternal gain." In the proof Harte found this observation: "Even in Yreka her chastity was conspicuous." Of course that word was a misprint for *charity,* but Harte didn't think of that; he knew a printer's mistake had been made, and he also knew that a reference to the manuscript would determine what it was; therefore he followed proof-reader custom, and with his pen indicated in the usual way that the manuscript must be examined. It was a simple matter, and took only a moment of his time; he drew a black line under the word *chastity,* and in the margin he placed a question-mark enclosed in parentheses. It was a brief way of saying "There is something the matter with this word; examine the manuscript and make the necessary correction." But there is another proof-reader law which he overlooked. That law says that when a word is not emphatic enough you must draw a line under it, and this will require the printer to reinforce it by putting it in italics. When Harte took up the paper in the morning and looked at that obituary he took only one glance; then he levied on a mule that was not being watched and cantered out of town, knowing well that in a very little while there was going to be a visit from the widower, with his gun. In the obituary the derelict observation now stood in this form: "Even in Yreka her *chastity* was conspicuous (?)"—a form which turned the thing into a ghastly and ill-timed sarcasm!

I am reminded, in a wide roundabout way, of another of Harte's adventures, by a remark in a letter lately received from Tom Fitch, whom Joe Goodman crippled in the duel—for Tom Fitch is still alive, although inhabiting Arizona. After wandering for years and years all about the planet, Fitch has gone back to his early loves, the sand, the sage-brush, and the jackass rabbit; and these things, and the old-time ways of the natives, have refreshed his spirit and restored to him his lost youth. Those friendly people slap him on the shoulder and call him—well, never mind what they call him; it might offend your ears, but it does Fitch's heart good. He knows its deep meanings; he recognizes the affection that is back of it, and so it is music to his spirit, and he is grateful. When "The Luck of Roaring Camp" burst upon the world Harte became instantly famous; his name and his praises were upon every lip. One day he had occasion to go to Sacramento. When he went ashore there he forgot to secure a berth for the return trip. When he came down to the landing, in the late afternoon, he realized that he had made a calamitous blunder: apparently all Sacramento was proposing to go down to San Francisco; there was a queue of men which stretched from the purser's office down the gangplank, across the levee, and up the street out of sight. Harte had one hope: inasmuch as in theatres, operas, steamboats, and steamships, half a dozen choice places are always reserved to be conferred upon belated clients of distinction, perhaps his name might procure for him one of those reserved places, if he could smuggle his card to the purser; so he edged his way along the queue and at last stood shoulder to shoulder with a vast and rugged miner from the mountains, who had his revolvers in his belt, whose great slouch hat overshadowed the whiskered face of a buccaneer, and whose raiment was splashed with clay from his chin down to his boot-tops. The queue was drifting slowly by the purser's wicket, and each member of it was hearing, in his turn, the fatal words: "No berths left; not even floor space." The purser was just saying it to the truculent big miner when Harte passed his card in. The purser exclaimed—passing a key—

"Ah, Mr. Bret Harte, glad to see you, sir! Take the whole stateroom, sir."

The bedless miner cast a scowl upon Harte which shed a twilight gloom over the whole region, and frightened that author to such a degree that his key and its wooden tag rattled in his quaking hand; then he disappeared from the miner's view, and sought seclusion and safety behind the life-boats and such things on the hurricane-deck. But nevertheless the thing happened which he was expecting—the miner soon appeared up there and went peering around; whenever he approached dangerously near, Harte shifted his shelter and hid behind a new one. This went on without unhappy accident for half an hour, but at last failure came: Harte made a miscalculation; he crept cautiously out from behind a life-boat and came face to face with the miner! He felt that it was an awful situation, a fatal situation, but it was not worth while to try to escape, so he stood still and waited for his doom. The miner said, sternly,

"Are you Bret Harte?"

Harte confessed it, in a feeble voice.

"Did you write that 'Luck of Roaring Camp'?"

Harte confessed again.

"Sure?"

"Yes"—in a whisper.

The miner burst out fervently and affectionately,

"*Son* of a ——— ! Put it there!" and he gripped Harte's hand in his mighty talons and mashed it.

Tom Fitch knows that welcome phrase, and the love and admiration that purge it of its earthiness and make it divine.

In the early days I liked Bret Harte, and so did the others, but by and by I got over it; so, also, did the others. He couldn't keep a friend permanently. He was bad, distinctly bad; he had no feeling, and he had no conscience. His wife was all that a good woman, a good wife, a good mother, and a good friend, can be; but when he went to Europe as Consul he left her and his little children behind, and never came back again from that time until his death, twenty-six years later.

He was an incorrigible borrower of money; he borrowed from all his friends; if he ever repaid a loan the incident failed to pass into history. He was always ready to give his note, but the matter ended there. We sailed for Europe on the 10th of April, 1878, and on the preceding night there was a banquet to Bayard Taylor, who was going out in the same ship as our Minister to Germany. At that dinner I met a gentleman whose society I found delightful, and we became very friendly and communicative. He fell to talking about Bret Harte, and it soon appeared that he had a grievance against him. He had so admired Harte's writings that he had greatly desired to know Harte himself. The acquaintanceship was achieved, and the borrowing began. The man was rich, and he lent gladly. Harte always gave his note, and of his own motion, for it was not required of him. Harte had then been in the East about eight years, and these borrowings had been going on during several of those years; in the aggregate they amounted to about three thousand dollars. The man told me that Harte's notes were a distress to him, because he supposed that they were a distress to Harte.

1878

Bret Harte continued: his visit to Newport; his several visits to Mr. Clemens in Hartford; once to borrow money, once to finish a story, once to write a play with Mr. Clemens; at the close of the latter visit Mr. Clemens gives him his opinion of his character.

Then he had what he thought was a happy idea: he compacted the notes into a bale, and sent them to Harte on the 24th of December '77 as a Christmas present; and with them he sent a note begging Harte to allow him this privilege because of the warm, and kind, and brotherly feeling which prompted it. Per next day's mail Harte fired the bale back at him, accompanying it with a letter which was all afire with insulted dignity, and which formally and by irrevocable edict permanently annulled the existing friendship. But there was nothing in it about paying the notes some time or other.

When Harte made his spectacular progress across the continent, in 1870, he took up his residence at Newport, Rhode Island, that breeding-place—that stud-farm, so to speak—of aristocracy; aristocracy of the American type; that auction mart where the English nobilities come to trade hereditary titles for American girls and cash. Within a twelvemonth he had spent his ten thousand dollars, and he shortly thereafter left Newport, in debt to the butcher, the baker, and the rest, and took up his residence with his wife and his little children in New York. I will remark that during Harte's sojourns in Newport and Cohasset he constantly went to dinners among the fashionables where he was the only male guest whose wife had not been invited. There are some harsh terms in our language, but I am not acquainted with any that is harsh enough to properly characterize a husband who will act like that.

When Harte had been living in New York two or three months he came to Hartford and stopped over night with us. He said he was without money, and without a prospect; that he owed the New York butcher and baker two hundred and fifty dollars, and could get no further credit from them; also he was in debt for his rent, and his landlord was threatening to turn his little family into the street. He had come to me to ask for a loan of two hundred and fifty dollars. I said that that would relieve only the butcher and baker part of the situation, with the landlord still hanging over him; he would better accept of five hundred, which he did. He employed the rest of his visit in delivering himself of sparkling sarcasms about our house, our furniture, and the rest of our domestic arrangements.

Howells was saying, yesterday, that Harte was one of the most delightful persons he had ever met, and one of the wittiest. He said that there was a charm about him that made a person forget, for the time being, his meannesses, his shabbinesses and his dishonesties, and almost forgive them. Howells is right about Harte's bright wit, but he had probably never made a search into the character of it. The character of it spoiled it; it possessed no breadth and no variety; it consisted solely of sneers and sarcasms; when there was nothing to sneer at, Harte did not flash and sparkle, and was not more entertaining than the rest of us.

Once he wrote a play with a perfectly delightful Chinaman in it—a play which would have succeeded if any one else had written it; but Harte had earned the enmity of the New

York dramatic critics by freely and frequently charging them with being persons who never said a favorable thing about a new play except when the favorable thing was bought and paid for beforehand. The critics were waiting for him, and when his own play was put upon the stage they attacked it with joy, they abused it and derided it remorselessly. It failed, and Harte believed that the critics were answerable for the failure. By and by he proposed that he and I should collaborate in a play in which each of us should introduce several characters and handle them. He came to Hartford and remained with us two weeks. He was a man who could never persuade himself to do a stroke of work until his credit was gone, and all his money, and the wolf was at his door; then he could sit down and work harder—until temporary relief was secured—than any man I have ever seen.

To digress for a moment. He came to us once, just upon the verge of Christmas, to stay a day and finish a short story for the New York *Sun* called "Faithful Blossom"—if my memory serves me. He was to have a hundred and fifty dollars for the story, in any case, but Mr. Dana had said he should have two hundred and fifty if he finished it in time for Christmas use. Harte had reached the middle of his story, but his time-limit was now so brief that he could afford no interruptions, wherefore he had come to us to get away from the persistent visits of his creditors. He arrived about dinner time. He said his time was so short that he must get to work straightway after dinner; then he went on chatting in serenity and comfort all through dinner, and afterward by the fire in the library until ten o'clock; then Mrs. Clemens went to bed, and my hot whisky punch was brought; also a duplicate of it for Harte. The chatting continued. I generally consume only one hot whisky, and allow myself until eleven o'clock for this function; but Harte kept on pouring and pouring, and consuming and consuming, until one o'clock; then I excused myself and said good night. He asked if he could have a bottle of whisky in his room. We rang up George, and he furnished it. It seemed to me that he had already swallowed whisky enough to incapacitate him for work, but it was not so; moreover, there were no signs upon him that his whisky had had a dulling effect upon his brain. He went to his room and worked the rest of the night, with his bottle of whisky and a big wood fire for comfort. At five or six in the morning he rang for George; his bottle was empty, and he ordered another; between then and nine he drank the whole of the added quart, and then came to breakfast not drunk, not even tipsy, but quite at himself, and alert and animated. His story was finished; finished within the time-limit, and the extra hundred dollars was secured. I wondered what a story would be like that had been completed in circumstances like these; an hour later I was to find out.

At ten o'clock the young girls' club—by name the Saturday Morning Club—arrived in our library. I was booked to talk to the lassies, but I asked Harte to take my place and read his story. He began it, but it was soon plain that he was like most other people—he didn't know how to read; therefore I took it from him and read it myself. The last half of that story was written under the unpromising conditions which I have described; it is a story which I have never seen mentioned in print, and I think it is quite unknown, but it is my conviction that it belongs at the very top of Harte's literature.

To go back to that other visit. The next morning after his arrival we went to the billiard room and began work upon the play. I named my characters and described them; Harte did the same by his. Then he began to sketch the scenario, act by act, and scene by scene. He worked rapidly, and seemed to be troubled by no hesitations or indecisions; what he accomplished in an hour or two would have cost me several weeks of painful and difficult labor, and would have been valueless when I got through. But Harte's work was good, and usable; to me it was a wonderful performance.

Then the filling-in began. Harte set down the dialogue swiftly, and I had nothing to do except when one of my characters was to say something; then Harte told me the nature of the remark that was required, I furnished the language, and he jotted it down. After this fashion we worked two or three or four hours every day for a couple of weeks, and produced a comedy that was good and would act. His part of it was the best part of it, but that did not disturb the critics; when the piece was staged they praised my share of the work with a quite suspicious prodigality of approval, and gave Harte's share all the vitriol they had in stock. The piece perished.

All that fortnight at our house Harte made himself liberally entertaining at breakfast, at luncheon, at dinner, and in the billiard room—which was our workshop—with smart and bright sarcasms leveled at everything on the place; and for Mrs. Clemens's sake I endured it all, until the last day; then, in the billiard room, he contributed the last feather: it seemed to be a slight and vague and veiled satirical remark with Mrs. Clemens for a target; he denied that she was meant, and I might have accepted the denial if I had been in a friendly mood, but I was not, and was too strongly moved to give his reasonings a fair hearing. I said in substance this:

"Harte, your wife is all that is fine and lovable and lovely, and I exhaust praise when I say she is Mrs. Clemens's peer—but in all ways you are a shabby husband to her, and you often speak sarcastically, not to say sneeringly, of her, just as you are constantly doing in the case of other women; but your privilege ends there; you must spare Mrs. Clemens. It does not become you to sneer at anybody at all; you are not charged anything here for the bed you sleep in, yet you have been very smartly and wittily sarcastic about it, whereas you ought to have been more reserved in that matter, remembering that you have not owned a bed of your own for ten years; you have made sarcastic remarks about the furniture of the bedroom, and about the table-ware, and about the servants, and about the carriage and the sleigh, and the coachman's livery—in fact about every detail of the house and half of its occupants; you have spoken of all these matters contemptuously, in your unwholesome desire to be witty, but this does not become you; you are barred from these criticisms by your situation and circumstances; you have a talent and a reputation which would enable you to support your family most respectably and independently if you were not a born bummer and tramp; you are a loafer and an idler, and you go clothed in rags, with not a whole shred on you except your inflamed red tie, and *it* isn't paid for; nine-tenths of your income is borrowed money—money which, in fact, is stolen, since you never intended to repay any of it; you sponge upon your hard-working widowed sister for bread and shelter in the mechanics' boarding-house which she keeps; latterly you have not ventured to show your face in her neighborhood because of the creditors who are on watch for you. Where have you lived? Nobody knows. Your own people do not know. But I know. You have lived in the Jersey woods and marshes, and have supported yourself as do the other tramps; you have confessed it without a blush; you sneer at everything in this house, but you ought to be more tender, remembering that everything in it was honestly come by and has been paid for."

Harte owed me fifteen hundred dollars at that time; later he owed me three thousand. He offered me his note, but I was not keeping a museum, and didn't take it.

Bret Harte continued: his contract with Bliss to write "Gabriel Conroy"—Two incidents: the miner of Jackass Gulch who borrowed a dollar of Mr. Clemens to give to the musical tramps; Bret Harte borrowed a dollar of Mr. Clemens to give to messenger for carrying manuscript to Parsloe's theatre.

Harte's indifference concerning contracts and engagements was phenomenal. He could be blithe and gay with a broken engagement hanging over him; he could even joke about the matter; if that kind of a situation ever troubled him, the fact was not discoverable by anybody. He entered into an engagement to write the novel, "Gabriel Conroy," for my Hartford publisher, Bliss. It was to be published by subscription. With the execution of the contract, Bliss's sorrows began. The precious time wasted along; Bliss could get plenty of promises out of Harte, but no manuscript—at least no manuscript while Harte had money, or could borrow it. He wouldn't touch the pen until the wolf actually had him by the hind leg; then he would do two or three days' violent work and let Bliss have it for an advance of royalties. About once a month Harte would get into desperate straits; then he would dash off enough manuscript to set him temporarily free, and carry it to Bliss and get a royalty-advance. These assaults upon his prospective profits were never very large, except in the eyes of Bliss; to Bliss's telescopic vision a couple of hundred dollars that weren't due, or hadn't been earned, was a prodigious matter. By and by Bliss became alarmed. In the beginning he had recognized that a contract for a full-grown novel from Bret Harte was a valuable prize, and he had been indiscreet enough to let his good fortune be trumpeted about the country. The trumpeting could have been valuable for Bliss if he had been dealing with a man addicted to keeping his engagements; but he was not dealing with that kind of a man, therefore the influence of the trumpeting had died down and vanished away long before Harte had arrived at the middle of his book; that kind of an interest once dead is dead beyond resurrection. Finally Bliss realized that "Gabriel Conroy" was a white elephant. The book was nearing a finish, but, as a subscription-book, its value had almost disappeared. He had advanced to Harte thus far—I think my figures are correct—thirty-six hundred dollars, and he knew that he should not be able to sleep much until he could find some way to make that loss good; so he sold the serial rights in "Gabriel Conroy" to one of the magazines for that trifling sum—and a good trade it was, for the serial rights were not really worth that money, and the book-rights were hardly worth the duplicate of it.

I think the sense of shame was left out of Harte's constitution. He told me once, apparently as an incident of no importance—a mere casual reminiscence—that in his early days in California when he was a blooming young chap with the world before him, and bread and butter to seek, he kept a woman who was twice his age—no, the woman kept him. When he was Consul in Great Britain, twenty-five or thirty years later, he was kept, at different times, by a couple of women—a connection which has gone into history, along with the names of those women. He lived in their houses, and in the house of one of them he died.

I call to mind an incident in my commerce with Harte which reminds me of one like it which happened during my sojourn on the Pacific coast. When Orion's thoughtful carefulness enabled my "Hale and Norcross" stock-speculation to ruin me, I had three hundred dollars left, and nowhere in particular to lay my head. I went to Jackass Gulch and cabined for a while with some friends of mine, surface-miners. They were lovely fellows; charming comrades in every way, and honest and honorable men; their credit was good for bacon and beans, and this was fortunate, because their kind of mining was a peculiarly precarious one; it was called pocket-mining, and so far as I have been able to discover, pocket-mining is confined and restricted on this planet to a very small region around about Jackass Gulch. A "pocket" is a concentration of gold-dust in one little spot on the mountain-side; it is close to the surface; the rains wash its particles down the mountain-side, and they spread, fan-shape, wider and wider as they go. The pocket-miner washes a pan of dirt, finds a speck or two of gold in it, makes a step to the right or the left, washes another pan, finds another speck or two, and goes on washing to the right and to the left until he knows when he has reached both limits of the fan, by the best of circumstantial evidence, to wit—that his pan-washings furnish no longer the speck of gold. The rest of his work is easy—he washes along up the mountain-side, tracing the narrowing fan by his washings, and at last he reaches the gold deposit. It may contain only a few hundred dollars, which he can take out with a couple of dips of his shovel; also it may contain a concentrated treasure worth a fortune. It is the fortune he is after, and he will seek it with a never-perishing hope as long as he lives. These friends of mine had been seeking that fortune daily for eighteen years; they had never found it, but they were not at all discouraged; they were quite sure they would find it some day. During the three months that I was with them they found nothing, but we had a fascinating and delightful good time trying. Not long after I left, a greaser (Mexican) came loafing along and found a pocket with a hundred and twenty-five thousand dollars in it on a slope which our boys had never happened to explore. Such is luck! And such the treatment which honest, good perseverance gets so often at the hands of unfair and malicious Nature!

Our clothes were pretty shabby, but that was no matter; we were in the fashion; the rest of the slender population were dressed as we were. Our boys hadn't had a cent for several months, and hadn't needed one, their credit being perfectly good for bacon, coffee, flour, beans and molasses. If there was any difference, Jim was the worst dressed of the three of us; if there was any discoverable difference in the matter of age, Jim's shreds were the oldest; but he was a gallant creature, and his style and bearing could make any costume regal. One day we were in the decayed and naked and rickety inn when a couple of musical tramps appeared; one of them played the banjo, and the other one danced unscientific clog-dances and sang comic songs that made a person sorry to be alive. They passed the hat and collected three or four dimes from the dozen bankrupt pocket-miners present. When the hat approached Jim he said to me, with his fine millionaire air,

"Let me have a dollar."

I gave him a couple of halves. Instead of modestly dropping them into the hat, he pitched them into it at the distance of a yard, just as in the ancient novels milord the Duke doesn't *hand* the beggar a benefaction, but "tosses" it to him, or flings it at his feet—and it is always a "purse of gold." In the novel, the witnesses are always impressed; Jim's great spirit was the spirit of the novel; to him the half-dollars were a purse of gold; like the Duke, he was playing to the gallery, but the parallel ends there. In the Duke's case, the witnesses knew he could afford the purse of gold, and the largest part of their admiration consisted in envy of the man who could throw around purses of gold in that fine and careless way. The miners admired Jim's handsome liberality, but they knew he couldn't afford what he had done, and that fact modified their admiration. Jim was worth a hundred of Bret Harte, for he was a man, and a whole man. In his little exhibition of vanity and pretense he exposed a characteristic which made him resemble Harte, but the resemblance began and ended there.

I come to the Harte incident now. When our play was in a condition to be delivered to Parsloe, the lessee of it, I had occasion to go to New York, and I stopped at the St. James Hotel, as usual. Harte had been procrastinating; the play should have been in Parsloe's hands a day or two earlier than this, but Harte had not attended to it. About seven in the evening he came into the lobby of the hotel, dressed in an ancient gray suit so out of repair that the bottoms of his trowsers were frazzled to a fringe; his shoes were similarly out of repair, and were sodden with snow-slush and mud, and on his head, and slightly tipped to starboard, rested a crumpled and gallus little soft hat which was a size or two too small for him; his bright little red necktie was present, and rather more than usually cheery and contented and conspicuous. He had the play in his hand. Parsloe's theatre was not three minutes' walk distant; I supposed he would say,

"Come along—let's take the play to Parsloe."

But he didn't; he stepped up to the counter, offered his parcel to the clerk, and said, with the manner of an earl,

"It is for Mr. Parsloe—send it to the theatre."

The clerk looked him over austerely and said, with the air of a person who is presenting a checkmating difficulty,

"The messenger's fee will be ten cents."

Harte said,

"Call him."

Which the clerk did. The boy answered the call, took the parcel and stood waiting for orders. There was a certain malicious curiosity visible in the clerk's face. Harte turned toward me, and said,

"Let me have a dollar."

I handed it to him. He handed it to the boy and said,
"Run along."
The clerk said, "Wait, I'll give you the change."
Harte gave his hand a ducal wave and said,
"Never mind it. Let the boy keep it."

Bret Harte continued: he avoids voting either for Tilden or Hayes because each has promised him a consulship; sends his son to John McCullough with letter of introduction; Mr. Clemens denounces him in the Players Club.

Edward Everett Hale wrote a book which made a great and pathetic sensation when it issued from the press in the lurid days when the Civil War was about to break out and the North and South were crouched for a spring at each other's throats. It was called "A Man Without a Country." Harte, in a mild and colorless way, was that kind of a man—that is to say, he was a man without a country; no, not man—man is too strong a term: he was an invertebrate without a country. He hadn't any more passion for his country than an oyster has for its bed; in fact not so much, and I apologize to the oyster. The higher passions were left out of Harte; what he knew about them he got from books. When he put them into his own books they were imitations; often good ones, often as deceptive to people who did not know Harte as are the actor's simulation of passions on the stage when he is not feeling them but is only following certain faithfully studied rules for their artificial reproduction. On the 7th of November 1876—I think it was the 7th—he suddenly appeared at my house in Hartford and remained there during the following day—election day. As usual, he was tranquil; he was serene; doubtless the only serene and tranquil voter in the United States; the rest—as usual in our country—were excited away up to the election limit, for that vast political conflagration was blazing at white heat which was presently to end in one of the Republican party's most cold-blooded swindles of the American people—the stealing of the Presidential chair from Mr. Tilden, who had been elected, and the conferring of it upon Mr. Hayes, who had been defeated. I was an ardent Hayes man, but that was natural, for I was pretty young at the time. I have since convinced myself that the political opinions of a nation are of next to no value, in any case, but that what little rag of value they possess is to be found among the old, rather than among the young. I was as excited and inflamed as was the rest of the voting world, and I was surprised when Harte said he was going to remain with us until the day after the election; but not much surprised, for he was such a careless creature that I thought it just possible that he had gotten his dates mixed. There was plenty of time for him to correct his mistake, and I suggested that he go back to New York and not lose his vote. But he said he was not caring about his vote; that he had come away purposely, in order that he might avoid voting and yet have a good excuse to answer the critics with. Then he told me why he did not wish to vote. He said that through influential friends he had secured the promise of a consulate from Mr. Tilden, and the same promise from Mr. Hayes; that he was going to be taken care of no matter how the contest might go, and that his interest in the election began and ended there. He said he could not afford to vote for either of the candidates, because the other candidate might find it out and consider himself privileged to cancel his pledge. It was a curious satire upon our political system! Why should a President care how an impending Consul had voted? Consulships are not political offices; naturally and properly a Consul's qualifications should begin and end with fitness for the post; and in an entirely sane political system the question of a man's political complexion could have nothing to do with the matter. However, the man who was defeated by the nation was placed in the Presidential chair, and the man without a country got his consulship.

Harte had no feeling, for the reason that he had no machinery to feel with. John McCullough, the tragedian, was a man of high character; a generous man, a lovable man, and a man whose truthfulness could not be challenged. He was a great admirer of Harte's literature, and in the early days in San Francisco he had had a warm fondness for Harte himself; as the years went by, this fondness cooled to some extent, a circumstance for which Harte was responsible. However, in the days of Harte's consulship McCullough's affection for him had merely undergone a diminution; it had by no means disappeared; but by and by something happened which abolished what was left of it. John McCullough told me all about it. One day a young man appeared in his quarters in New York and said he was Bret Harte's son, and had just arrived from England with a letter of introduction and recommendation from his father—and he handed the letter to McCullough. McCullough greeted him cordially, and said,

"I was expecting you, my boy. I know your errand, through a letter which I have already received from your father; and by good luck I am in a position to satisfy your desire. I have just the place for you, and you can consider yourself on salary from to-day, and now."

Young Harte was eloquently grateful, and said,

"I knew you would be expecting me, for my father promised me that he would write you in advance."

McCullough had Harte's letter in his pocket, but he did not read it to the lad. In substance it was this:

"My boy is stage-struck and wants to go to you for help, for he knows that you and I are old friends. To get rid of his importunities, I have been obliged to start him across the water equipped with a letter strongly recommending him to your kindness and protection, and begging you to do the best you can to forward his ambition, for my sake. I was obliged to write the letter, I couldn't get out of it, but the present letter is to warn you, beforehand, to pay no attention to the other one. My son is stage-struck, but he isn't of any account, and will never amount to anything; therefore don't bother yourself with him; it wouldn't pay you for your lost time and sympathy."

John McCullough stood by the boy and pushed his fortunes on the stage, and was the best father the lad ever had.

I have said more than once, in these pages, that Harte had no heart and no conscience, and I have also said that he was mean and base. I have not said, perhaps, that he was treacherous, but if I have omitted that remark I wish to add it now.

All of us, at one time or another, blunder stupidly into indiscreet acts and speeches; I am not an exception; I have done it myself. About a dozen years ago, I drifted into the Players Club one night and found half a dozen of the boys grouped cosily in a private corner sipping punches and talking. I joined them and assisted. Presently Bret Harte's name was mentioned, and straightway that mention fired a young fellow who sat at my elbow, and for the next ten minutes he talked as only a person can talk whose subject lies near his heart. Nobody interrupted; everybody was interested. The young fellow's talk was made up of strong and genuine enthusiasms; its subject was praise—praise of Mrs. Harte and her daughters. He told how they were living in a little town in New Jersey, and how hard they worked, and how faithfully, and how cheerfully, and how contentedly, to earn their living—Mrs. Harte by teaching music, the daughters by exercising the arts of drawing, embroidery, and such things—I, meantime, listening as eagerly as the rest, for I was aware that he was speaking the truth, and not overstating it.

But presently he diverged into eulogies of the ostensible head of that deserted family, Bret Harte. He said that the family's happiness had one defect in it; the absence of Harte. He said that their love and their reverence for him was a beautiful thing to see and hear; also their pity of him on account of his enforced exile from them. He also said that Harte's own grief, because of this bitter exile, was beautiful to contemplate; that Harte's faithfulness in writing, by every steamer, was beautiful, too; that he was always longing to come home in his vacations, but his salary was so small that he could not afford it; nevertheless, in his letters he was always promising himself this happiness in the next steamer, or the next one after that one; and that it was pitiful to see the family's disappointment when the named steamers kept on arriving without him; that his self-sacrifice was an ennobling spectacle; that he was man enough, and fine enough, to deny himself in order that he might send to the family every month, for their support, that portion of his salary which a more selfish person would devote to the Atlantic voyage.

Up to this time I had "stood the raise," as the poker players say, but now I broke out and called the young fellow's hand—as the pokers also say. I couldn't help it. I saw that he had been misinformed. It seemed to be my duty to set him right. I said,

"Oh that be hanged! There's nothing in it. Bret Harte has deserted his family, and that is the plain English of it. Possibly he writes them, but I am not weak enough to believe it until I see the letters; possibly he is pining to come home to his deserted family, but no one that knows him will believe that. But there is one thing about which I think there can be no possibility of doubt—and that is, that he has never sent them a dollar, and has never intended to send them a dollar. Bret Harte is the most contemptible, poor little soulless blatherskite that exists on the planet to-day——"

I had been dimly aware, very vaguely aware, by fitful glimpses of the countenances around me, that something was happening. It was I that was happening, but I didn't know it. But when I had reached the middle of that last sentence somebody seized me and whispered into my ear, with energy,

"For goodness sake shut up! This young fellow is Steele. He's engaged to one of the daughters."

Bret Harte concluded—Newspaper item regarding his daughter—Mr. Clemens shows that she is not responsible for her unfortunate condition, as she inherited her temperament from her father; also shows that no one is responsible for his actions, because of the law of temperament: the lower animals are not responsible for their peculiar traits, why should human beings be responsible for theirs, when they inherit them from the lower animals?

Ten or twelve days ago, this Associated Press telegram appeared in the twenty-three hundred daily newspapers of the United States, and of course was cabled to Europe:

JESSAMY BRET HARTE A PAUPER

Daughter of Sierra Poet in the Poorhouse at Portland, Me.

PORTLAND, Me., Jan. 28.—Mrs. W. H. Steele, formerly Jessamy Bret Harte, daughter of the poet Bret Harte, has been sent to the Portland poorhouse, ill, penniless and apparently friendless.

It is alleged by her husband, who is now somewhere in the West, that his wife's tastes were so expensive that he couldn't keep her in funds. He says he sent her $15 a week but this wasn't enough.

About a year ago Mrs. Steele came here under the patronage of local society women to give readings from her father's works. Since that time she has borrowed and spent money freely until now she is hopelessly in debt.

She first lived at the Sherwood, a fashionable apartment house. Then she rented a summer cottage at Cape Elizabeth, which she had to give up for lack of funds. This winter she got apartments at the Lafayette, the biggest hotel in the city, but finally went away from there. A fashionable family had her as guest for a week until yesterday, when she became an object of charity.

She wants to go to London, but the city will pay her fare to New York only.

Who is to blame for this tragedy? That poor woman? I think not. She came by her unwise and unhappy ways legitimately; they are an inheritance; she got them from her father, along with her temperament. Temperament is a law, and that which it commands its possessor must obey; restraint, training, and environment can dull its action or suppress it for a time—long or short according to circumstances—but that is the most, and the best, that can be done with it; nothing can ever permanently modify it, by even a shade, between the cradle and the grave. Is this girl responsible for the results of her temperament? She did not invent her temperament herself; she was not consulted in the matter; she was allowed no more choice in the character of it than she was allowed in the selection of the color of her hair. Bret Harte transmitted his unfortunate temperament to her. Was he to blame for this? I cannot see that he was. He was not allowed a choice in the sort of temperament he was to confer upon her. To take up the next detail: was he to blame for the unhappy results of his own temperament? If he was, I fail to see how. He did not invent his temperament; he was not allowed a voice in the selection of it. Did he inherit it from his parents?—from his grandparents?—from his great-grandparents? If so, were they responsible for the results of their temperament? I think not. If we could trace Harte's unlucky inheritance all the way back to Adam, I think we should still have to confess that all the transmitters of it were blameless, since none of them ever had a voice in the choice of the temperament they were to transmit. As I have said, it is my conviction that a person's temperament is a law, an iron law, and has to be obeyed, no matter who disapproves; manifestly, as it seems to me, temperament is a law of God, and is supreme, and takes precedence of all human laws. It is my conviction that each and every human law that exists has one distinct purpose and intention, and only one: to oppose itself to a law of God and defeat it, degrade it, deride it, and trample upon it. We find no fault with the spider for ungenerously ambushing the fly and taking its life; we do not call it murder; we concede that it did not invent its own temperament, its own nature, and is therefore not blamable for the acts which the law of its nature requires and commands. We even concede this large point: that no art and no ingenuity can ever reform the spider and persuade her to cease from her assassinations. We do not blame the tiger for obeying the ferocious law of the temperament which God lodged in him, and which the tiger must obey. We do not blame the wasp for her fearful cruelty in half paralysing a spider with her sting and then stuffing the spider down a hole in the ground to suffer there many days, while the wasp's nursery gradually torture the helpless creature through a long and miserable death by gnawing rations from its person daily; we concede that the wasp is strictly and blamelessly obeying the law of God as required by the temperament which He has put into her. We do not blame the fox, the blue jay, and the many other creatures that live by theft; we concede that they are obeying the law of God promulgated by the temperament with which He provided for them. We do not say to the ram and the goat "Thou shalt not commit adultery," for we know that ineradicably embedded in their temperament—that is to say in their born nature—God has said to them "Thou *shalt* commit it."

If we should go on until we had singled out and mentioned the separate and distinct temperaments which have been distributed among the myriads of the animal world, we should find that the reputation of each species is determined by one special and prominent trait; and then we should find that all of these traits, and all the shadings of these many traits, have also been distributed among mankind; that in every man a dozen or more of these traits exist, and that in many men traces and shadings of the whole of them exist. In what we call the lower animals, temperaments are often built out of merely one, or two, or three, of these traits; but man is a complex animal, and it takes all of the traits to fit him out. In the rabbit we always find meekness and timidity, and in him we never find courage, insolence, aggressiveness; and so when the rabbit is mentioned we always remember that he is meek and timid; if he has any other traits or distinctions—except, perhaps, an extravagant and inordinate fecundity—they never occur to us. When we consider the house-fly and the flea, we remember that in splendid courage the belted knight and the tiger cannot approach them, and that in impudence and insolence they lead the whole animal world, including even man; if those creatures have other traits they are so overshadowed by those which I have mentioned that we never think of them at all. When the peacock is mentioned, vanity occurs to us, and no other trait; when we think of the goat, unchastity occurs to us, and no other trait; when certain kinds of dogs are mentioned, loyalty occurs to us, and no other trait; when the cat is mentioned, her independence—a trait which she alone of all created creatures, including man, possesses—occurs to us, and no other trait; except we be of the stupid and the ignorant—then we think of treachery, a trait which is common to many breeds of dogs, but is not common to the cat. We can find one or two conspicuous traits in each family of what we impudently call the lower animals; in each case these one or two conspicuous traits distinguish that family of animals from the other families; also in each case those one or two traits are found in every one of the members of each family, and are so prominent as to eternally and unchangeably establish the character of that branch of the animal world. In all these cases we concede that the several temperaments constitute a law of God, a command of God, and that whatsoever is done in obedience to that law is blameless.

Man was descended from those animals; from them he inherited every trait that is in him; from them he inherited the whole of their numerous traits in a body, and with each trait its share of the law of God. He widely differs from them in this: that he possesses not a single trait that is similarly and equally prominent in each and every member of his race. You can say the house-fly is limitlessly brave, and in saying it you describe the whole house-fly tribe; you can say the rabbit is limitlessly timid, and by that phrase you describe the whole rabbit tribe; you can say the spider is limitlessly murderous, and by that phrase you describe the whole spider tribe; you can say the lamb is limitlessly innocent, and sweet, and gentle, and by that phrase you describe all the lambs; you can say the goat is limitlessly unchaste, and by that phrase you describe the whole tribe of goats. There is hardly a creature which you cannot definitely and satisfactorily describe by one single trait—but you cannot describe man by one single trait. Men are not all cowards, like the rabbit; nor all brave, like the house-fly; nor all sweet and innocent and gentle, like the lamb; nor all murderous, like the spider and the wasp; nor all thieves, like the fox and the blue jay; nor all vain, like the peacock; nor all beautiful, like the angel-fish; nor all frisky, like the monkey; nor all unchaste, like the goat. The human family cannot be described by any one phrase; each individual has to be described by himself. One is brave, another is a coward; one is gentle and kindly, another is ferocious; one is proud and vain, another is modest and humble. The multifarious traits that are scattered, one or two at a time, throughout the great animal world, are all concentrated, in varying and nicely shaded degrees of force and feebleness, in the form of instincts, in each and every member of the human family. In some men the vicious traits are so slight as to be imperceptible, while the nobler traits stand out conspicuously. We describe that man by those fine traits, and we give him praise and accord him high merit for their possession. It seems comical. He did not invent his traits; he did not stock himself with them; he inherited them at his birth; God conferred them upon him; they are the law that God imposed upon him, and he could not escape obedience if he should try. Sometimes a man is a born murderer, or a born scoundrel—like Stanford White—and upon him the world lavishes censure and dispraise; but he is only obeying the law of his nature, the law of his temperament; he is not at all likely to try to disobey it, and if he should try he would fail. It is a curious and humorous fact that we excuse all the unpleasant things that the creatures that crawl, and fly, and swim, and go on four legs do, for the recognizably sufficient reason that they are but obeying the law of their nature, which is the law of God, and are therefore innocent; then we turn about and with the fact plain before us that we get all our unpleasant traits by inheritance from those creatures, we blandly assert that we did not inherit the immunities along with them, but that it is our duty to ignore, abolish, and break these laws of God. It seems to me that this argument has not a leg to stand upon, and that it is not merely and mildly humorous, but violently grotesque.

By ancient training and inherited habit, I have been heaping blame after blame, censure after censure, upon Bret Harte, and have felt the things I have said, but when my temper is cool I have no censures for him. The law of his nature was stronger than man's statutes and he had to obey it. It is my conviction that the human race is no proper target for harsh words and bitter criticisms, and that the only justifiable feeling toward it is compassion; it did not invent itself, and it had nothing to do with the planning of its weak and foolish character.

Monday, February 11, 1907

The Emperor's dinner in Berlin at which Mr. Clemens is chief guest, and feels that he may have offended the Emperor by a possible slight breach of royal etiquette—although the Empress Dowager and the reigning Empress afterwards invite him to breakfast, etc. Eleven or twelve years later, at a dinner given by the proprietor of the *Staats-Zeitung* for Prince Henry when he visited this country, Mr. Clemens was not seated at the state table.

Two months ago (December 6) I was dictating a brief account of a private dinner in Berlin, where the Emperor of Germany was host and I the chief guest. Something happened day before yesterday which moves me to take up that matter again. The additions which I shall now make can appear in print after I am dead, but not before. From 1891 until day before yesterday, I had never mentioned them in print, nor set them down with a pen, nor ever referred to them in any way with my mouth—not even to my wife, to whom I was accustomed to tell everything that happened to me.

At the dinner his Majesty chatted briskly and entertainingly along in easy and flowing English, and now and then he interrupted himself to address a remark to me, or to some other individual of the guests. When the reply had been delivered, he resumed his talk. I noticed that the table etiquette tallied with that which was the law of my house at home when we had guests: that is to say, the guests answered when the host favored them with a remark, and then quieted down and behaved themselves until they got another chance. If I had been in the Emperor's chair and he in mine, I should have felt infinitely comfortable and at home, and should have done a world of talking, and done it well; but I was guest now, and consequently I felt less at home. From old experience, I was familiar with the rules of the game, and familiar with their exercise from the high place of host; but I was not familiar with the trammeled and less satisfactory position of guest, therefore I felt a little strange and out of place. But there was no animosity—no, the Emperor was host, therefore according to my own rule he had a right to do the talking, and it was my honorable duty to intrude no interruptions or other improvements, except upon invitation; and of course it could be *my* turn some day: some day, on some friendly visit of inspection to America, it might be my pleasure and distinction to have him as guest at my table; then I would give him a rest, and a remarkably quiet time.

In one way there was a difference between his table and mine—for instance, atmosphere; the guests stood in awe of him, and naturally they conferred that feeling upon me, for, after all, I am only human, although I regret it. When a guest answered a question he did it with deferential voice and manner; he did not put any emotion into it, and he did not spin it out, but got it out of his system as quickly as he could, and then looked relieved. The Emperor was used to this atmosphere, and it did not chill his blood; maybe it was an inspiration to him, for he was alert, brilliant, and full of animation; also he was most gracefully and felicitously complimentary to my books,—and I will remark here that the happy phrasing of a compliment is one of the rarest of human gifts, and the happy delivery of it another. In that other chapter I mentioned the high compliment which he paid to the book, "Old Times on the Mississippi," but there were others; among them some gratifying praise of my description in "A Tramp Abroad" of certain striking phases of German student life. I mention these things here because I shall have occasion to hark back to them presently.

Fifteen or twenty minutes before the dinner ended the Emperor made a remark to me in praise of our generous soldier-pensions; then without pausing he continued the remark, not speaking to me but across the table to his brother, Prince Heinrich. The Prince replied, endorsing the Emperor's view of the matter. Then I intruded my own view of it. I said that in the beginning our Government's generosity to the soldier was clean in its intent, and praiseworthy, since the pensions were conferred upon soldiers who had earned them, soldiers who had been disabled in the war and could no longer earn a livelihood for themselves and their families; but that the pensions decreed and added later lacked the virtue of a clean motive, and had little by little degenerated into a wider and wider and more and more offensive system of vote-purchasing, and was now become a source of corruption which was an unpleasant thing to contemplate, and was a danger, besides. I think that that was about the substance of my remark; but, in any case, the remark had a quite definite result, and that is the memorable thing about it—manifestly it made everybody uncomfortable. I seemed to perceive this quite plainly. I had committed an indiscretion. Possibly it was in violating etiquette by intruding a remark when I had not been invited to make one; possibly it was in taking issue with an opinion promulgated by his Majesty. I do not know which it was, but I quite clearly remember the effect which my act produced, to wit: the Emperor refrained from addressing any remarks to me afterward; and not merely during the brief remainder of the dinner, but afterward in the kneip-room where beer and cigars and hilarious anecdoting prevailed until about midnight. I am sure that the Emperor's good-night was the only thing he said to me in all that time.

Was this lengthy rebuke studied and intentional? I don't know, but I regarded it in that way. I can't be absolutely sure of it, because of modifying doubts created afterwards by one or two circumstances. For example: the Empress Dowager invited me to her palace, and the reigning Empress invited me to breakfast, and also sent General von Versen to invite me to come to her palace and read to her and her ladies from my books. I was not able to do any of these things, because I was ailing, and was soon abed with an inflammation of my port lung which kept me there thirty-four days and came exceedingly near to closing my sojourn in this world; so near that when the physicians ordered me to leave Berlin and go to the Riviera I was reluctant to pay my railway fare in advance, because I did not believe I was going to live to finish the trip. I am aware that it would be most unlikely that the Kaiser's Empress would invite to breakfast with her a person who had acquired the Kaiser's disapproval—most unlikely—perhaps even impossible.

1891 All this was in 1891. Eleven or twelve years later Prince Heinrich came over and made a brilliant progress through America. At two of the dinners given in his honor, and where I was one of the guests, no speeches were made, but at another one the case was different. *1902* This was a prodigious banquet given by the wealthy proprietor of the *Staats-Zeitung* to newspaper men of distinction drawn from all large American cities. At that banquet I found myself placed, not at the state table with the other notorieties, as usual, but on the main floor among the human race. My vanity was profoundly hurt. The like of this had not happened to me for thirty-five years. By and by George W. Smalley came over and said to me,

"What are you doing here? Why aren't you up yonder?"

I said mournfully, "Because I was not invited."

"You don't mean it! What ass is engineering this affair?"

"I don't know which one it is, but I think it's Ridder."

"Oh no, Ridder would know better. It must be the blunder of a subordinate. What toast are you going to respond to?"

"None. I have not been invited."

"Oh come!"

"No—it is as I say. I have not been invited."

"Do you know, it has an incredible look. There isn't a man at that state table of any real distinction; they are second-rates and third-rates, every one; they are mere semi-notorieties, evanescents, and of no lasting consequence. Ridder's understudy seems to have raked the town to find artificial ornaments for his state table. Why have you been left out? How do you account for it?"

"Perhaps it's because I don't belong in that class. But it is as it should be, Smalley; I shouldn't feel at home in that inferior company."

This was light talk. But at bottom, my vanity was sharply wounded. I was ashamed to be seen down there among all those common people. They would go back home, all over America, and tell about it, and perhaps think they had found out that I was not as important a personage in New York as the country had been deceived into believing. Midway of the banquet I felt that I could not endure the situation any longer, I must go out and cry. So I got up and walked down the central aisle toward a distant door of refuge, and then a thing happened which filled me with joy, and enabled me to show off—and I would rather show off, any time, than save a human life: a multitude of those journalists rose up and flocked after me and crowded that place of refuge whither I went, and shook hands with me, and praised me, and made me ineffably comfortable and contented, for I knew that in that whole house there wasn't another person that could call out that demonstration except the chief guest, the Imperial Prince, brother of an emperor! I went back to my humble seat healed, comforted, satisfied, all my bitter venom turned to sugar and molasses. On my way up the aisle the Prince discovered me and sent an aide-de-camp to ask me to come up and see him, which I did. He was very cordial, very pleasant, and asked me to come to the withdrawing-room when the banquet should be over, and have a talk. I did it. But he never mentioned the Emperor, and didn't bring any messages. I judged that Ridder's blasphemous treatment of me was now explained. I judged that originally he must have placed my name among the speakers—he naturally would; that in accordance with royal etiquette the list would have to be submitted to the Prince; that the Prince had remembered the crime or crimes which I had committed so long before, in Berlin, and had crossed my name out with his blue-pencil.

Tuesday, February 12, 1907

Member of the tariff-revision commission brings message to Mr. Clemens from Emperor Wilhelm in regard to the dinner described in former chapter.

* * * * * * * * * * *

Those stars indicate the long chapter which I dictated yesterday, a chapter which is much too long for magazine purposes, and therefore must wait until this Autobiography shall appear in book form, five years hence, when I am dead: five years according to my calculation, twenty-seven years according to the prediction furnished me a week ago by the latest and most confident of all the palmists who have ever read my future in my hand. The Emperor's dinner, and its beer-and-anecdote appendix, covered six hours of diligent industry, and this accounts for the extraordinary length of that chapter.

A couple of days ago a gentleman called upon me with a message. He had just arrived from Berlin, where he has been acting for our Government in a matter concerning tariff-revision, he being a member of the commission appointed by our Government to conduct our share of the affair. Upon the completion of the commission's labors, the Emperor invited the members of it to an audience, and in the course of the conversation he made a reference to me; continuing, he spoke of my chapter on the German language in "A Tramp Abroad," and characterized it by an adjective which is too complimentary for me to repeat here without bringing my modesty under suspicion. Then he paid some compliments to "The Innocents Abroad," and followed these with the remark that my account in one of my books of certain striking phases of German student life was the best and truest that had ever been written. By this I perceive that he remembers that dinner of sixteen years ago, for he said the same thing to me about the student-chapter at that time. Next he said he wished this gentleman to convey two messages to America from him and deliver them—one to the President, the other to me. The wording of the message to me was:

> Convey to Mr. Clemens my kindest regards. Ask him if he remembers that dinner, and ask him why he didn't do any talking.

Why, how could I talk when he was talking? He "held the age," as the poker-clergy say, and two can't talk at the same time with good effect. It reminds me of the man who was reproached by a friend, who said,

"I think it a shame that you have not spoken to your wife for fifteen years. How do you explain it? How do you justify it?"

That poor man said,

"I didn't want to interrupt her."

If the Emperor had been at my table, he would not have suffered from my silence, he would only have suffered from the sorrows of his own solitude. If I were not too old to travel I would go to Berlin and introduce the etiquette of my own table, which tallies with the etiquette observable at other royal tables. I would say, "Invite me again, your Majesty, and give me a chance;" then I would courteously waive rank and do all the talking myself. I thank his Majesty for his kind message, and am proud to have it and glad to express my sincere reciprocation of its sentiments.

February 19, 1907

About thirty-five years ago (1872) I took a sudden notion to go to England and get materials for a book about that not-sufficiently-known country. It was my purpose to spy out the land in a very private way, and complete my visit without making any acquaintances. I had never been in England, I was eager to see it, and I promised myself an interesting time. The interesting time began at once, in the London train from Liverpool. It lasted an hour—an hour of delight, rapture, ecstasy—these are the best words I can find, but they are not adequate, they are not strong enough to convey the feeling which this first vision of rural England brought to me. Then the interest changed, and took another form: I began to wonder why the Englishman in the other end of the compartment never looked up from his book. It seemed to me that I had not before seen a man who could read a whole hour in a train and never once take his eyes off his book. I wondered what kind of a book it might be that could so absorb a person. Little by little my curiosity grew, until at last it divided my interest in the scenery; and then went on growing until it abolished it. I felt that I must satisfy this curiosity before I could get back to my scenery, so I loitered over to that man's end of the carriage and stole a furtive glance at his book; it was the English edition of my "Innocents Abroad!" Then I loitered back to my end of the compartment, nervous, uncomfortable and sorry I had found out; for I remembered that up to this time I had never seen that absorbed reader smile. I could not look out at the scenery any more, I could not take my eyes from the reader and his book. I tried to get a sort of comfort out of the fact that he was evidently deeply interested in the book and manifestly never skipped a line, but the comfort was only moderate and was quite unsatisfying. I hoped he would smile once—only just once—and I kept on hoping and hoping, but it never happened. By and by I perceived that he was getting close to the end; then I was glad, for my misery would soon be over. The train made only one stop in its journey of five hours and twenty minutes; the stop was at Crewe. The gentleman finished the book just as we were slowing down for the stop. When the train came to a standstill he put the book in the rack and jumped out. I shall always remember what a wave of gratitude and happiness swept through me when he turned the last page of that book. I felt as a condemned man must feel who is pardoned upon the scaffold with the noose hanging over him. I said to myself that I would now resume the scenery and be twice as happy in it as I had been before. But this was premature, for as soon as the gentleman returned he reached into his hand-bag and got out the second volume! He and that volume constituted the only scenery that fell under my eyes during the rest of the journey. From Crewe to London he read in that same old absorbed way but he never smiled. Neither did I.

It was a bad beginning, and affected me dismally. It gave me a longing for friendly companionship and sympathy. Next morning this feeling was still upon me. It was a dreary morning, dim, vague, shadowy, with not a cheery ray of sunshine visible anywhere. By half past nine the desire to see somebody, know somebody, shake hands with somebody and see somebody smile had conquered my purpose to remain a stranger in London, and I drove to my publisher's place and introduced myself. The Routledges were about to sit down at a meal in a private room up stairs in the publishing house, for they had not had a bite to eat since breakfast. I helped them eat the meal; at eleven I helped them eat another one; at one o'clock I superintended while they took luncheon; during the afternoon I assisted inactively at some more meals. These exercises had a strong and most pleasant interest for me, but they were not a novelty because, only five years before, I was present in the Sandwich Islands when fifteen men of the shipwrecked *Hornet*'s crew arrived, a pathetic little group who hadn't had anything to eat for forty-five days.

In the evening Edmund Routledge took me to the Savage Club, and there we had something to eat again; also something to drink; also lively speeches, lively anecdotes, late hours, and a very hospitable and friendly and contenting and delightful good time. It is a vivid and pleasant memory with me yet. About midnight the company left the table and presently crystallized itself into little groups of three or four persons, and the anecdoting was resumed. The last group I sat with that night was composed of Tom Hood, Harry Lee, and another good man—Frank Buckland, I think. We broke up at two in the morning; then I missed my money—five five-pound notes, new and white and crisp, after the cleanly fashion that prevails there. Everybody hunted for the money but failed to find it. How it could have gotten out of my trowsers-pocket was a mystery. I called it a mystery; they called it a mystery; by unanimous consent it was a mystery, but that was as far as we got. We dropped the matter there, and found things of higher interest to talk about. After I had gone to bed in the Langham Hotel I found that a single pair of candles did not furnish enough light to read by with comfort, and so I rang, in order that I might order thirty-five more, for I was in a prodigal frame of mind on account of the evening's felicities. The servant filled my order, then he proposed to carry away my clothes and polish them with his brush. He emptied all the pockets, and among other things he fetched out those five five-pound notes. Here was another mystery! and I inquired of this magician how he had accomplished that trick—the very thing a hundred of us, equipped with the finest intelligence, had tried to accomplish during half an hour and had failed. He said it was very simple; he got them out of the tail-coat pocket of my dress suit! I must have put them there myself and forgotten it. Yet I do not see how that could be, for as far as I could remember we had had nothing wet at the Savage Club but water. As far as I could remember.

In those days—and perhaps still—membership in the Lotos Club in New York carried with it the privileges of membership in the Savage, and the Savages enjoyed Lotos privileges when in New York. I was a member of the Lotos. Ten or eleven years ago I was made an honorary member of the Lotos, and released from dues; and seven or eight years ago I was made an honorary member of the Savage. At that time the honorary list included the Prince of Wales—now his Majesty the King—and Nansen the explorer, and another—Stanley, I think.

Monday, February 25, 1907

Recent disasters: the wreck of the steamboat *Larchmont* in the Sound, of the *Berlin* at the Hook of Holland, and of a fast train on the Pennsylvania Railroad—Newspaper clippings concerning them, and Mr. Clemens's comments upon them.

As I have said once or twice already, interesting news cannot grow stale; time cannot destroy that interest; it cannot even fade it; the eye-witness's narrative which stirs the heart to-day, will as surely and as profoundly stir it a thousand years hence. I wish to clip from the newspapers this morning some things for future generations to read. When they come upon them in this book a century hence they will not put them aside unread; they will not find them stale.

Within the last four or five days several striking things have happened, and I desire to speak of them, one at a time, and each in its turn. First came the *Larchmont* disaster. On the bitterest night of this winter, and the stormiest, the *Larchmont,* a steamboat crowded with passengers, was cut down in the Sound by a heavy-laden schooner. The sea was running high, the wind was blowing a gale, there was no life-saving station close at hand; during the few moments that elapsed before the steamer sank in fathomless water, a few of the passengers got away in the boats, but only to drift helpless a while, buffeted by the tempest, then freeze to death. The captain and several of the crew took early measures to save themselves, and succeeded, and are now in disgrace; the rest of that great company of men and women and children quickly perished. Among the steamer's passengers was a sailor and his wife. Being experienced and courageous, the sailor kept his head. He secured two places in a boat; he put his wife into one of the places and was about to occupy the other himself, when a woman who was a stranger to him appealed to him and he promptly gave his place to her and elected to go down with the steamer. Then his wife said she would go down with him, and she made him help her out of the boat. Then the other woman said she would die with these two new friends, and she made the sailor take her out of the boat. After a minute or two the hurricane-deck fetched away from the steamer, and these three, together with a score or two of other passengers, floated away upon it. One by one those scores succumbed to the cold, and the waves, and the gale, and died—every one. But the sailor allowed his two women no rest; he kept them on their feet; he marched them staggering up and down; he buffeted them with his hands; he kept their blood moving—all this during two hours—and he saved them alive. It was remarked by the thoughtful and the learned that this exhibition of the power and the compassion of an ever-watchful Providence was a wonderful thing, and a matter for our deepest awe and gratitude and worship.

Now we come to a yet more splendid and heroic rescue by Providence—assisted, as before, by a sailor-man. Three or four days ago there was a terrible disaster at the Hook of Holland. At dawn the steamer *Berlin,* with a hundred and forty-two passengers on board, was fighting her way into the entrance of that port in the face of a tremendous gale, with her efforts further obstructed by giant seas and a driving snow-storm. Suddenly something went wrong with the machinery and she was flung, a broken and helpless ruin, upon the rocks at the end of a long pier, and so situated that it was next to impossible for the life-saving service to get near her or afford any help. But no matter; that brave service went out in its boats and stuck to its gallant and almost useless labors, hour after hour, all day and all night, fighting the freezing storm and refusing to give up. During that day and night they rescued a few of the unfortunates and got them to the shore, albeit in an exhausted state, and with hands and feet frozen; meantime, more than a hundred of the passengers had been washed overboard, or had perished from the cold. It was now believed that no passengers remained alive in the ship; still the life-savers went on with their labors, but without avail. They could no longer get near the ship. They got near enough, however, to be able to report that there were still three survivors—women. These three, with thirteen already rescued by the life-saving service, were all that were still alive of the hundred and forty-two passengers. When two days and nights had passed since that poor ship had been flung upon the rocks, the captain of a ship lying in the port made up his mind to go, uninvited, and chance his life in an effort to save those women. This was yesterday. I will now tell the great tale of what followed as the cable tells it to us in this morning's papers. It has moved every reader, to-day, and its power of moving will not wither out of it by force of any lapse of time, however great.

LAST SURVIVORS RESCUED.

BRAVE MAN SWIMS TO BERLIN WRECK AND SAVES 3 WOMEN.

Terrible Sufferings Through Days of Cold and Hunger—Mother Clasped Body of Drowned Child—Sang Hymns to Keep Up Courage.

Special Cable Despatch to THE SUN.

A correspondent who was aboard the Wodan describes Capt. Sperling's heroic achievement. After arriving at the scene Capt. Sperling, who is an experienced diver, quietly completed his arrangements. Divesting himself of his oilskins and heavy sea boots, he descended into a dingey and, with three others, rowed toward the breakwater, pulling like demons.

When they arrived near the wreck Capt. Sperling plunged overboard into the surf, swimming strongly. The waves beat him back twice, but eventually he climbed on the end of the breakwater. He took a moment's rest and then began a terrible crawl along fifty yards of treacherous masonry. He was often hidden by the spray.

Clinging spider-like to anything available he reached the trestles beneath the wreck, stood up and uncoiled a rope which he carried and flung the end over the wreck. He then began a perilous climb slowly up the side of the wreck. He was buffeted by the waves, but finally with a mighty effort clutched the rail and sprang on the deck.

By this time one of the boatmen had climbed the piles near the wreck. Through the gloom those aboard the Wodan watched Capt. Sperling heave a rope to the man below and lower a bundle, which was laboriously dragged along the pier to another man who was standing amid the spray. In this way the bundle was slowly transferred to the rowboat. This was done three times. Those saved in the three bundles were deposited there.

Then Capt. Sperling began his perilous descent. Suspended from a rope, he gained the piles and battled his way back to the breakwater. The tide was rising rapidly and he had not a moment to lose. He rejoined his companions who had shared in the rescue work below and they plunged into the water and were dragged into the boat by comrades.

On arriving beside the tug the sailors tenderly got the women aboard. The poor creatures were quite helpless, sodden with wet and blue with the cold. They were just able to murmur prayers of gratitude for their rescuers.

All was ready for their reception below. There were doctors and nurses waiting and restoratives were applied and the poor women were wrapped in blankets. Then the Wodan made a triumphant return.

When Capt. Sperling boarded the Berlin he found the three women huddled together on the hurricane deck screaming and crying hysterically. They threw themselves on their rescuer and had to be soothed before anything could be done for them. They were unable to walk and clung to the necks of the tugboatmen, hampering their movements. Their clothing was nearly frozen and soaked with icy water.

The captain found Mrs. Wenneberg clasping her dead child to her breast. She refused to leave the ship without the corpse and the rescuers were compelled to use force.

Minna Ripler asked the men to save Miss Thiele first and Capt. Sperling carried her to the side, fastened her securely in a rope cradle, which he slung to the main hawser with a running knot. She was thus landed safely. The others were similarly landed. Mrs. Wenneberg was in a pitiable state. Miss Ripler was in better condition than her companions and was able to walk.

Capt. Sperling is not the captain of the Wodan but of a ship that is now lying in the harbor. He privately arranged with the captain of the Wodan, who is a friend of his, to attempt the rescue before the lifeboat went out this morning. He was accompanied on the tug by two nephews and a friend.

A great ovation was given to the lifeboat men on their return after forty-eight hours' battling with the seas. Their beards were covered with ice and they were suffering terribly from their long exposure.

Interviews with the men and women who were rescued last evening show that they passed the time on the wreck sitting in icy cold water, huddled together for warmth, great waves continually breaking over them. They sang hymns and songs and told stories until they were too exhausted by cold and hunger to do so any longer.

During their long ordeal they had only a few biscuits and scraps of food, which the crew shared with the passengers, and some peppermint lozenges. For the last twenty-four hours not a morsel passed their lips. They were horrified on Friday morning to find that some of them had been sitting on a man's corpse. The men gave the women all of their clothes possible. One woman was washed off by the waves just before the rescue.

In an interview with *Lloyd's News's* correspondent, after the rescue, Capt. Sperling, who was bruised and shivering and was just recovering from exhaustion, said:

"I thought I would never reach the wreck. It was a terrible fight and I was getting worn out, but I determined to reach them or go under. How can I tell what passed in my mind? I was struggling with the waves and climbing on the wreck. My only thought was whether any person was still alive.

"It gave me hope when I reached the rail and saw them move. No sooner was I on the deck than they seemed to wake out of a trance. All three rushed at me like wild creatures. They looked terrible, so gaunt and bedraggled, with their eyes starting out of their heads. The women seized me by the clothes. One of them flung her arms around my legs. I said: 'Keep as cool as possible, ladies.'

"They clutched me harder than ever. 'I implore you to be quiet,' I said, 'or we will all four be drowned.' Then they began to cry and that soothed them.

"My first business was to make fast the rope around what remained of the funnel. As I was doing this I noticed one of the ladies pointing with horror. I looked and saw about ten corpses huddled together in terrible attitudes, staring heavenwards. When I made the rope fast I flung the other end to my mate. Then I got another rope, tied it around the waist of a woman and lowered her by a slip loop down the first rope, which was taut.

"In this way I got the three off. It was a difficult job, for each clung to me. They did not want to go. Then I had a last look around and found that there was nobody else alive. I struggled back to the piles. When we got back to the port the beach was deserted."

Salvagers reached the wreck of the Berlin to-day and landed twenty-two bodies from below. No more corpses are believed to be on the wreck of the vessel.

Now I come to another stirring thing. It happened in our own country last night, a quarter of an hour before midnight, and this morning's newspapers have furnished us the details.

BOLT WRECKS 18 HOUR TRAIN.

TRACK ON STEEL TIES SPREADS UNDER PENNA. R. R. FLYER.

Train Rolls Down Embankment and Crashes Through Ice on Conemaugh River—Not One of the 100 Passengers Killed and Only One in Danger of Death.

PITTSBURG, Feb. 23.—The Pennsylvania special, the famous New York-Chicago eighteen hour train of the Pennsylvania Railroad, left the tracks at Mineral Point, near Johnstown, at 11:45 o'clock last night, rolled down sixty feet of embankment and crashed through the almost solid ice of the Conemaugh River, the stream that took such a tragic part in the flood of almost two decades ago.

The remarkable feature is that not one of the more than a hundred persons on the train was killed outright. Fifty of the injured are at the hospitals in this city, Altoona and Johnstown.

It was the most unexpected thing that happened.

A new piece of track had been put in at this point a short time ago. Instead of the ordinary wood crossties the track was supported on steel ties, to which the rails are bolted. One of these bolts, the railroad men say, gave way, the rails spread and the train, running around a curve at sixty miles an hour to make up lost time, was thrown to the river.

When the heavy train went over the embankment everything went before it, including the telegraph poles. For that reason it was hours before the outside world could be communicated with and assistance sent to the injured.

In the meantime they were huddled together, many of them devoid of any but night clothing, others with what clothing they did have soaked with the icy waters of the Conemaugh, and still others with blood from their wounds congealing over their bodies.

It did not seem out of place that when assistance did arrive and a special train was started for Pittsburg early this morning with the unhurt and those of the injured who were able to continue on their journey the Rev. Edgar Cope, rector of St. Simeon's Episcopal Church of Philadelphia, assembled all together in one car and there conducted one of the most solemn services of thanksgiving that has ever been held. Most of the passengers were still without clothing and were wrapped in blankets and bedclothes.

"Let us give thanks to the Lord our God that our lives have been spared," said the pastor as he opened the brief service. "Our presence here in the flesh at this time

> is nothing more than an act of Providence. So let us utter thanks to Him who has permitted us to live."
>
> Then down on their knees went the survivors and the fervent "amen" of the clergyman was heartily joined in by every person in the car just as the Union Station in this city was reached.

These eventful happenings engage our interest, and they also make us thoughtful. By the official statistics compiled by the United States Government, we find that within the brief compass of the year 1906 our railroads killed 10,000 persons outright and injured 60,000 others.

It has been said that the ways of Providence are wonderful, and past finding out, and this is true; but in a good many cases they do not seem so wonderful as are the ways of the pulpit, nor so curious, and obscure, and interesting, as are the results of its mental feats. The language of that clergyman in the train indicates that he fully believes that Providence is so all-comprehensively powerful that He can rescue from death and mutilation any of His children that are in peril by the simple exercise of His will, and at no inconvenience to Himself; also that Providence extended this grace to him and to his ninety-nine fellow-passengers, and that this was a most praiseworthy act and entitled to admiring applause, and to the deepest and humblest gratitude. It is as if a millionaire should contribute ten cents' worth of bread to a couple of his starving children and then sit down and admire his benevolence while the rest of his family pine supplicating around him and die of hunger. It is also as if this clergyman, being one of the rescued pair, found nothing to observe in these sorrowful circumstances except merely and solely the benefit which had accrued to him and his brother, and by that happy fortune was stricken so blessedly stone blind to the rest of the extraordinary episode that he could not even perceive its ghastliness, and stricken so dumb with gratitude for his own escape that he could not utter a word of criticism, reproach, or censure for the treatment which had been meted out to the rest of the family. Ten thousand killed and sixty thousand injured by the railroads; the *Larchmont*'s people allowed to go to their pitiful death unhelped by any but a poor sailor-man; the *Berlin*'s hundred and twenty-six allowed to go to their miserable doom without help from any but another good-hearted sailor-man and some brave and devoted life-saving crews—mere human beings, not all-powerful, but weak, and with lives to lose—and this clergyman in the train is dull enough, silly enough, indiscreet enough, to slander His Providence with grotesque compliments for doing an inexpensive kindness to one little handful of His earthly children while allowing all that multitude of others to drift into misery and death when a nod from Him could have saved them whole. I do not know what the pulpit's mind is made of. It takes a child's delight in theatrical exhibitions of the Creator's physical powers; no other thing so excites its eloquence; it can find opportunity for intemperate admiration where opportunity for sarcasm holds the better chance by a thousand to one.

In this connection I will remark that an elder sister of Harriet Beecher Stowe told me this anecdote a generation ago. One summer afternoon when Harriet was a little creature, she was playing about the room where her mother sat at work, when a storm came up, and presently a thunderbolt struck an apple-tree close by, accompanying the act with a prodigious burst of sound and scattering the abolished tree in fragments all over an acre of ground. The astonished child said,

"Mamma, who did that?"

"God," answered mamma, reverently.

"What did He do it for?"

"To show His power, my child."

Later the child reported the matter to the elder sister, who was surprised at one detail, and thought that perhaps she had misheard, so she said,

"What did mamma say He did it for?"

"To show off," answered Harriet.

The mother had not intended to utter a sarcasm; neither had the child, but both had done it.

Tuesday, February 26, 1907

Mr. Clemens describes the new club which he has started, called The Human Race—Another newspaper clipping concerning the wreck of the *Berlin*.

Last week I started a club. The membership is limited to four men; its name is The Human Race. It will lunch at my house twice a month, and its business will be to discuss the rest of the race. It is privileged to examine, criticise, and discuss any matter that concerns the race, and do it freely. In the matter of subjects and manner of treatment, there are no limitations. The reason that certain tender subjects are avoided and forbidden in all other clubs is because those clubs consist of more than four members. Whenever the human race assembles to a number exceeding four, it cannot stand free speech. It is the self-admiring boast of England and America that in those countries a man is free to talk out his opinions, let them be of what complexion they may, but this is one of the human race's hypocrisies; there has never been any such thing as free speech in any country, and there is no such thing as free speech in England or America when more than four persons are present; and not then, except the four are all of one political and religious creed. Whenever our club meets, its first duty will be to synopsize the performances of mankind as reported in the newspapers for the previous fortnight, and then discuss such of these performances as shall require our most urgent attention. After this stern duty shall have been accomplished the talk may wander whither it shall choose. Of a necessity, man will come in for more censures than compliments, more reproach than praise; but he will also have done some things during the fortnight of a sort to earn our commendation, and we shall confer it upon him in full and hearty measure. When we come to discuss the *Larchmont* and *Berlin* disasters we shall not forget the sailor-man and his wife, and their new acquaintance—great and fine characters, all three! neither shall we forget the

Dutch sailor-man and his three gallant satellites; nor the Dutch life-saving crew; nor the three heroic women on the wreck; nor the soldierly little servant maid. However, the little servant maid has not appeared prominently in the world's fifty thousand newspapers until this morning, therefore we will insert her prominently here, in order that future generations may still be reading about her, and caressing her name, and saying affectionate things of her, long after she shall have finished her pilgrimage and gone to her rest. On the shore, as will be noted, another sort of representatives of the human race were present and diligently exposing their kind; but Minna Ripler offsets them, and makes them show pallid and sallow in the white light that streams from her generous little soul. With the following cabled narrative of this morning we will close the fearful incident of the wrecked steamer.

HORRORS OF BERLIN WRECK.

WAVES BEAT MEN AND WOMEN TO DEATH ON THE DECK.

Last Survivors Nearly Crazed by Cold and Terror—Brave Servant, Who Stood by Her Mistress, Shows Best Progress—Heartless Throng of Gay Sightseers.

Special Cable Despatch to THE SUN.

LONDON, Feb. 24.—With the rescue, already described in the despatches to THE SUN, of the three women who after exactly forty-seven hours of indescribable suffering were the last to be taken alive from the wrecked steamer Berlin, the story of this terrible wreck comes to an end. Seldom has a sea tragedy, even when the loss of life has been greater, been so full of stories of poignant anguish.

Rescue or death as a rule comes with more merciful swiftness. The heroism of the rescued and the rescuers alike shows brighter in every descriptive line that comes from the Hook of Holland. Of the three women who were left until the last two remained rather than abandon the third, Mrs. Wenneberg, who was distraught from having seen her husband swept to death before her eyes and having her baby die in her arms, and who was also physically disabled by a dislocated arm.

She begged Miss Thiele and her sixteen-year-old maid, Minna Ripler, not to leave her, so Miss Thiele and the girl remained to give what comfort they could to their friend and mistress. The maidservant showed fine courage.

"Take the other two first; I am better off than they are and I don't mind if I am not saved if they are," said the girl, who alone of the three women was able to speak sensibly to the brave Dutchman Sperling when he reached them.

All three, however, were saved. Their lips were cut and bleeding, their faces frostbitten and bruised and their clothes almost torn from their bodies. There seemed but little life in them. Even now Mrs. Wenneberg, realizing the loss of her husband and child, seems not to care whether she lives or dies. Miss Thiele has relapsed into delirium, reiterating:

"The sea is coming over us."

The little maidservant, however, is recovering. She has seen some of her relatives for a few minutes, and given a short account of her last hours on the wreck. She said: "At the end we did not want to live; only to die. Hope had gone completely."

From the words of other survivors, who are now able to give some account of what they saw and felt, it is possible to picture the horror of those awful hours. They describe how men and women were dashed up and down the deck like pieces of cork. Some were caught in the tackle and hammered to a pulp. The women, some of whom were subsequently saved, were knocked all over the deck by the big seas, sometimes being carried forward, and again pitched with a thud against the woodwork. Within a few minutes several were stripped of their clothes and their naked forms were lashed by the waves.

One passenger, a Liverpool man of the name of Young, had a quarrel with a Frenchman in the face of death. He got to a part of the deck where the best shelter was afforded, and the Frenchman called out, asking him to give place for a lady. Young moved and the Frenchman took his place. Violent words followed, ending with Young slapping the Frenchman's face and threatening to throw him overboard.

A woman describes her hunger as being so intense that she was obliged to have something in her mouth. So she ate some paper and for drink tried to catch the sleet, snow and raindrops.

One of the stewards tells how the German ladies kept together in a little knot, taking quarter hour turns in sitting in each other's laps for warmth. He saw one old man washed overboard. Then a great wave dashed him back on deck, head first, and the top of his skull was literally sliced off. Some of the people were killed by wreckage that was carried back by the waves, striking like great spears.

Turning from the tale of suffering and heroism, which has not yet and never will be adequately told, it is somewhat of a shock to realize how throughout the day its scenes were converted into what might have been expected if a national holiday were being celebrated at the Hook of Holland. Every five minutes excursions trains arrived at the station discharging hundreds of sightseers.

The happy, laughing crowd for the most part were bent on enjoyment. All kinds of people arrived at the spot, which, as a rule, is a mere stage of arrival or departure. Even beggars arrived, the first for many years, who thought it a profitable adventure. The demand for refreshments was enormous and prices were doubled.

The office of the Great Eastern Railway Company was as thickly besieged as if lottery tickets were being sold. It was here that permits were given for admission to the temporary morgue. Nearly all the arrivals were armed with telescopes or racing glasses. Ladies brought opera glasses.

Helter skelter they made for the breakwater, which all day was a black ribbon of humanity. They ventured as far as possible along the slippery surface. Beyond was the storm swept area, with the dismembered wreck standing out in eloquent barrenness. Others, having secured permits, made a mad rush to the morgue, outside of which there was a queue like that at a theatre.

To-day the morgue was beautiful with flowers, including a large wreath from Queen Wilhelmina and her husband, Prince Henry. The walls were hung with black drapery. The strictest precautions were taken to prevent the incursion of the curious to the hotel, where the survivors are being cared for, and the crowds, despairing of any gratification of their curiosity there, proceeded to the jetty, where a steamboat left every half hour for the scene of the wreck.

Then, everything having been "done," there were mad rushes back for the trains.

Wednesday, February 27, 1907

Chapter dictated in Florence three years ago, about the first typewriter which Mr. Clemens saw and bought; Mr. Clemens the first person to apply the type-machine to literature—The introduction of the telharmonium music into Mr. Clemens's house on New Year's Eve, its first appearance in a private house—Newspaper clippings concerning the shooting of William Whiteley, in London; Mr. Clemens had had dealings with Whiteley, and inserts here a chapter of this Autobiography written in London seven years ago, which mentions Whiteley.

I am not a history maker, but I have been present two or three times when history was being made, and upon those occasions I furnished such help as I could. I have never been present at a great history-making battle on land or sea, but I have been present at civilizing and humanitarian victories achieved by the human mind which were of larger value and importance than have been ninety-nine out of every hundred of the immortal achievements of the sword. I wish to go back and bring forward to this place in my Autobiography a chapter which I dictated in Italy a trifle over three years ago.

1904. *Villa Quarto, Florence, January.*

Dictating autobiography to a typewriter is a new experience for me, but it goes very well, and is going to save time and "language"—the kind of language that soothes vexation.

I have dictated to a typewriter before—but not autobiography. Between that experience and the present one there lies a mighty gap—more than thirty years! It is a sort of lifetime. In that wide interval much has happened—to the type-machine as well as to the rest of us. At the beginning of that interval a type-machine was a curiosity. The person who owned one was a curiosity, too. But now it is the other way about: the person who *doesn't* own one is a curiosity. I saw a type-machine for the first time in—what year? I suppose it was 1871—because Nasby was with me at the time, and it was in Boston. We must have been lecturing, or we could not have been in Boston, I take it. I quitted the platform that season or the next.

But never mind about that, it is no matter. Nasby and I saw the machine through a window, and went in to look at it. The salesman explained it to us, showed us samples of its work, and said it could do fifty-seven words a minute—a statement which we frankly confessed that we did not believe. So he put his type-girl to work, and we timed her by the watch. She actually did the fifty-seven in sixty seconds. We were partly convinced, but said it probably couldn't happen again. But it did. We timed the girl over and over again—with the same result always: she won out. She did her work on narrow slips of paper, and we pocketed them as fast as she turned them out, to show as curiosities. The price of the machine was a hundred and twenty-five dollars. I bought one, and we went away very much excited.

At the hotel we got out our slips and were a little disappointed to find that they all contained the same words. The girl had economised time and labor by using a formula which she knew by heart. However, we argued—safely enough—that the *first* type-girl must naturally take rank with the first billiard player: neither of them could be expected to get out of the game any more than a third or a half of what was in it. If the machine survived—*if* it survived—experts would come to the front, by and by, who would double this girl's output without a doubt. They would do a hundred words a minute—my talking-speed on the platform. That score has long ago been beaten.

At home I played with the toy, repeating and repeating and repeating "The Boy Stood on the Burning Deck," until I could turn that boy's adventure out at the rate of twelve words a minute; then I resumed the pen, for business, and only worked the machine to astonish inquiring visitors. They carried off many reams of the boy and his burning deck.

By and by I hired a young woman, and did my first dictating (letters, mainly,) and my last until now. The machine did not do both capitals and lower-case (as now), but only capitals. Gothic capitals they were, and sufficiently ugly. I remember the first letter I dictated. It was to Edward Bok, who was a boy then. I was not acquainted with him at that time. His present enterprising spirit is not new—he had it in that early day. He was accumulating autographs, and was not content with mere signatures, he wanted a whole autograph *letter.* I furnished it—in type-machine capitals, *signature and all.* It was long; it was a sermon; it contained advice; also reproaches. I said writing was my *trade,* my bread and butter; I said it was not fair to ask a man to give away samples of his trade; would he ask the blacksmith for a horseshoe? would he ask the doctor for a corpse?

Now I come to an important matter—as I regard it. In the year '73 the young woman copied a considerable part of a book of mine *on the machine.* In a previous chapter of this Autobiography I have claimed that I was the first person in the world that ever had a telephone in his house for practical purposes; I will now claim—until dispossessed—that I was the first person in the world to *apply the type-machine to literature.* That book must have been "The Adventures of Tom Sawyer." I wrote the first half of it in '72, the rest of it in '73. My machinist type-copied a book for me in '73, so I conclude it was that one.

That early Boston machine was full of caprices, full of defects—devilish ones. It had as many immoralities as the machine of to-day has virtues. After a month or two I found that it was degrading my character, so I thought I would give it to Howells. He was reluctant, for he was suspicious of novelties and unfriendly towards them, and he remains so to this day. But I persuaded him. He had great confidence in me, and I got him to believe things about the machine that I did not believe myself. He took it home to Boston, and my morals began to improve, but his have never recovered.

He kept it three months, and then returned it to me. I gave it away twice after that, but it wouldn't stay; it came back. Then I gave it to our coachman, Patrick McAleer, who was very grateful, because he did not know the animal, and thought I was trying to make him wiser and better. As soon as he got wiser and better he traded it to a heretic for a side-saddle which he could not use, and there my knowledge of its history ends.

By means of a painstaking and rigidly accurate mathematical computation I find that the typewriter and the telephone, taken together, are worth more to the human race than twelve hundred and sixty-one battles and seventeen hundred and forty-two thousand barrels of blood. These figures have been examined by the mathematical authorities of Harvard and Yale universities, and found to be correct.

Two months ago it was my good fortune to assist at another bloodless historical birth: on New Year's Eve, at midnight, that extraordinary invention, the telharmonium, had its first experience in uttering music in a private house, and the house was mine. The utterance was clear and sweet and strong, and it broke upon the ears of the assembled company as a weird and charming surprise; there being no musical instruments in sight, they could not guess whence it came. It was brought over the telephone wire from three miles away, and it ushered in the New Year in a very moving and eloquent fashion.

The present plant cost only two hundred thousand dollars, yet with it it is proposed to furnish music, both night and day, to as many as twenty thousand subscribers at the phenomenally cheap rate of five dollars per month. It is claimed that within a few years nearly every person in Christendom will have this music in his house. If this shall turn out to be true, the telharmonium must take rank as educator and benefactor above all the great inventions so far produced by the human mind, excepting the movable types and the printing-press. I hold it a high distinction for me that it did its first home-work in my house.

The other day this cablegram appeared in the papers:

WILLIAM WHITELEY SHOT DEAD

LONDON'S "UNIVERSAL PROVIDER" KILLED IN HIS STORE.

By a Man Calling Himself His Son, Who Afterward Shot Himself—Family Doesn't Know Assailant—Panic Among Shoppers—Whiteley's Rise as a Merchant.

Special Cable Despatch to THE SUN.

LONDON, Jan. 24.—William Whiteley, known as "The Universal Provider," who established the great department store in Westbourne Grove, the first of its kind in London, was shot dead this afternoon by an unidentified man, who afterward attempted to commit suicide.

Mr. Whiteley was in his store, when the man, who was well dressed, entered and insisted on seeing him. The two men had a heated interview, which ended by Mr. Whiteley threatening to call the police. As he turned to reenter his office his assailant fired twice from a revolver into the back of Mr. Whiteley's head and then shot himself in the forehead, falling across his victim's body.

This interested me, because I had known Mr. Whiteley a little in years gone by. He was a very remarkable man. His death has called out several interesting communications in the newspapers, both here and abroad. I will insert one of them here:

WHITELEY, UNIVERSAL PROVIDER

How He Found a Wife for an Anglo-Indian Official in London on Furlough.

To the Editor of The Sun—Sir: With reference to the death of the great dry goods prince in London, Mr. William Whiteley, I should like to relate an incident which came under my own observation when I was in India many years ago. It was Mr. Whiteley's boast that you could get anything in his store, from a pin to a plough, and he endeavored to live up to his position as a "universal provider." In the '70s there was a civil officer in the Central Provinces who occupied the position of a commissioner, or chief civil officer of a division, and consequently he was prominent socially.

During a furlough in England he had patiently looked for a wife, but had not succeeded. When he was about to return to India he went to Whiteley's store and made some large purchases; and as he was leaving the store Mr. Whiteley accosted him and asked if he had found everything he wanted. The commissioner replied: "Yes, Mr. Whiteley, you have thoroughly supplied me with everything I want but one article, which it will be impossible for you to find." "Don't be so sure of that, sir!" replied the merchant. "State your wants, sir, and they shall be supplied." "Well, Mr. Whiteley, I am in search of a wife, and I scarcely think you can supply that article." Mr. Whiteley said: "Indeed I can. A young lady has just become a saleswoman in one of our departments, and she is altogether too highly educated and too refined for such a position. She is a clergyman's daughter and has been left an orphan. If you will allow me, I will introduce you to her, and I will take care that she does not know about the bargain!"

The commissioner went to the department and was introduced to the young lady, of whom he made large purchases. The result was that he eventually asked her to become his wife. They were married in due time and went to India. During my residence this lady was the leader of society in one of the divisions of the Central Provinces. It is said that after the marriage, and before he left England, the commissioner called on Mr. Whiteley and told him of his success, and asked how much was to pay. "Oh," he replied, "that is *con amore.* Simply a labor of love!"

ANGLO-INDIAN.

Mr. Whiteley is mentioned in a chapter of this Autobiography which I wrote in London seven years ago. I will bring it forward to this place.

Dollis Hill House, London, 1900. I spent eleven months in England, ending with June, '97; spent July, August and September in Weggis, Switzerland; spent twenty months in Vienna; then a month and a half in London, (1899); then two and a half months in the village of Sanna, Sweden; returned to London at the end of September, 1899, and have now been a detail of the world's metropolis for the past twelve months. By help of these now-and-then glimpses of London, I am able to realize that in some ways she undergoes changes, and that in many ways she doesn't.

In these latter ways she is what one must call—not slow, not sluggish, for those are not polite words—but conservative. Conservative is one of the most courteous and delicate words the etiquette-book contains. The telephone remains at about the stage in England which it had reached four years ago, from all I can see. In other enlightened countries one is hourly moved to use that handy servant, but not in England. In London, telephones are scarcer than churches. Perhaps it is because the service is substantially a monopoly in the hands of the Postal Department—a Department which is supernaturally and even superstitiously conservative.

If there is argument that the telephone is a great nuisance fifty-nine minutes in the hour, there is still no getting around the fact that in the remaining minute it is generally able to offset that bad record with a shining service which shall amply justify its right to exist. In my experience, life without the telephone is hampered, obstructed and difficult. Dollis Hill House comes nearer to being a paradise than any other home I have ever occupied. But it has no telephone, and that has sometimes made life in it a biting aggravation. There has never been a telephone in it. How did the occupant get along without it? I do not know; it is a riddle to me. Mr. Gladstone used to be a frequent guest of its owner a month or two at a time, and we know that he was able to superintend the Empire without it. It looks incredible. He used to sit in the shade of the trees, and read, talk, translate Homer, pace the lawn, and take his rest in serenity and comfort—all without a telephone. And yet there were times—times of upheaval in India or South Africa or some other corner of the Empire—when it was necessarily a heavy strain upon him to have to wait for news from Downing street per messenger, and he must have privately wished he had a telephone. We know that he did govern the Empire from Dollis Hill House without a telephone—that is, he did it as well as he could, in the circumstances, and also with tranquillity—but it would have made another man sweat blood. But was he always really tranquil within, or was he only externally so—for effect? We cannot know. We only know that his rustic bench, under his favorite oak, *has no bark on its arms.* Facts like this speak louder than words.

In England nothing is just as it is anywhere else. Dollis Hill House is not situated as is any other house on the planet. It is within a biscuit-toss of solid London; yet it stands solitary on its airy hill, in the centre of six acres of lawn, and garden, and shrubbery, and heavy-foliaged ancient trees; and beyond its wire fences the rolling sea of green grass still stretches away on every hand, splotched with shadows of spreading oaks in whose black coolness flocks of sheep lie peacefully dreaming. Dreaming of what? That they are in London, the metropolis of the world, Post-Office District N.W.? Indeed no. They are not aware of it. I am *aware* of it, but that is all; it is not possible to *realize* it. For there is no suggestion of city here; it is country, pure and simple, and as still and reposeful as is the bottom of the sea.

It will remain as it is. It, with the surrounding country, has been bought for a park, to be for all time a memorial to Mr. Gladstone, and two years from now the park will be thrown open and made free to the people.

No telephone. Twelve minutes' walk to the brick-and-mortar mass of London, thirty-five minutes' drive with a single horse to Piccadilly—and no telephone. But it is of no use to struggle with miracles, as a rule—some of them cannot be accounted for; raising the dead is one, and this is another. It gives us much discomfort sometimes. For instance, Whiteley serves us. Whiteley is one of those people, found only in London, I believe, who serve both cities and empires. His nearest establishment, on our side of London, is miles away. We can't telephone him, we can't telegraph him, we must do everything by letter—and give him a day and a half in which to fill the order. Our nearest telegraph office is two miles away, the postoffice which attends to our mails is further, the postman comes to us but twice a day—9 a.m., and 5 p.m. A letter sent to our pillar-box at any hour in the evening up to 11, will reach Whiteley next morning, but not earlier. Whiteley will send out the things next day at 1 p.m., per wagon. He will send you anything you want: a bishop, a cook, a cow, a kangaroo; set of furniture; beef, ham, butter, ice, any breed of eatable or drinkable the globe affords; an orchestra, a nigger show, a banquet, with table-ware, flowers, waiters, after-dinner speakers; a bride, a groom, bridesmaids, groomsmen, wedding-clothes, bridal presents; cradle, cat, dog, doctor, rat-poison, rats, whetstone, grindstone, tombstone, hearse, corpse—anything you want; but you must get your order to him a day and a half in advance, to make sure. And then the trouble begins! One or two articles are lacking, and they may be essentials of the last essentiality. It may be a bishop, it may be a ham; but whatever it is, it is nearly sure to be the very thing you most want. The driver has brought a list, and the missing thing is *in* it. Where is it, then, personally? He says he has brought everything that was given him; and washes his hands of the whole matter. By and by the week's bill comes, and in it the missing article is charged. The correspondence begins, now. You write Whiteley and say the missing article never arrived. Whiteley answers courteously that he will make inquiry. In time comes another letter: he has inquired of the driver, who is positive that he delivered everything that was given him. He has next inquired of the Head of the Ham Department—or of the Head of the Ecclesiastical Department, according to the nature of the missing link—who says he knows by the fact that the article is *in the list,* that he delivered it to the driver. That settles it. You have witnesses, Whiteley has witnesses—two on a side; but the court sits at Whiteley's, not at your house. So you pay. That is, Whiteley attends to that, himself; you have to keep a cash deposit with providers of his magnitude.

Next time, these proceedings are repeated; with the same result. You pay. The third time, it all happens as before. You pay. Then you give it up. After that, you enter no complaints, but pay the whole list, missings and all, and say no word. That is our experience. Why don't we go elsewhere? Because there isn't any elsewhere to go. Whatever you succeed in getting of Whiteley is up to standard; and while that is also the case with other world-providers like Harrod's and the Army and Navy Stores, their delivery-wagons do not come outside the cab limit, and we are as much as a hundred yards outside, I should say. Whiteley seems to be the only world-provider who provides everything on earth except a protection for his own repute and for his customer's pocket. The others will deliver to you no detail of your order without a signed receipt. It looks like obvious common sense. How Whiteley, without that rational little check, has been able to keep his gigantic business successfully flourishing all these years is to me a wonderful thing, another English miracle. Once we sent a hymn-book, or a corkscrew or some such furniture to the Army and Navy to be tinkered up and put in going order, and a month later we were going to have an entertainment and noticed that it was missing. The servants said they had not seen it since it went to the Army and Navy. I went over and laid the disaster before the presiding Admiral, and he rang up the responsible person, and did it just as calmly. He was not fluttered in the least; he knew he could find that thing. The responsible person brought his book, and exhibited his entries for May; whereby it appeared that on the 24th the missing article was received and repaired, and was dispatched by post three days later. The Admiral rang up a tracer and set him on. The tracer traced the article through the postoffice and into the responsibility of a maid in our house. "Oh, *that,*" she said; "yes, I remember about it, now; I know where it is." And she produced it. Whiteley would not have found it, here at Dollis Hill House, for he would have had no check upon our cook. It is my belief that our cook stole all those missing articles that we have been paying Whiteley for—or at least her fair share of them. Whiteley's system is calculated to make thieves of cooks and drivers—in fact is bound to do it.

Since writing the above paragraph the need of a telephone has come into evidence again. We are to pack up everything and begin a sea-voyage seventeen days hence, and must remove from this house eight days from now. Experience has taught us that if we want things done in other countries, that is one thing: in England it is another. In London you must not try to hurry the doer, you must give him time to turn around—time to turn around a good many times; time to turn around until he is dizzy; he cannot do anything until he is in condition. So we wrote the Army and Navy, three days ago, and asked them if they could send us a packer by 10 a.m. to-day. We mailed the letter at 3 p.m., within a mile of their establishment, and they probably had it before 5, for there are as many as eighteen postal-deliveries a day in their part of London. No answer the next morning. No answer the following day—yesterday. In the afternoon we telegraphed, asking an answer at our expense. No answer in the evening. All arrangements came to a standstill, and there was much of that kind of language which one only thinks, but does not utter, for piety's sake. There being no telephone, nothing could be done. At last a written answer came this morning, dated yesterday. They might have taken the trouble to send us a telegram of a single word, and thus saved us some of our language for next occasion, but they didn't. The letter was from their "Removals and Warehousing Department," as per its heading, and it confessed that "the pressure of quarter-day removals" had suffocated that Department; and that it would therefore "not be practicable to send a packer until after the 1st." A delay of thirteen days! This was serious. There being no telephone, we hitched up and took as prompt measures as we could, hurrying a messenger off to Harrod's. If it shall turn out that Harrod's, too, is smothered by the quarter-day pressure, what is to become of this family?

Fifteen minutes later—1.20 p.m. Telegram from the Army and Navy Stores: "Official calling this afternoon *re* packing."

Evidently something has happened; the suffocation of the Removals Department has been relieved, and thirteen days of it have vanished in a breath. "Official" coming; probably the Admiral himself. It was not as important as all that; a common packer from the anchor-watch would answer my purpose, and be less embarrassing, for I have nothing to do a salute with, and no way to pipe him over the side. Moreover, there will be two packers and two bills, now, for of course Harrod's man will come, he not being really expected but only invited.

7 p.m. Telegram from the Army and Navy to say that after all, they find it impossible to spare a packer before the 1st of October.

I shall probably have to pack that satchel myself.

Later. Probably not. Harrod's is going to send a competent person to-morrow, if possible; will send one anyhow, possible or impossible, if we cannot wait. We said we couldn't, and furnished reasons, some of which were true; the others I furnished, myself. So the packer is coming in the morning.

Next day. He came.

That we have had this bother and worry is our own fault, and is the fruit of heedlessness. We knew that London's "moving" days were like any other city's moving days—paralysing to all the transporting industries; and that one must do, here, what he would do in any other city: make arrangements well in advance, or suffer when the rush comes. When London moves, it is a world moving. For a month a million wise people have been engaging packers and movers and making dates, while we the unwise, have sat still and allowed them to corner the market. We should have done the same thing in New York in a May-"moving," and would have found the market cornered there, when we were ready to start.

It may be that we have imported the World-Provider since I have been away from home. I hope so, for he is a public benefactor, and a trustworthy one.

He is seldom "out" of anything; his goods are worth but a shade more than he asks for them; his time-limited things, such as fruits, vegetables, flowers, meats, eggs, bread, cakes, pastry, etc., are not stale, but fresh; he delivers everything at your door, and although you have to give him liberal time on your order when you are far away, it will at least arrive with certainty at the time promised—you can set your watch by his wagon. He has relieved life in London of four or five-sixths of its difficulties. After you have worn yourself out with a fortnight's railroading around London hunting for the right country house by help of an estate-agency, and are at last in despair, you go to the Army and Navy and they look at their list and find you a Dollis Hill in fifteen minutes. Also, the World-Provider furnishes you house-servants; also, carriage, coachman, horse and harness; also, the several kinds of horse-feed; and the supply is kept up from week to week without your knowing when it happens. We have had long experience of the Army and Navy, and Harrod's, and Whiteley's, and have come to regard them as the best friends the helpless and improvident can have. Each country has ideas that are worth borrowing by the others, and the world-provider idea is one which I think ought to be adopted and naturalised in all great cities.

The Army and Navy Co-operative Stores is an institution which was started by a small group of naval and military men thirty or forty years ago on a handful of capital—not as a speculation, but with the design of cheapening their current expenses. From that small seed it has grown, through its merits, to its present giant proportions and vast wealth. If the founders kept their stock they are well off now, even those who contributed but a month's pay. The small group of stockholders of their day has expanded to twenty thousand now, and their few dozen guineas have multiplied to millions.

I suppose it was a madman who invented the London system of indicating addresses. Obscuring them, is the exacter phrase. I suppose it must cause many cabmen and postmen to lose their reason every year. The town is a vast planless cobweb of criss-cross and helter-skelter streets which begin nowhere, end nowhere, and travel in no particular direction, but wander around aimless and indifferent. There are scores and scores of miles of them, and as a rule each of them is only three hundred yards long, and changes its name every time it turns a corner—which it is always doing. The tangle and confusion are bewildering beyond imagination; a stranger of my calibre cannot walk a quarter of a mile and find his way back again. There are eleven Queen streets, two or three dozen King streets, a library of Duke streets, and so on, and they are distributed far and wide over the town; so, if you want a particular one out of a litter of streets which bear the same name, you can go home and give it up, for you will never know where to look for it.

In some of the streets the houses are numbered, but there are great areas where the houses are merely named—like Dollis Hill House—not numbered. Sometimes a street is called a terrace, sometimes a lane, sometimes an alley, sometimes a place, sometimes a court, sometimes a garden, sometimes a crescent, sometimes a square, sometimes a circus, sometimes an avenue, and so on—anything that can protect it from being identified. One may wander block after block down a street of dwellings which display names only—no numbers: Idlewild, Horsechestnut Hall, Leslie Villa, Hollyhock Retreat, The Elms, The Oaks, The Pines, Windermere, Strawberry Cottage, Inglenook, Seafield House, Sanctified Rest, and so on. The postman has to learn all those names. Thousands of new ones are added annually. The cabman is worse off than the postman, for he has to know the whole town. He really does know it, though this seems unbelievable when one examines the map of London. To know it as he knows it must require a smart memory and an unusually retentive one, for there must be regions of it which he hardly sees twice a year. It is said that he cannot get a license until he has passed an examination. This must of course be so—one would know that, without being told it. I suppose that few pass and many fail. The cabman does know London, but he can never know the whole of its details—that is beyond the human possibilities. For instance, there are several cabmen who get into trouble when they try to find No. 7 Cromwell Gardens. They drive patiently up and down that great avenue hunting for No. 7, but they do not find it. This is because No. 7 Cromwell Gardens is not in Cromwell Gardens at all—it is around the corner, down another street. And when they try to find Albert Gate Mansions they are likely to fail, because that building is not in Albert Gate, it is in Knightsbridge. When they try to find Wellington Court they seek a court, quite naturally; but they are on the wrong scent, for it isn't a court, it is a house. You must learn to pronounce names as cabmen and policemen pronounce them—otherwise you create confusion. Cromwell is a name in point. You say "2 Cromwell Houses." The cabman looks dazed, but starts. By and by you find he is hailing other cabmen, as he goes along—asking questions evidently—and apparently not getting informing answers. Presently he stops and questions a policeman, and you put your head out and listen—noticing, at the time, that you are in a part of London which you have not seen before. The cabman tenders a name which vaguely resembles Cromwell, but is not familiar to you. The officer says there is no such place in London; then he steps forward and asks you to name the address. You say "2 Cromwell Houses." He studies a minute, then his face lights, and he says to the driver, "He means *Krumml*—Krummlowzez." In time I learned how to pronounce it properly, and was respected after that. If you wish to go to No. 9 Harley Gardens, you may start promisingly enough, but you will not arrive. You will arrive at Airley Gardens. I get this from experience. You must learn to distribute your *h*'s properly, then you will fare well, and have the driver's respect, besides. It is easy and simple: you ask for Airley when you want Harley, and for Harley when you want Airley.

Thursday, February 28, 1907

The Thaw trial, and Stanford White's character—Colonel Harvey's parable concerning the case, copied from *Harper's Weekly*.

The most lurid *cause célèbre* of modern ages is still before the court, but the most spectacular feature of it came to an end day before yesterday. This feature was the testimony of Mrs. Thaw, the slender and illustriously beautiful girl-wife of young Thaw, the fast youth who is charged with the murder of the gifted and famous architect, Stanford White. Daily, for many days, the girl has been under fire on the witness-stand, and hour after hour she has answered the questions of the lawyers, with the result that the whole Christian world is now as intimately acquainted with the past six years and a half of her life as she is herself. From the time that she was fifteen and a half, and was setting all the scoundrels of New York crazy with her matchless beauty, until now, when she is twenty-two, all the details of her comings and her goings have gone into print; in all the Christian communities of the globe these details have appeared daily in interminable cablegrams and Associated Press dispatches, and have been devoured by everybody, and commented upon by all the newspapers; no such banquet of cowardly crime and mephitic filth has ever before been spread before the world; the like banquets have always been local, before, and hardly heard of outside of the local limits—but all the kings and emperors, all the high and all the low, all the clean and all the unclean, have fed at this horrible Thaw banquet and passed their plates for more.

The girl's testimony exposes six years of Stanford White's career also. The witness charges the middle-aged architect—who was rich, of the first renown in his profession, and possessed of a middle-aged wife and a grown-up son—with eagerly and diligently and ravenously and remorselessly hunting young girls to their destruction. These facts have been well known in New York for many years, but they have never been openly proclaimed until now. On the witness-stand, in the hearing of a court room crowded with men, the girl told in the minutest detail the history of White's pursuit of her, even down to the particulars of his atrocious victory—a victory whose particulars might well be said to be unprintable; yet, with the exception of four abnormally hideous descriptive sentences, they were put in type in the daily newspapers and exhibited to the world.

New York has known for years that the highly educated and elaborately accomplished Stanford White was a shameless and pitiless wild beast disguised as a human being; and few, if any, have doubted that he ought to have been butchered long ago, by some kindly friend of the human race.

Under our infamous laws the seducer is not punished, and is not even disgraced, but his victim and all her family and kindred are smirched with a stain which is permanent—a stain which the years cannot remove, nor even modify. Our laws break the hearts and ruin the lives of the victim and of her people, and let the seducer go free. I am not of a harsh nature—I am the reverse of that—and yet if I could have my way the seducer should be flayed alive in the middle of the public plaza, with all the world to look on.

I have come into casual contact with Stanford White, now and then, in the course of the past fifteen or twenty years. He had a very hearty and breezy way with him, and he had the reputation of being limitlessly generous—toward men—and kindly, accommodating, and free-handed with his money—toward men; but he was never charged with having in his composition a single rag of pity for an unfriended woman. Notwithstanding his high and jovial spirits and his cordial ways, there was a subtle something about him that was repellent. I was not the only one that felt this; in times past others have mentioned this feeling to me. That splendid human being, Tom Reed, was one of these. When we were yachting in the West Indies with Henry Rogers several years ago, and were in the great lobby of the hotel in Nassau one day, the majestic figure of Stanford White appeared among the crowd, and he marched past with his gray-haired wife on his arm. Tom Reed said,

"He ranks as a good fellow, but I feel the dank air of the charnel-house when he goes by."

The question now before the country is, ought the newspapers to be allowed to print the dreadful particulars of such a trial as the one which I have been speaking of? Good arguments have been put forth on both sides, and I have read them thoughtfully, but I find myself unable to settle upon an opinion as yet. Therefore, for lack of a view of my own, I will here transfer from *Harper's Weekly* Colonel Harvey's parable, which I like because it justly and properly characterizes Stanford White.

The Man Who Ate Babies

THE President of the United States thinks that the papers that give "the full, disgusting particulars of the THAW case" ought not to be admitted to the mails. Perhaps not. Perhaps the country at large does not need all the particulars, but in our judgment New York does need most of them, and it would be not a gain, but an injury, to morals if the newspapers were restrained from printing them.

We will try to explain.

Once there was a man who had the incomparable misfortune to be afflicted with a mania for eating babies. He was an extraordinary man, of astonishing vigor, of remarkable talents, of many engaging qualities, and of prodigious industry. He had education and social position; he could earn plenty of money; and the diligent exercise of his intellectual gifts made him valuable to society. There was nothing within reasonable reach of a man of his profession which he could not have, but over what should have been a splendid career hung always the shadow of his remarkable propensity. The precise dimensions and particulars of it were not definitely known to many persons. A few men who had a mania like his doubtless knew absolutely; a good many other men knew well enough; and there was practically a public property in the knowledge that he had, and gratified, cannibalistic inclinations of much greater intensity and more curious scope than those that commonly obtained among careless men. There was an honest prejudice against him. Persons of considerable indulgence to eccentricities of deportment disliked to be in the same room with him. Sensitive stomachs instinctively rose against him. Yet he was tolerated, for, after all, nobody had ever seen him eat a baby.

One day another man—quite a worthless person—knocked him on the head, and let his pitiable spirit escape from its body. It made a great stir, for the man who was killed was very widely known, and his assailant was also notorious. There followed profuse discussion of the dead man's character, qualities, and achievements. His record was assailed, but it was also warmly extenuated. When it was averred that he was an ogre, the retort was that he was not a materially worse ogre than a lot of other men, and that we must take men as we find them, and make special allowances for men of talent. When it was whispered that he ate babies the answer was that that was absurd; that whatever his failings, he was the helpfulest, best-natured man in the world, and particularly fond of children and good to them; and that if he ever did eat babies he was always careful where he got them, avoiding the nurseries of his acquaintances, and selecting common babies of ordinary stock, who were born to be eaten, anyway, and would never be missed, and who, besides, were in many cases not so young as they made out.

So the discussion went on, and waxed and waned as the months passed. But one day there was set up a great white screen, big enough for all the world to see, and over against it was placed a lantern that threw a light of wonderful intensity, and then came a person named Nemesis, with something under her arm, and took charge of the lantern. And then there fluttered forth all day on the great screen the moving picture of the poor monomaniac and a baby—how he found her, enticed her, cajoled her, and finally took her to his lair, prepared her for the table, and ate her up.

Well; it was said that the picture was shocking, and that the public ought not to have been allowed to see it. Oh yes, it was shocking; never picture more so. But it was terribly well adapted to make it unpopular to eat babies.

EXPLANATORY NOTES

These notes are intended to clarify and supplement the Autobiographical Dictations in this volume by identifying people, places, and incidents, and by explaining topical references and literary allusions. In addition, they attempt to point out which of Clemens's statements are contradicted by historical evidence, providing a way to understand more fully how his memories of long-past events and experiences were affected by his imagination and the passage of time. Although some of the notes contain cross-references to texts or notes elsewhere in this volume and in Volume 1, the Index is an indispensable tool for finding information about a previously identified person or event.

All references in the notes are keyed to this volume by page and line: for example, 1.1 means page 1, line 1 of the text. All of Clemens's text is included in the line count except for the date titles of the dictations. Most of the source works are cited by an author's name and a date, a short title, or an abbreviation. Works by members of the Clemens family may be found under the writer's initials: SLC, OSC (Susy), CC (Clara), and JC (Jean). All abbreviations, authors, and short titles used in citations are fully defined in References. Most citations include a page number ("*L1,* 74," or "Derby 1884, 182–84"), but citations to works available in numerous editions may instead supply a chapter number or its equivalent, such as a book or act number. All quotations from holograph documents are transcribed verbatim from the originals (or photocopies thereof), even when a published form—a more readily available source—is also cited for the reader's convenience. The location of every unique document or manuscript is identified by the standard Library of Congress abbreviation, or the last name of the owner, all of which are defined in References.

Autobiographical Dictation, 2 April 1906

3.6–7 PROMOTION FOR BARNES, WHOM TILLMAN BERATED] The article that begins here was published in the New York *Times* on 1 April. Clemens provided his stenographer with a (partial) clipping of it and dictated the following instructions: "Miss Hobby, please paste this in at this point, in record of April 1st, but I may not comment on it until later." The clipping itself did not include the last two paragraphs of the original article, which contained background information about Benjamin Barnes and a comment about Senator Platt (see the note at 3.11–20). Clemens had discussed Mrs. Minor Morris's ejection from the White House, Barnes's part in it, and Senator Benjamin Tillman's response in his Autobiographical Dictations of 10 January, 15 January, and 18

January 1906 (*AutoMT1,* 256–59, 279–81, 292–93). He takes up his discussion of the incident in the next dictation, of 3 April.

3.11–20 MERRITT GETS NEW PLACE . . . succeeding the late Major James Low] President William McKinley appointed John A. Merritt (1851–1919) as postmaster of Washington in 1899, the same year that he made James Low collector of customs for the district of Niagara. Thomas Collier Platt (1833–1910), who had recommended Merritt for the postmastership, was a senator from New York and former Republican party leader ("New City Postmaster," Washington *Post,* 28 May 1899, 3; New York *Times:* "Presidential Nominations," 21 Jan 1899, 4; "John A. Merritt," 17 Oct 1919, 17).

4.1–2 Governor Nye was . . . politician, not statesman] James W. Nye (1815–76) had been a district attorney and judge in Madison County (New York), a lawyer in Syracuse, and president of the New York City Metropolitan Police Commission before Abraham Lincoln appointed him governor of Nevada Territory in 1861 ("Obituary. Gen. James W. Nye," New York *Times,* 28 Dec 1876, 4; see also the notes at 5.25–36 and 6.8–9).

4.40–5.5 The Governor's official menagerie . . . boarders and lodgers] In the first four chapters of *Roughing It* Clemens recalls Orion's appointment as secretary of Nevada Territory, and the "six pounds of Unabridged Dictionary" he brought along on their stagecoach trip west from Missouri. In chapter 21, he describes the Carson City boardinghouse at which he and Orion and Nye's "menagerie"—that is, his "Irish Brigade" of retainers—lived. It was run by "a worthy French lady by the name of Bridget O'Flannigan, a camp follower of his Excellency the Governor." Her real name was Margret Murphy (see *RI 1993,* 1–19, 141–46, 613).

5.5 the silver I had brought from home] Out of his earnings as a Mississippi River steamboat pilot, Clemens had paid his and Orion's $200 stagecoach fares from St. Joseph, Missouri, to Carson City, and had also provided about $800 for expenses (*RI 1993,* notes on 574–76).

5.7–8 a journalistic life on the Virginia City *Enterprise* . . . Carson City to report the legislative session] After about six weeks on the staff of the Virginia City *Territorial Enterprise,* Clemens was assigned to report the second session of the Nevada Territorial Legislature, held in Carson City from 11 November until 20 December 1862. None of his legislative dispatches has been recovered, but two of the weekly general letters he sent to the paper at the time survive (see *AutoMT1,* 251, 543 n. 251.31–38, and *MTEnt,* 9–10, 33–41).

5.15–21 I got the legislature to pass a wise and very necessary law . . . furnishing a certificate of each record] Clemens may be conflating two sessions of the Nevada Territorial Legislature. During the first session he served as Orion's clerk, and it is likely that he influenced the passage of a law on 29 November 1861 that permitted Orion to collect certain fees: thirty cents per hundred words for copying documents, one dollar for sealing and for filing them, and five dollars for appointing a commissioner of deeds (notary public). Another law was approved during the second session, on 19 December 1862, that required corporations to file official certificates (with no fee stated) and raised the copying fee to forty cents—the amount Clemens recalls here. No evidence has been found, however, that he was involved in the enactment of this second law (William C. Miller 1973, 3–5; *Laws* 1862, 310–11; *Laws* 1863, 94).

5.23–24 Very well, we prospered. The record-service paid . . . a thousand dollars a month, in gold] Orion's salary was $1,800 a year, paid quarterly, as set by the congressional act of 2 March 1861 which organized the Nevada Territory. Clemens earned $480 as Orion's clerk during the first session of the legislature, and evidently planned to do so in the second (1862) session. It is highly unlikely that the record-service was so lucrative. In fact, the Clemens brothers were frequently pressed for funds, in part because they were spending much of what they did have on working their several mining claims and speculating in mining stock (see 25 Oct 1861 to PAM and JLC through 26 May 1864 to OC, *L1,* 129–301 passim; *Laws* 1862, ix, xiv).

5.25–36 Governor Nye was often absent . . . as Acting Governor] For four years Nye was a driver for his brother's stagecoach line, hauling passengers and express on its Syracuse-Albany run, before studying law in Troy, New York, and being admitted to the New York State bar in 1839. Orion's longest stint as acting governor was between December 1862 and July 1863, while Nye was on one of his frequent political forays outside Nevada (Samon 1979, 16; OC and SLC to MEC, 29, 30, and 31 Jan 1862, *L1,* 145–46 n. 2).

5.42–6.1 He recklessly built and furnished a house at a cost of twelve thousand dollars] In November 1863 Orion paid George B. Cowing $1,100 for the plot of land at the northwest corner of Spear and Division streets in Carson City. There he built the two-story clapboard house which, somewhat renovated, still stands today. Shortly after it was completed in early 1864, the house and its furnishings were assessed at a taxable value of $3,250. Orion and his wife, Mollie, sold the property on 14 August 1866, after they had already left Nevada (Rocha 2000; Jeffrey M. Kintop [Nevada state archivist], personal communication, 3 Jan 2012, CU-MARK).

6.8–9 the people were willing . . . the Governor's game was made] Nevada voters approved statehood on 2 September 1863, and Nevada became the thirty-sixth state in late 1864. Nye was elected a Republican senator and served from 1864 to 1873 (19 Aug 1863 to JLC and PAM, *L1,* 265 n. 5).

6.10–12 Orion's game . . . disaster followed] For the details, see the Autobiographical Dictation of 5 April 1906. Clemens also describes Orion's personality in the Autobiographical Dictations of 28 March and 29 March 1906 (*AutoMT1,* 451–62).

Autobiographical Dictation, 3 April 1906

6.22–30 BARNES'S APPOINTMENT . . . Citizens Say Selection Is an Insult] Clemens made three brief notes on the clipping of this article from the New York *Times* of 3 April, to remind himself of what he wanted to say about it: "*The* representative American—the President" above the headline; "insolence" above the first subhead; and "Is it Pr. suicide?" above the third subhead.

6.34–36 a "carpetbag" appointment . . . an effort will be made to defeat the confirmation] The *Times,* while not condoning Barnes's part in the Morris incident, editorialized:

> Mr. BARNES is objected to as a "carpet-bagger," although he has been a virtual resident of Washington for eighteen years, while retaining a legal residence in New Jersey doubtless, very possibly for the purpose of securing his right to vote. If he does not know the local needs of the capital by this time, his ignorance is incurable. It is inconceivable that he would make a less good Postmaster of Washington for having been all these years a voter in New Jersey. ("The Washington Post Office," 4 Apr 1906, 4)

Efforts to prevent Barnes's confirmation were made in both houses of Congress—including a vituperative and partisan discussion of the Morris incident—but on 23 June his nomination was confirmed by the Senate by a vote of 35 to 16, with all but two of President Roosevelt's fellow Republicans in favor and the Democrats unanimously opposed (New York *Times:* "Penrose Calls Tillman an Ass in the Senate," 6 May 1906, 3; "Barnes Is Confirmed," 24 June 1906, 6).

7.45–46 the President's letter of some weeks ago. Maybe I inserted it] On 16 February 1906 Minor Morris had written to Roosevelt, complaining of the "damnable treatment" his wife had received at the White House. Roosevelt's reply was conveyed in a letter of 19 February from his secretary, William Loeb, Jr. Roosevelt had concluded that Mrs. Morris's arrest was "justified," that the force employed was "no greater than was necessary," and that "the kindest thing that could be done to Mrs. Morris and her kinsfolk was to refrain from giving any additional publicity to the circumstances surrounding the case" ("President Indorses Ejection of Mrs. Morris," New York *Times,* 22 Feb 1906, 5). Clemens did not insert the letter, or comment on it, at the time.

8.10–11 When Choate and I agreed to speak . . . Tuskegee Institute] For lawyer and jurist Joseph H. Choate, Booker T. Washington, and the Tuskegee Institute benefit, see the Autobiographical Dictation of 23 January 1906 (*AutoMT1,* 302–10 and notes on 572–73).

8.11–15 I at first took that thief and assassin, Leopold II . . . our Government's attitude toward Leopold and his fiendishnesses] Clemens probably agreed to speak at the Tuskegee Institute fundraiser when Washington called at his house on 13 December 1905. Two days earlier he had announced his intention to talk about Leopold II's atrocities in the Congo Free State at the Church of the Ascension in New York on the evening of 21 December—although he never did so. He and Washington were both vice-presidents of the Congo Reform Association, and for a time Clemens planned to make a similar speech at the 22 January 1906 fundraiser (Lyon 1905a, entry for 13 Dec; letterhead of Barbour to SLC, 23 Nov 1905, CU-MARK; Lyon *for* SLC to Twe, 11 Dec 1905, MS draft, CU-MARK). But by the time he formally accepted Washington's invitation in a letter of 8 January, he had decided to withdraw from public involvement in the Congo reform movement (see the note at 8.28–33). He never delivered a speech on the subject, and if he ever wrote out a Congo speech "in full," no text is known to survive. In his letter to Washington he wrote, "I will choose my subject *to suit myself;* & shall probably choose it *that night,* (22^{d}) *on the platform*" (DLC). He continued to express his outrage over the Congo situation privately, however: four days later, in his Autobiographical Dictation of 12 January, he condemns Leopold II's "slaughters and robberies," and he returns to the subject in several later dictations (see *AutoMT1,* 268, 557 n. 268.24–25; see also the ADs of 22 June, 25 June, 17 July, and 5 Dec 1906).

8.15–20 Twice I went to Washington . . . A final visit to the State Department settled the matter] Only one of the three trips to Washington Clemens mentions here has been documented: on 24–27 November 1905 he traveled there on copyright business, and it is likely that he visited the State Department then. He lunched at the White House with Roosevelt on 27 November and had "a private word with him on a public matter" that was on his "citizen-conscience"—almost certainly the United States position on Leopold II and the Congo (28 Nov 1905 to Edith K. Roosevelt, SLC copy in CU-MARK; Lyon 1905a, entries for 24, 27, and 28 Nov; 27 Oct 1905 to Barbour, ViU).

8.22–24 of the fourteen Christian Governments . . . our Government was not one] Clemens alludes to the General Act of Berlin of 26 February 1885, which concluded a conference that met from November 1884 through February 1885 and was attended by representatives of Austria-Hungary, Belgium, Denmark, France, Germany, Great Britain, Italy, the Netherlands, Portugal, Russia, Spain, Sweden, Turkey, and the United States. The act apportioned spheres of commercial influence in Central Africa, provided for free trade and navigation, established rules for future colonization, and committed the signatories to monitor the welfare of the native tribes and help in suppressing slavery. It also recognized the Congo Basin as the Congo Free State, under the personal control of Leopold II of Belgium, which effectively undermined the commitment to the native tribes. The United States signed the act, but did not ratify it.

8.28–33 I privately withdrew . . . the Government would of course do nothing] On 8 January 1906 Clemens wrote to Thomas S. Barbour, a member of the "Local Committee of Conference" of the Congo Reform Association in Boston, announcing that "I have retired from the Congo." He pleaded an inability to tie himself "to any movement of any kind, nor be officially connected with a movement of any kind, in a way which would lay duties & obligations upon me. . . . My instincts & interests are merely literary, they rise no higher; & I scatter from one interest to another, lingering nowhere. I am not a bee, I am a lightning-bug" (NN-BGC; letterhead of Barbour to SLC, 10 Jan 1906, CU-MARK). And in another letter to Barbour partially drafted around the same time, but evidently not sent in any form, he further explained:

> It has been my belief, ever since my last visit to the State Department, some weeks ago, that the American branch of the Congo Reform Association ought to go out of business, for the reason that the agitation of the butcheries can only wring peo-

ple's hearts unavailingly—unavailingly, because the American people unbacked by the American government cannot achieve reform in the Congo. (CU-MARK)

8.34 So I suppressed that speech and delivered one . . . on another subject] At the 22 January 1906 Tuskegee Institute fundraiser Clemens spoke on private and public morals (see *AutoMT1,* 305–8).

8.39 I did not throw the speech away, but saved it] A manuscript of this speech on manners, comprising thirteen leaves, survives in the Mark Twain Papers. Clemens left it untitled, but in 1923, in publishing it in *Mark Twain's Speeches,* Albert Bigelow Paine supplied the title "Introducing Doctor Van Dyke" (SLC 1923b, 296–301; also printed in Fatout 1976, 487–91). Henry van Dyke (1852–1933) was a Presbyterian clergyman, author, and professor of English literature at Princeton University.

9.11–14 I talked upon a text . . . my exposition of what the American gentleman should be got suppressed] Clemens spoke at New York's Majestic Theatre on the afternoon of 4 March 1906 to fifteen hundred members and friends of the West Side Branch of the Young Men's Christian Association. He did not entirely suppress his thoughts on "the American gentleman," but closed his speech with some remarks on that subject. For a text of the speech, as well as identification of the participants, see the Autobiographical Dictation of 15 March 1906 (*AutoMT1,* 409–12 and notes on 619–20).

9.31–36 Leonard Wood . . . "upholding the honor of the American flag."] For Clemens's extended remarks on this episode see the Autobiographical Dictations of 12 March and 14 March 1906 (*AutoMT1,* 403–9 and notes on 614–19).

10.5–7 MARK TWAIN LETTER SOLD. Written to Thomas Nast, It Proposed a Joint Tour] Clemens's letter, written on 12 November 1877, is quoted only in part in this article from the New York *Times* (for the original manuscript, see *Letters 1876–1880*). Nast (1840–1902), a well-known illustrator and editorial cartoonist, served on the staff of *Harper's Weekly* from 1862 to 1886. His work was highly influential in promoting the political causes he supported, including the Union side during the Civil War, the fight against New York City's Tweed Ring (see AD, 4 Apr 1906, note at 13.26), and numerous Republican candidates. He also created the enduring image of a plump and bearded Santa Claus, and the elephant and donkey as emblems of the Republican and Democratic parties. His reply to Clemens's proposal does not survive, and the two men never toured together.

10.30–32 It appears that four of my ancient letters were sold . . . twenty-nine dollars respectively] Clemens's source was probably the New York *Tribune* of 3 April, which published a fuller excerpt of his letter to Nast than did the *Times.* The *Tribune* reported:

> A friend of the Nast family, whose name was not given, paid $43 for a letter of the humorist to Mr. Nast, proposing a joint lecture tour. . . . Hitherto Mark Twain's autograph letters have not brought more than $5 or $6. The same man paid $28 and $27 respectively for two other Twain letters. A fourth was sold to another buyer for $29. ("For Twain Letter, $43," 7)

10.37–38 a letter of General Grant's sold at something short of eighteen dollars] "The highest price paid for any of several autograph letters of General Grant was $18" ("For Twain Letter, $43," New York *Tribune,* 3 Apr 1906, 7).

11.2 Dr. J. Ross Clemens] James Ross Clemens (1866–1948), one of Clemens's second cousins, was a native of St. Louis. He received his medical education at Cambridge University and the Royal College of Surgeons in London. Beginning in 1902 he practiced in St. Louis and was a professor of children's diseases at St. Louis University. From 1916 until 1918 he was dean of the Creighton University Medical School in Omaha. He also was a poet and playwright ("Dr. Clemens, Cousin of Mark Twain, Dies," St. Louis *Post Dispatch,* 19 July 1948, 3B).

11.12–15 "Say the report is greatly exaggerated." . . . it keeps turning up, now and then, in the newspapers] In a notebook entry for 2 June 1897 Clemens reported that his reply to the inquiry about his possible death was "in substance this: 'James Ross Clemens, a cousin, was seriously ill here two or three weeks ago, but is well now. The report of my illness grew out of his illness; the report of my death was an exaggeration. I have not been ill'" (Notebook 41, TS p. 28, CU-MARK). The remark was soon reported in newspapers around the world. Clemens inserted the word "greatly" when he revised the dictation for publication in the *North American Review* (NAR 2), and this is the best-known version of the quotation.

Autobiographical Dictation, 4 April 1906

11.28 MRS. MORRIS CASE IN SENATE] Clemens dictated the following instruction to his stenographer, who included it in her typescript of the dictation: "Under to-day's date, Miss Hobby, please paste in this clipping from the morning paper." Hobby attached a clipping of the article on Mrs. Morris's case from the New York *Times* of 4 April.

12.6–14 Mr. Barnes's successor as Assistant Secretary . . . These four men are prize-fighters] M. C. Latta was chosen to be Roosevelt's new assistant secretary. James J. Corbett (1866–1933) and James J. Jeffries (1875–1953) were former heavyweight champions; Robert P. Fitzsimmons (1862–1917) was a former middleweight, light-heavyweight, and heavyweight champion; Augustus Ruhlin (1872–1912) was a journeyman heavyweight, never a champion (New York *Times:* "Latta Gets Barnes's Job," 26 June 1906, 7; "Ruhlin Dies Suddenly," 14 Feb 1912, 9; "Robt. Fitzsimmons Dies of Pneumonia," 22 Oct 1917, 15).

12.18–19 differs from *all* other autobiographies, except Benvenuto's, perhaps] Cellini's was one of the autobiographical works that Clemens most admired (see *AutoMT1,* 5, 600 n. 378.32–34).

12.36 Here is some more about the Nast sale] The article "30 Cents for McCurdy Poem," from the New York *Times* of 4 April, continues the discussion that Clemens began in the Autobiographical Dictation of 3 April.

13.1–2 Theodore Roosevelt as Police Commissioner, Colonel of the Rough Riders, Governor, and President] Roosevelt was president of the New York Board of Police Commissioners in 1895–97. In 1898 he became colonel of the Rough Riders, the volunteer cavalry regiment he helped organize to fight in the Spanish-American War. He served as governor of New York in 1899–1900 and, as vice-president of the United States, became the twenty-sixth president on 14 September 1901, when William McKinley died eight days after being shot by Leon Czolgosz, an anarchist.

13.5 Richard A. McCurdy's autograph letter] McCurdy (1835–1916), president of the Mutual Reserve Life Insurance Company from 1885 to 1905, was one of the insurance executives whose illegal activities were uncovered by the New York State legislative investigation of 1905–6. See the Autobiographical Dictation of 10 January 1906 (*AutoMT1,* 257, 549 n. 257.6–9).

13.8 J. H. Manning, a son of the late Daniel Manning] Daniel Manning (1831–87) was a journalist and newspaper owner, prominent Democratic politician, and President Cleveland's first secretary of the treasury (1885–87). His son, James H. Manning (1854–1925), was a reporter and then the managing editor for the Albany (N.Y.) *Argus,* his father's paper, and was also an Albany banker and business executive who served two terms as that city's mayor (1890–94) (Reynolds 1911, 1:213–14; "Died," New York *Times,* 7 July 1925, 19).

13.11 I will be married on the 30th of June coming] General Philip H. Sheridan (see *AutoMT1,* 472 n. 67.5) was married in Chicago on 3 June 1875 to Irene Rucker, the twenty-two-year-old daughter of General D. H. Rucker, an assistant quartermaster general and a member of Sheridan's staff ("Gen. Sheridan's Wedding," New York *Times,* 4 June 1875, 1).

13.16 P.S. and M.I.] Postscript and, presumably in jest, military intelligence.

13.20–21 the dress of Laura Keene, worn on the night of Lincoln's assassination . . . the stain was made by his blood] Laura Keene (1826?–73) was a well-known actress and a pioneer female theater manager and producer. She was appearing in the popular comedy *Our American Cousin* at Ford's Theatre in Washington on 14 April 1865, when Abraham Lincoln was assassinated there.

13.22–24 Gen. W. T. Sherman's letter . . . Sumner, Greeley, Walt Whitman] General William Tecumseh Sherman (see *AutoMT1,* 473 n. 68.10); Charles Sumner (1811–74), senator from Massachusetts (1851–74), an organizer of the Republican party, and a fierce opponent of slavery and proponent of equal rights for all; Horace Greeley (see *AutoMT1,* 506 n. 145.1); and poet Walt Whitman (1819–92).

13.26 William M. Tweed and his companion, Hunt, under arrest] From the mid-1850s until his arrest in December 1871, William M. ("Boss") Tweed (1823–78) and his Democratic party Tammany Hall cohorts defrauded New York City of as much as $200 million through systematic graft and election fraud. Thomas Nast's scathing cartoons in *Harper's Weekly* were instrumental in bringing down the Tweed Ring. Tweed escaped from prison in December 1875 and fled, with one William Hunt, to Cuba and then to Spain. Identified by Spanish officials partly through a Nast cartoon in *Harper's Weekly,* Tweed was arrested, along with Hunt, in September 1876. He died in prison (Hershkowitz 1977, 280–99; see also AD, 9 Jan 1907, note at 362.13).

13.40–41 this morning's stirring news from Russia . . . clipping is about me] Clemens refers to a report of 4 April in the New York *Times* about the possibility of military conflict between Russia and China over the Russian presence in Manchuria ("Chinese-Russian Friction," New York *Times,* 4 Apr 1906, 4). The article about him that is inserted instead is from the same issue.

14.1 MARK TWAIN TALKS TO COLLEGE WOMEN] The article about Clemens's talk at the Women's University Club appeared in the New York *Times* on 4 April. The members of this social club were college graduates, and many of them were teachers ("The City's Women's Clubs," New York *Times,* 25 Nov 1894, 18).

14.41 On the 19th of this month, at Carnegie Hall] On 19 April 1906 Clemens spoke at Carnegie Hall on behalf of the Robert Fulton Memorial Association; see the Autobiographical Dictation of 20 March 1906 (*AutoMT1,* 425–28, 630–31 nn. 426.13–15, 426.20–21).

15.1 a yarn about a walking tour with the Rev. Joseph Twichell] The Reverend Joseph H. Twichell was pastor of the Asylum Hill Congregational Church in Hartford and Clemens's lifelong friend (*AutoMT1,* 479 n. 73.13). For the yarn see the note at 16.28–29.

15.3–4 *MARK TWAIN ADORED . . . AT WOMEN'S UNIVERSITY CLUB*] This second article about Clemens's club appearance was from the New York *World* of 4 April.

15.41 Miss Maida Castelhun, the President] Maida Castelhun (1872–1940) graduated from the University of California in 1894. She was a French and Norwegian translator as well as a novelist, poet, and biographer ("Miss Castelhun Becomes a Bride," San Francisco *Chronicle,* 25 May 1906, 1).

16.18 the Blue Jay story] One of Clemens's most frequent recitations, from chapters 2 and 3 of *A Tramp Abroad* (1880).

16.28–29 the story of Twichell and himself . . . hunted for a lost sock] The story is from chapter 13 of *A Tramp Abroad,* where Twichell figures as "Harris."

16.35–37 Susy's Biography shows . . . old goat who was President there] For the excerpts from Susy Clemens's biography of Clemens that describe their 1 May 1885 visit to Vassar and the poor treatment they received from Samuel L. Caldwell, the school's president, see the Autobiographical Dictation of 7 March 1906 (*AutoMT1,* 379, 394–95, 607 nn. 394.41, 395.12, 395.29–42). Clemens lectured at Smith College several years later, on 26 November 1888 and again on 21 January 1889 (*N&J3,* 435–36).

16.41–42 The occasion was a benefit arranged by Vassar . . . to aid poor students] The Vassar Students' Aid Society raised almost a thousand dollars with an afternoon event at the Hudson Theatre on 2 April 1906, which included dramatic and musical entertainment as well as a candy sale. The New York *Times* reported that "Mark Twain was the centre of one admiring group in a lower stage box" ("Three New Plays at Vassar Aid Benefit," 3 Apr 1906, 9).

17.21–22 I delivered a moral sermon to the Barnard girls . . . a few weeks ago] For the 7 March 1906 Barnard College lecture, see the Autobiographical Dictation of 8 March 1906 (*AutoMT1,* 396, 607–8 nn. 396.13–19, 396.22–25).

18.10 There was no Mrs. Faulkner among the *Quaker City*'s people] Clemens's memory was correct. For a complete list of passengers, see "Passengers and Crew of the *Quaker City,*" *L2,* 385–87.

Autobiographical Dictation, 5 April 1906

18.34–36 Miss Mary Lawton . . . will be a great name some day] It is not known when Clemens met actress Mary Lawton (1870?–1945), but by late 1905 he had begun to take an interest in her career: on 16 November he wrote to Charles Frohman, "Thank you very much for the appointment—I shall instruct Miss Lawton to arrive there on time" (Lyon draft in CU-MARK; see the note at 18.36–19.3). Within a few months Lawton was a regular guest at the Clemens home, and she became a special friend of Clara Clemens's. She began to appear regularly on the stage in 1906, and remained a success at least through the early 1920s, enacting both leading and supporting roles. She subsequently achieved equal, if not greater, notice as the author of a series of "as told to" memoirs, including *A Lifetime with Mark Twain: The Memories of Katy Leary, for Thirty Years His Faithful and Devoted Servant* (Lawton 1925, xii–xiii; Lyon 1906, entries for 3, 11, and 24 Mar).

18.36–19.3 Fay Davis . . . asked Charles Frohman if he would let Miss Lawton try that part] Davis (1872–1945), a comic and dramatic actress successful both in the United States and in London, began appearing on 12 February 1906 in *The Duel,* a play by Henri Lavedan, at the Hudson Theatre, one of the New York theaters managed by brother producers Daniel (1851–1940) and Charles (1860–1915) Frohman. Clemens's effort on behalf of Mary Lawton was partly successful (no text of his cablegram to Charles has been found). *The Duel* closed in New York on 14 April, but late that month or early the next, in the road company, Mary Lawton was given the part formerly played by Fay Davis. Despite excellent reviews she was quickly fired on the orders of Otis Skinner, the lead actor and head of the company. Clemens protested the firing in a vitriolic letter of 7 May to Skinner (possibly not sent), addressing him as "Dear little Otis" and calling him a "homunculus," not a man. He suggested that Skinner was jealous of the "outbursts of applause" Lawton had received, and condemned him for the contract imposed on her:

> Miss Lawton was to play a week for you on trial, & provide stage-clothes at her own expense. She saved you fifty dollars a day; her work was entirely satisfactory to your audiences; it won the praises of your troupe; it won the praises of your manager;

> it won your own praises, freely & frankly expressed. The trial-week completed, you hadn't the courage to dismiss her yourself, but put that humiliating office upon your manager.... You did not even offer to pay for the stage-clothes you had obliged her to buy. You knew, from the beginning—confess it!—that you intended to use her to save expenses, & then dismiss her. In other words, that you meant to rob her. Would you mind telling me what it feels like to be an Otis Skinner? (Photocopy in CU-MARK)

No answer from Skinner has been found (New York *Times:* "Amusements," 4 Feb 1906, X5, and 14 Apr 1906, 18; "Fay Davis Is Dead; Noted Actress, 72," 27 Feb 1945, 19; Hayman to SLC, 23 Apr 1906, CU-MARK).

19.4–7 Ellen Terry ... will retire in due form at a great banquet in London] Terry (1847–1928), who made her debut on 28 April 1856, achieved international renown for her acting in Shakespeare's plays as well as in works by the leading playwrights of her day. On 11 April 1906 the New York *Times* reported that "a movement was started recently in London for the celebration of Miss Ellen Terry's fiftieth anniversary on the stage, when the aim is to give a jubilee banquet in her honor on April 28, and also to raise a fund that will enable her to spend the remainder of her days in comfort." Mark Twain, the paper noted, was among those who "have declared themselves in full sympathy with the cause" ("Ellen Terry's Jubilee," 11). Her jubilee celebrations began at His Majesty's Theatre in London on the evening of 27 April 1906, following her performance in *The Merry Wives of Windsor,* and continued on her actual anniversary the next day (New York *Times:* "Ellen Terry's Jubilee," 28 Apr 1906, 7; "Ellen Terry's Anniversary," 29 Apr 1906, X8; "Ellen Terry Dies in Her 81st Year; Puts Ban on Grief," 22 July 1928, 1).

19.14 Age has not withered, nor custom staled] Compare *Antony and Cleopatra,* 2.2.

19.17–18 Sir Henry Irving ... thirty-four years ago in London] Irving (1838–1905), the internationally famous Shakespearean actor, was Ellen Terry's stage partner from 1878 to 1902. Clemens met Irving, and evidently Terry, in London in the fall of 1872, after seeing Irving perform at the Lyceum Theatre (6 July 1873 to Fairbanks, *L5,* 405 n. 6).

19.30–32 So I wrote Hammond Trumbull ... the learned man of America at that time] See *AutoMT1,* 272, 559–60 n. 272.31–32. Clemens discusses Trumbull further in the Autobiographical Dictation of 30 January 1907.

19.34–39 then his answer came ... was a Chinese one] The exchange that Clemens recalls occurred in July 1874 while he was writing *Colonel Sellers,* his popular play based on *The Gilded Age.* During the first week of that month, while on a business trip to Hartford from his family's summer residence at Quarry Farm near Elmira, he called on Trumbull to consult about his "splendid inspiration" for a novel ending to *Colonel Sellers.* He then followed up with a telegram to Trumbull (not known to survive), abandoning the idea. But on 22 July Trumbull wrote, complying with his request. The letter barely filled two pages, but did report four possible precedents for Clemens's idea, including a Chinese version and one borrowed "from the Sanskrit." On Trumbull's envelope, Clemens noted: "J. Hammond Trumbull, the Philologist. About the proposed 'dream' feature of my play of 'Col. Sellers.'" Nothing further has been learned about this "'dream' feature" (CU-MARK; link note following 28 June 1874 to Dickinson, *L6,* 170–71).

20.6–8 new State of Nevada . . . Nye was certain to get a Senatorship] See the Autobiographical Dictation of 2 April 1906, note at 6.8–9.

20.8–22 Orion was so sure to get the Secretaryship . . . He had not received a vote] Orion was not the only candidate nominated, nor did he avoid attending the Republican convention or fail to receive any votes. He was one of four candidates and came in a distant second in the voting on 11 October 1864. He may, however, have refused to do the saloon campaigning that was commonplace. On 7 November 1865 he was elected to the Nevada State Assembly, but served for only a few months (see Fanning 2003, 98–101, 104, 110–11). For details of Orion's religious vagaries, including his excommunication from the Presbyterian Church in 1879 and his attempt to publish a refutation of the Bible in 1880, see 9 Feb 1879 to Howells, *Letters 1876–1880; N&J2,* 209 n. 95; and Fanning 2003, 168, 174–78, 196–97.

20.23–24 His rich income ceased . . . He put up his sign as attorney at law] Orion was admitted to the Nevada bar on 14 March 1865 (Fanning 2003, 100; see also AD, 2 Apr 1906, note at 5.23–24).

20.31 I had taken up my residence in San Francisco] Clemens had "taken up residence" in San Francisco after leaving Virginia City, Nevada, at the end of May 1864 (link note following 28 May 1864 to Cutler, *L1,* 302).

20.32–35 Mr. Camp . . . told me to buy some shares in the "Hale and Norcross."] Herman Camp, whom Clemens had first known in Virginia City and San Francisco in the early 1860s, was one of the first locators on the Comstock Lode and an active speculator in Nevada mining stock. The Hale and Norcross Silver Mining Company operated a claim on the southern portion of the lode (13 Dec 1865 to OC and MEC, *L1,* 327 n. 1).

20.35–21.5 I bought fifty shares . . . when at last I got out I was very badly crippled] Clemens did own stock in the Hale and Norcross mine (almost certainly never as much as fifty shares), but his purchase and sales prices have not been documented. Although several of his surviving letters to Orion written in 1864–65 include mentions of the stock, they contain no requests for money. Clemens probably bought his shares when he visited San Francisco in May and June 1863, during which time their value rose precipitously from $915 to over $2,000. Certainly by May 1864, when he moved to San Francisco from Virginia City, he had some holdings. Over the next nine months the share price fluctuated dramatically, ranging from a low of $200 in August up to $1,000 in November and then back to under $300 by February 1865. Clemens evidently sold some of his shares before visiting Jackass Hill in the winter of 1864–65, but still owned two of them in the spring of 1865, when he was listed in an assessment delinquency notice. In 1868 he recalled, "Hale & Norcross, whereof I sold six feet at three hundred dollars a foot, is worth two thousand, now" (SLC 1868a; *L1:* 26 May 1864 to OC, 299, 300–301 n. 4; 13 and 14 Aug 1864 to OC and MEC, 309 n. 5; 11 Nov 1864 to OC,

319 n. 5; "San Francisco Stock and Exchange Board," San Francisco *Evening Bulletin*, issues of Jan–Feb 1865).

21.11–15 our Tennessee land . . . what Mr. Longworth thought of those Tennessee grapes] See "The Tennessee Land" and "My Autobiography [Random Extracts from It]" (*AutoMT1*, 61–63, 206, 208–9, 469 n. 61.1–3, 470–71 n. 63.14–16, 529 n. 206.19–20, 530 n. 208.37).

21.27–36 a gentleman arrived yesterday from Tennessee . . . the surviving heirs—the remaining third] These visitors have not been identified. About a year later, however, Clemens did join in a lawsuit relayed to him by his attorney, John Larkin, to secure an old claim to the Tennessee land. According to the "Declaration" filed on 15 May 1907, eight defendants had allegedly taken illegal possession of some four thousand acres of land in Tennessee that arguably belonged to the heirs of John M. Clemens. Clemens and his niece and nephew, Annie Moffett Webster and Samuel E. Moffett (the children of Pamela Moffett), joined suit with the Fentress Land Company to recover the land, worth more than $2,000, plus $5,000 in damages. When deposed on 7 and 8 June 1909, Clemens was asked to explain his assertion, published in two *North American Review* installments (NAR 12, NAR 13), that his family no longer owned any Tennessee land. (These installments were drawn from "My Autobiography [Random Extracts from It]" and the present dictation.) When questioned about the "Tennesseean gentleman" and the "well-to-do citizen of New York," Clemens could not recall their names, and referred all questions to Larkin. The litigation continued for more than three years. Most of the witnesses were questioned about the disputed boundary between Fentress and Overton counties, being asked to recall landmarks such as trees, stumps, streams, and structures. The surveyor who had run the most current county line, in 1896, was also deposed at length. Meanwhile, Moffett and Clemens had both died, leaving Annie Webster as the sole family plaintiff. The case was dismissed in December 1910 because the defendants proved that the land in question was in Overton County, where the court had no jurisdiction, and the plaintiffs were ordered to pay more than $400 in court costs. Clemens had anticipated this result, remarking to Isabel Lyon, his secretary, in September 1906: "Tennessee Lands going to be an expense after all. The almighty has been looking after it for 70 years, & he'll make it expensive" (Lyon Stenographic Notebook #1, CU-MARK; U.S. National Archives and Records Administration 1907–9, documents in Fentress Land Company et al. v. Bruno Gernt et al., Case 967: "Declaration," filed 15 May 1907; "Interrogatories for Saml. L. Clemens," filed 3 Apr 1909; "Deposition S.L. Clemens," filed 11 June 1909; "Deposition of Chas. R. Schenck," filed 17 Nov 1909; depositions of various witnesses, filed 28 Nov 1910; "Non-suit," filed 14 Dec 1910; "Fieri Facias," filed 8 Jan 1912; copies of these documents provided courtesy of Barbara Schmidt).

21.39–42 I came East in January 1867. Orion remained in Carson City . . . steamer for New York] Orion and Mollie Clemens actually returned East before Clemens. They left Carson City on 13 March 1866, but remained in California until 30 August, when they departed San Francisco for New York. Clemens left San Francisco on 15 December 1866 and arrived in New York on 12 January 1867 (22 May 1866 to MEC, *L1,* 342 n. 1; link note preceding 15 Jan 1867 to Hingston, *L2,* 1). The account here is the primary source for information about Orion's activities between 1866 and 1875. Additional details, drawn from family correspondence during this period, may be found in *L1–L6* and in Fanning 2003, 111–26, 131–51, 155–66.

22.7–8 I had bought my mother a house in Keokuk . . . They all lived together in the house] Clemens makes a chronological leap here. It wasn't until August 1882 that Jane Clemens went to Keokuk to live with Orion and Mollie. They occupied rented houses until January 1889, when Orion bought a house for $3,100, financing it with $1,100 in cash, most of it from a matured insurance policy, and a $2,000 loan. As his contribution to the purchase, Clemens helped pay for extensive repairs and improvements to make the house more comfortable for Jane, including the addition of an indoor "water closet." During this entire period and beyond, Clemens supported the Keokuk household with a monthly check (supplemented by cash gifts at Christmas and other times): at first he sent $125 ($75 for Orion and Mollie, $50 for Jane), then $150 (the additional $25 for Orion and Mollie), then $155 (the additional $5 to be passed on to a needy cousin, Tabitha Quarles Greening), and finally $200 (the additional $45 for an attendant for Jane, who by the late 1880s was suffering serious senile dementia as well as rheumatism). He continued the monthly $200 even after Jane's death on 27 October 1890, finally reducing it in 1891 to $110 ($10 of it for Tabitha Greening), and then by 1893 to $50, which he continued to send to Mollie after Orion's death on 11 December 1897 (OC to SLC, numerous letters in 1882–90, and 11 Dec 1897 to Whitmore, all in CU-MARK).

22.8–9 Orion could have had all the work he wanted . . . in the composing-room of the *Gate City*] Orion tried repeatedly to get editorial or compositorial work on the Keokuk *Gate City* and other newspapers, but was unable to do so on anything but a spot basis, and was usually unpaid for the few editorials he managed to publish.

22.10 his wife had been a Governor's wife] That is, when Orion, as Nevada territorial secretary, was standing in for the absent territorial governor (see AD, 2 Apr 1906, note at 5.25–36).

22.12–24 Orion got a job as proof-reader on the New York *Evening Post* . . . Rutland, Vermont] Clemens's chronology is inaccurate. Orion worked for the New York *Evening Post* in the fall of 1873, while Mollie stayed in Fredonia, New York, with Jane Clemens and Pamela Moffett (6 Nov 1873 to JLC, *L5,* 471 n. 1). His position on the Hartford *Evening Post* had lasted from about September 1872 until May 1873. Clemens's scheme for getting a job by first working without pay is the subject of his Autobiographical Dictation of 27 March 1906 (see *AutoMT1,* 446–51). In a letter to Olivia of 3 October 1872 Clemens implied that Orion had gotten the Hartford position by following his advice:

> Livy darling, it is indeed pleasant to learn that Orion is happy & progressing. Now if he can only *keep* the place, & continue to give satisfaction, all the better. It is

> no trouble for a man to get any situation he wants—by working at first for nothing—but of course to hold it firmly against all comers—after the wages begin—is the trick. (*L5,* 188)

By early May 1873 Orion had accepted the editorship of the Rutland *Globe,* remaining there until sometime in July (*L5:* 25 Sept 1872 to OLC, 182 n. 11; 5 May 1873 to OC and MEC, 363 n. 1).

22.36–39 his idea was to buy that place and start a chicken farm . . . and I sent the money] In May 1874 Clemens gave Orion and Mollie $900 to make a first payment on Mollie's father's chicken farm near Keokuk. But price negotiations stalled, the purchase was never completed, and Orion and Mollie merely rented the farm until sometime in 1876, when they gave up trying to make it pay and moved to Keokuk proper. There Orion tried, unsuccessfully, to practice law while Clemens supported him (*L6:* 23 Apr 1864 to OC, 110–14; 10 May 1874 to JLC, 141–42; 10 June 1874 to OC and MEC, 156 n. 3; 27 March 1875 to OC, 427–28; 25 Apr 1875 to JLC and PAM, 461, 462–63 n. 8; Fanning 2003, 164–67).

23.13–14 I found twenty-five dollars for pew-rent . . . sell the pew] On 26 July 1875 Clemens wrote to Orion:

> One item in your account strikes me curiously—"pew rent." You might as well borrow money to sport diamonds with. I am willing to lend you money to procure the needs of life, but not to procure so useless a luxury as a church pew. It would much better become a man to remain away from church than borrow money to hire a pew with. The *principle* of this thing is what I am complaining of—not the amount of money. (*L6,* 519)

Autobiographical Dictation, 6 April 1906

23.23 Renwick, the architect of the Roman Catholic Cathedral] James Renwick (1818–95), a graduate of Columbia College but self-trained as an architect, designed many prominent buildings in New York, including banks and hotels, luxurious private residences, and several churches. The most important of these was Saint Patrick's Cathedral, completed in 1879, except for the spires, which were added in 1888.

23.24–25 Katy, (the housekeeper,)] Katy Leary, who had been with the Clemens family for twenty-six years (see *AutoMT1,* 541 n. 242.22).

24.14–22 Etta Booth . . . Virginia City, Nevada] Booth was probably the daughter of Lucius A. Booth of Virginia City, owner of the Winfield Mill and Mining Company. In 1877 Clemens recalled seeing her at a ball in Virginia City when she was "8 years of age" (10 Sept 1877 to Booth, *Letters 1876–1880;* 12 July 1867 to JLC and family, *L2,* 73 n. 2).

25.4–5 poultry experiment . . . had then cost me six thousand dollars] Since the chicken farm was never actually purchased, it is unlikely that the two-year "poultry experiment" cost Clemens this much, even allowing for the regular support "loans" he made to Orion (see AD, 5 Apr 1906, especially the note at 22.36–39).

25.24 he invented a wood-sawing machine] This invention was one of many that Orion worked on but never successfully completed, such as an "Anti-Sun-Stroke hat" and a "flying machine" (7 June 1871 to OC and MEC, *L4,* 396; 4 Feb 1874 to OC, *L6,* 26–27, 28 n. 2).

25.29–31 fifty-thousand-dollar prize . . . Orion worked at that thing two or three years] In 1871 the New York legislature established a commission to test inventions to enable economical navigation on the state's canals by steam power rather than by "bank propulsion," that is, towage by draft animals. Prizes were offered in two categories—"degrees of perfection as to methods employed and results attained," and "successful operation and probable general adoption"—each paying $50,000 to a single winner, or the same amount divided among three winners (Whitford 1906, 1:281–82). At that time Orion was, in fact, working on his invention of a boat propelled by a paddle wheel (*L4:* 7 June 1871 to OC and MEC, 396 n. 3; 16 Sept 1871 to OC, 457–58).

26.4–14 he wrote me all about it himself . . . to the joy of every witness present] No letter of Orion's describing such an event has been found. During the presidential campaign of 1888, however, Orion assisted Keokuk Republicans despite being a supporter of the Democratic candidate, Grover Cleveland. In a letter of 31 August Orion described a torchlight event staged by African American residents that included "two tariff sentiments I furnished for the white folks Republican procession . . . though I expect to vote for Cleveland on that issue." And in a letter of 8 September he reported that "transparencies" bearing his tariff mottoes were used in both Republican processions, "white and colored." One of his slogans was "Protection is the eagle's wings that keep her out of the lion's mouth" (CU-MARK).

26.34–35 Bill Nye, poor fellow . . . is dead] Edgar Wilson (Bill) Nye (1850–96), the popular humorist and lecturer, suffered from chronic meningitis for many years before his death from that illness, at age forty-five.

27.15–16 Orion wrote his autobiography . . . he was constantly making a hero of himself] Clemens gives a similar account of Orion's autobiography in his Autobiographical Dictation of 23 February 1906 (see *AutoMT1,* 6, 378, 599–600 n. 378.25–27). Paine mined Orion's manuscript for details about Clemens's childhood while researching and writing his official (authorized) biography, and quoted from it in that work, published in 1912. He called "altogether unwarranted" Clemens's assertion that Orion "was constantly making a hero of himself." He judged Orion's work faithful to Clemens's "original plan," characterizing it as "just one long record of fleeting hope, futile effort, and humiliation. It is the story of a life of disappointment; of a man who has been defeated and beaten down and crushed by the world until he has nothing but confession left to surrender" (*MTB,* 1:24, 28, 44, 85, 89–93, 103–4, 107–8, 2:676–77).

27.21–22 I destroyed a considerable part of that autobiography] Today only a few pages of Orion's autobiography survive in the Mark Twain Papers. What befell the bulk of the manuscript that Lyon and Paine saw is unclear. In later years Paine himself reported, inconsistently, that it was buried "deep in the dusty obscurity of a safe deposit vault" and that it had been burned in keeping with "M.T.'s wish." According to Lyon, however, Paine lost the manuscript in Grand Central Station in July 1907 (Fanning 2003, 218–19; *MTHL,* 1:313).

27.22 Miss Lyon] Isabel Van Kleek Lyon (1863–1958) was the daughter of Giorgiana and Charles Lyon. Her father, an author of Greek and Latin textbooks, left his family impoverished when he died in 1883, and Isabel, after several other jobs, took a position as governess for the Franklin Whitmore family in Hartford. Clemens met her while playing whist at their home in the late 1880s. She came to work for the Clemenses as a secretary in the fall of 1902, despite her lack of typing or stenographic skills. She soon assumed some of Olivia's housekeeping duties and befriended Clara and Jean, on occasion serving as their chaperone. By the time the family went to Florence in the fall of 1903 she had become Clemens's amanuensis (Trombley 2010, 10–12, 19–28, 261).

27.23 I shall quote from them here and there and now and then, as I go along] In the remaining dictations, through 1909, Clemens only once quotes an excerpt from Orion's autobiography: into his dictation of 29 January 1907 he inserted the text of a letter he had written to Orion and Mollie on 6 February 1861, which Orion had transcribed into his manuscript.

27.24–25 in 1898 a cablegram came from Keokuk announcing Orion's death] Orion died on 11 December 1897. From Vienna, Clemens wrote Mollie the same day:

> We all grieve for you; our sympathy goes out to you from experienced hearts, & with it our love; & with Orion, & for Orion, I rejoice. He has received life's best gift.
>
> He was good—all good, and sound; there was nothing bad in him, nothing base, nor any unkindness. It was unjust that such a man, against whom no offence could be charged, should have been sentenced to live 72 years. It was beautiful, the patience with which he bore it. (IaCrM)

Autobiographical Dictation, 9 April 1906

27.36–28.8 a letter from a French friend of mine, enclosing . . . de la faire] This clipping from an unidentified French newspaper was sent to Clemens by Hélène Elisabeth Picard (b. 1872 or 1873) in a letter of 28 or 29 March 1906. In English it reads:

> **MARK TWAIN BANNED**
>
> New York, 27 March. *(By dispatch from our special correspondent.)*—The directors of the Brooklyn library have put Mark Twain's two latest books on the prohibited list for children under the age of fifteen, considering them unwholesome.

The celebrated humorist has written the officials a letter full of wit and sarcasm. These gentlemen have refused to publish it, under the pretext that they have not been given the author's permission to do so.

28.10–11 she wrote me about five years ago . . . friendly letters three or four times a year] The surviving correspondence between Clemens and Picard consists of thirty-one letters, written (with the possible exception of one undated postcard) between February 1902 and August 1909. Nineteen letters are by Picard (all in CU-MARK); twelve are by Clemens, of which nine survive only as transcriptions published in the *Ladies' Home Journal* of February 1912 ("Mark Twain's Private Girls' Club," 23, 54). In her 14 March 1902 letter to Clemens, Picard described herself as "Helene E. Picard—of a French Alsatian familly—aged 29—born in le Havre—tall, fair and plain looking, but not altogether too bad—living alone with her mother . . . in a very small town in the Vosges Mountains, quite near the frontier of Alsace.—Is very fond of books, delights in yours" (CU-MARK). For an account of the correspondence, with the texts of all Clemens's letters except for one he dictated to Isabel Lyon on 9 April 1906, see Schmidt 2011.

28.18–19 I have the constitution and by-laws somewhere] Clemens drafted the "Constitution and Laws of the Juggernaut Club" early in 1902. The only qualification for membership was "superior mentality, joined with sincerity and the spirit of good will"; inside the "imaginary Temple of Juggernaut, where the Club foregathers in the spirit . . . ranks cease, nationalities cease, no clan is represented there but the Human Race." The unspecified object of the club was to be "determined by the Membership" (draft in CU-MARK, 4–5, 7).

28.41–29.7 His temple is visited by pilgrims of all ranks . . . those pilgrims constitute a perfect democracy] The temple of Juggernaut, who was a form of the Krishna avatar of Vishnu (one of the most highly revered Hindu divinities), is in Puri in central India, on the Bay of Bengal. The cult of Juggernaut allows no caste distinctions.

29.11–19 Something in a newspaper . . . clean, clear ink] Apart from the enclosed newspaper clipping, this paragraph is the only part of Picard's letter that is known to survive.

29.22–24 When "Huck" appeared . . . the public library of Concord, Massachusetts, flung him out indignantly] For a detailed account of the Concord library's March 1885 expulsion, see *HF 2003,* 763–72.

29.28–29 Then the public library of Denver flung him out] In August of 1902, at the request of local clergymen who attacked *Huckleberry Finn* as immoral and sacrilegious, the Denver Public Library removed the book from its shelves (Denver *Post* to SLC, 12 Aug 1902, CU-MARK). In a letter of 14 August to the Denver *Post,* which had solicited his response, Clemens wrote, in part:

There's nobody for me to attack in this matter even with soft and gentle ridicule—and I shouldn't ever think of using a grown up weapon in this kind of a nursery. Above all, I couldn't venture to attack the clergymen whom you mention, for I have their habits and live in the same glass house which they are occupying. I am always reading immoral books on the sly, and then selfishly trying to prevent other people from having the same wicked good time. ("Mark Twain on 'Huck Finn,'" New York *Tribune,* 22 Aug 1902, 9)

Embarrassed by the controversy, the library reversed its decision and lifted its ban.

30.3 Brander Matthews's opinion of the book] Matthews, a leading critic and a friend of Clemens's (see *AutoMT1,* 548 n. 255.24), praised *Huckleberry Finn* at great length in the *Saturday Review* for 31 January 1885, soon after first publication. He saw the book as much more than just a sequel to *Tom Sawyer,* noting that "the skill with which the character of Huck Finn is maintained is marvellous. We see everything through his eyes—and they are his eyes and not a pair of Mark Twain's spectacles." Matthews called Clemens "a literary artist of a very high order," and especially appreciated "the sober self-restraint" with which he "lets Huck Finn set down, without any comment at all, scenes which would have afforded the ordinary writer matter for endless moral and political and sociological disquisition" (Matthews 1885, 153). And in a later essay, "The Penalty of Humor," published in *Harper's New Monthly Magazine* for May 1896, Matthews observed that "no one of our American novelists has ever shown more insight into the springs of human action or more dramatic force than is revealed in Huck Finn's account of the Shepherdson-Grangerford feud, and of the attempt to lynch Colonel Sherburn" (Matthews 1896, 900).

30.10–11 Seeing you the other night at the performance of "Peter Pan"] *Peter Pan,* based on the book by J. M. Barrie, opened a successful run at the Empire Theatre in New York on 6 November 1905. It starred the popular actress Maude Adams (1872–1953) in what became her most famous role. Clemens, who saw the play on 15 November, called it "consistently beautiful, sweet, clean, fascinating, satisfying, charming, and impossible from beginning to end" ("A Joyous Night with 'Peter Pan,'" New York *Times,* 7 Nov 1905, 9; "Samuel L. Clemens Interviews the Famous Humorist, Mark Twain," Seattle *Star,* 30 Nov 1905, 8, in Scharnhorst 2006, 528; Schmidt 2009; 16 Nov 1905 to Frohman, Lyon draft in CU-MARK).

30.13–14 "warn't no more quality than a mud cat."] "He was well born, as the saying is, and that's worth as much in a man as it is in a horse, so the widow Douglas said, and nobody ever denied that she was of the first aristocracy in our town; and pap he always said it too, though he warn't no more quality than a mud-cat, himself" (*HF 2003,* 142).

30.20 Asa Don Dickinson] After leaving the Brooklyn Public Library in 1906, Dickinson (1876–1960) worked as a librarian in New York, Kansas, Washington, and Pennsylvania before finishing his distinguished career at Brooklyn College. He also was a prolific author and anthologist. In 1935 he published "Huckleberry Finn Is Fifty Years Old—Yes; But Is He Respectable?" in which he gave a very brief account of how and when *Huck Finn* was written, as well as an account of his correspondence with Clemens (Asa Don Dickinson 1935).

30.27–29 21 Fifth Ave. . . . Dear Sir] The source of this letter text is Lyon's handwritten record copy of Clemens's original manuscript. In his 1935 article Dickinson published a facsimile of the holograph letter that he actually received (Asa Don Dickinson 1935, 184; see also the note at 30.38–40).

30.38–40 Huck's character . . . is no better than those of Solomon, David, Satan] In the holograph letter that Clemens sent to Dickinson, this passage reads: "Huck's character . . . is no better than God's (in the Ahab chapter & 97 others,) & those of Solomon, David, Satan" (Asa Don Dickinson 1935, 184). Clemens canceled "God's (in the Ahab chapter & 97 others,)"—the only revision he made—on Lyon's copy of this letter, which he inserted in the dictation.

31.24–25 report had sprung up that I had written a letter some months before to the Brooklyn Public Library] The report had probably "sprung up" because Dickinson—as he later explained—read the letter aloud at a librarians' meeting: "Needless to say, it fluttered the library dovecotes not a little, and all agreed that silence was golden. Mark Twain's name had a publicity value in those days only comparable to [Franklin] Roosevelt's in this. Public interest in his lightest word was unbounded and as uncontrollable as a prairie fire" (Asa Don Dickinson 1935, 183).

31.34–37 Miss Lyon . . . sent them away mightily pleased with her, but empty] In her diary entry for 27 March Lyon noted that

> all day reporters have been flitting in & out trying to get M[r]. Clemens to say something because Huck Finn & Tom Sawyer are reported as under ban in a Brooklyn library. M[r]. Clemens hasn't anything to say—he never does have—except from the depths of that glory of a bed & for private ears— Those reporters wanted to get hold of the letter he wrote to M[r]. Asa Don Dickinson—"a most characteristic & most damnedest letter"—but it would be a damaging letter. (Lyon 1906, entry for 27 Mar)

32.5–6 I wrote Mr. Dickinson . . . to be wise and wary] In a short letter of 26 March Clemens instructed Dickinson: "Be wise as a serpent & wary as a dove! The newspaper boys want that letter—don't you let them get hold of it. They say you refuse to allow them to see it without my consent. Keep on refusing, & I'll take care of this end of the line" (Lyon record copy, CU-MARK). In his article Dickinson quoted from this letter, which he said arrived with "a special delivery stamp" (Asa Don Dickinson 1935, 185). On 27 March, Clemens took care of his "end of the line" by releasing this statement about the Brooklyn library's treatment of *Huckleberry Finn* and *Tom Sawyer:*

> "It is all a matter of indifference to me. As I understand it, the librarian has not placed the books upon a restricted list, but has put them in the list of books for adults so grown up people can have the opportunity of reading them. They were heretofore given out to children only. Now they can be read by everybody.
>
> "The letter I wrote was a personal one, and I would not care to have it made public. I don't think my books are harmful to children, but I don't care to go into a discussion about that at this time." ("Topics in New York," New York *Sun,* 28 Mar 1906, 5, reprinting the Baltimore *Sun*)

32.39–40 where Choate and I made our public appeal in behalf of the blind] On 29 March 1906 Clemens and Joseph Choate spoke at the Waldorf-Astoria Hotel, at the inaugural meeting of the New York State Association for Promoting the Interests of the Blind (see *AutoMT1,* 649 n. 464.17–19).

Autobiographical Dictation, 10 April 1906

33.14–21 I find one from a little girl . . . the ocean] Clemens quotes a letter of 31 March 1906 (not from "twenty-one years ago") from Elizabeth Owen Knight (1894–1981) (CU-MARK; Rasmussen 2013, letter 164). He probably read aloud to his stenographer the portion of the letter he wanted to quote, but he substituted two different titles for the ones in the original: where the present text has "Huck Finn" and "Tom Sawyer," the original letter reads "Tom Sawyer" and "Tom Sawyer abroad."

33.28–29 Ambassador White's autobiography, and I find the book charming, particularly where he talks about me] Andrew Dickson White (1832–1918) was a preeminent educator and diplomat. Among other achievements, he was a cofounder, with Ezra Cornell, of Cornell University, and served as its first president (1868–85). Later he served as the U.S. minister to Russia (1892–94) and ambassador to Germany (1897–1902). In his two-volume autobiography, published in 1905, he recalled:

> My first visit to the upper Mississippi left an indelible impression on my mind. No description of that vast volume of water slowly moving before my eyes ever seemed at all adequate until, years afterward, I read Mark Twain's "Tom Sawyer," and his account of the scene when his hero awakes on a raft floating down the great river struck a responsive chord in my heart. It was the first description that ever answered at all to the picture in my mind. (Andrew Dickson White 1905, 2:379)

White was evidently recalling chapter 19 of *Adventures of Huckleberry Finn,* not *Tom Sawyer.* But it must have been this paragraph that charmed Clemens. White's other references to him are perfunctory (Andrew Dickson White 1905, 2:82, 203, 231).

34.3–9 Willard Fiske was a poor and untaught and friendless boy . . . Cornell University] Daniel Willard Fiske (1831–1904), a journalist, editor, and book collector, was a professor of Northern European languages and the head librarian at Cornell University from its inauguration in 1868 until his resignation in 1883. Clemens met him through their mutual friend, Charles Dudley Warner (see the note at 34.27–28; *AutoMT1,* 541–42 n. 239.23–24). Between 1845 and 1848 he had received schooling at Cazenovia Seminary, in Cazenovia, New York, and at Hamilton College, in Clinton, New York. According to his biographer, Fiske met Bayard Taylor (1825–78) in New York in 1850. In the summer of that year he went abroad to study Scandinavian languages and literature, and they apparently renewed their friendship in Europe sometime in the next few years (Horatio S. White 1925, 5, 10–16). Taylor, already a published poet and travel writer, later served as U.S. secretary of legation at St. Petersburg (1862–63) and U.S. minister to Germany (1878).

34.10–12 Mr. McGraw . . . had a lovely young daughter] John McGraw (1815–77), a founding trustee and great benefactor of Cornell University, made his fortune in the lumber industry. Clemens may have confused him with Ezra Cornell, the university's cofounder, who became wealthy through his partnership with Samuel Morse, inventor of the telegraph. Jennie McGraw (1840–81) was his only child.

34.27–28 she invited Fiske and Charles Dudley Warner and his wife to make a trip up the Nile] Warner, Clemens's Hartford neighbor and his collaborator on *The Gilded Age,* had been a fellow student and Psi Upsilon fraternity brother of Fiske's at Hamilton College, becoming his lifelong friend. Although he and his wife, Susan, visited Egypt during an 1874–76 excursion, they did not accompany Jennie McGraw and Fiske when they traveled there in the winter of 1880–81, after their marriage (3 Oct 1874 to Howells, *L6,* 248 n. 3; Horatio S. White 1925, 63, and Fiske to Andrew D. White, 27 Nov 1880, 426–27).

34.29 the old-fashioned dahabieh] A native sailing vessel, somewhat resembling a houseboat.

34.35–37 she wanted to marry Fiske . . . he was not willing to accept the fortune] Before his marriage in Berlin on 14 July 1880, Fiske signed a document renouncing his right to his wife's property (Morris Bishop 1962, 226). He later recalled:

> I declined, when I had the opportunity, by her own offer, to learn the contents of her will; I signed, without an instant's hesitation, the prenuptial contract, refusing to take any advantage hereafter of the rights that I might derive from the Prussian marriage laws . . . and when I saw her sad death weekly drawing nearer, I persisted in my resolution to make no suggestion which might pecuniarily benefit myself. I would not have exchanged the chance of losing one additional week of her life for all the money she had. (Horatio S. White 1925, 104)

34.42–35.2 Mrs. Fiske made a will . . . left the residue of the fortune to Cornell University] The estate of Jennie McGraw Fiske was estimated to be as much as $3 million. She bequeathed $300,000 to her husband, $550,000 to family members, and $290,000 to Cornell for the construction of three buildings; Cornell was also the sole residuary legatee (New York *Times:* "Trying to Annul a Will," 7 Sept 1883, 5; "Cornell Loses a Legacy," 20 May 1890, 9; Morris Bishop 1962, 227). Fiske assumed that the mansion under construction in Ithaca above Cayuga Lake—which the newlyweds had planned over the course of "many a pleasant Nile evening"—was bequeathed to him as well. In fact, the will "contained no provision for the completion of the house nor for its support" (Fiske to Boardman, 29 May 1890, Horatio S. White 1925, 105; "Two Millions Lost," San Francisco *Chronicle,* 4 June 1890, 3; Morris Bishop 1962, 227).

35.4–5 He could not live in the Ithaca house on any such income as that. He did not try to live in it] According to the historian of Cornell University, Fiske "realized that the income on $300,000 would not suffice to keep the house in proper style." White "saw it as his dream home for an Art Gallery. Everyone supposed that Fiske would occupy it, as custodian for the University," but that plan was never realized (Morris Bishop 1962, 227).

35.15 Charley Warner, who drew the will] Warner earned a law degree in 1858, but he made his career in journalism and literature. He did not draw Jennie Fiske's will, which was prepared by Douglass Boardman, the university's chief counsel and a justice on the state supreme court (Andrew Dickson White 1905, 1:419–20; "Two Millions Lost," San Francisco *Chronicle,* 4 June 1890, 3).

35.16–25 the University might claim the little palace . . . Fiske resisted the University's claim and the University brought suit] The executors asserted that Fiske was entitled to absolutely nothing beyond the $300,000 bequeathed him, claiming not only the house but its contents; according to some reports, these included Jennie Fiske's personal effects. It was actually Fiske who initiated the lawsuit, in 1883, in an attempt to break the will. After numerous conflicts with Boardman and the trustees (especially Henry W. Sage), he finally became "furiously indignant" when he learned of the university's deceit (see the note at 36.32–41; Fiske to Boardman, 29 May 1890, Horatio S. White 1925, 104–5). The case became a *cause célèbre* in the newspapers. Some of them represented Fiske as a fortune hunter carrying out a "diabolical and long-matured plot to win millions" (Morris Bishop 1962, 229–30). Others printed unsubstantiated (and no doubt exaggerated) reports of the university's cruelty, like this one in the San Francisco *Chronicle:*

> If he wished his wife's wedding-ring and his wife's wedding-dress he would have to buy them at the highest figure they would command, and in a similar manner and at a like rate he paid for every souvenir and present she had in her possession. Professor Fiske made a proposition to give Cornell University at his death every dollar he was worth if they would let him live in his wife's house, and he met with a scornful refusal. ("Two Millions Lost," San Francisco *Chronicle,* 4 June 1890, 3)

35.37 I furnished him the conditions in the same old way] Clemens's scheme for getting a job, by first working without pay, is the subject of his Autobiographical Dictation of 27 March 1906 (see *AutoMT1,* 446–51).

36.8 the young man of whom I have been talking] Charles P. Bacon (1859?–1916) was one of the Cornell students in whom Fiske took a special interest, and for several years he lived with Fiske and his mother on campus. He earned his degree in 1879. Clemens may have pointed him toward the Elmira *Gazette,* not the Hartford *Courant* (where Fiske had worked briefly). At any rate, it was the *Gazette* that Bacon edited during the journalistic phase of his career (New York *Times:* "Cornell Loses a Legacy," 20 May 1890, 9; "Charles P. Bacon," 20 June 1916, 11; "Two Millions Lost," San Francisco *Chronicle,* 4 June 1890, 3).

36.13–15 David B. Hill of Elmira . . . a very distinguished lawyer and a big politician] Hill (1843–1910) was the leader of the New York State Democratic party. He served briefly as mayor of Elmira (1882), then was state lieutenant governor (1882–85), governor (1885–91), and U.S. senator (1892–97).

36.32–41 young Bacon had this happy idea . . . It is the university, now, that has no show] At the time of Mrs. Fiske's bequest, White and Boardman were both aware of the restriction in the university's charter. But Boardman argued that it was "intended simply to prevent the endowment of corporations beyond what the legislature might think best for the commonwealth," and assured White that "if the attorney-general did not begin proceedings against us to prevent our taking the property, no one else could; and that he would certainly never trouble us" (Andrew Dickson White 1905, 1:419–21). Nevertheless, in 1882 the university amended its charter in an attempt to secure the bequest. Fiske "exploded" when he learned that

> the charter revision was designed (though ex post facto) to remove this disability, that according to state law no decedent having a husband could leave more than half her estate to charity, that Judge Boardman . . . had sedulously—and improperly—refrained from informing Fiske of his rights, and that the trustees in the know had surrounded Fiske with a wall of concealment. (Morris Bishop 1962, 228)

It was at this point, on the eve of his departure for Europe in 1883, that Fiske signed the papers initiating the suit.

37.1–4 Bacon won the case . . . that first lawsuit of his was also his last one] In 1890, after seven years of litigation, the case was decided by the U.S. Supreme Court, which awarded the entire estate to Fiske; his attorney received a fee of $180,000. Bacon remained close friends with David B. Hill, serving as his confidential adviser during Hill's term as governor of New York, and (despite Clemens's assertion that it was his first and only case) continued to practice law for many years (Morris Bishop 1962, 231–32; "Charles P. Bacon," New York *Times,* 20 June 1916, 11). Ultimately Cornell was not greatly injured by the loss of the lawsuit. Henry W. Sage, at one time John McGraw's partner in the lumber industry, donated over $200,000 for a new library building, together with an endowment of $300,000. And Fiske bequeathed his valuable book collection and nearly $600,000 (Horatio S. White 1925, 96–97, 237–38; "Mr. Sage's Gift to Cornell," New York *Times,* 24 May 1889, 1; for Sage see *AutoMT1,* 599 n. 377.14).

Autobiographical Dictation, 11 April 1906

37.19–20 I think it likely that in . . . "Roughing It" I have mentioned Frank Fuller] *Roughing It* makes no mention of Fuller. See the note at 37.27.

37.27 the Secretary of the Territory, Frank Fuller—called Governor, of course] Fuller (1827–1915) had not yet arrived in Utah Territory in the summer of 1861 when the Clemens brothers passed through on their way to Carson City. Alfred Cumming, the current governor, was a secessionist, and had returned to his native Georgia the previous May, knowing that President Lincoln would not reappoint him. He was replaced by Territorial Secretary Francis H. Wootton, who also soon resigned. Fuller, appointed by Lincoln to replace Wootton, became the acting governor upon his arrival in Salt Lake City on 10 September 1861 and held the position for three months, until the newly appointed governor arrived in December (New York *Times:* "Affairs in Utah," 17 June

1861, 5; 8 July 1861, 2). Clemens and Fuller actually met in Virginia City in 1862; they developed their acquaintance in San Francisco in 1863 or 1864 and then in New York in 1867, where Fuller acted as Clemens's lecture manager. They remained lifelong friends. After his time in Utah, Fuller, who had studied medicine and dentistry, had a varied career as a newspaperman, dentist, broker of mining stocks, railroad official, insurance agent, entrepreneur, and indefatigable speculator. In 1906 he was still proprietor of the Health Food Company, which he had established in New York in 1874, and reportedly a millionaire (*L2:* link note preceding 15 Jan 1867 to Hingston, 5; 23 Apr 1867 to Stoddard, 33–34 n. 7; *RI 1993,* notes on 591–92; Schmidt 2002; "Frank Fuller Dead," New York *Times,* 20 Feb 1915, 5).

38.6–11 I had spent several months in the Sandwich Islands for the Sacramento *Union* . . . on the platform in San Francisco] See *AutoMT1,* 128, 226–27, 501–2 n. 128.22–24, 536–37 nn. 225.29–31, 226.41–227.1.

38.15–20 I found Fuller there in some kind of business . . . matronly of aspect, and married] In January 1867 Fuller was vice-president of the Northern Pacific Railroad Company, with offices at 57 Broadway. He was married to his first wife, Mary F. Fuller (1829?–70); his daughters, Ida F. and Anna Cora, were about seventeen and thirteen, respectively (Fuller 1911; *Portsmouth Census* 1860, 679:740).

38.39–40 He would have the basement hall in Cooper Institute] Fuller booked the hall, in the Cooper Union for the Advancement of Science and Art, for 6 May 1867. This free educational institution had been established in 1859 by inventor, industrialist, and philanthropist Peter Cooper (1791–1883). Occupying an entire block between Third and Fourth avenues and Seventh and Eighth streets, in addition to its large basement lecture hall it included stores and offices, art galleries and studios, laboratories, and an extensive library, and offered diploma and degree programs for working-class men and women of all races. Today the Cooper Union continues its tuition-free tradition and is a leading college of art, architecture, and engineering (James Miller 1866, 49–50; Lossing 1884, 670–72; Cooper Union 2011).

39.1 Oh, he was all on fire with his project] In 1911 Fuller claimed that it was Clemens who was fired with the idea of a New York lecture and insisted upon Cooper Union as the venue. In 1895 Clemens recounted this episode in some detail for a lecture he wrote out but never gave, now published as "Frank Fuller and My First New York Lecture" (Fuller 1911; SLC 2009a, 5–17; for the contemporary details of this episode, including his letters at the time and reviews of the lecture, see *L2:* 23 Apr 1867 to Stoddard, 33–35 n. 7; 1 May 1867 to JLC and family through the link note preceding 14 May 1867 to Stanton, 38–44; and 28 Nov 1868 to OLL, 292–93, and "Enclosures with the Letters," 417–19).

40.18 That episode must have cost him four or five hundred dollars] Fuller recalled that "the expense of the lecture was a little over $600; the receipts were not quite $300" (Fuller 1911).

40.24–30 I put myself in Redpath's hands . . . whether it was the following year] Clemens did not undertake any lecture tour in the season of 1867–68, following his 6 May success at the Cooper Union and the *Quaker City* excursion, which took place from June to November. He did tour dozens of cities and towns in the Midwest and the East in 1868–69, but it was not until the following season that he signed with James Redpath's Boston Lyceum Bureau, for an eastern tour that ran from 1 November 1869 through 21 January 1870. For Clemens's 1898–99 accounts of his experiences on the lecture circuit see "Lecture-Times" and "Ralph Keeler" (*AutoMT1,* 146–49, 151–53, and notes on 506–12).

40.35–37 Last fall his wife's brother was murdered . . . beaten him to death with a club] Fuller's first wife died in 1870, and on 14 December of that year he married Annie Weeks Thompson (1840?–1906) (*Chatham Census* 1880, 792:65C; "Married," New York *Times,* 15 Dec 1870, 5). Her brother, Jacob Thompson (b. 1837?), exchange editor of the New York *Times* for nearly forty years, died on 8 September 1905. He had been found that morning, unconscious and severely injured, in his room at the Hotel St. James. The chambermaid who found Thompson reported that he "was almost covered with blood, which also stained the carpet around and spattered the wall above for about four feet" ("J. H. Thompson Found Dying in His Room," New York *Times,* 9 Sept 1905, 6). An autopsy revealed that Thompson had died of three severe skull fractures. It was soon determined that he had been robbed of a gold watch and several hundred dollars. The suspected murderer, a St. James bellboy, died on 31 October, before he could be apprehended, from stab wounds received in a domestic altercation (New York *Times:* "Mr. Thompson Slain and Probably Robbed," 10 Sept 1905, 5; "Mr. Thompson's Lights Burning All the Night," 12 Sept 1905, 2; "Seek Former Servant in Thompson Case," 15 Sept 1905, 5; "Death Beats Police in Thompson Case," 1 Nov 1905, 1).

41.6 She passed to her rest about three days later] Annie Fuller died on 10 February 1906. On 2 February Isabel Lyon wrote in her diary, "This afternoon a messenger came with a note from M^r^. Frank Fuller asking, M^r^. Clemens to call on M^r^. Fuller's ill ill wife. I telephoned to him that M^r^. Clemens would be happy to do so, & tomorrow afternoon at 5 has been set for the call." It seems likely that this visit is the same one that Clemens describes here. Lyon continued with a description of Fuller similar to the one in this dictation ("Died," New York *Times,* 11 Feb 1906, 7; Lyon 1906, entry for 2 Feb).

41.18 Homer Hawkins] A twenty-two-year-old timekeeper for the New York, New Haven and Hartford Railroad ("Learns His Life Secret in Plot to Blackmail," New York *World,* 12 Apr 1906, 2).

41.19–20 he is only the adopted son of Dr. Frank Fuller] Louis R. Fuller (b. 1878) was adopted at three months of age by Frank and Annie Fuller, after their own son died in infancy. Louis's birth mother was a sixteen-year-old woman from a family "equal in birth and breeding" to the Fullers, and young Louis later came to know her as a family friend ("Learns His Life Secret in Plot to Blackmail," New York *World,* 12 Apr 1906, 2).

41.23–24 Mr. Rowbotham, whose daughter is engaged to marry Fuller] George B. Rowbotham was president of the Bay State Belting Company in Boston ("Father of Fuller's Fiancee Says Wedding Will Take Place," New York *World,* 13 Apr 1906, 18).

41.26–27 Mrs. Ellen Faxon] No daughters of Fuller have been identified other than Ida and Anna (see the note at 38.15–20).

42.8 his uncle . . . was being educated at Yale] Louis Fuller was a 1905 graduate of Harvard University, not Yale (*Harvard Directory* 1910, 250).

43.1–2 I doubt if I have thought of Olive Logan . . . for a good thirty years and more] Clemens had written about Logan in an 1898–99 autobiographical essay, describing her in the same way he does here (see "Ralph Keeler," *AutoMT1,* 151–52, 512 n. 152.3–7).

43.4–7 the Anna Dickinson kind . . . could powerfully move an audience with their eloquence] Dickinson (1842–1932), a powerful and eloquent speaker on abolition and women's rights, was one of the best-paid performers on the lecture circuit, earning as much as $200 per appearance. She was a close friend of Clemens's in-laws, the Langdon family of Elmira, and became an acquaintance of his as well, although their opinions of each other were not entirely positive. Dickinson was one of several "women who had something to say" who were represented by Clemens's lecture manager, James Redpath, in the early 1870s (see *L3:* 12 Jan 1869 to Langdon, 30 n. 3; 22 Jan 1869 to Langdon, 63, 66 n. 2; "Enclosures with the Letters," *L4,* 550 n. 8).

43.27–29 world-famous Parisian male milliner, Worth . . . his new but prosperous rival, Savarin] Charles Frederick Worth (1825–95) was an Anglo-French designer of women's clothes, the leader of Paris fashion for many years. By "Savarin" Clemens presumably means the rival fashion house of L. Savarre (Thieme 1993, 2–3).

45.9–11 "Surf; or, Life at Long Branch," dramatized Wilkie Collins's "Armadale" . . . Francois Coppee's "Le Passant."] Logan's play *Surf,* a melodramatic farce, opened in New York in January 1870. Her dramatization of *Armadale,* a novel by English author Wilkie Collins, was first produced in New York in December 1866. She made a metrical translation of *Le Passant (The Stroller)* by French poetic dramatist François Coppée, which was staged in London in 1887.

45.21–22 "The Widow Bedott." . . . swept this continent with a hurricane of laughter] Frances Miriam Berry Whitcher (1812?–52) settled in Elmira with her minister husband in 1847. She began writing when very young, but didn't publish her first story until 1839, when she was nearly thirty. Between 1846 and 1850 she wrote a highly popular series of satirical magazine sketches featuring her comic creation, the Widow Bedott. They were first collected in book form in 1855 as *The Widow Bedott Papers,* which sold over 100,000 copies and was reprinted many times (Gowdy 2003, 392–95).

45.36 you see it is another tragedy] Despite the assistance of a friend, who settled her in a New York apartment, Logan returned to England, where she died in a "pauper lunatic asylum" in 1909 ("Olive Logan in an Asylum," New York *Times,* 27 Feb 1909, 5).

46.3–14 In this morning's paper . . . news that she is on her way to the cemetery] Accounts of these events appeared in several newspapers; the particular one that Clemens read has not been identified. The woman, Katherine B. Raymond of Los Angeles, who had shown signs of mental illness for years, recovered from her near asphyxiation and was committed to an insane asylum. Because of her condition, she was not prosecuted for murder (San Francisco *Chronicle:* "May Not Be Prosecuted for Her Son's Murder," 18 Apr 1906, 2; "Committed to Highlands," 28 Apr 1906, 1).

Autobiographical Dictation, 21 May 1906

46.23–25 Charles H. Webb . . . *The Californian*] Charles Henry Webb (1834–1905) was born in northern New York State. Inspired by reading *Moby-Dick* when it was first published (1851), he shipped on a whaler, where he served for more than three years. In 1860 he began a long career as a writer and journalist when he joined the staff of the New York *Times,* serving as its literary editor and, briefly, as a correspondent during the Civil War. In 1863 he went to California, where he worked as city editor of the San Francisco *Evening Bulletin.* In May 1864 he founded the *Californian,* alternating with Bret Harte as editor until mid-1866, when Webb left for New York (for Clemens's association with the *Californian* see *AutoMT1,* 509 n. 150.2–4). He published parodies and light verse in several journals, and corresponded for the New York *Tribune* under the pseudonym "John Paul." He was a successful inventor as well, and was granted patents on a cartridge-loading machine (which he sold to the Remington Arms Company) and an adding machine.

46.33–34 Artemus Ward passed through California . . . in 1865 or '66, I told him the "Jumping Frog" story] Clemens met, and enjoyed a convivial time with, popular humorist Artemus Ward (born Charles Farrar Browne, 1834–67) in December 1863, when the latter lectured in Virginia City. Ward soon recommended Clemens to the New York *Sunday Mercury* (which ultimately published nine Mark Twain sketches). Then in November 1864 he wrote to ask Clemens to contribute a story to his forthcoming book, *Artemus Ward; His Travels* (Charles Farrar Browne 1865). But Clemens did not see Ward's letter until February 1865, after his return from Angels Camp, where he first heard the "Jumping Frog" story, and by then he thought it was too late to comply. When Ward persisted, Clemens wrote at least two drafts of the story before sending the final draft, "Jim Smiley and His Jumping Frog," to New York in mid-October 1865. So Clemens never "told" Ward the story, although he did tell it to Bret Harte and others before he managed to write it out to his satisfaction (*L1:* 2? Jan 1864 to JLC, 267, 269–70 nn. 5–6; link note following 11 Nov 1864 to OC, 320–22; 20 Jan 1866 to JLC and PAM, 327–28, 330 n. 3; *ET&S2,* 262–65; *AutoMT1,* 515 n. 161.9–10).

46.35–47.1 his publisher, Carleton . . . didn't think much of it] George W. Carleton (1832–1901) began his publishing career as a humorous illustrator. In 1857 he cofounded a bookstore and publishing house in New York, becoming sole proprietor in 1861. By 1869 the firm was one of the most successful of its era, specializing in works of humor and popular fiction, encyclopedias, and self-improvement books. In addition to Ward, Carleton's list of authors included humorist Josh Billings (Henry Wheeler Shaw) and Thomas Bailey Aldrich, who for a time also served as his literary adviser (Murray 1986, 84–85; "Obituary. George W. Carleton," *Publishers' Weekly,* 19 Oct 1901, 857). In an 1895 interview Clemens gave a different (and apparently more accurate) account: he claimed that Ward's "volume was got out before 'The Jumping Frog' arrived" ("A Chat with Mark Twain," *New Zealand Mail* [Wellington], 12 Dec 1895, 51, quoted in Scharnhorst 2006, 259–60).

47.3–5 made Henry Clapp a present of it . . . joyous feature of the obsequies] Henry Clapp, Jr. (1814–75), a journalist, satirist, and brilliant wit, was the center of a group of New York "bohemians," writers and other artists who congregated at Pfaff's saloon to carouse and converse. In 1858 he founded the *Saturday Press,* a literary weekly of fiction, poetry, and critical commentary. It ceased publication in December 1860, but resumed in August 1865; "Jim Smiley and His Jumping Frog" appeared in the issue of 18 November 1865 (SLC 1865e). Although the magazine was in financial difficulty, it survived for seven more months. Elsewhere Clemens recalled that Carleton gave the story to Clapp "for nothing, which was lucky, as Henry Clapp never could pay for anything" ("A Chat with Mark Twain," *New Zealand Mail* [Wellington], 12 Dec 1895, 51, quoted in Scharnhorst 2006, 259–60). Clapp lived for many years in poverty, contributing occasionally to magazines and newspapers, and died from complications of alcoholism ("Obituary. Henry Clapp," New York *Times,* 11 Apr 1875, 7; "The Late Henry Clapp," New York *Daily Graphic,* 16 Apr 1875, unknown page; Mott 1938a, 38–40).

47.9 Webb undertook to collate the sketches] Bret Harte proposed to Clemens in January 1866 that they issue a joint collection of sketches, but they did not pursue the idea. Clemens did, however, gather clippings of some of his *Enterprise* and *Californian* sketches into a scrapbook, which he carried with him when he left San Francisco for New York in December 1866. It was there, in early 1867, that Webb persuaded him to reprint some of his sketches. The present account implies that Webb prepared the book, entitled *The Celebrated Jumping Frog of Calaveras County, and Other Sketches,* but it is clear that Clemens himself played a large role in selecting and revising the twenty-seven sketches included in the collection (20 Jan 1866 to JLC and PAM, *L1,* 328; for a detailed account of the editing process see *ET&S1,* 503–42).

47.33–34 I refused a book of yours] Carleton explained elsewhere that he had declined the manuscript "because the author looked so disreputable" (Ellsworth 1919, 222, quoted in *ET&S1,* 505 n. 8).

48.3–4 He made the plates . . . and published it through the American News Company] The book, issued in April 1867, was printed and bound by John A. Gray and Green and distributed by the American News Company; it sold for $1.50 (*ET&S1,* 543–45).

48.6–9 found a letter from Elisha Bliss . . . alternative of ten thousand dollars] Bliss's letter, written on 21 November 1867, is now lost, but when Clemens replied on 2 December he proposed a book based on the newspaper letters he had written during the *Quaker City* excursion, weeded "of their chief faults of con[s]truction & inelegancies of expression. . . . If you think such a book would suit your purpose, please drop me a line." Bliss accepted, and in late January 1868 they agreed that the author's royalty would be 5 percent of the retail price of the book (for Bliss, the *Quaker City* excursion, and the writing of *The Innocents Abroad,* see *AutoMT1,* 227–28, 537 n. 227.13–14, 596 n. 370.32–33; *L2:* 2 Dec 1867 to Bliss, 119; 24 Jan 1868 to JLC and PAM, 160, 162–63 n. 3; 27 Jan 1868 to Bliss, 169).

48.9 I consulted A. D. Richardson] Albert Deane Richardson (1833–69), journalist and traveler, worked on several newspapers in the East and Midwest before joining the staff of the New York *Tribune,* for which he corresponded during the Civil War. He was captured by the Confederates at Vicksburg, but escaped after eighteen months in prison. His books about his war experiences (*The Secret Service, the Field, the Dungeon, and the Escape,* 1865) and the Far West (*Beyond the Mississippi,* 1867), published by the American Publishing Company, sold 100,000 and 75,000 copies respectively (2 Dec 1867 to Bliss, *L2,* 120–21 n. 4).

48.12–13 Bliss provided a multitude of illustrations . . . contract date for the issue went by] *The Innocents Abroad* was published by the subscription method: agents solicited prepublication orders and delivered books when they came from the press. Clemens's contract, signed on 16 October 1868, stipulated that copies would be ready for the agents to deliver "very early next spring," which proved to be overly optimistic ("Contract for *The Innocents Abroad,*" *L2,* 421–22).

48.14–15 I was lecturing all over the country] Clemens was on tour from mid-November 1868 until mid-March 1869, delivering "The American Vandal Abroad," about the *Quaker City* excursion, more than forty times in the East and Midwest ("Lecture Schedule, 1868–1870," *L3,* 481–83).

48.28–34 One of the directors, a Mr. Drake . . . begged me to take away "The Innocents Abroad"] As a young man Sidney Drake (1811–98) was apprenticed to a bookbinder in Hartford, and in 1841 began his own bookbinding business, which—with various partners—endured for over fifty years. He was a director of the American Publishing Company from its inception in 1865, and president in 1869. Clemens gave a similar account of this incident in 1903, claiming that Drake begged him, "as a charity, to take the book away, because it was not serious enough and could finish the destruction of the Company" (SLC 1903a; "Death of Sidney Drake," Hartford *Courant,* 14 Feb 1898, 7).

48.38–41 I lost patience and telegraphed Bliss . . . sale within the required time] No such telegram has been found, but in a bitter letter of 22 July 1869 Clemens accused Bliss of deliberately causing "annoying & damaging delays" by promoting books by other authors. He claimed, sarcastically, that he desired only "to be informed from time to time what future season of the year the publication is postponed to, & why." Bliss explained that the book had initially been late because of the large number of illustrations; he had then decided to postpone it until the fall to increase sales. The copyright was registered on 28 July, and canvassing began in early August (*L3:* 22 July 1869 to Bliss, 284–85, 286 n. 1; 1 Aug 1869 to Bliss, 287 n. 1; 12 Aug 1869 to Bliss, 291–92, 292–94 n. 1; Hirst 1975, 255–57).

48.41–49.1 In nine months . . . seventy thousand dollars' profit to the good] In 1903 Clemens calculated that by "February or March" 1870 the American Publishing Company had earned about $91,000 net profit on *The Innocents Abroad,* $20,000 of which had gone to pay off debts. Calculations based on the company's bindery records suggest a slightly lower net profit in the first nine months of sales, about $85,000 (SLC 1903a; Hirst 1975, 314–17).

Autobiographical Dictation, 23 May 1906

49.21–24 I made my contract for "The Innocents Abroad" . . . forbidding me to publish books with any other firm] The contract for *The Innocents Abroad,* drawn up by Elisha Bliss and signed on 16 October 1868, contains no such exclusivity clause ("Contract for *The Innocents Abroad,*" *L2,* 421–22). The contract for *Roughing It,* however, made nearly two years later, stipulated that Clemens was "not to write . . . any other book unless for said company during the preparation & sale of said manuscript & book" ("Contract for *Roughing It,*" *L4,* 565–66).

49.31–33 that I should surrender to him such royalties as might be due me . . . eight hundred dollars cash] In late 1869 Clemens considered "prosecuting Webb in the N.Y. Courts" for an unspecified grievance involving the book; he hoped that Webb would "yield up the copyright & plates of the Jumping Frog, if I let him off from paying me money. Then I shall break up those plates" (22 Jan 1870 to Bliss, *L4,* 34, 35 n. 5). He decided against legal action, however, and negotiated a settlement with Webb a year later. In a letter of 22 December 1870 to Bliss he said, "I bought my Jumping Frog from Webb—gave him what he owed me ($600^{00},), and $800 cash, & 300 remaining copies of the book, & also took $128 worth of unprinted paper off his hands." The payment of $600 evidently represented a 10 percent royalty on 4,000 books: four days later he admitted that he had "fully expected the 'Jumping Frog[']' to sell 50,000 copies & it only sold 4,000." A statement prepared the same month by the printers, John A. Gray and Green, listed a total of 4,076 books printed (*L4:* 22 Dec 1870 to Bliss, 281, 282 n. 4; 26 Dec 1870 to Drake, 287; *ET&S1,* 545 n. 43).

50.11–14 bound and unbound "Jumping Frogs" . . . six hundred more that should have come to me on royalties] There is no evidence to support Clemens's claim that Webb owed him $600 in royalties for 4,000 "inherited" books (see the note at 49.31–33). The 1870 settlement had not satisfied him, however; in April 1875 he claimed that Webb had "swindled me on a verbal publishing contract on my first book (Sketches), (8 years ago) & now he has got caught himself & appeals to me for help. I have advised him to do as I did—make the best of a bad bargain & be wiser next time" (8 Apr 1875 to Webb, *L6,* 442–43 n. 1).

50.22–23 when I became notorious through the publication of "The Innocents Abroad,"] *The Innocents Abroad* was a huge success: eight years after publication, in 1877, 119,870 copies had been sold, earning Clemens royalties of approximately $21,876 (*RI 1993,* 891 n. 278). Clemens's reputation also spread to England, where two publishers—John Camden Hotten and George Routledge and Sons—sold nearly 200,000 copies of their editions.

50.42 About 1872 I wrote another book, "Roughing It."] The account that follows, in which Clemens describes his negotiations and agreements with Bliss and the American Publishing Company for the publication of *Roughing It* and *A Tramp Abroad,* essentially duplicates—with minor variations—the version he gives in the Autobiographical Dictation of 21 February 1906 (see *AutoMT1,* 369–72 and notes on 596–97).

52.14 Newton Case] See the Autobiographical Dictation of 24 May 1906, note at 53.19–20.

52.16–17 Sixty-four thousand copies . . . had been sold, and my half of the profit was thirty-two thousand dollars] These figures reflect sales and royalties of *A Tramp Abroad* for the entire first year (7 Mar 1881 to Osgood, MH-H, in *MTLP,* 133–34).

Autobiographical Dictation, 24 May 1906

53.7–9 I . . . proposed that the Company cancel the contracts] In late 1881 and early 1882 Clemens considered bringing a lawsuit against the American Publishing Company for charging him excessive costs in the manufacture of *A Tramp Abroad,* but his "bottom object" was "to frighten them into giving up all my copyrights to me." He believed that he could make his copyrights pay "$25,000 a year, right along. They now pay me less than $3,000" (26 Oct 1881 and 12 Apr 1882 to Webster, NPV, in *MTBus,* 173–74, 184–85).

53.19–20 I repeated it, and proceeded to say unkind things about his theological seminary] Newton Case (1807–90) established a printing business in Hartford in 1830, which he expanded over the years, with a series of partners, into one of the largest in New England. The firm prospered for decades under the name Case, Lockwood and Brainard, although Case retired from active participation in 1858 to pursue other commercial interests. A devout Christian and an original member of the Asylum Hill Congregational Church, Case was also a trustee of the Hartford Seminary and made generous donations to its library (Hartford *Courant:* "Obituary. Newton Case," 16 Sept 1890, 1; "Hartford Theological Seminary," 29 Apr 1890, 2).

53.28 Judge What's-his-name, a director] George Shepard Gilman (1825–86), a former Hartford city prosecuting attorney and judge of the Hartford police court, was an

American Publishing Company director in the 1870s and 1880s (Connecticut Historical Society 2012; 7 May 1870 to Bliss, *L4,* 127 n. 1; Geer 1882, 453; 1886, 556).

53.32–34 carried my next book to James R. Osgood of Boston . . . "Old Times on the Mississippi."] As in the previous dictation, Clemens substantially repeats his account in the Autobiographical Dictation of 21 February 1906 (*AutoMT1,* 369–72). He consistently refers to *Life on the Mississippi* (1883) as "Old Times on the Mississippi," the title of the series of articles in the 1875 *Atlantic Monthly* that were reprinted in chapters 4–17. It was not Clemens's "next book": see the note at 54.11–13.

54.11–13 I think that that was Osgood's first effort, not his third . . . after his failure with "The Prince and the Pauper,"] Clemens's first publication with Osgood was a booklet containing only two sketches: *A True Story, and the Recent Carnival of Crime* (1877). This was followed by *The Prince and the Pauper* (1881), a collection of sketches entitled *The Stolen White Elephant, Etc.* (1882), and *Life on the Mississippi* (see *AutoMT1,* 597 n. 372.25–27).

54.15–16 old and particular friend of mine unloaded a patent on me] In a June 1879 letter to Frank Bliss (son of Elisha), Clemens praised a patented process owned by Daniel Slote (1828?–82), a friend from the *Quaker City* excursion, which was used for printing illustrations. In this process, called Kaolatype, "the pictures are not transferred, but drawn on a hard mud surface. It looks like excellent wood engraving, whereas *all* these other processes are miserably weak & shammy" (10 June 1879 to Bliss [1st], *Letters 1876–1880*). The "mud surface" was a steel plate covered with kaolin (a type of clay), from which a mold was formed to make plates for printing. In February 1880 Clemens paid Slote $20,000 for four-fifths of the stock in the Kaolatype Engraving Company and became its president. He then hired a "young German" metallurgist named Charles Sneider to adapt the process for stamping book covers, wallpaper, and leather (*Letters 1876–1880:* 26 Feb 1880 to OC; 20 Mar 1880 to Bliss; 27 Nov 1880 to OC; Krass 2007, 108–10).

54.20–21 That raven . . . the dove didn't report for duty] Genesis 8:7–12.

54.21–22 After a time, and half a time, and another time] Revelation 12:14: "a time, and times, and half a time"; cf. Daniel 12:7.

54.22–23 put the patent into the hands of Charles L. Webster, who had married a niece of mine] In the spring of 1881, after a year of pouring money into the project, Clemens hired his nephew-in-law, Charles L. Webster (husband of Annie Moffett Webster, his sister Pamela's daughter), to manage the company and investigate Slote and Sneider (*N&J2,* 352–53, 390–91; for Webster see *AutoMT1,* 486 n. 79.21–22).

54.26 when I had lost forty-two thousand dollars on that patent] Webster proved that Sneider was a fraud, and that he and Slote were conspiring to swindle Clemens: the sample impressions that Sneider had supplied had not been created by Kaolatype. Clemens's belief in the process persisted, however. In 1882 he suggested it be used to produce the illustrations for *Life on the Mississippi,* but the artist found it unsatisfactory and refused. The invention proved a failure (*N&J2,* 392–93; 6 May 1881 and 24 Nov 1881 to Webster, NPV, in *MTBus,* 153–54, 178–79; Osgood to SLC, 5 June 1882, CU-MARK).

54.28 That same friend was ready with another patent] No additional patent promoted by Slote has been identified.

54.32–34 arrived with a wonderful invention . . . Mr. Richards] In 1877 Clemens's old friend Frank Fuller persuaded him to invest in a company that he managed, the New York Vaporizing Company, which was financing H. C. Bowers to develop a new type of steam generator. Bowers's machine was built, but did not run, and by early 1878 Clemens had lost $5,000. Charles B. Richards (1833–1919) was a mechanical engineer who had invented a pressure indicator for steam engines (*N&J2,* 12 n. 4, 459 n. 90, 491; Fuller to SLC, 15 May 1877, CU-MARK; Asher 2011).

55.9–11 I took some stock in a Hartford company . . . with a new kind of steam pulley] In early 1881 Clemens bought $14,500 worth of stock in the Hartford Engineering Company, which intended to build a factory for making steam-powered pulleys. In December 1887 the failed company settled with its creditors; Clemens recovered $1,897 (6 Mar 1881 to PAM, transcripts in CU-MARK; *N&J2,* 491; Bunce to SLC, 2 Dec 1887, CU-MARK).

55.14–16 I invented a scrap-book . . . in the hands of that old particular friend of mine] Clemens first mentioned his idea for a pregummed scrapbook in August 1872, and patented what he called "Mark Twain's Patent Self-Pasting Scrap Book" in June 1873. Slote, Woodman and Company began selling the book in several sizes in late 1876. Sales were brisk—for example, in the second half of 1877, 26,310 scrapbooks were sold, earning Clemens about $1,100 in royalties. On 5 June 1881 he told Webster, "The Scrapbook gravels me because while they have been paying me about $1800 or $2000 a year, I judge it ought to have been 3 times as much" (ViU). In February 1882, after Slote's death, he told Mary Mason Fairbanks that "Dan stole from me . . . he has swindled me out of many thousands of dollars." Although sales diminished in later years, the scrapbook remained his only profitable patent (21 Feb 1882 to Fairbanks, CSmH; Slote, Woodman and Company to SLC, 12 Jan 1878, Scrapbook 10:33, CU-MARK; *N&J2,* 12 n. 2).

54.23–24 They failed inside of three days] Slote, Woodman and Company failed in July 1878. After settling with its creditors for 30 cents on the dollar, the firm reorganized as Daniel Slote and Company and continued to market the scrapbook (20 Aug 1878 to Fuller, *Letters 1876–1880; N&J2,* 392 n. 119).

54.26–32 Senator John P. Jones was going to start a rival . . . we began business] Jones, a wealthy silver-mine owner, served as a U.S. senator from Nevada in 1873–1903. He organized the "rival" Hartford Accident Insurance Company in mid-1874, offering $200,000 of capital stock. He subscribed for $75,000, and Clemens for $50,000, 25 percent of which he was required to pay for immediately. George B. Lester (1827?–94), Jones's son-in-law, was actuary as well as secretary of the new company; both he and Clemens were on the board of directors. The company discontinued business in September 1876 ("Death Record," Los Angeles *Times,* 17 Jan 1894, 8; link note following 28 June 1874 to Dickinson, *L6,* 170–72; "The Hartford Accident Insurance Co.," Hartford *Courant,* 21 Sept 1876, 2; for Jones see *AutoMT1,* 496 n. 104.16–17; for Joseph T. Goodman, proprietor of the Virginia City *Territorial Enterprise* and Clemens's lifelong friend, see *AutoMT1,* 535 n. 225.3–5, 544 n. 252.32–253.1).

55.35–36 hotel which he had bought, (the St. James)] The St. James Hotel at Broadway and Twenty-sixth Street, built in 1859, was purchased in 1869 by "two gentlemen who were backed financially by Senator Jones of Nevada"; Lester was listed as its proprietor in 1876 ("Sale of St. James Hotel," New York *Times,* 15 Aug 1896, 9; Disturnell 1876, 287).

56.12–15 Jones had bought a piece of the State of California . . . in debt for these properties] In January 1875 Jones paid $150,000 for a two-thirds interest in a large rancho in Southern California. There he helped to lay out the town of Santa Monica, hoping to develop it into a major seaport. He built a railroad from Santa Monica to Los Angeles with plans to extend it to his mining interests in Inyo County, on the eastern side of the Sierra Nevada. In mid-1877, when his mines were played out and he had spent nearly a million dollars, his debts forced him to sell the line to the Southern Pacific Railroad (Ingersoll 1908, 144–45, 152–53).

56.23–29 Mr. Slee of our Elmira coal firm . . . There are not many John P. Joneses in the world] John D. F. Slee was the chief officer of the Langdon family's coal business. He—possibly accompanied by Clemens—met with Jones in New York in late March 1878 and persuaded him to make restitution. Shortly before that, Clemens recorded a less charitable view of Jones in his notebook, calling him a "lying thief" (*N&J2,* 54–55; *AutoMT1,* 578 n. 321.25–27).

56.34 General Hawley] Joseph Roswell Hawley was editor and part owner of the Hartford *Courant* (*AutoMT1,* 576 n. 317.23–24).

56.37–57.8 Graham Bell . . . *first* one that was ever used in a private house in the world] Alexander Graham Bell (1847–1922) obtained his first telephone patent in March 1876. In early 1877 only six telephones were actually in use, but by November of that year "three thousand telephones were leased with the apparatus needed for their practical use." When Clemens installed his line to the *Courant* office sometime in late December 1877 or January 1878, it was not the first in Hartford, but was quite possibly the first in a private home. On 24 January he wrote to a friend, "as the Courant is in the center of the business district this telephone is a great convenience to me when I want to send for something in a hurry; but the advantage is all on one side. I get all the benefit & they get all the bother" (24 Jan 1878 to Daggett, *Letters 1876–1880;* Thomas A. Watson 1926, 76, 134; "The Telephone," Hartford *Courant,* 5 June 1877, 2; Hubbard to SLC, 17 Dec 1877, CU-MARK).

57.15–18 We were gone fourteen months . . . his telephone stock was emptying greenbacks into his premises] The family returned in early September 1879, almost seventeen months after their departure. The National Bell Telephone Company, a consolidation of several previous companies, was formed in March of that year with capitalization of $850,000. In June its share price was about $110, but by December its value had risen to $995 (*N&J2,* 46–49; Thomas A. Watson 1926, 171; Fagen 1975, 30).

Autobiographical Dictation, 26 May 1906

57.27–28 Webster, from the village of Dunkirk, New York] Charles L. Webster was actually from Fredonia, New York, where in early 1870 Clemens had relocated his mother, sister, niece, and nephew (Jane Clemens, Pamela Moffett, and her children, Annie and Samuel) from St. Louis. Dunkirk, a busy port and railroad terminus on Lake Erie, was three miles north of Fredonia (21 Apr 1870 to OC, *L4,* 115 n. 2; *MTBus,* 239).

58.3 I had paid Bixby a hundred dollars, and it was borrowed money] Horace E. Bixby agreed to take on Clemens as an apprentice pilot in 1857 for a fee of $500. Clemens borrowed $100 from his brother-in-law, William A. Moffett, for a down payment; it is not clear how much of the total he ultimately paid (link note following 5 Aug 1856 to HC, *L1,* 70–71).

58.17–27 I erected Webster into a firm . . . Webster was his own sub-agent] Clemens has jumped ahead in his chronology by a year, skipping the events of late 1882 and 1883 entirely. In the fall of 1882, Clemens expanded Webster's duties to include acting as the New York general agent for subscription sales of his forthcoming book, *Life on the Mississippi,* which Osgood planned to publish the following spring. On 9 September Clemens told Webster, "Go to studying up the methods & mysteries of General-Agency right away," and Webster made plans to visit several agencies to learn the trade. On 19 September Clemens suggested that Osgood could "probably get some chap or girl for you who has served a General Agent in Boston—somebody who can help you, for wages, in New York, & teach you the methods," but no office staff has been identified (9 Sept 1882 and 19 Sept 1882 to Webster [1st], NPV, in *MTBus,* 195–96, 199). The man who "knew all about" subscription book sales may have been Howard N. Hinckley, a former general agent for the American Publishing Company who was now operating in Chicago. Hinckley was willing to give advice, and in addition—because he planned to leave the book business—he offered to sell the "lists of agents who have been employed on all the Twain books in this section for the past seven to ten years." Clemens agreed to buy the list for $500 (Hinckley to Webster, 2 Oct 1882, on verso of Webster to SLC, 5 Oct 1882, CU-MARK; Webster to SLC, 11 Oct 1882 and 24 Oct 1882, CU-MARK; 18 Oct 1882 to Osgood, ViU, in *MTLP,* 159 nn. 1–2). By October 1882 Webster had moved his office from Fulton Street to 658 Broadway, at the corner of Bond Street. Although over the next months he occasionally used stationery headed "Charles L. Webster, Publisher," he was in fact only a general agent. In early March he expanded his business by arranging to take charge of the New York sales of all of Osgood's publications. In 1883 Clemens grew dissatisfied with Osgood's handling of the sales of *Life on the Mississippi,* and wanted to publish his next book, *Adventures of Huckleberry Finn,* elsewhere. Although he briefly considered giving it to the American Publishing Company, by the end of February 1884 he had decided to establish his own company, with Webster as its titular head. Webster, no longer just a "general agent," was entrusted with managing the entire production of the book (Webster to American Publishing Co., 26 Oct 1882, ViU; Webster to PAM, 2 Mar 1883, CU-MARK; *HF 2003,* 697–98).

58.31–32 his friend Whitford] Like Webster, Daniel Whitford (1840–1923) was from Fredonia, where the two men had been friends. He practiced law in Buffalo, Chicago, and Fredonia before joining the New York firm of Alexander and Green in 1873. Webster hired him in May 1881 to help him investigate the Kaolatype business, and he remained Clemens's attorney for over a decade. In 1894, however, when Charles L. Webster and Company declared bankruptcy, Clemens concluded that Whitford was disloyal and untrustworthy ("Died," New York *Times,* 19 May 1923, 13; *Chautauqua County* 1904, 2:1130–32; Webster to SLC, 5 May 1881, CU-MARK; Harrison to SLC, 1 June 1894, CU-MARK, in *HHR,* 63 n. 3; *MTLP,* 365; see also AD, 29 May 1906).

58.34–35 I had tried to confer upon Webster a tenth interest in the business in addition to his salary, free of charge] The establishment of Charles L. Webster and Company was formalized by a contract drawn on 10 April 1884, which granted Webster a salary of $2,500 a year but no share of the profits (NPV).

59.5–8 Alexander and Green had a great and lucrative business . . . Life Insurance Companies] Charles B. Alexander was head of the law firm Alexander and Green and counsel for—and a director of—the Equitable Life Assurance Society. During the 1905 investigation into unethical practices in the insurance industry he was accused of using the society's assets for personal gain. Several other insurance company directors, including members of the Alexander family, were also implicated (*AutoMT1,* 549 n. 257.6–9; Chicago *Tribune:* "Loot Equitable Policy Holders," 14 Apr 1905, 5; "49 Defendants in Equitable Suit," 31 July 1905, 1).

59.25–26 I went off with George W. Cable on a four months' reading-campaign] Clemens toured with Cable, known for his stories of Creole life, from November 1884 through February 1885 (see *AutoMT1,* 488 n. 86.12).

59.29 pecuniary compulsions came, and I lectured all around the globe] See the Autobiographical Dictation of 4 June 1906 and *AutoMT1,* 521 n. 190.10–12.

59.32–33 lecture . . . for the benefit of the Robert Fulton Memorial Fund] See *AutoMT1,* 426–28, 630–31 nn. 426.13–15, 426.20–21.

Autobiographical Dictation, 28 May 1906

60.10 That was General Grant's memorable book] This account of the publication of Grant's *Personal Memoirs* by Webster and Company largely repeats what Clemens dictated to James Redpath in 1885, dictations that were not included in his *Autobiogra-*

phy. The dates and figures in the two accounts are slightly different, but there is only one major discrepancy, identified in the next note, at 60.13–18 (see "About General Grant's Memoirs" in *AutoMT1,* 75–98 and notes on 482–93).

60.13–18 two dim figures . . . permitted to overhear them] In his 1885 dictation, made when events were fresh in his mind, Clemens said that he and his wife "stumbled over" Richard Watson Gilder (editor of the *Century Magazine*) after the reading in Chickering Hall (New York), and were invited to a late supper at his house, where Gilder revealed that Grant "had written three war articles for the Century and was going to write a fourth," and "had set out deliberately to write his memoirs in full and to publish them in book form." If the different account in the present dictation describes an actual event, it would have to have occurred the following evening, when Clemens again lectured at Chickering Hall unaccompanied by his wife (*AutoMT1,* 77–78, 486 n. 77.27–31).

62.30–31 feed fat the ancient grudge I bore them] *The Merchant of Venice,* act 1, scene 3.

62.33–40 General Sherman had published his Memoirs . . . ought to have been published in that way] *Memoirs of General William T. Sherman* was first issued in two volumes in 1875 by D. Appleton and Company. According to the manager of the firm's subscription book department, Sherman "had a horror of book agents, and would neither patronize them nor have his book sold by them" (Derby 1884, 182–84). Clemens noted in 1887 that the *Memoirs* had earned Sherman $25,000, and claimed he could have "quadrupled that sale easily, and paid him $80,000 in royalties" (18 Sept 1887 to Webster and Co., NN-BGC, in *MTLP,* 234). Webster and Company later bought the rights to Sherman's *Memoirs* and reissued them in 1890–92.

64.10–12 that his salary be increased to thirty-five hundred dollars . . . I furnish all the capital required at 7 per cent] No contract on these terms has been found. It seems likely that it was soon "abolished" in favor of a "new one," as Clemens recounts in the Autobiographical Dictation of 29 May 1906. This "new" contract, dated 20 March 1885, is described in the note there at 65.30–38.

64.15–16 my brother-in-law, General Langdon] Olivia's younger brother, Charles Jervis Langdon (see *AutoMT1,* 578 n. 321.25–27).

64.28–29 quarters better suited to his new importance] Webster moved to larger quarters at 42 East Fourteenth Street in early March 1885, shortly after the contract with Grant was signed (Webster to SLC, 14 Mar 1885, CU-MARK; *MTB,* 2:806–7).

Autobiographical Dictation, 29 May 1906

65.23–29 George Evans . . . "I've never read any of his books, on account of prejudice."] As "George Eliot," English writer Mary Ann Evans (1819–80) was best known for her novels *Adam Bede, Daniel Deronda,* and *Middlemarch;* Clemens here combines her name with her pseudonym. Charles Webster's son, Samuel, said in 1946 that he did not believe this story, claiming that his father knew the author was a woman and owned a set of her works. It is not clear what Webster meant by "prejudice" (if he is quoted accurately), unless he was trying to ingratiate himself by echoing Clemens's own prejudice against Eliot. In 1885 Clemens said that he had "bored through Middlemarch during the past week, with its labored & tedious analyses of feelings & motives, its paltry & tiresome people, its unexciting & uninteresting story. . . . I wouldn't read another of those books for a farm" (21 July 1885 to Howells, NN-BGC, in *MTHL,* 2:533; *MTBus,* 364–65; see also Gribben 1980, 1:216–18).

65.30–38 Webster had suggested that we abolish the existing contract . . . I could not even make a suggestion] A contract drawn on 20 March 1885 provided Webster with the same salary as before ($2,500 a year), one-third of the net profits up to a limit of $20,000, and one-tenth thereafter. Clemens was granted 8 percent interest on the capital he advanced. Webster was not to be held responsible for any losses "over and above the amount which he may have received as profits during the continuance of said co-partnership." The clause that Clemens evidently objected to put Webster in charge of the "entire management of the active business of the said firm," including "the employment and discharge of clerks and other employees . . . and the making of all contracts for work or material." Clemens could "not be called upon to perform any service or to take any supervision of the said business." The only action that required Clemens's consent was the making of any "contract for the publishing of a book" (NPV; see *AutoMT1,* 486 n. 79.21–22). Webster defended himself against this accusation in December 1888, shortly after he retired. He told Whitford, "Mr. Clemens now complains of a clause (placing all business in my hands) which has appeared in every contract he ever made with me"—an accurate description of all four subsequent contracts (Webster to Whitford, 31 Dec 1888, *MTBus,* 391).

66.17 During the winter of 1884 . . . hurt himself] As Clemens correctly remembered in 1885, when dictating "Grant and the Chinese," this accident took place in December 1883 (*AutoMT1,* 72, 478 n. 72.7–9).

66.23–24 Shrady or Douglas; Douglas, I think—Douglas, I am sure] George F. Shrady (1837–1907) was a physician—second only to John H. Douglas—who attended Grant in his last days at Mount McGregor ("Another Quiet Day," New York *Times,* 25 June 1885, 4; for Douglas see *AutoMT1,* 487 n. 82.30).

67.41 the memorable 4th of March, 1885] See the Autobiographical Dictation of 31 May 1906, note at 70.20–23.

Autobiographical Dictation, 31 May 1906

68.10–11 Monadnock is so close by] Clemens and his household spent the summer and early fall of 1906—from mid-May to late October—at Upton House in Dublin, New Hampshire. His stay was punctuated by brief trips to New York and Boston.

69.21–23 Some people had a prejudice against Webster . . . that he was a Jew. I have no prejudices against Jews] Charles L. Webster was certainly not Jewish in religion, and nothing that is known of his family background suggests Jewish ancestry. The fullest scholarly account of Clemens's relation to the Jews is *Mark Twain's Jews* (Vogel 2006).

69.36 However] As originally dictated, this text read: "I said that if I had been at the Crucifixion—— However"; Clemens deleted the incomplete sentence on the typescript (see the Textual Commentary at *MTPO*).

70.3–9 one-word title, "General" . . . surrendered it to become President] When the title General of the Army was given to Grant in July 1866 it had previously been conferred only on George Washington. Grant surrendered it upon his election to the presidency in 1869, and it was passed to William T. Sherman (U.S. Army Center of Military History 2011; see *AutoMT1,* 472 n. 67.2–3, 482–83 n. 76.5–8).

70.20–23 news was dispatched to General Grant by telegram . . . exhibited itself in his iron countenance] Clemens was at the Grant residence on 4 March 1885 when a telegram arrived with the news that Congress had, after years of failed attempts, restored Grant's title as General of the Army on the retired list (*AutoMT1,* 485 n. 77.9–13).

70.27 This was in Chicago, in 1879] For Clemens's earlier account of this event see "The Chicago G.A.R. Festival," *AutoMT1,* 67–70 and notes on 472–75.

70.36–37 Schofield, Logan] John McAllister Schofield (1831–1906) held major commands during the Civil War and later was secretary of war (1868) and superintendent of West Point (1876–81); he remained in active service and retired as a lieutenant general in 1895. John Alexander Logan (1826–86) commanded the Army of the Tennessee and entered politics after the war, serving Illinois as a congressman and then a senator until his death.

Autobiographical Dictation, 1 June 1906

72.5–6 most telling speech I ever listened to . . . by the capable Depew] This speech has not been identified with certainty, but Depew (see the note at 72.23–25) himself described an occasion bearing some resemblance to the one that Clemens recalls here.

> I arrived at the dinner late and passed in front of the daïs to my seat at the other end, while General Grant was speaking. He was not easy on his feet at that time, though afterwards he became very felicitous in public speaking. He paused a moment until I was seated and then said: "If Chauncey Depew stood in my shoes, and I in his, I would be a much happier man."
>
> I immediately threw away the speech I had prepared during the six hours' trip from Washington, and proceeded to make a speech on "Who can stand now or in the future in the shoes of General Grant?" . . .
>
> The enthusiasm of the audience, as the speech went on, surpassed anything I ever saw. They rushed over tables and tried to carry the general around the room. When the enthusiasm had subsided he came to me and with much feeling said:

"Thank you for that speech; it is the greatest and most eloquent that I ever heard." (Depew 1924, 70–71)

According to another account, Depew used the "felicitous" keynote phrase repeatedly, each time listing another of Grant's victories, and the "effect was magical" (Marden 1907, 196).

72.23–25 Depew . . . is dying now, and under a cloud] Chauncey M. Depew had been a Republican senator from New York since 1899. The life insurance investigation of 1905 resulted in accusations that he used his political influence to promote corporate interests, especially those of the Equitable Life Assurance Society (which paid him a yearly $20,000 retainer) and the Vanderbilt railroad companies. Although he resisted pressure to resign, he did withdraw from many of the seventy-nine companies he served as a director or trustee. Although the newspapers reported that his health was poor, he lived until 1928 and died at the age of ninety-three (Los Angeles *Times:* "Recall Invoked for Depew," 3 Jan 1906, 1; "He Won't Resign," 4 Jan 1906, 1; "Friends Uphold Depew; Brackett Seeks Cover," New York *Times,* 4 Jan 1906, 5; "Senator Depew. Reasons Why He Should Withdraw from Public Life," San Francisco *Chronicle,* 5 Jan 1906, 6).

72.38–73.2 When I was entering the house, the Confederate General, Buckner . . . General Grant captured the fortress] Clemens did not encounter Buckner at Mount McGregor, the resort near Saratoga Springs, New York, where Grant spent his last days. When Buckner visited there, on 10 July 1885, Clemens was at Quarry Farm with his family. Two months earlier, he had already recorded in his notebook the anecdote he retails here (*N&J3,* 149–50). Simon Bolivar Buckner (1823–1914) of Kentucky attended West Point with Grant and fought in the same division in the Mexican War. After Grant resigned from the army in 1854, he borrowed money from Buckner in New York to pay his hotel bill. When Kentucky sided with the Union in the Civil War, Buckner reluctantly joined the Confederacy. In February 1862 Union forces captured Fort Donelson in Tennessee, the first major victory for the North. Grant's note to Buckner, "No terms except unconditional and immediate surrender can be accepted," earned him the nickname of "Unconditional Surrender" (for "U.S.") Grant. After the war Buckner edited the Louisville *Courier* and was governor of Kentucky in 1887–91 (Smith 2001, 89–90, 161–62, 165–66).

73.24–25 in the aggregate the book paid Mrs. Grant something like half a million dollars] The net profits on the book were divided between Mrs. Grant (70 percent) and the Webster firm (30 percent). Estimates of the total royalties paid to her vary somewhat, but Clemens's figure—equivalent in today's dollars to at least $8 million—is plausible (*AutoMT1,* 486–87 n. 80.35; see also AD, 2 June 1906, note at 74.38–75.1).

73.26 Webster was in his glory] In a self-aggrandizing 1887 interview Webster claimed that it was he who first approached Grant about writing his memoirs, several months before the incident that Clemens recalls here:

About the time of the Grant & Ward failure . . . I went to the General and represented that it would be advantageous for him to write a history of his career. He

> replied that John Russell Young and Adam Badeau had both written him up, and that he did not think, in justice to those gentlemen, he should take up the pen in his own behalf. I continued my solicitations, and the *Century* company also strove to induce him to write his life. I finally succeeded, and the first volume of the memoirs was given to the public.

He also gave an implausible account of his role in persuading Grant to dictate his book:

> He demurred at first, saying that he never had dictated a letter in his life. . . . I finally agreed to go to his house each day with a stenographer, remain while the general dictated for about two hours, go home with the stenographer and remain with him until he had delivered to me not only his notes but the complete text of the general's remarks. ("The Publisher of Grant's Book," Kansas City *Star,* 25 June 1887, 1)

Autobiographical Dictation, 2 June 1906

74.14 Charles L. Webster was one of the most assful persons I have ever met] This dictation about the ill fortunes of Webster and Company is one-sided and in many instances erroneous. Although some of the inaccuracies in the following account are pointed out in the notes, it is not possible to recover the actual events with any certainty. In *Mark Twain, Business Man,* Samuel Charles Webster records a more even-handed version of the interactions between Clemens and Webster, whose fundamentally incompatible personalities made conflict inevitable (*MTBus;* see also the note at 80.14–18).

74.22 on a level with Sherlock Holmes] Although Clemens himself employed the literary device of mysteries solved by clever deduction (usually for comic effect), he had no admiration for Arthur Conan Doyle's Sherlock Holmes, whom he considered a "pompous sentimental 'extraordinary man' with his cheap & ineffectual ingenuities" (8 Sept 1901 to Twichell, CtY-BR). His "Double-Barrelled Detective Story" is a parody of the genre in general and Sherlock Holmes in particular (SLC 1902a; for a discussion of Clemens's detective fiction see Lillian S. Robinson's "Afterword" in SLC 1996c).

74.38–75.1 Fred Grant . . . ordered another examination] Colonel Frederick Grant, the general's son, questioned Webster and Company's accounting in April 1887, complaining that legal fees had been improperly "charged" to Mrs. Grant. He asked his own accountant to examine the books, and in July reported the results in a five-page typed letter: the total net profits to date on the *Memoirs* were about $678,000; about $475,000 of this (70 percent) was due to Mrs. Grant, who had been paid $361,000. She was therefore owed $114,000, instead of the company's figure of $33,000. The dispute continued through the following winter, with Grant threatening a lawsuit and Webster and Company rejecting all demands. It is not clear how this matter was resolved, but no legal action followed (Webster to SLC, 23 Apr 1887, and Grant to Webster and Co., 22 July 1887, CU-MARK; *N&J3,* 319 n. 54).

75.10–20 expert found that Scott had stolen twenty-six thousand dollars . . . sent to the penitentiary for five years] Frank M. Scott (b. 1859?) was hired as a cashier and bookkeeper by Charles L. Webster and Company in July 1885. According to Clemens's notebook, Webster almost immediately began to receive anonymous letters claiming Scott was a thief. It is certain that by October 1886 Webster suspected him of embezzlement, but he waited for some months before commissioning an expert to investigate. Arrested in March 1887, Scott admitted he had been stealing from the start, covering up the shortfall with false entries in the books. He used the money to pay debts, to speculate in the stock market, and to buy jewelry for his wife; he also started to build a house. He was convicted of embezzling $26,000 and sentenced to six years' imprisonment. In late 1890 Clemens and Webster successfully petitioned the governor to have him pardoned for his family's sake. After his release he got a job as a cashier and bookkeeper for a printer, and again "misappropriated his employer's moneys to the extent of about $6,300" (S. Meredith Dickinson 1900, 344–49; *N&J3,* 283–84 n. 194, 314; New York *Times:* "A Weakness for Display," 13 Mar 1887, 2; "Confessions of a Thief," 18 Mar 1887, 5; Webster to SLC, 25 Mar 1887, CU-MARK; "City and Suburban News," 23 Apr 1887, 3).

76.2–7 pay to him his share of that loss . . . deficit of eighteen or nineteen thousand dollars could amount to four thousand] Scott's accounts showed a payout of $8,000 to Webster, who claimed he had drawn only $4,000. In a contract dated 1 April 1887 (NPV) Clemens raised Webster's salary by $800 a year for five years to compensate for his loss. He later regretted his generosity, and suggested that Webster "relinquish & sacrifice" his raise to pay the salary of a new employee (28 Dec 1887 to Webster, NPV, in *MTBus,* 389–90). Some of the stolen funds were recovered—an estimated $8,000—partly from the sale of the house that Scott had been building in his home town of Roseville, New Jersey (Webster to SLC, 29 Dec 1887, CU-MARK; *N&J3,* 315–16 n. 46, 322 n. 66, 323 n. 70; *MTBus,* 349).

76.10–16 ex-preacher, a professional revivalist . . . a gross sum of thirty-six thousand dollars, and Webster never got a cent of it] The Iowa agent, R. T. Root, was a member of the American Bible Society. A fellow member later described him as the embodiment of piety "to outward appearances," but in reality a swindler who paid his debts only when "it suited his conscience" (Antrobus 1915, 1:363; American Bible Society 1872, appendix, 9). In mid-1885 Clemens received a warning from his brother Orion (then living in Keokuk, Iowa) that Root was "a sharper," but replied with confidence that half of the general agencies "have made sales so greatly exceeding their contracts, that the other half could default, now, without hurting the book or me, either; but none of them will default. Such a thing is entirely out of the question" (OC to SLC, 21 Aug 1885, CU-MARK; 30 Aug 1885 to OC, CU-MARK). Orion was proved right, however, when Root defaulted on a debt to Webster and Company of about $30,000. In June 1888 Root offered to settle for $8,000, but was refused. In early 1889 a court judgment awarded the company the full amount, but only $9,000 was recovered, $7,000 of which was paid to Mrs. Grant for her share of the settlement (Hall to SLC, 8 June 1888, CU-MARK; *N&J3,* 390 n. 306).

76.30–33 Joe Jefferson wrote me and said . . . He simply ignored it] Joseph Jefferson (1829–1905) was born into a theatrical family and became a leading comedian of his day. His signature role was in *Rip Van Winkle,* adapted from the story by Washington Irving, which he played for forty years. He and Clemens had been acquainted since at least 1885. On 11 May 1887 Clemens wrote to Webster, "Joe Jefferson has written his Autobiography! You see, by George we've *got* to keep places open for great books; they spring up in the most unexpected places." Jefferson sent his manuscript to Clemens, who found it "delightful reading" (11 May 1887 and 28 May 1887 to Webster, NPV, in *MTBus,* 382, 383). Five months later Jefferson wrote to Webster:

> I presumed from the long silence that followed my correspondence with Mr. Clemens—to whom I am under many obligations—that you had given up the idea of publishing my book. Being under this impression I began negociations with another firm.
>
> Should the terms it may propose be unacceptable I will be pleased to write you on this subject. I would have replied to your letter before but have lately been acting in the West and your communication only reached me yesterday. (20 Oct 1887, NPV)

The Autobiography of Joseph Jefferson was published by the Century Company in 1890.

76.33–34 He accepted and published two or three war books that furnished no profit] The first of these war books was *McClellan's Own Story: The War for the Union,* by Major General George Brinton McClellan, published posthumously in December 1886. This was followed in 1887 by *The Genesis of the Civil War: The Story of Sumter 1860–1861,* by Brigadier General Samuel Wylie Crawford, and *Tenting on the Plains,* by Elizabeth B. Custer, widow of General George A. Custer (see also AD, 8 Oct 1906, note at 247.30). Finally, in 1888, the company issued the *Personal Memoirs* of General Philip Henry Sheridan (*N&J3,* 269 n. 141). According to a later recollection by Frederick J. Hall, Webster's successor, the "military memoirs" were initially successful, but sales rapidly declined (Hall 1947). Clemens's notebooks of the period are peppered with comments and calculations relating to the poor sales and diminishing profits of all the Webster and Company books (see, for example, *N&J3,* 303 n. 12, 310, 332, 429–31). Clemens himself had entertained high hopes for these books. But by October 1888 it was clear, according to Hall, that "*war literature of any kind and no matter by whom written is played out.* We have got to hustle everlastingly to get rid of 75,000 sets of Sheridan. I had set my mind on 100,000 sets but am forced to lessen this figure. There is not a man today who could write another book on the war and sell 5000 in the whole country" (15 Oct 1888 to SLC, CU-MARK).

76.40 It doesn't contain words enough for the price and dimensions] Clemens is probably referring to Almira Russell Hancock's book about her husband, *Reminiscences of Winfield Scott Hancock* (1887). This book was one-third as long as the other war books: even in large type it contained only three hundred and forty pages, and was padded with appendixes and full-page illustrations. According to Paine, it did not pay for the cost of manufacture (*N&J3,* 320 n. 60, 360 n. 191; *MTB,* 2:856).

77.7–17 he had agreed to resurrect Henry Ward Beecher's "Life of Christ" . . . money was eventually returned] Beecher, the famous liberal pastor of Plymouth Church in

Brooklyn, had published the first volume of his *Life of Jesus, the Christ,* in 1871 with J. B. Ford and Company, but the second volume remained incomplete. In January 1887 Beecher agreed to write his autobiography for publication through Webster and Company. First, however, he planned to finish the *Life of Jesus* so that Webster could publish a complete edition. Beecher received a $5,000 advance against royalties for both works, but died on 7 March before fulfilling his contract. After lengthy negotiations, his family returned the advance in December 1888 (Hall to SLC, 27 Dec 1888, and Webster to SLC, 26 Jan 1887, CU-MARK; 11 Jan 1889 to Hall, VtMiM, in *MTLP,* 252; *N&J3,* 276 n. 169). The "ruinous scandal" began in September 1872, less than a year after the first volume of the *Life of Jesus* appeared, when Beecher was accused of committing adultery with a parishioner (see AD, 10 Oct 1906, note at 253.17–22).

77.18–19 Webster kept back a book of mine, "A Yankee at the Court of King Arthur," . . . published it so surreptitiously] Clemens did not complete *A Connecticut Yankee* until the spring of 1889, and it was published later that year. By that time Webster had sold his interest in the business and retired, and it was his successor, Frederick J. Hall (see the note at 78.14–15), who produced the book on a lightning schedule (*CY,* 571–72, 577–89; 12 Nov 1888 to Hall [2nd], NN-BGC, in *MTLP,* 251 n. 3).

77.20–22 He suppressed a compilation made by Howells and me, "The Library of Humor," . . . there was such a book] Beginning in late 1880 Clemens developed a plan to collaborate on an anthology, *Mark Twain's Library of Humor,* with William Dean Howells and Charles Hopkins Clark, an editor with the Hartford *Courant* (Clemens discusses this book further in AD, 17 July 1906; for Clark see *AutoMT1,* 576 n. 317.33). They planned to publish it through James R. Osgood, but when his company failed in May 1885 the work had not yet been completed. Webster and Company bought the rights to all of Osgood's Mark Twain titles, including the *Library of Humor.* By the time Howells, the principal compiler, had completed the work in late 1885, he was under contract to Harper and Brothers and could not let his name appear "except over their imprint." Clemens paid him for his work, but decided to "pigeon-hole it & wait a few years & see what new notion Providence will take concerning it" (Howells to SLC, 16 Oct 1885, CU-MARK, in *MTHL,* 2:537; 18 Oct 1885 to Howells, NN-BGC, in *MTHL,* 2:538–39; for Howells see *AutoMT1,* 475 n. 70.19). In early 1887 Howells proposed giving the *Library of Humor* to Harpers. Webster objected, but admitted that he could not publish it until "we get some of the important pressing things off our hands," assuring Clemens that it "cannot get too old, it will always sell" (Webster to SLC, 17 Feb 1887, CU-MARK). By the summer of 1887 Clemens had become impatient, frustrated by the need to secure permissions and arrange for illustrations. Later that year he wrote in his notebook, "Lib Humor ought to have issued & sold 100,000, fall of '86, stead of being balled-up with Custer & Cox in the winter of 87–8" (*N&J3,* 360). The book was finally issued in 1888; its sales were good, but not as high as Clemens had hoped (3 Aug 1887 to Webster, NN-BGC, in *MTLP,* 221–22; 15 Aug 1887 to Hall and Webster, NN-BGC, in *MTLP,* 223–24; *N&J3,* 35–36 n. 67, 276 n. 172, 302–3 n. 10; *MTB,* 2:857;

for the later edition, published by Harpers, see AD, 17 July 1906; for the book by Sunset Cox, see AD, 18 Dec 1906, note at 318.39–40).

77.23–24 William M. Laffan told me that Mr. Walters, of Baltimore . . . illustrate in detail his princely art collection] William Mackay Laffan (1848–1909), a longtime friend of Clemens's, was born in Ireland and emigrated to America as a young man. From 1877 he wrote on art and drama for the New York *Sun,* with which paper he would be connected for the next thirty-two years, as publisher, general manager, and eventually proprietor. An authority on Chinese ceramics, he served as a trustee of the Metropolitan Museum of Art ("W. M. Laffan Dead of Appendicitis," New York *Times,* 20 Nov 1909, 11; Mitchell 1924, 352). William Thompson Walters (1819–94) was born in Pennsylvania and made his fortune in commerce, banking, and railroads. His collection had special strengths in French paintings and Asian ceramics; it became the core of the Walters Art Museum in Baltimore, which opened to the public in 1934.

77.31 you can make a fortune out of that without any trouble] In a letter of 13 January 1887 to Webster, Clemens estimated the "probable" profit to be $750,000. Webster was indeed dilatory in talking to Laffan. Clemens wrote him on 5 September 1887, and again on 17 October, urging him to meet with Laffan, who planned to depart soon for France to engage artists for his project (13 Jan 1887 to Webster, NPV, in *MTLP,* 213; 5 Sept 1887 to Webster, NPV, in *MTBus,* 385–86; 17 Oct 1887 to Webster and Co., NN-BGC, in *MTLP,* 236). The book was later postponed for other reasons, however, which did not involve Webster. In May 1888 Clemens explained to Hall:

> Laffan was to go to Europe & get the artists, *and* the man to write the letterpress (the mighty Wolf of Paris), & superintend clear till the plates were made & the books printed & placed in our hands—a matter of 2 or 3 years.
>
> But since then I have found a job for Laffan which will pay him $210,000 in ten or twelve months, & of course he wouldn't leave that till it is finished, to tackle the art book. In fact I could not *let* him. So we will leave the art book unmentioned for a year, & then maybe take another shy at it. (7 May 1888 to Hall, NN-BGC, in *MTLP,* 245–46)

The catalog, with a preface by Laffan, was ultimately published by D. Appleton and Company in 1897, after Walters's death: *Oriental Ceramic Art: Illustrated by Examples from the Collection of W. T. Walters.*

77.41 new German drug, phenacetine] This drug, also known as acetophenetidin, was introduced in 1888 as an analgesic and antipyretic by the Bayer company of Germany. Although widely used for many years, it is now known to have dangerous side effects—such as kidney damage and cancer—and has been superseded by acetaminophen, to which it is related.

78.12–13 Webster would be willing to put up with twelve thousand dollars and step out] In 1887 Webster, who suffered from a chronic condition diagnosed as acute neuralgia, found it increasingly difficult to participate actively in the business. Clemens recorded in his notebook in February 1888 that Webster had agreed to "retire from business, from all authority, & from the city, till April 1, 1889, & try to get back his health" (*N&J3,* 374). Webster never again acted as a member of the firm, and in December of 1888 his retirement became official when—after a series of offers and counteroffers—he agreed to sell his share for $12,000. He remained dissatisfied with the settlement, however, as he told Whitford on 31 December 1888: "I have sold out my interest for far less than I believe it to be worth but it is done and that is the end of it" (*MTBus,* 391). He lived quietly with his family in Fredonia until his death on 26 April 1891, at the age of thirty-nine, as a result of "an attack of grip, which led to peritonitis and hemorrhage and caused death" ("Grant's Publisher Dead," Columbus [Ga.] *Enquirer,* 29 Apr 1891, 1; *N&J3,* 298, 374, 374–75 n. 239, 615 n. 151, 625–26 n. 193).

78.14–15 understudy and business manager . . . Frederick J. Hall, another Dunkirk importation] Hall (1861–1926) was born in New York City and attended Peekskill Military Academy. Hired by Webster and Company in the spring of 1884 as a stenographer and office assistant, he gradually assumed further duties. In 1886 he was made a partner in the firm, with a salary of $1,500 a year and a one-twentieth share of the net profits on all books, excepting Grant's *Memoirs* (contract of 28 Apr 1886, NPV). During Webster's absences Hall took charge of the business, and assumed its management entirely when he bought out Webster's interest in December 1888. After the failure of the company in 1894 he continued his business career, eventually becoming vice-president of the Habirshaw Electric Cable Company. An enthusiastic golfer, he played once a week with John D. Rockefeller (Caldwell and Feiker 1919, 113; "Died," New York *Times,* 17 Oct 1926, E9; Hall 1947).

78.19–28 Stedman, the poet . . . thereby secured the lingering suicide of Charles L. Webster and Company] Clemens had known Edmund Clarence Stedman (1833–1908), an influential poet and critic, since the early 1870s (23 Feb 1872 to Redpath, *L5,* 47 n. 1). In 1887 Webster and Company paid $8,000 to W. E. Dibble, a Cincinnati subscription publisher, for plates of the first five volumes of the *Library of American Literature.* This proposed ten-volume anthology (to which an eleventh volume was ultimately added), comprising "selections of American literature, both in prose and poetry, from the earliest settlement in this country down to the present time," was being compiled by Stedman in collaboration with Ellen M. Hutchinson (1851–1933), a writer in the literary department of the New York *Tribune.* Webster enthusiastically promoted the work to Clemens, who replied, "I think well of the Stedman book, but I can't somehow bring myself to think *very* well of it" (1 Mar 1887 to Webster, NPV, in *MTLP,* 214); but Webster and Company acquired the *Library,* with Stedman and Hutchinson each receiving a 3 percent royalty. Sales of the series were good, but the slow receipt of installment payments could not offset the cost of producing the books. When Clemens was unable to furnish sufficient working capital, Hall was forced to borrow money to cover the expense (Webster to SLC, 25 Feb 1887, CU-MARK; Stedman and Hutchinson 1888–90; *N&J3,* 320 n. 62, 341 n. 123, 360–61 n. 195, 464 n. 195, 572, 612–13 n. 141; for Clemens's opinion of Stedman see AD, 3 July 1908).

78.30–31 a bank in which Whitford was a director] The Mount Morris Bank, located in Harlem, was one of the more persistent creditors of Webster and Company, refusing to renew notes when they became due. As of May 1894 the troubled firm owed the bank $29,500. Whitford was the bank's attorney, but it has not been confirmed that he was also a director (Harrison to SLC, 1 June 1894, CU-MARK, in *HHR,* 63 n. 3; 4 May 1894 to OLC, CU-MARK; "Business Troubles," New York *Times,* 19 Sept 1894, 11).

78.42 fearful panic of '93] The failure of the National Cordage Company on 4 May 1893 triggered a rapid decline in stock values; by the end of the year, over six hundred banks and fifteen thousand businesses had gone under. The panic led to a depression lasting five years, the country's worst up to then (Campbell 2008b, 168–69).

79.2–3 The property had cost a hundred and sixty-seven thousand dollars] This is the highest of the various estimates Clemens made of the house's cost, and it is probably too high. In 1877 the property was assessed for taxes at $66,650 (Courtney 2011, 107–8; bill enclosed with 7 July 1877 to Perkins [1st], *Letters 1876–1880*).

79.3 Henry Robinson] See *AutoMT1,* 560 n. 272.36–37.

79.7–9 Webster and Company failed . . . ninety-six creditors an average of a thousand dollars or so apiece] The company declared bankruptcy on 18 April 1894, after the Mount Morris Bank demanded repayment. According to the New York *Times,* its liabilities exceeded its assets by about $40,000 (excluding its debt to Olivia). Clemens ultimately paid some $15,000 to the Mount Morris Bank, which settled for 50 percent of its claim ("Business Troubles," New York *Times,* 19 Sept 1894, 11; *MTLP,* 365; *HHR,* 23–24; Rogers to SLC, 10 Dec 1897, CU-MARK, in *HHR,* 306 n. 1; Harrison to SLC, 11 Feb 1898, CU-MARK, in *HHR,* 322).

79.23–27 Mr. Rogers stepped in . . . they could not have my books; that they were not an asset of Webster and Company] Henry Huttleston Rogers, the wealthy vice-president of the Standard Oil Company, befriended Clemens in the fall of 1893 and guided him through the financial complexities of the bankruptcy. In an attempt to salvage Webster and Company he arranged for the sale of the *Library of American Literature* to his son-in-law, William Evarts Benjamin, for $50,000, and when bankruptcy became inevitable he transferred Clemens's personal assets, including the copyright on his books, to Olivia (*AutoMT1,* 192; *HHR,* 10–11).

79.39–80.4 We lectured and robbed and raided . . . creditors have all been paid] For details of this world lecturing tour see the Autobiographical Dictation of 4 June 1906. Clemens was accompanied by Olivia and his daughter Clara; Susy and Jean remained in the United States. After Susy died of meningitis in Hartford shortly after the end of the tour, the grieving family settled in London. There Clemens wrote his account of the trip, *Following the Equator.* The book was completed in May 1897 and published in November. In February 1898 Rogers's secretary, Katharine I. Harrison (who had handled the details of the financial settlements) wrote that only three claims remained, which would soon be paid (Harrison to SLC, 11 Feb 1898, CU-MARK, in *HHR,* 322).

80.6–7 "Put it in Federal Steel" . . . a profit of 125 per cent] Acting on Clemens's behalf, in October 1898 Rogers purchased preferred and common stock (heavily discounted) in the newly incorporated Federal Steel Company for $17,139.87. In December he sold it and reinvested in 712 shares of Federal's common stock, which soared in value through January 1899 on expectations that the company would combine with rival firms to form a giant steel trust—Rogers himself being one of the prime movers behind this consolidation. Rogers sold the stock on 21 January and reported a gain of $16,000. The U.S. Steel Corporation was founded in 1901, with Rogers as one of the directors and Clemens, once again, as a shareholder (Notebook 40, TS pp. 50, 54, 55, CU-MARK; New York *Times:* "The Great Steel Trust," 25 Dec 1898, 2; "Mr. Carnegie Sells Out," 5 May 1899, 1; "Steel Trust Officers," New York *Evening Tribune,* 2 Apr 1901, 1).

80.14–18 I was assisting in the work . . . The machine was a failure] Clemens gives a full account of this disastrous venture in "The Machine Episode" (*AutoMT1,* 101–6). In the present dictation he blames Webster almost entirely for the collapse of his publishing company, but the estimated $170,000 he invested in the typesetter was a contributing factor. In 1885, when the Grant *Memoirs* were in production, Clemens had nothing but praise for Webster, saying that he had a "tremendous season: but he has come through it with a superb record; & with all its array of business-inventions, -ingenuities & -triumphs, he has not made a single business-misstep" (30 July 1885 to Annie Webster, NPV). By 1888, Clemens's growing impatience with Webster had turned to dislike, and then to contempt. In a letter of 1 July 1889 to his brother Orion he admitted, "I have never hated any creature with a hundred thousandth fraction of the hatred which I bear that human louse, Webster" (CU-MARK).

80.19 It stands in Cornell University] A note in Volume 1 states that one machine survives at the Hartford House and Museum, and that the other was donated by the Mergenthaler Company to Cornell University and later used for scrap metal in World War II (*AutoMT1,* 644 n. 455 *footnote*). New information indicates that the Mergenthaler Company, which owned both prototypes of the machine, loaned one to Columbia University and one to Cornell. The Cornell machine was displayed from 1898 to 1921, and then returned to the Mergenthaler Company, which donated it to the Mark Twain House and Museum in 1957. The one at Columbia was melted down for scrap metal (Goble 1998, 14; information courtesy of Lance Heidig).

Autobiographical Dictation, 4 June 1906

81.7 I lecturing every night] Clemens facetiously represented these lectures as a lesson in morals, illustrated by examples from his writings. He prepared a working repertoire of some twenty-five selections, drawn from *The Innocents Abroad* (1869), *A Tramp Abroad* (1880), *Adventures of Huckleberry Finn* (1885), and several other works (*HF 2003,* 617).

81.33 accident which I have before mentioned in a previous chapter] That is, in the Autobiographical Dictation of 13 February 1906 (*AutoMT1,* 356).

81.34 We took No. 14 West 10th street] The family moved to this large furnished house, secured through Clemens's friend Frank N. Doubleday, on 1 November 1900 (JC 1900–1907).

82.4–9 Three months' repose and seclusion in the Adirondacks . . . York Harbor for the summer] From late June to mid-September 1901 the Clemenses stayed in a summer home on Lower Saranac Lake that they called "The Lair" (see the photographs following page 300). On 1 October they settled into a spacious home built on sixteen acres of river-front property in Riverdale (now known as Wave Hill), formerly the home of publisher William H. Appleton from 1866 until his death in 1899. The following summer, in late June 1902, they rented a cottage at York Harbor, Maine (see *AutoMT1,* 603 n. 387.6; *MTB,* 3:1135, 1141, 1176; Wave Hill 2011; "Personal Items," *The School Journal,* 7 June 1902, 651).

82.9–10 Mr. Rogers brought his *Kanawha,* the fastest steam yacht in American waters] Rogers bought the *Kanawha,* a 227-foot-long steam-powered yacht, in 1901. He allowed the Clemenses to use it for transport to York Harbor but was not present himself. Clemens wrote on 26 June 1902, while en route, "By George, you ought to have been along! The sail from Riverdale till night fell was charming & exalting & beautiful beyond all experience" (26 June 1902 to Rogers, Sotheby 2003, item 105; 5 July 1901 to Rogers, photocopy in CU-MARK, in *HHR,* 464 n. 1).

82.14 Jean's health was bad] Jean's epileptic seizures, which she had suffered since 1896, struck unpredictably and were preceded by black moods and fits of mental "absence" (see the Appendix "Family Biographies," p. 652; SLC 1899b; Ober 2003, 156–66).

82.22 we sailed to Fairhaven] In 1895 Rogers built an eighty-five-room mansion in Fairhaven, Massachusetts, which overlooked the bay in the southern part of town (Thomas and Avila 2003, 10).

82.31–36 Aix-les-Bains . . . there was nothing very serious the matter with her] Olivia was at Aix-les-Bains, France, in June and July 1891, and at Bad Nauheim from June to mid-September 1892. On 10 June 1892 Clemens wrote to Clara, "The best news of all, is that two doctors have pronounced Mamma's case curable, & *easily* curable. They say these baths will do it, & that these are the only baths in the world that can" (CU-MARK).

83.16–17 I at once wrote it out . . . and sent it to *Harper's Monthly.* I here append it] Clemens wrote in his notebook on 27 August 1902, "Send 'Heaven or Hell' to Harper?" Frederick A. Duneka (general manager of Harper and Brothers) replied on 18 September, "Thank you very much for Heaven or Hell. It is great." The story appeared in *Harper's Monthly* the following December (SLC 1902d; Notebook 45, TS pp. 24, 27, CU-MARK). Tear sheets from that issue, which Clemens attached to the typescript of this dictation, are the source of the text reproduced here.

Autobiographical Dictation, 6 June 1906

97.10–12 celebration in commemoration of . . . municipal self-constituted government on the continent of America] York, Maine, chartered as Gorgeana in 1642 and then rechartered and renamed in 1652, celebrated its 250th anniversary as "the first city in America" in August 1902 ("The Old Town of York," New York *Tribune,* 3 Aug 1902, "Illustrated Supplement," 2; Baxter 1904, 34, 38–43).

97.26–98.4 visitor was a lady . . . earn a living there by teaching] The visitor, Florence Hartwig, was a singer and voice teacher who had left America to study in Europe at the age of fourteen. She was married to Elias Hartwig, a German businessman living in Bucharest, where she became a lady-in-waiting and singer in the court of Elisabeth (1843–1916), queen of Romania. She visited the Clemenses in August 1902 bearing a letter of introduction from the queen, written on 9 May. Elisabeth of Romania was born in Germany and married at twenty-six to Prince Carol of Romania, who became king in 1881. Known for her benevolent and charitable works, she also wrote prolifically—poetry, fairy stories, plays, and novels—under the pseudonym "Carmen Sylva." She had been a friend and admirer of Clemens's since his sojourn in Vienna at the Hotel Metropole in 1897–98: in her letter she thanked him for "every beautiful thought you poured into my tired heart and for every smile on a weary way!" He was fond of one of her books, *A Real Queen's Fairy Tales,* and in an essay published in April 1902 in the *North American Review* he described her as a "charming and lovable German princess and poet" (SLC 1902b, 437; "A Favorite at Carmen Sylva's Court," Philadelphia *Inquirer,* 31 May 1903, "Woman's Magazine," 2; Elisabeth of Romania to SLC, 9 May 1902, CU-MARK, in *MTL,* 2:726–27; *MTB,* 2:1062; Gribben 1980, 1:218–19).

98.27–28 article by an Austrian prince on Dueling in Court and Military circles on the Continent of Europe] The article, "The Effort to Abolish the Duel" by Prince Alfonso Carlos of Bourbon and Austria-Este (1849–1936), appeared in the *North American Review* for August 1902 (Alfonso Carlos 1902).

98.36–37 poor woman's face was as white as marble! The French phrase stood translated] In her letter Queen Elisabeth explained that Hartwig's husband had been forced to leave "quite a brilliant situation" in Bucharest after he "refused to participate in une affaire onéreuse" ("a tiresome affair"). Evidently Hartwig's reaction to the article on dueling led Clemens to conclude that the phrase was equivalent to "une affaire d'honneur"—that is, a duel (Elisabeth of Romania to SLC, 9 May 1902, CU-MARK, in *MTL,* 2:726–27). In 1904 Clemens wrote a letter of endorsement for Hartwig, citing the queen's praise (16 Nov 1904 to "Whom It May Concern," photocopy in CU-MARK, in *MTL,* 2:727).

99.8 next sixty days were anxious ones for us] On 13 October Clemens wrote, "We thought it was heart disease, & for 4 weeks we had but little hope. But she will get well—they all say it. If we only *could* get home to Riverdale!" (13 Oct 1902 to Pears, CtY-BR).

99.16–19 We secured a special train . . . delivered us at our home, Riverdale] "We left York Harbor at about 9 yesterday morning in an invalid car & special train," Clemens wrote to Laurence Hutton 16 October, "& reached the Grand Central at 5.40; special engine rushed us up to Riverdale in 20 minutes—a long & rough journey for a sick person & terribly fatiguing" (16 Oct 1902 to Hutton, NjP-SC). He recorded in his notebook that the trip cost $339 (Notebook 45, TS p. 30, CU-MARK).

99.22 trained nurse] Margaret Garrety, who was hired on 28 September and discharged on 23 October; Clemens found her to be "vain, silly, self-important, untrustworthy, a most thorough fool, & a liar by instinct & training" (Notebook 45, TS pp. 29–30, 32, CU-MARK).

Autobiographical Dictation, 7 June 1906

100.12 Susy Crane] Susan Langdon Crane, Olivia's foster sister (see *AutoMT1,* 579 n. 324.32).

100.15 young Dodges] Clara and Jean were friends of the children of Cleveland H. Dodge (see the note at 107.19–20): Elizabeth (b. 1884), Julia (b. 1885), and their twin brothers, Bayard and Cleveland Earl (b. 1888) (*Riverdale Census* 1900, 1127:10A).

100.29 woman named Tobin] Unidentified.

100.34 Old Point Comfort] A spit of land on the Virginia shore of the Chesapeake Bay, known for its health resorts.

100.34 Katy] Longtime family servant Katy Leary.

101.8 I will here insert the Susy Crane letter] Clemens's preparations for this dictation go back to Florence in January 1904, when he asked Isabel Lyon to gather materials for a "Chapter which Livy must not see. Send to Susy Crane & Twichell for letters written at that time to be sent to Miss Lyon in my care" (Lyon transcript of SLC notes, CU-MARK). Both letters were obtained, and in 1906 Clemens pasted the manuscript letter to Crane into his dictation typescript; a typed copy of the letter to Twichell was made, and the original returned to him.

101.13 York Harbor experience] Susan Crane traveled from Elmira to York Harbor in mid-August 1902 to help nurse Olivia. Clemens wrote her on 15 August, "We try our best to keep hidden the doctor-secrets, but she is sharp, & penetrating, & hunts us through all our shifts & dodges, & worms everything out of us, & then the result makes her low-spirited. She wants you, & she is right" (15 Aug 1902 to Crane, CU-MARK).

101.17 Dr. Janeway] Dr. Edward Gamaliel Janeway (1841–1911) was a prominent specialist in nervous diseases and tuberculosis who had attended two presidents—McKinley and Cleveland—and was currently treating Cornelius Vanderbilt for typhoid fever (New York *Times:* "Mr. Vanderbilt's Condition," 24 Dec 1902, 1; "Worst Fears Realized," 14 Sept 1901, 1; "Cleveland Had His Left Jaw Removed," 21 Sept 1917, 9; "Dr. E. G. Janeway, Diagnostician, Dead," 11 Feb 1911, 11).

101.31 Mrs. Hapgood's luncheon] Emilie Bigelow Hapgood (1868–1930), a family friend, was the daughter of a Chicago banker; she married the author Norman Hapgood in 1896 ("Emilie Hapgood Dies of a Stroke," New York *Times,* 17 Feb 1930, 17; *Manhattan Census* 1900, 1115:1A).

102.5 Miss Sherry] Margaret Sherry was hired sometime after 23 October 1902, when Margaret Garrety was discharged (see AD, 6 June 1906, note at 99.22). Sherry accompanied the family to Italy in the fall of 1903; when she departed a month later Clemens noted, "We can never forget her, & shall always be grateful to her" (Notebook 46, TS p. 31, CU-MARK).

102.23 *feeding of the five thousand*] Matthew 14:13–21 (also in the other three gospels).

102.40 John Howells] John Mead Howells (1868–1959) was the son of William Dean and Elinor Howells. After studying at Harvard and the École des Beaux-Arts in Paris, he founded the architectural firm of Howells and Stokes in New York City. In 1906–8 he designed and supervised the construction of Stormfield (Clemens's house in Redding, Connecticut), in the style of an Italian villa. In later years he designed public buildings all over the country, including several at Harvard and Yale.

103.9 Mark Hambourg] Hambourg (1879–1960) was a Russian pianist who began his career as a child prodigy. After studying with renowned piano teacher Theodor Leschetizky, he made the first of many world tours in 1895. Clara met him in Vienna in the spring of 1898, when she too was a pupil of Leschetizky (it was then that she also met fellow student Ossip Gabrilowitsch, her future husband). Hambourg was currently performing in New York (CC 1938, 1–3; New York *Times:* "Mendelssohn Hall," 6 Jan 1903, 10; "Mark Hambourg's Recital," 11 Jan 1903, 14).

103.30 Letter to Reverend Joseph H. Twichell] See the note at 101.8.

103.42 "Was it Heaven? Or Hell?"] See the Autobiographical Dictation of 4 June 1906 and the note at 83.16–17.

105.6–7 I wish Clara . . . could take a pen and put upon paper all the details of one of her afternoons in her mother's room] On 31 December 1902, the same day that Clemens wrote his letter to Twichell, Clara wrote her friend Dorothea Gilder:

> Dear Me! I used to maintain that there was no use in lying because if you arranged the words well, even very well the expression of face still destroyed the possibility of success in deceiving—but I must take back that statement for my whole conversation with my mother is one long string of lies. . . . Jean is out coasting with the Dodges or at a matinee[,] visit a friend in New York etc. etc. I really get so confused trying to remember that I have been to a lesson in town instead of sitting near Jean's room all morning that I can't see why my mother doesn't detect my many slips & badly mended breaks. So far she has been successfully blinded but I do hope that Jean won't be long getting well. (TS of catalog, George Robert Minkoff Rare Books, 10 Dec 1998, CU-MARK)

105.18 Joe, don't let those people invite me—I couldn't go] Twichell had written Clemens from Hartford on 30 December: "If you are coming up here Jan. 21st you can make a speech at the Dinner—in the Foot Guard Armory—of the Sons of the Revolution; or if you prefer at the meeting of the Workingmens' Club in the Lafayette St Public School Hall. Or perhaps you might do *both* things. I have been requested to press both honors on your acceptance" (CU-MARK).

105.20–21 full report of that dinner*—issued by Colonel Harvey as a remembrancer . . . to all the guests] George Harvey—president of Harper and Brothers and editor of the *North American Review* and *Harper's Weekly*—hosted a dinner at the Metropolitan Club on 28 November 1902 for over fifty guests in celebration of Clemens's sixty-seventh birthday (for Harvey see *AutoMT1,* 557 n. 267.35). No "remembrancer" has been found, but *Harper's Weekly* printed the following poems read at the dinner: "A Double-Barrelled Sonnet to Mark Twain," by Howells; "Mark Twain (A Post-prandial Obituary)," by humorist John Kendrick Bangs (1862–1922); and "A Toast to Mark Twain!" by Henry van Dyke (*Harper's Weekly* 46 [13 Dec 1902]: 1943–44). Clemens also made a brief speech, in which he mentioned Twichell, saying in part:

> Another of my oldest friends is here—the Rev. Joe Twichell—and whenever Twichell goes to start a church I see them flocking, rushing to buy the land all around there. Many and many a time I have attended the annual sale in his church, and bought up all the pews on a margin and it would have been better for me spiritually and financially if I had staid under his wing. I try to serve him, I have tried to do good in this world, and it is marvelous in how many ways I have done good. ("When Twain Got His Say," New York *Times,* 30 Nov 1902, 10)

105.34 Fay Davis] In November 1902 Davis made a successful New York debut in the comedy *Imprudence,* by H. V. Esmond ("The Theatres Last Night," New York *Times,* 18 Nov 1902, 9; see AD, 5 Apr 1906, note at 18.36–19.3).

106.1 "The Death-Wafer,"] Early in 1902 Clemens's dramatization of his story "The Death-Disk" was staged at Carnegie Hall by the Children's Theatre ("News of the Theatres," New York *Times,* 7 Feb 1902, 6). For a description of the story see the Autobiographical Dictation of 30 August 1906, note at 197.40–198.8.

106.4 Mary Foote] Mary Hubbard Foote (1872–1968) was a cousin of the Clemens girls' former governess, Lilly Gillette Foote (see *AutoMT1,* 579 n. 326.13–21). Orphaned at age thirteen, she was raised by an aunt in Hartford and became an especially close friend of Susy's. In 1890 she enrolled in the Yale School of the Fine Arts, and then continued her studies in Paris. In 1901 she returned to New York, established her own studio in Washington Square, and found success as a portraitist. In the 1920s she began to withdraw from art and social life, moving permanently to Switzerland to be treated by Carl Jung, who convinced her to stop painting professionally (Fahlman 1991, 19–20; "Nook Farm Genealogy" 1974, Foote Addenda, vi).

106.45 unberufen!] Clemens frequently used this superstitious German interjection. In his own words: "If a German forgets himself & suddenly lets slip a strong desire, he immediately protects himself by exclaiming *'Unberufen!'*—otherwise, the evil spirits, having discovered the desire of his heart, would set themselves at work, right away, and smash it" (30 Aug 1881 to Norton, MH-H).

107.12 Judy] Julia Curtis Twichell (1869–1945), Joseph Twichell's oldest daughter, was called "Judy" by her family. She had been married to Howard Ogden Wood since 1892 (Twichell to SLC, 2 Feb 1892, CU-MARK; "Wood-Twichell," New York *Times,* 27 Apr 1892, 5).

107.19–20 William E. Dodge's house, or . . . at Cleveland Dodge's] William E. Dodge and his son, philanthropist and financier Cleveland H. Dodge (1860–1926), both owned estates in Riverdale. Their wealth derived from the family business, founded by William's father (of the same name), which dealt in metals ("Dodge Family Gets $20,000,000 Estate," New York *Times,* 28 July 1926, 21; *Riverdale Census* 1900, 1127:10A; *Social Register* 1902, 100; see *AutoMT1,* 558 n. 269.24–26).

107.20–21 George W. Perkins's house] Perkins (1862–1920), a partner in J. P. Morgan and Company and vice-president of the New York Life Insurance Company, was another Riverdale neighbor. In mid-1903 he bought the house the Clemenses were leasing; by then it was owned by Frank A. Munsey, who had purchased it in April 1902 from Appleton's heirs. In recent years Perkins had become one of the most important financiers on Wall Street, and was now purchasing contiguous properties on the Hudson River to create a large estate ("Perkins the Wonder," Los Angeles *Times,* 10 May 1903, B4; 30 June 1903 to Perkins, NRivd2; "Literary and Trade Notes," *Publishers' Weekly,* 26 Apr 1902, 1014; Wave Hill 2011).

107.29–30 I have already told a sufficiency of the history of our eight months' occupancy of that infamous place] See "Villa di Quarto" (*AutoMT1,* 230–49 and notes on 539–42).

Autobiographical Dictation, 11 June 1906

109.7 Franklin MacVeagh] MacVeagh (1837–1934) was a Chicago businessman, lawyer, and banker who later (in 1909–13) served as secretary of the treasury. In early June 1906 he went to Europe, returning to his summer home in Dublin in August. Clemens had socialized with him in Dublin the previous summer ("News of the Society World," Chicago *Tribune,* 20 May 1906, 13; Lyon 1906, entry for 25 Aug).

109.16 household consisting of six or eight persons] The Dublin household included Jean Clemens, Isabel Lyon, Albert Bigelow Paine, stenographer-typist Josephine Hobby, and the following staff: Jean's maid (Anna), a cook (Mary), a coachman (George O'Connor), and a "waitress" (Katherine). In addition, they enjoyed the company of Jean's dog (Prosper) and three kittens "rented" for the season (Lyon 1906, entries for 18 June, 30 Aug, and 18 Oct; JC 1900–1907, entry for 30 Apr 1906).

109.17–20 Alexander Selkirk . . . horrible place] Alexander Selkirk (1676–1721) was marooned for over four years on an uninhabited island three hundred and fifty miles off the coast of Chile. His ordeal, which is thought to have inspired Daniel Defoe's *Robinson Crusoe* (1719), is also the subject of William Cowper's "Verses Supposed to Be Written by Alexander Selkirk" (1782), which Clemens slightly misquotes here.

109.37–110.4 Early in April came the great irruption of Vesuvius . . . account by the Younger Pliny of the overwhelming of Herculaneum and Pompeii] A major eruption of Vesuvius began in 1905 and climaxed the following year. Between 5 and 18 April 1906 repeated eruptions destroyed several towns and killed hundreds of people. Detailed accounts of the disaster appeared daily in the New York *Times* (Banks and Read 1906, 338–50). Gaius Plinius Caecilius Secundus, known as Pliny the Younger (A.D. 62?–?113), was a prominent and wealthy Roman. From a location across the bay of Naples, he witnessed the eruption of Vesuvius which buried Herculaneum and Pompeii under volcanic debris in A.D. 79. Several years later he described the event in two letters to the historian Tacitus. On 10 April the New York *Times* published English translations of Pliny's letters ("When Vesuvius Buried Pompeii in A.D. 79," 2).

110.18 obliteration of San Francisco by earthquake and fire] The San Francisco earthquake of 18 April 1906, and the fires that erupted in its wake, destroyed over twenty-eight thousand buildings, killed some three thousand people, and rendered homeless more than half of the city's population. The damage totaled over $8 billion in today's dollars (Cherny 2008).

Autobiographical Dictation, 12 June 1906

111.18 One friend of mine] Unidentified.

111.21 a young couple] Unidentified.

111.27–29 thirty-eight years since I last saw San Francisco . . . chief and only reporter] Clemens describes his 1864 job at the *Morning Call* in the Autobiographical Dictation of 13 June 1906. He left San Francisco in December 1866, returning only once, for several months, in 1868 (*AutoMT1,* 509 n. 150.1–2).

111.35–112.14 husband of Madame Sembrich . . . little creature was not frightened] Marcella Sembrich (1858–1935), born in Austrian Poland, was a child prodigy on the piano and violin who ultimately became an operatic soprano. She performed at many European venues before making her New York debut in 1883, and sang with the Metropolitan Opera Company from 1898 to 1909. Her husband, Guillaume Stengel-Sembrich (1846–1917), was a pianist and one of Sembrich's teachers. The Metropolitan company arrived in San Francisco the day before their opening performance on 16 April, and were scheduled to present thirteen different operas in as many days ("Guillaume Stengel Dies at the Gotham," New York *Times,* 16 May 1917, 13; San Francisco *Chronicle:* "Amusements," 18 Mar 1906, 42; "Grand Opera Stars Arrive," 16 Apr 1906, 7). Clemens may have taken the details of his dictation from a story in the New York *Times* of 25 April, which reported Sembrich's account of her ordeal. She explained that during her first attempt to return to her room in the St. Francis Hotel she met a "second shock, which sent me hurrying to the street":

> But I could not stay out without some sort of wear other than my night clothes, and I went back a second time. It was a climb of six flights of stairs, and on the third floor the third shock came. I kept on and got this suit I have on and my jewels. . . . We bundled blankets, some crackers, and a little whisky into a wagon and went to the beach near the Presidio. Thousands of people had gathered there, and there were many animals. Among Chinese, Japanese, negroes, and all races we slept that night on the beach, nothing between us and the sky save our blankets. ("Conried's Singers Hug and Kiss Him," New York *Times,* 25 Apr 1906, 6)

Sembrich and Clemens were acquainted: the previous November she had written to congratulate him on his seventieth birthday. He thanked her, and wrote her again on 30 April, "Welcome back to life again, dear Madame Sembrich, after that stupendous adventure!" (1 Dec 1905 and 30 Apr 1906 to Sembrich, NBolS).

112.18–24 I was in what was called the "Great Earthquake" . . . because I was a newspaper reporter, and was thankful] On 8 October 1865 an earthquake caused significant damage to buildings not only in San Francisco but as far away as San Jose and Santa Cruz. At that time Clemens was corresponding for the Virginia City *Territorial Enterprise* and had just agreed to write dramatic criticism for the San Francisco *Dramatic Chronicle* (*ET&S2,* 289, 294, 297). He wrote several humorous sketches about the event: two letters to the *Enterprise* ("The Cruel Earthquake," SLC 1865b, and "Popper Defieth Ye Earthquake," SLC 1865c); a brief article in the *Dramatic Chronicle* ("Earthquake Almanac," SLC 1865d); and a longer account in the New York *Weekly Review* ("The Great Earthquake in San Francisco," SLC 1865f).

112.30–34 Professor William James . . . had no feeling of fright or fear] Psychologist and philosopher William James (1842–1910) taught at Harvard University from 1873 to 1907, and was a visiting lecturer at Stanford when the earthquake occurred. Clemens was familiar with at least two of his works: *The Principles of Psychology* (1890) and *The Varieties of Religious Experience* (1902) (Gribben 1980, 1:351). The two men had also corresponded in 1900 about the efficacy of Jonas Kellgren's treatments for heart disease, and they shared an interest in "mind cure" (17 Apr 1900 and 23 Apr 1900 to James, MH-H; AD, 21 Dec 1906, note at 330.34). The "published letter" Clemens alludes to here was an article entitled "On Some Mental Effects of the Earthquake," published in the *Youth's Companion* for 7 June 1906 (80:283–84). In it James described his reaction when the temblor was "shaking the room exactly as a terrier shakes a rat":

> The emotion consisted wholly of glee and admiration; glee at the vividness which such an abstract idea or verbal term as "earthquake" could put on when translated into sensible reality and verified concretely; and admiration at the way in which the frail little wooden house could hold itself together in spite of such a shaking. I felt no trace whatever of fear; it was pure delight and welcome. . . .

> I ran into my wife's room, and found that she, although awakened from sound sleep, had felt no fear, either. Of all the persons whom I later interrogated, very few had felt any fear while the shaking lasted. (William James 1983, 331–32)

113.7–20 "little Ward," . . . had reached the age of sixty-five] Lewis P. Ward (1837–1903) was a compositor on the San Francisco *Alta California* when Clemens shared a room with him in San Francisco in 1865. A Civil War veteran, he also taught gymnastics and performed in fencing exhibitions. When the two old friends corresponded briefly in 1888–89, Ward found Clemens to be the "same whole-souled, good fellow that you were when I last saw you, 24 years ago" (*San Francisco Census* 1900, 107:3A; Goodman to SLC, 2 Oct 1903, CU-MARK; National Park Service 2012; *CofC,* 223; Ward to SLC, 23 Feb 1889, CU-MARK; for Steve Gillis see *AutoMT1,* 569 n. 295.5–15).

113.21–23 Steve Gillis and his brother Jim . . . young sons and daughters of the family] Clemens mentions boarding with the Gillis family in San Francisco—in 1864 and again in 1865—in the Autobiographical Dictation of 19 January 1906. He became friends with Steve Gillis when working on the *Enterprise* in Virginia City, and stayed with Jim and Billy Gillis in their cabin at Jackass Hill in the winter of 1864–65 (see *AutoMT1,* 295, 569 n. 295.5–15).

113.38–114.4 I am the eldest son of the eldest of the Gillis sisters . . . he was thirty-seven] The eldest Gillis sister, Theresa Ann (1843–1929), married Henry Williams, a stockbroker born in England. In 1906, her eldest (and only surviving) son was Henry Alston Williams (1864–1941). The other Gillis sisters were Mary Elizabeth (Mollie, 1846–1916) and Francina California (1849–1916) (Evans, Gillis, and Williams 1970).

Autobiographical Dictation, 13 June 1906

114.23–26 I was a reporter on the *Morning Call* . . . Mr. Barnes's idea, and he was the proprietor] Clemens was the local reporter for the *Call* from June to October 1864. For George Barnes, see *AutoMT1,* 536 n. 226.36–37.

114.33–34 court interpreter . . . familiar with fifty-six Chinese dialects] Charles T. Carvalho (1834?–70), the official court interpreter, was a native of Java ("Death of Charles T. Carvalho," San Francisco *Bulletin,* 31 Jan 1870, 3; *CofC,* 76–77; *San Francisco Mortality Schedules* 1870, 74).

115.12 "Uncle Remus"] Author Joel Chandler Harris (*AutoMT1,* 532–33 n. 217.25–27; see also AD, 16 Oct 1906).

115.16–17 I took the pen and spread this muck out in words and phrases] Much of Clemens's local reporting is collected in *Clemens of the "Call";* for the theater and crime news described here see "The Stage" (*CofC,* 93–98) and "Part Two: Crime and Court Reporter" (*CofC,* 139–205).

115.38–39 The *Call* could not afford to publish articles criticising the hoodlums for stoning Chinamen] Clemens had previously described this incident in a May 1870 *Galaxy* article, "Disgraceful Persecution of a Boy": "Brannan street butchers set their dogs on a Chinaman who was quietly passing with a basket of clothes on his head; and while the dogs mutilated his flesh, a butcher increased the hilarity of the occasion by knocking some of the Chinaman's teeth down his throat with half a brick" (SLC 1870a, 723). Later in 1870 he used the attack in a *Galaxy* sketch entitled "Goldsmith's Friend Abroad Again," in which some jeering young men set a fierce dog on a Chinese man. Two policemen at first ignore him, then beat and arrest him for "being disorderly and disturbing the peace" (SLC 1870b, 571). In an 1880 letter to Howells Clemens recalled the "degraded 'Morning Call,' whose mission from hell & politics was to lick the boots of the Irish & throw bold brave mud at the Chinamen" (3 Sept 1880, *Letters 1876–1880*).

115.41–116.6 Day before yesterday's New York *Sun* . . . from one end of the United States to the other] Clemens describes a "special cable despatch" from the London correspondent for the *Sun,* published on the front page on 10 June 1906. The article, entitled "Blow to America Abroad," noted that recent revelations about Chicago meat packers "have come as a climax to a long series of exposures with which American telegrams to English and European papers have teemed for many months," citing the life insurance scandal in particular (see *AutoMT1,* 549 n. 257.6–9). The dispatch (the only one that has been found) made no specific reference, however, to the other instances of graft that Clemens mentions, in municipal government and the railroad industry. Stories about corruption in Philadelphia and St. Louis had been appearing in newspapers since at least early 1905. More recently, in May 1906, the officials of the Pennsylvania Railroad had come under scrutiny for granting lower freight charges to coal companies in return for gifts of stock (see, for example, New York *Times:* "Railroad Officials Got Rich Gifts of Stock," 17 May 1906, 1; "High Railroad Men Called," 22 May 1906, 6; Washington *Post:* "Responsibility for Ring Rule," 21 Apr 1905, 6; "Nation's Awakening," 25 Nov 1905, 5).

116.7–8 to-day's lurid exposure, by Upton Sinclair, of the . . . Beef Trust] Upton Sinclair (1878–1968) published his novel *The Jungle* in serial form in 1905, and it became a best-selling book in early 1906. Its horrifying description of the Chicago stockyards and revelations about the sale of tainted meat awakened public outrage against the Beef Trust (a conglomerate of the three largest Chicago meat-packing firms, Swift, Armour, and Morris). The *Sun*'s London correspondent commented that even "a cleaning of the Augean stables at Chicago" would not suffice "to restore European belief in American honesty" ("Blow to America Abroad," New York *Sun,* 10 June 1906, 1; "Report on Beef Trust," *Wall Street Journal,* 5 June 1906, 7). Clemens wrote to Sinclair on 22 June 1906: "In dictating the morning's chapter in my autobiography one day last week, I uttered a paragraph, which indicates that I realize the magnitude and effectiveness of the earthquake which 'The Jungle' has set going under the Canned Polecat Trust of Chicago"; he then quoted his own remarks from this dictation ("Mark Twain on 'The Jungle,'" Eau Claire [Wis.] *Leader,* 7 Aug 1906, unknown page).

116.8–10 an exposure which has moved the President . . . hands of the doctor and the undertaker] After reading *The Jungle* President Roosevelt ordered an investigation and forwarded the resulting report to Congress on 4 June, urging immediate action. The Meat Inspection Act, which he signed into law on 30 June, provided a permanent appropriation for the inspection of animals before and after slaughter, and established regulations to ensure the safety of meat products ("Report on Beef Trust," *Wall Street Journal,* 5 June 1906, 7; "Congress Passes Three Big Bills," Chicago *Tribune,* 30 June 1906, 1, 4).

116.10–12 According to that correspondent . . . an honest male human creature left in the United States] The *Sun* correspondent opined that "it becomes the duty, however painful, of any conscientious correspondent to inform his countrymen of the indictment which the world at large is bringing against them and to warn them that it is not corporate criminals alone who are being arraigned. It is the whole American people who stand to-day at the bar of public opinion before their sister nations" ("Blow to America Abroad," New York *Sun,* 10 June 1906, 1).

116.16–17 swore off my taxes] See *AutoMT1,* 573 n. 304.11.

116.39–40 He called him Smiggy McGlural] Clemens's colleague on the *Call* was William K. McGrew (1827–1903), who was also undoubtedly the man he recalls here. The nickname "Smiggy McGlural" was borrowed from the title of a humorous song popular in the early 1860s. McGrew was born to a wealthy family, but lost his inheritance in the financial panic of 1857. He took a position on the New York *Times,* but after the death of his wife he began a series of remarkable travels: he crossed the continent on foot three times and walked from Central America to San Francisco, supporting himself by playing the flute. In 1864 he was a relatively new *Call* employee, and he went on leave in the fall of 1865. He returned to his position intermittently until 1889, when he resigned to practice law (*San Francisco Census* 1900, 103:13B; *CofC,* 18–19, 304 nn. 62–63; *ET&S2,* 546; Waltz and Engle 2011; San Francisco *Chronicle:* "A Fatal Accident," 3 Oct 1893, 5; "Deaths," 1 May 1903, 13).

117.21–22 *Morning Call* building . . . nothing was left but the iron bones] The nineteen-story *Call* building (later known as the Spreckels building), erected in 1897 at Market and Third streets, was for many years the tallest edifice west of the Mississippi. It was badly damaged by the 1906 fire, but its steel frame remained intact, and the building, reconstructed and remodeled, still stands today (Himmelwright 1906, 231–34).

117.33–37 in the Magnalia . . . nothing left but the man himself] *Magnalia Christi Americana; or, The Ecclesiastical History of New-England, from Its First Planting in the Year 1620 unto the Year of Our Lord, 1698* was the greatest work of Puritan minister Cotton Mather (1663–1728). The work was first published in London in 1702; Clemens owned the first American edition, issued in 1820 in two volumes (Gribben 1980, 1:457). The passage that Clemens remembers has not been identified.

117.40–42 In those ancient times . . . Bret Harte as private secretary of the Superintendent] In 1864 the *Call* was located in a new brick building at 612 Commercial Street, next door to the United States Branch Mint. The superintendent of the mint, Robert B. Swain (1822–72), rented offices in the building; Harte worked as his secretary from 1863 to 1869, a position that left him ample time to write (*CofC,* 12, 227–28; 29 Dec 1868 to Langdon, *L2,* 363 n. 9; Scharnhorst 2000a, 18). Clemens describes Swain's patronage of Harte in the Autobiographical Dictation of 14 June 1906.

118.3–5 Harte was doing a good deal of writing for *The Californian* . . . I was a contributor] Harte edited the *Californian* from 10 September to 19 November 1864, and was probably responsible for accepting Clemens's first nine literary contributions to the journal (25 Sept 1864 to JLC and PAM, *L1,* 314 n. 5). Harte described his "Condensed Novels" as "a humorous *condensation* of the salient characteristics of certain writers" (Harte 1867). These parodies of well-known authors—such as James Fenimore Cooper, Charles Dickens, and Victor Hugo—were widely praised. The first two appeared in the *Golden Era* in August 1862, and the series continued in the *Californian* from July 1865 to June 1866. In 1867 Harte collected all fifteen pieces in *Condensed Novels. And Other Papers* (New York: G. W. Carleton and Co.) (Scharnhorst 1995, 83–84, 92–98; Scharnhorst 2000a, 25–26).

118.5–7 Charles H. Webb; also Prentice Mulford . . . Charles Warren Stoddard] For Webb see the Autobiographical Dictation of 21 May, note at 46.23–25; for Mulford and Stoddard see *AutoMT1,* 509–10 n. 150.2–4, 516 n. 161.27–30. Hastings has not been identified.

118.7–9 Ambrose Bierce, who is still writing acceptably for the magazines . . . *Golden Era,* perhaps] In 1905–6 Bierce wrote primarily for the New York *American* and *Cosmopolitan* magazine, to which he contributed a column called "The Passing Show." He was not in San Francisco in 1864 (he was fighting in the Union army), nor did he publish anything in the *Golden Era* until July 1868. Clemens is probably recalling his own last visit to the West Coast, in the spring and early summer of 1868: in March of that year, Bierce began contributing articles regularly to the San Francisco *News Letter and California Advertiser,* and he later stated that he first met Clemens in the offices of that newspaper (Morris 1995, 117, 238–40; Joshi and Schultz 1999, 75–76, 238–51; *AutoMT1,* 509–10 n. 150.2–4).

118.13–20 Harte had arrived in California . . . campers were satisfied with it and adopted it] Harte arrived in California in 1854—when he was seventeen—to join his mother, who had recently remarried. He is not known to have been in Yreka, which is in Siskiyou County. It is likely that Clemens confused "Yreka" with "Eureka" (see the note at 118.21–23). He makes the same error in the Autobiographical Dictation of 4 February 1907. "Yreka" is thought to derive from a Native American name for Mount Shasta (George R. Stewart 1931, 29–30; Gudde 1962, 353).

118.21–23 Harte taught school . . . Jackass Gulch (where I tarried, some years later, during three months)] In the summer of 1857 Harte left San Francisco to join his married sister in Union (or Uniontown, now Arcata), on the coast near Eureka in Humboldt County. He taught school, and then in December 1858 was hired as a printer's assistant on the town's newspaper, the *Northern Californian.* His sojourn at Jackass Hill, near the mining town of Jackass Gulch in Tuolumne County, predated his time in Uniontown: according to Jim Gillis, Harte stayed with him briefly in December 1855 in his cabin there. Clemens visited the area several years later, in the winter of 1864–65. He describes some of his experiences in the Autobiographical Dictations of 23 January and 4 February 1907 (George R. Stewart 1931, 52–53, 75–88; Gudde 1962, 13; O'Connor 1966, 32; Gillis 1930, 178–81; *AutoMT1,* 552–53 n. 261.21–24).

118.30–31 quaint dialect of the miner . . . until Harte invented it] Clemens also criticized Harte's unauthentic dialect in chapter 7 of *Is Shakespeare Dead?*

> I know the *argot* of the quartz-mining and milling industry familiarly; and so whenever Bret Harte introduces that industry into a story, the first time one of his miners opens his mouth I recognize from his phrasing that Harte got the phrasing by listening—like Shakespeare—I mean the Stratford one—not by experience. No one can talk the quartz dialect correctly without learning it with pick and shovel and drill and fuse. (SLC 1909c, 74–75)

Clemens had been sharply dismissive of Harte's use of dialect since at least 1873 (see *N&J1,* 553). He repeated his criticism in various (undated) marginalia on Harte's works. For example, in his own copy of *The Luck of Roaring Camp, and Other Sketches* he wrote, "Miggles is an excellent sketch. The girl's 'dialect' is not good, but it has at least *one* saving feature—it is difficult to explain *why* it isn't good, or point out the precise errors. It has a grand *general* badness" (Harte 1870a, 55; Clemens's marginalia in this volume are published in Booth 1954).

118.32–33 By and by he . . . got work in the *Golden Era* office] In February 1860, while substituting for the absent editor of the *Northern Californian,* Harte published an article condemning a local massacre of Native American women and children. He was allegedly forced to leave Uniontown, and returned to San Francisco. He had previously published some writings—both verse and prose—in the *Golden Era* in 1857–58, and he soon joined the staff as a compositor (O'Connor 1966, 42–47; Scharnhorst 1995, 3–4).

Autobiographical Dictation, 14 June 1906

118.36–37 Joe Lawrence] See *AutoMT1,* 509–10 n. 150.2–4.

119.32–36 he came East five years later, in 1870, to take the editorship . . . lamented absence] Harte had edited the highly successful *Overland Monthly* since 1868, and his publications in that journal had brought him instant celebrity (see the note at 120.6–17). Eager to establish his reputation in the East, he left San Francisco for Boston on 2 February 1871. In Chicago he was offered a position as editor and part owner of the newly conceived *Lakeside Monthly.* (The magazine was a relaunch of the *Western Monthly,* founded in 1869; it was fairly successful until the financial panic of 1873.) But he snubbed the backers of the new enterprise by failing to show up at a banquet in his honor and continued east. At the time, Clemens described Harte's journey as "a perfect torchlight procession of eclat & homage. All the cities are fussing about which shall secure him for a citizen" (3 Mar 1871 to Riley, *L4,* 338, 339 n. 6; Mott 1938b, 404–6, 413–16).

119.37–38 crossed the ocean to be Consul, first at Crefeld, in Germany, and afterwards in Glasgow] In mid-1877 Clemens heard that President Hayes was likely to award Harte a diplomatic post. He wrote to Howells:

> Three or four times lately I have read items to the effect that Bret Harte is trying to get a Consulship. To-day's item says he *is* to have one.
>
> Now if I knew the President, I would venture to write him, for he has said that in the matter of information about applicants for office he values the testimony of private citizens as well as that of Members of Congress.
>
> You *do* know him; & I think your citizenship lays the duty upon you of doing what you can to prevent the disgrace of literature & the country which would be the infallible result of the appointment of Bret Harte to any responsible post. Wherever he goes his wake is tumultuous with swindled grocers, & with defrauded innocents who have loaned him money. He *never* pays a debt but by the squeezing of the law. He borrows from all new acquaintances, & repays none. His oath is worth little, his promise nothing at all. He can lie faster than he can drivel false pathos. He is always steeped in whisky & brandy; he gets up in the night to drink it cold. No man who has ever known him, respects him. Harte is a viler character than Geo. Butler, for he lacks Butler's pluck & spirit.
>
> You know that I have befriended this creature for seven years. I am even capable of doing it still—while he stays at home. But I don't want to see him sent to foreign parts to carry on his depredations. He told me many months ago that he was to have a consulship under Mr. Tilden, but I gave myself no concern about the matter, taking it as a mere after-breakfast lie to whet up his talent for the day's villainies; & besides, I judged that his character was so well known that he would not be able to succeed in his nefarious design. But these newspaper items have an alarming look. Come, now, Howells, do a stroke for the honor of the guild. Put me under oath if you will. (21 June 1877 to Howells [1st], *Letters 1876–1880*)

Later the same day he withdrew his request, explaining that he had needed to "have an outlet" for his feelings. He knew Howells would find his request "disagreeable," because his wife was President Hayes's cousin. Howells nevertheless forwarded the letters to Hayes (21 June 1877 to Howells [2nd], *Letters 1876–1880; MTHL,* 1:186). In April 1878 Howells wrote an extremely candid letter about Harte to the president:

> I am reluctant to say anything about the matter you refer to me, but I will do so at your request. Personally, I have a great affection for the man, and personally I know nothing to his disadvantage. He spent a week with us at Cambridge when he first came East, and we all liked him. He was lax about appointments, but that is a common fault. After he went away, he began to contract debts, and was arrested for debt in Boston. (I saw this.) He is notorious for borrowing and *was* notorious for drinking. This is *report.* He never borrowed of *me,* nor drank more than I, (in my presence) and yesterday I saw his doctor who says his habits are good, now; I have heard the same thing from others. From what I hear he is really making an effort to reform. It would be a godsend to him, if he could get such a place; for he is poor,

> and he writes with difficulty and very little. He has had the worst reputation as regards punctuality, solvency and sobriety; but he has had a terrible lesson in falling from the highest prosperity to the lowest adversity in literature, and—you are good enough judge of men to know whether he will profit by it or not.
>
> *Personally,* I should be glad of his appointment, and I should have great hopes of him—and fears. It would be easy to recall him, if he misbehaved, and a hint of such a fate would be useful to him.
>
> —I must beg that you will not show this letter to anyone whatever, but will kindly return it to me at Cambridge. (Howells 1979, 194–95)

Harte was appointed in May as "commercial agent" (consul) at Crefeld (near Düsseldorf), and he departed for his post on 27 June ("Departures for Europe," New York *Times,* 27 June 1878, 3). Upon hearing the news, Clemens wrote Howells that Harte was "a sot, a sponge, a coward," and opined that the president had "simply pocketed his own ball" (27 June 1878 to Howells, *Letters 1876–1880*). Harte disliked Germany, and remained in Crefeld only two years before receiving a transfer to Glasgow, where he served as consul from 1880 to 1885.

119.39–40 When he died, in London . . . twenty-six years] See the Autobiographical Dictation of 4 February 1907, notes at 417.24–27 and 422.4–7.

120.6–17 he had written "The Heathen Chinee" for amusement . . . finer glory of "The Luck of Roaring Camp,"] The *Overland Monthly* was founded in 1868 by Anton Roman, a San Francisco bookseller and publisher, to replace the defunct *Californian.* Harte, its chief editor and a major contributor, published his "Luck of Roaring Camp" in the second issue, in August (Harte 1868). This tale of California miners was received without enthusiasm in the West, but its startling popularity in the East ensured the journal's success. In his own copy of *The Luck of Roaring Camp, and Other Sketches* Clemens noted, "This is Bret's very best sketch, & most finished—is nearly blemishless" (Harte 1870a, 18). Clemens misremembers the publication dates of the two sketches: Harte's best-known dialect poem, "Plain Language from Truthful James" (better known as "The Heathen Chinee"), followed "The Luck of Roaring Camp," appearing in the *Overland Monthly* in September 1870 (Harte 1870c; he made the same error in a letter to *Harper's Weekly* dated 5 Oct 1905, RPB-JH). Although Harte himself allegedly considered it "trash" and "the worst poem I ever wrote," it brought him immediate fame and was republished in countless journals and anthologies. Clemens later consented, reluctantly, to include it in *Mark Twain's Library of Humor* (1888). In March 1882 he wrote to Howells:

> I am at work upon Bret Harte, but am not enjoying it. He is the worst literary shoe-maker, I know. He is as blind as a bat. He never sees anything correctly, except Californian scenery. He is as slovenly as Thackeray, and as dull as Charles Lamb. The things which you and Clark have marked, are plenty good enough in their way, but to my jaundiced eye, they do seem to be lamentably barren of humor. Still I think we want some funereal rot in the book as a foil. (23 Mar 1882 to Howells, MH-H, in *MTHL,* 1:396)

The *Library of Humor* included three additional Harte selections: "A Jersey Centenarian," "A Sleeping-Car Experience," and "The Society on the Stanislaus" (SLC 1888, 89–92, 352–58, 642–48, 679–80; Scharnhorst 2000a, 36–43; for *Mark Twain's Library of Humor* see AD, 2 June 1906, note at 77.20–22).

120.17–22 "Tennessee's Partner," . . . "Gabriel Conroy,"] "Tennessee's Partner" was published in the *Overland Monthly* in October 1869 and collected in *The Luck of Roaring Camp, and Other Sketches.* In his copy of the book Clemens commented, "In this sketch the 'dialect' is much better done than is usual with Harte; but the gambling slang introduces 'bowers' into poker, where they do not belong." In addition, he noted that it was "much more suggestive of Dickens & an English atmosphere than 'Pike County'" (Harte 1869b, 1870a, 62, 71). For *Gabriel Conroy* see the Autobiographical Dictation of 4 February 1907 and the notes at 421.16–22 and 421.35–40.

120.38–41 undertook to give all the product of its brain . . . spent the money before the year was out] Harte wrote to James Osgood, publisher (with James T. Fields) of the *Atlantic Monthly* and *Every Saturday,* on 6 March 1871: "I accept your offer of $10,000 for the exclusive publication of my poems and sketches (not to be less than 12 in no.) in your periodicals for the space of one year commencing Mar. 1st 1871" (CU-BANC, in Harte 1997, 48). This generous fee was said to be the largest in the history of any American magazine. It took Harte a year and a half to fulfill his contract, but he had contributed twelve tales and poems to both publications by September 1872. They were not up to the standard of his earlier work, however, and even he acknowledged that at least one was "poor stuff" (Harte 1997, 61–62; O'Connor 1966, 145–46; Scharnhorst 2000a, 77–87; Scharnhorst 1995, 48–51, 132–34).

Autobiographical Dictation, 18 June 1906

122.6–10 and not to strangers, but to personal friends of mine . . . Mrs Williams] On the day of this dictation Isabel Lyon noted in her journal: "In an old sack of letters sent to SLC from Keokuk about 5 years ago he unearthed a batch of 5 letters this morning which are a romance & a tragedy. Today he dictated in the house & his topic was the 5 letters and their tragedy, a dictation to be published 500 years hence" (Lyon 1906, entry for 18 June). Two of the characters figuring in the drama that unfolds in the correspondence below were not "strangers," as Clemens claims: "Mrs Williams" is a pseudonym for Mollie Clemens, the wife of Clemens's brother Orion, who is referred to here as "Mr. W." Orion and Mollie were both dead, but even so, the opinion of her that Clemens admits to here is clearly too scornful for public expression. For example, at one point he says, "I feel disrespectfully toward that machine-made Christian who writes the second one. I think that *in her heart* she turned the friendless refugee and the baby into the street in the raw March weather" (126.37–40). (Clemens was momentarily confused. Although Mollie was the second in his cast of characters—"No. 2 is evidently elderly, and apparently has some education" [121.36–37]—she actually wrote the fourth letter. The first two were written by the same woman, Mrs. Griffiths.) Clemens usually carried out his self-censorship when revising the typescripts of his dictations. In this instance, however, he asked Lyon to alter the letter manuscripts even before they were transcribed, substituting "Williams" and "Detroit" for every mention of "Clemens" and "Keokuk." When he planned to publish the dictation in the *North American Review* (it never appeared there), he disguised the other names and cities. In the present text, the suppression of "Clemens" and "Keokuk" is accepted, but the other names are left as in the original manuscripts, since the second round of revision was carried out strictly for contemporary publication (for details see the Textual Commentary at *MTPO*). The letter manuscripts have been transcribed verbatim, with no correction of spelling or punctuation.

127.27–28 I shall finish with Bret Harte by and by] Clemens does not return to the subject of Harte until the Autobiographical Dictation of 4 February 1907.

127.29–40 he reminds me of God . . . only really important thing in it] On the typescript of the present dictation, Clemens noted that his remarks about God on the "last 2 pages must be postponed to the edition of A.D. 2406."

Autobiographical Dictation, 19 June 1906

128.3–4 Our Bible reveals to us the character of our God with minute and remorseless exactness] On 17 June Clemens wrote to Howells,

> To-morrow I mean to dictate a chapter which will get my heirs & assigns burnt alive if they venture to print it this side of 2006 A.D.—which I judge they won't. There'll be lots of such chapters if I live 3 or 4 years longer. The edition of A.D. 2006 will make a stir when it comes out. I shall be hovering around taking notice, along with other dead pals. You are invited. (NN-BGC, in *MTHL,* 2:810–12)

On 18 June he began to dictate the ideas about God and the Bible that he thought would get him "ostracized" if published before his death, but after only two paragraphs his interest was diverted, and he postponed his potentially offensive ideas until the following day. He continues to talk about religion in four more dictations, concluding with the Autobiographical Dictation of 25 June 1906.

129.25–26 seventy times seven times] Matthew 18:22.

Autobiographical Dictation, 20 June 1906

130.24 We borrow the Golden Rule from Confucius] In the nineteenth century Western commentators began to note that Confucius had given the equivalent of the "Golden Rule" (Matthew 7:12) five hundred years before Christ. Analects 15:23 reads, in part: "What you do not want done to yourself, do not do to others."

130.25–29 When we want a Deluge we go away back to hoary Babylon and borrow it . . . The flood is a favorite with Bible-makers] The story of a universal flood is present in a great number of the world's mythologies. A Babylonian myth of the flood was discovered in 1872, when George Smith, an assistant at the British Museum, deciphered a cuneiform tablet, later identified as part of the epic of Gilgamesh. On account of its parallels to Genesis, the Babylonian version caused a sensation, and its relevance for the dating and reliability of the biblical account became a subject of widespread debate. The Babylonian text is discussed from an atheist standpoint in *Bible Myths and Their Parallels in Other Religions* by T. W. Doane, a book that Clemens is likely to have read by the time of this dictation (Budge 1925, 267–68; Doane 1882, 19–32; Gribben 1980, 1:195).

130.33 Immaculate Conception] The Roman Catholic doctrine that Mary herself was conceived and born free of original sin. Clemens, however, refers to the doctrine that she conceived Jesus by divine intervention and not by natural procreation.

130.35–37 Hindoos prized it . . . Buddhists were happy when they acquired Gautama by the same process] In Hindu tradition, Krishna, the most important avatar of the god Vishnu, was miraculously conceived and saved from murder at birth through divine intervention. In one Buddhist tradition, a virgin conceived Siddhartha Gautama (the Buddha) after dreaming that a white elephant entered into her side. Both these miraculous conceptions are discussed by Doane (see the note at 130.25–29); Clemens's copy is heavily marked in the chapter on "The Miraculous Birth of Christ Jesus" (Doane 1882, 114–17, 280; Gribben 1980, 1:195).

131.5–7 Episcopal clergyman in Rochester . . . did not believe that the Savior was miraculously conceived] On 9 May 1906, Algernon Sidney Crapsey (1847–1927), minister of St. Andrew's church in Rochester since 1879, was convicted of heresy by an ecclesiastical court for views he had expressed in his sermons and published in *Religion and Politics* (1905). He denied "doctrines that Jesus Christ is God, the Saviour of the world; that He was conceived by the Holy Ghost; of His virgin birth, of His resurrection, and of the Blessed Trinity" (New York *Times:* "Dr. Crapsey a Heretic," 16 May 1906, 9; "Crapsey Verdict Reached," 10 May 1906, 1; "Crapsey Files an Appeal," 7 June 1906, 6). Having appealed the verdict without success, Crapsey renounced his ministry in November 1906. In his autobiography, *The Last of the Heretics,* he described himself as a "Pantheistic Humanist" (Crapsey 1924, 232, 272, 276, 292).

131.7–17 Rev. Dr. Briggs, who is perhaps the most daringly broad-minded . . . in a position to know] Charles Augustus Briggs (1841–1913) was a prominent clergyman, biblical and Hebrew scholar, and professor at Union Theological Seminary in New York from 1874 until his death. He was suspended from the Presbyterian ministry in 1893 after being convicted of heresy by an ecclesiastical court. Despite his continued espousal of radical views he was later ordained an Episcopal minister. A prolific author, he published at least two hundred books and articles and remained one of the most influential theologians of his day. The article on the virgin birth that Clemens cites, "Criticism and

Dogma," appeared in the *North American Review* for June 1906 (Briggs 1906). Part of Briggs's argument is that the angels who announced the coming birth must have been "reliable witnesses," and that Joseph and Mary could not have given false testimony because it would be "inconsistent with their character." Furthermore, the story "had the sanction of James and Jude of the family of Jesus" and was therefore "too near the birth of Jesus, in temporal, geographical and personal relations, to go astray in so important a matter" (865–66).

132.3–4 some addled Christian Scientist . . . Mother Eddy] See the Autobiographical Dictation of 22 June 1906, note at 136.10–12.

Autobiographical Dictation, 22 June 1906

132.35–133.3 For two years, now . . . the ultra-Christian Government of Russia has been officially ordering and conducting massacres of its Jewish subjects] In the early years of the century, the government of Tsar Nicholas II (who ruled from 1894 to 1918) promoted vicious anti-Semitism. In April 1903, at the instigation of both high-level and local officials, violence erupted in Kishinev at Passover. A Christian mob with the backing of the police and the army murdered about fifty Jews and injured five hundred. Thereafter the government participated in numerous pogroms, one of which occurred in Kishinev in October 1905, when rioters killed about twenty Jews.

133.11–12 Horrible details have been sent out by the correspondent of the Bourse Gazette, who arrived in Bialystok] Clemens had a clipping of this portion of the article, from the New York *Times* of 19 June, pasted into the typescript of this dictation. The pogroms of June 1906 in Bialystok (now in northeastern Poland), abetted both by local police and by higher authorities, resulted in the murder of as many as two hundred Jews.

134.4–5 massacre of the Albigenses] The Albigenses were members of a medieval religious sect in southern France, concentrated in the area of Albi. They were ascetics who practiced chastity and vegetarianism. Their exact creed is unclear, since it is described primarily by their enemies, but some of their doctrines were apparently of non-Christian origin, and they were persecuted by the Catholic Church as heretics. In 1208 Pope Innocent III ordered a crusade against them, in which many people were slaughtered, regardless of age, sex, or creed. The crusade led to an official Inquisition, and the sect became extinct.

134.7 Bartholomew's Day] On 24 August 1572, the feast of Saint Bartholomew, a group of Huguenot (Calvinist Protestant) leaders were assassinated in Paris at the instigation of Catherine de' Medici, mother of King Charles IX. These assassinations triggered a growing massacre, which during the following week spread to the provinces, where over the next two months Catholic mobs murdered thousands of Huguenots.

134.11 The Gospel of Peace] Romans 10:15 (paraphrasing Isaiah 52:7): "How beautiful are the feet of them that preach the gospel of peace."

134.13–16 George III reigned sixty years . . . public rejoicing in England] George III (1738–1820) reigned from 1760 until his death. Clemens witnessed Queen Victoria's celebration of her Record Reign and Diamond Jubilee in London in June 1897, and wrote three newspaper reports about it (*AutoMT1,* 501 n. 126.19).

134.17–18 for each year of the sixty of her reign . . . a separate and distinct war] The London *Standard* noted that during Victoria's sixty years on the throne "it would be possible to name sixty nations or races over whom the Queen's arms have triumphed; they have varied from civilised and powerful States to the naked savages of Africa and the Southern Seas, and these wars have been rewarded with an immense addition of territory and influence" ("The Queen's Wars," 22 June 1897, 2). Another news item, started by the radical *Reynolds's Newspaper* and widely reprinted in America, enumerated forty-two wars, from the Afghan War (1838–40) to the Bombardment of the Cretan Christians (1897) ("Always at War," 28 Feb 1897, 1).

134.28 Alexander VI] Pope Alexander VI (born Rodrigo Borgia, 1431–1503) was infamous for his corruption and moral turpitude. He imprisoned and murdered his enemies to confiscate their wealth, and gave away the church's assets to the children he fathered with several mistresses.

134.38–135.1 each Christian Government has played with its neighbors . . . We are in it, ourselves, now] In the late 1880s the major European powers began to build up their navies, increasing their production of battleships in an effort to intimidate the enemy and deter aggression. By the fall of 1905 Britain had in service, or under construction, sixty-six battleships; France had forty; and Germany had thirty-seven. The Russian fleet, however, had been reduced from twenty-seven to ten by what Clemens calls the "untaught stranger" (Japan) in the Russo-Japanese War of 1904–5. In 1906 Britain commissioned the *Dreadnought,* an innovative warship whose size, speed, and gun power made earlier models obsolete. The United States adopted the new design, immediately undertaking the construction of two battleships. This naval arms race significantly increased the tensions that led to the First World War (Sondhaus 2002, 102–8, 127, 131–35; Spears 1908, 305).

136.10–12 "Science and Health" . . . Mrs. Mary Baker G. Eddy] The Church of Christ, Scientist, is a denomination based on the theories set forth in *Science and Health* (1875) by Mary Baker Eddy (1821–1910). According to its tenets, material life is illusory, and only the spiritual realm is real; therefore disease is imaginary, and through Christian faith people can be healed. Clemens both praised and criticized Eddy. He believed to some extent in the curative power of the mind and acknowledged her organizational ability, but he found her writings ludicrous and largely incoherent, and possibly authored by someone else. Furthermore, he denounced her as a hypocritical and power-hungry fraud and deplored the growing popularity of her theology. Clemens owned (or at least consulted) as many as six different editions of *Science and Health,* ranging in date from 1881 to 1902; volume 2 of the 1884 edition, with his sparse marginalia, survives in the Mark Twain Papers (Eddy 1884; *WIM,* 271, 293, 339, 554–55, 575). He first attacked

Christian Science in an article in *Cosmopolitan* in 1899, and again in the *North American Review* in 1902–3. These articles were expanded and published as *Christian Science* in 1907 (SLC 1899c, 1902c, 1903b, 1903c, 1903d, 1907a). His views did not, however, deter his only surviving daughter, Clara, from becoming a Christian Scientist after experiencing more than one "miraculous" cure. In 1956 she described her conversion, and explained her father's views on Eddy, in *Awake to a Perfect Day* (CC 1956). Clemens returns to the subject in the Autobiographical Dictations of 5 October and 27 December 1906. For comprehensive discussions of the matter see: *WIM,* 20–28, 553–77; Stoneley 1992, 116–45; Wills's "Introduction: Twain and Eddy" and Hill's "Afterword" in SLC 1996a; see also Gribben 1980, 1:212–13.

Autobiographical Dictation, 23 June 1906

137.31–38 Mr. Garfield lay near to death . . . died, just the same] President James A. Garfield (b. 1831) was shot on 2 July 1881 by Charles J. Guiteau (b. 1841). Destitute and unemployed, Guiteau had written a campaign speech that he claimed entitled him to a diplomatic post. While Garfield lingered with a bullet lodged near his pancreas, reports of prayers offered for his recovery appeared in the newspapers (see, for example, Washington *Post:* "The People's Prayers," 4 July 1881, 4; "Invoking Divine Aid," 22 Aug 1881, 4). He suffered from repeated infections before dying of a heart attack on 19 September. Guiteau was hanged in June 1882.

137.40–138.21 Boer population was a hundred and fifty thousand . . . confidence in the righteousness and intelligence of God impaired] The Second Boer War (1899–1902) was fought between Britain and the Dutch (Boer) colonies in southern Africa. Hostilities began when British gold miners in Boer territories protested being denied equal rights. British troops were sent to defend them, and the Boers declared war. At first the Boers were victorious, but began to lose ground when additional British forces arrived. The Boers continued to wage guerrilla warfare, but were ultimately overcome by the British, who prevailed by imprisoning (and thereby often killing) thousands of Boer civilians in concentration camps. By the time a peace treaty was signed in May 1902, British troops numbered three hundred and fifty thousand, while the Boers had only sixty thousand. The ideas that Clemens expresses here echo those in "The War-Prayer," written in March 1905. Clemens submitted this brief tale to *Harper's Bazar,* but the editor, Elizabeth Jordan, returned it on 22 March 1905 "with regret," explaining that it was "admirable, but not quite suited to a woman's magazine, in my opinion" (CU-MARK). On 30 March Clemens told Dan Beard, "I don't think the prayer will be published in my time. None but the dead are permitted to tell the truth" (DLC). It was not published in full until 1923, when Paine included it in *Europe and Elsewhere* (SLC 1923a, 394–98).

138.42–139.6 spider was so contrived . . . chew her legs off at their leisure] Clemens had previously discussed his view of "Nature's infernal inventions for the infliction of needless suffering" in his 1895 notebook: "Nature's attitude toward all life is profoundly vicious, treacherous & malignant" (Notebook 34, TS p. 31, CU-MARK). He probably learned about the cruel behavior of the parasitic wasp in Darwin's *Origin of Species,* and was no doubt aware that Darwin mentioned it when describing his own struggle to believe in a beneficent Deity. *The Life and Letters of Charles Darwin* (which, according to Isabel Lyon, Clemens borrowed from the library in late 1905) includes a letter of 22 May 1860 from Darwin to Asa Gray, which reads in part:

> With respect to the theological view of the question. This is always painful to me. I am bewildered. I had no intention to write atheistically. But I own that I cannot see as plainly as others do, and as I should wish to do, evidence of design and beneficence on all sides of us. There seems to me too much misery in the world. I cannot persuade myself that a beneficent and omnipotent God would have designedly created the Ichneumonidae with the express intention of their feeding within the living bodies of Caterpillars, or that a cat should play with mice. (Darwin 1887, 2:105)

Clemens reiterates this idea, again citing the example of the wasp, in the Autobiographical Dictation of 4 February 1907 (5th section) (Darwin 1884, 234, 415; Gribben 1980, 1:176; Lyon 1905b, entry for 17 Oct).

Autobiographical Dictation, 25 June 1906

142.14 Man is not to blame for what he is] Many of Clemens's remarks in this Autobiographical Dictation reprise his philosophy in *What Is Man?*—an essay in dialog format that he printed anonymously, for private distribution, in 1906. At the time of this dictation, he was revising and proofreading the text, which was printed by the De Vinne Press. Clemens discusses the work further in the Autobiographical Dictations of 4 September 1907 and 2 November 1908 (*WIM,* 11–20).

Autobiographical Dictation, 17 July 1906

143.8–10 Five or six weeks ago . . . third publisher] See the Autobiographical Dictations of 21 May through 2 June 1906.

143.22 Mr. Duneka] Frederick A. Duneka (1859–1919), a native of Kentucky, was a colleague of George Harvey's on the New York *World,* serving as its city editor. When Harvey became president of Harper and Brothers in 1900, he installed Duneka as secretary of the board of directors and general manager. Duneka had editorial dealings with Clemens, Howells, Henry James, and Theodore Dreiser, among many others. He was named vice-president of Harpers in 1915, but illness soon forced him into retirement (Colby 1920, 461; "Frederick A. Duneka Dead," New York *Times,* 25 Jan 1919, 11; Curtis 1890; Exman 1967, 187–88, 209, 211; see also the note at 146.6–9).

143.30–31 Bliss captured my thirty thousand dollars, but I made it cost him a quarter of a million thirteen years afterward] Clemens describes negotiating the *Rough-*

ing It contract with Elisha Bliss in the Autobiographical Dictation of 23 May 1906. His conviction that Bliss had cheated him of $30,000 is based on his conjectural estimate of "half profits" on a sale of 150,000 copies—a figure he claimed came from Bliss himself. Clemens's remark "I made it cost him a quarter of a million" refers to Francis E. Bliss (1843–1915), who had succeeded his father in 1880 as president of the American Publishing Company. The estimated profits are those Frank could have had, hypothetically, from *Huckleberry Finn,* published in 1885 by Clemens's own firm of Charles L. Webster and Company (*AutoMT1,* 370–71; SLC 1903a).

143.34–144.5 Harpers had half of them, and the American Publishing Company . . . had changed his mind] By the terms of a contract made in 1895, the American Publishing Company retained the rights to the seven books it had originally published, while Harpers had the rights to eight books and *Mark Twain's Library of Humor*—works originally published by James R. Osgood or by Charles L. Webster and Company. In 1896 the two companies reached an agreement allowing the American Publishing Company to publish uniform sets of Clemens's collected works—the Autograph, Royal, and Riverdale editions, among others—which included the books owned by Harpers. Over the course of 1903, the purchase of the rights to Clemens's American Publishing Company books—amounting in effect to the purchase of the entire company—was considered first by Clemens himself, then by P. F. Collier and Son, and finally by Harpers. Clemens's summary of these negotiations is generally accurate so far as it can be verified. It is unclear why Harpers should have been deterred, as Clemens says they were, by Collier's offer to publish a subscription set, but by August it had become clear that Harpers intended to be Mark Twain's exclusive publisher: as Frank Bliss wrote in his diary, they "wanted to get the whole business & had blood in their eyes" (Schmidt 2010, chapter 6). Harpers realized that ambition by the terms of contracts signed in October 1903 (*HHR,* 534 n. 3, 671–77, 678–81, 691–99, 700–708; *AutoMT1,* 596–97 n. 371.35–372.2; Bliss to SLC, 27 June 1903, ViU; Harper and Brothers [London] to Chatto and Windus, 2 Nov 1903, UkReU).

144.7–10 I wrote some Christian Science articles . . . that announcement was made] Clemens published four articles on Christian Science in the *North American Review,* in December 1902, January and February 1903, and April 1903. Harpers announced the volume *Christian Science* in *Publishers' Weekly* on 21 March 1903 (772) (SLC 1902c, 1903b, 1903c, 1903d; see also AD, 22 June 1906, note at 136.10–12).

144.24–27 Mr. Duneka said . . . publication had been postponed until the fall] In a letter drafted at the time of these events, Clemens said this ruse was his own idea:

> The form agreed upon with Mr. Duneka was carefully chosen—& of course departed from. It was, "too late, now, for a spring book, therefore *postponed until autumn.*" This was to save my face, & was my suggestion: I did not want the fact exposed that a book of mine had been (in effect) declined.
>
> The situation is not barren of humor: I had been doing my very best to show in print that the X-Scientist cult was become a power in the land—well, here was

proof: it had scared the biggest publisher in the Union! (On or after 20 Apr 1903 to Anderson, CU-MARK)

144.32–39 *Publishers' Weekly* of April 11th, 1903 . . . a Pittsburgh bookseller sent it to me] Remarkably, Clemens remembered the exact date of the announcement. On 24 June 1906 he had asked Isabel Lyon to find the 1903 *Publishers' Weekly* for "some time in April, about the 11th an insulting advertisement signed by the Harpers" (Lyon Stenographic Notebook #1, CU-MARK). The announcement read: "Neither Harper & Brothers nor the *North American Review* will publish in book form Mark Twain's papers on 'Christian Science.' All orders for the book now on file will be cancelled" (*Publishers' Weekly,* 11 Apr 1903, 984). No letter from a "Pittsburgh bookseller" has been found.

145.9–10 Duneka . . . would make that book volume XXIV of my Collected Works] In April 1905 Duneka wrote to Clemens (in a letter no longer extant) outlining his plan to add *Christian Science* to Harpers' collected editions of Mark Twain's works. This was not done, however, and in 1906, believing that Harpers had no plans to publish *Christian Science,* Clemens demanded the return of the manuscript; Harpers did not publish the book until 1907 (11 Apr 1905 to Morel, Wuliger 1953, 235–36; 13 June 1906 to Rogers, CtHMTH, in *HHR,* 610; *WIM,* 22–23).

145.17–19 I wrote an unfriendly article about the Butcher, King Leopold . . . publish it as soon as possible] In late 1904 Clemens promised Edmund Dene Morel, the secretary of the British Congo Reform Association, a magazine article exposing the depredations of King Leopold II in the Congo Free State. He finished "King Leopold's Soliloquy" in February 1905. The *North American Review* rejected it as too controversial, so Clemens published it the following September as a pamphlet, with the profits going to the association (Hawkins 1978, 153–56; 11 Apr 1905 to Morel, Wuliger 1953, 235–36; SLC 1905a; for Clemens's other comments on King Leopold see AD, 3 Apr 1906).

145.19–24 he had employed Mr. Nevinson . . . Mr. Nevinson's first article appeared] Harvey sent British journalist Henry Woodd Nevinson (1856–1941) to Portuguese West Africa (now Angola) in late 1904 to report on the practice of plantation slavery there. Nevinson's findings were published in a series of seven articles in *Harper's Monthly* between August 1905 and February 1906 (Satre 2005, 2–12; Exman 1967, 251).

145.36–146.2 short story called "A Horse's Tale," . . . he did not explain what the trouble was] Clemens wrote "A Horse's Tale" in late 1905, and it was published in *Harper's Monthly* in August and September 1906. He describes the impetus for writing it in the Autobiographical Dictation of 29 August 1906. In a letter of 8 May 1906, Duneka told him that "A Horse's Tale" was a "greater story" than his essay about Howells (scheduled for the July issue), and no evidence has been found that he objected to anything in it (CU-MARK; SLC 1906g, 1906h). The manuscript of the story (now at NN-BGC) does not contain any passage about priests hurrying to "see the butcheries" in the bullring; but there is a passage omitted from the final version, almost wholly anticlerical, which survives in the Mark Twain Papers. In this fragment of six sheets, a horse relates that the bullring's "principal boxes are reserved for the clergy," with other remarks about the participation of priests in the bullfight (MS in CU-MARK, 114D-E-F).

146.6–9 Last summer, Mr. Duneka wanted . . . that priest reformed or left out] In July 1905 Duneka visited Clemens at his summer retreat in Dublin, New Hampshire. Lyon recorded his reaction to "No. 44, the Mysterious Stranger," the fourth and last version of the story: "Mr. Duneka shrivelled up over the first part of Forty Four because there is that evil priest Father Adolph in it" (Lyon 1905a, entry for 12 July; *MSM,* 221–405). After Clemens's death Duneka and Paine undertook to publish *The Mysterious Stranger: A Romance* (1916), using as the basis of their text the earliest version, "The Chronicle of Young Satan," in which the profane priest Father Adolf also appears; Duneka and Paine eliminated him, replacing him with an astrologer of their own invention (SLC 1916; Tuckey 1963, 19–20; see also AD, 30 Aug 1906, note at 196.39–42).

146.18–21 My contract with the Harpers of three years ago puts all my books permanently in their possession . . . "Mark Twain's Library of Humor."] The 1903 contract is described in the Autobiographical Dictation of 7 August 1906, note at 160.32–36. For the *Library of Humor,* published by Charles L. Webster and Company in 1888, see the Autobiographical Dictation of 2 June 1906, note at 77.20–22.

146.37–147.9 Mr. Duneka said that he had heard that a "pirate" out West . . . I wrote him and consented to that] In October 1905 Duneka proposed to Clemens that Harpers reissue the book to foil some "more or less obscure publishers in the West" who were "threatening" to publish an unauthorized edition: "This we would do not only for the purpose of selling it but with a view to preventing any other person from using the title or issuing a similar book. . . . What we are looking for chiefly is protection of your name in the first place, rather than profits which are of secondary importance in this matter." Clemens replied three days later, "Go ahead & issue the Library & pay me what you think is fair in the way of a royalty" (Duneka to SLC, 6 Oct 1905, CU-MARK; 9 Oct 1905 to Duneka, NN-C; for the pirate "out West" see AD, 31 July 1906, and the note at 152.28). Duneka wrote that because the *Library* was "not matter which you have written yourself" there was not "much money in it in the way of royalty"; he offered 3 percent, which Clemens accepted (Duneka to SLC, 11 Oct 1905, CU-MARK; contract in CU-MARK).

147.17–18 That detail privileges Mr. Duneka to . . . "bring it up to date."] Duneka assigned the task of creating a revised and expanded edition to a young Harper subeditor, Burges Johnson, who later recalled that he was charged with "keeping all of the old contents, but adding enough new matter to bring it up to date and spread it out into several volumes" (Burges Johnson 1952, 65). Each of the new volumes was roughly one-quarter material from the old *Library,* the balance being new matter chosen by Johnson.

147.24–35 About the end of last April, Mr. Duneka began to vomit . . . nor have I ever edited a line of it] Three volumes of the Harper *Library of Humor* were published in February, April, and May 1906; a fourth was in preparation—and already advertised—when Clemens at last examined the new series. On 4 June 1906 he dictated an indignant letter to Duneka: "I find that this 'Library of Humor' is not the one which was compiled by me, but is a new book, in whose compilation I have had no part." In addition, it was a real publication, not the "ostensible" one he had agreed to, and—at $1.50 per volume—was overpriced as well. Clemens demanded a halt to sales of the volumes already published and the destruction of the plates. He did not send the letter, however, but forwarded it to Henry Rogers for his review (4 June 1906 to Duneka *per* Lyon, MFai; 6 June 1906 to Rogers [1st], MFai, in *HHR,* 609–10). Clemens had, in fact, agreed to an editorial revision and expansion of the original *Library of Humor;* the "detail" he did not notice in his 19 October 1905 contract with Harpers was a clause that gave the publishers "the right to omit portions therefrom, and to add any new material thereto" (*BAL,* 2:3666–69; SLC 1906b, 1906c, 1906d, 1906e; "Notes among the Publishers," Springfield [Mass.] *Republican,* 12 July 1906, 11; contract in CU-MARK).

147.36–37 When an author is wholly unknown... 20 per cent] This estimate of royalty entitlements recapitulates Clemens's long-standing opinion—as given, for example, in "About General Grant's Memoirs" (1885)—and conforms to early twentieth-century American practice (*AutoMT1,* 78; Maurice 1908, 338; "Literary Chat," *Munsey's Magazine* 18 [Oct 1897]: 151–56).

148.14 my legal counsel] Edward Lauterbach (see AD, 30 July 1906, note at 149.11–17).

Autobiographical Dictation, 30 July 1906

149.11–17 Edward Lauterbach... the Harper lawyer, Larkin] Lauterbach (1844–1923) was a prominent New York corporate lawyer specializing in railroad cases; he was also active in the Republican party. Clemens retained him in 1904–6 and was impressed: "If I had had him 30 yrs ago I shd not have been swindled so often" (Notebook 46, TS p. 24, CU-MARK; "Edw. Lauterbach, Lawyer, Dies at 78," New York *Times,* 5 Mar 1923, 15). John Larkin (1862?–1935) was a New York lawyer specializing in copyright law. He was general counsel for Harper and Brothers for much of his professional life, serving also on the board of directors. During 1906–7 he represented Clemens in copyright, tax, and real estate affairs ("John Larkin Dead; Noted Lawyer, 73," New York *Times,* 19 Sept 1935, 25).

149.38–150.1 an early sweetheart of mine... New Orleans as guest of a relative of hers who was a pilot] Clemens met and courted Laura Mary Wright (25 December 1844–23 February 1932) between 16 and 18 May 1858, when he spent several days in New Orleans while serving as a cub pilot on the *Pennsylvania;* she was aboard the *John J. Roe* as a guest of her uncle, pilot William C. Youngblood, a friend of his (see the notes at 150.1–17 and 150.26–28). Clemens was twenty-two and she was fourteen. Despite the impression Clemens gives here that he knew Laura for only these few days, it is clear that the two corresponded for some time, and probably saw each other at least once again (see the note at 151.12–13). Evidently, at some point Laura ceased to reply to his letters; Clemens thought their correspondence had been intercepted, but in later years Laura intimated that she had broken it off: "*I* understand why Mr. C. *thought* his letters were intercepted" (Laura M. Dake to Paine, 26 Jan 1917, photocopy in CU-MARK; see AD, 29 Jan 1907). In 1862 she married lawyer Charles T. Dake (1839–96). She held several educational positions in Dallas before moving to California, where in the early twentieth century she wrote historical and mystical fiction and taught school (Edgar M. Branch, personal communication, 23 Jan 1986, CU-MARK; 6 Feb 1861 to OC and MEC, *L1,* 114 n. 7; *Dallas Census* 1880, 1299:105C; "My Sutherland-Wright Ancestry" 2011, entries for Laura Mary Wright and Charles T. S. Dake; *Missouri Marriage Records* 2011; Payne 2007, 40–43; see also the note at 151.14–20).

150.1–17 the *John J. Roe,* a steamboat whose officers I knew . . . I saw him four years ago] Clemens was a cub pilot ("steersman") on the *John J. Roe* from 5 August to 24 September 1857, plying the river between St. Louis and New Orleans. Zebulon Leavenworth (1830–77) was still an active pilot as late as 1867; his brother Mark (1827?–66), the boat's captain, became a banker in 1864 (link note following 1 June 1857 to Taylor, *L1,* 74; *Missouri Death Records* 2011; 23 Apr 1867 to Stoddard, *L2,* 31 n. 2). Sobieski (Beck) Jolly (1831–1905) piloted steamboats from 1846 to 1885; during the Civil War he steered Union steamboats on the Mississippi and its tributaries. Clemens's last meeting with him was in May 1902, on the St. Louis stop of his final trip to Missouri (28 Mar 1874 to Thompson, *L6,* 100 n. 3; Ferris 1965, 14–16; "Mark Twain's Visit," St. Louis *Globe-Democrat,* 30 May 1902, 9). Clemens mentions three pilots working on the *John J. Roe* in May 1858 (Youngblood, Zeb Leavenworth, and Jolly); the typical crew included only two (see also AD, 31 Aug 1906, where Youngblood is again mentioned as one of the pilots).

150.26–28 steering for Brown, on the swift passenger packet . . . presently blew up and killed my brother Henry] Clemens began his service as steersman under pilot William Brown on the *Pennsylvania* in November 1857; the disaster that killed Henry Clemens occurred in June 1858: see Clemens's full account in the Autobiographical Dictation of 13 January 1906 (*AutoMT1,* 274–76 and notes on 560–61).

151.12–13 "I never saw her afterward. It is now forty-eight years . . . no word has ever passed between us since."] Clemens evidently did make at least one trip to Laura's home town of Warsaw, Missouri. And he also had news of her in the spring of 1880, when he received a letter from Wattie Bowser, a Dallas schoolboy. Bowser wrote to request information for his school newspaper, and he mentioned that his teacher, Mrs. Dake, had known Clemens when he was "a little boy" (Murray to SLC, 8 May 1880, CU-MARK; Bowser to SLC, 16 Mar 1880, CU-MARK). Clemens replied:

> No indeed, I have not forgotten your principal at all. She was a very little girl, with a very large spirit, a long memory, a wise head, a great appetite for books, a good mental digestion, with grave ways, & inclined to introspection—an unusual girl. How long ago it was! Another flight backward like this, & I shall begin to realize that I am cheating the cemetery. (20 Mar 1880 to Bowser, TxU-Hu)

Time and distance did not diminish Laura's importance to Clemens. He dreamed about her throughout his life; as recently as January 1906 he had described her as "that unspoiled little maid, that fresh flower of the woods & the prairies" (24 Jan 1906 to the Gordons, photocopy in CU-MARK). His memory of Laura is also reflected in several of his literary works. She contributed to his characterization of the young Laura Hawkins in *The Gilded Age* (1873–74), and was the "sweetheart" Clemens says he dreamed about in "My Platonic Sweetheart," a sketch he wrote in 1898 which was not published until after his death, and then only in Paine's heavily censored version (SLC 1898; see Baetzhold 1972 for a discussion of Laura's presence in Clemens's works).

151.14–20 I reached home from Fairhaven last Wednesday and found a letter from Laura Wright . . . in need of a thousand dollars, and I sent it] This passage is the only known evidence that Laura sought help for her "disabled son." Her first 1906 letter to Clemens has been lost or destroyed, but his account of it here is supported by what he wrote to Susan Crane on the day he received it: "She is poor, is a widow, in debt, & is in desperate need of a thousand dollars. I sent it" (27 July 1906 to Crane, photocopy in CU-MARK). On 12 August, however, Laura wrote again, stating that she had received no reply and feared her earlier letter had been lost. This time she identified the object of charity as "a young friend of mine who is making an effort for higher things" (CU-MARK). None of the obituaries or other records found so far indicates that she had any offspring. Laura later refused to exploit her relationship with Clemens, despite her need for money, because she chose not to have their correspondence made public. According to C. O. Byrd, who knew her at the end of her life, she turned down offers "from several magazines" who wanted to buy Clemens's letters. She asked Byrd to destroy them after her death, because they had been written "to her and for her" and "were not to be published." Byrd evidently complied: none of them is known to survive (Byrd to Charles H. Gold, 25 Feb 1964, CU-MARK). Clemens reminisces about Laura again in the Autobiographical Dictations of 31 August 1906 and 29 January 1907.

151.21–22 her father was an honored Judge of a high court in the middle of Missouri] Foster P. Wright (1809–87) was appointed a circuit court judge in 1837 and was on the bench of a series of Missouri courts for the rest of his career ("My Sutherland-Wright Ancestry" 2011, entry for Foster Pellatier Wright).

Autobiographical Dictation, 31 July 1906

152.8–9 I shall insert Clara's compliment here, where it can't get lost] The balance of Clara's letter did in fact "get lost"; the extract transcribed here—presumably from the original—is the only portion of it known to survive.

152.18–24 your Howells article which I have just this minute read . . . extract from "Venetian Days"] In his appreciation of Howells, published in the July 1906 issue of *Harper's Monthly,* Clemens wrote: "For forty years his English has been to me a continual delight and astonishment. In the sustained exhibition of certain great qualities—clearness, compression, verbal exactness, and unforced and seemingly unconscious felicity of phrasing—he is, in my belief, without peer in the English-writing world." Citing Howells's description of winter in Venice from chapter 3 of his *Venetian Life,* a travel memoir first published in 1866, Clemens concluded that his "pictures are not mere stiff, hard, accurate photographs; they are photographs with feeling in them, and sentiment, photographs taken in a dream, one might say." He concluded the article with a humorous description of other authors' "stale and overworked stage directions," contrasting them with Howells's "fresh ones" (SLC 1906g).

152.28 The western pirate . . . has really published his book] The pirated book was not, as Duneka and Clemens had feared, the Webster and Company *Library of Humor* (see AD, 17 July 1906, note at 146.37–147.9). It may have been *Hot Stuff by Famous Funny Men.* This volume, with its illustrated cloth boards depicting Mark Twain lecturing to a theater audience, was a reprint of an anthology originally published in 1883, edited by Eli Perkins (Melville D. Landon). In 1900 this was reissued under the title *Library of Wit and Humor by Mark Twain and Others,* with Clemens's portrait on the cover; he sued the book's distributor for infringement of trademark, and planned to sue the publisher as well as "every large store in New York" (21 Dec 1900 to Gurlitz, photocopy in CU-MARK; Landon n.d.; Landon 1898; "Mark Twain, Plaintiff," New York *Times,* 27 Mar 1901, 6; *BAL,* 5:11220).

152.29 my copyright lawyer] John Larkin.

152.37 George Ade and Dooley] George Ade (1866–1944) became famous for his "Fables in Slang," originally written for the Chicago *Record* and published, starting in 1899, in a series of books; he went on to write successful works of fiction, plays, and musicals. One of his last works is a memoir of his 1902 meeting with Mark Twain (Gribben 1980, 1:10–11; Ade 1939). For "Dooley" (humorist Finley Peter Dunne) see the Autobiographical Dictation of 22 January 1907 and the note at 377.3. Howells hailed both Ade and Dunne as leading figures in the "Chicago School of Fiction" (Howells 1903, 739–46).

152.40–41 my visit to the cemetery in Hannibal, Missouri, four years ago] Clemens visited Hannibal, and its cemetery, in 1902, when he made his final trip to Missouri: see *AutoMT1,* 613 n. 401.30–34.

153.3–17 Nasby, Artemus Ward . . . the "Disbanded Volunteer,"] For Artemus Ward and "the Pfaff crowd" see the Autobiographical Dictation of 21 May 1906 and the notes at 46.33–34 and 47.3–5; see *AutoMT1* for Petroleum V. Nasby (David Ross Locke, 506 n. 146.1–5), George Derby (476 n. 71.9–18), and Josh Billings (Henry Wheeler Shaw, 508 n. 148.21). "Yawcob Strauss" is a figure in several poems in Pennsylvania Dutch dialect by Charles Follen Adams (1842–1918). The most popular work of Robert J. Burdette (1844–1914) was his lecture "The Rise and Fall of the Moustache," which he is said to have delivered more than five thousand times. "Eli Perkins" was the pseudonym of humorist Melville D. Landon (1839–1910). The "Danbury News Man," so called from his column in the Danbury (Conn.) *News,* was James Montgomery Bailey (1841–94).

"Orpheus C. Kerr" (i.e., *office-seeker*) was journalist Robert Henry Newell (1836–1901). There was no American humorist named "Smith O'Brien"; Clemens may have meant the Irish-born writer Fitz-James O'Brien (1828–62), confusing his name with that of Irish patriot William Smith O'Brien (1803–64). "Ike Partington" is a character in the stories of B. P. Shillaber (1814–90). "Q. K. Philander Doesticks" was the pen name of journalist Mortimer Thomson (1831–75). The "Disbanded Volunteer" was the fictive persona of Joseph Barber (1808?–74) in a series of Civil War letters ("Suburban News," New York *Times,* 15 Apr 1874, 8).

153.36–42 letters of the late John Hay, copies of which I enclose . . . Chas. Orr] The letters were written to Alexander Gunn (1837–1901), a Cleveland industrialist, by Clemens's friend John Hay, who had died on 1 July 1905 (see *AutoMT1,* 534 n. 222.9). Charles Orr (1858–1927), superintendent of the Cleveland public schools, sent the copies; he was preparing the letters for publication in a short article. Orr had been shown the letters by their owner at that time (1906), lawyer and patron of the arts Frank H. Ginn (1868–1938). The work by Clemens that is discussed in them (and in the dictation that follows) is *Date 1601,* a ribald pastiche of Elizabethan speech and manners. Clemens initially showed the sketch, composed in 1876, only to trusted male friends. But it attained a wider circulation in 1880 through Hay, who took the manuscript to Cleveland. There it was appreciatively read by his literary circle, the Vampire Club, and privately printed in an anonymous edition of perhaps six copies (Kohn 1957; SLC 1880a, 1996b; Orr 1906; *BAL,* 2:3388; Barnes 2009; 19 July 1880 to Twichell, transcript in CU-MARK; Hay to SLC, 15 Aug 1880, CU-MARK; Rhodes 1922, 120–21).

154.16 The Globe has not yet recovered from Downey's inroad] Hay refers to a recent occurrence in Washington, D.C. On 12 April 1880 Stephen W. Downey, a congressional delegate from Wyoming Territory, introduced a bill that began with a recital of the Apostles' Creed and went on to propose that $500,000 be appropriated to decorate the Capitol walls with scenes from "the birth, life, death and resurrection of our Saviour, Jesus Christ." Downey also obtained permission to have additional "argument" in support of his bill published in the *Congressional Record* (which Hay casually calls by the name of its predecessor, the *Congressional Globe*). When the *Record* appeared on 22 April, readers were surprised to find that Downey's "argument" was a religious-mythological poem over twenty-five hundred lines in length. The affair occasioned much mockery of Downey and debate about the abuse of the *Congressional Record* (Washington *Post,* 23 Apr 1880: "Downey's Immortal Ode," 1; "Downey Invades the Record," 2; Downey 1880).

154.34 I replied to Mr. Orr as follows] Isabel Lyon recalled that she took down Clemens's dictation of his letter to Orr as he lay in bed "roaring, and chuckling, and smoking and rejoicing" (note by Lyon, NN-BGC, TS in CU-MARK).

155.13–15 sumptuous edition . . . was made by Lieut. C. E. S. Wood at West Point—an edition of 50 copies] The so-called West Point edition of *1601* was printed in 1882 by Lt. Charles Erskine Scott Wood—with Clemens's active consent—at the little press of

West Point Military Academy. At least fifteen copies remained in Clemens's hands at the time of his death and are now in the Mark Twain Papers. Wood (1852–1944), a polymath from Pennsylvania, was the adjutant to the superintendent of West Point, the director of the press, and a personal friend of Clemens's. Pirated editions began to appear in 1901, but not until this correspondence with Orr did Clemens acknowledge to anyone outside his group of intimates that he was the author of the sketch (for a facsimile of the West Point edition, see SLC 1939; Barnes 2009; Kohn 1957; SLC 1882a, 1996b).

156.16–17 ten-mile walk to Talcott Tower and back] Bartlett Tower, a wooden lookout on the ridge of Talcott Mountain near Hartford, was about eight miles from the Nook Farm neighborhood where Clemens and Twichell lived. Built in 1867 by Matthew Henry Bartlett, it was part of a tourist resort with picnic tables, swings, and refreshments for sale (Brenda J. Miller 2012; Courtney 2008, 148–50).

156.26–34 Dean Sage . . . got a dozen copies privately printed in Brooklyn] Sage (1841–1902), the son of wealthy lumber merchant Henry W. Sage, was Clemens's close friend and occasional financial adviser. He was well known as a writer on angling and collected books on the subject. No evidence has been found that he sponsored or printed any edition of *1601* (*AutoMT1,* 599 n. 377.14; 28 Mar 1875 to Sage, *L6,* 431 n. 1).

156.34–35 He sent one to David Gray, in Buffalo; one to a friend in Japan] David Gray, a poet and the longtime editor of the Buffalo *Courier,* and journalist Edward H. House, who in 1880 returned permanently from a ten-year stay in Japan, both received copies of the 1882 West Point edition of *1601* from C. E. S. Wood (see *AutoMT1,* 594 n. 363.32–33, 598 n. 375.23; Wood to SLC, 25 July 1882, CU-MARK).

156.35 Lord Houghton] Richard Monckton Milnes, first Baron Houghton (see *AutoMT1,* 634 n. 433.27–35).

156.38–157.3 learned rabbi said it was a masterpiece . . . *'He wrote the immortal "1601".'*] The rabbi in Albany has not been identified. When Clemens repeated this anecdote to a friend in 1907, he made it clear that the quoted remark about the epitaph was the rabbi's, as "delivered" by Gray (Lyon to Owen, 19 Jan 1936, NN-BGC).

157.7–8 Rudolph Lindau, of the Foreign Office] Rudolf Lindau (1829–1910) was a German diplomat and novelist. Clemens became acquainted with him during the winter of 1891–92, when the Clemenses were living in Berlin. He tells a story about Lindau, disguising him as "Smith," in the Autobiographical Dictation of 6 December 1906.

157.9 Mommsen] Theodor Mommsen (1817–1903), the great historian of Rome, was Germany's preeminent academic, a liberal politician, and a noted public figure. While living in Berlin, Clemens wrote in his notebook, "Been taken for Mommsen twice. We have the same hair, but upon examination it was found that the brains were different" (Notebook 31, TS p. 27, CU-MARK).

157.9–10 William Walter Phelps, who was our minister at the Berlin court] See *AutoMT1,* 527 n. 204.25–26.

157.13–17 In 1890 I had published in *Harper's Monthly* a sketch called "Luck," . . . it is Lord Wolseley] This sketch was written in April 1886, the purported facts of the case deriving, according to Clemens, from Twichell's report of an acquaintance's story. The sketch, built around the revelation that a renowned British military hero was in reality "an absolute fool," is slight, and Clemens did not publish it until what Paine called "the general house-cleaning which took place after the first collapse of the [Paige typesetting] machine"; it was published in *Harper's New Monthly Magazine* in August 1891 (*MTB,* 2:1106; *N&J3,* 226; SLC 1891b). As Clemens tells the story, he was later informed that in "Luck" he had unwittingly retailed the personal history of Garnet Wolseley, first Viscount Wolseley (1833–1913), the foremost British soldier of his day. Born into a poor family with military traditions, Wolseley rose through the ranks, campaigning in Burma, the Crimea, and Africa; he was made a peer in 1882 and commander in chief in 1895. Regarded as an intellectual and a professionalizing force within the army, he was publicly acclaimed as "our only general" and inspired the "very model of a modern major general" in Gilbert and Sullivan's *Pirates of Penzance.* He does not, however, fit the details of the tale very closely, and the protagonist of Clemens's sketch may be a composite of more than one military figure (Beck 2005). Clemens tells this anecdote again, with variations, in the Autobiographical Dictation of 27 December 1906.

157.23–24 In 1900, in London, I went to the Fourth of July banquet . . . Choate was presiding] Clemens did attend the American Society's Independence Day dinner in London in 1900; Choate and Wolseley were also present ("London's Fourth," New York *Daily People,* 5 July 1900, 5).

157.31–38 he asked me for a copy of "1601," . . . see whether it really is a masterpiece or not] Having recovered his store of copies, Clemens did eventually offer one—rather tentatively—to Wolseley. Writing on 17 April 1909, he correctly recalled the occasion of their meeting, but not the book's exact title (UkBrH):

> My dear Lord Wolseley:
>
> It is long ago—8 or 9 years. I arrived late—it was a Fourth of July dinner & the last speakers were gasping out their feelings to half a crowd & many empty & emptying seats, & you halted me on my way & I sat down & had a pleasant chat with you. You see I am trying to identify myself.
>
> With this purpose in view: to inquire if you asked me for a copy of *"1603?"* I *believe* it was your very self, but truly & sincerely I am not *charging* it, & would not charge it upon any innocent man, since the classic I speak of, being a quite free conversation between Queen Elizabeth, Shakspeare, Raleigh, etc., is not a proper thing to charge any unoffending person with wanting.
>
> When I came home I ransacked this country & searched several foreign countries where it had been republished in the dark, but I failed to find a copy. I had promised three copies while in England, & I had to fall short of those promises.
>
> Was your lordship one of the three? I am merely a well-meaning person who is trying to keep his word, so I know you will forgive me if I am off the right track. Perhaps I ought not to have written "1603," but I was young then (34 years ago)

& familiar with misdoing. Once I expurgated it, but then—well then there wasn't anything left, of course.

With the pleasantest recollections of that now ancient Fourth of July chat, I am

Your lordship's
Obedient servant to command,
Mark Twain

Autobiographical Dictation, 6 August 1906

158.4–7 Let us go back three months, now, and take up—no, let him wait . . . boil him in oil] Clemens never identifies this person. At the end of the Autobiographical Dictation of 7 August 1906 he calls him "No. 14 in the blatherskite gallery," and once again postpones his indictment.

158.10 feeding fat my ancient grudges in the cases of only thirteen deserving persons] *The Merchant of Venice,* act 1, scene 3. For a conjectural list of the "deserving persons" see *AutoMT1,* 22–23.

158.28–38 resume where we left off . . . debt left behind by the dead Webster firm] Clemens discusses his disastrous investments, the financial panic of 1893–94, and his debts in the Autobiographical Dictation of 2 June 1906.

158.38–39 I stumbled accidentally upon H. H. Rogers . . . Dr. Clarence C. Rice] Rice (1853–1935), who practiced medicine in New York City, became the Clemenses' family physician in 1885, sometimes visiting them in Hartford. Clemens was a guest at Rice's house at 123 East 19th Street at the start of his 1893–94 stay in New York. His claim that he and Rice "stumbled accidentally upon H. H. Rogers" is belied by contemporary correspondence: Rice brought them together deliberately. Clemens wrote of Rice to Olivia on 17 September 1893: "He told me he had ventured to speak to a rich friend of his who was an admirer of mine about our straits. I was very glad" (CU-MARK; Clarence C. Rice 1925; 1 May 1893 to OC, transcript by PAM in CU-MARK; *N&J3,* 332 n. 92).

159.11–12 decorating the globe's circumference . . . in the interest of the Webster creditors] See the Autobiographical Dictation of 2 June 1906, note at 79.39–80.4, and the Autobiographical Dictation of 4 June 1906.

159.21–22 We had paid a hundred cents on the dollar, and owed no one a penny] In his original dictation Clemens admitted, "I am a weak sister, and I could probably have been persuaded to let the Webster assets pay what they could of the indebtedness and stop there. But no persuasions could ever have been compiled out of the dictionary that would have moved Mrs. Clemens." He deleted the remark when revising his typescript (see the Textual Commentary at *MTPO*).

160.3–8 the books had revived . . . generous support for my children] In the course of revising this account of his income from royalties, Clemens rewrote several sentences, substituting general terms for specific dollar amounts. In his original dictation he explained that his royalties soon amounted to "twenty thousand dollars a year," and sometimes "ten or twenty thousand above it"; in fact, they were sometimes "as high as fifty-seven thousand dollars in a year, and will go well beyond that in the next twelve months, counting old books, new books, and magazine stuff" (see the Textual Commentary at *MTPO*).

Autobiographical Dictation, 7 August 1906

160.28–29 Mr. Rogers gave a part of his time . . . to the straightening out of my Paige entanglements] For Rogers's role in dealing with the failure of the Paige typesetting machine see *AutoMT1,* 497–98 n. 106.23–24.

160.29–30 an agreement between the American Publishing Company and the Harpers . . . issued by the former Company] See the Autobiographical Dictation of 17 July 1906, note at 143.34–144.5.

160.32–36 three years ago . . . servant to only one—the Harper Corporation] In October 1903 Harpers bought the American Publishing Company for $50,000, half of it paid by Harpers and half by the Clemenses. Harpers agreed to pay the Clemenses a royalty of 20 percent on individual titles and 17 percent on uniform editions (*HHR,* 691–99, 700–708). Clemens wrote in his notebook at the time:

> The contract . . . concentrates all my books in Harper's hands, & now at last they are valuable: in fact they are a fortune. They *guarantee* me $25,000 a year for 5 years, but they will yield twice as much [as] that for many a year, if intelligently handled. Four months ago I could not have believed that I could ever get rid of my 30-years' slavery to the pauper American Publishing Co—a worthless concern which always kept a blight upon the books. (Notebook 46, TS p. 15, CU-MARK)

162.9–11 Federal Steel . . . more than twice the figure he had paid for it] See the Autobiographical Dictation of 2 June 1906, note at 80.6–7.

Autobiographical Dictation, 8 August 1906

163.18 forlorn hope] In military language, a detachment of soldiers, usually volunteers, selected to perform some especially perilous service.

164.8 'Lohengrin'] Clemens saw a performance of this opera by Richard Wagner in Mannheim in 1878, which he described in chapter 9 of *A Tramp Abroad* as a "shivaree" (Gribben 1980, 2:731).

165.12–14 Papa went to Europe to lecture . . . reading with Mr. G. W. Cable] Susy made a leap in time here. Clemens and Olivia took Susy to England, Scotland, and Ireland from May to October 1873; Clemens lectured in London near the end of the trip. The reading tour with Cable took place over the winter of 1884–85.

166.2 the nurse] Rosina Hay (see AD, 3 Oct 1906, note at 242.34).

166.11 Aunt Clara Spaulding] A dear childhood friend of Olivia's (see *AutoMT1,* 593–94 n. 363.23–25).

166.15 Frank Warner] Frank (1867–1931), then aged seventeen, was the son of George H. and Elisabeth (Lilly) Gillette Warner, Nook Farm neighbors. George was the brother of Charles Dudley Warner ("Nook Farm Genealogy" 1974, 30; *AutoMT1,* 580 n. 327.14).

166.28–29 I have already described that monumental night in an earlier chapter of this autobiography] See the Autobiographical Dictation of 6 February 1906 for Clemens's earlier description of this occasion, which took place on 14 March 1885 (*AutoMT1,* 334–36, 583 n. 335.18–21).

166 *footnote* at dinner the other night . . . Sir Henry Irving] Clemens added many such footnotes to Susy's original manuscript. He dined with the renowned British actor Sir Henry Irving (1838–1905) at The Players club on 10 November 1901 (Notebook 44, TS p. 17, CU-MARK).

Autobiographical Dictation, 10 August 1906

167.5 This morning's mail brings me this clipping from the *Westminster Gazette*] The undated clipping was sent by George Harvey of Harpers, enclosed in a letter of 9 August. On it he wrote, "What ho! GH" (CU-MARK).

167.9 "Diary of Eve"] *Eve's Diary* was written in July 1905 and published as a book in June 1906 (16 July 1905 to Duneka, NN-BGC; SLC 1906a; *BAL,* 2:3489).

168.25–30 At last we have heard from Higbie . . . he proposed to pass his manuscript through my hands] Calvin Higbie was Clemens's cabinmate in the mining camp of Aurora in 1862. His letter of 15 March 1906, in which he proposed to write an account of his experiences in the West, is transcribed in the Autobiographical Dictation of 26 March 1906 (*AutoMT1,* 445–46, 640 n. 445.4–13).

169.4–5 Robinson Crusoe] Clemens owned a 1747 edition of Daniel Defoe's novel, one of his favorite books to read to his children (Gribben 1980, 1:181; CC 1931, 25). See also the Autobiographical Dictation of 11 June 1906, note at 109.17–20.

169.18–20 "A Little Experience in Nevada and Surrounding Country in the Early Sixties, Leading up to My Acquaintance with Samuel L. Clemens, 'Mark Twain.'"] Higbie's essay is in the Mark Twain Papers, in two forms (both purchased in 2002): the original manuscript, and a typed copy of it bearing Clemens's revisions. It remained unpublished at Higbie's death in 1914, but was quoted extensively in a 1920 *Saturday Evening Post* article (Higbie 1906; Phillips 1920).

169.33–34 I have written Higbie the following letter] Only Hobby's typed transcription of this letter is extant; the original sent to Higbie has not been found.

170.6 You have invented some new things—such as . . . the ball] Higbie's essay describes a ball celebrating the opening of a saloon:

> It was a queer combination five ladies and a thousand men, and in the nature of things the sets were composed allmost entirely of men, and very picturesque they were. All sorts and conditions; very few wore coats, miners with red shirts, pants outside of boots, with gun knife or both strapped to their waist. . . . [Sam] was all animation and making great play to entertain his partner, bowing and scraping at a great rate but paying not the slightest attention to the music or prompter calling off the figures. (Higbie 1906, TS pp. 15–16)

170.26 I here append his flap-jack episode] The "episode" is an extract from the original typescript of Higbie's essay, on which Clemens made one spelling correction and added several paragraph breaks (Higbie 1906, TS pp. 11–12).

Autobiographical Dictation, 11 August 1906

172.7–8 in this morning's paper is a note which I wrote to Andrew Carnegie some years ago] Clemens wrote this letter to Carnegie on 6 February 1901 (DLC), and it was soon widely printed in the newspapers. Carnegie replied two days later, "Nothing less than a two dollar & a half hymn book *gilt* will do for you. Your place in the Choir (celestial) demands that & you shall have it" (CU-MARK). If Hobby did indeed transcribe a clipping "from this morning's newspaper," it has not been found, but the present text corresponds closely to the one published in *Everyday Housekeeping* for August 1906 (23:1005). Whatever the exact source, its textual history must have included a British reprinting, for Clemens's "dollar & a half" has been turned into "six shillings."

172.26–34 Peace Palace . . . eighty million dollars' worth of free libraries] The Palace of Peace, in The Hague, was funded by Carnegie to house the Permanent Court of Arbitration, the first global court for the settlement of international disputes; the building was completed in 1913, at a cost of $1.5 million. The Carnegie Institute of Pittsburgh, founded in 1896, comprised a group of cultural and educational departments, including a museum, a music hall, and several technical schools that ultimately developed into Carnegie Mellon University. By 1906 Carnegie's gifts to the institute totaled more than $8 million. The Carnegie Foundation for the Advancement of Teaching was founded in 1905 as a pension fund for American and Canadian teachers aged sixty-five or over with at least twenty-five years of service; to his original $10 million gift Carnegie added $5 million in 1906. His expenditure on free public library buildings, by the end of his life, is estimated at over $60 million (Carnegie Endowment 1922, 3–8, 127–35, 274–77, 311; "Comment," *Harper's Weekly* 50 [11 Aug 1906]: 1123).

172.40–173.1 In a previous chapter I have told how John T. Lewis saved the lives of a rich man's wife and daughter] There is no such "chapter" in the *Autobiography,* but the anecdote was one that Clemens was fond of recounting, as he had done three years earlier in the *Ladies' Home Journal* (see the note at 173.19–20). John T. Lewis (1835–1906) was born in Carroll County, Maryland, where he lived as a black freeman. He settled in Elmira in 1864, working as a coachman for Jervis Langdon, then as a blacksmith, then as the ten-ant farmer at Quarry Farm. Clemens described the events of 23 August 1877 in a letter to the Howellses (the entire letter, written on 25 and 27 August, is in *Letters 1876–1880*):

> Day before yesterday was a fine summer day away up here on the summit. Aunt Marsh & Cousin May Marsh were here visiting Susie Crane & Livy at our farm house. By & by mother Langdon came up the hill in the "high carriage" with Nora the nurse & little Jervis (Charley Langdon's little boy)—Timothy the coachman driving. Behind these came Charley's wife & little girl in the buggy, with the new, young, spry gray horse—a high-stepper. Theodore Crane arrived a little later.
>
> The Bay & Susie were on hand with their nurse, Rosa. I was on hand, too. Susie Crane's trio of colored servants ditto—these being Josie, housemaid; Aunty Cord, cook, aged 62, turbaned, very tall, very broad, very fine every way (see her portrait in "A True Story Just as I Heard It" in my Sketches); Chocklate (the laundress,) (as the Bay calls her—she can't say Charlotte), still taller, still more majestic of proportions, turbaned, very black, straight as an Indian——age, 24. Then there was the farmer's wife (colored) & her little girl, Susie.
>
> Wasn't it a good audience to get up an excitement before? Good excitable, inflammable material?
>
> Lewis was still down town, three miles away, with his two-horse wagon, to get a load of manure. Lewis is the farmer (colored.) He is of mighty frame & muscle, stocky, stooping, ungainly, has a good manly face & a clear eye. Age about 45—& the most picturesque of men, when he sits in his fluttering work-day rags, humped forward into a bunch, with his aged slouch hat mashed down over his ears & neck. It is a spectacle to make the broken-hearted smile.
>
> Lewis has worked mighty hard & remained mighty poor. At the end of each whole year's toil he can't show a gain of fifty dollars. He had borrowed money of the Cranes till he owed them $700—& he being conscientious & honest, imagine what it was to him to have to carry this stubborn, hopeless load year in & year out.
>
> Well, sunset came, & Ida the young & comely (Charley Langdon's wife) & her little Julia & the nurse Nora, drove out at the gate behind the new gray horse & started down the long hill—the high carriage receiving its load under the porte cochère. Ida was seen to turn her face toward us across the fence & intervening lawn—Theodore waved goodbye to her, for he did not know that her sign was a speechless appeal for help.
>
> The next moment Livy said, "Ida's driving too fast down hill!" She followed it with a sort of scream, "Her horse is running away!"
>
> We could see two hundred yards down that descent. The buggy seemed to fly. It would strike obstructions & apparently spring the height of a man from the ground.
>
> Theodore & I left the shrieking crowd behind & ran down the hill bareheaded & shouting. A neighbor appeared at his gate—a tenth of a second too late!—the buggy vanished past him like a thought. My last glimpse showed it for one instant, far down the descent, springing high in the air out of a cloud of dust, & then it disappeared. As I flew down the road, my impulse was to shut my eyes as I turned them to the right or left, & so delay for a moment the ghastly spectacle of mutilation & death I was expecting.
>
> I ran on & on, still spared this spectacle, but saying to myself "I shall see it at the turn of the road; they never can pass that turn alive." When I came in sight of that

> turn I saw two wagons there bunched together—one of them full of people. I said, "Just so—they are staring petrified at the remains."
>
> But when I got amongst that bunch, there sat Ida in her buggy & nobody hurt, not even the horse or the vehicle. Ida was pale but serene. As I came tearing down she smiled back over her shoulder at me & said, "Well, you're alive yet, *aren't* you?" A miracle had been performed—nothing less.
>
> You see, Lewis,-the-prodigious, humped upon his front seat, had been toiling up, on his load of manure; he saw the frantic horse plunging down the hill toward him, on a full gallop, throwing his heels as high as a man's head at every jump. So Lewis turned his team diagonally across the road just at the "turn," thus making a V with the fence—the running horse could not escape that but must enter it. Then Lewis sprang to the ground & stood in this V. He gathered his vast strength, and with a perfect Creedmoor aim he siezed the gray horse's bit as he plunged by & fetched him up standing!

In recognition of Lewis's deed, the Cranes made him gifts of money and forgave all of his debt to them, Ida Langdon bought him an engraved gold watch, and Clemens gave him some inscribed copies of his own works. By 1902, however, Lewis was again in financial difficulties, and Clemens arranged a pension for him, to which both he and Rogers contributed. In his fiction, Clemens reworked Lewis's feat of rescue twice: in *Pudd'nhead Wilson* (in a passage omitted from the finished novel) and in chapter 52 of *Life on the Mississippi* (McKeithan 1961, 23–25; 9 Aug 1876 to Howells, n. 4, *Letters 1876–1880; MTB,* 2:599–600). "Creedmoor aim" refers to a famous long-range rifle match that took place in 1874 on the Creed farm in upstate New York.

173.19–20 I got myself spaciously photographed alongside of John T. Lewis] The photograph was taken in July 1903 by Thomas E. Marr as part of a pictorial article in the *Ladies' Home Journal,* "Three Famous Authors Outdoors" (20 [Nov 1903]: 1, 36–37; 17 July 1903 to Bok, ViU). It is reproduced following page 300.

173.37 Lewis was a Dunker Baptist] The Church of the Brethren—known as the Dunkers—is an anabaptist church with origins in eighteenth-century Germany. Their distinctive theological tenet is baptism of adults by triple immersion (otherwise the faith resembles that of the Mennonites, who sprinkle). Never numerous, American Dunker congregations are found primarily in the mid-Atlantic and midwestern states.

175.20 Lewis's last estate reminds me of David Gray's] See *AutoMT1,* 375, 598 n. 375.7.

175.26–28 This morning's cables contain a verse or two from Kipling . . . the conquered Boers] Great Britain defeated the Boers in southern Africa in 1902 and annexed their lands (see AD, 23 June 1906, note at 137.40–138.21). The Boers still outnumbered the British, however, and when the Liberal party came to power in 1905, its decision to enfranchise them inflamed Kipling (see the note at 175.33–37). His poem "South Africa," published in the London *Standard* on 27 July 1906, brands the government's proposal as treachery ("A Kipling Political Poem," New York *Times,* 27 July 1906, 1). Clemens is, however, unlikely to have seen the poem in "this morning's cables," as he claims here; it was news from two weeks earlier. A more probable source is the excerpt and comment in *Harper's Weekly* of 11 August (Gilmour 2002, 196–99; "Comment," *Harper's Weekly* 50 [11 Aug 1906]: 1123).

175.33–37 He came over and traveled about America . . . up to Quarry Farm in quest of me] From March to October 1889, Rudyard Kipling (1865–1936), at the time an obscure journalist, traveled from India to Britain by an eastward route: crossing the Pacific to San Francisco, he made his way overland to Pennsylvania (to visit friends) before taking ship for Liverpool. Along the way he sent back travel letters to the Allahabad *Pioneer,* collected later in *From Sea to Sea* (1899). The day Kipling visited the Clemenses in Elmira was probably 15 August 1889; his article about the visit, however, was not published until a year later (New York *Herald,* 17 Aug 1890, 5, in Scharnhorst 2006, 117–26). By that time Kipling—still only twenty-four years old—had become well known in Britain and America for his stories and poems. Clemens frequently alluded to the sudden, overwhelming quality of Kipling's rise to fame; in 1898 he wrote, "In those days you could have carried Kipling around in a lunch basket—now he fills the world" (Notebook 40, TS p. 62, CU-MARK). Clemens's anti-imperialist commitments never kept him from reading and praising Kipling's works. Isabel Lyon recorded that Clemens explained Kipling's reactionary views as the result of "his training that makes him cling to his early beliefs; then he loves power & authority & Kingship" (Lyon 1907, entry for 22 Jan). See also the Autobiographical Dictation of 13 August 1906 (Graver 1992; Gilmour 2002, 87–97; Krauth 2003, 209, 248–57; Gribben 1980, 1:375–82).

Autobiographical Dictation, 13 August 1906

176.10 Eric Ericsons] Norwegian mariners Eric the Red and his son Leif Ericson explored Greenland and Vinland (variously identified as Labrador, Newfoundland, or New England) in the second half of the tenth century.

176.31–32 He was a stranger . . . universally known] See the Autobiographical Dictation of 11 August 1906, note at 175.33–37.

177.2–16 "Plain Tales," . . . "Kim"] Kipling's short story collection *Plain Tales from the Hills* (1888); *The Jungle Book* and *The Second Jungle Book* (1894, 1895); and his novel *Kim* (1901).

Autobiographical Dictation, 15 August 1906

177.24–25 Mrs. Horr taught the children . . . Mr. Sam Cross taught the young people of larger growth] Elizabeth Horr (1790?–1873), born in New York, was Clemens's first schoolteacher. Samuel Cross (1812–86), born in Ireland, moved to Missouri in 1837 and by 1840 was a teacher in Hannibal. Clemens attended his school in the mid-1840s. In the spring of 1849 Cross led a party of Hannibal citizens to California and settled in Sacramento, where he practiced law and eventually became a judge (*Inds,* 326, 316).

178.7–8 Jim Dunlap] There was a James Dunlap among Clemens's Hannibal contemporaries; however, "Dunlap" was one of Clemens's stock names for disguising or inventing villagers, and on the evidence of a 1902 notebook entry it was Ed Stevens who gave him his "first whipping" (Notebook 45, TS p. 16, CU-MARK; *AutoMT1,* 627 n. 420.17; *Marion Census* 1850, 293B).

178.18–20 I prayed for gingerbread. Margaret Kooneman . . . brought a slab of gingerbread to school every morning] In notes made in Switzerland in 1897, Clemens planned to make use of the baker, his daughter, and her gingerbread in "Tom Sawyer's Conspiracy," transferring the episode to Huck Finn: "Old Koonemann, & make him talk broken English. Make a great character of this kind-hearted garrulous old thing. (baker) Margaret K used to bring gingerbread to school & Huck used to pray for it" (Notebook 41, TS p. 59, CU-MARK; *Inds,* 289). And in a note made around 1905 he assigned a deeper importance to the gingerbread episode in a note headed "Prayer":

> Why should one laugh at my praying for gingerbread when I was a child? What *would* a child naturally pray for?—a child who had been lied to by teachers & preachers & a lying Bible-text?
>
> My prayer failed. It was 65 years ago. I remember the shock yet. I was as astonished as if I had caught my own mother breaking a promise to me.
>
> Was the doubt planted then, which in 50 years grew to a certainty: that the X & all other religions are lies & swindles? (Autobiographical Fragment #146, CU-MARK)

Autobiographical Dictation, 27 August 1906

179.3–4 Several weeks ago, in Chapter XLI, I spoke of how rare a thing a good memory for names and faces is] Unless this refers to the remarks on James W. Nye (AD, 2 Apr 1906), there is no such passage. The last time Clemens is known to have used chapter numbers for parts of his autobiography was in 1903 (*AutoMT1,* 17–18). He never used them for the dictations begun in 1906, and his reference here has not been explained.

179.5–7 I received a distressed letter from my London publisher . . . tax due upon my English copyrights] This contretemps arose in 1887, when Clemens's London publishers, Chatto and Windus, informed him: "We have been having a 'brush' with the commissioners of H. M. Inland Revenue, who have been putting the screw to us to obtain income tax from our payments to authors residing abroad." Clemens requested further documentation, which he received, and kept—"because I might want to print some nonsense on the subject some time, when I've got an idle hour" (Chatto and Windus to SLC, 24 Aug 1887, UkReU; 19 Sept 1887 to Chatto, UkReU).

180.12–13 Harpers applied to me for some nonsense, and I sent . . . "An Open Letter to the Queen."] Clemens's exercise in lèse-majesté, "A Petition to the Queen of England," appeared in *Harper's New Monthly Magazine* for December 1887; its content is largely recreated in the present dictation. When Chatto and Windus read the article, they wrote to him, "We are sorry we did not have a copy of it in time that we might have sent the Inland Revenue instead of the cheque for £47.19.4 which we reluctantly paid on your account" (Chatto and Windus to SLC, 25 Nov 1887, CU-MARK; SLC 1887).

180.29 flight of Saxon arrows at the battle of Senlac] The Battle of Hastings (14 October 1066) took place at Senlac Hill, but it was the Normans, not the English, who used archers in their attack.

180.38 "Mr. President, I am embarrassed—are you?"] Clemens told this story in an 1885 dictation, "The Chicago G.A.R. Festival" (*AutoMT1,* 67–68), which he never published, as well as in chapter 2 of *Following the Equator* (1897). For a sorting out of the actual timing and circumstances of his several meetings with Grant, see *AutoMT1,* 472–73 nn. 67.6–13, 67.17–19, 68.1, 68.4–5.

181.4–5 In an earlier chapter I have already told how Chicago was packed and jammed with people] See the Autobiographical Dictation of 31 May 1906.

181.31–36 In 1891 or '92 . . . he asked me if I would like to meet the Prince of Wales] The Clemenses spent the summer of 1892 at Bad Nauheim, being joined by Joseph and Harmony Twichell in August. Nauheim is less than twenty miles from Bad Homburg, where on 21 August 1892 Clemens was introduced to the Prince of Wales, Albert Edward (1841–1910; later King Edward VII), by British ambassador Sir Edward Malet (Notebook 32, TS pp. 19–20, CU-MARK, original at TxU-Hu; Courtney 2008, 244–45).

182.25 W. W. Jacobs's "Dialstone Lane."] William Wymark Jacobs (1863–1943) was a British writer mostly of comic fiction, but he is best remembered for his tale of horror "The Monkey's Paw" (1902). Clemens frequently recommended Jacobs's 1904 novel *Dialstone Lane* (Gribben 1980, 1:348).

Autobiographical Dictation, 28 August 1906

182.35 Higbie's reply has come] See the Autobiographical Dictation of 10 August 1906.

183.34 Bar Harbor] A bay off Mount Desert Island, Maine.

183.37–38 Fellow-Craftsmen's Club, and I attended its first banquet] The Fellowcraft Club, an organization of New York journalists and illustrators with a membership of over two hundred, was founded in 1888 with Richard Watson Gilder as president. "One of the principal features," wrote Gilder, "is a monthly dinner, which begins with a little informal speech-making, and goes on into music, story-telling, etc. A peculiar point of this dinner is its informality, and the fact that although the room is full of reporters the speeches are not reported" (Gilder 1916, 185). In the present dictation, Clemens describes the dinner of 15 November 1889. The Fellowcraft Club was defunct by 1892 (*N&J3,* 522 n. 132, 530 n. 148; "The Fellowcraft Club," New York *Times,* 19 May 1888, 5; King 1892, 503; for Gilder see *AutoMT1,* 486 n. 77 *footnote*). Clemens returns to the subject of "spontaneous oratory" in the Autobiographical Dictations of 31 August and 3 September 1906.

183.42–43 Major J. B. Pond was alive in those days] James B. Pond died in 1903 (see *AutoMT1,* 600 n. 381.14, and AD, 20 Nov 1906, note at 280.17–20).

186.34 Daguerre's monumental invention] Artist and inventor Louis Daguerre (1757–1851) introduced the first commercially successful photographic process, the daguerreotype, in 1839.

187.25 General Horace Porter] See *AutoMT1,* 631 n. 427.29–30.

Autobiographical Dictation, 29 August 1906

189.5–6 Chapter XXXI, where we quoted . . . a wronged and grieving western girl] See the Autobiographical Dictation of 18 June 1906. Like the earlier reference to "Chapter XLI" (AD, 27 Aug 1906), this mention of a chapter number has not been explained.

189.13 Soldier Boy's story] "A Horse's Tale," discussed in the note at 189.43–190.4.

189.20 your story of the poor dog] "A Dog's Tale," which appeared in *Harper's Monthly* in December 1903 (SLC 1903f).

189.32 (Mrs) Lillian R. Beardsley] Lillian Robinson Beardsley (1867–1925) was born in Coventry, Connecticut; her husband was a clerk in a custom house (Rasmussen 2013, letter 165).

189.43–190.4 The "Horse's Tale" . . . distributed abroad in Spain] Clemens began "A Horse's Tale" in September 1905 at the request of the actress and animal rights activist Minnie Maddern Fiske (1865–1932), who wrote:

> I have lain awake nights very often wondering if I dare ask you to write a story of an old horse that is finally given over to the bull-ring. The story you would write would do more good than all the laws we are trying to have made and enforced for the prevention of cruelty to animals in Spain. We would translate and circulate the story in that country. (Fiske to SLC, 15? Sept 1905, *MTB,* 3:1245–46)

"I shall certainly write the story," Clemens replied, and it was soon written—"not manufactured calmly but with an eight-day drive & rush," as he told Clara. "For an 8-day job it isn't a bad tale. Profitable, too—an average of $700 a day—for it is to go into the magazine—Jan. & Feb. numbers of Harper's" (18 Sept 1905 to Fiske, CU-MARK; 1 Oct 1905 to CC, photocopy in CU-MARK; 6 Oct 1905 to CC, CU-MARK). Publication in *Harper's Monthly* was delayed to August and September of 1906; the story was reprinted as a book in 1907 (see AD, 17 July 1906, note at 145.36–146.2). No Spanish translation or printing has been found, although Mrs. Fiske apparently "had thousands of 'The Horse's Prayer' [*sic*] printed on water-proof paper and distributed" in Cuba (W.C.T.U. 1913, 205; SLC 1906h, 1907b).

190.10–14 editor of *Harper's Bazar* projected a scheme for a composite story . . . would take an interest in it or not] Elizabeth Jordan (1867–1947) was the editor in charge of *Harper's Bazar,* but it was Howells who initiated the idea for the collaborative novel

The Whole Family. Serialized from December 1907 to November 1908, it almost realized an interest Howells and Clemens had shared for many years. In 1876 they planned a "Blindfold Novelette"—or "Skeleton Novelette"—in which several writers would independently work up a story from the same basic outline and publish the results serially in the *Atlantic Monthly,* then edited by Howells. In April 1876 Clemens wrote out his treatment of the plot, which he called "A Murder, a Mystery, and a Marriage," and eventually handed it in to Howells. It remained unpublished, however, because Howells could not persuade enough authors to join the scheme. Clemens nevertheless couldn't "seem to give up that idea," as he told Howells in 1879, and in 1893 he wrote Olivia, "I mean to change the plan of the skeleton novelettes, & throw in a new detail or two which will be an improvement, I think. Pity, too; for if I kept to the old plan, my story is already written, & lies in pigeonholes at home" (15 Apr 1879 to Howells, *Letters 1876–1880;* 20 Oct 1893 to OLC, photocopy in CU-MARK). In May 1906, more than twenty years after their first discussions, Howells pitched *The Whole Family* to editor Jordan, offering to contribute the chapter in the persona of "the Father" and suggesting that Clemens "do the Small Boy" (Howells 1928, 2:224; June Howard 2001, 1, 13–15).

190.23–32 Mr. Howells began the composite tale . . . Thus far, the boy has not applied to me] Clemens at first consented to contribute to *The Whole Family,* telling Jordan that the idea was "excellent" but that he would first need to see some of the other authors' installments (notes by Lyon on Jordan to SLC, 29 May 1906, CU-MARK). Howells's chapter was dispatched to him, as well as the second chapter—"The Maiden Aunt"—written by Mary E. Wilkins Freeman (1852–1930), a widely published author of novels and tales of New England life. But inspiration did not strike, and on 4 August Clemens resigned his charge. Jordan begged him to leave the matter open, however, and in December 1906 *Harper's Bazar* was still advertising Mark Twain as one of the authors of *The Whole Family* (SLC 2001, 70–75; 4 Aug 1906 to Jordan, CU-MARK; Jordan to SLC, 10 Aug 1906, CU-MARK; June Howard 2001, 16–17).

190.37–191.8 letters which were handed to me by a neighbor yesterday . . . letter No. 1] These semiliterate letters were shown to Clemens in August 1906 by Sumner B. Pearmain (1859–1941), a Boston stockbroker and Clemens's neighbor in Dublin, New Hampshire (Roswell F. Phelps 1941; Lyon 1906, entries for 17 June and 29 Aug). Pearmain had excised the names of the writer (Jennie Allen) and the addressee (Anne Stockbridge). For the complete story, see the Autobiographical Dictation of 5 October 1906.

191.11 Shevyott] That is, cheviot, a kind of wool cloth.

191.12 passy menterry] That is, passementerie, decorative trimming or edging.

192.15–18 Captain Ned Wakeman . . . I made two voyages with him, and we became fast friends] Edgar Wakeman (1818–75), once described by Clemens as "a splendidly uncultured old sailor, but in his own opinion a thinker by divine right," was born not at sea (as Clemens claims at 192.24), but in Westport, Connecticut (24 Apr 1901 to Phelps, CtY-BR). He went to sea at the age of fourteen, and from 1850 was a steamship captain based in San Francisco. Clemens made just one journey with Wakeman, in 1866, on the *America* going from California to Nicaragua on the way to New York, and saw him thereafter only once, in 1868. But Wakeman was to inspire a whole crew of fictional or semifictional sea captains in Mark Twain's works: Captain Waxman in his December 1866 letters to the San Francisco *Alta California,* Captain Ned Blakely in chapter 50 of *Roughing It,* Hurricane Jones in "Some Rambling Notes of an Idle Excursion" (1877–78), the Admiral in "The Refuge of the Derelicts" (1905–6), and Eli Stormfield, the hero of the long-gestating "Captain Stormfield's Visit to Heaven" (see the note at 193.39–194.2). In December 1872 Clemens was instrumental in a successful campaign to relieve the ailing seaman's financial distress; and he tried to help Wakeman find a publisher for his book, eventually issued posthumously as *The Log of an Ancient Mariner* (Edgar Wakeman 1878, 21, 30–31, 119–37; *N&J1,* 241–43; *RI 1993,* 331, 677–78 n. 331.10; *FM,* 157–248).

192.37–38 he brought the murderer of his colored mate to trial in the Chincha Islands] Clemens's notebook entry made during his 1866 voyage with Wakeman reads "Hanging the negro in the Chinchas." This alludes to an incident of March 1858 when Wakeman was commanding the clipper ship *Adelaide,* anchored at Elide Island, off Mexico. A black sailor, William Williams, was accused of murdering the second mate, a white man; Wakeman was part of a group of ships' officers and crewmen who sat in judgment on Williams and hanged him. (The Chinchas, off Peru, are guano islands, like Elide Island.) Clemens used the same phrase in an August 1868 letter to the Chicago *Republican.* Four years later, adapting Wakeman's experience in chapter 50 of *Roughing It,* Clemens swapped the ethnicities of the accused and the dead man. Thereafter, he consistently recalled that Wakeman "hung the mate . . . for killing the negro," rather than the other way around (18 Mar 1874 to OC, *L6,* 82–84). Wakeman was noted for his involvements with summary justice; he was a prominent vigilante in San Francisco's early days, and was remembered in connection with more than one lynching (*N&J1,* 253, 336; SLC 1868b; *RI 1993,* 677 n. 331.10; "Tragedy at Elide Island. Homicide of Thomas P. Lewis and Lynching of William Williams," San Francisco *Bulletin,* 12 Apr 1858, 3; "Coroner's Inquest," San Francisco *Alta California,* 14 June 1851, 4; "Our Ocean Commandery, No. 3. High-Handed Work of Capt. Wakeman," Boston *Journal,* 2 Aug 1890, 5).

193.7–24 When he was fifty-three . . . then the nautical paradise was complete] Wakeman was thirty-six when he met and married Mary E. Lincoln, one of the passengers aboard his ship, the SS *New Orleans,* en route from San Francisco to Panama. By his own account in *The Log of an Ancient Mariner,* his words on seeing the young lady sleeping in an armchair on deck were: "'Gentlemen,' I replied, 'that is my wife; if, when she opens her eyes, she be not swivel-eyed and with all her head-rails rotted out, I shall marry that girl, if I kill eleven men before breakfast to get up an appetite.'" They were married on 24 December 1854. In 1862 Wakeman built with his own hands the house in Brooklyn, California (later part of Oakland), where Mary and he would raise five children ("Births, Marriages and Deaths in California," New York *Times,* 31 Jan 1855, 1; Edgar Wakeman 1878, 171–76, 227–28; Robert P. Wakeman 1900, 292; Bishop 1877, 450).

193.31–37 when he died he left his family . . . Ralston, the banker, took the matter up and raised it in an hour] In 1872, when Clemens's help was enlisted, Captain Wakeman had not died, but had suffered a disabling stroke. Clemens's public appeal for $5,000 to pay off the mortgage on the Wakemans' house was published on the front page of the San Francisco *Alta California* on 14 December 1872. The money was raised in a few days, thanks to the energetic solicitation of H. D. Bacon; banker William C. Ralston, mentioned by Clemens, also contributed (Ray B. Browne 1961, 322–24; "Success of the Wakeman Subscription," San Francisco *Bulletin,* 27 Dec 1872, 3).

193.39–194.2 he once told me of a visit which he had made to heaven . . . Howells and he said, "Publish it."] In 1906 Clemens had been working on "Captain Stormfield's Visit to Heaven" for at least thirty-seven years, off and on, and considering (and rejecting) publication for nearly as long. Clemens said in an August 1868 letter to the Chicago *Republican* that he had heard Wakeman tell "his remarkable dream" while visiting with him in Panama City, sometime in late July (SLC 1868b). This precludes his having started to write his own version "in the first quarter of 1868," but the first quarter of 1869 is plausible. Clemens worked on the tale fitfully until March 1878, at which time Howells urged publication of a newly reconceived version (with the addition, he suggested, of a preface by the dean of Westminster). In 1878–81, the bulk of the story (chapters 3 and 4) was written. Sometime in the 1880s, according to Joe Goodman, Clemens showed him those chapters and expressed the fear that publishing the story "might hurt his literary reputation; that the public wasn't yet advanced enough for that sort of thing" (Goodman to Tufts, 12 July 1908, CU-MARK). The manuscript stayed "pigeonholed" until 1905–6, when Clemens added chapters 1 and 2, along with other passages whose intended position within the whole is unclear (23 Mar 1878 to OC, *Letters 1876–1880;* Baetzhold and McCullough 1995, 129–38).

194.3–4 "The Gates Ajar," a book which had imagined a mean little ten-cent heaven] *The Gates Ajar,* by Massachusetts author Elizabeth Stuart Phelps (1844–1911), was published in November 1868 and, according to Clemens, went "straight to the hearts of all the sentimental people with limited imaginations in the land" (SLC 1901–2). The afterlife is portrayed in this novel as an extension and perfection of earthly life—a conception that was criticized as unorthodox and materialistic; Bret Harte sneered, in a review which Clemens reprinted in the Buffalo *Express,* that Phelps's heaven was "a place where little boys find the balloons that they lose on earth" (Harte 1869a, 293). *The Gates Ajar* was a tremendous commercial success, selling nearly 70,000 copies in its first decade and spawning three sequels (Elizabeth Stuart Phelps 1964, 124–25; *BAL,* 8:20865; 25 Aug 1869 to Stoddard, n. 2, *Letters NP1;* "The Great Novel of the Year!" *Publishers' Weekly,* 13 Oct 1877, 449).

194.17–18 I mean to put it into this Autobiography now.† It is not likely to see the light for fifty years, yet] On the typescript of this dictation Paine noted, "He changed his mind a year later—Stormfield was published both in j⌊our⌋nal & book form in 1907–8." This would not necessarily preclude the text's incorporation into the *Autobiography;* but in subsequent Autobiographical Dictations, Clemens's references to "Captain Stormfield" assume that the reader has not read (or indeed heard of) it. The inference must be that at some point he rescinded his order to insert it; consequently it is not included in this edition (for the fullest text of "Captain Stormfield's Visit to Heaven" see Baetzhold and McCullough 1995, 129–88). At the time he made the present dictation, it is clear that Clemens had not decided what to do with "Stormfield." The footnote in which he says he has "just burned the closing two-thirds of it" is contradicted by the next day's dictation (AD, 30 Aug 1906). His intention as declared here to let the work remain unpublished "for fifty years, yet" is at odds with the fact that he offered it at this time to George Harvey as an article for *Harper's Monthly.* Harvey rejected the story as too controversial for religious sensibilities, and mildly scolded Clemens: "I'm sure it wouldn't do to print it now and I guess you're sure too, if you'll tell the truth." Yet a year later Harvey published it in *Harper's Monthly* after all, and in 1909 the same text became Mark Twain's last published book (Harvey to SLC, 7 Sept 1906, NNC; SLC 1907–8, 1909b).

194.31–195.2 His guess was right, and the two men were inseparable . . . I have printed it in full in one of my books] In August 1874 Twichell traveled from New York to Peru, accompanying his friend Yung Wing, who was on a diplomatic mission. On 22 August he wrote Clemens from a steamship approaching Panama that he had met Captain Wakeman on board (CU-MARK):

> What a delicious old misanthrope he is—what an entertaining denunciator! And, oh Mark, what a titanic commentator on the Old Testament!! . . . The thought that you had heard the same fascinating and unspeakably amusing talk, added to my relish of it. But I mean to tell him before I say goodbye, or *when* I say goodbye that I am a minister. I think it will tickle him to recall certain of his remarks on the profession.

Drawing on Twichell's account of his conversations with Wakeman, Clemens worked up the rationalizing exposition of 1 Kings 18 (Elijah's contest with the prophets of Baal), which he attributed to Captain Hurricane Jones in the second chapter of "Some Rambling Notes of an Idle Excursion." This sketch, first published in the *Atlantic Monthly,* was included in the collection *The Stolen White Elephant, Etc.* in 1882 (Courtney 2008, 151–52; SLC 1877–78, 1882b, 36–105).

Autobiographical Dictation, 30 August 1906

196.12–19 I had reached the middle of "Tom Sawyer" . . . When the manuscript had lain in a pigeon-hole two years] Clemens had reached the end of what was ultimately chapter 18 when "the story made a sudden and determined halt." On 4 September 1874 Clemens wrote to John Brown:

> I have been writing fifty pages of manuscript a day, on an average, for some time, now, on a book, (a story). . . . But night before last I discovered that that day's chapter was a failure, in conception, moral, truth to nature & execution—enough blemishes to impair the excellence of almost any chapter—& so, I must burn up the

> day's work & do it all over again. It was plain that I had worked myself out, pumped myself dry. (SLC and OLC to Brown, *L6,* 221–25)

Clemens canceled the last paragraph on manuscript page 500 (not 400 as claimed in this dictation) and destroyed the remainder of the chapter. He resumed work on the manuscript eight or nine months (not two years) later, completing it by 5 July 1875 (*TS,* 10–12, 505, 583 n. 148.30).

196.28–32 "The Prince and the Pauper" struck work in the middle . . . a story of mine called "Which Was It?"] The composition of *The Prince and the Pauper* began in 1877 but was broken off in early 1878 when the Clemenses went to Europe; it was not resumed until 1880. A "dry interval of two years" in *Connecticut Yankee* has not been identified; work on the novel was intermittent between 1885 and 1889. The first phase of work on "Which Was It?" was in the summer and fall of 1899 while Clemens was living in London and Sanna (Sweden); he resumed work on it in 1900–1903, then abandoned it (*P&P,* 3–7; *CY,* 1–13; *WWD,* 177–78).

196.39–42 "The Refuge of the Derelicts." . . . "The Mysterious Stranger."] "The Refuge of the Derelicts" and "Three Thousand Years Among the Microbes" are substantial but unfinished novels, written in 1905–6 and 1905 respectively, and left in manuscript at Clemens's death (they have been published in *FM,* 157–248, and *WWD,* 430–553). "The Mysterious Stranger" is Clemens's fourth and last attempt at a story about a boyish supernatural being who visits earth. The earliest treatment is discernible embedded in the second, which takes place in eighteenth-century Austria ("The Chronicle of Young Satan," 1897–1900); the third is set in nineteenth-century Missouri ("Schoolhouse Hill," 1898). The last attempt, entitled in full "No. 44, The Mysterious Stranger," takes place in a fifteenth-century Austrian village and print shop. It was incomplete at the time of the present dictation; Clemens would add more than a hundred pages to the manuscript in 1908, but he still left it in an unfinished state (Tuckey 1963; *MSM,* 1–34).

197.4–7 I carried it as far as thirty-eight thousand words . . . Tom Sawyer and Jim were the heroes of it] Clemens seems to allude to a story he worked on when his family was staying at York Harbor, Maine, in 1902. The manuscript is not extant and is known only from his correspondence, notebooks, and stray references. Set as usual in a fictionalized Hannibal, the book's first section would take place during Huck and Tom's youth; the second section was to portray them and their contemporaries fifty years later. Howells records that in August or September 1902 Clemens read aloud to him from "an admirable story" which was populated with "characters such as he had known in boyhood," but which he later denied having written (Howells 1910, 90; Howells to SLC, 20 Oct 1902, CU-MARK, in *MTHL,* 2:747–48). From his notebooks it is clear that Clemens planned to work into this novel many of his own memories which had been, or would be, used in the *Autobiography* (Notebook 45, TS pp. 2, 13, 21, CU-MARK).

197.18–19 an offer of sixteen thousand dollars a year . . . as editor of a humorous periodical] The offer referred to may have been from Robert Barr (1849–1912), who in

1892 founded *The Idler,* a London monthly. At that time he offered Clemens the position of nominal coeditor, with no duties attached; no agreement was reached (reportedly because Clemens's requested share of the profits was too high), and the coeditorship went to humorist Jerome K. Jerome, author of the popular *Three Men in a Boat.* Clemens did however assist in launching *The Idler,* serializing in its pages his novel *The American Claimant,* and acting as the magazine's American distributor through his firm of Charles L. Webster and Company. In 1895 Barr quarreled with Jerome and lost editorial control of *The Idler;* but in 1897 Jerome was forced out, and Barr, as sole proprietor, tried to relaunch the magazine. He again offered Clemens a place on the masthead and was refused: "No, bedad I dasn't be either editor or associate. It is a pity, too, for I think you will make your scheme succeed. Go ahead—you are young & full of energy—& grand prosperity attend you! I am old, & will get me to a nunnery" (29 Sept 1897 to Barr, photocopy in CU-MARK; Oxenham 1946, 36–37; Ashley 2006, 93–100; SLC 1892b).

197.40–198.8 six attempts to tell a simple little story . . . "The Death-Wafer."] Inspired by a passage that Clemens read in 1883 in *Oliver Cromwell's Letters and Speeches,* "The Death-Disk" is the story of three soldiers who are convicted of exceeding their orders; one of them is to be selected by lot for execution. The daughter of one soldier innocently hands him the disk of sealing wax that condemns him to death. Clemens initially planned it as a tragedy to be written in collaboration with Howells, but after his 1899 conversation with Robert McClure (brother of S. S. McClure, and London agent for *McClure's Magazine*), he decided to supply a happy ending. The story was published in the 1901 Christmas issue of *Harper's Monthly* (20 Dec 1883 to Howells, MH-H, in *MTHL,* 2:455–59; *N&J3,* 14–15; Rasmussen 2007, 1:100–101; "Find R. B. M'Clure Suicide in His Home," New York *Times,* 31 May 1914, 1; SLC 1901; see also AD, 7 June 1906 and the note at 106.1).

Autobiographical Dictation, 31 August 1906

200.6 Messrs. Brush and Smith] George de Forest Brush (1855–1941) was a painter associated with the American Renaissance movement of the turn of the century; Joseph Lindon Smith (1863–1950), likewise a painter, was an enthusiast of amateur theatricals. Both were residents of the artists' colony of Dublin, New Hampshire (University Art Galleries 1985, 77–79, 115–16).

200.16–28 forty years ago, in San Francisco . . . That anecdote is in one of my books] A contemporary report of Clemens's second San Francisco lecture, on 16 November 1866 at Platt's Hall, said:

> The lecturer commenced with a story he had heard about the Overland Mail service, and didn't want to hear any more, for he had read it in the *Tribune,* in Bayard Taylor's letter, in the letters of Ross Browne, and in the letters of every other person who had ever crossed the mountains and knew that there were such persons as Horace Greeley and Hank Monk. ("Amusements, Etc.," San Francisco *Alta California,* 17 Nov 1866, 1)

Clemens used this anecdote in chapter 20 of *Roughing It.* For Horace Greeley, Hank Monk, and John Ross Browne, see *RI 1993,* 608–12, and *L1,* 370 n. 6.

200.29–30 I had been a reporter on one of the papers] The *San Francisco Morning Call* (see AD, 13 June 1906 and notes).

202.20–25 there was to be an Authors' Reading at Chickering Hall . . . James Russell Lowell] Clemens resurrected this Monk-Greeley anecdote for the Chickering Hall reading of 28 November 1887. The speakers also included George Washington Cable and James Whitcomb Riley. The chairman was James Russell Lowell (1819–91), eminent man of letters and Harvard professor of modern languages and literature. He edited the *Atlantic Monthly* (1857–62) and the *North American Review* (1864–72), later serving as the American minister to Spain and ambassador to Great Britain ("Authors Have a Matinee," New York *Times,* 29 Nov 1887, 5).

203.26–30 The pictures which Mr. Paine made . . . I am sending half a dozen of these sets to friends] Paine, who in his youth had been a professional photographer, took these photographs on the porch of Clemens's summer rental (Upton House, Dublin, New Hampshire) on 25 June 1906, the day before Clemens departed for New York. After his return to Dublin he ordered and inscribed them as a series: "I like them ever so much. Mr. Paine made 7 negatives in the hope of getting one satisfactory one; & when the samples came back from the developer they were *all* good. It seemed to me that a progressive thought was traceable thru them, & after arranging the series in varying order several times I discovered what it was" (4 Sept 1906 to CC, CU-MARK). He sent out many sets of the pictures (certainly more than "half a dozen") to friends and family that summer; in September he arranged for the pictures to be published in the Christmas number of *Harper's Weekly* (*AutoMT1,* 542 n. 250.19–21; Lyon 1906, entries for 25 and 26 June; *MTB,* 3:1316; 27 Sept 1906 to Ashcroft, photocopy in CU-MARK; SLC 1906j).

211.1–6 my long-vanished little fourteen-year-old sweetheart . . . has written a charming letter] Laura Wright Dake's letter of 27 August 1906 thanked Clemens effusively for the $1,000 check he had sent her (see AD, 30 July 1906):

> Oh, *how* can I thank you! How can I, except to ask the Lord, every night as I commend myself to his care, to bless you and yours. You see, after having run the gauntlet of nearly every "ism" and speculative philosophy that has turned the modern mind towards Baal, I have gone back, baffled, to the simple faith—trusting it *all* to the Divine Intelligence and accepting what is sent, for weal or woe, without question. When, on a sudden impulse I wrote to you, hoping to reach Mr. Carnagie's heart through yours, not knowing where I could find him, I sealed the letter with a fervent "As God wills it!" and lo! He has answered me.
>
> I did not dream, my dear old friend, that *you* would respond personally, else I would not have presumed to ask such a thing. . . . However, it is not *so much* the generous response that enables me to carry into execution my heart's desire (and that is more than mere words can tell you—) but it is the finding out that the adulation of a world has left unchanged the sweet nature of the friend of long ago. Few, oh so few come from this crucible untainted! (CU-MARK)

211.9–14 the *John J. Roe* . . . Youngblood, one of the pilots] See the Autobiographical Dictation of 30 July 1906.

212.28 Lyell's "Geology,"] Charles Lyell's three-volume *Principles of Geology,* first published in 1830–33 and revised frequently until the author's death in 1875, established geology among the sciences and introduced its methods and vocabulary to a wide audience (Gribben 1980, 1:430).

Autobiographical Dictation, 3 September 1906

214.11–12 George Brush and Joseph Smith] See the Autobiographical Dictation of 31 August 1906, note at 200.6.

214.20 Professor Henderson] Ernest Flagg Henderson (1861–1928), who earned his doctorate in history at the University of Berlin, had by 1906 published three books on Germany: *Select Historical Documents of the Middle Ages* (1892), *A History of Germany in the Middle Ages* (1894), and *A Short History of Germany. Volume 1: 9 A.D. to 1648 A.D.* (1902). The Clemenses had known Henderson and his wife, the former Berta von Bunsen (1862–1942), in Berlin in the early 1890s. The Hendersons, with their six children, regularly spent their summers in Dublin, New Hampshire ("Mrs. Bertha Henderson," New York *Times,* 5 Mar 1942, 23; Lyon 1905a, entries for 9 Aug and 6 Oct; U.S. National Archives and Records Administration 1877–1907, Roll 55, passport application for Ernest Flagg Henderson, issued 4 Nov 1903).

215.1–4 Brush assumed the character and manner of an old German professor . . . effective] Jean Clemens reported in her diary that the club "was *packed.* All the doors & windows were as full of men & women as they could possibly hold." She recounted Brush's argument:

> Mr. Brush said there were several women in the audience that he loved very dearly, but that even so he didn't consider that men should be obliterated and to prove that men were better people to have on the earth than women, he went on to say "how felicitously what he had just been saying was proved by the following statement" of Mr. Pumpelly's who told how when he had recently been on an archaeological expedition in the Orient, he had found bones twenty thousand years old. The men's bones were good & hard & would take on a good polish whereas the women's were all spongy and of no account whatever, which showed their greater weakness. (JC 1900–1907, entry for 1 Sept 1906)

Professor Raphael Pumpelly (1837–1923), an eminent geologist, was also a summer resident of the Dublin area.

215.5–7 Mr. Smith assumed the precise and ornate style . . . of an established reputation] Jean Clemens also reported Smith's argument:

> Then Joe Smith got up and showed that while he, too, thought that women were kindlier and better-hearted people than men & therefore better to have about, still

men were more capable business people so that he found it very difficult to reach a decision. "How felicitously what I have just been saying is illustrated by the following anecdote" & then Mr. Smith went on to relate a story about a man who had been ordered by his physician to walk to his business & never to ride in an automobile or an electric car. The man was famous for his stinginess & he was thankful that while improving his health, he would also be saving the price of gasoline or his car-fare. The first morning he started out to walk, he came across an old woman crying bitterly in front of the Cathedral, with a tiny baby in her arms. The man stopped and asked what the trouble was, & the woman, still crying, said she wanted to have the baby christened in the Cathedral. "Well, why don't you go in and have it done?" "Oh! it costs, & I haven't got the money." "And how much does it cost?" "Three dollars." The man fumbled in his waist-coat pocket a moment and then drew forth a ten-dollar bill, which, with a pleased smile he handed the woman. "And is that for me?!" she exclaimed, too delighted to believe it possible. "Yes. And I'll wait here while you get the child christened and bring me the change!" So the woman went in & then brought the man the seven dollars.

When he reached his office, his partner noticed that he looked better & brighter & considerably more cheerful. He asked what had happened to him & said he must surely be feeling better. The man told him that four good things had happened to him that day. The walk had made him feel stronger already; he had saved the expense of the gasoline; he had saved a child from Satan and he had gotten rid of that counterfeit ten-dollar bill & had seven dollars back from it! He was a competent business man!! (JC 1900–1907, entry for 1 Sept 1906)

215.18–19 over-impassioned recitations of "Curfew Shall Not Ring To-night,"] This poem, written by sixteen-year-old Rose Hartwick (later Thorpe) in 1867 and first published three years later, describes a young woman who stopped the bells at Chertsey Abbey to prevent the execution by Cromwell's men of her lover, falsely accused of being a Cavalier spy during England's civil war. It became a standard of nineteenth-century public recitation, popular but also much parodied, and was a particular favorite of Queen Victoria's (George Wharton James 1916, 5, 7–9, 14–15, 18–19).

216.26–28 She . . . jumped on his back and rode him all over the farm] In a letter to Clemens of 1 August 1886, Olivia (at Quarry Farm) reported a visit from Clara Spaulding. Clara had brought her dog Rob with her, and "although we had a good visit, Rob did not because as soon as he appeared in front of the house Sour Mash jumped onto his back and planted her claws so securely into his nose that he bled well, it is a wonder that she did not scratch his eyes out" (CU-MARK). "Brave Sour Mash!" Clemens replied, "Splendid Sour Mash! to furnish Rob Spaulding her autograph, without stamp, card, envelop, or any of the other requirements" (2 Aug 1886 to OLC, CU-MARK).

217.13 Cadichon] The Clemens children adopted the name of their donkey from *Les Mémoires d'un âne* (1860) by Sophie Rostopchine, comtesse de Ségur. They had a copy of the 1880 English translation (Gribben 1980, 2:620).

218.23 General Beale recently outlined his great, simple, beautiful nature] Beale's remarks were quoted in a "Special" report from Washington to the Chicago *Tribune,* and were probably printed in other newspapers as well ("A Tribute. Gen. Beale's Recollections of the Dying General," 2 Apr 1885, 1). Edward Fitzgerald (Ned) Beale (1822–93), a close friend of Grant's, was a former naval officer, California militia general, surveyor general of California and Nevada, and superintendent of Indian affairs for California and Nevada, as well as a millionaire rancher in California and Hyattsville, Maryland, near Washington. He served as ambassador to Austria-Hungary under President Grant (1876–77).

218.30–219.4 And when Sir Ector . . . put spear in rest] The quoted passages are from Sir Thomas Malory's *Le Morte d'Arthur,* book 21, chapter 13.

Autobiographical Dictation, 5 September 1906

222.28–30 It is years . . . little chaps] Clemens and Olivia began "the Children's Record," which Clemens titled "A Record of the Small Foolishnesses of Susie & 'Bay' Clemens (Infants)," in August 1876, when Susy was four years old and Clara was two; Jean was not yet born. The last entry was dated 7 June 1885 (SLC 1876–85). The seven anecdotes given in this dictation, however, are not all from the "Record": two closely follow an 1884 manuscript headed "At the Farm" (CU-MARK), while one other has not been found in any document.

224.2–3 Mr. Darwin said that nothing was necessary . . . statute of limitations] Darwin, in his "Biographical Sketch of an Infant," described his young son's beginning to lie:

> I met him coming out of the same room, and he was eyeing his pinafore which he had carefully rolled up; and again his manner was so odd that I determined to see what was within his pinafore, notwithstanding that he said there was nothing and repeatedly commanded me to "go away," and I found it stained with pickle-juice; so that here was carefully planned deceit. As this child was educated solely by working on his good feelings, he soon became as truthful, open, and tender, as anyone could desire. (Darwin 1877, 292)

224.30 Clara will make her public début as a singer . . . seventeen days hence] See the Autobiographical Dictations of 3 October and 4 October 1906.

224.35 Will Gillette] The actor and dramatist, brother of Lilly Gillette Warner (see *AutoMT1,* 336, 584 n. 336.18).

224.37–38 Mrs. Leslie and her daughters. Elsie Leslie . . . a great celebrity on the stage] Evelyn Lyde (b. 1849) became known as Mrs. Leslie after her daughters' stage names, Elsie and Dora Leslie. Elsie Leslie Lyde (1879–1966) and her sister Eda (Dora) O. Lyde (b. 1873) joined the theatrical company of Joseph Jefferson, a family friend, in 1885 after the failure of their father's business. Jean met Elsie sometime in 1889; by that time Elsie had become famous for her role in *Editha's Burglar* (1887), which she first played on Broadway and then (with William Gillette as the burglar) in the traveling company; and for her lead role in *Little Lord Fauntleroy* (1888). She became a friend of the Clemens family's and in early 1890 appeared on Broadway in the dual role of the Prince and Tom Canty in Abby Sage Richardson's dramatization of *The Prince and the*

Pauper, in which her sister also appeared as Princess Elizabeth (U.S. National Archives and Records Administration 1795–1905, Roll 468, passport applications for Evelyn and Eda Lyde, issued 26 May 1896; *Newark Census* 1880, 779:224C; Lyde 1889, 372, 374; RGB/CL 2011; Odell 1927–49, 14:263–64).

225.9 Rosa] Rosina Hay.

Autobiographical Dictation, 7 September 1906

225.39–226.1 the banquet, last winter . . . the Ends of the Earth Club] According to the New York *Times,*

> The Ends of the Earth Club, of which Mark Twain is the honorary head, with Rudyard Kipling and Admiral George Dewey as members of the Honorary Council, was formed three years ago by globe trotters of New York and everywhere else in the world, whose idea was to dine together once every twelve months and exchange felicitations. ("Ends of the Earthers Foregather Here Again. And Astonish Mark Twain with Some Very Brief Reports," 17 Feb 1906, 9)

The club's third annual dinner was held on 16 February 1906 at the Savoy Hotel in Manhattan. For Clemens's brief speech, about writing *The Gilded Age* and his 1867 lecture at the Cooper Union in New York, see Fatout 1976, 485–86.

226.1–2 chairman, a retired regular army officer of high grade] General James H. Wilson (1837–1925), the toastmaster and unofficial chairman, served in both the Civil War and the Spanish-American War. The words that Clemens quotes here have not been found in the newspaper reports of his speech, but according to the New York *Tribune,* "The eventual domination of the Anglo-Saxon race was the burden of many of the remarks" at the banquet ("From Ends of Earth," New York *Tribune,* 17 Feb 1906, 7).

226.11–14 the old-time picture in the almanac . . . needs sewing up right away] Nineteenth-century almanacs typically included the figure of a naked man surrounded by the signs of the zodiac. The purpose of this "anatomy," or "man of signs," was to correlate the parts of the body with the astrological signs that governed them. Often the man was shown with his abdomen cut open and his intestines exposed—either to facilitate linking them to their star-sign (Virgo) or because the abdominal flaps helped to conceal his genitals (Scorpio). The "man of signs" is found in English and American almanacs dating back to the

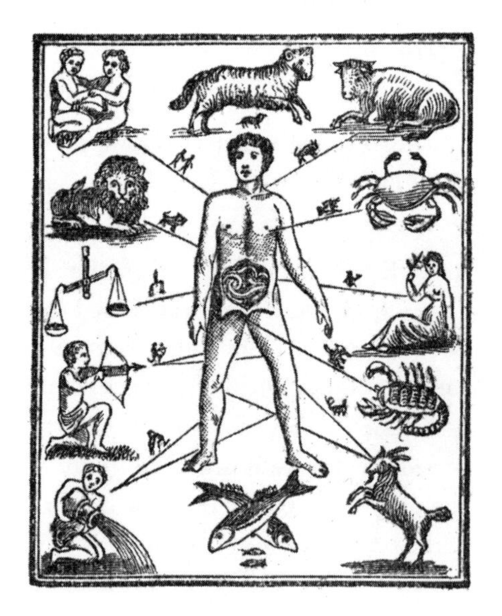

seventeenth century; the image is based on classical and medieval astrology (Kittredge 1904, 53–61).

227.6 "Come, *step* lively!"] The standard exhortation from train conductors such as those of the Manhattan Elevated Railway to move passengers off and onto the trains (see *AutoMT1,* 620 n. 411.5–6).

227.25–26 British Premier Campbell-Bannerman celebrates seventieth birthday to-morrow] Sir Henry Campbell-Bannerman (1836–1908) was born Henry Campbell in Kelvinside, near Glasgow, Scotland, on 7 September. He reluctantly changed his surname to Campbell-Bannerman after a conditional inheritance of property in 1871 (Wilson 1973, 46–47). See the note at 227.34–37.

227.28–33 To His Excellency . . . Mark Twain] Clemens sent this telegram to the London *Tribune*'s New York correspondent, Luther E. Price, who had made the request (Price to SLC, 6 Sept 1906, VtMiM).

227.34–37 A great and brave statesman . . . we lived in the same hotel for a time] Clemens probably first met Campbell-Bannerman at Marienbad in August 1891. In October 1898 they could have met "daily" at Vienna's Hotel Krantz, where he and his wife, Sarah Charlotte Bruce (d. 1906), often stayed after their annual six-week visit to Marienbad. Campbell-Bannerman began his career in the House of Commons in 1868 as the Liberal member for Stirling Burghs. He became known as an advocate of universal elementary education, free trade, Irish home rule, anti-imperialism, and improved social conditions. Although not a compelling speaker, he was famously principled in dealing with provocative opposition even within his own party. He served as secretary of state for war in 1886 and again in 1892–95. He was knighted by Queen Victoria in 1895, and in 1905 King Edward VII appointed him premier (the first to be called prime minister) and first lord of the treasury, a position he resigned in early April 1908, about two weeks before his death (John Wilson 1973, 137, 140, 149, 446, 634–42; "Premier's Wife Dead," New York *Times,* 31 Aug 1906, 9).

228.5–6 Labouchere . . . that picturesque personality] After two years at Trinity College, adventures in South America and Mexico, six months in an Ojibwe Indian camp, ten years as an attaché in Washington, D.C., and Europe, and two short stints in Parliament as a Liberal member for Windsor and Middlesex in the late 1860s, Henry du Pré Labouchere (1831–1912) worked as a theater owner, theatrical producer, journalist, editor, and publisher. He was known for his cynical wit, his brilliance, his combativeness, and his adventurous life. His magazine, *Truth,* which regularly exposed fraud and reported inside information about the court and prominent politicians, was several times sued for libel. In 1880 Labouchere returned to Parliament as a Liberal member for Northampton and served until 1906.

228.8–11 his wife, in the throng of medicinal-water drinkers . . . had been a great actress in her time] Actress Henrietta Hodson (1841–1910) lived with Labouchere, served as his hostess, bore him a child, and eventually married him, after the death of her estranged husband, Richard Walter Pigeon, in 1887. Ellen Terry said she was "a brilliant burlesque actress, a good singer, and a capital dancer" with "great personal charm" (Terry 1908, 47). She had a very successful career, primarily in comic roles, in Bristol and London, where she became manager of the Royalty Theatre, introducing the innovation of having the orchestra in a pit below the stage. In 1877 she had a public feud with W. S. Gilbert, whose dictatorial behavior when she was part of the cast for his *Pygmalion and Galatea* prompted her to attack him in a pamphlet addressed to the profession, and in 1878 she retired from acting. Clemens probably saw her in Bad Homburg in August 1892, possibly on the same day he met the Prince of Wales (23 Aug 1892 to OC and MEC, CU-MARK; see AD, 27 Aug 1906, note at 181.31–36).

228.20–21 the Nestor of Parliament of that day] Unidentified.

228.21–22 Sir William Vernon Harcourt, leader of the Opposition] Harcourt (1827–1904), a lawyer, journalist, and Liberal member of Parliament, served as home secretary and chancellor of the exchequer under Gladstone before becoming Leader of the Opposition in 1896–98, when a Conservative-Unionist government was in power.

228.31 death of William IV] On 20 June 1837.

228.38–39 the Prince of Wales . . . was to receive in state the deed of a vast property which had been conferred upon the nation by a wealthy citizen] A manuscript fragment in the Mark Twain Papers reads in part, "tell about lost deed to the new national gallery"; this note's proximity to notes on Sir William Harcourt makes it probable that the opening of the Tate Gallery is meant, and that it was Harcourt himself who told the story. He was a prime mover in the foundation of the gallery, and assisted at the ceremony on 21 July 1897 at which Henry Tate presented the Prince of Wales with the deeds to the property and the building (Autobiographical Fragment #148, CU-MARK; "The Prince of Wales and the Tate Gallery," London *Times,* 22 July 1897, 7).

Autobiographical Dictation, 10 September 1906

229.17–18 not yet finished about the British Premier and his seventieth birthday, but I will let that go over until another day] Clemens again mentions Campbell-Bannerman in the Autobiographical Dictation of 1 October 1907, but does not return to the subject of his birthday.

230.1–2 In a chapter which I dictated five months ago . . . dates of their occurrence] See the Autobiographical Dictation of 29 March 1906 (*AutoMT1,* 455–62).

230.4–6 I edited one issue . . . several weeks to quiet down and pacify the people whom my writings had excited] When in September 1852 Orion was obliged to be out of town, he asked his brother to edit one issue of the Hannibal *Journal,* a weekly. Clemens, aged sixteen, took on the 16 September issue and part of the following week's as well. In three of the five sketches he wrote he signed himself "W. Epaminondas Adrastus

Blab" or "W.E.A.B.": "Historical Exhibition—A No. 1 Ruse" (about a humiliating hoax perpetrated by a local merchant); "Editorial Agility" (aimed at Joseph P. Ament, editor of the rival Hannibal *Missouri Courier,* under whom he had served an apprenticeship from May 1848 to January 1851); and "Blabbing Government Secrets!" (satirizing the debate in the Missouri legislature over the allocation of land grants to the railroads). But the article that caused a real commotion was "'Local' Resolves to Commit Suicide," which he signed "A Dog-be-Deviled-Citizen." It ridiculed (without naming him) the local editor, J. T. Hinton, of the Hannibal *Tri-Weekly Messenger,* who it was rumored had tried and failed to drown himself because he had been jilted. Clemens illustrated his brief article with a woodcut he carved himself, showing the local editor holding a lantern and walking into the stream, intent on "feeding his carcass to the fishes of Bear Creek.... Fearing, however, that he may get out of his depth, he *sounds the stream with his walking-stick.*" Hinton protested such rough treatment in his own local column, but Clemens followed up on 23 September with "Pictur' Department," also signed "A Dog-be-Deviled-Citizen," containing two more woodcuts and further ridicule. Orion tried to defuse the situation in the same issue, saying the work was "perpetrated in a spirit of fun, and without a serious thought, no attention was expected to be paid to them, beyond a smile at the local editor's expense." But Hinton the same day responded at some length, dismissing the articles as "the feeble eminations of a puppy's brain." In 1871 Clemens published a sketch describing, and no doubt embroidering, these events, "My First Literary Venture," in the *Galaxy* (*ET&S1,* 71–75, 78; 4 Mar 1870 to Walden, *L4,* 86 n. 1; SLC 1852a, 1852b, 1852c, 1852d, 1852e, 1871).

230.6–7 I did not meddle with a pen again, so far as I can remember, until ten years later—1859] Texts of more than seventy newspaper letters and sketches by Clemens written between 1849 and 1859 have been recovered. Most were published in his brother's various small-town newspapers: the Hannibal *Western Union,* the Hannibal *Journal,* and the Muscatine (Iowa) *Journal.* But a handful were published in journals like the Boston *Carpet-Bag,* the Philadelphia *American Courier,* the Hannibal *Missouri Courier,* the St. Louis *Missouri Republican,* and the New Orleans *Crescent,* while still other writings, like "Jul'us Caesar" (SLC 1855–56) and various poems for his friends' albums, remained unpublished.

230.21–27 The pilots handed my extravagant satire ... nor ever used his nom de guerre again] Clemens's satire was an untitled sketch made up of an "editor's" introduction and a letter giving river information signed "Sergeant Fathom." It was published in the daily "River Intelligence" column of the New Orleans *Crescent* on 17 May 1859, less than six weeks after he got his pilot's license (SLC 1859). Two days after it appeared the editor wrote that "the letter which appeared in the river column of the Crescent of Tuesday morning was handed to us by Mr. B. W. S. Bowen, pilot of the steamer A. T. Lacey" (*ET&S1,* 128 n. 10). At the time Barton S. Bowen was copilot with Clemens on the *Lacey* ("Steamboat Calendar: Clemens's Piloting Assignments, 1857–1861," *L1,* 389). Clemens "told all about this" in chapter 50 of *Life on the Mississippi.* No evidence has yet been found that Isaiah Sellers (1803?–64) ever used "Mark Twain" to sign his contributions to newspapers (24 June 1874 to Unidentified, *L6,* 166–67 n. 1; Kruse 1992, 2–25).

230.30–32 I wrote no literature until 1866, when . . . "The Jumping Frog" was published in a perishing literary journal in New York] Clemens is distinguishing between journalism and literature. But much of his writing for the *Enterprise* must be considered something other than reportage—"Ye Sentimental Law Student," written in 1863, for instance—and even before he was hired as a local reporter in 1862 he had volunteered the so-called "Josh" letters (no longer extant), which included at least one memorable burlesque. In addition, he wrote dozens of newspaper letters containing humorous sketches, as well as several literary articles for the *Californian* and the *Golden Era,* before "Jim Smiley and His Jumping Frog" was published in the New York *Saturday Press* for 18 November 1865 (SLC 1863b, 1865e; *ET&S1,* 13–14, 16–17; see AD, 21 May 1906, especially the note at 47.3–5).

230.40 Mr. Alden, editor of *Harper's Monthly*] Called the "true genius of the magazine," Henry Mills Alden (1836–1919), first hired by Harpers in 1862, was made editor of *Harper's New Monthly Magazine* in 1869, a position he held for fifty years, although he retired from active management some years before his death. He insisted from the beginning of his tenure that he be "first reader" of submitted manuscripts, and although he worked closely with writers and wrote numerous editorials as well as "The Editor's Study," his contribution was little known outside of the magazine, in part because the editorship was mostly associated in the public's mind with William Dean Howells and George William Curtis, authors, at different times, of "The Editor's Easy Chair." On Alden's seventieth birthday, Clemens said of his "dear and ancient friend": "You bear a kind heart in your breast, and the sweet and winning spirit that charms away all hostilities and animosities, and makes of your enemy your friend and keeps him so" ("Henry Mills Alden's 70th Birthday," *Harper's Weekly* 50 [15 Dec 1906]: 1813–14; Howells 1919; New York *Times:* "Henry Mills Alden" and "Henry Mills Alden of Harper's, Dies," 8 Oct 1919, 18, 19).

230.41 Mr. Thomas Rees] Thomas Rees (1850–1933) was the publisher of the Springfield (Ill.) *State Register* and the son of William S. Rees (d. 1859), publisher of the Keokuk *Post* ("Death of William S. Rees, the Street Preacher," New York *Times,* 12 Oct 1859, 8).

231.11–12 an affidavit sworn to by Mr. Rees, Sr.] The affidavit may have been in the hand of Thomas Rees's elder brother, George, who was assistant editor of the *Post* until their father's death in 1859, when he became editor (*Keokuk City Directory* 1859; *MTB,* 1:112; Rees 1908, 399–401).

233.40–41 a few columns of solid bourgeois] That is, text that is typeset in a font of medium size (9 point) with no additional line spacing.

234.2–3 a Philadelphian, Homer C. Wilbur, a regular and acceptable contributor to *Sartain's Magazine*] *Sartain's Union Magazine of Literature and Art* was published in Philadelphia between 1849 and 1852 by John Sartain (1808–97), a "master" of mezzotint engraving and a colleague and friend of Edgar Allan Poe's. Among its prominent contributors were Poe, Longfellow, Thoreau, James Russell Lowell, Bayard Taylor, Harriet Martineau, William Gilmore Simms, Richard H. Stoddard, and George W. Bethune (Nichols 2004, 1, 12, 15). No contributions to the magazine by Homer C. Wilbur have been found.

235.7 Burkes and Hares] William Burke and William Hare were convicted of entrapping and murdering seventeen victims in Edinburgh in 1827–28 and selling their corpses for dissection to Dr. Robert Knox, a private anatomy lecturer, who taught students of the Edinburgh Medical College.

235.20–22 when the affidaviter says that there was a *contract,* and that I was *paid* for the work, those two statements are plain straightforward falsehoods] Clemens wrote three Thomas Jefferson Snodgrass travel letters and published them in the Keokuk *Post* in 1856 and 1857: "Correspondence," "Snodgrass' Ride on the Railroad," and "Snodgrass, in a Adventure" (SLC 1856a, 1856b, 1857). He may have been correct that there was no written contract, but clearly there had been an agreement, if only verbal, to publish the letters. Thomas Rees, who knew of only two of the three letters, wrote his version of events in 1908, asserting that Clemens had indeed been paid:

> The firm of Rees & Son arranged with the young man to write some articles for publication in the Keokuk Post, which they mutually agreed would be worth five dollars each. . . . After writing the first, he concluded that he ought to have seven dollars and a half apiece for his articles, and the publishers met him at that price, so he wrote the second article, which was published, after which he thought his talent was worth ten dollars per article. As the publishers had reached the limit, having already invested twelve dollars and a half, which I am certain was the first money ever paid Mr. Clemens for writing, and which represented the profits of about two years' publication of that daily paper, the negotiations were broken off and the series of articles ended at that point. . . .
>
> At the present time I have, locked up in the safe in my office, typewritten copies of these two articles, taken from the files of my father's paper. Each one has an affidavit attached showing the genuineness of the publication and the circumstances under which it was written by Mr. Clemens. . . .
>
> I thought that I would insert these two articles in this letter, but they are such crude attempts at humor and are of such inferior composition as compared with Mr. Clemens' more recent writings, that, notwithstanding the affidavits, some persons might imagine that I had written them myself, and after all these long years even Mr. Clemens himself would, perhaps, doubt that he was the author of them. (Rees 1908, 400–401)

Autobiographical Dictation, 2 October 1906

235.33–34 banquet-speech in New York on the 19th of September] Clemens's speech, at the annual dinner of the Associated Press in the Waldorf-Astoria Hotel, was "an appeal to the nations in behalf of the simplified spelling" ("Spelling and Pictures and Twain at Dinner," New York *Times,* 20 Sept 1906, 4). The text is included in the Autobiographical Dictation of 19 November 1906. According to Isabel Lyon, Clemens originally began to prepare a different speech, on a topic suggested by Melville Stone, the general manager of the Associated Press:

> When I went to my study later, on the desk I found 8 closely written pages of Ms. A speech—Mr. Clemens explained to me a[t] dinner—a speech to be given at a press banquet sometime in Sept. A speech in which he is taking up cudgels for the Standard Oil. It seems that when he was in N.Y. Mr. Melville Stone asked him to do just this thing & as Mr. Rogers's intimate friend Mr. Clemens felt that he could not do it, and brought forward many sane reasons for not doing it, but Mr. Stone could see only the fact that he wanted Mr. Clemens to make that speech & make it so that it would attack the press for "muckraking" every corporation. (Lyon 1906, entry for 28 July)

235.34–35 visit to Norfolk, Connecticut, to witness my daughter Clara's début as a singer] Clemens returns to this topic at greater length in the Autobiographical Dictations of 3 October and 4 October 1906.

236.1–6 young woman in New York . . . what she regarded as a great service] Clemens alludes to Charlotte Teller (1876–1953), a writer and socialist who had earned a degree from the University of Chicago. (Teller used her maiden name as a *nom de plume;* she had separated from her first husband, Frank Minitree Johnson, when she met Clemens, but continued to call herself "Mrs. Johnson"; in 1912 she married Gilbert Hirsch and adopted his surname.) She lived with her grandmother and a group of fellow writers at 3 Fifth Avenue, and was therefore a close neighbor of Clemens's. In his Autobiographical Dictation of 30 March 1906 Clemens recalled their meeting, when she brought Nikolai Chaykovsky, the leader of the Socialist Revolutionary Party, to seek support for his cause (*AutoMT1,* 462, 647 n. 462.12). One of her works in progress, a play about Joan of Arc, caught his interest, and the two soon formed a warm friendship. Clemens was so impressed with her talent that he offered to read her manuscripts. On 13 April he wrote her, "If you yourself have had any doubts, brush them away; for there is greatness in you, Charlotte,—more of it than you suspect, I think. You are going to surpass your utmost anticipations" (NN-BGC). While on a trip to New York in late September he met with Joseph H. Sears to discuss a novel she had written, *The Cage:*

> Mrs. Johnson was one of the happiest persons in America last night. I sent for Sears, (President & Manager of Appletons) yesterday afternoon, & he came here at once & we talked an hour. He likes her book & is going to publish it; & I asked him to sell the serial rights for her, & he said he would do it with pleasure & give it to the magazine that offers the most. He also said it is his policy to secure a dozen authors permanently—a new book per year—& he believed she was going to be one of them. (25 Sept 1906 to Lyon and JC, photocopy in CU-MARK)

The "great service" was Clemens's offer to endorse *The Cage,* in the form of a letter addressed to the actress Maude Adams (famous for her role in *Peter Pan*). He described the novel as

> the story of the heart of a woman so big that all worldly forms are gladly ignored for the love of one man. That is what a real woman would do; & in so doing she would really make the man, too, if he had character to start with. And all of this takes place amidst the familiar surroundings of the Chicago of to-day. It is a strong book, Peter Pan, & if you once begin it you will not be able to leave this man & woman until you have finished the story. (24? Sept 1906 to Adams, draft not sent, CU-MARK)

But in late October Lyon relayed a rumor that alarmed Clemens (Lyon 1906, entry for 22 Oct; Teller to SLC, 24 Oct 1906, CU-MARK). Many years later Teller described what occurred:

> It was only a few days after that that Mr. Clemens, much agitated, told me he had heard people were gossiping about his seeing so much of me. He was at that time, as I remember, two years older than my grandmother who was living with me in New York. When I insisted on knowing just what the gossip was, he sent for his secretary, Miss Lyons, who said that someone at the Players' Club had asked Mr. Paine (whom I never met,) who this Miss Teller was that Mark Twain was seeing so much of.
>
> I did not see any reason for his being disturbed, but he was always peculiarly sensitive to public opinion. . . . He asked me if I would be willing to leave 3 Fifth Ave. with my grandmother, and live somewhere else conspicuously so he could come to see me; but I was unwilling to take that much notice of this gossip, nor did I think it was worthy of his position to give that much credence to what was an indifferent rumor. I asked him if he was worried about the letter he had given Mr. Seers which was to be photographed and used as advance notice, and while he did not ask that I should give it back to him, I insisted upon doing so, and I did not see him again. (Teller 1925, 5–6)

The rumor did not soon die away, however. Nearly a year later, on 2 July 1907, the San Francisco *Morning Call* reported that Clemens's marriage to Teller was "considered a possibility" ("Mark Twain and Charlotte Teller," 8). Then, even worse, on 4 July the New York *Herald* claimed that Clemens was engaged to Lyon. He responded with the following telegram from London: "I have not known, and shall never know, anyone who could fill the place of the wife I have lost. I shall not marry again" ("Mark Twain Will Not Marry Again," Washington *Post,* 6 July 1907, 6). Lyon blamed Teller for the second rumor, but Clemens later came to believe that Lyon herself was responsible. Teller and Clemens exchanged several letters in 1907–9, but never resumed their friendship (Trombley 2010, 137–38; Hill 1973, 172–73, 230; Schmidt 2009). *The Cage,* published in 1907 by D. Appleton and Company, received mixed reviews (see, for example, Peattie 1907 and "The Haymarket Riots," New York *Times,* 9 Mar 1907, BR142).

236.16–22 I believe that only one command has ever been issued . . . from that day to this] This "philosophy" became the basis of Clemens's essay "The Turning Point of My Life," published in 1910 (SLC 1910).

237.30 My father died] The account that begins here, of Clemens's early career before his years in the West, repeats the one he gave in the Autobiographical Dictations of 28 March and 29 March 1906 (see *AutoMT1,* 454–62 and notes on 644–47).

238.10 one of the pilots of the *Paul Jones*] Horace E. Bixby (see *AutoMT1,* 646 n. 461.16–17).

238.24 drifting toward the ministry] Although Clemens's remarks about the ministry may seem entirely facetious, he told his brother Orion in October 1865—evidently in earnest—that he had wanted to become a preacher:

> I never had but two **powerful** ambitions in my life. One was to be a pilot, & the other a preacher of the gospel. I accomplished the one & failed in the other, **because** I could not supply myself with the necessary stock in trade—*i.e.* religion. I have given it up forever. I never had a "call" in that direction, anyhow, & my aspirations were the very ecstasy of presumption. But I *have* had a "call" to literature, of a low order—*i.e.* humorous. It is nothing to be proud of, but it is my strongest suit. . . .
>
> But as I was saying, it is **human nature** to yearn to be what we were never intended for. It is singular, but it is so. I wanted to be a pilot or a preacher, & I was about as well calculated for either as is poor Emperor Norton for Chief Justice of the United States. (19 and 20 Oct 1865 to OC, *L1,* 322–23)

238.27–31 By and by I went out to the Humboldt mines . . . my muscles so incompetent] After silver and gold were discovered in the West Humboldt Mountains in 1860, the area became a center of mining activity. Clemens's trip there lasted from early December 1861 until late January 1862. For highly readable accounts of this adventure see chapters 26–33 of *Roughing It* and the letter to Jane Clemens dated 30 January 1862 (*L1,* 146–52). In early April Clemens departed for Aurora, in the Esmeralda mining region in southern Nevada; he worked briefly at Clayton's quartz mill in late June (see *AutoMT1,* 251, 543 n. 251.32–38).

238.38 Chief Justice Turner] George Enoch Turner (1828–85), an Ohio attorney, was appointed chief justice of Nevada Territory in 1861. He resigned that post in 1864, after the Nevada press accused him—and the rest of the judiciary—of corruption (Turner and SLC to OC, 18–30 Sept 1861, *L1,* 128–29 n. 2).

238.41–42 'the honey of the bees of Hymettus,'] Hymettus, a mountain southeast of Athens, was renowned in the ancient world for its exceptional honey.

238.42–239.1 'Whom the gods would destroy they first make mad,'] This Latin saying is sometimes misattributed to Euripides (Householder 1936; Bartlett 1980, 78:1, 134:21).

239.1 'Against the stupid, even the gods strive in vain.'] From *The Maid of Orleans* (1801) by Friedrich Schiller: "Mit der Dummheit kämpfen Götter selbst vergebens" (act 3, scene 6).

239.11–13 It was published in the *Enterprise* . . . I was offered his place for that interval] The burlesque was in one of several letters he signed "Josh" and sent gratis to the Virginia City *Territorial Enterprise,* probably beginning in April 1862, several months before he was hired as a local reporter. No text for any of the "Josh" letters has been found, but in 1893, Rollin Daggett, a colleague of Clemens's on the staff of the newspaper, described this particular burlesque as a "bogus Fourth of July oration purporting to have been delivered near Owens's Lake, where Mark was engaged in prospecting," and he recalled that owner and editor Joseph T. Goodman "decided at once that the writer was a man worth cultivating" (*ET&S1,* 13, 15, 17). Clemens traveled to Virginia City to begin his new job in September 1862 (for Daggett see *AutoMT1,* 568 n. 294.28; for William Wright, the "paper's city editor," see *AutoMT1,* 543 n. 251.32–38).

239.18–21 I had to go to Carson City . . . I signed these letters 'Mark Twain.'] Clemens corresponded for the *Territorial Enterprise* during the second session of the Territorial Legislature, held from 11 November to 20 December 1862. Only two of his reports are known to survive, written on 5 and 12 December, but neither is signed "Mark Twain" (SLC 1862a, 1862b). Although Clemens may have used the pseudonym in work now lost, Joe Goodman reported that he first signed "Mark Twain" on "Letter from Carson City," probably written on 31 January 1863 and published in the *Enterprise* a few days later. Goodman also remembered that the "first special article" signed "Mark Twain" was "Ye Sentimental Law Student," published on 19 February (SLC 1863a, 1863b; *MTEnt,* 48; *ET&S1,* 18, 192–93, 215–16).

239.25–28 accident which gave me a correspondence-job . . . Sandwich Islands for the Sacramento *Union*] Clemens was fired from the *Call* in October 1864 (see AD, 13 June 1906). Joe Goodman of the *Territorial Enterprise* agreed to pay him for a daily letter from San Francisco in September or October 1865, which he wrote until he left for the Sandwich Islands in March 1866.

Autobiographical Dictation, 3 October 1906

240.6–8 I went up to Norfolk, Connecticut . . . She had sung in public once before, but that was in Italy] In late 1898 Clara changed her musical study from piano to voice, hoping to pursue a professional career as a mezzo-soprano. She gave her first recital on 22 January 1901 in Washington, D.C.; it went badly, one sympathetic reviewer blaming "stage fright" and "partial paralysis of the vocal cords" ("Music and the Drama," Chicago *Tribune,* 23 Jan 1901, 7). The Italian concert Clemens mentions took place in Florence, on 8 April 1904. Clemens wrote Rogers that Clara "astonished the house—including me—with the richness & volume of her voice, & with her trained ability to handle it. It was a lone hand quite triumphantly played. The congratulations have been abundant & cordial" (12 Apr 1904 to Rogers, Salm, in *HHR,* 561). Clara's Norfolk, Connecticut, performance of 22 September 1906 was her professional debut. She continued to give concerts (largely bankrolled by her father) over the next several years, but never pursued a professional career (5 Mar 1899 to James R. Clemens, CtHMTH; Hartford *Courant:* "Miss Clemens's Debut," 23 Jan 1901, 8; "Miss Clemens's Success," 3 May 1904, 5; "Miss Clemens Well Received," 24 Sept 1906, 10; Shelden 2010, 173–75, 231–32, 345–46, 382).

241.12 Polish wet-nurse] Julia Koshloshky (22 Apr 1882 to OLC, CU-MARK).

241.36 George, the colored butler] George Griffin (see *AutoMT1,* 583 n. 335.28–32).

241.41–242.1 we have always set a high value on the three which I have described] The first two incidents that Clemens describes occurred on 2 and 9 January 1881 (9 Jan 1881 to JLC, NPV). The third incident, involving the barber, is not mentioned in any 1881 letters.

242.9–14 on the third floor of a hotel in Baden-Baden . . . her small body through the pillars] This incident took place at the Hotel de France, where the Clemenses stayed in late July and early August 1878. Clara later reported the she had been on the sixth floor (*N&J2,* 113–14, 367; CC 1931, 6).

242.34 she married a young farmer] Rosina Hay (1852?–1926) came to work for the Clemenses in 1874, and left on 16 August 1883 to prepare for her wedding. On 4 September she was married in Elmira's Park Church to Horace K. Terwilliger. In 1909 he was a committee clerk for the New York State Assembly (*N&J2,* 365 n. 33; *Hartford Census* 1880, 97:117C; Staver 1938, 34; Koenig 1909, 591; *AutoMT1,* 607 n. 394.15–18).

Autobiographical Dictation, 4 October 1906

243.9 Clara was to sing in Norfolk on the 22d] See the Autobiographical Dictation of 3 October 1906, note at 240.6–8.

243.10–12 some of them printed Clara's portrait . . . but put "Mark Twain's daughter" in very large letters] The Boston *Journal,* for example, printed a portrait under the headline "Twain's Daughter to Make Debut as Singer" (14 Sept 1906, 7). The drawing appears to be a stock image, however, and is not an accurate likeness.

243.23 our old Katy] Katy Leary.

243.27 Mrs. R. W. Gilder] Helena de Kay Gilder (1846–1916), who married Richard Watson Gilder in 1874, was an accomplished artist who had studied under Winslow Homer. Many of her illustrations appeared in the *Century Magazine* and in her husband's books of poetry. The Gilder home in New York became a gathering place for the most talented artists, writers, and musicians of the day. Clemens and his daughters frequently attended their regular Friday night soirées (McNay 2011; "R. W. Gilder's Widow Dies," New York *Times,* 29 May 1916, 11; Lyon 1906, entries for 3, 16, 23, 30 Mar, and 6 Apr).

243.35 Mr. Luckstone] Isidore Luckstone (1861–1941) was Clara's vocal coach and accompanist. He began his professional career as a pianist at age fifteen, and within a few years had become a conductor as well. He accompanied many famous singers and instrumentalists, including Enrico Caruso, Fritz Kreisler, and Marcella Sembrich, and composed a number of songs. In recent years he had given up most of his work as an accompanist to focus on teaching voice, for which he was greatly in demand. Clara first sang for him in March 1906. Isabel Lyon noted in her journal, "Mr. Luckstone gave his verdict & it was that C.C.'s breath is not as it should be. Luckstone is strong & breezy & Norsemanlike & competent—& his explanations were illuminating & inspiring" (Lyon 1906, entry for 16 Mar).

244.6 Rodman Gilder] After his graduation from Harvard in 1899, Rodman Gilder (1877–1953), son of Richard Watson and Helena Gilder, worked as a freelance journalist for the New York *Evening Sun* and the *Criterion.* In 1904–11 he was employed by the Crocker-Wheeler Electric Company (manufacturers of motors), first as publicity manager and then as secretary. In 1911 he married Louise Comfort Tiffany, daughter of Louis Comfort Tiffany.

244.21 Miss Gordon] Clara J. Gordon, a nurse at the New York sanatorium where Clara stayed after her mother's death, had become her good friend (Hill 1973, 97).

244.42–245.1 My talk was reported in the newspapers] A review of the concert in the New York *Sun*—entitled "Twain's 'First Appearance.' At His Daughter's Singing Debut He Tells How Stage Fright Once Gripped Him"—included a complete text of Clemens's speech, in which he "recalled the agony of his own first appearance upon a public stage," in San Francisco in October 1866. The reviewer said nothing about Clara's performance until the last paragraph, where he noted that she "displayed some nervousness in her opening number," but then "acquitted herself with coolness and effect" in performing works by Grieg, Schubert, and Haydn, among others (24 Sept 1906, 3). For a text of Clemens's speech see Fatout 1976, 528–29.

Autobiographical Dictation, 5 October 1906

245.26–27 Several weeks ago I injected into one of these chapters a couple of odd and comical letters] Clemens included the texts of two "odd and comical" letters in the Autobiographical Dictation of 29 August 1906.

245.36–246.1 I used one of them in a speech before the Associated Press . . . The speech was published] Clemens used the first letter in his speech at the Associated Press dinner on 19 September, which was printed in the New York *Times* the following day and is inserted into the Autobiographical Dictation of 19 November 1906 ("Spelling and Pictures and Twain at Dinner," New York *Times,* 20 Sept 1906, 4; see AD, 2 Oct 1906, note at 235.33–34, and AD, 19 Nov 1906).

246.9–10 Miss Anny Stokbridge] Anne W. Stockbridge (b. 1854), a music teacher, was the principal of Stockbridge Hall, a girls' boarding school in Yarmouth, Maine (*Freeport Census* 1900, 590:21A; Patterson 1908, 96).

246.11–12 Mr. Stockbridge of the University Club, Boston] William H. Stockbridge (b. 1844), a music teacher (*Freeport Census* 1900, 590:5B). The University Club was an athletic and social club founded in 1891.

246.33 Miss Grace Donworth] Donworth (1857–1945) was the historian of the Machias chapter of the Daughters of the American Revolution (*Machias Census* 1900, 602:10A; *D.A.R. Directory* 1908, 45; Flagg 1966, 97–98).

246.43 Very truly yours] In the top margin of Stockbridge's letter Clemens wrote, "Tell her I will find a publisher when I get to New York." He replied to her on 4 October, offering his assistance (NN-BGC):

Dear Miss Stockbridge (if she really exists):
257 Benefit Street (if there is any such place)

Yes, I should like a copy of that other letter. This whole fake is delightful, & I tremble with fear that you are a fake yourself & that I am your guileless prey. (But never mind, it isn't any matter)

Now as to publication. I shall be going home to New York 8 days hence—
21 Fifth Avenue
Suppose you send me, there, type-written copies of as many of "Jennie's" letters as Miss Donworth has thus far forged, & I will show them to a magazine editor & put him in correspondence with you if he thinks well of them.

For they ought to be *serialized* in a magazine FIRST.

I think that the swindle that they are genuine ought to be maintained. This is a sin, but that is nothing. The newspapers will attack their genuineness, & this will furnish good & cheap advertising. The Christian publisher likes that.

Sincerely Yours
S. L. Clemens.

In 1907 the "Jennie Allen" letters ran serially in the *Ladies' Home Journal;* Donworth admitted authorship only when she published them in book form the following year (*MTB,* 3:1318–20; Donworth 1908).

247.2–3 Chatterton deceived Horace Walpole with his Rowley inventions] Thomas Chatterton (1752–70) was born in Bristol and grew up in relative poverty. At the age of sixteen he began forging manuscripts in a pseudo-medieval diction. Seeking the patronage of Horace Walpole (1717–97), the fourth earl of Orford and famed man of letters, Chatterton sent him a supposed treatise on early English painters, ostensibly the work of a fifteenth-century poet-monk named Thomas Rowley. Initially, Walpole was taken in, asking to see the poems; but further reflection and advice from literary friends convinced him of the fraud. Chatterton continued to create Rowley's works, but died in 1770 of an overdose of arsenic and laudanum; he was not yet eighteen. In the decade after his death, his "Rowley poems" began to be published and admired; immediately the question of their authenticity sparked a public controversy, in the course of which his fakery was proved, and his precocity acknowledged.

247.4 The Ireland forgeries were accepted by astute Shaksperean scholars] William-Henry Ireland (1775–1835) was the illegitimate son of a Shakespeare-worshiping London artisan. To please his father, and in emulation of Chatterton (see the note at 247.2–3), Ireland began in 1794 to produce forged documents, supposedly in Shakespeare's hand, which he claimed were from a cache of the playwright's personal papers. Ireland's early attempts were modest—a deed and a promissory note—but soon he was forging letters and dramatic manuscripts, including the complete play *Vortigern.* Ireland's father exhibited his son's "finds" to literary gentlemen, many of whom (including James Boswell) signed a "Certificate of Belief" in their genuineness. Upon publication of a collection of these papers in 1795, the fraud was exposed by Edmond Malone, the preeminent Shakespearean scholar of the age. Acclaim turned to abuse; *Vortigern* was "howled off the stage"; and the elder Ireland died in 1800, still refusing to accept that his son's documents were forgeries (Schoenbaum 1991, 132–67).

247.9–10 Book of Mormon, engraved upon metal plates . . . by Joseph Smith] Smith (1805–44) claimed to have found the metal plates, engraved with ancient characters he called "Reformed Egyptian," after seeing their location in several visions. He translated them by means of "seer" stones to create the Book of Mormon. The plates had been buried under a stone near Manchester, in western New York State (*RI 1993,* 601 n. 107.5–10). Clemens dictated "the State of New York" but later revised that to "Canada" on the typescript. The reason for this is unclear.

247.14 Brother Quimby] Phineas Quimby (1802–66), the first practitioner of mental healing in the United States, used hypnotism to treat Eddy in the 1860s. From his teaching she derived her belief in the power of the mind to cure illness, later developing his ideas into the religious doctrine that became the foundation of the Church of Christ, Scientist (see AD, 22 June 1906, note at 136.10–12).

Autobiographical Dictation, 8 October 1906

247.28 various entries, covering a month] In these entries Susy records her parents' visit to Onteora Park, a colony of artists and writers in the Catskills, from 24 to 29 August 1885, while she and her sisters remained at Quarry Farm in Elmira. Clemens continues to talk about his experiences there in the Autobiographical Dictations of 9 October and 10 October 1906.

247.29 General Grant, the sculptor Gerhardt] In the spring of 1885 Karl Gerhardt had sculpted a bust of the dying Grant that greatly pleased his family. At Clemens's suggestion, he tried to win a commission to make a statue of Grant—a bid that was ultimately unsuccessful (*N&J3,* 157; for Gerhardt, and Clemens's account of his work on the Grant bust, see *AutoMT1,* 86–91, 480 n. 74.2–7).

247.29 Mrs. Candace Wheeler, Miss Dora Wheeler] Candace Wheeler (1827–1923), a pioneering decorative artist and an associate of Louis Comfort Tiffany, helped to decorate the Clemenses' Hartford house in 1881. In 1883 she was one of the founders of Onteora Park. Dora (1857–1940), Candace's daughter, was an artist and portrait painter. The Clemenses met them through their mutual friend Dean Sage and began a "long and enjoyable friendship" (Wheeler 1918, 324; *N&J3,* 178, 212, 221, 562).

247.30 Mr. Frank Stockton, Mrs. Mary Mapes Dodge] See the Autobiographical Dictation of 9 October 1906, notes at 250.29 and 250.30.

247.30 widow of General Custer] Elizabeth B. Custer (1842–1933) married General George A. Custer in 1864 and thereafter accompanied him wherever he was stationed, including the front lines during the Civil War. After his death at Little Bighorn in 1876, she glorified his memory in lectures and books. In 1887 Webster and Company issued

Tenting on the Plains, her account of their experiences at military forts in Texas and Kansas in 1865–67.

249.42–250.4 I made a brave experiment . . . I made a talk before a full house, in the village, clothed like a ghost] Clemens described the "experiment" in a letter to Mary Rogers:

> The night of the great storm I drove to the village through the deluge & talked, in the basement of the church, to a housefull of wet farmers & their families (it's a gratis monthly function instituted by the ladies of the church) all clothed in sombre colors; & my spectral costume was the only cheerful object in that place. I meant to explain my clothes, but as I was passing to the platform Miss Fanny Dwight—summer-resorter, friend of ours, a person of extraordinary taste & wonderful judgment—halted me & whispered, "Mr. Clemens, you look just too sweet for anything!" I whispered back, "Miss Fanny, I was going to explain & justify these clothes, but in my opinion they don't need it now." My, but some girls do have the clear eye! (11–16 Oct 1906, NNC, in Leary 1961, 69–75)

250.9 I hope to get together courage enough to wear white clothes all through the winter] Clemens first wore his now-famous white suit to speak to a congressional committee on copyright in Washington on 7 December 1906 (see AD, 26 Dec 1906, where his speech is reprinted). He had appeared in the suit during interviews earlier in the day, giving several reporters a preview of the coming spectacle. Howells recalled:

> Nothing could have been more dramatic than the gesture with which he flung off his long loose overcoat, and stood forth in white from his feet to the crown of his silvery head. It was a magnificent *coup;* but the magnificent speech which he made, tearing to shreds the venerable farrago of nonsense about non-property in ideas which had formed the basis of all copyright legislation, made you forget even his spectacularity. (Howells 1910, 96)

He began to wear the suit so regularly, both in private and for public appearances, that on 1 May the Washington *Post* called it his "copyrighted white flannel suit" ("Mark Twain in Gloom," 5; for an excellent discussion of the white suit phenomenon see Shelden 2010, xvii–xxiv and notes on 433–35).

250.19–20 what Choate said last March] Clemens and Choate spoke at the 29 March 1906 meeting of the New York State Association for Promoting the Interests of the Blind (see *AutoMT1,* 649 n. 464.17–19). Choate's remarks, as reported in the New York *Times,* did not include any comments about life after seventy; they were probably expressed in a private conversation ("Twain and Choate Talk at Meeting for Blind," 30 Mar 1906, 9).

Autobiographical Dictation, 9 October 1906

250.29 Mr. Frank Stockton] Francis R. Stockton (1834–1902) worked for *Scribner's Monthly,* and later served as assistant editor of *St. Nicholas,* a magazine for young people. His numerous stories and novels for children were known for their clever humor.

250.30 Mrs. Mary Mapes Dodge] Dodge (1831–1905) became an author after she was widowed in 1858. Her most famous work is the children's novel *Hans Brinker; or, The Silver Skates* (1865). She edited *St. Nicholas* magazine from 1873 until her death.

250.36 Rip Van Winkle's time] Washington Irving's famous story, first published in 1819, takes place in the Catskills both before and after the Revolutionary War.

Autobiographical Dictation, 10 October 1906

251.28–29 Laurence Hutton, Charles Dudley Warner, and Carroll Beckwith] Clemens's friendship with drama critic and editor Laurence Hutton (1843–1904) probably began in 1883, when Hutton invited Clemens to join the Kinsmen, an informal club of writers, artists, and actors. James Carroll Beckwith (1852–1917), a famous artist and teacher, painted a portrait of Clemens in 1890; it is now at the Mark Twain House and Museum in Hartford (*AutoMT1,* 498–99 n. 113.10; *N&J3,* 10 n. 10; for Warner see AD, 10 Apr 1906, note at 34.27–28).

251.31 Dean Sage] See the Autobiographical Dictation of 31 July 1906, note at 156.26–34.

251.32–33 Susy is in error . . . we were her guests] Clemens apparently conflates two different visits to Onteora. Susy described the first one, which took place in August 1885 (see AD, 8 Oct 1906, note at 247.28), but the Clemenses returned for a nearly three-month stay in the summer of 1890—as the marginal date Clemens provides here indicates. The dinner hosted by Mary Mapes Dodge must have occurred in 1890, because she did not build her Onteora summer home until 1888.

252.11 Chicago, eleven years ago, to witness the Grant festivities] Clemens described the banquet held in General Grant's honor at the convention of the Grand Army of the Republic in 1879 in "The Chicago G.A.R. Festival" (*AutoMT1,* 67–70).

252.13 Mr. Medill, proprietor of the Chicago *Tribune*] Joseph Medill (1823–99) was a founder of the antislavery Republican party, a strong Lincoln supporter, and a radical Reconstructionist after the Civil War. He bought an interest in the Chicago *Tribune* in 1855, and after becoming a majority stockholder in 1874 he remained the active manager of the newspaper until his death (Mott 1950, 284, 347–48).

253.4–14 Dean Sage . . . He and Reverend Joe Twichell had been classmates in college] Sage and Twichell were already close friends when Clemens met them in the late 1860s, but no record of Sage's attending Yale has been found. He earned his law degree at Albany Law School in 1861 (Courtney 2008, 141–42; *Yale Alumni Directory* 1920).

253.17–22 In '73, when Reverend Henry Ward Beecher was being tried . . . guest in the Sage mansion] Beecher was accused of committing adultery with Elizabeth Tilton, a parishioner, and in August 1874 her husband, Theodore, sued him for alienation of affection. The newspapers reported daily on the trial, which ended in a hung jury in

July 1875 (see *AutoMT1,* 575 n. 314.38–315.1). The Sage family had a special interest in the case because Henry W. Sage had been a trustee of Beecher's Plymouth Church for many years, and employed Beecher's son William in his lumber business. On 13 April 1875 Clemens and Twichell arrived at the Sages for a two-night stay, and they attended Beecher's trial together the following day (*L5:* MEC and SLC to JLC and PAM, 26 Nov 1872, 231 n. 3; 3 Dec 1872 to OLL, 237–38, nn. 7–11; *L6:* 29? July 1874 to Twichell, 202–3 n. 2; link note preceding 18 Apr 1875 to OLC, 446, 448–49).

253.27 Along about 1873 Sage fell a victim to an attack of dysentery] Clemens recorded an incomplete version of the following anecdote at the end of the manuscript of "My Autobiography [Random Extracts from It]," written in Vienna in 1897–98. He deleted the passage when revising the manuscript in 1906 for inclusion in the autobiography (see the Textual Commentary for that sketch at *MTPO*).

Autobiographical Dictation, 11 October 1906

255.16 I saw a rather disparaging paragraph the other day] The author and exact date of this newspaper article have not been identified. The "disparaging paragraph" to which it refers, however, probably appeared in the New York *Sun* on 1 August 1885. It claimed that the "man heavily enriched by Grant's death is Mark Twain," who would earn "a quarter to one-third of a million dollars" by publishing the *Personal Memoirs.* It said erroneously that the profits would be split evenly with Grant's heirs, but in fact Webster and Company's portion was only 30 percent. Clemens gave various estimates of the royalties paid to Mrs. Grant. In the latest, in the Autobiographical Dictation of 1 June 1906, he claimed her total was "half a million dollars"—which would make his share about $215,000 ("Mark Twain's Big Speculation," Scrapbook 22:62, CU-MARK; *AutoMT1,* 486–87 n. 80.35; see also AD, 2 June 1906, note at 73.24–25).

255.17–18 Grant obsequies. I was at the Fifth Avenue Hotel . . . mob of American celebrities] Grant's funeral took place on 8 August 1885 in Manhattan. His coffin was escorted from City Hall north to Riverside Park, overlooking the Hudson River, in a cortege of some fifty thousand dignitaries and members of the armed forces. (Grant's body was placed in a temporary tomb in Riverside Park, but in 1897 it was moved elsewhere in the park to the large granite and marble mausoleum known as Grant's Tomb.) Grant's family—without his wife, who did not attend—stayed at the Fifth Avenue Hotel, where they received numerous friends and celebrities offering their condolences, including Clemens himself, who traveled to New York for the occasion ("Mighty in Death. Grant Followed to the Tomb by Thousands," New York *Express and Mail,* 8 Aug 1885, Scrapbook 22:78–83, CU-MARK; 6 Aug 1885 to OLC [3rd], CU-MARK).

255.35–256.4 He was one of Ossawatomie Brown's right-hand men in the "bleeding Kansas" days . . . "jayhawkers," who were pro-slavery Missourians] The passage of the Kansas-Nebraska Act of 1854, which granted those two territories the right to determine their own slavery policy, led to bloody conflicts between Kansas free-state settlers and proslavery "border ruffians" from western Missouri. John Brown, who with his sons and other followers sought to defend and protect the settlers, earned the nickname "Ossawatomie" from violent skirmishes with such ruffians near the Kansas town of that name. Redpath, an ardent abolitionist, worked as a journalist in Kansas from 1855 to 1858, writing in support of the antislavery cause. For a time he published his own newspaper, the Doniphan *Crusader of Freedom.* In mid-1856 he interviewed Brown and briefly joined his armed band, occasionally participating in military actions. Redpath wrote a sympathetic (and consequently controversial) biography of Brown, published in 1860. "Jayhawkers" were not—as Clemens claims—proslavery. The term was actually applied to the antislavery guerrillas like Brown and his men; the proslavery "border ruffians" were also called "bushwhackers" (McKivigan 2008, 7–42, 47, 51–54; for Brown see *AutoMT1,* 512–13 n. 154.27–31).

Autobiographical Dictation, 12 October 1906

256.8 dare-devil guerrilla who led the jayhawkers] This guerrilla leader—correctly called a "bushwhacker," not a jayhawker—has not been identified.

Autobiographical Dictation, 15 October 1906

257.28 George] George Griffin.

258.29–33 I was trying to tame an old-fashioned bicycle . . . Twichell and I took lessons every day] Clemens and Twichell tried to master bicycle riding in the spring of 1884. Clemens described his experience in "Taming the Bicycle," which he considered submitting to the New York *Sun.* After deciding that he "didn't like it *at all,*" he tore up his manuscript, but he had already sent a copy to Charles Webster, who had it typed (31 May 1884 and 6 June 1884 to Webster, NPV, in *MTBus,* 258). A manuscript (presumably the copy sent to Webster) survives at Vassar, and an incomplete typescript, which Clemens revised, is in the Mark Twain Papers (SLC 1884; *N&J3,* 55 n. 123).

259.5 Pond's Extract] A popular patent medicine made of witch hazel, marketed since 1846 as a topical remedy for bruises, cuts, burns, and a variety of other ailments.

259.21–26 Papa will be fifty years old tomorrow . . . I will put the poem and paragraphs in here] Into her biography Susy pasted a clipping from *The Critic* of 28 November 1885 (253), which contained a poem and three letters written in honor of Clemens's fiftieth birthday. Clemens included two of these tributes, letters from Stockton and Warner, in the present dictation; he postponed the other two—a poem by Holmes and a letter from Harris—until the Autobiographical Dictation of 30 October 1906. Warner and Harris are described in the Autobiographical Dictation of 16 October 1906; for Stockton see the Autobiographical Dictation of 9 October 1906, note at 250.29.

259.40 Frank R. Stockton] Clemens thanked Stockton for his good wishes on 29 November 1885 (Pforzheimer):

> My Dear Mr. Stockton:
> Ah, but I am like the man who polished the pin-points: I am not going to repeat. For a different reason though: he could but wouldn't, I would but can't. And yet I thank you for the generous wish, all the same, & I value it to the utmost, coming from you.
>
> Sincerely Yours
> S. L. Clemens

The "man who polished the pin-points" is an allusion to Stockton's story "His Wife's Deceased Sister," first published in the *Century Magazine* in January 1884. One of its characters is a writer who cannot repeat an early success and so ends up earning his living by "grinding points to pins."

Autobiographical Dictation, 16 October 1906

260.13–14 Warner is gone. Stockton is gone. I attended both funerals . . . nineteen years afterward] Warner died in October 1900 (twenty-nine years after the Clemenses settled in Hartford). His funeral took place in the Asylum Hill Congregational Church; Clemens was an honorary pallbearer, and the Reverend Joseph Twichell officiated. Frank Stockton died in April 1902, and his funeral was held at his sister's home in Philadelphia; Clemens was again an honorary pallbearer ("Funeral of Mr. Warner," Hartford *Courant,* 24 Oct 1900, 4; "Frank R. Stockton's Funeral," New York *Times,* 25 Apr 1902, 3).

260.24–26 Uncle Remus still lives . . . photograph of him in the public prints within the last month or so] Clemens probably saw a photograph of Joel Chandler Harris taken by Underwood and Underwood that was published in the Washington *Post* on 15 July 1906 (17) and possibly elsewhere. Harris was fifty-seven years old (see the photograph following page 300; *AutoMT1,* 532–33 n. 217.25–27).

260.29–30 It is just a quarter of a century since I have seen Uncle Remus . . . our home in Hartford] Harris made a long-promised visit to Hartford in the spring of 1883 (12 Dec 1881 and 5 Sept 1882 to Harris, GEU; Harris 1918, 191–92).

261.1–3 in an earlier chapter I have already introduced him . . . memorable adventure with the cats] See "Scraps from My Autobiography. From Chapter IX" (*AutoMT1,* 159–61).

Autobiographical Dictation, 30 October 1906

263.28–29 Susy inserts a poem by Oliver Wendell Holmes and a greeting from Uncle Remus (Joel Chandler Harris)] Holmes's poem and the letter from Harris are from a clipping of *The Critic* of 28 November 1885 which Susy pasted into her biography (see AD, 15 Oct 1906, note at 259.21–26).

264.25 Oliver Wendell Holmes] Clemens expressed his gratitude in the following letter to Holmes, probably written on 29 November 1885 (*MTL,* 2:466):

Dear Mr. Holmes,—I shall never be able to tell you the half of how proud you have made me. If I could you would say you were nearly paid for the trouble you took. And then the family: If I can convey the electrical surprise and gratitude and exaltation of the wife and the children last night, when they happened upon that *Critic* where I had, with artful artlessness, spread it open and retired out of view to see what would happen—well, it was great and fine and beautiful to see, and made me feel as the victor feels when the shouting hosts march by; and if you also could have seen it you would have said the account was squared. For I have brought them up in your company, as in the company of a warm and friendly and beneficent but far-distant sun; and so, for you to do this thing was for the sun to send down out of the skies the miracle of a special ray and transfigure me before their faces. I knew what that poem would be to them; I knew it would raise me up to remote and shining heights in their eyes, to very fellowship with the chambered Nautilus itself, and that from that fellowship they could never more dissociate me while they should live; and so I made sure to be by when the surprise should come.

Charles Dudley Warner is charmed with the poem for its own felicitous sake; and so indeed am I, but more because it has drawn the sting of my fiftieth year; taken away the pain of it, the grief of it, the somehow *shame* of it, and made me glad and proud it happened.

With reverence and affection,

Sincerely yours,
S. L. Clemens.

265.12 Joel Chandler Harris] Clemens also wrote to Harris on 29 November 1885 (GEU):

Dear Uncle Remus:

I thank you cordially; & particularly for the good word about Huck, that abused child of mine who has had so much unfair mud flung at him. Somehow *I* can't help believing in him, & it's a great refreshment to my faith to have a man back me up who has been where such boys live, & knows what he is talking about.

May you never be fifty till you've got to be, & then may we all be there to say the kind word that will mollify the affront of it.

Sincerely Yours
S L Clemens

In addition to thanking his friends individually, Clemens wrote to them as a group via *The Critic,* also on 29 November (CLU-SC):

My dear Conspirators:

It was the pleasantest surprise I have ever had, & you have my best thanks. It reconciles me to being fifty years old; & it was for you to invent the miracle that could do that—I could never have invented one myself that could do it. May you live to be fifty yourselves, & find a fellow-benefactor in that time of awful need.

Sincerely Yours
S. L. Clemens

No individual letter thanking Warner for his tribute in *The Critic* is known to survive (see AD, 15 Oct 1906; "Mark Twain Surprised," *The Critic,* 4 Dec 1885, 271).

265.21 James Russell Lowell] Lowell turned fifty on 22 February 1869, almost a year before Clemens met Howells in December 1869.

265.30–34 Major General Franklin, who had been one of McClellan's favorite generals in the Civil War . . . Monday Evening Club] William Buel Franklin served under General George B. McClellan. Clemens discusses Franklin, McClellan, and the Monday Evening Club in the Autobiographical Dictations of 12 and 13 January 1906 (*AutoMT1,* 269–72, 273, 558 n. 269.1–6, 560 n. 273.3–5).

265.41 rout at the first Bull Run] The First Battle of Bull Run, fought near Manassas, Virginia, on 21 July 1861, ended with the Union forces retreating in panic.

Autobiographical Dictation, 7 November 1906

266.17 The first time I was in Egypt a Simplified Spelling epidemic had broken out] This dictation was first published in *Letters from the Earth,* edited by Bernard DeVoto (1962), who suggested that it had been "interpolated in a dictation" of 7 November 1906 but was "certainly written before that day" (*LE,* 159–63, 291). The suspicion is natural; yet Hobby made her standard notation on the typescript that it took two hours to dictate, and Clemens wrote on the same day to Mary Rogers that he had "dictated a while, this morning—the first time for 19 days. On Simplified Spelling" (NNC). No manuscript has been found, but it is likely that Clemens had written it as a speech to be delivered in Egypt, where, during a burst of enthusiasm in late October 1906, he had been planning to spend the winter. But he canceled his plans on 31 October, and perhaps sought to salvage his Egyptian-themed speech by reading it into the *Autobiography.* Andrew Carnegie agreed to financially support the Simplified Spelling Board in January 1906, believing that the irregular orthography of English was impeding its adoption as "the world language" ("Carnegie Assaults the Spelling Book," New York *Times,* 12 Mar 1906, 1). Clemens agreed to be a member of the board, and he publicized Simplified Spelling in various speeches and articles. In this dictation, he alludes to Carnegie under the name of "Croesus," and to Theodore Roosevelt as "the Khedive." Twelve days later, in the Autobiographical Dictation of 19 November 1906, he goes on to discuss the origins of the Simplified Spelling movement and Roosevelt's ill-fated support for it (Lyon 1906, entries for Oct 27–31; *MTB,* 3:1325–26; "Simple Spellers Start with 300 Pruned Words," New York *Times,* 13 Mar 1906, 6).

268.22–23 The trouble is not with the spelling . . . it is with the *alphabet*] Clemens developed this line of thought in a speech at a banquet honoring Andrew Carnegie on 9 December 1907 and in one of his manuscripts, "A Simplified Alphabet" ("Mark Twain Jeers at Simple Spelling," New York *Times,* 10 Dec 1907, 2; SLC 1909a; for a text of the speech see Fatout 1976, 597–600; see also AD, 10 Dec 1907).

Autobiographical Dictation, 8 November 1906

269.28–29 he has been publishing Gen. Grant's book] See the Autobiographical Dictation of 28 May 1906.

270.4–5 he published without her knowledge that article in the "Christian Union"] See the Autobiographical Dictation of 21 December 1906.

270.17–18 Jean has been absent . . . at a Sanatorium in the country] Clemens had arranged for Jean to stay at the private sanatorium operated by her doctor, Frederick Peterson, at Katonah, New York. She left on 25 October 1906; for the next three years, her life would be spent in sanatoriums, rented lodgings, and clinics, until Clemens brought her to Stormfield in April 1909 (Lystra 2004, 83–85).

270.20–22 Mrs. Kate Douglas Wiggin Riggs . . . Mr. Riggs] Author and educator Kate Douglas Wiggin (1856–1923), whose best-known book is *Rebecca of Sunnybrook Farm* (1903), had married businessman George Christopher Riggs in 1895. Dorothea Gilder (1882–1920) was the eldest daughter of Richard Watson Gilder, and a friend of Clara's. For Norman Hapgood and his wife see *AutoMT1,* 598 n. 375.2, and the Autobiographical Dictation of 7 June 1906, note at 101.31.

271.14 Gulliver in Lilliput] From Jonathan Swift's *Gulliver's Travels* (1726).

271.32 my five or six unfinished books] See the Autobiographical Dictation of 30 August 1906, notes at 196.39–42 and 197.4–7.

271.39–272.5 F. Hopkinson Smith . . . auction this time was of original manuscripts] Clemens had told this story some twelve years earlier in a letter to Olivia written on 12 February 1894, two weeks after the event it describes (CU-MARK):

> And did I tell you about Mrs. Kate Douglas Wiggin & the sale of manuscripts? You see they had a great gathering at Sherry's in aid of the kindergartens, & they had music, & then it was announced that Hopkinson Smith & Mrs. Wiggin would read unpublished articles & each sell the other's MS. at auction.
>
> Smith ran Mrs. Wiggin's up to $85—a nice good figure. Of course Mrs. W. wanted to do as well; but when she mounted the auctioneering rostrum she found that Smith's was nothing but a type-written MS. But she wrought brightly & well, & scattered wit in all directions; & although she had a formidable job she stuck bravely to it till she captured the same sum secured for her own *genuine* MS.
>
> Mary Mapes Dodge, talking with her, said—
>
> "It was shabby of him to put off a type-written MS on you to sell. It would have been perfectly fair for you to resent it. Of course you were angry?"
>
> "Inside—*yes.* Boiling, in fact. Oh, I *wanted* to resent it, badly enough."
>
> "Then why didn't you?"
>
> "Oh, well, I am a lady, & I have to be so damned polite!"

The auction was held at Sherry's Restaurant on 29 January 1894 for the New York Kindergarten Association, a project of Wiggin's. F. Hopkinson Smith (1838–1915) was an author, painter, and engineer, and may be best remembered for having built the foundation for the pedestal of the Statue of Liberty. Clemens first met him at a Tile

Club dinner in New York on 20 December 1880. Eight years later he characterized him as "a well known water-color artist, civil engineer, architect, designer of railway bridges, magazine writer, after-dinner speaker, public reader, jack-of-all-trades & master of them all, & he is moreover an old & special friend of mine" (27 Dec 1888 to Gripenberg, FiH2; 11, 12, 13 Feb 1894 to OLC, CU-MARK; "Notes," *The Critic,* 3 Feb 1894, 84; *N&J2,* 360 n. 14).

272.31 Chase's spacious and sumptuous studio] The Tenth Street studio in New York of painter William Merritt Chase (1849–1916) was described by art critic Arthur Hoeber as "the sanctum sanctorum of the Aesthetic fraternity" (Gallati 1995, 39–42).

Autobiographical Dictation, 19 November 1906

273.19–25 pleading for the life of the culprit sentence . . . that it would get by the expergator alive] See the Autobiographical Dictation of 9 February 1906 *(AutoMT1,* 349). The long passage in the *Huckleberry Finn* manuscript in which Jim describes his midnight encounter with a cadaver in a medical school dissecting room, which Clemens deleted before publication, was probably one of the "delightfully dreadful" passages (*HF 2003,* 531–38).

273.28–274.5 Andrew Carnegie started this storm . . . The indignant British Lion rose] Clemens was one of many literary men who signed the pledge circulated by spelling reformers in May 1905 to adopt simplified forms of twelve common words such as *program, prolog,* and *thru.* Andrew Carnegie's financial support was contingent upon the gathering of these pledges. Satisfied, in early 1906 he organized the Simplified Spelling Board under the leadership of critic Brander Matthews. The board soon issued an amplified list of three hundred recommended spellings. On 27 August, Roosevelt ordered the government printer to use the simplified system in all publications of the executive departments. American response was bemused, but the British response was unexpectedly fierce. The *Pall Mall Gazette* called Roosevelt an anarchist, and the *Evening Standard* reminded him that the English language "was ours while America was still a savage and undiscovered country." The *Globe* vowed that British resistance to spelling reform would be tougher than Filipino resistance to American rule, while the *Leader* said: "Of kors if Ruzvelt, backed up by Karnegi, sez we hav got to reform our speling we shal hav to, and that wil be the end of it, for Karnegi has awl the dollers and Ruzvelt has awl the branes" ("England in Fury Yelps at Ruzvelt," Chicago *Tribune,* 26 Aug 1906, 1). Against this tide of anti-American, anti-Roosevelt feeling, Carnegie protested that spelling reform was neither American nor Roosevelt's: it was an international movement and the reformed spellings had all been recommended in 1883 by an Anglo-American committee. But American support was also lacking: on 13 December the House of Representatives went on record against Roosevelt's presidential order, and he promptly rescinded it (Scott 1905; New York *Times:* "Carnegie Assaults the Spelling-Book," 12 Mar 1906, 1; "Spelling Changes Came from England—Carnegie," 7 Sept 1906, 1; Matthews to SLC, 21 May

1905, CU-MARK; U.S. Government Printing Office 1906, 5–6; "New Spelling Dies," Washington *Post,* 14 Dec 1906, 1).

274.31–32 speech . . . before the Associated Press delegates, last September] See the Autobiographical Dictation of 5 October 1906, note at 245.36–246.1.

275.16–17 In 1883, when the Simplified Spelling movement first tried to make a noise] In 1883 the Philological Society of London and the American Philological Association joined in recommending three thousand standardized spellings ("Spelling Changes Came from England—Carnegie," New York *Times,* 7 Sept 1906, 1).

Autobiographical Dictation, 20 November 1906

277.38–278.6 Georgia Cayvan . . . had taken lessons in the Delsarte elocutionary methods] Cayvan (1857–1906) was born in Bath, Maine. She studied at the Lewis B. Monroe School of Oratory, which taught the system of expressive gestures created by French musician and teacher François Delsarte (1811–71), and embarked on a career as a professional reader and reciter (Gagey 1971, 2:314–15; "Georgia Cayvan Dead," New York *Tribune,* 20 Nov 1906, 7; Wilbor 1887, 256–57).

278.10 Miss Porter's celebrated school] Sarah Porter's boarding school for girls in Farmington, Connecticut, established around 1843, offered instruction in Latin, German, French, natural philosophy, rhetoric, mathematics, chemistry, geography, history, and music in a noncompetitive fashion that dispensed with grades and examinations and allowed each student to progress at her own pace. No record of Georgia Cayvan's visit to the school, or Clemens's, has been found (*N&J3,* 444 n. 121).

278.15–28 The stage was her dream . . . her mind was affected] Cayvan made a great success as Jocasta in an 1881 production of *Oedipus Tyrannus.* She reached the zenith of her career as the leading woman of New York's Lyceum Theatre in 1887–94, but in the latter year she entered a period of ill health and inactivity. In 1898 she was named as co-respondent in a sensational divorce case. Although she was exonerated, it was reported that the scandal had deranged her mind. She was placed in a sanatorium in 1900, where she eventually became blind and passed into a vegetative state; news reports leave little doubt that her disease was syphilis ("Miss Cayvan Exonerated," New York *Times,* 4 Jan 1899, 7; "Georgia Cayvan Childish," Hartford *Courant,* 17 July 1902, 10; "Georgia Cayvan Dead," New York *Tribune,* 20 Nov 1906, 7; "Georgia Cayvan Dead," New York *Sun,* 20 Nov 1906, 1).

278.30–31 The profession flocked to her relief] In 1903 Cayvan's personal wealth had been exhausted, and Broadway's most prominent actors and managers staged a benefit performance on her behalf ("Benefit for Georgia Cayvan," Fort Worth *Star-Telegram,* 13 Jan 1903, 6).

279.24–26 I first met Helen Keller . . . at Laurence Hutton's house] See the Autobiographical Dictation of 30 March 1906 (*AutoMT1,* 464–67, 650 n. 465.6–7).

279.30–31 Miss Sullivan was a pastmaster of Dr. Howe's methods] Samuel Gridley Howe (1801–76) was an American teacher specializing in the education of the blind, the deaf, and the mentally disabled. He taught language to the blind and deaf Laura Bridgman by means of two tactile methods: first, using cards printed with embossed letters, and later, with a manual alphabet (finger spelling). Anne Sullivan, Keller's teacher, graduated from Howe's school for the blind (the Perkins Institute); she studied his notes of the Bridgman case before she went to Alabama to teach Keller (for Sullivan see *AutoMT1,* 650 n. 465.9).

279.39–280.1 I was sojourning in London . . . leaving Helen and Miss Sullivan destitute] In November 1896 the Clemenses were in deep seclusion, mourning Susy's death, when Eleanor Hutton wrote that Keller's wealthy patron, John S. Spaulding, had died without making provision for her, thus casting in doubt her ability to attend Radcliffe. On 26 November Clemens replied to Mrs. Hutton:

> There is only one reason why I do not turn out at once & try to interest rich Englishmen in Helen's case: I go nowhere, I see no one, I keep my address strictly concealed. I must not get discovered, or my work on my long book would be disastrously interfered with, straightway.
>
> But I have written to Mrs. Rogers & asked her to persuade her husband to lay the case before the other Standard Oil chiefs & ask them to contribute a temporary *annual* fund, to continue while Helen is in college; something to supply the essential immediate need, & give you time to work out your plan for achieving a *permanent* fund. I do hope my suggestion will bear fruit. I remarked that Laurence would be close by & handy at Harper's when wanted.
>
> I would suggest to you that whenever a person declines to subscribe to your permanent fund, you strike him for a $25. *annual* subscription, & let him off with less, if you must. For many years Mrs. Clemens & I did the annual thing to the amount of $2,300—the interest on $40,000, you see; & it didn't hamper us—but it would have made us shudder if we had been asked to put up the $40,000. (NjP-SC)

Rogers himself wrote Clemens a month later that "the Helen Keller matter has been adjusted satisfactorily with Mrs. Hutton for the time being, at any rate." He then described "a singular coincidence in connection with that matter." Having conversed with Laurence Hutton at a recent Lotos Club dinner, he learned of Helen Keller's situation and offered to help:

> Monday morning at the breakfast table I received a letter from Mrs. Hutton and Mrs. Rogers received a letter from you; they were both on the same subject, viz: Helen Keller. Mrs. Rogers went that day to call on Mrs. Hutton and had a very pleasant talk, and the arrangement that I before referred to was consummated. I do not know whether you would bring that coincidence into your mental telegraphy business or not, at any rate, I thought I would tell you about it, and knew it would please you to say the least. (Rogers to Clemens, 24 Dec 1896, CU-MARK, in *HHR,* 256–58)

In a letter of 4 January 1897 Clemens agreed, saying the coincidence "is more easily explained as an instance of telegraphy than in any other way" (Salm, in *HHR,* 258–60). Rogers supported Keller's education at Radcliffe, and he left her an annuity at his death in 1909 (Herrmann 1999, 94, 108–9; Keller 2005, 113).

280.17–20 When J. B. Pond, the lecture agent, died . . . Pond's little boy] James B. Pond (see *AutoMT1,* 600 n. 381.14) died of heart failure on 21 June 1903, after an operation to remove a gangrenous leg. His son, James B. Pond, Jr., was thirteen at the time. William Webster Ellsworth (1855–1936) was principally a publisher but was also an author and lecturer, one of Pond's clients. Clemens answered his appeal in late June 1903: "A fund? Raise it? It is easier to raise the dead. A *pension* is the thing. I have tried it, & I know. Get people to put up a monthly sum" (late June 1903 to Ellsworth, extract in CU-MARK; *Hudson Census* 1900, 979:10A; New York *Times:* "Major J. B. Pond Is Dead," 22 June 1903, 1; "Wm. W. Ellsworth, Lecturer, 81, Dies," 19 Dec 1936, 19).

280.28–33 Sir Henry M. Stanley . . . finding and rescuing Emin Pacha] Explorer-author Henry M. Stanley (1841–1904) was born John Rowlands, in Wales. His mother abandoned him at birth, and his father died a short time later. After the death of his grandfather, he was in foster care, then at age six was sent to a workhouse, where he was brutally treated. He ran away at age fifteen, and in 1859 emigrated to New Orleans. There he was adopted by a merchant, Henry Morton Stanley, whose name he assumed. His successful career as a journalist began after the Civil War, during which he fought for—and deserted from—both sides. In 1869 he received an assignment from the New York *Herald* to search for the Scottish missionary David Livingstone, who had disappeared in Africa several years earlier. After enduring great hardship, he succeeded in November 1871 ("Dr. Livingstone, I presume"), and returned to Europe, where his writings and lectures made him famous. In 1879 Stanley explored the Congo and founded the Congo Free State on behalf of King Leopold II of Belgium. He went back to Africa in 1887 as head of a mission to relieve Emin Pasha, the European-born governor of a province of the Sudan, who was holding out against the Mahdist rebellion which had overrun the rest of the country. But Emin, when located in 1888, wanted supplies, not rescue; he accompanied Stanley to the east coast, only to return to the interior, where he was later killed by slave traders. The relief expedition failed of its object and its casualties were enormous; but Stanley's lecture tour of America, under the management of James B. Pond, was highly successful (November 1890–April 1891), as was his book *In Darkest Africa* (1890), which Clemens tried without success to acquire for Webster and Company. Stanley settled in England, served in Parliament, and was knighted in 1899 (25 Oct 1872 to OLC, *L5,* 201–2 n. 4; Chicago *Tribune:* "Henry M. Stanley Starts on His Long Lecturing Tour," 14 Nov 1890, 2; "Henry M. Stanley to Sail Next Week," 11 Apr 1891, 2; *N&J3,* 304–5 n. 19).

280.37–38 he stenographically reported a lecture of mine in St. Louis] Stanley was a staff reporter for the St. Louis *Missouri Democrat* when he reported Clemens's 26 March 1867 lecture on the Sandwich Islands (20 Dec 1870 to Judd, *L4,* 278–80 n. 8).

Autobiographical Dictation, 21 November 1906

281.32–282.10 Father Hawley . . . one of these annual assemblages] David Hawley (1809–76) was a farmer until 1851, when he was hired by the City Mission Board to do humanitarian work in Hartford. For the next twenty-five years he concerned himself with the "ministration of temporal charities," devoting much of his time to visiting the poor. Hawley reported on his work at annual meetings of the City Missionary Society. Clemens twice gave lectures in Hartford for the benefit of Hawley's mission: on 31 January 1873 and on 5 March 1875 (28 Jan 1873 to the Public, *L5,* 287–90; 6 Mar 1875 to Seaver, *L6,* 402–3; "City Missions," Hartford *Courant,* 8 Dec 1873, 2).

282.16 Wendell Phillips] Phillips (1811–84) first won fame in the late 1830s for his eloquent and impassioned antislavery speeches. After the Civil War he advocated a wide variety of reforms, including voting rights for freedmen, equal rights for women, temperance, and better treatment of Native Americans. Clemens met him at the Langdon house in Elmira on 18 March 1869, and that evening he and Olivia probably attended Phillips's lecture on Irish political leader Daniel O'Connell. Later, Clemens and Phillips were both clients of James Redpath's Lyceum Bureau (link note following 13 Mar 1869, *L3,* 174–75).

Autobiographical Dictation, 22 November 1906

283.25–284.16 he went to Washington . . . I supported the Chace Bill] At the invitation of the American Copyright League, which was sponsoring the "Hawley bill" on international copyright, Clemens went to Washington in January 1886 to testify before the Senate Committee on Patents. He was not, however, in perfect accord with the league's official stance, and his testimony was diffident. At the hearing of 28 January, Clemens, upset by differences between himself and the league's leaders, excused himself from speaking; at the next day's hearing, urged by George Walton Green, the league's secretary, to "speak right out like a little man," he lent qualified support to the Hawley bill. In his remarks, Clemens advocated the adoption of what he called the "printing clause," which would protect the interests of publishers, printers, and manufacturers by requiring that books be domestically produced (Fatout 1976, 206–9; Robert Underwood Johnson 1923, 267). The rival bill introduced by Senator Jonathan Chace of Rhode Island, a member of the Committee on Patents, did include such a clause, but Clemens refrained from mentioning the Chace bill explicitly. Also mentioned in the newspaper clipping inserted by Susy are General Joseph Hawley; the International Typographical Union, which represented workers in the printing industry in the United States and Canada; and James Russell Lowell, president of the American Copyright League since 1885 (Seville 2006, 217–24, 299; for Hawley see *AutoMT1,* 576 n. 317.23–24; for the Chace bill see also AD, 18 Dec 1906, note at 318.21–22).

284.27–28 Somewhere about 1888 or '89 . . . author of "Struwwelpeter."] The author and illustrator of *Der Struwwelpeter* (1845) was Heinrich Hoffmann (1809–94), of Frankfurt. Clemens may have met him during his visit to Frankfurt in October 1891. On 27 October he wrote his publisher, Fred Hall, from Berlin that he had just spent "3 days & nights" translating *Der Struwwelpeter* into English and was about to send him the text. He wanted Hall to publish his translation "on the blank page facing the corresponding picture & the corresponding *German verses,*" and to have the book "on the American market Dec. 10 to catch the holidays." But the very next day he again wrote Hall, this time from Frankfurt, to say that he had been trying and failing to acquire the plates of the German edition, which he wanted to reproduce in his own book (CSmH, in *MTLP,* 287–89; Wecter 1941). Clemens's translation, which he never published, goes unmentioned in this 1906 dictation. His 1891 manuscript preface begins:

> STRUWWELPETER is the best known book in Germany, & has the largest sale known to the book trade, & the widest circulation. For nearly fifty years it has had its home in every German nursery. No man can divine just where its mysterious fascination lies, perhaps, but that it *has* a peculiar & powerful fascination for children is a fact that was settled long ago. (SLC 1891a)

285.40–286.3 five years from now my copyrights will begin to expire . . . another twenty-eight years' copyright] In 1906 United States law conferred copyright on original works for twenty-eight years, reckoned from the date of publication, and a renewal term of fourteen years. Under this law, *The Innocents Abroad,* first published in 1869, if renewed, would have gone into the public domain in 1911, to be followed in due course by Clemens's other works. For his plan to extend the copyright of his books by republishing them with the Autobiographical Dictations included as running footnotes, see *AutoMT1,* 23–24 (Draper 1901, 40).

Autobiographical Dictation, 23 November 1906

286.10–11 Thorvald Solberg, Register of Copyrights] Solberg (1852–1949), a member of the American Copyright League, served as the register of copyrights from 1897 until 1930. He played a large role in formulating the Copyright Act of 1909 (see the note at 286.12–13; "T. Solberg Dead; Copyright Expert," New York *Times,* 16 July 1949, 13).

286.12–13 Senate and House . . . pending Copyright Bill on December 7th and 8th] A bill "to amend and consolidate" United States copyright law had been introduced on 31 May 1906 and referred to the House and Senate Committees on Patents. A first round of public hearings was held in June; at a subsequent hearing (on 7 December 1906), Clemens was one of the speakers (see the ADs of 18, 19, and 26 December 1906). The bill was eventually ratified as the Copyright Act of 1909, which provided a copyright term of twenty-eight years from the date of publication, renewable for a further twenty-eight years ("The Copyright Campaign," *Publishers' Weekly,* 3 July 1909, 22–24; 7 Dec 1906 to JC, photocopy in CU-MARK).

286.21–36 Thirty-five years ago, an idea, in the line of international copyright . . . cruelly and cordially] A bill requiring the United States to recognize the copyrights of foreign authors was introduced in the House in December 1871, but languished in committee and was finally reported unfavorably, in February 1873. In December 1872

Clemens drafted his first attempt at a petition in favor of international copyright, which perhaps was never circulated (20–22 Dec 1872 to Twichell, *L5,* 255–58). In 1875 he framed a new petition and, in early November, went to Boston "to see some of the literary big guns about the copyright project" (27 Oct 1875 to Howells, *L6,* 576–78). Clemens expected Holmes's (qualified) support: "Holmes will sign," he had written to Howells on 18 September, "he said he would if he didn't have to stand at the head." But after this visit to Boston, and the obloquy which Holmes evidently rained on the project, Clemens dropped his petition and, for a time, his efforts toward copyright reform (see 18 Sept 1875 to Howells with the enclosed petition, *L6,* 536–39).

Autobiographical Dictation, 24 November 1906

288.18 Lord Thwing] The family name of Henry, first Baron Thring (1818–1907), appears consistently in the typescripts as "Thwing," leaving very little doubt that Hobby understood Clemens to be saying "Thwing." Clemens did not correct that spelling; in fact, when Hobby once typed "Thring" in a later dictation he "corrected" it to "Thwing" (AD, 26 Dec 1906).

289.4–13 statements made to them by Stephenson . . . twelve miles an hour!] English engineer George Stephenson (1781–1848), the "father of the railways," appeared before a House of Commons committee in 1825 to support a proposed railway between Liverpool and Manchester. The story of his testimony became a commonplace of nineteenth-century journalism. Clemens's considerably elaborated version may ultimately derive from the popular account of Samuel Smiles:

> In his strong Northumbrian dialect, he [Stephenson] struggled for an utterance, in the face of the sneers, interruptions, and ridicule of the opponents of the measure, and even of the Committee, some of whom shook their heads and whispered doubts as to his sanity, when he energetically avowed that he could make the locomotive go at the rate of twelve miles an hour! (Smiles 1857, 231)

In *A Connecticut Yankee in King Arthur's Court,* Clemens placed Stephenson in the company of Gutenberg, James Watt, and Alexander Graham Bell, "the creators of this world—after God" (*CY,* 369).

289.33–35 Macaulay . . . trivial and jejune in its reasonings] During the House of Commons debates on what would become the Copyright Act of 1842, Thomas Babington Macaulay (1800–1859) made two renowned speeches (on 5 February 1841 and 6 April 1842) against proposed copyright schemes. In his first speech he claimed that copyright was equivalent to a monopoly and opposed an attempt to extend it to sixty years after an author's death. His second stressed the justice and fairness of an equal term of copyright for all books and proposed the law that was ultimately passed: see the note at 290.17–19. Macaulay's biographer (and nephew), G. O. Trevelyan, called this speech "as amusing as an essay of Elia, and as convincing as a proof of Euclid." Clemens was very familiar with the works of Macaulay, one of his favorite writers, these strictures on the copyright speeches notwithstanding (Trevelyan 1876, 2:134–36; Gribben 1980, 1:434–36, 2:712).

290.17–19 in London seven years ago . . . add eight entire years to the copyright limit, and make it fifty] On 3 April 1900, five members of a Select Committee of the House of Lords heard Clemens's testimony on the two copyright bills that were then before Parliament. Since 1842 Britain had recognized copyright in a literary work for a term of the author's lifetime plus seven years, *or* forty-two years from the date of publication, whichever proved longer. One bill under consideration proposed a term of the author's lifetime plus thirty years. Clemens read a written statement in which he argued for perpetual copyright, and was then questioned by the committee (Draper 1901, 40, 45; "Mark Twain on Copyright," *The Publishers' Circular,* 7 Apr 1900, 367–68; "Mark Twain," New York *Times,* 21 Apr 1900, BR7; SLC 2002, 112 n. 3).

290.19–20 One of the ablest men in the House of Lords did the most of the question-asking—Lord Thwing] In this dictation Clemens takes considerable liberties with the facts as they appear from the published minutes of the committee session. In particular he inflates the role of Lord Thring, making him his chief interlocutor; in fact, it appears that all the statements and questions that Clemens attributes to Lord Thring were made by others or not made at all (House of Lords 1900).

291.4–8 New and Old Testaments had been granted perpetual copyright . . . the press of Oxford University] In the United Kingdom, copyright in the Authorized Version of the Bible is vested in perpetuity in the Crown, which delegates it to the King's Printer and the presses of Oxford and Cambridge universities. The situation for the Book of Common Prayer is analogous. In the Autobiographical Dictation of 30 July 1907, Clemens identifies publisher John Murray as the source of his information (Bentley 1997, 372, 386).

Autobiographical Dictation, 30 November 1906

293.24–34 a new version of "There is a happy land" . . . I heard Billy Rice sing it in the negro-minstrel show] This song burlesques the first verse of a hymn written in 1838 by Andrew Young (*N&J3,* 38 n. 76):

There is a happy land,
  Far, far away,
Where saints in glory stand,
  Bright, bright as day.
O, how they sweetly sing,
"Worthy is our Saviour King,
Loud let His praises ring,
  Praise, praise for aye."

The author of the burlesque version is unknown; it became popular around 1876. Billy Rice (stage name of William H. Pearl, 1844–1902) was an exceptionally popular minstrel-show performer whose career lasted over thirty years ("A Boarding House Hymn," New York *Commercial Advertiser,* 18 July 1876, 1; "Fact and Fancy," Macon [Ga.] *Telegraph,* 3 Nov 1877, 4; Edward Le Roy Rice 1911, 163).

293.39–40 Billy Birch, David Wambold, Backus . . . made life a pleasure to me forty years ago] William Birch (1831–97), with Charles Backus (1831–83), Dave Wambold (1836–89), and William H. Bernard (1830–90), formed the famous San Francisco Minstrel Troupe, which Clemens enjoyed in his California days. In an 1867 letter to the *Alta California,* Clemens wrote from New York: "Our old San Francisco Minstrels have made their mark here, most unquestionably. . . . The firm remains the same—Birch, Backus, Wambold and Bernard. They have made an extraordinary success" (SLC 1867c). With variations in personnel, the Birch and Backus troupe had an eighteen-year residency in New York that ended only with the untimely death of Backus in 1883 (*ET&S1,* 316, 490 n. 316.19; Edward Le Roy Rice 1911, 68–71).

294.13 the first negro-minstrel show I ever saw] The earliest minstrel troupe that has been documented as visiting Hannibal was G. Bancker's Sable Brothers, mentioned in a letter written by "Lorio"—almost certainly Orion Clemens—and published in the St. Louis *Reveille* of 30 April 1847 (Scharnhorst 2010, 277–79).

296.5–6 "Buffalo Gals," "Camptown Races," "Old Dan Tucker,"] These three songs were written for, or featured in, minstrel shows. "Buffalo Gals" derives from the song "Lubly Fan" (1844), written by the minstrel performer Cool White; "Camptown Races" was written by Stephen Foster (1850); "Old Dan Tucker" was published in 1843 by the minstrel Dan Emmett (Mahar 1999, 274; Gribben 1980, 1:222, 238).

296.6–8 "The Blue Juniata," . . . "The Larboard Watch,"] The songs mentioned here are: "The Blue Juniata" by Marion Dix Sullivan (1844); "Ellen Bayne" (1854) and "Nelly Bly" (1849) by Stephen Foster; "A Life on the Ocean Wave" by Epes Sargent (1838); and "The Larboard Watch" by Thomas E. Williams (Gribben 1980, 1:238, 2:603, 678, 774).

296.18 Aunt Betsey Smith] Elizabeth W. Smith (b. 1794 or 1795), an old friend of the Clemens family's in Hannibal, was remembered by Annie Moffett Webster, Clemens's niece, as a frequent and welcome visitor in St. Louis. She served as the model for minor characters in "Those Extraordinary Twins" (SLC 1892c), "Hellfire Hotchkiss" (1897, in *Inds,* 109–33), and "Schoolhouse Hill" (1898, in *Inds,* 214–59; 3? Oct 1859 to Smith, *L1,* 94–95 n. 2).

296.40 the Christy minstrel troupe] The minstrel troupe led by E. P. Christy (1815–62), active from 1843 to 1855, was one of the first to enjoy widespread fame. After Christy retired in 1855, various troupes, led by his sons or associates, continued to perform under the Christy name (Brown 2005).

Autobiographical Dictation, 1 December 1906

297.32 Mr. Clemens's early experiments with mesmerism] The texts of 1, 2, and 3 December were not in fact dictated, but were written out in Clemens's normal longhand in 1903 and inserted here in 1906.

297.33–34 I think the year was 1850. As to that I am not sure . . . it was May] Clemens may be describing events that occurred in May 1847, when two mesmerists named Sparhawk and Layton performed in Hannibal, conducting "experiments" every night for two weeks. According to the Hannibal *Gazette,* their "subject (who resides in the city) seemed fully under the magnetic influence." The performances were also described in a letter written by "Lorio" (probably Orion Clemens) to the St. Louis *Reveille,* published on 20 May (see Scharnhorst 2010, 279–80, which quotes the *Gazette*).

298.17 Hicks, our journeyman] Urban East Hicks (1828–1905) evidently worked from the mid-1840s as a journeyman printer on Henry La Cossitt's Hannibal *Gazette* (where in 1847 Clemens was briefly a printer's devil and errand boy), and then in 1848–50 on the Hannibal *Journal.* Probably in the fall of 1850 he moved to Orion Clemens's Hannibal *Western Union,* where by early January 1851 Clemens and Jim Wolf were apprenticed. Later that year Hicks set out for the Pacific Northwest, where he taught school and worked as a printer. In 1855–56 he was a volunteer officer in the Yakima and Klikitat Indian Wars, and thereafter he served the Washington territorial government in various capacities. After 1861 he serially edited and published several newspapers in Washington and Oregon. In 1886 Clemens wrote to a mutual friend, "I remember Urban E. vividly & pleasantly; & also the fencing-matches with column-rules & quack-medicine stereotypes. . . . If I could see Hicks here I would receive him with a barbecue & a torchlight procession, & put the entire house at his disposal" (17 Jan 1886 to Himes, MoPeS; *Inds,* 324; Hicks 1886, 20; *AutoMT1,* 515 n. 159.30, 645 n. 459.22–23, 651).

300.35–40 old Dr. Peake, who was the ringleader . . . person in the community] Humphrey Peake (1773–1856) grew up on his family's Virginia estate, which bordered on Mount Vernon; his father had been a hunting companion of George Washington's. He was a surgeon in the Virginia Militia in 1812, a justice of the peace in 1813, and the collector of the port of Alexandria from 1820 to 1830. He moved to Missouri in the middle 1830s and then to Hannibal, where in 1839 he bought land, opened a medical office, and became a friend of John Marshall Clemens's. In 1847, at age seventy-four, he was still practicing at the same office. In 1897 Clemens described him as a "courtly gentleman of the old school," and in 1898 based the character of Dr. Wheelwright, the "stately old First-Family Virginian and imposing Thinker of the village," upon him in "Schoolhouse Hill" (*Inds,* 104, 238, 296; *U.S. and International Marriage Records* 2011; "Medical Notice," Hannibal *Journal,* 1 July 1847, unknown page; Hannibal *Courier-Post* 2011; Jim Boulden, personal communication, 23 Aug 2011, CU-MARK). In 1902 Clemens told a newspaper reporter that he remembered old Dr. Peake better than almost any of the Hannibal citizens of fifty years ago. He described Dr. Peake as a Virginian who, on state occasions, wore knee breeches and large silver buckles on his low cut shoes, and wore a wig. He . . . and the elder Clemens, Sam's father, were subscribers for the Weekly National Intelligencer, published at Washington, D.C., and it was their custom to discuss the speeches made in Congress from the time the paper was received until the next copy came to hand. ("Good-bye to Mark Twain," Hannibal *Courier-Post,* 3 June 1902, 1)

300.42 I rejoiced without shame] Clemens's 1880 working notes for *Huckleberry Finn* show that he considered making use of his encounter with the mesmerizer: "Do the mesmeric foolishness, with Huck ~~& the king~~ for performers" (*HF 2003,* 486). And again in 1897 he considered using his experience in "Tom Sawyer's Conspiracy": "The mesmerizer—Tom gets no pay, yet was superior to Hicks, who got $3 a week" (Notebook 41, p. 58, CU-MARK). In the end, neither story used the "mesmeric foolishness."

Autobiographical Dictation, 2 December 1906

301.1 Mr. Clemens's experiments in mesmerism, continued] Like the previous day's text, this one and the next are in fact 1903 manuscripts inserted in 1906.

301.2–6 large white house on the corner of Hill and Main . . . Dr. Grant's] The Clemens family moved in with Dr. Orville R. Grant (1815–?54) and his family in 1846, occupying the flat above his drugstore. They boarded the Grant family in exchange for their lodging, after it became clear that all of the Clemens property would be sold to pay a debt (see *AutoMT1,* 62–63, 454). John Marshall Clemens died several months later, in March 1847. Grant was born in Kentucky, received his Doctor of Medicine "on the Modus Operandi of Medicines" at the Louisville Medical Institute in March 1838, and evidently spent time in Virginia before setting up shop in Hannibal, where he served as a physician, surgeon, and pharmacist for nearly a decade (Yandell 1838). In 1845 he attended the dying Sam Smarr, who had been shot in the street in front of the drugstore by William Owsley—an incident that Clemens used in chapter 21 of *Huckleberry Finn.* And Clemens remembered, in 1867, that when Jimmy Finn, one of the town's drunkards, died the same year, "his body went to Dr. Grant" (SLC 1867b). Clemens had seen the house when he was last in Hannibal, from 29 May to 3 June 1902, a year before writing this manuscript (Wecter 1952, 133; *Inds,* 318–19, 339–40; *Kanawha Census* 1850, 954:101A).

301.6–7 Dr. Grant and Dr. Reyburn argued a matter on the street with sword-canes] In August 1845, a report on the incident appeared in the newspaper exchanges, which named another assailant: "An affray took place in Hannibal on last Friday week, in which a man by the name of Railey stabbed Dr. Orville R. Grant through the left lung, with a spear attached to his cane" ("Affray at Hannibal, Mo.," Philadelphia *North American,* 26 Aug 1845, 1).

301.13 Mrs. Crawford, Mrs. Grant's mother] Orville Grant married Miriam M. McFarland (1820–53) in 1837 in Charleston, West Virginia. Her mother, Lethe Reynolds McFarland (1800–1882), was the first of her father's four wives. No confirmation has been found that she ever took the name Crawford (Little 1893, 149–50; Atkinson 1876, 273).

301.14–15 the Richmond theatre burned down thirty-six years before . . . that memorable tragedy] On the night of 26 December 1811, during a pantomime afterpiece entitled "Raymond and Agness, or the Bleeding Nun," fire engulfed the Richmond Theatre "with electric velocity," spreading from a chandelier onstage to the entire building in only ten minutes. Despite all efforts to rescue those who were trapped inside, fifty-four women and eighteen men died out of an audience of six hundred (Richmond Then and Now 2011).

302.34–35 General Sherman used to rage and swear over "When we were marching through Georgia,"] In 1865 Henry Clay Work wrote "Marching through Georgia" to celebrate Major General William Tecumseh Sherman's March to the Sea at the end of 1864, which left a wide path of destruction and hastened the end of the Civil War.

302.41–42 Thirty-five years after those evil exploits . . . I had not seen for ten years] Clemens probably confessed his deception to his mother in January 1885, when he stopped in Keokuk on his reading tour with George Washington Cable. The last time he had seen her was in August 1874, when he and Olivia visited her in Fredonia, New York, where she was living with Pamela Moffett (14 Jan 1885 to OLC, CU-MARK; link note following 1–3 Aug 1874 to Dickinson, *L6,* 205).

304.2 Carlyle said "a lie cannot live."] Thomas Carlyle's *French Revolution* was one of Clemens's favorite books, but he was familiar with other works as well. "Nature admits no lie," Carlyle wrote in "The Stump-Orator," but no closer version of the quotation has been found (Gribben 1980, 1:128–29; Carlyle 1864, 180).

Autobiographical Dictation, 3 December 1906

304.5 Mesmerism continued—The Baron F. incident] This text, like those of 1 and 2 December, is from a 1903 manuscript inserted here in 1906.

304.6–14 dined with the C.'s, (in Vienna, in 1897) . . . across the table at a Mr. B.] The people mentioned in this paragraph have not been identified.

304.35–305.1 mesmerism—as it was then called . . . by Charcot under its other name of hypnotism] The term "mesmerism" derived from the name of Franz Mesmer (1734–1815), one of the earliest researchers to experiment with the phenomenon. Mesmer theorized that a force called "animal magnetism"—a transference of energy from one animate or inanimate object to another—produced the unusual effects he witnessed. In 1842 a Scottish physician, James Braid (1795–1860), concluded that the cause was instead "a peculiar condition of the nervous system, induced by a fixed and abstracted attention of the mental and visual eye, on one object, not of an exciting nature," and he proposed the term "hypnotism" to replace the scientifically derided "mesmerism" (Braid 2008, 10, 31). Jean-Martin Charcot (1825–93), an eminent French neurologist, turned a Paris asylum for women into a renowned research and teaching hospital; he became world famous for his public lectures and demonstrations in which hypnotized patients reproduced symptoms such as temporary paralysis of the limbs, deafness and muteness, amnesia, heightened or lost sensitivity of the skin, hallucinations, somnambulism, and fits of contortions, flailing, and seizures (Hustvedt 2011, 10–12, 58–63, 90–93, 106–13).

Autobiographical Dictation, 5 December 1906

307.23–31 not so cruel, not so pitiful, as is life in Russia to-day . . . so long as the Czardom continues to exist] Clemens published the bitter "Czar's Soliloquy" in 1905 and expressed similar sentiments about the "insane and intolerable slavery" of the Russian people and the tsar's "medieval barbarisms" in a public protest the same year (SLC 1905c; see *AutoMT1,* 648 nn. 462.36–37, 463.2).

307.35 *SELLING WIVES FOR BREAD*] This dispatch appeared in the New York *Sun* on 5 December. The 1906 famine in Russia was one of the worst in the country's history: an estimated twenty million people were threatened with starvation ("20,000,000 Face Famine," New York *Times,* 4 Dec 1906, 4).

308.6–7 John Cadwalader, a distinguished lawyer of Philadelphia, furnished me such a note] John Cadwalader (1843–1925) practiced law in state and federal courts throughout his career ("John Cadwalader Dies at 81 Years," New York *Times,* 13 Mar 1925, 19). Clemens heard this story from him when they dined together on 28 August 1902 (Notebook 45, TS p. 20, CU-MARK).

308.9–12 the illustrious John Marshall, Chief-Justice of the United States Supreme Court . . . a monument to commemorate the event] John Marshall (b. 1755) died on 6 July 1835. The following day, the Bar Association of Philadelphia met to establish the monument fund (U.S. Government Printing Office 1884, 81–82).

308.22–23 the young subscription-gatherer already mentioned died in the harness . . . undistinguished lawyer] Peter McCall (1809–80) was the last surviving member of the committee. After graduating from Princeton with high honors in 1826, McCall studied law under the lawyer and statesman Joseph R. Ingersoll and was admitted to the Philadelphia bar in 1830, the beginning of what was in fact a distinguished career. Among his more famous clients was Samuel Morse, whom he successfully represented in several cases regarding infringements of his telegraphic patents. A member of Philadelphia's Select Council between 1840 and 1848, McCall served as mayor in 1844–45 (U.S. Government Printing Office 1884, 91; Wilson and Fiske 1887–89, 4:75; "Obituary. Death of Hon. Peter McCall, a Well-Known Citizen," Philadelphia *North American,* 1 Nov 1880, unknown page).

308.41–309.1 Philadelphia's most revered, beloved, and illustrious old lawyer, Daniel O'Dogherty] Daniel Dougherty (1826–92), a native of Philadelphia whose early years were spent in poverty, was admitted to the bar in 1849. He soon became celebrated not only for his courtroom appearances but for the brilliance of his oratory, often in support of political causes. He worked for Lincoln's reelection in 1864, and gave the presidential nomination speeches for General Winfield Scott Hancock at the Democratic Convention in 1880 and for Grover Cleveland in 1888 ("Daniel Dougherty Dead," New York *Times,* 6 Sept 1892, 2; Young 1892; Wilson and Fiske 1887–89, 2:210–11).

309.14–15 to raise this fifty thousand dollars is happily not necessary—it is already raised!] The initial $2,557 raised in 1835 from members of the bar in Pennsylvania and other localities—with the stipulation that no individual contribution should exceed $10—had grown to almost $20,000 in 1880. In 1882, "Congress, in order that the nation might join the bar in honoring the memory of the great man to whom so much was due, added another $20,000 to the lawyers' fund" (U.S. Government Printing Office 1884, 3, 12–13, 23–25, 90).

309.18 The resulting Marshall monument is in the Capitol grounds at Washington] The bronze statue was sculpted in 1883 by William Wetmore Story (1819–95), son of Justice Joseph Story, Marshall's friend and colleague on the Supreme Court. It was installed on the west plaza of the Capitol and formally unveiled on 10 May 1884; in 1981 it was moved to the basement of the Supreme Court building, where it remains.

Autobiographical Dictation, 6 December 1906

310.2–3 each stitch that he took made Clara wince slightly, but it shriveled the others] Clemens may be conflating two incidents. In July 1880 he made note of both in "A Record of the Small Foolishnesses of Susie & 'Bay' Clemens." The first occurred in about 1877, when Clara was three years old, and had "the end of her forefinger crushed nearly off—she was full of interest & comment while the doctor took his stitches, & hardly winced." In the second incident, which he described as occurring "last spring," Clara had

> an angry & painful boil on her hand, & mamma made preparation to cut into it. Bay was serene, Susie was full of tremors & anxieties. As the cruel work progressed, Bay was good grit, & only winced, from time to time. Susie kept saying, *"Isn't* she brave!"—& at last a compliment was even wrung from mamma, who said, "Well you *are* a brave little thing!" Bay placidly responded, "*There ain't anybody braver but* God!" (SLC 1876–85, 69, 71)

310.12–20 a command from the Emperor of Germany to come to dinner . . . to get acquainted with but God] The dinner took place in Berlin on 20 February 1892 at the house of Clemens's third cousin, Alice Clemens von Versen, and her husband, Maximilian, a Prussian cavalry general (see *AutoMT1,* 456, 645 n. 456.25–26, where the city is misidentified as Vienna). On 24 January Clemens had been forced by "congestion of lungs & influenza" to decline an earlier invitation she had conveyed from the emperor, Kaiser Wilhelm II, to visit the palace:

> Frau von V. came again that day or the next & said the Emperor had commanded her to prepare dinner for him & me in her house—the date of the dinner to be the day that I sh[d] be well enough.
>
> A day or two ago, Jean was overheard to say—after some talk about this approaching event—"I wish I could be in papa's clothes"—pause & reflection—"but it wouldn't be any use, I reckon the Emperor wouldn't reconnize me." (Notebook 31, TS p. 21, CU-MARK)

310.24 Prince Heinrich, and six or eight other guests] Prince Heinrich of Prussia was the emperor's brother (see AD, 11 Feb 1907, note at 432.15–18). The other guests included Prince Hugo von Radolin (1841–1917), the former Count Radolinski, soon to be appointed the German ambassador at Constantinople, and two of Clemens's friends from the German ministry: Franz von Rottenburg (1845–1907), undersecretary in the Ministry of the Interior, and Rudolf Lindau (see AD, 31 July 1906, note at 157.7–8, and the notes at 310.35–37 and 312.19–20 in this dictation; Notebook 31, TS p. 31, CU-MARK; *MTB,* 2:940; London *Morning Post:* "Germany," 22 Apr 1891, 7; "Germany," 2 July 1892, 5; "Death of Dr. Von Rottenburg," London *Times,* 15 Feb 1907, 7).

310.32–34 he said that my best and most valuable book was "Old Times on the Mississippi." . . . presently] Clemens mentions the emperor's praise of *Life on the Mississippi,* and some of his other works, in the Autobiographical Dictations of 17 December 1906, 11 February 1907, and 12 February 1907.

310.35–37 An official who was well up in the Foreign Office . . . Smith, I will call him] "Smith" was in fact Clemens's friend Rudolf Lindau, who had been chief of the press department of the Foreign Office under Otto von Bismarck (1815–98), first chancellor of the German Empire. He was one of Bismarck's "most trusted subordinates" from 1878 until 1890, when Wilhelm II replaced Bismarck with Count Georg Leo von Caprivi (1831–99), and he retained the same office under Caprivi until his "vacation" in Constantinople beginning in 1892 ("The German Emperor and Prince Bismarck," London *Standard,* 28 Sept 1897, 5).

312.19–20 Eight years later Smith was passing through Vienna . . . no interruption of his vacation] Clemens last saw Lindau in Vienna in 1898, and in 1901 recounted his memories of the Berlin dinner in a letter:

> How well I remember the night when you told me to watch the Emperor and count how many seconds he conversed with you, so that I might know if the seconds reached sixty it would be a sure sign that he was satisfied with you and that you would get your vacation in Constantinople; and I also remember that he put his hand on your shoulder and that when he was done with you the watch had marked twelve minutes, so I knew that you could stay as long in Constantinople as you pleased and boss the German Embassy there if you chose. Ten years have gone by since that night and there you have been luxuriating in the Turkish capital ever

> since. You have been leading an ideal life there, and we all hope you will be able to transport the charm of it to Heligoland. (24 Apr 1901 to Lindau, ViU)

After his years in Constantinople, in part working as a director of the Tobacco Board of the Anatolian Railway, Lindau retired to the island of Heligoland, near Germany in the North Sea (Lindau 1917).

Autobiographical Dictation, 13 December 1906

312.23–24 As regards the coming American monarchy . . . chairman of the banquet] The occasion for Clemens's remarks was a banquet in honor of Secretary of State Elihu Root (1845–1937), held at the Waldorf-Astoria on 12 December by the Pennsylvania Society (see the note at 312.25–26). Clemens returned to New York from a trip to Washington on the afternoon of the banquet, but there is no evidence that he actually attended it (see AD, 18 Dec 1906; Lyon 1906, entries for 10–12 Dec). The source of the present text is a manuscript, into which Clemens copied a series of quotations excerpted from Root's speech as reported in the New York *Times* the following morning. The chairman was James Hampden Robb (1846–1911), a retired banker and former state assemblyman and senator (New York *Times:* "Root, Crying for Power, Meets a Judge's Reply," 13 Dec 1906, 1–2; "J. Hampden Robb, Ex-Senator, Dead," 22 Jan 1911, 11).

312.25–26 that such a man as you, Mr. Root, is chief adviser of the President] After a distinguished legal career of over thirty years in New York City, Elihu Root served in 1899–1904 as secretary of war under William McKinley, and since 1905 had been secretary of state under Theodore Roosevelt. He later served as a U.S. senator from New York (1909–15), and was a prominent figure in international law and diplomacy, for which he was awarded the Nobel Peace Prize in 1912.

312.32–33 He did not say . . . unavoidable replacement of the republic by monarchy] Root made an appeal for the centralization of power in the federal government, arguing that the contradictory laws of the individual states were often inconsistent with national interests. The applause for Root's speech was "comparatively slight," while the rebuttal delivered by John Hay Brown, a justice on the supreme court of Pennsylvania, was enthusiastically received; he argued that it was the role of the federal judiciary to "save the country from the consequences of legislative wandering beyond constitutional limits" ("Root, Crying for Power, Meets a Judge's Reply," New York *Times,* 13 Dec 1906, 1–2).

313.42 *The end is not yet*] This quote from Matthew 24:6 (or Mark 13:7) was not reported as part of Root's speech, but was supplied by Clemens.

314.6 ship-money] The English Crown had the right, in wartime, to collect ships (or, in place of ships, money) from seaport towns. King Charles I's innovation in collecting this "ship-money" nationwide and in peacetime made it effectively a perpetual tax, levied without the consent of Parliament.

Autobiographical Dictation, 17 December 1906

315.11 "Old Times on the Mississippi" got the Kaiser's best praise] See the Autobiographical Dictation of 6 December 1906.

315.12 when I reached home] In February 1892 the Clemens family was lodging at the Hotel Royal in "six chambers & one dining room & one parlor" on Berlin's Unter den Linden (Notebook 31, TS p. 20, CU-MARK).

316.15 my twenty-three volumes] The authorized collected editions of Mark Twain's works stood at twenty-three volumes from 1903 to late in 1906. Clemens forgets that *The $30,000 Bequest and Other Stories* had recently been added as volume 24 of Harper's Hillcrest Edition (Schmidt 2010, chapters 6 and 26).

317.12–16 I took up the *Sun* . . . crediting the meat and marrow of his conclusions to me] The (unsigned) editorial in the New York *Sun,* entitled "The Millionaire in Overalls," concluded:

> This essential and undeniable philosophic distinction between work and work-play, or play-work, is not ours. It belongs to our white robed young friend the Hon. MARK TWAIN; yet we dare say that you can find it a hundred times among the ancient Greeks, who made other folks work for them and "went in for" gymnastics; and it must have been old when NOAH was a sailor.
>
> Work for work's sake is a superstition and a delusion. The best that can be said for it is that it perpetuates a great mistake. If it has become almost a law of the human race, why should anybody go into raptures over it? Gravitation is a good deal more impressive and a universal law. Does anybody feel called upon to thank GOD for gravitation when a brick hits him? (17 Dec 1906, 8)

317.17 the whitewashing of the fence in "Tom Sawyer."] At the end of chapter 2, containing this famous scene, Mark Twain wrote:

> Tom said to himself that it was not such a hollow world, after all. He had discovered a great law of human action, without knowing it—namely, that in order to make a man or a boy covet a thing, it is only necessary to make the thing difficult to attain. If he had been a great and wise philosopher, like the writer of this book, he would now have comprehended that Work consists of whatever a body is *obliged* to do and that Play consists of whatever a body is not obliged to do. (*TS,* 50)

Autobiographical Dictation, 18 December 1906

317.26–28 I went to Washington, a fortnight ago . . . Mr. Paine made the trip with me] Clemens and Paine arrived in Washington on 6 December, in the evening. The joint copyright hearings before the Senate and House Committees on Patents took place from 7 to 11 December (see AD, 23 Nov 1906, note at 286.12–13). For Paine's detailed account of the trip see *MTB,* 3:1343–50.

317.29–36 League Committee . . . something connected with a railroad] Robert Underwood Johnson (1853–1937), secretary of the American Copyright League in 1906, became an associate editor of the *Century Magazine* in 1881, and in that capacity had edited several of Clemens's works that appeared there in full or in part. At the time of this dictation he had published *The Winter Hour and Other Poems* (1892), *Songs of Liberty and Other Poems* (1897), and *Poems* (1902). William Worthen Appleton (1845–1924) succeeded his father, William H., in 1899 as president of the firm of D. Appleton and Company, best known for its popular travel and reference books such as *Appleton's Cyclopaedia of American Biography* (1887–89). In 1906 he was president of the American Publishers' Copyright League. George Haven Putnam (1844–1930) became a partner in his father's publishing business, Wiley and Putnam, in 1866. Upon his father's death in 1872, Putnam and his brothers established G. P. Putnam's Sons in New York, which was known for its publication of popular fiction and the writings of American statesmen. He was a founding member, in 1887, of the American Publishers' Copyright League, and the author of several books on international copyright. Richard R. Bowker (1848–1933) was second vice-president of the American Copyright League in 1906. In 1879 he bought *Publishers' Weekly,* becoming its editor in 1884. He wrote several works on economics and politics, and in 1886 he published the comprehensive reference work *Copyright: Its Law and Its Literature.* He did not publish his first poetry collection, *From the Pen of R. R. B.,* until 1916. Clemens alludes to Bowker's vice-presidency of the De Laval Steam Turbine Company of New York, founded in 1901. The De Laval turbine generated electrical power to produce lighting for railroad trains (Garrison 1904, 4).

318.12–16 When I went to Washington sixteen years ago . . . Mr. Lowell appeared just once] Clemens conflates two separate trips to Washington, saying mistakenly that they both occurred "sixteen years ago" (at 318.12 and 318.38). On the first occasion, in January 1886, he and James Russell Lowell both spoke and answered questions before the Senate Committee on Patents when it was debating two international copyright bills (see AD, 22 Nov 1906, note at 283.25–284.16). The second occasion occurred in 1889 (see the note at 318.39–40).

318.18 Edward Everett Hale] See the Autobiographical Dictation of 4 February 1907, note at 424.10–13.

318.21–22 The international bill was passed, and became law] The International Copyright Act of 1891, the first U.S. law to recognize the copyrights of foreign authors, was based on the Chace bill, which Clemens had supported in 1886.

318.22–23 This victory was attributed to Johnson . . . Legion of Honor for it] The cross of the Legion of Honor was awarded not only to Johnson, but to Putnam as well ("Notes and Announcements," London *Publishers' Circular* 54 [2 May 1891]: 448).

318.39–40 Sunset Cox smuggled me in on the floor of the House] On 31 January 1889 Clemens went to Washington with Johnson to lobby for the international copyright bill; he described his efforts in a speech given to the Washington Ladies' Literary Association on 2 February. The bill was killed by filibuster, never coming to a vote. Clemens had known Samuel Sullivan (Sunset) Cox (1824–89) since 1870, and in 1887 his publishing firm, Charles L. Webster and Company, had published a book by him, *Diversions of a Diplomat in Turkey.* A Democrat, Cox served in Congress for nearly thirty years, first representing Ohio (1857–65) and then New York (1869–89) (6 July 1870 to OLC, *L4,* 164–66; *N&J3,* 332 n. 91, 445 n. 123; "'Mark Twain's' Speech," Washington *Post,* 4 Feb 1889, 2).

319.1–2 Mr. John D. Long supplied me with Republicans] John Davis Long (1838–1915) had been the Republican governor of Massachusetts in 1880–82. At the time of Clemens's visit in February 1889 he was in the last month of his third term as the U.S. congressman from Massachusetts.

319.18–22 He and Bowker appeared . . . next day's sitting, at five in the afternoon, and spoke] Underwood, Bowker, and Clemens all spoke at the second session of the copyright hearings, which was held on the afternoon of the first day (7 December); Clemens's speech is included in the Autobiographical Dictation of 26 December 1906. Among the others who made statements at that session were artist Francis D. Millet, and authors Edward Everett Hale and Thomas Nelson Page ("Plead for Copyright," Washington *Post,* 8 Dec 1906, 4; U.S. Congress 1906, 77–98, 114–21; for Millet and Page see *AutoMT1,* 548 n. 255.28–29, 602 n. 385.1–3).

319.32 Mr. Speaker Cannon] Joseph Gurney Cannon (1836–1926), a Republican from Illinois, served forty-six years in the House of Representatives, from 1873 to 1923 (with two hiatuses), becoming Speaker of the House in 1903. Clemens wrote him on 7 December 1906, asking for his help: "It is imperatively necessary that I get on the floor for 2 or 3 hours & talk to the members, man by man, in behalf of the support, encouragement & protection of one of the nation's most valuable assets & industries—its Literature. I have arguments with me—also a barrel. With liquid in it" (MS facsimile, Chapple 1910, 301).

319.37–38 Neal has served a procession of Speakers of the House . . . for forty years] Henry Neal (1850–1921) was appointed doorkeeper and messenger in 1876 by Speaker Samuel J. Randall. The "efficient, affable, and diligent" Neal, who had served for thirty-one years under seven Speakers of the House when he helped Clemens in 1906, retained his position until his death ("Petty Spoils," Washington *Post,* 21 Jan 1911, 6). A member of the Masons, the Colored Personal Liberty League, and the Oldest Inhabitants Association, Neal "knew practically every man prominent in public life. He knew many secrets of the nine speakers under whom he served, was trusted by them and invariably proved himself, both in honesty and diplomacy, equal to any situation that arose" ("Henry Neal Gets Final Message," Chicago *Defender,* 8 Oct 1921, 1; "Liberty League Banquet," Washington *Post,* 31 Mar 1899, 2; *Washington Census* 1900, 164:7A).

320.6–7 chairmen of the Senate and House Committees that had the bill in charge] Senator Alfred B. Kittredge of South Dakota (1861–1911) and Congressman Frank D. Currier of New Hampshire (1853–1921) (U.S. Congress 1906, 2).

320.12 mine] Clemens added, and then deleted, the following comment: "*Note.* 300 publishers interested to the extent of several million dollars a year, and a dozen authors interested to the extent of next to nothing at all, so far as money is concerned."

Autobiographical Dictation, 19 December 1906

322.32–33 The clause in the Constitution . . . which denies perpetual property in an author's book] Section 8 of the U.S. Constitution empowers Congress to "promote the Progress of Science and useful Arts, by securing for limited Times to Authors and Inventors the exclusive Right to their respective Writings and Discoveries."

323.1–11 The late Baron Tauchnitz was the only publisher . . . not a pirate it is Tauchnitz's son] Christian Bernhard von Tauchnitz (1816–95) founded his Leipzig publishing house in 1837, originally publishing only translations from Greek and Latin. In 1841 he began a new series in English, the Collection of British (later British and American) Authors. Despite the absence of an international copyright law, Tauchnitz offered authors what they considered generous payment for the privilege of republishing their works, which won him much gratitude and loyalty from authors such as Dickens, George Eliot, Carlyle, Longfellow, Thackeray, and Trollope. In 1876 Tauchnitz approached Clemens through Bret Harte for permission to add *The Adventures of Tom Sawyer* to the series. Clemens responded, "That you have recognized my moral right to my books gratifies me but does not surprise me, because I knew before that you were always thus courteous with authors" (14 Sept 1876 to Tauchnitz, *Letters 1876–1880*). In part for his efforts to make English literature popular in Germany, Tauchnitz was granted the title Freiherr (Baron) in 1860 by Ernest II, duke of Saxe-Coburg-Gotha (the brother of Prince Albert, husband of Queen Victoria). After Tauchnitz's death, his son, Baron Christian Karl Bernhard von Tauchnitz (1841–1921), continued to publish Clemens's books under the same arrangement (Meyer 1929, 1339; Reece 1937, 27; "Baron Tauchnitz's Service Told," London *Daily Telegraph,* 1 Sept 1895, 28; "Death of Baron von Tauchnitz," New York *Times,* 15 Aug 1895, 5).

323.31 "The glory that was Greece, and the grandeur that was Rome"] From Edgar Allan Poe's revised version of "To Helen," published in the 1845 edition of *The Raven and Other Poems.*

Autobiographical Dictation, 20 December 1906

324.13 "What Cheer,"] The What Cheer House, at the corner of Sacramento Street and Leidesdorff, opened in 1852. A temperance hotel for men, it was frequented mainly by miners, sailors, and farmers. Its popular and inexpensive basement restaurant allegedly served as many as four thousand meals a day, charging five cents a dish in the 1860s. It burned down in the aftermath of the 1906 earthquake (Craig 2003; Conlin 1986, 140–42).

324.14–15 "Miners' Restaurant." . . . good food on the cheapest possible terms] The Miners' Restaurant, on Commercial Street near the San Francisco *Call* offices, was known for its "square meals," evidently paying more regard to "quantity than quality." It was demolished in October 1863 ("An Old Land-Mark Gone," Virginia City *Evening Bulletin,* 24 Oct 1863, 4; *RI 1993,* 702–3 n. 408.27–409.1).

Autobiographical Dictation, 21 December 1906

327.3–6 an article came out in the "Christian Union" . . . by the mother of the child] "What Ought He to Have Done?" was published in the *Christian Union* on 11 June 1885 (31:13). The article was reprinted from the May issue of *Babyhood* magazine, where it had appeared as a letter to the editor signed "X" (1:180–81). The author recounts an incident in which a young boy throws a paper from his father's desk on the floor, refuses to pick it up again, and persistently defies his parents. The father spanks him "until—he—picks—that—paper—up—with—his—hands"; when the boy instead picks it up with his teeth, the author asks what the father should have done. It is not clear why Clemens assumed that the author was the boy's mother.

327.41 paper cutter] A letter opener, at that time usually made of bone or wood.

329.4–5 When the Christian Union reached the farm and papa's article in it] Clemens's article—also in the form of a letter to the editor—was published under the title "'What Ought He to Have Done?': Mark Twain's Opinion" in the 16 July 1885 *Christian Union* (SLC 1885b). After calling the boy's father a ludicrous ass for spanking his child to make him obey, he praises Olivia's approach to disciplining their children: she did not spank them "for spite, or ever in anger," but only after "an hour or two. By that time both parties are calm, and the one is judicial, the other receptive." His article was reprinted under the same title in the August 1885 issue of *Babyhood,* along with a letter from the child's father justifying his own actions ("John, Senior, Speaks," 1:275–77).

329.21–27 letters began to come in to papa crittisizing it . . . (he was the baby's father)] Several letters about Clemens's article, most of them complimentary, survive in the Mark Twain Papers. The "very worst" was written by someone who signed his name "Thomas Twain"; Clemens noted on the letter that it was "evidently from 'John Senior,'" the boy's father, but that seems unlikely. The writer, who was appalled by Livy's delayed punishment of the children, describes a sadistic fantasy in which he imagines himself torturing her:

> Your wife must be a solemn ass, a prig, a calvinistic schoolmistress of three generations back. I hate the very idea of her perambulating around thinking of the "duty" i.e. treat to come, and then with her damned "calmness" executing the 'sentence,' and requesting the child to see that it is in love and not in "anger"—Oh—damn the woman! I had such a mother, and being my mother I shall say nothing disrespectful of her except this that neither my two brothers nor myself shed a tear for her when she died, and although our sister did cry in a feminine way,

she rapidly reconciled herself to the loss of the admirable disciplinarian with her irrevocable sentences, her hours of torturing delay, her calm 'execution,' and her hateful embraces and humbug afterwards which made hypocrites of all of us. It gives me pleasure to damn your wife. I feel she deserves it, and it relieves me. When our father married a second time some three years after our mother's death, our young step mother won all our hearts. No damned crocodile calmness about her. She had little bits of temper, she could give and take with her tongue, sometimes she would give us a little slap, but everything in that way was soon forgotten, she was joyous, kind, charitable, indulgent, good— She believed in bright example and good humor, & any hastiness of temper was only a summer cloud— She knew children, she loved them, she understood our minds and our imperfect point of view. She was worth 20 cartloads of stereotyped, drill sergeant mothers with their d—d organized discipline—

When you were at it, Mr Mark Twain, why did not you make a little money by a graphic description of the "scene of torture," and a full account of the modus operandi. I'll be bound admirable Mrs Twain has some special method, or weapon of her own, which she has calmly thought out and given some mind to. I'll be bound also she knows all the soft spots of a child's anatomy, and carefully notes and studies the effects as she calmly exerts herself in the "scene of torture"— Torture! Good God, and by a Christian mother! . . .

Your admirable wife be damned, Mr Twain. I only wish I had her in a room quietly by myself and free of interruption for half an hour. I would tie her hands, I would strap her on a table, her feet on the floor, making a fine half crescent at a certain part of her body, convex side upper-most, I would bare her to the skin, and then proceed to ply a stout leather strap with knotted tails to her buttocks. Heavens! I enjoy the very idea of it! There would be no delay between sentence and execution. I would consider my anger righteous. But in the tempest, torrent, whirlwind of my passion I would beget a calmness of scientific application. I would study the torture and I would rejoice with exceeding joy as I saw the blisters and welts accumulating under my scientific handling. Then I would untie M[rs] Twain, and lead her to the sofa, and then in less time than it takes to tell it "love her back into happy heartedness and a joyful spirit"! (21 July 1885, CU-MARK)

330.29–32 Mr. Laurence Barrette and Mr. and Mrs. Hutton . . . he was staying with us] The actor Lawrence Barrett (1838–91) and the drama critic Laurence Hutton—with his wife of one year, Eleanor Varnum Mitchell Hutton (1848–1910)—stayed with the Clemenses on 3 and 4 March 1886. Clemens had met Barrett briefly in San Francisco, but became better acquainted with him in 1874, when he offered him the part of Colonel Sellers in his *Gilded Age* play (link note following 10 May 1874 to Haddon, *L6,* 148–49). Barrett, who had brought his repertory company to Hartford after a successful month-long engagement in New York, appeared on 3 March in the role of Lanciotto, the deceitful hunchback husband, in George H. Boker's verse tragedy *Francesca da Rimini* (after Dante), and on 4 March he played the role of the title character in Victor Hugo's *Hernani* (New York *Times:* "Died," 17 Nov 1910, 9; "Mr. Lawrence Barrett," 18 Feb 1886, 5; "Notes of the Week," 28 Feb 1886, 6; Hartford *Courant:* "Lawrence Barrett This Evening," 3 Mar 1886, 2; "Lawrence Barrett in 'Hernani,'" 5 Mar 1886, 3; Barrett to SLC and OLC, 27 Feb 1886, CU-MARK; Hutton to Winter, 4 Mar 1886, JIm; U.S.

National Archives and Records Administration 1795–1905, Roll 227, passport application for Eleanor V. Mitchell, 10 Feb 1879).

330.32 Mrs. ———] Perhaps Susy meant Susan Warner (Mrs. Charles Dudley Warner), whose name she left blank elsewhere in her biography (*AutoMT1,* 587 n. 346.9).

330.34 "Mind Cure" theory] In the late nineteenth century the terms "mind cure" and "mental cure" were used in a general way for the belief that disease was the result of negative thoughts, and could therefore be cured by mental effort alone. Mary Baker Eddy's *Science and Health,* published in 1875, was just one of the many books that promoted this idea. Clemens said in 1894 that Lilly Gillette Foote, Susy and Clara's governess since about 1880, was (at least by the early 1890s) an "eloquent enthusiast upon mind-cure," and it may have been she who encouraged the family to experiment with it (3 Aug 1894 to OLC, CU-MARK; Ober 2003, 210–18; for Foote see *AutoMT1,* 579–80 n. 326.13–21). Clemens remained fascinated with the healing power of the mind until the end of his life, despite his skepticism about Christian Science and other religious applications of the philosophy. He returns to the subject in the Autobiographical Dictation of 27 December 1906.

331.1–2 Miss Holden the young lady who is doctoring in the "Mind Cure" theory] Unidentified.

331.3 Mrs. George Warners] Lilly Gillette Warner (see AD, 8 Aug 1906, note at 166.15).

331.39–41 We have just had our Prince and Pauper pictures taken . . . the lady Jane scene was perfect] The photographs were taken by Horace L. Bundy of Hartford, exactly one year after the Clemens children first performed their version of the play (see AD, 8 Aug 1906). The group picture that Susy calls the "Interview," with Margaret (Daisy) Warner as the pauper (Tom Canty) and herself as the prince (Edward VI), is published in the photo gathering of Volume 1 (*AutoMT1,* following page 204). The "lady Jane scene," with Clara as Lady Jane Grey and Daisy Warner as the pauper in the prince's clothing, can be found in this volume, following page 300.

332.28–30 Fifteen years were to pass before . . . re-utter that daring opinion and print it] Howells commented in print on Clemens's underlying earnestness and philosophical seriousness as early as 1875, in his review of *Sketches, New and Old:* "There is another quality in this book which we fancy we shall hereafter associate more and more with our familiar impressions of him, and that is a growing seriousness of meaning in the apparently unmoralized drolling, which must result from the humorist's second thought of political and social absurdities" (Howells 1875, 749). His reviews of *A Tramp Abroad, The Prince and the Pauper,* and later works were even more emphatic about this serious vein (Howells 1880, 1881).

332.35–36 Two years after she passed out of my life I wrote a philosophy . . . three persons who have seen the manuscript] Between April and July 1898 Clemens wrote the first draft of *What Is Man?* in Vienna and Kaltenleutgeben, and continued to work on it through at least September 1905. In December 1906, when this text was dictated,

What Is Man? had actually been printed and privately distributed; his reference to it as a "manuscript" that only "three persons" have seen reflects his use here of earlier material—his manuscript footnotes to Susy's biography (SLC 1901–2a; see AD, 25 June 1906, note at 142.14).

333.3 Mr. Jesse Grant] Ulysses S. Grant's youngest son (*AutoMT1,* 482 n. 76.1).

333.28 Miss Corey] Susan (Susy) Corey (b. 1865?), a graduate of the Stuttgart Conservatory in 1884, taught music and piano to Susy and Clara Clemens in Hartford in the mid-1880s and also participated in—sometimes as a teacher or coach—the German classes that Olivia and the girls attended. She was the daughter of Ella J. Corey (b. 1841?), an old friend of Olivia's from Elmira (Buffalo *Courier:* "Musical Personals and Miscellany," 22 Aug 1885, and "Social Topics," 13 Sept 1885, unknown pages; *N&J3,* 631; OLC to SLC, 14 Nov 1884 and 16 Jan 1885, CtHMTH; 17 and 18 May 1869 to OLL, *L3,* 243 n. 4; *Chemung Census* 1870, 914:302A).

333.38 Mamma and papa Clara and Daisy have gone to New York to see the "Mikado."] The four left for New York on Friday, 16 April 1886, and saw one of the final performances of Gilbert and Sullivan's *Mikado* by the D'Oyly Carte Opera Company at the Fifth-Avenue Theatre ("Amusements," New York *Times,* 16 Apr 1886, 7; *N&J3,* 234; 12 Apr 1886 to Howells, MH-H, in *MTHL,* 2:553).

334.11–13 at my side was Cable . . . seven grandchildren in stock, and a brand-new wife] On 24 November 1906 sixty-two-year-old George Washington Cable married his second wife, Eva Colegate Stevenson of Kentucky (d. 1923), "a woman of forty-eight, of charming social accomplishments, a beautiful musician, large in mind and heart, of a mirthful temper and ardent affections," as he wrote to Andrew and Louise Carnegie (Turner 1956, 335–36; "Mrs. Eva Stevenson Cable," New York *Times,* 8 June 1923, 19). Louise Stewart Bartlett Cable (b. 1846), his first wife and the mother of his children, had died in 1904, after thirty-five years of marriage (Rubin 1969, 249–50).

Autobiographical Dictation, 26 December 1906

334.17–18 a letter from England from a gentleman whose belief in phrenology is strong] The letter, dated 7 December 1906, was from Frederic Whyte (1867–1941), a former Reuters correspondent, editor at Cassell and Company (1889–1904), and prolific writer and translator (Archives Hub 2011). Whyte wrote, "I have induced the Editor of the *Daily Graphic* to open the columns of that journal to a discussion of the subject not merely by men of science but also by other writers and observers whose views will be of interest and value," and "I am most anxious to have a few lines from you" (CU-MARK).

334.24–26 In London, 33 or 34 years ago . . . I went to Fowler under an assumed name] Lorenzo N. Fowler (1811–96) was an active phrenologist, lecturer, and author. He and his older brother, Orson Squire Fowler (1809–87), both graduated from Amherst College. In addition to the books they coauthored (see the note at 335.1–3), Lorenzo wrote *Synopsis of Phrenology and Physiology* (1844) and *Marriage: Its History and Philosophy, with Directions for Happy Marriages* (1846). After leaving the family's New York publishing house in 1863, he moved to London, but continued to write for the firm's *Phrenological Journal.* Throughout the 1870s he conducted examinations in his Fleet Street offices near Ludgate Circus (Stern 1969, 210; 1971, 188). No record of Clemens's 1872–73 visits, other than this account, has been found.

335.1–3 Fowler and Wells stood at the head . . . publications had a wide currency] Lorenzo and Orson Fowler coauthored and published their first book, *Phrenology Proved, Illustrated, and Applied,* in 1836. Two years later they began the *Phrenological Journal* in Philadelphia, and in 1842 they founded a publishing firm in New York. In 1844 Orson continued the business with his brother-in-law, Samuel R. Wells (1820–75), establishing the firm of Fowler and Wells. Their dozens of books, written primarily by Orson, were hugely popular; among them were *Physiology, Animal and Mental* (1842), *Self-Culture and Perfection of Character* (1843), *Love and Parentage Applied to the Improvement of Offspring* (1844), *Amativeness; or, Evils and Remedies of Excessive and Perverted Sexuality* (1844), and *A Home for All; or, The Gravel Wall, and Octagon Mode of Building* (1849). By 1850 there were probably almost half a million of their "various productions . . . in the hands of the American public" (Stern 1971, 84). In 1863 the Fowler brothers withdrew from the firm, which was continued by other family members, under a series of names, until 1904.

335.27 the voice of the doubter was not heard in the land] A play on Song of Solomon 2:12, "The flowers appear on the earth; the time of the singing of birds is come, and the voice of the turtle is heard in our land."

336.32–337.2 William T. Stead made a photograph . . . was totally destitute of the sense of humor] The character "estimates" were solicited by William T. Stead (1849–1912), a radical journalist, political reformer, and spiritualist. In 1890 he had given *A Connecticut Yankee in King Arthur's Court* an enthusiastic review in his new journal, the *Review of Reviews,* which proved to be one of the few positive notices to appear in Britain. He corresponded with Clemens at that time, and after meeting him by chance on an Atlantic crossing in March 1894, he recruited Clemens's assistance in the palm-reading experiment. He published prints of Clemens's hands in the July 1894 issue of his psychical research quarterly, *Borderland,* and invited "experts" to read and respond. The readings of four palmists were published in October 1894; that issue of the magazine has not been found, but Clemens saw a copy and commented on them in a letter to Stead. He gave the palmists limited praise, noting that only one of them "claims that the sense of humor exists in my make-up; the other three are silent as to that" (30 Nov 1894 to Stead [2nd], ViU; Stead 1895; *CY,* 26–27; Baylen 1964).

337.3–4 six professional palmists of distinguished reputation here in New York City] The readings of three of these palmists are included in the Autobiographical Dictation of 28 January 1907.

337.11–12 The speech which I made before the copyright committees . . . in a Congressional document] Clemens's speech of 7 December 1906 was published in the Government Printing Office's *Copyright Hearings, December 7 to 11, 1906* (SLC 1906i). See the Autobiographical Dictation of 18 December 1906.

337.23 "Sufficient unto the day."] From the Sermon on the Mount, Matthew 6:34.

337.34 The Decalogue] The Ten Commandments.

338.41–42 I was to be called before the Copyright Committee of the House of Lords] See the Autobiographical Dictation of 24 November 1906, note at 290.17–19.

339.26 Lord Thwing] Henry, first Baron Thring. See the Autobiographical Dictation of 24 November 1906, note at 288.18.

339.39–41 it was recognized that books had perpetual copyright . . . in Queen Anne's time] Edward Everett Hale, who spoke immediately before Clemens, said, "The whole business of copyright law came in in Queen Anne's time by statute, when they supposed they were giving a benefit to authors" (Hale 1906, 114; for Hale see AD, 4 Feb 1907, note at 424.10–13). The Statute of Anne, effective from 1710 to 1842, was the first governmental regulation of copyright. Previously, copyrights had been enforced by the Stationers' Company, a printers' guild, and were vested in publishers, who purchased them in perpetuity from authors. The new law established the first term limit of copyright, granting it to authors for fourteen years, renewable for another fourteen.

340.17 Cape-to-Cairo Railway] Cecil Rhodes's projected railroad and steamer line, stretching for about three thousand miles from Cape Town at the southern tip of Africa to Cairo in the north, was never completed. In 1906 about two-thirds of the route was in service ("From the Cape to Cairo," New York *Times,* 20 Aug 1906, 3).

340.19 William Penn, who bought for forty dollars' worth of stuff the giant area of Pennsylvania] William Penn (1644–1718) developed land in the American colonies granted to him by King Charles II, and purchased more from the indigenous people, in 1682–84. Clemens seems to be confusing him with Peter Minuit, who—according to legend—bought Manhattan in 1626 for about twenty-four dollars.

340.38–39 like that of 1714, under Queen Anne] Queen Anne died in 1714; Clemens alludes to the statute of 1710 (see the note at 339.39–41).

341.1 Lord Macaulay, who made a speech on copyright] See the Autobiographical Dictation of 24 November 1906, note at 289.33–35.

341.10–11 Mrs. Stowe's two daughters . . . they had their living very much limited] Harriet Beecher Stowe's *Uncle Tom's Cabin* (1852) was phenomenally successful; about 310,000 copies had been printed by early 1863, and it continued to earn her regular payments of several thousand dollars a year. In 1893, however, the copyright expired. Her royalty payment, which in 1892 had been $6,694, fell to only $697 in 1895. In "Concerning Copyright. An Open Letter to the Register of Copyrights," published in January 1905, Clemens noted, "The profits on 'Uncle Tom's Cabin' continue to-day;

nobody but the publishers get them—Mrs. Stowe's share ceased seven years before she died; her daughters receive nothing from the book. Years ago they found themselves no longer able to live in their modest home, and had to move out and find humbler quarters" (SLC 1905b, 3–4; Winship 2012; *AutoMT1,* 574 n. 310.37–38). Stowe's twin daughters, Harriet Beecher Stowe (1836–1907) and Eliza Tyler Stowe (1836–1912), never married. They lived with (and cared for) their parents in a cottage neighboring the Clemenses' house on Forest Street in Hartford. After the author's death in 1896, they moved to Simsbury, Connecticut, to be near their brother Charles (Beecher Stowe Center 2011).

341.27 perpetual copyright upon the Old and New Testaments] See the Autobiographical Dictation of 24 November 1906, note at 291.4–8.

Autobiographical Dictation, 27 December 1906

342.12 Mind Cure] See the Autobiographical Dictation of 21 December 1906 and the note at 330.34.

345.28–36 Fourth of July dinner . . . Lord Wolseley] See the Autobiographical Dictation of 31 July 1906 (and the note at 157.13–17), in which Clemens first relates this anecdote about "Luck" and meeting Lord Wolseley at the 1900 Fourth of July dinner.

Autobiographical Dictation, 28 December 1906

346.22–27 "Whoop Says She." . . . from one of Charles Reade's books, I think] The original typescript of this dictation attributes this anecdote to "Charles Reid"—evidently the stenographer's error for Charles Reade (1814–84), the popular British novelist. Clemens had been acquainted with Reade since 1872 and had read and liked many of his books, including *The Cloister and the Hearth* (1861); the "Whoop Says She" anecdote, however, is not by him. It derives from chapter 30 of *Miss Van Kortland,* published anonymously in 1870 by American novelist Frank Lee Benedict (1834–1910) (Benedict 1870; *MTB,* 1:462; Gribben 1980, 2:571–73).

347.30 Like Gargery Wot larks] "What larks" was Joe Gargery's catchphrase in *Great Expectations.*

348.1–3 Andrew Lang's affectionate hand-shake . . . painstaking care] This birthday tribute to Mark Twain by Andrew Lang (1844–1912), a Scottish novelist, poet, folklorist, and literary critic, was published in his column, "At the Sign of the Ship," in the February 1886 issue of *Longman's Magazine* (Andrew Lang 1886). If this was Susy's source, she made minor alterations and omitted most of the following passage from the introductory paragraph: "When he gets among pictures and holy places perhaps we all feel that he is rather an awful being. But on a Mississippi boat, or in a bar-room, or editing (without sufficient technical information) an agricultural journal, or bestriding a Celebrated Mexican Plug, or out silver-mine hunting, or on the track of Indian Joe, Mark is all himself."

348.7–8 For Booth Dinner. (This speech was given to Susy, and never used or printed] Clemens's claim that this speech was "never used" conceals one of his rare failures as an after-dinner speaker. He had delivered this speech at a Players club dinner honoring Edwin Booth (1833–93), held at Delmonico's Restaurant on the evening of 30 March 1889. The club hosted the event in gratitude for Booth's having given it the deed to his Stanford White mansion at 16 Gramercy Park (New York *Times:* "The Players' Clubhouse," 1 Jan 1889, 5; "The Booth Supper," 1 Apr 1889, 4). Brander Matthews, who was present, recalled: "he did not say a word about the distinguished guest; he actually took for his topic the long clam of New England—and what was worse, this inappropriate offering was read from manuscript!" "We hung our heads," wrote another guest, "hoping that it would soon be over" (Matthews 1922, 273; Morgan 1910, 69–70). The speech does not appear in Susy's biography, which ends with an entry written on 4 July 1886.

348.8 Long Clam] The long-necked clam, *Mya arenaria.*

349.28–29 I consider Depew the Long Clam of the great world of intellect and oratory] See the Autobiographical Dictation of 1 June 1906.

349.32 Pilla] The nickname of Mildred Howells (1872–1966), the Howellses' youngest child, who in later life became a successful poet, watercolor artist, and illustrator ("Mildred Howells," New York *Times,* 20 Apr 1966, 47).

349.35–350.3 in "Silas Lapham" he wrote a sentence about a Jew . . . decided to take out the sentence] Howells received three letters from Jewish readers while *The Rise of Silas Lapham* was being serialized in the *Century Magazine* from November 1884 to August 1885. One of these, by Cyrus L. Sulzberger, editor of the *American Hebrew,* urged him to remove a passage in chapter 2 before the novel was published as a book. In it, Silas asserts that although "there aint any sense in it," Jews "send down the price of property" when they move into a neighborhood. Sulzberger claimed the remark was "unworthy of the author," could serve no literary purpose, and that "the sentiment is violently dragged in for no other ascertainable reason than to pander to a prejudice against which all educated and cultured Jews must battle." Howells replied on 17 July 1885, "I supposed that I was writing in reprobation of the prejudice of which you justly complain, but my irony seems to have fallen short of the mark." Despite his annoyance at being misunderstood, he did remove the passage—and a similar one later in the chapter—before the book was published (Arms and Gibson 1943, 119–22; Howells 1884, 22–23, 25; Howells 1980, 124–25).

350.5–22 Mr. Wood an equantance of his, new a rich Jew who read papa's books . . . always well taken care of] Charles Erskine Scott Wood's "equantance" was Morris W. Fechheimer (1844–86), who had remarked that Clemens never ridiculed or satirized Jews in his writings. Clemens wrote Wood on 22 January 1885, "I have never felt a disposition to satirize the Jews. . . . We do not satirize people whom we singularly respect—one would do it but indifferently well, and be ashamed of it when done," and gave as his reasons essentially what Susy reports here (photocopy of TS in CU-MARK; "Morris W. Fechheimer," *The West Shore,* Apr 1886, 115; for Wood see AD, 31 July 1906, note at 155.13–15). After seeing the letter, Fechheimer replied to Clemens on 5 February:

> I have noticed comments at various times upon the fact that Scott in Ivanhoe and Lessing in Nathan the Wise were the first authors in their respective countries, who in modern times had represented a Jew in other than the most contemptible light. Now, to me it seems that what under the circumstances you failed to do, is equally as noteworthy as what they did do. (CU-MARK)

350.23–32 once the ladies of a orphans home wrote him . . . everything that was needed to make it comfortable] Clemens delivered his "American Vandal Abroad" lecture on 22 January 1869 for the Cleveland Protestant Orphan Asylum, earning $564 for a bathtub and other expenses. In a pitch for further contributions, Clemens said at the end of his speech:

> Don't be afraid of giving too much to the orphans, for however much you give you have the easiest end of the bargain. Some persons have to take care of those sixty orphans and they have to *wash* them. [Prolonged laughter.] Orphans have to be washed! And it's no small job either for they have only one wash tub and it's slow business! They can't wash but one orphan at a time! They have to be washed in the most elaborate detail, and by the time they get through with the sixty, the original orphan has to be washed again. Orphans won't stay washed! I've been an orphan myself for twenty-five years and I know this to be true. ("Mark Twain," Cleveland *Leader,* 23 Jan 1869, 4)

The asylum, founded in 1853, was located on Woodland Avenue near Cleveland's Jewish Orphan Asylum for the orphans of Jewish Civil War veterans, which opened in 1868, underwritten by the Independent Order of B'nai B'rith (*L3:* 7 Jan 1869 to Fairbanks et al., 15–17; 23 Jan 1869 to Twichell and family, 68 n. 5; 5 Feb 1869 to Fairbanks, 87–88 n. 4; *Cleveland Directory* 1871, 542; Rose 1950, 246, 351).

352.13 Many years have gone by, and the pegs have disappeared] Clemens devised the history game at Quarry Farm in Elmira in July 1883, first setting pegs on the road on 18 July. Two days later he wrote Howells that he had also figured out a way to play it indoors with a cribbage board (NN-BGC, in *MTHL,* 1:435–36).

352.33–34 one of the first two written by me . . . twelve or fifteen years old] Probably *The Innocents Abroad* (1869) or *Roughing It* (1872). It seems unlikely that Clemens counted *The Celebrated Jumping Frog* (1867) as his first book, since he had been at some pains to destroy its plates and prevent its being reprinted (see AD, 23 May 1906, note at 49.31–33).

353.10–19 I did not want the authorship to be known . . . they put my name to it, with my consent] "Personal Recollections of Joan of Arc," ostensibly translated by "the Sieur Louis de Conte . . . out of the ancient French into modern English from the original unpublished manuscript in the National Archives of France, by Jean François Alden," was serialized in *Harper's New Monthly Magazine* in 1895–96. After the first installment was published in April 1895, Clemens's authorship was almost immediately suspected and confirmed. On 11 April the Hartford *Courant* wrote, "It is now known for a fact that Mr. Clemens is the author" ("Those 'Personal Recollections,'" 8). Although his name was never attached to the serial version, "Mark Twain" is on both the cover and the spine of the 1896 book edition (SLC 1895–96, 1896; Rood 1895; "News Notes," *Bookman,* Apr 1895, 145).

353.24–26 Two years ago, I wrote in a carefully disguised fashion . . . anybody would know me by] On 21 August 1905 Clemens wrote to George Harvey, "I am publishing anonymously an article in an outside paper, in the hope that the authorship will not be detected" (Willis F. Johnson 1929, 81). The "outside paper" was *Collier's Weekly,* and the article was "Christian Citizenship," a brief plea for the voter to heed "his Christian code of morals" in the upcoming civic elections and to reject New York's Tammany Hall government. The article appeared in the issue of 2 September, credited to "a great creative artist whose reasons for anonymity seem sufficient to us as to himself" (SLC 1905f; Lee to SLC, 13 Sept 1905, CU-MARK; Louis J. Budd, unpublished TS in CU-MARK).

353.30–38 when Thomas Bailey Aldrich succeeded Mr. Howells . . . I did write the article, and I'll cash the check] Aldrich, who succeeded Howells at the *Atlantic Monthly* in early 1881, published the untitled and unsigned piece, about a western obituary with "rhetorical blemishes," in the November 1881 "Contributors' Club." Clemens wrote him on 2 November, "I *did* write that article, after all. The check for it has come; so I know I wrote it" (MH-H; SLC 1881).

355.2–3 Mrs. Clemens's instinct had been correct; Jean had been dangerously ill] This incident took place in late November 1890, when Olivia was called to Elmira to be with her dying mother, Olivia Lewis Langdon. Clemens and Olivia both went, leaving Clara and Jean with the servants. Jean was ten years old. Susy was at Bryn Mawr (26–27 Nov 1890 to OLC, *Twainian* 35 (Sept–Oct 1976): 2–3; 27 Nov 1890 to Howells, MH-H, in *MTHL,* 2:633–34).

356.3–6 Bessie Stone said . . . it must be on account of those pleadings that Mary came to be a child of prayer] Bessie Stone's first letter to Clemens, of 1870 or 1871, is not known to survive, but she wrote again in 1883 that Jesus "has just come to several of my friends, and found an entrance; and I, who have not ceased to pray for you these twelve years, am expecting Him to come to you now." Clemens wrote on the envelope "D—d fool." In 1890 she sent birthday greetings to Clemens, alluding to Mary Jane Wilks's vow to Huckleberry Finn in chapter 28 that she would pray for him, and adding, "As you sent that extraordinary passage out into the world, weren't you hiding in it a hint to your small friend that you still cared for my prayers?" (Stone to SLC, 13 Feb 1883 and 30? Nov 1890, CU-MARK; *HF 2003,* 244).

Autobiographical Dictation, 29 December 1906

357.31–32 I went West to attend my mother's funeral] Jane Lampton Clemens died on 27 October 1890; she "was borne by her children to Hannibal and laid to rest" beside her husband (*MTB,* 2:901). In his moving tribute to her, "Jane Lampton Clemens," Clemens concluded, "She always had the heart of a young girl; and in the sweetness and serenity of death she seemed somehow young again. She was always beautiful" (*Inds,* 82–92).

358.4–19 a Medical Convention took place in a river town . . . a secret which she had carried in her heart for more than sixty years] Clemens apparently heard his mother's "secret" in 1886 from Pamela Moffett, who had visited Jane, Orion, and Mollie in Keokuk in April, then stopped over in New York and Hartford on her way back to Fredonia. Jane Clemens had first told Orion, then Pamela during her April visit, and finally Mollie, enjoining each to secrecy. The doctor (whose name both Clemens and Mollie reported as "Barrett"—not "Gwynn"—at the time) was Richard Ferril Barret (1804–60), who had lived in nearby Green County, Kentucky, when Jane married John Clemens in 1823. He studied medicine in Cincinnati and at Transylvania University in Lexington, Kentucky, between 1824 and 1827, and married Maria Buckner in 1832. In 1840 he was a cofounder, with Dr. Joseph Nash McDowell, of the Medical Department at Kemper College (later Missouri Medical College) in St. Louis. He was later described as "eminently noble and engaging,—a figure tall, graceful, and courtly, and a countenance of the Roman model. . . . His pride of race and scholarly habits made him appear exclusive and aristocratic, but his impulses were ardent, and his manners polite and engaging" (Scharf 1883, 1:677). His son, Richard Aylett Barret (b. 1834), who became a successful doctor, lawyer, and journalist, lived much of his life in St. Louis. Clemens told a somewhat different—and probably more accurate—version of his mother's story to Howells in May 1886. He said that Orion had accompanied Jane to "a convention of old settlers of the Mississippi Valley in an Iowa town" (not a "Medical Convention," as he recalls here); when she was told that Dr. Barret had "returned to St. Louis," they "went straight back to Keokuk" (19 May 1886, NN-BGC, in *MTHL,* 2:566–68). The event may have been the "Tri-State Old Settlers' Reunion," which was held in Keokuk in September 1885; no convention in Burlington, or another "Iowa town," has been documented. And if there was a Dr. Barret at the reunion, it was the son of the one Jane had known, who had died in 1860 (letters in CU-MARK: PAM to Samuel Moffett, 2 Apr 1886 and 21 May 1886; MEC to SLC and OLC, 3 Feb 1887; and OC and MEC to SLC and OLC, 23 Feb 1887; *Inds,* 300–301; Conard 1901, 1:160–63; Scharf 1883, 1:676–77; Carolyn D. Palmgreen, personal communication, 30 Dec 1985, CU-MARK; Varble 1964, 113–14, 351–52).

359.5–8 Aaron Burr, old, gray, forlorn, forsaken . . . ship that bore all his treasure, his daughter] Theodosia Burr Alston (1783–1813), daughter of former Vice-President Aaron Burr, was a child prodigy who knew several languages, including Latin and Greek. After her mother's death, when she was eleven, she served as hostess in her father's house. In 1801 she married Joseph Alston (1779–1816) of South Carolina, who was elected governor in 1812. In 1807 Aaron Burr was arrested for what came to be known as the Burr Conspiracy, but was acquitted on a technicality and retreated to Europe for four years before resuming his legal career in New York. In December 1812, in ill health and depressed over the death of her ten-year-old son, Theodosia boarded the schooner *Patriot* in Georgetown, South Carolina, bound for New York. For weeks, Burr daily walked the Manhattan pier watching in vain for the ship, whose fate remains unknown (Lomask 1982, 361–63; Parmet and Hecht 1967, 56, 67, 88–90, 163, 300–304, 328–30; Côté 2012).

Autobiographical Dictation, 6 January 1907

359.27–28 Reverend Joseph H. Twichell is with me . . . my last visit to Bermuda] Clemens, Twichell, and Isabel Lyon left New York for Bermuda aboard the RMS *Bermudian* on 2 January; they arrived in Hamilton two days later and registered at the Princess Hotel. They departed for New York, again on the *Bermudian,* on 7 January. Miss Hobby did not accompany them (Lyon 1907, entries for 2, 4, 7, and 9 Jan; Hoffmann 2006, 69–78). For this dictation and probably the first part of the next (9 January), Lyon took down Clemens's words in longhand (she did not know shorthand), and Hobby subsequently created the typescript from Lyon's notes, which have not survived. Clemens, accompanied by Twichell, had last visited Bermuda from 20 to 24 May 1877. His account of the trip, "Some Rambling Notes of an Idle Excursion," appeared in four installments in the *Atlantic Monthly,* from October 1877 through January 1878 (SLC 1877–78; for the notebook he kept during the trip, see *N&J2,* 8–36).

360.3–8 Twichell's school days in Hartford . . . "Olney's Geography"] *A Practical System of Modern Geography,* by Jesse Olney (1798–1872), was first published in 1828. Innovative in its presentation of world geography, and far from neutral in its characterization of ethnic groups, for thirty years it was used in virtually every school in the United States. Revised and enlarged many times, it ran through ninety-eight editions. Olney was a teacher in New York State, and from 1821 to 1831 served as a school principal in Hartford. In 1834 he moved to Southington, where Twichell was born (in 1838) and spent his boyhood. Although Olney thereafter devoted much of his time to writing textbooks, he worked to establish a system of public schools in Connecticut and opened his own "select school" (Timlow 1875, 450; Baker 1996; Courtney 2008, 8–17).

360.13 "Kirkham's Grammar!"] *English Grammar in Familiar Lectures,* by Samuel Kirkham, first published in 1824, was issued in dozens of editions by several publishers. An 1835 Baltimore edition, designated the "one hundred and fifth," is now in the Mark Twain Papers, and may have belonged to Clemens during his Hannibal youth (Kirkham 1835; for a discussion of its provenance and authenticity, see Gribben 1980, 1:383–84).

360.17–18 Miss Kirkham . . . was still keeping boarders] Emily Kirkham and her widowed mother, Mary Ann (d. 1894), had run the boardinghouse where Clemens and Twichell stayed in 1877. Emily was then twenty-five (Hoffmann 2006, 35, 74).

360.21–22 the day on which her only nephew was born] Clemens had recorded the birth in his 1877 notebook: "Mrs. Kirkham had a grandchild born to her in the middle of the night—that is, 1 Thursday morning, the Queen's birthday, May 24" (*N&J2,* 32).

360.24–31 Twichell (bearing the assumed name of Peters) . . . name is not Wilkinson—that's Mark Twain] Twichell traveled on the ship to and from Bermuda under his own name. A "Reverend Mr. Peters" figures in the second installment of "Some Rambling Notes of an Idle Excursion," but he is not Twichell, who is referred to throughout the series as "the Reverend." Clemens used his middle name, Langhorne, as his alias during most of the trip (Bermuda *Royal Gazette* [photocopies in CU-MARK, courtesy of Donald Hoffmann]: "Passengers Arrived," 22 May 1877, 2; "Passengers Sailed," 29 May 1877, 2; "'Mark Twain,' the very amusing author . . . ," 29 May 1877, 2; Twichell 1874–1916, entry for 28 May 1877; Hoffmann 2006, 26, 72).

360.40 swiftly developing possibilities of aerial navigation] Orville and Wilbur Wright had made their first powered flights on 17 December 1903. In early 1908 the War Department awarded them a contract to produce a biplane for $25,000 which could fly a distance of 125 miles at 40 miles per hour.

360.41–361.1 those striking verses of Tennyson's which forecast a future when airborne vessels of war shall meet and fight] These lines from "Locksley Hall," first published in 1842, were frequently quoted in the first years of the twentieth century when aerial navigation was becoming a practical reality (Tennyson 1842, 2:104):

> For I dipt into the future, far as human eye could see,
> Saw the Vision of the world, and all the wonder that would be;
>
> Saw the heavens fill with commerce, argosies of magic sails,
> Pilots of the purple twilight, dropping down with costly bales;
>
> Heard the heavens fill with shouting, and there rain'd a ghastly dew
> From the nations' airy navies grappling in the central blue.

At the time of this dictation, George Harvey had just quoted these lines in his "Editor's Diary" in the *North American Review* for 21 December 1906 (Harvey 1906, 1330–33).

361.2–5 something which I had read . . . kill 10,000 persons outright and injure 80,000] These figures derive ultimately from the annual report by the Interstate Commerce Commission, which had been submitted to Congress on 19 December 1906. When revising this dictation, Clemens increased his original number of people injured; he evidently made the change sometime after 10 January, when he "bought a world almanac & read Railroad accidents in the U.S. for the past nine years." He repeats the original number—60,000—in his Autobiographical Dictation of 25 February, and although he revised that dictation, he did not correct the number there ("Commerce Commission Reports," *Wall Street Journal,* 20 Dec 1906, 7; Thompson 1907, 3–8, 44–45; Lyon 1907, entry for 10 Jan).

Autobiographical Dictation, 9 January 1907

362.13 no Tammany] The Democratic political machine in New York City, named for the Delaware Indian chief Tamanend. Incorporated in 1789, it reached its height of power, and corruption, in the mid-nineteenth and early twentieth centuries, and remained a factor in New York politics into the 1960s.

362.16 W.C.T.U.] The Woman's Christian Temperance Union was founded in 1874 to oppose the use of alcohol, particularly because of its destructive effects on families. Today, as "the oldest voluntary, non-sectarian woman's organization in continuous existence in the world," it has a wider agenda of social concerns, including women's rights (W.C.T.U. 2011). Clemens's mother and sister were among the earliest members of the organization, and he was initially supportive of its temperance efforts, but soon repudiated the goal of total abstinence (see *L6:* 12 Mar 1874 to the Editor of the London *Standard,* 66–73; 23 July 1875 to PAM, 515–16).

363.13 As concerns interpreting the Deity] The ultimate source of the remainder of this day's dictation is "Interpreting the Deity," a manuscript that Clemens had written in June 1905. Jean Clemens typed a copy of the manuscript, probably by the end of August 1905, and her typescript is the immediate source of the text here (SLC 1905e; Lyon 1905a, entries for 17 Sept, 23 Sept, 1 Oct, and 21 Oct).

363.14–15 Rosetta stone . . . Champollion] This basalt slab, found in 1799 by Napoleon's troops in northern Egypt, was inscribed by priests affirming the cult of Ptolemy V, king of Egypt (205–180 B.C.). Their text was in the three scripts then in use: hieroglyphic (used for priestly documents), demotic (the ordinary native script), and Greek (used by the government). The Greek inscription provided the key to the decipherment of hieroglyphics by pioneer Egyptologist Jean François Champollion (1790–1832), who published his first translation in 1822–24. The hieroglyphs reproduced here (like the demotic characters and the "Dighton" petroglyphs on page 364) are in Clemens's own hand. Although most of them appear on the Rosetta stone, his actual source is not known. He evidently selected a variety of signs and arranged them in a random order.

363.21–24 Grünfeldt . . . Gospodin] Both names are fictitious. "Gospodin" is Russian for "sir" or "Mr."

363.29 Rawlinson] Sir Henry Creswicke Rawlinson (1810–95) was a distinguished British soldier, diplomat, and scholar, best known for his decipherment, in 1844–46, of Akkadian cuneiform writing, not hieroglyphics.

364.2 Flight from Elba] Napoleon Bonaparte escaped in February 1815 from the island of Elba, where he had been exiled in May 1814 after his defeat in the Peninsular War.

364.16–17 two little lines of hieroglyphs among the figures grouped upon the Dighton Rocks] The Dighton Rock is a forty-ton boulder in the Taunton River near Berkley, Massachusetts, probably deposited during the last Ice Age, some ten thousand years ago. For over three hundred years scholars and the general public have been studying the mysterious inscriptions on it, which at various times have been thought to be Phoenician, Roman, Norse, Chinese, Japanese, Portuguese, or Native American. Clemens's drawings of petroglyphs are not copies of these inscriptions. In 1963 the rock was moved from the riverbed, and a museum was built around it (Massachusetts Historical Society 2011).

365.3 *Bohn's Suetonius*] *The Lives of The Twelve Caesars,* by C. Suetonius Tranquillus, as translated by Alexander Thomson, was part of Bohn's Classical Library. The 1876 edition that Clemens owned, annotated, and quotes three times in this dictation survives in the Mark Twain Papers. In one of his marginalia, Clemens remarked that it was "Translated into Cowboy English." Paine noted in it, "This was a favorite book of Mark Twain's—one of the very last that he tried to read." And in his biography of Clemens, he reported that this volume was one of the works that Clemens had with him on his deathbed (Suetonius 1876; *MTB,* 3:1576–77).

365.6 Caesar Augustus] Gaius Octavius (63 B.C.–14 A.D.), who as Augustus reigned as the first Roman emperor (27 B.C.–14 A.D.).

365.37–366.1 King Henry is dead . . . to steal the throne from Henry's daughter] Henry I (1068–1135) reigned from 1100 until his death. His nephew, Stephen of Blois (1097?–1154), then dispossessed Henry's daughter, the widowed Empress Matilda of Germany (1102–67), and seized the English throne. Stephen had previously sworn allegiance to Matilda as Henry's rightful successor. Their violent contention for power, with Matilda occupying the throne for six months in 1141, continued until 1153, when Stephen accepted Matilda's son, later Henry II (reigned 1154–89), as his heir.

366.2 Henry of Huntingdon . . . his Chronicle] Henry, archdeacon of Huntingdon (1084?–1155), wrote *Historia Anglorum,* a chronicle "Comprising the History of England, from the Invasion of Julius Caesar to the Accession of Henry II." Clemens used the 1853 edition in Bohn's Antiquarian Library; his annotated copy is now in the Huntington Library (CSmH; Gribben 1980, 1:308).

366.3–5 wherefore the Lord . . . he died within a year] Henry of Huntingdon 1853, 262.

366.8–9 The kingdom . . . in every quarter] Henry of Huntingdon 1853, 273.

367.13–19 King David of Scotland . . . the despair of the living] Henry of Huntingdon 1853, 266–67.

367.21–23 Then the chief . . . like a cobweb] Henry of Huntingdon 1853, 269.

367.33–368.2 In the month of August . . . through all ages] Henry of Huntingdon 1853, 282–83. Both Marmion (d. 1143) and Geoffrey de Mandeville (d. 1144, mistakenly called Godfrey in the *Chronicle*) were excommunicated for desecrating church property.

368.28–31 the just God . . . brought to his end; (p. 400)] This quotation is not from Henry's text, but from an anonymous work, *The Acts of Stephen, King of England and Duke of Normandy,* which was included with the 1853 edition that Clemens read (Henry of Huntingdon 1853, 321–430).

368.36 Robert F. . . . had committed unprintable crimes] Fitzhildebrand was "a soldier of experience, though of low extraction," whose "military virtues were stained by lust and drunkenness." In about 1141 the countess of Anjou sent him with a troop of soldiers to assist William de Pont de l'Arche in a struggle against the bishop of Winchester. Fitzhildebrand proceeded

> to debauch William's wife; and, by a horrible and abominable plot concerted between them, William was bound in fetters and thrown into a dungeon. Having thus obtained possession of his castle, his treasures, and his wife, Robert spurned the alliance of the countess, to whom he owed his honourable mission, and entered into league with the king and bishop. (Henry of Huntingdon 1853, 399–400)

369.6–10 .... about to come ... all will come to pass] A quotation from a letter written by Pope Gregory I (540–604) to Ethelbert, the king of Kent (552?–616) (Henry of Huntingdon 1853, 74–75).

369.11–12 sent before ... the impending judgment] Henry of Huntingdon 1853, 75–76.

369.21 GOD BEHIND THIS WAR] This article appeared in the New York *Times* on 12 June 1905. The conflict was the 1904–5 Russo-Japanese War, a major defeat for Russia (see *AutoMT1,* 647–48 nn. 462.33–36, 462.36–37).

369.24–25 Rev. Dr. Newell Dwight Hillis] Hillis (1858–1929) was pastor of the Plymouth Congregational Church in Brooklyn from 1899 until 1924 and a prolific author of inspirational works.

370.4 the hungry and oppressed Russian millions] Clemens comments more fully on the deplorable events in Russia in the Autobiographical Dictations of 22 June and 5 December 1906.

370.8 Brooklyn praise is half slander] Proverbially, "self-praise is half slander" (Mieder, Kingsbury, and Harder 1992, 531).

Autobiographical Dictation, 15 January 1907

370 *title* Tuesday, January 15, 1907] This dictation follows a gap of five days. On at least two of these days, however, Clemens evidently did prepare dictations. In her journal on Thursday, 10 January, Isabel Lyon noted that he had dictated that morning on the subject of railroad accidents—a topic he had already touched on in his dictation of 6 January. And on Sunday, 13 January, she noted that he was planning to read "Friday's dictation which Hobby should have sent yesterday & didn't" (Lyon 1907). Nothing further is known of the 10 and 11 January dictations.

371.17–18 process which will turn our republic into a monarchy] Clemens addresses the question of the "coming American monarchy" in his discussion of Elihu Root's speech in the Autobiographical Dictation of 13 December 1906.

371.42–372.15 we granted deserved pensions ... Grand Army of the Republic] Initially, only Union army veterans who had suffered disabilities as a result of the Civil

War were granted pensions. By the terms of the Disability Pension Act of 1890, however, any Union soldier who had served for ninety days and was incapacitated for any reason was entitled to a pension, regardless of income. Furthermore, any veteran's widow, even if born and married after the war, was likewise eligible. The Grand Army of the Republic, a politically powerful fraternal organization of Union veterans, was formed in 1866, and at its peak in 1890 had more than 400,000 members. One of its chief purposes was to campaign for pension benefits, and the Republicans in Congress who passed the 1890 Disability Pension Act were assured of the G.A.R.'s votes. In addition, special pension bills were routinely passed by the "vote-hunters in Congress," according to the Louisville *Courier-Journal,* which claimed in 1900 that the practice had become "the most gigantic machine for robbing the government that ever existed under a so-called free republic" ("The Pension Roll," Washington *Post,* 14 Aug 1900, 4, reprinting the Louisville *Courier-Journal;* Glasson 1918, 219–21, 233–38; for additional remarks on generous pensions see the ADs of 28 Jan and 11 Feb 1907).

372.29 the immortal Executive Order 78] This military pension order, issued by President Theodore Roosevelt, had gone into effect on 13 April 1904. It broadened the terms of the Disability Pension Act of 1890 (see the note at 371.42–372.15) by adding advanced age as a pensionable disability: any Union veteran who had served for ninety days and reached the age of sixty-two was entitled to $6 a month and increasing amounts thereafter. The cost of Executive Order 78 was estimated to be as high as $15 million annually; it was seen by Roosevelt's critics as his "bid for the pension vote" in an election year, and as a typical instance of his "transcending the constitutional limits of Executive authority." The order's addition of advanced age as a disability was incorporated into law by congressional acts of 24 April 1906 and 4 March 1907 ("Mr. Roosevelt's Pension Order," New York *Times,* 18 Sept 1904, 6; Glasson 1918, 246–49; see also AD, 29 May 1907, where Clemens lists "illegal Order 78" in his roster of Roosevelt's sins).

372.35–36 communication in this morning's *Sun* signed "A Union Veteran."] This letter to the editor of the New York *Sun* was published on 15 January under the heading "Service Pensions." Clemens redacts and quotes about half of it in this dictation.

372.37 I see that the Senate has passed the service pension bill] "Union Veteran" responded to the New York *Sun*'s 12 January 1907 report of a bill passed the previous day. It awarded pensions ranging from $12 a month at age sixty-two to $15 at age seventy—amounts significantly higher than stipulated in Executive Order 78. Identical pensions were also authorized for veterans of the Mexican War. The unanimous vote came after some debate on whether the war between the states was a rebellion or a civil war. The latter was agreed upon ("Was Civil War a Rebellion?" New York *Sun,* 12 Jan 1907, 4; "No Rebellion in '61, Declares the Senate," New York *Times,* 12 Jan 1907, 2; Glasson 1918, 249–50).

373.15 from Bunker] The Battle of Bunker Hill, on 17 June 1775.

373.19–20 A few years after the war Congress gave to all veteran soldiers an additional bounty of $100] In the years following the Civil War bounties of various amounts were paid to Union army veterans, according to when they joined up and how long they served. Soldiers who had enlisted between 12 April 1861 (the start of the Civil War) and 24 December 1863, and served honorably for three years, received a bounty of $100. A congressional act passed on 28 July 1866 paid them an additional bounty of $100 (Lamphere 1881, 112).

374.18–19 The veteran . . . pensions be now extended to the Confederate soldiers] "Union Veteran" wrote, "The war is over and the country reunited in bonds growing stronger and stronger and knitting us more closely daily. Why not finish the business at a stroke by having Union and Confederate veterans share alike in the benefits of the service pension?" ("Service Pensions," New York *Sun,* 15 Jan 1907, 6). Confederate veterans were never eligible for pensions from the federal government, but they did receive some benefits from the Southern states.

Autobiographical Dictation, 17 January 1907

374.24–25 Helen Keller dined with us . . . Mrs. Macy became her first teacher] On 16 January Isabel Lyon noted in her journal:

> Helen Keller came tonight. At half past seven she arrived with Mrs Macy—& when the King who had been pacing up & down the room, went to the library door to meet her as she came in with short, hesitating steps, she threw her arms around him & buried her head in his neck, & felt of his hair[;] when Mrs Macy told her that he was still wearing his halo—the King wept. (Lyon 1907)

Keller was twenty-six at the time of this visit. For further details of Clemens's friendship with her and her teacher and companion, Annie Sullivan Macy (wife of writer John Macy), see *AutoMT1,* 465–66, 531 n. 209.42–210.1, 650 n. 465.9.

375.1–2 equipped with a . . . complete university education] Keller was a 1904 honors graduate of Radcliffe College.

375.23 Susan Coolidge] The pen name of Sarah Chauncey Woolsey (1835–1905), best known as a popular author of stories for young people, but also a much-published poet, magazine writer, and editor. Her poem "Helen Keller," which Clemens goes on to quote, was included in her posthumously published *Last Verses,* a copy of which Clemens owned (Woolsey 1906, 3–4; Gribben 1980, 2:786).

376.17–21 my secretary began to play on the orchestrelle . . . beat the time and follow the rhythm] In her journal on 17 January, Lyon described Keller's demeanor, in particular her response to music:

> I didn't expect to find her as she is. I believed she would be blasée & spoiled a little—because of her great fame; but she isn't spoiled a bit. The signs of her great

> afflictions are always present, because she is so dependent upon others— She waits with a sweet, almost breathless attention, while Mrs Macy spells with inconceivable rapidity, the sentence or remark that has just been uttered, & when it is finished her face ripples with delight & she gives a sweet little shiver of pleasure, & in her expression you can see that she has understood perfectly. Helen & Mrs Macy are the guests of Mrs Laurence Hutton, & while we were waiting for Mr Macy who is staying some other place, to appear, it was suggested that I play something on the orchestrelle to see if Helen could detect the musical vibrations— I took The Erlkönig, & at the first deep trembling of the bass, she turned instantly to Mrs Macy & said "Music." She was fully conscious of its shadings—for she said that it reminded her of the rising & falling of winds or waves. She wore a white gown trimmed with a great deal of soft lace, & a string—a long double string of coral beads. Her face, particularly the left side of it, is very noble. . . . I had been struck with the nobility, & the womanliness, & the great play of intellect & affection & emotion & seriousness that make it what it is. The King says of her that "she is a mine.[”] (Lyon 1907)

Franz Schubert composed his "Der Erlkönig," for solo voice and piano, in 1815, setting a poem of that title by Goethe. Clemens's Aeolian Orchestrelle was an imposing and ornate foot-pumped roll-operated reed organ, standing approximately eight feet tall, which he had purchased for $2,600 in 1904, along with sixty rolls of music. Playing it was one of Lyon's tasks (for a full, illustrated discussion of the orchestrelle, see Richards 1983, 42–46; for Mrs. Hutton see the ADs of 20 Nov 1906, note at 279.39–280.1, and 21 Dec 1906, note at 330.29–32).

Autobiographical Dictation, 22 January 1907

376.27 In an earlier chapter I inserted some verses beginning "Love Came at Dawn"] In the Autobiographical Dictation of 2 February 1906 (see *AutoMT1,* 325, 579 n. 325.15–25).

376.31–33 Stedman was not able to determine the authorship . . . William Wilfred Campbell] In a letter of 17 January 1907 Frank Nicholls Kennin identified Campbell as the author of the poem, entitled "Love" (CU-MARK). Kennin had seen Clemens's mistaken attribution to Susy Clemens in an excerpt from the 2 February 1906 Autobiographical Dictation published in the *North American Review* on 5 October 1906 (NAR 3). Isabel Lyon noted in her journal that Clemens was glad to have the correction, for

> he would not want Susy to be claiming from the Grave, a thing that was not hers. He went on to say that the particular reason for his dislike of Stedman is due to the fact that the King wrote him just after we came home from Italy, asking if he could tell him who wrote the verses, & Stedman wrote him such an indifferent letter, one claiming all honor for Stedman the Anthologist, & evincing no interest for anyone[']s but Stedman's poems. (Lyon 1907, entry for 20 Jan)

For Stedman see the Autobiographical Dictation of 2 June 1906, note at 78.19–28. His "indifferent letter," evidently written in July or August 1904, is not known to survive.

376.33–34 his book called "Beyond the Hills of Dream."] Campbell's book was published in 1899, three years after Susy's death. "Love" had also appeared in the *Century Magazine* for October 1891, where Susy presumably saw it. On the 17 January letter from Kennin, which provided the title of Campbell's book, Lyon noted Clemens's instruction to "send & get the book" (CU-MARK). It is not known if she succeeded.

377.1–2 author's name,* and it has been added to the verses upon the gravestone] The inscription on Susy Clemens's headstone, in Woodlawn Cemetery in Elmira, New York, now reads:

> "Warm summer sun
> Shine kindly here,
> Warm southern wind
> Blow softly here,
> Green sod above
> Lie light, lie light—
> Good night, dear heart,
> Good night, good night."
> Robert Richardson

The lines are the Clemenses' adaptation of the last stanza of "Annette," by Robert Richardson (1850–1901), from his 1893 collection, *Willow and Wattle* (Jerome and Wisbey 1977, 165; Robert Richardson 1893, 33–35; see also Gribben 1980, 2:577–78).

377.3 Last night, at a dinner party . . . Mr. Peter Dunne Dooley] Finley Peter Dunne (1867–1936) was the author of several popular collections of social and political commentary spoken in the voice of Martin Dooley, an Irish bartender. He and Clemens had met in London in 1899. The 21 January dinner party was at the home of publisher Robert J. Collier (1876–1918). In her journal Lyon noted that Clemens "came home at 10.30 with freesia in his button hole, & smoking a long thick cigar. He dropped into his big brown chair & told how M[r] Dooley was there, [&] what a pleasant time it was" (Lyon 1907; Ellis 1941, 126–27).

377.7–9 Dooley . . . stands at the head of all the satirists of this generation] The admiration Clemens felt for Dunne was more than reciprocated during their decade-long friendship. And in 1935, upon the centenary of Clemens's birth, Dunne wrote that "if any centennial anniversary should be celebrated it is that of our unequaled humorist. Emerson and Clemens our greatest writers; Emerson and Clemens, Hawthorne, Poe, Whitman, Abraham Lincoln. No 'centenary' can be too vivacious, no monument too high for him and his fame" (Dunne 1963, 240).

377.24–25 My game was caroms] Carom billiards is played on a pocketless table with two white cue balls and one red object ball. To score a point, a player must make a shot in which the cue ball caroms (hits and rebounds off of) each of the other two balls. If his shot fails to hit either one, he loses his turn, or "run."

377.33 Mr. Dillon called on my brother-in-law, on a matter of business] Olivia Clemens's younger brother, Charles J. Langdon, had succeeded their father, Jervis, as head of the family coal business after the latter's death in 1870 (see *AutoMT1,* 578 n. 321.25–27). Dillon has not been identified. For the *North American Review* version of this dictation, published on 5 April 1907 (NAR 15), Clemens changed "Dillon" to the fictional name "Dalton."

377.35–36 I had played with him many times at the club] Probably the Elmira City Club.

378.14–15 Mr. George Robinson] George M. Robinson, an Elmira furniture manufacturer and dealer, was a longtime friend and billiards partner of Clemens's (Boyd and Boyd 1872, 183–84; Towner 1892, 185–86; *N&J2,* 430; *N&J3,* 578). Clemens altered his name to "Robertson" for publication in the *North American Review* installment of 5 April 1907.

380.2–3 Twichell and I walked to Boston and he had the celebrated conversation with the hostler] The incident occurred on the evening of 12 November 1874, after the first day of the comically abortive "pedestrian excursion" that Clemens and Twichell made from Hartford to Boston. In 1882 Clemens included a nineteen-page account of the ostler's "crimson lava-jets of desolating & utterly unconscious profanity" in the manuscript of chapter 34 of *Life on the Mississippi,* but cut it before the book was published. That account did not see print until 1940, when Bernard DeVoto published it in *Mark Twain in Eruption,* in the mistaken belief that it was an early autobiographical sketch. In 1907, therefore, the conversation was "celebrated" only among friends, who doubtless had heard Clemens recount it (12 Nov 1874 to OLC [1st and 2nd], *L6,* 277–79; *AutoMT1,* 8 n. 21; SLC 1882c, 431, 437; *MTE,* 366–72).

380.4 Patrick] Patrick McAleer, the Clemens family's coachman from 1870 until 1891 (*AutoMT1,* 579 n. 322.31–42, 621 n. 412.41–42).

380.24 *P.S. Saturday.* He has been here. Let us not talk about it] In her journal Lyon reported on Dunne's billiards visit on Friday, 25 January:

> The King says "I am just thirsting for blood & Mr Dooley is going to furnish it!"— Billiards!— Mr Dooley is coming for luncheon. But the King is walking up & down the billiard room with quick light eager steps—ready for dictation, but readier for the blood of Mr Dooley—
>
> Later:—He got the blood, for he & Mr Dooley played all the afternoon—& while M^r^ D isn't a good billiardist, he is good company, & the King was quite happy I think— (Lyon 1907)

Evidently recalling this same occasion, Paine noted that Dunne's defeats "continued until Clemens had twenty-five dollars of Dunne's money, and Dunne was sweating and swearing, and Mark Twain rocking with delight" (*MTB,* 3:1367). Nevertheless, given that Clemens's postscript suggests that the billiards contest was not to his satisfaction, this may also have been the occasion on which—according to Dunne's biographer—he played his

> trick of introducing one white billiard ball that was not quite round, and watching the consternation of his opponent as he tried to use it as his cue ball. But Dunne was either forewarned or quick to detect the imperfection; for he ignored it until Twain's back was turned, and then he reversed the white balls and the shoe was on the other foot. (Ellis 1941, 195)

Autobiographical Dictation, 23 January 1907

380.28 George] George M. Robinson.

380.34–35 More than forty years ago . . . office staff adjourned] If the year Clemens supplies here—1865—is correct, then he refers to his work for the San Francisco *Dramatic Chronicle:* between October and December of that year he contributed several dozen unsigned items to that paper. He was the local reporter for the San Francisco *Morning Call* from June to October 1864 (see AD, 12 June 1906, note at 112.18–24, and AD, 13 June 1906).

381.37–38 A quarter of a century ago I arrived in London . . . Dickens readings in America] See *AutoMT1,* 516 n. 161.24–27, 517 n. 162.6.

383.16–19 Mr. Clemens . . . Bateman's Point] The insertion here of a summary paragraph (typically found only at the beginning of a dictation) marks the beginning of a new section. Despite the absence of a new dateline, the two sections were evidently created on different days: according to Hobby's typed notes, each one took two and a half hours to dictate, a typical time for one morning's work.

384.16–19 Jackass Gulch, California . . . in my time it had disappeared] Clemens refers to his visit to the "Southern mines" at Angels Camp and Jackass Hill in the winter of 1864–65. The whole economy of the area had declined after the rich placer deposits discovered in 1848 were exhausted, leaving opportunity only for the "pocket mining" practiced by his friends Jim Gillis and Dick Stoker. For Clemens's fictional representation of the rickety saloon and pool table in the decaying city of "Boomerang," written in September 1865 just months after leaving the area, see "The Only Reliable Account of the Celebrated Jumping Frog of Calaveras County" (SLC 1865a; see also the ADs of 13 June 1906 and 4 Feb 1907; Herbert O. Lang 1882, 3–4).

384.32–34 Last winter, here in New York, I saw Hoppe and Schaefer and Sutton . . . contend against each other] Clemens attended three matches of the world-championship billiards tournament held in Madison Square Garden in the early spring of 1906: on 9 April with Rogers, on 11 April with Paine, and on 18 April (no companion identified). On the first two occasions the audience applauded him spontaneously. According to a report in the New York *Times* after the third match, he occupied "his usual seat at one side of the table" to watch the game, a type of carom billiards with balklines drawn eighteen inches from each cushion (which he calls the "eighteen-inch game" below at 385.1). In addition, on 24 April (the day after the tournament ended) he spoke briefly at a billiards exhibition, a benefit for the San Francisco earthquake victims (for a text see Fatout 1976,

520–21; Lyon 1906, entry for 10 Apr; New York *Times:* "Hoppe Defeats Cutler; Schaefer Wins Easily," 12 Apr 1906, 7; "Sutton Beats Slosson by Superior Billiards," 19 Apr 1906, 14; "Billiard Benefit Plans," 23 Apr 1906, 12; "Sutton Beats Schaefer," 24 Apr 1906, 12). William F. Hoppe (1887–1959) was only eighteen at the time of the tournament, but had already won his first world title. He earned fifty more before retiring in 1952. Jacob Schaefer, Sr. (1855–1910), called the "Wizard," was known for his versatility, becoming a champion of several different types of games. George H. Sutton (1870–1938) graduated from medical school before becoming a professional billiards player. Despite losing both his arms to the elbow in a sawmill accident at the age of eight, he astonished observers with his remarkable skill. In the April 1906 tournament, Sutton placed second, followed by Schaefer and Hoppe. The winner was George F. Slosson of New York; the other contenders were Louis Cure (of Paris), Albert G. Cutler, and Orlando E. Morningstar (Gamo 1908, 309; Hoppe 1975, vii, 4, 88, 97, 105–9; New York *Times:* "Schaefer, the Wizard, Dead," 9 Mar 1910, 9; "'Handless' Sutton, Billiard Player, 68," 16 May 1938, 17).

385.9–10 Twenty-seven years ago . . . at Bateman's Point, near Newport, Rhode Island] The Clemens family stayed at this popular summer resort, built on an old farm by proprietor Seth Bateman, from 31 July to 8 September 1875 (*L6:* link note following 29? July 1875 to Redpath, 521–22; 1 Sept 1875 to Milnes, 531).

Autobiographical Dictation, 28 January 1907

387.8–10 particular friend . . . take me to a dinner at the Union League Club] The Union League Club of New York was a private social club of wealthy and influential businessmen, lawyers, and statesmen. It was formed in 1863 to support the Union cause, and after the war it dedicated its efforts to civic service of all kinds. Clemens dined at the clubhouse at Fifth Avenue and East Thirty-ninth Street on 26 January with William Evarts Benjamin (1859–1940), a member of the club since 1902. Benjamin, a book collector and publisher, was married to Anne Engle Rogers, Henry H. Rogers's oldest daughter (New York *Times:* "Dinner to Senator Clark," 27 Jan 1907, 13; "Union League Club May Quit Fifth Avenue," 14 Oct 1905, 1; Lyon 1907, entry for 26 Jan; Union League Club 1916, 57; *HHR,* 736).

387.17 Senator Clark of Montana] William A. Clark (1839–1925) accumulated his considerable fortune through gold and copper mining in Montana and Arizona, and later through banking. He lost two bids to become a Democratic senator, in 1889 (when Montana became a state) and in 1893, and was finally elected in 1899, but not seated. See the note at 387.35–388.5.

387.26 We have lately sent a United States Senator to the penitentiary] Joseph R. Burton (1852–1923), a Republican senator from Kansas, was convicted of accepting $2,500 from a company whose "get-rich-quick business" had been "barred from the mails," in return for pleading its case with the Post Office Department. He resigned in

June 1906 after his conviction was upheld on appeal by the Supreme Court, and served five months in prison ("Burton Must Go to Jail Supreme Court Decides," New York *Times,* 22 May 1906, 2).

387.29–31 They all rob the Treasury . . . to keep on good terms with the Grand Army of the Republic] See the Autobiographical Dictation of 15 January 1906 and the note at 371.42–372.15.

387.31–32 Grand Army of the Republic, junior . . . Grand Army of the Republic, junior, junior] Clemens alludes to two allied organizations: Sons of Veterans of the United States of America (founded in 1881) and National Auxiliary to Sons of Union Veterans of the Civil War (founded in 1883).

387.35–388.5 Clark of Montana . . . most disgusting reptile that the republic has produced since Tweed's time] In January 1900 a Senate investigative committee concluded that Clark was not entitled to the seat he had won in 1899 because he had bought the votes of the Montana legislators who elected him. Although he denied any wrong-doing, he admitted to spending nearly $140,000 on his campaign, and resigned before he could be tried and punished. Clark's bribery of the Montana legislature was instrumental in bringing about the passage of the Seventeenth Amendment to the Constitution, ratified in 1913, which requires senators to be elected directly by voters instead of by their state legislatures (Rossum 2001, 2, 190, 214). In early 1901 Clark was vindicated when he was again elected to the Senate (without resorting to bribes), where he served for a full term. Clemens's animosity was no doubt magnified by his friendship with Henry Rogers, vice-president of Standard Oil, which had long sought to control the copper industry in Montana. Rogers and Clark were bitter political enemies, each accusing the other of corruption. Standard Oil's reputation for unscrupulous business practices and its harsh labor policies contributed to Clark's 1901 victory (Foor 1941, 136, 150–59, 251–56, 259–62, 266–71; for Tweed see AD, 4 Apr 1906, note at 13.26).

388.10–13 Mr. Clark had lately lent to the Union League Club . . . European pictures for exhibition] Clark had loaned "thirty canvases . . . representing $1,000,000 in value" ("Dinner to Senator Clark," New York *Times,* 27 Jan 1907, 13). His collection included works by Titian, Degas, Van Dyck, Rembrandt, and Gainsborough, among others. In 1926 he bequeathed more than eight hundred works to the Corcoran Gallery of Art in Washington, which form the core of its holdings of European art (Corcoran Gallery 2011).

388.19–20 Clark's income . . . was thirty million dollars a year] Clark was by far the wealthiest senator, with a fortune of $100 million. Chauncey Depew, the fourteenth on the list, was worth a mere $2 million (William K. Howard 1906).

388.28–38 late Jay Gould . . . was the noblest thing in American history, and the holiest] In September 1879 Gould telegraphed $5,000 to the Howard Association of Memphis to help it care for the city's yellow fever victims, and he directed it to "keep on at your noble work till I tell you to stop and I will foot the bill." This generosity was reported widely in the newspapers, and was even remembered after his death in 1892, in a letter to the editor of the Washington *Post* ("Watching Yellow Fever," New York *Times,* 6 Sept 1879, 1; "Jay Gould's Good Deeds," Washington *Post,* 8 Dec 1892, 4; see *AutoMT1,* 594 n. 364.19).

388.39 President of the Art Committee of the club] Unidentified.

389.9–10 President of the Union League] Financier George R. Sheldon (1857–1919) was elected president on 10 January 1907 (New York *Times:* "Sheldon Beats Odell's Man," 11 Jan 1907, 2; "Geo. R. Sheldon Dies of Mine Injuries," 15 Jan 1919, 11).

390.4–6 Palm Readings . . . prints of my hands to several New York palmists] "Palm Readings," which comprises the remainder of this day's text, is a manuscript that Clemens wrote in 1905, interleaving typed copies of the three palmists' reports, followed by his own comments (see the note at 391.21). In the Autobiographical Dictation of 29 January 1907 he explains that the palm readings were arranged by George Harvey, editor of *Harper's Weekly* and president of Harper and Brothers. The sketch remained unpublished during Clemens's lifetime, but in 2010 excerpts appeared in *Playboy* (SLC 2010b).

390.8–16 Mr. Stead tried it nine years ago . . . destitute of the sense of humor] One of the four palmists commented that Clemens had "a strong and a fine sense of humour"; the complete text of the reading has not been found, but these words were quoted by Stead in the January 1895 issue of *Borderland* (Stead 1895, 61): see the Autobiographical Dictation of 26 December 1906, note at 336.32–337.2.

391.16 in London, once, I went to Fowler] See the Autobiographical Dictation of 26 December 1906, note at 334.24–26.

391.21 Reading by Niblo] The three experts who examined the prints of Clemens's palm in 1905, and whose readings are interpolated into this dictation, were all active at the turn of the twentieth century. "Professor Niblo" (real name Marshall Clark) was based in San Francisco, where he advertised himself in local newspapers as an "Astro-Trance Clairvoyant." He attained brief notoriety in 1909 when a young heiress's hypnotic trance revealed to him that she was destined to marry him (he was already married). John William Fletcher (1852–1913) was a medium and lecturer, who in his last years practiced as a palm reader in New York. (Clemens would subsequently meet him in person: see the AD of 12 Feb 1907.) In 1913 Fletcher had a fatal heart attack when policemen visited him with a warrant for his arrest. The third palmist, Carl Louis Perin, rejected the label of spiritualist, calling himself a "scientific palmist" and claiming to have graduated from the "Oriental Occult College of India." If he performed this reading after 24 February 1905, he was violating a court order not to practice palmistry and potentially forfeiting a bond of $500 (Melton 2001, s.v. "Fletcher, John William"; "Clairvoyants," San Francisco *Call,* 16 Aug 1905, 10; "Niblo, Mystic, Also Author," Chicago *Tribune,* 18 Jan 1910, 5; "Says He Is a Clairvoyant," Washington *Post,* 25 Mar 1900, 16; "Sleuths Fooled the Wizard," New York *Times,* 25 Feb 1905, 16).

392.7–8 "The World turns aside to let him pass who knows whither he is going"] From *The Call of the Twentieth Century: An Address to Young Men* by David Starr Jordan, a naturalist and president of Stanford University from 1891 to 1913 (Jordan 1903, 48).

392.39 Mr. Spencer] Herbert Spencer (1820–1903), English philosopher and polymath.

393.13 Henry A. Butters of Long Valley] Clemens believed that Butters had swindled him out of $12,500 in 1905 by causing the bankruptcy of the Plasmon Company, in which he had invested. In addition to a mansion in Piedmont, California, Butters owned a cattle ranch in Long Valley, Lassen County (California), on the eastern slope of the Sierra Nevada (*AutoMT1,* 586–87 n. 342.33; "Big Deal Made Yesterday," Reno *Nevada State Journal,* 12 July 1903, 1; "Oakland Capitalist Succumbs to Pneumonia," San Francisco *Chronicle,* 27 Oct 1908, 4).

394.9 within one gasp of drowning *nine* different times] Clemens was consistent in saying that he had nearly drowned nine times. See the Autobiographical Dictation of 9 March 1906 (*AutoMT1,* 401–2; 2 Jan 1895 to Rogers, CU-MARK, in *HHR,* 115; SLC 1899a, 2).

397.6 Mount of Venus proves his love for home] On the typescript of Perin's reading Clemens deleted the following remark: "In judging from the formation of this mount I should say that this man is married and happy" (see the Textual Commentary at *MTPO*).

399.29–31 I wrote a philosophy six years ago . . . hidden away in a secret place] Clemens alludes to *What Is Man?* (see AD, 25 June 1906, note at 142.14, and AD, 21 Dec 1906, note at 332.35–36).

400.19–20 attached his reading of Queen Marguerite's to the Countess Raybaudi-Massiglia's prints] If this incident actually occurred, nothing further has been learned about it. Margherita Maria Teresa Giovanna of Savoy (1851–1926) was married to King Umberto I of Italy. After he was assassinated in 1900, her son, Vittorio Emanuele III, assumed the throne, and she became known as the Queen Mother. (Her reputed favorite pizza was named "Margherita" after her.) The Countess Raybaudi-Massiglia was the owner of the Villa di Quarto near Florence, where the Clemens family lived from late 1903 until Olivia's death in June 1904. Clemens despised her for her obnoxious demeanor, petty cruelties, and adulterous relationship with her steward (*AutoMT1,* 540–41 n. 231.13).

Autobiographical Dictation, 29 January 1907

401.3–6 an acquaintance up town . . . clairvoyant was a portly middle-aged gentleman] Isabel Lyon recorded that on the afternoon of 23 January 1907 Clemens went to the home of social worker and suffragist Maud Nathan (1862–1946) "to see a clever clairvoyant Prof. Bert Rees, a big-faced German who read the contents of folded bits of paper in quite a wonderful way. He told the King among other things that he would live to be 98 years ten months & 2 days old—& the King wants to swap off some of those years & months & days" (Lyon 1907). "Prof. Bert Reese" (W. Berthold Riess, 1840–1926) was a native of Prussia who moved to New York around 1890. He traveled in America and Europe as a professional psychic entertainer, achieving fleeting notoriety in 1910 when Thomas Edison bore witness to his clairvoyant powers. Reese was a "billet-reader": his audience wrote questions on slips of paper and folded them; Reese would read the questions clairvoyantly and would also answer them. Harry Houdini said that "of all the clever sleight-of-hand men, he is the brainiest I have ever come across" (Ernst and Carrington 1932, 120–23; Marshall 1910; "W. Bert Reese Dies; Famed Clairvoyant," New York *Times,* 11 July 1926, E9).

403.1–4 a chapter of this Autobiography . . . all about my marriage and my children] Clemens apparently refers to his Autobiographical Dictation of 28 March 1906, part of which appeared in the 18 January 1907 issue of the *North American Review* (NAR 10). Neither it nor the chapter "which preceded it," in the 4 January issue (NAR 9), incorporating his dictations of 1, 2, and 13 December 1906, gives all the family details he recalls here.

403.30–32 death of Mrs. Hooker . . . being residents of Hartford for so many years] Isabella Beecher Hooker (1822–1907) was the half-sister of Henry Ward Beecher. John and Isabella Hooker, whom Clemens had met in early 1868 through Olivia's family, were among the original residents of the Nook Farm community in Hartford. The Clemenses rented their house for three years (from October 1871 to September 1874) while building their own home nearby. Isabella Hooker, a lifelong champion of women's rights, died on 25 January (8 Jan 1868 to JLC and PAM, *L2,* 146 n. 4; 20 Sept 1874 to Parish, *L6,* 236–37; "Last of Beecher Family Is Dead," Hartford *Courant,* 25 Jan 1907, 1).

403.34–35 Dr. Hooker . . . pall-bearer at his mother's funeral] Edward Beecher Hooker (1855–1927) was a physician and president of the American Institute of Homeopathy. Clemens served as an honorary pallbearer at his mother's funeral, which took place on 28 January in Hartford ("Homeopaths Elect Officers," Washington *Post,* 14 Sept 1906, 3; "Dr. Edward Beecher Hooker," New York *Times,* 24 June 1907, 23; "Mrs. Hooker's Funeral," Hartford *Courant,* 29 Jan 1907, 6).

403.36–37 my secretary] Isabel Lyon.

404.6 my brother Orion's autobiography] See the Autobiographical Dictation of 6 April 1906, note at 27.15–16.

404.14–15 Mrs. Holliday, who was always consulting fortune-tellers and believing everything they said] Mrs. Richard Holliday (born Melicent S. McDonald in about 1800) was the model for the character of Widow Douglas in *Tom Sawyer* and *Huckleberry Finn* (*Inds,* 325). In 1897 Clemens described her in "Villagers of 1840–3": "Well off. Hospitable. Fond of having parties of young people. Widow. Old, but anxious to marry. Always consulting fortune-tellers; always managed to make them understand that she had been promised 3 [husbands] by the first fraud. They always confirmed the prophecy. She finally died before the prophecies had a full chance" (*Inds,* 96).

404.24–25 chapter which I dictated . . . lately published in the *North American Review*] Clemens refers to the Autobiographical Dictations of 28 March, 29 March, and 2 April 1906 (*AutoMT1,* 451–55, 455–62). He originally selected a series of excerpts from these three dictations to comprise a single chapter in the *North American Review.* Starting with the issue of 4 January 1907, however, the magazine had a shorter format, and the proposed chapter was split in two: half appeared in the 18 January 1907 issue (NAR 10), and the other half in the most recent issue, of 1 February (NAR 11).

405.3–5 The sweetheart was Laura Wright . . . had not heard for forty-seven years] See the Autobiographical Dictation of 30 July 1906, note at 149.38–150.1.

405.8 I have just received the following letter from Sam] Orion added this remark to the top of Clemens's letter before forwarding it to his mother and sister in St. Louis. Clemens had directed the letter to Orion in Memphis, Missouri, where he was living with his wife and daughter and attempting to set up a law practice. The letter text inserted here has been lightly censored, presumably by Clemens on the now missing copy that Orion made of the original letter. Clemens says that Orion "copied it faithfully, word for word" (as Orion asserts in his appended notes), so it is a fair presumption that the departures from the original are not Orion's. The original undoctored manuscript was published in *Mark Twain's Letters, Volume 1* (107–16), and all of that volume's texts and notes are available at *MTPO.* The thorough annotation supplied there supplements the notes here.

405.13–14 Madame Caprell] Madame Caprell worked as a fortune teller from 1857 to 1861 in St. Louis as well as in New Orleans. She undoubtedly drew some of her information about the Clemens family from her conversations with Mrs. Holliday, one of her clients (6 Feb 1861 to OC and MEC, *L1,* 112–13 n. 1).

409.4–7 mother's mother . . . father died at 48] Clemens's forebears, in the order mentioned, are: Margaret (Peggy) Casey (mother's mother, 1783–1818); Jane Lampton (mother, 1803–90); Benjamin Lampton (mother's father, 1770–1837); William Lampton (mother's grandfather, 1724–90) and Martha (Patsy) Schooler (mother's grandmother, 1741–1811); Samuel Clemens (father's father, 1770–1805, killed by a falling log at a house raising); John Marshall Clemens (father, 1798–1847); Pamelia Goggin (father's mother, 1775–1845) (Lampton 1990, 23, 30, 79, 88).

409.10 Cook's pills] This drug, a combination of several strong laxatives (dried aloe juice, rhubarb, calomel, and soap powder), was formulated by John Esten Cooke (1798–1853) of Virginia and popularized—as "Cook's pills"—by John C. Gunn in his *Domestic Medicine* (1830). It was used to treat a variety of ailments (Swiderski 2009, 140–41; Hiss and Ebert 1910, 560).

Autobiographical Dictation, 30 January 1907

409.28–31 It takes a Cromwell . . . to pull them down into the mud again] Oliver Cromwell (1599–1658) was the Puritan political and military leader of the parliamentary forces during the English civil wars (1642–51), which led to the overthrow of the English monarchy. As Lord Protector of the newly established republican Commonwealth, he promoted moral and spiritual reform. The monarchy was restored after his death, and King Charles II (1630–85) placed on the throne.

409.39 "The press is the palladium of our liberties."] The full quotation—"The liberty of the press is the *Palladium* of all the civil, political, and religious rights of an Englishman"—is from the dedication in *Letters* by Junius (fl. 1770), the pseudonymous English polemicist.

410.3–8 Mr. Guggenheim . . . he is not aware that he has been guilty of even an indelicacy, let alone a gross crime] Simon Guggenheim (1867–1941), like his father and seven brothers, made a fortune in mining and smelting. He was elected as a Republican senator from Colorado by the state legislature on 15 January. When accused of buying the members' votes, he replied, "The money I have contributed has helped to elect these men, and naturally they feel under obligation to vote for me. It is done all over the United States to-day" ("Guggenheim Is Scored," Washington *Post,* 15 Jan 1907, 1; "Guggenheim for Colorado," Los Angeles *Times,* 16 Jan 1907, 15). Although no formal action was brought against Guggenheim, his reputation for dishonesty persisted: in July 1907 a Denver judge, Ben B. Lindsey, was reported as saying, "Not the senate chamber but the penitentiary or the gallows is the place for Guggenheim" ("Advises Gallows for Guggenheim," Chicago *Tribune,* 16 July 1907, 1).

410.11–21 It is true that Mr. Guggenheim . . . will of the people] The date of this article from the Denver *Post* has not been identified.

410.20 Tom Patterson] Thomas MacDonald Patterson (1839–1916) had served as a Democratic senator from Colorado since 1901 and was in the last year of his term.

410.24–26 they offered a motion to inquire . . . actually *sponged it from the records*] On 11 January a resolution was introduced in the Colorado legislature that provided for the appointment of a committee to investigate Guggenheim's "alleged purchase of the United States Senatorship." The resolution was tabled, and by a "viva-voce vote" the matter was "expunged from the records" ("Guggenheim Vindicated," Los Angeles *Times,* 12 Jan 1907, 17).

410.32–411.23 The Reverend Elliot B. X. . . . establishing its authenticity] In 1886 Frank M. Bristol, a Chicago minister and book collector, found, supposedly in Nevada, a copy of the second (1632) folio edition of Shakespeare's plays. On a flyleaf was pasted a slip of paper bearing an apparent Shakespeare signature. The book also contained the signature of John Ward. Since this was the name of a seventeenth-century vicar of Stratford-on-Avon, it seemed to lend credibility to the Shakespeare signature. Bristol acquired the book and sold it to the wealthy Chicago book collector Charles F. Gunther. The signature was soon recognized as a forgery, an imitation of one of the signatures on Shakespeare's last will and testament. Clemens himself would ignore it in *Is Shakespeare Dead?* (1909), where he enumerates the five signatures then extant ("Literary Notes," New York *Tribune,* 18 Feb 1886, 6; Vining 1887; Rolfe 1890; "The Gunther Autograph," *New Shakespeareana* 4 [Apr 1905]: 56–62; SLC 1909c, 33–34; Tannenbaum 1927, 149, 152–53).

412.36–38 copy of the Eliot Indian Bible . . . Mr. Trumbull would know the book's value] Missionary John Eliot (ca. 1604–90) translated the Bible into Natick, a dialect of the

Massachusett-Naragansett tribe in the Algonquian family. A thousand copies of it—the first Bible published in the Americas—were printed in Cambridge, Massachusetts, in 1660–63. By 1881 the preeminent historian and linguist James Hammond Trumbull (a Hartford acquaintance of Clemens's) was said to be the only man living who could read it. He spent his last years working on a Natick dictionary, which he left nearly complete when he died in 1897. It was published posthumously in 1903 by the Bureau of American Ethnology of the Smithsonian Institution (Library of Congress 2011; "Eliot's Indian Bible," Chicago *Tribune,* 17 Apr 1881, 24; "Key to Eliot's Bible," New York *Times,* 15 Aug 1903, BR13).

413.3–9 poverty-stricken sister, or other female relative of Audubon . . . boast about it afterwards] The original folio edition of John James Audubon's *Birds of America,* published in London in 1827–38, comprised four volumes of plates; five volumes of text were issued in 1831–38. Clemens described this incident, and contrasted it with Trumbull's sale of the Eliot Bible, in a eulogy he published in the *Century Magazine* in 1897: "James Hammond Trumbull. The Tribute of a Neighbor" (SLC 1897).

Autobiographical Dictation, 1 February 1907

413.12–22 Last summer I dictated some remarks . . . spelt as only Susy could spell] Clemens discusses the correspondence pertaining to the "western girl" in the Autobiographical Dictation of 18 June 1906; Ned Wakeman's letter is in the dictation of 29 August 1906; and a passage from Susy's biography of Clemens is excerpted and praised in that of 8 August 1906.

413.28–37 letter which has come to my hands . . . Miss Sullivan (Mrs. Macy,)] Clemens received—presumably from Helen Keller and Anne Sullivan—a typed copy of this letter by B. B. Page (of whom nothing has been learned beyond what is in the letter itself). Keller had published *The Story of My Life* in 1903 (see the ADs of 20 Nov 1906 and 17 Jan 1907).

414.34–35 I see in the Kansas City Star . . . he ought to take a good Wash] In May 1903 President Charles William Eliot of Harvard was reported as saying that western delegates to an upcoming Boston conference should visit Revere Beach because "a bath may be good for them" ("Do Westerners Need Baths?" Kansas City *Star,* 22 May 1903, 1).

414.42 Miss Francis Wilard] Frances Willard (1839–98) was a nationally known political figure, espousing temperance reform, labor rights, and women's rights.

414.44 your little Black plamate Marthy Washington] Helen Keller was unable to remember the real name of the childhood companion she called Martha Washington in *The Story of My Life,* an African American girl who was adept at understanding Keller's wishes before she had any language (Keller 1903, 10–13; 2005, 79).

415.1–3 that Duke told King Edward he was ingadged to Miss May Golet . . . Ingland neded her money] The engagement of the impoverished duke of Roxburghe to

May Goelet, reputedly America's richest heiress, was announced in September 1903. The Los Angeles *Times* reported that King Edward VII "regards all such marriages with high approval, being painfully aware that English society needs money more than anything to keep it alive" ("Duke to Wed May Goelet," Chicago *Tribune,* 3 Sept 1903, 5; "'Well Done Roxburghe,' Says the King," Los Angeles *Times,* 14 Sept 1903, 2).

415.16–17 Lue Dilen beet the World record . . . Name her *Driver*] Lou Dillon, a trotting mare, covered a mile in exactly two minutes at Readville, Massachusetts, on 24 August 1903, setting a world record. Her driver was Millard Saunders ("Lou Dillon Trots a Mile in Two Minutes," New York *Times,* 25 Aug 1903, 1).

Autobiographical Dictation, 4 February 1907

415 *title* Monday, February 4, 1907] This Autobiographical Dictation is actually a series of five dictations strung together under the single date of 4 February. The fifth dictation was probably written no later than 9 February: it includes a clipping from a 29 January newspaper, published—according to Clemens—"Ten or twelve days ago" (427.8).

415.27–28 lively gold-mining camp of Yreka . . . editing the little weekly local journal] Harte lived for a time in Union, a town near Eureka (not Yreka), which served as a port for the gold fields in the mountains to the east (see AD, 13 June 1906, notes at 118.13–20 and 118.21–23; George R. Stewart 1931, 61–62).

416.16–18 Tom Fitch, whom Joe Goodman crippled in the duel . . . has gone back to his early loves] Clemens describes the duel between Fitch, editor of the Virginia City *Union,* and Goodman, editor of the rival *Territorial Enterprise,* in his Autobiographical Dictation of 19 January 1906 (*AutoMT1,* 294–96, 568 n. 294.29–33). Fitch told Clemens in his letter of 14 January 1907 (CU-MARK) that after the duel he and Goodman "became warm friends." Fitch also explained that after leaving Nevada he worked in thirty-four law offices "between New York and Honolulu," and was "on the roll of Supreme Court lawyers in 9 states, 3 territories and in the District of Columbia." He finally established a law office in Tucson, Arizona, where he enjoyed the "brooding stillness, the reaches of space, the lavender mountains, and the electric air of the desert."

416.23–24 When "The Luck of Roaring Camp" burst upon the world] See the Autobiographical Dictation of 14 June 1906, note at 120.6–17.

417.24–27 His wife was all that a good woman . . . never came back again from that time until his death] Harte was married in San Rafael, California, in 1862 to Anna Griswold (1832–1920), a contralto whom he had met in Thomas Starr King's First Unitarian Church in San Francisco. Over the next thirteen years she bore him four children: Griswold (1863–1901), Francis King ("Frank," 1865–1917), Jessamy (1872–1964), and Ethel (1875–1964). The two were not well suited, however. Anna was a demanding—even domineering—wife who preferred life in a hotel without domestic responsibilities, while Harte yearned for a peaceful home. Neither was good at managing money, and they soon found it difficult to live within their means. They were separated when Harte sailed for Europe in June 1878; he corresponded regularly with his family, but their occasional plans for a reunion—either in America or in Europe—were never realized. Frank visited his father in England in 1884, and again in 1888; in 1893 he settled at Weybridge (Surrey) with his wife, and five years later Anna and Ethel Harte joined his household. Harte occasionally spent time with Frank as well, and especially enjoyed seeing his grandchildren. But by then he and his wife were permanently estranged, and they never lived together again (Scharnhorst 2000a, 20–23, 33, 87, 114, 140–41, 165, 195, 215, 227, 232; Harte 1997, 44 n. 3; George R. Stewart 1931, 204, 282–83, 307).

417.31–32 Bayard Taylor . . . Minister to Germany] The banquet honoring Taylor was held at Delmonico's on 4 April 1878. Like the Clemens family, he sailed on the SS *Holsatia,* which departed New York for Hamburg on 11 April (*N&J2,* 43, 53 n. 19, 63 n. 41; for Taylor see AD, 10 Apr 1906, note at 34.3–9).

417.32–34 I met a gentleman whose society I found delightful . . . grievance against him] Harte's benefactor was Thomas B. Musgrave (d. 1903), head of a New York brokerage firm (Scharnhorst 2000b, 213; "Thomas B. Musgrave Dead," New York *Times,* 1 May 1903, 9).

418.12 When Harte made his spectacular progress across the continent, in 1870] See the Autobiographical Dictation of 14 June 1906, note at 119.32–36.

418.23–30 he came to Hartford . . . accept of five hundred, which he did] Harte visited the Clemenses on 13–14 June 1872. After returning to New York, he wrote that he had received a check and paid one of his creditors the next day (15 June 1872 to Howells, *L5,* 103, 105 n. 2; Harte to SLC, 17 June 1872, CU-MARK, in Harte 1997, 67–68).

418.40 Once he wrote a play with a perfectly delightful Chinaman in it] Clemens saw Harte's play, *Two Men of Sandy Bar,* in early September 1876, shortly after it opened in New York. He told Howells, "Harte's play can be doctored till it will be entirely acceptable & then it will clear a great sum every year. . . . The play entertained me hugely, even in its present crude state" (14 Sept 1876 to Howells, *Letters 1876–1880*). The play drew on two of Harte's California short stories, "Mr. Thompson's Prodigal" and "The Idyl of Red Gulch," with the addition—for comic effect—of the laundryman Hop Sing. This "delightful Chinaman" was on stage for a few minutes and delivered only nine lines (Harte 1869c, 1870b, 1870c; Scharnhorst 2000a, 118, 124).

418.41–419.5 Harte had earned the enmity of the New York . . . critics were answerable for the failure] On opening night the audience was "good-humored and indulgent," but the critics were for the most part merciless. For example, the reviewer for the *Times* declared, "Its sentiment is maudlin and mushy, its plot shallow, its pathos laughable, and its wit lachrymose"—all in all, a "dismal mass of trash" ("Amusements," New York *Times,* 29 Aug 1876, 5). No earlier charges by Harte against drama critics have been found, but he had "never been popular with the press," according to Stuart Robson, the star of the production ("Mr. Bret Harte's Critics," Baltimore *Gazette,* 12 Oct 1876, 1). After his play's New York premiere, Harte engaged in an acrimonious public quarrel with the reviewers. It began when he published, in the New York *Herald,* a letter he had received from Robson charging that critics were known to be influenced by the "largest purse" to write the "longest and strongest editorials." A nasty article in the San Francisco *Chronicle* described the incident:

> We find Mr. Harte openly accusing "representatives of the most prominent New York papers" of being blackmailers, and demanding money for favorable criticisms. The *Sun* and the *Spirit of the Times* loudly importune him for the names of the mercenary critics, but as yet they are not forthcoming. On the other hand, the dramatic critics of the *Sun* and *Tribune* have asserted their innocence, and denounced the falsity of the charge. Mr. Harte has damaged his reputation forever, and attracted notice to himself from all classes of persons, many of whom would otherwise never have cared whether he was a gentleman or not. That he possesses talent none will deny; so does a performing mule. . . . His quondam friends despise him, his creditors credit him to loss, and his publishers find no profit in him. . . . California consigns Francis Bret Harte, with his shuffling ways, his debts, his ingratitude and his other brilliant qualities to the mercies of the East, where, Heaven grant! he may always stay. ("Francis Bret Harte," San Francisco *Chronicle,* 6 Oct 1876, 6)

After five weeks in New York, Robson took the play on the road to a dozen other cities, performing it last in San Francisco in 1878. He later acknowledged that he had badly misjudged the play, admitting that "its gifted author violated every law of successful dramatic construction" (quoted in Scharnhorst 2000a, 121). He allegedly lost $10,000 on the production (Harte to the editors of the New York *Herald, Sun,* and *Graphic,* 2, 13, and 21 Sept 1876 respectively, Harte 1997, 128–31, 135–37, 139–41; Scharnhorst 1995, 186).

419.5–8 he proposed that he and I should collaborate in a play . . . remained with us two weeks] Clemens wrote to Howells on 11 October 1876:

> Bret Harte came up here the other day & asked me to help him write a play & divide the swag, & I agreed. I am to put in Scotty Briggs (see Buck Fanshaw's Funeral, in Roughing It), & he is to put in a Chinaman (a wonderfully funny creature, as Bret presents him—for 5 minutes—in his Sandy Bar play.) This Chinaman is to be *the* character of the play, & both of us will work on him & develop him. Bret is to draw a plot, & I am to do the same; we shall use the best of the two, or gouge from both & build a third. My plot is built—finished it yesterday—six days' work, 8 or 9 hours a day, & has nearly killed me. (*Letters 1876–1880*)

Harte stayed in Hartford to work on the play, *Ah Sin,* for two weeks in late October. It was by no means finished, however, when he departed. Clemens continued to revise it, even traveling to Baltimore in late April and early May 1877 to oversee the rehearsals before its premiere in Washington on 7 May (27 Apr 1877 and 1 May 1877 to Howells, *Letters 1876–1880*).

419.11–12 He came to us once . . . "Faithful Blossom"] Harte returned to Hartford on 5 December and stayed at least four days. During his visit he worked on the later installments of "Thankful Blossom," serialized in the New York *Sun* on four Sundays, from 3 to

24 December (Harte to Osgood, 5 Dec 1876, Harte 1997, 142–143; Harte 1876). On 5 December Clemens wrote to George Bentley, editor of the English journal *Temple Bar:* "Mr Bret Harte has been reading to me his charming little love story. As I consider it the best piece of literary work he has ever done, I wanted it to go to Temple Bar. I said if it got there in time and was otherwise useable in the magazine, you would pay him whatever was fair for such use of it" (*Letters 1876–1880*). The story did not appear in *Temple Bar.*

419.14 Mr. Dana] Charles A. Dana (1819–97) was the editor and part owner of the New York *Sun* from 1868 until his death.

419.25 George] George Griffin.

419.35–36 young girls' club—by name the Saturday Morning Club—arrived in our library] This club was organized in the spring of 1876 at the suggestion of Boston publisher James T. Fields. It had a charter membership of nineteen or twenty young women who met regularly on Saturday mornings to engage in discussions and debates and listen to invited speakers. Clemens was a frequent speaker and host. In 1881 he presented the women with membership pins that he commissioned from Tiffany and Company in New York. The meeting described here must have taken place on 9 December 1876 (Saturday Morning Club 1976, 7–12, 59; *N&J2,* 370–71 n. 49).

420.10–11 After this fashion we worked . . . and produced a comedy that was good and would act] *Ah Sin* was first staged briefly in Washington in May 1877, and was well received. Before its opening in New York, however, Clemens had already grown disatisfied with it, especially Harte's contribution. He told his mother on 12 July:

> It took Bret Harte & me 14 working days (long ones, too) to plot out that play of ours ("Ah Sin",) in skeleton; it took the two of us 8 days to write it after it was plotted out. We didn't trim & polish it at all—& we shall live to repent it, too. It was not my fault; it was wholly that of that natural liar, swindler, bilk, & literary thief, Bret Harte, son of an Albany Jew-pedlar. I shall shed no tears if that play should fail, in October. It *ought* to—I know *that* pretty well. (*Letters 1876–1880*)

420.11–14 His part of it was the best . . . The piece perished] *Ah Sin* opened in New York on 31 July. The audience response was favorable, as Clemens wrote Howells on 3 August, alluding to *Colonel Sellers,* his dramatization of *The Gilded Age,* first produced in 1874:

> "Ah Sin" went a-booming at the Fifth Avenue. The reception of Col. Sellers was calm compared to it. If Bret Harte had suppressed his name (it didn't occur to me to suggest it) the play would have received as great applause in the papers as it did in the Theatre. The criticisms were just; the criticisms of the great New York dailies are just, always intelligent, & square & honest. (*Letters 1876–1880*)

The critical reception was mixed. The New York *Herald* declared the play "a popular success," but believed that "it cannot be justly called a good play." The *Tribune* noted that the dialog was "sparkling with wit," while the *Sun* declared the plot "weak, commonplace, and not at all original . . . and the characters are mere sketches. . . . As a piece of dramatic work the play is beneath criticism. As an entertainment it is laughable and lively, owing to the clever manner in which it is played" (reviews quoted in SLC 1961, xiii, xv). But Clemens's opinion of Harte's contribution had not improved, as he told Howells in his 3 August letter:

> I have been putting in a deal of hard work on that play in New York, & have left hardly a foot-print of Harte in it anywhere. But it is full of incurable defects: to-wit, Harte's deliberate thefts & plagiarisms, & my own unconscious ones. I don't believe Harte ever had an idea that he came by honestly. He is the most abandoned thief that defiles the earth. (*Letters 1876–1880*)

After a brief unsuccessful road tour in the fall Clemens finally pronounced the play "a most abject & incurable failure" and withdrew it from the stage (15 Oct 1877 to Howells, *Letters 1876–1880;* Duckett 1964, 158; for the text of the play see SLC 1961).

420.40–421.1 you sponge upon your hard-working widowed sister . . . creditors who are on watch for you] Harte's older sister, Eliza C. T. Harte (1831–1912), married Frederick Knaufft (1810–92) in 1851. The couple maintained a residence in New York at 45 Fifth Avenue and ran a boardinghouse, or family hotel, in Morristown, New Jersey. The Hartes moved frequently in the 1870s, often staying at one or the other of these residences. In addition, Harte borrowed a substantial sum of money from Knaufft, which he had difficulty repaying, and was perpetually in debt. While touring on the lecture circuit he often sent money to his sister to cover his overdue bills, but he tried to avoid paying his tailors and haberdashers even after they had won court judgments against him (Scharnhorst 2000a, 87, 115; Harte to SLC: 25 July 1872, 8 Aug 1874, 24 Dec 1875, and 16 Dec 1876, CU-MARK, in Harte 1997, 69–70, 97–99, 125–27, 143–45; Scharnhorst 2000b, 200, 204–5, 208–9, 216–17).

421.6 Harte owed me fifteen hundred dollars at that time] In an attempt to recover some of the money he was owed, Clemens wrote to his attorney the following summer: "Mine & Bret Harte's shares from the new play 'Ah Sin' will come to you. . . . Please place both shares to my credit at Bissell's & tell me the amount. Harte shan't have a cent until his entire indebtedness to me is paid" (3 Aug 1877 to Perkins [2nd], *Letters 1876–1880*). It is not clear when—or even if—Clemens delivered the scathing rebuke he recalls here. The rupture in his friendship with Harte did not occur until March 1877; in the meantime, they had discussed another collaboration. On 1 March Harte replied angrily to a letter from Clemens (now lost): "Had I written the day after receiving your letter, I hardly think we would have had any further correspondence or business together." Later in the letter he added, "No, Mark, I do not think it advisable for us to write another play together." On the back of the letter Clemens wrote, "I have read two pages of this ineffable idiotcy—it is all I can stand of it" (Harte to SLC, 1 Mar 1877, CU-MARK, in Duckett 1964, 134–37).

421.16–22 He entered into an engagement to write the novel, "Gabriel Conroy," . . . for an advance of royalties] At the request of Elisha Bliss, Clemens persuaded Harte to publish a book through the American Publishing Company. In September 1872 Bliss drew up a contract with Harte for a six-hundred-page novel, paying him an advance of

$1,000. The manuscript for the book, *Gabriel Conroy,* was not completed until June 1875, two and a half years after the stipulated date of delivery (contract dated 8 Sept 1872, CLU-SC; Scharnhorst 2000a, 116; Duckett 1964, 101–3).

421.35–40 He had advanced to Harte thus far . . . book-rights were hardly worth the duplicate of it] By the end of 1875 Bliss had paid Harte "between $3 & $4000" (Harte to SLC, 24 Dec 1875, CU-MARK, in Harte 1997, 125–26). Bliss had by then recovered some of this outlay by selling the serialization rights to *Scribner's Monthly* for $6,000, which he split with Harte. The novel appeared in ten installments, beginning in November 1875, and was issued as a book shortly afterward. Its few merits—several memorable scenes and some shrewd social commentary about the misperception and mistreatment of Chinese immigrants—were not enough to rescue its preposterous plot, which involved several love stories interwoven with improbable coincidences, impersonations, seduction, suicide, fraud, and intimations of cannibalism. *Gabriel Conroy* was a critical and commercial failure in America, selling fewer than 3,500 copies in the first two years. (It was translated into several languages, however, and became quite popular in Germany.) Harte was convinced that Bliss had failed to market the book aggressively, and he complained that his requests for accurate royalty statements were ignored (Scharnhorst 2000a, 116–17; Scharnhorst 1995, 144, 198; Duckett 1964, 106, 109; APC 1866–79, 90). Harte held Clemens partly to blame for Bliss's behavior, and devoted more than five pages of his 1 March 1877 letter to airing his grievance:

> Even Bliss' advances of $6,000 cannot cover the loss I shall have from respectable publishers by publishing with *him.* Now, this is somewhere wrong, Mark, and as my friend you should have looked into Bliss's books and Bliss's methods, quite as much with a desire of seeing justice done your friend, as with the desire of seeing what chance you had of recovering any possible advance of $500 on our mutual work, if it failed. (CU-MARK, in Duckett 1964, 125)

422.4–7 he kept a woman who was twice his age . . . in the house of one of them he died] Only one of these women has been identified: Hydeline de Seigneux Van de Velde (1853–1913). Fluent in three languages, she was by all accounts a charming hostess and brilliant conversationalist who collaborated with Harte on several plays. She became to some extent his patron, fostering his talent and providing "surroundings and conditions to stimulate his powers" ("Broadway Note-book," New York *Tribune,* 26 Aug 1883, 4, quoted in Harte 1997, 302–3 n. 2). In 1882 Harte explained his situation to his wife:

> I suppose I am most at ease with my friends the Van de Veldes in London. A friendship of four years has resulted in my making their comfortable London home my home when I am in London. . . . There are nine children in all and nearly as many servants. It is the most refined, courteous, simple, elegant and unaffected household that can be imagined. The father and mother are each foreigners of rank and title; Madame is the daughter of Count de Launay the Italian Ambassador at Berlin. Sir Arthur Van de Velde is the Chancellor of the Belgian Legation. They have adopted me into their family,—Heaven knows how or why—as simply as if I had known them for years. (Harte to Anna Harte, 11 Oct 1882, Harte 1997, 291–92)

Not only were Mrs. Van de Velde's attitudes and comportment unconventional, she was reportedly still married to her first husband; her association with Harte therefore provided an entrée into literary and social circles that would otherwise have been closed to her. The gossip and speculation about the nature of their relationship increased after Mr. Van de Velde's death in 1892, when she and Harte moved together to a new residence. There is little doubt that at some point their friendship evolved into something more intimate: in 1895 they traveled together for six weeks, leaving England separately and reuniting in Switzerland. Harte died in 1902 from throat cancer at her country home in Camberley, in Surrey (Scharnhorst 2000a, 163–65, 169–74, 197–99, 204–6, 228–29; Harte to Hydeline Van de Velde, 10 Sept 1880, Harte 1997, 271–73).

422.9–10 Orion's thoughtful carefulness enabled my "Hale and Norcross" stock-speculation to ruin me] See the Autobiographical Dictation of 5 April 1906, note at 20.35–21.5.

422.11–12 I went to Jackass Gulch and cabined for a while with some friends of mine, surface-miners] Clemens's mining comrades were Jim and Billy Gillis and their partner, Dick Stoker (*AutoMT1,* 552–53 n. 261.21–24; see AD, 12 June 1906, note at 113.21–23, and AD, 23 Jan 1907, note at 384.16–19).

422.28–29 These friends of mine had been seeking that fortune . . . they had never found it] The miners' luck was not entirely bad; in January 1864 Billy Gillis had discovered a "pocket from which, in the next three days, we panned out seven thousand dollars" (Gillis 1930, 10–11).

423.20 Parsloe, the lessee of it] Clemens and Harte persuaded Charles T. Parsloe (1836–98), the celebrated comic actor who had portrayed Hop Sing in Harte's *Two Men of Sandy Bar,* to enact the title role of the Chinese laundryman in *Ah Sin.* They hoped that Parsloe could repeat the popular and financial success of John T. Raymond in *Colonel Sellers.* Parsloe leased the play and was given "sole right for the entire world" (29 Dec 1876 to Conway *per* Fanny C. Hesse, *Letters 1876–1880;* "Death List of a Day," New York *Times,* 23 Jan 1898, 7).

423.26 gallus] From "gallows," meaning "rakish, dashing" ("Mark Twain's 1872 English Journals," *L5,* 598 n. 23).

424.10–13 Edward Everett Hale . . . "A Man Without a Country."] Hale (1822–1909) was a Unitarian minister, editor, and the author of numerous novels, histories, and stories. "The Man without a Country," a patriotic parable published anonymously in the *Atlantic Monthly* in December 1863 (not when the Civil War was "about to break out"), brought him world-wide fame and inspired support for the Union cause (Hale 1863).

424.26–29 one of the Republican party's most cold-blooded swindles of the American people . . . I was an ardent Hayes man] The presidential election of 7 November 1876 was the second in history in which the defeated candidate, Samuel J. Tilden (Democratic governor of New York), received more popular votes than the winner, Rutherford B. Hayes (Republican governor of Ohio). On 9 November Clemens sent a jubilant telegram to Howells to celebrate Hayes's apparent early victory (*Letters 1876–1880*). Hayes was not officially declared the winner, however, until March 1877, after an electoral commission created by Congress awarded him 185 electoral votes to Tilden's 184. As part of a compromise between the parties, the Republicans agreed to withdraw federal troops from the South, which brought Reconstruction to an end. It is not known when, or why, Clemens changed his opinion and came to view the election as a "cold-blooded" swindle.

425.9 the man without a country got his consulship] See the Autobiographical Dictation of 14 June 1906, note at 119.37–38, for more information about Harte's appointment.

425.10–11 John McCullough, the tragedian] See the Autobiographical Dictation of 16 January 1906 (*AutoMT1,* 284, 564–65 n. 284.31).

425.18–38 One day a young man appeared in his quarters . . . John McCullough stood by the boy] Harte contacted the noted playwright, actor, and producer Dion Boucicault (1820–90) as well as McCullough on behalf of his son Frank. In a letter of 15 December 1882 he wrote to Frank:

> Mr. Boucicault left or was to leave London on the 8th inst. for New York. I had another interview with him regarding your affairs a few days ago. He said he would see you whenever you could call or make an appointment with him, and that he would give you his advice frankly, and, in case he thought you were fit for an immediate engagement, would do all in his power to help you to it. Whether this means that he will be ready to take you *himself* in hand, I cannot say; he is a man immersed in his own business, but as that is dramatic, theatrical, and managerial, your interests may come together. Of one thing you can count surely; I believe he will be frank with you; not to discourage you solely, if you are not all that you think you are, but to show you what you can do in the way of a beginning. This is what McCullough said he would do for you, at my request—and *not,* as your mother writes to me that he said to you—'be rude to you, if necessary, to keep you off the stage.' It is scarcely worth while repeating that I never *could* nor *did* say anything of the kind or write anything like it to McCullough. I told him that if it were true that you were physically not up to the active requirements of the stage, he ought to dissuade you from it. (Harte 1926, 220)

Despite what Harte wrote to McCullough, it is clear that he had doubts about his son's acting ability. Frank nevertheless secured a position playing small parts with Boucicault's troupe; in 1885–86 he worked with Lawrence Barrett, and then returned to Boucicault; in 1887–88 he acted in Edwin Booth's company. After four years on the stage Frank abandoned his acting career, and by 1889 he was working as a secretary in Boucicault's acting school. In 1895 Harte wrote his wife, "I fail also to see where Frank 'has suffered'; during his whole misplaced career on the stage, he had advantages that the greatest actors have never had, and availed him nothing" (Harte to Anna Harte, 15 Feb 1884, 15 June 1884, 3 Apr 1886, 30 Mar 1895, and 15 Feb 1889, Harte 1997, 308–10, 313–15, 332–34, 355–57, 396–97; Harte to Anna Harte, 16 Nov 1885 and 15 July 1887, and Harte to Frank Harte, 28 Dec 1885, Harte 1926, 290–91, 294–95, 317–19; "Faithless Wives," San Francisco *Chronicle,* 28 Nov 1889, 1).

426.11–12 arts of drawing] Jessamy Harte was an artist of modest talent; she exhibited her work at the Chicago World's Fair in 1892–93 (Harte to Anna Harte, 19 Nov 1893, Harte 1997, 388–90).

426.31–34 Possibly he writes them . . . he has never sent them a dollar] Clemens had no personal contact with Harte after 1878. He relied on gossip and reports in the press for most of his information, which is inaccurate in several ways. In fact, Harte sent regular payments to his family. From Crefeld, he sent an average of $150 a month; from Glasgow he forwarded his entire consular salary, $3,000 a year. In addition, he provided money for Christmas gifts, and whatever additional sums he could scrape together for expenses like vacations, relying on his writing for his own meager income. According to his grandson, in his first fifteen years abroad Harte sent home over $60,000. It is true that he seemed ambivalent about reuniting with his wife, telling her soon after his arrival about the discomforts of living in Germany and discouraging Frank from visiting because he could not provide a home, but on more than one occasion in 1883–84 he invited his family to come to Glasgow, which they declined to do. He rarely saw his wife again, despite writing long, affectionate letters regularly to her and his children, and eagerly awaiting their replies (Harte to Anna Harte, 4 Aug 1883, 16 Oct 1878, 17 Sept 1883, and 15 June 1884, Harte 1997, 191–96, 300–302, 313; Duckett 1964, 184–85, 200–201, 232).

426.41–42 Steele . . . engaged to one of the daughters] Jessamy Harte married Henry Milford Steele (1866?–1917) in June 1898. At one time Steele served as art editor of *Scribner's Monthly,* and later was involved in financial enterprises in Denver as well as oil and mining operations in California. When the couple divorced in 1910, Steele accused Jessamy of desertion, and she charged him with "extreme cruelty" (New York *Times:* "Bret Harte's Daughter Weds," 28 June 1898, 7; "Mrs. Harte-Steele Divorced," 2 Jan 1910, 4; "Widely-Known Oil Man Passes Away," Los Angeles *Times,* 27 Feb 1917, I10).

427.10 *JESSAMY BRET HARTE A PAUPER*] This article appeared on the front page of the New York *Sun* on 29 January; the name of Jessamy's husband is incorrect in the article (see the note at 426.41–42).

427.27 She wants to go to London, but the city will pay her fare to New York only] The prominent actress Eleanor Robson organized a benefit performance for Jessamy Harte. On 14 February she and her company performed a stage adaptation of Harte's story "Salomy Jane's Kiss." They hoped to raise at least $5,000 but the benefit realized only $800 (Harte 1898; "Aid Daughter of Bret Harte," San Francisco *Chronicle,* 31 Jan 1907, 9; "Mrs. Steele in New York," Washington *Post,* 7 Feb 1907, 13; "Benefit for Mrs. Steele Raises $800," New York *Times,* 15 Feb 1907, 11). In a letter of 29 January Robson asked for Clemens's participation (CU-MARK). His initial response is recorded in Isabel Lyon's Stenographic Notebook #2: "It might be better taste to leave me out. For the past 30 years we were not friends. In the circumstances I do not want a prominent place—never heard of any member of the family who differed much from Bret Harte. I despised him— If there are going to be a lot of names, then well & good" (CU-MARK).

Clemens did not attend the benefit, although he did provide a testimonial for public use:

> I feel that the American people owe a debt of gratitude to Bret Harte, for not only did he paint such pictures of California as delighted the heart, but there was such an infinite tenderness, such sympathy, such strength, and such merit in his work that he commanded the attention of the world to our country, and his daughter is surely deserving of our sympathy. ("Aid for Harte's Daughter," New York *Times,* 30 Jan 1907, 18)

According to Lyon, Clemens gave his permission to use his name to promote the benefit, then revoked it: "He sees through the whole thing as being mainly an advertisement for Eleanor Robson. He is so impulsive, & continually has to withdraw from propositions that he has gone into with enthusiasm" (Lyon 1907, entries for 29 and 30 Jan). In early 1907 Jessamy was already showing signs of the mental illness that led to her commitment to a psychopathic ward in 1915; she remained hospitalized until her death in 1964 at age ninety-two ("Mrs. Steele in New York," Washington *Post,* 7 Feb 1907, 13; Scharnhorst 2000a, 232).

428.9–19 We find no fault with the spider . . . miserable death by gnawing rations from its person daily] See the Autobiographical Dictation of 23 June 1906, note at 138.42–139.6.

429.40 Stanford White] See the Autobiographical Dictation of 28 February 1907, note at 454.3–7.

Autobiographical Dictation, 11 February 1907

430.24–25 Something happened day before yesterday] See the Autobiographical Dictation of 12 February 1907.

431.21–22 my description in "A Tramp Abroad" . . . of German student life] Mark Twain discussed German student life in chapters 4–7 and appendix C of *A Tramp Abroad* (1880), drawing on his family's residence in Heidelberg in May–July 1878.

431.25–33 our generous soldier-pensions . . . offensive system of vote-purchasing] See the Autobiographical Dictation of 15 January 1907 and the notes at 371.42–372.15, 372.29, and 372.37.

431.37–39 I had committed an indiscretion. Possibly . . . in taking issue with an opinion promulgated by his Majesty] In the Autobiographical Dictation of 29 March 1906, Clemens claims that his offense on this occasion was an ill-timed exclamation concerning a potato (*AutoMT1,* 456).

432.15–18 Prince Heinrich came over . . . prodigious banquet given by the wealthy proprietor of the *Staats-Zeitung*] Prince Heinrich of Prussia (1862–1929), the brother of Kaiser Wilhelm II, toured the United States in February–March 1902 and was lavishly entertained. Clemens claims to have attended three dinners in the prince's honor, but only two have been identified: one given by Mayor Low of New York on 25 February, and the one described at length in this dictation, given on 26 February by Herman Ridder (1851–1915), publisher and editor of the *New-Yorker Staats-Zeitung,* America's foremost German-language newspaper. Ridder's banquet, at the Waldorf-Astoria Hotel, was attended by more than twelve hundred editors and publishers (New York *Times:* "Prince Guest of Mayor," 26 Feb 1902, 2; "Press of America Honors Prince Henry," 27 Feb 1902, 1).

432.22 George W. Smalley] Smalley was the U.S. correspondent of the London *Times* (*AutoMT1,* 635 n. 434.1).

Autobiographical Dictation, 12 February 1907

433.27–28 prediction furnished me a week ago by . . . all the palmists] Isabel Lyon recorded that on 26 January Clemens visited the palmist John William Fletcher: "At 4 o'clock he came home full of the amusement of it. Fletcher told him that he was to live close onto a century" (Lyon 1907). Fletcher had read a print of Clemens's palm two years earlier (see AD, 28 Jan 1907, note at 391.21).

433.31–33 A couple of days ago a gentleman called . . . tariff-revision] S. N. D. North, the head of an American delegation to Germany concerning tariffs, visited Clemens in New York on 10 February, carrying a message from Wilhelm II (Lyon 1907, entry for 10 Feb; "German Tariff Prospects," New York *Times,* 28 Jan 1907, 5).

434.10 "held the age,"] In draw poker as played in the nineteenth century, the player to the dealer's left was said to "hold the age," and had to bet before any of the other players could do so.

Autobiographical Dictation, 19 February 1907

434 *title* February 19, 1907] The real date of this dictation is not known; Clemens's vague chronological statements in the text, taken literally, yield dates ranging from 1904 to 1907. The text survives in a typescript by an unidentified typist; the date adopted here was written at the top by Isabel Lyon. In correspondence with his friend British librarian John Y. W. MacAlister, Clemens identified this essay as a dictation for the *Autobiography.* MacAlister, a fellow member of the Savage Club, wrote to him on 6 February 1907 (CU-MARK), seeking an original contribution to a volume celebrating the club's fiftieth anniversary. Clemens replied on 21 February:

> There has been no time at my disposal in which to write something special, so I have taken this out of my vast pile of autobiographical MS. It will appear after my death, along with the rest of my Memoires. It lacks smoothness in spots, but I seldom apply an after-polish, for dictated things are *talk,* & talk is all the better & all the more natural when it stumbles a little here & there. (NN-BGC)

The piece was printed in the Savage Club volume as "Mark Twain's Own Account" (Aaron Watson 1907, 131–35; for the Savage Club, see the note at 435.36).

434.24–25 About thirty-five years ago (1872) . . . to go to England and get materials for a book] Acting on a suggestion from Joseph Blamire, the New York agent of his London publisher, George Routledge and Sons, Clemens visited England in August–November 1872, and made extensive notes for a travel book that he never completed. On 21 August he sailed from New York on the *Scotia* and arrived at Liverpool ten days later, traveling by train from Liverpool to London on 2 September (*L5:* 21 July 1872 to Blamire, 128–31 n. 3; 11 Aug 1872 to OC, 144–45 n. 1; link note following 1 Sept 1872 to OLC, 153).

435.28 I drove to my publisher's place . . . The Routledges] The first English edition of *The Innocents Abroad* was published in 1870 by John Camden Hotten. In the absence of international copyright agreements, he paid Clemens nothing for the privilege. He divided the text into two volumes, *The Innocents Abroad* and *The New Pilgrim's Progress.* Three years earlier, in 1867, the firm of George Routledge and Sons had reprinted *The Celebrated Jumping Frog of Calaveras County,* also without permission or payment; its sales were promising, and they began to seek exclusive rights to Clemens's books in England. In mid-1871, as Clemens was about to publish *Roughing It* through the American Publishing Company, he wrote Elisha Bliss, "Have you heard anything from Routledge? Considering the large English sale he made of one of my other books (Jumping Frog,) I thought may be we might make something if I could give him a secure copyright" (21 June 1871, *L4,* 410–11). English copyright could be secured on a book by publishing it in England just before it appeared in the United States. This was done with *Roughing It,* and in early September 1872, when Clemens was going to visit the Routledges in London, they had just published their own two-volume edition of *The Innocents Abroad.* They became Mark Twain's favored British publishers, producing authorized English editions of the *Jumping Frog, Mark Twain's Sketches, A Curious Dream, The Innocents Abroad, Roughing It,* and *The Gilded Age.* In 1876, with *The Adventures of Tom Sawyer,* Clemens transferred his loyalties to Hotten's successors, Chatto and Windus (*ET&S1,* 546–55, 586–610; *RI 1993,* 876–77).

435.34–35 I was present in the Sandwich Islands . . . hadn't had anything to eat for forty-five days] In 1866 Clemens was in Honolulu when the survivors of the *Hornet* reached the Sandwich Islands after forty-three days adrift at sea. He promptly interviewed the emaciated crew and wrote up the story for the Sacramento *Union.* Later that year he also wrote "Forty-three Days in an Open Boat," published in the December issue of *Harper's New Monthly Magazine* (SLC 1866a, 1866b). More than thirty years later, in 1898, he wrote about this early experience as an author in "My Debut as a Literary Person," calling it "Chapter XIV of my unpublished Autobiography" (*AutoMT1,* 127–49 and notes on 501–6).

435.36 In the evening Edmund Routledge took me to the Savage Club] Edmund Routledge (1843–99) became a partner in his father's publishing company in 1865.

Clemens's first visit to the Savage Club was not on his first day in London, but about three weeks later, on 21 September (his after-dinner speech on that occasion is printed as the enclosure with 22 Sept 1872 to Conway [2nd], *L5,* 172–78). The Savage Club was founded in 1857 as a private and informal club for authors, journalists, and artists. Some believed that the club took its name from poet and playwright Richard Savage (d. 1743), best known from Samuel Johnson's biography of him. Journalist and novelist George Augustus Sala, on the other hand, asserted that "we dubbed ourselves Savages for mere fun" and "practised a shrill shriek or war-whoop, which was given in unison at stated intervals" (Aaron Watson 1907, 21; *L5:* 21 Nov 1873 to OLC, 480 n. 2; 22 Sept 1872 to OLC, 169–70 n. 3).

435.41–42 Tom Hood, Harry Lee, and . . . Frank Buckland] Clemens mentions the following Savage Club members: Tom Hood (1835–74), poet, journalist, anthologist, and son of poet and humorist Thomas Hood (1799–1845); Henry S. Lee (1826–88), self-educated naturalist and author of popular works on marine life; and Francis Trevelyan Buckland (1826–80), physician and prominent natural historian and pisciculturist.

436.1–15 five five-pound notes . . . tail-coat pocket of my dress suit] On 22 September 1872 Clemens reported the loss of bank notes worth thirty or forty pounds (but not their recovery) in a letter to his wife (*L5,* 169–70).

436.20–22 I was a member of the Lotos . . . honorary member of the Savage] Clemens was elected to membership in the Lotos Club in 1873; he became a life member in 1895. He seems to have become an honorary member of the Savage Club in 1897 (Pardee to SLC, 13 Feb 1873, CU-MARK; "Mark Twain a Life Member of the Lotos," New York *Tribune,* 25 Apr 1895, 11; Notebook 40, TS p. 19, CU-MARK).

436.23–24 the King—and Nansen the explorer, and another—Stanley] The Prince of Wales (later King Edward VII) had been elected to honorary life membership in 1882. Henry M. Stanley received that honor in 1890. Norwegian explorer Fridtjof Nansen (1861–1930) was elected in 1897, after his historic effort to reach the North Pole in April 1895 ("The Savage Club," London *Morning Post,* 13 Feb 1882, 3; Aaron Watson 1907, 135; "Stanley a Savage," Boston *Herald,* 26 Feb 1890, 2; for Stanley's life and exploits see AD, 20 Nov 1906, note at 280.28–33).

Autobiographical Dictation, 25 February 1907

436.36–437.7 First came the *Larchmont* disaster . . . the rest of that great company of men and women and children quickly perished] On the night of 11 February, the Joy Line steamboat *Larchmont,* bound from Providence to New York, collided with a schooner in Block Island Sound. Nearly all of its estimated one hundred and sixty passengers were killed; fourteen of them froze to death in a lifeboat. Captain George W. McVay and the other *Larchmont* officers were accused of cowardice for their inadequate rescue efforts. The New York newspapers all printed detailed reports of the disaster;

Clemens's particular source has not been identified (New York *Times:* "Probably 150 Lost in Wreck," 13 Feb 1907, 1; "How Survivors Escaped," 14 Feb 1907, 2; "Another Larchmont Victim," 16 Feb 1907, 3; "Did All I Could for Others—M'Vay," 17 Feb 1907, 4).

438.4 LAST SURVIVORS RESCUED] This article is from the New York *Sun* of 24 February.

440.8 BOLT WRECKS 18 HOUR TRAIN] This article appeared in the New York *Sun* on 24 February.

441.7–9 official statistics . . . our railroads killed 10,000 persons outright and injured 60,000 others] See the Autobiographical Dictation of 6 January 1907 and the note at 361.2–5.

441.39 an elder sister of Harriet Beecher Stowe] Either Catharine Beecher (1800–1878) or Mary Beecher Perkins (1805–1900), both of whom lived in Hartford's Nook Farm neighborhood (Andrews 1950, 17).

Autobiographical Dictation, 26 February 1907

442.17–18 I started a club . . . its name is The Human Race] On 6 February 1907 Clemens composed an invitation to William Dean Howells, George Harvey, and Finley Peter Dunne, summoning them to the first meeting of The Human Race on 15 February (CtHMTH). The club's full name was "The God Damned Human Race," as is shown by Clemens's inscription, on 7 February, of a copy of *Christian Science* to Isabel Lyon in her capacity as "Hon. Sec. G. D. H. R." (NN-BGC).

444.42 Queen Wilhelmina and her husband, Prince Henry] Wilhelmina (1880–1962), daughter of King William III of the Netherlands, was married to Prince Henry of Mecklenburg-Schwerin (1876–1934). She reigned from 1890 (at first under a regency) until she abdicated in 1948.

Autobiographical Dictation, 27 February 1907

445.17 1904. *Villa Quarto, Florence, January*] This account of Clemens's first typewriter was dictated in Florence in 1904; Hobby presumably copied a now-lost typescript made at that time by Jean Clemens, who transcribed longhand notes made by Isabel Lyon (see *AutoMT1,* 19–23).

445.26–27 I saw a type-machine for the first time . . . I suppose it was 1871—because Nasby was with me] Clemens saw and purchased his first typewriter in the course of a visit to Boston in November 1874. He and Twichell had attempted to walk to that city from Hartford, but gave up at Webster, Massachusetts, and completed the journey by rail. There is no mention of Petroleum V. Nasby (David Ross Locke) either in Clemens's letters or in Twichell's journal account of the Boston visit, although Nasby was in fact lecturing in Boston at the time. The typewriter was delivered to Hartford, where Clemens typed his first letter on 9 December (*L6:* 9 Dec 1874 to OC, 308–10; 13 Nov 1874 to Redpath, 281; for Locke see *AutoMT1,* 506 n. 146.1–5).

446.8–9 "The Boy Stood on the Burning Deck,"] The first line of Felicia Hemans's poem "Casabianca" (1826), ubiquitous in school recitations (see *Tom Sawyer,* chapter 21).

446.13–15 I hired a young woman, and did my first dictating . . . Gothic capitals] Clemens conflates this early period and typewriter with later events and a later typewriter. In Hartford in 1882 Clemens hired a woman typist, whose name is not known, to take down his dictated letters in shorthand and type up her notes. Both the 1874 and the 1882 machines produced all-capital "Gothic" (sans-serif) letters (*HF 2003,* 687 n. 75; A. A. Stewart 1912, 91; see also the note at 446.29–31).

446.16 the first letter I dictated . . . was to Edward Bok] Bok (1863–1930) was born in the Netherlands and came to the United States at the age of six. Educated in the Brooklyn public schools, he worked his way into the publishing business. He founded and edited the *Brooklyn Magazine* (later *Cosmopolitan*) and, as editor of the *Ladies' Home Journal,* piloted that magazine to unprecedented popularity. From the great personal fortune he amassed as a publisher and syndicate owner, he funded philanthropic activities and promoted social reforms. The letter Clemens recalls was dated 24 February 1882 (Bok 1922, 204–5):

> I HOPE I SHALL NOT OFFEND YOU; I SHALL CERTAINLY SAY NOTHING WITH THE INTENTION TO OFFEND YOU. I MUST EXPLAIN MYSELF, HOWEVER, AND I WILL DO IT AS KINDLY AS I CAN. WHAT YOU ASK ME TO DO, I AM ASKED TO DO AS OFTEN AS ONE-HALF DOZEN TIMES A WEEK. THREE HUNDRED LETTERS A YEAR! ONE'S IMPULSE IS TO FREELY CONSENT, BUT ONE'S TIME AND NECESSARY OCCUPATIONS WILL NOT PERMIT IT. THERE IS NO WAY BUT TO DECLINE IN ALL CASES, MAKING NO EXCEPTIONS, AND I WISH TO CALL YOUR ATTENTION TO A THING WHICH HAS PROBABLY NOT OCCURRED TO YOU, AND THAT IS THIS: THAT NO MAN TAKES PLEASURE IN EXERCISING HIS TRADE AS A PASTIME. WRITING IS MY TRADE, AND I EXERCISE IT ONLY WHEN I AM OBLIGED TO. YOU MIGHT MAKE YOUR REQUEST OF A DOCTOR, OR A BUILDER, OR A SCULPTOR, AND THERE WOULD BE NO IMPROPRIETY IN IT, BUT IF YOU ASKED EITHER OF THOSE FOR A SPECIMEN OF HIS TRADE, HIS HANDIWORK, HE WOULD BE JUSTIFIED IN RISING TO A POINT OF ORDER. IT WOULD NEVER BE FAIR TO ASK A DOCTOR FOR ONE OF HIS CORPSES TO REMEMBER HIM BY.
>
> MARK TWAIN.

The letter to Bok was probably not the first letter that Clemens dictated. Three earlier typed letters survive from February 1882, and it seems unlikely that he typed them himself.

446.25–27 In a previous chapter . . . first person in the world that ever had a telephone in his house] See the Autobiographical Dictation of 24 May 1906 and the note at 56.37–57.8.

446.29–31 "The Adventures of Tom Sawyer." . . . so I conclude it was that one] Clemens scrambles the facts about his unnamed typist (see the note at 446.13–15). *The Adventures of Tom Sawyer* was written in 1872–75, but none of it was copied on the typewriter. The book that "the young woman copied a considerable part of" was *Life on the Mississippi.* Harry M. Clarke (and Jakob B. Coykendall) had typed "a great portion" of the book in Elmira during the summer of 1882 (24 Apr 1883 to "Whom It May Concern," Freedman; *TS,* 503–4). The young woman took over typing the remainder when Clemens returned to Hartford in late September, but fell ill with scarlet fever three months later and could not complete the work. This was Clemens's first book to be sent to the publisher in typescript (*HF 2003,* 688–89).

447.5–6 New Year's Eve, at midnight, that extraordinary invention, the telharmonium . . . in a private house] The Telharmonium, invented by inventor Thaddeus Cahill (1867–1934), was an electrical device for making music (an early synthesizer) and transmitting it over telephone lines. Operated by two players working at a fiendishly complex console, it could simulate dozens of different instruments. It was powered by large generators located at a "central station," which sent an electric signal to any number of "translating instruments" (speakers). Cahill patented his device in 1897 and demonstrated a working model in 1901; in the summer of 1906 a much larger instrument weighing two hundred tons was installed at "Telharmonic Hall" in New York (Broadway and Thirty-ninth Street). Demonstrations were given; Telharmony was piped into certain New York restaurants and museums, and press coverage was copious. Clemens, having read a newspaper report, was given a private demonstration on 21 December, and immediately arranged for a New Year's Eve "concert" in his home at 21 Fifth Avenue. Since he lived about three-quarters of a mile below the southern reach of the Telharmonium cables, a special extension was installed to make the connection. About sixty guests—including several newspaper reporters—attended the party, at which the Telharmonium was a featured attraction. Clemens wrote to Jean on New Year's Day:

> At 11.55 there was a prepared surprise: lovely music—played on a *silent* piano of 300 keys at the corner of Broadway a mile & a half away, & sent over the telephone wire to our parlor—the first time this marvelous invention ever uttered its voice in a private house. Two weeks from now it will go by wire 1,000 miles to Chicago & furnish the music for the Electrical Convention, & within a year or two the artist will play on those dumb keys & deliver his music into 20,000 homes—& cheap as water; only 20 cents an hour, & shut it off when you please, like the gas. (ViU)

The public service, begun in 1907, failed to attract enough subscribers, and the Telharmonium was shut down the next year (Weidenaar 1995, 5, 28–35, 63–69, 121–33, 142, 198–99, 222–24, 267; "Twain and the Telephone," New York *Times,* 23 Dec 1906, 2; Lyon 1906, entries for 21 and 31 Dec, and an entry dated 31 Dec written on the datebook page for 1 Dec; Shelden 2010, 3–8).

447.32–38 was shot dead this afternoon by an unidentified man . . . shot himself in the forehead] Whiteley (1831–1907) opened a shop in the London suburb of Westbourne Grove in 1863, selling ribbons and "fancy goods." By the 1880s the business had grown immensely, and the wealthy Whiteley adopted the title of "Universal Provider." His murder came about as the result of more than one adulterous entanglement. Whiteley and a friend, George Rayner, had affairs with a pair of sisters who lived at Brighton, Emily and Louisa Turner. The murderer was born out of wedlock to Emily Turner in 1879; he was raised under the name of Horace Rayner, but his mother told him (he later said) that Whiteley was his father. Hoping for financial assistance, Rayner approached Whiteley in his store on 24 January 1907 and, when rebuffed, shot him and then unsuccessfully tried to kill himself. He was tried and, after ten minutes' deliberation by the jury, convicted of murder and sentenced to death. Despite Rayner's reported claim that he wanted to "get the whole business over and done with," a petition to commute his sentence to life imprisonment was successful. In Parkhurst Prison he again attempted suicide, a criminal act punished by two weeks in solitary confinement. He was released in 1919 (London *Times:* "The Murder of Mr. Whiteley," 23 Mar 1907, 6; "The Convict Rayner," 1 Apr 1907, 8; "Attempted Suicide of Mr. Whiteley's Murderer," 23 Oct 1907, 8; "The Convict Rayner," 21 Nov 1907, 6).

448.36 *Dollis Hill House, London,* 1900] Clemens wrote this sketch on or about 19 September 1900, judging from internal evidence; Hobby transcribed his manuscript. Dollis Hill House was built in 1825 near Willesden, at that time a rural area outside London. From 1881 the house was the summer residence of the earl of Aberdeen, and after he was appointed governor-general of Canada in 1897, the property was sold to the local district council for use as a public park. The house was still occupied, however, and rented to the Clemenses, who moved in on 2 July. Its proximity to London suited their requirements, as Jean was being treated by osteopath Dr. Jonas Kellgren and visited his nearby Belgravia offices three times a week. Clemens's first impression of the house was not favorable. "It is certainly the dirtiest dwelling-house in Europe—perhaps in the universe," he wrote in his notebook on taking possession; but it improved upon cleaning and further acquaintance (Notebook 43, TS p. 20, CU-MARK). The Clemenses inhabited Dollis Hill House throughout the summer of 1900, enjoying the country seclusion. They left for New York on 6 October on the SS *Minnehaha,* having been assured that Jean's treatment could be continued by an American osteopath. The grounds of Dollis Hill House were opened to the public as Gladstone Park on 25 May 1901; but over the course of the twentieth century, the house itself became dilapidated. Closed to the public in 1994, it was demolished in January 2012, despite the protests of locals who campaigned to save it (Dollis Hill House Trust 2011; 31 July 1900 to Rogers, Salm, in *HHR,* 448; 7 June 1900 to Baldwin, UkOxU; 4 Oct 1900 to Pond, NN-BGC; Ober 2003, 157–61; "Opening of Gladstone Park," London *Times,* 27 May 1901, 10; Brady 2012).

449.13–16 Mr. Gladstone used to be a frequent guest . . . translate Homer] For British Prime Minister William Gladstone, see *AutoMT1,* 499 n. 119.29–30. Educated at Eton and Oxford, Gladstone was an able classical scholar. His productions in this line included a verse translation of the *Iliad* (unpublished during his lifetime), seven volumes of studies on Homer, a thesaurus of Homeric Greek, and a translation of the *Odes* of Horace.

450.32–33 Harrod's and the Army and Navy Stores] Harrods opened in Knightsbridge in 1849; by 1900 it had grown to contain eighty departments in a building occupying thirty-six acres. The Army and Navy Stores began in 1871 as a cooperative formed by a group of junior officers to supply their provisions at reduced cost. The first store opened in London in 1872, and expanded into an emporium with branches elsewhere in England as well as in India (Falk and Campbell 1997, 69; John Richardson 2001, 3–4).

451.27 quarter-day removals] In traditional British usage, "quarter days" marked off the quarters of the year. Tenancies began and ended on these days (in the fall, the day was Michaelmas, on 29 September), so moving companies were exceptionally busy.

451.38 anchor-watch] The minimal crew required to remain aboard while a ship is at anchor and the rest of the crew are off duty.

Autobiographical Dictation, 28 February 1907

454.3–7 most lurid *cause célèbre* . . . gifted and famous architect, Stanford White] On 25 June 1906, the millionaire Harry K. Thaw (1871–1947) fatally shot renowned architect Stanford White (1853–1906) as he sat watching a play at the rooftop theater of Madison Square Garden. Thaw had a history of sexual violence, drug abuse, and mental instability. His trial for murder began in January 1907, Thaw claiming he had been tormented by thoughts of White's earlier intimacy with Evelyn Nesbit (1884–1967), the artist's model and chorus girl with whom both men had had affairs, starting when she was sixteen years old, and whom Thaw had married in 1905 at age twenty-one. Evelyn Nesbit Thaw was called to the stand on 7 February; in twenty days of testimony she put forward the case that White was a seducer who had plied her with drugs. Thaw's lawyers argued that he suffered from "dementia Americana," a previously unknown ailment wherein zealousness in defense of female chastity turns into uncontrollable violence. The trial ended with a deadlocked jury on 12 April. In a second trial the next year, Thaw was found not guilty by reason of insanity; he was committed to a hospital for the criminally insane, from which he escaped in 1913. He was captured and tried for conspiracy; yet two years later he was pronounced sane and released (Mooney 1976, 22–28, 244–62, 266–73, and passim).

454.28–29 with the exception of four abnormally hideous descriptive sentences] These "hideous" sentences have not been recovered. Clemens could have heard them repeated by any of several friends who were involved in the case, such as District Attorney William T. Jerome, the prosecutor, or Martin W. Littleton, who later became Thaw's chief attorney at his second trial, in 1908 (*MTB,* 3:1406–7; Mooney 1976, 244, 266).

454.34–37 Under our infamous laws . . . the seducer go free] In a 1903 article published in *Harper's Weekly* ("Why Not Abolish It?") Clemens had given vent to his view that the age of consent should be abolished, arguing that it shifts the burden of guilt from the males (who seduce) to the females (who are seduced). He returns to this theme in the Autobiographical Dictation of 20 April 1907 (SLC 1903e).

455.8–9 splendid human being, Tom Reed . . . we were yachting in the West Indies with Henry Rogers] In April 1902 Clemens sailed to the Bahamas on Rogers's yacht, the *Kanawha;* among the other guests was Thomas B. Reed (1839–1902). Reed was trained in the law and served as a Republican congressman from Maine from 1877 to 1899, and as the very powerful Speaker of the House for much of that time, resigning when President McKinley decided to go to war with Spain. Clemens enjoyed Reed's company, calling him a "delightful & irresistible old bullfrog," and they passed much of their time on the cruise playing poker and arguing about politics (7 Aug 1902 to Rogers, CU-MARK, in *HHR,* 496; *MTB,* 3:1162–63).

455.19–21 Colonel Harvey's parable . . . The Man Who Ate Babies] George Harvey, the president of Harper and Brothers as well as the editor of *Harper's Weekly,* published his parable in the March issue of that magazine (Harvey 1907).

APPENDIXES

SAMUEL L. CLEMENS: A BRIEF CHRONOLOGY

1835 Born 30 November in Florida, Mo., the sixth child of John Marshall and Jane Lampton Clemens. Of his six siblings, only Orion, Pamela, and Henry lived into adulthood. (For details, see "Family Biographies.")

1839–40 Moves to Hannibal, Mo., on the west bank of the Mississippi River; enters typical western common school in Hannibal (1840).

1842–47 Spends summers at his uncle John Quarles's farm, near Florida, Mo.

1847 On 24 March his father dies. Leaves school to work as an errand boy and apprentice typesetter for Henry La Cossitt's Hannibal *Gazette.*

1848 Apprenticed to Joseph P. Ament, the new editor and owner of the Hannibal *Missouri Courier.* Works for and lives with Ament until the end of 1850.

1851 In January joins Orion's newspaper, the Hannibal *Western Union,* where he soon prints "A Gallant Fireman," his earliest known published work.

1853–57 After almost three years as Orion's apprentice, leaves Hannibal in June 1853. Works as a journeyman typesetter in St. Louis, New York, Philadelphia, Muscatine (Iowa), Keokuk (Iowa), and Cincinnati.

1857 On 16 February departs Cincinnati on the *Paul Jones,* piloted by Horace E. Bixby, who agrees to train him as a Mississippi River pilot.

1858 Henry Clemens dies of injuries from the explosion of the *Pennsylvania.*

1859 On 9 April officially licensed to pilot steamboats "to and from St. Louis and New Orleans." By 1861 has served as "a good average" pilot on at least a dozen boats.

1861 Becomes a Freemason (resigns from his lodge in 1869). Works as a commercial pilot until the outbreak of the Civil War. Joins the Hannibal Home Guard, a small band of volunteers with Confederate sympathies. Resigns after two weeks and accompanies Orion to Nevada Territory, where Orion will serve until 1864 as the territorial secretary. Works briefly for Orion, then prospects for silver.

1862 Prospects in the Humboldt and Esmeralda mining districts. Sends contributions signed "Josh" (now lost) to the Virginia City *Territorial Enterprise,* and in October becomes its local reporter.

1863–64 On 3 February 1863 first signs himself "Mark Twain." While writing for the *Enterprise* he becomes Nevada correspondent for the San Francisco *Morning Call.* To escape prosecution for dueling, moves to San Francisco about 1 June 1864 and for four months works as local reporter for the *Call.* Writes for the *Californian* and the *Golden Era.* In early December visits Jackass Hill in Tuolumne County, Calif.

1865 Visits Angels Camp in Calaveras County, Calif. Returns to San Francisco and begins writing a daily letter for the *Enterprise.* Continues to write for the *Californian.* "Jim Smiley and His Jumping Frog" published in the New York *Saturday Press* on 18 November.

1866 Travels to the Sandwich Islands (Hawaii) as correspondent for the Sacramento *Union,* to which he writes twenty-five letters. In October gives his first lecture in San Francisco.

1867 His first book, *The Celebrated Jumping Frog of Calaveras County, and Other Sketches,* published in May. Gives first lecture in New York City. Sails on *Quaker City* to Europe and the Holy Land. Meets Olivia (Livy) Langdon in New York City on 27 December. In Washington, D.C., serves briefly as private secretary to Senator William M. Stewart of Nevada.

1868 Lectures widely in eastern and midwestern states. Courts and proposes to Livy, winning her consent in November.

1869 *The Innocents Abroad* published. With Jervis Langdon's help, buys one-third interest in the Buffalo *Express.*

1870 Marries Olivia on 2 February; they settle in Buffalo in a house purchased for them by Jervis Langdon. Son, Langdon, born prematurely on 7 November.

1871 Sells *Express* and the house and moves to Hartford, Conn. For the next two decades the family will live in Hartford and spend summers at Quarry Farm, in Elmira, N.Y.

1872 Daughter Olivia Susan (Susy) Clemens born 19 March; son Langdon dies 2 June. *Roughing It* published in London (securing British copyright) and Hartford. Visits London to lecture in the fall.

1873 Takes family to England and Scotland for five months. Escorts them home (Livy is pregnant) and returns to England alone in November. *The Gilded Age,* written with Charles Dudley Warner, published in London and Hartford.

1874 Returns home in January; daughter Clara Langdon Clemens born 8 June. The family moves into the house they have built in Hartford.

1875–76 *Mark Twain's Sketches, New and Old* (1875) and *The Adventures of Tom Sawyer* (1876) published.

1878–79 Travels with family in Europe.

1880 *A Tramp Abroad* published. Daughter Jane (Jean) Lampton Clemens born 26 July.

1881 Begins to invest in Paige typesetting machine. *The Prince and the Pauper* published.

1882 Revisits the Mississippi to gather material for *Life on the Mississippi,* published 1883.

1884–85 Founds publishing house, Charles L. Webster and Co., named for his nephew by marriage, its chief officer. Reading tour with George Washington Cable (November–February). *Adventures of Huckleberry Finn* published in London (1884) and New York (1885). Publishes Ulysses S. Grant's *Memoirs* (1885).

1889 *A Connecticut Yankee in King Arthur's Court* published.

1891–94 Travels and lives in France, Switzerland, Germany, and Italy, with frequent business trips to the United States. Henry H. Rogers, vice-president of Standard Oil, undertakes to salvage Clemens's fortunes. In 1894 Webster and Co. declares bankruptcy, and on Rogers's advice Clemens abandons the Paige machine. *The Tragedy of Pudd'nhead Wilson* published serially and as a book in 1894.

1895 In August starts an around-the-world lecture tour to raise money, accompanied by Olivia and Clara; lectures en route to the Pacific Coast and then in Australia and New Zealand.

1896 Lectures in India, Ceylon, and South Africa. *Personal Recollections of Joan of Arc* published. On 18 August Susy dies from meningitis in Hartford. Jean is diagnosed with epilepsy. Resides in London.

1897 *Following the Equator* published in London and Hartford. Lives in Weggis (Switzerland) and Vienna.

1898 Pays his creditors in full. Lives in Vienna and nearby Kaltenleutgeben.

1899–1901 Resides in London, with stays at European spas. The family returns to the United States in October 1900, living at 14 West 10th Street, New York, then in Riverdale in the Bronx. Publishes "To the Person Sitting in Darkness" (February 1901).

1902 Makes last visit to Hannibal and St. Louis. Olivia's health deteriorates severely. Isabel V. Lyon, hired as her secretary, is soon secretary to Clemens.

1903 Moves family to rented Villa di Quarto in Florence. Harper and Brothers acquires exclusive rights to all Mark Twain's work.

1904 Begins dictating autobiography to Lyon; Jean types up her copy. Olivia dies of heart failure in Florence on 5 June. Family returns to the United States. Clemens leases a house at 21 Fifth Avenue, New York.

1905 Spends summer in Dublin, New Hampshire, with Jean. Writes "The War-Prayer."

1906	Begins Autobiographical Dictations in January. Excerpts will appear in the *North American Review,* 1906–7. Rents Upton House, Dublin. Commissions John Mead Howells to design a house to be built at Redding, Conn. *What Is Man?* printed anonymously for private distribution.
1907	*Christian Science* published. Hires Ralph W. Ashcroft as business assistant. Travels to England to receive honorary degree from Oxford University.
1908	Moves into the Redding house (called first "Innocence at Home," then "Stormfield").
1909	Dismisses Lyon and Ashcroft. Jean rejoins Clemens at Stormfield. Clara marries Ossip Gabrilowitsch, pianist and conductor, on 6 October. Jean dies of heart failure on 24 December.
1910	Suffers severe angina while in Bermuda; with Paine leaves for New York on 12 April. Dies at Stormfield on 21 April.

For a much more detailed chronology, see *Mark Twain: Collected Tales, Sketches, Speeches, & Essays, 1852–1890* (Budd 1992a, 949–97).

FAMILY BIOGRAPHIES

Biographies are provided here only for Clemens's immediate family—his parents, siblings, wife, and children. Information about other relatives, including Olivia Clemens's family, may be located through the Index.

John Marshall Clemens (1798–1847), Clemens's father, was born in Virginia. As a youth he moved with his mother and siblings to Kentucky, where he studied law and in 1822 was licensed to practice. He married Jane Lampton the following year. In 1827 the Clemenses relocated to Jamestown, Tennessee, where he opened a store and eventually became a clerk of the county court. In 1835 he moved his family to Missouri, settling first in the village of Florida, where Samuel Clemens was born. Two years later he was appointed judge of Monroe County Court, earning the honorific "Judge," which young Clemens unwittingly exaggerated into a position of great power. In 1839 he moved the family to Hannibal, where he kept a store on Main Street and was elected justice of the peace, probably in 1844. At the time of his death, he was a candidate for the position of clerk of the circuit court, but died some months before the election. He was regarded as one of the foremost citizens of the county, scrupulously honest, but within his family circle he was taciturn and irritable. A contemporary reference to John Clemens's "shattered nerves," together with his extensive use of medicines, may point to some chronic condition. His sudden death from pneumonia in 1847 left the family in genteel poverty. When his father died Clemens was only eleven; he later wrote that "my own knowledge of him amounted to little more than an introduction" (*Inds,* 309–11; 4 Sept 1883 to Holcombe, MnHi).

Jane Lampton Clemens (1803–90), Clemens's mother, was born in Adair County, Kentucky. Her marriage to the dour and humorless John Marshall Clemens was not a love match: late in life she confided to her family that she had married to spite another suitor. She bore seven children, of whom only four (Orion, Pamela, Samuel, and Henry [1838–58]) survived at the time of her husband's death in 1847. The widowed Jane left Hannibal, Missouri, and between 1853 and 1870 lived in Muscatine, and possibly Keokuk, Iowa, and in St. Louis, Missouri, initially as part of Orion Clemens's household and then with her daughter, Pamela Moffett. After Clemens married and settled in Buffalo, New York, in 1870, Jane set up house in nearby Fredonia with the widowed Pamela. In 1882 she moved to Keokuk, Iowa, where she lived with Orion for the rest of her life. She was buried in Hannibal's Mount Olivet Cemetery, alongside her husband and her son Henry. Her Hannibal pastor called her "a woman of the sunniest temperament, lively, affable, a general favorite" (Wecter 1952, 86). She was the model for Aunt Polly in *Tom Sawyer* (1876), *Huckleberry Finn* (1885), and other works. After her death in 1890 Clemens wrote a moving tribute to her, "Jane Lampton Clemens" (*Inds,* 82–92, 311).

Orion (pronounced Ó-ree-ən) Clemens (1825–97), Clemens's older brother, was born in Gainesboro, Tennessee. After the Clemens family's move to Hannibal, Missouri, he was apprenticed to a printer. In 1850 he started the Hannibal *Western Union,* and the following year became the owner of the Hannibal *Journal* as well, employing Clemens and Henry, their younger brother, as typesetters. In 1853, shortly after Clemens left home to travel, Orion moved with his mother and Henry to Muscatine, Iowa. There he married Mary (Mollie) Stotts (1834–1904), who bore him a daughter, Jennie, in 1855. He campaigned for Lincoln in the presidential election of 1860, and through the influence of a friend was rewarded with an appointment as secretary of the newly formed Nevada Territory (1861). Mollie and Jennie joined him there in 1862; Jennie died in 1864 of spotted fever. That year Nevada became a state, and Orion could not obtain a post comparable to his territorial position. Over the next two decades he struggled to earn a living as a proofreader, inventor, chicken farmer, lawyer, lecturer, and author. From the mid-1870s until his death in 1897, Orion was supported by an amused and exasperated Clemens, who said that "he was always honest and honorable" but "he was always dreaming; he was a dreamer from birth" (*Inds,* 311–13; see *AutoMT1,* 451–55 and notes on 643–44).

Pamela (pronounced Pə-meé-la) A. (Clemens) Moffett (1827–1904), also known as "Pamelia" or "Mela," was Clemens's older sister. Born in Jamestown, Tennessee, after the Clemens family's move to Hannibal she attended Elizabeth Horr's school and in November 1840 was commended by her teacher for her "amiable deportment and faithful application to her various studies." Pamela played piano and guitar, and in the 1840s helped support the family by giving music lessons. In September 1851, she married William Anderson Moffett (1816–65), a commission merchant, and moved to St. Louis. Their children were Annie (1852–1950) and Samuel (1860–1908). From 1870 Pamela lived in Fredonia, New York. Clemens called Pamela "a lifelong invalid"; she was probably the model for Tom's cousin Mary in *Tom Sawyer, Huckleberry Finn,* and other works (*Inds,* 313).

Olivia Louise Langdon Clemens (1845–1904), familiarly known as "Livy," was born and raised in Elmira, New York, the daughter of wealthy coal merchant Jervis Langdon (1809–70) and Olivia Lewis Langdon (1810–90). The Langdons were strongly religious, reformist, and abolitionist. Livy's education, in the 1850s and 1860s, was a combination of home tutoring and classes at Thurston's Female Seminary and Elmira Female College. Always delicate, her health deteriorated into invalidism for a time between 1860 and 1864. "She was never strong again while her life lasted," Clemens said in 1906. Clemens was first introduced to the shy and serious Livy in December 1867; he soon began an earnest and protracted courtship, conducted largely through letters. They married in February 1870 and settled in Buffalo, New York, in a house purchased for them by Livy's father; their first child, Langdon Clemens, was born there in November. In 1871 they moved, as renters, to the Nook Farm neighborhood of Hartford, Connecticut, and quickly became an integral part of the social life of that literary and intellectual enclave. They purchased land and built the distinctive house which was their home from 1874 to 1891. Young Langdon died in 1872, but three daughters were born: Olivia Susan (Susy) in 1872, Clara in 1874, and Jane (Jean) in 1880. Clara later recalled her mother's "unselfish, tender nature—combined with a complete understanding, both intellectual and human, of her husband"; she took "care of everything pertaining to house and home, which included hospitality to many guests," and made "time for lessons in French and German as well as hours for reading aloud to my sisters and me" (CC 1931, 24–25). To her adoring husband, whom she addressed fondly as "Youth," Livy was "my faithful, judicious, and painstaking editor" (*AutoMT1,* 354–59). In June 1891, with their expenses mounting and Clemens's investments draining his earnings as well as Livy's personal income, they permanently closed the Hartford house and left for a period of retrenchment in Europe; thenceforth Livy's life was spent in temporary quarters, hotel suites, and rented houses. When Clemens was forced to declare bankruptcy in April 1894, the family's financial future was salvaged by the expedient of giving Livy "preferred creditor" status and assigning all Clemens's copyrights to her. In 1895–96 she and Clara accompanied Clemens on his round-the-world lecture tour. The death of her daughter Susy in 1896 was a blow from which she never recovered. She died of heart failure in Italy in June 1904.

Olivia Susan Clemens (1872–96), known as "Susy," was Clemens's eldest daughter. Her early education was conducted largely at home by her mother and, for several years starting in 1880, by a governess. Her talents for writing, dramatics, and music were soon apparent. At thirteen, she secretly began to write a biography of Clemens, much of which he later incorporated into his autobiography; it is a charming portrait of idyllic family life. Susy accompanied her parents to England in 1873 and for a longer stay abroad in 1878–79. In the fall of 1890 she left home to attend Bryn Mawr College in Pennsylvania, but completed only one semester. In June 1891, the Clemenses closed the Hartford house, and the family, including Susy, left for a period of retrenchment in Europe that would last until mid-1895. Susy attended schools in Geneva and Berlin and took language and voice lessons, but increasingly she suffered from physical and nervous complaints for which her parents sought treatments including "mind cure" and hydrotherapy. After the European sojourn Susy chose not to go with her father, mother, and sister Clara on Clemens's lecture trip around the world (1895–96); she and her sister Jean stayed at the Elmira, New York, home of their aunt Susan Crane. In August 1896, while visiting her childhood home in Hartford, Susy came down with a fever, which proved to be spinal meningitis. She died while her mother and sister were making the transatlantic journey to be with her. "The cloud is permanent, now," Clemens wrote in his notebook (Notebook 40, TS p. 8, CU-MARK; see *AutoMT1,* 323–28).

Clara Langdon Clemens (1874–1962), called "Bay," was Clemens's second daughter. Born in Hartford, Connecticut, she was mostly educated at home by her mother and governesses. During the family's sojourn in Europe between 1891 and 1895, Clara enjoyed more independence than her sisters, returning alone to Berlin to study music. She was the only one of Clemens's daughters to go with him and Livy on their 1895–96 trip around the world. The death of her sister Susy, and the first epileptic seizure of her other sister, Jean, both came in 1896: "It was a long time before anyone laughed in our household," Clara recalled (CC 1931, 179). The family settled in Vienna in 1897. Clara aspired to be a pianist, studying under Theodor Leschetizky, through whom she met the young Russian pianist Ossip Gabrilowitsch (1878–1936). By 1898 Clara's vocation had changed from pianist to singer, a career in which she found more indulgence than acclaim. After her mother's death in 1904 Clara suffered a breakdown and was intermittently away from her family at rest cures in 1905 and 1906. She was financially dependent on her father but spent less and less time in his household, traveling and giving occasional recitals. Increasingly suspicious of the control exerted by Isabel V. Lyon and Ralph Ashcroft over her father and his finances, Clara convinced Clemens to dismiss the pair in 1909. She married Gabrilowitsch in 1909; their daughter, Nina Gabrilowitsch (1910–66), was Clemens's last direct descendant. Between 1904 and 1910 Clara lost her mother, her sister Jean, and her father; at the age of thirty-five, she was sole heir to the estate of Mark Twain, which was held in trust for her, not to be disposed in its entirety until her own death. For the rest of her life she used her influence to control the public representation of her father. Gabrilowitsch died in 1936; in 1944 Clara married Russian conductor Jacques Samossoud (1894–1966). Her memoir of Clemens, *My Father, Mark Twain,* was published in 1931. She spent the last decades of her life in Southern California. Clara's bequest of Clemens's personal papers to the University of California, Berkeley, in 1962, formed the basis of the Mark Twain Papers now housed in The Bancroft Library.

Jean (Jane Lampton) Clemens (1880–1909), Clemens's youngest daughter, was named after his mother but was always called Jean. Like her sisters, she was educated largely at home. In 1896, however, she was attending school in Elmira, New York, when she suffered a severe epileptic seizure. Sedatives were prescribed, and for the next several years her anxious parents tried to forestall the progress of her illness, even spending the summer of 1899 in Sweden so that she could be treated by the well-known osteopath Jonas Kellgren. Her condition, which worsened after her mother's death in 1904, and the household's frequent relocations, gave Jean little chance to develop an independent existence. In late 1899 she began teaching herself how to type so that she could transcribe her father's manuscripts. She also loved riding and other outdoor activities, and espoused animal and human-rights causes. In October 1906 Jean was sent to a sanatorium in Katonah, New York, and remained in "exile" until April 1909, when she rejoined her father at Stormfield, in Redding, Connecticut. Over the next months she enjoyed a close, happy relationship with him and took over Isabel Lyon's duties as secretary. Jean died at Stormfield on 24 December 1909, apparently of a heart attack suffered during a seizure. Over the next few days Clemens wrote a heart-breaking reminiscence of her entitled "Closing Words of My Autobiography."

PREVIOUS PUBLICATION

Below is a list of each piece in this volume, identifying its earliest publication, if any. Separate publications of the various writings that Clemens incorporated into the *Autobiography,* such as speeches, letters, and literary works, are not tracked, unless the published text was based on the autobiographical dictation. The designation "partial" may mean publication of anything from an excerpt to a nearly complete piece. Short quotations from the typescripts in critical or biographical works are not accounted for. Charles Neider, the editor of *The Autobiography of Mark Twain (AMT),* reordered and recombined excerpts to such an extent that all publication in his volume is considered "partial." At the end of this appendix is a list of the "Chapters from My Autobiography" published in installments in *North American Review* (NAR) between 7 September 1906 and December 1907. All works cited by an abbreviation or short title are fully cited in References.

Autobiographical Dictations, April 1906–February 1907

2 April 1906: NAR 11, 229–32, partial; *MTA,* 2:303–10; *AMT,* 103–6.
3 April 1906: NAR 2, 459–60, partial; *MTE,* 33–34, 252–53, partial.
4 April 1906: *MTA,* 2: 310–16, partial.
5 April 1906: NAR 12, 337–41, partial; *MTA,* 2:316–25, partial; *AMT,* 106–7, 218–21.
6 April 1906: NAR 12, 341–44, partial; *MTA,* 2:325–32, partial; *AMT,* 221–24.
9 April 1906: *MTA,* 2:332–40, partial.
10 April 1906: *MTA,* 2:340–49.
11 April 1906: *MTA,* 2:349–57, partial; *AMT,* 170–74.
21 May 1906: NAR 2, 449–53; *MTE,* 143–48; *AMT,* 152–54, 158–59.
23 May 1906: *MTE,* 148–55; *AMT,* 159–61, 225–27.
24 May 1906: *MTE,* 155–65; *AMT,* 227–33.

26 May 1906: *MTE,* 165–70; *AMT,* 233–36.
28 May 1906: *MTE,* 170–79; *AMT,* 236–41, 245–46.
29 May 1906: *MTE,* 179–82, partial; *AMT,* 246–48.
31 May 1906: *AMT,* 248–51.
1 June 1906: *MTE,* 182–86, partial; *AMT,* 251–54.
2 June 1906: *MTE,* 186–95, partial; *AMT,* 254–58, 263–64.
4 June 1906: SLC 1902d, partial; *AMT,* 325–28.
6 June 1906: *AMT,* 328–32.
7 June 1906: *AMT,* 332–43.
11 June 1906: previously unpublished.
12 June 1906: SLC 2009b.
13 June 1906: SLC 1922a, 455–58, partial; *MTE,* 254–63; *AMT,* 119–24.
14 June 1906: SLC 1922a, 458–60, partial; *MTE,* 263–68; *AMT,* 124–27.
18 June 1906: previously unpublished.
19 June 1906: SLC 1963, 332–35.
20 June 1906: SLC 1963, 335–38; *AutoMT1-RE,* 411–14.
22 June 1906: SLC 1963, 338–43.
23 June 1906: SLC 1963, 343–49.
25 June 1906: SLC 1963, 349–52.
17 July 1906: previously unpublished.
30 July 1906: *AMT,* 79–81.
31 July 1906: *MTE,* 200–211, partial; *AMT,* 268–71, 272–74.
6 August 1906: previously unpublished.
7 August 1906: previously unpublished.
8 August 1906: *AMT,* 284–86.
10 August 1906: previously unpublished.
11 August 1906: *MTE,* 35, 309–10, partial; *AMT,* 286.
13 August 1906: *MTE,* 310–12; *AMT,* 286–88.
15 August 1906: *MTE,* 107–10; *AMT,* 31–33.
27 August 1906: SLC 2009c.
28 August 1906: previously unpublished.
29 August 1906: *MTE,* 243–49, partial; *AMT,* 275–78.
30 August 1906: SLC 1922b, 310–12, partial; *MTE,* 196–200, partial; *AMT,* 264–67; SLC 2004, 46–47, partial.
31 August 1906: *AMT,* 81–83, 143–47.
3 September 1906: previously unpublished.
4 September 1906: SLC 2010a, 181–86.
5 September 1906: NAR 19, 247–51.
7 September 1906: *MTE,* 380–83, partial; *AMT,* 345–47.
10 September 1906: *MTE,* 228–39.
2 October 1906: *MTE,* 384–93, partial.
3 October 1906: previously unpublished.

4 October 1906: previously unpublished.
5 October 1906: previously unpublished.
8 October 1906: NAR 15, 673–77.
9 October 1906: NAR 24, 327–28.
10 October 1906: NAR 22, 8–12; *AMT,* 309–13.
11 October 1906: NAR 24, 330, partial; *AMT,* 162.
12 October 1906: NAR 24, 330–31; *AMT,* 162–63.
15 October 1906: NAR 17, 1–4, partial; SLC 2010a, 186–87, partial.
16 October 1906: NAR 24, 328–30; *MTE,* 136–39; *AMT,* 47–48.
30 October 1906: *MTE,* 139–42, partial; *AMT,* 48–50.
7 November 1906: *LE,* 159–63.
8 November 1906: NAR 21, 689–91, partial.
19 November 1906: NAR 19, 243–45, partial.
20 November 1906: previously unpublished.
21 November 1906: previously unpublished.
22 November 1906: previously unpublished.
23 November 1906: previously unpublished.
24 November 1906: *MTE,* 372–80; *AMT,* 279–83.
30 November 1906: NAR 19, 245–47, partial; *MTE,* 110–18, partial; *AMT,* 58–63.
1 December 1906: NAR 9, 5–9; *MTE,* 118–25; *AMT,* 50–54.
2 December 1906: NAR 9, 9–14; *MTE,* 125–31; *AMT,* 54–58.
3 December 1906: *MTE,* 131–36.
5 December 1906: *MTE,* 211–13, partial; *AMT,* 271–72.
6 December 1906: NAR 14, 561–65.
13 December 1906: NAR 9, 1–5; *MTE,* 61–66.
17 December 1906: NAR 14, 565–67, partial.
18 December 1906: previously unpublished.
19 December 1906: previously unpublished.
20 December 1906: NAR 22, 17–21.
21 December 1906; NAR 18, 113–18, 119–22, partial; NAR 19, 241–43, partial.
26 December 1906: *AMT,* 63–67.
27 December 1906: previously unpublished.
28 December 1906: Harnsberger 1948, 48–50, partial.
29 December 1906: previously unpublished.
6 January 1907: NAR 21, 695–98.
9 January 1907: previously unpublished.
15 January 1907: *MTE,* 66–70, partial; SLC 2007, 95–101, partial.
17 January 1907: previously unpublished.
22 January 1907: NAR 15, 677–82.
23 January 1907: NAR 20, 471–74, partial; NAR 24, 331–36, partial; *AMT,* 130–38.
28 January 1907: *MTE,* 70–77, partial; SLC 2010b, partial.
29 January 1907: previously unpublished.

30 January 1907: *MTE,* 81–83, 91–96.
1 February 1907: previously unpublished.
4 February 1907: *MTE,* 268–92, partial; *AMT,* 127–29, 294–309.
11 February 1907: NAR 14 (misdated 10 February), 567–68, partial; *MTB,* 2:940–43, partial.
12 February 1907: NAR 14, 568–70.
19 February 1907: Aaron Watson 1907, 131–35.
25 February 1907: previously unpublished.
26 February 1907: previously unpublished.
27 February 1907: SLC 1905d, 391, partial.
28 February 1907: previously unpublished.

"Chapters from My Autobiography" in the *North American Review,* 1906–1907

The texts listed below in italic type were published in full or nearly so—that is, with no more than a paragraph or occasional sentence omitted.

Installment	*Published*	*Contents*
NAR 1	7 Sept 1906	AD, 26 Mar 1906 (Introduction); My Autobiography [Random Extracts from It] (first part)
NAR 2	21 Sept 1906	AD, *21 May 1906;* Scraps from My Autobiography. From Chapter IX (first part); [*Robert Louis Stevenson and Thomas Bailey Aldrich*]; AD, 3 Apr 1906
NAR 3	5 Oct 1906	ADs, 1 Feb 1906, 2 Feb 1906, 5 Feb 1906
NAR 4	19 Oct 1906	ADs, 7 Feb 1906, *8 Feb 1906*
NAR 5	2 Nov 1906	ADs, *9 Feb 1906, 12 Feb 1906*
NAR 6	16 Nov 1906	ADs, 26 Feb 1906, *7 Mar 1906,* 22 Mar 1906
NAR 7	7 Dec 1906	ADs, 5 Mar 1906, 6 Mar 1906, 23 Mar 1906
NAR 8	21 Dec 1906	AD, 19 Jan 1906
NAR 9	4 Jan 1907	ADs, *13 Dec 1906, 1 Dec 1906, 2 Dec 1906*
NAR 10	18 Jan 1907	ADs, 28 Mar 1906, 29 Mar 1906
NAR 11	1 Feb 1907	ADs, 29 Mar 1906 (misdated 28 Mar in the NAR), 2 Apr 1906
NAR 12	15 Feb 1907	[John Hay]; ADs, 5 Apr 1906, 6 Apr 1906
NAR 13	1 Mar 1907	My Autobiography [Random Extracts from It] (second part)
NAR 14	15 Mar 1907	ADs, *6 Dec 1906,* 17 Dec 1906, 11 Feb 1907 (misdated 10 Feb in the NAR), *12 Feb 1907,* 17 Jan 1906

NAR 15	5 Apr 1907	ADs, *8 Oct 1906, 22 Jan 1907*
NAR 16	19 Apr 1907	ADs, 12 Jan 1906, 13 Jan 1906, 15 Jan 1906
NAR 17	3 May 1907	AD, 15 Oct 1906; Scraps from My Autobiography. From Chapter IX (second part)
NAR 18	17 May 1907	ADs, 21 Dec 1906, *28 Mar 1907*
NAR 19	7 June 1907	ADs, 21 Dec 1906 (with note dated 22 Dec), 19 Nov 1906, 30 Nov 1906, *5 Sept 1906*
NAR 20	5 July 1907	*Notes on "Innocents Abroad";* AD, 23 Jan 1907
NAR 21	2 Aug 1907	ADs, 8 Nov 1906, 8 Mar 1906, *6 Jan 1907*
NAR 22	Sept 1907	ADs, *10 Oct 1906,* 19 Jan 1906 (dated 12 Mar 1906 in the NAR, with note dated 13 May 1907), *20 Dec 1906*
NAR 23	Oct 1907	ADs, 9 Mar 1906, *16 Mar 1906,* 26 July 1907, 30 July 1907
NAR 24	Nov 1907	ADs, *9 Oct 1906, 16 Oct 1906,* 11 Oct 1906, *12 Oct 1906,* 23 Jan 1907
NAR 25	Dec 1907	ADs, 11 Jan 1906, *3 Oct 1907*

NOTE ON THE TEXT

The present volume consists of 104 autobiographical dictations, arranged chronologically by the date of their creation, continuing the series begun in Volume 1. It starts with the dictation of 2 April 1906 (Volume 1 ended with that of 30 March 1906), and it concludes with a dictation made on 28 February 1907, two years before the author ceased to add dictations to his text. The history of Mark Twain's work on his autobiography, from the preliminary manuscripts and dictations he produced between 1870 and 1905 through the dictation series that began in early 1906, is given in the Introduction to Volume 1 (pp. 1–58). The editorial rationale for choosing between variants and for correcting errors is given in the Note on the Text to Volume 1 (pp. 669–79). Both are also available in the electronic edition published at Mark Twain Project Online (*MTPO*).

In this volume the source documents begin to present a textual situation not found earlier in the *Autobiography:* the existence of ribbon and carbon copies of a single typescript. It is not known for certain when Josephine Hobby began to make carbon copies, but it was probably in late May or early June 1906. Her original practice of retyping Mark Twain's revised copy, generating the successive typescripts TS1, TS2, and TS3, did not entirely disappear until August 1906. After that, there is only a single typed text for any given dictation, although often either the ribbon or the carbon copy is now missing.

Mark Twain's revision of these documents poses a minor problem. Beginning with the Autobiographical Dictation of 31 July, a pattern emerged in which he revised one copy (usually the ribbon) and transferred his changes to the other (usually the carbon), which he then further revised, often with contemporary (selective) publication in mind. Sometimes he had his revisions transferred by his secretary, Isabel Lyon. The transfer process was, as a rule, carried out accurately. But occasionally Clemens or Lyon neglected to transfer all of the originally inscribed changes. In all but a handful of cases, these variants between ribbon and carbon copy were inadvertent, and it is therefore necessary to accept all of them, regardless of where they were inscribed. In a few cases, however, Clemens seems to have deliberately altered a revision in the process of transferring it, in which case the version judged to be the later of the two has been adopted.

For some dictations Hobby, having made a typescript with a carbon copy, later made erasures and typed corrections of her own. In cases where, through omission or inattention, she created discrepancies, we follow her corrected (or first-corrected) version.

As with Volume 1, each dictation is supplied with a Textual Commentary, available only at *MTPO,* which spells out in detail how the editors have chosen between variants, and how and where they have corrected the text. Commentaries also identify and explain any necessary departures from the general policy.

WORD DIVISION IN THIS VOLUME

The following compound words that could be rendered either solid or with a hyphen are hyphenated at the end of a line in this volume. For purposes of quotation each is listed here with its correct form.

6.1–2	sage-brush
47.2–3	waste-basket
52.12–13	stockholders
56.7–8	bricklayers
100.24–25	hard-worked
150.11–12	good-natured
162.3–4	book-making
164.38–39	long-winded
165.30–31	clothes-basket
178.35–36	heart-broken
191.3–4	earthquake
196.1–2	unbusinesslike
198.28–29	headquarters
227.25–26	to-morrow
244.42–245.1	newspapers
275.27–28	railroad
296.26–27	camp-meetings
342.13–14	near-sightedness
353.32–33	handwriting
360.9–10	school-books
432.34–35	semi-notorieties
443.37–38	frostbitten
446.30–31	type-copied
448.21–22	saleswoman

REFERENCES

This list defines the abbreviations used in this volume and provides full bibliographic information for works cited by an author's name and a date, a short title, or an abbreviation. Works by members of the Clemens family may be found under the writer's initials: SLC, OSC (Susy), CC (Clara), and JC (Jean).

AD. Autobiographical Dictation.

Ade, George. 1939. *One Afternoon with Mark Twain.* Chicago: Mark Twain Society of Chicago.

Alfonso Carlos, Prince of Bourbon and Austria-Este. 1902. "The Effort to Abolish the Duel." *North American Review* 175 (August): 194–200.

American Bible Society. 1872. *Fifty-sixth Annual Report of the American Bible Society, Presented May 9, 1872.* New York: American Bible Society.

AMT. 1959. *The Autobiography of Mark Twain.* Edited by Charles Neider. New York: Harper and Brothers.

Anderson, Frederick, and Kenneth M. Sanderson, eds. 1971. *Mark Twain: The Critical Heritage.* New York: Barnes and Noble.

Andrews, Kenneth R. 1950. *Nook Farm: Mark Twain's Hartford Circle.* Cambridge: Harvard University Press.

Antrobus, Augustine M. 1915. *History of Des Moines County Iowa and Its People.* 2 vols. Chicago: S. J. Clarke Publishing Company.

APC (American Publishing Company). 1866–79. "Books received from the Binderies, Dec 1st *1866* to Dec 31. *1879,*" the company's stock ledger, NN-BGC.

Archives Hub. 2011. "Frederic Whyte Papers." http://archiveshub.ac.uk/data/gb186fw. Accessed 8 December 2011.

Arms, George, and William M. Gibson. 1943. "'Silas Lapham,' 'Daisy Miller,' and the Jews." *New England Quarterly* 16 (March): 118–22.

Asher, Robert. 2011. "Connecticut Inventors." http://www.ctheritage.org/encyclopedia/topicalsurveys/inventors.htm. Accessed 11 January 2011.

Ashley, Mike. 2006. *The Age of the Storytellers: British Popular Fiction Magazines, 1880–1950.* London: British Library.

Atkinson, George W. 1876. *History of Kanawha County.* Charleston, W.Va.: Printed at the office of the West Virginia *Journal.*

AutoMT1. 2010. *Autobiography of Mark Twain, Volume 1.* Edited by Harriet Elinor Smith, Benjamin Griffin, Victor Fischer, Michael B. Frank, Sharon K. Goetz, and

Leslie Diane Myrick. The Mark Twain Papers. Berkeley and Los Angeles: University of California Press. Also online at *MTPO.*

AutoMT1-RE. 2012. *Autobiography of Mark Twain, Volume 1.* Reader's Edition. Edited by Harriet Elinor Smith, Benjamin Griffin, Victor Fischer, Michael B. Frank, Sharon K. Goetz, and Leslie Diane Myrick. Berkeley and Los Angeles: University of California Press.

Baetzhold, Howard G. 1972. "Found: Mark Twain's 'Lost Sweetheart.'" *American Literature* 44 (November): 414–29.

Baetzhold, Howard G., and Joseph B. McCullough, eds. 1995. *The Bible According to Mark Twain: Writings on Heaven, Eden, and the Flood.* Athens: University of Georgia Press.

Baker, Simon. 1996. "Jesse Olney's Innovative Geography Text of 1828 for Common Schools." *Journal of Geography* 95 (January–February): 32–38.

BAL. 1955–91. *Bibliography of American Literature.* Compiled by Jacob Blanck. 9 vols. New Haven: Yale University Press.

Banks, Charles Eugene, and Opie Read. 1906. *The History of the San Francisco Disaster and Mount Vesuvius Horror.* N.p.

Barnes, Tim. 2009. "C. E. S. Wood (1852–1944)." *The Oregon Encyclopedia.* http://www.oregonencyclopedia.org/entry/view/c_e_s_wood. Accessed 25 January 2011.

Bartlett, John. 1980. *Familiar Quotations: A Collection of Passages, Phrases and Proverbs Traced to Their Sources in Ancient and Modern Literature.* 15th ed., rev. and enl. Edited by Emily Morison Beck. Boston: Little, Brown and Co.

Baxter, James Phinney. 1904. *Agamenticus, Bristol, Gorgeana, York.* York, Me.: Old York Historical and Improvement Society.

Baylen, Joseph O. 1964. "Mark Twain, W. T. Stead and 'The Tell-Tale Hands.'" *American Quarterly* 16 (Winter): 606–12.

Beck, Hamilton. 2005. "Mark Twain on the Crimean War." *The Victorian Web.* http://www.victorianweb.org/history/crimea/beck/1.html. Accessed 19 October 2011.

Beecher Stowe Center. 2011. "Stowe's Family." http://www.harrietbeecherstowecenter.org/hbs/stowe_family.shtml. Accessed 16 December 2011.

Benedict, Frank Lee. 1870. *Miss Van Kortland. A Novel. By the Author of "My Daughter Elinor."* New York: Harper and Brothers.

Bentley, G.E., Jr. 1997. "The Holy Pirates: Legal Enforcement in England of the Patent in the Authorized Version of the Bible ca. 1800." *Studies in Bibliography* 50:372–89.

Bishop, D.M., and Co., comp. 1877. *Bishop's Oakland Directory for 1877–8.* San Francisco: B.C. Vandall.

Bishop, Morris. 1962. *A History of Cornell.* Ithaca, N.Y.: Cornell University Press.

Bok, Edward W. 1922. *The Americanization of Edward Bok.* New York: Charles Scribner's Sons.

Booth, Bradford A. 1954. "Mark Twain's Comments on Bret Harte's Stories." *American Literature* 25 (January): 492–95.

Boyd, Andrew, and W. Harry Boyd, comps. 1872. *Boyds' Elmira and Corning Directory:*

Containing the Names of the Citizens, a Compendium of the Government, and Public and Private Institutions . . . 1872–3. Elmira, N.Y.: Andrew and W. Harry Boyd.

Brady, Tara. 2012. "Campaigners' Dismay as Listed Mansion Falls to the Bulldozers." Brent and Kilburn (England) *Times,* 19 January, 14.

Braid, James. 2008. *The Discovery of Hypnosis: The Complete Writings of James Braid, "The Father of Hypnotherapy."* Edited by Donald Robertson. Studley, England: National Council for Hypnotherapy.

Briggs, Charles Augustus. 1906. "Criticism and Dogma." *North American Review* 182 (June): 861–74.

Brown, T. Allston. 2005. "Early History of Negro Minstrelsy." http://www.circushistory.org/Cork/BurntCork3.htm. Accessed 12 July 2011.

Browne, Charles Farrar [Artemus Ward, pseud.]. 1865. *Artemus Ward; His Travels.* New York: G. W. Carleton and Co.

Browne, Ray B. 1961. "Mark Twain and Captain Wakeman." *American Literature* 33 (November): 320–29.

Budd, Louis J., ed.

1992a. *Mark Twain: Collected Tales, Sketches, Speeches, & Essays, 1852–1890.* The Library of America. New York: Literary Classics of the United States.

1992b. *Mark Twain: Collected Tales, Sketches, Speeches, & Essays, 1891–1910.* The Library of America. New York: Literary Classics of the United States.

Budge, E. A. Wallis. 1925. *The Rise and Progress of Assyriology.* London: Martin Hopkinson and Co.

Caldwell, O. H., and F. M. Feiker. 1919. "Gossip of the Trade." *Electrical Merchandising* 22 (August): 109–16.

Campbell, Ballard C.

2008a. *American Disasters: 201 Calamities That Shook the Nation.* Edited by Ballard C. Campbell. New York: Checkmark Books.

2008b. "1893: Financial Panic and Depression." In Campbell 2008a, 168–71.

Carlyle, Thomas. 1864. *Collected Works.* Volume 13, *Latter-Day Pamphlets.* London: Chapman and Hall.

Carnegie Endowment. 1919. *A Manual of the Public Benefactions of Andrew Carnegie.* Washington, D.C.: Carnegie Endowment for International Peace.

CC (Clara Langdon Clemens, later Gabrilowitsch and Samossoud).

1931. *My Father, Mark Twain.* New York: Harper and Brothers.

1938. *My Husband, Gabrilowitsch.* New York: Harper and Brothers.

1956. *Awake to a Perfect Day: My Experience with Christian Science.* New York: Citadel Press.

Chapple, Joe Mitchell. 1910. "Affairs at Washington." *National Magazine* 32 (June–July): 285–310.

Chatham Census. 1880. *Population Schedules of the Tenth Census of the United States, 1880. Roll T9. New Jersey: Morris County, Chatham Township.* Photocopy in CU-MARK.

Chautauqua County. 1904. *The Centennial History of Chautauqua County.* 2 vols. Jamestown, N.Y.: Chautauqua History Company.

Chemung Census. 1870. *Population Schedules of the Ninth Census of the United States, 1870. Roll M593. New York: Chemung County, Elmira.* Photocopy in CU-MARK.

Cherny, Robert W. 2008. "1906: San Francisco Earthquake and Fire." In Campbell 2008a, 198–200.

CHi. California Historical Society, San Francisco.

Cleveland Directory. 1871. *Cleveland Directory, 1871–72. Comprising an Alphabetical List of All Business Firms and Private Citizens; A Classified Business Directory; and a Directory of the Public Institutions of the City.* Compiled by A. Bailey. Cleveland: W. S. Robison and Co.

CLU-SC. University of California, Los Angeles, Department of Special Collections, Los Angeles, Calif.

CofC. 1969. *Clemens of the "Call": Mark Twain in San Francisco.* Edited by Edgar M. Branch. Berkeley and Los Angeles: University of California Press.

Colby, Frank Moore, ed. 1920. *The New International Year Book: A Compendium of the World's Progress for the Year 1919.* New York: Dodd, Mead and Co.

Conard, Howard L., ed. 1901. *Encyclopedia of the History of Missouri.* 6 vols. New York: Southern History Company.

Conlin, Joseph R. 1986. *Bacon, Beans, and Galantines.* Reno: University of Nevada Press.

Connecticut Historical Society. 2012. "A Guide to the Gilman Family Papers at the Connecticut Historical Society." http://www.chs.org/finding_aides/finding_aids/gilmf1787.html. Accessed 10 April 2012.

Cooper Union. 2011. "The Cooper Union." http://cooper.edu/about-us. Accessed 10 May 2011.

Corcoran Gallery. 2012. "A Love of Europe." http://www.corcoran.org/past_exhibitions/past/a_love_of_europe_highlights-from-the-william-a.-clark-collection. Accessed 10 July 2012.

Côté, Richard N. 2012. "Theodosia Burr Alston: Portrait of a Prodigy." http://www.bookdoctor.com/corinthian/cote/theodosia.html. Accessed 23 January 2012.

Courtney, Steve.

2008. *Joseph Hopkins Twichell: The Life and Times of Mark Twain's Closest Friend.* Athens: University of Georgia Press.

2011. *"The Loveliest Home That Ever Was": The Story of the Mark Twain House in Hartford.* Mineola, N.Y.: Dover Publications.

Craig, Christopher. 2003. "Woodward, R(obert) B(lum): Hotel and Amusement Resort Proprietor." In *Encyclopedia of San Francisco.* http://www.sfhistoryencyclopedia.com. Accessed 12 October 2011.

Crapsey, Algernon Sidney. 1924. *The Last of the Heretics.* New York: Alfred A. Knopf.

CSmH. Henry E. Huntington Library, Art Collections and Botanical Gardens, San Marino, Calif.

CtHMTH. Mark Twain House and Museum, Hartford, Conn.

CtHSD. Stowe-Day Memorial Library and Historical Foundation, Hartford, Conn.

CtY-BR. Yale University, Beinecke Rare Book and Manuscript Library, New Haven, Conn.

CU-BANC. University of California, The Bancroft Library, Berkeley.

CU-MARK. University of California, Mark Twain Papers, Berkeley.

Curtis, David A. 1890. "In and About New York." Kalamazoo (Mich.) *Gazette,* 24 May, 6.

CY. 1979. *A Connecticut Yankee in King Arthur's Court.* Edited by Bernard L. Stein, with an introduction by Henry Nash Smith. The Works of Mark Twain. Berkeley and Los Angeles: University of California Press.

Dallas Census. 1880. *Population Schedules of the Tenth Census of the United States, 1880. Roll T9. Texas: Dallas.* Photocopy in CU-MARK.

D.A.R. Directory. 1908. *Directory of the National Society of the Daughters of the American Revolution.* Compiled by Order of the Sixteenth Continental Congress. Washington, D.C.: n.p.

Darwin, Charles.

1877. "A Biographical Sketch of an Infant." *Mind: A Quarterly Review of Psychology and Philosophy* 7 (July): 285–94.

1884. *On the Origin of Species by Means of Natural Selection.* New York: D. Appleton and Co.

1887. *The Life and Letters of Charles Darwin, Including an Autobiographical Chapter.* Edited by Francis Darwin. 2 vols. New York: D. Appleton and Co.

Depew, Chauncey M. 1922. *My Memories of Eighty Years.* New York: Charles Scribner's Sons.

Derby, J. C. 1884. *Fifty Years among Authors, Books and Publishers.* New York: G. W. Carleton and Co.

Dickinson, Asa Don. 1935. "Huckleberry Finn Is Fifty Years Old—Yes; But Is He Respectable?" *Wilson Bulletin for Librarians* 10 (November): 180–85.

Dickinson, S. Meredith. 1900. *Reports of Cases Decided in the Court of Chancery, and, on Appeal, in the Court of Errors and Appeals, of the State of New Jersey, Volume 13.* Newark: Soney and Sage.

Disturnell, John, comp. 1876. *New York as It Was and as It Is.* New York: D. Van Nostrand.

DLC. United States Library of Congress, Washington, D.C.

Doane, T. W. 1882. *Bible Myths and Their Parallels in Other Religions.* 4th ed. New York: Commonwealth Company.

Dollis Hill House Trust. 2011. "Dollis Hill House: Our History." http://www.dollishillhouse.org.uk/history.htm. Accessed 17 August 2011.

Donworth, Grace. 1908. *The Letters of Jennie Allen to Her Friend Miss Musgrove.* Boston: Small, Maynard and Co.

Downey, Stephen W. 1880. *The Immortals. Argument of Hon. Stephen W. Downey, of Wyoming Territory, in the House of Representatives, Tuesday, April 13, 1880, on a Bill Providing for Certain Paintings on the Walls of the National Capitol.* Washington, D.C.: n.p.

Draper, Warwick H. 1901. "Copyright Legislation." *Law Quarterly Review* 17 (January): 39–55.

Duckett, Margaret. 1964. *Mark Twain and Bret Harte.* Norman: University of Oklahoma Press.

Dunne, Finley Peter [Martin Dooley, pseud.]. 1963. *Mr. Dooley Remembers: The Informal Memoirs of Finley Peter Dunne.* Edited with an introduction and commentary by Philip Dunne. Boston and Toronto: Little, Brown and Co.

Eddy, Mary Baker G. 1884. *Science and Health; with a Key to the Scriptures.* 10th ed. 2 vols. Cambridge: published by the author. SLC copy of volume 2 in CU-MARK.

Ellis, Elmer. 1941. *Mr. Dooley's America: A Life of Finley Peter Dunne.* New York: Alfred A. Knopf.

Ellsworth, William Webster. 1919. *A Golden Age of Authors: A Publisher's Recollection.* Boston: Houghton Mifflin Company.

Ernst, Bernard M. L., and Hereward Carrington. 1932. *Houdini and Conan Doyle: The Story of a Strange Friendship.* New York: Albert and Charles Boni.

ET&S1. 1979. *Early Tales & Sketches, Volume 1 (1851–1864).* Edited by Edgar Marquess Branch and Robert H. Hirst, with the assistance of Harriet Elinor Smith. The Works of Mark Twain. Berkeley and Los Angeles: University of California Press.

ET&S2. 1981. *Early Tales & Sketches, Volume 2 (1864–1865).* Edited by Edgar Marquess Branch and Robert H. Hirst, with the assistance of Harriet Elinor Smith. The Works of Mark Twain. Berkeley and Los Angeles: University of California Press.

Evans, Peter A., William R. Gillis, and Henry Alston Williams. 1970. Gillis family genealogy, unpublished manuscript documents, photocopy in CU-MARK.

Exman, Eugene. 1967. *The House of Harper: One Hundred and Fifty Years of Publishing.* New York: Harper and Row.

Fagen, M. D., ed. 1975. *A History of Engineering and Science in the Bell System: The Early Years (1875–1925).* N.p.: Bell Telephone Laboratories.

Fahlman, Betsy. 1991. "Women Art Students at Yale, 1869–1913: Never True Sons of the University." *Woman's Art Journal* 12 (Spring–Summer): 15–23.

Falk, Pasi, and Colin Campbell. 1997. *The Shopping Experience.* London: Sage Publications.

Fanning, Philip Ashley. 2003. *Mark Twain and Orion Clemens: Brothers, Partners, Strangers.* Tuscaloosa: University of Alabama Press.

Fatout, Paul. 1976. *Mark Twain Speaking.* Iowa City: University of Iowa Press.

Ferris, Ruth. 1965. "Captain Jolly in the Civil War." *Missouri Historical Society Bulletin* 22 (October): 14–31.

FiH2. Suomalaisen Kirjallisuuden Seura (Finnish Literature Society), Helsinki, Finland.

Flagg, Mildred Buchanan. 1966. *Boston Authors Now and Then: More Members of the Boston Authors Club, 1900–1966.* Cambridge: Dresser, Chapman and Grimes.

FM. 1972. *Mark Twain's Fables of Man.* Edited by John S. Tuckey. Text established by Kenneth M. Sanderson and Bernard L. Stein. Berkeley and Los Angeles: University of California Press.

Foor, Forrest LeRoy. 1941. "The Senatorial Aspirations of William A. Clark, 1898–1901: A Study in Montana Politics." Ph.D. diss., University of California, Berkeley.

Freedman. Collection of Samuel N. Freedman.

Freeport Census. 1900. *Population Schedules of the Twelfth Census of the United States, 1900. Roll T623. Maine: Cumberland County, Freeport Township.* Photocopy in CU-MARK.

Fuller, Frank. 1911. "Utah's War Governor Talks of Many Famous Men." New York *Times,* 1 October, 5:10.

Gagey, Edmond M. 1971. "Cayvan, Georgia Eva." In *Notable American Women, 1607–1950: A Biographical Dictionary.* Edited by Edward T. James, Janet Wilson James, and Paul S. Boyer. 3 vols. Cambridge: Belknap Press of Harvard University Press.

Gallati, Barbara Dayer. 1995. *William Merritt Chase.* New York: Harry N. Abrams.

Gamo, Benjamin. 1908. *Modern Billiards: A Complete Text-Book of the Game.* New York: Brunswick-Balke-Collender Company.

Garrison, Charles. 1904. "The De Laval Steam Turbine." *National Engineer* 8 (April): 1–4.

Geer, Elihu, comp.

1882. *Geer's Hartford City Directory and Hartford Illustrated; for the Year Commencing July 1st, 1882.* Hartford: Elihu Geer.

1886. *Geer's Hartford City Directory; July 1, 1886: Being a Fifteen-Fold Directory of Hartford.* Hartford: Elihu Geer.

GEU. Emory University, Atlanta, Ga.

Gilder, Rosamond, ed. 1916. *Letters of Richard Watson Gilder.* Boston: Houghton Mifflin Company.

Gillis, William R. 1930. *Gold Rush Days with Mark Twain.* New York: Albert and Charles Boni.

Gilmour, David. 2002. *The Long Recessional: The Imperial Life of Rudyard Kipling.* New York: Farrar, Straus and Giroux.

Glasson, William H. 1918. *Federal Military Pensions in the United States.* Edited by David Kinley. New York: Oxford University Press.

Goble, Corban. 1998. "Mark Twain's Nemesis: The Paige Compositor." *Printing History: The Journal of the American Printing History Association* 18 (36): 2–16.

Gowdy, Anne Razey. 2003. "Frances Miriam Berry Whitcher, 1812?–1852." In *Writers of the American Renaissance: An A–Z Guide.* Edited by Denise D. Wright. Westport, Conn.: Greenwood Publishing Group.

Graver, William J. 1992. "Rudyard Kipling and Mark Twain: A Literary Friendship." *The Kipling Journal* 66 (September): 13–30.

Gribben, Alan. 1980. *Mark Twain's Library: A Reconstruction.* 2 vols. Boston: G. K. Hall and Co.

Gribben, Alan, and Nick Karanovich, eds. 1992. *Overland with Mark Twain: James B. Pond's Photographs and Journal of the North American Lecture Tour of 1895.* Elmira, N.Y.: Center for Mark Twain Studies.

Gudde, Erwin G. 1962. *California Place Names: The Origin and Etymology of Current Geographical Names.* 2d ed., rev. and enl. Berkeley and Los Angeles: University of California Press.

Hale, Edward Everett.

1863. "The Man without a Country." *Atlantic Monthly* 12 (December): 665–79.

1906. "Statement of Rev. Edward Everett Hale." Speech made on 7 December before the Senate and House Committees on Patents. In U.S. Congress 1906, 114–15.

Hall, Frederick J. 1947. "Fred J. Hall Tells the Story of His Connection with Charles L. Webster & Co." *Twainian* 6 (November–December): 1–3.

Hannibal *Courier-Post.* 2011. "About Us." http://www.hannibal.net/contact. Accessed 4 August 2011.

Harnsberger, Caroline Thomas, ed. 1948. *Mark Twain at Your Fingertips.* New York: Beechhurst Press.

Harris, Julia Collier. 1918. *The Life and Letters of Joel Chandler Harris.* Boston and New York: Houghton Mifflin Company.

Harte, Bret.

1867. "Preface." In *Condensed Novels. And Other Papers.* New York: G. W. Carleton and Co.

1868. "The Luck of Roaring Camp." *Overland Monthly* 1 (August): 183–89.

1869a. "Current Literature." *Overland Monthly* 3 (September): 292–96.

1869b. "Tennessee's Partner." *Overland Monthly* 3 (October): 360–65.

1869c. "The Idyl of Red Gulch." *Overland Monthly* 3 (December): 569–74.

1870a. *The Luck of Roaring Camp, and Other Sketches.* Boston: Fields, Osgood, and Co. SLC copy in CU-MARK.

1870b. "Mr. Thompson's Prodigal." *Overland Monthly* 5 (July): 91–95.

1870c. "Plain Language from Truthful James." *Overland Monthly* 5 (September): 287–88. Also known as "The Heathen Chinee."

1876. "Thankful Blossom: A Romance of the Jerseys, 1779." New York *Sun:* 3 December, 1–2; 10 December, 1–2; 17 December, 1–2; 24 December, 1–2.

1898. "Salomy Jane's Kiss." New York *Sun,* 22 May and 29 May, sec. 3, 7.

1926. *The Letters of Bret Harte.* Edited by Geoffrey Bret Harte. Boston: Houghton Mifflin Company.

1997. *Selected Letters of Bret Harte.* Edited by Gary Scharnhorst. Norman: University of Oklahoma Press.

Hartford Census. 1880. *Population Schedules of the Tenth Census of the United States, 1880. Roll T9. Connecticut: Hartford County.* Photocopy in CU-MARK.

Harvard Directory. 1910. *Harvard University Directory: A Catalogue of Men Now Living Who Have Been Enrolled as Students in the University.* Cambridge: Harvard University.

Harvey, George.

1906. "The Editor's Diary." *North American Review* 183 (21 December): 1321–36.

1907. "The Man Who Ate Babies." *Harper's Weekly* 51 (2 March): 296.

Hawkins, Hunt. 1978. "Mark Twain's Involvement with the Congo Reform Movement: 'A Fury of Generous Indignation.'" *New England Quarterly* 51 (June): 147–75.

HC. Henry Clemens.

Henry of Huntingdon. 1853. *The Chronicle of Henry of Huntingdon. Comprising the History of England, from the Invasion of Julius Caesar to the Accession of Henry II. Also, The Acts of Stephen, King of England and Duke of Normandy.* Translated and edited by Thomas Forester. Bohn's Antiquarian Library. London: Henry G. Bohn.

Herrmann, Dorothy. 1999. *Helen Keller: A Life.* Chicago: University of Chicago Press.

Hershkowitz, Leo. 1977. *Tweed's New York: Another Look.* Garden City, N.Y.: Anchor Press/Doubleday.

HF 2003. 2003. *Adventures of Huckleberry Finn.* Edited by Victor Fischer and Lin Salamo, with the late Walter Blair. The Works of Mark Twain. Berkeley and Los Angeles: University of California Press. Also online at *MTPO.*

HHR. 1969. *Mark Twain's Correspondence with Henry Huttleston Rogers.* Edited by Lewis Leary. The Mark Twain Papers. Berkeley and Los Angeles: University of California Press.

Hicks, Urban E. 1886. *Yakima and Clickitat Indian Wars, 1855 and 1856. Personal Recollections of Capt. U. E. Hicks.* Portland, Ore.: Himes the Printer.

Higbie, Calvin H. 1906. "A Short Description Leading up to my Acquaintance with Saml. L. Clemens, Mark Twain." Two versions survive: Higbie's original MS of forty-six leaves, and a TS, by an unidentified typist, of thirty-four leaves (the version mailed to SLC, with his revisions); CU-MARK.

Hill, Hamlin.

1964. *Mark Twain and Elisha Bliss.* Columbia: University of Missouri Press.

1973. *Mark Twain: God's Fool.* New York: Harper and Row.

Himmelwright, A. L. A. 1906. *The San Francisco Earthquake and Fire: A Brief History of the Disaster.* New York: Roebling Construction Company.

Hirst, Robert H. 1975. "The Making of *The Innocents Abroad:* 1867–1872." Ph.D. diss., University of California, Berkeley.

Hiss, A. Emil, and Albert E. Ebert. 1910. *The New Standard Formulary.* Chicago: G.P. Engelhard and Co.

Hoffmann, Donald. 2006. *Mark Twain in Paradise: His Voyages to Bermuda.* Columbia: University of Missouri Press.

Hoppe, Willie. 1975. *Thirty Years of Billiards.* Edited by Thomas Emmett Crozier. New York: Dover Publications.

Householder, Fred W., Jr. 1936. "Quem Deus Vult Perdere Dementat Prius." *The Classical Weekly* 29 (April): 165–67.

House of Lords. 1900. *Report from the Select Committee of the House of Lords on the Copyright Bill [H. L.] and the Copyright (Artistic) Bill [H. L.]; Together with the Proceedings of the Committee, Minutes of Evidence, and Appendix. Session 1900.* London: Her Majesty's Stationery Office.

Howard, June. 2001. *Publishing the Family.* Durham, N.C.: Duke University Press.

Howard, William K. 1906. "Twenty-five United States Senators Estimated to Be Worth $171,000,000." Washington *Post,* 27 May, SM3.

Howells, William Dean.

1875. "Recent Literature." *Atlantic Monthly* 36 (December): 748–60. Reprinted in Appendix E, "Howells's Review of *Mark Twain's Sketches, New and Old,*" *L6,* 655–58.

1880. "Mark Twain's New Book." *Atlantic Monthly* 45 (May): 686–88.

1881. "New Publications. A Romance by Mark Twain." New York *Tribune,* 25 October, 6.

1884. "The Rise of Silas Lapham." *Century Magazine* 29 (November): 13–26.

1903. "Certain of the Chicago School of Fiction." *North American Review* 176 (May): 734–46.

1910. *My Mark Twain: Reminiscences and Criticisms.* New York: Harper and Brothers.

1919. "Editor's Easy Chair. In Memoriam." *Harper's Monthly Magazine* 140 (December): 133–36.

1928. *Life in Letters of William Dean Howells.* Edited by Mildred Howells. 2 vols. Garden City, N.Y.: Doubleday, Doran and Co.

1979. *W. D. Howells, Selected Letters, Volume 2: 1873–1881.* Edited and annotated by George Arms and Christoph K. Lohmann. Textual editors Christoph K. Lohmann and Jerry Herron. Boston: Twayne Publishers.

1980. *W. D. Howells, Selected Letters, Volume 3: 1882–1891.* Edited and annotated by Robert C. Leitz III, with Richard H. Ballinger and Christoph K. Lohmann. Textual editor Christoph K. Lohmann. Boston: Twayne Publishers.

Hudson Census. 1900. *Population Schedules of the Twelfth Census of the United States, 1900. Roll T623. New Jersey: Hudson County, Jersey City.* Photocopy in CU-MARK.

Hustvedt, Asti. 2011. *Medical Muses: Hysteria in Nineteenth-Century Paris.* New York: W. W. Norton and Co.

IaCrM. Iowa Masonic Library, Cedar Rapids.

Inds. 1989. *Huck Finn and Tom Sawyer among the Indians, and Other Unfinished Stories.* Foreword and notes by Dahlia Armon and Walter Blair. The Mark Twain Library. Berkeley and Los Angeles: University of California Press. Also online at *MTPO.*

Ingersoll, Luther A. 1908. *Ingersoll's Century History: Santa Monica Bay Cities.* Los Angeles: Luther A. Ingersoll.

InU-Li. Indiana University Lilly Rare Books, Bloomington.

James, George Wharton. 1916. *Rose Hartwick Thorpe and the Story of "Curfew Must Not Ring To-night."* Pasadena, Calif.: Radiant Life Press.

James, William. 1983. *Essays in Psychology.* Edited by Frederick H. Burkhardt, Fredson Bowers, and Ignas K. Skrupskelis, with an introduction by William R. Woodward. Cambridge: Harvard University Press.

JC (Jean Lampton Clemens). 1900–1907. *Diaries of Jean L. Clemens, 1900–1907.* 7 vols. MS, CSmH.

Jerome, Robert D., and Herbert A. Wisbey, Jr. 1977. *Mark Twain in Elmira.* Elmira, N.Y.: Mark Twain Society.

JIm. Iwaki Meisei University, Iwaki, Fukushima, Japan.

JLC. Jane Lampton Clemens.

Johnson, Burges. 1952. "A Ghost for Mark Twain." *Atlantic* 189 (May): 65–66.

Johnson, Robert Underwood. 1923. *Remembered Yesterdays.* Boston: Little, Brown and Co.

Johnson, Willis F. 1929. *George Harvey, "A Passionate Patriot."* Boston: Houghton Mifflin Company.

Jordan, David Starr. 1903. *The Call of the Twentieth Century: An Address to Young Men.* Boston: Beacon Press.

Joshi, S. T., and David E. Schultz. 1999. *Ambrose Bierce: An Annotated Bibliography of Primary Sources.* Westport, Conn.: Greenwood Press.

Kanawha Census. 1850. *Population Schedules of the Seventh Census of the United States, 1850. Roll M432. Virginia: Kanawha County.* Photocopy in CU-MARK.

Keller, Helen.

1903. *The Story of My Life.* New York: Doubleday, Page and Co.

2005. *Helen Keller: Selected Writings.* Edited by Kim E. Nielsen. New York: New York University Press.

Keokuk City Directory. 1859. *Lee County Genealogy History.* Submitted and transcribed by Salli Griswold. http://iagenweb.org/lee/data/1859/1859–5.htm. Accessed 13 May 2011.

King, Moses.

1892. *King's Handbook of New York City: An Outline History and Description of the American Metropolis.* Boston: Moses King.

1893. *King's Handbook of New York City: An Outline History and Description of the American Metropolis.* 2d ed. Boston: Moses King.

Kirkham, Samuel. 1835. *English Grammar in Familiar Lectures, Accompanied by a Compendium; Embracing a New Systematick Order of Parsing, a New System of Punctuation, Exercises in False Syntax, and a System of Philosophical Grammar in Notes: To Which Are Added an Appendix, and a Key to the Exercises: Designed for the Use of Schools and Private Learners.* 105th ed. Baltimore: John Plaskitt.

Kittredge, George Lyman. 1904. *The Old Farmer and His Almanack.* Boston: William Ware and Co.

Koenig, Samuel S., comp. 1909. *Manual for the Use of the Legislature of the State of New York.* Albany: J. B. Lyon Company.

Kohn, John S. Van E. 1957. "Mark Twain's *1601.*" *Princeton University Library Chronicle* 18 (Winter): 49–54.

Krass, Peter. 2007. *Ignorance, Confidence, and Filthy Rich Friends: The Business Adventures of Mark Twain, Chronic Speculator and Entrepreneur.* Hoboken: John Wiley and Sons.

Krauth, Leland. 2003. *Mark Twain and Company: Six Literary Relations.* Athens: University of Georgia Press.

Kruse, Horst H. 1992. "Mark Twain's *Nom de Plume:* Some Mysteries Resolved." *Mark Twain Journal* 30 (Spring): 1–32.

L1. 1988. *Mark Twain's Letters, Volume 1: 1853–1866.* Edited by Edgar Marquess Branch, Michael B. Frank, and Kenneth M. Sanderson. The Mark Twain Papers. Berkeley and Los Angeles: University of California Press. Also online at *MTPO.*

L2. 1990. *Mark Twain's Letters, Volume 2: 1867–1868.* Edited by Harriet Elinor Smith, Richard Bucci, and Lin Salamo. The Mark Twain Papers. Berkeley and Los Angeles: University of California Press. Also online at *MTPO.*

L3. 1992. *Mark Twain's Letters, Volume 3: 1869.* Edited by Victor Fischer, Michael B. Frank, and Dahlia Armon. The Mark Twain Papers. Berkeley and Los Angeles: University of California Press. Also online at *MTPO.*

L4. 1995. *Mark Twain's Letters, Volume 4: 1870–1871.* Edited by Victor Fischer, Michael B. Frank, and Lin Salamo. The Mark Twain Papers. Berkeley and Los Angeles: University of California Press. Also online at *MTPO.*

L5. 1997. *Mark Twain's Letters, Volume 5: 1872–1873.* Edited by Lin Salamo and Harriet Elinor Smith. The Mark Twain Papers. Berkeley and Los Angeles: University of California Press. Also online at *MTPO.*

L6. 2002. *Mark Twain's Letters, Volume 6: 1874–1875.* Edited by Michael B. Frank and Harriet Elinor Smith. The Mark Twain Papers. Berkeley and Los Angeles: University of California Press. Also online at *MTPO.*

Letters 1876–1880. 2007. *Mark Twain's Letters, 1876–1880.* Edited by Victor Fischer, Michael B. Frank, and Harriet Elinor Smith, with Sharon K. Goetz, Benjamin Griffin, and Leslie Myrick. *Mark Twain Project Online.* Berkeley and Los Angeles: University of California Press. [To locate a letter text from its citation, select the "Letters" link at http://www.marktwainproject.org, then use the "Date Written" links in the left-hand column.]

Letters NP1. 2010. *Mark Twain's Letters Newly Published 1.* Edited by Victor Fischer, Michael B. Frank, Sharon K. Goetz, and Harriet Elinor Smith. *Mark Twain Project Online.* Berkeley and Los Angeles: University of California Press. [To locate a letter text from its citation, select the "Letters" link at http://www.marktwainproject.org, then use the "Date Written" links in the left-hand column.]

Lamphere, George N. 1881. *The United States Government: Its Organization and Practical Workings.* Philadelphia: J. B. Lippincott and Co.

Lampton, Lucius Marion. 1990. *The Genealogy of Mark Twain.* Jackson, Miss.: Diamond L Publishing.

Landon, Melville D. [Eli Perkins, pseud.].

1898. *Library of Wit and Humor by Mark Twain and Others.* Chicago: Thompson and Thomas.

n.d. *Hot Stuff by Famous Funny Men: Comprising Wit, Humor, Pathos, Ridicule,*

Satires, Dialects, Puns, Conundrums, Riddles, Charades, Jokes and Magic. Chicago: Reilly and Britton Company.

Lang, Andrew. 1886. "At the Sign of the Ship." *Longman's Magazine* 7 (February): 445–46. Reprinted in Anderson and Sanderson 1971, 146–47.

Lang, Herbert O. 1882. *A History of Tuolumne County.* San Francisco: B. F. Alley.

Lanier, Henry Wysham, ed. 1938. *The Players' Book: A Half-Century of Fact, Feeling, Fun and Folklore.* New York: The Players.

Laws.

1862. *Laws of the Territory of Nevada, Passed at the First Regular Session of the Legislative Assembly.* San Francisco: Valentine and Co.

1863. *Laws of the Territory of Nevada, Passed at the Second Regular Session of the Legislative Assembly.* Virginia City: J. T. Goodman and Co.

Lawton, Mary. 1925. *A Lifetime with Mark Twain: The Memories of Katy Leary, for Thirty Years His Faithful and Devoted Servant.* New York: Harcourt, Brace and Co.

LE. 1962. *Letters from the Earth.* Edited by Bernard DeVoto. With a preface by Henry Nash Smith. New York: Harper and Row.

Leary, Lewis, ed. 1961. *Mark Twain's Letters to Mary.* New York: Columbia University Press.

Library of Congress. 2011. "The Eliot Indian Bible: First Bible Printed in America." Library of Congress Bible Collection. Ongoing exhibition, opened 11 April 2008. http://myloc.gov/exhibitions/bibles/pages/objectlist.aspx. Accessed 25 August 2011.

Lindau, Rudolf. 1917. *Morgenland und Abendland.* Mit einer Einleitung von Wilhelm Rath, einem Bilde des Verfassers und 11 Zeichnungen von Franz Müller-Münster. Hamburg-Grossborstel: Verlag der Deutschen Dichter-Gedächtnis-Stiftung.

Little, Mrs. C. M. 1893. *History of the Clan MacFarlane.* Tottenville, N.Y.: Mrs. C. M. Little.

Lomask, Milton. 1982. *Aaron Burr: The Conspiracy and Years of Exile, 1805–1836.* New York: Farrar, Straus, Giroux.

Lossing, Benson J. 1884. *History of New York City, Embracing an Outline Sketch of Events from 1609 to 1830, and a Full Account of Its Development from 1830 to 1884.* New York: A. S. Barnes and Co.

Lyde, Elsie Leslie. 1889. "My Stage Life." With an added note by Lucy C. Lillie. *Cosmopolitan* 6 (February): 372–77.

Lyon, Isabel V.

1903–6. MS journal of seventy-four pages, with entries dated 7 November 1903 to 14 January 1906, CU-MARK.

1905a. Diary in *The Standard Daily Reminder: 1905.* MS notebook of 368 pages, CU-MARK. [Lyon kept two diaries for 1905, this one and Lyon 1905b; some entries appear in both, but each also includes entries not found in the other.]

1905b. Diary in *The Standard Daily Reminder: 1905.* MS notebook of 368 pages, photocopy in CU-MARK. [In 1971 the original diary was owned by Mr. and Mrs.

Robert V. Antenne and Mr. and Mrs. James F. Dorrance, of Rice Lake, Wisconsin; its current location is unknown. Lyon kept two diaries for 1905, this one and Lyon 1905a; some entries appear in both, but each also includes entries not found in the other.]

1906. Diary in *The Standard Daily Reminder: 1906.* MS notebook of 368 pages, CU-MARK.

1907. Diary in *Date Book for 1907.* MS notebook of 368 pages, CU-MARK.

Lystra, Karen. 2004. *Dangerous Intimacy: The Untold Story of Mark Twain's Final Years.* Berkeley and Los Angeles: University of California Press.

Machias Census. 1900. *Population Schedules of the Twelfth Census of the United States, 1900. Roll T623. Maine: Washington County, Machias Township.* Photocopy in CU-MARK.

Mahar, William J. 1999. *Behind the Burnt Cork Mask: Early Blackface Minstrelsy and Antebellum American Popular Culture.* Urbana: University of Illinois Press.

Manhattan Census. 1900. *Population Schedules of the Twelfth Census of the United States, 1900. Roll T623. New York: Manhattan.* Photocopy in CU-MARK.

Marden, Orison Swett, ed. 1907. *The Consolidated Library.* Volume 14, *The Ethics of Business and Inspiration of Daily Life.* Rev. ed. New York: Bureau of National Literature and Art.

Marion Census. 1850. *Population Schedules of the Seventh Census of the United States, 1850. Roll 406. Missouri: Marion, Mercer, Miller, and Mississippi Counties.* National Archives Microfilm Publications, Microcopy no. 432. Washington, D.C.: General Services Administration.

Marshall, Edward. 1910. "Wizard with Amazing Powers Astounds Scientists." New York *Times,* 13 November, SM1–2.

Massachusetts Historical Society. 2011. "Seth Eastman on Dighton Rock." http://www.masshist.org/objects/2011march.php. Accessed 7 September 2011.

Matthews, Brander.

1885. "Huckleberry Finn." *Saturday Review* 59 (31 January): 153–54. Reprinted in Anderson and Sanderson, 121–25.

1896. "The Penalty of Humor." *Harper's New Monthly Magazine* 92 (May): 897–900.

1922. "Memories of Mark Twain." In *The Tocsin of Revolt and Other Essays,* 253–94. New York: Charles Scribner's Sons.

Maurice, Arthur Bartlett. 1908. "The Author's Full Dinner Pail." *Bookman* 28 (December): 326–39.

McKeithan, Daniel Morley. 1961. *The Morgan Manuscript of Mark Twain's "Pudd'nhead Wilson."* Essays and Studies on American Language and Literature, 12. Uppsala: A.-B. Lundequistska Bokhandeln.

McKivigan, John. 2008. *Forgotten Firebrand: James Redpath and the Making of Nineteenth-Century America.* Ithaca: Cornell University Press.

McNay, Dan. 2011. "Helena de Kay Gilder." http://helenadekaygilder.org/index.htm. Accessed 18 May 2011.

MEC. Mary E. (Mollie) Clemens.

Melton, J. Gordon, ed. 2001. *Gale Encyclopedia of Occultism and Parapsychology.* 2 vols. Detroit: Gale Research.

Meyer, Hermann Julius. 1929. *Meyers Lexikon, Band 11.* 7 Auflage. Leipzig: Bibliographisches Institut.

MFai. Millicent Library, Fairhaven, Mass.

MH-H. Harvard University, Houghton Library, Cambridge, Mass.

Mieder, Wolfgang, Stewart A. Kingsbury, and Kelsie B. Harder, eds. 1992. *A Dictionary of American Proverbs.* New York: Oxford University Press.

Miller, Brenda J. 2012. "Bartlett's Tower." http://www.ctvisit.com/travelstories/details/bartlett-s-tower/81. Accessed 6 April 2012.

Miller, James, comp. 1866. *Miller's New York as It Is.* New York: J. Miller. Citations are to the 1975 reprint edition, *The 1866 Guide to New York City.* New York: Schocken Books.

Miller, William C. 1973. "Samuel L. and Orion Clemens vs. Mark Twain and His Biographers (1861–1862)." *Mark Twain Journal* 16 (Summer): 1–9.

Missouri Death Records. 2011. *Missouri Death Records, 1834–1910* [online database]. http://ancestry.com. Accessed 3 October 2011.

Missouri Marriage Records. 2011. *Missouri Marriage Records, 1805–2002* [online database]. http://ancestry.com. Accessed 10 September 2011.

Mitchell, Edward P. 1924. *Memoirs of an Editor: Fifty Years of American Journalism.* New York: Charles Scribner's Sons.

MnHi. Minnesota Historical Society, St. Paul.

Mooney, Michael Macdonald. 1976. *Evelyn Nesbit and Stanford White: Love and Death in the Gilded Age.* New York: William Morrow and Co.

MoPeS. St. Mary's Seminary, Perryville, Mo.

Morgan, James Appleton. 1910. "Concluding Chapter of Dr. Morgan's Autobiography." *New Shakespeareana* 9, nos. 2–3 (May–September): 42–78.

Morris, Roy, Jr. 1995. *Ambrose Bierce: Alone in Bad Company.* New York: Crown Publishers.

Mott, Frank Luther.

1938a. *A History of American Magazines, 1850–1865.* Cambridge: Harvard University Press.

1938b. *A History of American Magazines, 1865–1885.* Cambridge: Harvard University Press.

1950. *American Journalism: A History of Newspapers in the United States through 260 Years, 1690 to 1950.* Rev. ed. New York: Macmillan Company.

MS. Manuscript.

MSM. 1969. *Mark Twain's Mysterious Stranger Manuscripts.* Edited by William M. Gibson. The Mark Twain Papers. Berkeley and Los Angeles: University of California Press.

MTA. 1924. *Mark Twain's Autobiography.* Edited by Albert Bigelow Paine. 2 vols. New York: Harper and Brothers.

MTB. 1912. *Mark Twain: A Biography.* By Albert Bigelow Paine. 3 vols. New York: Harper and Brothers. [Volume numbers in citations are to this edition; page numbers are the same in all editions.]

MTBus. 1946. *Mark Twain, Business Man.* Edited by Samuel Charles Webster. Boston: Little, Brown and Co.

MTE. 1940. *Mark Twain in Eruption.* Edited by Bernard DeVoto. New York: Harper and Brothers.

MTEnt. 1957. *Mark Twain of the "Enterprise."* Edited by Henry Nash Smith, with the assistance of Frederick Anderson. Berkeley and Los Angeles: University of California Press.

MTH. 1947. *Mark Twain and Hawaii.* By Walter Francis Frear. Chicago: Lakeside Press.

MTHL. 1960. *Mark Twain–Howells Letters.* Edited by Henry Nash Smith and William M. Gibson, with the assistance of Frederick Anderson. 2 vols. Cambridge: Belknap Press of Harvard University Press.

MTL. 1917. *Mark Twain's Letters.* Edited by Albert Bigelow Paine. 2 vols. New York: Harper and Brothers.

MTLP. 1967. *Mark Twain's Letters to His Publishers, 1867–1894.* Edited by Hamlin Hill. The Mark Twain Papers. Berkeley and Los Angeles: University of California Press.

MTPO. Mark Twain Project Online. Edited by the Mark Twain Project. Berkeley and Los Angeles: University of California Press. [Launched 1 November 2007.] http://www.marktwainproject.org.

MTTB. 1940. *Mark Twain's Travels with Mr. Brown.* Edited by Franklin Walker and G. Ezra Dane. New York: Alfred A. Knopf.

Murray, Timothy D. 1986. "G. W. Carleton (New York: 1861–1871); G. W. Carleton and Company (New York: 1871–1886)." *Dictionary of Literary Biography, Volume 49: American Literary Publishing Houses, 1638–1899. Part 1: A–M.* Edited by Peter Dzwonkoski. Detroit: Gale Research Company.

"My Sutherland-Wright Ancestry." 2011. Privately compiled genealogy, photocopy in CU-MARK.

N&J1. 1975. *Mark Twain's Notebooks & Journals, Volume 1 (1855–1873).* Edited by Frederick Anderson, Michael B. Frank, and Kenneth M. Sanderson. The Mark Twain Papers. Berkeley and Los Angeles: University of California Press.

N&J2. 1975. *Mark Twain's Notebooks & Journals, Volume 2 (1877–1883).* Edited by Frederick Anderson, Lin Salamo, and Bernard Stein. The Mark Twain Papers. Berkeley and Los Angeles: University of California Press.

N&J3. 1979. *Mark Twain's Notebooks & Journals, Volume 3 (1883–1891).* Edited by Robert Pack Browning, Michael B. Frank, and Lin Salamo. The Mark Twain Papers. Berkeley and Los Angeles: University of California Press.

NAR 1. 1906. "Chapters from My Autobiography.—I. By Mark Twain." *North American Review* 183 (7 September): 321–30. Galley proofs of the "Introduction" only (NAR 1pf) at ViU.

NAR 2. 1906. "Chapters from My Autobiography.—II. By Mark Twain." *North American Review* 183 (21 September): 449–60. Galley proofs (NAR 2pf) at ViU.
NAR 3. 1906. "Chapters from My Autobiography.—III. By Mark Twain." *North American Review* 183 (5 October): 577–89. Galley proofs (NAR 3pf) at ViU.
NAR 4. 1906. "Chapters from My Autobiography.—IV. By Mark Twain." *North American Review* 183 (19 October): 705–16. Galley proofs (NAR 4pf) at ViU.
NAR 5. 1906. "Chapters from My Autobiography.—V. By Mark Twain." *North American Review* 183 (2 November): 833–44. Galley proofs (NAR 5pf) at ViU.
NAR 6. 1906. "Chapters from My Autobiography.—VI. By Mark Twain." *North American Review* 183 (16 November): 961–70. Galley proofs (NAR 6pf) at ViU.
NAR 7. 1906. "Chapters from My Autobiography.—VII. By Mark Twain." *North American Review* 183 (7 December): 1089–95. Galley proofs (NAR 7pf) at ViU.
NAR 8. 1906. "Chapters from My Autobiography.—VIII. By Mark Twain." *North American Review* 183 (21 December): 1217–24. Galley proofs (NAR 8pf) at ViU.
NAR 9. 1907. "Chapters from My Autobiography.—IX. By Mark Twain." *North American Review* 184 (4 January): 1–14. Galley proofs (NAR 9pf) at ViU.
NAR 10. 1907. "Chapters from My Autobiography.—X. By Mark Twain." *North American Review* 184 (18 January): 113–19. Galley proofs (NAR 10pf) at ViU.
NAR 11. 1907. "Chapters from My Autobiography.—XI. By Mark Twain." *North American Review* 184 (1 February): 225–32. Galley proofs (NAR 11pf) at ViU.
NAR 12. 1907. "Chapters from My Autobiography.—XII. By Mark Twain." *North American Review* 184 (15 February): 337–46. Galley proofs (NAR 12pf) at ViU.
NAR 13. 1907. "Chapters from My Autobiography.—XIII. By Mark Twain." *North American Review* 184 (1 March): 449–63. Galley proofs (NAR 13pf) at ViU.
NAR 14. 1907. "Chapters from My Autobiography.—XIV. By Mark Twain." *North American Review* 184 (15 March): 561–71.
NAR 15. 1907. "Chapters from My Autobiography.—XV. By Mark Twain." *North American Review* 184 (5 April): 673–82. Galley proofs (NAR 15pf) at ViU.
NAR 16. 1907. "Chapters from My Autobiography.—XVI. By Mark Twain." *North American Review* 184 (19 April): 785–93.
NAR 17. 1907. "Chapters from My Autobiography.—XVII. By Mark Twain." *North American Review* 184 (3 May): 1–12. Galley proofs (NAR 17pf) at ViU.
NAR 18. 1907. "Chapters from My Autobiography.—XVIII. By Mark Twain." *North American Review* 185 (17 May): 113–22.
NAR 19. 1907. "Chapters from My Autobiography.—XIX. By Mark Twain." *North American Review* 185 (7 June): 241–51. Galley proofs (NAR 19pf) at ViU.
NAR 20. 1907. "Chapters from My Autobiography.—XX. By Mark Twain." *North American Review* 185 (5 July): 465–74.
NAR 21. 1907. "Chapters from My Autobiography—XXI. By Mark Twain." *North American Review* 185 (2 August): 689–98. Galley proofs (NAR 21pf) at ViU.
NAR 22. 1907. "Chapters from My Autobiography.—XXII. By Mark Twain." *North American Review* 186 (September): 8–21.

NAR 23. 1907. "Chapters from My Autobiography.—XXIII. By Mark Twain." *North American Review* 186 (October): 161–73.

NAR 24. 1907. "Chapters from My Autobiography.—XXIV. By Mark Twain." *North American Review* 186 (November): 327–36. Galley proofs (NAR 24pf) at ViU.

NAR 25. 1907. "Chapters from My Autobiography.—XXV. By Mark Twain." *North American Review* 186 (December): 481–94. Galley proofs (NAR 25pf) at ViU.

National Park Service. 2012. *The Civil War Soldiers and Sailors System* [online database]. http://www.nps.gov/civilwar/soldiers-and-sailors-database.htm. Accessed 11 July 2012.

NBolS. Marcella Sembrich Memorial Studio, Bolton Landing, N.Y.

Newark Census. 1880. *Population Schedules of the Tenth Census of the United States, 1880. Roll T9. New Jersey: Essex County, Newark.* Photocopy in CU-MARK.

Nichols, Heidi L. 2004. *The Fashioning of Middle-Class America: "Sartain's Union Magazine of Literature and Art" and Antebellum Culture.* New York: Peter Lang.

NjP-SC. Princeton University, Princeton Special Collection, Princeton, N.J.

NN-BGC. New York Public Library, Albert A. and Henry W. Berg Collection, New York, N.Y.

NNC. Columbia University, New York, N.Y.

NNPM. Pierpont Morgan Library, New York, N.Y.

"Nook Farm Genealogy." 1974. TS by anonymous compiler, CtHSD.

NPV. Jean Webster McKinney Family Papers, Francis Fitz Randolph Rare Book Room, Vassar College Library, Poughkeepsie, N.Y.

NRivd2. Wave Hill House, Riverdale, Bronx, N.Y.

Ober, K. Patrick. 2003. *Mark Twain and Medicine: "Any Mummery Will Cure."* Columbia: University of Missouri Press.

OC. Orion Clemens.

O'Connor, Richard. 1966. *Bret Harte: A Biography.* Boston: Little, Brown and Co.

Odell, George C. D. 1927–49. *Annals of the New York Stage.* 15 vols. New York: Columbia University Press.

OLC. Olivia (Livy) Langdon Clemens.

OLL. Olivia (Livy) Louise Langdon.

Orr, Charles. 1906. "An Unpublished Masterpiece." *Putnam's Monthly and The Critic* 1 (November): 250–51.

OSC (Olivia Susan [Susy] Clemens).

1885–86. Untitled biography of her father, MS of 131 pages, annotated by SLC, ViU. Published in OSC 1985, 83–225; in part in *MTA,* vol. 2, passim; and in Salsbury 1965, passim.

1985. *Papa: An Intimate Biography of Mark Twain.* Edited by Charles Neider. Garden City, N.Y.: Doubleday and Co.

Oxenham, Erica. 1946. *Scrap-Book of J. O.* London: Longmans, Green and Co.

PAM. Pamela Ann Moffett.

P&P. 1979. *The Prince and the Pauper.* Edited by Victor Fischer and Lin Salamo with the

assistance of Mary Jane Jones. The Works of Mark Twain. Berkeley and Los Angeles: University of California Press.
Parmet, Herbert S., and Marie B. Hecht. 1967. *Aaron Burr: Portrait of an Ambitious Man.* New York: Macmillan Company.
Patterson, Homer L. 1908. *Patterson's College and School Directory of the United States and Canada.* Chicago: American Educational Company.
Payne, Darwin. 2007. "Literary Connections: Mark Twain, Katherine Anne Porter, William A. Owens, and Tennessee Williams." *Legacies: A History Journal for Dallas* 19 (Spring): 40–51.
Peattie, Elia W. 1907. "Socialistic Romance with Haymarket Riot as Culmination." Chicago *Tribune,* 16 March, 9.
Pforzheimer. Collection of Walter L. Pforzheimer.
Phelps, Elizabeth Stuart. 1964. *The Gates Ajar.* Edited by Helen Sootin Smith. The John Harvard Library. Cambridge: Belknap Press of Harvard University Press.
Phelps, Roswell F. 1941. "Sumner B. Pearmain, 1859–1941." *Journal of the American Statistical Association* 36 (December): 545–46.
Phillips, Michael J. 1920. "Mark Twain's Partner." *Saturday Evening Post* 193 (11 September): 22–23, 69–70, 73–74.
Portsmouth Census. 1860. *Population Schedules of the Eighth Census of the United States, 1860. Roll M653. New Hampshire: Rockingham County, Portsmouth Township.* Photocopy in CU-MARK.
Rasmussen, R. Kent.
2007. *Critical Companion to Mark Twain: A Literary Reference to His Life and Work.* 2 vols. New York: Facts on File.
2013. *Dear Mark Twain.* Berkeley and Los Angeles: University of California Press.
Reece, John Holroyd. 1937. *The Harvest: Being the Record of One Hundred Years of Publishing, 1837–1937.* Leipzig: Tauchnitz.
Rees, Thomas. 1908. *Sixty Days in Europe and What We Saw There.* Springfield, Ill.: State Register Company.
Reynolds, Cuyler, ed. 1911. *Hudson-Mohawk Genealogical and Family Memoirs.* 4 vols. New York: Lewis Historical Publishing Company.
RGB/CL. 2011. "Essay on Chase's 'Little Lord Fauntleroy.'" Spanierman Gallery, New York. http://www.spanierman.com/Chase,-William-Merritt/essay/top/Essay. Accessed 10 March 2011.
Rhodes, James Ford. 1922. *The McKinley and Roosevelt Administrations, 1897–1909.* New York: Macmillan.
RI 1993. 1993. *Roughing It.* Edited by Harriet Elinor Smith, Edgar Marquess Branch, Lin Salamo, and Robert Pack Browning. The Works of Mark Twain. Berkeley and Los Angeles: University of California Press. [This edition supersedes the one published in 1972.]
Rice, Clarence C. 1925. "Mark Twain's Doctor Tells How Wit Won Humorist His Wife." Boston *Sunday Globe,* 29 November, unknown page.

Rice, Edward Le Roy. 1911. *Monarchs of Minstrelsy, from "Daddy" Rice to Date.* New York: Kenny Publishing Company.

Richards, James Howard. 1983. "Music and the Reed Organ in the Life of Mark Twain." *American Music* 1 (Fall): 38–47.

Richardson, John. 2001. *The Sorcerer's Apprentice: Picasso, Provence, and Douglas Cooper.* Chicago: University of Chicago Press.

Richardson, Robert. 1893. *Willow and Wattle: Poems.* Edinburgh: John Grant.

Richmond Then and Now. 2011. "Richmond Theatre Fire." http://richmondthenandnow.com/Newspaper-Articles/Richmond-Theatre-Fire.html. Accessed 5 August 2011.

Riverdale Census. 1900. *Population Schedules of the Twelfth Census of the United States, 1900. Roll T623. New York: Bronx Borough, Riverdale.* Photocopy in CU-MARK.

Rocha, Guy. 2000. "Sell the Sizzle and Not the Steak: Mark Twain in Carson City." http://nsla.nevadaculture.org/index.php?option = com_content&task = view&id = 726&Itemid = 418. Accessed 3 January 2012.

Rolfe, W. J. 1890. "The So-Called Gunther Autograph of Shakespeare." *The Critic,* 8 March, 117.

Rood, Henry Edward. 1895. "New York Letter." *Literary World* 26 (6 April): 104–5.

Rose, William Ganson. 1950. *Cleveland: The Making of a City.* Cleveland: World Publishing Company.

Rossum, Ralph A. 2001. *Federalism, the Supreme Court, and the Seventeenth Amendment: The Irony of Constitutional Democracy.* Lanham, Md.: Lexington Books.

RPB-JH. Brown University, John Hay Library of Rare Books and Special Collections, Providence, R.I.

Rubin, Louis D. 1969. *George W. Cable: The Life and Times of a Southern Heretic.* New York: Pegasus.

Salm. Collection of Peter A. Salm.

Salsbury, Edith Colgate, ed. 1965. *Susy and Mark Twain: Family Dialogues.* New York: Harper and Row.

Samon, Jud. 1979. "Sagebrush Falstaff: A Biographical Sketch of James Warren Nye." Ph.D. diss., University of Maryland.

San Francisco Census. 1900. *Population Schedules of the Twelfth Census of the United States, 1900. Roll T623. California: San Francisco.* Photocopy in CU-MARK.

San Francisco Mortality Schedules. 1870. *U.S. Federal Census Mortality Schedules, 1850–1885. Roll T655. California: San Francisco.* Photocopy in CU-MARK.

Satre, Lowell J. 2005. *Chocolate on Trial: Slavery, Politics, and the Ethics of Business.* Athens: Ohio University Press.

Saturday Morning Club. 1976. *One Hundred Years of the Saturday Morning Club of Hartford.* Hartford: Saturday Morning Club.

Scharf, J. Thomas. 1883. *History of St. Louis City and County, from the Earliest Periods to the Present Day.* 2 vols. Philadelphia: Louis H. Everts and Co.

Scharnhorst, Gary.
1995. *Bret Harte: A Bibliography.* Scarecrow Author Bibliographies, no. 95. Lanham, Md.: Scarecrow Press.
2000a. *Bret Harte: Opening the American Literary West.* Volume 17 in *The Oklahoma Western Biographies,* edited by Richard W. Etulain. Norman: University of Oklahoma Press.
2000b. "'I Do Not Write This in Anger': Bret Harte's Letters to His Sister, 1871–93." *Resources for American Literary Study* 26 (no. 2): 200–222.
2006. *Mark Twain: The Complete Interviews.* Tuscaloosa: University of Alabama Press.
2010. "The 'Lorio' Letters to the *St. Louis Daily Reveille:* On Mark Twain, Minstrelsy, Mesmerism, and McDowell's Cave." *Resources for American Literary Study* 33:277–84.
Schmidt, Barbara.
2002. "Frank Fuller, *The* American, Revisited." *Twainian* 58 (March): 1–3.
2009. "Mark Twain's Angel-Fish Roster and Other Young Women of Interest." http://www.twainquotes.com/angelfish/angelfish.html. Accessed 20 May 2009.
2010. "A History of and Guide to Uniform Editions of Mark Twain's Works." http://www.twainquotes.com/UniformEds/toc.html. Accessed 19 November 2010.
2011. "Mark Twain's Juggernaut Club Correspondence—The Helene Picard Letters." http://www.twainquotes.com/picard.html. Accessed 12 April 2011.
Schoenbaum, S. 1991. *Shakespeare's Lives.* New ed. Oxford: Clarendon Press.
Scott, Charles P. G. 1905. "A Declaration of Independence: A Promise as to Twelve Words." N.p.
Seville, Catherine. 2006. *The Internationalisation of Copyright Law: Books, Buccaneers and the Black Flag in the Nineteenth Century.* Cambridge: Cambridge University Press.
Shelden, Michael. 2010. *Mark Twain, Man in White: The Grand Adventure of His Final Years.* New York: Random House.
SLC (Samuel Langhorne Clemens).
1852a. "Blabbing Government Secrets!" Hannibal *Weekly Journal,* 16 September, 2.
1852b. "Editorial Agility." Hannibal *Weekly Journal,* 16 September, 2.
1852c. "Historical Exhibition—A No. 1 Ruse." Hannibal *Weekly Journal,* 16 September, 2. Reprinted in *ET&S1,* 78–82.
1852d. "'Local' Resolves to Commit Suicide." Hannibal *Weekly Journal,* 16 September, 2. Reprinted in *ET&S1,* 72–75.
1852e. "Pictur' Department." Hannibal *Weekly Journal,* 16 September, 2. Reprinted in *ET&S1,* 72–74, 76–77.
1855–56. "Jul'us Caesar." MS of fourteen pages on four folios, NPV. Published in *ET&S1,* 110–17.
1856a. "Correspondence." Letter dated 18 October. Keokuk *Saturday Post,* 1 November, 4. Reprinted in SLC 1928, 3–16.

1856b. "Snodgrass' Ride on the Railroad." Letter dated 14 November. Keokuk *Post,* 29 November, 2, and Keokuk *Saturday Post,* 6 December, 4. Reprinted in SLC 1928, 19–33.

1857. "Snodgrass, in a Adventure." Letter dated 14 March. Keokuk *Post,* 10 April, 2, and Keokuk *Saturday Post,* 18 April, 4. Reprinted in SLC 1928, 37–48.

1859. "River Intelligence." New Orleans *Crescent,* 17 May, 7. Reprinted in *ET&S1,* 126–33.

1862a. "Letter from Carson City." Letter dated 5 December. Virginia City *Territorial Enterprise,* 8? December, clipping in Scrapbook 1:60, CU-MARK. Reprinted in *MTEnt,* 35–38.

1862b. "Letter from Carson City." Letter dated 12 December. Virginia City *Territorial Enterprise,* 15? December, clipping in Scrapbook 1:60, CU-MARK. Reprinted in *MTEnt,* 39–41.

1863a. "Letter from Carson City." Letter dated "Saturday Night" (31? January). Virginia City *Territorial Enterprise,* 3? February, clipping in Scrapbook 4:11, CU-MARK. Reprinted in *ET&S1,* 192–98.

1863b. "Ye Sentimental Law Student." Virginia City *Territorial Enterprise,* 19 February. Reprinted in *ET&S1,* 215–19.

1865a. "The Only Reliable Account of the Celebrated Jumping Frog of Calaveras County." MS of eleven leaves, written between 1 September and 16 October, NPV. Published in *ET&S2,* 262–78.

1865b. "The Cruel Earthquake." Gold Hill *News,* 13 October, 2, reprinting the Virginia City *Territorial Enterprise* of 10–11 October. Reprinted in *ET&S2,* 289–93.

1865c. "Popper Defieth Ye Earthquake." Virginia City *Territorial Enterprise,* 15–31 October, clipping in the Yale Scrapbook, CtY-BR, 38A–39. Reprinted in *ET&S2,* 294–96.

1865d. "Earthquake Almanac." San Francisco *Dramatic Chronicle,* 17 October, 3. Reprinted in *ET&S2,* 297–99.

1865e. "Jim Smiley and His Jumping Frog." New York *Saturday Press* 4 (18 November): 248–49. Reprinted in *ET&S2,* 282–88.

1865f. "The Great Earthquake in San Francisco." New York *Weekly Review* 16 (25 November): 5. Reprinted in *ET&S2,* 300–310.

1866a. "Letter from Honolulu." Letter dated 25 June. Sacramento *Union,* 19 July, 1. Reprinted in *MTH,* 335–47.

1866b. "Forty-three Days in an Open Boat." *Harper's New Monthly Magazine* 34 (December): 104–13.

1867a. *The Celebrated Jumping Frog of Calaveras County, and Other Sketches.* Edited by John Paul. New York: C. H. Webb.

1867b. "Letter from 'Mark Twain.'" Letter dated 16 April. San Francisco *Alta California,* 26 May, 1. Reprinted in *MTTB,* 141–48.

1867c. "Letter from 'Mark Twain.'" Letter dated 17 May. San Francisco *Alta California,* 16 June, 1. Reprinted in *MTTB,* 167–79.

1868a. "Letter from Mark Twain." Letter dated 2 May. Chicago *Republican,* 31 May, 2.
1868b. "Letter from Mark Twain." Letter dated 17 August. Chicago *Republican,* 23 August, 2.
1869. *The Innocents Abroad; or, The New Pilgrims' Progress.* Hartford: American Publishing Company.
1870a. "Disgraceful Persecution of a Boy." *Galaxy* 9 (May): 722–24.
1870b. "Goldsmith's Friend Abroad Again." *Galaxy* 10 (October): 569–71.
1871. "Memoranda." *Galaxy* 11 (April): 615–18. Includes: "Valedictory," "My First Literary Venture," "About a Remarkable Stranger."
1873–74. *The Gilded Age: A Tale of To-day.* Charles Dudley Warner, coauthor. Hartford: American Publishing Company. [Early copies bound with 1873 title page, later ones with 1874 title page: see *BAL,* 2:3357.]
1876–85. "A Record of the Small Foolishnesses of Susie & 'Bay' Clemens (Infants)." MS of 111 pages, "begun in August 1876 at 'Quarry Farm,'" ViU.
1877–78. "Some Rambling Notes of an Idle Excursion." *Atlantic Monthly* 40 (October–December 1877): 443–47, 586–92, 718–24; *Atlantic Monthly* 41 (January 1878): 12–19.
1880a. *[Date, 1601.] Conversation, as It Was by the Social Fireside, in the Time of the Tudors.* [Cleveland: privately printed.]
1880b. *A Tramp Abroad.* Hartford: American Publishing Company.
1881. "—He is gone. . . ." Untitled piece in "The Contributors' Club." *Atlantic Monthly* 48 (November): 716–17.
1882a. *Date 1601. Conversation, as It Was by the Social Fireside, in the Time of the Tudors.* [West Point, N.Y.]: Done att Ye Academie Presse.
1882b. *The Stolen White Elephant, Etc.* Boston: James R. Osgood and Co.
1882c. "Twichell and the profane ostler." MS of nineteen leaves, numbered 429–47, deleted by SLC from chapter 34 of *Life on the Mississippi,* CU-MARK. Published in *MTE,* 366–72, mistakenly identified as "one of the random pieces that preceded Mark's sustained work on the *Autobiography.*"
1883. *Life on the Mississippi.* Boston: James R. Osgood and Co.
1884. "Taming the Bicycle." MS of eighty leaves, NPV. Published in SLC 1917, 285–96.
1885a. *Adventures of Huckleberry Finn.* New York: Charles L. Webster and Co.
1885b. "'What Ought He to Have Done?': Mark Twain's Opinion." *Christian Union* 32 (16 July): 4–5.
1887. "A Petition to the Queen of England." *Harper's New Monthly Magazine* 76 (December): 157–58. Reprinted in Budd 1992a, 922–26.
1888. *Mark Twain's Library of Humor.* New York: Charles L. Webster and Co.
1891a. "Struwwelpeter or Happy Tales and Funny Pictures. Freely Translated by Mark Twain." From the German of Heinrich Hoffmann. MS of twenty-six leaves, CtY-BR. Published in SLC 1935.

1891b. "Luck." *Harper's New Monthly Magazine* 83 (August): 407–9. Reprinted in SLC 1892a.

1892a. *Merry Tales.* New York: Charles L. Webster and Co.

1892b. *The American Claimant.* New York: Charles L. Webster and Co.

1892c. "The Tragedy of Pudd'nhead Wilson and the Comedy Those Extraordinary Twins." MS of 124 leaves, NN-BGC, and MS of six leaves rejected from the longer MS, NNPM.

1895–96. "Personal Recollections of Joan of Arc." *Harper's New Monthly Magazine* 90 (April): 680–99; (May): 845–58; 91 (June): 82–94; (July) 227–39; (August): 456–67; (September): 543–55; (October): 743–53; (November): 879–94; 92 (December): 135–50; (January): 288–306; (February): 432–45; (March): 585–97; (April): 655–73.

1896. *Personal Recollections of Joan of Arc.* New York: Harper and Brothers.

1897. "James Hammond Trumbull. The Tribute of a Neighbor." *Century Magazine* 55 (November): 154–55.

1898. "My Platonic Sweetheart." MS of fifty-eight leaves, written in July, CU-MARK. Published in *Harper's Monthly Magazine* 126 (December 1912): 14–20 and Budd 1992b, 284–96.

1899a. "Samuel Langhorne Clemens." MS of fourteen leaves, notes written in March for Samuel E. Moffett to use in preparing a biographical sketch, NN-BGC.

1899b. "Jean's Illness." Untitled MS of nine leaves, written 5 August, CU-MARK.

1899c. "Christian Science and the Book of Mrs. Eddy." *Cosmopolitan* 27 (October): 585–94.

1901. "The Death-Disk." *Harper's Monthly Magazine* 104 (December): 19–26.

1901–2a. "Footnotes to Susy's Biography." Untitled MS of thirty-two leaves, ViU.

1901–2b. Untitled MS of one leaf, excised from SLC 1901–2a ("Footnotes to Susy's Biography"), CU-MARK.

1902a. "A Double-Barrelled Detective Story." *Harper's Monthly Magazine* 104 (January–February): 254–70, 429–41.

1902b. "Does the Race of Man Love a Lord?" *North American Review* 174 (April): 433–44.

1902c. "Christian Science." *North American Review* 175 (December): 756–68.

1902d. "Was It Heaven? Or Hell?" *Harper's Monthly Magazine* 106 (December): 11–20.

1903a. "As Regards the Company's Benevolences." TS of four leaves, CU-MARK. Published in *HHR,* 533–34.

1903b. "Christian Science—II." *North American Review* 176 (January): 1–9.

1903c. "Christian Science—III." *North American Review* 176 (February): 173–84.

1903d. "Mrs. Eddy in Error." *North American Review* 176 (April): 505–17.

1903e. "Why Not Abolish It?" *Harper's Weekly* 47 (2 May): 732. Reprinted in Budd 1992b, 550–53.

1903f. "A Dog's Tale." *Harper's Monthly Magazine* 108 (December): 11–19.

1905a. *King Leopold's Soliloquy: A Defense of His Congo Rule.* Boston: P. R. Warren Company. Reprinted in Budd 1992b, 661–86.
1905b. "Concerning Copyright. An Open Letter to the Register of Copyrights." *North American Review* 180 (January): 1–8. Reprinted in Budd 1992b, 627–34.
1905c. "The Czar's Soliloquy." *North American Review* 180 (March): 321–26.
1905d. "From My Unpublished Autobiography." *Harper's Weekly* 49 (18 March): 391. Reprinted as "Mark Twain Was Pioneer in Use of Typewriter," Atlanta *Constitution,* 3 April, 6, and as "The First Writing-Machines" in SLC 1906f, 166–70.
1905e. "As Concerns Interpreting the Deity." MS of thirty-two leaves and TS of twenty-four leaves, written in June and typed later in the summer, CU-MARK. Published in SLC 1917, 265–74, and *WIM,* 109–20.
1905f. "Christian Citizenship." *Collier's, The National Weekly,* 2 September, 17. Reprinted in Budd 1992b, 658–60.
1906a. *Eve's Diary: Translated from the Original MS.* New York: Harper and Brothers.
1906b. *Mark Twain's Library of Humor: A Little Nonsense.* New York: Harper and Brothers.
1906c. *Mark Twain's Library of Humor: Men and Things.* New York: Harper and Brothers.
1906d. *Mark Twain's Library of Humor: The Primrose Way.* New York: Harper and Brothers.
1906e. *Mark Twain's Library of Humor: Women and Things.* New York: Harper and Brothers.
1906f. *The $30,000 Bequest and Other Stories.* New York: Harper and Brothers.
1906g. "William Dean Howells." *Harper's Monthly Magazine* 113 (July): 221–25. Reprinted in Budd 1992b, 722–30.
1906h. "A Horse's Tale." *Harper's Monthly Magazine* 113 (August–September): 327–42, 539–49.
1906i. "Statement of Mr. Samuel L. Clemens." Speech made on 7 December before the Senate and House Committees on Patents. In U.S. Congress 1906, 116–21.
1906j. "Mark Twain Soliloquizes on 'Being Good' and Decides to Let 'Good Enough' Alone." *Harper's Weekly* 50 (15 December): 1790–91.
1907a. *Christian Science, with Notes Containing Corrections to Date.* New York: Harper and Brothers. Reprinted in *WIM,* 215–397.
1907b. *A Horse's Tale.* New York: Harper and Brothers.
1907–8. "Extract from Captain Stormfield's Visit to Heaven." *Harper's Monthly Magazine* 116 (December 1907): 41–49; (January 1908): 266–76.
1909a. "A Simplified Alphabet." MS of fifteen leaves, CU-MARK. Published in SLC 1917, 256–64.
1909b. *Extract from Captain Stormfield's Visit to Heaven.* New York: Harper and Brothers.
1909c. *Is Shakespeare Dead? From My Autobiography.* New York: Harper and Brothers.

1910. "The Turning Point of My Life." *Harper's Bazar* 44 (February): 118–19. Reprinted in Budd 1992b, 929–38, and *WIM,* 455–64.
1916. *The Mysterious Stranger: A Romance.* New York: Harper and Brothers.
1917. *What Is Man? And Other Essays.* New York: Harper and Brothers.
1922a. "Unpublished Chapters from the Autobiography of Mark Twain: Part II." *Harper's Monthly Magazine* 144 (March): 455–60.
1922b. "Unpublished Chapters from the Autobiography of Mark Twain." *Harper's Monthly Magazine* 145 (August): 310–15.
1923a. *Europe and Elsewhere.* With an appreciation by Brander Matthews and an introduction by Albert Bigelow Paine. New York: Harper and Brothers.
1923b. *Mark Twain's Speeches.* With an introduction by Albert Bigelow Paine and an appreciation by William Dean Howells. New York: Harper and Brothers.
1928. *The Adventures of Thomas Jefferson Snodgrass.* Edited by Charles Honce, with a foreword by Vincent Starrett, and a note on "A Celebrated Village Idiot" by James O'Donnell Bennett. Chicago: Pascal Covici.
1935. *Slovenly Peter (Struwwelpeter), or Happy Tales and Funny Pictures, Freely Translated by Mark Twain.* From the German of Heinrich Hoffmann. New York: Harper and Brothers.
1939. *Mark Twain's Conversation as It Was by the Social Fireside in the Time of the Tudors.* Embellished with an Illuminating Introduction, Facetious Footnotes and a Bibliography by Franklin J. Meine. Chicago: privately printed for the Mark Twain Society of Chicago.
1961. *"Ah Sin." A Dramatic Work by Mark Twain and Bret Harte.* Edited by Frederick Anderson. San Francisco: Book Club of California.
1963. "Reflections on Religion." Edited by Charles Neider. *Hudson Review* 16 (Autumn): 329–52.
1996a. *Christian Science.* Foreword by Shelley Fisher Fishkin. Introduction by Garry Wills. Afterword by Hamlin Hill. The Oxford Mark Twain. New York: Oxford University Press.
1996b. *1601, and Is Shakespeare Dead?* Foreword by Shelley Fisher Fishkin. Introduction by Erica Jong. Afterword by Leslie A. Fiedler. The Oxford Mark Twain. New York: Oxford University Press.
1996c. *The Stolen White Elephant and Other Detective Stories.* Foreword by Shelley Fisher Fishkin. Introduction by Walter Mosley. Afterword by Lillian S. Robinson. The Oxford Mark Twain. New York: Oxford University Press.
2001. *A Murder, a Mystery, and a Marriage.* Foreword and afterword by Roy Blount, Jr. New York: W. W. Norton and Co.
2002. "Copyright in Perpetuity." *The Green Bag,* 2d ser., 6 (Autumn): 109–15.
2004. *Mark Twain's Helpful Hints for Good Living: A Handbook for the Damned Human Race.* Edited by Lin Salamo, Victor Fischer, and Michael B. Frank. Berkeley and Los Angeles: University of California Press.

2007. *Mark Twain's Civil War.* Edited by David Rachels. Lexington: University Press of Kentucky.
2009a. *Who Is Mark Twain?* Edited, with a note on the text, by Robert H. Hirst. New York: HarperStudio.
2009b. "Hell or San Francisco: In Which the Author Recalls the 'Great Earthquake of 1865' in the Wake of a Much Greater One in 1906." *California* 120 (March–April): 28–29.
2009c. "The Prince and the President: In Which the Author Recalls Meetings with Edward, Prince of Wales and Ulysses S. Grant." *California* 120 (March–April): 43–46.
2010a. *Mark Twain's Book of Animals.* Edited by Shelley Fisher Fishkin. Berkeley and Los Angeles: University of California Press.
2010b. "The Palm Readers." *Playboy* 57 (December): 84–86.

Smiles, Samuel. 1857. *The Life of George Stephenson, Railway Engineer.* London: John Murray.

Smith, Jean Edward. 2001. *Grant.* New York: Simon and Schuster.

Social Register. 1902. *Social Register, Summer 1902.* New York: Social Register Association.

Sondhaus, Lawrence. 2002. *Navies of Europe, 1815–2002.* London: Longman.

Sotheby. 2003. *The Mark Twain Collection of Nick Karanovich.* Sale of 19 June. New York: Sotheby and Co.

Spears, John R. 1908. *A History of the United States Navy.* New York: Charles Scribner's Sons.

Staver, Addie Johnstone, comp. 1938. "Marriage Records. Copy of the Original Records of Marriage by Rev. Thomas K. Beecher of Park Church, Elmira, New York, from 1854 to 1900." Copied for Chemung Chapter of Daughters of the American Revolution. Photocopy in CU-MARK.

Stead, William T. 1895. "Character Reading by Palmistry and Otherwise." *Borderland* 2 (January): 60–64.

Stedman, Edmund Clarence, and Ellen Mackay Hutchinson, comps. and eds. 1888–90. *A Library of American Literature from the Earliest Settlement to the Present Time.* 11 vols. New York: Charles L. Webster and Co.

Stern, Madeleine B.
1969. "Mark Twain Had His Head Examined." *American Literature* 41 (May): 207–18.
1971. *Heads and Headlines: The Phrenological Fowlers.* Norman: University of Oklahoma Press.

Stewart, A. A., comp. 1912. *The Printer's Dictionary of Technical Terms.* Boston: School of Printing, North End Union.

Stewart, George R., Jr. 1931. *Bret Harte: Argonaut and Exile.* Boston: Houghton Mifflin Company.

Stoneley, Peter. 1992. *Mark Twain and the Feminine Aesthetic.* Cambridge: Cambridge University Press.

Suetonius Tranquillus, C. 1876. *The Lives of The Twelve Cæsars. By C. Suetonius Tranquillus; to Which Are Added, His Lives of the Grammarians, Rhetoricians, and Poets.* Translated by Alexander Thomson. Revised and corrected by T. Forester. Bohn's Classical Library. London: George Bell and Sons. SLC copy in CU-MARK.

Swiderski, Richard M. 2009. *Calomel in America: Mercurial Panacea, War, Song and Ghosts.* Boca Raton: BrownWalker Press.

Tannenbaum, Samuel A. 1927. *Problems in Shakspere's Penmanship: Including a Study of the Poet's Will.* New York: Century Company, for the Modern Language Association of America.

Teller, Charlotte. 1925. *S.L.C. to C.T.* New York: privately printed.

Tennyson, Alfred. 1842. *Poems.* 2 vols. London: Edward Moxon.

Terry, Ellen. 1908. *The Story of My Life: Recollections and Reflections.* New York: McClure Company.

Thieme, Otto Charles, et al. 1993. *With Grace and Favour: Victorian and Edwardian Fashion in America.* Cincinnati: Cincinnati Art Museum.

Thomas, Joseph D., and Jay Avila, eds. 2003. *A Picture Postcard History of Fairhaven.* New Bedford: Spinner Publications.

Thompson, Slason. 1907. *Railway Statistics of the United States of America for the Year Ending June 30, 1906. Compared with the Official Reports of 1905 and Recent Statistics of Foreign Railways.* Chicago: Gunthorp-Warren Printing Company.

Timlow, Heman R. 1875. *Ecclesiastical and Other Sketches of Southington, Conn.* Hartford: Case, Lockwood and Brainard Company.

Towner, Ausburn [Ishmael, pseud.]. 1892. *Our County and Its People: A History of the Valley and County of Chemung from the Closing Years of the Eighteenth Century.* Syracuse, N.Y.: D. Mason and Co.

Trevelyan, G. Otto. 1876. *The Life and Letters of Lord Macaulay.* 2 vols. London: Longmans, Green and Co.

Trombley, Laura Skandera. 2010. *Mark Twain's Other Woman: The Hidden Story of His Final Years.* New York: Alfred A. Knopf.

TS. Typescript.

TS. 1980. *The Adventures of Tom Sawyer; Tom Sawyer Abroad; and Tom Sawyer, Detective.* Edited by John C. Gerber, Paul Baender, and Terry Firkins. The Works of Mark Twain. Berkeley and Los Angeles: University of California Press.

Tuckey, John S. 1963. *Mark Twain and Little Satan.* West Lafayette, Ind.: Purdue University Studies.

Turner, Arlin. 1956. *George Washington Cable: A Biography.* Durham, N.C.: Duke University Press.

Twichell, Joseph H. 1874–1916. "Personal Journal." MS of twelve volumes, Joseph H. Twichell Collection, CtY-BR.

TxU-Hu. Harry Ransom Humanities Research Center, University of Texas, Austin.

UkBrH. Brighton and Hove Libraries, Rare Books and Special Collections, Hove, Sussex, England.

UkOxU. Oxford University, Bodleian Library, Oxford, England.

UkReU. University of Reading Library, Whiteknights, Reading, Berkshire, England.

Union League Club. 1916. *The Union League Club of New York.* New York: Knickerbocker Press (G. P. Putnam's Sons).

University Art Galleries. 1985. *A Circle of Friends: Art Colonies of Cornish and Dublin.* Durham: University Art Galleries, University of New Hampshire.

U.S. and International Marriage Records. 2011. *U.S. and International Marriage Records, 1560–1900* [online database]. http://ancestry.com. Accessed 4 August 2011.

U.S. Army Center of Military History. 2011. "U.S. Army Five-Star Generals." http://www.history.army.mil/html/faq/5star.html. Accessed 21 January 2011.

U.S. Congress. 1906. *Copyright Hearings, December 7 to 11, 1906. Arguments before the Committees on Patents of the Senate and House of Representatives, Conjointly, on the Bills S. 6330 and H.R. 19853.* Washington, D.C.: Government Printing Office.

U.S. Government Printing Office.

1884. *Exercises at the Ceremony of Unveiling the Statue of John Marshall, Chief Justice of the United States, in Front of the Capitol, Washington, May 10, 1884. . . . With the Proceedings of the Philadelphia Bar Relating to the Monument to Chief Justice Marshall.* Washington, D.C.: Government Printing Office.

1906. *Simplified Spelling. For the Use of Government Departments.* Washington, D.C.: Government Printing Office.

U.S. National Archives and Records Administration.

1795–1905. *Passport Applications.* Microfilm Serial: M1372. Photocopy in CU-MARK.

1877–1907. *Emergency Passport Applications (Passports Issued Abroad).* Microfilm Serial: M1834. Photocopy in CU-MARK.

1907–9. *Fentress Land Co. et al. v. Bruno Gernt et al.* Civil Case No. 967, Circuit Court of the United States for the Southern Division of the Eastern District of Tennessee, Southeast Region Archives, Morrow, Ga.

Varble, Rachel M. 1964. *Jane Lampton Clemens: The Story of Mark Twain's Mother.* Garden City, N.Y.: Doubleday and Co.

Vining, E. P. 1887. "The Gunther Folio and Autograph." *Shakespeariana* 4:154–59.

ViU. University of Virginia, Charlottesville.

Vogel, Dan. 2006. *Mark Twain's Jews.* Jersey City, N.J.: KTAV Publishing House.

VtMiM. Middlebury College, Middlebury, Vt.

Wakeman, Edgar. 1878. *The Log of an Ancient Mariner. Being the Life and Adventures of Captain Edgar Wakeman.* Edited by Minnie Wakeman-Curtis. San Francisco: A. L. Bancroft and Co.

Wakeman, Robert P. 1900. *Wakeman Genealogy. 1630–1899.* Meriden, Conn.: Journal Publishing Company.

Waltz, Robert B., and David G. Engle. 2011. "The Traditional Ballad Index: An Annotated Bibliography of the Folk Songs of the English-Speaking World." http://www.csufresno.edu/folklore/BalladSearch.html. Accessed 21 March 2011.

Washington Census. 1900. *Population Schedules of the Twelfth Census of the United States, 1900. Roll T623. Washington: District of Columbia.* Photocopy in CU-MARK.

Watson, Aaron. 1907. *The Savage Club: A Medley of History, Anecdote and Reminiscence . . . With a Chapter by Mark Twain.* London: T. Fisher Unwin.

Watson, Thomas A. 1926. *Exploring Life. The Autobiography of Thomas A. Watson.* New York: D. Appleton and Co.

Wave Hill. 2011. "A Brief History of Wave Hill: 1843–1903." http://wavehill.org/about/history.html. Accessed 8 March 2011.

W.C.T.U.

1913. *Report of the Ninth Convention of the World's Woman's Christian Temperance Union.* N.p.

2011. "Early History." http://www.wctu.org/earlyhistory.html. Accessed 17 August 2011.

Wecter, Dixon.

1941. "Mark Twain as Translator from the German." *American Literature* 13 (November): 257–63.

1952. *Sam Clemens of Hannibal.* Boston: Houghton Mifflin Company, Riverside Press.

Weidenaar, Reynold. 1995. *Magic Music from the Telharmonium.* Metuchen, N.J.: Scarecrow Press.

Wheeler, Candace. 1918. *Yesterdays in a Busy Life.* New York: Harper and Brothers.

White, Andrew Dickson. 1905. *Autobiography of Andrew Dickson White.* 2 vols. New York: Century Company.

White, Horatio S. 1925. *Willard Fiske, Life and Correspondence: A Biographical Study.* New York: Oxford University Press.

Whitford, Noble E. 1906. *History of the Canal System of the State of New York Together with Brief Histories of the Canals of the United States and Canada: Supplement to the Annual Report of the State Engineer and Surveyor of the State of New York for the Fiscal Year Ending September 30, 1905.* 2 vols. Albany: Brandow Printing Company.

Wilbor, Elsie M., ed. 1887. *Werner's Directory of Elocutionists, Readers, Lecturers and Other Public Instructors and Entertainers.* New York: Edgar S. Werner.

Wilson, James Grant, and John Fiske, eds. 1887–89. *Appletons' Cyclopaedia of American Biography.* 6 vols. New York: D. Appleton and Co.

Wilson, John. 1973. *CB: A Life of Sir Henry Campbell-Bannerman.* London: Constable and Co.

WIM. 1973. *What Is Man? And Other Philosophical Writings.* Edited by Paul Baender. The Works of Mark Twain. Berkeley: University of California Press.

Winship, Michael. 2012. "Uncle Tom's Cabin: History of the Book in the 19th-Century United States." http://utc.iath.virginia.edu/interpret/exhibits/winship/winship.html. Accessed 14 February 2012.

Woolsey, Sarah Chauncey [Susan Coolidge, pseud.]. 1906. *Last Verses.* Boston: Little, Brown, and Co.

Wuliger, Robert. 1953. "Mark Twain on *King Leopold's Soliloquy.*" *American Literature* 25 (May): 234–37.

WWD. 1967. *Mark Twain's Which Was the Dream? and Other Symbolic Writings of the Later Years.* Edited by John S. Tuckey. The Mark Twain Papers. Berkeley and Los Angeles: University of California Press.

Yale Alumni Directory. 1920. *Alumni Directory of Yale University (Graduates and Non-graduates).* Compiled by Lottie G. Bishop. New Haven: Yale University.

Yandell, L. P. 1838. "Louisville Medical Institute." *American Medical Intelligencer* 2 (2 April): 14.

Young, John Russell. 1892. "More Than Eloquent. John Russell Young Tells of Thirty Years' Friendship with Daniel Dougherty the Orator." Pittsburgh (Pa.) *Dispatch,* 18 September, 9.

INDEX

Boldfaced page numbers indicate principal identifications or short biographies. All literary works are by Clemens unless otherwise noted: his major writings are listed only by title; the minor ones are listed both by title and under "Clemens, Samuel Langhorne: WORKS." Other literary works are found only under their authors' names. Place names are indexed only when they refer to locations SLC lived in, visited, or commented upon. Newspapers are listed by city, other periodicals by title. Bullets (•) designate people and places represented in the photographs following page 300.

Adams, Charles Follen, 153, **534**
Adams, Maude, 475, 564–65
Ade, George, 152, **534**
Adelaide (clipper ship), 549
"The Adventures of a Microbe" ("Three Thousand Years Among the Microbes"), 196, 552
Adventures of Huckleberry Finn: banned by libraries, 28, 29–33, 473–76; contract and publication, 58–59, 492–93, 651; deleted passages, 273, 580; inspiration for, 332; mesmerist episode considered, 590; Mississippi River description, 477; praised, 30–31, 33, 265, 347, 475, 477, 577; praised by SLC, 355; sales and royalties, 59, 528; shooting episode, 590
CHARACTERS: Mary Jane Wilks, 356, 609; prototypes, 626, 653–54; SLC's defense of Huck, 30–31, 476
The Adventures of Tom Sawyer: banned by libraries, 28, 29–33, 473–76; composition, 196, 446, 551–52, 645; inspiration for, 332; prototypes for characters, 626, 653–54; publication, 53, 599, 641, 650; readers' responses, 16, 33; whitewashing fence episode, 317, 321, 596
African Americans: Helen Keller's playmate, 414–15; political events, 472; Quarry Farm servants, 542; servant of Speakers of the House, 319, 598; Wakeman's execution of, 192–93, 549. *See also* Lewis, John T.; Minstrel shows
Ah Sin (SLC and Harte): collaboration, 419–20, 632–34; lead actor, 423, 636; reviews, 633–34; SLC's opinion, 633–34
Aircraft, 360–61, 612
Albigenses, 134, 524
•Alden, Henry Mills, 230–31, **562**
•Aldrich, Thomas Bailey, 318, 339, 353, 485, 609
Alexander, Charles B., 493
Alexander the Great, 330
Alexander and Green (law firm), 59, 493. *See also* Whitford, Daniel
Alexander VI (Rodrigo Borgia; pope), 134, 525
Alfonso Carlos (prince of Bourbon and Austria-Este), 98, 507
Allen, Jennie. *See* Donworth, Grace
Alonzo Child (steamboat), 405
Alston, Theodosia Burr (Aaron Burr's daughter), 359, **610–11**
Ament, Joseph P., 561, 649
America (steamboat), 549
American Bible Society, 499
The American Claimant, 553
American Copyright League, 317–18, 584–85, 597
American Missionary Society, 297

American News Company, 48, 49–50, 485
American Philological Association, 581
American Publishers' Copyright League, 597
American Publishing Company (Hartford): directors and staff, 48, 52–53, 486, 488–89, 492; Grant's *Personal Memoirs,* 61–62; Harpers' agreement, 160, 539; Harte's contract, 421, 634–35; Richardson's books, 486; rights to SLC's books, 143, 160, 528; SLC's contracts and disputes, 49–53, 143, 147, 487–88, 527–28; SLC's split from, 52–53, 488–89. *See also* Bliss, Elisha, Jr., *and* Bliss, Francis E.
PUBLICATION OF SLC'S WORKS: *Following the Equator,* 504, 651; *The Gilded Age,* 53, 650; *Huckleberry Finn* (considered), 492–93; *The Innocents Abroad,* 48–51, 53, 486–88, 650; *Mark Twain's Sketches, New and Old,* 53, 650; *Pudd'nhead Wilson,* 651; *Roughing It,* 50–51, 53, 143, 147, 488, 527–28, 641, 650; *Tom Sawyer,* 53, 650; *A Tramp Abroad,* 51–52, 488, 651
"The American Vandal Abroad," 48, 486, 608, 650
Angels Camp, 484, 621, 650
Anna (Jean's maid), 511
Anne (queen of England), 339–40, 605
Appleton, William H., 506, 597
Appleton, William Worthen, 317, **597**
Army and Navy Stores, 450–52, 647
Army of the Tennessee, 70, 181, 496
Arthur, Chester A., 70
Arthur (king), 218, 307
"As Concerns Interpreting the Deity," 363–70, 613–15
Ashcroft, Ralph W., 652, 655
Associated Press: on Clara's début, 243, 568; on Jessamy Harte, 427; SLC's speech at banquet, 245–46, 274–77, 563–64, 569; on Thaw case, 454
Astrology, 226, 558–59
Atlantic Monthly: editors and publishers, 353, 521, 548, 554, 609; Harte's writing, 120, 521; Hale's writing, 636; SLC's writing, 353, 489, 549, 551, 609, 611
"At the Farm," 557
Audubon, John James, 413, 629
Augusta Victoria of Schleswig-Holstein (empress of Prussia), 432
Augustus (Gaius Octavius; emperor of Rome), 365, **614**
Austria: dueling, 98, 507; Clemenses' stay in Marienbad, 227–28, 559; Clemenses' stay in Kaltenleutgeben, 602, 651. *See also* Vienna
Autobiography (SLC): daily dictation time, 621; remarks about form and content, 12, 127, 162, 172, 229–30, 243, 522, 640; written as from the grave, 68–69, 116, 121, 153, 158, 169–70, 172, 344, 357, 430, 522. *See also* Florentine Dictations; "Chapters from My Autobiography"

B., Mr. (unidentified), 304–6
Babyhood (periodical), 600
Backus, Charles, 293–94, **588**
Bacon, Charles P., 36–37, **479**–80
Bacon, Francis, 155, 333
Bacon, H. D., 550
Bahamas, 455, 648
Bailey, James Montgomery ("Danbury News Man"), 153, **534**
Bancker, G., 588
Bangs, John Kendrick, **510**
Bar Association of Philadelphia, 308–9, 592
Barber, Joseph ("Disbanded Volunteer"), 153, 534–35
Barbour, Thomas S., 461–62
Barnard College, 15, 17, 466
Barnes, Benjamin F.: appointed postmaster, 3, 6–8, 11–12, 460; Morris incident, 3, 7–9, 11–12, 457–58, 460
Barnes, George Eustace, 114–17
Barr, Robert, **552–53**
Barret, Richard Aylett, **610**
Barret, Richard Ferril (called Dr. Gwynn), 358, **610**
Barrett, Lawrence, 330, **601**, 637
Barrie, J. M., 30, 475
Bartlett, Matthew Henry, 536
Bartlett Tower (Talcott Mountain), 156, 536
Bateman, Seth, 622
Bateman's Point resort (Newport, R.I.), 385–87, 622

Bay. *See* Clemens, Clara Langdon
Bayer and Company, 502
Bay State Belting Company, 483
Beale, Edward Fitzgerald (Ned), 218, 556, **557**
Beard, Dan, 526
Beardsley, Lillian Robinson, 189–90, **547**
•Beckwith, James Carroll, 251, **573**
Beecher, Catharine, **643**
Beecher, Henry Ward: family, 501, 574, 626; proposed autobiography, 501; scandal and trial, 253, 501, 573–74; WORK: *Life of Jesus, the Christ*, 77, 500–501
Beecher, William, 574
Beef Trust, 116, 515
Belgium. *See* Leopold II
Bell, Alexander Graham, 56–57, 491–92, 586
Benedict, Frank Lee, 346, **606**
Benjamin, Anne Engle Rogers, 622
Benjamin, William Evarts, 387, 389, 504, **622**
Bentley, George, 633
Berlin: Clemenses' visits, 82, 157, 310, 315–16, 432–33, 536, 555, 584, 596, 655; SLC's dinner with Wilhelm II, 310–12, 315, 431–34, 593–95; SLC's illness, 432, 593–94
Berlin disaster (1907), 437–44
•Bermuda, 359–63, 611–12, 652
Bermudian (ship), 611
Bernard, William H., **588**
Bethune, George W., 563
Bible: copyright, 291, 341, 587; corrupting influence on children, 30, 135; Natick translation, 412–13, 628–29; school opened with reading, 178; stories shared with other religions, 130–31, 522–23; unreliable as evidence, 131–32, 140–41; Wakeman's explanation of miracles, 192, 194–95; mentioned, 109, 236, 360, 374. *See also* Christianity; *Eve's Diary;* God
REFERENCES: "After a time, and half a time . . ." (Revelation), 54, 489; "Ask and ye shall receive" (Matthew), 178; Decalogue (Ten Commandments), 337, 605; Elijah and prophets of Baal (1 Kings), 551; "The end is not yet" (Matthew), 313, 595; "feeding of the five thousand" (Matthew), 102, 509; "Golden Rule" (Matthew), 130, 522; "how beautiful are the feet . . . gospel of peace" (Romans), 134, 524; "seventy times seven times" (Matthew), 129, 522; "sufficient unto the day" (Matthew), 337, 605; Noah's flood (Genesis), 54, 130, 489, 523; "the voice . . . heard in the land" (Song of Solomon), 335, 604
Bierce, Ambrose, 118, 517
Bicycling (SLC), 258–59, 575
•Billiards, 53, 149, 161, 346, 377–85, 619–22
Billings, Josh (Henry Wheeler Shaw), 153, 485, 534
Birch, William (Billy), 293–94, **588**
Bismarck, Otto von, 310, **594**
Bixby, Horace E., 58, 238, 492, 566, 649
"Blabbing Government Secrets," 561
Blamire, Joseph, 641
Blind, associations for, 32, 477, 582. *See also* Keller, Helen
"Blindfold Novelette" (planned by SLC and Howells), 548
•Bliss, Elisha, Jr.: characterized by SLC, 50, 52, 54, 60; death, 52; "swindles" SLC, 50–53, 143, 147, 527–28; *A Tramp Abroad* published, 51–52, 488. *See also* American Publishing Company
•Bliss, Francis E., 52, 62, 143–44, 489, **528**
B'nai B'rith, 608
Boardman, Douglass, 479–80
Boer War (second, 1899–1902), 137–38, 526, 543
Bohn's Classical Library, 365–66, 614
Bok, Edward, 446, **644**
Boker, George H., 601
Bonaparte, Napoleon, 364, 613
Book of Common Prayer, 587
Book of Mormon, 247, 571
Booth, Edwin, 348, **607**
Booth, Etta, 24–25, 471
Booth, Lucius A., 24, 471
Borderland (periodical), 604, 624
Borgia, Rodrigo (Pope Alexander VI), 134, 525
Boston (Mass.): courteous cabmen, 362; pedestrian excursion, 380, 620, 643; press dinner, 256; SLC's visits, 445, 495,

Boston (Mass.) *(continued)*
586, 643; typewriter purchased, 445–46, 643–44
Boston *Carpet-Bag,* 561
Boston *Journal,* 568
Boston Lyceum Bureau. *See* Redpath, James
Boswell, James, 570
Boucicault, Dion, 637
Bowen, Barton S., 561
Bowen, William, 405
Bowers, H. C., 490
Bowker, Richard R., 317, 319, **597**–98
Bowling, 380–81, 385–87
Bowser, Wattie, 532
Boyle, B. Butler, 213
Braid, James, 591–92
Bridgman, Laura, 582
Briggs, Charles Augustus, 131, **523**–24
Bristol, Frank M. (Rev. Mr. X.), 410–12, **628**
British Congo Reform Association, 529
British Empire: Anglo-Saxon superiority, 225–27; Boer War (second), 137–38, 526, 543; wars and depredations in name of Christianity, 134–35, 525. *See also* Great Britain
British Inland Revenue Office, 179–80, 545
British Parliament: and copyright law, 288–90, 291, 586–87; SLC's testimony, 290–92, 338–41, 587
Brooklyn Magazine, 644
Brooklyn Public Library, *Huckleberry Finn* and *Tom Sawyer* banned, 28–33, 473–76
Brown, John (doctor), 551–52
Brown, John ("Ossawatomie"; abolitionist), 255–56, 574–75
Brown, John Hay, 595
Brown, William, 150, 532
Browne, Charles Farrar (Artemus Ward), 46, 153, **484**–85
Browne, Ross, 553
Bruce, Sarah Charlotte, 559
Brush, George de Forest, 200, 203, 214–15, **553**, 555
Buckland, Francis Trevelyan, 435, **642**
Buckner, Simon Bolivar, 72–73, **497**
Buddhism, 130, 131, 523
Buffalo (N.Y.), 650, 653–54
Buffalo *Courier,* 536
Buffalo *Express,* 550, 650
Bunce, Edward M., 346
Bundy, Horace L., 602
Bunker Hill battle and monument, 257, 373, 616
Burdette, Robert J., 153, **534**
Burke, William, 235, 563
Burr, Aaron, 359, **610–11**
Burton, Joseph R., 387, 622–23
Bushwhackers, 575
Butters, Henry A., 393, 399, **625**
Byrd, C. O., 533

Cable, Eva Colegate Stevenson, **603**
Cable, George W.: author's reading, 554; reading tour with SLC, 59, 66, 165, 333–34, 493, 539, 591, 651; second marriage, 334, 603
Cable, Louise Stewart Bartlett, **603**
Cacography (and semiliterate letters as literature): from Higbie to SLC, 182–83, 188–89; from Jennie Allen to Stockbridge, 191–92, 246–47, 276–77, 548, 570; from Page to Helen Keller, 413–15, 629–30; from and about the "western girl," 121–27, 521–22; from Wakeman to Twichell, 192, 195, 413. *See also* Clemens, Olivia Susan, biography of SLC
Cadwalader, John, 308–9, **592**
Caesar, Julius, 71–72
Cahill, Thaddeus, **645**
Caldwell, Samuel L., 16, 465
California. *See* Angels Camp; Jackass Hill; San Francisco
Californian (periodical): contributors, 118; Harte's editing and writing, 118, 484, 517; replaced by *Overland Monthly,* 520; SLC's writing, 485, 562, 650; Webb's founding and editing, 46, 484
Caligula, 128
Cambridge University Press, 587
Camp, Herman, 20–21, **468**
Campbell, William Wilfred, 376–77, 618–19
Campbell-Bannerman, Henry, 227–28, **559**, 560

Cannon, Joseph Gurney, 319, **598**
Caprell, Madame (fortune teller), 404–8, 627
Caprivi, Georg Leo von, 310–11, 594
"Captain Stormfield's Visit to Heaven," 193–95, 269, 549–51
Carleton, George B., 46–47, **484–85**
Carlyle, Thomas, 304, 591, 599
Carnegie, Andrew: dinner with SLC, 334; letters from SLC, 172–73, 541, 603; philanthropy, 172, 541, 554, 578; and Simplified Spelling (as "Croesus"), 266, 273, 578, 580; wealth, 116, 266, 578
Carnegie Foundation for the Advancement of Teaching, 541
Carnegie Hall: SLC's "The Death-Disk," 105–6, 510; SLC's speech for Robert Fulton Memorial Association, 14, 15, 59, 465; SLC's speech for Tuskegee Institute, 8, 460–62
Carnegie Institute of Pittsburgh, 172, 541
Carnegie Mellon University, 541
Carson City (Nev.): SLC's and Orion's journey to, 458, 480, 649; SLC's and Orion's residence, 5–6, 21, 458–59, 469; SLC's reportage of Territorial Legislature, 5, 239, 458, 567
Carvalho, Charles T. (court interpreter), 114, **514**
Case, Newton, 52–53, **488**
Casey, Margaret (Peggy; SLC's mother's mother), 409, **627**
Castelhun, Maida, 15, **465**
Catholic Church, 134, 145–46, 523–24
Catskill Mountains. *See* Onteora Park
Cayvan, Georgia, 277–78, **581**
The Celebrated Jumping Frog of Calaveras County, and Other Sketches: attempt to destroy plates, 49, 487, 608; authorized English edition, 641; contract dispute, 49–50, 487–88; pirated edition, 641; price and sales, 48, 49, 485, 487; publication, 47–48, 485, 650; title story, 46–47, 230, 484–85, 562, 650
Cellini, Benvenuto, 12, 463
Censorship: *Huckleberry Finn* and *Tom Sawyer* banned from libraries, 28, 29–33, 473–76
Central Africa. *See* Congo
Century Company, 60–63, 280, 500
Century Magazine: contributors, 61–62, 568, 576, 607, 619; editors, 317, 494, 597; SLC's writing, 629
ARTICLES: Campbell's "Love," 619; Grant's Civil War articles, 61–62; Howells's *Silas Lapham* serialized, 607; SLC's tribute to Trumbull, 629; Stockton's "His Wife's Deceased Sister," 576
Chace, Jonathan, 283, 584
Chace Bill, 283–84, 584, 597
Champollion, Jean François, 363, 365, **613**
"Chapters from My Autobiography" (*North American Review*), 404, 463, 469, 522, 618, 620, 626–27, 652, 656–60
Charades, 164–65, 333
Charcot, Jean-Martin, 304–5, 591, **592**
Charles I (king of England), 595
Charles II (king of England), 409, 605, 627
Charles L. Webster and Company: book acquisitions and rejections: 76–78, 494, 499–503, 583; bookkeeper's embezzlement, 73–76, 498–99; failure, 78–80, 158–59, 162, 493, 498, 500, 504–5, 538, 651; general agent's default, 76, 499; Olivia as creditor, 79, 159, 654; organization and offices, 57–59, 64–66, 76, 78, 492–95, 500, 502–3, 651. *See also* Hall, Frederick J.; Webster, Charles L.
WORKS PUBLISHED: Custer's *Tenting on the Plains,* 500, 571–72; Cox's *Diversions of a Diplomat,* 598; Crawford's *The Genesis of the Civil War,* 500; Grant's *Personal Memoirs,* 63–65, 69, 71, 73–76, 493–94, 497–99, 505, 574; *McClellan's Own Story,* 500; Sheridan's *Personal Memoirs,* 500; SLC's books, 58–59, 77, 492–93, 501, 528, 530, 534, 651; Stedman's *Library of American Literature,* 78, 503–4; *The Idler* (periodical; distributor), 553
Charlotte (laundress), 542
Chase, William Merritt, 272, **580**
Chatterton, Thomas, 247, **570**
Chatto, Andrew, 179
Chatto and Windus, 545–46, 641
Chaucer, Geoffrey, 277

Chaykovsky, Nikolai, 564
"The Chicago G.A.R. Festival," 546
Chicago (Ill.): banquet for Grant, 70–71, 181, 252, 255, 573; "School of Fiction," 534
Chicago *Republican,* 549–50
Chicago *Tribune,* 252, 556, 573
Chickering Hall (N.Y.), 60, 202–3, 494, 554
"Children's Record." *See* "A Record of the Small Foolishnesses of Susy & 'Bay' Clemens (Infants)"
Childs, George W., 63–64
China, 13, 465
Chincha Islands, 192–93, 549
Choate, Joseph H.: at benefits with SLC, 8, 32, 259; 460, 477, 572; at Fourth of July banquet, 157, 345, 537; handsomeness, 161; on privileges of age, 250
"Christian Citizenship," 353, 609
Christianity: "automatic," 292–93; as cause of wars and depredations, 132–35, 524; demise, 135–36; futility of prayer, 138, 178, 526; 545; modern vs. medieval, 306–7; minister's heresy, 131, 523–24; virgin birth/divinity of Jesus, 131–32, 140–42, 523–24. *See also* Bible; Christian Science; God; Morality; Religion
DENOMINATIONS: Catholics, 134, 145–46, 523–24; Congregationalists, 253, 465, 488, 574, 576, 615; Dunker Baptists, 173–75, 543; Episcopalians, 131, 523; Mormons, 247, 571; Presbyterians, 117, 131, 175, 462, 468, 523–24
Christian Science (Church of Christ, Scientist): believers characterized, 132, 136, 247; SLC's writings, 144–45, 525–26, 528–29, 643, 652; tenets, 343, 525, 571, 602
"Christian Science" (articles), 144, 525–26, 528
Christian Science (book), 144–45, 526, 528–29, 643, 652
Christian Union (periodical), 270, 327–29, 600–601
Christy, E. P., and minstrel troupe, 296–97, 588
"The Chronicle of Young Satan," 530, 552
Church of the Brethren (Dunkers), 173–75, 543
City Missionary Society (Hartford). *See* Hawley, David
Civil War (1861–65): beginning, 616; Hale's "Man without a Country," 424, 636; Mississippi River steamboats shut down, 238; Nast's illustrations, 462; pensions for veterans, 371–74, 387, 431–32, 615–17; Sherman's march through Georgia, 302, 591; SLC's service, 649; unprofitable books about, 76, 500. *See also* Grand Army of the Republic; Grant, Ulysses S.
BATTLES: Bunker Hill, 373, 616; First Bull Run, 265–66, 578; Fort Donelson, 73, 497
Clairvoyance. *See* Fortune telling and divination
Clapp, Henry, Jr., 47, **485**
Clark, Charles Hopkins, 146, 501, 520. See also *Mark Twain's Library of Humor*
Clark, Marshall (Professor Niblo), 391–93, 396, **624**
Clark, William A., 387–89, 410, **622**–23
•Clemens, Clara Langdon (Bay; SLC's daughter): biographical information, 650, 654, **655**; characteristics, 99, 103, 224–25, 240–41, 309, 328, 332; friendships, 466, 473, 508–9, 569, 579; SLC's difficulty in remembering face, 270; and SLC's writing, 152, 328–29, 343–44, 353; mentioned, 542, 609
CHILDHOOD: accidents, illnesses, and injuries, 240, 242, 309–10, 331, 568, 593; 602; education (general), 218, 310, 654–55; education (musical), 603; family pets, 217–18, 224; Harris's visit, 260; Kipling's visit, 175; "mark twain" call, 357; mind cure, 342, 602; Olivia's discipline, 327–28; playacting English history, 333; playacting *The Prince and the Pauper,* 165–66, 331, 602; solitaire playing, 331; tennis playing, 218. *See also* Clemens family amusements
LATER YEARS: around-the-world trip, 79, 81, 162, 244, 504, 651, 654–55; as Christian Scientist, 526; correspon-

dence, 151–52, 509, 547; daughter, 655; Fifth Avenue house selection, 23; gift of SLC's papers, 699; health, 569, 655; letters from SLC, 506, 547; lying, 99–107, 509; marriages, 509, 652, 655; music studies, 224, 240, 509, 567–68, 655; as Olivia's nurse, 99–107, 509; opinion of SLC's speaking, 244–45; praises SLC and Olivia, 152, 654; relationship with SLC, 243–45; singing career, 224, 235, 240, 243–44, 567–68, 655; telephone conversation, 199
WORKS: *Awake to a Perfect Day,* 526; *My Father, Mark Twain,* 655
Clemens, Henry (SLC's brother), 150, 237, 532, 649, 653
Clemens, James Ross (SLC's second cousin), 11, **463**
•Clemens, Jane Lampton (SLC's mother): biographical information, **653**; ancestors, 409, 627; belief in mesmerism, 302–4; characteristics, 358, 393, 406, 545, 653; children, 402, 649; Clemenses' visits, 356–58, 591; comforts SLC, 178; death and funeral, 25, 357, 609–10; early romance, 357–58, 61, 653; ends SLC's schooling, 409; fondness for entertainment, 296–97; health, 357–58, 394, 470; letters from SLC, 566, 627, 633; marriage, 357–58, 610, 652–53; namesake of Jean Clemens, 356, 655; prototype for Aunt Polly, 653; residences, 470, 492, 591, 610, 652–53; SLC's support, 22, 25, 408, 470; SLC's tribute, 610, 653; W.C.T.U. membership, 613
•Clemens, Jean (Jane Lampton; SLC's daughter): biographical information, **655–56**; birth and death, 651–52, 654; characteristics, 222–24; friendships, 224, 473, 508, 557; language abilities, 223–24, 264; letters from SLC, 218, 645; SLC's difficulty in remembering face, 270; SLC's reminiscence, 656; mentioned, 247, 504, 557, 609, 655
CHILDHOOD: characterizes SLC and Olivia, 224; education, 218, 257, 310, 654–55; family pets, 218, 224, 511; health, 342, 355; love of animals, 223, 292; mind cure, 342, 602; playacting English history, 333; playacting *The Prince and the Pauper,* 165–66, 331; rescued from fire, 241; on SLC's meeting Wilhelm II, 310, 594; and SLC's writing, 224–25, 343–44, 355; solitaire playing, 331. *See also* Clemens family amusements
LATER YEARS: diary, 555–56; Dublin stay, 511, 651; health, 82, 100–107, 270, 506, 509, 579, 609, 646, 651, 655–56; hobbies and interests, 100–101, 105–6, 509, 655; Italy visit, 108; Lewis's pension, 173; relationship with SLC, 656; as SLC's typist and secretary, 101–2, 613, 643, 651, 656; "spontaneous oratory" debate noted, 555–56; Stormfield residence, 652, 656
Clemens, Jennie (SLC's niece), **653**
Clemens, John Marshall (SLC's father): biographical information, 627, **652**; characteristics, 357–58, 394, 653; children, 649, 652–53; death, 237, 301, 406, 408–9, 590, 649, 652; education and occupations, 652; marriage, 357–58, 653; self-medication, 408–9, 627, 652; Tennessee land, 21, 469; mentioned, 589
Clemens, Langdon (SLC's son), 650, 654
•Clemens, Mary Eleanor Stotts (Mollie; Orion's wife): birth and death, 24, 521, 653; California residence, 469–70, characteristics, 5, 22, 25; daughter, 653; Fredonia stay, 470; Hartford stay, 26; hears Jane Clemens's account of early romance, 357, 610; Keokuk residence, 22–23, 25, 470–72, 610; letters from SLC, 473; marriage, 653; Memphis (Mo.) residence, 627; Muscatine residence, 653; Nevada residence, 5–6, 21–22, 459, 469–70, 653; New York City visit, 470; Orion's death, 473; portrayed by SLC as Mrs. Williams, 121–27, 521–22; SLC's support, 470–72
•Clemens, Olivia Louise Langdon (Livy, Mousie; SLC's wife): biographical information, **654**; around-the-world trip, 79, 81, 162, 504, 651, 654–55;

Clemens, Olivia Louise Langdon *(continued)*
characteristics, 82, 97, 107, 224, 538, 654; charitable activities, 278–79, 582; Clara's nursing, 99–107, 509; closeness to SLC, 28; courtship and marriage, 239, 565, 650, 654; death, 80–81, 108, 251, 260, 651, 654; education, 654; friendships, 250–51, 260, 330, 483, 509, 540, 557, 571–72, 603; Harte's visits, 419–20; health, 41, 81–83, 97–108, 506, 654; household and social burdens, 81–82, 97, 654; intuition, 354–55, 609; letters from SLC, 470–71, 548, 579; letter to SLC, 556; mother's death, 353, 609; Onteora visits, 250–53, 571, 573; runaway horse incident, 542; Webster and Company creditor, 79, 159–60, 504, 654; mentioned, 352. *See also* Clemens family residences
AS MOTHER: births and deaths of children, 650, 654; concern for children, 309, 331, 342, 353–55, 609; disciplinary measures, 223–24, 327–29, 600; education of children, 218, 257, 310, 654–55; family pets, 218; house-fly killing scheme, 257–58; mind cure, 331, 342–43, 602; solitaire playing, 331. *See also* Clemens family amusements
SLC'S WRITING: autobiography, 508; "The Death-Disk" ("The Death-Wafer"), 106; *Huckleberry Finn,* 273; *The Innocents Abroad,* 352, 608; "Luck," 343–44; *The Prince and the Pauper,* 165–66, 353; *Roughing It,* 352, 608; SLC's copyrights, 79, 159–60, 504, 654; as SLC's editor, 197, 270, 273, 350, 508, 654; SLC's enjoying his own book, 352, 608; SLC's reputation, 197; SLC's speeches, 97; "'What Ought He to Have Done?': Mark Twain's Opinion," 328–29, 600–601
•Clemens, Olivia Susan (Susy; SLC's daughter): biographical information, **654–55**; birth, 650, 654; characteristics, 223–24, 258, 328–30, 332, 654; gravestone inscription, 376–77, 618–19; illness and death, 81, 504, 582, 651, 654, 655; remembered and missed, 258, 359; Vassar College visit, 16–17, 465
CHILDHOOD: education (general): 218, 310, 654–55; education (musical), 218, 241, 603; Harris's visit, 260; Kipling's visit, 175–77; lying, 223–24; mind cure, 330–31, 342–43, 602; nearsightedness, 331, 342–43; Olivia's discipline, 223–24, 327–28; playacting English history, 333; playacting *The Prince and the Pauper,* 165–66, 216, 331, 602; poem misattributed, 376–77, 618–19; promenading with SLC, 269, 271; rescued from fire, 241; mentioned, 225. *See also* Clemens family amusements
Clemens, Olivia Susan, biography of SLC: Cable's visit, 333–34; characterizes Clara, 309, 332; characterizes Elizabeth Custer, 250; characterizes Jean, 224; characterizes self, 309, 332; excerpts, 165–66, 215–19, 247, 250, 255, 257–60, 263–65, 269–70, 273, 283–84, 292–93, 306, 309, 327, 330–32, 342–43, 346–47, 349–52, 356, 358; Howellses' visit, 349; parents' relationship, 269–70, 273, 328–29; people given passing mention, 247; secrecy of writing, 654; SLC's footnotes, 165–66, 218, 255, 269, 332, 350, 540; SLC's praise, 166, 257, 292, 330, 413–14; spelling, 273, 333, 348, 413; "There is a happy land," 292, 293; unfinished, 358–59; visits to Elmira, 216, 327; visit to Keokuk, 356, 358; visit to Onteora, 250; visit to Vassar College, 16–17, 465; written for family, 257
FAMILY ANECDOTES AND ACTIVITIES: arithmetic problem, 215–16; blowing soap bubbles, 258; Clara's injuries, 309, 331; family pets, 216–18, 247–48, 257; favorite stories, 346; games, 347; Jean and ducks, 292–93; Jean and insects, 257; mind cure, 331, 342; playacting *The Prince and the Pauper,* 165–66, 216, 331, 602; SLC's history game, 351
REMARKS ABOUT OLIVIA: characteristics, 224, 330; disciplining children, 327; occupations, 218; opinion of SLC's writing, 329, 343; relationship with children, 218, 257, 309, 331, 342, 654–55
REMARKS ABOUT SLC: characteristics, 16, 166, 253, 269–70, 330–32; chess scheme, 333; *Christian Union* article,

270, 326, 328–29; copyright opinion, 283–84; cure for colds, 330; enjoying his own book, 352, 608; fiftieth birthday and tributes, 258, 259–60, 263–65, 347–48, 575; Howells and Jews, 349–50, 607; lecturing, 165; literary plans, 269; "Luck," 343–44; as publisher, 269; reading manuscripts to family, 273, 306, 343–44; Redpath's compliment, 255; tribute and assistance to Grant, 218–19, 255; trip to England and Scotland, 165; writings, 217, 273, 328–29, 332, 343–44, 348–49, 352, 608

•Clemens, Orion (SLC's brother): biographical information, **653**; autobiography, 27, 404, 472–73; death, 24, 27, 473, 521; described by fortune teller, 404, 406, 407–8; employs SLC, 230, 237, 560–61, 653; finances, 5–6, 20–23, 25, 458–59, 470–71, 653; Hartford bathtub incident, 26; hears Jane Clemens's account of early romance, 610; letters from SLC, 21, 23, 404–9, 468, 471, 473, 505, 566, 627; letters to SLC, 472, 499; marriage and family, 653; politics, 20, 26, 468, 472, 653; religion, 20, 26, 393, 468, 471; SLC's support, 22–23, 25, 238, 458, 470–72, 653; temperance opinions, 20–21, 468; Tennessee land, 21; trip west with SLC, 37–38, 238, 458, 649; warning about book agent, 499

CHARACTERISTICS: changeability, 6, 20–21, 26, 393, 407, 472; depression, 393; as dreamer, 653; honesty, goodness, and kindness, 5, 20, 25–26, 47, 653; ineffectuality, 5, 22; patience, 473

OCCUPATIONS: author, 27, 404, 468, 472–73, 588–89, 653; chicken farmer, 22–23, 25, 471–72, 653; inventor, 25, 472; lawyer, 20, 22, 25, 407, 468, 471, 653; lecturer, 653; mining investor, 20–21, 422; Nevada territorial and state official, 5–6, 20–22, 37, 238, 458–59, 468–70, 649, 653; newspaperman, 22, 25–26, 230, 233–34, 470–71, 560–61, 653; printer, 237, 261, 653

RESIDENCES: California, 469–70; Hartford, 22, 26, 470; Keokuk, 22–23, 470–72, 499, 610, 653; Memphis (Mo.), 627; Muscatine, 653; Nevada, 5–6, 21, 458, 469, 653; New York City, 470; Rutland, 471; St. Louis, 653

Clemens, Pamela A. (SLC's sister). *See* Moffett, Pamela A.

Clemens, Samuel (SLC's father's father), 627

•Clemens, Samuel Langhorne (SLC): biographical information (life chronology), **649–52**; appearance, 249–50, 572; attitude toward life and death, 68–69, 473; Civil War service, 649; eyesight, 342–43; family biographies, 652–56; first sweetheart (*see* Wright, Laura Mary); forebears, 627; images and photographs, 161, 173, 203, 204–10, 543, 554, 573; reported death, 11, 463; sale of letters, 10, 462–63; writing method, 195–96. *See also* Clemens family residences

AMUSEMENTS: bicycling, 258–59, 575; billiards, 53, 149, 161, 346, 377–85, 619–22; bowling, 380–81, 385–87; chess, 333; "Quaker" (card game), 382–83; solitaire, 331. *See also* Clemens family amusements

BIRTHDAY ACTIVITIES: fiftieth birthday and tributes, 258–60, 263–65, 575–78, 606; sixty-seventh birthday dinner and tributes, 105, 510; seventy-first birthday, 285; centenary, Dunne's tribute, 619

BUSINESS AND FINANCIAL MATTERS: bankruptcy, 78–80, 158–60, 197, 493, 503–4, 538–39, 654; failure to buy telephone stock, 56–57, 489–90; Federal Steel Company, 80, 162, 505; Hale and Norcross mine, 18, 20–21, 422, 468; Hartford Accident Insurance Company, 55–56, 490–91; Kaolatype, 54, 489–90; Lyon and Ashcroft's influence, 655; miscellaneous inventions, 54–55, 489–90; Paige typesetting machine, 80, 158–60, 505, 537, 539, 651; Plasmon Company, 625; royalty income, 55, 159–60, 487–88, 490, 538–39; support for mother and brother, 22–23, 25, 238, 408, 458, 470–72, 653; taxes, 21, 116, 179–80, 504, 516, 545. *See also* American Publishing Company; Charles L. Webster and Company; Rogers, Henry H.

Clemens, Samuel Langhorne (SLC) *(continued)*
CHARACTERISTICS: characterized by Jean, 224; characterized by Susy, 16, 166, 253, 269–70, 330–32; charitable, forgiving, and gentle nature, 75, 368, 392, 491; college-girl habit, 15–17; dignity, 212–13; excitability, 299; fashion sense, 249–50, 572; generosity, 255; grudge-bearing, 158; honesty and lying, 116, 298, 302–4; imagination, 298–99; laziness, 37, 46, 51, 115, 170, 196; love of cats, 216–18, 224, 247–49, 331, 393, 429; mercifulness, 222; representative of human race, 383; temper, 198, 226, 251, 430; vanity, 10, 16–17, 243–44, 291, 300, 387, 432–33. *See also* Fortune telling and divination; Palmistry; Phrenology
CHARITABLE ACTIVITIES: advice for fundraisers, 281–83; appearances, lectures, and speeches, 8–9, 14–17, 32, 59, 350, 460–62, 465–66, 477, 493, 572, 584, 608; influencing contributors, 193, 279–81, 582–83, 639; pension scheme for charities, 279–81, 582–83; personal contributions, 211, 278–80, 582
CHILDHOOD AND YOUTH: early experiences as author, 230–35, 238–39, 560–63, 649; education and schoolteachers, 177–78, 233, 237, 360, 409, 544–45, 649; health, 408–9; mesmerism experiments, 297–304, 589–90; mischief, 177–78; 237, 262–63; parental relationship observed, 357–58; schoolmates, 178, 545
JOURNALISM: *Golden Era,* 562, 650; Hannibal *Journal,* 560–61; Hannibal *Western Union,* 561, 589, 649, 653; Keokuk *Post,* 230–35, 563; Muscatine *Journal,* 561; New Orleans *Crescent,* 561; New York *Weekly Review,* 513; San Francisco *Alta California,* 549, 588; San Francisco *Dramatic Chronicle,* 513, 621; *Saturday Press,* 47, 485, 562, 650. See also *Californian;* Sacramento *Union;* San Francisco *Morning Call;* Virginia City *Territorial Enterprise*
LECTURES AND SPEECHES: after Clara's début, 243–45, 569; on American manners, 8–9, 462; "The American Vandal Abroad," 48, 486, 608, 650; around-the-world tour, 79–81, 159, 162, 244, 504, 651, 654–55; Associated Press banquet, 235, 245–46, 274–77, 563–64, 569; "The Babies," 180–81; Barnard College, 17, 466; Booth banquet, 348–49, 607; Carnegie banquet, 578; Carnegie Hall, 8, 14–15, 59, 105–6, 460–62, 465; Chickering Hall, 60, 202–3, 494, 554; City Missionary Society (Hartford), 584; Cleveland Protestant Orphan Asylum, 350, 608; Cooper Union, 38–40, 481–82, 558; on copyright, 284, 319, 337–42, 572, 584–85, 587, 597–98, 605; Delmonico's Restaurant, 607; drunken man anecdote, 186–87, 342; early lecture tours, 40, 48, 482, 486, 650; Ends of the Earth Club, 558; on *The Gilded Age,* 558; Grant banquet, 180–81; Hudson Theatre, 16–17, 465–66; Jessamy Harte benefit declined, 638–39; lecturing speed, 446; on Leopold II (undelivered), 8, 460–62; long-necked clam, 348–49, 607; lost-sock anecdote, 16, 465; Majestic Theatre, 8–9, 462; on marriage engagements, 187; on men and women, 214; Monk-Greeley anecdote, 200–203, 553–54; on morals, 17, 462, 505; New York State Association for Promoting the Interests of the Blind, 32, 477, 572; pedestrian excursion anecdote, 14–15, 465; plan to quit speaking for money, 14–15, 59, 212; Platt's Hall, 200–202, 553; on *Quaker City* excursion, 48, 486, 608, 650; reluctance to speak, 316; Robert Fulton Memorial Association, 14, 15, 59, 465, 493; Sandwich Islands lecture, 38–40, 200–202, 239, 280, 481–82, 553, 558, 569, 583, 650; Savoy Hotel, 558; Simplified Spelling, 245–46, 266–69, 274–77, 563–64, 569, 578; SLC-Cable reading tour, 59, 66, 165, 333, 493, 539, 591, 651; Smith College, 16, 465; "spontaneous oratory" scheme, 184–88, 200, 203, 213–15, 555–56; stage fright, 569; talk distinguished from speech, 244–45; tour with Nast proposed, 10, 462; Tuskegee

Institute, 8, 460–62; Vassar College, 16–17, 465–66; at Waldorf-Astoria Hotel, 32, 477, 563–64; Washington Ladies' Literary Association, 597–98; Women's University Club, 14–18, 465; for Young Men's Christian Association, 8–9, 462

LETTERS. *See* Letters from SLC; Letters to SLC

OCCUPATIONS: authorial history, 230–35, 238–39, 560–63, 649–52; clerk for Orion in Nevada, 458–59, 649; editorship turned down, 197; errand boy, 649; inventor, 55, 351–52, 490, 608; miner and mining speculator, 20–21, 118, 168–69, 238, 422–23, 459, 468, 566, 621, 636, 649; ministry considered, 238, 566; printer, 561, 589, 649, 653; quartz-mill laborer, 238, 566; steamboat pilot, 58, 150–51, 230, 238, 264, 405–8, 458, 492, 531–32, 561, 566, 649

ORGANIZATIONAL ACTIVITIES AND MEMBERSHIPS: Congo Reform Association, 8, 460–62, 529; Ends of the Earth Club, 225–27, 558; Fellowcraft Club, 183–87, 546; Freemasonry, 649; The God Damned Human Race club, 442–43, 643; Juggernaut Club, 28–29, 474; Kinsmen, 573; Lotos Club, 436; Monday Evening Club, 265, 578; The Players club, 426, 540, 565, 607; Saturday Morning Club, 419, 633; Savage Club, 435–36, 640–42; Tile Club, 579–80

PET SCHEMES (SLC's advice): employment, 34–37, 470–71, 479; "graduated blush," 188; pension, for charities, 279–81, 582–83; "spontaneous oratory," 184–88, 200, 203, 213–15, 546, 555–56

PSEUDONYMS: A Dog-be-Deviled Citizen, 561; Blab, 560–61; Josh, 562, 566–67, 649; Mark Twain, 239, 353, 356–57, 567, 650; Sergeant Fathom, 561; Snodgrass, 230–35, 563

READING: *The Acts of Stephen,* 614; Bible (as child), 30, 135; Briggs's "Criticism and Dogma," 131, 523–24; Carlyle's *French Revolution,* 591; Darwin's *On the Origin of Species,* 527; Defoe's *Robinson Crusoe,* 540; Doane's *Bible Myths,* 523; dueling essay, 98, 507; English history, 155–56; friends' literary offerings, 162–63; Hartwick's "Curfew Shall Not Ring To-night," 215, 556; Henry of Huntingdon, 366–69, 614; his own dictations, 158; humorists, 153, 534–35; Jacobs's *Dialstone Lane,* 182; William James's works, 513; Joseph Jefferson's autobiography, 76, 500; Kipling, 176–77, 544; laughing at own books, 346, 352–53, 355; Macaulay, 586–87; *Oliver Cromwell's Letters and Speeches,* 553; Phelps's *The Gates Ajar,* 194, 550; Pliny the Younger, 110, 512; Poe's "To Helen," 323, 599; Reade's *The Cloister and the Hearth,* 606; reading aloud to family, 273, 306, 343–44, 540; reading in German, 248; SLC's marginalia, 518, 521, 525, 573, 614; Suetonius, 365, 614; White's autobiography, 33, 477. *See also names of other authors and titles of newspapers*

WORKS: "The Adventures of a Microbe," 196, 552; *The American Claimant,* 553; "As Concerns Interpreting the Deity," 363–70, 613–15; "At the Farm," 557; "Blabbing Government Secrets," 561; "Blindfold Novelette," 548; "Captain Stormfield's Visit to Heaven," 193–95, 269, 549–51; "Chapters from My Autobiography" (*North American Review*), 404, 463, 469, 618, 620, 626–27, 652, 656–60; "The Chicago G.A.R. Festival," 546; "Christian Citizenship," 353, 609; "Christian Science" (articles), 144, 525–26, 528; *Christian Science* (book), 144–45, 526, 528–29, 643, 652; "The Chronicle of Young Satan," 530, 552; "Closing Words of My Autobiography," 656; *Colonel Sellers,* 467–68, 601, 633, 636; "Concerning Copyright," 605–6; *A Curious Dream,* 641; "The Czar's Soliloquy," 592; "The Death-Disk" ("The Death-Wafer"), 106, 197–98, 510, 553; "Disgraceful Persecution of a Boy," 515; "A Dog's Tale," 189, 547; "A Double-Barrelled Detective Story," 498; "Editorial Agility," 561; *Eve's Diary,* 167–68, 540; *Following the Equator,* 504, 546, 651; "Forty-three Days in an Open Boat,"

Clemens, Samuel Langhorne (SLC)
WORKS *(continued)*
641; *The Gilded Age* (with Warner), 53, 467, 478, 533, 558, 601, 633, 641, 650; "Goldsmith's Friend Abroad Again," 515; "Hellfire Hotchkiss," 588; "Historical Exhibition—A No. 1 Ruse," 561; "A Horse's Tale," 145, 188–90, 529–30, 547; *Is Shakespeare Dead?*, 518, 628; "James Hammond Trumbull," 629; "Jim Smiley and His Jumping Frog" ("The Jumping Frog"), 46–47, 230, 484–85, 562, 650; "Josh" letters, 562, 566–67, 649; "Jul'us Caesar," 561; "Kiditchin," 217; "King Leopold's Soliloquy," 145, 529; "'Local' Resolves to Commit Suicide," 561; "Luck," 157, 343–45, 537; "Mark Twain's Own Account," 434–36, 640–41; *Mark Twain's Sketches, New and Old,* 53, 542, 602, 641, 650; "A Murder, a Mystery, and a Marriage," 548; "My Autobiography [Random Extracts from It]," 469, 574, 659; "My Debut as a Literary Person," 641; "My First Literary Venture," 561; "My Platonic Sweetheart," 533; *The Mysterious Stranger: A Romance,* 530; "No. 44, The Mysterious Stranger," 146, 196–97, 530, 552; "Old Times on the Mississippi," 489; "The Only Reliable Account of the Celebrated Jumping Frog of Calaveras County," 621; *Personal Recollections of Joan of Arc,* 197, 353, 608–9, 651; "A Petition to the Queen of England," 179–80, 545–46; "Pictur' Department," 561; "Prayer," 545; *Pudd'nhead Wilson,* 543, 651; "A Record of the Small Foolishnesses of Susie & 'Bay' Clemens (Infants)," 222–25, 330, 557, 593; "The Refuge of the Derelicts," 196, 198, 549, 552; "River Intelligence," 561; "Schoolhouse Hill," 552, 588, 589; "Scraps from My Autobiography," 576, 659–60; "A Simplified Alphabet," 578; "Snodgrass" letters, 231–35, 563; "Some Rambling Notes of an Idle Excursion," 549, 551, 611–12; *The Stolen White Elephant, Etc.,* 54, 489, 551; "Taming the Bicycle," 575; *The $30,000 Bequest and Other Stories,* 596; "Those Extraordinary Twins," 588; "Three Thousand Years Among the Microbes," 196, 552; "Tom Sawyer's Conspiracy," 545, 590; "To the Person Sitting in Darkness," 651; *Tom Sawyer Abroad,* 477; *A True Story, and the Recent Carnival of Crime,* 489; "A True Story, Repeated Word for Word as I Heard It," 542; "The Turning Point of My Life," 565; "Villagers of 1840–3," 626; "The War-Prayer," 526, 651; "Was it Heaven? Or Hell?," 83–96, 103–4, 107, 506; "'What Ought He to Have Done?': Mark Twain's Opinion," 328–29, 600–601; "Which Was It?," 196, 552; "Why Not Abolish It?," 647–48; "Ye Sentimental Law Student," 562, 567. See also *Adventures of Huckleberry Finn; The Adventures of Tom Sawyer; Ah Sin; The Celebrated Jumping Frog of Calaveras County; A Connecticut Yankee in King Arthur's Court; Date 1601; The Innocents Abroad; Life on the Mississippi; Mark Twain's Library of Humor; The Prince and the Pauper; Roughing It; A Tramp Abroad; What Is Man?*

Clemens family amusements: arithmetic problem, 215–16; charades, 164–65, 333; croquet, 347; Olivia's reading aloud, 218, 654; playacting English history, 333; playacting *The Prince and the Pauper,* 165–66, 216, 331, 540, 602; SLC's history game, 351–52, 608; SLC's reading aloud, 260, 273, 306, 343–44, 540; soap-bubble blowing, 258; solitaire, 331; songs and poems, 217, 293–94; storytelling, 346–47; tennis, 218; theatergoing, 333, 603

•Clemens family pets: children's responses to kitten's death, 224; at Quarry Farm, 216–18, 247–48, 257, 556; SLC's love of cats, 216, 224; at Upton House, 248–49, 511

NAMES: Ashes (cat), 248–49, 511; Cadichon (Kiditchin, donkey), 216–18, 556; Famine (cat), 217; Motley (kitten), 224; Old Minnie (cat), 217; Prosper (dog), 511; Rob (dog), 556; Sackcloth (two cats),

248–49, 511; Sour Mash (cat), 216–17, 247–49, 257, 556; "Stray Kit" (cat), 331
•Clemens family residences: 14 West 10th Street (N.Y.), 80, 81–82, 506; Hartford house, 79, 504, 626, 654; Riverdale (now Wave Hill), 82, 99–107, 506–8, 511, 651; Stormfield (Redding, Conn.), 509, 579, 652, 656; 21 Fifth Avenue (N.Y.), 23, 32, 111, 149, 447, 645, 651; vacation houses rented, 82, 97, 101, 183, 187, 506–8, 546, 552. *See also* Dublin (N.H.); Florence; London
•Clemens family servants: Anna (Jean's maid), 511; George Griffin (butler), 241, 257, 419, 567; George O'Connor (coachman), 511; Julia Koshloshky (wet nurse), 241, 567; Katherine (waitress), 511; Lilly Gillette Foote (governess), 510, 602; Margaret Sherry (nurse), 102, 104, 107, 509; Mary (cook), 511; Miss Tobin (nurse), 100, 101–2, 103, 508; Patrick McAleer (coachman), 292–93, 380, 446, 620. *See also* Hay, Rosina; Leary, Katy
Cleveland, Grover, 472, 508, 593
Cleveland Protestant Orphan Asylum, 350, 608
"Closing Words of My Autobiography," 656
Collier, Robert J., 619
Collier's Weekly, 609
Collins, Wilkie, 45, 483
Colonel Sellers, 467–68, 601, 633, 636. See also *The Gilded Age*
Colorado: corrupt legislature, 409, 410, 628; *Huckleberry Finn* banned by Denver library, 29, 474–75. *See also* Denver *Post*
Colt Arms Factory, 54
Columbia University, 505. *See also* Barnard College
"Concerning Copyright," 605–6
Concord (Mass.) Public Library, 29, 33, 474
Confucius's "Golden Rule," 130, 522
Congo. *See* Leopold II
Congo reform associations, 8, 460–62, 529
Congregationalists, 253, 574
Congressional Record (formerly *Congressional Globe*), 154, 535
A Connecticut Yankee in King Arthur's Court: composition and publication, 77, 196, 501, 552, 651; great inventors praised, 586; reviews, 604; theme, 306–7
Cooke, John Esten, 627
Cook's pills, 409, 627
Coolidge, Susan (Sarah Chauncey Woolsey), 375–76, **617**
Cooper, James Fenimore, 339, 517
Cooper, Peter, **481**
Cooper Union for the Advancement of Science and Art (N.Y.), 38–40, 481–82
Cope, Edgar, 440–41
Coppée, François, 45, 483
Copyright: and German law, 285; international, 283–84, 286–88, 318, 584, 585–86, 597; legislators' ignorance, 288–90, 318–19; SLC's argument for perpetual, 290–92, 338, 339–41, 587; SLC's testimony for Parliament, 290–92, 338–41, 586–87
ON SLC'S BOOKS: Harpers and American Publishing Company, 143–44, 146, 528; transferred to Olivia, 159–60, 504, 654. *See also titles of works*
AND U.S. LEGISLATION: in 1886, 283–84, 318, 584, 585–86, 597; in 1889, 317–20, 596–98; in 1906, 286, 320–24, 337–42, 585, 599
Copyright Act (U.K., 1842), 586
Copyright Act (U.S., 1909), 286, 585
Corbett, James J., 12, **463**
Corey, Ella J., **603**
Corey, Susan (Susy), 333, **603**
Cornell, Ezra, 477, 478
Cornell University: cofounders, 477; Fiske-McGraw marriage and consequent lawsuit, 33–37, 478–79; Paige typesetting machine, 80, 505
Cosmopolitan, 517, 526, 644
Cowing, George B., 459
Cowper, William, 109, 512
Cox, Samuel Sullivan (Sunset), 318–19, 501–2, 597–**98**
•Crane, Susan Langdon (Aunt Susy; Mrs. Theodore Crane): letters from SLC, 100, 101–3, 508, 533; letter to SLC, 174–75; and Lewis, 173, 174–75, 542; mentioned, 328, 655. *See also* Quarry Farm

Crane, Theodore, 542
Crapsey, Algernon Sidney, 131, **523**
Crawford, Samuel Wylie, 500
Criterion (periodical), 568–69
The Critic (periodical), 259–60, 263–65, 575–78
Cromwell, Oliver, 106, 409, 553, 556, **627**
Cross, Samuel, 177, **544**
Cumming, Alfred, 480
Cure, Louis, 622
A Curious Dream, 641
Currier, Frank D., 598
Curtis, George William, 562
Custer, Elizabeth B., 247, 250, 500, 501, **571–72**
Cutler, Albert G., 622
Cutting, Miss (university woman), 15
"The Czar's Soliloquy," 592
Czolgosz, Leon, 464

Daggett, Rollin, 566–67
Daguerre, Louis, 186, 547
Dake, Charles T., 532
Dake, Laura. *See* Wright, Laura Mary
Dana, Charles A., 419, 633. *See also* New York *Sun*
Dante, 601
D. Appleton and Company, 494, 502, 564–65, 597
Darwin, Charles, 223–24, 527, 557
Date 1601, 153–57, 535–38
David I (king of Scotland), 367, 614
Davis (mate on *John J. Roe*), 211–12
Davis, Fay, 18–19, 105, **466**, 510
"The Death-Disk" ("The Death-Wafer"), 106, 197–98, 510, 553
Defoe, Daniel, 169, 512, 540
De Laval Steam Turbine Company, 597
Delmonico's Restaurant (N.Y.), 607, 631
Delsarte, François, 278, 581
Denver *Post,* 410, 474–75
Denver (Colo.) Public Library, 29, 474–75
Depew, Chauncey M., 71, 72, 349, 387, 496–97, 623
Derby, George, 153, 534
Determinism: consequences of Adam's first act, 236–39, 240–41; of God/Nature, 127–28, 138–39, 141–43, 427–30
DeVoto, Bernard, 578, 620
Dewey, George, 558
Dibble, W. E. (Cincinnati publisher), 78, 503
Dickens, Charles, 119–20, 381, 408, 517, 521, 599, 606, 621
Dickinson, Anna, 43, **483**
Dickinson, Asa Don, 29–32, **475**–76
Dighton Rock (Berkley, Mass.), 364, 613
Dillon, Mr. (unidentified), 377–78, 619–20
Disability Pension Act (U.S., 1890), 616
"Disgraceful Persecution of a Boy," 515
Doane, T. W., 523
Dodge, Bayard, 100, 103, 105, **508**, 509
Dodge, Cleveland Earl, 100, 103, 105, **508**, 509
Dodge, Cleveland H., 107, 508, **511**
Dodge, Elizabeth, 100, 103, 105, **508**, 509
Dodge, Julia, 100, 103, 105, **508**, 509
•Dodge, Mary Mapes, 247, 250–53, 272, **573**, 579
Dodge, William E., 107, **511**
Doesticks, Q. K. Philander (Mortimer Thomson), 153, **535**
"A Dog's Tale," 189, 547
Dolby, George, 381–82
•Dollis Hill House (London), 448–53, 646
Doniphan (Kans.) *Crusader of Freedom,* 575
Donworth, Grace (Jennie Allen), 191–92, 246–47, 276–77, 548, **569**–70
Dooley, Martin. *See* Dunne, Finley Peter
"A Double-Barrelled Detective Story," 498
Doubleday, Frank N., 506
Dougherty, Daniel (called O'Dogherty), 309, **593**
Douglas, John H., 66, 495
Downey, Stephen W., 154, 535
Doyle, Arthur Conan, 74, 498
Drake, Sidney, 48, **486**
Dreadnought (battleship), 525
Dublin (N.H.): artists' colony, 553; Clemenses' acquaintances, 548, 553, 555; Clemenses' stay at Upton House, 46, 68, 108–9, 148, 151, 495, 511, 530, 554, 651; "Interpreting the Deity" written, 363–70; letters by SLC, 154, 169–70, 189–90; photographs of SLC, 203, 204–10, 554; talent shows for residents, 199–200, 203, 214–15, 555–56; white suit worn, 249–50

Dueling, 98, 416, 507, 630, 650
•Duneka, Frederick A.: biographical information, **527**; characterized by SLC, 143–49, 530–31; *Mark Twain's Library of Humor* and piracy concerns, 146–49, 152, 530–31, 534; opinion of SLC's works, 144–46, 506; 528–30. *See also* Harper and Brothers
Dunker Baptists, 173–75, 543
Dunlap, Jim (James), 178, 545
"Dunlap," use of name, 545
Dunne, Finley Peter (Martin Dooley), 152, 377, 379–80, 534, **619**, 620–21, 643
Dwight, Fanny, 572

École des Beaux Arts (Paris), 509
Ecyot, 218
Eddy, Mary Baker G.: biographical information, **525**, 571; *Science and Health,* 136, 247, 525, 602; SLC's opinion, 132, 136, 247, 525–26
Edison, Thomas, 625–26
"Editorial Agility," 561
Edward I (king of England), 352
Edward VII (king of England; formerly prince of Wales): anecdote about property deed, 225, 228–29, 560; on Anglo-American marriages, 415, 629–30; as Savage Club member, 436, 642; SLC's meeting, 180–82, 546; mentioned, 559
Egypt: Rosetta stone, 363–64, 613; Simplified Spelling sketch, 266–69, 578; SLC's proposed visit, 578; mentioned, 186, 371, 478
Eliot, Charles William (president of Harvard), 414, 629
Eliot, George (Mary Ann Evans), 65, 494–95, 599
Eliot, John, 412–13, **628–29**
Elisabeth (Carmen Sylva; queen of Romania), 97–98, **507**
Elizabeth I (queen of England), 154–56, 333, 537
Ellsworth, William Webster, 277, 280–81, **583**
Elmira (N.Y.). *See* Langdon family; Quarry Farm
Elmira *Gazette,* 479
Emerson, Ralph Waldo, 233, 339, 619
Emin Pasha, 280, 583
Emmett, Dan, 588
Empire Theatre (N.Y.), 30, 475
Employment. *See* Clemens, Samuel Langhorne: PET SCHEMES
Ends of the Earth Club, 225–27, 558
England. *See* Great Britain; London
Equitable Life Assurance Society, 493, 497
Ericson, Eric the Red, 176, 544
Ericson, Leif, 544
Erie Canal, boat design competition, 25, 472
Ernest II (duke of Saxe-Coburg-Gotha), 599
Evans, Mary Ann (George Eliot), 65, 494–95, 599
Everyday Housekeeping (periodical), 541
Every Saturday (periodical), 521
Eve's Diary, 167–68, 540
Executive Order 78 (Roosevelt), 372, 616

F., Baron (unidentified), 304–6, 591
•Fairhaven (Rogers's mansion at): construction, 506; SLC's visits, 82, 149, 151, 173, 235
Faxon, Ellen, 41–42, 483
Faxon, Frank, 41
Fechheimer, Morris W., **607–8**
Federal Steel Company, 80, 162, 505
Fellowcraft Club, 183–87, 546
Fentress Land Company, 469
Fields, James T., 521, 633
Fields, Osgood and Company, 53. *See also* Osgood, James R.
Fifth Avenue Hotel (N.Y.), 255, 574
Fifth-Avenue Theatre (N.Y.), 603, 633
Financial panics: of 1857, 516; of 1873, 518; of 1893–94, 78–79, 158–59, 504
Finn, Jimmy, 590
Fish, James D., 61, 66
Fiske, Daniel Willard: biographical information, 34–35, **477**, 478; Cornell University lawsuit, 35, 36–37, 479–80
Fiske, Jennie McGraw, 34–35, **478**, 479
Fiske, Minnie Maddern, **547**
Fitch, Thomas, 416, 417, **630**
Fitzhildebrand, Robert, 368, **614–15**
Fitzsimmons, Robert P., 12, **463**
Fletcher, John William, 394–96, **624**, 640

Florence: Clara's public singing, 240, 243, 567; Olivia's illness and death, 80–81, 82,100, 107–8, 651; Villa di Quarto landlady, 625
Florentine Dictations, 80, 445–46, 503, 643
Florida (Mo.), 649, 652
Following the Equator, 504, 546, 651
Foote, Lilly Gillette, 510, 602
Foote, Mary Hubbard, 106, **510**
Fortune telling and divination: augury in ancient Rome, 364–65, 369–70; SLC's experience with Madame Caprell (1861), 404–8, 627; SLC's experience with clairvoyant Professor Riess (1907), 401–3, 625–26. *See also* Palmistry; Mental telegraphy
"Forty-three Days in an Open Boat," 641
Foster, Stephen, 588
Fowler, Lorenzo N., 334–36, 337, 391, **603**, 604
Fowler, Orson Squire, **603**, 604
France: Clemenses' stay at Aix-les-Bains, 82, 506; *Huckleberry Finn* news item, 27–29, 32; Huguenots assassinated, 134, 524; naval fleet and statesmanship, 134–35, 525; SLC destroys manuscripts, 197
Franklin, William Buel, 265–66, 578
Fredonia (N.Y.): home of Jane Clemens and Pamela Moffett, 470, 492, 610, 653; home town of Webster and Whitford, 492, 493, 503; SLC's visit, 591
Freeman, Mary E. Wilkins, 548
Free speech, 442
French Revolution, 227
Frohman, Charles, 19, **466**
Frohman, Daniel, 19, **466**
Fuller, Annie Weeks Thompson, 40–42, **482**
Fuller, Frank: biographical information, **480-81**; as acting governor of Utah Territory, 37–38; adopted and biological sons, 41–42, 482–83; daughters, 42, 481, 483; SLC's lecture, 38–40, 481; SLC's meeting, 481; steam generator company, 54–55, 490; wife's death, 40–41
Fuller, Louis R., 41–42, **482**–83
Fuller, Mary F., **481**

Gabrilowitsch, Clara Clemens. *See* Clemens, Clara Langdon
Gabrilowitsch, Nina (SLC's granddaughter), **655**
Gabrilowitsch, Ossip (Clara's husband), 509, 652, **655**
Galaxy (periodical), 515, 561
Garfield, James A., 137, **526**
Garrety, Margaret, 508, 509
General Act of Berlin (international agreement, 1885), 461
George III (king of England), 134, 352, 525
George Routledge and Sons: authorized SLC editions, 488, 641; New York agent, 641; SLC's meeting (1872), 435–36. *See also* Routledge, Edmund
Gerhardt, Karl, 247, 333, **571**
Germany: Clemens family activities, 225; copyright law, 284–85; Harte as consul, 119, 519, 520, 635; Harte's *Gabriel Conroy* popular, 635; naval fleet, 525; SLC's translation project, 584–85; SLC's travels with Twichell, 181–82, 546; SLC's works published, 316, 599; U.S. tariff negotiations, 433, 640; Wagner's *Lohengrin*, 539. *See also* Wilhelm II
PLACES: Baden-Baden, 242, 568; Bad Homburg, 181–82, 228, 546, 560; Bad Nauheim, 181, 506, 546; Frankfurt, 584–85; Hamburg, 417, 631; Mannheim, 539. *See also* Berlin
Gilbert, W. S., 333, 537, 560, 603
The Gilded Age (SLC and Warner), 53, 467, 478, 533, 588, 601, 633, 641, 650. See also *Colonel Sellers*
Gilder, Dorothea, 270, **509**
Gilder, Helena de Kay, 243, **568**
Gilder, Louise Comfort Tiffany, 569
Gilder, Richard Watson: as *Century Magazine* editor, 494; family, 243, 244, 568–69, 579; as Fellowcraft Club member, 183–84, 186, 546; Friday night soirées, 568
Gilder, Rodman, 244, **568–69**
Gilgamesh epic, 130, 523
Gillette, Elisabeth (Lilly; Mrs. George Warner), 331, 540, 557
Gillette, William Hooker, 224, 557
Gillis, William (Billy), 514, 636
Gillis, Francina California, 514

Gillis, James (Jim): clothing, 422; Harte's stay, 518; liberality, 423; "pocket mining," 422, 621, 636; safe after earthquake, 113, 114; SLC's stay, 514
Gillis, Mary Elizabeth (Mollie), 514
Gillis, Stephen E. (Steve), 113, 114, 514
Gillis, Theresa Ann (Mrs. Henry Williams), 514
Gilman, George Shepard ("Judge What's-his-name"), 53, **488–89**
Ginn, Frank H., **535**
Gladstone, William, 449, 560, **646–47**
God: characterized by SLC, 127–30, 136–40; Clara's comments, 309–10, 593; creation of man, 288–89; man's interpretation of intentions, 365–79; as Providence, 117, 292–93, 380, 382, 440–42; SLC's reluctance to discuss frankly, 121, 522. *See also* Bible; Determinism; Christianity; Religion
The God Damned Human Race (club), 442–43, 643
Goelet, May, 415, 629–30
Goggin, Pamelia (SLC's father's mother), 627
"Goldsmith's Friend Abroad Again," 515
Golden Era (periodical), 118, 119, 517, 518, 562, 650
Goodman, Joseph T.: on "Captain Stormfield's Visit to Heaven," 550; duel with Fitch, 416, 630; on insurance stock, 55, 56; safe after earthquake, 113; SLC hired, 567
Gordon, Clara J., 244, **569**
Gould, Jay, 116, 388, 409, 623–24
G. P. Putnam's Sons, 597. *See also* Putnam, George Haven
Grand Army of the Republic: allied organizations, 623; annual convention, 372; banquet for Grant, 70–71, 181, 252, 573; founding and goals, 615–16; influence on Congress, 387. *See also* Pensions
Grant, Frederick, 60–61, 62, 64, 74–75, 498
Grant, Jesse, 333, 603
Grant, Julia: Grant's funeral, 574; proceeds from Grant's *Memoirs*, 73, 74, 75–76, 255, 497, 498, 499, 574
Grant, Miriam M. McFarland, 301, 590–91
Grant, Orville R., 301, **590**, 590–91
Grant, Ulysses S.: Chicago banquet, 70–71, 180–81, 252, 496, 573; Civil War articles, 61–62, 494; death and funeral, 73, 255, 574; Gerhardt's bust, 571; illnesses, 65, 66, 72, 495; names and faces remembered, 181; Nast's sketch, 13; pension and title restored, 70–71, 496; popularity of Roosevelt compared with, 9; presidential appointments, 45, 556–57; sale of letters, 10, 463; SLC's meeting, 180, 546; SLC's tribute, 218–19; "Unconditional Surrender" nickname, 497; Ward's swindling, 61, 62, 66–67. See also *Personal Memoirs*
Grant and Ward (brokerage firm), 61, 62, 66–67, 497
Gray, David, 156–57, 175, 536
Great Britain: Clemenses' travel (1872–73), 165, 539, 650; copyright law, 284, 288–89, 291, 318, 339–41, 586–87, 605, 641; free speech absent, 442; and international copyright, 287–88; naval fleet and statesmanship, 134–35, 525; pirated editions of SLC's works, 641; Simplified Spelling opposed, 274, 580; SLC's history game, 351–52, 608; tax on foreign copyright owners, 179–80, 545. *See also* British Empire; British Parliament; London
Great Eastern Railway Company, 444
Greece (ancient), 130–31, 168, 323, 371
Greeley, Horace: Nast's sketch, 13; SLC's anecdote, 199, 200–203, 553, 554; mentioned, 464
Green, George Walton, 584
Greening, Tabitha Quarles, 470
Gregory I (pope), 369, 615
Griffin, George, 241, 257, 419, 567
Griffiths, Mrs. William, 122–23, 126–27, 521–22
Griswold, Anna (Mrs. Francis Bret Harte), 420, 426, **630–31**
Guggenheim, Simon, 410, **628**
Guiteau, Charles J., **526**
Gunn, Alexander, 153–54, **535**
Gunn, John C., 627
Gunther, Charles F., 628

Gutenberg, Johannes, 586
Gwynn, Dr. *See* Barret, Richard Ferril

The Hague, Palace of Peace, 172, 541
Hale, Edward Everett, 318, 338–40, 424, 598, 605, **636**
Hale and Norcross Silver Mining Company, 20–21, 422, 468
Hall, Frederick J.: biographical information, **503**; *A Connecticut Yankee,* 501; Hoffmann's *Der Struwwelpeter,* 584–85; management of Webster and Company, 78, 500–503; military memoirs and war literature, 500; Walters's *Oriental Ceramic Art,* 502
Hambourg, Mark, 103, **509**
Hancock, Almira Russell, 500
Hancock, Winfield Scott, 500, 593
Hannibal (of Carthage), 330
Hannibal (Mo.): cemetery, 152–53, 534; Clemenses' living arrangements, 301, 590; Clemenses' move, 649, 652; Jane Clemens's departure, 653; mesmerist, 297–300, 589; minstrel show, 294, 296, 588; phrenologist's visit, 335; schools and teachers, 177–78, 544; SLC's last visit, 534, 590, 641; stabbing affray, 301, 590; story about Huck and Tom's later years, 552
Hannibal *Gazette,* 589
Hannibal *Journal:* Orion's ownership, 230, 560, 653; serial story sought, 233–34; SLC's sketches, 230, 560–61; staff, 260–61, 589
Hannibal *Missouri Courier,* 561, 649
Hannibal *Tri-Weekly Messenger,* 561
Hannibal *Western Union,* 561, 589, 649, 653
Hapgood, Emilie Bigelow, 101, 102, 270, **509**, 579
Hapgood, Norman, 270, 509, 579
Harcourt, William Vernon, 228, **560**
Hare, William, 235, **563**
Harper and Brothers: American Publishing Company purchase, 160, 539; *Christian Science* published, 144–45, 529; Howells's contract, 501; legal counsel (*see* Larkin, John); *Mark Twain's Library of Humor,* 146–49, 151, 530–31; rights to SLC's books, 143–44, 528; SLC's contract, 146–47, 531, 539, 651. *See also* Duneka, Frederick A.; Harvey, George
Harper's Bazar, 190, 526, 547–48
Harper's Monthly, Nevinson's articles on Portuguese West Africa, 145, 529; SLC's tribute to Howells, 152, 533–34
SLC'S WORKS: "Captain Stormfield's Visit to Heaven," 550–51; "The Death-Disk," 553; "A Dog's Tale," 189, 547; "A Horse's Tale," 145, 189–90, 529, 547; "Was it Heaven? Or Hell?," 83–96, 100, 103–4, 107, 506
Harper's New Monthly Magazine: Alden as editor, 562; *Huckleberry Finn* reviewed, 475; Snodgrass letters, 230–31, 562
SLC'S WORKS: "Forty-three Days in an Open Boat," 641; "Luck," 157, 344, 537; "Personal Recollections of Joan of Arc," 608–9; "A Petition to the Queen of England," 179–80, 545–46
Harper's Weekly: Harvey's parable about White, 455–56, 648; on Kipling, 543–44; Nast's cartoons of Tweed Ring, 462, 464–65; palm readings arranged by editor, 337, 390, 400, 624. *See also* Harvey, George
SLC'S WORKS: series of photographs, 204–10, 554; "Why Not Abolish It?," 647–48
•Harris, Joel Chandler (Uncle Remus): age, 260; expression "dry gripes," 115; letter from SLC, 577; photograph mentioned, 576; praise for *Huckleberry Finn,* 265, 577; tribute for SLC's fiftieth birthday, 259, 263, 264–65, 575
Harrison, Katherine I., 504
Harrods (London), 450–52, 647
Harte, Anna Griswold (Mrs. Francis Bret Harte), 420, 426, **630–31**
Harte, Eliza C. T. (Mrs. Frederick Knaufft; Bret's sister), 420, **634**
•Harte, Bret: death, 422, 636; marriage and family, 417, 630–31, 638; mistresses, 422, 635–36; move to East, 119, 120, 518–19; treatment of son, 425, 637; mentioned, 484, 599
CHARACTERISTICS: debts, 417–18, 420–21, 634; "Howells's opinion, 519–20; "man without a country," 424–25; pre-

tense of wealth, 423–24; SLC's opinion, 119–20, 127, 417–18, 420–21, 425–26, 519; temperament, 427–28, 430; treachery, 425
LITERARY CONCERNS: anecdote of Osborn's adventure, 324–26; dialects used in writing, 118, 518, 520, 521; fame, 416–17; literary contracts, 120, 421, 635; on Phelps's *The Gates Ajar*, 550; playwriting, 418–20, 631–32 (see also *Ah Sin*); proposed book of sketches with SLC, 485; writing process, 118–19
OCCUPATIONS: compositor, newspaper and magazine editor, 118, 415–16, 517; schoolteacher, 118, 415, 517–18; secretary at U.S. Mint, 117–18, 516–17; U.S. consul, 119, 424–25, 519–20. See also *Californian; Golden Era; Overland Monthly*
RELATIONSHIP WITH SLC: Hartford visits, 418, 419–20, 424, 631, 632–33; ruptured friendship, 634, 635; SLC's loans, 418, 421, 423–24, 634
WORKS: *Condensed Novels,* 118, 517; *Gabriel Conroy,* 120, 421, 634–35; "The Idyl of Red Gulch," 631; *The Luck of Roaring Camp, and Other Sketches* (including title story), 120, 416–17, 518, 520–21; "Mr. Thompson's Prodigal," 631; "Plain Language from Truthful James" ("The Heathen Chinee"), 120, 520; "Tennessee's Partner," 120, 521; "Thankful Blossom" (called "Faithful Blossom"), 419, 632–33; *Two Men of Sandy Bar,* 418–19, 631–32, 636. See also *Ah Sin*
Harte, Ethel (Bret's daughter), 426, **630–31**
Harte, Francis King (Frank; Bret's son), 425–26, **630–31**, 637
Harte, Griswold (Bret's son), **630–31**
Harte, Jessamy (Bret's daughter), 426, 427, **630–31**, 638–39
Hartford Accident Insurance Company, 55–56, 490–91
Hartford *Courant,* 35–36, 56–57, 146, 479, 491, 609
Hartford Engineering Company (steam-powered pulleys), 55, 490
Hartford *Evening Post,* 22, 26, 470–71
Hartwick, Rose (Mrs. Thorpe), 215, 556
Hartwig, Elias, 507
Hartwig, Florence, 97–98, **507**
•Harvey, George: biographical information, **510**; "Captain Stormfield's Visit to Heaven" accepted, 551; *Eve's Diary* review clipping sent, 540; as club member, 643; hires Duneka, 527; letter from SLC, 609; palm readings arranged, 337, 90, 400, 624; parable about White, 455–56, 648; and SLC's sixty-seventh birthday dinner, 105, 510; Tennyson lines quoted, 612; travels, 149, 151. *See also* Harper and Brothers
Hastings (writer), 118, 517
Hawkins, Homer, 41–42, 482
Hawley, David, 281–83, **583–84**
Hawley, Joseph Roswell, 56, 283, 491
Hawley Bill, 284, 288, 584
Hay, John, 153–55, 535
Hay, Rosina (Mrs. Horace K. Terwilliger; nurse): children rescued, 240–42, 568; in Germany with family, 225; marriage, 242, 568; mentioned, 539, 542
Hayes, Rutherford B., 424–25, 519–20, 636–37
Heinrich (prince of Prussia): SLC as guest at dinner, 310, 594; U.S. visit, 432–33, 639–40; on veterans' pensions, 431
"Hellfire Hotchkiss," 588
Hemans, Felicia, 644
Henderson, Berta von Bunsen, 555
Henderson, Ernest Flagg, 214, **555**
Henry (prince). *See* Heinrich
Henry I (king of England), 351, 365–67, 614
Henry II (king of England), 614
Henry III (king of England), 352
Henry V (king of England), 352
Henry of Huntingdon, 366–69, 614
Henry of Mecklenburg-Schwerin (prince), 444, **643**
Hervy, Miss (university woman), 15–16
Hicks, Urban East, 298–99, 300, **589**, 590
Hieroglyphics: alphabet vs., 266–69; mock translations, 363–64, 613
Higbie, Calvin: biographical information, **540**; manuscript sent for SLC's criticism, 168–71, 182–83, 188, 541

Higgins (bowler), 385–86
Hill, David B., 36–37, **479**, 480
Hillis, Newell Dwight, 369–70, **615**
Hinckley, Howard N., 492
Hinduism, 130, 131, 474, 523
Hinton, J. T., 561
Hirsch, Gilbert, 564
"Historical Exhibition—A No. 1 Ruse," 561
•Hobby, Josephine (stenographer-typist): clippings pasted in typescript, 457, 463; Dublin stay, 511; and Simplified Spelling dictation, 578; SLC's letter to Carnegie, 541; transcriptions, 540, 586, 615, 643, 646, 661; typing of Lyon's notes, 611
Hodson, Henrietta (Labouchere's wife), 228, **559–60**
Hoeber, Arthur, 580
Hoffmann, Heinrich (doctor): entertainment for sick children, 284–85; WORK: *Der Struwwelpeter,* 284, **584**–85
Holden, Miss (mind cure practitioner), 331, 602
Holliday, Melicent S. McDonald, 404, 405, 626
Holmes, Oliver Wendell: and father's misplaced paper, 354, 356; letter from SLC, 577; life of books, 339; reaction to SLC's copyright ideas, 286–88, 586; SLC's opinion, 339; tribute for SLC's fiftieth birthday, 259, 263–64, 575; mentioned, 233
Holsatia (ship), 631
Hood, Thomas, 435–36, **642**
Hooker, Edward Beecher, 403, **626**
Hooker, Isabella Beecher, 403, **626**
Hooker, John, 626
Hoppe, William F., 384, 621, **622**
Hornet (ship), 435, 641
Horr, Elizabeth, 177–78, 233, **544**, 653
"A Horse's Tale": composition and publication, 529–30, 547; Duneka's opinion, 145–46; reader's letter (and SLC's reply), 188–90
Hot Stuff by Famous Funny Men (Perkins, ed.), 534
Hotten, John Camden, 488, 641
Houdini, Harry, 626
Houghton, Richard Monckton Milnes, Lord, 156, 536
House, Edward H. (friend in Japan), 156, 536
House-flies. *See* Insects
Howe, Samuel Gridley, 279, **582**
Howells, Elinor Mead, 509, 542–43, 607
Howells, John Mead, 102, **509**, 652
Howells, Mildred (Pilla), 349, **607**
•Howells, William Dean: as club member, 643; hears story of Jane Clemens's early romance, 610; and Jews, 349–50, 607; letters from SLC, 151–52, 495, 501, 515, 519, 520, 522, 542–43, 548, 586, 608, 631–34; letter to Hayes, 519–20; SLC's opinion, 339; SLC's tribute, 152, 533–34; summer visit with Clemenses, 80, 83; tribute to SLC, 510; typewriter gift, 446; mentioned, 527, 578
LITERARY CONCERNS: "Chicago School of Fiction," 534; collaborative story idea, 190, 547–48; and copyright hearings, 318–19; as editor of *Atlantic Monthly* and *Harper's New Monthly Magazine,* 353, 548, 562, 609; novelettes and play planned with SLC, 548, 553
TOPICS DISCUSSED: age, 265; Harte, 418, 519; invalid story, 83 (*see also* "Was it Heaven? Or Hell?"); SLC's character, 332, 602; SLC's white suit, 572; SLC's works, 194, 550, 552, 602
WORKS: "A Double-Barrelled Sonnet to Mark Twain," 510; *The Rise of Silas Lapham,* 349–50, 607; *Venetian Life,* 152, 534. See also *Mark Twain's Library of Humor*
Howells and Stokes (architectural firm), 509
Huckleberry Finn. See *Adventures of Huckleberry Finn*
Hudson Theatre (N.Y.), 16–17, 466
Hugo, Victor, 517, 601
Huguenots, assassinated on Bartholomew's Day, 134, 524
Human race: advance to perfection, 134; cats compared with, 248–49; character evidenced in letters, 121–27; easily deceived, 247; as ephemeral as soap bubbles, 258; exception to generalities about, 412–13; extreme behaviors juxtaposed, 307; free speech abominated by,

442; God's disappointment, 288; and God's two halves, 128–30; greed, 234–35; hopes for heaven, 140; house-fly's mastery, 219–22; impossibility of irreverence, 167–68; law of temperament, 427–28, 429–30; love for titles, 37–38, 70, 314, 652; naïve self-appreciation, 18, 142; SLC's study of self as representative, 383–84, 412; unchangeable nature, 370–72; vanity, 171; yearnings, 566. *See also* Determinism
The Human Race (club), 442–43, 643
Humor: about baldness, 26; of alcohol's effects, 186; characteristics, 153; contagiousness of laughter, 297; early newspaper satire by SLC, 560–61; first humorous woman's book, 45, 483; humor magazine editorship declined, 197, 552–53; as independent from facts, 167–68; Jacobs's *Dialstone Lane* as perfect story, 182, 546; of maxims, 361; in minstrel shows, 295–96; newspaper satire, 6–7; phrenologists and palmists on SLC's sense of humor, 336–37, 390–91, 397, 399–400, 624; publisher's concern about humor in *Innocents Abroad,* 48; repetition of Monk-Greeley anecdote, 200–203; SLC's disinterest, 332n; in tributes for SLC's fiftieth birthday, 259–60. *See also* Practical jokes
Hunt, Sylvia M., 122–27, 521–22
Hunt, William, 13, 464–65
Hutchinson, Ellen M., **503**
•Hutton, Eleanor Varnum Mitchell, 330, 582, **601**, 618
•Hutton, Laurence: biographical information, **573**, 601; as guest at Onteora, 251; and Helen Keller, 279–80, 582; letter from SLC, 507–8; Susy on visit, 330
Hymettus (Greek mountain), 238, 566
Hypnotism. *See* Mesmerism

The Idler (periodical), 553
India: and Kipling, 175–77; SLC's travel, 81, 651. *See also* Hinduism
Indians. *See* Native Americans
Ingersoll, Joseph R., 592
"In God We Trust" motto, 226–27
The Innocents Abroad: authorized and pirated English editions, 641; contract and publication, 48, 49, 486, 487, 650; copyright registered, 487, 585; delivery of manuscript, 180; Gray's opinion, 156–57; invitation to write, 239; pictures noted, 14; *Quaker City* passengers, 17–18, 466; readers' responses, 351, 434–35; sales and royalties, 48–49, 487, 488; SLC's subsequent notoriety, 50, 488; Wilhelm II's appreciation, 434. See also *Quaker City* excursion
Insects: house-flies, 139, 219–22, 257–58, 428–29; mosquitoes and fleas, 220, 221, 428–29; spider, 138–39, 221, 428–29, 526–27; wasps and Jim Wolf, 261, 262–63; wasps' nature, 139, 428–29, 526–27
Insurance industry: graft, 115–16, 515; investigations, 59, 464, 493, 497; SLC's investment, 55–56, 490–91
International Copyright Act (U.S., 1891), 597
International Typographical Union, 283, 584
"Interpreting the Deity," 363–70, 613–15
Interstate Commerce Commission, 612
Inventions and patents: all born of ideas, 291–92, 339–40; daguerreotype, 186, 547; Kaolatype, 489–90, 493; lawyer for infringements, 592; Orion's, 25, 472; Paige typesetting machine, 80, 158–60, 505, 537, 539, 651; self-pasting scrapbook (SLC), 55, 490; steam generator, 54–55, 490; steam-powered pulley, 55, 490; Telharmonium, 447, 645; typewriter, 445–47, 643–45. *See also* Telephone
Ireland, William-Henry, 247, **570–71**
Irving, Henry, 19, 166, 467, 540
Irving, Washington, 250, 339, 500, 573
Is Shakespeare Dead?, 518, 628
Italy. *See* Florence; Rome

Jackass Hill (or Gulch, Calif.): billiard playing, 384–85; Harte's stay, 118, 517–18; SLC's stay, 422–23, 468, 514, 621, 636, 650
Jackson, Andrew, 9
Jacobs, William Wymark, 182, 546
James, Henry, 527

James, William, 112–13, **513**, 513–14
James I (king of England), 352
"James Hammond Trumbull," 629
"Jane Lampton Clemens," 610, 653
Janeway, Edward Gamaliel, 101, **508**
Japan: *Date 1601* privately printed, 155–56; war with Russia (1904–5), 369–70, 525, 615
Jayhawkers, 256, 574–75
Jefferson, Joseph, 76, **499–500**, 557–58
Jeffries, James J., 12, 463
Jerome, Jerome K., 553
Jerome, William T., 647
Jewish Orphan Asylum (Cleveland), 350, 608
Jews: attitudes toward, 69, 350, 496, 607–8; as "chosen," 129, 136; Howells and, 349–50, 607; orphan homes, 350, 608; Russian pogroms, 132–34, 524; Webster's Jewish ancestry suggested, 69, 496
"Jim and the Strainin' Rag" (recitation), 346–47
"Jim Smiley and His Jumping Frog," 46–47, 230, 484–85, 562, 650
Joan of Arc: in others' writing, 564, 566; in SLC's writing, 197, 353, 608–9, 651; mentioned, 28
John A. Gray and Green (printer), 485, 487
John J. Roe (steamboat), 150–51, 211, 531–32
John Marshall Monument Fund, 308–9, 592–93
Johnson, Burges, 530
Johnson, Frank Minitree, 564
Johnson, Robert Underwood, 317–18, 319, **597**, 598
Johnson, Samuel, 642
Jolly, Sobieski (Beck), 150, **532**
Jones, John P., 55–56, 490–91
Jonson, Ben, 155
Jordan, David Starr, 392, 624
Jordan, Elizabeth, 526, 547–48
"Josh" letters, 562, 566–67, 649
Josie (housemaid), 542
Judaism. *See* Jews
Juggernaut Club, 28–29, 474
"Jul'us Caesar," 561
"The Jumping Frog." *See* "Jim Smiley and His Jumping Frog"; *The Celebrated Jumping Frog of Calaveras County*
Jung, Carl, 510

Kaiser. *See* Wilhelm II
Kanawha (Rogers's steam yacht): Bahamas trip, 455, 648; Clemenses' travel aboard, 82, 506; Rogers's character aboard, 161; SLC's living aboard, 149; and "spontaneous oratory" scheme, 183, 187–88
Kansas City *Star*, 414, 629
Kansas-Nebraska Act (1854), 255–56, 574–75
Kaolatype Engraving Company, 489–90, 493
Katherine (waitress), 511
Katonah (N.Y.), 579, 656
Keene, Laura, 13, **464**
Keller, Helen: cowboy's letter to, 413–15, 629; Lyon's description, 617–18; raising support for, 280, 582; SLC's dinner with, 374–76; SLC's meeting, 279, 581
Kellgren, Jonas, 513, 646, 656
Kennin, Frank Nicholls, 618–19
Keokuk (Iowa): Clemenses' visit, 356–58; mother's home, 22, 25, 237–38; 469, 470, 591, 653; Orion's chicken farm, 22–23, 25, 471–72; SLC's home, 237, 649; SLC's 1885 visit, 591; mentioned, 27
Keokuk *Gate City*, 22, 470
Keokuk *Post*, 562, 563
Kerr, Orpheus C. (Robert Henry Newell), 153, **535**
"Kiditchin," 217
"King Leopold's Soliloquy," 145, 529. *See also* Leopold II
Kinsmen (club), 573
Kipling, Rudyard: biographical information, **544**; in Ends of the Earth Club, 558; visit to SLC and America, 175, 176–77, 544; mentioned, 274; WORKS: *The Jungle Book* and *The Second Jungle Book*, 177; *Kim*, 177; *Plain Tales from the Hills*, 177; "South Africa," 543
Kirkham, Emily, 359, 360, **611**
Kirkham, Mary Ann, 359, 360, **611**
Kirkham, Samuel, 360, **611**

Kittredge, Alfred B., 598
Knaufft, Eliza C. T. Harte (Mrs. Frederick Knaufft; Bret's sister), 420, **634**
Knaufft, Frederick, 634
Knight, Elizabeth Owen, 477
Kooneman, Margaret, 178, 545
Koshloshky, Julia (wet nurse), 241, 567

Labouchere, Henry du Pré, 228, **559**
Lacey (steamboat), 561–62
La Cossitt, Henry, 589
Ladies' Home Journal, 474, 541, 543, 570, 644
Laffan, William Mackay, 77, **502**
Lakeside Monthly, 119, 120, 518–19
Lampton, Benjamin (SLC's mother's father), 627
Lampton, Jane. *See* Clemens, Jane Lampton
Lampton, William (SLC's mother's grandfather), 627
Lancaster (ship), 325
Landon, Melville D. (Eli Perkins), 153, 534
Lang, Andrew, 347–48, **606–7**
Langdon, Charles Jervis (Olivia's brother), 64, 239, 377, 494, 619–20
Langdon, Ida B. Clark (Charles's wife), 542–43
Langdon, Jervis (little Jervis), 542
Langdon, Jervis (Olivia's father), 377–78, 541, 619, 650, **654**
Langdon, Julia, 542–43
Langdon, Olivia Lewis (Olivia's mother), 176, 542, 609, **654**
Langdon, Olivia Louise. *See* Clemens, Olivia Louise Langdon
Langham Hotel (London), 334, 436
Larchmont disaster (1907), 436–37, 441–43, 642–43
Larkin, John, 149, 469, **531**
Latta, M. C., 12, 463
Launcelot, 218
Lauterbach, Edward, 149, **531**
Lavedan, Henri, 466
Lawrence, Joe, 118–19
Lawton, Mary, 18–19, 466–67
Layton (mesmerist), 589
•Leary, Katy (housekeeper): and Clara's début, 243; examines Fifth Avenue house, 23; and Jean's illness, 100, 102, 105, 107, 353–55; length of service, 471; memoir, 466; at Olivia's death, 108
Leavenworth, Mark, 150, **532**
Leavenworth, Zebulon, 150–51, **532**
Lee, Henry S., 435–36, **642**
Leonard (doctor), 99
Leopold II (king of Belgium): crimes, 8, 134, 141, 145, 307, 393, 460–62, 529; SLC's article on, 529; and Stanley's exploration of Congo, 583
Leschetizky, Theodor, 509, 655
Leslie, Dora (Eda O. Lyde), 224, **557**–58
Leslie, Elsie (Elsie Leslie Lyde), 224, **557–58**
Leslie, Mrs. (Evelyn Lyde), 224, **557**–58
Lester, George B., 55–56, 490–91
Letters from SLC: destroyed after Laura Wright's death, 533; sold at auction, 10, 12–13, 462; typewritten, 446, 644
TO FAMILY MEMBERS: Clara, 506, 547; Jane Lampton Clemens, 566, 627, 633; Jean, 645; Mollie (Orion's wife), 473; Olivia, 470–71, 538, 548, 556, 579, 602; Orion, 21, 23, 404–9, 468, 471, 473, 499, 505, 566, 627; Susan Crane, 100, 101–3, 508, 533
TO OTHER PEOPLE: Maude Adams, 564–65; Thomas S. Barbour, 461–62; Robert Barr, 553; Lillian Robinson Beardsley, 189–90; George Bentley, 633; Elisha Bliss, 486–87, 641; Frank Bliss, 489; Edward Bok, 446, 644; John Brown, 551–52; Joseph Cannon, 598; Andrew Carnegie, 172, 541; Chicago *Republican* editor, 549, 550; Denver *Post* editor, 474–75; Asa Don Dickinson, 30, 476; Charles Frohman, 19, 466; Joel Chandler Harris, 577; George Harvey, 609; Calvin Higbie, 169–70; Oliver Wendell Holmes, 577; William Dean Howells, 151–52, 495, 501, 515, 519, 520, 522, 548, 586, 608, 631–34; William Dean and Elinor Howells, 542–43; Eleanor Hutton, 582; Laurence Hutton, 508; Rudolf Lindau, 594–95; Thomas Nast, 10; Charles Orr, 154–55; Henry Huttleston Rogers, 567; Mary Rogers, 572,

Letters from SLC
TO OTHER PEOPLE *(continued)*
578; Upton Sinclair, 515; Otis Skinner, 466–67; Thorvald Solberg (register of copyrights), 605–6; Anne W. Stockbridge, 569–70; Frank Stockton, 576; Bessie Stone, 355–56, 609; Charlotte Teller, 564; Ellen Terry, 19; Joseph Twichell, 103–7, 155, 498; Victoria (queen of England), 179–80, 545–46; Lord Wolseley, 537–38; Frederick Whyte, 334, 603; Charles E. S. Wood, 607–8
Letters to SLC: about *Christian Science,* 144–45; about *Christian Union* article, 329, 600–601; Lyon asked to locate for autobiography, 508; opposing ban on *Huckleberry Finn,* 29–32, 33; SLC's burden of correspondence, 81–82
FROM FAMILY MEMBERS: Clara, 152; Olivia, 556; Orion, 472, 499; Susan Crane, 174–75
FROM OTHER PEOPLE: Henry Mills Alden, 231; Lillian Robinson Beardsley, 189; B. Butler Boyle, 199, 213; George W. Cable, 334; Andrew Carnegie, 541; Susy Crane, 174–75; Asa Don Dickinson, 29–30, 31, 32; Morris Fechheimer, 608; Minnie Maddern Fiske, 547; Thomas Fitch, 415, 630; Bret Harte, 634, 635; George Harvey, 551; Calvin Higbie, 182–83; William Dean Howells, 501; Charles Orr, 153; Hélène Elisabeth Picard, 28, 29, 473–74; Henry Huttleston Rogers, 582; "John Senior," 600–601; Anne W. Stockbridge, 246; Frank R. Stockton, 259; Bessie Stone, 355–56, 609; J. Hammond Trumbull, 467–68; Joseph Twichell, 510, 551; Laura Wright, 151, 211, 553, 554
•Lewis, John T.: biographical information, **541–42**; death, 173–75; pension, 172–73, 175; rescue of women, 542–43; on Sour Mash (cat), 216
Library of Humor. See *Mark Twain's Library of Humor*
Library of Wit and Humor by Mark Twain and Others (anthology), 152–53, 534
Lies and lying: Carlyle quoted, 304, 591; Clara's lies to Olivia, 99–103, 104–7, 509; SLC's mesmerism deception, 298–302; Susy's lies in childhood, 223–24; truth perceived as, 302–4, 381–82. *See also* "Was it Heaven? Or Hell?"
Life on the Mississippi: contract, 53; German porter's appreciation, 315–16; Lewis's rescue of women recounted, 543; origin of "Mark Twain" pseudonym, 230, 356, 561; profane ostler anecdote, 380, 620; publication, 52, 53–54, 489, 492, 651; typewritten copy, 645; Wilhelm II's appreciation, 310, 315, 431, 594
Lincoln, Abraham: assassination, 13, 464; Gettysburg Address compared to Malory, 218; letter and memorabilia sold at auction, 13; political appointments, 458, 480, 653; political supporters and tribute, 573, 593, 619
Lindau, Rudolf (called Smith): biographical information, **536**; copy of *Date 1601* promised, 157; letter from SLC, 594–95; vacation (or resignation) request, 311–12, 594–95; work schedule, 310–11
Lindsey, Ben B., 628
Literature: amateur offerings from friends, 162–63, 168–71; children's writing, 166 (*see also* Clemens, Olivia Susan, biography of SLC); detective stories, 74, 498; journalism vs., 230, 562; most prodigious asset of a country, 323–24; popular recitations by others, 556; right form for a story, 197–98; writing from the heart, 127, 183, 188–90, 413–15. *See also* Autobiography (SLC)
Littleton, Martin W., 547
Livingstone, David, 583
Lloyd's News, 439–40
"'Local' Resolves to Commit Suicide," 561
Locke, David Ross (Petroleum V. Nasby), 153, 445–46, 643–44
Loeb, William, Jr., 460
Logan, James O'Neill, 44–45
Logan, John Alexander, 70, **496**
Logan, Olive, 43–46, 483
London: American Society's Independence Day dinner, 157, 537; billiard playing, 381–82; Clemenses' stay in Tedworth

Square (1896–97), 10–11, 81; Clemenses' stay at Dollis Hill House (1900), 81, 448–53, 646; house addresses puzzling, 452–53; merchants, 447–48, 449–52, 645–46; phrenology readings, 334, 335–36, 391, 604; rumor of SLC's death, 11; Simplified Spelling rejected by press, 580; SLC's first visit (1872), 434–36, 641; SLC's meeting of Campbell-Bannerman, 227–28; SLC's meeting of Wolseley, 157, 345; SLC's testimony before Parliament, 290–92, 338–41, 587; Terry's jubilee celebrations, 19, 467. *See also* Chatto and Windus; George Routledge and Sons
London *Evening Standard,* 580
London *Globe,* 580
London *Idler* (monthly), 553
London *Leader,* 580
London *Pall Mall Gazette,* 580
London *Standard,* 525, 543
London *Tribune,* 227, 559
London *Westminster Gazette,* 167, 540
London *World,* 177
Long, John Davis, 319, **598**
Longfellow, Henry Wadsworth, 563, 599
Longman's Magazine, 606
Longworth, Nicholas, 21
Lord's Prayer, 175, 267, 269
Lotos Club (N.Y.), 436, 582, 642
"Lou Dillon" (mare), 415, 630
Louisville *Courier-Journal,* 616
"Love" (William Wilfred Campbell), 376–77, 618, 619
Low, James, 3, 458
Low, Seth, 640
Lowell, James Russell: biographical information, **554**; at copyright hearings, 283–84, 318, 584, 597; fiftieth birthday, 265–66, 578; and Monk-Greeley anecdote, 202–3, 554; mentioned, 233, 563
•Lower Saranac Lake (N.Y.), 82, 506
"Luck," 157, 343–45, 537
Luckstone, Isidore, 243–44, **568**
Lyceum Theatre (London), 467
Lyceum Theatre (N.Y.), 581
Lyde, Eda O. (Dora), 224, **557**
Lyde, Elsie Leslie, 224, **557–58**
Lyde, Evelyn (Mrs. Leslie), 224, **557**–58
Lyell, Charles, 212, 555
Lyon, Isabel Van Kleek (secretary): biographical information, **473**, 651, 652; Bermuda trip, 611; Clara's suspicions, 655; errands for Olivia, 101, 102; Harpers' *Christian Science* advertisement, 529; "Hon. Sec." of The Human Race (club), 643; Orion's autobiography, 27, 473; playing the orchestrelle, 376, 618; reporters handled, 31–32, 476; SLC's letters gathered, 508; telephone conversation, 198–99
TOPICS AND EVENTS RECORDED: Annie Fuller, 482; clairvoyant reading, 625; Dublin household, 511; Duneka's reaction to "No. 44," 530; Helen Keller, 617–18; Jessamy Harte benefit, 638–39; Kipling, 544; Luckstone (music teacher), 568; missing autobiographical dictations, 615; old letters unearthed, 521–22; palm readings, 640; poetry misattributed to Susy, 618, 619; proposed speech on Standard Oil, 564; rumors that SLC will remarry, 565; SLC's dinner and billiards with Dunne, 619, 620; SLC's letter to Orr, 535; Tennessee land, 46
MacAlister, John Y. W., 640
Macaulay, Thomas Babington, Lord, 289, 341, **586–87**
MacVeagh, Franklin, 109, **511**
Macy, Annie Sullivan: biographical information, **582**; cowboy's praise, 413–15; in need of support, 279–80, 582; as SLC's dinner guest, 374–75, 617–18
Macy, John, 374, 617, 618
Madison Square Garden (N.Y.), 384–85, 621–22, 647
Majestic Theatre (N.Y.), 8–9, 462
Malet, Edward (British ambassador), 181, 546
Malone, Edmond, 570
Malory, Thomas, 218–19
Mandeville, Geoffrey de (called Godfrey), 367–68, 614
Manners, 8–9, 362, 462
Manning, Daniel, 13, **464**
Manning, James H., 13, **464**
Margherita Maria Teresa Giovanna of Savoy (queen of Italy), 400, **625**

"Mark Twain (A Post-prandial Obituary)" (Bangs), 510
"Mark Twain" pseudonym: Isaiah Sellers's use, 230, 561–62; meaning, 356–57; SLC's first use, 239, 567, 650
Mark Twain House and Museum, 505, 573
Mark Twain in Eruption (DeVoto), 620
Mark Twain's Library of Humor: 1888 edition, issued by Webster and Company (SLC, Howells, and Clark, eds.), 77, 146, 501, 520–21, 528, 530, 534; 1906 edition, issued by Harpers, 146–48, 149, 530–31
"Mark Twain's Own Account," 434–36, 640–41
"Mark Twain's Patent Self-Pasting Scrap Book," 55, 490
Mark Twain's Sketches, New and Old, 53, 542, 602, 650
Mark Twain's Speeches (Paine), 462
Marmion, Robert, 367–68, 614
Marr, Thomas E., 543
Marsh, Mrs. E. L., 542
Marsh, May, 542
Marshall, John, 308–9, 592–93
Mary (cook), 511
Mary (queen of Scots), 333
Massachusetts: Dighton Rock (Berkley), 364, 613; *Huckleberry Finn* banned by Concord library, 29, 33. *See also* Boston; Fairhaven
Massiglia, Countess (Frances Paxton), 399, 400, 625
Mather, Cotton, 117, 516
Matilda (queen of England), 614
•Matthews, Brander, 30, 273–74, 475, 580, 607
McAleer, Patrick, 292–93, 380, 446, 620
McCall, Peter, **592**
McClellan, George B., 265, 500, 578
McClure, Robert, 197–98, 553
McClure, S. S., 553
McCullough, John, 425, 637
McCurdy, Richard A., 13, **464**
McFarland, Lethe Reynolds (called Mrs. Crawford), 301, 590–91
McGlural, Smiggy. *See* McGrew, William K.
McGraw, Jennie (Mrs. Daniel Willard Fiske), 34–35, **478**, 479
McGraw, John, 34, **478**
McGrew, John L., 12
McGrew, William K. (Smiggy McGlural), 116–17, 118, 119, **516**
McKinley, William, 9, 458, 464, 508, 595, 648
McVay, George W., 642
Meat Inspection Act (U.S., 1906), 116, 516
Medici, Catherine de', 524
Medill, Joseph, 252, **573**
Mental telegraphy, 198, 582
Mergenthaler Company, 505
Merritt, John A., 3, 7, **458**
Merwin-Clayton Company, 10, 12–13
Mesmer, Franz, **591**
Mesmerism: and Baron F. incident, 304–6; SLC's confession not believed, 302–4; SLC's experience in Hannibal, 297–302; theory, 591–92
Metropolitan Club (N.Y.), 105, 510
Mexican War (1846–48), 497, 616
Millet, Francis D., 598
Mind cure, 330–31, 342–43, 513, 602, 655
Miners and mining interests: corporate charters and fees, 5, 458–59; Esmeralda region, 168–69, 238, 540, 566, 649; Hale and Norcross mine, 18, 20–21, 422–23, 468; and Harte, 118, 415, 517–18, 630; Humboldt region, 238, 566, 649; Jackass Hill (or Gulch), 118, 384, 422, 514, 621, 636. *See also* Higbie, Calvin
Miners' Restaurant (San Francisco), 324, 600
Minnehaha (ship), 646
Minstrel shows, 293–97, 587–88
Missouri: "border ruffians" and Kansas-Nebraska Act, 255–56, 574–75; SLC born in Florida, 649, 652; SLC's satire of legislature, 561; *See also* Hannibal; St. Louis
Moffat, Dr., 99
•Moffett, Annie (Mrs. Charles L. Webster; SLC's niece), 21, 469, 489, 492, 494, 588, **653**
•Moffett, Pamela A. Clemens (SLC's sister): biographical information, **653–54**; characterized by SLC, 393; Fredonia home with Jane Clemens, 470, 492, 591,

653; hears Jane Clemens's account of early romance, 610; prototype for Tom Sawyer's cousin Mary, 653–54; W.C.T.U. membership, 613
Moffett, Samuel E. (SLC's nephew), 21, 469, 492, **653**
Moffett, William A., 492, **653**
Mommsen, Theodor, 157, **536**
Monadnock, Mount, 68, 108–9
Monarchy, 312–15, 371–72, 595
Monday Evening Club, 265, 578
Monk, Hank, 200–202, 553–54
Montana, 387–88, 622–23
Morality: "Christian Citizenship," 609; copyright violation as theft, 287–88, 322–23, 622–23; corrupting power of wealth, 370–71; commercial graft, 115–17, 515–16; government graft, 72, 116, 372–74, 387–88, 409–10, 464, 497, 623; insurance company investigations, 59, 464, 493, 497, 515; "moral purpose" photographs, 203, 204–10, 554; public vs. private, 226–27, 287–88; SLC's lectures, 17, 462, 465, 505. *See also* Lies and lying
Morel, Edmund Dene, 529
Mormon Church, 247, 571
Morningstar, Orlando E., 622
Morris, Minor, 460
Morris, Mrs. Minor, 3, 7, 9–12, 457–58, 460
Morse, Samuel, 478, 592
Mount McGregor (Saratoga Springs resort), 72–73, 495, 497
Mount Morris Bank (N.Y.), 504
Mulford, Prentice, 118, 517
Munsey, Frank A., 511
"A Murder, a Mystery, and a Marriage," 548
Murphy, Margret, 458
Murray, John, 587
Murray Hill Hotel (N.Y.), 224–25
Muscatine (Iowa), 237, 649, 653
Muscatine *Journal,* 561
Musgrave, Thomas B. (Harte's benefactor), 417, 631
Music: Aeolian Orchestrelle (organ), 376, 618; and Clemens children, 103, 224, 240, 567, 603, 654, 655; and Helen Keller, 617–18; in mining camp, 423; in minstrel shows, 293–96, 587–88; and Pamela Moffett, 653; SLC as singer, 248; SLC's passion, 400; Telharmonium, 447, 645
"My Autobiography [Random Extracts from It]," 469, 574, 659
"My Debut as a Literary Person," 641
"My First Literary Venture," 561
"My Platonic Sweetheart," 533
"The Mysterious Stranger," 146, 196–97, 530, 552
The Mysterious Stranger: A Romance, 530

Nansen, Fridtjof, 436, 642
Nasby, Petroleum V. (David Ross Locke), 153, 445–46, 534, 643–44
Nast, Thomas, 10, 12–13, **462**, 464–65
Nathan, Maud, 625
National Auxiliary to Sons of Union Veterans of the Civil War, 623
National Bell Telephone Company, 491–92
National Cordage Company, 504
Native Americans: Natick translation of Bible, 412–13, 628–29; petroglyphs, 364, 613
Neal, Henry, 319–20, **598**
Nero, 128
Nesbit, Evelyn (Mrs. Harry K. Thaw), 454, **647**
Nevada: Chief Justice Turner, 238–39, 566; Governor Nye, 4–6, 20, 37, 458–59, 468, 545; Orion as secretary, 3, 5–6, 20, 238, 458–59, 653; Senator Jones, 55–56, 490–91; Senator Stewart, 180–81; statehood, 6, 459, 468. *See also* Carson City; Miners and mining interests; Virginia City; Virginia City *Territorial Enterprise*
Nevada State Assembly, 468
Nevada Territorial Legislature: laws, 5, 458–59; SLC's reporting, 3, 5, 239, 458, 567
Nevinson, Henry Woodd, 145, **529**
Newell, Robert Henry (Orpheus C. Kerr), 153, 535
New Hampshire. *See* Dublin (N.H.)
New Orleans (ship), 549
New Orleans *Crescent,* 561
New Orleans *True Delta,* 230
Newport (R.I.): Bateman's Point resort,

Newport (R.I.) *(continued)*
383, 385–87, 622; community of aristocrats, 418
Newspapers: "the palladium of our liberties," 409–10, 628. *See also* Associated Press *and titles of newspapers*
New York (state): Clemenses' stay at Lower Saranac Lake, 82, 506; Clemenses' visit to Onteora, 250–53, 571, 573; SLC's visit to Mount McGregor, 72–73, 497. *See also* Fredonia; Quarry Farm
New York *American,* 517
New York City: SLC's arrival from San Francisco, 38, 46; Tweed Ring and Tammany Hall, 13, 362, 388, 462, 464–65, 609, 612–13. *See also* Clemens family residences
PLACES: Chase's Tenth Street studio, 272, 580; Chickering Hall, 60, 202–3, 494, 554; Cooper Union, 38–40, 481–82; Delmonico's Restaurant, 607, 631; Madison Square Garden, 384–85, 621–22, 647; Metropolitan Club, 105, 510; Murray Hill Hotel, 158, 224–25; The Players club, 426, 540, 565, 607; Savoy Hotel, 558; St. James Hotel, 42, 55–56, 423, 482, 491; Telharmonic Hall, 645; Union League Club, 387–90, 410, 622, 622–24. *See also* Carnegie Hall
New-Yorker Staats-Zeitung, 432, 640
New York *Evening Post,* 22, 470
New York *Evening Sun,* 11, 568–69
New York *Herald,* 32, 168, 170, 565, 583, 632, 633
New York Kindergarten Association, 272, 579–80
New York *Saturday Press,* 47, 485, 562, 650
New York State Association for Promoting the Interests of the Blind, 32, 477, 572
New York *Sun:* on *Berlin* disaster, 438–40, 443–44, 643; on Clara's début and SLC, 569; on famine in Russia, 307–8, 592; editorial mentioning SLC, 317, 596; Harte's "Thankful Blossom," 419, 632–33; on Jessamy Harte, 427, 638; London correspondent on U.S. corruption, 115–16, 515–16; on Pennsylvania Railroad wreck, 440–41, 643; proprietors, 502, 633; on SLC and Grant's *Memoirs,* 574; on SLC and Harte's *Ah Sin,* 633–34; veteran's letter, 372–74, 616–17; on Whiteley's death, 447
New York *Sunday Mercury,* 484
New York *Times:* on Barnes, 3, 6–7, 11–12, 457, 459–60, 463; editorial staff, 484, 516; on Ends of the Earth Club, 558; on Harte's *Two Men of Sandy Bar,* 631; on letters sold at auction, 10, 12–13, 462, 463; Root's speech on government, 595; on Russian pogroms, 133, 524; on Russo-Japanese War, 369, 615; on San Francisco earthquake, 512–13; on SLC at billiards tournament, 621; SLC's Associated Press speech, 246, 569; on SLC's speech to college women, 14–15, 465; on Terry's jubilee celebrations, 467; on Vassar benefit, 466; on Vesuvius eruption, 512; on Webster and Company bankruptcy, 504
New York *Tribune,* 10, 462, 484, 486, 503, 558, 633
New York Vaporizing Company, 490
New York *Weekly Review,* 513
New York *World,* 11, 15–16, 41–42, 465, 527
New Zealand, 81, 651
Nicaragua, 38, 549
Nicholas II (tsar), 134, 307–8, 524, 592
"No. 44, The Mysterious Stranger," 146, 196–97, 530, 552
Nora (nurse), 542–43
Norfolk (Conn.), Clara's singing début, 235, 240, 243, 567
North, S. N. D. (tariff-revision commissioner), 433–34, 640
North American Review (NAR): Briggs on virgin birth of Jesus, 131, 523–24; "King Leopold's Soliloquy" rejected, 145, 529; Lowell as editor, 554; publication of autobiography chapters, 404, 463, 469, 522, 618, 620, 626–27, 652, 656–60; SLC on Christian Science, 144, 526, 528–29; SLC on Elisabeth of Romania, 507; SLC's reading of dueling essay, 98, 507; Tennyson lines quoted, 612. *See also* Harvey, George

Nye, Edgar Wilson (Bill), 23, 26, **472**
Nye, James W., 4–6, 20, 37, **458**–59, 545

O'Brien, Fitz-James (possibly called Smith O'Brien), 153, **535**
O'Brien, William Smith, **535**
O'Connor, George, 511
"Old Times on the Mississippi," 489. See also *Life on the Mississippi*
Olney, Jesse, 360, **611**
"The Only Reliable Account of the Celebrated Jumping Frog of Calaveras County," 621
•Onteora Park (N.Y.), 250–53, 571, 573
Orr, Charles, 153–54, **535**–36
Osgood, James R., 53–54, 489, 492, 501, 521
Overland Monthly, 120, 518, 520, 521
Owsley, William, 590
Oxford University, 291, 341, 587, 652
Oyster, D. William, 7

Page, B. B., 413–15, 629
Page, Thomas Nelson, 598
Paige, James W., 74, 80, 158–60, 505, 537, 539
Paine, Albert Bigelow: and billiards, 620–21; on "Captain Stormfield's Visit to Heaven," 550–51; at copyright hearings, 317, 596; on Hancock's *Reminiscences,* 500; on "Luck," 537; and Orion's autobiography, 472–73; as photographer of SLC, 203, 204–10, 554; as posthumous editor of SLC's works, 526, 530, 533, 462; shin-skinning coincidence, 403–4; on SLC's reading of Suetonius, 614; mentioned, 511, 565, 652
Palace of Peace (The Hague), 172, 541
Palmistry: readings of SLC arranged by Stead, 336–37, 604; readings of SLC arranged by Harvey, and "Palm Readings" manuscript, 390–401, 624, 640; SLC's longevity predicted, 392, 395, 396, 400, 640; SLC's sense of humor discussed, 336–37, 390–91, 397, 399–400, 624. *See also* Fortune telling and divination; Phrenology
Panama City, 549
Parsloe, Charles T., 423–24, **636**
Patents. *See* Inventions and patents
Patterson, Thomas MacDonald, 410, **628**
Paul Jones (steamboat), 238, 566, 649
Peake, Humphrey, 300–303, **589**, 590
Pearl, William H. (Billy Rice), 293–94, 587, **588**
Pearmain, Sumner B., 246, **548**
Penn, William, 340, **605**
Pennsylvania (steamboat), 150–51, 531, 532
Pennsylvania Railroad, 116, 436, 440–41, 515
Pennsylvania Society, 595
Pensions: for Grant, with title restored, 68, 70–71, 496; for Lewis, 173, 175, 543; SLC's scheme for providing, 279–81, 582–83; for teachers, 541; for veterans, 371–74, 387, 615–17
Perin, Carl Louis, 396–400, 624
Perkins, Eli (Melville D. Landon), 153, **534**
Perkins, George W., 107, **511**
Perkins, Mary Beecher, **643**
Perkins Institute, 582
Perry, R. Ross, 7
Personal Memoirs (Ulysses S. Grant): Caesar's "Commentaries" compared, 71–72; contract negotiations, 60–64, 493–94; publication and sales, 65, 73, 505, 651; royalties paid to Mrs. Grant, 73–76, 255, 497–99, 574; mentioned, 69, 269, 503
Personal Recollections of Joan of Arc, 197, 353, 608–9, 651
Peterson, Frederick, 579
"A Petition to the Queen of England," 179–80, 545–46
Petroglyphs, 364, 613
Pets. *See* Clemens family pets
P. F. Collier and Son, 143–44, 528
Phelps, Elizabeth Stuart, 194, **550**
Phelps, William Walter, 157, 536
Philadelphia *American Courier,* 561
Philadelphia Bar Association, 308–9, 592
Phillips, Wendell, 282, **584**
Philological Society of London, 581
Phrenology, 334–36, 391, 603–4
Picard, Hélène Elisabeth, 28–29, 473–74, **474**

"Pictur' Department," 561
Pigeon, Richard Walter, 560
Plasmon Company, 625
Platt, Thomas Collier, 3, 387, 457, 458
Playboy (periodical), 624
The Players club (N.Y.), 426, 540, 565, 607
Pliny the Younger (Gaius Plinius Caecilius Secundus), 110, 512
Poe, Edgar Allan, 323, 339, 563, 599, 619
•Pond, James B., 183–84, 280, 547, 583
•Pond, James B., Jr., 280, 583
Pool. *See* Billiards
Porter, Horace, 187, 547
Porter, Sarah, 278, 581
Practical jokes: Sage's joke on Twichell, 251, 253–55; SLC's joke on Jim Wolf, 262–63; SLC's opinion, 4, 262, 263
"Prayer" (SLC note), 545
Presbyterians, 117, 175, 462, 468, 523
Price, Luther E., 559
•*The Prince and the Pauper:* children's playacting (and photographs noted), 165–66, 216, 331, 540, 602; composition, 155–56, 196, 552; family's opinion, 332, 353; publication, 52, 54, 353, 489, 651; readers' opinions, 14, 16; review by Howells, 602; stage production, 557–58
Pseudonyms (SLC): "A Dog-be-Deviled-Citizen," 561; Josh, 562, 566–67; Sergeant Fathom, 561; Thomas Jefferson Snodgrass, 231, 563; W. Epaminondas Adrastus Blab (W.E.A.B.), 560–61. *See also* "Mark Twain" pseudonym
Publishers. *See* American Publishing Company; Bliss, Elisha; Bliss, Francis E.; Carleton, George B.; Charles L. Webster and Company; Chatto and Windus; George Routledge and Sons; Harper and Brothers; Hotten, John Camden; Osgood, James R.; P. F. Collier and Son, 143–44, 528; Tauchnitz, Christian Bernhard von; Webb, Charles H.
Publishers' Weekly, 144–45, 528–29, 597
Pudd'nhead Wilson, The Tragedy of, 543, 651
Pumpelly, Raphael, 555
Punishment: of Clemens children, 223–24, 327–29, 600; Darwin's opinion, 223–24, 557; by God/Providence, 117, 130, 138–39, 142–43; of SLC in childhood, 177–78, 237, 545
Putnam, George Haven, 317, **597**
Pyrrhus, 330

Quaker City excursion: 17–18, 48–49, 239, 466, 482, 486–87, 489. See also *The Innocents Abroad*
"Quaker" (game), 382–83
•Quarry Farm (Elmira, N.Y.): daily routine, 218; *Date 1601* written, 155; Kipling's visit, 175–77, 544; Lewis's rescue of women, 173–74, 542–43; pets and other animals, 216–18, 223, 247–48, 257, 556; servants, 542; SLC conceives play idea, 19, 467; SLC's history game, 351–52, 608; mentioned, 46, 242, 353, 497, 571, 650. *See also* Clemens family amusements
Quimby, Phineas, 247, **571**

Rabelais, François, 155–56
Radolin, Hugo von (prince, formerly Count Radolinski), 594
Railey, Dr. (called Reyburn), 301, 590
Railroads: accidents, 359, 361, 436, 440–41, 612, 615; in Africa, 340, 605; invalid's car for Olivia, 99, 507–8; and Stephenson, 289, 586
Raleigh, Walter, 155, 537
Ralston, William C., 193, 550
Randall, Samuel J., 598
Rawlinson, Henry Creswicke, 363–65, **613**
Raymond, John T., 636
Raymond, Katherine B., 46, 484
Rayner, George, 646
Rayner, Horace, 447, **646**
Reade, Charles, 346, **606**
"A Record of the Small Foolishnesses of Susie & 'Bay' Clemens (Infants)," 222–25, 330, 557, 593
•Redpath, James: as abolitionist, 255–56, 574–75; as lecture agent, 40, 43–44, 256, 482, 483, 584; on SLC's character, 255; and SLC's Grant dictations, 493–94
Reed, Thomas B., 455, **648**
Rees, George, 562
Rees, Thomas, 229, 230–33, **562**, 563

Rees, William S. (elder Rees), 234–35, **562**, 563
Reese, "Professor" Bert (German clairvoyant), 401–3, **625–26**
"The Refuge of the Derelicts," 196, 198, 549, 552
Religion: changing constantly, 135–36, 371; mythologies shared, 130–31, 522–23. *See also* Bible; Christianity; God; Morality
Renwick, James, 23, **471**
Review of Reviews, 604
Rhodes, Cecil, 605
Rice, Billy (William H. Pearl), 293–94, 587, **588**
Rice, Clarence C., 158–59, **538**
Richards, Charles B., 54, **490**
Richardson, Abby Sage, 557–58
Richardson, Albert Deane, 48, **486**
Richardson, Mason W., 7
Richardson, Robert, 376–77, **619**
Richmond Theatre (Richmond, Va.), 301–3, 591
Ridder, Herman, 432–33, **640**
Ridout, John, 7
Riggs, George Christopher, 270, 579
Riggs, Kate Douglas Wiggin, 270–72, **579**, 580
Riley, James Whitcomb, 554
Ripler, Minna, 439, 443
Riverdale, 82, 99–107, 506–8, 511, 651
"River Intelligence," 561
Robb, James Hampden, **595**
Robert Fulton Memorial Association, 14, 15, 59, 465, 493
Robinson, George M., 378–80, **620**
Robinson, Henry, 79
Robson, Eleanor, 638–39
Robson, Stuart, 631–32
Rockefeller family, 116
Rogers, Anne Engle (Mrs. William Evarts Benjamin), 622
Rogers, Emilie Augusta Randel Hart, 582
Rogers, Mary (Mrs. William R. Coe), 572, 578
•Rogers, Henry Huttleston: Bahamas trip with SLC, 455, 648; bankruptcy advice for SLC, 79–80, 159–60, 162, 504; characterized by SLC, 161–62; and Helen Keller's support, 582; and Lewis's pension, 171, 172–73, 175; and *Library of Humor,* 149, 531; political enemy of Clark, 623; SLC's meeting, 158–59; and SLC's investments, 80, 505, 539. *See also* Fairhaven; *Kanawha;* Standard Oil Company
Roman, Anton, 520
Rome: ancient, 323–24, 364–65, 369, 372, 614; modern, 344, 157
Roosevelt, Theodore: biographical information, **464**; Barnes and Morris incident, 3, 6–8, 11–12, 460; called worst president, 9; food safety, 116, 516; pensions for veterans, 372, 616; and Simplified Spelling, 266, 274, 578, 580; SLC's visit, 461; mentioned, 13, 312, 463, 476, 595
Root, Elihu, 312–14, **595**
Root, R. T., 76, **499**
Rosa (nurse). *See* Hay, Rosina
Rosetta stone, 363–64, 613
Rostopchine, Sophie, comtesse de Ségur, 556
Rottenburg, Franz von, 594
Roughing It: contents and characters, 458, 549, 566, 632; contract and publication, 50–53, 143, 487, 488, 527–28, 608, 641, 650; English edition, 641, 650; and Fuller, 37, 480; Higbie's use, 169–70; Monk-Greeley anecdote, 200–203, 554; praised, 351
Routledge, Edmund, 435–36, **641–42**. *See also* George Routledge and Sons
Rowbotham, George B., 41, **483**
Rowley, Thomas, 247, 570
Roxburghe (duke of), 415, 629–30
Royalty Theatre (London), 560
Rucker, D. H., 464
Rucker, Irene (Mrs. Philip H. Sheridan), 464
Ruhlin, Augustus, 12, **463**
Russia: Chinese conflict, 13, 465; oppression and famine, 307–8, 592; pogroms, 132–34, 524;
Russo-Japanese War (1904–5), 134–35, 369–70, 525, 615
Rutland (Vt.) *Globe,* 22, 470–71

Sable Brothers (minstrel troupe), 588
Sacramento *Union,* 38, 239, 481, 567, 641, 650

Sage, Dean: biographical information, **536**, 573; acquaintances, 251, 271; and Beecher trial, 574; practical joke on Twichell, 253–55, 574; and SLC's *Date 1601,* 156
Sage, Henry W., 479, 480, 536, 574
Saint Bartholomew's Day, 134, 534
Sala, George Augustus, 642
Salt Lake City (Utah), 37–38
Samossoud, Clara Clemens. *See* Clemens, Clara Langdon
Samossoud, Jacques, 655
Sanders, Burton, 325–26
Sandwich Islands: and *Hornet* disaster, 435, 641; SLC's lectures, 38–40, 200, 280, 481–82, 553, 583; SLC's letters for Sacramento *Union,* 38, 239, 567, 650
San Francisco: restaurants, 324, 599–600; SLC's acquaintances and activities, 113, 118, 380–81, 514, 588; SLC's arrival and departure, 20–21, 38, 46, 468, 470, 512; SLC's experience of earthquake (1865), 112, 513; SLC's journalism, 111–17, 239, 513–15, 549, 567, 588, 621; SLC's lectures, 38, 200, 481, 553; SLC's visit (1868), 512; treatment of Chinese, 115, 515; U.S. Mint, 117–19, 517. *See also* San Francisco earthquake and fire (1906)
San Francisco *Alta California,* 193, 514, 549, 550, 588
San Francisco *Chronicle,* 479, 632
San Francisco *Dramatic Chronicle,* 513, 621
San Francisco earthquake and fire (1906), 110–14, 117, 191–92, 245–46, 512–14, 516, 599, 621
San Francisco *Evening Bulletin,* 46, 484
San Francisco Minstrel Troupe, 588
San Francisco *Morning Call:* building, 117–18, 516–17; rumor of SLC's second marriage, 565; SLC as local reporter, 114–17, 239, 514–15, 567, 621
San Francisco *News Letter and California Advertiser,* 517
Sargent, Epes, 588
Sartain, John, **562–63**
Sartain's Union Magazine of Literature and Art, 234, 562–63
Saturday Evening Post, 540
Saturday Morning Club, 419, 633
Saturday Press, 47, 485, 562, 650
Saturday Review, 475
Saunders, Millard, 630
Savage, Richard, 642
Savage Club (London), 435–36, 640–41, 642
Savarre, L. (called Savarin), 43, 483
Savoy Hotel (N.Y.), 558
Schaefer, Jacob, Sr., 384, **622**
Schiller, Friedrich, 566
Schofield, John McAllister, 70, **496**
Schooler, Martha (Patsy; SLC's mother's grandmother), **627**
"Schoolhouse Hill," 552, 588, 589
Schubert, Franz, 618
Scipio, Publius Cornelius Africanus, 330
Scotia (ship), 641
Scott, Frank M., 73–76, 498–99
Scovel (telephone man), 198–99
"Scraps from My Autobiography," 576, 659–60
Scribners (Charles Scribner's sons, publishers), 62, 148
Scribner's Monthly, 572, 635, 638
Sears, Joseph H., 564
Selkirk, Alexander, 109, **512**
Sellers, Isaiah, 230, **562**
Sembrich, Marcella, 111–12, **512**, 513
Senlac, battle of, 180, 546
Seventeenth Amendment (U.S. Constitution), 623
Shakespeare, William: folio edition discovered, 410–12, 628; Ireland's forgeries, 247, 570–71; and palmistry, 390; and SLC's *Date 1601,* 155–56, 537; and spelling, 277
REFERENCES: "age has not withered . . ." (*Antony and Cleopatra*), 19; "feed fat the ancient grudge . . ." (*The Merchant of Venice*), 62, 158, 494, 538
Shaw, Henry Wheeler (Josh Billings), 153, 485, 534
Sheldon, George R. (president of the Union League), 389, 624
Sheridan, Irene Rucker, 464
Sheridan, Philip Henry, 13, 70, 181, 464, 500
Sherman, William Tecumseh, 62, 13, 70, 302, **464**, 494, 496, 591

Sherry, Margaret (nurse), 102, 104, 107, 509
Sherry's Restaurant (N.Y.), 272, 579
Shillaber, B. P., 153, 535
Shrady, George F., 66, 255, **495**
Sikes, William Wirt, 45
Simms, William Gilmore, 563
Simmons (mesmerist), 298–300
"A Simplified Alphabet," 578
Simplified Spelling: early movement (1883), 275, 581; later movement (1906), 273–74, 578, 580; SLC's sketch set in Egypt, 266–69, 578; SLC's speech to Associated Press, 245–46, 274–77, 563–64, 569
Sinclair, Upton, 116, **515**–16
1601. See *Date 1601*
"Skeleton Novelette" (planned by Howells and SLC), 548
Sketches, New and Old, 53, 542, 602, 641, 650
Skinner, Otis, 466–67
Slavery: abolitionists, 255–56, 464, 573–75, 584; African, 461, 529; undesirable work as, 316–17
Slee, John D. F., 56, 491
Slosson, George F., 622
Slote, Daniel, 55, **489**–90
Slote, Woodman and Company, 55, 490
Smalley, George W., 432, 640
Smarr, Sam, 590
Smiles, Samuel, 586
Smith, Elizabeth W. (Aunt Betsey), 296–97, **588**
Smith, F. Hopkinson, 271–72, **579–80**
Smith, George, 523
Smith, Joseph (Mormon), 247, **571**
Smith, Joseph Lindon, 200, 203, 214–15, **553**, 555–56
Smith, Roswell, 61, 63
Smith College, 16, 17, 465
Smoking, 66, 258, 405–6, 409
Sneider, Charles, 489
Snodgrass letters, 231–35, 563
Socialist Revolutionary Party, 564
Solberg, Thorvald, 286, **585**
"Some Rambling Notes of an Idle Excursion," 549, 551, 611–12
Sons of Veterans of the United States of America, 623
South Africa, 81, 175, 543. *See also* Boer War
Spain, 145, 189–90, 547
Sparhawk (mesmerist), 589
Spaulding, Clara L., 166, 225, 540, 556
Spaulding, John S., 582
Spelling. *See* Cacography; Simplified Spelling; Clemens, Olivia Susan, biography of SLC
Spencer, Herbert, 392, **625**
Spenser, Edmund, 277
Sperling, Capt., 438–40, 443
"Spontaneous oratory." *See* Clemens, Samuel Langhorne: PET SCHEMES
Standard Oil Company, 159, 161, 504, 564, 582, 623, 651
Stanley, Henry M., 280, 436, **583**, 642
Stationers' Company (London), 605
Statute of Anne (Britain, 1710), 605
Stead, William T., 336–37, 390, **604**, 624
•Stedman, Edmund Clarence, 78, 376, **503**, 504, 618
Steele, Henry Milford, 426, **638**
Stengel-Sembrich, Guillaume, 111–12, **512**
Stephen of Blois (later king of England), 351, 365–67, **614**
Stephenson, George, 289, **586**
Stevens, Ed, 545
Stewart, William M., 180–81
St. James Hotel (N.Y.), 42, 55–56, 423, 482, 491
St. Louis (Mo.): Barret family home, 609–10; government corruption, 116, 525; James Ross Clemens home, 11, 463; Moffett family home, 492, 588, 627, 653; newspapers and journals mentioned, 230, 561, 588, 588–89 (*see also titles of newspapers*); SLC's last visit, 532, 651; SLC's lecture (1867), 280, 583; SLC takes mother to minstrel show, 296–97; mentioned, 10, 237, 408, 532, 649
St. Louis *Missouri Democrat,* 280, 583
St. Louis *Missouri Republican,* 561
St. Louis *Reveille,* 588, 589
St. Nicholas (periodical), 572, 573
Stockbridge, Anne W., 246, 548, **569**, 570
Stockbridge, William H., 246, **569**

Stockton, Francis R., 247, 250, 259, 260, **572**, 575–76
Stoddard, Charles Warren, 118
Stoddard, Richard H., 563
Stoker, Dick, 621, 636
The Stolen White Elephant, Etc., 54, 489, 551
Stone, Bessie, 346, 355–56, 609
Stone, Melville, 564
Stormfield (Clemenses' house in Redding, Conn.), 509, 579, 652, 656
Story, William Wetmore, **593**
Stowe, Charles, 606
Stowe, Eliza Tyler, 341, **606**
Stowe, Harriet Beecher, 225, 339, 341, 441–42, 605–6
Stowe, Harriet Beecher (Harriet's daughter), 341, **606**
Suetonius, 365, 614
Sullivan, Annie. *See* Macy, Annie Sullivan
Sullivan, Arthur, 333, 537, 560, 603
Sullivan, Marion Dix, 588
Sulzberger, Cyrus L., 607
Sumner, Charles, 13, **464**
Sutton, George H., 384–85, **622**
Swain, Robert B., 118, 119, 517
Swift, Jonathan, 271, 579
Switzerland, 225, 651
Sylva, Carmen (Elisabeth of Romania), 97–98, **507**

Talcott Mountain (Bartlett Tower), 156, 536
"Taming the Bicycle," 575
Tammany Hall, 362, 464, 609, 612–13. *See also* Tweed, William M.
Tate, Henry, 560
Tate Gallery (London), 560
Tauchnitz, Christian Bernhard von (father), 323, **599**
Tauchnitz, Christian Karl Bernhard von (son), 323, **599**
Taylor, Bayard, 34, 417, **477**, 553, 563, 631
Telephone: scarcity in London, 448–49; SLC's first, in Hartford house, 56–57, 354, 491–92; trouble with, 98–99; value as invention, 446–47
Telharmonium, 447, 645
Teller, Charlotte (Mrs. Johnson, later Mrs. Hirsch), 236, **564–65**
Tennessee land, of Clemens family, 21, 469
Tennyson, Alfred, Lord, 360–61, 612
Terry, Ellen, 19, **467**, 560
Terwilliger, Horace K., 568
Thaw, Evelyn Nesbit, 454, **647**
Thiele, Miss, 439, 443
The $30,000 Bequest and Other Stories, 596
Thompson, Annie Weeks (Mrs. Frank Fuller), 40–42, **482**
Thompson, Jacob H., 40, 42, **482**
Thomson, Mortimer (Q. K. Philander Doesticks), 153, **535**
Thorpe, Rose Hartwick, 215, 556
"Those Extraordinary Twins," 588
"Three Thousand Years Among the Microbes," 196, 552
Thring (called Thwing), Henry, Lord, 288, 290–91, 339, 341, **586**–87
Tiffany, Louis Comfort, 569, 571
Tiffany, Louise Comfort (Mrs. Rodman Gilder), 569
Tiffany and Company, 633
Tilden, Samuel J., 424–25, 519, 636–37
Tile Club, 579–80
Tillman, Benjamin, 3, 12, 457–58
Tilton, Elizabeth, 573
Tilton, Theodore, 573–74
Timothy (coachman), 542
Tobin, Miss, 100–102
Tom Sawyer. See *The Adventures of Tom Sawyer*
Tom Sawyer Abroad, 477
"Tom Sawyer's Conspiracy," 545, 590
"To the Person Sitting in Darkness," 651
The Tragedy of Pudd'nhead Wilson, 543, 651
A Tramp Abroad: contents and characters, 16, 465, 539, 639; contract and publication, 51–52, 488, 651; Howells's review, 602; sales and royalties, 52, 488; Wilhelm II's appreciation, 431, 433–34
Travelers Accident Insurance Company, 55
Tremont Hotel (Boston), 256
Trevelyan, G. O., 586
A True Story, and the Recent Carnival of Crime, 489
"A True Story, Repeated Word for Word as I Heard It," 542

Trumbull, James Hammond: characterized by SLC, 412–13, 629; and SLC's idea for a play, 19–20, 467–68
Turner, Emily, 646
Turner, George Enoch, 238–39, **566**
Turner, Louisa, 646
"The Turning Point of My Life," 565
Tuskegee Institute, 8, 460–62
Tweed, William M. ("Boss"), 13, 388, 462, 464–65. *See also* Tammany Hall
•Twichell, Joseph H.: biographical information, 465, 511; bicycling, 258, 575; Clara visited by, 152; and *Date 1601,* 155–56; handsomeness, 161; officiating at funerals, 108, 576; "Peters" alias, 194, 360, 612; Sage's practical joke, 253–55, 574; school days, 360, 611; and Wakeman, 192, 194–95, 551
FRIENDSHIP WITH SLC: Bermuda trips, 359–60, 611–12; correspondence, 103–7, 508, 510, 551; SLC's gratitude, 160; SLC's "Luck" based on report, 157, 344, 537; SLC's sixty-seventh birthday dinner, 105, 510; travels in Germany, 15, 16, 181–82, 465, 546; walk to Bartlett (Talcott) Tower, 156, 536; walk to Boston, 380, 620, 643–44
Twichell, Julia Curtis (Judy), 107, **511**
Twichell, Julia Harmony Cushman, 546
Typewriter, 445–47, 643–45

Underwood Johnson. *See* Johnson, Robert Underwood
Union League Club (N.Y.), 387–90, 410, 622, 622–24
Uniontown *Northern Californian,* 518
Upton House. *See* Dublin (N.H.)
U.S. Congress (House and Senate): Barnes's appointment, 6, 11–12, 460; direct election of senators, 623; Grant's pension and title restored, 70, 496; John Marshall Monument Fund authorized, 593; pension bills, 372–74, 431, 615–17; presidential election (1876), 636–37; Simplified Spelling, 580; SLC's opinion of senators, 55–56, 387–88, 409–10, 490–91, 497, 622–23. *See also* Copyright
U.S. Constitution, 314, 322, 337, 599, 623
U.S. Mint (San Francisco), 117–19, 517
U.S. State Department, 8, 461
U.S. Steel Corporation, 505
U.S. Supreme Court, 308–9, 480, 592–93, 621–22
Utah Territory, 37–38

Vanderbilt family, 116
Van de Velde, Arthur, 635–36
Van de Velde, Hydeline de Seigneux, **635–36**
van Dyke, Henry, **462**, 510
Vassar College, 15–17, 465–66
Versen, Alice Clemens von, 593–94
Versen, Maximilian von, 432, 593–94
Vesuvius, Mount, 109–10, 512
Victoria (empress dowager of Prussia), 432
Victoria (queen of England): favorite recitations, 556; Jubilee, 134, 525; SLC's "Petition," 179–80, 545–46; mentioned, 352, 559, 599
Vienna (Austria): Clara's piano study, 509, 655; Clemenses' stay, 27, 80, 81, 162, 448, 651, 99, 162, 473, 507; Hotel Krantz, 227–28, 559; Hotel Metropole, 507; and Lindau, 312, 594; mesmerism incident, 304–6, 591–92; SLC's works composed, 574, 602
Villa di Quarto. *See* Florence
"Villagers of 1840–3," 626
Virginia: letter from SLC admirer, 351; Old Point Comfort resort, 100, 107, 508; Richmond Theatre burned, 301–3, 591; Virginians living in Hannibal, 301–3, 590
Virginia City (Nev.): ball, 24, 471; SLC's acquaintances, 481, 484, 514; SLC's arrival and departure, 468, 567
Virginia City *Territorial Enterprise:* SLC as reporter, 5, 238–39, 458, 567; SLC's "Josh" letters, 562, 566–67, 649; SLC's sketches, 485, 513. *See also* Goodman, Joseph T.
Virginia City *Union. See* Fitch, Thomas

Wagner, Richard, 164, 294, 539
•Wakeman, Edgar (Ned): biographical information, 193, **548–49**; as inspiration for SLC's writing, 192–94, 198, 549–

Wakeman, Edgar *(continued)*
51; SLC's appeal for financial aid, 193, 550; spelling, 195, 413; and Twichell, 192, 194–95, 551; WORK: *The Log of an Ancient Mariner*, 549
•Wakeman, Mary E. Lincoln, 193, 549
Waldorf-Astoria Hotel (N.Y.), 32, 477, 563–64, 595, 640
Walpole, Horace, 247, **570**
Walters, William Thompson, 77, **502**
Walters Art Museum (Baltimore), 502
Wambold, David, 293–94, **588**
Ward, Artemus (Charles Farrar Browne), 46, 153, **484**, 484–85
Ward, Ferdinand, 61–62, 66–67
Ward, John, 411, 628
Ward, Lewis P., 113, **514**
Warner, Charles Dudley: death, 260, 576; family, 540; and the Fiskes, 34–35, 477–49; guest at Onteora, 251; on Susy and Clara, 224; tribute for SLC's fiftieth birthday, 259, 260, 575, 577, 578; WORK: *The Gilded Age* (with SLC), 533, 641, 650
Warner, Elisabeth Gillette (Lilly; Mrs. George H. Warner), 331, 540, 557, 602
Warner, Frank, 166, 333, **540**
Warner, George H., 165–66, 176–77, 540
Warner, Susan (Susy; Mrs. Charles Dudley Warner), 34, 251, 330, 333, 478, 602
•Warner, Margaret (Daisy), 333, 602
"The War-Prayer," 526, 651
Washington (D.C.): Clara's public singing, 567; John Marshall Monument, 306, 308–9, 592–93; proposed murals for Capitol, 535; SLC's visits, 8, 180, 461. *See also* Copyright; U.S. Congress
Washington, Booker T., 8, 414–15, 460–61
Washington, George, 9, 335, 496, 589
Washington *Evening Star,* 6–7, 12
Washington Ladies' Literary Association, 597–98
Washington *Post,* 572, 576
"Was it Heaven? Or Hell?," 83–96, 103–4, 107, 506
Wasps. *See* Insects
Watt, James, 586
W.C.T.U. (Woman's Christian Temperance Union), 362, 613
Webb, Charles H.: biographical information, **484**; *Californian* contributions, 118; *The Celebrated Jumping Frog* published, 46–48, 49–50, 143, 485, 487–88
•Webster, Annie Moffett (SLC's niece), 21, 469 , 489, 492, 494, **653**
•Webster, Charles L.: biographical information, 21, 77–78, 492, 496, 502–3; and bookkeeper's embezzlement, 73–76, 499; books acquired or rejected, 76–77, 78, 499–502; characterized by SLC, 58–59, 64–66, 68, 73–77, 497–98, 505; Jewish ancestry suggested, 69, 496; salary, 54, 57–58, 64, 65, 493, 494, 495, 499; and SLC's patents, 54, 57, 489–90. *See also* Charles L. Webster and Company
Webster, Samuel Charles, 494–95, 498
Wells, Samuel R., 335, **604**
Wenneberg, Mrs., 439, 443
West Point Military Academy, 72, 155, 157, 496, 497, 535–36
What Cheer House (San Francisco), 324, 599
What Is Man?: composition and publication, 332, 399, 527, 602–3, 625, 652; SLC dictation that reprises philosophy, 140–43, 527
"'What Ought He to Have Done?': Mark Twain's Opinion," 328–29, 600–601
•Wheeler, Candace, 247, **571**
•Wheeler, Dora, 247, **571**
"Which Was It?," 196, 552
Whitcher, Frances Miriam Berry (Widow Bedott), 45, **483**
White, Andrew Dickson, 33, **477**, 478, 479–80
White, Cool, 588
White, Stanford, 429, 454–56, 607, **647**
Whiteley, William, 447–52, **645–46**
Whitford, Daniel: biographical information, **493**; characterized by SLC, 59, 66, 75, 493; and Webster's employment contracts, 58, 59, 64, 78, 495, 503
Whitman, Walt, 13, 464, 619
Whittier, John Greenleaf, 339
The Whole Family (collaborative novel), 190, 547–48

"Why Not Abolish It?," 647–48
Whyte, Frederic, 603
Wiggin, Kate. *See* Riggs, Kate Douglas Wiggin
Wilbur, Homer C., 234, **562–63**
Wiley and Putnam, 597. *See also* Putnam, George Haven
Wilhelm II (emperor of Germany and king of Prussia): appreciation of SLC's books, 310, 315, 431, 433–34; SLC's dinner with, 309, 310–12, 430–32, 593–95
Wilhelmina (queen of the Netherlands), 444, **643**
Wilkerson (fictional name of palm reader), 403, 404
Willard, Frances, 414, **629**
William I (the Conqueror; king of England), 351
William IV (king of England), 228, 560
William Rufus (king of England), 351–52
Williams, Henry (father), 514
Williams, Henry Alston (son), **514**
Williams, Richard, 113–14, 514
Williams, Theresa Ann Gillis, **514**
Williams, Thomas E., 588
Williams, William, 549
Wilson, James H. (Ends of the Earth Club chairman), 226, **558**
Wolf, Jim, 260–63, 589
Wolseley, Garnet Joseph, Lord, 157, 344–45, **537**, 537–38
Woman's Christian Temperance Union (W.C.T.U.), 362, 613
Women's University Club, 14–18, 465–66
Wood, Charles Erskine Scott, 155, 350, 535–36, **536**, 607
Wood, Howard Ogden, 511
Wood, Leonard, 9, 462
Woolsey, Sarah Chauncey (Susan Coolidge), 375–76, **617**
Wootton, Francis H., 480
Wordsworth, William, 347
Work, Henry Clay, 591
Worth, Charles Frederick, 43, **483**
Wright, Foster P. (judge), 151, **533**
Wright, Laura Mary (Mrs. Charles T. Dake), **531–32**; fortune teller on romance with SLC, 404–5, 407, 408; letters to SLC (1906), 151, 211, 405, 533, 554; SLC's reminiscences, 149–51, 211, 531–33
Wright, Orville and Wilbur, 612

"Ye Sentimental Law Student," 562, 567
York Harbor (Maine), 82, 97, 101, 506–8, 552
Young, Andrew, 587
Young, Warren, 12
Youngblood, William C., 211, 531, 532
Young Men's Christian Association, 8–9, 462
"Yreka," source of name, 118, 415, 517. *See also* Harte, Bret
Yung Wing, 551

Zodiac (astrology), 226, 558–59

The Mark Twain Project is housed within the Mark Twain Papers of The Bancroft Library at the University of California, Berkeley. The Papers were given to the University by Mark Twain's only surviving daughter, Clara Clemens Samossoud, and form the core of the world's largest archive of primary materials by and about Mark Twain. Since 1967 the Mark Twain Project has been producing volumes in the first comprehensive critical edition of everything Mark Twain wrote, as well as readers' editions of his most important texts. More than thirty-five volumes have been published, all by the University of California Press.

The Mark Twain Papers and *The Works of Mark Twain*
are the ongoing comprehensive editions for scholars.
Full list of volumes in the Papers at
http://www.ucpress.edu/books/series/mtp.php
Full list of volumes in the Works at
http://www.ucpress.edu/books/series/mtw.php

The Mark Twain Library
is the readers' edition that reprints texts and notes from the Papers and Works volumes for the benefit of students and the general reader.
Full list of Library volumes at
http://www.ucpress.edu/books/series/mtl.php

Mark Twain Project Online
is the electronic edition for the Mark Twain Project. *Autobiography of Mark Twain, Volumes 1* and *2,* are now published there. All volumes in the Papers and Works as well as the Library will eventually be made available at
http://www.marktwainproject.org

Jumping Frogs: Undiscovered, Rediscovered, and Celebrated Writings of Mark Twain
brings to readers neglected treasures by Mark Twain—stories, tall tales, novels, travelogues, plays, imaginative journalism, speeches, sketches, satires, burlesques, and much more.
Full list of Jumping Frogs volumes at
http://www.ucpress.edu/books/series/jf.php

Editorial work for all volumes in the Mark Twain Project's Papers, Works, and Library series has been supported by grants from the National Endowment for the Humanities, an independent federal agency, and by donations to The Bancroft Library, matched equally by the Endowment.

DESIGNER: SANDY DROOKER
TEXT: 10.75/14 GARAMOND PREMIER PRO
DISPLAY: AKZIDENZ GROTESK
COMPOSITOR: BOOKMATTERS, BERKELEY CA
PRINTER AND BINDER: THOMSON-SHORE, INC.